THE

BRIGAND;

OR,

THE MOUNTAIN CHIEF.

A Romance.

BY THE AUTHOR OF "ELA, THE OUTCAST," "GIPSY BOY," "GILDEROY," "GALLANT

TOM," "THE SMUGGLER KING,"

"THE DEATH SHIP," "MANIAC FATHER," "FLORIAN, THE DUMB BOY," &c., &c.

LONDON:

PUBLISHED BY E. LLOYD, SALISBURY-SQUARE, FLEET-STREET.

MDCCCLI.

PREFACE.

UPON arriving at the conclusion of this, one of the most successful of his productions, the Author deems it necessary to offer a few explanatory observations at parting with his kind readers. His object has been to amuse; and that, the extraordinary favour with which "THE BRIGAND" has been received by the public affords him the gratifying conviction has been achieved. He wishes, however, to inform the reader that his narrative, though interpolated with the romance of fiction, is founded on facts.

To use the words of George Daniels (D. G.) "Allesandro Massaroni, the Italian Robin Hood, was one of those daring spirits that seem to have been created to correct the unequal distribution of good and evil. Chief of a lawless band infesting the mountains near Rome, his name spread terror throughout Italy. No place was secure from his emissaries; and so skilful were his acts of disguise, that he was often made the confident of plots laid by his enemies to entrap him. He was a strict dispenser of moral justice; if he made free with the rich, he was the almoner of the poor, and never did he resort to violence but when a tempting booty or a stout resistance stood in his way. Like the famous freebooter of merry England, he mingled mirth with his malefactions, and those who paid the dearest for his pranks were often the first to laugh at his humour.

"A mystery hung over his birth. His mother was a young Florentine, who, having been seduced and deserted by some 'puppy unknown,' had died of a broken heart, and the only family record he possessed was her miniature, which, even in the wildest moments of disorder and rapine, produced in him certain compunctious visitings of nature, that showed he was deserving of a better fate. Such was Massaroni—nurtured by banditti—once their comrade, afterwards their chief!"

It may, in conclusion, not be considered out of place to inform the public that the author of "THE BRIGAND" has now publishing, in weekly numbers, another romance, founded upon an equally celebrated character, teeming with incident, entitled "GILDEROY; OR, THE FREEBOOTER OF SCOTLAND."

London, January, 7th, 1851.

THE BRIGAND

OR THE

MOUNTAIN CHIEF

CHAPTER I.

THE LIBERTINE AND HIS VICTIM.—THE TALE
OF SORROR.—THE BRIGAND CHIEF.

"HE will not come—he will not come—
and my heart misgives me. It is long past the
hour at which he appointed to meet me, and if
he should now fail, my last hope is gone. Oh
Alberti, should you deceive me—but no, I
will not entertain the thought, for that would
drive me to madness, after I have sacrificed all
for your dear sake. No—no—yon sweet
innocent pledge of our affections must bind
you to your promise. You cannot now desert me

and your offspring ; you will not leave us to the tender mercies of the heartless world. And yet, methinks your manners have been colder of late than they were wont to be when you vowed that I was the chief, nay, the only charm of your very existence. Oh, that sad feeling again! Alberti, dearest Alberti, on whom my very soul is rivetted, if the poor foundling girl was worthy of your love, high even as is your rank and station, why, oh, why was she not your bride ere now ?"

Such were the words that were uttered in silvery tones of the most melancholy plaintiveness by the lovely Olympia as she anxiously gazed from the lattice of the humble but comfortable room in which she was seated. Her fair bosom heaved with the contending passions which at that moment struggled within it, and tears trembled on her long dark silken eyelashes. Pity that tears should ever dim such sparkling eyes; or that sorrow and anguish should ever adorn that beauteous countenance. Hope, and joy, and content, should ever be the guests of that breast in which so many noble virtues are implanted. With what indescribable grandeur the golden monarch of the day now sinks to rest in the bosom of the blue waters of the Mediteranean, and gilding the lofty domes of the many noble buildings with his departing rays, how sublimely does the glorious orb retire from one of the loveliest days with which it had ever gladdened fair Italy. What various hues of azure, purple, and gold, adorn the western sky, and reflect upon the surface of the deep. How solemn and impressive is the hour. What can equal the heavenly splendour of that scene? But although Olympia's eyes seemed fixed on it, it was lost upon her, for all her thoughts were fixed upon the one in whom all her hopes of happiness were involved ; and agony and suspense made her view every object around with a jaundiced eye.

" He will not come, he will not come!" she once more sighed forth, and arising from her seat, she turned disconsolately away from the lattice and approached her sleeping infant.

All a young mother's fondness was evinced in the kisses she bestowed upon the poor babe, and her scalding tears flowed fast upon its innocent face, whilst agonizing sobs escaped her distracted bosom.

" Sweet offspring of my affection and dishonour ;" she ejaculated, "thy cruel father loves us not; he will leave us to the mercy of the pitiless world; oh, it were better that we were both dead, than to have to encounter the miseries that appear to be in store for us. Alberti, Alberti, oh, canst thou have the heart to consign us to such a fate ?"

At that moment there was a knock at the door, and with a palpitating heart Olympia started from the seat she had taken by the side of her slumbering infant.

" 'Tis he," she ejaculated, in a tremulous voice, " oh, Heaven be thanked, and forgive me, dear Alberti, for having wronged thee by my hasty suspicions."

With trembling haste, she made her way to the door, which she opened, but starting back with a faint shriek of alarm and disappointment, when instead of him she expected to behold, a stranger presented himself. It was a man dressed in the humble garb of a peasant, who supported himself by a stout stick, and whose features were almost concealed by huge black whiskers, and a long flowing beard. Olympia trembled and retreated to the further end of the room, but the stranger retained his position, and fixing his eyes, which were peculiarly expressive and penetrating full upon her, he said, in the most respectful accents—

" Be not alarmed, fair signora, I am a poor traveller who am weary and footsore, and merely request you to allow me to rest myself for a few moments in your dwelling."

Olympia's alarm and confusion increased, and with difficulty she faltered out:

" Stranger, I am a lone woman, and propriety——"

" And would the fair and gentle Olympia refuse a fellow-creature the rights of hospitality ?" demanded the man in a different voice.

" Ah! know you then my name ?" she said.

" Even so;" replied the man, walking deliberately into the room, and closing the door after him. Olympia shrunk from him, and could scarcely refrain from screaming aloud, especially when the stranger approached nearer towards her, and gazed at her for a moment or two with the most intense earnestness.

" Lovely signora," he said ; " again I beg of you not to alarm yourself, for no harm can come to you while I am here."

" Who are you?" asked Olympia, in a faint voice.

" Your friend, and the mortal enemy of your betrayer, Count Alberti d'Amalfi."

" Gracious Heaven!" cried the astonished Olympia ;—"how know you this? and what is your purpose here?"

" I come to warn you. The count has appointed to meet you this evening; you expected him ere this; you start, but do I not speak the truth ?"

" Alas, you do. But by what means has this come to your knowledge, and why should you take such an interest in what concerns me ?"

" It matters not. I have told you I am your friend, and when you know me better you will find that I am not a friend to be despised. Alberti has promised that he will this night finally fix the day when he will render you justice by making you his bride. Oh, signora, be not deceived by him; treachery lurks in his guilty breast. Not only does he mean to abandon you and your innocent offspring, but he would fain get rid of you altogether."

"Great God of Heaven!" cried the horrorstruck Olympia, "stranger, can you speak the truth?"

"You need not doubt me, signora; by an artful tale he will endeavour to persuade you to quit this neighbourhood for the present, so that he may the better be enabled to carry his diabolical plans to get rid of you and your child altogether, into effect. Count Alberti d'Amalfi will never make the poor foundling girl of his parents' bounty his bride."

"Ah!" ejaculated Olympia, with increased astonishment, "you know my history?"

"I do, signora. It is briefly this. Some twenty years ago a tender child of about two years of age was found at the portico of the Villa Nova, and kindly taken in by the Count Alberti's father, and as its parents could never be discovered, it was brought up and cherished in the family with the same care as if it had been one of their own. That child was you, Signora Olympia. Years flew on, and your charms inspired a passion in the young count's breast, which you too fondly and confidingly returned. But he was noble, and could not think of allying himself to a poor unknown girl. With subtle arts, with flattering promises, and honeyed accents, he triumphed o'er your woman's weakness, and in a fatal hour you became his unfortunate victim."

"Alas! alas!" sobbed the blushing Olympia, averting her looks from those of the stranger, with feelings of the most inexpressible agony.

"To conceal the baseness of his conduct, he persuaded you to leave the shelter of that roof beneath which you had ever found a home, and to seek refuge here, solemnly promising that he would at some future period snatch you from that shame into which he had plunged you. Is not this correct, signora?"

"Would to Heaven it were not," groaned Olympia; "but tell me who are you that are so well acquainted with my unfortunate history?"

"That you will shortly know. My business here is to protect you from the danger which now threatens you, and you will find that I have the power as well as the will to perform what I say. But, hist, I hear footsteps approaching the house. It is probably he!"

"Good God! what will become of me, stranger, should he find you here?" exclaimed the agitated Olympia. "Hark, the footsteps approach nearer!—A knock!—All is lost if you do not instantly fly. I pray you:—you can escape by the back door, but there is not a moment to lose."

The knock was repeated.

"I must not leave the place," said the stranger in a low voice; "I will conceal myself in yonder room, fear not."

Immediately he darted into the apartment beyond, and cautiously closed the door after him, and Olympia endeavouring to subdue the violence of her emotion which this extraordinary adventure had excited in her breast, with a trembling hand opened the outer door and gave addmission to the Count Alberti.

"Dear Olympia," said the count, embracing her, "why this delay in admitting one whom I thought you would be waiting to see with such anxious impatience? But you are pale and agitated, you have been weeping; why do you shrink from my embrace? Is this the reception that an ardent lover should expect from his mistress?"

"I—I—feared you would not come, dear Alberti;" faltered out Olympia, in a faint voice, and scarcely daring to fix her eyes upon the handsome countenance of him to whom she had sacrificed her whole affections, and who she feared was now about so cruelly to deceive her. "But," she added, brightening up, and struggling with her feelings, "pardon me, dear Alberti, you arenow present, and I will endeavour to be happy." He led her to a chair, and taking a seat by her side, placed his arm around her slender waist, and drew her with apparent tenderness towards him. Olympia could not help shuddering when she remembered what the stranger had told her. She pointed to the infant, and in a tremulous voice ejaculated:

"Dear Alberti, see our little one sleeps in innocence and tranquillity. Oh, may kind Heaven decree that she shall never experience a moment's sorrow; and may it guard her from the snares and vices of the world; but should she never know a father's tender care; should she live to know her unfortunate origin——"

She paused, for her emotions would not suffer her to proceed. The count felt confused, and it was also several minutes before he could return any reply, and at length he said:—

"Come, Olympia, you must not give way to these sad feelings, I thought to find you all smiles and joyful expectation, considering the important business I was to meet you upon this evening."

"Beloved Alberti," said Olympia, hope reviving in her breast; "you have not then forgotten your promise, you will name the blissful day when I may call you my lawful lord, and set the world's reproach and scandal at defiance! Oh, what happiness will then be mine: But what mean those looks?—Dear Alberti, do you not share in the sanguine hopes that animate my breast?"

"Yes, yes," faltered out the count in a confused manner, "but my sweet Olympia must somewhat subdue the ardour of her feelings, and listen to me with calmness and patience

You know the fervour of the love I bear you, which neither time nor circumstances can subdue, and how proud and happy I should be to make you my lawful bride, I had hoped to have been able to name the day of our nuptials on this occasion, but—but——"

"But what?" gasped forth Olympia, her heart sinking within her, and fixing her beautiful eyes upon him with an expression that ought to have penetrated to his very soul : " oh, Alberti, what can be the meaning of your hesitation ! Do not, oh, do not, I beseech you, keep me in suspense."

" Be calm, Olympia, circumstances over which I have no control, and which I cannot now explain, unfortunately render it impossible for me to fulfill my promise for some months to come, and in the meantime I wish you to retire to the house of an amiable signora at Fondi, who will behave to you and our child with the greatest kindness and attention. I will make ample provision for you, and——"

" Oh, God ! oh, God !" interrupted the distracted Olympia, clasping her hands together with the most inexpressible agony, " then my worst, my most horrible fears are realized, and I am indeed one of the most wretched of human beings. Oh, Alberti, for whom I have sacrificed virtue, the world's esteem, everything ; how have I merited this? But you cannot mean it ; no, no, I will not believe that you can so cruelly deceive me, after all the solemn promises you have made. Alberti I love you, I adore you, I worship you more than I can express by words or actions, our little innocent claims the protection of a father, do not then, oh, I implore you, do not thus abandon me to the blackest despair. You may find many of noble rank and station, but none who will love so fondly as the poor foundling girl, who now kneels at your feet, and begs you to look down with pity upon her !"

" Cease these paroxysms, Olympia," returned the count; " of what avail are they ? You accuse me wrongfully of wishing to deceive you. What reason have you ever had to doubt my love ? I say again that it is impossible for me to fulfil my promise for some months to come, but then, when all the obstacles that are at present thrown in my way are removed, if you comply with my wishes, I will. But you must leave this neighbourhood and retire whither I have mentioned."

" Leave you, Alberti," sobbed Olympia; " oh, never, never, my heart would break in doing so,"

" You talk madly, Olympia," said Alberti, impatiently ; " You also do me wrong by doubting my honour. If you thus oppose my wishes, I must adopt another course."

" And can this be that man to whom I have devoted my heart, my very soul; for whose sake, I would willingly endure anything ! Alas ! alas! unhappy Olympia, death would then be mercy to you."

" This is but a waste of time," said the count, coldly, " are you ready to comply with my wishes?"

" Oh, I cannot, dear Alberti ; to be separated from you would be more dreadful to me than the most lingering death of torture."

" Then farewell, our interview is at an end;" said the count advancing towards the door.

" No, no, you shall not leave me thus;" cried Oylmpia, clinging distractedly to him; "Alberti, my soul's idol, have mercy on me and your child, and do not thus cruelly abandon us to misery and despair. You have solemnly vowed in the face of high heaven to make me your lawful bride, and you cannot thus heartlessly and recklessly break your oath !"

" I will not be detained," said the count, " you have heard my decision, and must abide by it."

With these words he violently released himself from the wretched woman's hold, and was about to hasten from the house, when the stranger suddenly darted from the room in which he had been concealed, and stood before him.

" Hold, villain !" he exclaimed, in a commanding voice; " I must have a few words with you before you depart from hence."

Nothing could exceed the rage and astonishment of the count at this unexpected interruption, and he fixed a malicious look upon the trembling Olympia, who covered her face with her hands and sobbed with agony and terror.

" Nay," said the unknown, " blame not this unfortunate woman for my appearance here; she knew not of my coming, and I am a perfect stranger to her."

" Insolent intrusion !" cried the count passionately, " for what purpose do you presume to appear before me ?"

" Pr'ythee do not ruffle your temper signor," said the stranger, with a smile, and in tones of the most studied politeness ! " for I can assure you that harsh words are entirely thrown away upon me. I came here to see justice done to Signora Olympia, and you shall render it too ere you quit this place."

" Ah ! dare you threaten?"

" Yes, I dare threaten a score such men as he that stands before me ;" replied the unknown, with a scornful laugh.

" Stranger, forbear ;" supplicated Olympia, in a faint voice ; " and leave this place ; your interference can effect no good."

" Indeed, fair lady," replied the man, " I regret that I cannot comply with your request."

" Insolent varlet," exclaimed the count, as he drew forth his stiletto, and rushed upon the stranger, " this to punish you for your daring."

The stranger, however, wrenched the weapon

from the count's grasp with the greatest ease, and hurling him to the other side of the room, he laughed aloud,

"Dog!" cried the enraged nobleman, "know you not that it is the Count Alberti d'Amalfi upon whom you commit this outrage?"

"Yes," replied the other with a smile, but I will not return your flattering compliment. However, you may be desirous to know the name of him who has dared to intrude himself upon you?"

"I demand to know it!"

"It is not to your demand I yield, Count Alberti," returned the stranger, "but in compliance with my own will; you have been pleased to inform me of that I knew before, namely, that you are the Count Alberti d'Amalfi, and I am——"

"Who?" eagerly asked the count and and Olympia, in a breath.

"Allessandro Massaroni, the Brigand Chief!" was the reply; and throwing by his peasant's dress, and removing the false whiskers and beard which had concealed his features, that daring man stood confessed before them!

CHAPTER II.

THE EXTORTED OATH.—THE COMPACT.—THE SUDDEN ATTACK ON MASSARONI.

OLYMPIA uttered a cry of horror on this unexpected discovery, and the astonishment and alarm of the count for some time deprived him of the power of speech. The brigand removed his carbine, which had been slung to his back beneath his peasant's dress, and placing his elbow upon the butt end of it, gazed at the count with an ironical smile of triumph. The brigand chief was a remarkably handsome man, apparently about thirty years of age, and there was a wicked smile constantly playing over his bronzed features which showed the natural daring yet withal infinite humour of his character. His figure was a perfect model of manly grace, and the characterestic costume he wore added much to the interest of his appearance. His dress consisted of a rich green velvet jacket, and breeches of the same; red striped waistcoat, and a large sash of the brightest red encircled his waist. He wore canvass stockings with sandals. His head was surmounted by a high Spanish hat, decorated with feathers and ribbons; round his neck hung a loose handkerchief, and he wore a profusion of jewellery; a cross suspended by a gold chain—several orders, watches, &c. His belt was well provided with pistols and stiletto's for he was always well prepared for self defence upon all occasions. Never was a more daring or reckless spirit than Allesandro Massaroni, who has been justly called the Robin Hood of Italy, innumerable and romantic

were his exploits, wonderful his hair breadth escapes, but they will be fully brought forward in the course of our tale. Chief of a lawless band infesting the mountains near Rome, his name spread terror throughout Italy. No place was secure from his emissaries; and so skilful were his arts of disguise, that he was often made the confidant of plots formed by his enemies to entrap him. But Massaroni was a lover of moral justice, and dispensed it strictly; if he made free with the rich, he was the almoner of the poor, and never did he resort to violence, but when a tempting booty and stout resistance stood in his way. Like the famous freebooter of merry England, he mixed mirth with his malefactions, and those who paid the dearest for his pranks were often the first to laugh at his humour. His manners were gentlemanly, and his character was full of chivalry and romance. To the ladies he was particularly gallant, and many were the fair damsels who had celebrated his exploits in their songs. A mystery hung over our hero's birth, which will be unravelled in the course of our tale. His mother was a young Florentine, who having fallen the victim of some one unknown, and who afterwards deserted her, had died of a broken heart; and the only family record which he possessed was her minature, which in his wildest moments of disorder and rapine, produced in him certain compunctious visitings of nature, that showed he was deserving of a better fate. Such was Allessandro Massaroni the brigand chief at the period from which we date the commencement of our tale.

"Well, Count Alberti," said the brigand smilingly, after a pause, "what think you now of the dog, eh? Ha, ha, ha! I must apologize for not having given you notice of my intended visit, but I was fearful that you might be induced to make too many friendly preparations for my reception, and I am a man who detests anything in the shape of ceremony or ostentation. Pray be seated, count, for I have much to say to you before we separate."

"Massaroni;" exclaimed Olympia, "I implore you to forbear and to retire from this place. Do not, oh, do not proceed to any desperate lengths."

"Sweet lady," replied the brigand, with the greatest politeness, "I request that you will not alarm yourself; Allessandro Massaroni never wages war against your lovely sex, neither does he shed blood unless he is compelled to do so in self-defence.

"What is it then you demand?" asked the count, sullenly.

"Justice to the fair Signora Olympia;" replied Massaroni. "I am fully aware of all your designs, Count Alberti, and I am resolved to defeat them. You have brought Olympia to shame and misery, and the only atonement you can make to her, is by requiting the love she bears you by making her your bride, which you have promised so solemnly to do. I demand that you fulfil that promise."

"You demand!" returned the count, with a look of scorn, and biting his lips with rage.

"Yes, I, Alessandro Massaroni, the brigand chief;" was the reply; "and perhaps I need not remind you that I am not used to disobedience?"

"And what are the terms you would exact?"

"That you bind yourself by a solemn oath and a no less solemn compact, to make Olympia your wife, within a period of three months from this date, or forfeit to her the sum of two hundred thousand ducats."

"Oh, no; not for the world!" exclaimed the lovely Olympia; "I should despise myself if I could ever give my sanction to such a course being forced upon the count under such circumstances."

"Be calm, I beg, signora," said the brigand, "and suffer me to proceed without interruption. "What say you to my demand, Count Alberti?"

"A very modest one, truly;" replied the young nobleman, with a half scornful laugh; "and what if I refuse?"

"Unless you are mad, you will not."

"What for?" asked Alberti.

"Because," replied Massaroni, "in the event of that I must insist upon the honour of your company with me to my mountain retreat, until you have had time to reflect more coolly and maturely upon my proposition."

"Indeed! then I tell you at once that neither will I enter into the compact you wish to intimidate me to, nor accept of your other polite invitation."

"We shall see, count;" said the brigand, walking to the window, which he opened, and applying a whistle to his lips, blew a signal, which was immediately answered.

The count was now seriously alarmed, and Olympia throwing herself at the brigand's feet, with the most impressive looks, supplicated his forbearance. Massaroni raised her with the utmost respect, and again desired her not to be alarmed.

"Massaroni," said the count, "I caution you to forbear; what would you do?"

"I have merely summoned a few of my trusty attendants, who generally accompany me on business;" replied our hero; "see, they are here."

Massaroni opened the door, and the room was immediately filled with his daring associates.

"You see, Count Alberti," remarked the brigand, "that I have not come unprepared to put my designs into execution. Are you now ready to comply with my demands?"

"By Heaven! this is past all human endurance;" said the young nobleman; "am I to be thus falsely entrapped?"

"No one seeks to entrap you;—did you nor solemnly promise to make Signora Olympia your wife?"

"I will not be forced into an unlawful fulfilment of that promise."

"Enough;" said Massaroni; "comrades then you know what to do."

"Oh, mercy, mercy, spare him!" shrieked Olympia, as the brigands gathered round the count. "What madness is this. Think you that I would ever consent to become his wife on such terms as those you propose? Or do you believe that the count would consider a compact obtained in such a manner as at all binding?"

"But Alessandro Massaroni would take care that he fulfilled it to the very letter," replied the brigand; "there is no escaping me, fair lady, and justice will sanction the course I am pursuing. Besides I cannot help thinking that the count would hereafter be ready to acknowledge the injustice of his present conduct, and have reason to thank me for having assisted him to so much happiness. Come, count, I once more urge you to yield; here are writing materials, and I have the document with me which only requires filling up, and your signature prefixed to it."

The count hesitated.

"Is there no way to escape?" he half muttered to himself.

"Not any," said Massaroni; "of that you may rest satisfied. Come, my time is precious; I can no longer delay."

"I yield;" said the count sullenly; "but bear witness, Olympia, that this compact is exacted from me by intimidation."

"Alas, dear Alberti," replied Olympia, "can I say more than I have, to show how I disapprove of it? But oh, if you had kept your promise, the solemn promise you made to me, this would never have happened."

"Come," said the brigand, "we waste time; here is the document; I will read it to you."

He did so; and it ran as follows:—

"I, Alberti, Count d'Amalfi, do solemnly pledge myself of my own free will, and according to a promise previously made, that three months after the present date, I will make Signora Olympia my lawful wife, or forfeit the sum of two hundred thousand ducats on demand."

With feelings of the greatest indignation and mortified pride, the count signed the compact, and then the brigand turning towards him, with an insinuating smile, said:

"I thank you, Count Alberti; you have acted on the wisest plan, depend upon it. I will keep this document in my possession, where it will be most secure, and fear not but I will be punctual in my demand on behalf of the signora, if you break the other part of the compact."

The count bit his lips with vexation, and could not return any answer; but he knew it would be useless to attempt to offer any resistance, and he was therefore forced to submit.

"And now for the oath;" said Massaroni, removing the cross which was suspended from his neck.

"What necessity is there for that?" demanded the count; "is not that compact sufficient?"

"No;" replied the brigand, "I must trouble you to take the oath I am about to administer to you."

The count knelt down, and taking the cross in his hand, took the solemn oath which Massaroni repeated to him.

"And, now are you satisfied?" demanded the count sternly.

"Perfectly so, count," was the answer; "but mark me, beware how you seek to deceive me or to act with injustice towards Signora Olympia, for my vengeance is as sure as it is terrible, and I take a particular interest in her fate. She loves you, and is worthy of a prince. Beauteous Olympia, I pray you pardon me if I have appeared bold or presumptuous in this proceeding. Farewell, and rest assured that Massaroni, the brigand chief, will keep careful watch over your safety. Come, count, as Olympia is not in a state of mind to hold further converse with you to-night, we will escort you part of the way home."

"Dear Alberti;" said Olympia, " will you not say to me one word of kindness at parting? You will not, you cannot blame me for what had taken place. See our little one awakes and smiles upon you; can you resist that invitation to affection?"

Moved by the earnestness of her manner, the count did for a moment relent, and returning her embrace, whispered the words, Good night, and suffered himself to be escorted by Massaroni and his comrades out of the house.

Olympia went to the door and followed their receding forms with her eyes as long as the light of the moon would admit her, and then returning into the room she threw herself upon a seat with mingled feelings of anguish, fear, and disappointment. The brigand chief and his daring comrades took the most unfrequented way, and having got to some distance from the residence of Olympia, Massaroni having again cautioned the count as to his behaviour towards that lovely woman, politely bade him good night, and suffered him to depart.

"Quick, comrades," said the chief, "we must reach our mountain retreat as soon as we can, for I have important business for to-morrow, and we shall require rest."

They hurried on their way, and proceeding in this manner for about half an hour, they were suddenly startled by hearing the heavy tramp of horses' hoofs behind them, and looking back, they beheld by the light of the moon, which was shining brilliantly in a clear sky, a number of persons galloping towards them.

"We are pursued," said the brigand ; "the count has given the alarm, and these are probably some of the soldiers of the Prince Bianchi, who is so anxious to apprehend me; we had better avoid a collision if possible, for they seem to outnumber us, and being mounted might prove more than a match for us. Quick, comrades, we will take this narrow defile, whither they cannot follow us, and by that means we may escape them."

They did, but when they reached the termination of the defile, they perceived that their pursuers were close upon them.

"Stand firm, comrades," said Massaroni; " there is nothing left for us but fighting, and it is strange to me indeed if we suffer ourselves to be shamefully defeated."

The brigands drew themselves up in a line, and with looks of determination awaited the approach of those who were in pursuit of them, and who they could now closely perceive were some of the soldiers of the Prince Bianchi, who had tried every stratagem to apprehend Massaroni, but had hitherto failed. Seeing the determined attitude of the brigands, the soldiers hesitated, and seemed to consult with each other; our hero took advantage of this, and darting forward with his daring band, they opened a heavy fire upon their adversaries, which had a most destructive effect, and threw them into confusion. The combat was a brief but a bloody one, both parties fighting with great bravery and resolution; but notwithstanding the soldiers far outnumbered them, the brigands were triumphant, and after several of their companions had been slain, the soldiers fled in all directions, amid the exulting shouts of their desperate opponents.

"Well done, my brave comrades;" said Massaroni; " the prince is once more disappointed, and he must await the gratification of his desire a little longer, though perhaps he may see me much sooner than he expected."

None of the brigands were killed, and only two or three of them slightly wounded, and they therefore pursued their way, and were soon far beyond the reach of danger.

CHAPTER III.

THE MOUNTAIN RETREAT OF THE BRIGANDS. —THE NIGHT WATCH.—THE BRIGANDS.— THE SURPRISE. —THE TRAVELLERS.

ABOUT a week has elapsed since the occurrance of the events recorded in the previous chapters, and the scene of action is changed. We must now direct the reader's imagination to the lofty summit of the Guadagnola, and wild and picturesque was the prospect commanded from it. In the distance was indistinctly seen through the grey mist of opening day, the Mediterranean, and on every side were large masses of rocks intermingled with trees, shrubs, and underwood. On the brink of a frightful precipice stood a large oak tree, whose thickly foliaged branches stretched far over the abyss. On a fragment of rock beneath the tree, reposed the mountain chief, fatigued after a weary night march from Velletri. One of the brigands was on guard, and by the side of Massaroni, anxiously watching him, was seated Maria Grazie, the brigand's wife. She was indeed a handsome woman, a beautiful brunette, whose piercing black eyes spoke the masculine daring of her spirit, and proved her a fit companion for the bold and reckless man with whom she had joined her fate. Her figure was tall and commanding, and distinguished by every grace which can render woman charming. The grey mists of night now gradually dispersed, and the first bright blush of morn appeared in the eastern horizon, gilding o'er the ocean and tinging the summit of the mountains with its golden beams, and directly afterwards the rest of the brigands might be seen slowly winding their way up the mountain's side, headed by Massaroni's daring lieutenant, Rubaldo, towards the spot where their chief was reposing.

"Comrades, comrades," said Rubaldo, when they were all assembled; "see, the morn is breaking, we must up and away."

The sound of his voice aroused Massaroni—he started up ; and seizing his hat and carbine, greeted his bold band most cordially, while their shouts of "Evviva Massaroni!" rent the air.

"My Maria," said the brigand chief, tenderly addressing his wife, "you have not slept, and how will you be able to bear the fatigue of the day ?"

"Think not of me, Allesandro," replied his devoted wife; "I have strength to endure fatigue, and I felt not inclined for repose ; but why have we made this night's march from Velletri ?"

"I will tell you," answered Massaroni; "for no doubt you and our comrades are anxious to know. Listen: The Neapolitan Ambassador leaves Rome this morning on a private visit to the Villa Covisma, where a celebrated cantatrice is suffering from the effects of a severe cold, caught while attending the rehearsal of a new opera, in which she had a secondary part to perform. His excellency, who shares in the national and general despair of Rome upon this occasion, carries with him a large share of that golden balsam which has

ever been found an infallible remedy for the hoarseness of a prima donna, and travels alone in his cabriolet upon this important mission. Rubaldo, you will receive his excellency at the foot of the mountain with a guard of honour ; accost him with the respect due to his exalted rank and inviolable character; suggest to him that the signora is rich enough already, and that we wish to become so. His lordship has too much good sense not to perceive immediately the justice of your observations."

"Ay, ay," replied Ribaldo, "I warrant we will convince him."

"This offers a far more profitable prospect than your late adventure with Olympia and Count Alberti Allesandro," said his wife. "I never could see the wisdom of that proceeding, where there was nothing to be gained."

"Say not so, Maria," returned Massaroni; "was there not that to be obtained which is far more gratifying to me than even the richest booty ; namely, justice to an injured woman ?"

"True, true," coincided Maria ; "but, think you, is it at all likely that the count will obey the compact he has entered into with you ?"

"If he be wise he will; if he do not he must take the consequences. He will find that Massaroni, the brigand chief, is a man of his word. You cannot wonder, my Maria, that I take so deep an interest in the fate of the fair Olympia when you remember her history, which in many respects is so similar to my own. But enough of this. I expect that this will be a rare day of business with me. A singular piece of information has already reached me with respect to the steward of the college of St. Arnulph : he is accustomed to traverse this mountain on his road to collect the rents of the college, in the disguise of a beggar, and, for better security on his return with the money, he goes nearly two leagues about, by a more frequented route, carrying generally from nine to ten thousand ducats, ingeniously concealed in—but it matters not, I have his secret, he will pass anon, and I have formed a mad scheme, which I have no doubt will lure the old fox this way home again. Away, Rubaldo, to meet the ambassador. Leave me to take care of the worthy steward—the rest vanish."

The brigands obeyed, and immediately disappeared, and Massaroni and his wife were left alone. Maria for a few moments seemed wrapped in thought, but suddenly turning to her husband, she said,—

"Allesandro, you have other reasons for leaving Velletri."

"Are not those I have given sufficient ?" asked Massaroni.

"For the band, perchance," replied the brigand's wife, "but not for Maria Grazie. The Prince Bianchi, your inveterate enemy, is at

Villa Rosa; you contemplate a descent upon the Palazzo, perhaps?"

"What?" exclaimed Massaroni, "risk the safety of the whole band for a few pictures? For rich and ostentatious as the old voluptuary may be, he is too wise to keep his treasure without the walls of Rome."

"But," observed Maria, "to seize his person and carry him off to the mountains."

"Ha! ha! ha!" laughed the brigand chief, "that would, indeed, be a rare trick, and might win us a heavy ransom; but that is not my motive for approaching so near the city. List ye, girl; what think you of laying hands upon a cardinal—a prince of the church!—and demanding, in lieu of ransom, an unconditional pardon and absolution from the Pope?"

"What?" said Maria, ironically, "to wipe out old sins and commence a new score upon a clear conscience?"

"Not so," returned Massaroni, in accents which were unusual to him; "no, Maria, I am weary of this watch-dog life. Another stroke of good fortune, and my booty will amount to a sufficient sum to enable me to quit the mountains, purchase a villa, and pass the rest of my days in Tuscany or Savoy, rich, noble, and as honest, per chance, as the prince who plunders his own subjects, or the marquis who draws his income from a faro table. If my deeds have been lawless, let the punishment fall upon his head who abandoned me, the victim of his lust, and her innocent offspring, to the scorn of the world and the temptations of despair. He! he!—they told me he was noble."

He took a miniature from his breast and gazed with feelings of the most powerful emotion upon it, as he ejaculated—

"My mother!—my poor injured mother!—why did thy dying lips conceal the villain's name? I would have carried thy corse into the banquet-hall, and placed it at the festive board beside. Ay, made his shuddering guests do honour to the lady of the mansion, fairer in her grave clothes than her seducer in his perfumed embroidery."

"Allesandro!" said his wife, in a voice of alarm.

"Ay! ay!" replied the brigand chief, arousing himself, and returning the miniature to his bosom—"'tis past! Some wine, Maria—my countess that shall be."

"I will be none," said Maria; "I am a brigand's daughter, I will die a brigand's wife!"

"A brigand's wife!" repeated Massaroni; "a brigand's widow rather, an' Prince Bianchi's pleasure be consulted. The wine, I say."

Maria went to the rock and quickly produced a flask. She filled a horn and presented it to her husband.

"To the health of his highness," said Massaroni, "his anxiety for my safe keeping demands my respect."

"Hush!" said Maria, cautiously, and looking down the mountain; "I hear a footstep."

Massaroni followed the direction of her eyes, and then observed—

"It is the worthy steward of St. Arnulph's, that I have been speaking of. Quick!—my peasant's hat and cloak."

Maria fetched them instantly, from beneath the shrubs behind the rock, where they had been concealed, and assisted her husband on with them.

"Away," said Massaroni, "and watch the issue of Rubaldo's expedition."

Maria obeyed, and Massaroni watched the approach of his intended victim.

"The dress—the staff," he said; "yes, all agrees with the description. Now to tickle this holy trout."

He took his seat at the rock, underneath the tree, and, taking a dice box from his pocket, began playing. Nicolo, the old steward, now arrived at the spot, disguised as a mendicant, and supporting himself on a long staff, and weary with his journey, he paused to rest himself a while.

"Six for thee, holy St. Eustace," said Massaroni.

At the sound of his voice the steward started, and gazed with astonishment upon him.

"Eh, what's that?" he exclaimed.

"And four for me," said the brigand, throwing again; "my old luck haunts me still."

Nicolo's amazement increased.

Why, what's that fellow about?" he said, "playing at dice by himself?"

"Five for thee, and three for me," continued Massaroni, not appearing to notice the steward. Cospetto!—were it not I played with a saint, I would swear the devil were in the dice."

Nicolo now advanced towards the brigand chief, and, addressing him in a kind voice, said—

"My son, thou seemest disturbed, what ails thee?"

"Silence, man," returned Massaroni; "don't speak to me just as I'm throwing:—ten for Saint Eustace, for me, nine!—Maladizzione!" he added, passionately, and throwing the dice aside.

"Swear not, my son," said Nicolo; "what has befallen thee?"

"Befallen me!" repeated Massaroni "why, Corpo di Bacco! here hath St. Eustace won a matter of two hundred ducats from me since sunrise."

The steward stared at him with astonishment.

"St. Eustace win of thee?" he cried,

"Ay," replied Massaroni," I play with him four or five times a day upon this stone, and out of three thousand ducats my father left me, two months ago, I have already lost more than half. Never, never, by any accident, do I rise a winner."

"The fellow's mad," thought Nicolo; "some broken gambler, whose wits have turned with a run of bad luck, and still raves of dice and ducats."

"I'll have one chance more for my money," said the brigand; "double or quits—come, friend, see fair play."

Nicolo thought it was advisable not to provoke him, and he therefore replied—

"Well, I wish you good fortune, friend."

"I'll throw first this time," said Massaroni, "seven—come, viva Maria, I have a chance for it now."

"Poor wretch," muttered Nicolo to himself; 'how earnestly he plays."

Massaroni threw again.

"Nine!" he cried; "look you there now," he said, "it's no use. Four hundred ducats gone in a morning."

"Well, well," returned the steward, "never mind; St. Eustace will not press for payment, I'll answer for him."

"Not press for payment," repeated Massaroni, "what mean you by that? It's a debt of honour, and shall be paid were it my last scudo."

"And to whom do you pay it, signor?" asked Nicolo—scarcely able to suppress a laugh; "to the hermits of Monterella, near his chapel."

"No, I do not," replied the brigand, "he sends me his receiver."

"His receiver!" repeated Nicolo, and he added aside—"he's stark mad, but very harmless seemingly. And who may that be, signor?" he said aloud.

"Some poor soul, to whom the money is an object," answered Massaroni; "thyself, for instance; for now I look at thee, thou seemest poor enough. I warrant me St. Eustace has sent thee for his winnings."

This aroused the cupidity of the steward.

"By the mass," he muttered to himself, "if I thought he had the money to pay, I would not be long answering the question."

"Here, my friend," said Massaroni, giving him a purse, "here are two hundred ducats; all I have about me at present. I must be thy debtor till sundown of the other half."

"How!"

"Oh, you need not trouble yourself to count it," said the brigand, as Nicolo with greedy and delighted eyes was examining the contents of the purse; "the sum is there; and the rest shall be on this stone before sunset. I'll pay honestly and promptly while my money lasts; when I am broken, there's an end on't."

With wonder and delight the old steward eyed the glittering gold, and the temptation was so strong within him to keep it, that he could not resist it.

"Well," said Massaroni, "why do you hold them as if they would bite you? They are your's, I say; I have lost them and paid them; and you shall find the other two hundred ducats here by sundown."

"Many thanks to you, noble signor," said Nicolo, pocketing the purse, "and send you better fortune another time."

"Enough, enough!" returned Massaroni, "begone."

The old steward, chuckling at his extraordinary good fortune, bowed obsequiously to Massaroni, and fearful that he might change his mind, he hastily departed.

"Ha, ha, ha!" laughed the brigand when he was gone; "the hook is in the old shark's gills, and if I land him not, I will turn Jesuit myself, and sell my carbine for a rosary."

He threw off his disguise, and at that moment Maria re-appeared hastily, and seemed to be much alarmed.

"How now, Maria?" demanded Massaroni, "why this haste? Has anything happened?"

"To arms! to arms!" said Maria; "Rubaldo is in danger. The story of the ambassador was but a snare—the soldiers are upon us—two of our men have fallen, the rest are hotly pursued!"

Massaroni placed his whistle to his lips and blew it loudly, and a number of his bold associates were quickly on the spot.

"My carbine—follow!" cried the brigand, rushing down the mountain followed by the whole of his comrades. Maria sprung upon a jutting rock, under the oak tree, grasping with her left hand one of the branches which overhung the precipice, and gazed anxiously down the mountain to watch the progress of her husband and his daring followers.

"To the right, to the right! through the thicket!" she shouted, "now they see them. San Antonio!"

And now the soldiers and the brigands were fiercely engaged, and the latter seemed determined to yield only with their lives. Massaroni fought desperately, and in a few moments several of the enemy, including their leader, had fallen by his hands. But for some time the battle continued with the greatest bravery and determination on both sides. At length, however, the soldiers began to waver, and Massaroni taking advantage of the circumstance, at the head of his daring band rushed boldly upon them, and they fled in all directions, in the greatest disorder.

"Viva Massaroni!" shouted Maria, as she rushed into the arms of her husband, who had not received the slightest injury in the battle, though several of his men had fallen, and others were severely wounded.

"Viva Massaroni!" was re-echoed by the brigands, as they gathered round their chief.

"Bravely done, my gallant comrades," said Massaroni; "the prince, I imagine, will not be much gratified at the result of this expedition. Wine, wine!—we need some refreshment after this morning's work."

The brigands retired into their mountain retreat, and wine being produced, they regaled themselves freely.

* * * *

We must now conduct the reader to the beautiful ruins of a Roman Temple, and from which was commanded a romantic view of the distant country. The sun was now riding majestically in a clear Italian sky, and nothing could be more lovely or tranquil than the hour. Suddenly two young men entered the ruins, who seemed fatigued, as if they had been walking a long way. One of them was a particularly handsome man, but with rather a melancholy expression of countenance, while that of his companion was gay and animated, and his whole demeanour was that of a person upon whom the cares of the world had never been suffered to make much impression.

"How beautifully the light falls upon this ruin," said the latter gentleman; "stay, stay, Florio, I must positively make another sketch."

"Be quick, then," said his companion. "We shall scarcely reach the Villa Rosa by dinner time, and you know the prince receives company this evening."

Theodore, for such was the name of the other, opened his portfolio, and stooping down on one knee, commenced his sketch, talking all the time.

"We have made a long round this day certainly," he said; "but then what glorious scenery have we gazed on! Vanity apart, I do almost believe that I want but a glimpse of that same banditti your Melina talks so much about, to make me a second Salvator."

"The anxiety that Melina will labour under if we are beyond our time," remarked Florio, "is an additional reason for my requesting dispatch. Though we are in no danger here. Massaroni has never yet thought proper to push his advanced posts so near to Rome."

"I should like to see that fellow amazingly," said Theodore; "he does things with a high hand by accounts, and his language and manners, they tell me, are far superior to those of his companions."

"He is the Robin Hood of Italy," said Florio, "taking from the rich to give to the poor—generous, daring, and fond of frolic—he has never been known to shed blood but in his own defence, and in addition to the usual anomalies which compose the character of an Italian brigand, he is renowned for a sense of justice, which makes him the umpire upon all occasions of dispute amongst the peasantry,

who seek him for council, assistance, and revenge."

"You have caught the enthusiasm of Melina," said Theodore, "respecting him. Egad! Florio, you are a lucky dog to have inspired the niece of Prince Bianchi with a tender passion. You, a poor devil of a painter, with nothing but your twelve hundred francs per annum to depend on!"

At this moment Maria entered the ruins, and seeing them, she drew aside to listen.

"Ah," said Florio, with a sigh, "I am indeed happy in having won the heart of the lovely Melina; but, alas! I am truly miserable when I remember the disparity of our stations, and reflect upon the improbability of the prince ever giving his consent to our union."

"Oh," said Theodore, "do not give way to despair, my dear fellow, he will not refuse anything to Melina, and you are so great a favourite with him since you restored the picture of the lady he keeps curtained up in the sala. But there, I have finished my sketch, and filled my book all but one leaf, for a group of brigands, which it seems I must paint from imagination."

Maria during this space had retired to apprize the brigands.

"Then, now you are ready to depart, I suppose," said Florio.

"Yes, onward as fast as you please," said Theodore.

They were about to depart, but they had only just emerged from the ruins, when Maria, Rubaldo, and two more brigands crossed their path, and prevented them from proceeding further.

"Stand!" commanded Rubaldo.

"Robbers," said Theodore aside to his companion, "I have my wish at any rate."

"What would you?" demanded Florio.

"Can't you guess?" replied Rubaldo, "money."

"They are but three," whispered Theodore, the woman counts for nothing; knock down that fellow."

Florio immediately made a rush at one of the brigands, Theodore seized the carbine of Rubaldo, and the other brigand and Maria drew forth their stilettos. The consequences must have been fatal to the two young men, but at that critical moment Massaroni, with two or three more of his band, rushed to the spot, and beating up the carbine of Rubaldo, who having overthrown Theodore, had levelled the deadly weapon at his head, exclaimed in a commanding voice—

"Hold, hold, Maria—Rubaldo! two unarmed travellers! Why the skirmish with the prince's troops has put your blood up with a vengeance. Pardon, young gentlemen, the hasty temper of my friends here: some of them have been roughly handled in a little ambuscade this morning, and it has disturbed the natural serenity of their dispositions."

"Why here is a thief of quality now!" said Theodore aside; "a gentlemanly high-wayman, who will hear reason I'll warrant. Your name, signor, is——"

"Massaroni!" replied the brigand chief.

"As I suspected;" remarked Theodore to his companion—"there's a head for a study!"

"Your custom," said Florio, addressing himself to Massaroni—"your custom is, I believe, to make prisoners and demand ransoms? What sum do you fix upon for our's?"

"You are artists, apparently?"

"Students of the French Academy," replied Theodore, "and as poor as Job."

"But you have friends, I dare say," said Massaroni, "who will not grudge two thousand scudi for you? In the meantime I must request your company to my retreat in the mountains, an excellent situation, and a salubrious air; we will find a peasant to convey your letter, by and by."

"They are the friends of Prince Bianchi," said Maria angrily, "two thousand scudi are insufficient."

"Friends of the prince!" said Massaroni; "nay, then, gentlemen, I must treble the sum at least. I could not so offend his highness as to take a common ransom for any one he honours with his friendship, particularly after the merry jest he played upon me this morning. You will desire the Prince Bianchi to send me immediately six thousand scudi."

"No, no ransom," cried Rubaldo; "the friends of the prince are our deadliest foes. They shall not live!"

As the fellow thus spoke he presented his carbine at Theodore, Maria standing near him with a drawn dagger, while the other brigands showed evident symptoms of revolt.

"Who says they shall not live?" demanded Massaroni authoritatively. "They shall not live who dare dispute the will of Massaroni! Rubaldo, I saved you this morning from a short shrift and a sharp axe in the Piazza del Popolo. Back! or I'll balance accounts by putting a brace of bullets through that ox head of thine! Back, all of ye, I say! Are ye mad, that you would make me bid you twice?"

Rubaldo and the others obeyed sullenly, and Theodore, who had recovered, said aside to Florio—

"There's a pose!—if he would but keep so for five minutes." He sketched hurriedly as he spoke, Massaroni not observing him.

"Massaroni, hear me," said Florio; "you have saved our lives, and we will be frank with you. The Prince Bianchi esteems me, and would not, under other circumstances, grudge the sum you demand for my liberty and that of my friends—but I know him well. On the receipt of my letter he would not send money but soldiers—"

"Indeed!" said Massaroni, scornfully—"the soldiers of Rome! Ha! ha! ha—he sent some this morning—they have galloped back to the eternal city faster and fewer than they left it. Say you this," he added sternly, "to intimidate Massaroni?"

"No," replied Florio, "for I know him brave, as I am told he is generous. You fix our ransom at six thousand scudi; let me go and seek them."

"Your companion then will remain our hostage?"

"No; his absence would awake the suspicion of the prince. Money, I repeat, you would receive none, and surely the murder of that youth would be a poor recompense for the loss of his ransom. Give us our liberty, and by that holy sign upon your breast, I swear to send a faithful servant to any spot you may appoint before midnight."

"And what security have I that you will keep faith with a brigand?" asked Massaroni.

"Let the belief in your generosity," replied Florio, "which has inspired so novel a proposition, be the pledge of the sincerity with which it is made. That and his oath, are all a poor foundling has to offer."

"A foundling," said Massaroni, starting; "abandoned by your parents! Enough, I will trust you; but mind, no messenger, no confidant: before midnight I will send these to Villa Rosa who shall receive the ransom or bring you back again."

"I consent;" said Florio.

"You are answerable for your friend?"

"With my life."

"Your name?" demanded Massaroni.

"Florio Clairville."

"You may depart;" said the brigand chief.

"Depart!" said Rubaldo hastily, and with a look of anger.

"Silence!" commanded Massaroni, sternly.

"I rely on your promise;" he said, addressing himself to Florio.

"Free!" said Theodore, closing his book, "you don't say so."

"To the mountains," commanded Massaroni, speaking to the brigands. Remember, young gentlemen, the vengeance of Massaroni is sweeping as it is sure. Adio."

With these words he departed, with his wife and his associates.

"Evviva Massaroni!" exclaimed Theodore; "what have you promised?"

"To pay six thousand scudi to his messenger before midnight, or return his captive;" replied Florio.

"Oh, the devil!" said Theodore, with a look of disappointment, "I thought he had let us off scot free; but no matter, we'll raise the sum, I'll be bound, and here's a portrait from the life, my boy, that, when transferred to canvas, will sell for half the money."

"You must to Rome instantly," said Florio. "We will find a horse at the next village. Go to our patrons, to the academy; I will account for your absence at the villa; I have fifteen hundred scudi there—the rest must be raised at any sacrifice. Hasten!"

With these words they hurried away.

CHAPTER IV.

THE STEWARD AND THE BRIGAND AGAIN. —THE NIGHT ATTACK.—A PLOT.

AT the hour stated, Massaroni, disguised in his peasant's dress, was once more seated in the same spot, and occupied in the same manner as Nicolo had seen him in the morning, and, punctual to the moment, the old man made his appearance.

"There he is, sure enough," he muttered to himself, "and at play still. Oh, if the saint has made good use of his time? I almost feared to return this way, for it is whispered that the brigands have been seen somewhere in this neighbourhood; not that my presence is promising enough to provoke their attack, but should they have heard of my errand——"

"Viva Maria!" cried Massaroni, at that moment, and seeming to be quite unconscious of the presence of the old steward. "Viva Maria! that was a noble cast! double or quits? Nay, now the tide is turning. I'll not throw at all. Double or quits be it."

"Signor Gamester," said Nicolo, advancing towards him, "I'm here according to——"

"Silence—silence, man," interrupted Massaroni, "I have a heavy stake upon the cast. Six for St. Eustace; now, now for it—twelve! Evviva! I have won!—I have won!"

"Won!" repeated Nicolo, staring at him with amazement.

"Ay," returned the brigand, "I have won ten thousand ducats!"

"Poor fool," thought the steward; "I give you joy, signor," he remarked, aloud, "you give St. Eustace long credit, of course."

"Long credit," replied Massaroni, "not an hour, he is as punctual in his payments as I am in mine."

"And in what coin, pray?"

"The coin of the realm to be sure," said the brigand, "honest gold and silver. Oh, 'tis all arranged; when I lose he sends his receiver, some poor devil who is glad of the money; when I win, he sends his paymaster, some rich old hunks or another, whose gold, hardly wrung from the needy, is weighing his s down to perdition."

"He is very mad indeed," muttered the old man to himself, "I don't like his looks."

"For instance, now," continued Massaroni, "this morning, when I lost, he threw in my way a beggarly-looking personage, who, I believe, had not a scudi about him; but this afternoon, like an honest saint as he is, he sends me the grasping steward of St. Arnulph's with upwards of nine thousand ducats to pay my fair winnings."

A strange misgiving came over the old man when Massaroni made these observations, and he sincerely wished that he was far away from the spot; for the eye of the brigand chief was fixed upon him in a peculiar manner, and there was a wicked smile upon his countenance that made Nicolo feel anything but comfortable.

"I don't understand, signor," he said, "I wish you good day—I——"

"Nay," interrupted Massaroni, detaining him, "Nay, nay, master steward, I think I speak plainly enough. Come, fulfil the intentions of the most holy and honourable St. Eustace. Nine thousand eight hundred ducats is my due; let us see how nearly you can make up the sum; I will not haggle with you for a few scudi."

Very disconcerted did the poor old steward appear as the brigand chief thus addressed him. He would have very much liked to have made his exit in an abrupt and unceremonious manner, but there was something about the appearance of the person, and in the expression of his countenance, which suggested to him that such a course might probably not be exactly safe, and he therefore adopted the more prudent plan of submission and conciliation, with a slight tincture of hypocracy to make up the mixture.

"Most worthy signor," he said, "I call St. Eustace to witness you are mistaken, I have not a scudi upon my person. Search me, noble signor, and satisfy yourself."

"You are very crafty, master steward," said Massaroni, with a laugh, "but I flatter myself that you cannot exactly deceive me. You say you have not a scudi upon your person, and I grant you that; but this staff——"

And as he said so, the brigand chief snatched the staff out of the old man's hands, at which he set up a hideous howl of—

"Murder! thieves!—I am ruined! Oh, had I but arms!"

"Oh," returned Massaroni, "if that is all you require—only arms, master steward, perchance I can furnish you with some."

As he said so, Massaroni applied his whistle to his lips, and quick at the signal his trusty band rushed to the spot, and the wretched old man dropped on his knees in terror and dismay.

"Mercy, mercy!" he ejaculated; "gentlemen, I—I—I believe you to be gentlemen; but—but—you are surely only joking."

"Exactly so," replied Massaroni, "we ar only joking, truly, and a very pleasant joke, on our side, I imagine it will turn out to be Comrades," he continued, turning to his band "give thanks to the worthy steward of St Arnulph's, who presents, in the name of his college, ten thousand ducats to the troops of Allesandro Massaroni."

"Massaroni!" re-echoed the terrified Nicolo; "oh, most noble signor, I crave your mercy."

"You have your request," replied the brigand chief, "and I the losings of St. Eustace."

As he spoke, he broke the staff across his knee, and out poured a goodly stream of glittering ducats, at sight of which the brigands laughed most lustily, whilst the poor steward groaned with agony.

"Most illustrious major domo," said Rubaldo, bowing with mock obsequiousness to the discomfited steward, "allow me to acknowledge, in the name of my friends, our just appreciation of your kindness and liberality. Be pleased to present our compliments to the college, and to inform the heads thereof that we shall be most happy to see you, their representative, similarly provided on any future occasion. Adio, Signor Nicolo."

"Diavolo!" exclaimed the bewildered steward, as he started to his feet, and without waiting to exchange another word, but glad to have escaped with his life, darted down the mountain's side, and was out of sight in a much shorter space of time than could have been imagined in a person at his advanced period of life.

Loud were the shouts of laughter that burst from the lawless and reckless band as the steward made his precipitate retreat, and Massaroni having placed himself in the centre of them, by a motion of his hand commanded silence, and then observed—

"Comrades, St. Eustace has been good to us on this occasion, and we must do full honour to the Saint's beneficence. Let the song and the flask freely circulate. Let us give way to sport and revelry till the bright sun declines behind the mountains, and then to business. And see our worthy peasant friends toil up the neighbouring rock to join us, and to swell our stock of fair Genevano's racy wine."

As he spoke, numerous peasants, male and female, toiling up the craggy path, approached the spot, each carrying with them a basket of provisions, which they distributed among the brigands, and received in return a no less supply of money and trinkets. The scene now became particularly animated. Some of the brigands chose from the bright-eyed maids partners, and entered into the merry mazes of the dance; others drank, sung, and laughed, in cheerful

and rollicksome revelry, and every person seemed bent upon enjoying himself in the best possible manner. At length the bell of a distant convent in the most solemn and impressive tones rung forth the Angelus, and the brigands and the peasants paused in their sports, and showed the utmost devotion to the sacred hour. The sun went down, and the revellers, almost exhausted with their sports, were about separating, when the sound of a postilion's whip was heard, and Rubaldo jumped upon the rock under the oak tree to reconnoitre.

"A carriage wheels round the mountain road," he said.

Massaroni rushed up to the spot, and looked eagerly down the mountain.

"Ah," he said, "it is a noble-looking carriage, and but badly attended. There is some rare booty in the very appearance. Load, load, comrades."

The brigands obeyed the order on the instant, and Massaroni seized his carbine, which he had placed against the side of a rock, whilst his wife hastily loaded his pistols and placed them in his belt.

"They come, they come," said Massaroni, in an undertone, as the carriage wheels were heard slowly ascending the difficult path; "away with ye," he added, addressing himself to the peasants, "to your dwellings, all of ye. Comrades, conceal yourselves."

Quick in obedience to those commands, the peasants stole cautiously away, and the brigand chief and his daring associates crouched behind the rocks and shrubs in every direction, with their carbines levelled, to await the arrival of the traveller or travellers. They were not long kept in suspense. The carriage arrived at the spot, and the gentleman whom it contained ordered the postilion to stop, and immediately afterwards alighted himself. He was a very handsome man, and of commanding figure, while the splendour of his dress and his dignified bearing showed him to be a man of the noblest station. He folded his hands, and gazed with enthusiastic admiration upon the wild and diversified prospect commanded from the summit of that majestic mountain.

"Now," he soliloquized, "if I had but time to spare from the festivities of the Villa Rosa, how could I linger to contemplate this delightful scene. Oh, Italy, dear Italy, land of my birth, thou art indeed the fairest of——."

"Welcome, Monsignore!" said Massaroni, suddenly appearing before him, and gracefully bowing as he spoke. The traveller started. "Be not alarmed, signor," said the brigand chief; "there is no danger to be apprehended, if you do not forget the courtesy due from one gentleman to another. I will trouble you to favour me with your name?"

"And pray who are you that thus rather rudely demands it?" asked the traveller.

"That you shall know," returned Massaroni, "when you have replied to my question."

"Well, it is rather an odd question to put to a stranger," said the traveller with a smile, "but as you seem, signor, to be something of an eccentric, I will answer you candidly. I am the Count di Strozzi, colonel in the Austrian service."

"Very good. And the place of your present destination?"

"The Villa Rosa, to join the festivities given by his highness the Prince Bianchi, in honour of his niece's, the fair Melina's, birthday."

"Aye, a lovely maiden, I have been told," said the brigand. "Methinks I will pay my respects to the lady and her august uncle myself; but as my equipage is not ready, I will take the liberty of borrowing your's, count."

"How!" exclaimed that nobleman, placing his hand upon the hilt of his sword.

"Nay, signor," said Massaroni, with the utmost coolness and *sang froid*, "you cannot surely have any objection to so reasonable a request? But I have a further favour to beg, and that is, that you permit me to assume your dress and your name for a short time, on condition, that I mitigate the sum that I should otherwise have demanded for your ransom."

"Ransom!" exclaimed the count, starting and looking alarmed. "You are then——"

"Allesandro Massaroni, the brigand chief, and these, signor, are my faithful attendants, who are as anxious as myself to pay their dutiful respects to you."

As Massaroni thus spoke, he beckoned to his comrades, and they came forward from the different places where they had been concealed, and surrounded the astonished and alarmed count and his carriage.

"Massaroni," he said, "forbear! You would not take my life?"

"No," replied the brigand; "Allesandro Massaroni is no common cut-throat; but he feels inclined for a simple joke whenever the opportunity is afforded him. I am aware that his Highness the Prince Bianchi has a particular wish to see me, and as you have arrived so opportunely, and moreover, as I have a little business at Villa Rosa, I will do myself the honour of gratifying his wish this very evening. I am sorry to deprive your lordship of the pleasure you anticipated, but really I cannot any longer delay paying my respects to his highness, particularly after the marked intimation of the friendship and esteem he bears towards me, which I heard this morning."

"Hear me, Massaroni," said the count. "All that I have at present in my possession I will freely give you, and any ransom you may think proper to demand, but I must be allowed to proceed on my journey."

"I am sorry to be compelled to dissent from so very courteous a gentleman," said Massaroni; "but really I must insist that you tarry here in my mountain retreat for a short time, while I repair to Villa Rosa, where, as Count di Strozzi, I no doubt shall be received with all due honour and respect."

"Diavolo!" cried the count; "that my unlucky stars should have guided me hither." Will nothing prevail upon you, Massaroni?"

"You have heard my determination, and you must submit to it. Come, my lord count, allow me to conduct you to a place where we may perform our toilette, and then, having partaken of a glass of wine together, we must part company for a few hours. My faithful adherents will see to the security of your carriage. Come, count, come!"

Thus saying, the brigand chief took the arm of the astonished and bewildered Count di Strozzi with the utmost politeness, and led him from the spot, followed by a portion of his daring band.

CHAPTER V:

THE FESTIVAL AT VILLA ROSA.—THE REMORSE OF CONSCIENCE.—THE VOLUPTUARY.—THE PORTRAIT.—THE DISCOVERY.—THE ESCAPE.

ALL was gaiety at the Villa Rosa, where the Prince Bianchi was at present staying, for it was the anniversary of the birth-day of his niece Melina. And in truth Melina was a most lovely maiden; one who was formed in every way to captivate, and whose amiable manners not only won for her the admiration but the esteem of all. She was not more than eighteen, and had for more than four years been left an orphan, under the protection of the prince, her uncle, from whom she experienced the affectionate care and attention of a parent. Prince Bianchi was a man who felt the full dignity of his exalted station, and looked upon his inferiors with superlative contempt; but, although haughty, tyrannical, and withal a voluptuary from his earliest youth, he was not without some redeeming qualities. His general demeanour was gay and volatile, but he had his moments of sadness, his fits of gloom, and at those times every person was afraid to approach him. In the sala of Villa Rosa was a picture which was always kept concealed by a red curtain, and in respect to which much interest and curiosity was excited. It was the portrait of a lady eminently beautiful, and before this the prince had more than once been surprised, kneeling and evidently absorbed in the deepest anguish, but no one had been able to fathom the particulars of the history connected with that painting. Possessing such charms as Melina did it is natural to expect that she had numerous suitors as well as admirers, and amongst the former was the young Count Alberti D'Amalfi, whom we have introduced in a previous chapter, and of whom the Prince Bianchi approved, and hoped to see the day when he should become the husband of his niece. But did Melina love him?—Oh, no, she could admire many of the graces and accomplishments of his mind, but at the same time she was no stranger to his vices; she had heard of his intrigue with the unfortunate Olympia, and she despised and hated him for it, and was resolved that, whatever might be the consequences, nothing should ever induce her to become his bride. Moreover she loved the young painter, Florio Clairville, whose virtues presented such a glowing contrast to the vices of Count Alberti. We must now conduct the reader to the terrace of Villa Rosa, from which was commanded one of the most magnificent views that the imagination could form. Old Nicolo, the steward, who had been invited to the festival, was standing in company of Prince Bianchi, to whom he had been relating in the most doleful terms his adventure with the brigand chief; to which his highness listened with much delight, and, much to the horror and discomfiture of the steward, laughed most heartily.

"Ha! ha! ha!" laughed the prince, when he had concluded, "of all the tricks I ever heard, this is the most amusing."

"Your highness will pardon me," observed Nicolo, gravely, "but really I am unable to perceive the joke."

"Perceive the joke," returned Prince Bianchi, "you never could see a joke in your life, Nicolo; all my best things are thrown away upon you. I tell you it's capital—give you two hundred ducats at daybreak to receive ten thousand by noon! By the dome of St. Peter's, but all the Jews in Rome ought to worship him, for raising the rate of usance; and a shy old fox like you to be so entrapped!"

"But, monsignore," said the steward, "this is no answer to my complaint; will you see justice done to the college or not?"

"Cospetto! master steward," returned the prince, "what would you have me do? I can't hang the fellow till I catch him. I'm sure I take trouble enough to do it; I threw out a bait for him this morning, but he was too much bent upon a game at dice with St. Eustace to bite at it, but we peppered a few of his people though."

"But, excellenza!" said Nicolo.

"But, master steward," interrupted the prince, "as you have the honour of a personal acquaintance with this facetious gentleman, you will do me the favour to return this evening after dusk and conduct a large detachment of the soldiers to the place of your encounter. I will lose no time in striving to take the

rascal living. I am sorry to disappoint the good people of Rome of the spectacle of his execution, but if my soldiery can get within gun shot, they shall cut the matter as short as possible. Fabio!" he added, addressing himself to a servant who was in waiting.

"Yes, excellenza," replied that individual.

"A glass of tokay, for master steward," said the prince. Fabio's countenance became overcast as he faltered out—

"Of—of tokay, excellenza?"

"Of tokay—aye, of the pannier that came from Rome this morning, that you brought yourself—or have my orders been neglected?"

"No, excellenza," answered Fabio.

"Then why stand you there?" demanded his highness. "Bring me the pannier here immediately; let me see if——"

"Pardon, excellenza," interrupted Fabio, in a tremulous voice, "I can bring you the pannier certainly, if you please, but as for the wine—"

"The wine, what of the wine, villain?"

"It's all drunk, your highness."

"Drunk!" cried the prince, "who should dare to drink my choice tokay?"

"Those who dare do anything, excellenza," replied Fabio.

"Explain, scoundrel!"

"I—I—," stammered Fabio, "put the wine up myself, as your highness desired, and had been half way to the villa, when the day being hot, I sat down under a tree by the road side to rest a minute, and somehow I fell asleep, and——"

"Go on, sirrah!" passionately commanded the prince. "And when I awoke," continued Fabio, "I saw twelve brigands, armed to the teeth; each with a bottle of your highness's tokay, which they drained to the health of your highness, and bade me carry the empty pannier back, with Massaroni's duty to your highness."

"Malpesta! maladizzione!" angrily cried the prince, "drink my tokay!"

"Ha! ha! ha!" laughed the steward; "I crave pardon, excellenza, but that is a capital joke—I do see that."

"Oh, you do see that?" returned the prince; "a pannier of the first tokay in the world!—the present of his highness!—you call that a joke, eh? "Begone, fellow," he said, speaking to Fabio, "get out of my sight, scoundrel. I'll send a messenger to Rome to double the number of troops—to surround Guadagnola— to —to— don't stand grinning there, you old tottering mumskull! Get to your college, sir, and ask leave to return this evening, and guide the soldiers to the haunt of this audacious ruffian, who robs the church and state. laughs at the laws of the holy city, and——"

"And," added Nicolo, as he retired, "drinks

its governor's tokay! Ha! ha! I'm gone, excellenza."

"Drinks my tokay!" repeated the prince; "by the body of Bacchus——"

At that moment a fair hand was laid upon his shoulder, and looking up he beheld the fair Melina standing by his side.

"My dear uncle," she said, "you seem ruffled."

"Ruffled!" he repeated; "I'm rifled,

THE BRIGAND'S WIFE.

robbed, plundered, and insulted; but that villain Massaroni shall suffer for it."

"Massaroni!"

"Yes," replied the prince, "your heroical robber. The polite assassin, you and your lady friends are so enchanted with, who takes your snuff-box with the same air he would beg a pinch from it; pockets your watch with as many excuses as if he only stopped to ask you what o'clock it was, and cuts a throat in so gentlemanly a manner, that the most fastidious traveller was never heard to complain of it afterwards."

"My uncle," said Melina, "I am sure I

never defended the lawless acts of the brigand chief, or denied the necessity of repressing them; but I have more than once had occasion to admire his generosity, his unequalled contempt of danger, and the flashes of honourable and high feeling which occasionally gleam through the cloud of crime around him. Now, my dear uncle, remember his behaviour to the poor peasant girl, Ottavia. Did he not seize the lordly seducer, and carry him up into the mountains, compel him to marry her, and settle the heavy ransom he demanded upon the mother and child he would so barbarously have abandoned? And then, did he not—what is the matter, sir?"

The prince evinced the greatest possible emotion, and turning away, he ejaculated—

"Nothing, nothing; this cursed gout—an ugly twinge."

"Surely you, sir," continued Melina, "whose kind and noble spirit must rise indignantly against the wanton liberties of the heartless seducer, whose cheek I have seen grow pale when—dear uncle, you are in pain, much pain!"

"In torture!" said the prince, endeavouring to conceal the emotion which her observations excited in his breast; "don't talk to me, girl! I can't bear it! you know I can't, and yet there you stand, chatter, chatter, chatter, while you see me writhing under this infernal malady. Why do you look at me," he added wildly, "as if you doubted my words? The pain is here, in my hand, I tell you! It's true:—it goes to my heart, like a knife—like a knife! But you care not—you see me suffer, and add to my pangs by taunts and sarcasms!"

"I—I taunt you, sir?"

"Ha! ha!" laughed the prince, in the same wild strain; "threaten him, compel him to marry her at the dagger's point! What, could the stiletto of an assassin strike terror into the heart of one who had seen unmoved the victim of his treachery grovelling at his feet, with clasped hands and streaming eyes, imploring death in lieu of desertion? Was the pointed knife sharper than her last cry, when he broke from her grasp, and saw the long dark hair he had doated on scattered by handsful to the winds of Heaven. that howled after him in scorn? If he could bear that——"

"Dear sir," said the astonished and horrified Melina, "I beseech you to be calm."

"Thirty years!—thirty years!" continued the prince, not seeming to notice her; "thirty years, and the thing is as strong as ever. Must I go down to the grave with the barb in my heart? Penance can't pluck it out, nor purchased pardon deaden the throb."

Overcome by the power of his feelings, he sunk in a chair, and the beauteous Melina, kneeling affectionately by his side, said in her most tender accents—

"What words are these—uncle, dear uncle?"

The prince aroused himself.

"Melina, good girl," he said; "psha! I grow old—old and feeble; I cannot bear pain; don't mind my pettish words—dry your eyes, silly girl; when this tyrant gout afflicts me, I do say harsh things, but I don't mean them, child;—I've a birthday present for you. Baubles, mere baubles, but girls are pleased with them; and egad! I think they'd hit the taste of your friend Massaroni, if he could get a peep at them: but I have some bracelets of another description for him; ha! ha! I'm easy now, and can laugh again; but it is plaguy sharp while it lasts, wench, I can promise you. Ha! ha! ha!"

So saying, with a forced laugh, he quitted her.

"My poor uncle," said Melina, when he was gone, "I never saw him so moved before; but what is this he has given me? Bracelets, did he say? What superb brilliants! Dear, kind old man! he lavishes a fortune on me. What a pity, so good, so generous a creature could ever know a moment's pain; I'm sure he cannot deserve to suffer—I must run after him and give him a hundred kisses for his splendid present."

She turned round to depart, and beheld Florio by her side.

"A hundred kisses, Melina," he said; "the present must be splendid indeed that deserves so rich an acknowledgment."

"Ah, Florio," said the damsel, blushing, "you have come, then; I began to think that you had forgotten it was my birthday."

"Theodore would make so many sketches," replied Florio, "I threatened at last to leave him on the road."

"And have you done so, as he is not with you?" asked Melina.

"No; he has ridden to Rome on some business, but will return shortly."

"See, this is the present I spoke of," said Melina, showing him the jewels.

"Magnificent indeed!" he remarked.

"With this, and the necklace my mother gave me, I shall look as fine as the lady in the picture that Theodore calls the queen of diamonds: by the bye, Florio, you promised to tell me why there is always a curtain drawn before that portrait."

"Oh, 'tis a common custom so to preserve choice paintings: there is a Guido, you know, in the Farnese Palace, that——"

"Nay, nay," interrupted Melina, "you said there was a story about it; and I remember once I saw my uncle looking at it, and when he saw me he dragged back the curtain, and was so agitated, so furious."

"Why then," said Florio, after some hesitation, "I have heard, but I know not how truly, that it is the portrait of a young Florentine peasant, to whom the prince was much attached: some circumstances prevented their union, and she died, I believe—but the rumour is so vague: however, he certainly was fond of her, for when I restored the parts which the damp had injured, he desired I would alter the dress from the simple costume of Florence to the richest robes and ornaments that a princess could wear. 'Such,' he added, with a deep groan, 'such should have been her rank, and even as such she shall now be painted.'"

"Poor uncle!" said Melina, "it is, no doubt, her loss that preys so heavily at times upon his spirits. But I must go and thank him for this new proof of his kindness—will you come with me?"

"I'll follow you upon the instant," said Florio, pressing her hand to his lips, and she immediately departed.

"I am all anxiety for the return of Theodore," said Florio, when she was gone; "should he not be able to raise the sum, what other resource is there left? The governor—I dare not trust him—he would laugh my scruples to scorn—and the forfeit of my word might bring destruction on his head and my beloved Melina. 'The vengeance of Massaroni is sweeping as it is sure!' Those were his parting words."

The guests approach; all was festivity in the villa; the soft strains of music were heard; while here and there, in the beautiful grounds which surrounded it, numerous persons might be seen merrily and gracefully, "treading the mazy windings of the fantastic dance." Nothing could be more gay and animated than the joyous scene, and everything betokened a delightful day; the prince had been most lavish in the expenses; magnificent and extensive were the preparations that had been made, and the noble guests, as they thronged to the villa, showed by their countenances that they were determined to do full honour to the auspicious occasion. While Florio stood still, meditating in what way it would be possible for him to raise the ransom demanded, the sound of carriage wheels smote his ears.

"The guests still continue to arrive," he said; "if amongst them I could find a friend——"

He was interrupted by the entrance of a nobleman, magnificently attired in full dress, and preceded by three servants. His figure was commanding, his deportment graceful, and his whole appearance seemed to bespeak an individual of the most eminent distinction and rank in society.

"Whom shall I have the honour to announce, signor?" said one of the servants, bowing obsequiously.

"The Count di Strozzi," answered the visitor, and he crossed over to the spot where Florio was standing.

"The Count di Strozzi!" said the young painter, starting at the sound of the voice; "Heavens!" he added, "can I believe my sight?"

"And why not, my young Raphael?" returned the brigand chief, for he it was, as the reader will doubtless have guessed. "I said I would send those, ere midnight, who should receive your ransom, or take you back again. I know not any of my band so fit to be trusted as myself."

"But do you know where you are?" asked Florio.

"Cospetto!" replied Massaroni; "to be sur. I do. In the Villa Rosa, the property of his highness Prince Bianchi, the governor of Rome, a gay, noble-hearted old gentleman, whom I respect sincerely, notwithstanding his rigorous measures against me—he would hang me, if he could catch me, it is his duty to do so—I do not quarrel with him for that—but I do not choose to be hanged, if I can help it, and that vexes him, and makes him say sometimes harsh things of me, I am told but that is no reason why I should not pay him a visit of ceremony."

"I cannot conquer my astonishment!" said Florio.

"Corpo di me!" ejaculated the brigand, looking around him; "but he is too well lodged here. The governor!—I have never before examined his villa so closely."

"Fly, wretched man," said Florio, anxiously, "I save your life, and cannot see you thus madly walk into the very mouth of destruction. Should the prince recognise you—"

"He!—fear nothing!—we have never yet met."

"But he receives friends to-night, and amongst them—"

"Ha! ha! ha!" laughingly interrupted Massaroni. "You do me the honour to suppose I now and then see good company. I will risk the meeting of a few old acquaintances—they will not dream of seeing me here, and you and your friend, I know, will not betray me."

"Massaroni!" eagerly demanded Florio, "mean you wrong or violence to the prince, or his niece Melina? If so, not e'en my oath—"

"Be satisfied," answered the brigand; "unless you fail in your promise, I am here only as Count di Strozzi's Colonel in the Austrian service, and this day arrived at Rome from Naples on my way back to Milan."

He walked boldly forward, and in his comportment, acted the part of the Count di Strozzi with the ease and gentlemanly bearing of one born to the high estate he then but temporarily filled. He was formally introduced to the Prince Bianchi, and the other noble guests who had arrived before him, and was cordially welcomed, and received the homage due to the exalted office he then held. During the entertainment, he made himself so agreeable and prominent, by his songs and anecdotes, that he soon became the general favourite of the assembly, especially with the ladies who were struck with his manly beauty, and regularly chiselled features. The prince, too, seemed much attached to his new guest, and could not account for a feeling which caused him to feel more than common friendship towards the young count. He said—

" Are you an Austrian, count ?"

" No," replied Massaroni; " although I wear the uniform of the Austrian arms, I am a native of Florence, and have but recently adopted the insignia of the Austrians."

The prince seemed evidently moved at the mention of his being a Florentine, and appeared in deep thought, and seemed to be writhing under some mental affliction. Massaroni, seeing that the prince's mind was abstracted, turned his attention to the ladies, and was not long before he engaged them in merry chat, which continued for some time. The voices of his new guest and the ladies, roused the prince from his lethargy. Soon as an opportunity occurred, he again commenced conversing with Massaroni, by asking him the state of the country through which he had passed, and if he had seen anything of the brigands he was so anxious to bring to execution. He said that the country seemed tranquil at present, but he feared that, unless relief were granted to the peasants of some of the districts, there would be a revolt.

" It shall be prevented," said the prince; ' I will send one of our people to the authorities at —— with two thousand ducats to relieve their immediate wants."

" Excellenza," said Massaroni, " I will, with your permission, save you the inconvenience, by carrying it myself to its destination."

" I am much beholden to you," said the prince, " and shall esteem it a favour."

The money was sent for, and carefully locked in carpet bags, for the greater convenience of the count; after which, the assembled guests began to be merry again, and desired Massaroni to oblige them by singing a Florentine song, as he was a native of that country. He complied, by singing a pathetic song in tones that would outrival the nightingale. He had not proceeded far before the prince seemed paralyzed, and endeavoured to say something, but was unable to articulate a syllable. He was led from the room uttering incoherent sentences, amongst which might be heard, " The same words—the same subject—the same time—all corresponds; but yet, it cannot be—it cannot be. The eyes, too, bear such a semblance. Thirty years have now elapsed—it cannot be." He remained quiet for a few minutes, and then

said, " Oh, this gout will drive me mad some day. I say very foolish things when it attacks me severely; but no one takes notice of them." He was brought into the banquet-hall again, and apologised for his hasty departure to those who were near him, requesting them to convey his apology from one to the other till each had received it. From the time he returned till the party were about to separate, he scarcely once took his eyes off Massaroni. The time was drawing on apace for the party to separate, therefore Massaroni sought out the young painter, Theodore, who was to pay him the ransom. The object of his search was soon discovered, and the amount settled for. During the lapse of time that had taken place since the brigand's arrival, he had been enabled to make up the amount. As soon as he had transacted his business with the artist, he ordered his carriage to be drawn round to the entrance, while he returned to the hall, to bid adieu to the assembled guests, who had done him so much honour during his brief sojourn amongst them. While he was speaking to the prince, two gentlemen might be observed in close converse together, and who scrutinised the brigand narrowly.

" It is he," said one, " I know him by his voice. I thought so when I first entered, but was afraid to accuse the prince of entertaining the greatest desperado in Italy. He robbed me a month ago, and if I mistake not, the person who now assumes the name of the Count di Strozzi, is the same person."

" That cannot be," said the other, " for I saw him arrive in his carriage from the direct Naples road, and moreover, he was attended by servants in livery."

" Very true," rejoined the other, " but he might have robbed the Count di Strozzi, and taken possession of his carriage and clothes, and the clothes of his servants. He must not be permitted to pass from this hall before the prince is made acquainted of the suspicions that are entertained of his favourite guest. You endeavour to engage him in conversation when he leaves the prince, while I communicate my doubts."

They agreed to adopt this method, and immediately Massaroni turned from the prince, one of the gentlemen crossed the path of the brigand chief, and endeavoured to keep him in conversation; but suspecting that all was not right, he moved, while speaking, as near to the door as possible. The countenance of the prince underwent various changes during the time the communication was being made, and he made several impatient gestures, indicative of a wish to end the communication, in order that he might act immediately. When he saw that the supposed count had left the hall, he summoned a few of his most intimate friends together, and requested them to accompany him to the carriage that was in waiting, and assist him in ascertaining the truth or falsehood of the statement he had recieved, which was conveyed to them as briefly as possible. He began to fear that he should lose the money that he intended for the relief of his peasants, and not only that, he would be made the laughing-stock of the world, which was, to the feelings of the governor of Rome, more full of horrors than anything that had as yet entered his imagination.

"Come, my friends," he said, "do not delay a moment longer; if it be the brigand in disguise, we will give the people of Rome a treat in witnessing his speedy execution."

Melina, who had been an anxious listener to all that had passed, cried—

"No, no, uncle; you will not disgrace your rank by committing yourself so far; he is a count, and deserving of the esteem you have been pleased to honour him with this evening; if you listen to these ungrounded assertions, you will tarnish your name, and probably the reputation of an innocent nobleman."

"Go to, girl. It is my bounden duty to be convinced of his innocence, or how far the assertions of my friends are true or without foundation."

He urged his adherents to prepare themselves for an encounter, if it should be the brigand. In the meantime, Melina made her way to the entrance of the Villa Rosa, where the carriages of her uncle's guests were ranged, and in a few minutes found the one in which the count had just entered. He knew her, and called her by name, although it was rather dark.

"Flee." she said, "you are suspected of being the brigand chief, Massaroni, and my uncle, with a large force, is even now on the way to your carriage. If you be the Count di Strozzi, do not suffer the degradation of being put into confinement for a single hour; and if you be the brigand, flee, and get safe to your retreat in the mountain."

She was not able to say more before the Prince Bianchi and his party arrived. The coachman, in accordance with previous instructions, drove through the party who accompanied the prince, unknown; as the carriage passed the group, the brigand threw out a card, on which was written,—"Massaroni's compliments to the Prince Bianchi, and returns thanks for the entertainment afforded him during the evening." The card was picked up by one of the party, but there was not sufficient light to read it. A light was procured, and it was handed to the prince, who grew furious at the trick that had been played upon him. He ordered instant pursuit to be set on foot by an armed body of soldiers, and wended his way back to the mansion. He was accompanied by Melina, who endeavoured all in her power to soothe him, but in vain. He raved at her as

being the means of the brigand's escape, and darted passionately out of the room, and left her to herself. For a few minutes after he was gone Melina stood absorbed in agony of grief, and her mind completely bewildered and distracted by the extraordinary and exciting events of the night. She felt her uncle's anger keenly, but still, in spite of his lawless character, she could not but sympathize with Massaroni, and felt satisfied at his escape from an untimely and fearful death. The personal appearance of the brigand chief, and his accomplished manners, had made a deep impresion upon her, and she felt a more than ordinary interest in his fate.

"What a pity," she sighed, "that so bright a mind should be stained with crime, and become a curse to that society it is so well formed to ornament and improve. Oh, destiny, how inexplicable are thy decrees. What cruel fate has placed this man in the degrading situation he now occupies? Surely he has been precipitated into it by no vicious propensities of his own."

She was surprised to find herself dilating upon such a theme, and yet she wished not to destroy the sympathy which Massaroni had excited in her breast. With melancholy feelings she entered her chamber, and before she retired to rest she knelt down and invoked a blessing upon the head of the prince her uncle, and fervently besought heaven to preserve the life of the brigand chief, and to recal him from his present lawless and desperate pursuits. When Prince Bianchi retired to his chamber, he paced the room for some time, giving vent to his feelings of rage and disappointment at the escape of Massaroni.

"To be so duped," he cried—" to absolutely become the entertainer of the rascal I have so long been anxious to bring to the scaffold, or to shoot down like a dog; to allow myself to bandy jokes with and to flatter him; nay, more, to permit him to plunder me of no less a sum than two thousand ducati on the very night when I thought I had arranged my plans so nicely to entrap him. Malpesta maladizione! I, the Prince Bianchi, the governor of Rome, shall be brought into contempt!—I shall be laughed at!—I can never show my head in society again. But, by the dome of St. Peter's, I will though, and my apperance shall be accompanied by the head of that same daring brigand chief;—And yet —what means this sickly sensation?—There was an expression in Massaroni's countenance when he stated he was a native of Florence, that struck a pang to my heart;—his features, too, the eyes especially—psha! I am growing childish! Away with these gloomy thoughts! Years ought to have buried them in oblivion. Valencia!—that name! Oh, God—oh, God— there is a time when Thou makest Thy creatures think, in spite of all their efforts to the contrary. Valencia!—lovely, innocent, gentle Valentia! Beauteous, confiding Zitella, too, where art thou?—Where is that innocent babe, the offspring of our illicit intercourse, whom I confided to—Jesu Maria! what distracting thoughts are these that now scorch and madden my brain?—Let me rush away from them—for they stalk before my imagination like so many grim and ghastly spectres, howling hideous tales in mine ears, and bidding me despair. Within there—Wine! wine! to drown these maddening thoughts. Slaves! do you not hear me, or dare you disobey me?"

Wildly the wretched man—wretched, in the midst of all the superabundance of wealth and splendour—looked around him, and then sunk exhausted in a chair, and buried his face in his hands.

"Oh, conscience! conscience! What a terrible monitor art thou!

For several minutes the wretched prince remained in a state of apathy; but anon strange ideas and forms flitted before his imagination, and riveted his whole attention. Was he asleep or waking?—Whether or not, those scenes and forms appeared as palpable before his eyes as if they were reality. The past, the guilty past, was re-enacted to his tortured vision, and prominent amongst those forms that were depicted to his imagination, was that of the Brigand Chief Massaroni. He tried to arouse himself from the spell that enchained his faculties, but could not. And now what voice is that which salutes his ear, breathing tones so melancholy, so impressive, so plaintive, and unearthly? What is the melody of that song? What are the words? God! they are the same! The perspiration rushed from every pore, the veins upon his temple swelled to bursting, and yet he was unable to move from the chair on which he was seated; he was fixed, paralyzed, rivetted, as if he had been a statue! He tried to place his fingers in his ears to shut out the words of that song he had sung many, many years ago; he endeavoured to drown the heavenly voice—the well-remembered voice which now sung them, but as well might he have endeavoured to stop the progress of the mighty ocean, or command the tempest to cease in its fury. The ballad was a simple one, and beautifully impressive in its effects. These were the words that vibrated on the ears of the prince:—

Maiden of Florence, oh! listen to me,
  Nor think that I seek thy fond heart to en-
    snare;
If e'er I deceive thee, accurs'd may I be,
  And my bosom be plunged in the darkest
    despair!

Maiden of Florence, my soul most reviles,
  The wretch who'd the innocent damsel be-
    tray;

Maiden of Florence, more bright are thy smiles
  To me than the radiant orb of the day.

Maiden of Florence, I liken thine eyes,
  That now with such lustre are beaming on
    me,
To the stars that so brilliantly shine in the
    skies,
  And I love them not, dearest, more than I
    love thee.

Can I deceive thee? never!—oh, never!
  Let no such thought in thy bosom have
    birth;
May I, if false to thee, curs'd be for ever,
  Wandering hated, despised, o'er the earth!

Maiden of Florence, oh, listen to me,
  Nor think that I seek thy fond heart to en-
    snare;
If I deceive thee accurs'd may I be,
  And my bosom be plunged in the darkest
    despair.

As the last tones of this song died away, the prince aroused from the torpor in which he had been wrapped, and started to his feet, with the perspiration standing upon his temples in large drops, and altogether in a most violent state of horror and agitation. How long he had been in that state of stupefaction we cannot say, but it was evident that it had lasted some time, for his lamp was burnt out, and the morn shone brightly through the window. Was it reality, or only the effects of a terrified imagination? As he gazed vacantly around the room, a shadowy form seemed to flit past his eyes, and vanish immediately by an opposite door, though it was secured by both lock and bolt. God! how he trembled, and the blood seemed to freeze in his veins! He was rivetted to the spot, and still his eyes remained fixed upon that part of the chamber where he imagined the form had disappeared. At length the power of speech was restored to him, and he shouted aloud, and in a voice of terror—

"What, ho! within there! Lights!—lights! Varlets, are ye deaf? Lights, I say!"

Thus he continued to shout at the very top of his voice, and his cries at length reached the ears of some of the servants who had not yet retired to rest, and they rushed to the chamber, but when they entered it, they were surprised and alarmed to behold the prince extended on the floor in a strong fit. With all possible dispatch they raised him; they summoned a female attendant, and sent her to make Melina acquainted with the circumstance. Melina was very much shocked when she was made acquainted with her uncle's alarming situation, and lost no time in repairing to his chamber, when she found the prince supported in the arms of two of his attendants, and staring wildly about him. She tenderly approached him, and took his hand, but he shrunk from her, and gazed vacantly upon her.

"Dear uncle," said the fair girl, looking earnestly into his face with her fine full eyes, "do you not know me?"

"Pursue that form!" ejaculated the prince, without appearing to comprehend what Melina had said. "Am I thus to be braved and taunted? Pursue her, I say!"

"My poor, dear uncle," sobbed Melina, throwing her fair arms around his neck; "oh, what is it that has affected you thus? Some fearful dream—but, heed it not."

"Dream! dream!" repeated the prince, tearing himself roughly, in the excitement of his feelings, from the embrace of his niece; "who says it was a dream? It was stern reality! Did she not sing the song?—Yes, the ballad I—Ah! there she stands now, and by her side the brigand chief: she points affectionately at him, and appeals to me—and now! Do you not see her?—Zitella! Have I no command here, that the dead should thus arise in judgment against me, without one of those whom I employ, and to whom I have ever been a friend, attempting to repudiate the foul aspersions with which they will stigmatize my character? Cowards! slaves! do not hold me! They are standing there.—They mock my agony. Release me!—release me! I am the Prince Bianchi, governor of Rome, and will trample them into their native dust, though a whole legion of devils opposed me!"

With these wild and incoherent expressions, the unhappy and conscience-stricken prince tore himself from the hold of Melina, and those who had come to her aid, and rushed wildly towards the spot where he imagined the objects of his terror stood. He staggered half way—his hands grappled with the air—and with a hysterical laugh he sank into the arms of his attendants, in a state of utter insensibility. All those present were completely appalled by what they had seen and heard, but they placed the prince upon his couch, and immediately summoned his medical attendant. But who shall describe the consternation—the agony of poor Melina? She sunk in a chair, and could scarcely preserve herself from fainting; but a flood of tears came to her relief, and approaching the bed on which her uncle had reclined, and leaning with affectionate solicitude over him, she sighed—

"Dear, dear uncle, what can have caused this dreadful excitement? Surely it cannot have been the escape of Massaroni! Oh, I will never more mention the name of that wretched man in his presence, if it must produce such terrible results as these. But it must have been some frightful dream that has thus disturbed him, from the effects of which he will soon recover, and—ah, Signor Priuli," she said, as the medical gentleman entered the chamber, "my poor uncle is ill—very ill; for Heaven's sake do your best to recover him, and my blessings shall attend you."

"Fair signora," replied Signor Priuli, "you may depend on me; I will use my best exertions with his highness. Do not alarm yourself; he has suffered some little excitement, probably from the events of the night, which, I trust, will soon pass away. But I must request you, signora, to retire to your chamber, and endeavour to compose your feeling. Should any serious symptoms take place, you shall be immediately apprized."

Melina felt more tranquillized by Signor Priuli's assurances, and having imprinted an affectionate kiss upon the lips of her insensible uncle, retired from the chamber supported by her waiting woman. We must now follow the footsteps of Massaroni and his daring band. Brilliantly shone the moon over the romantic scenery around, as they pursued their rapid flight from the place of their late desperate encounter.

"Cospetto!" exclaimed Massaroni, suddenly pausing to take breath, "but this has been a busy night. I have had a narrow escape, thanks to our young friends the Frenchmen. But we are now far away from the Villa Rosa, and I think I have spoilt their festivities for the remainder of the night."

"Aye, aye," returned Rubaldo, "but have you got the ransom?"

"Certainly," said Massaroni, "and what is more, upwards of two thousand ducati from his highness. But we must hasten from our present retreat, for no doubt, if we stay, an overwhelming force will be sent against us. Who did you leave in charge of the Count de Strozzi?"

"Carlotzi and Sangrino," replied Rubaldo.

"It would be most unfortunate if he should escape," remarked the brigand chief.

"Escape!" replied Rubaldo; "oh, there is no fear of that; we can depend upon our comrades."

"And where was Maria?"

"We thought she would have accompanied us; but she had some secret mission to go upon, and left the mountains about half an hour before we did."

"That is unfortunate," said the brigand chief; "for she would have had a vigilant eye upon the prisoner; truth to say, I rather doubt the sincerity of Carlotzi and Sangrino. But should they dare to have played us any acts of treachery, they shall pay dearly for it."

"They shall," said the brigands; "death to those who would deceive Allesandro Massaroni, the brigand chief!"

"Thanks, thanks, my old comrades," said Massaroni, "but on, on—we have no time to lose; before the sun rises upon another day we must be far from the Guardagnota."

"But do you not intend to have revenge upon the Prince Bianchi, for the good intentions he has towards us?" asked Rubaldo.

"Aye—aye," replied Massaroni, in an abstracted manner; "but we will talk of that anon. I have seen that to-night which has aroused fresh feelings within my breast. Almighty powers!" he added with the greatest emotion —"that portrait!—should it be!—mother—dear sainted mother, thank heaven, thy deserted son yet lives to avenge thy wrongs."

Onward they proceeded, but there was a gloom, a heavy gloom upon the spirits of the brigand chief, which his comrades had never witnessed before, and he frequently muttered incoherent sentences to himself which they were at a loss to comprehend. Torturing and various, indeed, were the thoughts of Massaroni as they made their way towards their mountain retreat. The portrait he had accidentally seen at the Villa Rosa was still vividly present to his mind's eye, and brought with it all the melancholy associations of the past; that mother whom he had so fondly loved while living, and whose memory, even in his most guilty moments, he so deeply venerated. He could almost imagine that she stood before him, and that he heard her voice urging him on to avenge her's and his own wrongs upon the head of her betrayer; that man who had promised love and protection, and gave her ruin, shame, misery, and an untimely grave. That man who had broken the heart of the poor confiding girl who was so faithful to him, at whom scandal dare not point the finger of scorn and reproach, until he crossed her path, and left the offspring of their unfortunate intercourse to become an outcast from society, and an object of terror to his fellow creatures. Oh, yes, these were strong reasons for vengeance.

"Spirit of my mother," muttered Massaroni to himself, "and I will have it too, before I die. Oh, should the suspicions that the adventure of this night have aroused prove correct!—But let me be calm, and weigh this solemn business in my mind deliberately."

Thus meditating, the brigand and his companions continued on their way, and in the course of another hour they arrived at the place of their destination. Massaroni found his wife anxiously watching his return, and when she beheld him and his bold companions approaching, she flew to meet him, and rushed fondly into his arms.

"Massaroni!" she ejaculated.

"Maria, my wife!—the faithful partner of my desperate fortunes!" he replied with unusual emotion.

"You have returned safe, Allesandro," said the brigand's wife, "and I am satisfied. But I have had some strange and fearful misgivings of this night's expedition, and—how is this? You came not back with the same state as that in which you left. You seem agitated too; what has happened?"

"In truth, Maria," returned Massaroni, "I have had a narrow escape with my life."

"Ah! were you then recognised?"

"Aye, that confounded old steward of St. Arnulph's was near consigning me to the tender mercies of his highness the prince; but we will talk upon this subject at another time: we must depart from here immediately."

"So soon?" said Maria Grazie.

"Aye, or we shall have our enemies down upon us with an overwhelming force," answered Massaroni.

"And you have the ransom?"

"Yes, and much more."

"That is well; however, I never approved of this last adventure; there was too much risk, with very little prospect of gain."

"I do not regret it," said Massaroni, "for I have learnt that—but no matter—where is the Count di Strozzi, our prisoner?"

"No longer our prisoner," answered Maria.

"How!" exclaimed Massaroni, starting.

"'Tis even so," returned his wife. "I was compelled to go to the relief of one of our humble sick friends, the peasant Ninetta, and in the meantime, Carlotzi and his companion, by some accident or other, which they will best be able to explain, suffered the count to escape."

"Escape! Diavole!" cried the brigand. "The knaves!—the traitors! But they shall suffer for it. What explanation did they give?"

"That, having partaken rather too freely of some of the tokay taken from the servant of the Prince Bianchi, they fell asleep, and when they awoke the Count di Strozzi had taken his departure."

"The lying rascals," said Massaroni; "but they shall not deceive me by such a tale. Rubaldo, bring them before me."

Rubaldo and the other brigands obeyed this command, and in a few minutes Carlotzi and Sangrino were brought into the presence of their enraged chief.

"So, the Count di Strozzi has escaped?" said Massaroni.

"Accidentally he has done so, Massaroni," replied Carlotzi.

"Accidentally!" repeated the brigand chief, "and think you to deceive me by such a tale? Traitors! I have always had my suspicions of your fidelity; you have taken the count's gold and suffered him to escape; answer me, is it not so?"

"No—no," hastily replied Sangrino, who was the most alarmed of the two; "Carlotzi and I were to blame for partaking so freely of the Prince Bianchi's wine; but—but—had we really connived at the escape of the Count di Strozzi, it is not likely that we should have continued here."

"And think you that answer will satisfy me?" said Massaroni, sternly; "search them, Rubaldo."

Rubaldo obeyed, and immediately produced two well filled purses from the person of Carlotzi.

"Here is a confirmation of your guilt," said Massaroni; "a goodly sum, truly; the count has paid a noble sum for his ransom. Do you any longer dare deny your guilt?"

"No, no," replied the poor trembling wretches, in a breath, and sinking on their knees at the same time; "mercy! mercy!"

"Why, you cowardly varlets," returned Massaroni, "who have the audacity to become traitors, but not the courage to meet the con-

MELINA.

sequences. Remain where you are. Comrades," he continued, addressing himself to Rubaldo and the others, "what is the punishment of those who act with treachery towards Allesandro Massaroni, the brigand chief?"

"Death!" was the unanimous reply.

"Mercy! mercy!" again supplicated the two unfortunate wretches.

"Do your duty, comrades," commanded Massaroni.

The contents of half-a-dozen carbines were immediately discharged at the miserable men, and bounding in the air, they sank dead upon the earth.

"So perish all who would prove false to Allesandro Massaroni!" said the brigand chief. "We will leave the carcases of these fellows as a legacy to our enemies. Wine! wine! and then we must away, for, no doubt, the affair of this night will arouse our foes to the most energetic course of action, and it would not be prudent to wait here to receive the numerous troops that will, no doubt, be sent against us."

The bodies of the two brigands who had thus been so summarily executed were dragged aside, and, the wine being brought, Massaroni quaffed a glass, and then seated himself by the side of his wife, and became lost in meditation.

"Why are you so thoughtful, Massaroni?" she asked; "something seems to oppress your mind."

"Ah, Maria," answered the brigand, in melancholy tones that were unusual to him, "I am, indeed, borne down by the weight of conflicting and agonizing thoughts; but let us change the subject."

"Nay, Allesandro, have I not always been the partner of your cares and anxieties, and do you now deem me unworthy of your confidence?"

"Not so, Maria; you wrong me by such a suspicion, but——"

"But what, Massaroni?"

"I am not now in the mood to detail the adventures of this night."

"Your hesitation but increases my curiosity," said the brigand's wife; "it must have been something very particular indeed, that has occurred to agitate you thus. Tell me, Massaroni, do not keep me in suspense."

"Would you have me, then, recall the dismal past to my memory?"

"Has this that now weighs upon your mind any reference to it?"

"It has—it has. But you shall know all, and in as few words as possible, for before long the sun will commence its diurnal course, and we must depart from hence."

Massaroni then related to her all those particulars with which the reader has been made already acquainted, and to which she listened with the most profound attention and interest."

"And are you certain that the portrait you mention," she said, when he had concluded, "so strangely resembles your mother? or did you suffer your imagination, and the excitement you was labouring under at the time, to deceive you?'

"Deceive me, Maria!" repeated Massaroni, "that were impossible. It is her very counterpart; I could almost persuade myself while I gazed upon it that she were still living before me, and that I again heard her sweet voice breathing blessings upon my head. And then the distracting scene of her death-bed rushed

upon my recollection, and drove me to madness. I could have knelt before that portrait in reverence for ever, had not danger pressed so closely upon me, and had not the thought rushed upon my brain of what would become of you, my faithful partner, were you deprived of my protection."

"Not for me alone, Massaroni," said the brigand's wife; "you must live for vengeance!"

"Aye, for vengeance on the head of the base and heartless betrayer of her who gave me being! Should I discover him, I should forget that he were my father; I should think only of the wrongs of my mother, and that he had made me what I am, and satiate my hatred in his life's blood. Hitherto Massaroni has never taken human life but in self-defence, but in such a case he would glory in becoming a murderer. Oh, Maria, had you but seen my poor mother in her last moments, when she knew that the scene of her mortal career was fast closing, and that she was about to leave me a poor, helpless, friendless boy, unprovided for, unprotected in the wide world, it would never have been banished from your memory. Young as I was at that time, I registered an oath in Heaven to redress her wrongs if ever I had the opportunity; and, by all my hopes here and hereafter, that oath shall not be broken."

"Suspect you the Prince Bianchi?"

"I dare not trust myself to come to that conclusion until I have had farther proof," replied Massaroni.

"But how came the portrait of which you have been speaking, in his possession?" asked his wife. "And what can be his motive for keeping it concealed so carefully?"

"It is that I want to discover," replied Massaroni, "and then I shall be decided in what manner to act."

"It was strange that your mother always refused to tell you the name of her seducer."

"She loved him still, fondly, devotedly, although he had acted so cruelly towards her; and doubtless it was the fear that I should at some future time seek to revenge her wrongs, that prevented her."

"And you never saw him?"

"No, no, I have told you so frequently," said Massaroni; "I was but an infant when he deserted her."

"But you understood from her that he was of noble rank, did you not?" asked Maria.

"I did. But no more of this; this melancholy suits not the brigand chief. I must devote my attention to other business for the present. His highness shall not have the gratification of hanging or shooting me just yet, and I think the defeat he has had by me this night, and at the very time when he flattered himself that he had me quite secure, will rather daunt his courage, and be a source of no little vexation and disappointment to him. Ha! ha! ha!—I feel myself again. Only to think that I should be seated in his company and cheating him at cards, at the very time he was talking about me, and boasting of the plans he had laid for my capture. Oh, it is a good joke—an excellent joke. Ha! ha! ha! But see, the shades of night are fast disappearing, and warn us to depart. Let us proceed."

"Whither do you now intend to direct our course?" asked Maria.

"We will talk of that on the road. Comrades, are you ready?"

"We are," replied Rubaldo.

"Then follow!" commanded Massaroni; "and let us concoct our plans for future exploits of daring. Massaroni has given his highness the prince the slip, and will live to play him many a trick yet."

"Evviva Massaroni!" shouted the brigands; and then, shouldering their carbines, they rapidly followed their chief down the lofty mountain's side, singing the following chorus:—

Merry brigands all are we,
    And 'tis our maxim wise and bold,
With the wealthy to make free,
    And ease them of their yellow gold.
Banish every weaker feeling,
    Let the bigot prate of crime;
Time from all is daily stealing,
    We but do as teaches Time.
        Li lara, li lara, lira la!

This rude chorus gradually died away upon the air, and the brigands were soon far away from the majestic mountain of the Guadagnola.

CHAPTER VI.

THE SUFFERINGS OF OLYMPIA.—THE VILLAINOUS PLOT.—HER ABDUCTION.

THE reader will probably now be anxious to know what became of the fair but unfortunate Olympia after the exciting circumstances which were related at the commencement of this tale. For some time after the departure of the count, in the custody of Massaroni and his daring band, she remained in a state bordering upon insensibility. Her brain was so bewildered that she had but a confused recollection of what had taken place; it was so extraordinary and unexpected that it appeared more like a wild dream; but at length the whole truth flashed upon her recollection, and she burst into a convulsive flood of tears. She sank on her knees, and with clasped hands and upraised eyes, she mentally invoked the protection of Heaven; but she was unable for some time to articulate a single syllable. The singular appearance of the brigand chief, his extraordinary behaviour, and the remarkable interest he seemed to take in her fate, was a source of the most unqualified astonishment to her; and the

singular promise he had extorted from her seducer filled her at once with amazement, embarrassment, and alarm. How had he become acquainted with her melancholy history, and by what means had it come to his knowledge that the Count Alberti had appointed to meet her that evening? She was lost in astonishment, and it was useless for her to attempt to fathom these mysteries and incongruities, for it only involved her still deeper in perplexity the more she reflected on them. She lamented the appearance of Massaroni, for what construction might not be put upon the circumstance by those who were so prejudiced against her? Besides, was it not offering Count Alberti an excuse for his cruel desertion of her? It was not for a moment to be supposed that the count would be intimidated by the threats of the brigand chief; that he would fulfil the compact that had been exacted from him; neither would she have consented to become his wife under such circumstances. She would have despised herself if she could so have descended, and what happiness could she expect from such a union? Then, how could Massaroni think to serve her by such means? No, it was the love of Alberti that she principally sought, and that she was now convinced she possessed not, and that he was only too anxious to get rid of her and her innocent offspring, to conceal his shame and villany, in order that he might pay his addresses to some more favoured and wealthy maiden. The thought was an agonising one, but after what he had said that evening, it was quite impossible that she could reject it. And what would be the course he would now adopt towards her? Had she not everything to fear from him, for he would be stimulated to revenge for the outrage which Massaroni had committed against him, and would be too ready to believe, however preposterous and improbable the idea, that she was connected with that desperate and daring man. She dreaded, yet longed to see him again, that she might remove any such prejudice from his mind, and once more on her knees implore his pity and sympathy. As these thoughts crowded in rapid succession upon the brain of Olympia, her heart sickened, and her bosom swelled with anguish.

"The die is cast," she sighed; "my worst fears are realized; my fate is sealed. He has cast me from him; deserted me and my tender infant, and there is nothing left for me but to wander o'er the earth a degraded being. I cannot remain here, and whither can I go? Who will pity or shelter me? By what means can I support myself and child, and with all this weight of care upon my mind? Oh, Alberti, Alberti, for whom I have sacrificed everything, how have I deserved this? Would that me and my poor child were at rest in the silent grave; for what hope, alas! is there now for both of us? And why should I continue to live?" she added after a pause with a frenzied look. "In a moment I can put an end to my earthly troubles, and save Alberti from the shame he dreads. Why should I hesitate? What is there now to tempt me to live? All is still around, there is none to interrupt me! The child sleeps, and——"

The wretched Olympia paused, hesitated; a thousand tumultuous feelings were rushing through her bosom at that moment; despair had driven her to a state of madness. There was an expression in her beautiful countenance which had never distorted it before. For an instant she cast a glance of unutterable affection upon her sleeping babe, and her resolution wavered. The dark, the desperate passions which cruelty and injustice, despair, and misery had engendered in her breast, for the moment, yielded to the better feelings of her gentle nature, and she shuddered with horror at the dreadful double crime she had thought of penetrating; but again the black and hideous perspective of the future miseries which were in store for her and that slumbering innocent, rushed like a foul vision before her disordered imagination, destroying reason, rendering her again frantic in her despair and utter wretchedness, and she was no longer the gentle Olympia that nature had formed her, but the determined suicide, the murderess of herself and her child! It was a moment of horror; such an one as even the stoutest hearts could not look back upon without the most harrowing feelings. All was silent and solemn as those awful few moments that form the prelude to the closing scene of a beloved friend or relative. There was scarcely a whisper even in the breeze, whilst the gentle queen of the night shed her mellow tints into the chamber of the wretched woman, as if she would soothe her to composure and hope. Composure and hope! There was none for that poor deceived, abandoned, and distracted woman. All was storm, and darkness, and misery before her mind's eye. Again she looked at her slumbering babe, and when she reflected upon the horrors to which it might be exposed; the career of crime into which it might be plunged; the scorn, the contumely, which might be heaped upon its head; frenzy once more lit her eye, and despair nerved her arm. There was a knife lying upon the table. The eye of Olympia suddenly fell upon it, and she grasped it with terrible determination. For the moment the very world itself seemed to be shut out from her vision. She seemed to be moving in another sphere; to be urged on by some inscrutable power—certainly she had lost all control over her reason and her better feelings. Hideous forms appeared to flit before her—grin upon her—taunt her with pusillanimity—point to the terrible perspective of the future earthly torments, and disgrace, and misery, in store for her and her child, if they continued to live; and

there was no friendly voice at hand to whisper in her ear the eternal torments which must attend her soul if she perpetrated so horrible a crime. And now, to her bewildered imagination, appeared the form of her seducer, smiling and exulting in her misery and despair. And, oh God! what form was that by his side, whom he so fondly embraced, but who yet turned from him with an expression of loathing and disgust? It was that of Melina—her whom she had reared, and had every reason to believe he loved, and for whom he now sought, after the most solemn promises that could ever escape the lips of human being, not to abandon her and her child. Her brain whirled round!—she grasped the knife more firmly, and advanced towards the bed upon which her beauteous little one was slumbering in all unconscious innocence of the dreadful misery, the awful thoughts, which were at that moment raging within its wretched mother's breast.

"I will do it," she said, in a tone of voice that was quite unearthly, as she stooped over the infant with the knife upraised in her hand. "But one blow from this friendly knife, and thy short career in life, my cherub, will be ended in innocence, and thou wilt be restored to thy native heaven!—far better, far better than thy father's hatred, and the world's scorn. God of Heaven! pardon me the deed. But one kiss, my little one, and then——"

At that moment the infant smiled beautifully in its sleep, and a change immediately came over the feelings of the wretched mother; reason again resumed its seat, and throwing the knife from her, she sank upon her knees, and clasping her hands together in an agony indescribable, she ejaculated—

"All merciful Father! forgive me the dreadful, the unnatural crime, my madness and despair would have urged me to perpetrate! Oh, guide me—teach me how to act in this trying hour, I humbly supplicate Thee! My child!—my sweet little innocent!" she added, starting from her knees, and once more approaching the couch on which it slumbered, "we will yet live to battle with the world's vicissitudes, and trust to mercy from that Power which we cannot expect from its creatures."

The distracted mother stooped down over her child, and covered it with her caresses. Then she once more sank on her knees, and returned thanks to Heaven for having preserved her from the perpetration of the horrible crimes of self-destruction and infanticide, which in the phrenzy of her despair she had contemplated.

"Oh, Alberti!" she sighed; "would that thou couldst see me at this moment. Methinks thou must be moved to pity, and urged to render me and thine innocent offspring the justice that is due to us. But, alas! thou toldest me that unless I complied with thy wishes I had nothing to hope—that thou would'st abandon me for ever—and what can I expect should I accede to thy wishes? The assertions of the brigand, Massaroni, appear too well founded in truth; it is but a scheme to get rid of me and the offspring of our unfortunate intercourse for ever. But can he, whom I have ever looked upon as the most perfect, the most honourable of human beings, really be so great a villain? For villain he must be, and that of the blackest dye, who could contemplate such an odious deed! My heart revolts at the idea, and the blood congeals in my veins. Alberti! Alberti! still dear Alberti, may Heaven reform thee if thou hast suffered such dark thoughts to enter thy mind."

She pressed her fair hands upon her burning temples, the tears streamed between her long and taper fingers, and she sobbed convulsively; but nothing could relieve the leaden weight of anguish which pressed upon her heart.

"He loves the fair Melina!" she sighed, after a pause; "I have seen the flush of confusion mantle in his cheeks when her name has been accidentally mentioned, and scrupulously he has evaded the questions which my jealous fears have put to him. Yes; he loves her! I am convinced he does, and for that reason he wishes to rid himself of the poor victim of his deceit, after all the solemn vows of love and constancy he has pledged to her. She is very beautiful—she is amiable—she is rich. Presumptuous fool that I must be to imagine for a moment that he would ever make me, a poor, friendless, unknown woman, his wife! But she loves him not! Her heart, I know, is fixed upon the young painter, Florio Clairville, and therefore must I blame her not. Oh, it is impossible that she, or any other maiden, could ever love him with that intensity, that perfect adoration of feeling, that I do. I—I—I will seek her presence—I will unburthen to her my soul—I—I—will on my knees supplicate her to swear— No—no, Olympia," she added, whilst a feeling of shame and woman's pride came over her, "what would'st thou do? Would'st thou degrade thyself, and he to whom thine affections are devoted, and call the blush of shame and offended modesty upon that fair one's cheek? Away with such thoughts as these. Whatever my sufferings may be, I will bear them alone, and the world shall have reason to say that, although Olympia had fallen, she was still a woman!"

She sank on a chair, and burying her face in her hands, for some moments became completely absorbed in the intense agony of the torturing thoughts which rushed with such rapidity upon her brain. Then the form and the observations of the brigand chief arose to her recollection, and excited the most extraordinary and unaccountable emotions in her breast. What could be his real character? And why should he take such a remarkable interest in her fate? His manners, too, so accomplished and noble;—surely there must be something better inherent in that mind than the guilty propensities which had led him on to the perpetration of those daring and lawless deeds which had rendered his name so notorious and dreaded. There was something, too, in the expression of his features which had made the deepest impression upon her mind, and which, even amidst all the terrible cares which at that moment oppressed her, haunted her like a vision. She could not but feel surprised at these thoughts occurring to her, but she could not shake them off. Why should he so warmly espouse her cause? And how had he become so minutely acquainted with all the melancholy facts of her history? She was lost in amazement and perplexity. But Massaroni had declared that he was the enemy of Count Alberti, and his conduct on this particular and important occasion, proved that he was indeed so; and she earnestly prayed to Heaven that he might experience no danger from the vengeance of that desperate and much dreaded man. The deep toned bell of St. Peter's sounding the hour of eleven aroused her from her meditations, and exhausted with thinking, and the excitement she had undergone, she slowly arose, and having once more looked out upon the night, which was calm and lovely, she closed the door, and throwing herself upon the couch, and pressing her child with all a young mother's fondness to her bosom, she endeavoured to compose herself to sleep. For some time this was a completely useless task, but at length the drowsy god descended upon her eyelids, and shortly after the poor sufferer became insensible to her cares. But this was not permitted to last long. Even in her sleeping moments the cares and anxieties of the unfortunate Olympia were renewed, and visions of the most torturing description were conjured up before her disordered imagination. The cruel words which Alberti had made use of towards her again rang in her ears, and she heard him utter the most dreadful threats, whilst rage and hatred flashed from those eyes in which she had ever looked for the fondest affection. She heard curses and reproaches breathed from those lips which before had uttered naught but words of love and adoration. At one time he held a poniard to her breast and threatened her with death; and then she saw her infant writhing in his grasp, whilst all the deadly passions of the most inhuman fiend distorted the features of Alberti, and made that hideous and disgusting which she had hitherto worshipped as all that was noble, and manly, and handsome. Then she imagined herself in a strange wild place, surrounded by ferocious looking men, who laughed at and reviled her anguish. Dreadful imprecations were thundered in her ears, and Alberti stood by, and seemed to exult in the tortures she was enduring, and encouraged the wretches by whom she was surrounded to fresh inflictions. The horrors of this vision were too much for her, and she awoke, and starting from the bed, and sinking on her knees, she shrieked piteously for mercy! For some minutes, such was the powerful effect that these dreams had taken upon her senses, she was quite unconscious of where she was; but she was soon aroused to a state of sensibility by a loud knocking at the outer door. She staggered to her feet, and, panting for breath, she trembled with fear. Who could it be that thus sought admission to her dwelling at that unseasonable hour of the night? For it must now be long past midnight! She was riveted to the spot, and feared almost to breathe; but how to act she knew not. Some vague ideas of of the brigand chief, and that some outrage was intended her, rushed upon her mind, and she trembled more violently than before. The knocking was repeated with much greater vehemence, and it appeared evident that the applicant, whoever he was, and whatever might be his designs, was determined to enter. With a faltering step Olympia approached the door, and in a faint voice demanded who was there, and what they wanted.

"Open the door immediately," replied the well-known voice of Alberti; "open the door, I say, or I will dash it from its hinges; I must see thee."

"Alberti!" gasped Olympia; "at such an hour! Oh, merciful powers, protect me! What means this?"

"Do not delay!" returned the count, in tones of stern authority, "for I am already tired of waiting."

The distracted Olympia withdrew the bolt, and the Count Alberti stalking into the room, she sank at his feet, and with her looks, for she could not articulate a syllable, she implored his pity and forbearance. His countenance was ghastly pale, his lips were compressed, his eyes looked sternly upon her, and his whole demeanour bespoke the utmost rage and guilty determination.

"Rise, woman!" he commanded, in accents which she had never heard him assume before, and which, as she recalled the circumstances of her dream to her recollection, struck a sensation of the most indescribable horror to her heart. "Rise, woman!" he repeated; "none of this affected foolery to me, for it will no longer make the least impression on me. My time is but brief, but that must not be wasted n useless words. This night seals your fate."

"Oh, Alberti!" shrieked the horrified Olympia, clinging to his knees, and looking up piteously and imploringly in his face; "for the love of heaven, what would you do? I cannot hear aright. Alberti! Alberti! this must be some frightful dream."

"Indeed it is not," he answered, with a bitter smile, "and so you will shortly discover. So, then, the delicate, the bashful Olympia, the foundling dependent on mine and my parents' bounty; she whom I condescended to honour with my love, and even promised to make my wife, I discover, after all, is the paramour of the daring robber and assassin, Massaroni."

"Alberti!" cried the horror-struck Olympia, "you cannot mean what you say. You will not, dare not think me so degraded, so fallen. Oh, be not so unjust, if you no longer love me, and would cast me from you! By all my hopes here and hereafter, I never saw the desperate man you mention before this night, and I knew not of his coming here."

"'Tis false!" retorted the count, passionately; "think not to deceive me; how should he know of the appointment I had made to meet you? By what means did he become acquainted with all our secrets? and why should he take such a particular interest in your fate?"

"Alberti!" solemnly replied Olympia, "by the Great God who rules above, I swear I know not. He came to the door of my dwelling in the disguise in which you saw him, and craved refreshment, and to rest a few minutes, as he had travelled far. I would fain not have relieved him, and urged him to be gone, but he would take no denial, and——"

"Bah!" interrupted the Count Alberti, "a most probable story, truly, but you are much mistaken if you think to persuade me to believe it. And so I am to be forced into a marriage with you by this brigand chief; compelled to sign a document, and the most daring threats held out to me if I do not fulfil it. Mighty fine forsooth; but he and you, too, will find yourselves much mistaken. He has, this night, escaped me, and defeated the troops that were sent against him; but it will be my turn to triumph yet, and to make him quail before the power of the insulted Count Alberti. And you, his paramour——"

"Forbear! forbear!—spare me, Alberti, if you would not see me a corpse at your feet," interrupted Olympia, her fair bosom swelling and heaving with agony; "oh, surely you cannot believe me so depraved, so abandoned;—I repudiate all that Massaroni has done or said on this melancholy occasion;—I would accept your hand on no such degrading and compulsory terms, if even you were inclined to submit to them;—no, by Heavens, I again swear that I am perfectly innocent of that of which you so cruelly accuse me. Abandon me, if I no longer possess your love, but oh, do not thus unjustly accuse me of that at which my very soul recoils with horror."

"Your protestations are all lost upon me," replied the count, "my mind is made up, and my purpose is fixed. This night, this very hour shall settle all."

"God of Heaven!" shrieked Olympia. "Alberti, what would you do?"

"Rid myself of that which has ever become an intolerable burthen to me," he answered.

"Would you, then, murder me and our innocent offspring?"

"No, I am no assassin; but I would protect myself from annoyance and degradation."

"Oh, Alberti," sobbed the wretched woman, "did I ever expect it would come to this?— But let your dagger's point pierce my heart, and that of my poor child;—it would be a mercy to us both, since we have become so hateful to you. With my dying words I will still bless you, and pray to heaven that you may find one who will prove as faithful to you, or love you half as ondly, as the wretched abandoned Olympia."

The count remained unmoved; he had evidently made up his mind to some desperate purpose, therefore he was completely insensible to the tears and supplications of the unfortunate victim of his lust.

"Your words will not make the least impression upon me," he said sternly; "I will not again suffer myself to be deceived by you; come, prepare yourself, for you and your child must instantly quit this place."

"You cannot mean what you say," she cried, still clinging to his knees, and sobbing as if her heart would break. "Oh, reflect, reflect, Alberti, before you proceed to extremities, which may afterwards fill your bosom with the bitterest remorse, and blight all your hopes of happiness. On my knees I supplicate you, and once more solemnly declare, in the name of High Heaven, that I am innocent—innocent as your slumbering infant, of that which you accuse me."

"Psha!" returned the count; "this is a waste of time. What ho! there!"

"Merciful God, protect me and my child!" exclaimed Olympia; "what is your dreaded intention towards me?"

"You will soon see," replied the Count Alberti, and Olympia shrank appalled with horror, when several fierce-looking men, well armed, made their appearance at the door, and entering the room on the command of the count, surrounded her.

"Alberti!—Alberti!" she shrieked; "you cannot be so inhuman;—how have I deserved this?—Oh, mercy!—mercy!—spare me!— Save me!—Those ferocious men! Whither would they convey me?—What is the fate you have in store for me and our poor helpless offspring?—Oh, Alberti, think of the love I have borne you, of the sacrifice I have made for you, and relent, relent!—Nay, do not turn away from me in scorn! You cannot be so monstrous!— Hear me, Alberti, as you hope for mercy here

and hereafter, do not proceed in your cruel and guilty plot."

"Away with her!" commanded the count, "heed not her cries; you know my instructions, and as you obey them, so will you be rewarded."

The ruffians seized Olympia, but she struggled desperately, and succeeding in releasing herself from their hold, she once more threw herself at the count's feet, and in frantic accents, and with looks of anguish and despair which were sufficient to move the most stubborn heart to pity, she implored his mercy; but he turned away from her, he was deaf to her supplications, and at length, completely exhausted by the power of her emotions, the hapless Olympia uttered one appalling shriek and fainted.

"Quick!—quick!" ordered the count; "bear her and the child to the carriage, and convey them to the place of their destination, where you will await my further orders. The hour is favourable to your designs, and you need not apprehend any interruption; but if you should meet with any, you are armed sufficiently to resist it."

"Aye, aye, signor," returned one of the fellows, "we are fully prepared for anything that may take place, though there is not much fear of it. When may we expect to see you at our cavernous retreat in the mountains?"

"In a day or two," replied the count; "here is gold for you—now away."

The men bore the insensible form of Olympia to a vehicle which they had in waiting, and then one of them returned for the child, which having wrapped in a mantle, he also conveyed to the carriage. The young count eagerly watched them depart, and he then re-entered the house, and for some minutes he paced the room wrapped in deep meditation.

"So," he soliloquised, "I have at last got rid of Olympia and the child, and I have made such arrangements as will, I think, prevent them from troubling me again, whilst no one will suspect me as having been the cause of their disappearance. And yet," he continued, after a brief pause, "this is cruel to one who so fondly loves me, and to whom I have uttered such solemn vows. But, psha! let me not think thus. She must have been mad to imagine that ever I would make her my wife. No, no, the fair and wealthy niece of the Prince Bianchi is her to whom my ambition soars, and if I judge rightly by the marked respect with which he has ever treated me, he will not be unfavourable to my suit. I am rather doubtful whether or not I may meet with the same success with Melino herself: the plebeian Florio, I know, loves her, and I believe that she returns his passion; but they can never be mad enough to imagine that the prince will ever consent to such an unequal match. No, no; I will rest myself contented that she will be mine, and with that hope endeavour to forget Olympia and her offspring. I have no doubt that I may yet find her a husband among some of the peasantry, who, for the sake of a goodly sum in gold, will be very glad to accept of the match, and to do his duty by her too. Oh, yes, only let me have time, and I dare say I shall be able to arrange matters to the satisfaction of us all."

But although the young count thus attempted to argue with himself, he felt far from satisfied; he could not reconcile to his conscience the crime of which he had that night been guilty, and the base part he had taken towards the affectionate and too confiding Olympia: she who had sacrificed her income to her devoted love for him, and who was willing to lay down her very life to serve him. How basely, how cruelly had he deceived and betrayed her; how recklessly he had broken all the solemn vows he had pledged to her; and could he expect that such black-heartedness and inhumanity would be suffered to go unpunished? Notwithstanding, he attempted to treat the threats of the brigand chief with indifference, and to imagine that he would never have the daring to attempt to put them into execution, when he thought of the desperate character of the man, the subtle means he had of carrying out his plans; the bold exploits of which he had been the hero, and the number of years which he had set the laws at defiance, he could not but feel some considerable alarm at having him for an enemy. Should he also hear of the abduction of Olympia—which there could be very little doubt that he would—he would be sure to seek revenge, after the deep interest he had seemed to take in her fate. But why he should take that interest he was at a loss to imagine, and how he had become so minutely acquainted with the particulars of her history. Filled with these thoughts, the young count slowly left the late residence of the unfortunate Olympia, and sought his palazza—but not to sleep—no, his mind was far too much disturbed to admit of that, and in order to seek to drown the racking and reproachful thoughts which crowded upon his brain, he quaffed deeply of the wine cup, but that only added to the excitement of his mind. He now regretted the desperate and guilty course he had adopted, and was half resolved to retrace his steps, and, restoring Olympia to liberty, seek her forgiveness.

"But no," he said, after a pause, "I have gone too far to retrace my steps; and how could I ever dare hope to receive her forgiveness after the atrocious outrage I have committed against her?—what other atonement could I make her than by bestowing upon her my hand? And would she even now accept of that? No; she must now despise and hate me, and the base

conduct I have pursued towards her must arouse in her hitherto gentle bosom, the dark feelings of revenge. Psha! Why do I torture myself thus? Let me arouse myself from these gloomy thoughts and become once more a man. Since I have thus boldly dared, I must continue in my daring, or I shall be laughed at, degraded, and despised. My whole thoughts must henceforth be devoted to the beauteous Melina, and I must use all my endeavours to supplant this plebeian Frenchman in her affections, though I have no doubt that will be no easy task to accomplish. However, I flatter myself that my wealth and rank will prevail with the prince, her uncle, independent of the esteem in which I know he holds me. My intrigue with Olympia is not likely to prejudice him against me, for, if report speaks truly, and I have no doubt it does, he has been guilty of many such practices himself, and he will therefore be the more likely to excuse me, if he does not even applaud me for it. In a few days I will ease my doubts, and see how far my hopes may extend. Olympia and her child, the greatest obstacles of all, are removed, and I will therefore flatter myself that success will crown my wishes."

Having endeavoured to come to this satisfactory conclusion; the count at last retired to bed, but busy conscience was at work, and when he did sleep, the forms of the much wronged Olympia and her innocent child were constantly before his eyes; and he frequently started from his sleep and gazed around the room, as strange voices, to his disordered imagination, seemed to mutter curses in his ears, and to reproach him for that of which he had that night been guilty.

CHAPTER VII.

OLYMPIA IN THE ROBBERS' CAVE.—THE ANNIHILATION OF HOPE.

THE parents of the young Count Alberti had been dead about a twelvemonth before these events took place, so that he was left entirely his own master, with no one to place the least restraint upon his actions, and that before his passions were sufficiently matured and subdued by age and experience. Possessed of almost unbounded wealth, and descended from one of the noblest families of Rome, he possessed advantages which few young men could boast of. Added to which, being handsome, accomplished, and insinuating, it will not be wondered at that he should be looked upon with admiration and regard by the most lovely of the opposite sex. But there was one who ever beheld him with timidity, and doubt, and suspicion, and that one was the beauteous Melina, and his amour with the poor foundling girl Olympia, the reader may be sure, did not tend to raise him in her estimation. His manners, too, towards her, whenever accident brought them together, excited a feeling of uneasiness in her breast, and therefore it was with no small regret, and even alarm, that she beheld the marked attention of the prince, her uncle, always paid him, and to hear the flattering elogism he seemed to delight to pass upon him at every opportunity. This caused her many an hour of anguish and dread, and the advances of the count daily become more bold, her uneasiness increased, and she avoided his society as

[Allesandro Massaroni, the Brigand Chief.]

much as possible. Her affections were entirely placed upon Florio, and if they had even not been so, she felt satisfied that the Count Alberti could never have been the man of her choice. But still she consoled herself under all these reflections with the convictions that the prince was too good and generous, and loved her too affectionately, ever to wish her to become the wife of any man on whom she could not bestow her heart as well as her hand. The count was not so blind that he could not penetrate Melina's thoughts, and read the opinion she entertained of him, which was anything but flattering to his vanity; however, as has been shown, he did not give way to despair, as the behaviour of the prince towards him convinced him that he would find a warm friend and advocate in him; and as for supposing that he would ever give his sanction to an alliance between his niece and the poor painter, Florio Clairville, that he imagined would be preposterous in the extreme. He therefore determined to persevere, and he had not the least doubt that he would be crowned with success, and, moreover, that in time he should even be able to overcome the scruples of Melina. But we must now return to the ill-fated Olympia. It was not till the vehicle had got a considerable distance from her late residence, that she was restored to sensibility, and she had then but a vague recollection of what had taken place. Her horror at her situation may be easily conceived, but her first thought was her child, which she snatched frantically to her bosom, and bedewed its innocent face with her tears of agony. Two of the ruffians were seated in the carriage with her, and their fierce looks convinced her that she had nothing to hope from them. The rest of the fellows rode on either side of the vehicle, which was pursuing its way at a rapid rate through a most wild and unfrequented part of the country, and along a dismal road which, on each side, as far as the eye could stretch, was enclosed by stupendous mountains, whose summits were buried in the clouds, and whose steep sides it seemed impossible for human foot to venture to ascend. The gloom and silence of the hour was unbroken by the slightest sound, and the moon only at intervals showed its bright face from behind the clouds, making the horrors still more visible. Olympia felt her heart hang like a leaden weight within her bosom; every faculty for the time was paralysed and bound up in horror, and she could not articulate a syllable; but even had she been able to utter the least cry for help, there was none to be obtained, and the threatening looks of her ferocious companions filled her breast with the most unspeakable terror. But oh, how maddening were her feelings, when she thought of the cruel, the inhuman conduct of that man to whom she had sacrificed her honour and her peace of mind. She could scarcely persuade herself that it was true, or that one whom she had loved to adoration, and who had pretended to return her passion with equal fervour, and had so frequently promised that none other but her should ever become his bride. could ever have acted with such base treachery and cruelty towards her. And what were now his designs against her?—For what purpose had he taken her from that humble home which he had provided for her for the purpose of concealing his own shame and guilt?—Could he be monster enough to consign her to the murderous knife?

—Oh, no, she could not believe that he could ever become so lost to every feeling of humanity as to be guilty of such an atrocious act; and yet it would have been a mercy to her and her child after what had taken place. To drag on a wretched life of captivity, surrounded by miscreants who probably were associated with every crime, would be worse than a hundred deaths; and fervently she prayed to Heaven to rescue her from so horrible a fate. Her heart sickened at the thought, and the scalding tears flowed fast down her cheeks.

"For pity's sake tell me," she at length found power to ejaculate, "whither are you conveying me?"

"Oh, to a very snug retreat among the mountains, signora," replied one of the ruffians, "several leagues from this place. We must hurry on our way, or we shall not reach there before daylight, which would be rather inconvenient."

"Why, in the first place, signora," answered the man, "we are gentlemen who make merry by lightening the overburthened purses of the wealthy; and, in the next place, we have the orders of the most noble Count Alberti to hold you in security until we have received further instructions from him."

"Brigands!" said Olympia, with a look of terror.

"Why, you can call us so if you think proper, signora," said the ruffian, "though we do not exactly aspire to that title. We do not pretend to compete exactly with Massaroni and his daring band; though we have at times performed some exploits that even they might not be ashamed of."

"Good God!" exclaimed Olympia; "and is it possible that Count Alberti can so have debased himself as to become associated with such desperate men?"

"Even so; you see, signora, your fine noblemen can descend at times, when they want their turns served. They are not over particular as to the instruments they employ."

Olympia shuddered with horror, and averted her gaze from the countenances of the ruffians, and pressed her infant more closely to her bosom.

"Is there no hope?" she said, at length; "will nothing move you to take pity on a poor friendless and deeply injured woman?"

"We must obey the orders of the count, signora," replied the fellow, "or we shall not get the reward he has promised us; and we do not wish to offend him on any account whatever. But make your mind perfectly easy, for we will behave to you with all that gallantry and respect due to so fair and gentle a signora."

"Heaven help me!" sighed Olympia; "for without its aid I am lost! Oh, my sweet unconscious babe, little do you know the dangers to which we are now exposed, or the pangs which rend thy wretched mother's bosom; and 'tis well thou dost not. Oh, Alberti! Alberti! little did I imagine that thou couldst ever have been guilty of such cruelty as this, and towards one whom you professed to love to adoration. God forgive him, or surely he will be fearfully punished for this."

She wrung her hands in despair, and then, sinking back in the vehicle, gave herself up entirely to the anguish of her feelings. The men took no notice of her, but conversed together freely, recounting, with triumph, the many daring and lawless deeds in which they had been engaged at different times, and laughing boisterously all the while. The vehicle continued to dash along with unabated speed, but the aspect of the scenery was not changed, unless it was to become more wild and gloomy the further they proceeded. The spirits of poor Olympia became more and more depressed, and all hope was entirely banished from her bosom. There was no alternative for her but to endeavour to resign herself to her fate, whatever it might be, and to trust to Providence; for to attempt to move the wretches in whose power she was, to compassion, would have been sheer madness. With heart-rending agony she thought upon Alberti, and she now found, to her bitter cost, how perfectly, how fatally true were the assertions of the brigand chief, though by what means he had obtained his knowledge of the count's designs, she was at a loss to imagine. But surely, she thought, Alberti would relent, and taking pity on her, restore her to liberty, though he could never make her a sufficient atonement for the cruel outrage he had perpetrated against her, or restore her to happiness. No; whatever might be the future fate that was in store for her—that was blasted for ever. She felt that she could almost have borne anything rather than this last act of monstrous cruelty on the part of Alberti; even the horrors of his deceit and desertion would have been bad enough to endure, but to find that he was so lost to shame, humanity, and honour, as to associate himself with villains of the blackest dye for the purpose of depriving her of liberty, perhaps of life, was a blow far too great, a shock too powerful for human nature to support with any degree of patience or fortitude. As the horses were much jaded with the speed at which they had been driven, the men stopped a few minutes to give them rest; and the ruffians who were in the vehicle with Olympia then partook of some liquor out of a flask, and, filling a horn, offered it to her; she, however, declined it, and remained absorbed in the same gloomy train of thought which had so long occupied her mind. She looked from the window of the vehicle, but nothing whatever met her gaze to inspire her with the least ray of hope. All was gloom and cheerlessness;

not a human being was to be seen in that dreary part of the country, and at that untimely hour, and the barren and rugged scenery around seemed to frown despair upon her, and to mock her sufferings. She recalled to her memory all the melancholy circumstances of her short, but eventful life, and her tears flowed fast at the dreary retrospective. It seemed as if she had been sent into the world for no other purpose but to experience the most bitter and unmitigated misfortunes, and how deeply she regretted that it had not been the will of Providence that she should expire in her infancy. While the late Count and Countess D'Amalfi were living, she had experienced the same kindness and affection from them as if she had been their own offspring; to them she was indebted for all the happiness she had ever experienced; for moral culture, education, everything, and when she had, by the earnest solicitations of her seducer, so abruptly quitted the paternal shelter of their roofs to conceal her own and his shame from their knowledge, she felt convinced that it must have caused them a pang which they little expected, and so ill-deserved, to experience. But had they been living, the dreadful misfortunes which had now befallen her, she felt satisfied would never have happened; they would have pardoned her for her weakness, and even, she was convinced, at the risk of everything, would have compelled their son to have rendered her justice. Oh, it was one of the greatest calamities that had ever befallen her when those excellent, those amiable individuals expired. The horses having now rested for about a quarter of an hour, they resumed their journey, through the same dismal and mountainous tract of country; and the further they proceeded, the more did despair seem to close in around the persecuted and broken-hearted Olympia. The men continued their conversation, but never addressed themselves to her, and did not seem inclined to interrupt her meditations; for this she seemed thankful, and remained silent, pressing her infant with maternal fondness to her bosom, and bedewing its cheeks with her tears. She felt faint and fatigued for the want of rest, and the unusual excitement she had undergone, but still she felt certain that under any circumstances she could not sleep in her present state of mind. They now diverged towards the left, into a more open part of the country, but whose features presented the same rude and cheerless aspect as the dismal way they had been travelling, and in the distance appeared another chain of lofty mountains, towards which they seemed to be directing their course.

"Have we much further to go?" Olympia at length ventured to inquire, in a faint voice.

"Not more than two leagues and a half, signora," replied the man to whom she had addressed her question; yonder mountains will bring us to the termination of our journey, and glad enough I am of it, for see, the first streak of dawning day appears in the eastern horizon."

Olympia shuddered as she gazed towards the mountains. Was it then in those gloomy regions she and her poor child were to be held in captivity? Oh, Alberti—false, treacherous Alberti—surely thy cruelty could extend no further. They proceeded on their way with increased speed, and two of the men who were on horseback hurried on before them, no doubt with the intention of preparing their comrades for their arrival. Another half hour brought them to the foot of this lofty chain of mountains, and here the carriage stopped, and the two ruffians descending from the vehicle, assisted Olympia and her child to alight. She looked despairingly around her, and wrung her hands in agony; but one of the men proceeded to blindfold her, and she then inquired, in a terrified voice, what they were going to do with her.

"Do not be alarmed, signora," answered the man, "we do not intend to harm you, for our orders are strictly to the contrary. Spinotti, take the carriage round to old Jacopo from whom we hired it."

The arms of Olympia were now taken by the two men who rode with her in the vehicle, and she was hurried on at a quick pace. They seemed to be taking a circuit of one of the mountains, and not a word was spoken during the time they proceeded. Notwithstanding the assurances of the ruffians, the heart of Olympia misgave her, and she again asked what they intended to do with her, and what had become of her child.

"The child is here, by your side, signora," replied one of the men; "come, come, no more useless questions, but rest assured you are safe enough."

Olympia did feel a little more satisfied at the assurances of the men, and uttered not another word. At length, as her rude conductors desired her to stoop they seemed to be passing through some opening, probably the entrance to some cavern in the mountain, and soon afterwards she found herself being hurried down a rugged flight of steps; which having descended, they seemed to be traversing a long passage, and she could hear the voices of men in the distance. They approached the sounds nearer, and they became more distinct. At length they halted, and one of the men gave three loud and peculiar knocks on what appeared to be a door. It was immediately opened, and Olympia being hurried into the place beyond, could hear the murmurs of several voices, as the persons to whom they belonged seemed to gather round her and her rude conductors.

"All right!" said one of the men, "we have arrived safe at last; remove the bandage from the signora's eyes."

The fellow to whom this was addressed obeyed, and Olympia sank appalled and amazed on her knees at the scene which was presented to her eyes. She found herself in a spacious cavern lighted by two lamps suspended from the arched roof, and which shed a sickly glare upon the savage countenances of the numerous men who filled the place, and who were all armed in the most formidable manner. There were several women and children scattered about, whose features were scarcely less repulsive than those of the men, and who also carried stilettos and pistols in their belts. In the centre of the cavern was a long table on which was spread a plentiful repast, and which was surrounded by seats, on which many of the robbers were seated, and most of whom from their flushed faces and their boisterous mirth, seemed to have partaken most freely of the intoxicating contents of the flask. The walls were hung round with carbines, swords, and numerous other deadly weapons, and in various recesses were piled casks of gunpowder. The robbers were gazing with rude curiosity upon Olympia, and whispering among themselves. She shuddered with terror, and snatched her child to her breast, sinking on a seat completely overpowered by the violence of her emotions. The ruffian who had principally addressed himself to Olympia while on their journey, took his place at the head of the table; he appeared to be the captain of this daring band, and rising he said:—

"Comrades! welcome to our mountain home, the fair Signora Olympia, the late mistress of the most noble Count d'Amalfi."

"Welcome to the Signora Olympia!" shouted the robbers, in a breath.

A deadly sickness came over Olympia, and she trembled with disgust and horror.

"Theresina," said the captain, speaking to one of the women who was standing near him, "conduct the signora to a seat at our festive board, and let her partake of refreshment, which she must so much require after the fatigue of the journey."

The woman approached her, but Olympia shrank in terror from her, and in a voice half stifled with anguish ejaculated—

"No, no, for the love of Heaven do not urge me;—oh, if you are indeed a woman, and are insensible to every feeling of humanity towards one of your own sex, take pity on me, and do not seek to add to my misery, by insulting me in my misfortunes."

"Signora," replied Theresina, as she had been called, in rather more respectful accents than Olympia had expected, "there is no one here who will attempt to offer you any insult, so make your mind perfectly easy upon that point. But had you not better partake of some refreshment ?"

"Alas ! no," said Olympia, "my heart is too much oppressed to permit me to eat ; suffer me to retire from the presence of these men, and to brood in solitude upon my unmerited sorrows."

Theresina returned to the captain, and held a brief conversation with him.

"Be it so," he said aloud ; "Signora Olympia, you may retire. Theresina will attend you to the place prepared for your reception. Good morning."

Olympia could make no reply, and Theresina taking up a hand lamp which stood in a corner, again approached her and motioned her to follow. With trembling footsteps Olympia did so, and the robber's wife (for Theresina was the wife of the captain,) led the way towards a small door in one corner of the cavern, which she opened, and disclosed a winding passage, which appeared to have been excavated out of the solid rock. Pursuing their way along this, they at last arrived at another door, strongly bolted, and Theresina having unfastened it, they entered a small apartment, or cell, and which contained no other furniture than a couple of chairs, rudely formed out of the branches of a tree, a table, and a trussel bedstead on which was laid a mattress, covered with a couple of rugs. Theresina lighted a lamp which was standing on the table, by the one she carried, and then turning to Olympia, said—

"The accommodation here, signora, I dare say is not so good as that you have been used to ; but it is the best that in our mountain home we are able to provide for you. I would advise you to endeavour to snatch a few hours' repose, for you look fatigued, and you need not fear anything, for no one will attempt to intrude upon you."

"Oh, for what cruel purpose am I brought hither ?" said Olympia : "you do not appear to be entirely destitute of humanity. Tell me then, I beseech you, what are the intentions of the robbers respecting me ?"

"They can only act according to the instructions of the Count Alberti, signora," answered Theresina ; "but I can assure you that no personal harm is is intended you or your infant, and that you shall be treated with every mark of respect."

"And is there no hope of escape from this ?" asked Olympia.

"None, lady."

"Alas !—alas ! How terrible is the prospect before me ; but tell me, has the Count Alberti long been acquainted with your band ?"

"I know not, signora," replied Theresina ; "but I believe he has not. Adieu, signora, and fear not."

Thus saying, without giving Olympia time to put any further questions to her, Theresina left the cell, and when Olympia heard the door locked and bolted upon her, her heart sank within her bosom, and she remained for a few moments immersed in an agony of grief and despair. That Alberti could behave thus inhumanly towards her was a thought which drove her almost to distraction, and she wrung her fair hands in an agony of unutterable grief.

"God forgive him !" she sighed, " for surely a terrible retribution will overtake him for conduct so monstrous and unjust. Alberti, if I have sinned, it is thou that hast been the tempter. I could willingly have laid down my life to serve thee. Oh, cursed was the hour when I first beheld thee. But to be left to the mercy of these guilty men, whose very looks strike terror to my breast ; Heaven help and watch over me and my innocent offspring, or we are lost !"

As she thus gave vent to her feelings, she knelt down, and supplicated the mercy and protection of the Supreme ; then she arose and endeavoured to compose her little one, who was crying bitterly. There was a small aperture in one side of the cell which admitted light and air, and beneath that Olympia, who was oppressed with heat, seated herself, and felt great relief from the current of air that passed through it. The voices of the robbers, who were singing and laughing tumultuously, reached her ears, and added to her terror and apprehension. But at length they ceased altogether, and silence reigning through the cavernous retreat, the fear of Olympia became somewhat appeased. She laid her infant, which had again fallen asleep, on the bed, and seating herself beside it, watched it with the most anxious solicitude.

"My sweet babe," she sighed, "to what troubles art thou destined in maturer years ? If I thought that thou wert doomed to experience a similar bitter fate to that of thine hapless mother, though thou art mine only comfort, I should wish thee dead, for better would it be that Heaven should take thee in thine innocence than that thou shouldst live to experience the temptations, the troubles, the treachery, and the vices of the sinful world. And must thou never be suffered to repeat a father's name, or to receive a blessing from his lips ? Dreadful fate—how have we merited it ?"

Exhausted at last, and imagining, from the silence which reigned around, that the robbers had retired to rest, and that there was nothing more to fear from them, Olympia once more fervently invoked the protection of Heaven, and endeavouring to resign herself to her fate, horrible as it was, she threw herself on the bed by the side of her child, and endeavoured to compose her mind to sleep. Nature was exhausted, and at length slumber closed her eyelids ; her sleep was more tranquil than might have been expected, under the circumstances, and she did not awake for several hours, when she felt much refreshed in body, but still labouring under the same intense agony of mind. She had not long arisen when Theresina entered the cell, bringing with her some provisions of which she requested her to partake, and with which she complied, but her appetite and the anguish of her mind would only allow her to eat sparingly.

"Fair signora," said Theresina, "I assure you that, although I am a robber's wife, and have for so many years been used to this lawless life, I can feel for your situation, and trust that something will shortly occur to release you from it. But be comforted, and rest assured that I will do all that lies in my power to render your confinement as little irksome as possible."

"Thanks, thanks!" ejaculated Olympia; somewhat tranquillized by these assurances; "thank Heaven, that I have at least one near me who is not quite insensible to every feeling of humanity. Have you been long in this degrading situation?"

"Nearly twenty years, signora," replied Theresina, with a melancholy look, and sighing.

"It is a long period to pass in so lawless and hazardous a career."

"Ah! signora, it is; but I must never leave it, I am bound to it for the rest of my life."

"How so?" asked Olympia, whose thoughts were for the moment diverted from her own sorrows, and her curiosity greatly excited by the manner of Theresina.

"I am the wife of the captain of this band," replied Theresina, "who brought you hither, signora."

"Ah, how could you become connected with such a man?" asked Olympia.

"It was love, signora."

"Love?"

"Aye, Rinaldo was not always what you now see him," replied Theresina.

"What a pity it is that a woman of your mind should be placed in such a degrading position," remarked Olympia; "what could have brought you into such a degrading situation?"

"It is a sad story, signora," replied Theresina; "but some time or other, if you feel disposed to hear it, I will relate it to you. But I must leave you, lady, as I have business to attend to. Keep up your spirits, and depend upon it that no farther harm is intended you than your detention."

Olympia again thanked her, and Theresina retired.

CHAPTER VIII.

THE PROPOSITION.—COUNT ALBERTI AND MELINA.—THE DISTRACTED LOVERS.—THE DESPAIR AND DEPARTURE OF FLORIO CLAIRVILLE.

It was several days before the Prince Bianchi was sufficiently recovered to leave his chamber, and his beauteous niece Melina watched him with the most anxious solicitude and affection. It was totally in vain that he tried to banish from his mind the impression which the stirring and alarming events of the night of the festival at Villa Rosa had made on it, or to persuade himself that it was only the effect of his perturbed imagination which had conjured up the shadowy form which he had seen in his chamber, and the longer he reflected on it, the stronger became his conviction that he had not been mistaken. The escape of Massaroni also served to harass his feelings, and he swore that he would yet capture the brigand chief at all hazards and at any costs. As soon as he was sufficiently restored to health, he collected a large body of troops together, such as he thought must be able to overwhelm any force they might have to encounter, and despatched them to the Guadagnola with strict injunctions to allow the brigands no quarter, and to bring Massaroni back with them either dead or alive. This expedition was headed by the Count di Strozzi, who was anxious to have revenge on the brigand chief for the trick he had played him. As the reader is already aware, however, the Prince Bianchi was doomed to experience another disappointment, for on the arrival of the Count di Strozzi and the troops at Guadagnola, Massaroni and his band had taken their departure several days, and all that they found were the festering carcases of the two guilty wretches who had suffered the count to escape, and who paid for their treachery with their lives. The rage of the prince at this fresh disappointment exceeded all bounds, and it was some time before he could in the slightest degree regain his equanimity. Still, in the midst of all this anxiety to apprehend and bring to justice Massaroni, there was a feeling would come over him at times, when he recalled the mountain chief to his memory, which he was at a loss to comprehend, and which he found very difficult to subdue. The Count Alberti having been called away from home on some important business, had been unable to be present at the festival got up at the Villa Rosa to celebrate Melina's birth-day, and the indisposition of the prince prevented him for some days from making the visit he was so anxious to pay. The count had at last formed the resolution to make Prince Bianchi acquainted with the sentiments the charms of Melina had excited in his breast; and to endeavour to prevail upon him to sanction his addresses; and with that design in view, about a week after the prince had been entirely restored to convalescence, he made his way to the Villa Rosa, and had a private audience of the Prince Bianchi. What transpired at that interview it is needless to mention ; it may be sufficient to state that when the Count Alberti left the Villa the satisfied expression of his countenance fully testified that he had not been unsuccessful

"Melina, my love," said the prince to his niece, the following day, "I have something of a most important nature for your private ear ; attend me."

Melina curtseyed and followed her uncle to his library. He handed her a chair and took a seat by her side. Taking her hand within his, he looked affectionately in her face, as he said—

"You know, my dearest Melina, that your happiness has always been one of the principal studies of my life."

"Oh, my beloved uncle," replied Melina, "you have always been most kind, most considerate, and indulgent to me, and I trust that my conduct has been such as to convince you of the affection I bear towards you, and of the unbounded gratitude I feel for all the blessings you have so bountifully lavished upon me."

"True, my sweet niece," returned the prince. "And I have to thank Heaven for sending me such a comfort in my declining years. But there is a time, my dear Melina, when the fondest must part ; and it behoves us, while we have health and strength, and all the faculties of our mind are unimpaired, to make provision for that solemn occasion to which I have alluded."

"Oh, my lord," said Melina, with an inward shudder, "I beseech you do not talk in that melancholy strain ; it fills my breast with the most dismal forebodings to hear you."

"Nay, Melina, I am an old man ; I cannot expect to live many years longer, and Heaven knows how I may be taken from you ; how would it then embitter my last moments knowing I had left you unprotected."

"Dear uncle !" said Melina, "it tortures my heart to hear you talk thus ; distant, oh, far, far distant may be the time when it shall please God to visit me with such a calamity. Oh, my lord, what has put such sad ideas in your mind?"

"Melina, I must be brief and candid with you ; the time has arrived when it it is absolutely necessary that you should be united to one who is worthy of you, and who is calculated to make you happy."

Melina trembled, blushed ; and modestly averting her looks, she waited in the greatest possible suspense for her uncle to continue.

"My sweet Melina," resumed the prince, after a pause, "think not by what I have said that I am tired of the charge which Heaven has so long entrusted to me ; no, my love, you are far more precious to me than ever—'tis only your future welfare that is the subject of my most earnest anxiety."

The prince again paused, and Melina awaited in the most trembling suspense and anxiety to hear what would be the result of this interview, but her heart at the same time throbbed violently, and some fearful misgivings tortured her mind.

"I would see you united to a man," continued the prince, "who, in addition to all the graces, accomplishments, and virtues of mind, should possess rank, wealth, and station equal to your own ; to such a man, and no other, must my Melina be united. But you are pale—you tremble, dear Melina—what is the matter?"

"Nothing—nothing—my lord," faltered out the agitated maiden ;—"it was only a momentary faintness—it is over now—it—it was very childish—pray proceed, my dear uncle."

"Such a man as I have described," resumed her uncle, "is alone worthy of the possession of a treasure so inestimable as my Melina. Such a man I have in my mind's eye, and——"

"My lord !" interrupted the blushing girl, and her emotions increased, while she dreaded yet longed to hear the conclusion of what he had begun.

"Do not agitate yourself, my sweet niece," said the prince, with an encouraging smile ; "for I trust that what I have to disclose to you, you will not find by any means alarming. The Count Alberti D'Amalfi——"

"The Count Alberti D'Amalfi !"

"Aye, he is young, handsome, noble, and accomplished ; in fact, he is all that I have described the man whom I should wish to see united to my Melina ;—yesterday he acknowledged to me that you have inspired in his breast sentiments of the warmest description. He, in fact, made proposals to me for your hand, and, to sum up all in a few words, as I felt convinced you would feel honoured by the preference he has shown you, I gave him my permission that he should pay his addresses to you."

Melina uttered a faint shriek of agony, and would have sank insensible on the floor, had not the prince caught her in his arms. Alarmed, he immediately summoned the attendance of her waiting women, and having resigned her to their care, he hastily quitted the room in a state of the greatest agitation.

"It is plain she loves him not," he said, when he was alone, and pacing the room backwards and forwards with disordered steps. "Are then my hopes to be thus disappointed? —By Heaven, they shall not be !—The count is noble, wealthy, handsome, and accomplished ; what then can be her objections to him?—Can it be because of his amour with the girl, Olympia? Psha !—That was merely a youthful indiscretion of which most young men are guilty, and though, for the sake of his own credit, he found it necessary to abandon her and the child—Abandon them !" he added, with a look of agony ;—" ah ! that pang !—Why do I suffer myself to wander upon such a subject ?—It will arouse the demon once more within my breast !—Oh, Valencia !—Oh, Zitella !"

He groaned with the intensity of his feelings, and sinking into a chair, remained for a few moments completely overpowered by the strength of his emotions. At length he aroused himself, and again he ejaculated—

" Away with such thoughts—they only serve to madden me, 'tis past now, and cannot be recalled, and why should I still continue to torture myself by reviving it in my memory ?— But, Melina !—Ah, I see it all now ; had I not been blind, I must have observed it before, and should have taken steps to guard against it. She loves the young Frenchman, Florio Clairville, and he returns her passion. I might have noticed it from the first, their every look, their every action, when in each other's society, bespeak it, and the agitation of Melina, when I mentioned the proposal of the Count Alberti, confirmed it. Confusion—how imprudent have I been to give him such encouragement, and to have offered him and Melina so many opportunities of being in each other's company. Florio Clairville is handsome, accomplished, and I believe strictly honourable ; but he is poor, and cannot therefore aspire to the hand of the niece and heiress of the Prince Bianchino, no, it must not be ;—Melina, I regret to be obliged to cause one pang to agitate your gentle bosom, but never can I encourage a passion, an alliance, so far as birth and station go, so unworthy of you. I must lose no time in seeking Florio, and checking his presumptuous thoughts. And yet, it is a source of infinite regret to me to have to annihilate the hopes of two individuals, who, as far as intrinsic pretensions go, are every way so worthy of each other. Psha ! it is weakness to entertain these thoughts. My own dignity and that of Melina demand that I should act with determination. The proposal of the young Count Alberti is by far too flattering and advantageous to be idly rejected ; and after all, Melina, by the attentions of the count, may in time learn to forget her girlish love, and to smile upon his suit ; and Florio Clairville may meet with one whom he can love, perhaps, as sincerely, though not so ardently, as Melima, and who may be worthy of his great merits. The principal obstacles to Alberti's addresses are removed—Olympia and her offspring have quitted the neighbourhood, and will probably never again trouble him, and as for the threats of that impudent rascal, Massaroni, the young count, I think, may well laugh them to scorn ;

my power and his may surely set that desperate brigand at defiance, and if I do not shortly have him secure, either dead or alive, I am not the Prince Bianchi."

Having come to this conclusion, he endeavoured to rest satisfied, but he was far from being able to do so ; in spite of all his efforts to the contrary, he could not persuade himself otherwise than that he was acting with injustice and cruelty towards his beauteous and affectionate niece, in thus annihilating all her young hopes, and in seeking to force her into a marriage with a man whom he rested assured she did not, and never could love, if even she could esteem him, which he much doubted after his behaviour towards the ill-fated Olympia, the unfortunate victim of his treachery and deceit ; and as these thoughts arose to his imagination, and he recalled the past errors of his own life, conscience again goaded him on to madness. With disordered footsteps he traversed his apartment, and became wavering and undecided how to act.

" She will never consent," he said ; " her agitation on the bare mention of the count's name, and the proposals he has made, convince me of that, and of the disgust, if not the utter hatred, she entertains towards his character. And shall I, who have ever looked upon her with the same affection as if she were my own child, and to whom she has ever been so gentle, so tender, so beautiful, and submissive, force her into an alliance which is so hateful to her feelings ? My heart revolts at the idea ; and yet I cannot make up my mind to offend the Count Alberti by rejecting his suit, or consent to Melina's becoming the bride of one so far beneath her in rank and station as the poor painter, Florio Clairville. No, that must not be ; no plebeian blood must circulate with that of the noble and illustrious house of Bianchi. It is true that I could make him noble, but that would not alter the meanness of his origin, or stop the voice of busy scandal. Patience—patience, and the voice of reason and persuasion, may have all the effect which I wish them to have upon her. Heaven knows, my sweet Melina, how anxious I am for your happiness, but I cannot allow you to sacrifice the dignity of station to misplaced love.'

Excessive pride, it will be seen, was one of the most predominant passions of the prince's breast, and that urged him on in his harsh and ungenerous determination. Melina, on recovering her senses, was aroused to a full consciousness of all that the prince, her uncle, had stated to her, and to the misery that was in store for her. Love the Count Alberti ! the heartless betrayer of confiding innocence—he who had abandoned the victim of his lust, and the offspring of their illicit connexion to want and wretchedness !—Oh, never ! never ! There was something most revolting even in the very idea. She felt that she could sooner endure a thousand lingering deaths than submit to such a disgusting sacrifice. And could she abandon all hopes of the noble-minded Florio—he who had, by his numerous virtues, won her most ardent affections! The thought was agonizing, and she felt that to do so would be utterly impossible! And could her uncle, who had ever treated her with such indulgence upon all occasions, with such unbounded affections persist in forcing her into a union which was in every way so repugnant to her feelings?

[OLYMPIA IMPLORES ALBERTI NOT TO DESERT HER.]

Could he wish to sacrifice her to a man, who, after his conduct towards the unfortunate Olympia, she could not even esteem? She could not fully persuade herself that the prince would endeavour to do so.

"Oh, no," she soliloquised, "I know his generous nature too well; his affectionate regard for me, and his anxious solicitude for my happiness, to believe him capable of doing so. He will not turn a deaf ear to my prayers and supplications; he cannot view with indifference and obdurate insensibility my tears of anguish—he will not, cannot thus annihilate all my hopes, my prospects of happiness, by forcing me to grant my hand to one who has proved himself so unworthy as the Count Alberti. Even though he may refuse to sanction the love of Florio, he surely cannot remain determined to force me into a marriage with one whom I must ever despise, if I do not entirely loathe him. I will be calm, and still hope."

She did endeavour to tranquillize her feelings, but it was all in vain. She well knew the pride of the Prince Bianchi, and therefore the influence that the wealth, the rank, and station of Count Alberti D'Amalfi were likely to have over him, and again her heart sank within her, and she abandoned herself to despair. Oh, what would be the agony of Florio Chairville when he should be made acquainted with the melancholy, the torturing particulars. She well knew the strength and ardour of Florio's love, and the encouragement which the marked respect the Prince Bianchi had ever shown towards him had given to his hopes, and she feared that this bitter disappointment was more than he would be able to find fortitude to support with patience. With Florio she could have been content to live in the humblest cottage, and even to endure all the trials of poverty, but a palace and Count Alberti she felt would be the most cruel fate she could possibly be destined to; and she shuddered with horror at the bare contemplation of it. It was some time before the distracted damsel could regain the least composure, or look forward to the future with any other feelings than those of misery and despair; but at last she did become a little more composed, and sought to prepare herself to meet her uncle, where he should seek her presence again with firmness and determination. In the course of a couple of hours, a servant entered the room with a message from the prince, in which he stated that it was his desire to have another interview with her, if she was in a condition to see him. She trembled; but mustering all her courage and resolution to her aid, she desired the servant to inform him that she was ready to receive his highness whenever he thought proper. In a few minutes afterwards Prince Bianchi entered the room, and advancing affectionately towards her, took her hand, while he said—

"How is my sweet niece, now?—I regret that anything I should have occasion to communicate to her should cause her so much emotion; but I trust that it was only temporary, and that the good sense of Melina will convince her that what I said was only with a sincere wish for her future happiness."

"Oh, my dear uncle," replied Melina, "I am well aware of the love you bear towards me, and the anxious solicitude you feel for all that concerns my happiness. It is that certainty which inspires me with the hope that you will not persist in urging me upon a subject which is so repugnant to my feelings.'

"Nay, Melina," said the prince, "I cannot allow you to come to any hasty conclusions. The Count Alberti deserves more respectful treatment at your hands, and I must not have his proposal treated so lightly."

"My lord—my lord," supplicated Melina, "I beseech you to spare my feelings on this painful subject. I fully appreciate the honour which Count Alberti intends me; but—but I must candidly acknowledge that I have no heart to bestow upon him; I cannot love him."

"And why not, dear Melina?" said the prince, impatiently. "Is he not noble, accomplished, virt——"

"Oh no, no, no!" interrupted Melina; "not virtuous, my lord; remember his base conduct towards the poor girl Olympia, and then I am sure you cannot, will not praise him for his virtue. Oh! my dear uncle, can you wonder that I cannot look upon the count with any other feelings than those of terror and disgust, after such heartless treachery as this towards one whom he vowed to love and promised to make his bride?—Never, never, can I willingly enter into so dishonourable a connection."

"Melina," said the prince, who nevertheless felt the full justice of her observations, "you censure the conduct of the Count Alberti too severely; it is true that he erred, but I am convinced that he now sincerely repents, and would willingly make all the atonement in his power to Olympia. But she has deceived him, she has proved herself unworthy of his regard or attention. Has she not become connected with Massaroni? The deep interest that desperate man has evinced in her fate, and the outrage he committed against the count proves it; and has she not now fled, no doubt, to join the brigand chief, and with him to concoct some scheme of vengeance?"

"Fled!" repeated Melina, shaking her head incredulously; "oh, no, I do not believe that she would willingly do so. It is my firm opinion that——"

"That what, Melina?" hastily demanded the prince.

"That her sudden disappearance from the place of her late residence, with her innocent child, has been caused by the count, who now has her somewhere confined, where she can no longer annoy him," replied Melina.

"Melina," said the prince angrily, "you do Count Alberti an injustice, I am certain, by supposing him capable of such conduct. But dismiss those prejudices from your mind, and permit me to return an encouraging answer to him."

"Oh, no, no; not for the world," returned the damsel in a voice of the greatest agitation; "my heart revolts at the bare idea. Oh, my dear uncle, you have ever been so kind, so affectionate to me, do not, I implore you, urge me further upon so hateful a subject. You have ever found me dutiful and submissive, but indeed I cannot upon this occasion give my consent to that in which my happiness is involved. The bare idea of becoming the wife of the Count Alberti is far more horrible to me than even the most torturing, the most lingering death. Have pity on me, and do not force me into that which must plunge me into the deepest misery and despair."

The prince paced the room for a few minutes in a state of the greatest disorder. He could not deny the force and truth of Melina's arguments, and the injustice, if not cruelty, of his own behaviour, but still his pride prevailed over the natural affection he bore towards his niece, and he determined that whatever the consequences might be, the count's suit should not be so easily and abruptly rejected.

"Melina," he said, turning towards her, "you have, as you say, found me ever kind and indulgent, and most studious of your happiness; but on this important subject, I cannot yield to what I cannot call by any other term than your false prejudices. But answer me, and that candidly and truly—is your heart entirely disengaged? Have you not suffered the image of another man to make a fatal impression upon it?"

Melina blushed and trembled, and for a few moments so great was her agitation, that she was unable to articulate a syllable in reply. The prince watched her narrowly, and his suspicions were confirmed by the confusion she evinced.

"Alas! my dear uncle," she sighed at last, "why do you put such a question? Does it follow that because I cannot love the Count Alberti, that any other man should possess my affections?"

"Nay, Melina," returned the prince, in accents of displeasure, "this is equivocating. Tell me, and as you value my love, do not seek to deceive me, have you not suffered Florio Clairville to make a favourable impression upon your heart?"

Poor Melina hung down her head, blushed deeply, but was unable to reply.

"Enough!" said the prince, "your silence convinces me that I am right in my conjectures, and that you love the plebeian Florio. But mark me, Melina, your passion is hopeless, and you must banish it from your breast, for never can I consent to encourage the love of one so far beneath you in rank. Florio Clairville, the painter, is not the husband for the niece of the Prince Bianchi."

"Oh, my lord." sobbed the hapless damsel,

"why torture me thus? What are rank and title, compared with the noble qualities that Florio Clairville possesses?—I do acknowledge that his virtues have won my utmost esteem, nay more, my love, and that, if I am not destined to become his wife, no man can ever supplant him in my affections. For pity's sake bear with me, my dear uncle, and pardon me for the first time having acted in opposition to your wishes."

"Melina," returned the prince, in a tone of anger which she had never before heard him assume, "this is a weakness which I could not have thought you capable of. Where is that becoming pride which should characterize your station?—Would you, the illustrious niece and heiress of the Prince Bianchi, wed a beggar! But 'psha! I tell you again, you must banish Florio from your mind, for he can never become your husband."

"Then mark me, my lord," replied Melina firmly and resolutely, "no other man shall ever possess my heart or my hand. Sooner would I endure the greatest earthly misery, even your displeasure, than I would submit to so horrible a destiny as to become the wife of a man, upon whom I now look with feelings almost amounting to those of hatred."

"Beware!—beware! Melina," said the prince, passionately; "you have found me hitherto indulgent almost to a fault; but in this instance I have made up my mind, and I will be obeyed. Remember what I have said, and as you value my love, and fear my everlasting displeasure, do not remain foolishly obstinate. Florio Clairville and you must never meet again."

"Oh, my lord!" sobbed Melina in the greatest agony.

"Nay, I have said it," continued her uncle, resolutely, "and you will find that I will keep my word. Florio Clairville, the poor French painter, who has not a friend in the world, to have the presumption to aspire to the hand of the niece of the Prince Bianchi!—bah! the idea is monstrous. I have been a fool to honour him with my friendship, and to encourage his frequent visits to my pallazzo; but I never suspected that he would take so ungenerous, so ungrateful an advantage of my kindness."

"Oh, hear me, my dear uncle," sighed Melina, sinking on her knees at his feet, and looking up in his face with supplicating looks; —"hear me, I beseech you, and act with forbearance towards me and Florio; I——"

"I have heard enough," interrupted the prince, impatiently. "The Count Alberti honours you with his addresses; I approve of him, and command you to receive him with that respect which is due to him. I must suffer no childish prejudices to stand in the way of your future welfare."

"Then, my lord," replied Melina, sobbing

violently, "you condemn me to the most abject misery, than which, death to me would be far more preferable. But no, I cannot believe that you will act with such cruelty towards me. I know your noble and generous nature too well to entertain such a thought. In everything else that you may command me, I will cheerfully, willingly obey you, but in this, I cannot. Oh, spare me—have pity on me; and if you will not encourage the love of Florio Clairville, at least, do not endeavour to force me into a marriage which is odious to me."

"You will think better of this, Melina," said her uncle, after a brief pause; "and I will give you time to reflect on it. The Count Alberti must not be treated with scorn or contempt; it is to my interest to retain his friendship, and, by the saints, I know of no man who is so well worthy to become the husband of my niece. Nay, Melina, it is useless to supplicate me further; my mind is made up, and it is your duty to conquer this unreasonable repugnance, and learn to act in obedience to my wishes."

Having thus spoken, the Prince Bianchi stalked from the room, and left Melina in the most agonizing state of mind. She arose from her knees, and sinking into a chair, she gave herself up entirely to the intensity of her grief. She could not think of the Count Alberti without feelings fast approximating to those of horror; but to view him in the character of her future husband, was more than she could find fortitude to do. The more she reflected upon his conduct towards the unfortunate Olympia, the stronger became her disgust towards him, and the more she shuddered at the idea of beholding him, and of being compelled to listen to his odious vows. But that her uncle should come to so cruel and unnatural a determination, surprised her more than all, and she wept bitterly when she recalled to her mind his observations. She had hitherto had reason to believe him to be incapable of doing anything that might cause her the least unhappiness, but his present resolution showed too plainly to what lengths he might suffer his pride to urge him, and filled her mind with the greatest dread, and the gloomiest misgivings as to the future. And should she then never be permitted to see Florio again? Must all the hopes, which in the innocence and sincerity of their love, had been encouraged, be doomed thus suddenly to be annihilated? The thought distracted her brain; but it was too probable to be rejected, and her anguish every moment increased. To banish Florio from her bosom would be utterly impossible, for he had gained too strong a hold upon her affections, and she was convinced that though distance might separate them, though seas might divide them, let whatever fate might befall them, nothing whatever could subdue the mutual passion which

glowed in their breasts for each other, but that, on the contrary, time and separation could only serve to strengthen the flame. The anguish of the poor girl's mind was so great, that she almost sank under it; but she was quite unable to leave her chamber for the remainder of the day, and passed the time in the most painful meditation, and gloomy anticipations of the future. The Prince Bianchi was not at all disappointed at the manner in which Melina had received the proposals of the Count Alberti, but still he was greatly vexed and chagrined at her obstinacy, and was fully determined to persist in compelling her to receive that young nobleman's addresses, let the consequences be whatever they might. He felt his pride insulted by what he considered the presumption of Florio Clairville in inspiring to the love of his niece, and he was exceedingly mortified at the impression which Melina acknowledged he had made upon her heart; but he resolved to annihilate their hopes at once, and to remove the object of danger, by taking the earliest opportunity of banishing Florio from the villa, and not permitting his visits for the future. He had only just come to this resolution, when a servant entered the room, and informed him that Florio Clairville was waiting below, and requested an audience with him.

"'Tis well," said the prince, "this arrival is almost opportune; "show Monsieur Clairville up stairs."

The servant departed, and in a few minutes afterwards Florio entered the room, and was received with formal politeness by the Prince Bianchi, who requested him to be seated. Florio obeyed, but felt rather confused at the unusual coldness of the prince's manner.

"I am happy to see you, Signor Clairville," he said, "you have arrived in very good time, for I am anxious to talk with you on matters of serious import."

"Indeed, your highness," said Florio, "you do me great honour by condescending to consult me on any subject."

"Tut, tut, tut!" said the prince, impatiently, "this is foreign to the subject, and as I never like to waste words in useless prefatory remarks, we will come at once to the point. Signor Clairville, I believe you have ever found me act with friendship and esteem towards you?"

"Oh, yes, my lord; your highness has ever treated me with more condescension than any humble pretensions of mine could have aspired to, and—"

"Believe me, Florio," interrupted the prince, "that I shall ever entertain the same feeling of esteem towards you, because I believe you worthy of it; but circumstances render it necessary that from this day intimacy must cease. I will do anything that may forward your future interests most willingly, but I must desire that you discontinue your future visits to the villa.''

"My lord !" exclaimed the astonished and bewildered Florio, scarcely believing the evidence of his senses; in what way have I been so unfortunate as to incur your highness's displeasure?"

"You and my niece, Melina, love each other," said the prince, abruptly.

Florio started, and looked most confused.

"Nay, it is useless to deny it, Signora Clairville," remarked Prince Bianchi; "I have long suspected it, but I have this day received confirmation of the painful truth from the lips of Melina herself."

"Oh, my lord," replied the agitated Florio, "what can I say in answer to your observations? Candour and truth have ever been my principal characteristics, and I will therefore confess that the transcendant charms and glowing virtues of your noble niece have excited in my breast sentiments which I have found it utterly impossible to subdue, and which must continue while——"

"Hold! signor," interrupted the prince, with a look of anger; "I must not listen to this; you have presumed too much on my friendship. Florio Clairville, the poor student, should have paused ere he dared to raise his thoughts to the noble niece of the Prince Bianchi, and inspired her with a passion which he must beware could never be gratified, and could only be productive of pain and annoyance to all parties interested."

"Pardon me, my lord," said Florio; "I do admit that I must appear presumptuous in having sought the love of so peerless a damsel as the Countess Signora Melina; but, oh, who could behold so fair and amiable a maiden without loving, without worshipping her? He must have been less than man could he have done so. I do again acknowledge myself her slave, and though years may intervene, though we may never be destined to meet again, I must ever continue to be so. Her image is so deeply enshrined in my heart, is so wrapped up with my very existence, that by Heaven——"

"Cease, bold, presumptuous youth, I command you !" exclaimed the prince, with indignation; "I have been mistaken in you, and from henceforth will hold no further communication with you. You have heard my will, and I charge you at your peril not to dare to disobey it. Melina and you must never meet again, and I warn you not to attempt to see her, or to correspond with her, as you dread my vengeance."

Florio beat his breast with an agony of despair, and looked imploringly at the prince.

"I beseech you, my lord,' he said, "to hear me but for one minute."

"No more," replied his highness, impatiently, "you have heard my decision, and be the consequences upon your own head if you attempt to oppose it. Our interview is at an end, and remember, this is the last time you will be received at the villa. Farewell."

Having thus spoken, the prince waved his hand in an authoritative manner, and, retiring from the room, left the bewildered and distracted Florio to his own reflections. For some minutes he was in such a violent state of agitation and excitement that he scarcely knew how to act, or where he was. The mandate of the prince came like a thunderbolt upon him, and quite unnerved him.

"All my hopes are, then, at one fell blow crushed," he said, "and I am driven as though I were something loathsome or contagious from the presence of that beloved being for whom alone I wished to live. Oh, cruel fate !—But am I not justly punished for my presumption? Ambitious fool that I was, to dare to raise my thoughts to one so far above me in rank and intrinsic merits ! But she loves me !—she loves me! —and even in the midst of my blackest despair that assurance will afford me some consolation. Oh, why did fortune not bless me with her choicest gifts, or place Melina on an equality with my own lowly station, then might I indeed hope to possess her ! And must we never meet again? That thought alone is sufficient to drive me to madness. Life is now hateful to me, since I can no longer hope to share it with Melina."

He sighed deeply as these thoughts occurred to him, and then, with the most disconsolate air, he slowly quitted the room, and with a heart worn down by the weight of care which oppressed it, he departed from the villa. He lingered for a few minutes outside the house, loth to leave it, and with the vain hope of catching a parting glance of Melina at one of the windows, but he was disappointed, and, with feelings of anguish we cannot find language to pourtray, he hurried away, he scarcely knew whither. He had not proceeded far when he met one of the female attendants, who was the principal confidant of Melina, and from her he elicited all the particulars of her situation, and of the proposition of the Count Alberti.

"Ah!" he ejaculated, his bosom swelling with indignation, "and can the Prince Bianchi think of sacrificing his beautiful and innocent niece to such a man as this Count Alberti, the betrayer of the unfortunate Olympia? Is it for such a man as him that I am rejected? And shall Melina be forced into a union that must be so repugnant, so odious to her feelings? By heaven ! it must not, shall not be ! A just God will never, surely, permit it."

His emotions nearly overpowered him, but a

sudden thought occurred to him, which would afford him some melancholy consolation, and he determined to put it into execution; he would write a farewell note to Melina, and he had no doubt that he could prevail upon this confidential servant to deliver it into her hand. He questioned her upon the subject, and she willingly agreed to comply with his request. Tearing a leaf from his sketch-book, he took his pencil and hastily wrote a most affectionate and eloquent epistle, in which he fully expressed the feelings that at that time agitated his breast, and at the same time lamenting their cruel destiny, and repeating his vows of eternal constancy, although fate frowned upon their sentiments, he bade her adieu for ever. Having delivered this letter to the servant, at the same time strictly enjoining her to secresy, and informing her where he might be communicated with if it should be the wish of Melina to return him an answer, with a burst of anguish which he could not repress, he hurried on his way, completely reckless as to what might now become of him. Almost unconscious of what he did, he wandered towards the residence of his noble rival, the Count Alberti. The gate which opened into the extensive gardens of the pallazzo was unfastened, and without any defined object in view, he entered. Arriving at a spot where he might be concealed from observation, he threw himself on the ground, and gave himself up to the most gloomy meditation.

"Are all my hopes to be thus crushed?" he muttered to himself; "and shall this noble libertine be permitted to triumph, and to bear away that lovely prize for which monarchs might contend, and whose virtues entitle her to the happiest fate that can attend human beings? Short-sighted, ungenerous prince to condemn thy fair niece to so cruel a fate. Where is now that affection which thou hast ever professed towards her? Alas! alas! dearest Melina, how dark is the prospect which is now spread before thee. Thou canst never, I know, feel any other sentiments towards the heartless betrayer of the too confiding Olympia but those of loathing and disgust. But to be compelled to become his wife! Oh, there is madness in the thought. But it shall not, must not be! By Heaven I will prevent it, though I bring down upon my head the bitterest hatred and revenge of the prince thine uncle. I know that thou wouldst prefer any fate rather than be forced into an union with the Count Alberti, and at every risk, even that of my own degradation, I will frustrate his ambitious wishes."

He looked up at the different windows of the pallazzo, thinking that he might behold the count, but he appeared not, and he therefore imagined that he was from home. In this manner several hours passed away, and Florio thought not of departing. He seemed as if he were riveted to the spot, and the tumult of his feelings increased every minute. Thoughts took possession of his mind which had never entered it before, among which a feeling of hatred and revenge towards the Count Alberti was predominant.

"By all my hopes!" he exclaimed, in the distraction of his feelings, "he shall never become the husband of Melina. Sooner shall his life be sacrificed."

He shuddered to find himself entertaining such ideas, which were so foreign to his nature.

"What would the ardour of my love for Melina tempt me to do?" he said; "would I become the secret and cowardly assassin? And would she not loathe and despise me for it? The weight and anxiety of my disappointment has driven me mad. Reflect, reflect, Florio, and become calm. Thou hast never yet been guilty of anything that could call the blush of shame in thy face, and shalt thou now precipitate thyself into crime? No, no; I will endeavour to wait patiently, and to trust in the goodness of Providence to save my beloved Melina from the fate with which she is threatened, and which would, I know, be worse to her than even the most lingering death."

Night had now spread its dark mantle around, and Florio arose from the earth and prepared to depart from the garden, when the sound of approaching footsteps saluted his ears, and the moon at that moment emerging from behind a cloud, he was enabled by its light to behold the persons who where advancing. It was the Count Alberti, and he was accompanied by a tall, ferocious looking man, enveloped in a large black mantle, and altogether of suspicious appearance. They seemed to be engaged in deep and earnest conversation, and to take no notice of anything around them. Florio concealed himself as well as he could, determined to watch their actions. His feelings were greatly excited, but he struggled to subdue them as well as he could, and succeeded better than could be expected. They advanced towards an alcove, which they entered, and behind which Florio was concealed, and so situated that he could hear every word that passed between them without the least fear of being discovered himself. His curiosity was excited to the utmost degree, and he listened attentively. The count was the first that spoke.

"Rinaldo and your comrades have acted well, Spinotti," he remarked. "So, Olympia is quite secure in the cavern of the mountains?"

"Perfectly secure, signor," replied Spinotti, "and Rinaldo, our captain, only wishes to know your further orders respecting her and the child?"

"I have not made up my mind as to their ultimate fate," said the count; "but at present 'tis my wish that they should be kept confined in the cavern; but that no unnecessary severity should be practised towards them. Do you understand me, Spinotti?"

"Perfectly well, my lord. Before long, I presume, we may expect a visit from you?"

"Why, I have not yet made up my mind as regards that," answered the count; "I am not over anxious to meet Olympia again, for I know that she will heap upon me her reproaches whenever she sees me. How does she comport herself?"

"At first she was distracted," answered Spinotti; "but through the attentions of Theresina, Rinaldo's wife, she quickly recovered herself, and is now as quiet and resigned as can be expected.

"I am glad to hear it," said Count Alberti, "and think I could not have adopted a better plan to rid myself of her and her child."

"Certainly not, signor. No doubt she will soon reconcile herself entirely to her new situation, when she finds that there is not the least chance of her escaping."

"Exactly so. And hark you, Spinotti; methinks she would make an excellent wife or mistress for one of your daring band."

"Capital, my lord—capital!"

"And I should not grudge a good dowry," added the count. "Bear that in mind."

"I will, my lord."

"By that means I should rid myself of her entirely, and prevent her from having any further claim upon me," observed the count.

"Exactly so, signor," coincided Spinotti. "Then I have the whole of your lordship's commands?"

"Yes. Should I require the assistance of your band at any time, I suppose I can have it?"

"Certainly. We are pledged to obey you upon all occasions."

"'Tis well. You will convey this bag of gold to your captain, and tell him that probably in a few days he may see me at the cavern."

"I will do so, my lord," replied Spinotti, placing the bag in his pocket. "And now, I suppose, we had better separate, for I presume that you have no wish that you and I should be seen together by any of your servants?"

"Unquestionably not," returned the count, "for that would excite suspicion. But stay: have you any knowledge of the present retreat of the brigand chief, Massaroni?"

"I do not know it exactly," answered Spinotti, "but I have been given to understand that it is somewhere near the Appenine Mountains. He is no friend of your lordship's, I believe?"

"No; he has taken a most extraordinary interest in the fate of Olympia, and has threatened me with his deadliest vengeance if I break a compact he extorted from me under the most remarkable and unexpected circumstances."

"And Massaroni is one, signor, who, I think you are aware, never fails to keep his word."

"Very true; I would give a fortune could that desperate and fearful man be secured and brought to punishment."

"No doubt of it, signor," said Spinotti; "and so would many others beside yourself; but Massaroni is more than a match for all that ingenuity can devise to entrap him. He will, I firmly believe, never die by the hands of the executioner. We dare not offend him, for we have not the power to resist his vengeance. The name of Allesandro Massaroni itself is sufficient to daunt the stoutest heart."

"And yet I am determined that he shall not escape my power," said the count; "the daring outrage he committed against me calls for vengeance, and I will have it yet, let the consequences be whatever they may."

"I would have your lordship be cautious what you say," remarked the robber; "for Massaroni is no common foe; he is here, there and everywhere; you are never safe from him, he has his spies, and is himself in every place when the least expected. Nothing escapes his knowledge, and woe to those who attempt to thwart him or to set his power at defiance."

"Very true, Spinotti; but, notwithstanding all this, he may yet be defeated," replied Count Alberti; "and it shall be no fault of mine if he is not. But I have communicated to you all my wishes, and will now bid you farewell."

"Farewell, signor," said Spinotti; "I will communicate all that you have told me to Rinaldo."

With these words the count and the robber separated, and the former passing by the spot where Florio was concealed, without observing him, passed into the pallazzo.

"And this is the man," remarked Florio, when the count had disappeared—"this, the libertine, the associate of robbers, who dares to aspire to the hand of the amiable, the gentle, and beauteous Melina! Oh, monstrous idea! But it shall not, must not be! No, by Heaven, though I lose my own life in the attempt, I will prevent it. Unfortunate Olympia, thou too must be rescued from the power of those wretches, and yet bring shame and misery upon the head of thine heartless seducer! Massaroni is near the Appenines. Would that I could meet with him, and make him acquainted with what I have over heard; I am certain he would wreak his vengeance upon the head of his dastardly enemy, and frustrate his plans against the happiness of Melina and Olympia. He is indebted to me for the preservation of his life, and well knowing that he is never ungrateful, I have sufficient reason to believe he is my friend. I will endeavour to find him, and place my dependence upon his advice."

Having come to this resolution, Florio hastily departed from the gardens of the count's pallazzo, and notwithstanding the night was now considerably advanced, he did not return home, but wandered on in a state of mind of which the reader may form a very proper conception. He continued walking all night, and by the time the morning dawned, he had advanced far on his way towards the mountains of the Appenines, with a full determination to obtain an interview with the brigand chief if possible.

CHAPTER LX.

MSSARONI'S RETREAT NEAR THE APPE-NNIES.—THE OLD COTTAGER.—THE MYS-TERY.—THE MEETING WITH FLORIO.—THE MIDNIGHT ATTACK ON THE PALLAZZO AND THE CAPTURE OF COUNT ALBERTI.

THE brigand chief, as has been intimated, was now located in a romantic wood near the lofty Appenines, where he might bid defiance to detection, or to any enemy that might be set to apprehend him. The country between this wood and the mountains was much intersected by ravines, water falls, and rocks covered with the mountain ash and Lombardy poplars; the whole presenting a most wild appearance well according with the character of the brigand and his bold band. The scene was indeed most picturesque, and might have created a feeling of admiration in even the most indifferent breast. Frequently the woody glades re-echoed with the sounds of the brigands' revelry, but the traveller avoided its precincts with the utmost caution, and no one ventured to intrude upon what might be truly called the dominions of Allesandro Massaroni, the brigand chief. Since the events which had taken place at the Villa Rosa, however, Massaroni had been subject to frequent fits of melancholy and abstraction, from which his wife Marie in vain endeavoured to arouse him. He would at such times withdraw himself for hours from his band, and no one knew whither he wandered or concealed himself. The portrait he had seen at the Villa Rosa continually haunted his imagination, and he sought in vain to banish it from his thoughts. It was constantly present to his eyes—it pursued him like a vision; and the more he strove to hide it from his gaze, the stronger became the impression it made upon him. Not far from the place of Massaroni's retreat, there resided in a cottage an old man name Montaldi, whose appearance and secluded manners particularly attracted the attention of the brigand chief, and when his mind was in the troubled state which we have described, having insinuated himself into his friendship, but without Mon-

taldi's having the least idea as to who he was, he would frequently pay him a visit. In listening to the old man's religious conversation and advice, Massaroni found a soothing balm that nothing else imparted to his mind, and in return he gave Montaldi a paper with strict injunctions not to open it unless his life or property were in danger. But there was another circumstance that more particularly attracted Massaroni to the cottage. Residing with old Montaldi was a woman apparently between forty and fifty years of age, whose intellects were deranged, and who was not only in no way related to Montaldi, but although she had resided with him for several years, he did not even know her name, or where she came from. He had found her perishing at his cottage door on a cold winter's night, and had kindly taken her in and supported her out of charity ever since. This unfortunate creature excited the deepest interest in Massaroni's breast, and he felt the greatest curiosity to become acquainted with her history, but at present there seemed to be not the least probability of his being able to do so while her mind was in the distracted state it was. Ottavia (for so Montaldi called her, not knowing her proper name,) was still a remarkably handsome woman, and had evidently once been very beautiful, nor were the graces of her person less captivating than the charms of her countenance. There was something particularly striking and commanding in her figure, and her features bore a most striking resemblance to one whom he had seen before, but where he could not at that time call to mind. Ottavia would frequently wander from home for hours together, and when she was seated in the cottage she seemed to be unconscious of what was passing around her, and seldom spoke a word. Every day did Massaroni become more anxious to be made acquainted with this unfortunate woman's history, but still with not the most remote prospect of his being able to do so, and he was therefore compelled to give up the idea in despair. It happened that on one occasion when Massaroni was visiting Montaldi, and was seated in conversation with him, a loud demand for admittance was heard at the cottage door.

"Ah!" exclaimed the brigand, rising from his seat; "who are these that would thus unceremoniously intrude themselves upon our privacy? Look out, Montaldi."

Montaldi obeyed, and looking from the casement informed Massaroni that it was two men, who, from their being armed, he thought were officers of justice.

"But how is this, signor?" added the old man; "you seem agitated. Surely you have nothing to fear?"

"No—no—Montaldi," replied the brigand, somewhat confused; "but—but I have a particular aversion for strangers, and I know not who these fellows may be."

"Well, then, signor," remarked Montaldi, "retire into an inner apartment until I have ascertained their business, and got rid of them."

Massaroni obeyed, and retiring into the room which the old man pointed out, the latter opened the door and gave admittance to two of the worst of Massaroni's band.

"Now, signors," said Montaldi, "your business?"

FLORIO SENDS A LETTER BY NURSE.

"It is briefly stated," said one of the ruffians; "you must hand over to us, without a moment's delay, the whole of your money."

"Money!" replied the old man, "I have none, I am miserably poor."

"Do not attempt to deceive us!" said the villain, "we will have every scudi you possess or your life. Quick! for we have no time to wait while you are making up your mind."

"Spare me, I beseech you," said Montaldi, "I am but a poor old man, and surely, signors, you will not be cowardly enough to——"

"No more of this nonsense," said the other fellow, presenting his carbine at the head of Montaldi—"Your money, I say, or your life!"

"Hold! but a moment," said the old man, suddenly recollecting the paper which the brigand chief had given him, and which he produced and delivered to the ruffian who had spoken last.

On beholding it one of the fellows was for obeying it, but the other snatched it from Montaldi's hand, and tearing it in a hundred pieces, stamped upon it with contempt.

"Think not to save yourself by this," he observed, "you see the value and importance I set upon it, and I repeat, if you do not deliver up your money without a moment's mere hesitation, I will send a bullet through your head."

"Villains!" cried Massaroni, rushing from the place of his concealment, and grasping them by their collars; "is it thus you despise the orders of your chief, and outrage those whom it is his will to protect?"

With these words, he hurled them to each side of the room, and drawing a brace of pistols from his belt, he was on the point of discharging their contents at them, when they shrunk on their knees in the most abject manner, and shrieked aloud for mercy; and Montaldi, who was astonished and alarmed at finding in Massaroni the terrible brigand chief, also interceded for them.

"'Tis well you have found a friend in the man you would have so basely plundered," he said; "begone to the rendezvous, and there I will decide what punishment shall be inflicted on you."

The brigands hastened away without another word, and Massaroni, turning to Montaldi, said—

"No doubt you are surprised and alarmed at discovering who I am, but you have nothing to fear, I have promised you my friendship, and I never break my word, it is not the poor who are the victims of Allesandro Massaroni, the brigand chief."

"Alas! Massaroni," said Montaldi, "what a pity it is that one who is possessed of so many good qualities should lead such a lawless life. Oh, what can have driven you to it?"

"Wrongs deep as ever were inflicted upon human being," answered Massaroni; "it is not the fault of myself that I have become an outcast from society, but that of him who should have protected me, and who cruelly deserted me and my unfortunate mother, and left her to die of a broken heart. I live alone for vengeance, Montaldi, and when I have obtained that I shall be at peace."

"Unfortunate man," said Montaldi, "your's seems to have been indeed a hard destiny. But is the author of your being still living?"

"I know not," answered Massaroni, "but I have every reason to believe he is. I have heard that he is rich and noble, but my mother ever refused to reveal to me his name."

At that moment Ottavia, who had hitherto been seated in one corner of the room, staring vacantly around her, and apparently unconscious of what was passing, uttered a faint shriek, and starting from her chair, advanced towards the spot where Massaroni and Montaldi were standing.

"Who talks of innocence betrayed?" she ejaculated in wild accents; "who mentioned the name of the deceiver? Yes, he was rich and noble, his victim poor and friendless! He deserted her, but oh, it was most cruel to rob her of her child! To snatch the little innocent from her breast, and bear it, Heaven only knows whither. Oh, he was then young and handsome: even like you," she added, addressing herself to Massaroni; "and oh, how honied were his accents, and solemn were the promises he made to her. Did you ever hear the song he used to sing to her? These are the words—

"Maiden of Florence, oh, listen to me,
　Nor think that I seek thy fond heart to ensnare;
If I deceive thee accurs'd may I be,
　And my bosom be plunged in the darkest despair.

Maiden of Florence, my bosom reviles
　The wretch who'd the innocent damsel betray;
Maiden of Florence, more bright are thy smiles
　To me, than the radiant orb of the day.

Maiden of Florence, I liken thine eyes,
　That now with such lustre are beaming on me,
To the stars that so brilliantly shine in the skies,
　And I love them not, dearest, more than I love thee.

Can I deceive thee? oh, never! oh, never!
　Let no such thought in thy bosom have birth;
May I, if false to thee. cursed be for ever,
　Wandering hated, despised, o'er the earth.

Maiden of Florence, oh, listen to me,
　Nor think that I seek thy fond heart to ensnare;
If I deceive thee accurs'd may I be,
　And my bosom be sunk in the darkest despair."

In a voice of the most plaintive sweetness and melancholy, the hapless Ottavia sang these words, and Massaroni and Montaldi listened to her with the deepest interest and attention. When she had concluded, she burst into a wild hysterical laugh, and rushing from the room entered the inner apartment.

"Unfortunate woman!" said the brigand chief, "I feel more interested in her than ever. It is but too evident that she has also been the victim of some heartless seducer, and the similarity of her fate to that of my deeply wronged mother, excites my utmost sympathy. Watch over her tenderly, Montaldi, and at some future period her senses may be restored to her, and we may then be made acquainted with her history; and Massaroni swears that if ever he has the opportunity, he will redress her wrongs."

Massaroni now renewed the protection he had given to Montaldi, and then taking his leave, he departed to the rendezvous to rejoin his comrades. It was a beautiful evening; the silver lamp of night was shining brilliantly in the heavens, and the rich foliage of the trees glittered in its beams. In order to dissipate the gloomy thoughts which had taken possession of his mind, Massaroni joined the revelry and boisterous mirth of his band, and the song, the jest, and the dance were freely indulged in, making the green wood resound again, and forming altogether a scene of the most striking, picturesque, and romantic description. For more than an hour the brigands continued their sports, in their woodland retreat, and beneath, the bright beams of Luna; but at length during a brief interval of silence, loud cries of help saluted their ears, and which seemed to proceed from no great distance off.

"Follow me!" cried Massaroni, seizing his carbine; "some one needs our aid, and it must never be denied to the unprotected."

As he thus spoke he rushed from the spot in the direction of the place from whence the cries proceeded, followed by two or three of his band. The cries were repeated, and it was evident there was no time to lose. Forcing his way through a thicket, Massaroni came upon a more open space, and beheld at a short distance from him a man on one knee, whilst two of the brigands had raised the butt ends of their carbines in the air, and were apparently in the act of felling him to the earth, the traveller being totally unarmed.

"Hold, villains!" shouted Massaroni, darting towards them. "Cowards! would you strike a defenceless man? Hold! I say! Who dares to disobey the commands of Allesandro Massaroni?"

The brigands started back at the voice of their chief, and the traveller jumped to his feet with an exclamation of mingled astonishment and delight.

"Ah! what my young Raphael," said Massaroni; "is it possible we meet again? What strange accident has led your footsteps to this place?"

"Massaroni," replied Florio, for he it was, "I am glad to see you, for I have much to say to you, and need your advice upon a very delicate subject, and which I doubt not you will grant to me."

"Indeed!" said Massaroni; "but what has brought you so far from Rome, and how did you discover the place of my retreat?"

"It was entirely by accident," answered Florio; "but I will tell you all, if you will listen to me."

"Most willingly," said the brigand chief; "and if I can serve you in anything, you will find me most ready to do so, for I do not forget that to you I am indebted for the preservation of my life. Costello! but that was a narrow escape, and I have no doubt that his highness the prince was greatly vexed and disappointed to think that I should have been in his company all the night, and that after all I should manage to slip through his fingers."

"Yes, he was greatly enraged," remarked Florio; "but that is not the subject upon which I wish to talk with you, Massaroni. Oh, no, it is one which to me is of far greater importance."

"Indeed!" said the brigand chief, "I shall be most happy to listen to you. Follow me, signor."

Florio Clairville obeyed in silence, and Massaroni led the way to that part of the wood in which his cave was situated, and motioning him to be seated, requested him to disclose what he wished. Florio sighed.

"Massaroni," he said after a brief pause, "you see before you one of the most miserable of men."

"Miserable!" repeated Massaroni, "and yet possessing the love of the fair Melina, the noble niece of the Prince Bianchi? It is impossible, signor."

"Alas!" sighed Florio, "it is even so. 'Tis true that the beauteous and amiable Melina has honoured me by placing on me her affections; but our hopes are all at an end."

"How so, my young friend?"

"The Prince Bianchi frowns upon our love. He has reproached me for my presumption in aspiring to the hand of his niece; he has banished me from her presence, and has declared that we must never meet again."

"Ah!" said Massaroni, "this is indeed bad news, signor, and I deeply sympathise with you. Has he destined her for some other wealthy rival?"

"He has," answered Florio, "and one whom Melina cannot but loathe and despise."

"His name?"

"The Count Alberti!"

"The Count Alberti! the base and treacherous seducer of Olympia, to whom he is pledged to give his hand?"

"'Tis too true, Signor Massaroni; "the count has made proposals for the hand of Melina, and the prince sanctions his addresses, and seems determined to compel his niece to become his wife."

"Diavolo!" exclaimed the brigand chief; "and will the count dare to set the compact he has entered into with me at defiance?"

"No doubt of it," replied Florio.

"We shall see," remarked Massaroni; "should he do so, my most terrible vengeance shall descend upon his head. Woe to those who attempt to deceive Allesandro Massaroni. I tell thee, Signor Florio, and mark me, I will keep my word; the Count Alberti D'Amalfi shall never become the husband of the beauteous Melina. But what of Olympia? Know you aught of her, signor?"

"She has been forced from her late residence," answered Florio, "and is at present confined somewhere by the count's orders."

"The villain!" cried Massaroni, "has he then so dared? Is it thus he scorns my threats? But how know you this, signor?"

"I will tell you, Massaroni," returned Florio; and he then related those particulars of the conversation he had overheard in the gardens of the palazzo between the count and Spinotti with which the reader is already acquainted.

"I will be revenged for this," said the brigand chief, when Florio had concluded; "The Count Alberti shall deeply repent his conduct. Olympia must be released. But could you not ascertain where she is confined?"

Florio answered in the negative.

"No matter," remarked Massaroni, "I will extort the secret from the count's own lips. I am glad, Signor Florio, that chance has led you to my retreat; but whither do you now intend going?"

"I know not," replied Florio, "all places are now alike to me. Alas!" he added, with a deep sigh, "this annihilation of my hopes has rendered me perfectly reckless as to what becomes of me. And yet, I must admit that I have been most presumptuous in daring to raise my thoughts to that peerless maiden, so far, so very far exalted above me."

"Nay, Signor Clairville," remarked Massaroni, clapping him encouragingly on the shoulder, "you must not suffer yourself to give way entirely to despair. There is a good old English maxim that 'faint heart ne'er won fair lady,' and I must say that I quite agree with the aphorism. I repeat, that I owe to you a debt of gratitude which I am most anxious to repay; and although you probably may not consider yourself very highly flattered by the compliment, coming as it does from the so much dreaded brigand chief, I assure you that I feel the most sincere friendship towards you, and would most gladly render you any service that may be in my power. Moreover, I highly esteem the fair and amiable object of your passion, and consider you worthy of each other. The Prince Bianchi, I admit, seems to me to deserve very little favour at my hands, seeing that he has always shown himself so anxious to consign me to the hands of justice. I would foil him in his designs, more especially, when I find that when, totally regardless of his gentle niece's

happiness, he would not hesitate to sacrifice her to the heartless and unprincipled betrayer of the unfortunate Olympia. Take the word of Allesandro Massaroni, Florio—the Count Alberti D'Amalfi shall never become the husband of Melina."

"Massaroni," said Florio, "I thank you for your good wishes, and the generous sympathy you express in the fate of myself and Melina; but mark me, I can never consent to become a party to any act which might bring dishonour upon my hitherto unsullied name, or endanger the life of my rival, the Count Alberti."

"Fear not, Florio, Massaroni has too much regard for his own honour, too great a respect for human life to shed the blood of even his bitterest enemy excepting in his own defence. No, the mountain chief, whose daring exploits have obtained for him, perhaps, so unenviable a notoriety, is not a reckless assassin. No, he possesses feelings, that, had not cruel destiny placed him in his present situation, might have given him a better title to the term Christian than many of those who so pompously arrogate to themselves the name, and condemn and stigmatize all those who probably by their vices have alone been plunged in infamy and disgrace. There is no sympathy for the wretched outcast who has been hunted from the peace of society by the very being to whom he had a right to look up for support and protection. But this is a dismal theme that suits me not. The innocent demand that justice shall be rendered to them, and never shall it be said that Massaroni refused his utmost aid when it was in his power. The Count Alberti has set me at defiance, has dared to violate the solemn compact he entered into with me, and he must be taught that great and powerful though he be, he must not be allowed to do such things with impunity."

"What course would you adopt towards him, Massaroni?" demanded Florio, anxiously.

"Seize his person," answered the brigand, "and hold him in safe custody until he chooses to divulge the place where he has Olympia confined, and fulfils the terms of the agreement he has entered into with me."

"Are you sufficiently aware of his power, combined with that of the Prince Bianchi?"

"Fully, and set them both at perfect defiance. I think they have both had a sufficient taste of the quality of Allesandro Massaroni, to know that he is a man who is not to be trifled with. By the break of day, I will with my bold companions, be on my way to the palazzo of the count, and I have no doubt that the secret attack I shall make will be crowned with every success. In the meantime, my young friend, you will find every security by remaining here and witnessing the result of my expedition."

"Massaroni," said Florio, with a look of

uneasiness and suspicion, you will not compromise me in this business?"

"No," replied the brigand, "I have given you my word, and I will not forfeit it; you may depend upon me. Come, my comrades await me; let us join them, and seek to banish the gloomy thoughts which at present occupy your mind, Florio. Come, come."

Florio obeyed, but in spite of all his efforts he was most sad at heart. They entered the inner cavern, where the brigands usually assemble to carouse, and Massaroni, placing the young painter at his right hand, had refreshments placed before him, of which he urged him to partake, and after some pressing he prevailed upon him. Florio gazed around him at the rude retreat, and the wild determined aspects of these lawless men, and he felt anything but comfortable. The brigand's wife and Rubaldo, together with several of the others, eyed him with looks of jealousy and suspicion, which rendered him still more timid, but Massaroni, by his observations, and the authority he possessed over his band, encouraged him, and in a short time he became more at his ease. Having partaken freely of the repast which was so abundantly spread upon the board, the brigands gave themselves up to mirth and revelry, and Massaroni having given "Success to the mountain band," Rubaldo sang the following rude but characteristic song, the whole of his comrades joining and making the spacious caverns resound again:

Evviva Massaroni! Evviva Massaroni!
Hail to the chief so daring and bold,
Whose name is a passport wherever 'tis heard
    To the coffers of wealth, to the bright yellow
        gold   Evviva Massaroni!
                CHORUS.
Dance, drink, and sing, play at dice, play at
        mora,
    Laugh at the laws from our erie secure;
Round with the bottle, ancora! ancora!
    Wine is of all earthly evils a cure!

Evviva Massaroni! Evviva Massaroni!
    Free as the eagle when soaring on high;
Dauntless and brave as the lion in the desert,
    Formed ev'ry power on earth to defy.

                CHORUS.
Dance, drink, and sing, play at dice, play at
        mora,
    Laugh at the laws from our erie secure;
Round with the bottle, ancora! ancora!
    Wine is of all earthly evils a cure!

This song and chorus had a peculiar effect, and Florio could not help but feel amused and interested by it; but still his mind was disturbed by the most torturing thoughts, and fatigued with his travelling, for he had stopped but little to rest on the road, and he was anxious to snatch a few hours' repose. Massaroni perceived this, and at the conclusion of the song he arose from his seat, and said—

"Signor Clairville, I see that you are worn out with travelling, and therefore would advise you to seek repose. I wish to see you at an early hour in the morning, to talk farther of the important business which so deeply concerns us both. Follow me, signor, if you please."

Massaroni took up a lamp, and Florio having bowed to Maria Grazie and the brigands, and bade them good night, followed the mountain chief from the cavern along a dark and narrow passage, until they arrived at a smaller vault or cave, in which was a table and a stool, and in one corner a mattress.

"This is but a rough lodging, signor," said Massaroni, "but here you are perfectly safe. In the morning I must depart with a portion of my band on my expedition to the Count Alberti, but here you may rest in security till my return."

"Massaroni!" said the young painter, anxiously, "you again give me your word that you will use no more violence than is absolutely necessary?"

"I do," answered the brigand chief.

"I would rather even now you would abandon your intentions."

"Nonsense, signor, what have you to fear? I take the whole responsibility upon myself."

"Know you not the danger you may involve yourself in?"

"Cospetto, signor, of course I do. Allesandro Massaroni is not to be thwarted in his plans, or daunted by any thoughts of danger. The hapless Olympia pines in confinement; for aught I know she may be consigned to death by her heartless seducer;—I have sworn to protect her, and I will not break my oath; she must be rescued, and the Count Alberti be compelled to render her justice. Good night, signor."

"Good night," repeated Florio, and the brigand having lighted a lamp which was standing on the table, left him to himself.

Massaroni, on his return to the cavern, found his wife and the brigands consulting deeply together, and the peculiarity of their looks afforded him anything but satisfaction.

"Come, comrades!" he said, "to rest, to rest, the night has far advanced, and we shall have to travel many leagues before the set of sun to-morrow evening."

"Why, how is this, Massaroni?" demanded Maria, in a dissatisfied tone; "what brings this young man to our retreat?"

"Accident, but he seeks my help, and I am resolved that he shall not seek it in vain."

"Another mad-brained design, Massaroni," said his wife, "fraught with all the danger that surrounded you, and from which you so narrowly escaped at the Villa Rosa. I like it not, especially when the prospect of gain may be so little. Remember that treachery is abroad to entrap you."

"And this Signor Florio, with his smooth tongue and friendly bearing," remarked Rubaldo, "may he not be a spy? And——"

"Hold, Rubaldo," interrupted Massaroni, sternly, "you are always too ready with your suspicions. I am satisfied that you wrong Signor Clairville by such a surmise. Am I not indebted to him for the preservation of my life?"

"And against whom is this expedition directed?" asked Maria.

"The Count Alberti D'Amalfi."

"The Count Alberti?"

"Aye! he has broken the compact he entered into with me."

"Indeed!" said his wife, scornfully, "and were you mad enough to suppose that he would ever fulfil it?"

"By all my hopes!" exclaimed Massaroni, resolutely, "I will compel him to do so. I will seize upon his person and bring him hither, and see then whether he dare defy the Brigand Chief. He has torn the fair Olympia and her infant from their home, and now has them confined. Be it my task to restore them to liberty, and if my hitherto good fortune does not forsake me, I shall succeed."

"You appear to take a peculiar interest in the fate of this *fair* Olympia, Massaroni," said his wife with a look which bespoke the feelings of jealousy that were fast gaining ascendancy in her bosom. "Time was when you had no eyes, no thoughts for any woman, but the devoted partner of your wild fortunes."

"Maria," demanded Massaroni, "what mean you? Can you for a moment doubt the love and constancy of Allesandro? Oh, how cruelly do you wrong me if you do. No other woman but the Brigand's wife, Maria Grazie, the faithful companion of all his cares and dangers, can ever possess her husband's love. 'Tis true that I feel no common interest in the fate of the Count Alberti's unfortunate victim; the oppressed and injured ever excite my commiseration and anxious care, and shall I deny them to one who has so powerful and just a claim upon my sympathies?—Nay, more, has she not like myself been thrown an outcast upon the wide and cheerless world, without a friend to advise or cherish her? Bethink yourself, Maria, and let your better feelings prevail. But no more of this; comrades, retire, and prepare to meet me as soon as the first streak of day shall gild the summits of the eastern mountains."

The brigands dispersed, and Massaroni and his wife, after some further conversation, retired to rest.

CHAPTER X.

DESPERATE CONFLICT IN THE PALAZZO OF THE COUNT ALBERTI.—THE BRIGANDS TRIUMPHANT.

THE golden sun had scarcely mounted the bright chariot of the day, and the birds were sweetly carolling their morning song, making the green woods resound again with their mellifluous notes, when Massaroni entered the cavern in which Florio had been reposing, and found him already risen, and traversing the place apparently deeply immersed in thought. The languid expression of his countenance showed plainly that he had rested but little during the night, and that his mind was now in the most distressed and agitated state.

"Come, Signor Florio," remarked Massaroni, "you must arouse yourself from this state of gloom and despondency, and look forward with hope to the future. Rest satisfied that I am your friend, and you may yet learn that even the friendship of Allesandro Massaroni, the Brigand Chief, is not to be despised. I promise you again that the Count Alberti D'Amalfi, the seducer of Olympia, shall never be the husband of her whom you love."

"Alas! alas!" sighed Florio, "how can I venture to encourage hope, poor and friendless as I am, and after the stern and fixed determination of the Prince Bianchi? I must be a presumptuous idiot were I to do so."

"Not so," returned Massaroni; "but come, the morning repast awaits us, and then me and my band must depart, for even by the most expeditious travelling it will be night before we can possibly reach the palazzo."

"Massaroni," said Florio, still hesitatingly, "I would much rather that you would abandon your designs, which I much fear cannot be productive of any good result."

"Tut, tut, tut!" replied Massaroni, impatiently; "let's hear no more of this. My mind is made up, and nothing will alter my mind. But you will promise me, Signor Clairville, that you will not depart from this cavern till my return?"

"I will," said Florio, after a pause; "but what will the world, what will Melina think of me, should it become known that I am in any way connected with you?"

"Fear not," answered Massaroni; "that shall ever remain a profound secret. Come, follow me."

Florio obeyed without making use of any further observation, and accompanied Massaroni into the cavern, where Maria Grazie and the brigands were assembled. They greeted him with sullen looks, but Massaroni by a glance awed them into silence, and treated him with the utmost respect and attention.

The meal over, Massaroni arose from the

table, and addressing himself to those who were to accompany him, commanded them to prepare to depart, and communicated to them his instructions.

It was arranged that they were to disguise themselves, and travelling by different routes towards the palazzo, meet at a given point, and there decide upon the method of their attack; but Massaroni strictly enjoined them not to endanger the life of the count, his only object being to secure his person.

Having commanded his wife and the rest of the brigands who were to be left behind to guard the cavern, and to see to the safety and comfort of Florio, Massaroni assumed the dress of an old man, and his companions having likewise disguised themselves in such a manner as would render it impossible for any person to have the least suspicion of their real characters, Massaroni shook Florio by the hand, and telling him to be of good cheer, they quitted the cavern, and separating in the wood, the brigand chief pursued his way alone, leaning on a staff, and in every respect bearing the appearance of a decrepid old man. Prince Bianchi had endeavoured to conceal from the Count Alberti the feelings with which his niece Melina had received his proposals, but he could not, and although the count was greatly enraged, and his pride severely mortified, he was by no means disappointed. The prince also endeavoured to encourage him to hope, and expressed his authority to conquer Melina's repugnance, and to make her receive his addresses with a favourable eye; he, however, advised him to defer seeking an interview with Melina for a day or two, until her feelings should be more composed, and she might feel disposed to give him a reception in accordance with his (the prince's) wishes.

"So, the proud beauty scorns me," he said when the prince had left him; " she loathes, she despises me!--'Tis no more than I expected; the beggar Florio Clairville possesses her heart, but I have found favour in her uncle's eyes, and, even though I cannot win her love, she shall become my bride. I will not so easily resign my proud pretensions. No, fair Melina, thy doom is sealed, and no earthly power shall avert it. Olympia and her child are secured, and therefore they can present no obstacle to the gratification of my wishes; they shall never trouble me again."

And in spite of all his efforts to the contrary, the count could not reconcile his villanous conduct towards Olympia and her innocent child to his conscience, and many were the bitter thoughts and painful self-upbraidings it caused him. Although he had taken such pains to conceal the fate to which he had consigned them from the knowledge of every one, he could not help thinking that he was looked upon with universal suspicion, and he had no doubt that

that was the principal cause of Melina's being so prejudiced against him. He heartily wished that they were both dead, and yet he revolted from the idea of taking their life. In order to banish these thoughts he rushed into society as much as possible, and entertained large parties at his own castle or palazzo; but it was all to no purpose, and he became, amidst all his wealth, and all the ambitious hopes he had formed, truly miserable. Notwithstanding, also, he had endeavoured to treat the threats of Massaroni with contempt, and to banish them from his recollection, they continually haunted his imagination, and kept him in a constant state of dread and uneasiness. On the evening of the intended attack of the brigand chief and his band upon the palazzo, the count had entertained a few select friends, among whom was the Prince Bianchi; but feeling suddenly indisposed and spiritless, the party broke up and dispersed at an early hour, and left him alone to his own thoughts. A sensation, however, came over the Count Alberti, which prevented him from retiring to rest, and he sat buried in gloomy meditation until the hour of midnight rapidly approached. Massaroni and his band met at the place they had appointed, and when darkness entirely obscured the horizon, they made their way to the castle. There was not a human being to be seen near the spot, and all around was perfectly silent. The night too was particularly dark, so that objects were not distinguishable at any distance.

"All is favourable to our designs," said Massaroni, "and if fortune does not frown upon us, success is certain. But now to gain admittance."

"We shall find that no easy task, I fancy," remarked Rubaldo; "for you see the castle is surrounded by a moat, the bridge over which is drawn up."

" That is awkward," said Massaroni, surveying the castle; " but we have no time to deliberate. Ah! this tree may assist us."

On one part of the bank was a willow tree, the boughs of which overhung the water, and this it was which had attracted the attention of Massaroni.'

" By a leap from that tree," he remarked, " I think I might reach the bank within."

" It would be a desperate attempt," said Rubaldo.

"Ay," answered the brigand chief, " but not more desperate than the occasion. I will boldly venture it."

As he thus spoke, bold and active, Massaroni mounted the tree, and standing on the strongest branch, he made a spring. The elastic nature of the wood gave him an additional impetus, and threw him on the bank, stunned with the fall. He soon recovered himself, and gazing eagerly around him, he beheld the sentinel at the gate. In order for him to accomplish his plans, there was nothing left for him to do but to sacrifice the life of this unfortunate man, though it was not without the greatest repugnance he was driven to such a necessity. Massaroni crept on close by the walls, until he reached the gate. The sentinel's back at that moment was turned towards him, and taking advantage of the opportunity, the brigand chief plunged his stiletto to the hilt in the unfortunate wretch's body, and he sunk at his feet a corpse, without giving utterance to the slightest cry. This done, without the least noise, Massaroni let down the drawbridge and gave admittance to Rubaldo and the rest of his bold associates.

"Conceal yourselves behind yonder trees," ne said, "there is a door open, and lights proceed from the windows of the apartment beyond it. When I give the signal, hasten to my assistance, and not before. I will enter the castle alone."

"Why, what madness is this!" remarked Rubaldo; "know you not the danger you may rush upon?"

"Obey my orders," commanded Massaroni peremptorily, "and question not my will."

Thus saying, he cautiously stole into the castle by the open door, and crept with silent footsteps towards the apartment, from the windows of which he had seen the lights, and which he supposed to be the sitting room of the Count Alberti, who, he imagined, had not yet retired to rest. When he arrived at the door he paused to listen, but hearing no person stirring, he ventured to open it slowly, and to look cautiously in. The count was seated at the further end of the apartments with his head resting on his hand, and apparently wrapped in the deepest meditation. Massaroni stepped into the room with a pistol in each hand, and was hastily advancing towards his intended prisoner, when his toe came in contact with something that was lying on the floor, and stumbling, the noise he made aroused the count, who started to his feet and gazed with the utmost astonishment and alarm towards him.

"Ah!" he exclaimed, "what means this intrusion?—Who are you, fellow, that thus dares to break upon my privacy, and what is your purpose?—What ho! there!—Help, help!"

"Silence!" commanded Massaroni, in a determined voice, "or you are a dead man."

"Ah! by Heaven!" cried the count, as he recognised that man whom he had so much cause to fear, and upon whom his thoughts had been fixed only a few minutes before;—"it is the brigand Massaroni! Villain! what would you?"

"Justice for Olympia and her innocent offspring, whom you now hold in your power!"

replied Massaroni. "It is useless for you to attempt to resist me; you are my prisoner!"

"Liar!" exclaimed the count as he rushed desperately upon the brigand chief and tried to wrest the pistols from his grasp; "help! help!"

The count was a powerful man as well as Massaroni, and the latter could not release himself from his grasp, while the count continued to shout lustily for help, and Massaroni could hear footsteps hastily approaching the apartment, but he had no means of giving the signal to his associates. It was a moment of great danger, and they both of them became desperate; but in the struggle that ensued one of the pistols accidentally exploded, and gave the alarm to the brigands outside, who came rushing into the room just at the same instant that a number the count's vassals, all well armed, entered by an opposite door. Massaroni had now succeeded in felling his antagonist to the earth, and had placed one of his feet on his chest, and presented the loaded pistol at his head, threatening him with instant death if he did not yield. The brigands attacked the vassals fiercely and kept them at bay, though they fought with great determination, and Massaroni's life was several times placed in the utmost jeopardy. The noise and confusion that now reigned in the castle was perfectly terrific, and the vassals of the count rent the air with the name of Allesandro Massaroni. But now another calamity added to the horrors of the scene; a portion of the rich drapery of the apartment caught fire, and the flames spread with astonishing rapidity, destroying everything in their progress, and hissing and crackling frightfully. The smoke soon became suffocating, and the combatants could not distinguish each other. The vassals, however, at length began to give way, and as the conflagration spread on every side, the consternation that prevailed became indescribable.

"Secure the count!" shouted Massaroni, "and away with him. The triumph is ours."

Two of the brigands immediately seized Alberti, and in spite of his struggles and the dreadful threats and maledictions that escaped his lips, when he saw his noble castle fast falling a prey to the devouring element, they forced him from the room. The vassals rallied again, and pursued the brigands to the drawbridge, where the combat became fiercer than ever, and the sacrifice of human life that took place was terrific. Wherever the danger was the greatest, there was Massaroni, and many were those that fell beneath his dauntless arm. But at length the vassals, finding that resistance was useless, many of them fell back, while the others, more determined, continued the combat over the bridge and to some distance from the castle, until all hope was at an end, and they fled in all directions to alarm the neighbours, to get others to assist them, and to go in pursuit of the brigands.

"Quick! quick!" cried Massaroni, "to the wood, and we may set pursuit and further resistance at defiance."

"Oh, villain! atrocious villain!" exclaimed the infuriated nobleman; "you shall dearly repent this monstrous, this dastardly outrage."

"Away with him!" commanded Massaroni, "and heed not his ravings. My lord, the wrongs of Olympia and her child shall be amply avenged. Massaroni the brigand chief never

promises that which he is not competent to perform."

"Miscreant!" cried the unhappy count, "may the deadliest curses pursue thee and thy atrocious associates."

Massaroni returned no other answer than an exulting and scornful laugh, and the ruffians hurrying the count along, they soon entered the wood. The shouts of the affrighted people in the neighbourhood of the burning castle still rang in their ears, and imparted the utmost agony to the bosom of the Count

Alberti, who now gave himself up entirely to despair, and could have offered no more resistance than a child, if even it had not been completely useless. The castle was evidently now one mass of flames, and was doomed to entire destruction, and the lurid reflection from it spread far over the horizon, rendering the scene at once one of the most sublime and awful that could be imagined. The brigands continued their flight with increased speed, and in the course of another hour were far beyond the danger of pursuit. It was at this point that they arrived at a vehicle, with which Massaroni had ordered two of his band to be in waiting at a certain hour. The count, whose arms were pinioned, was lifted into it, Massaroni and Rubaldo followed, and it was driven off at a rapid rate towards their retreat, the rest of the brigands following in the rear. The count remained for some time buried in silence, and seemed to have given himself up to the most abject despair, but at length turning to the brigand chief, he said—

"Oh, Massaroni, what have I done to merit this cruel treatment?"

"You have broken faith with me!" replied Massaroni; "you have dared to set my power at defiance, and those who know me are well aware that I will not suffer any man to do so with impunity, let his rank or station be ever so exalted. Did I not tell you what would be the consequences if you dared attempt to deceive me?—You cannot say that I have acted without giving you fair and timely warning, and you have got yourself to blame alone for all that has taken place. You have played the part of a dastardly villain, and justice demands that you should make atonement for it."

"A villain!" repeated the young count, his eyes flashing with indignation and offended pride.

"Aye, of a villain!" said the brigand chief; "I always call things by their right names, and ask your own conscience whether or not I speak the truth?"

"What mean you?" demanded Alberti, in a faint and faltering tone of voice.

"Psha!" replied Massaroni, impatiently, "it is worse than childish to plead ignorance of that to which I allude. Where is Olympia? Where is your child?"

"I know not," stammered out Alberti, in a hesitating voice; "Olympia left her home of her own accord, and I know not whither she has gone."

"Tis false! and you know it," said Massaroni, indignantly. "Think you to deceive me thus? Beware, Count Alberti, for I am not a man to be trifled with, as by this time you are properly convinced. You know that Olympia and her child were forcibly taken away from their home by villains in your pay, and in your presence; and that at this moment they are held in confinement in some distant part of the country."

"How know you this?"

"Can you deny that it is true?"

The count looked confused, but returned no answer.

"Your silence is an admission of your guilt," said Massaroni, "Oh, what a consummate, what a heartless scoundrel you must be, thus to act towards those whom it is your duty to love and cherish. You call me miscreant robber; be it so; but Allesandro Massaroni would despise and hate himself if he could ever become the betrayer of female innocence, and afterwards add to her misery by the most refined cruelty and oppression. However, I have sworn to protect Olympia and her child, and I will not fail to keep my word, you may depend upon it."

"Massaroni," said the count, in accents of alarm, "if I have erred, have you not already had a terrible revenge? My noble castle and all it contains has become a prey to the destructive flames, myself in the power of you and your lawless band;—pause before you proceed to farther extremities—what are your intentions towards me?"

"You will know that," replied the brigand chief, "when we arrive at the place of our destination."

"Will nothing induce you to set me at liberty?"

"Oh, yes."

"Name the terms?"

"You shall know them anon."

"Why keep me in suspense?" demanded the count, with an expression of fear and suspicion.

"To punish you for the contempt with which you have treated me and my threats. I would convince you of the power of Allesandro Massaroni, which you have affected to consider so insignificant. And so, you, the seducer of Olympia, have even dared to raise your thoughts to the fair and peerless Signora Melina, the niece of my much respected friend, his highness the Prince Bianchi?—You would force her to become your bride, though she can never entertain any other feelings towards you than those of hatred and disgust!"

"By what means have you become acquainted with this, Massaroni?" asked the astonished Alberti.

"Oh," replied the brigand, with a laugh, "there are few things that do not come to the knowledge of Massaroni, to the confusion of the tyrant and oppressor. The prince may favour your suit, but I tell you that Melina shall never be forced into a marriage with one who is so unworthy of her, and whom she so utterly loathes."

"And who will prevent it?" haughtily demanded the count.

"I will," replied Massaroni; "Melina shall become the wife of the man on whom she has bestowed her affections."

"And who may that highly favoured individual be?" demanded Alberti, scornfully.

"Signor Florio Clairville."

"The poor painter?"

"The same, Count Alberti."

"Psha! Massaroni, you do but jest."

"Indeed I do not," replied the brigand; "and so you will find to your confusion and disappointment."

"And think you that the Prince Bianchi will ever consent to bestow the hand of his niece upon a mere beggar?"

"Consent or not, she shall become his wife."

"And why take you so deep an interest in the fate of this man?"

"Massaroni is always the friend of the unfortunate, and Signor Clairville possesses my esteem."

"Ah, then," observed the count, "Florio Clairville, the affected paragon of virtue and honour, is connected with the lawless mountain chief and his daring band?"

"In any of my proceedings he is not," replied the brigand; "Signor Clairville is no hypocrite; he is, I am convinced, all that he has represented himself to be—noble-minded, honourable: beware then, Count Alberti, how you seek to stigmatise his character."

"Massaroni," again supplicated the count, after a pause, "I beseech you to pause in what you are doing, and which can only bring down a terrible retribution upon your head."

"I scorn, I defy it!" said Massaroni; "think you, that after all my years of daring, I am to be so easily intimidated?"

"Will no offer of gold induce you to set me at liberty?" said the count.

"Not at present," replied Massaroni; "so you may as well rest your mind contented. We are now far beyond the reach of pursuit, and in a short time we shall arrive at my secret retreat, where no doubt you will receive a most cordial welcome"

"Do not hurt me, Massaroni."

"It is my delight to taunt and torture the guilty oppressor," answered the brigand chief.

"I have never injured you."

"But you have those whom I esteem, and that is all the same to me. Recollect that you have brought this all upon yourself."

"How so?"

"By your acts of villany, and in breaking the solemn compact you entered into with me."

"And was not that extorted from me by threats and intimidation?"

"Be it so, but justice sanctioned it, and I am fully determined that you shall abide by it. But it is useless for us to prolong this discussion—you are now in my power; you have heard my determination, and cannot help yourself."

"Depend upon it, Massaroni," said the count, "that this atrocious outrage will but serve to hasten your own destruction. My friends will not fail to pursue you even to the furthest limits of the globe, and to wreak upon you their vengeance."

"Ha! ha! ha!" laughed the brigand chief, scornfully, "what cares Massaroni for those idle threats?—Your friends, most noble Count Alberti, will have a long chase ere they find me; and should they succeed in doing so, they will meet with a much warmer reception than they may perhaps calculate upon. At any rate, I shall hold you in security, and depend upon it that if I fall, you at any rate shall perish also."

"Would you take my life?"

"In self-defence only; I repeat that I am no reckless murderer, and woe to them who dare to give me that title. Recollect the maxim of Allesandro Massaroni, and beware of what you say; the vengeance of Massaroni is as sweeping as it is sure."

The count made no reply, but threw himself back in the vehicle in despair, and gave himself up to the most gloomy thoughts, for he saw that he was completely in the power and at the mercy of the brigand chief, and that he had no means of helping himself. They continued their journey at a rapid pace, and the silence remained unbroken. The darkness that prevailed was solemn and impressive; and wild and frightful was the scenery through which they travelled, which added to the melancholy and misery of the count's reflections.

CHAPTER XI.

THE CONSTERNATION AT THE DISAPPEARANCE OF THE COUNT ALBERTI, AND THE DESTRUCTION OF HIS CASTLE.—THE STINGS OF A GUILTY CONSCIENCE.

FLORELLA, the waiting maid of Melina, to whom Florio had entrusted his letter on his departure from the Villa Rosa, faithfully delivered it to her mistress, whom she found completely overwhelmed with grief and despair. With eager but trembling hand Melina took the precious epistle, and her tears fell fast as she gazed upon the well known characters. She unfolded it and proceeded to peruse the contents, but her agitation was so great that she could with difficulty decipher the words. How deeply affecting and eloquent was the language in which that epistle was couched, and how agonizing was the effect it had upon the hapless damsel's heart. Florio repeated all those ardent vows of love he had so frequently uttered in her ear, deplored the cruelty of their destiny, and bade her farewell for ever.

"For ever!" she sighed; "oh, that dreadful word; but it must not, cannot be. Oh, Florio, I feel that thou art now dearer to me than ever, and should fate ordain that we should never be united, life will become an insupportable burthen to me. But to become the wife of the libertine Alberti, the heartless betrayer of female innocence! Oh, the idea is monstrous! I will sooner die than submit to so revolting a fate! Alas! my uncle, you have ever behaved to me with such kindness and indulgence, and on whom I have ever lavished the same affection as if you had been my own parent, can you have the heart to wish to consign me to such a cruel and disgusting fate? Can you be so totally regardless of my future happiness? Surely you cannot be so lost to all sense of shame or honour as to encourage the addresses of the base betrayer of the unfortunate Olympia. I will not, cannot believe that you will ever be so unjust and ungenerous."

She was startled from this soliloquy by a hand being placed upon her shoulder, and looking round, her astonishment, emotion, and confusion may be conceived when she beheld the Prince Bianchi standing by her side, and his eyes fixed upon her with a look of displeasure.

"Give me that letter, Melina, that you was this moment so fondly perusing," he sternly and peremptorily demanded.

"Oh, my dear uncle," sighed the trembling damsel, "I beseech you bear patiently with my grief. You, to whom I have ever looked for indulgence and affection—whom it has been my constant study to please, and whose will I have never disobeyed by thought or deed. Oh, why seek to torture me thus, and to annihilate all my bright and youthful hopes?"

"Give me the letter, I say," again commanded the prince, at the same time snatching it from her hands.

Melina sunk on her knees at his feet, and looked up imploringly in his face. Bitter sobs escaped her bosom, but she could not give utterance to a word. The prince hastily glanced over the contents of the letter, and his countenance became more stern.

"And has he thus dared, after what passed between us at our last meeting?" he said. "The presumptuous beggar! to persist in his bold addresses to one who is placed so far above him in rank and station. He, the poor friendless plebeian, whom I honoured with my esteem, little thinking that he would take so mean an advantage of it, to aspire to the hand of the niece of the Prince Bianchi, the Governor of Rome. Let him beware, or, by heaven, he shall feel the full weight of my wrath! Thus do I treat his daring epistle."

He tore the letter into a thousand fragments as he spoke, and then fixed his eyes still more severely upon the pale countenance of his trembling and deeply agitated niece.

"Melina," he said, "I solemnly charge you, as you value my love; never to receive any more communications from, or to hold any future correspondence with this presumptuous man, but to prepare yourself to obey my wishes in every respect. Where are your proper feelings of pride, girl? Away with this weakness. Banish Florio from your thoughts, and prepare to receive the Count Alberti as your future husband."

"The Count Alberti as my husband!" ejaculated Melina, with a shudder of horror; "oh, never! never!—my heart revolts at the base idea. Oh, my dear uncle, you cannot be so cruel as to seek to sacrifice me to such a man. Condemn me to a life of celibacy, to perpetual confinement, but do not force me to become the wife of one whom I must ever despise and hate."

"Be not obdurate, Melina," returned the prince, "for it will avail you nothing, and will only excite my wrath. I have hitherto found you obedient to my will, and if you would continue to possess my affection, you must be so on the present occasion. My determination is fixed, and nothing whatever can move me from it."

"God of Heaven help me then!" groaned Melina, "for you have consigned me to a fate that is far too horrible to contemplate. Oh, in mercy, my dear uncle, reflect and relent. Do not, oh, do not compel me to bestow my hand upon one whom I can never look upon but as a villain."

"A villain!" repeated the prince, with a frown.

"Yes, my lord!" said the damsel; "harsh as the word may seem, is not the Count Alberti fully deserving of it?—Has he not basely betrayed the fair Olympia, and now abandoned her and her offspring to misery? Oh, my uncle, you who have ever had such a high sense of honour and virtue, surely cannot sanction or excuse the acts of the heartless and unprincipled libertine, the——"

"Hold! hold, Melina!" interrupted the prince in a voice of extreme agitation;—"why talk to me upon a theme which you know always drives me mad?—why recall to my memory the guilty past?—why reproach me for deeds which——"

"Reproach you, dear uncle," said Melina, with a look of astonishment; "oh, what can you mean?—Why this violent agitation?—Your face is pale, and your eyes glare wildly upon me. What have I said to excite you in this fearful manner?"

"Girl!" replied the prince, in the same agitated manner, "you torture me!—Am I ever to be reminded of the faults of my youthful days?—Who dares accuse me of being the betrayer of female innocence?—Who says that I deserted my victims and their offspring?—'Tis false!—'Tis a vile calumny got up to blast my fair fame and reputation. But—but—" he added, appearing to recollect himself;—"I am mad!—I knew not what I say!—Melina, heed me not, but, as you value my love, venture not again to speak to me upon that hated subject."

'Dear uncle," said his niece, looking up affectionately into the pale face of the prince; "what is the meaning of this?—I never saw you so agitated before. Tell me——"

"Question me not, girl!" interrupted the prince passionately; "you see that I am in pain—this confounded gout, and—and yet you seem to delight to torture me more. But—but—I must leave you; farewell, Melina—reflect well upon what I have said, and learn to obey my will. Remember, the plebeian Clairville and you must never meet again, or correspond with each other; Count Alberti honours you with his love, and I command you to receive his addresses with favour. No other than he shall become the husband of the niece of Prince Bianchi."

Melina covered her face with her hands in an agony of grief and despair, and sobbed as if her heart would break, but she could not give utterance to a word. The prince, still greatly excited, without making use of another observation, quitted the room.

For a few minutes after his departure, his niece remained completely absorbed in grief, and her tears flowed fast and uncontrolled.

"He will remain obstinate," she sighed at length, "and there is no hope for me. Oh, this determination is most cruel and unjust, and never could I have believed that my uncle could have been guilty of it. Oh, Heaven help me under this dreadful trial, which I never expected to experience. And shall we not meet again, dear Florio?—Oh, no, such is my uncle's stern decree, and nothing will move him from it. Alas! whither have you now gone, Florio?—and what will in future become of you?—What vicissitudes may it not be your hard lot to endure, poor and friendless as you are. I shudder at the thought."

She wrung her hands in the anguish of her feelings, and in vain sought for consolation. Alas! there was none for her under the painful circumstances, and every moment her agitation increased. The strange emotions and mysterious observations of the prince perplexed her greatly, and she in vain endeavoured to comprehend them. It seemed, however, evident to her that something weighed heavily on his conscience, and she began to fear that he had not always been the virtuous and honourable being she had thought him to be; and his present determination to sacrifice her to such a man as the Count Alberti, greatly lowered him in her esteem; and anticipating the troubles that were in store for her, she became truly wretched. The Prince Bianchi, on leaving Melina, retired to another apartment, in a most agitated state of mind. He threw himself into a chair, and gave himself up to the anguish of his thoughts.

"I cannot banish the remembrance of the guilty past from my recollection!" he cried. "And why is this girl constantly touching a chord which drives me to distraction?—She knows not my secret; and, yet it would seem that she suspects me, by her so frequently alluding to that painful subject. By Heaven, this is unendurable!—Oh, what can drown the memory of the past?—And now, since I have seen the brigand Massaroni, my tortures have increased. What can this mean?—why should I associate the name of that daring chief with those who became the victims to my guilty passions? My brain is bewildered and distracted as those thoughts rush upon it. The features of Massaroni are constantly present to my imagination; they haunt me sleeping or waking; and nameless feelings come over me when I recall his name to my memory. I dread, yet long to have him in my power, that I may behold him again. How is this?—has age impaired my intellects? Psha! I will shake off this weakness, which so ill becomes me. What have I to fear?"

Having thus given vent to his feelings, he arose from his seat and walked to the other side of the apartment. Suddenly raising his eyes, they fell upon the mysterious portrait which was usually kept concealed by the curtain, as before described, but was now uncovered. He trembled violently as he gazed upon it, and his face became ghastly pale.

"Ah! he exclaimed, in a hoarse voice, "what prying eye has dared to wander here?—Who has presumed to obtrude upon the sanctity of this place? Oh, Valencia! deeply wronged Valencia, can I, who brought thee to shame and misery, dare to look upon thy resemblance? Even more beautiful than this didst thou look in life; and yet I could become the heartless wretch to deceive and abandon thee! Oh, I deserve a severe punishment, and methinks I hear thy solemn and impressive voice invoking it on my head. I could almost imagine that I hear thy curses ringing in my ears. Oh, what dreadful torture is this! But away with thought. Let me shut thee from my sight and my memory for ever!"

Hastily he drew the curtain over the portrait, and then again flung himself upon a seat in a state of the utmost excitement. In spite of all the efforts he made, the most agonizing thoughts continued to harass his mind, and he was unable, although anxious, to leave the apartment.

Conscience was busy at work, and he in vain tried to stifle its upbraiding voice. Many, many years had fled since he had been guilty of the crimes with which he now reproached himself; but nothing had ever been able to banish them from his recollection. He had sought the wine cup—he had courted the gayest society, but still it was all to no purpose; the dark deeds of old were constantly present to his thoughts, and made him wretched in the midst of all his wealth. Some dreadful fate seemed to be in store for him, which it would be impossible for him to avoid, and he contemplated the future with the most torturing apprehensions. Although it was now night, the prince was so entranced, rivetted by those dark and painful thoughts, that he could not move from the room; everything around seemed to be wrapped in unwonted silence and gloom, and such was the powerful influence that his feelings had obtained over him, that he almost feared to look around him lest his eyes should encounter the ghastly forms which his timid imagination had conjured up. He sunk into a deep lethargy, from which he was not aroused until the hour of eleven tolled from the sonorous bell of St. Peter's. He started up with a sudden feeling of terror, and scarcely knew where he was. The lights in the apartment burnt dimly, but he involuntarily cast his eyes to that side of the room where the portrait was suspended, but started back with an exclamation of horror, and trembled in every limb. Merciful Powers! what form was that which presented itself to his imagination, standing immediately beneath the portrait, with its ghastly eyes fixed stedfastly upon him, and her hand pointing menacingly towards him? It was that of Valencia, the unfortunate original of the painting. The blood seemed to congeal in his veins, his eyes dilated with terror, but still he could not remove them from that ghastly form, which it could only have been his troubled and guilty conscience that had conjured up. Was he labouring under mental delusion? Was he asleep or awake? No, there it still stood in the same attitude. He could not be mistaken.

"Shade of the deeply wronged Valencia!" cried the wretched and deluded man, "why dost thou appear before me? Avaunt—avaunt! I must not—dare not gaze upon thee. I do repent me of the injuries I did thee; then why, oh, why does not thy soul rest in peace?"

He staggered forward, as he spoke, towards the spot where he supposed that the form was standing, but it faded from his sight; and overcome by the power of his terrors, the conscience-stricken prince sunk on the floor in a state of insensibility. Such is the earthly perdition that the guilty create for themselves. In this state the prince was found by his attendants, and by them conveyed to his chamber; and the remainder of the night he passed in the greatest agony and fear. It was two or three days before the prince could entirely recover himself from the shock which this imaginary apparition had given to his feelings, and during that time Melina was left to the privacy and seclusion of her own apartment, and deep indeed was the anguish of her thoughts, when she thought upon the uncertainty of what had befallen Florio, and to what he might be driven in the frenzy of his despair. Could she have been certain that he was safe, and that he was enabled to bear his bitter disappointment with fortitude, she would have been more content; but as it was, the most painful doubts and apprehensions beset her mind, and kept her constantly miserable. When her uncle had recovered and again sought her society, she had the anguish to find that he still remained firm in his cruel determination, and that neither tears nor supplications could move him; and he also bade her prepare for an interview with Count Alberti in a day or two, who would then make a formal declaration of his love, and he (the prince) cautioned her, as she feared his indignation, to receive him with favour. Melina saw it was useless to appeal to him, and she therefore gave herself up to the most absolute despair. Thus matters went on till the eventful evening on which the seizure of the Count Alberti, and the destruction of his castle by Massaroni and his band, took place. We have before stated that the prince was one of the guests whom the count had invited that evening, but that he returned home at an early hour in consequence of the sudden indisposition of Alberti. But he did not feel inclined to retire to rest, and sat for some time in his chamber, buried in deep meditation. Suddenly he was aroused from these reflections by beholding immense flames of fire and showers of sparks proceeding from that part where the castle of the count was situated; and the distant shouts from numerous voices smote his ears. He started from his seat and gazed from the window with the utmost anxiety. The conflagration was now at its height, and a lurid glare overspread the horizon for miles around. Every object was as clearly visible as at noon-day, and the longer the Prince Bianchi gazed, the more he became convinced that it was the castle of the Count Alberti which was fast falling a prey to the devouring element.

"What devil's work is going on there?" he exclaimed; "is this an accident, or the work of some base incendiary?"

He had scarcely given utterance to these words, when he beheld two of the vassals of the Count Alberti running with the utmost speed, and apparently in a state of great consternation, towards the villa, and his worst apprehensions were then confirmed. He summoned an attendant, and ordered them to be immediately ushered into his presence; and a few minutes afterwards the men made their appearance, with looks of the greatest alarm and excitement.

"How now, Pietro, tell me quickly," demanded the prince; "what is the meaning of all this? what has happened?"

"Oh, your highness," replied Pietro, "there has been dreadful work; the castle is in flames, and our noble master, the Count Alberti——"

"Ah!" interrupted the prince, in an agitated voice, "what of the count? Speak! do not keep me in suspense; he has not perished in the flames?"

"No, your highness, but he is gone; forced away by ruffians, who overpowered us by numbers, and we were unable to rescue him."

"Forced away!" cried the prince, starting with astonishment and consternation; "who are the wretches who have dared to commit this atrocious outrage?"

"Massaroni, the terrible brigand chief, and his desperate band, your highness," answered Pietro.

"Massaroni!" exclaimed the prince, with an oath, "the villain! But he must not be suffered to escape; the count must be rescued from his power at all hazards. Which way did the brigands take?"

"They fled towards the wood, my lord,' said Pietro; "but I fear it is now too late to overtake them."

"They must be pursued," said the Prince, "or the unfortunate count will fall a victim to their vengeance."

Quickly he ordered the whole of his vassals to arm themselves, and then in spite of the entreaties of Melina, who had become acquainted with what had taken place, and had hastened to her uncle's apartment, the prince mounted his horse and galloped off at the head of his attendants in pursuit of Massaroni and his associates. When he had departed Melina sunk upon her knees, and with clasped hands she fervently prayed that Massaroni might escape, though she sincerely hoped that no particular harm would befall the count, from whom she was at present at any rate released, and that fact removed a great weight of fear and anxiety from her mind. The prince and his followers in the meantime rode on with all the speed they possibly could in pursuit of the brigands, and reaching the wood, they scoured it in every direction, but to no purpose; they were too late, and after more than a couple of hours spent in this useless search without being able to discover any traces of Massaroni and his companions, enraged and disappointed he returned to the Villa, where Melina was awaiting him in the greatest anxiety. In the meantime the once proud castle of the Count Alberti was reduced to a pile of smoking ruins. This unexpected and important event excited the deepest feelings of astonishment and emotion in the bosom of Melina. She could not but experience a certain degree of satisfaction, while the indomitable courage and daring of the brigand chief overrated her most unqualified wonder and admiration. She had no doubt that Massaroni has adopted the course to avenge the wrongs of Olympia, and the contempt with which the count had treated his threats; but although she could feel no sympathy with one whom she had every reason to fear and detest, she trusted that the brigand would not make any attempt upon his life, but would merely detain him a prisoner until the time he should think proper to comply with his demands, the fate of Olympia ascertained, and herself and her child restored to liberty. So great was the excitement under which the Prince Bianchi laboured that he could scarcely restrain himself within the bounds of reason. He could not think of retiring to rest, but continued to pace his chamber with unequal steps during the remainder of the night, muttering curses long and deep against the brigand chief and his bold as ociates, and vowing terrible revenge.

"Shall this atrocious marauder for ever triumph and set all the laws and every person at defiance," he said. "By the saints he shall not while there is a soldier left in Rome, or I can raise a hand in defence of peace, order, and honesty. How much longer will this miscreant be permitted to escape the halter, and to perpetrate deeds of reckless daring, and unequalled magnitude, which might almost lead one to suppose he was something superhuman? I will have a terrible revenge, but in the meantime while I am endeavouring to find out his secret haunts, what may not be the fate of the unfortunate Count Alberti? I shudder at the thought. And this is the gentlemanly robber and cutthroat, whom foolish romantic girls like Melina so greatly admire, and celebrate his daring deeds in their silly ballads. Bah! I have no patience in such folly! And no doubt my niece is now exulting in the seizure of the count, flattering herself that she will now be released for ever from his importunities. But she shall find herself mistaken. Alberti shall be released from the power of the villain, though it cost me my fortune to achieve it. If gold can tempt any one to betray Massaroni, it shall not be wanting, and I will then send such a force against him as must overwhelm him. There is no time to be lost, and I will immediately set about putting my designs into execution. He will not, surely attempt to take the life of the count, since that would arouse the vengeance of the whole country against him, and they would never rest until he and the who e of his ferocious band were exterminated."

Thus the prince continued to soliloquise at intervals during the remainder of the night, and as soon as the morning dawned, he set about putting his plans into effect for the detection and apprehensions of Massaroni and the deliverance of the Count Alberti. He first visited the scene of devastation, and awful, indeed, was the spectacle the blackened ruins presented. There was not one portion of that once noble building left entire. The work of destruction had been complete; all the magnificent furniture, rare articles of vertu, valuable paintings, the choice and extensive library, and everything that the castle had contained were now smouldering amid the heterogenous mass of ruins that were piled around. Vast numbers of people had congregated round the scene of the conflagration, and various were the remarks they made upon the calamity, and shuddered with terror while they whispered the name of Massaroni. The emotion of the prince increased, and addressing the people, he enjoined them to assist him and the military in the apprehension of the brigands, and the restoration of the Count Alberti, while at the same time he offered a reward of ten thousand ducats to any one who should be enabled to obtain information of the place of Massaroni's retreat. The people could do nothing more than promise obediedience to the prince's wishes, though they all stood too much in terror of the brigand chief to wish to have anything to do in his apprehension; besides, although he committed such extensive depredations on the rich, and those who had offended him, to them he had ever been a friend; and while they admired his heroism, they could but likewise esteem him for his generosity. On the contrary, the character of the young Count Alberti was almost universally despised; his treacherous conduct towards Olympia had aroused their indignation, independantly of his oppressive conduct towards his tenantry and dependents; they believed him to be the cause of the disappearance of Olympia and her child, if he had not absolutely sacrificed their lives, and that he was justly punished for that which he had been guilty. The prince busied himself during the day in laying his plans for the discovery of Massaroni, and the restoration of the count to liberty, though he entertained the greatest fears as to the fate that would befal him in the power of so desperate and determined a man as the brigand chief; nor could he divest himself of the strange and unaccountable feelings that would come over him whenever he thought upon his name, and remembered the striking character of his features. The prince lost no time in despatching spies to the different parts of the country to endeavour to find out the locality of the brigands, or to ascertain the route they had taken on their flight from the scene of the conflagration; but all these endeavours were ineffectual, for the inhabitants either could not, or most probably would not give them any information, and the prince was doomed to remain in the same state of doubt, anxiety, and perplexity, and was at a perfect loss what future course to pursue; he began to fear that the fate of the count was inevitable. Melina experienced almost as much anxiety as her uncle, but it was more on account of her lover, Florio, who was now a wanderer no one knew whither, and who, although she might be released from the hateful suit of the count, it was more than probable she would never behold again. Her tears flowed fast as these dismal thoughts arose to her mind, and she gave herself up almost entirely to the most absolute despair. Had she but been acquainted with the place of his destination, and knew that he was safe, she might have been more content; but when she reflected that the anguish of his feelings might lead him to the perpetration of some rash act, she gave way to the most torturing and gloomy apprehensions, and considered herself one of the most miserable and unfortunate of human beings. The alarming events of the last few days had so irritated the prince, that she now dreaded his society as much as she had before delighted in it, and she avoided his presence as much as she possibly could, keeping herself secluded in her own apartments, and giving free indulgence to the melancholy thoughts which constantly oppressed her. The wealth and splendour which surrounded her became irksome and hateful to her, since it shut out all her hopes; how gladly would she have resigned it all, for the humblest cottage and the lowliest station, had she been permitted to become the wife of the man of her heart. But we must now pursue the progress of the brigands and their prisoner towards their romantic retreat in the wood.

CHAPTER XII.

THE MEETING.—THE RIVALS.—THE MANIAC AND THE SEDUCER.

THROUGH the same wild tract of country, and in the same gloomy silence, which was only interrupted at intervals by the roaring of a distant cataract, as it rushed with frightful velocity down the rocky steep into the frightful abyss beneath, the brigands and their captive pursued their way, and the farther they advanced the more the young count's despair increased, and which the horrors by which they were surrounded did not serve to diminish. Sometimes they wended their weary way through frightful mountain passes, and along narrow defiles, which none but those who were inured to the wild mountain life of

Massaroni and his band could have traversed. Anon their pathway lay along the very verge of hideous precipices, down which the eye could not venture to look lest the brain should turn giddy with the fathomless horrors beneath; then again they fearlessly walked between immense piles of overhanging rocks, which seemed to threaten every moment to topple down and crush them beneath their ponderous weight, and from whose lofty summits and hollow cavities the night birds sent forth their dismal shrieks, which were answered

OLYMPIA'S FATE IS OVERHEARD BY FLORIO.

by a thousand echoes, like the horrid cries of the damned in purgatory. By and by they entered a black and impervious wood, where it seemed impossible that the light of heaven could ever have penetrated, and which seemed alone calculated for the pepetration of deeds of blood and rapine. Among the thick foliage the wind now howled in hollow gusts, and to the affrighted imagination it seemed as though the wood was peopled with fiends, who were uttering their curses upon the daring traveller who ventured to intrude themselves

No. 9.

upon their infernal precincts. In spite of all his efforts to the contrary, the count could not help shuddering with fear, and looked anxiously at Massaroni, who had lighted his silver pipe, and was smoking with the utmost composure and enjoyment; occasionally trolling snatches of some romantic ballad which was common amongst the brigands, or the peasantry whom they befriended, and with whom they associated.

"Whither are you taking me?" demanded the count, in a tremulous voice, "and why do you keep me in this state of suspense?"

"Oh, your anxiety will soon be at an end, signor," replied Massaroni; "make your mind easy, we shall reach the place of our destination very shortly now, and you will find that Allesandro Massaroni has a very comfortable and secure retreat, and plenty of accommodation for those whom he may honour by making his guests."

"This is a frightful place to travel through," said the count, "fit only for deeds of darkness. Massaroni, I again caution you to beware what you do, for most assuredly this outrage will not go unavenged should you not relent."

"Cospetto! signor," returned the brigand chief, "are you still so foolish as to waste your breath in threats against Massaroni? Methinks you ought by this time, at any rate, to see the utter uselessness of them."

"It is not too late to repent, Massaroni," said the count, "restore me to liberty, and even after the terrible outrage you have this night committed, and which surely ought most amply to satiate your vengeance, I will forgive you."

"A very generous promise, truly, signor," returned our hero, "but it strikes me it is too liberal to be sincere, and consequently I must beg most respectfully to decline it. But you seem dull, signor;—hark, my companions are amusing themselves with a song, which, perhaps, may serve to wear away some of the tediousness of the journey."

The count threw himself back in the vehicle in despair, while the brigands made the woods resound with the following rude chorus—

"O'er the mountain, up the rock,
   Through the glen, or forest drear,
The daring brigands take their way,
   Scorning danger, mocking fear.

See, black clouds obscure the sky,
   Fierce the tempest howls around,
But its fury they defy,
   So that booty can be found.

Tra la! tra la! the brigand's life
   Is a life of mirth and glee;
With ev'ry wild enjoyment rife,
   Who so happy, gay, and free?"

In that lonely place, where echo opened a thousand responses, this rude chorus had a re-markable and impressive effect; but the heart of Alberti sickened, and he remained silent, giving himself up to the agony of his own thoughts. At length they emerged from the forest, and entered upon a scene which was equally cheerless. It was a narrow glen which seemed to be a very appropriate theatre for deeds of murder and rapine, as it was overhung on each side by frowning precipices (partly overgrown with stunted brushwood), up which it would be impossible to escape. They came to the end of this narrow gorge, and the country then presented a less cheerless and savage appearance. The dark mists of night also gradually dispersed, and the first flush of day appeared in the eastern skies. In a short time the aspect of the country was entirely changed, and they were pursuing their way through a track of that luxuriant and romantic scenery with which Italy so richly abounds. They passed by the ruins of several of those architectural monuments of its ancient splendour, with which the country is interspersed, and, notwithstanding his situation, the count could not help surveying with feelings of admiration the magnificence of the prospect that was spread before him. The golden beams of the rising sun were shedding their glories upon a noble stream that expanded to the breadth of a lake in the extreme distance, and pursued its devious course through a thickly wooded country, in which for some miles it was buried from the traveller's eyes, and then flowed within a few hundred yards of his feet. Here and there amongst the woodlands were scattered the castles and palaces of the ancient nobility, and the temples of classic times, lifting their tall summits into the sunshine above the trees, and imparting a scene of grandeur to the whole, of which none but those who have gazed upon an Italian landscape can form an adequate conception. A faint ray of hope stole into the bosom of the count as he gazed around him, and the probability of his meeting with some assistance presented itself to his imagination. Massaroni, however, who had watched the expression of his countenance narrowly, penetrated his thoughts, and he quickly undeceived him.

"The peasantry who inhabit this part of the country are all my friends," he remarked; "they esteem the brigand chief, and seek his advice and assistance whenever they need it. You will therefore perceive, signor, that you have nothing to hope for from them. You may as well rest your mind contented, count, for we shall soon arrive at our journey's end, where I will introduce you to the rest of my brave comrades, who no doubt will give you a most hearty welcome."

"Massaroni, I perceive too well that I am entirely in your power, and that it would be useless to attempt to resist you."

"A very sensible and prudent conclusion to come to, signor."

"But I beg of you to deal mercifully towards me."

"That will all depend upon yourself. As you deal out mercy and justice to others, so will the brigand chief apportion it to you."

The count made no reply, but resigned himself to his fate, and in a short time they approached near the romantic retreat of Massaroni and his companions. He suddenly ordered the vehicle to stop, and turning to the count, said—

"Signor, should you any longer doubt the power or importance of Allesandro Massaroni, wherever he goes, and how well he is prepared to defend himself from every attack that might be made upon him, I will now convince you. Should you even effect your escape from me at this moment, before you could reach the base of this mountain you would be food for vultures. Do not scorn what I say ; should I allow you to make the attempt, and bid you run for your life, and not suffer one of those who are now with me to fire upon you, I would advise you to look well at the bushes, for there would be a rifle barrel peeping at you from every one of them. Nay, if you still doubt me, I will e'en convince you that I speak the truth at once."

He raised his whistle to his lips as he thus spoke and blew the well-known signal, and immediately they were surrounded by the remainder of the brigands with their rifles levelled. The count started and trembled at the sight, and Massaroni beheld his astonishment and alarm with exultation.

"You seem surprised, Count Alberti," he said, "and almost to disbelieve the evidence of your eyes. Do you imagine that these are mere automatons, incapable of doing harm? By the cross, they are men of flesh and blood, and many of your nobles have known the same long since to their cost. Is not this a hardy and daring band, capable of bidding defiance to all the Roman soldiers that my respected friend, his highness the Prince Bianchi, may send to your rescue, should he discover my retreat? They are rovers of wood and wild, capable of enduring any fatigue and fearless of every danger. Allesandro Massaroni is proud of his daring band, and with them would face even a legion of devils."

"Evviva, Massaroni! Evviva, the mountain chief!" shouted the brigands, and they immediately prepared to escort the brigand chief to his cavernous retreat.

"Calvetti," said Massaroni, addressing one of the band, "is all prepared for our reception?"

"All, captain," replied Calvetti.

"Is Maria at the cavern?"

"She is not; she left it at the break of day to visit Ottavia at the cottage of Montaldi, as she understood that she was rather indisposed."

"And where is my friend? You understand who I mean?" demanded Massaroni.

"He had not arisen when we left the cavern. So, you have met with success, captain?"

"Aye, when did Massaroni fail in accomplishing anything upon which he had fixed his mind? But away to our retreat."

They moved on, and winding their way down the lofty mountain's side, they entered the romantic wood, and soon arrived at the cavern, into which the count was conducted, and gazed with astonishment at the unusual scene which met his eyes, and was so bewildered that he could not give utterance to a word. Massaroni waved his hand to Brunaldo and the other brigands as a signal that he wished to be alone, and they immediately withdrew, and Massaroni folding his arms across his chest, stood contemplating his prisoner for a few moments with looks of exultation and satisfaction. The young nobleman shrunk beneath his gaze, and with a sickly feeling at his heart he sunk on a seat, and awaited for the brigand to address him.

"Welcome, Count Alberti D'Amalfi," at length he said, "to the retreat of Signor Allesandro Massaroni, the brigand chief. Here you will find every accommodation, though perhaps not quite so costly as that to be met with in your late noble castle, the best of fare, and jovial company withal. Once more I bid you welcome."

"Massaroni," returned the count, biting his lips with indignation, "do not mock me, if you are a man, and possess any spark of generosity. It ill becomes you to triumph over a fallen foe."

"Well, well, be it so," said Massaroni; "however we shall, doubtless, understand each other better by and by."

"You will not persist in detaining me?" said the count.

"Indeed, signor, but I shall, you may depend, until you comply with my demands, and give me a sufficient guarantee that you will never again venture to set me at defiance. What I insist upon is that you render justice, or such justice as it is now in your power to render, to the victim of your treachery, Signora Olympia."

"How am I to do so," said Alberti, "since I know not where she is?"

"Do not attempt to deceive me, or to trifle with me, signor," said Massaroni, sternly, "or you will have bitter cause to repent your boldness. You know that you speak falsely, and that Olympia and her offspring were conveyed away by your orders, and that they are at present confined by your instructions. You look confused, my lord; nay, it is useless to deny the truth to me."

"What proof have you of that which you so boldly assert?" demanded the count, in a faltering tone.

"Such as you cannot repel," answered the brigand chief; "but all in good time, signor; are you prepared to reveal the place where you have so villanously concealed them, that they may be snatched from the power of the fellows whom you have employed to do your nefarious work?"

"You ask me that which I cannot perform," replied Alberti.

"Liar!" exclaimed Massaroni, passionately; "have you still the effrontery to deny your guilt? I again caution you to beware, and to think of the danger you incur by your obstinacy. Know you a ruffian called Spinotti?"

The count started.

"You look amazed, signor," continued the brigand, "but, by and by, I will furnish you with further proof that the full extent of your guilt is well known to me, and that it would be worse than madness for you to persist in denying it. At present we will talk no more upon this subject. I give you time to collect yourself, and for mature reflection; but remember, that on no other conditions than those which I have mentioned shall you be restored to liberty. You have already set my threats at defiance, and treated my authority with contempt—that alone is worthy of death; but Massaroni can be merciful as well as just, and that mercy he is disposed to extend to you, if you comply with his demands; but should you remain obdurate, be the consequences on your own head. Here are refreshments, of which you are welcome to partake."

The count was about to decline this invitation and again to remonstrate with Massaroni, when the door of the cavern opened, and Maria Grazie, the brigand's wife, suddenly entered, followed by the unfortunate Ottavia, who would persist in accompanying Maria to her husband's retreat.

The fine commanding figure of the brigand's wife; the handsome expression of her countenance and full dark eyes, and the romantic elegance of her costume, completely revetted the attention of the young nobleman; whilst Maria folded her arms and eyed him with mingled looks of contempt and indignation. A wild exclamation from Ottavia diverted his attention to her, and no sooner did he fix his eyes upon the features of the poor maniac, than he gave an involuntary start, turned pale, trembled violently, and exclaimed in a voice of extreme emotion—

"Good God! that resemblance! Who is this brought here to torture me?"

"What is it that alarms you thus, signor?" said Massaroni, "surely it cannot be the sight of this poor unfortunate, from whose brain reason has been unseated?"

"Let me retire," said the count, in an agitated manner, unable to remove his gaze from the countenance of Ottavia; "the—the

events of the last few hours have overcome me, I —I need rest."

"Does your conscience disturb you, signor?" said the brigand's wife with a bitter sneer; "no doubt it is a severe monitor, and one whose voice will not be easily stifled."

"Hold, Maria," said Massaroni, angrily, "this is not the time for remarks such as these."

"Maria Grazie," she replied, proudly, "although a brigand's wife, is still a woman, and has not forgot the feelings of her sex. And so, this is the noble betrayer of fond confiding innocence!—the artless deserter of her and their helpless offspring."

A loud shriek from Ottavia made them all start back with amazement, and she rushed forward and fixed her eyes upon the features of the count with an expression which it would be difficult to describe.

"Who talks of confiding innocence betrayed!" she cried in wild accents; "who is it that pities the poor abandoned wretch and her murdered child? 'Tis mockery all! there is no pity for her! And where is he?—the villain, the deceiver, with his perjured vows and honied accents. If he lives, tell him that she—so gentle now—seeks revenge, a terrible revenge! Ah! who art thou who standest in mockery thus before me? He once was like you, fair and noble to look upon, but possessed of the heart of a demon. Still you gaze upon me with ironical smiles! you mock my sufferings! Nay! then—thus!—thus!—do I avenge myself!"

As she thus spoke, the wretched woman suddenly snatched a dagger from the girdle of Maria, and rushing upon the astonished and bewildered Alberti, she would have plunged it to the hilt in his breast, had not Massaroni darted forward and arresting the arm of Ottavia forced the deadly weapon from her; and, overpowered by the excitement of her feelings, the poor maniac sunk inanimate on the earth. Massaroni raised her from the ground, and placing her in the arms of his wife, said—

"Take the unfortunate creature away, Maria, and see to her recovery."

Maria fixed a look upon the trembling count which filled him with confusion and dismay, and obeyed; and Alberti again sunk on a seat, overcome by his emotions.

"What is the meaning of this, Massaroni?" he said at length, "and who is that wretched woman?"

"I know not, signor," answered the brigand; "she inhabits a cottage not far from this cave, and you must have perceived that her mind wandered, and that she is not accountable for her actions. It is my belief that her's has been a similar melancholy history to the victim of your treachery. Why were you so agitated when you beheld her?"

"I know not," said the count; "but—but suffer me to retire, Massaroni, in order that I may endeavour to compose myself."

"Be it so, signor," returned Massaroni; "but remember what I have said, and reflect seriously upon it, as you value your future liberty, and dread my vengeance. Follow me."

The count arose and with trembling footsteps obeyed, and the brigand chief led the way into one of the inner caverns which had been prepared for his reception; where, after a few more observations he left him, and Alberti, throwing himself on a rude couch, gave himself up to the most racking thoughts. Massaroni returned to the cavern he had just quitted, and was soon after joined by his wife, whose countenance expressed anything but pleasure.

"How now, Maria?" he asked; "has the unfortunate Ottavia recovered?"

"She has," replied Maria, "and two of the band have escorted her home."

"This is a most extraordinary circumstance, Maria," said Massaroni.

"'Tis even so," returned his wife; "it is fortunate for this young man that you were present, or Ottavia would have stretched him dead at her feet. You must have observed the extreme agitation of his manner the instant he beheld her."

"I did."

"And did you remark the observations he made use of, respecting her resemblance to some one whose name he did not mention?"

"Undoubtedly I did," replied the brigand. "To whom can he allude?"

"I know not, unless it be Olympia."

"Ah!" ejaculated Massaroni; "it must be so; and now I recollect that I have frequently thought a most extraordinary likeness did exist between Ottavia and that unfortunate woman."

"Massaroni," observed Maria, "the Count Alberti is a villain."

"Have I not always said so? But now I have got him in my power, and I am determined that he shall make atonement for the wrongs he has done to Olympia, and the contempt and defiance with which he dared to treat my threats."

"Did you have much difficulty in accomplishing his seizure?" asked his wife.

"Why, yes; a determined resistance was offered to us, but nothing could stand against the bravery of my invincible band. The castle is now a heap of ruins."

"Ah!" ejaculated Maria, with a look of surprise, "what made you proceed to such a desperate extremity as that, Massaroni?"

"It was not my intention to have done so?" replied the brigand, "nor after all was it the work of my hands; the conflagration took place entirely by accident. But listen, and I will relate to you the whole particulars."

Maria did listen with profound attention; but her looks evinced anything but satisfaction as he proceeded.

"I admire not this adventure, Massaroni," she remarked, when he had come to a conclusion.

"And why not, Maria?"

"Because it will arouse the indignation of the whole country, and such plans may be laid for our detection that we may find it impossible to escape."

"Nay—Maria, you, the brigand's bride, who have hitherto ever evinced such indomitable courage and heroism, facing danger in its most appalling form, will surely not give way to idle fears."

"Maria Grazie knows not fear," she replied, proudly, "but she likes not running unprofitable risks. You have had an excellent opportunity for pillage to an unlimited extent, but you have let it slip, and what advantage do you expect to gain by having got this Count Alberti in your power?"

"Psha! Maria," said Massaroni, impatiently, "think you not that the count will yield to my demands, whatever they may be, rather than remain my prisoner for the remainder of his days? Besides, I have sworn to compel him to render justice to the injured Olympia, and I will not break my oath. Florio Clairville also saved my life, and I owe him a debt of gratitude which I am anxious to repay. He loves the fair Melina, and she returns his passion, but the Prince Bianchi frowns upon their love, and would sacrifice her to the heartless betrayer of Olympia; by the cross, Maria, this shall never be!"

"Melina is the niece of your deadliest enemy; of that man who would consign you and all of us to the scaffold."

"But she is young—she is gentle, amiable, and beauteous," said Massaroni, warmly; "she is the victim of oppression, and therefore must be the object of the brigand's sympathy and care."

"Methinks you suffer your enthusiasm to go rather too far, Massaroni, when speaking of the niece of Prince Bianchi," said Maria, whilst an expression of jealousy overspread her features.

"Indeed I do not, Maria," replied her husband; "and even you, my wife, could not contemplate her without admiration. Olympia is fair, but the charms of Melina far transcend her's. Olympia is like the pale queen of Heaven, when she sheds her silvery radiance over nature's carpet, darting glory, effulgence, and transport around her; but Melina is like the rising sun, glorious, golden, and majestic; imparting warmth, grandeur, and bliss, as she approaches. Or like a bower of roses, all perfume and loveliness."

"Massaroni!" exclaimed his wife, with a look of astonishment and anger.

"Nay, Maria," said the brigand, laughing, "you surely are not jealous at my eloquent description of two pretty women; you know I love and admire the whole of the sex, but none like my own faithful Maria, my mountain bride—the affectionate partner of all my vicissitudes, dangers, and wild fortunes, and—and—Signor Florio, art thou here?"

Florio, who had overheard the latter part of the conversation between Massaroni and his wife, now came forward.

"Massaroni," he remarked, "I have to thank you for the flattering eulogiums you have just passed upon the beauteous Melina, and those who have seen that amiable and lovely being must admit that the compliments you have bestowed upon her are even far short of what she merits."

"Cospetto!" returned the brigand chief, "but you are right, my young Raphael; and it shall be no fault of mine if she does not unite her fate to one who possesses her heart, and who is worthy of so inestimable a treasure. Maria, I would be alone, for a short time, with Signor Clairville, I will rejoin you shortly."

Maria made no reply to this, but casting a hasty glance of suspicion upon Florio, she immediately quitted the cavern.

"So, my young friend," said Massaroni, "you see I have returned safe from my expedition to the castle of Count Alberti."

"Aye," replied Florio, "I am glad of it; but," he added, impatiently, "what have been the results of your adventure?—What of the count?"

"He is at present my prisoner," replied the brigand.

"Ah!" cried Florio, eagerly, "where?"

"In this very retreat. Yes, here I have your rival secure, and he can only hope to be released from my power by an unqualified compliance with my demands."

"Massaroni," said Florio with a look of alarm, "I shudder at the consequences this daring outrage may bring upon you and your associates."

"Nay, signor, fear not for me. Massaroni, the brigand chief, is not apt to be intimidated by the anticipation of consequences."

"I would rather you had not have persisted in your design, Massaroni," said Clairville; "alas! it cannot surely advance my wishes—Melina can never become mine; and, however painful the task, I must endeavour to resign my hopes of her, and submit to my fate."

"But indeed you will do no such thing, signor. Mark my words, Melina shall never become the bride of any other man than him to whom her affections are devoted. This do I not only promise you in consideration of the service you rendered me when I was so near being entrapped at the Villa Rosa, but likewise in order to gratify my revenge."

"Massaroni," said Florio, still more alarmed,

"you will not go to extreme acts of violence with respect to the Count Alberti?"

"That will depend entirely upon himself."

"You have given me your word."

"And I will not break it, if he does not compel me to it by the obstinacy of his conduct. He has the means of purchasing his liberty and future safety, and if he acts wisely he will avail himself of it."

"But is he aware that I am an inmate of this cavernous retreat?" asked Florio.

"He is not," answered the brigand; "but listen to me, and I will relate to you all the particulars of the count's seizure."

Florio paid the greatest attention, but he evinced the utmost agitation as Massaroni proceeded, particularly when he came to that part which described the destruction of the castle.

"Ah," he cried, "this is a most unfortunate circumstance, Massaroni, and one that I fear will bring down upon you, and all connected with you, the most terrible and signal vengeance."

"Be not alarmed, signor, for the brigand chief is not. I regret the destruction of the count's castle, but it was no fault of mine; it was entirely by accident that it occurred."

"Accident or not," returned Florio, "it will be sure to excite a universal feeling of indignation. Massaroni, I regret that fate ever guided my footsteps to your secret haunts. My life has hitherto been passed in honour, and no one ever dared to cast an aspersion on my character; but should it now become known that I have suffered myself to become in any way associated with you, I shall be looked upon as a villain, and hunted from society as such. Will not Melina also despise me, and——"

"Upon my word, Signor Clairville," interrupted Massaroni, "you do not compliment me very highly. However, I am not disposed to quarrel with you; when you have reflected more maturely upon this subject, I am inclined to think you will judge more fairly of my motives. The brigand chief is no villain, although a portion of mankind may consider him as such. He is a lover of justice, the stern enemy of oppression and tyranny, and the staunch defender of the wronged and innocent. However, I am disposed to suffer every person to enjoy their own opinion, though I do not despair of yet being placed in my proper position, to the confusion of my enemies."

"Massaroni, nature never formed you for this lawless and perilous life."

"True, true."

"What could have driven you to it?"

"Cruelty and treachery from him to whom I had a right to look for love and protection—the vile author of my being. May every curse pursue him both in this world and the next!"

"Forbear, forbear! Massaroni; language such as this, when speaking of your own parent!"

"Aye," exclaimed Massaroni, greatly excited, "what language can I find sufficiently powerful to express my thorough hatred and disgust for such a miscreant? He abandoned me and the hapless victim of his lust to every earthly misery; left her to perish of a broken heart, and me to become a despised outcast and a robber, hunted from place to place like some wild beast. And think you, signor, that I can ever forgive these deep, these unmerited wrongs? Oh, had you but seen my poor mother in her last moments, could you marvel at the spirit of revenge that inspires my bosom against her heartless seducer? Had you seen her throw her thin emaciated arms around the neck of her lovely boy, and breathe her last in a blessing upon his head. Had you known the months of misery, privation, and scorn we endured together, wandering shelterless, in the bleak wind, and amid the howling tempest, till exhausted nature could endure no more, and we have thrown ourselves upon the cold earth with the pitiless storm pelting upon us, and prayed for death to come to our relief from such insupportable, such unparalleled misery. By Heaven, the very thought drives me to madness! and yet you wonder that I should express such feelings of deadly hatred towards the monster who was the cause of it all. You marvel that I should so deeply sympathise with those who have met with a similar fate to that of my unfortunate mother!"

Massaroni walked to and fro as he thus gave utterance to his feelings, and Florio could not but sympathise with him.

"And is your guilty parent still living, Massaroni?" he asked.

"I know not," replied the brigand chief; "but something ever seems to whisper to me that he is, and I shall never rest contented until I have discovered him, and demanded justice for mine and my poor mother's wrongs."

"But know you not his name?"

"No; that I am also ignorant of. My mother ever declined to reveal it to me, and the secret died with her."

"'Tis strange," observed Florio.

"'Tis true," said Massaroni. "He was of noble rank, I was given to understand; but more I know not."

"And your mother's name?"

"Pardon me, signor," replied our hero, "but that, for particular reasons, I must decline to reveal. Behold, this is the likeness of her who gave me being. Is it not most lovely?"

As Massaroni thus spoke, he drew from his bosom the miniature of his mother, and presented it to the gaze of Florio; but no sooner did the latter behold it, than he started, and exclaimed—

"Gracious Heaven! why this is an exact counterpart of the young Florentine damsel, in the Villa Rosa!"

"It is," said Massaroni; "and strange thoughts have haunted my imagination ever since the night when that mysterious portrait met my gaze. Tell me, Signor Florio, know you the name of the fair being whom that painting represents?"

"I do not. I never had the boldness to inquire of the Prince Bianchi, and he always became most violently agitated whenever the subject was alluded to."

"And know you anything of her history?" asked the brigand.

"No more than that I have already revealed to you," answered Clairville.

Massaroni folded his arms across his chest, traversed the cavern, and seemed to be communing with himself for a few minutes. At length he turned to Florio, and in a more composed tone of voice, said—

"We will talk no further upon the subject at present, signor. Remember what I have said, and, depend upon it, all will yet turn out as well as your most sanguine hopes can wish."

Florio shook his head.

"Massaroni," he remarked, "I must repeat that I feel far from comfortable in my present situation. I feel obliged to you for the interest you have taken in my affairs, and the friendship you have expressed towards me; but I must be permitted to depart from this place, and trust to Providence for what may in future befall me."

"Nonsense, signor," returned Massaroni, "you cannot mean what you say. I tell you again that you shall run no danger by your association with me, and that my only wish is to serve you."

"I do believe you, Massaroni," said Florio, "and beg to repeat my acknowledgments for the trouble you have taken, and the risk you have run on my account; but, indeed, I cannot remain here; and you surely will not compel me to do so against my will."

"And whither would you go?"

"I know not."

"Foolish young man—do not act precipitately; here you may find a safe asylum, and I promise you that in no respect will I compromise your honour. The Count Alberti has only to comply with my demands—reveal the place where Olympia and her child are confined, render them that justice which is in his power, promise to abandon his hated designs against the fair object of your love, and he shall be immediately restored to liberty."

"And should he refuse?"

"Why, then the consequences must rest upon his own head. However, he will not be mad enough to do so, I am convinced of that; for he must be well aware that Allesandro Massaroni, the brigand chief, is not the man to be trifled with, and that what he promises he never fails to perform. But we have talked long enough upon this subject at present. Another time you will, perhaps, be more collected, and better disposed to listen to reason."

Massaroni and Florio now separated, and the former hastened to rejoin his wife, whose observations had caused him no inconsiderable share of uneasiness.

CHAPTER XIII.

COUNT ALBERTI IN CONFINEMENT.—HIS RAGE AND DESPAIR.—THE INTERVIEW BETWEEN HIM AND MASSARONI.—THE FLIGHT OF FLORIO.

THE reader may be able to form a pretty adequate idea of the emotions of the Count Alberti, when he found himself so securely in the power of Massaroni, and knew that he had little or nothing to hope for from his mercy and forbearance. For some time after the brigand had left him, he traversed the gloomy cavern in which he was confined, giving vent to his feelings of rage and despair, and unable to feel the least portion of comfort.

"What a cursed fate is mine!" he cried, "to thus become the victim of this desperate man, whom no laws can intimidate or dangers appal, and how can I hope to escape from the fate with which he has threatened me, without complying with his demands, however monstrous they may be? Curses light upon him and all connected with him! My noble castle, too, and all it contained, destroyed by his hands; a a princely fortune gone at one fell swoop! Oh, the bare thought is enough to drive me to madness! How came the villain so well acquainted with my affairs? How knew he that Olympia and her child's disappearance were the work of my hands, and that they are at present in the power of the robbers? There must have been some treachery amongst those whom I trusted; and yet had there been so, would they not also have revealed the place of their concealment? He shall never know it from my lips, though he should endeavour to extort the secret from me by the most excruciating tortures. He will not dare to proceed to extremities, notwithstanding the threats he has held out to me. The Prince Bianchi, and my other friends, will lose no time in tracing out the place of my confinement, and in wreaking their vengeance on the head of the brigand Massaroni and his daring associates. Yes, yes; it will be so, and I will not therefore give myself up entirely to despair."

But it was in vain that the count tried to console himself with these ideas; every moment that he reflected showed him the greater danger of his situation, and his mind became completely distracted. The power of the brigands was even much greater than he had ever imagined it to be, and with such consummate skill did they manage their affairs that they might almost safely set detection at defiance. Massaroni, he was aware, had places of concealment in all parts of the country, and he had also secret spies working in every direction, so that he was apprised of any movement that might be set on foot against him, and enabled to concert plans for his own safety accordingly. What chance, therefore, had any government against such a man? And should he hear of any force being sent to his (the count's) rescue, would it not be the immediate signal for his death? The count became distracted as these thoughts racked his brain, and he threw himself disconsolately on a seat, and for some time gave himself up to all the anguish of despair. And now the features of the maniac Ottavia, and her strange and alarming conduct and observations, recurred to his recollection, and excited in his breast feelings of the most extraordinary and unaccountable description.

"Who can she be?" he ejaculated; "and why should the sight of me excite her so powerfully? And then her extraordinary resemblance to Olympia! By heaven! had it not been for the difference in their years, I could almost have imagined that it was Olympia who stood before me! Has everything conspired to torture me? Have I become the complete sport of evil destiny? Curses light on all! How am I to find patience to endure this accumulation of misery?"

Again he arose from his seat and traversed the damp cave with disordered steps. Nothing could be more gloomy and cheerless than the place in which he found himself, and which received no other light than from a small lamp placed on the table, and which cast a sickly glare upon the few objects around. The count could not help shuddering when he reflected that here he might be destined to pass the residue of his days; that this might be his future tomb, and that no one would become acquainted with the fate that had befallen him. There were provisions on the table, but the count felt too agitated to partake of them, and he turned from them with a sickening feeling of disgust. In this manner two or three hours passed away, and no one offered to interrupt him. The dreariness of his situation became intolerable, and various were the terrified thoughts that crowded upon his busy and distracted imagination. Although the unusual events of the night, and the great length of the journey had much fatigued him, he could not think of endeavouring to snatch a few hours' repose, which might have served to refresh him and to revive his spirits, but he continued alternately to traverse the cavern, and to give utterance to his feelings in the wildest exclamations of despair. At length, quite worn out, he stretched himself upon the mattress which was placed there for his accommodation, and after a while, tossing about in a restless manner, he fell asleep, but it was disturbed by frightful dreams, and he was even more wretched than in his waking moments. He was aroused by the withdrawal of the rusty bolts, and presently afterwards the door was opened, and one of the brigands entered, bringing with him a fresh lamp for the night, a flask of wine, and some more provisions. These the man placed on the table and retired without saying a word, and the count was once more left to the gloom and agony of his own thoughts. Every moment his despair increased, and he gave vent to his

MASSARONI SURPRISES ALBERTI IN HIS PRIVACY.

feelings in the most bitter exclamations. He had no means of ascertaining the time, for his watch had stopped, and even this circumstance, simple as it was, added to the gloom and despondency of his mind. Ever and anon he could hear the voices of the brigands, as they gave vent to their hilarious feelings by boisterous shouts of mirth; and then all would become silent again as the grave.

"And how long am I fated to remain in this terrible situation?" he exclaimed; "by all my hopes, this is even worse than death! There is no chance of my deliverance, unless Massaroni should relent, for it is impossible that any of my friends can discover me in this secret retreat, and in such a distant part of the country. I shall go mad! Oh, may every torture pursue the wretch who has been the cause of this. Why did not my vassals pursue the villains in their flight? Cowards! They have permitted me to be sacrificed. Olympia, thou art indeed most terribly avenged."

In this manner the guilty count continued to rave for several hours, and obtain not a moment's repite from his anguish; but at length, quite exhausted, he again threw himself on the mattress and slept till morning. He arose somewhat more composed than he had been the day before, but his mind still the abode of anguish and suspense, and undetermined in what manner to act, whether to yield to the demands of the brigand chief, or to remain obstinate and brave the worst. But to acknowledge himself to be the guilty being Massaroni had accused him of being, and to reveal the place where Olympia was confined, was so repugnant to his feelings that he could not entertain the idea with any degree of patience.

"No, by all my hopes, I will not be intimidated into any such degrading submission," he cried, after a pause; "let the consequences be whatever they may, I will brave them. If this Massaroni is the generous being he is represented to be, and which he boasts of being himself, he will not persist in his designs, or surely money may tempt him to abandon them. I will, at any rate, try what resistance and persuasion will avail, and if I can only obtain delay, by some fortunate circumstance in the meantime my friends may be able to discover the place of my concealment, and hasten to my deliverance."

This thought, sanguine and preposterous as it was, revived his hopes, and he became more tranquil. He now partook of the refreshments, and feeling more confident, he prepared himself to meet the brigand chief again, whenever he should think proper to visit him. It was not long ere the young count heard the bolts of the door again withdrawn, and Massaroni entered, with a polite bow, and a smile of triumph upon his countenance. Alberti received him with haughty dignity, and could scarcely restrain the feelings of resentment and mortified pride which struggled for vent in his bosom.

"Good morning, signor," said the brigand, in his usual careless manner. "I trust you are in good health and spirits, though, to be sure, you are not quite so comfortably domiciled as you were in your own castle. I would not disturb you yesterday, because I thought that you would be fatigued after your journey. I hope you have rested well, and now feel refreshed."

"Massaroni," said the count, "come you here to mock me? Begone, and leave me to my own meditations."

"I am sorry to be compelled to interrupt you, Count Alberti, in your ruminations," said the brigand, "but I must claim the indulgence of a few minutes' conversation with you, upon that subject which is so important to us both."

"What would you of me?"

"I would know whether or not you have reflected upon what I have said?"

"I have," replied the count, sullenly.

"And what is your determination?"

"I cannot accept liberty upon the terms you propose."

"Beware!" said Massaroni, sternly; "I need not tell you that my vengeance will be sure to follow your obstinacy. Tell me at once, for it is useless to waste time in words, are you resolved not to reveal the place where Olympia is confined?"

"I cannot; I know not myself where she is."

"And think you, Signor Alberti," said Massaroni, angrily, "think you to deceive me by such a palpable falsehood as this? No trifling, signor, or you may bitterly repent it when it is too late. I have sufficient proof of your guilt."

"I dare you to produce it," said the count, boldly.

"I could this instant do so, to your utter confusion," returned Massaroni; "but at present it would not serve my purpose. Do you still persist in your impudent assertion?"

"I do," replied Alberti, firmly; "and even should your accusation be just, what right have you to question my conduct?"

"The right of every man to protect the injured and the innocent, and to punish the guilty. Do you still despise the power and authority of Allesandro Massaroni? Once more I caution you, and it will be well for you if you do not treat my warning lightly. Prouder spirits than the Count Alberti D'Amalfi have been forced to succumb to the will of the brigand chief, and I am no conjurer if you will not be glad enough to do so ere long."

"Massaroni," said the count, somewhat quailing beneath his stern glance, "why should you pursue me with such bitter animosity? I never did you wrong?"

"But you have done wrong to those whom I esteem, and I am determined to have satisfaction ere I again lose sight of you. Such obstinate resistance to my will is sheer madness, and can only tend to exasperate me to vengeance."

"Massaroni," said the count, "if it is money that you demand for my liberation; name the sum and it shall be yours."

"Bah! what is the use of endeavouring to evade the subject in this manner?" said the brigand; "you know well that I not only demand money, but the restoration of Olympia and her child to liberty. You know that I insist upon your making her all the atonement in your power, and moreover, that I command you to abandon all your hopes of the fair niece of the Prince Bianchi. It is to insist upon these that I have brought you hither, and until you submit, you must remain my prisoner without the least chance of escaping."

"Very modest, truly," said the count, with an ironical smile; "but what if I beg leave to decline?"

"Have I not just informed you, count," said Massaroni, with a frown, "you affect to treat my threats with scorn and indifference; but once more, I would have you beware, or you may find that arousing the indignation of the brigand chief is not so trifling an affair as you seem to imagine. I am no miscreant, seeking to bathe my hands in the blood of my fellow creatures, merely to gratify my sanguine propensities; but insult and obduracy I never fail to punish, however exalted the station of the offender may be."

"If I have offended you," remarked Alberti, "you surely have had a sufficient and terrible revenge in the destruction of my castle, and probably of all the valuable property it contained. But if that is not enough, again I demand you to name any ransom you may desire for my liberty, and it shall be paid to you."

"Of that we will talk anon, signor," replied Massaroni; "but think not that I part with my friends so easily, especially when they have anything to divulge which I am anxious to be made acquainted with. It will be time enough for you to talk about terms when you have confessed where Olympia and her child are confined, and they are restored to liberty."

"Diavolo!" passionately exclaimed the count, biting his lips, and pacing the cavern backwards and forwards with disordered steps; "am I to be thus braved and intimidated, outraged, and insulted by a lawless robber, a——"

"Better language, signor," interrupted Massaroni, proudly, "or it may cost you much more than you expect. You have heard my demands, and I repeat, are you ready to comply with them?"

"Never!" replied Alberti, boldly.

"Are you mad?"

"I am determined."

"Be it so, and so am I, and you must e'en take consequences. We shall see who will yield first. I leave you, Count Alberti, to your own reflections."

"Stay, Massaroni," cried the prisoner, in a more subdued tone, and somewhat alarmed by the threats of the brigand chief; "will you not listen to reason?"

"When you learn to be honest, count."

"And has Allesandro Massaroni, the terror of Italy, the presumption to talk of honesty?"

"And has Count Alberti, the seducer of female innocence, the effrontery to boast of honour? You know my terms, and it is for you to decide whether you will accept or reject them. Until Olympia's place of concealment is divulged, and her and her innocent offspring are restored to that liberty of which you have so cruelly deprived them, you remain my prisoner. You may flatter yourself with the hope that your friends may discover you, and release you from my power, but I defy them to do so; and you will find, signor, that I am no empty boaster. However, this interview has lasted long enough, and for the present I bid you farewell; when next we meet, I trust to find you in a different frame of mind, and that you are awakened to reason and a sense of justice."

Thus saying, without giving his prisoner time to say a word in reply, Massaroni quitted the cave. For several minutes after the departure of the brigand chief, Count Alberti remained absorbed in the most torturing thought, and beat his breast in the rage and excitement of his feelings. If he could possibly have entertained any doubt before, he now saw that his situation was a most alarming and desperate one—that Massaroni was determined; and he was undecided how to act. To remain a prisoner in this wretched place, surrounded by desperate men, inured to every lawless deed, and at the mercy of the brigand chief, was a a terrible prospect; but yet he recoiled with disgust and indignation from a compliance with his demands, and the degradation of acknowledging his guilt, and revealing the place in which his unfortunate victims were confined. At such a distance from any of his friends, and without their having the slightest knowledge of the secret haunts of Massaroni and his band, what hope was there of his deliverance? None whatever, and the thought worked so powerfully upon his imagination, that she was almost driven to a state of frenzy. Massaroni, on leaving the count and returning to the cavern in which he and his bold associates usually assembled, found his wife seated there alone, and attentively perusing a paper which she held in her hand, and her countenance and whole demeanour exhibited no little excitement. On hearing him approach, she looked up, and there was an expression in her full black eyes of mingled vexation and agony.

"How now, Maria?" hastily demanded Massaroni; "you seem agitated."

"I am agitated, Allesandro," she replied, "but still what has happened is no more than I expected."

"What mean you? And what is that paper which so earnestly engages your attention?"

"I found it here on my entrance," answered Maria; "read it, Massaroni, and no doubt it will afford you much gratification."

"The brigand chief hastily took the paper from his wife's hand, but he had no sooner perused the first line than his countenance underwent a change, and he exclaimed—

"Florio gone—absconded from the cavern, after the friendship I have evinced towards him? Nay, now, this is most ungrateful and annoying."

"Aye," said Maria, "did I not caution you against him? What dependence can you place upon him, the friend of your bitterest enemy, the Prince Bianchi? No doubt he will take advantage of the knowledge he possesses to betray you, with the hope of once more being able to ingratiate himself in the favour of his highness."

"No, Maria," returned Massaroni, "I am convinced you wrong Signor Clairville by such a supposition. Had it been his wish to betray me, would he not have done so at the Villa Rosa on the night of the festival, when I was surrounded by every danger, instead of aiding me in my escape?—But you have always been prejudiced against him from the first moment you beheld him."

"Because, with all his plausible exterior, I do believe him to be a spy upon our actions."

"Nay, Maria," remarked her husband, "this is ungenerous, and unworthy of you. I regret that Signor Florio has thought proper to leave us, but still I do not believe that he intends us any harm. I place the strictest reliance on his honour."

"On his honour!—ha, ha!" laughed Maria, ironically;—"of course, the gold, and the favour of the Prince Bianchi, with the hope of being still permitted to pay his addresses to the fair Melina, are not likely to have any effect upon a poor friendless painter?"

Massaroni frowned, and traversed the place for a minute or two with an air of vexation.

"Maria," he said at last, "enough of this; you know that I am ever ready to acknowledge your penetration, and to receive your advice, but on this occasion I cannot."

"Be it so, Allesandro," returned the brigand's wife, with a look of dissatisfaction. "However, look to it well!—or, perhaps, you may find that the opinion of Maria Grazie is not so erroneous or contemptible as you may seem to believe it."

Having thus spoken, she retired, and left her husband considerably agitated at what had taken place. The abrupt departure of Florio was a great source of vexation and disappointment to him; but still he placed the utmost confidence in his honour, and anticipated no unfortunate result from it, though he determined to be on his guard, and prepared to give his enemies a warm reception, should any attack be made.

CHAPTER XIV.

THE WOUNDED BRIGAND.—THE EXPEDITION. THE CONFLICT.

As day after day elapsed, and still, in spite of all the extraordinary efforts that were made

and the strong temptations which were held out, not the least clue could be obtained to the retreat of the brigands, or the fate which had befallen the Count Alberti d'Amalfi, the chagrin of the Prince Bianchi increased, and his patience became completely exhausted; and this state of feverish, of distracting excitement, was not the least diminished by the upbraidings of his own conscience, and the recollection of the phantom which that guilty conscience led him to imagine he had seen. He avoided the apartment which contained the mysterious portrait with a feeling of dread which he could not conquer, and strictly enjoined his domestics not to enter it on any pretext whatever. The misery of Melina was most intense, and melancholy were the hours she passed in the solitude of her own chamber, though she felt a great relief in not so frequently being obtruded upon by her uncle. She could not help looking upon the prince now with a feeling almost amounting to dread; for his manners had become severe and morose towards her, and he appeared to heap upon her head and that of Florio all the fault of the disappearance of the Count Alberti, and even at times threw out insinuations which surprised and shocked her, which she could never have thought him capable of. Her principal, though melancholy pleasure, was now in recalling to her mind all the fond things that her lover had ever said to her, in re-perusing the various epistles she had at different times received from him, or in contemplating with the fondest transport a miniature likeness of himself he had once presented to her, and which she had ever since kept carefully concealed within her bosom. As she gazed upon that dear resemblance, and thought upon the cruelty of their destiny, her tears would flow fast, and she would give herself up to the most abject and insupportable despair.

"Oh, where art thou now, my beloved Florio?" she would sigh, wringing her fair hands at the same time in an agony of grief, "whither has evil destiny guided thy footsteps? and what are the vicissitudes that thou at now in all probability enduring? Is it ordained that we shall indeed never meet again? If it is, oh, why does the Almighty permit me to exist another minute?"

Sometimes the dreadful idea would rush upon her disordered imagination that he was no more, that he had perished by the stiletto of the secret assassin, or that he had, in the frenzy of his despair, laid violent hands upon himself; and in such terrible moments as these her agony of feeling was perfectly indescribable, and she was almost tempted to commit that which at other times she would have shuddered at barely contemplating. The roses faded from the poor girl's cheeks, the fire that had before lighted her expressive eyes was extinguished, the sunny smiles that had before irradiated her lovely countenance no longer beamed there, and, in fact, she had became altogether but a sickly phantom of her fo mer self. There were moments, too, when thoughts of a still more desperate and alarming character would force themselves upon her brain. Home had become hateful to her since he, to whom her whole soul's affections were devoted, was driven from it; and she was almost tempted to abandon it, and, in disguise to seek out her lover, and to resign her fate into his hands, whatever the consequences might be. Anxious as she was to ascertain the fate of the Count Alberti, and deeply as her sensitive and gentle bosom would have regretted to hear that any untimely fate had befallen him, she dreaded his restoration to liberty; for then she was convinced that it would only hasten the consummation of her misery, and the total annihilation of her hopes. Her uncle was completely inexorable, and notwithstanding the utter aversion she had expressed towards Alberti, she felt satisfied that he would compel her to become his wife, a fate of far greater horror than any her imagination could depicture; the most lingering death of torture would be bliss compared with it. The Prince Bianchi was one evening sitting in his private apartment, brooding upon the various exciting events that had recently taken place, when he was aroused from his lethargy by hearing a confused noise below, and immediately summoned a domestic to inquire into the cause.

"A wounded brigand, your highness," replied the man, "and who appears to be dying, has just been discovered in the neighbourhood and brought to the villa; he requests to see your excellence, as he has something of importance to communicate, and there is not a moment to be lost."

The prince waited to hear no more, but immediately hastened to the room to which the wounded stranger had been conveyed. He was a ferocious looking man, upon whose savage features the ghastly impress of death was already stamped, and who was bleeding profusely from a frightful wound in his side, which seemed to have been inflicted by a stiletto. He was groaning awfully, and his end was rapidly approaching. As the prince eagerly approached him, and leant over him, he raised his eyes towards his countenance, and endeavoured to speak, but his voice failed to give articulation to a single syllable, and he sunk back in the arms of those who were supporting him, apparently almost exhausted. The anxiety of the prince increased, he ordered a cordial to be applied to the dying man's lips, and that somewhat revived him; he rallied a little, but it was clear that he was sinking fast.

"You sent for me," said Prince Bianchi, impatiently; "exert yourself;—what is it you have to communicate to me?"

The wretched man opened his lips, and struggled hard to give expression to his wishes, but for a moment or two not a word could escape him; at length, with much difficulty, he faltered out in a voice scarcely audible—

"Massaroni—the Count Alberti—near the Appenines—they—oh!"

That word was his last, for he sunk back a ghastly corpse in the arms of those who supported him.

"How unfortunate is this," said the prince; "had he been discovered but a few minutes before, he might have been able to divulge all that he wished. Search the body, and see if anything can be discovered which may lead to any further explanation."

The attendants obeyed, while the prince looked on with the utmost anxiety; but nothing was discovered to throw any further light upon the mystery, and after giving instructions as to the disposal of the corpse, his highness again departed to the apartment from which he had been so hastily summoned, filled with a variety of conjectures of the most conflicting nature.

"How torturing is this," he muttered to himself; "this man is, doubtless, of the band of the villain Massaroni, and could have given me all the information I seek, had he only been discovered a few minutes sooner. However, he has said enough to put me upon the brigand's track, and I will lose no time in despatching an expedition in search of him. It appears evident that Massaroni, holding the Count Alberti a prisoner, is secreted somewhere near the Appenines, and if I do not succeed in finding him out and hunting him from his lair, say I am not the Prince Bianchi."

The prince lost no time in summoning one of the the principal officers of the troops into his presence, and consulting with him upon what was best to be done, as it was evident that unless they acted with promptitude they could not expect to meet with success, and it was finally arranged that a strong force should be despatched with all possible speed towards the Appenines with the hope of their being there able to obtain such information as would lead to the discovery of the secret haunt of the brigands, and that taking them by surprise the conquest would be an easy one. The prince was anxious to have headed them himself, for he was fearless of danger, but he was too weak and ill from recent excitement to do so, and after giving them the strictest commands not to return until their search had been crowned with success, and they had secured the persons of Massaroni and the Count Alberti, he dismissed them on their perilous expedition.

"I shall triumph—I shall triumph yet!" said the prince as he traversed his chamber that night, his mind too busily occupied with thought to suffer him to retire to rest. "The Count Alberti shall be restored to liberty, and Massaroni, the daring brigand chief, who has so long been the terror of the country, and bid defiance to the laws, shall at length be in my power, and suffer the penalty due to his crimes. Ah, what sweet revenge it will be to me to witness his excruciating agonies beneath the hands of the executioner, to——"

He paused, and started, for at that moment a deep groan seemed to vibrate on his ear, and then suddenly to die away on the midnight air. His limbs trembled, and his heart palpitated violently against his side. He looked fearfully around the room, but nothing but his own dark shadow on the wainscot met his gaze. Still he could not divest himself of the impression which that imaginary sound had made upon his mind. He shuddered to be alone, and the universal silence which reigned at that solemn hour added to his fear.

"What a weak fool I am!" he muttered at length; "have I become a child again, to be frightened at my own shadow?—Psha! why should such gloomy thoughts and apprehensions rise to my mind whenever the name of the brigand chief recurs to my memory?—I should think of him with no other feelings but those of disgust and abhorrence; and yet, I know not how it is, I cannot think of him without experiencing certain sentiments of an inexplicable nature, for which I am a loss to account. What can it mean?—Why should I suffer such a feeling to overcome me?"

He threw himself into a chair, and leaning his head upon his hand, gave himself up entirely to the extraordinary reflections that rose in such rapid and torturing succession upon his imagination. Time passed on; day began to dawn, and still the Prince Bianchi sat in the same deep lethargy of thought, from which nothing seemed to have the power to arouse him, and he attempted not to seek his couch. Melina had become acquainted with all that had taken place on that night, and we need scarcely say that it deeply interested her, and excited a variety of conjectures in her breast. Much as she regretted the errors of Massaroni, she earnestly hoped that he might not fall into the power of her uncle, who seemed determined to hunt him to the death, with a fierceness of revenge that made her shudder, and of which she could not have believed him capable. There was something so noble in the appearance of the brigand chief, so elegant in his manners, and so generous in many of his actions, that she was inclined to believe that it was some cruel injustice that had precipitated him into his present lawless and perilous career of life, and that he was worthy of a better fate. But more than all, the damsel dreaded the restoration of the Count Alberti to liberty, for then she knew he could resume his odious suit with tenfold energy, and she had not the least doubt, from all her uncle had said, he would not hesitate to force her into a union, the pure thought of which made her shudder with a feeling of horror which she could not surmount. These thoughts kept her waking nearly the whole of the night, and she arose at an early hour in the morning, and walked to the window of her chamber in order to endeavour to divert her ideas by watching the rising sun. While she was thus occupied, she beheld the troops, who were going upon the hazardous expedition against the brigands, wend their way past the Villa, and at the sight a sickly sensation of nameless dread came over her, which she found it impossible to subdue. She watched them till they were completely out of sight, and she then left the window, and sinking on her knees, supplicated the protection of Heaven. She even felt a greater depression of spirits than she had lately done, and the most dismal forebodings of some additional approaching calamity haunted her mind, and rendered her anguish almost insupportable.

"Almighty Father!" she fervently ejaculated, "save me from any danger that may threaten me, I beseech Thee, and suffer me not to fall a sacrifice to that man whom I must ever loathe and despise. Oh, watch over, too, and guard from every danger the unfortunate Florio, and if it is Thy will that we should never meet again, let him enjoy all the tranquillity and happiness I know he can ever hope to experience in this world without his poor Melina."

Her tears fell fast, and bitter sobs choked her utterance, and for some time she happily remained in almost an utter state of unconsciousness. She was aroused from this state by the entrance of Floretta, her attendant, who came to summon her to the presence of the prince, her uncle, who was awaiting her to join him at the morning repast. Alas! the bare mention of that name which once used to fill her bosom with feelings of delight, now made her tremble with fear, especially on this occasion, and glad would she have been had she been able to excuse herself from meeting him. However, she endeavoured to tranquillize her feelings as much as possible, and with a timid step she bent her way to the room in which he was awaiting her. She found him looking very pale and disordered, and it was very evident that he had had but little, if any, rest the night before; however, he arose and greeted her with much apparent affection, and handing her to a seat by his side, gazed at her earnestly in silence for a few moments.

"You look pale and ill, child," he observed, at length; "it is not the same, sweet, playful, rosy Melina that it was a short time since. Come, come, this must not continue; you must exert yourself, and dissipate the melancholy thoughts which you have suffered to take possession of your mind; they agree badly with your youth and natural vivacity of spirits. Arouse yourself, my dear Melina; smile again, as you were wont to do, and make your fond guardian happy ."

"Happy! my dear uncle," replied Melina; "oh, can you for a moment doubt my anxiety to do so? Can you for an instant imagine that my happiness is centered in your own ?"

"I know it, my love, but still I cannot be insensible to the feelings that are passing in your mind. You think me harsh and cruel because I cannot sanction your love for one who, however worthy his virtues may render him to you, and I do not for a moment dispute them, is so far beneath you in rank, in wealth, and station."

Tears gushed to the eyes of Melina at this allusion to her lover, but convulsive sobs prevented her giving utterance to a word in reply. The prince watched her very narrowly, and a slight expression of displeasure passed over his countenance.

"I see how it is, Melina," he remarked, "my fears are but too well founded, and, much as it grieves me to cause you a single pang, I must insist that you conquer this weakness, which is so visibly preying upon your health, to banish Florio Clairville from your thoughts, and to forget that such a being ever existed."

"Oh, my dear uncle," sighed Melina, "how hard is the task you would impose upon me!"

"It must be accomplished, Melina; Florio and you must henceforth be strangers to each other. The Count Alberti, I have reason to hope, will soon be rescued from the power of the villains who have committed so atrocious an outrage upon him, and you must then be prepared to receive him and look upon him as your future husband."

"The Count Alberti!" gasped forth Melina, in a faint voice.

"Aye," replied the prince, "why do you repeat his name with such a look of loathing and disgust ?"

"Oh, my lord!" ejaculated the deeply agitated damsel, "why will you persist in urging me upon a subject which I acknowledge is so hateful to me! Already have I sufficiently expressed to you my sentiments as regards the count, and nothing can ever alter them; and if you would not render me one of the most miserable of human beings, you will not insist upon compelling me to that which my heart abhors."

The prince arose from his seat, and walked up and down the room for a minute or two, in a state of great excitement. Melina trembled and covered her face with her hands.

"Melina," at length said her uncle, in an impressive voice, "this obstinacy excites my utmost anger, and is what I never expected from you. I have set my mind upon this alliance, every way so desirable, and I must not, will not suffer the foolish caprices of a thoughtless girl to disappoint me in my wishes. I expect, nay, command your implicit obedience to my will."

"Then," said Melina, bursting into an hysterical flood of tears, "may the great God of Heaven look down with pity upon me, for you have doomed me to greater earthly misery than I can ever find strength to endure. Oh! my uncle, you never was harsh and cruel before, and why should you now seek to consign me to a fate which must break my heart? Suffer me to remain as I am. and I will continue to love and bless you, and be subservient to your every wish, as I trust I have hitherto been; but do not—oh! do not, I implore you, sacrifice me to such a man as the Count Alberti."

"Grant me patience!" cried the prince, passionately; what a child hast thou become, Melina, to talk thus? But—but—I will be calm, for I know that your good sense will shortly convince you of the folly, nay, the downright perverseness and ingratitude of your present conduct. I repeat that we have obtained a clue to the haunt of the brigand Massaroni; in a few hours he will, doubtless, be surrounded, and, being taken by surprise, will be easily captured. The Count Alberti will then be released from his present dangerous situation, and flying on the wings of love, throw himself at the feet of her who is the sole empress of his affections. '

"For Heaven's sake spare me," with difficulty gasped forth Melina, "you cannot, you will not be so cruel, my lord, my uncle, as to sanction the addresses of one who has proved himself to be a miscreant of the blackest dye——"

She was about to proceed when the prince interrupted her passionately—

"A miscreant, say you, Melina?" he observed.

"Yes," she replied, regaining fortitude, and her woman's indignation coming to her aid : "a miscreant, I repeat, of the blackest dye. Can you term the wretch—I will not dignify him with the name of man—any other than a miscreant, who deliberately insinuates himself into the affections of a young and guileless unsuspecting girl, and——"

"Has hell itself conspired against me?" interrupted the prince, rising to his feet with a fury and vehemence that perfectly startled Melina; while his countenance evinced the most powerful mental agitation, and every limb trembled with the extraordinary excitement of his feelings;—"has hell itself conspired against me?" he repeated, "that I am thus constantly to be reminded of the past?—Girl, where have you gained your information? What dastard wretch has dared to pry into my secrets?—What cowardly eaves-dropper has poured his poison into your ears?—Who dares to call the Prince Bianchi miscreant, seducer, the deserter of his victims, the——"

"My lord, my lord, my dear uncle," said the astonished and terrified damsel, "oh, tell me, I beseech you, what have I said that should excite you thus?"

"You have said that," replied the prince, in the same wild manner, and staring wildly about him, "which whole centuries of compunction and regret could not eradicate. You have aroused a thousand demons which are now preying upon my brain. Girl—No, you are no niece of mine. Get you gone!—away with you!—I discard you!—I cur—"

"Uncle!" shrieked the horror-struck Melina, sinking upon her knees.

"No, I own you not," he continued in the same wild strain, and his whole demeanour becoming absolutely ferocious;—"who told you of Valentia and Zitella, girl?—Who is the reptile—let me know him that I may crush him. Who whispered in your too ready ear that I was their seducer, and afterwards abandoned them?—God of Heaven! have I lived to these years to be now reminded by her that I thought all loveliness, gentleness, and submission, of the errors of my youthful days?—Is it not enough that I should endure the stings of conscience?—that my nights should be restless, that my days should wear the blackest gloom of midnight, with all its attendant horrors, but that I must now have one in whom I have placed my whole affections, to whom I have granted every indulgence, on whom I looked as the prop and comfort of my declining years, seeking every means to add to my torture, and mocking my suffering?—Girl, I hate thee, I discard thee, I cur—"

"For the love of heaven!" again interrupted the distracted Melina, as the curse was upon the old man's lips—"for the love of heaven forbear!—Oh, my lord, my uncle, what have I said, what have I done to cause this extraordinary, this fearful excitement?—But you know not what you say; I am convinced you do not. Some strange infatuation has seized upon your brain. Suffer me, I implore you, to retire, until you have collected yourself. I pry into your secrets!—oh, my good lord, you must be mad, or you would never accuse me of such turpitude of conduct, of such degrading meanness of spirit. I have but spoken the candid sentiments of my heart; perhaps you may consider too boldly, but what I have said has been dictated by truth and honesty, and wherefore should I blush? God knows I wish not to sport with your feelings, or to triumph in your disappointment; I would not willingly impart a single pang to your breast; but at the same time I must, and will repeat, that I must ever look upon with scorn and loathing, with dis-

gust, with the most inexpressible hatred, the base, the cowardly, the unmanly seducer of Olympia, the Count Alberti; nay more, hear me—you may discard me, you may banish me from your doors, send me forth a wandering outcast upon the face of the earth, even heap your heaviest curses upon my head, but I swear by the Almighty Power that rules our actions, and holds the power alone to raise or crush us, that I will never become that villain's wife—no, not if all the world were arranged in power to compel me."

It would be impossible to describe the energy with which Melina gave utterance to these words, but overpowered by her feelings and her extraordinary exertions, she sank down in her seat and was almost ready to faint. The prince was completely astounded. He could scarcely believe that it was the same gentle and submissive girl, whom he had hitherto thought had no other will than his own. He was aroused as if from a dream, and for a few moments he gazed at her with the most indescribable astonishment, scarcely believing the evidence of his senses, and totally incapable of giving utterance to a syllable. Then the observations she had given utterance to went to his heart, and with their force of truth made him absolutely recoil within himself. He found that he had betrayed himself; that he had debased himself in the eyes of that fair being, to whom he wished to appear as one almost immaculate; and moreover, he found that he had a woman of noble spirit to contend with, and who, while she respected and practiced every gentle and generous virtue, would not tamely submit to tyranny and oppression, or yield to that against which her passions were opposed, let the consequences be to her whatever they might; let the peril of disobedience be ever so great. We say that the prince was astounded, but that is too mild a term—he was bewildered, distracted, degraded, and abashed. He had not the power to give utterance to a word. He felt at the moment debased; he hated himself, while at the same moment the poor trembling and almost insensible girl before him appeared as something superior to human beings. He traversed the room for a few minutes in a state of the utmost perturbation, and at last again venturing to approach his beauteous niece, who was weeping bitterly, he said—

"Melina, I may have been wrong, I may have been too hasty, apparently too harsh, too severe; but—but, my child, you should make some allowances for my age and consequent infirmities, and believe at the same time that I am ever studious of your happiness."

"My lord," replied the maiden, looking up through her tears, and in a calm and steady voice, "I make all those allowances, believe me, I do; I am the same gentle and submissive Melina that you have ever found me to be; but

I cannot—nay, I will not, in this single instance, dear uncle, comply with your wishes."

"You will not consent to receive the Count Alberti as your future husband?"

"I would sooner die a thousand deaths first," replied Melina.

"And you still cherish your love for the plebeian, Florio Clairville?"

"Yes, and while the stream of life continues to circulate through my veins, I ever shall.

"By Heaven!" cried the prince, unable to contain himself; "this is too much. Obsti-

FLORIO'S LETTER TO MELINA DEMANDED BY PRINCE BIANCHI.

nate girl, you may repent this opposition to my will. However, it shall avail you nothing; —I have made up my mind, and nothing shall alter it."

"And since you compel me to say so, my lord," said Melina, rising with a fierceness and dignity that perfectly astonished the prince, "I have also made up mine, and that is never, upon any consideration, to be forced into a marriage with a man who is worthy only of the detestation of every virtuous individual. The base betrayer of the unfortunate Olympia shall never become the husband of Melina. Nay more, should he have the boldness and presumption to insult my ears with his odious addresses, I will ring such a tale in his ears as will make even him shudder. But you, my lord, to endeavour to gloss over the crimes of the heartless libertine and profligate, the seducer of——"

"Girl! Girl!" interrupted the prince fiercely, and with an aspect which it would be no easy task to describe; "are you determined to drive me to madness?—To recall to my memory the dark deeds of the past, which many years of sorrow and contrition should have buried in oblivion?—Who is there living that dare accuse me of being a libertine, a seducer, a profligate?—Who says that I deserted my unfortunate confiding victims and their innocent offspring to misery and shame?—'Tis false, false as hell!—and——"

"Uncle!" again interposed the astonished and terrified Melina, " I never accused you of that of which I am thoroughly convinced you must ever have been incapable. Your mind is distracted, you know not what you say."

"Know not what I say!" repeated the prince, still wandering; "yes, I do, and it is that which drives me to madness. Even the dead arise from their graves to confront me and add to my anguish, and you, with bitter mockery, reproach me with my former crimes."

"Good God! my dear uncle," ejaculated Melina, looking at him with a mingled expression of dread and compassion; "what fearful words are these to which you are giving utterance?—Your mind must be bewildered—pray calm yourself."

"Yes," continued the prince, apparently taking no notice of what Melina said, "the silent graves yield up their dead to stalk in ghastly array before the eyes of those who so cruelly injured them while living. 'Twas but the other night I saw her, as plainly as when she was in existence."

"Who—who—dear uncle?"

"Her of whom you have been speaking," replied the prince in the same wandering and incoherent strain; "her of whom you have been speaking, girl, I repeat—Valentia. Oh, she was most lovely;—she was innocent, she was confiding, and I loved her, but she was poor; she was only a poor Florentine maid, and I—I was the Prince Bianchi, and could it be expected that I could sacrifice my dignity to my sense of honour?—Bah! the idea was preposterous, and yet if all the world knew this, they would be apt to despise me and call me villain, especially when they knew that she and her child were not my only victims. No, no, there was Zitella and her innocent offspring;—but—but I did not murder it—no—no, I only——"

"Dear uncle," interrupted the horror-struck Melina, "what frightful ideas are these that

have stolen your brain? You are not well. Come, come, endeavour to divert your thoughts, and let us converse on subjects more congenial to us both."

The prince was suddenly aroused to reason, and looking earnestly at his niece, he ejaculated—

"What have I said, that you should talk to me thus?"

"Nothing, nothing, dear uncle, only some feverish wanderings, to which we are all liable at times."

"You are certain I divulged nothing?" demanded the prince, sternly, and fixing a penetrating look upon her countenance.

"Why should you thus question me, my lord?" asked the trembling Melina.

"Enough, enough," he replied, "I am getting old and crazy; and—and you tantalize me, girl, by opposing my wishes."

"Heaven forbid that I should do so in anything that virtue should command me," returned Melina. "No, my lord, you have ever found me affectionate and dutiful, as I should be to one who, since the demise of my poor parents, has been my best, my only friend—but pardon me if I may appear too bold; there are certain limits even to duty and obedience, and those I cannot, will not go beyond."

"I understand you," said the prince, with a frown, "you will not accept the Count Alberti as your lover?"

"The thought is odious—I will court the most violent death rather."

"Obstinate girl, you will have reason to repent this."

"I trust not, my lord," replied Melina, firmly.

"The Count Alberti will be restored to liberty, and the day that marks the execution of the miscreant Massaroni, shall make you his bride."

"That day," returned Melina, in a tone, and with a look which completely startled her uncle, "I will never live to see."

"Melina!" exclaimed the prince, "know you what you say?"

"I do, my lord," answered the damsel calmly, "and mark me, I will fulfil my promise. But, oh, my dear uncle, you will relent; again I implore you to do so, to consign me to a nunnery, to any other fate rather than that one which I cannot even contemplate without feelings of horror."

"Do you then still love Florio Clairville?"

"I do," replied Melina faintly, and blushing deeply, "and ever must."

"And know you where he is at present?" demanded the prince, with a scrutinizing eye.

"By Heaven, I do not," answered Melina, solemnly.

"You have received no further communication from him since the one which I secured?"

"None. Can you suspect me of deceiving you, my lord?"

"It will be well for you that you do not," returned the prince, sternly, "but once more I command you to banish the beggar from your thoughts; to forget that you have ever seen such an individual."

Melina shook her head and sighed.

"You evidently scorn my mandates," said the prince, again frowning—"beware, beware! Cospetto! shall the niece of the Prince Bianchi, the Governor of Rome, condescend to encourage the addresses of a poor friendless dauber of canvas? Girl, have you no pride? No sense of your own dignity and value?"

"Pardon me. my lord," suggested Melina, modestly, but firmly, "my devotion to one, who though poor and humble, is honourable and virtuous, surely cannot deteriorate from either of those qualities."

"Psha! the girl is mad," said the prince, passionately. "But I will not suffer my temper to be again ruffled; you have heard my determination, and let whatever may be the consequences, I will not swerve from it."

"And since it is so, my lord," retorted Melina, with boldness of spirit, which took him completely by surprise, for he had never witnessed it in her before, "hear also mine—at every risk, even that of your everlasting displeasure, I will resist every attempt to compel me into a marriage which is so hateful to me; neither will I flatter the man whom I so thoroughly despise by holding out hopes to him which my sentiments will never allow me to realize. Believe me, my lord, that nothing can more sincerely afflict me than to act in any way contrary to your wishes, but you compel me to it, and I have no choice. Oh, my dear lord, do not be ungenerous; I have too great an opinion of the affection you bear me to imagine that you would wish to see me miserable, or to throw an overwhelming blight upon all my youthful hopes and future prospects. I repeat that the Count Alberti, by his conduct to Olympia and the innocent offspring of their illicit intercourse, has forfeited all claim even to my friendship or esteem; but to look upon him in the character of my future husband, is an idea so monstrous, so revolting to my feelings, that I find it impossible to give adequate expression to my sentiments upon the hateful subject. Thus far have I been bold enough to express my candid thoughts to you, and I am, moreover, fully prepared to meet the consequence of my disobedience to your will."

Nothing could exceed the vexation of the prince as his beauteous niece thus gave expression to her feelings; he looked at her with astonishment, and such was the modest firmness of her demeanour, and the immoveable determination that flashed from her fine intelligent eyes, that he could scarcely believe it was her. Two or three times he essayed to speak, but passion choked his utterance, and he traversed the apartment in a state of the greatest possible excitement. Melina, however, remained undaunted; and her bosom felt the greatest possible relief now that she had thus given utterance to her feelings, and as she had said, she was fully prepared to abide the consequences, whatever they might be.

"And is this the docile, gentle, affectionate, and submissive being, that I have loved and cherished with the same fondness and care as if she had been my own child?" said the prince, at last. "Oh, how bitterly have I been deceived, how shamefully have I been duped."

"Deceived! duped!" repeated Melina. "Oh, my lord, you surely cannot mean to accuse me of deception, of duplicity? Recal those harsh and unmerited words, I beseech you, for never were words so unjustly, so unkindly applied."

"Away, girl!" commanded the prince, sternly, "I will no longer listen to you; but remember that your obstinacy will have no other effect on me than to excite my utmost indignation. You must submit to my will, or my heaviest curse shall descend upon your head."

"Uncle—dearest uncle," sobbed fo th the agitated damsel, "hear me, I implore you."

"No more," replied the prince, in the same stern and forbidding tone;—begone, I say, to your chamber, and venture not again into my presence until you have learnt reason and obedience to my will."

Melina fixed upon him one look of supplication, and then with a bursting heart she quitted the room. It was a considerable time ere the prince could assume anything like a degree of composure when he was left alone, so great was his vexation at what he considered the obstinacy of Melina; but he was fully resolved, let what might be the result, that she should be forced to yield to his wishes, and then he would visit her with his sorest displeasure if she ventured to receive the addresses of the Count Alberti with that hatred and disdain which she had so freely expressed to him. The boldness and determination of her manner had taken him completely by surprise, and added to his rage and bewilderment, for hitherto he had looked upon her as a gentle and submissive creature who had no other will but his; but he now found that she had a spirit, which when properly called into action, it would be no easy task to subdue, and that he might experience far greater trouble with her than he had calculated upon. The observations she had made use of respecting the character and crimes of the count, he could not deny the force and justice of; they had sunk deep into his soul, and had made an impression which he would find it no easy task to banish, but still he reproached himself for suffering his conscience to overpower his prudence in the manner it had done, and to cause him to give utterance to words which must have excited the astonishment and suspicion of Melina, and which were so near disclosing that guilty secret which had been so long confined within his own breast, and which, if known, would not only degrade him in her estimation, but in the eyes of the whole world.

"But no matter," he muttered to himself, "in spite of all her resistance she must, she shall be forced to yield to my wishes, even at any cost. 'Sdeath! am I to be opposed and braved by a silly girl, and one who is entirely dependent upon me?—I should esteem myself worse than an idiot, were I to be moved from my purpose by her foolish prejudices. The count is wealthy, accomplished, and handsome; and what would Melina have more? It is true he has been guilty of folly and imprudence, but what young man has not?—and is he constantly to be upbraided for errors which are merely venial? The count loves her, and will make her a good and affectionate husband; and I have no doubt that, in time, Melina will be enabled to overcome the repugnance she now expresses towards him, and that she will make him a right dutiful wife. Could I only persuade her to banish Florio from her thoughts, all would go as well as I could wish it. It must, it shall be so, and I will take especial care that they never meet again. Should Florio Clairville again have the presumption to obtrude upon her presence, he shall deeply rue it, though I must acknowledge that I still esteem him for the natural good qualities he possesses, and have no wish to do him any harm. I wish I could discover whither he has directed his footsteps, that I might keep a strict watch upon his actions: but, no matter, I have nothing to apprehend from him; he will not dare incur my anger, for he must be well aware how dangerous the consequences would be to himself. I will, therefore, make my mind perfectly easy upon that subject."

He paused for a moment, and reflected, and then added—

"I am all impatience till I know the result of this expedition I have sent against the brigands: should they fail to discover their retreat, and to secure Massaroni, and restore the young count to liberty, I know not how I shall be able to support the disappointment. But they must succeed; something seems to assure me that they will; and I will look forward to the result with confidence. Oh! when I have the daring brigand chief, who has so long set my authority at defiance, in my power, my hopes will be accomplished, and all my fears set at rest. But there is a certain mystery about the character and actions of that lawless man, which I am most anxious to penetrate, and it shall be no fault of mine if I do not do so. His manners bespeak those of a man of superior birth, and there is something so noble in the expression of his features, and his general demeanour, that I am unable to do away with the impression they have made upon me. How is this?—I cannot account for it. Why should this robber and assassin excite such an extraordinary interest in my bosom, that whenever his name arises to my thoughts, I feel a certain sensation come over me, for which I am totally unable to account?—Bah! this is folly, and I must not suffer myself to give way to it, or it may prevent me from the administration of that stern justice which his numerous and reckless crimes demand."

He again paused, for as these thoughts occurred to him, a strange trembling feeling came over him, and a voice seemed to whisper in his ear "Forbear!" He started and looked around, almost expecting to encounter some ghastly object, but he was quite alone, and he chided himself for his folly and weakness. In order to compose his thoughts, he walked forth from the Villa, and strolled amongst the romantic scenery in the neighbourhood; but in spite of the fineness of the morning, and the beauty of all around him, the same torturing and conflicting thoughts pursued him, and rendered him doubtful, suspicious, discontented, and uneasy. Unconsciously his footsteps led him to the scene of the late conflagration, and he contemplated those blackened ruins of that once noble edifice with feelings of regret and rage.

"Massaroni," he ejaculated, "if it were only for this, I would pursue thee to destruction. I will never rest until I see thee in the hands of the executioner, and the inhuman deeds thou hast committed fully atoned for by a death of torture."

He was about to retire slowly from the spot, when he was astonished to hear his name pronounced in an unknown voice, and a man suddenly emerged from the ruins and stood before him. The prince started back a few paces with no little amazement and some alarm, and gazed at the man with the greatest curiosity. He was a coarse vulgar looking fellow, very meanly clad, and having the appearance of having travelled far. His countenance was almost concealed beneath huge black whiskers, and his features were of the most savage and repulsive character. His eyes, which were small but flashing, were overshadowed by black shaggy eye-brows, which imparted a still more forbidding aspect to his countenance. His form was powerful and robust, and he was armed with a stile to and a brace of pistols, which not a little added to the alarm of the prince, who had no weapon with him by which he could defend himself from any attack which the stranger might contemplate making upon him. The man noticed the surprise and uneasiness of the prince with a sinister grin, and then bowed with the utmost familiarity to him, and remained fixed in the same attitude, from which he seemed not disposed to move in a hurry.

"How now?" at length demanded the prince, "who are you, fellow?—why do you cross my path so abruptly, and what is your business with me?"

"Your highness and I are very old acquaintances," replied the man, with the utmost coolness, "though we have not met before for many years."

"Insolent!" exclaimed the prince, with haughty indignation, "know you not who it is you are addressing, or have you no fears for the consequences of your boldness?"

"None whatever, excellenza," answered the stranger, in the same bold and familiar tone; "your highness must respect me too much to wish to do me any harm, besides it would be very bad policy on your part to endeavour to do so."

The prince was more and more astonished, and looked at the man more narrowly than he had done before, but he had not the least recollection of his features.

"Speak!" he demanded, "who are you, and what would you have of me?"

"Money, my lord."

"Money!" repeated the prince, starting; "are you then a robber?"

"Why I do a little in that way sometimes, monsignore, but business has been very dull for some time; so, as I have a trifling claim upon your purse, I thought I would take the liberty of calling upon you."

"Daring scoundrel, I——"

"Nay, my lord," interrupted the man, "it is sheer folly in you to use such epithets towards one who has rendered you good service, and whose tongue it would be more prudent for you to endeavour to keep quiet."

"I never beheld you before."

"Indeed, but you have; I repeat that we have often met before, though many years have elapsed since we had that mutual pleasure, and time and travelling, I dare say, have changed my features."

"Who are you, then?" asked the prince, with increased wonder.

"A word in your ear, signor," replied the man, "for there might be listeners whom it would not be advisable should hear what I say."

The man approached nearer to the prince and whispered a few words in his ear, which he no sooner heard than he started and turned pale, and his whole demeanour evinced the violence of his agitation.

"Good God!" he exclaimed, "is it possible?"

"It is true," answered the man.

"What brings you here?—I thought you dead years ago."

"No doubt of it, and I dare say you are not a little disappointed, my lord," remarked the fellow, with a disagreeable and ironical grin.

"For mercy's sake, Malvolio," said the prince, in a voice of extreme emotion, "tell me, what did you do with the tender charge I committed to your care?"

"I did not murder it, my lord."

"Thank Heaven!"

"No, I had not the heart to do that, villain though I was."

"What did you with it? Tell me, and ease the agony of my suspense."

"Oh, I placed it in excellent quarters."

"Where? where? Tell me where?"

"Nay, that, my lord, I do not think proper to do at present."

"Oh, why not?" demanded the prince eagerly.

"Because," answered the man, "I wish to secure the patronage of your highness, which I might lose if I were to divulge too many of my secrets."

"Malvolio, you may depend upon my keeping faith with you, for, alas! you hold me in your power."

"I am glad to find that your highness is fully sensible of that," returned Malvolio.

"That matters not; I dare say you will see me as often as you wish."

"Tell me, Malvolio," faltered out the prince, "does that unfortunate child still live?"

"I believe she does."

"My God!" exclaimed the prince, "and shall I ever again behold her?"

"Why, it is not unlikely you may, my lord, if you wish it."

"No, no—I could not, dare not acknowledge her," said the prince, "I could not bear to gaze upon her countenance; I——"

"Does, then, your conscience so keenly reproach you, my lord?" said Malvolio, with an ironical grin.

"Oh, Malvolio," said the prince, "you can little imagine the years of remorse and bitter suffering I have endured since that unfortunate event; but the assurance that you did not take the unconscious innocent's life has removed a weight of care and anxiety from my mind, which at times drove me to madness. But you will not betray me, Malvolio?"

"I have not done so hitherto, and all depends in future upon yourself."

"You shall have no cause to complain, Malvolio. Here is gold, and when that is exhausted, I shall be ready to supply your demands."

"That is enough," said Malvolio, pocketing the purse with a look of satisfaction.

"When shall we meet again?"

"Oh, I will not fail to call upon you when my purse needs replenishing, answered Malvolio, "and I will always send you word where we may meet in secrecy. But mind—no treachery, my lord."

"You may depend upon me, Malvolio," replied the prince.

"Very well; then, while you continue to keep faith with me your secret is safe, but the moment I suspect that you seek to play me false, I will publish your guilt to the world; and bring forward such proof as will render all refutation impossible."

"You may be certain that I will not deceive you," said his highness.

"'Tis well, then," returned Malvolio, "so we understand each other."

"We do; but will you not tell me how you disposed of the child, and where she is at present?"

"No; be satisfied with what I have already revealed to you, more you must not know at present."

"I cannot perceive the necessity of this secrecy. Malvolio," remarked the prince.

"Probably not," answered the former; "however, I have my reasons, and let that suffice."

"There is another question I must ask you, Malvolio."

"Name it, my lord."

"Zitella—my lips tremble as I repeat the name of that deeply injured woman—know you whether she still lives?"

"I do not," answered Malvolio, "she made her escape from the convent in which she was placed by your lordship's orders, and what became of her I could not ascertain."

The prince evinced much emotion when he heard this, and continued for a few moments silent, and buried in thought.

"This is most unfortunate," he said at length, "and until I discover her fate I shall always remain in a state of doubt, suspense, and apprehension. Malvolio, will you not assist me to endeavour to find out whether she still lives, and the place of concealment?"

"I will, my lord. But you have nothing to fear from her, I should imagine. She did not know your name, I believe?"

"She did not," replied the prince.

"And after the lapse of so many years, should she behold you again, it is not very likely that she would recognise you."

"Probably not," coincided the prince, "but still I should not like to venture to encounter her; and my mind would be more at ease could I but ascertain that she was in a place of security, and where she would not be likely to discover me."

"Very true, my lord," observed Malvolio, "and I will do all I can to find her out."

"By doing so you will be rendering me a great service, and I will not fail to reward you handsomely for it."

"That is enough, so long as your highness is not churlish of your gold, you may always depend upon the service and secrecy o Malvolio."

"I am satisfied," said the prince, "but one thing I must impress upon your mind."

"And what is that, excellenza?"

"That whenever you wish to see me, you will forward me timely notice of the same, that our meetings may be conducted in secrecy, and without exciting the suspicions of prying curiosity."

"I will attend to the injunctions of your highness," replied Malvolio; "have you any further commands for me?"

"None."

"Then it will be as well to close this interview, lest we should be observed; and I must confess that my appearance is not at all calculated to excite any very favourable impression upon the mind of the beholder; however, you will find a change in me for the better when next we meet, my lord."

"I trust I shall," remarked the prince, eyeing the forbidding countenance of Malvolio with a look of suspicion and inward disgust.

"Then I have the honour to bid your highness farewell," said Malvolio, bowing obsequiously, and with affected politeness. The prince returned no answer, and the ruffian departed, leaving his wealthy employer in a state of the greatest confusion and excitement.

"What an unexpected meeting is this," he muttered to himself, as he slowly bent his way from the ruins, after looking carefully around him, fearful that they might have been watched;—"I had hoped that Malvolio was dead years ago, and that there was no one living who knew of my guilt. He holds me at his mercy, and too well do I know the villain's character, to believe that he will fail to take every advantage of it. I shall be in constant fear of him, and must yield to all his demands, however monstrous they may be, or I may be well assured what the consequences will be. But he did not sacrifice the life of the child, and my concience is therefore relieved from that weight of guilt. And she still lives!—Where?—What are her circumstances?—Oh, how I long, yet dread to behold her. Zitella, too, the unhappy victim of my lust, may still be in existence; and should she discover me!—the thought is distracting, let me try to banish it from my mind."

But in vain he tried to do so; the most painful thoughts continued to distract his brain as he proceeded on his way home, and when he arrived there he immediately locked himself up in his own room, and would not allow the intrusion of any one. Melina, when she found herself in her own room, after her painful interview with her uncle, gave herself up to all the violence of the grief which agonized her bosom, and in vain endeavoured to find hope or consolation. The harsh language of the prince smote her to the heart ; for she saw plainly that he was fully determined to carry his unfeeling project into execution, and that all her remonstrances or supplications would fail to have any effect on him. She might offer all the resistance in her power to this hated union, but of what use would that be?—She had no means to help herself, since the prince, her uncle, was resolved; and to the Count Alberti's sense of pity or honour she knew it would be equally futile to appeal ; what, then, could be more wretched or disheartening than the prospects before her ? She shuddered at the contemplation, and wrung her hands in the intensity of her grief. And if the troops which had been sent in search of Massaroni should prove successful, in a few hours she might expect the return of the count, and in a very short time she would be subjected to the misery of his odious addresses. She could not reflect upon this without the greatest alarm.

"Oh, Florio, dear Florio," she sighed, "how terrible would be your anguish did you but know the danger with which I am surrounded, and the misery I am enduring. But it is well that thou dost not, or thou mightest be tempted to fly to my rescue, and thus involve thyself in the most imminent peril. Heaven help me, and watch over and protect thee from every harm. But surely the Almighty will not suffer me to be sacrificed to a man who is every way so unworthy of me. I will not believe it, and, in spite of all that my uncle has said and insists upon, I will still encourage hope. The prince surely cannot ever remain obdurate ; I am convinced he loves me as fondly as if I were his own daughter, and he will not therefore compel me to become the wife of that man, whom the more I think upon the more I loathe and despise. But my uncle has threatened me with his heaviest malediction if I refuse to yield to his wishes, and can I think upon that without feelings of the most unbounded horror. Oh, God ! instruct me how to act, and avert the terrible evils that threaten me."

In this state of mind she continued throughout the day, but saw no more of her uncle, which was a great relief to her, as, after their late interview, she trembled at the idea of again entering his presence.

* * *

It was mid-day, and the sun was shining brilliantly in the heavens, while the whole face of nature bore a gay and animated appearance. A gentle breeze waved the green foliage of the trees, and the light air was redolent of the most refreshing fragrance. Beneath the canopy of some lofty trees near the entrance to their cavernous retreat, Massaroni, his wife, and several of the brigands were leisurely reclining, engaged in playing at cards, dice, and the Roman game of mora, and festivity and happiness seemed to be the order of the hour. At length Massaroni arose, and looked through an opening among the trees anxiously, as if expecting the arrival of some one.

"Rubaldo and his companions tarry," he said ; "I hope no accident has befallen them. I expected them to have returned some hours since."

"Oh, fear not," said Maria, "Rubaldo is too experienced to fall into danger easily. He has probably scented out some other profitable business, which he is waiting to execute."

"Aye, that may be it," said Massaroni, "and I only hope that he may come upon the track of that traitor Carlotzi, who has absconded from us, no doubt with the intention of making known to the authorities the place of our concealment."

"Yes," said Maria, "I had always my suspicions of Carlotzi, but you would never listen to them. With my will he should have been prevented from doing mischief long since."

"Well, well," remarked Massaroni, "it is useless to regret it now. All that we have to do is to be upon our guard against any danger that may threaten us, and we are fully prepared to resist any attack."

"Is the Count Alberti secure ?" asked the brigand's wife.

"Perfectly so."

"And he still remains obstinate ?"

"He does."

"Ah, Massaroni, you will find that his capture is not worth the risk you have run, and the trouble you have been at to secure it."

"Psha! Maria," returned her husband, "you talk erroneously; trust me, I will yet find a way to tame and subdue his obstinate and haughty spirit. He must yield, for he must be well aware that he has no child to trifle with in Allesandro Massaroni. I have given him three days to make up his mind, and if at the expiration of that period he still persists in refusing to reveal the place where he has Olympia and her child confined, he must e'en take the consequences."

"And of what service would his death be to you ?" demanded Maria.

"Hist! hist !" said the brigand chief, suddenly, "I hear the clattering of horses' hoofs approaching this way. Conceal yourselves."

The brigands obeyed, and presently the sounds approached nearer, and a shrill whistle resounded through the wood.

"It is Rubaldo and our other comrades," said Massaroni, and he instantly replied to the signal. Immediately afterwards Rubaldo and three of the brigands, disguised as peasants, came in sight, and galloped up with great haste to the spot.

"How now, Rubaldo ?" demanded Massaroni; "you are late."

"Yes," replied Rubaldo, hastily dismounting from his horse, "and yet we have ridden hard. But let us into the cavern, I have something of importance to communicate to you."

Massaroni led the way into the cavern without delay, and the others followed.

"Now, Rubaldo," said the brigand chief, when they had entered their secret retreat, "what news? You seem flurried."

"Danger threatens us," said Rubaldo, "and we have no time to lose in making preparations to defend ourselves against it."

"Ah!" exclaimed Massaroni, "what is the danger to which you allude?"

"The Prince Bianchi has gained some clue to the place of our retreat, and a powerful force is on its way towards the Appenines, with the hope of discovering us and taking us by surprise."

"Cospetto!" exclaimed Massaroni, "is it so?—then my respected friend, the Prince Bianchi, is still resolved to suffer another defeat in his very laudable and humane anxiety to hand me over to the executioner. Well, be it so, I will receive his troops with the same cordiality I have ever done, never fear. But ow know you this, Rubaldo?"

"Listen," replied the lieutenant, "and I will tell you all the particulars. In the first place I must inform you that our attack upon the travellers, of whom we went in quest, was entirely successful, and we obtained a far greater booty, with little or no resistance, than we expected."

"That is not bad news, at any rate; but proceed."

"Where we made the attack," continued Rubaldo, "was not far from the Villa Rosa, and the shades of evening had fallen ere our task was completed. We turned our horses' heads towards home, but we had not proceeded far when, by the light of the moon, we beheld the figure of a man approaching rapidly towards us. His person, as well as I could distinguish it, seemed familiar to me, and when I perceived that on beholding us he struck into a different path, and increased his speed, my suspicions were excited. We pursued him and called upon him to stop, but he ran the faster, and appeared terribly frightened. We approached him nearer, and I then discovered, to my no small amazement and satisfaction, that it was no other than the traitor Carlotzi."

"Ah!" ejaculated Massaroni, "that was indeed fortunate. But what followed? Of course, he could not escape you?"

"No," answered Rubaldo, "but, unable to control my rage at the sight of the traitor, I levelled my carbine, and stretched him upon the earth."

"That was hasty and imprudent," remarked the brigand chief; "but what then?"

"He appeared to be quite dead, so, fearful

that the report of my carbine might have given the alarm, we galloped from the spot with all the speed we could make. It was long after the hour of midnight when we reached the black forest, and our horses being completely jaded, and ourselves fatigued, we determined to rest for an hour or two, as we considered ourselves perfectly safe in that lonely and unfrequented place. We dismounted in a most secluded spot, and fastening our horses to the adjacent trees, we stretched ourselves on the grass and soon fell asleep.

"I was awakened by hearing the clattering of numerous horses' hoofs, and then found that it was broad daylight. I became alarmed, and aroused my companions and apprised them of the danger which threatened us, but advised them to lie still. They did so; and crawling cautiously towards an opening in the forest, I hastily climbed into the topmost branches of one of the loftiest trees, and then had a full view of the persons who were approaching, and immediately perceived that it was a troop of the prince's soldiers travelling at a rapid rate. The officers who headed them were talking loudly, and as they approached I could easily distinguish every word they said.

"Aye, aye, Signor Marcelli," observed one of them, "I do not entertain much doubt of our success; we shall find them somewhere in the neighbourhood of the Appenines, and as they will have no suspicion of our approach, the capture will be an easy one. Massaroni and his daring band will be in our power before many hours have elapsed."

"I hope they may," replied the person to whom this was addressed, "but it is a pity that the wounded brigand did not live long enough to give the prince a more particular description of the retreat of his comrades."

"Ah!" exclaimed Massaroni, "then it was the villain Carlotzi, whom you thought you had slain on the spot where you discovered him, that gave the information?"

"No doubt of it," replied Rubaldo, "but these observations were all of any consequence that I could overhear; the soldiers galloped on, and were soon out of sight. Me and my companions then mounted our horses and made our way hither by another route as fast as we could."

"Ha! ha! ha!" laughed the brigand chief, exultingly, "so his highness the prince makes sure of entrapping me on this occasion, at any rate. It is a pity that I should be compelled to disappoint him. It is a fortunate thing that you tarried on your journey, Rubaldo, and thus became acquainted with these particulars or we might indeed have been surprised and overpowered, but as it is, they shall yet find the brigand chief more than a match for all the troops they can send against him. It will be nightfall before they can reach the Appenines; I will immediately depart to meet them, so disguised that I will defy them to have the least suspicion of me. Be in readiness at my summons, near the 'Golden Flask.'"

The brigands obeyed, and immediately all was activity and preparation, and Massaroni having placed a strong guard over the count, in one of his most clever disguises, departed from the cavern alone.

*   *   *   *   *

The sun had sunk behind the mountains, and the soldiers had yet some distance to travel, and

OCTAVIA ATTEMPTS REVENGE ON COUNT ALBERTI D'AMALFI.

they were completely unacquainted with the way. They were worn out with fatigue, and were most anxious to meet with a house where they might procure some refreshment and a brief period of rest, but nothing of the kind met their gaze, and they became disheartened. To add to their discomfort, heavy clouds suddenly obscured the horizon, and gave token of a coming storm.

"Diavolo!" exclaimed one of the officers, "this is not altogether a very pleasant situation to be in, and I begin to find that this is is not quite such an agreeable expedition as I anticipated. Ah! there is a light yonder; Heaven send it may proceed from some hospitable place where we may obtain a shelter and something to cheer our drooping spirits as well. Why, by the cross, the light seems approaching this way."

It came nearer and nearer, and it soon became evident that it was a lantern carried by some traveller.

"Well, that may answer every purpose," observed Marcelli, "for this person, whoever he is, will, doubtless, be able to direct us to some place of shelter and refreshment."

They halted, and the person, who was whistling merrily, soon came up with them, and made a dead stop, apparently much alarmed at the sight of the soldiers. He was a coarse looking rustic, and the vacant stare he fixed upon the soldiers had a ludicrous effect by the light of the lantern he carried.

"Be not alarmed, my man," said one of the officers, "we are not robbers, though we are in search of some, and hope to capture the rascals in a few hours. Can you direct us to any house where we can receive accommodation?"

"What will you give me, signor?" asked the rustic, with a broad grin.

"Oh, fear not but we will reward you handsomely for your trouble: can you be our guide to any house of the description we require?"

"Yes, signor, indeed I can," replied the man; "and a capital house it is; not more than half a league from here, and near the foot of one of the Appenine mountains."

"The Appenine mountains!" repeated Marcelli; "that is the very place we want to go to."

"Then follow me, signor," said the peasant, "and I will conduct you safely."

The man now led the way, whistling as he proceeded, and the soldiers followed. At length they reached the house, which was a very agreeable sight to them; and the soldiers being accommodated in the best manner they could in the stables and out-houses, the officers entered a comfortable room, in which was a roaring fire, and invited their guide to partake of some refreshment with them, which he accepted very willingly; and after they had plied him with a glass or two of wine, they entered into conversation with him, especially as he seemed inclined to be communicative, and they thought they might obtain some information from him.

"I understand," said Marcelli, "that these mountains are infested with banditti: is it so?"

"Are you in search of them, signor?" asked the man.

"Why, yes; we are in search of the brigand Massaroni, who, we have been informed, is secreted somewhere near this spot."

"Well, I believe he is," answered the peasant, "and I only wish you may catch him; though

I warn you, signor, that that will be no easy task."

"We are soldiers, and do not shrink from the danger. I am determined to have the rascal before many hours have elapsed. When did you last hear of him, my good man?"

"Oh, only a few days since," replied the peasant, "and I'll be bound to say that you will hear from him before daylight."

"Humph!" said the captain, "that is a very welcome assurance: I am anxious to encounter him and his lawless band, so that I may teach them such a lesson as they never experienced before."

"And I have no doubt you will find Allesandro Massaroni a most apt scholar, signor," remarked the peasant.

"At any rate, Massaroni will find me a severe master," said Captain Marcelli. "By the cross, I long to encounter him single-handed, that I may chastise the rascal for the outrage he has committed on my friend, the Count Alberti d'Amalfi."

"Do not talk too loudly, signor," cautioned the rustic, "for Massaroni is here, there, and everywhere, though invisible. He may, even now, be nearer to you than you imagine; and should he overhear what you say, you may see him and his band much sooner than may be welcome to you."

"Psha!" exclaimed Marcelli, "I am not to be intimidated by the stories that are related of his prowess. I do believe him to be a mere empty boaster, whom Fortune has hitherto favoured; but he will find more than his match, I'll warrant, when he has to encounter me."

"Again, signor," observed the rustic, "I would advise you not to speak too loud, or to treat the brigand chief with contempt. There are many who, like you, I have heard, have expressed as great anxiety to meet with him, but when their wishes have been gratified, they would have given their very ears to have been fifty leagues away from him."

"Why, you seem to be very well acquainted with him, my good man."

"Yes, I believe there are very few that know him better."

"Then, I'm sorry I cannot compliment you on the respectability of your acquaintance."

"Indeed, signor, why so?"

"Because he is one of the most consummate villains in existence!"

"Hold, signor," said the rustic, "I cannot hear the character of Massaroni calumniated in this way. Although a robber he is a man, much more worthy of the name than many who boast of being noble and honourable. To the poor he is a generous friend and benefactor, and to the suffering and oppressed a champion and protector."

The man uttered these words in such a different tone of voice to that in which he had spoken before, that Captain Marcelli and his companions started, and stared at him with amazement.

"By the dome of St. Peter's," said Marcelli, "methinks if you were the brigand chief himself, you could not advocate his cause with greater warmth and energy."

"I give him no greater credit than is his due," said the man boldly, "and he is a coward, a liar, and a villain who dares to utter anything to the contrary!"

"How!" exclaimed Marcelli and his companions in a breath, and starting to their feet. "What is the meaning of this?"

"What I have said, Captain Marcelli," replied the man.

"Ah, know you my name?"

"Yes, and that of your proud master, the Prince Bianchi."

"A spy! a spy!" cried Marcelli. "You leave not this room, you must submit to become our prisoner."

"Who dare attempt to detain me?" shouted the supposed peasant, in a commanding voice.

"So daring!" cried Marcelli. "Speak, fellow—who are you?"

"The villain, the empty boaster, you were so anxious to see—Allesandro Massaroni, the brigand chief!"

He threw back his disguise, and revealed his brigand dress as he spoke, and the officers were completely thunder-struck at the unexpected meeting. In a moment, however, they recovered from their confusion, and drawing their swords, rushed towards him.

"Yield, villain! robber!" cried Marcelli.

"Yield yourself, empty braggart!" replied the brigand chief, at the same time discharging the contents of one of his pistols at the unfortunate captain, which took effect in his side, and he fell bleeding and insensible on the floor. He then sprang from the window and joined his associates, who were engaged with the soldiers outside. The combat was a savage one, but Massaroni soon found that he had been too precipitate, for the troops were too powerful for them, and finding that defeat had now become inevitable, much to his vexation he was compelled to retreat at the head of his band, after leaving many of the enemy dead and wounded behind. The troops pursued them some distance, but, unacquainted with the mountain passes, the brigands easily eluded them, and regained the cavern in safety. This defeat was a source of the greatest mortification to Massaroni, but he was determined that he would yet have revenge, and knowing that it would be almost impossible for the soldiers to find out the place of his concealment, he resolved to lose no time in putting his plans into execution. The soldiers being

now convinced that Massaroni and his band were concealed somewhere in the neighbourhood, were determined, notwithstanding the great loss they had sustained, especially in the death of Captain Marcelli (for the wound he had received proved mortal in a few hours), that they would not leave the place until they had discovered them, rescued the Count Alberti from their power, and brought them to justice. But they could not help feeling seriously alarmed for the fate of the count, fearing that Massaroni, after what had taken place, would lose no time in sacrificing him to his vengeance. They encamped themselves near the inn, and having despatched a messenger to the Prince Bianchi, informing him of what had taken place, and applying for a reinforcement, they lost no time in making their arrangements, and were most sanguine in their expectations of success. The indignation of the Prince Bianchi on hearing of the daring of Massaroni, and his escape for the present, may be readily imagined, but still he flattered himself that, as the troops were so close upon his track, their ultimate success was certain. But he feared, notwithstanding, that when the brigand chief found he was so closely pursued, he would wreak his vengeance on the head of his prisoner by sacrificing his life, and he knew not what plan to adopt to prevent it.

"How torturing is this suspense," he said; "can no plan be devised to rescue the count from his power? Alas! even now he may be no more—he may have perished by the villain's hands, and if so, all the hopes I have formed will be annihilated. But no, I cannot bear to encourage that dreadful thought. Massaroni will never have the daring to commit such a wanton and atrocious deed."

But, notwithstanding all his efforts, it was perfectly in vain that the prince tried to persuade himself to this, and as the critical situation of the Count Alberti became more apparent, his apprehensions increased, and he formed all kinds of fearful and alarming, yet too probable conjectures as to the fate which it was not at all unlikely had already befallen him; and to the infliction of which, Massaroni would be farther stimulated by a feeling of revenge for the annoyance to which he had been put by the various attacks which had been made upon him. Again the prince wavered, and hesitated how to act; he could not but see that the advantage was on the side of the brigand chief, holding as he did the unfortunate young nobleman entirely at his mercy, and secure as he appeared to be in his impregnable secret retreat. However, there was no alternative to choose; let it be as it would, the life of Alberti was at stake, and a determined effort must be made to rescue him, and to crush the power of Massaroni, which for many years had spread universal terror over the country, and who so boldly and so recklessly set all the authorities at defiance.

"By the mass!" ejaculated the prince, "the rascal must and shall be stopped in his lawless career, or there is no power in the eternal city. Shall a reckless robber be permitted to ride rough-shod over the nobility of the country, and to perpetrate such atrocious outrages with impunity? Are the lives and liberties of the people of Italy to be constantly placed in jeopardy by him and his ferocious band? The idea is monstrous. Man or devil, he must by some means be exterminated."

The reinforcement was accordingly raised with as little delay as possible, and departed to the assistance of their comrades; the Count Di Strozzi, who was anxious to revenge himself for the outrage and indignity Massaroni had committed against him, undertaking the command of the troops.

CHAPTER XV.

THE PROGRESS OF THE EXPEDITION.—THE DECOY.—THE MOUNTAIN PASS.—THE SURPRISE.

THE troops waited the arrival of the reinforcement with the utmost anxiety, but in the meantime they kept up a strict look-out, in order to guard against any surprise and sudden attack from the brigands, whilst they had scouts in various parts of the neighbourhood to endeavour to discover the exact place where they were located, and to prevent, if possible, their having an opportunity to escape. The persons at the "Golden Flask," who, as may be expected, were connected with Massaroni, had made their escape in the conflict that had ensued, and although a strict examination was made of the premises, nothing material was discovered to gratify their curiosity or to throw any light upon the mystery. At length the reinforcement having joined them, they determined to lose no time in endeavouring to put their plans into execution, and accordingly made preparations to ascend the mountains among which they imagined Massaroni and his band were concealed.

"This is a difficult task," said Count di Strozzi, "and I am afraid we shall never be able to accomplish it, unacquainted as we are with the secret and intricate passes. Could we but procure a guide."

"I am afraid, colonel," said one of the men, "that we could not place much dependence on the guides we might find in this part of the country. The peasants are all attached to Massaroni, to whom they say he is a friend and benefactor, and they would be more likely to betray us than him."

The speaker had no sooner given utterance

to these words than the report of a rifle was heard, and the unfortunate man sunk dead upon the earth. The Count di Strozzi and the men under his command looked around in amazement and alarm, but no one was to be seen. They advanced a few paces further, and two or three other shots were fired, which took effect in like manner, but still the persons who discharged them were nowhere to be discovered. Their situation was now most desperate, and the Count di Strozzi was at a loss how to act.

"It will never do to proceed in this manner," he said, "or the destruction which our secret enemies will thus be able to effect among us may prove fatal. We must endeavour to find a guide, and we have it in our power to prevent him from betraying us or leading us astray. We had better retrace our steps, for there is no knowing the danger in which we may involve ourselves, ignorant as we are of these mountain passes."

They turned back accordingly, but, to add to their difficulty and discomfiture, the sky at that moment became suddenly overcast by ponderous black clouds, the thunder rolled awfully among the mountains, and torrents of rain deluged the earth. The soldiers became dispirited, and were evidently in no condition for any attack that might be made upon them; but still the Count di Strozzi flattered himself that if the brigands should venture to come to an open engagement with them, they must overwhelm them by the superiority of their numbers. They proceeded with caution, keeping a strict watch around them; but still every now and then two or three of their comrades were brought down by a well directed fire from unknown hands, whilst amidst the pauses in the tempest, they could imagine that they heard shouts of derision proceeding from various parts of the mountains. The confusion and rage of the count increased, the more so as he had no means of preventing these attacks upon his men, and he knew not how much deeper they might not be involving themselves in danger every minute. The storm increased in fury, and it had a most terrific effect in that wild part of the country. It was almost as dark as midnight, and it was only by the aid of the vivid flashes of lightning that they were at all enabled to trace their way. At length, after much labour, and encountering many dangers, they once more gained the valley at the base of the mountains, and, completely worn out with fatigue, drenched to the skin, and vexed and disappointed, they returned to their quarters, having no alternative but to abandon their designs for that day with the hope that by the following morning they might be able to prevail upon some one, by the offer of a liberal reward, to act as a guide. The watch was set, and every precaution taken to guard against surprise, and the storm having at last totally subsided, the Count di Strozzi, accompanied by a chosen few of his troops, ventured to some distance from the quarters, with the hope of meeting with some individual who might answer their purpose. After walking for some distance without meeting with a single individual, they came upon a lowly hut, in a sequestered spot, and leaving his men at the door, the count entered, and found in the humble room no other persons but an old woman and a lad, about fourteen years of age, who seemed much startled by his appearance, but quickly recovered themselves, and made him a low obeisance, and the old woman requested to know his pleasure.

"I require a guide over the mountains, my good woman," replied the count, "can you tell me of any one in whose honesty I can depend, and who, for a liberal reward, would be willing to undertake the task?"

The old woman paused, and eyed the count narrowly.

"Ah! signor," she said, at length, "that is a very dangerous business to undertake, and especially at the present time."

"And why so?" demanded the count.

"Because Massaroni, the brigand chief, is at present secreted there, signor."

"You know the brigand, then?"

"Aye, by the saints do I, and fear him?"

"It is he and his lawless band of whom I am in search," said the count.

"Ah, signor," said the old woman, speaking in a low voice, and looking around her as though she was fearful that Massaroni or some of his associates might be at hand to overhear her, "I—I sincerely wish that that desperate man could be taken; for it is enough to frighten one out of their wits to hear of his daring deeds, though they do say he is a friend to the poor. That may be, but I never experienced it, and Heaven forbid that I should ever receive the smallest portion of that which is obtained by rapine and plunder."

"Well spoken, my good woman," remarked the count. "Have you no husband? have you no one but this lad?"

"He is my grandson, signor; but I have a husband, and a kind, honest man is old Pietro."

"And what is he?"

"A shepherd, signor."

"You seem to be very poor."

"Aye, poor enough, God knows, but still we are content."

"Would you not like to better your condition?" asked the count, "to procure the means of rendering the remainder of your days comfortable?"

"Ah, signor," replied the old woman, "but that is not to be our lot, and it is no use to murmur."

"You shall have the means if you will only comply with my wishes."

"What mean you, signor?"

"As your husband has lived for so many years in this neighbourhood, no doubt he is thoroughly acquainted with all the mountain passes?"

"Oh, yes, signor, there is not an inch of the ground but is perfectly familiar to him."

"'Tis well, then he is just the man I want," said the count; "do you think he would be willing to become my guide?"

"Why, signor," replied the old woman, "Pietro is old and feeble, and I am afraid he would not be able to accomplish the task; besides, would he not incur the vengeance of Massaroni or some of his band?"

"He would have nothing to fear," said the count, "I will protect him from every danger, besides, if my designs should succeed the brigands will be secured from committing future harm. When do you expect your husband to return home?"

"I expected him before now, signor," answered the woman, "but if your excellenza wishes to see him, I will send Pablo in search of him."

The count expressed a wish that she would do so, and Pablo was accordingly sent on the errand, and Di Strozzi awaited with impatience, but confidence, the arrival of the old man. He came at last, and the count was much struck by his appearance. He seemed to be very aged, long grey hair hung upon his shoulders, and he supported himself upon a staff. The count quickly made him acquainted with his wishes, offered him a large reward if he would undertake the task, and questioned him minutely as to his knowledge of the various passes, the whole of which old Pietro answered in the most satisfactory manner.

"I am not at all unwilling to become your guide, signor," he said, "but you see that I am very infirm, and I am almost afraid that the undertaking may prove too great for my strength."

"Put on a good resolution," replied the count, "and I have very little doubt that you will not fail. Come, the offer I have made you is one which is not easily to be rejected. Do you agree?"

"When do you propose to start on your expedition, signor?"

"To-morrow morning by the break of day."

"I will undertake the task, signor."

"I may depend on your fidelity?"

"If you doubt me, signor, there is no harm done; you can decline my services."

"No, no, I will trust you," returned Di Strozzi, "but you will have no objection to accompany me to-night to my quarters, where you will be in readiness for the morning."

Pietro did not seem altogether satisfied with this arrangement.

"You still appear to doubt me, signor," he said, "but what should you fear from a poor helpless old man like me? Will it not be satisfactory if I meet you by the break of day at the foot of the mountains?"

"No," answered the count, "I must urge upon you a compliance with my request."

"Well," observed Pietro, after a minute or two's hesitation, "I consent. I am ready to attend you, signor."

The count presented the old woman with a purse containing the reward which had been agreed upon, and Pietro having bade his wife and grandson good night departed from his hut in company with the count and the soldiers. On their way Di Strozzi put several questions to his companion respecting Massaroni and his daring associates, which he answered in the most satisfactory manner, and it was evident that he was thoroughly acquainted with all the desperate exploits of the brigand chief, and he flattered himself that he could not have found a man better calculated to assist him in his designs.

"And know you the exact place where Massaroni is concealed?" asked the count.

"Aye, signor," replied Pietro, "no one knows it better; and if you will promise to protect me from all danger, I will conduct you and your troops in safety to it."

"You may depend upon my word," said the count; "and, moreover, if you faithfully perform your promise, I will double the reward I have already given you."

"Ah, you are most liberal, signor," remarked the old man; "what a fortunate thing it is for me and my old Jacintha that we have met with you, for we may now end our few remaining days in comfort and peace."

"You may; and you will always find friends in me and his highness the Prince Bianchi."

"Ah, his highness is a great and a good man, I believe."

"Where can there be one of more exalted rank and character than the Governor of Rome?"

"Yes, signor," observed Pietro, "and it is well worthy of him to wish to rid the country of such a pest as Allesandro Massaroni."

"His highness owes him no good will for the tricks he has played him, independent of his other crimes. Cospetto! he even had the assurance to assume my character, and thus to gain admittance to the presence of the prince, to rob him at cards, and moreover to drink his health in his highness's own choice tokay."

"Ha! ha! ha!" laughed the old man, "what an impudent varlet, to be sure."

"Aye, you may say that. But the time is not far off. I rather imagine, when he will be amply rewarded for all his tricks. It will be a glorious day for Italy when he is placed in the hands of the executioner."

"Ah, most glorious, signor," coincided the old man, "and what a triumph for the prince;—what satisfaction for the loss of his ducats and his choice tokay! Ha! ha! ha! ha!"

"The idea seems to amuse you, Pietro."

"Oh, vastly, signor; I could not enjoy the joke more if I were personally interested in it."

They had now arrived at the place of their destination, where refreshments were provided for old Pietro, of which having partaken, he was permitted to retire to rest, a guard being placed at the door of the chamber in which he slept to prevent any treachery, should he contemplate it. The Count di Strozzi, now most sanguine as to the success of his designs against the brigand chief, could sleep little during the night, and by the first blush of day he and the soldiers were up and ready for their departure to the mountains, and old Pietro was summoned into the presence of the colonel.

"Now, Pietro," demanded the former, "are you ready?"

"Quite, signor," replied the old man; "I await your commands."

"Lead the way, then," said the count, and they immediately departed.

The morning was hazy, dark, and cheerless, and as they proceeded on their way the rain began to descend rapidly, and everything gave token of a miserable day. Having reached the mountains, they proceeded to ascend them, which Pietro did apparently with much difficulty, and several times paused to rest himself.

"This is a gloomy path you have taken, Pietro," observed the count; "it is a very fit haunt for robbers and murderers."

"True, signor," he replied, "and so, no doubt, Massaroni and his band find it. But it is the sure way to lead to them, and so, I dare say, you will find ere long."

They went on with much difficulty, and at every step they took the path grew wilder and more dark, until nothing could exceed the horror of the scene. The count at length halted, and called upon Pietro to stop, who instantly obeyed.

"This is an awful place, old man," he said;—"are you sure you have not mistaken the way—that you are leading us right?"

"Oh, quite, signor," replied Pietro; "there is no one better acquainted with these mountains than I am, not even Massaroni himself, I'll be bound. Hark! signor."

The count listened, and very distinctly heard the voices of men in the distance, singing a wild chorus.

"Those are the brigands," he observed.

"True, signor," answered the man; "we are close upon their retreat, and you will soon have the pleasure of being introduced to them. Come on, signor ; you could not have selected a better guide to Massaroni and his daring band than old Pietro."

Again they proceeded, and the way became still more gloomy and frightful, and strong misgivings came over the mind of the count. He again paused, and looked narrowly and suspiciously upon Pietro.

"How much farther have we to go?" he demanded.

"Not far, signor."

"Old man," said the count, "I begin to doubt you."

"Doubt me! doubt poor old Pietro, signor! oh, dear!"

"Beware!—Attempt not to play us false, or you will dearly repent it."

"Dear!—dear!" said Pietro, with much apparent simplicity, "you surely cannot mean what you say, signor."

"But I do: mark me, old man—if I see anything to strengthen my suspicions, I will stretch you lifeless on the earth."

"Nay, colonel; you a soldier, and thus to threaten a poor defenceless old man?'

"Beware, Pietro," said the count, " for, by the dome of St. Peter's, I will not fail to keep my word, should you attempt to act with any treachery towards us."

Pietro returned no answer to this, but again led the way ; and at length they entered a wild and dark glen, which was overhung on either side by frowning precipices, the bare aspect of which was sufficient to strike terror into the breast of the beholder. Arriving at the end of this, they found that it was entirely blocked up by a massy wall of rock, and the worst apprehensions of the count were now all but confirmed.

"Whither have you led us?" he demanded, hastily ; "and which way are we now to proceed?"

"Which way are you to proceed?" replied the guide, standing erect, and no longer speaking in the querulous tones of age which he had done before. "My errand is at an end, and the only advice I can give you is to proceed through the rock, to be sure."

"Traitor!" cried the count, as he hastily levelled his pistol at the supposed guide, and fired ; but to his complete amazement, and that of his companions, the singular being merely raised his hand, with a laugh of scorn, caught the bullet, and, returning it to the count, he cried—

"Fool! what pistol shot has the power to harm Allesandro Massaroni?"

As he gave utterance to these words, he seemed to sink into the earth, and instantaneously disappeared; and as he did so, the brigands suddenly covered every surrounding hill, while an immense body of them appeared in the rear, and every means of retreat seemed to be cut off. Massaroni now again appeared, having divested himself of his disguise, and advancing towards the Count di Strozzi, he said—

"You see, my lord, that it requires better generals than the Count di Strozzi to capture Massaroni and his bold band. The glorious day for Italy has not yet arrived, when the brigand chief will be handed over to the tender mercies of the executioner ; neither will his highness, the Prince Bianchi, at present gain very ample satisfaction for the loss of his gold at the card-table, or the drinking of his choice tokay. Ha! ha! ha!—On to the dastard knaves, my brave comrades, and suffer not one of them to survive the story of their defeat. Thus does Allesandro Massaroni avenge himself on those who dare to seek to hunt him from his lair. My lord count, I will honour you by chastising you, for your presumption, on the spot."

Dreadful was the slaughter that ensued. Hemmed in on all sides by the brigands, the unfortunate troops had but little chance to escape, until Massaroni, tired of the bloodshed, and having inflicted a mortal wound on the Count di Strozzi, gave the word to his band to cease and to withdraw, and suffer the small number of soldiers that survived the dreadful affray to make good their retreat.

CHAPTER XVI.

THE BRIGAND AND HIS PRISONER. — THE CONFESSION. — THE RAGE OF PRINCE BIANCHI.—THE LOVERS.—THE INTERRUPTION.—THE SEIZURE.

EXULTING in their triumph, Massaroni and his associates quitted the mountains, and once more retired to their cavernous retreat in the forest, where they were confident they were secure from discovery, and there for some time they abandoned themselves to the most boisterous mirth and revelry at the success which had attended them, and the utter defeat, through the clever contrivances of the brigand chief, of the force which had been sent against them.

"What a terrible blow will this be to the Prince Bianchi," said Massaroni; "methinks it will be some time ere he will venture to renew the attack, and should he dare to do so, he may find himself in far closer proximity to me than will be altogether agreeable to him. As he seems so anxious for my society, I may e'en accommodate him by escorting him to my retreat, where we can again amuse ourselves with *ecarte*, and I may revive his drooping spirits with a few glasses of as choice tokay as any he has got in his own cellar. Ha! ha! ha!"

There are one or two circumstances connected with what we have related in the previous chapter which, perhaps, it may be proper to explain, as we wish not to assign any superhuman powers to the hero of our tale. For instance, in respect to his mysteriously returning of the bullet to the Count di Strozzi, which he discharged at him; that was accomplished by a stratagem of the most simple but infallible nature, namely, by reversing the charge of the unfortunate colonel's pistol, well knowing that, if the bullet be put in before the powder, it will fall perfectly harmless against the person fired at. This he effected while they were in the hut, and while his attention was drawn off him. His sudden disappearance was caused by his sinking into a cavity, which the lank grass concealed, and from which there was a rugged pathway to the mountains; and his sudden appearance on which, so soon afterwards, was enough to create the idea that it could not be effected by any other means than those of magic. The Count Alberti, during the time these events were taking place, was in a state of the most painful anxiety and suspense, he having ascertained from the brigands who were placed to guard him, the intended attack of the Prince Bianchi's troops; and a secret hope sprang up in his breast that the brigands would be defeated, and that he should once more be restored to liberty; but when they returned to the cavern, and he heard their noisy revelry, he became convinced that the triumph was theirs, and his bosom once more became the abode of the deepest despair.

"And must I for ever become the prisoner of this lawless and desperate man," he said, "or submit to all his infamous demands? How torturing is that thought, but how can I help myself? Curses light upon Olympia, I say; would that I had never beheld her. And shall I resign all my hopes of Melina, merely at the bidding of this robber and assassin? By Heaven, I will not! 'Tis true she, I know, scorns and hates me—she loves the beggar, Florio Clairville; but the prince, her uncle, favours my suit and is anxious for my alliance, and therefore she must yield; however cheerless my present prospects are, I will not banish all hope from my bosom—she must, she shall be mine. Something will yet occur to rescue me from my present torturing and perilous situation, and to bring my enemies to punishment, and then my triumph will be complete."

He was interrupted in the midst of this soliloquy by hearing the key turn in the lock and immediately afterwards the door was thrown back on its hinges, and Massaroni stood before him. The brigand chief eyed his prisoner with an expression of triumph, but Alberti averted his gaze with a haughty look of scorn and defiance, and awaited what he had to say to him with as much calmness and determination as he could summon on the occasion.

"I came to bring you news, Count Alberti, though I question whether you will be much gratified to hear it. The soldiers of the Prince Bianchi, who were sent to rescue you from my power, and to drag me to the scaffold, have suffered a shameful defeat by me and my heroic band; but few of them have been suffered to return to tell the tale, and their commander, the most illustrious Count de Strozzi has fallen a victim to his daring and presumption. Fools!—think they that Massaroni can be so easily conquered? How many more times will he have to convince them of his power?"

"Monster!" cried Alberti, with a look of disgust.

"Beware, young man," returned the brigand with a frown; "you forget that you are at my mercy, or you would not dare to apply such epithets to me. Submission and humility would better become you."

"Submission, humility, to you!" repeated the count. "Never! by all my hopes!"

"You talk boldly, signor," returned Massaroni."

"I speak my firm determination."

"Then you know the consequences."

"I am fully prepared to meet them."

"Indeed!" said the brigand with a sneer, "but methinks you will change your mind."

"Not all the tortures you can inflict upon me shall induce me to do so," replied the count boldly."

"Psha!" cried Massaroni, "this is mere empty boasting. Are you not still convinced that you cannot escape from my power? Are you mad enough to suppose that your obstinacy will have any other effect than revenge upon me? Think you that I shall be induced to abandon my designs? Know you not that it is my determination to see full justice done to the injured Olympia and her child, and yet dare you presume to brave me?"

"All this I know," said the count in reply, "but nothing shall intimidate me."

"Madman! do you still obstinately refuse to reveal to me the place where you have confined the victims of your cruelty?"

"I do."

"Oh, then," said Massaroni, fixing upon him a penetrating look, "you do admit what you have hitherto so obstinately denied, namely—that Olympia and her innocent offspring are confined by your orders?"

Alberti returned no answer to this, and he seemed greatly confused and undecided what to say. He had been taken off his guard, and had never intended to make the acknowledgment which Massaroni had so acci dentally elicited from him. His perplexity and irresolution increased; he folded his arms across his chest, and paced backwards and forwards in the greatest disorder, muttering incoherent sentences to himself. It was quite evident that the obduracy and determination he had hitherto evinced was fast evaporating. The inflexible and desperate character of the brigand chief presented itself to his imagination in the most vivid and alarming colours. He felt convinced that if he, by an obstinate resistance, exasperated him, he could expect no

MASSARONI. "BEHOLD! THIS IS THE LIKENESS OF HER WHO GAVE ME BEING."—PAGE 71.

mercy from him; that he would be certain to carry his threats into effect, and how could he help himself?—The defeat of the prince's troops, and the death of the Count di Strozzi, added to his dismay, and made him feel the more acutely his own alarming situation. But to yield to the commands of the brigand, especially after the serious injury he had done him by the destruction of his noble castle, and all the rich property it contained, was most repulsive and degrading to his feelings, and he still hesitated how to act. Again he reflected that, were he to comply with the demands of Massaroni, extravagant and humiliating though they were, and he should be restored to liberty, promises extorted under such circumstances, he considered, were not binding, nor would he for a moment hesitate to break faith with an outlaw and a robber; and when he was once more released from his power he should have every means of gratifying his revenge to the fullest extent, and might easily rid himself of an enemy whom he had so much cause to dread. Massaroni marked his hesitation, and penetrated his thoughts with much satisfaction, but he did not offer to break in upon his reflections for a few minutes.

"You do not answer my question, my lord," he said, at length.

"Massaroni," replied the count, "what is it you require?"

"Justice to Olympia," replied the brigand; "it was idle of you to put such a question. You have admitted, indirectly, that her and her child are confined by your orders; are you willing to give up the place of their concealment, and to trust to my honour and sense of justice for your future disposal?"

"_Your_ honour, _your_ sense of justice!" replied Alberti, with a look of scorn.

"Aye, _my honour, my sense of justice_, Count Alberti," repeated Massaroni, in a dignified tone which quite abashed that young nobleman; "you seem to insinuate some doubts of both; it will be well for you not to test them."

"Massaroni," said the count, greatly subdued by the determination and observations of the brigand, "can money purchase my liberty?"

"No."

"What then do you demand?"

"I have already told you."

The count once more folded his arms across his chest, and walked backwards and forwards across the cavern in a state of the greatest agitation, but completely, as before, undecided how to act.

"We waste time, signor," at length said Massareni; "again I ask of you—are you prepared to divulge the place where you have your innocent victims confined?"

"Why do you take such an interest in their fate?" asked Alberti.

"That is my business," was the reply; "yours is to decide whether or not you will comply with my demands?"

"And supposing I should refuse?"

"You have had sufficient opportunity of seeing how Allesandro Massaroni carries his threats into effect; he will not deviate in the slightest degree from that rule in your case, therefore you can form your own decision. That is, I should think, a sufficient, though perhaps not a satisfactory, answer to your question, signor."

The count again became silent, and reflected deeply. It was evident that the determination of Massaroni alarmed him, and that it was only his feelings of pride which prevented him from immediately yielding to his demands. The brigand chief observed all this; nothing could escape his penetrating eyes, and he chuckled in exultation to himself at his triumph over his lordly enemy.

"It seems, signor," he remarked, with a smile upon his handsome countenance, "that Massaroni is not exactly the insignificant or irresolute being that you and most of your class are apt to consider him. What he promises he never fails to perform. It would have been well for you, my lord, had you, in your transactions with the too confiding Olympia, done the same. You have admitted that she was torn from her home by your commands; are you prepared to inform me where she is imprisoned? That is the simple question; if you, like a madman, obstinately refuse to answer it to my satisfaction, you must take the consequences."

"And what will they be?"

"Need you inquire? I could inflict death; but I would first try the experiment of torture, more exquisite than you can form the least conception of."

"Good God!" exclaimed Count Alberti, passionately, "am I to be thus bullied, intimidated into that which my feelings repudiate?"

"I have nothing to do with your lordship's feelings, which your conduct proves to be none of the best, my lord," retorted Massaroni, with a satirical smile; "you have heard my determination, and it is for you to use your discretion as to the manner in which you will act. But this is only a waste of time; once more I put the question to you—will you tell me where Olympia and her child are confined?"

"You will give me some time to consider before I answer that question, Massaroni?"

"I have already given you enough."

"I am confused—unsettled; I would crave a little longer."

"I will grant you three hours; no more."

"And what then?"

"If you refuse to yield to all I demand, although Allesandro Massaroni is not naturally cruel, you will find that he can, in cases of emergency, exact obedience to his will by such means as would make the stoutest heart shrink appalled. Think of this, Count Alberti, and remain not an obstinate idiot."

"Massaroni," said the count, "you have already surely had ample revenge for any injuries you may imagine that I have done you, though I know of none whatever, in the destruction of my property, and the misery and anxiety you have plunged my friends into by the detention of my person, and the uncertainty you have kept them in as regards my fate. All this, however, I promise to forgive you, and likewise to keep secret your retreat, and to award you any reasonable sums of money you may think proper to demand, if you will but permit me to go at liberty, and——"

"Psha!" interrupted Massaroni, impatiently; "you have heard my decision, and of what use is it to trifle thus? Allesandro Massaroni, I repeat, is not the man to say one thing and mean another. I leave you now for three hours, and at the expiration of that time I shall expect that answer which will decide your fate."

"Will nothing prevail upon you?"

"Nothing but truth and justice?"

"And if I were to yield to your demands, and disclose to you the place where Olympia and her child are confined, should I then be at liberty to depart?"

"Do you deem me a fool, Count Alberti?" said Massaroni with a sarcastic smile.

"What mean you?"

"Need you ask the question? put it to your own good sense, count."

"I do not understand you."

"Bah! you do not think it convenient to appear to do so; but it is quite sufficient that I thoroughly understand you, and for fear I may not have been explicit or lucid enough with you, allow me to assure you that you quit not this place until you have been confronted with Olympia, and she is safe in my keeping, and moreover, not until you have fully acceded to all my demands, however monstrous and extravagant they may seem to be. Do you hear that, my lord?"

The young count bit his lips and muttered a curse between his teeth, but his discomfiture made no other impression upon the brigand chief than to excite a laugh of derision.

"Have you no fear of the consequences that may follow this conduct?" at last demanded Alberti.

"Fear!" replied Massaroni, with a look of scorn; "it is unknown to me; I leave that for the acquaintanceship of such dastard knaves and villains as the Count Alberti d'Amalfi and his highness Prince Bianchi, the most noble and much-to-be-valued Governor of Rome, whose troops met with so cordial a reception from me this morning. Ha! ha! ha! For three hours I bid you farewell, my lord, and wish you much pleasure in your reflections."

"Do not taunt me, Massaroni."

"It delights me to do so towards every presumptuous braggadocia who dares to defy the power of the brigand chief. You have yet but experienced a simple sample of what it is my humour to inflict when I am aroused to it: you had better beware how you excite that comic vein to its fullest current of facetiæ."

"Massaroni! Massaroni!" again ejaculated the Count Alberti, with much emotion, "will you not listen to reason?"

"Yes," answered the brigand chief, "I am every way prepared to hear it when you have learned to speak it. Once more I impress upon you what I have observed, and leave you to weigh it in your mind, with the final assurance that nothing whatever shall tempt me to swerve from my determination. In three hours I will return to you, and upon your answer then depends your fate. Olympia and her child must be free, and safe under my protection; terms such as I shall dictate in her presence, must be acceded to, and a solemn promise on your part to abandon all further thoughts of the fair Melina will be exacted from you, ere you can hope for liberty. Nay, you may frown, my lord count, but I heed not your indignation; such is my will, and you must yield to it, or take the consequences. Of course your reason and superior sense will tell you which it is best, under all your present promising circumstances, for you to do."

With these words Massaroni abruptly quitted the cavern, and left his unhappy prisoner to his own reflections, which the reader may readily imagine were none of the most pleasant description. For some time he traversed the gloomy place of his confinement in a state of mind which bordered upon frenzy,—beating his breast and giving utterance to the bitterest maledictions against his hard destiny. The power of Massaroni, however much in his presence he might affect to despise it, he was compelled to acknowledge; he felt convinced that he was, as he had said, not to be trifled with; that he would not fail to carry out to the fullest extent all that he had threatened, and again and again he cursed his folly and incautiousness in having admitted the fact of Olympia's being confined by his commands, for he now saw plainly that the brigand had him, if possible, more than ever in his power, and that there was not the least chance of his deliverance but by revealing the truth, and submitting to all the consequent degradation. That his friends would have the opportunity of rescuing him from the fangs of so powerful an enemy, he now entirely despaired of, and therefore, what other alternative was there left to gain than to yield to all the demands of the mountain chief, however extravagant and humiliating they might be? But to have Olympia again at liberty;—all his vices to be exposed to the world;—to be compelled to encounter her reproachful eye;—to see her triumph in his misery;—these were thoughts that were almost past all human endurance; and he bit his lips and gnashed his teeth in very rage and despair.

"And shall I be thus triumphed over?" he exclaimed, as he paced the cavern; "shall I thus become the absolute bond slave of a robber and a murderer?—Are there no means to escape the degradation? Has Fortune abandoned me altogether? Must I do the bidding of this lawless and daring chief, let him dictate whatever he may?—Must I, at his will, abandon all my hopes of the beauteous but scornful Melina, and leave her to throw herself into the arms of the beggar Clairville, mocking the anger of her uncle, the prince? Perish such a thought!—I will still be firm, and set his powers at defiance, let the consequences be whatever they may."

He paused and ruminated.

"But," he said at length, "I talk madly; am I not in his power, and what can all my obstinacy or resistance avail? He has threatened me with tortures if I do not comply with his demands, and after what I have already experienced of his character, can I any longer doubt that he will carry out his promises to the fullest extent? No entreaties, no promises of reward will prevail upon his stern and inflexible nature, and I feel myself but as a child in his hands, and entirely at his mercy."

He was interrupted in these reflections by hearing a most impressively plaintive female voice, apparently in the adjoining cell or cavern, singing a wild melody, in such tones and with such feelings as immediately rivetted his whole attention.

"That voice," he muttered to himself—"I have surely heard it before; but where? Good God! how much like Olympia's. But the words of the song she is singing; let me listen to them."

He did so with almost breathless attention, and in a few seconds more he distinctly heard the following—

> Where shall the deceiver fly
> To hide his shame from mortal eye,
> Shall he seek the halls of mirth,
> Or hide in the bowels of the earth?
> Let him wander anywhere,
> His companion shall be black despair!
>
> Shall the deceiver's conscience sleep,
> Shall he ever cease to weep?
> He may assume the jocund smile,
> But will his conscience rest the while?
> No, the prey to every care,
> Pursued for ever by despair!
>
> Let him linger—linger on,
> As his wretched victim's done,
> Praying death, which will not come—
> Such be the deceiver's doom.
> Restless, wretched, everywhere,
> Haunted by the fiend—Despair.

The words sank deep into the heart of Alberti, and they were rendered more impressive by the tones in which they were sung, and which were so painfully familiar to him. The voice ceased for a few minutes, and then again it saluted his ears singing this pathetic ballad, with which the reader is already acquainted, but which it is necessary to repeat here, for the better furtherance of the plot of our tale.

> Maiden of Florence, oh, listen to me,
>   Nor think that I seek thy fond heart to ensnare;
> If I deceive thee accurs'd may I be,
>   And my bosom be plung'd in the darkest despair.
>
> Maiden of Florence, my bosom reviles
>   The wretch who'd the innocent damsel betray;
> Maiden of Florence, more bright are thy smiles
>   To me, than the radiant orb of the day.
>
> Maiden of Florence, I liken thine eyes,
>   That now with such lustre are beaming on me,
> To the stars that so brilliantly shine in the skies,
>   And I love them not, dearest, more than I love thee.
>
> Can I deceive thee? Oh, never! no never!
>   Let no such thought in thy bosom have birth;
> May I, if false to thee, curs'd be forever.
>   Wandering hated, despised, o'er the earth.
>
> Maiden of Florence, then listen to me,
>   Nor think that I seek thy fond heart to ensnare;
> If I deceive thee, accursed may I be,
>   And my bosom be plunged in the darkest despair.

The voice ceased, but still its melancholy and plaintive tones seemed to vibrate in the Count Alberti's ears. He traversed the place of his confinement in the most disordered manner, and longed, yet dreaded, to behold the singer.

"But why should I be thus agitated by the mere words of songs, which might apply to any other person as well as myself?" he ejaculated; "it is but an artifice contrived by Massaroni to taunt and torture me, and to elicit from me the confession he seeks. Let me be firm, and come to some decision. But of what avail will that be?—the villain knows that he holds me securely in his power at his mercy, and what utility will be all the resistance that I can offer to him?—What degradation, what torture is this! and I have no means of helping myself. Oh, curses light upon the misfortune which created me an enemy, where I least expected to find one, in the brigand chief Massaroni! And should I even yield to his demands, and promise compliance to his will, can I then calculate upon my future safety? Should I break my word with him, I may guess what the consequences will be. I have already experienced how dangerous it is to incur his wrath, and to break faith with him, and until his power is entirely annihilated I shall never be secure. I know not how to act."

Again he paused, and throwing himself into a seat, gave himself up to the most racking thoughts. Then he listened attentively, thinking again to catch the tones of that melancholy voice which had excited so deep an interest in his mind; but all was profoundly still, and he might almost have imagined that he was the only solitary inmate of that cavernous retreat. His despair increased every moment, and the only way in which he could at all give vent to his feelings of mingled rage and despair, was in the wildest exclamations. But yet he had not been able to make up his mind as to the way in which he should act. Were he to attempt to deceive Massaroni, by giving him a false account of the place where Olympia and her child were confined, that would not avail him, as he was determined to keep him in his custody until they were restored to liberty, and were under his protection; but, on the contrary, it would only have the effect of bringing down upon him his utmost vengeance. He saw no other means of escaping from the brigand's fangs than by yielding to his commands, but yet his proud spirit revolted at the bare idea of any such submission, and again and again he cursed the hard destiny to which he was exposed, while at the same time his soul thirsted for revenge against the daring man who held him in his power.

"I, the Count Alberti," he said, "to be treated worse than the veriest dog by this robber chief! To be held a prisoner, subservient to his will, and forced to endure all his taunts, however bitter they may be!—By heaven it is more than human patience can brook! What have I done to merit such a fate?—Am I not master of my own actions?—Am I to be accountable for my deeds to a robber and a murderer? —And is he still to be permitted to set every force that may be sent against him at defiance?—By all the powers, such a thought of itself is enough to drive a person to madness. And why should he take such an extraordinary interest in the fate of Olympia?—It perfectly bewilders and astounds me. They must be connected by other means than I am acquainted with, or what brought him to her residence on that eventful night when I had appointed to meet her?—How knew he of my secret designs, my very thoughts; and by what means could he have become familiar with every particular of her history?—They must have met before, and have together conspired to work my ruin. Curses light upon her, and the hour in which I committed myself by yielding to the temptation of her transcendant charms. Would to Heaven that she had never existed, or that we had never met. Had we never known each other, this calamity would not have befallen me, and I might have aspired to the hand of the lovely Melina with some hope and confidence of winning her heart; but as it is, though she may be forced to become my bride, I can never expect her to view me with any other feelings than those of loathing and disgust. No matter, let me but regain my liberty, and mine she shall be the triumph in spite of all."

In this manner the time wore on until the three hours which Massaroni had granted him to make up his mind, were expired, and he had not yet come to any decision. His feelings of pride revolted at the idea of submitting to the brigand's demands, and yet he saw no means of resisting them, for it was quite evident that he would not be tampered with, and that he would not hesitate to perform all that he had promised. There were no means of evading the danger with which he was threatened, but by a ready compliance, and to this he could not make up his mind, although the consequences of his disobedience were so apparent to him. While these thoughts were still distracting his brain, he heard the bolts of the door being withdrawn, and immediately afterwards Massaroni once more stood before him. There was an expression of triumph and confidence on his countenance, but Alberti met him with a haughty demeanour, and seemed determined to resist his demands to the last; but the truth was, that his heart sunk within him, and he knew perfectly well that he was entirely at the will and mercy of the brigand chief, and that all he could say would have not the least effect in moving that inflexible man.

"You see I am punctual," said Massaroni; "the three hours have expired, and I presume you have made up your mind, my lord?"

"I have," answered the count haughtily.

"'Tis well," remarked Massaroni; "what is your decision?"

"Not to comply with your daring and insolent demands."

"I am afraid you have made very bad use of the time I granted you, signor," said Massaroni; "you had better reflect again for a few minutes before you return me a positive answer."

"I have already reflected sufficiently," replied the count, "and see no occasion to alter the decision I have expressed."

"Remember that your obstinacy will be followed by the most degrading punishment. We have whips to chastise refractory prisoners, however exalted their rank may be, and methinks that even the Count Alberti would quail beneath the lash. What think you, my lord?"

"You would not dare to inflict such an indignity, Massaroni!" said the count, with much excitement.

"Think you so, signor," returned the brigand, "but if you are wise you will not be rash enough to try me. Once more I ask you, are you willing to reveal to me the place where your victim is confined?"

Alberti returned no immediate answer; the observation of the determination of Massaroni's manner had daunted him; he saw that there was no chance of his being able to move him to relent, and yet he hesitated.

"Massaroni," he at length said, 'will nothing induce you to forego your monstrous designs?"

"This is trifling, count," replied Massaroni; "it is sheer nonsense; have I not already given you sufficient proof that I am not the sort of man to be easily moved from any purpose upon which I have fixed my mind? I have given you plenty of time to consider, and you have only to answer decidedly yes or no, and according to your decision you will most undoubtedly find me act as I have promised."

"Name any sum that you may think proper to demand," said the count, "and, however exorbitant it may be, it shall be yours, if you abandon your present designs, and restore me to liberty."

"Not all the fortune that you possess, my lord, princely though it be, should induce me to yield to your wishes;" returned the brigand; "nothing less than justice to Olympia, and a full compliance with all my demands, will satisfy me."

"Obdurate man," ejaculated the young nobleman in accents of despair, "what injury have I ever done you that you, should thus visit me with your vengeance?—What is Olympia to you, that you should thus take such an interest in her fate?"

"The injured and oppressed always find a friend and protector in Massaroni," replied the brigand; "but these are idle questions; my patience is exhausted, and I ask of you, for the last time, whether or not you will comply with my wishes?"

The count again hesitated, and paced the cavern in the greatest disorder; he saw too plainly that it was useless to attempt to shake the resolution of Massaroni, and the idea of the indignities that would be inflicted on him, should he remain obstinate, appalled him, and at length, turning to Massaroni, he said—

"I find that it will be useless to contend with a man of your obdurate character, Massaroni. It is true that you hold me at your mercy, and that I have no means of helping myself; I have already experienced the terrible lengths to which your vengeance may carry you, and therefore there is no alternative left me ——"

"But to yield, signor," rejoined Massaroni; "and a very prudent resolution too. It is no use to tamper with me in the lion's den."

"But if I submit, you will faithfully perform your promise, will you not?" asked Alberti.

"You need not doubt me, Count Alberti; the brigand chief would scorn to break his word, even with his greatest enemy."

"And when I have revealed to you the place of Olympia's confinement, and agreed to pay to you any sum, so long as it is at all reasonable, you will suffer me to depart?"

"Not so, signor," replied Massaroni, with a smile, "I do not separate from my friends quite so readily; you have heard my conditions, and they must be complied with to the very letter, ere I permit you to leave this place. Olympia must be safe under my protection, and you must have rendered her that justice I demand of you, before you and I part company. There must be no false play between us. You understand me, signor!"

"What are the terms you would exact from me?" demanded the count, in a voice of trepidation.

"That you will know when you are brought into the presence of Olympia," replied Massaroni.

Alberti trembled, and shuddered at the idea of meeting the victim of his cruelty and injustice.

"Massaroni," he said, at length, "why not spare me this degradation?"

"And think you your conduct deserves any mercy, count?" demanded the brigand; "do you shrink with the feelings of a coward from confronting the unfortunate object of your cruelty and injustice?—But you have heard my firm resolution, and however repugnant the meeting may be to your feelings, however mortifying to your pride, you cannot avoid it. Not all your powers of persuasion can move me from my purpose. Nay more, I again tell you that you must abandon all your hopes of Melina; she shall never become your wife."

"Insolent!" exclaimed the count, haughtily.

"Aye, you may deem me so, signor," returned Massaroni, "but it matters not; I have sworn it, and you will find that I will not break my oath. But we waste time in useless words; are you ready to reveal the place where you have concealed Olympia and her child?"

Again the young nobleman hesitated, and bit his lips in the rage and excitement of his feelings. However, to oppose the will of Massaroni, humiliating as his demands were, was all to no purpose, and after a brief pause, he said—

"I yield, Massaroni, since I have no power to help myself; but at the same time I solemnly and indignantly protest against the whole proceeding; whatever my conduct may have been, at any rate, I have no right to be accountable for it to you."

"That is a mere matter of opinion, my lord," said the brigand chief, with perfect indifference; "however, you see I have taken to myself that power, and it is of little or no use questioning it. Now, count, the confession?"

It was not without the greatest difficulty that the count could suppress his rage at the authoritative manner in which the brigand addressed him, but he knew it would not serve his purpose to express his feelings, and he therefore prepared, with the best grace he could assume, to give him the information he required. Massaroni listened to him with feelings of the utmost resentment, and when he had concluded, he said—

"So, my lord, and this you consider to be conduct worthy of a man of honour? Oh, most virtuous Count Alberti—he who is so ready to slander his fellow creatures— not contented with seducing and betraying a helpless and too confiding woman, but he must afterwards tear her and her innocent offspring from the world, and place them at the mercy of wretches who are ready to perform his bidding, let the crime be ever so atrocious. Oh, most immaculate Count Alberti!—most worthy aspirant to the affections of the amiable and peerless Signora Melina!"

The count frowned, and his cheeks became flushed with indignation. Massaroni observed his indignation, and he exulted at the same, while he determined to have an ample revenge for the crimes of which his prisoner had been guilty.

"Massaroni," at last said the count, "I have complied with your demands, why, then, delight to taunt me thus?"

"It is no more than your crimes merit," replied the brigand chief; "what atonement can you make to the hapless Olympia for the injuries you have done her? Was it not enough for you that you triumphed over her innocence, that you should have abandoned her and her child to misery and shame, but that you must afterwards consign them to a fate in comparison with which death would probably be a mercy? But she shall shortly be restored to liberty, to your utter shame and confusion, and your guilt shall be fully published to the world. Here, for the present, you must remain, and should I find that you have dared to deceive me in the slightest particular, be the consequences on your own head."

"I have told you the truth, Massaroni," returned the count, "why should you still doubt me?"

"Well, a short time will prove all, and it will be well for you to have indeed told me the truth. For the present I leave you to your own reflections."

Thus saying the brigand chief abruptly quitted the cavern, and left the count in a more excited state than ever. He saw plain enough that he had everything to apprehend from his vengeance, but he looked forward with more dread than ever to the restoration of Olympia to liberty, and to meet her again. He almost regretted that he had been intimidated into an acknowledgment of the place where she was confined, since he knew not to what length Massaroni might be tempted to go. But of what use would it have been to remain obstinate, since he was entirely in his power and at his mercy, and he would have been safe to have punished him severely had he not have yielded compliance with his demands. He endeavoured to flatter himself with the hope that something would yet occur to rid him of so terrible an enemy, and likewise to relieve him from Olympia and her child. The love of the fair and gentle Melina he could never hope to obtain, indeed he had every reason to believe that she viewed him with the most thorough disgust and abhorrence, but still the prince gave the greatest encouragement to his suit, and therefore all Melina's opposition would be of no avail. He tried to await patiently the issue of events, but this was a task not easy of accomplishment, and the deeper he reflected the more uneasy he became. Massaroni having elicited the secret from his prisoner, determined to lose no time in hastening to the haunts of the robbers, in order that he might complete his laudable design of setting Olympia at liberty, and of taking her and her child under his future protection. With a chosen number of his fearless band thoroughly disguised, and prepared for any emergency that might arise, as soon as the darkness of night veiled the earth, he took his departure from the cavern, and for the present we will leave him to pursue his route, and once more return to the Villa Rosa. With the utmost impatience and anxiety the Prince Bianchi awaited the return of the Count di Strozzi and the soldiers under his command, and he gave way to mingled hopes and fears as to the result of the expedition, though he fully flattered himself with the idea, that if the haunt of the brigands should be ascertained, and they were taken by surprise, it could scarcely fail, with such an overwhelming force, of being successful. Still he could not help feeling the greatest uneasiness as to the fate of the young Count Alberti, who might already have fallen a victim to the rage and vengeance of Massaroni, and thus if even that desperate man should be captured and brought to justice, his principal object would not be accomplished, and all the hopes he had formed of an alliance between him and his beauteous and amiable niece would be totally annihilated—a disappointment which he felt it would be difficult for him to endure with anything like any degree of patience. And then what a triumph would it be for Melina, whose obstinate rejection of the young count's addresses, and the undisguised opinion she had expressed of his character excited his utmost indignation. Haughty, proud, and overbearing, the prince could brook no opposition to his will, and even the affection which he really felt for his lovely relative, yielded to that cruel determination which he had permitted to take such powerful possession of his mind. Melina read his thoughts with the deepest anguish and regret, and she could not but anticipate the greatest trouble to herself from his fatal resolution; but in spite of what the consequences might be, she was resolved to resist to the last, for never could she willingly bestow her hand upon one whom so far from holding any place in her affections, she could not look upon with the ordinary feelings of esteem and respect. Need it be wondered at that a man who had been guilty of such base conduct as Alberti, could ever be looked upon in any other character than that of a most despicable villain by so virtuous and gentle a maiden as Melina? The idea of an union with such a man inspired her with sentiments of the deepest disgust, and she fervently prayed that Heaven, rather than consign her to such a horrible fate, would bring her to a premature grave, for life, under such circumstances, would become insupportable. Scalding tears would chase each other down her cheeks whenever she thought of Florio, and when was he absent from her memory? How could she ever dwell upon his image without feelings of adoration and the deepest sorrow? Alas! most dismal were the apprehensions she entertained as to the fate which had befallen him; and her agony increased when she reflected upon the impossibility of her ever learning what had become of him. Sometimes the picture her imagination drew of the probable misery of his present situation was almost too frightful for endurance, and she would shrink from it appalled, and endeavour, but in vain, to divert her thoughts into some other channel. She awaited in the greatest anxiety and trepidation the result of the expediton which had been sent against the brigands, for, though she heartily wished that no danger might happen to the Count Alberti, she dreaded the idea of his restoration to liberty, well convinced as she was, that that would be the beginning of her persecution, and that she would be subjected to a trial which she might find it almost impossible to bear up against. Encouraged as he would be by the prince, her uncle, it was not likely he would abandon his addresses, but would even become more bold and importunate; and what could she, a poor helpless girl, oppose to the will of the prince, and the obstinate determination of Alberti? She must fall a sacrifice, for she had no power to save herself, and her uncle had already sufficiently convinced her that nothing would move him to relent. What, then, could be more dismal than her prospects? where could she look for one ray of consolation or of hope? The Prince Bianchi was seated in his study towards the evening, ruminating upon the probable success or failure of his plans, when he was interrupted by the entrance of a servant, who informed him that one of the officers who had attended the late expedition in search of the brigands was waiting below, apparently in a state of considerable excitement, and requested an audience of him immediately. The prince started from his seat in doubt and alarm, and fearful misgivings came over his mind.

"Ah!" he demanded hastily, "where is the Count di Strozzi? How is it he is not here? What fresh disappointment is in store for me? Usher the signor into my presence immediately."

The servant bowed and departed, and immediately afterwards Captain Corvetti, the officer alluded to, made his appearance, and the prince saw directly from the expression of his countenance that he had some unpleasant intelligence to communicate.

"How now, Signor Corvetti," asked the prince hastily, "what brings you here alone? You are agitated? Where is the Count di Strozzi?"

"Alas! your highness," replied the captain, with a doleful expression of countenance.

"Nay, nay, no hesitation, man," said the prince impatiently, "do not keep me in suspense, but let me know the worst at once."

"Ah, your highness," said Corvetti, "I almost tremble to tell you the fatal news. We have been betrayed, suffered a terrible defeat, and the unfortunate Count di Strozzi has perished by the hand of the brigand chief."

"My troops again defeated!" exclaimed the prince in a voice half stifled with passion; "the Count di Strozzi slain, and the villain Massaroni and his ferocious band again escaped! Curses! the bitterest curses light upon this misfortune. Coward! how have ye suffered this?"

"Pardon me, your highness," remarked Captain Corvetti, indignantly, "you do myself and my brave comrades an injustice by applying so unmerited an ephithet to us. I pray you be calm and listen to me, and then you will find that, however great the misfortune, we, at any rate, have not been to blame. There seems to be no possibility of guarding against the artifices of Massaroni, and one might almost be tempted to suspect that he is possessed of some superhuman power."

The prince traversed the room in a state of the greatest rage.

"Tell me all the particulars," he demanded impatiently, "by what devil's means have the miscreants again triumphed? And is the Count Alberti still in their power?"

"Alas! he is, my lord," answered Corvetti.

"Diavolo!" cried the prince, "this is too torturing to endure. But proceed—proceed, and let me know the full extent of this infernal calamity."

Captain Corvetti complied, but the prince was frequently compelled to interrupt him during the course of his narrative in order to give vent to his feelings of rage and disappointment.

"This defeat is worse than all," he remarked, when Signor Corvetti had concluded, "the unfortunate Di Strozzi, too, to perish thus! Oh, I shall burst with rage. The villain Massaroni will doubtless wreak his vengeance upon the head of the Count Alberti, and shall he be suffered to escape punishment altogether?

What is to be done? I am distracted and bewildered. Now would I give one half my fortune to have the rascals in my power! But they set me at defiance, mock me, laugh me to scorn. By all my hopes, this is too much, and I swear that I will never rest until I have had

PRINCE BIANCHI INTERROGATES THE DYING BRIGAND.

a terrible revenge, and Massaroni has paid the penalty for all."

"I would advise your highness to endeavour to calm your feelings," said Corvetti, "and to try to devise some future scheme to get these desperate men in your power. Stratagems may

effect that which we have hitherto not been able to accomplish by force."

"Oh, no," replied his highness, "what stratagem can defeat the subtle artifices of Massaroni? His power every day becomes more manifest. How shall we ever be able to penetrate his secret haunts? I still think that you could not have acted with due caution, or you surely must have had your suspicions excited by the manners of your supposed guide."

"Indeed, my lord, there was nothing to excite our suspicions until he had completely lured us into his snare, and we had no power to help ourselves, hemmed in as we were on all sides by his daring band."

The prince again gave expression to his feelings of rage in the most violent language, and Corvetti in vain sought to calm him. It was no more than he had expected, and he was very glad when his highness dismissed him from his presence. For some time after he was left alone, the prince locked himself in his apartment, which he traversed in the most distracted manner, and gave utterance to the bitterest curses. The apprehensions he now entertained for the fate of the Count Alberti were almost past endurance, and his agony and suspense became the more intolerable, as he was unable to come to any decision as to what course, in this desperate emergency, it would be best to adopt with the least possible chance of failure. The death of the Count di Strozzi was also a source of great grief to him, for in him he had lost a powerful coadjutor, and the triumph of the brigand chief was rendered the more complete.

"Surely he must be some fiend in human shape," he ejaculated, "that he is enabled to perform such daring deeds, and laugh to scorn all the attempts made to defeat him. And that he should have been permitted to escape when he was alone, under my own roof, on the night of the festival, and I was surrounded by my friends! Who pointed out to him the sliding panel, by which he effected his escape from the villa? There must have been some treachery amongst the guests. I have frequently heard Florio speak rather warmly in extenuation of his conduct, and I remember that he did so more particularly on the occasion to which I allude. Could it be he, urged on by that silly romantic girl, my niece, who connived at his escape? Could I but obtain proof of this, Clairville should pay dearly for his conduct. Why did I not think of this before—Florio should not have been allowed to depart so easily."

Thus the prince continued to distract his brain with conflicting thoughts for several hours, but without being able to come to any satisfactory conclusion, and his mind was too confused to allow him to consult his friends, or to take any immediate steps in the business. Melina had been made acquainted with all the particulars of the disastrous results of the expedition by Florella, and the reader may easily conceive the sensation it excited in her breast, and the mingled feelings of doubt and hope it gave rise to. But, notwithstanding she felt satisfied at the triumph of Massaroni in one sense of the word, and that she would not be annoyed by the presence of the Count Alberti for the present, she could not but experience some anxiety for the fate of that misguided young nobleman, and sincerely hoped that the brigand chief would not be induced, from motives of revenge, to sacrifice his life; thinking that something might yet bring him to repent of his past conduct, and to abandon all his ambitious hopes of her, especially when he must every day become the more convinced that she could never look upon him with any other sentiment than that of abhorrence, and that if she was forced into a marriage so detestable and revolting to her, it could have no other effect than to make her one of the most wretched of human beings, and to bring her to an untimely grave. The Prince Bianchi passed a restless night; in fact, his mind was so disturbed, that he could not think of retiring to his couch, but continued to pace the chamber and to give vent to his feelings in the most distracted and violent expressions. The morning found him scarcely more composed, but at length he saw the absolute necessity of no longer delaying a moment in seeking to derive some means for the apprehension of Massaroni, to avenge the defeat of his troops, and the death of the Count di Strozzi, and to restore Alberti to liberty, if he should not already have fallen a victim to the vengeance of the brigand. The defeat of the prince's troops soon became generally known, and caused the greatest sensation throughout the city. The prince summoned a council of some of the principal nobility, and the friends of the Count Alberti, to consult upon what was best to be done. Various plans were suggested, but almost immediately rejected as impracticable; and it was some time before they could come to anything like a satisfactory decision. A proclamation was issued, offering an immense reward to any one who could give any secret and useful information which might lead to the discovery and arrest of the brigands, and the recovery of Alberti. Every inquiry was speedily set on foot that reason could suggest, and spies sent to all parts of the country to endeavour to elicit intelligence of the retreat of Massaroni and his associates, but for some time without the least prospect of success. It was well known that the peasants were his friends, and that although they might be thoroughly acquainted with all his secret haunts, nothing whatever would prevail upon them to betray him. Several of these people were apprehended on suspicion of aiding him in his concealment, but neither threats nor promises of reward could induce them to divulge anything concerning him, and they were accordingly discharged after suffering various terms of imprisonment, and undergoing several most searching examinations. As day after day elapsed without the least satisfactory intelligence transpiring, the patience of the prince was quite exhausted, and he gave himself up to despair. He became morose and sullen, and Melina trembled to enter into his presence, much more to attempt to calm his feelings.

"You mock me," he said to her one day, " by pretending to sympathize with me in my anxiety upon this torturing business. No doubt you inwardly exult, girl, at the disappearance of the Count Alberti, and the probable fate that has befallen him."

Melina looked at him with astonishment, and tears started to her eyes.

"Oh, my lord," she replied, " what have I done to excite this cruel and unjust opinion in your mind? Although the count can never hope to possess my love, Heaven forbid that I should ever become so lost to every sense of virtue and humanity as to wish any danger to befall him. Indeed, my dear uncle, you cannot know what you say. You can never believe me capable of harbouring such a thought."

"You cannot deceive me," said the prince, "I know your thoughts are still constantly fixed on the beggar Clairville, in spite of the injunctions I have given you."

Melina blushed and sighed deeply.

"Those blushes, those sighs confirm me in my opinion, girl," said her uncle angrily. "Disobedient! have you no fear of my wrath? Would you still obstinately seek to oppose my will?"

"Dear uncle," sobbed the damsel, "Heaven forbid that I should do or say anything that my duty or affection towards you should not sanction ; but who shall control the heart's warm feelings when they are devoted to a worthy object. Florio is poor, but he is good and honourable, and why should I hesitate to say that I find it impossible to banish him from my memory?—that his image is deeply engrafted in my heart my very soul, and that while that heart shall continue to beat, no other man can ever supplant him in my affections."

"Bold, obdurate girl," returned the prince, sternly, "this to me? your only relative and protector—I, that ever have treated you with the affection and indulgence of a parent?"

"And have I not returned your love, my dear uncle? Have I ever been unmindful of your affectionate care? Has it not been my constant study to please you and contribute to your happiness? Alas, what an unfortunate being I am thus to incur those cruel, those unmerited reproaches."

"No more, girl," cried the prince, "I have not patience to listen to you ; your obstinacy angers me. Away to your chamber, and do not venture again into my presence until you have learnt obedience."

"Uncle, dear uncle," sobbed poor Melina, "you will not suffer me to leave you thus?'

"Begone, I say, I must be alone."

Melina fixed upon him a look which should have penetrated to his soul, and then with a bursting heart and trembling footsteps she staggered from the room. On reaching her own apartment she burst into a convulsive flood of tears and wrung her hands in agony. Never had she before felt so truly forlorn and wretched. The cruel observations of her uncle had sunk deep into her soul, and nothing but the blackest despair gathered around her. It was some time before she could gain the least composure, and then she sank upon her knees and prayed the Supreme to guide and protect her in her future actions, and also invoked His choicest blessings upon the head of Florio, and implored that He would guard him from every harm ; though she could not help entertaining the most dismal forebodings that some fearful and untimely fate had befallen him. Could she but have been convinced that he was safe, although she was certain that he could never be happy, she might have been comparatively content and resigned ; but, alas! there were no means of her doing so, and the longer her thoughts dwelt upon the melancholy subject, the more miserable she became. There seemed no probability that they would ever meet again, and therefore what hope was there left for her in this world? The whole of this night Melina passed in the most wretched manner ; sleep only descended upon her eyelids at broken intervals, and then all the anguish that had haunted her in her waking moments was renewed to her in the most torturing dreams. She was glad when daylight again dawned, and she sat at the window of her apartment painfully ruminating upon the wretchedness of her situation, and recalling to her memory the unfeeling observations which her uncle had made to her the evening before. She was afraid to disobey his stern commands by venturing again into his presence, until she had his permission to do so, and, indeed, while her mind was in its present distracted state, she dreaded to meet him. Florella supplied her meals to her in her own apartment, and exerted herself as well as she could to tranquillize her feelings, but with very little if any success. The day wore tediously away, evening again approached, and Melina was aroused from her painful cogitations by Florella once more entering her room. This time the faithful attendant looked confused and agitated, and it might easily be perceived that she had something particular to impart. She placed her finger significantly on her lips, and enjoining her mistress to silence, cautiously closed the door after her, and approached nearer.

"What is the meaning of all this caution, Florella?" inquired Melina, anxiously.

"Speak low, signora, I pray you," replied Florella.

"I have something particular to communicate to you—a surprise for you, and I rather suspect it will be an agreeable one too, but I would not for the world that we should be overheard, for if we were to be, I know not what might be the consequences."

"For goodness sake, Florella," said Melina, "do not keep me in suspense ; what is it you have to say that requires so much precaution?"

"Will you promise me, signora, that you will not be too violently agitated?"

"Yes, yes, proceed."

Florella placed her lips close to Melina's ear as she said in a whisper—

"Signor Clairville is in the neighbourhood."

Melina turned ghastly pale and sunk back in her chair, in a state of the utmost agitation, as Florella made this startling and unexpected announcement.

"Florio once more returned!" she said. "Good God! is it possible? How know you this, Florella?"

"Speak low, signora, I beg of you. I have seen him, spoken to him, and he begged of me, in a manner that I could not resist, to deliver to you this letter, on your answer to which, he said, depended his very life."

Melina eagerly snatched the letter from the hand of her faithful attendant, and pressed it repeatedly and vehemently to her lips, while her tears flowed fast, and the most indescribable emotions swelled her bosom. Florella cautiously locked the room door, to prevent any sudden intrusion, and then retired a short distance from her mistress, while she proceeded with a trembling hand to break the seal and to unfold the precious epistle, but a mist seemed to gather before her eyes, and for some moments prevented her being able to decypher a syllable. At length her feelings became more calm, and she was then able to peruse the contents, which were in the following words :—

"Dearest Melina, for such you must ever be to me, while the warm current of life shall continue to flow in my veins, even though cruel fate should ordain that we should never come together once more, despair drives me to break through the stern decree of the prince, your uncle, and to presume to address that angelic being who is the idol of my soul, and whom it would be madness for me to seek to forget. Oh, my Melina, can you pardon the wretched Florio for having thus dared? Oh, yes, I know your gentle and amiable spirit too well to doubt that you will.

Alas! can I depicture to you in language sufficiently forcible the anguish I have suffered since last we met—the dreadful agony, the unspeakable despair I am now enduring? Oh no, I need not, I am sure, seek to convince you of all that I have undergone; no, my ever loved Melina, fully conscious am I how faithfully your own fond and sympathising nature can depicture that which I fain would describe. Oh, Melina, what a cruel destiny is ours. Alas! alas! in thus addressing you, I may be deemed presumptuous. Perhaps, happily for you, you have forgotten that such a being as Florio Clairville ever existed. Pardon me, most amiable of women, for recalling the name of one so humble, so insignificant, to your memory. I have tried to forget—I have sought to rush from thought—to endeavour, in my solitary wanderings, to imagine that I was entering upon a new existence, and that the past was only a dream, too blissful, too flattering to assume the shape of reality. Alas! how futile those efforts; your dear form, Melina, has been ever present to my imagination; it has been the constant companion of my thoughts, sleeping or waking, and but one hope has enabled me to support that life which has now become a misery and a burthen to me ; that hope is, beloved Melina, that we should meet again. Yes, that again I might have the transport of gazing upon you, of listening to the heavenly music of your voice, though fate has ordained that you shall never be mine. And *shall* we meet again? Upon your answer depends my fate. If you will, in spite of all consequences, grant this request, probably the last that I shall ever venture to make, you will meet me to-morrow evening in ' *The Lover's Grove*,' at the hour of eight, should you be able to escape the watchful and jealous eye of the prince, your uncle. Florella will receive your answer, and convey it to me at the place I have appointed to meet her. Trembling with hope and fear, ever your devoted slave and fondest lover,

"FLORIO."

Oh, how vain would be the task to endeavour to pourtray the intense emotions which swelled the gentle bosom of the lovely Melina as she perused this affectionate epistle. Her heart palpitated with a feeling that almost overpowered her, and pearly tears chased each other in rapid succession down her cheeks. With what fond extacy did she press the letter to her lips, while, for a few minutes, her brain was so distracted that she knew not what to say, or how to act. At length, by a powerful effort, somewhat recovering herself from her emotion, she turned to Florella and said—

"Ah, Florella, what an unexpected event is this. How shall I act? To what decision can I come? Can I refuse his request, probably the last he will ever make, and by so doing drive him to the most absolute despair? And

Yet shall I dare to disobey the injunctions of my uncle, stern and ungenerous though they be? Dear Florio, how dreadful is the barrier that is thus placed between our affections, our our hopes, our happiness."

"Dear signora," replied the faithful Florella, "pray endeavour to compose your feelings and to reflect calmly upon what is best to be done. Oh, had you seen how anxious, how careworn he looked, signora, I am certain you could never have forgotten it."

Melina sighed and remained silent for a few moments. The thoughts which still agitated her bosom were of the most torturing description.

"And where did you meet him, Florella?" she at last eagerly enquired.

"Only a short distance from the villa, signora," replied Florella; "he was so disguised that I should not have known him had he not accosted me; and it was evident that he was waiting near this place with the hope of seeing me, for he had the letter already prepared in his possession."

"And did he not inform you where he is staying, Florella?"

"He did not, signora, but he told me that he had only returned to the neighbourhood yesterday, and that since he had been banished by his highness the prince from the villa, he had been a melancholy wanderer for many weary miles."

Melina again sighed, but for a time she returned no answer.

"Dear, unfortunate Florio," she at length ejaculated, "too well can I imagine what your sufferings have been; but what hope or consolation can I impart to you? Kind Heaven, instruct me how to act. Should I dare to disobey the commands of my uncle, and he should discover it, how fearful might be the consequences to both Florio and myself. Florella, when and where did you promise to meet Signor Clairville with my answer?"

"In the morning, signora," answered Florella, "and in the same place where I encountered him this evening. But will you not comply with his request, my sweet lady?"

"I know not how to act," said Melina; "affection urges me to do as he so earnestly supplicates, while duty to my uncle peremptorily forbids it. Alas! what a painful trial is this to my feelings."

"You do not blame me, signora, for yielding to Signor Florio's solicitations in bringing you the letter, do you?"

"Oh, no, Florella, it would have been cruel indeed to have refused him."

"Yes, signora," remarked her faithful attendant, "so I thought, and I well knew how anxious you were, notwithstanding the injunctions of the prince, to hear from him again."

"Alas! alas!" sighed Melina. "Florella, I believe I may safely confide in you?"

"Oh yes, signora," replied Florella, earnestly, "indeed I would willingly lay down my life to serve you."

"Thanks, thanks, my good girl; I do believe you, for I have ever found you faithful and affectionate. But leave me for the present to reflect upon the course it would be prudent for me to adopt, and return to me in an hour or two, when I shall, most likely, have been able to come to some decision."

Florella curtseyed and obeyed, and Melina, flinging herself on a seat, became absorbed in the most conflicting and painful thoughts. Again she perused the letter of her lover, and her tears flowed faster than ever, as her eyes dwelt eagerly upon every treasured sentence. How anxious was she once more to behold that amiable youth, whom neither time nor circumstance could banish from her heart, and yet she trembled at the consequences that would be almost certain to accrue to her and Florio should the Prince Bianchi discover her disobedience. Upon the head of her lover he would be sure to shower his utmost indignation, and he had also threatened her with his heaviest malediction if she failed to comply with his stern injunctions. From such an idea she could not help shrinking appalled, and still was she completely bewildered and undecided how to act. And how could she leave the villa without the knowledge of her uncle? She felt quite confident that he kept a strict watch upon her actions, and any attempt of the kind might be fraught with the greatest danger, and the more she reflected, the greater that danger appeared to be. Thus did her mind for some time continue racked and unsettled.

"But oh, my dearest Florio," she ejaculated at length, whilst the tears still continued to chase each other down her cheeks, "how can I refuse you that to which my heart so urgently prompts me? How can I, by my refusal, drive you to madness and despair? It may probably be the last time that we shall ever have the opportunity of meeting, and shall I deny you the melancholy consolation of a farewell interview? Would you not consider me false and cruel were I to do so? You must, you would; and that would add to the deep despair which already oppresses me and is bearing me down. Yes, I will yield to your request, let the consequences be whatever they may."

She felt her mind more at ease when she had been able to come to this resolution; and when Florella returned to her apartment she was gratified to find her so much more composed.

"Florella," she said, "may Heaven pardon me if I act wrong, but I have made up my mind."

"I am glad to hear you say so, signora," returned her attendant; "then you will meet Signor Clairville?"

"Yes, Florella, let whatever may be the result, I cannot forego that melancholy consolation. Alas! it may be the last time that ever we may be destined to meet in this world."

"Oh, my sweet lady," replied Florella, "I trust sincerely that it will not, but that every happiness may be yet in store for you both. The prince, your uncle, will surely relent. He cannot have the heart to annihilate all your fondest hopes, and to doom you to perpetual misery. I have too good an opinion of my noble master to believe him capable of such cruelty towards one on whom he has ever hitherto lavished such unbounded affection. But I have some information for you which I think will afford you much satisfaction, and banish from your mind all apprehensions of discovery."

"What do you mean, Florella?" asked her mistress, eagerly.

"Why, signora," Florella replied, "I have just heard that his highness goes from home to-morrow on a visit, and is not expected to return till a late hour of the evening."

"Ah!" ejaculated Melina, joyfully, "that is indeed most welcome news; fortune favours us, my dear Florio; oh, may it be the harbinger of future happiness. We may, therefore, leave the villa unobserved by any of the domestics."

"True, signora; but do you wish me to accompany you?"

"Oh, yes, I dare not think of venturing forth alone."

"Be it so, my lady, I am at your command'; and as a further precaution against discovery, I would recommend that we should so disguise our persons that it may be impossible for any one to recognize us."

"A prudent suggestion, Florella," remarked her mistress, "I will leave everything to your management, and may the Almighty protect us from every harm. By the morning I will have my answer for Signor Clairville prepared."

After some further conversation, Florella retired, and left Melina to her busy reflections. She wavered not, however, in her resolution, and she looked forward to the following evening with feelings of the utmost anxiety and impatience. The intended absence of the prince from home afforded her much satisfaction, still, at intervals, the most dismal forebodings occurred to her mind, and the danger of what she was about to undertake became more apparent to her. At length, having by dint of perseverance become more tranquil, she took up her pen and commenced writing her answer to Florio, which was written in the most affectionate and fervid style, and was every way calculated to convince him that the sentiments she still entertained towards him were as ardent as ever, and that, let whatever fate might be in store for them, he must continue to hold possession of her heart, until that heart should cease to beat. Many were the tears the poor girl shed

while she was engaged in writing this letter, and frequently her feelings so far overpowered her that she was compelled to lay down the pen and to give free indulgence to them; but at length the painful task was completed, and a weight of anxiety was removed from her mind. She now sought her pallet, but her mind was too busily occupied to permit her to sleep, and she lay tossing about on her pillow in the most restless manner during the greater portion of the night. In the morning, on Florella attending upon her at breakfast, she received from her the letter she had written in answer to the request of Florio, with the strictest injunctions for her to use every precaution in its delivery, and to avoid being observed by any of the domestics, which instructions Florella promised implicitly to obey, and watching her opportunity, when there was no one about, she took her departure on her important mission. Melina, being now left alone, gave herself up to the most anxious thoughts, and awaited her return with the greatest impatience. At times she almost regretted what she had done, and strange misgivings tortured her mind. She dreaded lest her uncle should wish to see her before he left the villa, lest she should betray herself in his presence, and evince such emotion as would urge him to demand an explanation which she would not then have the power to avoid; but her mind was relieved from this apprehension, when, as she looked from the window of her room, she beheld the prince, attended by his retinue, depart from the villa. Soon after this Florella returned, and immediately sought the presence of her mistress, who eagerly arose to meet her.

"Speak, Florella," she said, in an agitated voice; "what success has attended your mission? Have you seen him?"

Florella replied in the affirmative, and added—

"And oh! my dear signora, had you but witnessed his feelings of transport when he perused your letter, you could never have forgotten them. He pressed it to his lips a hundred times, invoked Heaven's choicest blessings on your head, and, with tears in his eyes, begged me to assure you of his lasting love and gratitude, and that he would not fail to be punctual to the moment at the place of appointment this evening."

Melina raised her eyes, humid with tears, towards Heaven, and supplicated its protection, and she then questioned Florella minutely as to every word her lover had uttered, which she listened to with mingled feelings of sorrow and delight.

"Oh, Florio!" she cried, "why has Fate thrown so cruel and insurmountable a barrier between our hopes?—Alas! and after all, what can this meeting be productive of to us both but the deepest sorrow and regret, since we know that it must only be to bid each other farewell for ever ?—Would to God that we had never seen each other, since all our hopes are doomed to be so cruelly annihilated. I almost regret that I have consented to this interview, since I fear that the trial will be too great for us both."

"Nay, my dear signora," observed Florella, "do not give way to such melancholy thoughts, for who knows what kind Fortune may yet have in store for you?—Collect all your fortitude, and rest assured that this interview will be but the forerunner of many years of happiness to both you and Signor Clairville."

Melina shook her head despondingly, as she replied—

"Alas! my good Florella, it is useless to seek to buoy me up with false hopes; my uncle is inflexible, and I feel convinced that nothing will ever move him from his purpose."

"But should not the Count Alberti be restored to liberty, signora, or should he be so, might he not abandon his importunities, when he finds that it is entirely impossible for him ever to make a favourable impression upon your heart ?"

"Oh! no," replied Melina, "I know the character of Alberti too well, for a moment to entertain such an idea. Besides, if he should, the pride of the prince, my uncle, would never permit him to give his sanction to the addresses of one he considers so much beneath me as Florio. There is no hope for me, Florella, and I must be mad to encourage one on such a subject."

Thus they continued to converse for some time, and at length, by the exertions of Florella, Melina became inspired with more confidence, and endeavoured to await the hour appointed for her meeting with her lover with patience and resignation. Florella had taken care to procure disguises for them both, namely, a couple of large mantles, which would entirely conceal their persons, and hoods to correspond, and which would render all suspicion of their sex almost impossible. The day wore tediously away: Melina thought she had never experienced so long and dreary a one in her life, and mingled hopes and fears alternately beset her mind. But Florella tried her utmost to keep up her spirits, and she succeeded much better than she had expected. At length evening approached, and a calm and lovely one it was, well suited to the fond meetings of lovers. The queen of night shone forth in the Heavens with a mellow lustre, and added to the beauty of every object around. The emerald foliage of the trees gently quivered in the soft refreshing breeze, and all was so serene and balmy, that it lulled the senses in tranquil delight, and gave a sweet respite to the heart borne down with sorrow. Melina looked forth from the window of her room upon the beauty of the evening

with feelings of hope and hesitation; but Florella encouraged her, and offering up a prayer to Heaven, Melina became prepared for anything which might happen. The time for their departure now rapidly approached, and having assumed their disguises, they listened to hear whether there was any one moving in the villa; but all was perfectly still, as if they were the only individuals in the house. The dead and sonorous bell of St. Peter's chimed half-past seven, and warned them that they had no time to lose. Melina again committed herself to the care of Providence, and then prepared to follow her faithful attendant. They quitted the room with noiseless steps, and traversing a gallery, they descended a flight of stairs at the extremity, and which led to a less frequented part of the villa. They were not many minutes in arriving at a door which was at the back of the house, and the next moment found themselves in the open air, and as far as their eyes could stretch in the bright moonlight, perceiving that the coast was quite clear, Melina acquired more confidence, and walked on in silence by the side of her companion towards the place of their destination. As they approached it nearer, the heart of Melina palpitated so violently against her side, that she was forced to pause to recover herself; and then she looked fearfully around her, to see that no one was watching them; but there was no one near, and they again proceeded on their way. And now they came in sight of "The Lover's Grove," a romantic and sequestered spot, well adapted for such meetings as that they were going upon, and now the agitation of Melina increased every step they advanced, and a sickly presentiment of, she knew not what, came over her. Such was the impression this made on her, that, notwithstanding she had advanced so far, had she been alone she would have turned back, but Florella again encouraged her by every means in her power, and they once more proceeded on their way. At length they entered the grove. All was silent around; but they had not advanced far, when they perceived the dark shadow of a figure approaching towards them, which was evidently that of a man. He seemed to observe them at the same moment, and hastened towards them with agitated footsteps.

"My love! my life! my Melina!" he exclaimed in accents of delirious transport, and the next instant she sank almost fainting in the arms o her lover, unable to utter a syllable.

With what unspeakable feelings of rapture did Florio clasp the sylph-like form of the beauteous Melina to his throbbing heart; with what mingled sensations of extacy and grief did he gaze upon those lovely features he had feared he should never behold again, and press chaste kisses on her balmy lips! What a world of bliss was there in that one moment! And

Poor Melina, too ; what were her emotions of mingled transport and sorrow as she raised her eyes, in which beamed an expression of the most indescribable affection, to the countenance of her lover, and observed the melancholy ravages which care and anxiety had already wrought upon it ? Her heart was full to bursting, and her feelings could only find vent in the most convulsive sobs.

"Great God, I thank Thee for even this indulgence," at length exclaimed Florio ; "my beloved Melina, and am I then again permitted to hold thee to my throbbing bosom ; to press warm kisses of affection on thy dear lips ; and to hear the music of thy voice, as I was wont to do in happier days, and when I dreamt not of the sorrow that was in store for us both ? Melina—dear, dear Melina, speak to me ; let me be convinced that I am not labouring under the influence of a dream, that I——"

"Florio!" gasped forth Melina, in a voice of such impressive tenderness that it was enough to ravish the senses ; but she had not the power to say more, and the lovers for several minutes remained silent, and gave themselves up entirely to the powerful and almost overwhelming emotions which agitated their bosoms.

"Oh, my Melina," at last said Florio, "how can I ever express my gratitude to you for having thus hazarded so much for my sake ? It convinces me that you still love me, if ever I could have entertained a thought to the contrary, and though this may be destined to be our last interview, I will endeavour to find some consolation in that blessed assurance. Beauteous girl, can you, will you pardon me for having thus presumed, and for having broken through the harsh injunctions of the prince, your uncle ? Oh, yes, my heart tells me you will, and I will endeavour to submit with patience and resignation to my fate, though happiness must henceforth be a stranger to my breast. Death is now all that the wretched Florio can anxiously look forward to."

"Florio," ejaculated Melina, "if you would not make me more miserable than I am already —if you would not drive me to madness, oh, talk not, for the love of Heaven, talk not thus. I have no control over the cruel destiny that pursues us, or God knows how eagerly I would exercise it ; with what pleasure I would contribute everything in my humble power to banish the sorrow that now afflicts your bosom."

"Beloved girl!" cried Florio, "what can I say in answer to that transporting avowal ; I, who am so unworthy of the love of one so fair and amiable as the peerless niece of the noble Prince Bianchi ? Oh, Melina, I must have perished had I not beheld you again, and so have ascertained from your own lips that the humble Florio was still not forgotten by you."

"Forget you, Florio!" sighed the blushing damsel, with a look of gentle reproach ; "oh! how could you do me the injustice to harbour such a thought ? Alas! you have read my heart but badly indeed, if you could think so lightly of the vows I have so repeatedly uttered, and which Heaven knows sprang alone from purity and sincerity of feeling."

"Pardon me, most lovely, most innocent of human beings, for what, in the anguish of my despair, I was induced almost unconsciously to give utterance to," replied Florio ; "oh, what exquisite torture it is to think that fate should throw such cruel obstacles in the way of our happiness ; that this is probably the last time we shall be permitted to meet on this earth, and that you, the very idol of my soul, are destined to become the wife of another man, and that man a villain, who by his base conduct has rendered himself worthy only of the disgust and hatred of his fellow creatures."

"Forbear! forbear! Florio," cried Melina, with a look of horror ; "harrow not my feelings by such a monstrous supposition. I can die, I can boldly, resignedly meet with any other fate, let it be ever so dreadful, but never, never will I become the bride of the detested Count Alberti !"

"Noble minded girl!" ejaculated Florio, again clasping her to his bosom, with a feeling which it would be no easy task to describe, "how can I thank you for that promise ; what a weight of care does it remove from my breast. Here, then, in the bright face of Heaven, let us vow that though it may be the will of Fate that we should never come together, we will never be united to those who cannot share our affection."

"Villain! presumptuous, treacherous villain !" at that moment exclaimed a fierce voice, and immediately the infuriated Prince Bianchi stood revealed before them, accompanied by several of his attendants.

Melina uttered a cry of terror and dismay, and stood petrified to the spot ; whilst Florio was so thunderstruck and confused, that he had not the power to move or to utter a word. The countenance of the Prince was inflamed with excitement, and his eyes flashed with rage.

"Cowardly reptile!" he cried, "and is it thus you set my authority at defiance, and seek to seduce into crime a weak and obstinate girl ? Seize him, and drag him to a dungeon, and there let him await the certain punishment due to his guilt !"

"Mercy! mercy! my lord !" shrieked the distracted Melina ; "harm him not, I beseech you, unless you would see me dead at your feet !"

"By the infernal host !" furiously cried the prince, drawing his sword, " this is too much ! Mind not this mad girl's cries, but sieze him, I command !"

"Hold!" once more cried the poor girl, rushing in between her and the prince; but before she could give utterance to another word, the prince accidentally staggered forward, and the point of his sword entering her breast, she sank bleeding and senseless to the earth. The con-fusion which was caused by this unexpected catastrophe rivetted all parties to the spot for a moment, and then the attendants released Florio from their grasp, and proceeded to assist in raising poor Melina from the ground.

MASSARONI REVEALS HIMSELF TO THE BOASTING SOLDIERS.

CHAPTER XVII.

THE HORROR AND DESPAIR OF THE PRINCE.—FLORIO CONVEYED TO PRISON.—THE DANGEROUS SITUATION OF MELINA.

THE Prince gazed on with stupified amazement, and seemed scarcely able to convince himself of the truth of the terrible catastrophe.

"Wretched old man," cried the distracted Florio, "what have you done?—Melina! dear, unfortunate Melina, oh, speak to me!"

"Ah!" exclaimed the unhappy prince, apparently for the first time aroused to consciousness, and gazing at the awful work of his hands with the most unbounded horror and despair.—"My Melina! my innocent child!—She bleeds!—

What means this?—But it is only some hideous dream—Melina! Melina!—it is your poor uncle, the prince, who speaks to you. She hears me not!—Wretch!—how dare you presume to hold her in your arms?—It is you who are the cause of this! Seize the villain, I command, and away with him to prison; but, my Melina! my—oh, God! oh, God!"

He covered his face with his hands and groaned aloud. In spite of the desperate resistance of Florio, the insensible form of Melina was forced from his hold, he was secured by two of the domestics, and dragged away crying frantically on the name of his lover. Melina was raised in the arms of two of the men, and conveyed with all possible despatch to the villa, followed by the unhappy prince, who seemed scarcely conscious of the terrible catastrophe that had taken place. Poor Florella, who was completely horrorstruck, had fled before them as fast as her limbs would carry her, to the villa, to apprise the inmates of what had happened, and to procure immediate assistance; and nothing could equal the astonishment and consternation which prevailed. The mournful cavalcade shortly afterwards arrived at the villa, and the prince, apparently not knowing what he did, immediately rushed like a madman into his own room, and locked himself in, seemingly ashamed and afraid to meet the gaze of any one. It was found, on examination of the wound, that it was not a very deep one; that no vital part had been injured, and the surgeon was of opinion that with proper care and attention there would be no danger to be apprehended from it. None was more thankful to hear this than Florella, who blamed herself for being indirectly the cause of the dreadful accident, and deeply regretted she had encountered Florio at all, or been induced by him to convey the letter to Melina. She never, for a moment, left the side of her mistress's couch, but watched her with the most anxious solicitude. It was some time before Melina was restored to sensibility, and she was then too weak, from loss of blood, to speak, but her looks sufficiently evinced the great mental and bodily anguish she was enduring; and indeed her whole thoughts were fixed on Florio; how anxious was she to know what had become of him, although she had too much reason to apprehend the worst. She made several attempts to speak, in order to put the question to Florella, but her strength failed her, and Florella also begged of her to be composed, and that she should be made acquainted with everything by-and-by. With this answer the poor girl was obliged to rest satisfied, for she saw that it would be useless to attempt to elicit anything at present. The wretched prince remained for some time after this alarming event secluded in his own room, and would not permit the intrusion of any one. To seek to describe the maddening agony of his mind would be

a fruitless task, and yet he was half unconscious of the stern reality of what had taken place. Confused thoughts distracted his brain, and rendered, if possible, his agony the more intense.

"What have I done?" he exclaimed, looking wildly around him, "have I become a murderer? No, no, why should I thus unjustly accuse myself? I saw her fall bleeding in the arms of Florio, but it was not my sword that inflicted the cruel blow. I could not be the inhuman monster to shed the innocent blood of her I have ever loved and cherished as my own child. No, it must be all a hideous dream. Who dare say that I have committed the frightful crime? They are liars, more false than hell itself—who dare accuse me of it? But—but was she not false? Did she not deceive me, and against my solemn injunctions fly to meet the presumptuous beggar who would have persuaded her to have abandoned me altogether, and to resign her future fate into his hands? Did I not overhear the voice of the wily tempter, and her willing responses to his base proposals? I did—I did. Oh, that I should live to see the day when my authority is set at defiance by a poor miserable worm, whom one word of mine would crush, would totally annihilate;—and to find her on whom I have lavished every care and attention, recklessly, obstinately disobey my will. But I will triumph yet; Florio is in my power, and shall pay dearly for his presumption, while Melina—Oh, God! should she die! Ah! the damning truth now rushes upon my memory. It was my sword that pierced her fair and innocent bosom? Yes, yes, I could never have contemplated so hideous a deed! Oh, God!—oh, God; I shall surely go mad!"

Thus the unhappy nobleman continued to rave, and could find very few minutes of composure. Yet he had not the fortitude to see any one, or to make any inquiry into the condition of Melina. He threw himself on a couch, and there gave himself up to the most maddening feelings of despair. All the errors of the past crowded upon his disordered memory with their attendant horrors, magnified by the present sickly state of his mind, and he viewed himself as one of the greatest of villains that had ever existed.

"Yes, yes," he once more wildly cried, "I have been a monster of the blackest dye, or I could never have perpetrated the crimes of which I have been guilty. Where are the victims of my lust, Valentia and Zitella? Where are their innocent offspring? Did I not tempt them with the honeyed accents of love and constancy, and then heartlessly betray them, and abandon them to misery and shame? I did—I did, and conscience now is severely punishing me for the deed. How should I, who have so grossly sinned, dare to hope for peace or prosperity? Fool! I merit the punishment of the damned, and such is now pursuing me! Where is Malvolio? Should he betray me, denounce me to the world in my true colours, what becomes of the character of the powerful and illustrious Prince Bianchi? Would that the wretch had perished years ago, then might my crimes have been hidden from the public eye. But he told me that he had not murdered the off-spring of Zitella, whom I committed to his power; that he had every reason to suppose that she still lived, and if so, my conscience is, at any rate, relieved of one crime that would press me down to destruction. But can I, dare I believe him? May he not only have told me this to quiet my suspicions, to answer his own purpose; to explore my guilt when I am the least prepared for it, and thus to render his own triumph the more complete? I feel myself standing on the brink of a precipice, down which I know not how soon I may be plunged. Oh, Heaven! this is misery the most exquisite."

As he uttered these wild and broken sentences, he beat his breast in the greatest agony, and the most terrific thoughts continued to rush upon his brain, until he was indeed in a state verging upon madness. He was interrupted by a knock at his door, and starting up, he sternly demanded who was there?

" It is I, Spilotti, your highness," answered the voice.

" Begone fellow!" returned the prince, " how dare you presume to disturb me?"

" Pardon me, excellenza," said the servant, " but I must beg of you to admit me to say a few words to you."

" Another time!—another time!" said the prince, angrily, " I am not now in the vein; another time, I say—begone, I will not be intruded upon."

" But, your highness," said Spilotti, " I have something to communicate to you respecting the Signora Melina."

" Ah!" exclaimed the prince, startled by the bare mention of that name, and aroused to a full sense of all that had happened, at the same time that a feeling of the most indescribable horror came over him, when he imagined that she probably might be dead; " what of her? I must hear you."

He unlocked the door and admitted Spilotti accordingly.

" Now, now, Spilotti," he demanded, eagerly, " what of my niece? She is not dead?"

" No, your highness, Heaven forbid."

" Thank God! thank God! But proceed. Do not keep me in suspense."

" The signora is not mortally wounded, though she is in a most alarming state," answered Spilotti.

" But has she asked for me? Has she mentioned my name?"

" Yes, my lord, and with the utmost affection and solicitude. She wishes to see your highness."

" Who is in attendance upon her?" asked the prince.

" Florella, my lord."

" Ah! the treacherous jade, it was she who assisted her and Clairville in their plot. Had it not been for her, all this would not have happened. But she shall pay dearly for it. Spilotti, my niece does not accuse me of having attempted her life, does she?"

" No, my lord, but——"

" But what, fellow?"

" Pardon me, excellenza; you must be aware that it was your sword which accidentally inflicted the wound."

" Liar!" cried the prince, passionately, and seizing him by the collar, " dare to repeat those words, and I will slay you on the spot."

Spillotti trembled, and ventured not to make any reply, but the passion of the prince having in some degree abated, he said—

" Enough, enough, Spilotti, I am perhaps too hasty. True, true, it was an accident. The blow was intended for the presumptuous villain Clairville; but have you anything further to communicate?"

" No, my lord," replied Spilotti, " but will not your highness see the Signora Melina?"

" No, no." said the prince, in an agitated voice, " not at present; I dare not—I will not. But where is Florio? Is he secure?"

" He is, my lord," said Spilotti; " he was conveyed to prison by your highness's orders."

" 'Tis well," remarked the prince, with a look of revengeful satisfaction; " then I have, at least, nothing more to apprehend from him. He shall pay dearly for his presumption. Would that the miscreant Massaroni was as securely in my power. Leave me, Spilotti, and do not offer to interrupt me again."

Spilotti obeyed, and the prince was once more left to his own troubled thoughts. He paced the apartments with hasty strides, and muttered incoherent sentences to himself. To hear that Melina was not dangerously wounded, however, and that she did not reproach him for his conduct, was no inconsiderable relief to his mind. But it was impossible that, under all the circumstances, he could rest himself contented. At length, he threw himself upon the bed, and sunk into a troubled sleep. But the visions which flitted before his disordered imagination, were even more torturing than his waking moments. The scene of the evening was re-enacted with redoubled horror. He again beheld his beauteous niece sinking to the earth, pierced by his deadly weapon, and the blood streaming from the gaping wound in her fair bosom, in a purple stream. He imagined that her dying eyes were fixed upon him with an expression of the most melancholy reproach; he knelt down to supplicate her forgiveness for the crime that he had so unintentionally committed, but she spurned him from her, and died with a curse upon her lips. Then that scene gradually faded away, and he fancied himself wandering in the dreary and ghastly precincts of a charnel house, amongst mouldering relics of the dead. Strange murmurings, and solemn music vibrated in his ears; his whole feelings were bound up in indescribable horror; he wanted to escape, but could not; whenever he attempted to approach the outlet from this awful place, frightful forms would rise from the earth to obstruct his path, and to grin hideously upon his torture. Then again he heard that plaintive song which we have often quoted, sung in tones such as it was impossible could proceed from any human being, and found himself quite incapable of closing his ears against them. Suddenly two shadowy and ghastly forms appeared before him—they were those of his two unfortunate victims, Valentia and Zitella. How awful was the expression of their countenances, how fearful were the looks they fixed upon him from their filmy and supernatural eyes. And now what form is that which arises between them? By Heaven! it is the brigand chief, Massaroni! Yes, there he stands, the ghastly shades of Valentia and Zitella pointing significantly towards him, and Massaroni smiling triumphantly upon him. Bursting with rage, as he imagined, he drew his sword and rushed toward him, but it fell powerless from his hand, and he sunk at his feet, while the dismal place resounded with the most terrific and appalling cries. Overpowered with horror the spell was broken; he awoke, and starting from the bed, gazed around him, with the large drops of perspiration standing upon his quivering temples, and such was the influence it had upon him, that it was several moments before he was conscious of where he was, or could persuade himself that what he had so recently witnessed were only the effects of a disordered imagination. The night was far advanced, it was now the most solemn hour; the light from the lamp was dimly flickering in the socket, and everything around tended to increase the horrors of his feelings. He trembled to find himself alone, and was half inclined to summon the attendance of some of his servants, but fear of the exposure of his weakness withheld him, and he sunk helplessly in a chair, and covering his face with his hands, abandoned himself to the most agonising thoughts. The deathlike silence that reigned throughout the villa added to the horror of his feelings. Oh, how he longed for daylight, that he might walk into the open air and endeavour to rush from thought.

"Oh, conscience! conscience!" he exclaimed, "what a terrible enemy art thou to cope with. In vain may guilty men attempt to stifle thy solemn voice, it will be heard sleeping or waking, or in the moments of thy wildest revelry. Alas! alas! with all my wealth, with every luxury at my command, what a miserable wretch I am. And will not years of suffering obliterate the past? Valentia! Zitella! Why do ye continue thus to haunt me? I do acknowledge the deep, the irreparable injury I did ye; but Heaven knows how bitter is the remorse I feel, and have for years experienced, and why am I not now permitted to rest in peace? Peace! oh no, there is none for me, and I feel too keenly that I deserve it not."

He paused, and smote his breast in the agony of his feelings.

"But why," he resumed after awhile, "does the form of the brigand chief, Massaroni, so constantly appear before my imagination, and under such remarkable circumstances? What is he to me, any more than my greatest enemy? I have never injured him, and why then should this feeling of horror and reproach come over me, whenever I recall even his name to my memory?"

But in spite of all his efforts to the contrary, a trembling sensation of the most unmitigated horror seized upon all his faculties, when he remembered all the awful circumstances of his dream. He feared to attempt to go to sleep again, if that had been possible, and yet he shuddered to be awake, it was so appalling at the solemn hour of the night, and in his present state of mind. At length, much to his relief, the sombre mists of night disappeared, and the morning dawned. He unlocked the door of his chamber and stole cautiously out, as if fearful of being observed by any one. He left the house, and when he found himself in the open air he felt himself more at his ease. The reader may perhaps be anxious to know by what means the prince had become acquainted with the intended meeting of Florio and Melina, and we will therefore proceed briefly to inform him. It happened that Spilotti had accidentally observed the meeting between Florio and Florella, and concealing himself in a convenient place, he was enabled to overhear all that passed between them. This intelligence he immediately conveyed to the prince, his master, whose astonishment and indignation may very readily be imagined. He, however, determined to remain silent and cautious until he had seen the full extent of the plot, and had the means of amply gratifying his revenge. Little did Melina suspect that at the very time that Florella was imparting to her the secret of her having encountered Florio, and that on the morning when she delivered to her the answer to his letter, consenting to meet him at the place appointed in the evening, the prince, concealed in an adjoining apartment where he could overhear everything, was an attentive listener to all that passed between them, and was thus enabled to adopt his plans accordingly. It is needless to add that his departure from the villa on that day was merely a *ruse*, to take them by surprise. How fatally it succeeded has been already shown. But we will now return to Melina. We have stated that after a time she was restored to consciousness, but was unable to give utterance to a word, although she made the most powerful efforts to do so, but the anguish of her mind, it would be a perfectly fruitless task to endeavour to describe, as the truth of all that had taken place rushed more vividly to her recollection. Florella attended to her with the most exemplary kindness, and tried by every means in her power to alleviate the anguish of her mind; but she earnestly enjoined her to silence, as she was fearful that if she exerted herself at present it would be attended with the most dangerous consequences.

"Thank Heaven, my dear signora," she said, "that fearful as this calamity is, it is no worse. The wound you have received has been pronounced not to be mortal, or even dangerous, and no doubt, with proper care and attention, you will soon recover. Ah, how bitterly must his highness, the prince, reproach himself for the imminent danger in which he accidentally placed your life."

Melina shuddered when Florella made use of these observations, and once more made a powerful effort to speak, but it was several minutes before she could succeed; at length, however, she said eagerly—

"My good, my faithful Florella, it is not for myself I care, and most freely do I forgive my uncle for the pain he has inflicted on me; but oh, tell me—Florio, was he not seized by the servants of the prince? What has become of him?"

"Do not urge me, signora, to answer that question for the present," replied Florella.

"Nay, for the love of Heaven," supplicated Melina, do not keep me in suspense, it is far more terrible to me than certainty. Reveal all you know, and however dreadful it may be, I trust that I shall find strength to bear it. Tell me, did the unfortunate Florio fall a victim to the indignation of my uncle?"

"Rest your mind contented on that subject, signora," returned Florella, "for, thank Heaven, he did not."

"God! I thank Thee for this!" cried Melina, raising her eyes towards heaven, and tears of gratitude streaming down her cheeks;—"but oh, tell me what became of him? Do not

hesitate, for my mind is on the rack, and will continue to be so until I know the whole truth. Was he so fortunate as to be able to make his escape?"

Florella shook her head, with a melancholy expression of regret.

"Ah!" gasped forth Melina, "your looks confirm my worst apprehensions. Florio is a prisoner, and will be made to feel all the resentment of my uncle, unless my supplications should move him in his favour. Answer me candidly, Florella, is it not so?"

"Alas! it is too true, signora," sighed Florella. "But pray compose yourself, for the prince is surely too merciful, and loves you too fondly to visit Signor Clairville with any severe punishment."

Melina clasped her hands vehemently together, and her tears fell faster than before, as she ejaculated—

"Unfortunate Florio, what will become of you? and what will be the agony you will endure at the uncertainty of my fate? Oh, would to God that you had never sought this fatal interview; for then, although you might never again have been happy, you would still have been at liberty."

"Do not give way to unnecessary fears, signora," remarked her attendant, "for his highness will certainly not proceed to extremities, especially in your present deplorable situation. He will not persist in detaining Florio in his power."

"Alas!" sighed Melina, "to what may not his resentment urge him?—Too well do I know his inflexible temper, and after his behaviour to me, I can have but little hope that my tears or supplications will have the power to move him to relent. Florio, dear Florio, the cruel fates have conspired against us, and unfortunate was the day that we ever became acquainted with each other. But I must see the prince, my uncle, immediately."

"I pray you, my dear signora, to defer the interview until you are somewhat more composed," said Florella.

"No, Florella," returned her mistress, eagerly, "if you love me, you will immediately apprize the prince of my wish to see him. There is not a moment to be lost; and until I have seen him, and learnt the fate of Florio from his own lips, my mind will continue in a state of agony that is worse than death, and will certainly drive me to madness."

"But the prince, signora, has locked himself in his chamber, and has strictly commanded that no one shall venture to obtrude upon him."

"He will not, cannot refuse to grant my request. Will you do as I desire, Florella?"

"It is my duty to obey you, signora," replied her attendant, "but indeed I sincerely wish that you would postpone the meeting till some other time, if only for a few hours. Your feelings are too much excited at present to enable you to undergo it, and the prince cannot be in any state of mind to see you."

But it was in vain that Florella tried to persuade her, and seeing the anguish of mind she was enduring, she left the room, and meeting Spilotti on the stairs, she communicated to him the wishes of her mistress, and requested him to make them known to the prince. The result will be shown. The refusal of the prince increased the anguish of Melina to the most alarming degree, and all the endeavours of her faithful attendant to pacify her, proved completely ineffectual.

"He pities me not," she said; "notwithstanding my present situation, he is still inexorable. He is goaded on by resentment, and poor Florio is doomed to feel all the terrors of his wrath. I can never, never support this severe trial; would to Heaven that death would put a period to my sufferings, for there is no future hope of happiness for me in this world."

"Oh, my dear signora!" said the kind-hearted Florella, "I beseech you do not talk thus, nor give yourself entirely up to despair. His highness cannot be so cruel; he cannot remain inexorable, he will relent. Surely his resentment must be already sufficiently gratified by what has taken place."

"Ah, no, Florella," sighed Melina, "in vain you seek to encourage me with that hope; it is fallacious. There is nothing but misery for me, and therefore the sooner that it pleases Heaven to take me the better."

For the remainder of the night the poor girl thus continued to lament the hard fate of Florio and herself, and to experience the most dismal forebodings; and all the efforts of Florella to tranquillize the feelings of Melina were to no purpose, and towards morning she was alarmed to perceive the change that had come over her for the worse, and to find that her wound had become considerably irritated and inflamed by the excitement of her feelings; that her mind wandered, and she was in a high state of fever, which she was apprehensive would be attended with the most fatal consequences. A servant was again despatched to the apartment of the prince, to make him acquainted with the alarming situation of his niece, and once more to request his attendance; but the servant quickly returned and informed her that the prince had quitted the villa, and no one had seen him go out, or knew whither he had gone. Melina was now insensible to all that was passing around her; she raved wildly of Florio, and all the symptoms became so alarming that the doctor was fearful that the most fatal results would follow. And scarcely less poignant were the sufferings of Florio, as he paced his gloomy dungeon. A thousand times he cursed his cruel fate, and bitterly reproached himself for having been the cause of the dreadful calamity which had befallen his beloved Melina, who, he apprehended, would never recover the serious wound she had received. He beat his breast in the utmost agony of despair, and for some time was unable to tranquillize his feelings in the least.

"Alas! my Melina," he sighed, "that you should be brought to so dreadful a fate, young, lovely, and innocent as you are. Why did Heaven ever permit us to meet?—had we not done so, this never would have happened, and you would now have been happy. Rash fool that I have been, I am the cause of all by tempting her to disobey the stern injunctions of her uncle. I can never, never forgive myself, and care not what becomes of me—what fate attends me, since all my hopes of happiness are entirely annihilated by this dreadful blow. Cruel prince, surely remorse will touch your inexorable heart after this, the fearful work of your hands; but I crave not your mercy towards me. No, you may inflict upon me the most horrible tortures that your resentment can suggest, and you will not find me quail. Death will be a mercy to me, since all that I loved on earth is destroyed."

Thus he continued to give vent to the agonised feelings of his bosom, and in vain sought to obtain the least consolation or fortitude. Nothing could divest his mind of the dreadful impression that Melina was no more; and her bleeding form, and the ghastly expression of her countenance continued to haunt his imagination in the most vivid colours. In vain did he try to persuade himself that it was all a frightful dream; the more he sought to do so, the more dreadful became the reality to his distracted mind. He recalled to his memory all that she had ever said or done—the many hours of happiness they had passed together in each other's society, and torturing was the regret that seized upon his heart, and drove him to a perfect state of frenzy. Never in his life had he experienced such a night of suffering and horror, and the morning brought with it no alleviation to his anguish. This was increased, when, on the appearance of his jailor, he was unable to elicit from him any information as to the fate of Melina, for the man positively and brutally refused to answer his questions. His anxiety and anguish now became insupportable, and if he had had the means in his possession, he would have been tempted in the frenzy of his despair to have laid violent hands upon himself. He beat his breast and tore his hair, and gave utterance to the most piteous exclamations.

"The wretches have murdered her," he groaned; "they have murdered one of the most lovely and innocent of Nature's works, and surely the most terrible vengeance of the Almighty will overtake them for it. Oh, Melina, idol of my soul! little did I think it would ever come to this. Why did I ever presume to aspire to the hand of one placed so far above me? I have been the indirect cause of all, and severely am I now suffering for it. Why should I still live to endure such misery as this? Welcome, welcome, death, come in whatever shape you may."

In the intense anguish of his feelings, he dashed his head against the wall of his dungeon with a violence that completely stunned him, and he remained in a state of utter insensibility for some time afterwards. Happy would it have been for him had he continued in that state of unconsciousness; but at length he recovered to a clear and fuller sense of the horrors of his situation; and he groaned aloud in the frenzy of his despair. At length, quite exhausted, he threw himself on the coarse pallet of straw which was provided for him, and abandoned himself entirely to the dreadful thoughts that distracted his mind. Strange, unearthly voices seemed to murmur in his ears, and to mock his sufferings; and such was the impression that this idea made upon his mind, that he could not shake it off. Thus dismally wore away the day, and Florio saw no one but his jailor, who remained in the same taciturn and dogged humour, and repulsed all the efforts of his unfortunate prisoner to elicit any information from him. Night came again, and brought with it, if possible, redoubled horrors to the mind of Florio. Not the least ray of hope was permitted to dawn upon him; which ever way he turned his eyes, the most awful prospects opened upon his distempered imagination. Could he but have ascertained the truth—could he only have learnt the fate of the unfortunate Melina, he thought that he might, perhaps, in time bring his mind to some little degree of resignation, but as it was, what could he do but give way to the most dismal apprehensions? The silence of his jailor, and the non-appearance of the prince, all but convinced him that the wound Melina had received had proved fatal, and therefore did his agony of mind become every moment the more excruciating. How he longed for a knife, or some deadly poison, that he might put a period at once to his wretched existence; and then he again invoked curses upon the head of every one who had been in the least degree the cause of this calamity. Under such painful circumstances as those in which the unfortunate Florio was placed, what a blessing is sleep—what a sweet respite, if even only transitory, from those corroding cares which are far too powerful for even the greatest fortitude to bear up against. But could Florio sleep? Oh, no; it was madness to attempt to do it. 'Tis true, he threw himself upon his rude pallet, and pressing his hands upon his burning eyelids, endeavoured to sink into forgetfulness, but in vain;

and the more he made the effort the more intense became his agony—the more palpable all the misery of his fate. The hour of midnight now tolled from the solemn prison bell, and every tone of it sunk into the soul of the hapless prisoner with double effect to that which it would have done on any ordinary occasion. Had it been the knell of death, he would have greeted it with pleasure. The small lamp suspended from the roof of his dungeon reflected but a faint and ghastly light upon its blackened walls, rendering the horrors of the place still more fearful. The awful silence that reigned throughout the gloomy building was enough of itself to create the most dreadful thoughts, and to drive the strongest mind to a state of frenzy. Florio started from his mattress, his blood-shot eyes protruding from their sockets, and every limb quivering with unconquerable emotion. To his disordered imagination there were dark shadows stalking upon the walls in which ever way he turned his distracted gaze. A legion of hideous forms flitted before him, exulting in his agony, and howling despair in his ears. He tried to shut them from his gaze, to drown their fearful mutterings—but could not; and then he threw himself upon the damp, cold paving of his dungeon, and rolled to and fro in a frantic state of mind, which it would be utterly impossible to describe. In this lamentable condition the ill-fated youth remained for some time, when again, as a sudden thought occurred to him, he started to his feet, and approached immediately under the lamp. In happier times he had taken a miniature likeness of Melina, which he always carried about him. It was a life-like resemblance; one of the best efforts of the skilful young artist. Those who gazed upon it, might almost imagine that the painting breathed, so wonderfully true to nature were all its minutest details executed. The eyes bore that expression which penetrated to the very soul, and the lips were gently parted, so that you might almost persuade yourself that you heard the silvery tones of the fair original addressing you, and it would be difficult to divest yourself of the illusion. This treasured miniature Florio now drew from his bosom, and as he gazed upon the lovely features which had been so skilfully delineated by his own hand, who shall seek to describe the powerful feelings that convulsed his breast?

"Yes," he ejaculated, pressing the miniature frantically to his lips, "so she looked in our moments of happiness, when we little dreamed that such unparalleled tortures as the present were in store for us. Oh, my Melina, and art thou indeed no more? Are those bright eyes closed for ever in the awful darkness of death? Are those cheeks that ever wore the roseate bloom of health and innocent vivacity, now pale and livid in the livery of the grave? Those lips, round which a smile was ever playing, for ever insensible to the chaste kiss of affection? That Heavenly voice, whose every accent imparted nameless transport to the soul, hushed for ever? My God! it cannot be true, and I still living! It must be some bitter mockery, a delusion, got up by fiends to torture me! And yet, did I not hold thee in my arms, while the purple current of life fast poured from thy fair bosom? Did I not hear thy last sigh, and then—and then they tore thy dear, inanimate form from my embrace, and dragged me hither! Yes, yes, the dreadful truth is too apparent. It is no dream! Thou art dead, my Melina! savagely murdered, and I have been the principal, though unintentional cause of thine untimely end! Come then tortures the most excruciating; let them tear me limb from limb; I will not writhe or murmur under the infliction, for it is only a just retribution for the monstrous, the frightful crime of which I have been guilty! But will you forgive me, my sainted Melina? Will your gentle spirit pardon the unfortunate wretch who has been the indirect cause of your dreadful and untimely death? Heaven spare me, for alas! I have greatly sinned! Shade of my Melina, I see thee now! You frown upon me; you—oh, horror! horror!"

With an hysterical laugh of madness, the unhappy Florio sunk upon the earth, and became insensible to everything.

CHAPTER XVIII.

COUNT ALBERTI—A FRIEND WHEN LEAST EXPECTED.—THE ESCAPE.

THE course of our narrative now compels us to leave Florio Clairville for the present, and to return to another prisoner of not less importance, namely, the young Count Alberti D'Amalfi, in the cavernous retreat of the brigand chief, Massaroni. We have fully described the agonised state of the count's mind after he had divulged the place where Olympia and her child were confined, and it is therefore unnecessary that we should say anything more particular upon that subject. So far from his anxiety abating, after the departure of Massaroni, it increased, and he formed the most fearful conjectures as to what would be his future destiny. In the assurances of the brigand chief he placed no confidence, and he firmly believed that he should never be able to obtain his liberty unless it was by some fortunate accident, or by submitting to a species of degradation from which his feelings of pride indignantly revolted. In fact, Massaroni, upon that point, had not attempted to deceive him, and he therefore had no other alternative than to endeavour

to make up his mind for the worst. But the thought of meeting with Olympia, of listening to her bitter reproaches, and having his villany fully exposed, was worse than all, he shuddered at the idea, he trembled at the thought of his victim's triumph, and now regretted that he had not boldly withstood all the threats of Massaroni, and refused to comply with his demands. To be thus coerced and dictated to by a robber and assassin, was a degradation at which his proud spirit recoiled, and he accused himself of even worse than cowardice in having submitted to it. How drearily the hours passed away, what a multiplicity of thoughts crowded upon Alberti's brain, and how vainly he sought to obtain any relief to his mind. The fates seemed to have conspired against him, all the world seemed leagued together to oppose and crush him, and he abandoned himself to the most absolute despair. And Melina too!—during his confinement what might become of her? Might not all his hopes regarding that peerless beauty be annihilated; might not Prince Bianchi, whose affection towards her he well knew, have been tempted to yield to her tears and supplications; and even if he should be liberated from his present situation, might it not be only to find her the bride of another man, nay even of that same Florio Clairville, whose plebeian origin he affected so much to despise. This thought was more torturing than all, but he found it quite impossible to reject it, so much probability and reason was there about it. The repeated defeats which the prince's troops had suffered from Massaroni, also all tended to increase the uneasiness of Alberti, and to excite the worst apprehensions in his mind. He could not help thinking that his highness would be intimidated, and would be constrained to yield to necessity what he would not do to choice, and if so, he (the count) would be abandoned to his fate. Such was the impression that every moment obtained fresh ascendancy in the mind of Alberti, and rendered his situation the more intolerable; and what added to his agony was, that he saw no possible means of helping himself; that he was entirely at the mercy of the brigand chief, and that he must, in spite of himself, yield to his terms, whatever they might be. There was no other alternative left him, for all that Massaroni had promised he was thoroughly convinced he was fully prepared to carry into effect to the very letter. Resistance, on his part, would be worse than childish, for he had candidly told him what would be the consequences if he still remained obstinate, and he already experienced enough of his determined character to doubt for a moment that he would not fail to keep his word. In this state of mind the count traversed the gloomy place of his confinement, and obtained but little rest. He awaited the return of Massaroni with the greatest anxiety, and at times the hope would spring up in his breast that his expedition would be unsuccessful, that some accident might occur which would place him in the hands of the authorities, and lead to his (Alberti's) release. But this idea was only transient, and he quickly became plunged in his former despair. Sometimes he would listen with feelings of mingled terror and disgust to the boisterous mirth of the brigands, which frequently saluted his ears, and presented more vividly to his imagination the hopelessness of his situation, and the utter

THE SURPRISE.—PRINCE BIANCHI'S SOLDIERS DEFEATED BY THE BRIGANDS.

impossibility of his ever being able to effect his release, and then all kinds of frightful ideas would rush upon his brain, which tortured and distracted him beyond expression. In this manner passed the second day after the departure of the brigands, without anything occurring worthy of being recorded. It was night, and the count was seated in one corner of his gloomy cell, pondering on the misery of his fate, and anticipating the sufferings and degradations which in all probability were in store for him, when he was suddenly aroused from this lethargy of thought by hearing the bolts of the door being withdrawn cautiously, and the next instant one of the brigands entered, bearing in his hand a lanthorn, and apparently apprehensive of being watched. He closed the door silently after him, and secured it on the inside, and he then approached nearer towards Alberti, but without uttering a word, at the same time placing his finger on his lips, signifying that the count should remain silent. Alberti could not help feeling a momentary sensation of dread, for the mysterious behaviour of the man was every way calculated to excite his suspicion, but it soon evaporated, and he then examined the features of the brigand more narrowly, and perceived that he was not the same who had hitherto brought him his provisions, and he had no recollection of ever having seen him before. The brigand placed the lanthorn on the table, and then approaching close to the count, he said in a low voice, scarcely beyond a whisper—

"Be not alarmed; I am a friend."

"A friend!" repeated Alberti, with a look of astonishment, and a feeling of hope springing up in his breast.

"Aye, a friend," returned the man; "that is, if you accede to the terms on which alone I am disposed to assist you, and restore you to liberty before Massaroni and his associates return."

"Ah!" ejaculated the count eagerly, "are you sincere? or is this only some fresh device to torture me?"

"I am sincere," answered the brigand, "but speak low, signor, for should we be overheard, the destruction of us both would be inevitable."

"Proceed, for Heaven's sake!" said Alberti; "if you will only render me the inestimable service you have promised, you will find me ready to submit to any terms you may think proper to demand from me."

"Enough," said the man. "No doubt, then, we shall soon understand each other. I have long been tired of my present course of life, and wish to escape from it. What I require of you is, a promise to ensure me a free pardon for my past misdeeds, and money sufficient to enable me to retire to some foreign country, where I may end my days in honesty and repentance, and be secure from the vengeance of Massaroni."

"Most willingly do I agree to these conditions," replied Alberti; "perform but your promise, and not only do I guarantee to you a free pardon for all your past offences, but I will so reward you that you may be able to pass your future days in comfort and independence."

"'Tis well," remarked the brigand, "but do you not know me, Count Alberti?"

The count again looked narrowly at the man's features, and shook his head.

"I have not the slightest recollection of you," he replied. "Have we then met before?"

"Aye, signor, under very different circumstances."

"Explain yourself."

"Do you not remember Storaldi, who once lived in the service of your late noble father, my lord?" demanded the man.

"I do. He was for some years a most faithful servant, but in an evil moment he was tempted to commit an act of robbery, and absconded from the castle."

"True, signor; I am that guilty man."

"You!" cried the count with a look of surprise.

"Time has doubtless changed my features, but once more I assure you that I am that same Storaldi."

"Most extraordinary that we should meet thus."

"Pardon me, signor, but it is most fortunate for you. On leaving the castle, I indulged myself in every extravagance while my ill-gotten booty lasted, and when that was exhausted, I wandered about the country in a state of the greatest misery, and was reduced to the most desperate condition. It was at this time that I encountered Massaroni, and it needed very little or no persuasion to induce me to join his band. I have remained with him ever since, though I have long been disgusted with this lawless life, and only longed for an opportunity to escape from it."

"Which opportunity is now presented to you, if you only remain faithful to the promise you have made to me," observed the count.

"You may place every reliance in me, signor," answered Storaldi; "from the first moment you were brought hither I was determined to rescue you if ever I had a chance, and I will do so at every risk."

"Ah! when?"

"This very night; any delay would be fraught with danger."

"But what chance have you of accomplishing your designs?" eagerly demanded Alberti.

"A good opportunity this night presents itself, of which I am resolved to avail myself."

"What is it?"

"Listen, my lord," replied Storaldi, in the same low accents. "Ronaldi, the man who has hitherto brought you your provisions, is taken suddenly ill, and I am appointed to his place."

"Well."

"Hear me out, signor, without interruption. Maria Grazie, the brigand's wife, is at present absent from the cavern in attendance upon the mad woman, Ottavia, as she is called, at the cottage of old Montaldi."

"Ah! and is this Ottavia the same woman whom I saw when I was first brought to this place?" asked Alberti.

"She is," replied Storaldi, "but to proceed. Most of the brigands are going forth on a predatory expedition this night, and those who remain behind I will engage at the festive board. I will take good care to mix a powerful drug with their drink, and when it shall have taken effect on them, I will return to you, and we can quit this secret retreat together without any fear of obstruction."

In the gratitude of his feelings the young count pressed the brigand's hand.

"Thanks, thanks, Storaldi, for this," he ejaculated, "act faithfully, and you shall meet with a reward far beyond your most sanguine expectations. But is there no fear of the success of the plot?"

"Not the least; leave everything to me," answered Storaldi.

"And when may I expect to see you again?"

"At the hour of midnight."

"Without fail?"

"Without fail. Prepare yourself to act with firmness and resolution, and before the dawn of another day I promise you that we will be far away from this place."

"I will be guided entirely by you, Storaldi," said Alberti.

"Then you have nothing to fear."

"At the hour of midnight, then——"

"You may expect to see me again without fail. I must begone, or I may not have an opportunity of putting my designs into execution. Be confident, signor, and success is certain. Farewell for the present."

Placing his finger once more upon his lips to enjoin silence, Storaldi retired. What a remarkable revolution was now wrought in the feelings of the young Count Alberti. Despair had given way to the most sanguine hope, and the thoughts of liberty inspired him with such emotions of delight and gratitude that he could scarcely contain himself. He had every confidence in the promises of Storaldi, for what interest could he have in deceiving him, while on the other hand he had every inducement for him to remain faithful. The plot seemed to be so admirably arranged that he thought it was almost impossible it could fail to succeed, and he therefore prepared himself for the journey he would shortly have to undertake with the most flattering anticipations. He awaited the hour of midnight with the utmost impatience: never had the time before appeared to him half so long or so tedious. He listened attentively, and he could hear the voices of the brigands as they shouted in noisy mirth. This inspired him with fresh hope, for he imagined that the plot was progressing, and that Storaldi had kept his word. By degrees the sounds became fainter and fainter, until at length they ceased altogether, and a profound silence reigned throughout the cavernous retreat.

"The drug has taken its effect," muttered the count to himself; "the important moment has arrived."

A brief interval ensued, which was one of the most intense agony and suspense Alberti ever remembered to have experienced, but at length he once more heard the bolts of the door being cautiously withdrawn, and Storaldi again entered, bringing with him a brace of pistols, a stiletto, a large mantle, and a brigand's hat.

"Now, Storaldi," said the count in a breathless voice, "what success?"

"All that could be wished, signor," was the reply.

"The brigands' senses are steeped in unconsciousness, and there is nothing to impede our progress to liberty. Come, my lord, assume this disguise, and let us not delay a moment in making our departure. I can procure horses a short distance from this place, and we may soon be beyond the reach of pursuit."

"Storaldi," said Alberti, "once more must I express to you my unbounded thanks for this inestimable service, and——"

"Nay, signor," interrupted Storaldi, "do not let us waste time in useless words; reserve what you have to say until we have escaped from this place, and are fairly on our journey. Quick! quick!"

The count said not another word, but wrapping himself in the mantle, and assuming the brigand's hat, with a firm step he followed Storaldi out of the cavern. They soon reached the cavern where the band were accustomed to assemble, and there found the four brigands, wrapped in a complete state of insensibility, with their heads reclining on the table. They had to pass them closely in their way out, and Alberti, in spite of himself, could not help feeling a slight trepidation; but his companion encouraged him by a significant look, and they soon emerged from the cavern, and after traversing the various intricate passages and windings of that subterranean retreat, and ascending a rude flight of steps, hewn out of the earth, they found themselves at liberty. The sudden entrance into the open air, after the dreary confinement he had for some time experienced, had such an effect upon Alberti, that it almost overpowered him, but Storaldi took his arm and urged him forward, and they made their way from the spot rapidly as their limbs could carry them.

"Quick! quick! my lord," said Storaldi, "for although we are now safe from the cavern, there is no knowing how soon the brigands may recover from the effects of the drug I have administered to them, and we have therefore no time to lose."

The count said not a word, and they continued their flight towards the most dismal and unfrequented part of the country, and where

Storaldi knew there was no fear of encountering the brigands who were absent from the cavern. It was not until they had proceeded to some considerable distance from the cavern, that they ventured to pause to take breath, and here Alberti once more expressed to his companion his feelings of gratitude for the service he had rendered him.

"Henceforth, Storaldi," remarked Alberti, "whatever your past crimes may have been, I must now look upon you as my best friend."

"Nay, signor," returned Storaldi, "I am not so presumptuous as to aspire to your friendship. All that I require are the means to live in peace and retirement. As soon as I have seen your lordship safe among your friends, I must lose no time in making my escape from the country, for Massaroni would be sure to scent me out if I ventured to remain here, and to visit me with his deadliest vengeance."

"Fear not, Storaldi," observed the count, "now I am again restored to liberty myself and my friends will lose no time in adopting such steps as will bring this daring brigand chief to justice, and I have not the least fear that we shall fail to succeed."

"I much doubt that, signor," replied Storaldi, "Massaroni is no common man, as all Italy must know by this time, and so secretly does he carry out his designs, that even his own associates are unable to comprehend them. But come, my lord, let us proceed."

"The journey is a long one," said the count, "and it will take us a long while to travel it on foot. Besides such a course might be fraught with danger."

"True," coincided Storaldi; "but I told you, signor, that I could procure horses not far from hence, and you will find that I will keep my word. I have already made arrangements for that purpose with a man in whom I can confide, and on the promise of an ample remuneration he has agreed to supply us."

"'Tis well," returned the count, "I am satisfied; so let us at once proceed on our way."

The night was very dark; the moon was observed behind murky clouds, and everything was favourable to concealment. Alberti felt his confidence strengthen every step they proceeded, and after walking for about another half hour, they perceived a light glimmering at a short distance, which evidently proceeded from some human habitation.

"It is the dwelling of the man I have told you of, signor," said Storaldi, in answer to a question from the count. "He is true to his promise, and evidently awaits our arrival."

In a few minutes they arrived at the house, which stood by itself, and Storaldi having given a particular signal, the light immediately disappeared from the window, and shortly afterwards the door was opened by an elderly man whom Storaldi saluted by the name of Paulo. He eyed the count with some little degree of curiosity, and then, without speaking a word, he led the way into the house, where in one of the inner rooms a comfortable fire was blazing on the hearth, and some refreshments were spread upon the table, of which old Paulo requested the count and his companion to partake, which they did, but sparingly. Paulo then brought forth a couple of peasants' dresses, which he desired Alberti and Storaldi to assume for security, and having hastily attired themselves in this costume, and the count having mentioned to his satisfaction the reward he was to give him for his services, Paulo led the way to a shed at the back of the house, where the horses were in readiness; they mounted them, and darting off at a smart speed, were soon far away from the danger of pursuit.

*   *   *   *

It was not until more than a couple of hours after the flight of the count and Storaldi from cavern, that the brigands recovered to a state of consciousness, and they then stared at each other with stupid amazement, but with a vague idea that all was not exactly right.

"By the mass!" said one of them, rubbing his eyes and looking upon his companions with an expression of doubt and suspicion, "our potations must have been very deep, or the wine we drank was unusually strong, for we all appear to have slept remarkably sound, and for a considerable time. Diavolo! what a confounded head-ache I have got."

"For my own part," observed another of the fellows, "I have not the slightest idea as to what has taken place. I may have been asleep for a month or an hour for what I know. Drink is not apt to overcome me in this manner. Where is Storaldi?"

"Ah! where is Storaldi?" said the others in a breath, as some slight fears and suspicions flashed upon their minds: "it was he who plied us so liberally; it is seldom that he is to be found in such a convivial mood."

"And now I recollect," remarked the first speaker, "that he drank but sparingly himself. My suspicions are beginning to be aroused."

"Suspicions! what of?" demanded the others.

"That Storaldi had some secret motive for this conduct; where is he now?"

"Oh, probably with the prisoner," replied one of the brigands.

This suggestion did not appear to be an improbable one, and they immediately repaired to the cavern in which the Count Alberti had been confined, but what was their consternation to behold the door standing wide open, and the place entirely deserted.

"By the infernal host!" exclaimed the brigand who had spoken first, "Storaldi has turned traitor! He and the Count Alberti have escaped—we are ruined. What is now to be done?''

No one could reply, and they stared at each other with looks of the utmost astonishment and alarm. An active search was made in every part of the cavernous retreat, but, of course, without the least success; it was quite evident that the count and Storaldi had fled, and the fears of the brigands increased every moment. The vengeance of their chief they well knew would be certain to descend upon them; and for some time they were completely at a loss how to act. One or two of them were for taking to immediate flight, but they could not finally make up their minds upon that point, and while they were still discussing the subject, Maria Grazie suddenly and unexpectedly made her appearance among them.

"How now!" she peremptorily demanded; —" what is the meaning of this scene of confusion?—Why do you look so alarmed. What has happened?''

None of them ventured to return any answer, but shrunk appalled beneath the stern and penetrating looks of the brigand's wife, whom they looked upon with as much awe and submission as Massaroni himself.

"Why do you not answer me?" she again haughtily demanded; "know ye not that it is Maria Grazie who addresses ye? Do ye dare to treat the wife of your chief with silent contempt? Again I demand what has happened to disturb ye thus?''

"We scarcely dare to inform you, Maria," at length faltered out one of the brigands.

"Speak!" cried Maria, impatiently; "why do you thus hesitate? Do not trifle with me or keep me in suspense, or, by the dome of St. Peter's, it shall be worse for you.''

"We are none of us to blame for what has taken place," stammered out the brigands together.

"What has taken place, ye trembling knaves, that you fear to divulge it to a woman?''

"It is the traitor Storaldi who is the cause of all.''

"Storaldi, what of him?''

"He has fled, and the Count Alberti has escaped with him.''

"Ah!" cried Maria, in a tone of the greatest excitement, "Alberti, escaped!—Villains! how is this?''

In a trembling voice one of the brigands related such facts as he was acquainted with, and as he proceeded, the fine handsome countenance of the brigand's wife evinced the utmost indignation.

"Traitors! cowards!" she exclaimed, when he had concluded; "and is this the way in which you guard the interests of that chief who has sacrificed so much for ye?—Think ye that Allesandro Massaroni, that Maria Grazie will be deceived by such a tale as this? Oh, but this night's work shall cost ye dear.''

The brigands looked significantly upon each other, and muttered something themselves; but nothing could daunt the haughty spirit of the brigand's wife. She drew from her belt a brace of pistols, and levelling them at them with a determined air, in a voice which made even those daring men tremble, she cried—

"Villains! dare ye murmur? Dare ye threaten Maria Grazie, woman only though she be? Back! back! all of ye, cowardly dogs, or, by the holy cross, the first who dares to disobey my commands shall perish on the spot!—In, I say to confinement until the return of your chief, to whom you will have to render a severe account for your conduct!''

The brigands looked upon each other perfectly abashed and confounded, but they ventured not to disobey, although they might easily have overpowered the daring woman. Like so many children, she drove them before her into the cavern which the Count Alberti had so recently occupied, and locking and bolting the door upon them, had them securely prisoners. She then threw herself on a seat, and gave her self up to meditation.

"And so," she soliloquized, "thus are the prospects of Massaroni frustrated, thus is he rewarded for all the danger he has run, for all the blood that has been shed. The Count Alberti has escaped without the payment of so much as a single scudi in ransom, and probably for the future will be able to set him at complete defiance! Bah! he has not acted with his usual wisdom and judgment on this occasion, and it will be well if he does not yet have cause to repent it. And all this has been caused through the extraordinary interest he takes in the fate of Olympia. He never speaks of her, too, but he is most eloquent on her beauty, her virtues, her gentle and amiable qualities. Time was when Massaroni had no eyes for any other woman than Maria Grazie, his mountain bride, the partner of all his toils, the willing partaker of all his dangers! Her who would willingly lay down her life to serve him. Can it be that time has changed those sentiments in his bosom, that he looks upon me with indifference, that the love he once so ardently professed for me is extinguished? No, away with such thoughts! Massaroni, I do thee an injustice, a cruel injustice, by entertaining them for a moment. Can I think so despicably of myself as to believe that any other woman, be she ever so lovely, can ever supersede me in the affections of my own loved brigand chief?''

She stifled the feelings of jealousy which for a brief period she had suffered to take possession of her bosom, and her countenance reassumed its usual expression. In order to compose her feelings, she walked to the entrance of the cavern and paced backwards and forwards in the night air. Her thoughts were all fixed upon her husband ; she waited anxiously his return from the perilous expedition he had gone upon, and anticipated with no little apprehension the consequences of the escape of the Count Alberti. Daylight found her still watching, and unable to seek a respite from anxious thought in sleep.

CHAPTER XIX.

THE SUFFERINGS OF OLYMPIA IN THE ROB-BERS' CAVE.—THERESINA'S TALE OF SORROW.

BUT how was the deeply wronged and persecuted Olympia during the time the events we have been recording, situated? What was her anguish, her despair, as she looked upon the noisome walls of her dungeon, and pressed her poor innocent unconscious babe to her bosom? But it was not the confinement, or the probability of the fate that was in store for her, that tortured her the most, but the base, the cruel, and heartless treachery of that man for whom she had sacrificed everything ; to whom her whole soul was devoted, for whom she would freely have undergone any punishment, nay, laid down her very life, which probed her heart, and drove her brain to madness. But still, after all that he had done, she felt no spark of animosity towards her betrayer. She still loved him with all that strength and fervour that woman alone can feel, and was prepared and anxious to pardon him the injustice he had rendered her, if he would now release her from confinement, and make her all the atonement in his power. She languished only for the continuance of his love, she coveted not his hand, had he the justice in his nature to offer it to her ; after his recent conduct, her woman's pride would have rejected it. But, oh, what tortures wrung her heart, when she recalled to her memory the vows he had so frequently uttered, and reflected upon the brutal manner in which he had broken them.

"Oh, Alberti," she would ejaculate, "what have I done that you should thus so cruelly deceive me—that you should thus so remorselessly treat me? Was it not enough that you broke those solemn vows, after making me a degraded being, hateful to myself and despised by all mankind, but that you must not only desert me and your innocent offspring, but consign us to a fate, the extent of the misery of which it is impossible for me to comprehend, Am I to remain for ever confined in this fearful place, surrounded by wretches who would not shrink from the perpetration of any crime, and who are ready at any moment to do thy bidding? Oh, God! and art thou, whom I thought all perfection—whom my very soul idolized ; the man to whom I resigned all that should be valuable to woman, in the vain hope of thy being sincere, the author of all this? Art thou the associate and friend of thieves and murderers? Horrible idea! And yet not more horrible than true. Alas! alas! what a foolish fond estimate have I formed of your character."

With such wild thoughts as these, would the unfortunate Olympia continue to torture herself, until her confinement, acquiring tenfold horror from the agony of her mind, became insupportable. For hours and hours together she would pace the narrow limits of the place of her confinement with disordered footsteps, and invoke curses, long and deep, upon the hard destiny that pursued her. Sometimes she was wound up to such a pitch of distraction, almost approaching to insanity, that thoughts which in her more reasonable moments would have smote her heart with horror, would rush upon her mind like hideous demons, urging her on to something frightful. In such moments she would gaze with ghastly looks upon her little innocent, and although, perhaps, a cherub smile at the time would glisten on its features, she was almost tempted to press her fingers in its throat, and at once to terminate that existence which she had at present every reason to believe would only be fraught with similar misery to that which she had herself experienced. There were moments when she could have dashed her own head and that of her infant against the rocky wall of her dungeon, and thus have put an end to their earthly sufferings; but an inscrutable Power interposed to save her from the perpetration of so hideous a crime, and she still continued to live to suffer, suffer on. Busy, indeed, were her thoughts in that terrible situation, and the extraordinary conduct of Massaroni formed the principal feature of them. Why should he, whom she had never seen before the evening, the eventful evening of her appointment with her seducer, take such a remarkable interest in her fate?—Why should he, whose name she had ever been accustomed to think upon with dread, interpose in her behalf? How had he not only become acquainted with her history, but also with those immediate secrets which she had supposed were only known to herself and Alberti? It was a mystery she found it impossible to penetrate, and the longer she reflected on it, only the deeper did she become involved in perplexity. But connected with this was another feeling, for which she could in nowise account. She felt her heart drawn towards the brigand chief with a sentiment almost amounting to affection. There was something in his features, in his observations, in his general demeanour, which had made an indelible impression upon her, and could she have persuaded herself that they would never meet again, she would have been more truly wretched, if possible, than she was at present. Although Olympia had never seen Massaroni before that occasion to which we have alluded, his features, to her imagination, seemed as familiar to her as if they had been constant companions from the earliest days of childhood, and she longed to gaze upon them again. Even the simplest tones of his voice still seemed to vibrate in her ears, and to conjure up scenes which her memory failed to supply her with, and which there was not a probability of ever having occurred. What could be the cause of this ?—She was at a loss to imagine, and the longer she endeavoured to do so, the more did she become entangled in the intricate mazes of uncertainty and bewilderment. If anything could have afforded her consolation in her present wretched situation, it would have been the behaviour of the robber's wife, Theresina, and the sympathy which she evinced in her misfortunes. She attended scrupulously to her utmost wishes, and was as much as possible in her company, seeking to banish the gloomy thoughts that constantly haunted her mind, and to inspire her with hope. Theresina was indeed no common woman. She was one that possessed an elevated mind, a finely cultivated taste, and great conversational powers, which, being always influenced by the utmost intelligence, rendered her a being who must always be interesting, if not absolutely fascinating. She still retained the traces of former beauty, and her whole appearance and behaviour showed evidently that she had at one time moved in no common sphere of society. What a pity it was that such a woman should now be placed in her present degrading situation. And what could have brought her to it ? This was the question that Olympia frequentlly put to her; but it always seemed to cause her the most intense mental anguish, and she evaded it as sedulously as she could. Olympia made frequent appeals to her to aid her in her escape, but although Theresina expressed her utmost abhorrence of the character of the Count Alberti, and condemned the conduct of her husband, Rinaldi, in becoming the instrument of his vile purposes, she regretted her inability to accede to Olympia's wishes, but sincerely trusted that something would yet occur to restore her to liberty and happiness.

"Happiness !" sighed Olympia, "alas, that can never again be mine, even though liberty and wealth should be at my command. He to whom I have devoted my utmost affections—to whom I have sacrificed my honour, everything that is valuable to a woman, has rendered that impossible. While I laboured under the delusion that he loved me, I was indeed happy; but now that the mist is dispelled from before mine eyes, what a truly miserable, degraded wretch do I feel myself; how unworthy to live,

and yet how unfit to die. Alas! Theresina, I am indeed a wretched creature."

"Say not so signora," said Theresina, in soothing and sympathising accents; "dark as your present days may appear to be, brighter prospects, depend upon it, are in store for you."

"Would that I could think so," replied Olympia, with a melancholy look; "I might then find courage to support my present trials with some degree of patience and resignation."

"Endeavour to do so, signora."

"Alas! it would be a vain task."

"Put your trust in Heaven."

"Heaven help me!" ejaculated Olympia; "but have I not reason to fear that it has deserted me ?"

"Heaven," replied Theresina, "never deserts those who have not willingly offended against its laws."

Olympia looked at her with astonishment.

"And is it possible," she said, "that a woman possessing the noble and amiable feelings you have just now expressed, can be placed in such a degraded situation ; the wife of a robber, the common associate of the worst of miscreants ?"

"Ah, signora," replied Theresina, with a sigh, "did you but know all, you would, I am convinced, consider that I am much more to be pitied than blamed. God knows the many pangs I endure—the suffering I have undergone—but nothing can ever subdue the devotion I feel towards that man with whom I have joined my fate."

"You say that he was once good and virtuous ?" said Olympia, with much curiosity.

"Noble, generous, honourable, and humane," replied Theresina, energetically.

"And what can have driven him to his present abandoned course of life ?" asked Olympia, with the deepest interest.

"Misfortunes the most unprecedented, unforeseen, and unavoidable," answered her companion. "Time was, signora, when Rinaldi would have shuddered at the bare idea of crime ; but trouble and oppression work revolutions in our nature."

"Very true," coincided Olympia.

"Ah! signora," continued Theresina; "could we have any knowledge of the trials it may be our hard fate to experience in the world, what miserable wretches we should be. But Providence has wisely ordained that we should not, and how grateful ought we to be for it. I was myself one of the happiest of the happy, born to the brightest prospects, with not a single care upon my mind. All around me was calm and sunshine. Tranquillity rested upon my slumbers, and morning awoke me to cheerfulness, hope, and content."

"Alas! and what occurred to break the charm of this existence ?"

"One fell blow annihilated all my hopes,

and those of Rinaldi, and rendered us what you
see us now," answered Theresina.

"It must have been a severe one," said
Olympia, "to bring about so deplorable a
change."

"It was, indeed; so deplorable, that I often
marvel to myself that I had strength sufficient
to bear up with it. But we know not what we
can endure, signora, until we are put to the
trial."

"True, that—very true," replied Olympia;
"but at the time when the misfortunes to
which you allude occurred, was Rinaldi your
husband?"

"He was not," returned Theresina.

"And not engaged in his present lawless
course?"

"Oh, no, lady. Had you known Rinaldi
at that time, you could never have supposed
that he and the robber chief are identical. As
I have before said, he was then good and
honourable, but unmerited misfortune made
him a villain; hard necessity drove him from
the path of virtuous and civilized society, and
plunged him into crime."

"Unfortunate man!" ejaculated Olympia,
"indeed I pity him and you."

"Indeed you may do so, signora," remarked the robber's wife, "for all that has
followed was entirely unmerited on our part."

"I do believe you, and compassionate you."

"Thank you, signora, and from what I state
you may probably congratulate yourself with
the reflection, that, however wretched your
own situation, there are still others in the
world whose troubles have been equal, if not
greater than your own."

"But surely the means are now in your
power of extricating yourselves from your
present perilous and degrading situation, and
of returning to the paths of rectitude and
honour?" observed Olympia.

"Ah, no, lady," replied Theresina, "tho
time has gone by, there is no hope for us; we
must be content to remain as we are, trusting
for mercy from that Supreme Judge, which we
cannot hope for from mankind."

"What a strange contradiction are your
words to your actual principles," said Olympia.

"They may appear to be so, signora,"
returned Theresina, "but nevertheless I speak
nothing but the truth. Are you disposed to
listen to my melancholy tale?"

"Oh, most readily," answered Olympia, "it
will serve to divert my thoughts for a time
from my own sorrows."

"It may, lady, and at the same time afford
me some relief in being able to give vent
to my feelings, to one who I know can and
will sympathise with me. It is but a brief
and simple story but nevertheless I doubt not
that it will possess the less interest in your
mind."

"I wait impatiently to hear it, Theresina,"
observed the fair prisoner; "and such poor
consolation and advice as it is in the power of
such a humble and unfortunate individual as
myself to offer you, you may freely command."

"Consolation, signora," returned Theresina
with a sigh, "alas! mine is a fate that will
admit of none. However, I will not regret,
it is the will of an all wise Providence that it
should be so, and it is not for poor insignificant
mortals like us to murmur at its decrees."

"What a pity it is," ejaculated Olympia,
"that one possessing such sentiments as those
you have just now expressed, and every way
calculated to shed a lustre upon any society in
which you might mingle, should be placed in
the melancholy situation in which you are.
Surely it is not too late to extricate yourself
from it?"

Theresina shook her head, with a melancholy expression of countenance, as she
replied—

"Alas! signora, it *is* my fate, and I must
submit—I cannot escape from it. My fate is
joined to that of Rinaldi—I am the faithful
partner of all his perils and his faults, and I
must, I will remain so, in spite of everything,
until death."

"But surely," said Olympia, with a look of
surprise and doubt, "your husband cannot have
become so depraved as not to wish to return to
the paths of rectitude and honour, if he had the
opportunity?"

"Signora," replied her companion, "my husband
is a proscribed man; he has not a being in the
world whom he could hail as a friend. All old
associations are buried in oblivion; he is hated
and despised—he is looked upon as a monster of
the blackest dye—hunted from society like
some wild beast—a price is set on his head, and
all are anxious to obtain the reward of blood.
What opportunity has he then of escaping from
his present course of life?—none. Evil destiny
has plunged him into crime; time has inured
him to his present wild and predatory life, and
he must continue to pursue it till that life is
terminated."

"Sad destiny indeed," said Olympia; "sincerely do I pity him and you."

"Thanks, signora," returned Theresina:
"but let us no longer dwell upon this part of
the subject. You say that you are willing to
listen to the melancholy story I have to relate?"

"Yes, Theresina," answered Olympia; "but
if by so doing you should increase the misery
of your thoughts by recounting the dreary events
of the past, still keep the painful narrative confined to your own breast."

"No, signora, as I before said, it will afford
me temporary relief by thus being allowed to
give vent to my feelings. Heaven knows how

c

constantly the fearful tale is uppermost in my secret thoughts, and how often I have prayed for the opportunity to communicate it to one who could sympathise with me, and who would not entirely condemn me for the present unfortunate position in life in which I am placed.

Such an individual are you, signora, I feel convinced."

"You do me no more than justice, Theresina, by that opinion," observed Olympia; "proceed for I am all attention."

"But a minute," said the former, "while I

FLORELLA DELIVERS FLORIO'S LETTER TO MELINA.

collect my thoughts. It is many years since the events which I am about to record happened, and although the painful truth is too powerfully impressed upon my memory ever to be effaced, my mind at times wanders, a mist seems to have descended upon my brain, and I

know not what I say—the horrid past overwhelms my brain."

Theresina paused, and placing her hand upon her forehead, as if to collect her scattered ideas, she reflected deeply for a few minutes, and Olympia, whose interest and curiosity were excited by the observations she had made use of, did not offer to interrupt her.

NARRATIVE OF THE ROBBER'S WIFE.

"How often," commenced Theresina, "in the bitterness of my anguish, when pondering o'er my past history, have I regretted that I have had no kindred being near me to whom I could confide my sorrows, and from whom I might expect commiseration. What a relief I felt it would be to my overburthened bosom to meet with a sympathizing friend in the midst of my solitude, especially one of my own sex. That wish is now gratified; you, signora, who have yourself experienced so many troubles and vicissitudes, and who possesses so tender and gentle a nature, will, I am confident, not fail to compassionate me, and to view with a lenient and charitable eye any errors of which, in the course of my eventful life, you may consider I have been guilty.

"Time was when I was the gayest of the gay, happiest of the happy. No pang of anxiety or care corroded my heart, no thought of sorrow disturbed the sweet dream of my youth; the aspect of everything around me was cheerful and lovely to my buoyant imagination; I had not a wish that was ungratified, no thoughts beyond my happy home and my beloved parents, of whom I was the only child, and who lavished upon me every fondness, whilst they took great pains to instil into my mind all those principles of virtue which should render me a comfort and a blessing to them in their declining years, and an ornament to that society in which I might be destined to move. How far I profited by their excellent precepts and example, of course it would be egotistical in me to say; but still I must be permitted to observe that I studied night and day to please them—to profit by their advice; and it is a consolation for me to reflect that never from their lips did I receive a word of reproof; never did I willingly cause them a moment's uneasiness, or venture to disobey their mild and virtuous injunctions.

"My parents were not in affluent, but independent circumstances, and they were regarded with universal esteem, and honoured with the friendship of some of the first families in the neighbourhood. But they saw but little company, for retirement suited their tastes and habits much better, and they had few wishes beyond their own immediate domestic circle.

"In the immediate vicinity of the place of our residence stood a noble castle, the possessor of which I shall call Count Manfredoni. He was a weak-minded nobleman, haughty and overbearing in his behaviour towards his inferiors, and scarcely less unbending even to those who moved in the same elevated station of life as himself; towards my parents, however, the count ever behaved with the most marked respect, and frequently invited them to his castle, and showed them on all occasions the utmost deference. I was likewise an especial favourite with him, and he seemed never so pleased as when listening to my innocent and artless conversation.

"At the time of which I am speaking, the Countess Manfredoni had been dead about three years, leaving her lord with two sons, Rudolphi, and he who is now my husband, and who is known by no other name than that of Rinaldi, the robber-chief."

"And is it possible," interrupted Olympia, with a look of surprise, "that your husband could have been born to such noble prospects, and that he should now become so disgraced?"

"It is true, signora," sighed Theresina; "alas! our's has been a terrible destiny; but what will not injustice, cruelty, and misfortune drive a person to?"

"Very true—true," coincided Olympia, "and more's the pity that it should be so. It is terrible to view these fearful revolutions in the circumstances and principles of our fellow-creatures."

"Ah; signora," returned Theresina, "had any one predicted the dreadful fate that was in store for us, with what horror and disgust should I have scouted the idea. Oh, what could be more happy and bright than our prospects were at that time? But villany brought about the change, and blighted all our hopes for ever."

"Believe me, Theresina," observed Olympia, "that I sincerely pity you, and trust that, even situated as you now are, happier days will yet dawn upon you."

Theresina shook her head.

"I'm obliged to you, signora," she said, "for your sympathy and good wishes, but it would be madness to encourage such hopes; our fate is sealed, it is now too late to avoid it and it is useless to murmur at it. But suffer me to proceed."

"Pardon me, Theresina," said Olympia, "for this interruption. I am anxious to listen to your melancholy but interesting narrative."

The robber's wife resumed in the following words—

"Rudolphi was his brother's senior by about two years, and his father's favourite, who had encouraged him in every childish caprice, while he treated Rinaldi with the utmost rigour, and was very ready to swell his most simple and venial errors into offences of the greatest magnitude, and to punish them accordingly. The consequence was that Rudolphi from his earliest period evinced a tyrannical, obstinate, and generally vicious disposition, treated his brother with every possible mark of disrespect, if not with absolute hatred, and took every opportunity to prejudice his father against him, to misrepresent his conduct in the most shameful manner, and, in fact, to annoy and injure him in every shape and form. It would seem as if he delighted to render him miserable, and the Count Manfredoni lent too ready an ear to his calumnies.

"But Rinaldi never murmured at this unjust and unnatural treatment; he bore it all with the most exemplary meekness and submission, for his disposition was the very reverse of that of his brother, and although it cost him many a pang in secret, he was still determined to bear it all with patience and forbearance, and trusted that time would bring his father to a full sense of the injustice and cruelty of his conduct.

"At this time Rinaldi and his brother were both extremely fine young men, highly accomplished, and excelling in every manly sport. But it needed no very deep penetration to discover the extraordinary difference in the dispositions of the brothers, and Rinaldi was the favourite wherever he went.

"I have before said that my parents were frequently invited to the castle of the Count Manfredoni, and, of course, whenever they went thither I always accompanied them. From the earliest days of childhood I had been the companion and playmate of Rinaldi and his brother, but I need scarcely say that the former was always my especial favourite, though Rudolphi showed me the most marked attention and respect. In this too, he showed the jealous feelings he entertained towards Rinaldi—feelings that strengthened as time wore on, and which were ultimately productive of such fatal and dreadful consequences.

"Rinaldi seemed never so happy as when he was in my society, and he constantly studied to contribute to my pleasure and amusement. These attentions, so delicately paid, I need not say were highly gratifying and flattering to me, and I looked upon Rinaldi with the same affection as if he had been my own brother.

"Years wore away, and this sentiment, almost unconsciously to myself, gradually ripened to one of a far more tender nature in my breast, nor could I conceal it from the object who had inspired it; it was a virtuous passion—I knew Rinaldi was good and honourable; I had every reason to believe that he loved me ardently in return, and why, therefore, I reflected to myself, should I seek to stifle a passion which sprang from so pure a source? Rinaldi read my thoughts in my eyes; eloquently he revealed his mind to me, and acknowledged himself one of the happiest of human beings.

"Rudolphi was not long in discovering the understanding that existed between me and his brother, and all his worst passions were inflamed in consequence, but he endeavoured to conceal them from me; he was always most plausible in his demeamour towards me, and treated me with more marked respect and attention than he had even done before; he also affected by his manner to be highly gratified at the passion which, too evidently for him, existed between us, and his behaviour towards his brother became remarkably changed. But we were neither of us to be deceived; beneath all this spacious garb we could discover the lurking fiend, who only waited the opportunity to gratify his feelings of hatred and revenge against Rinaldi, and to plunge us both into irrecoverable misery and despair. Alas! that diabolical and unnatural end he accomplished too successfully, as you will find, the farther I progress with my tale of woe.

"My father and mother had been no strangers to the sentiments which myself and Rinaldi had long entertained for each other, and therefore, when we ventured to acknowledge to them the truth, feeling satisfied that we were formed to make each other happy, they willingly gave their sanction to our addresses, providing that we could gain the consent of the Count Manfredoni; though of that, they told us candidly, they almost despaired.

"All this time Rudolphi was not idle in forwarding his evil designs; his object was to get rid of his brother, so that he might be the more at liberty to carry out his plans against me, and, alas! he too well succeeded. Rinaldi was suddenly astounded by a command from his father to prepare himself to depart from the castle immediately, as it was his determination that he should travel for two or three years for the improvement of his education.

"I need not seek to pourtray the agony of Rinaldi's mind on this unexpected announcement, and I could only see in it the forerunner to the greatest misfortunes. Too fatally were these presentiments realized, as you will find as I proceed.

"Rinaldi in vain sought to remonstrate with his father, and to persuade him to give him a few months' more grace; he was deaf to all his expostulations, so he well knew the crafty and insidious villain Rudolphi worked his fatal influence upon his mind. He would listen to no excuses; he even reproached Rinaldi for disobedience to his will, and commanded him, on pain of his everlasting displeasure, to submit without murmuring to his injunctions.

"What was Rinaldi to do? He was driven now to desperation and despair; he saw plainly through the evil designs of his brother, and he shuddered at the thought of leaving me behind to his tender mercies, and with the probability that some villanous scheme would be concocted to prevent the possibility of our ever meeting each other again. And yet he was completely powerless to oppose the will of his father, and he was distracted and bewildered as to the course it would be most advisable, under these painful circumstances, to pursue.

"In this dilemma, he consulted my parents, repeated his assurance of the unalterable affection he entertained towards me, and implored them to advise him how to act.

"The only counsel they could give him, was

to make a candid avowal of the sentiments we felt towards each other, to his father, and to throw himself on his mercy, although, too well knowing the pride and obstinacy of the count, and the influence which Rudolphi held over him, they had, and they freely confessed it, but little hopes that he would succeed in making a favourable impression upon him.

"It was a painful, and even humiliating task for Rinaldi; he shrank from it, but still it was the only reasonable course he could perceive, and he at last made up his mind to pursue it.

"He therefore seized the earliest opportunity of throwing himself at the feet of his father; confessing, with all the eloquence at his command, the mutual passion that existed between us; and fervently implored him not to annihilate all our youthful hopes, and doom us to everlasting misery, by refusing his consent to the encouragement of our views.

"Our worst apprehensions were realised; the Count Manfredoni heard Rinaldi with impatience. Rudolphi had gained complete ascendancy over him. He not only commanded Rinaldi to banish all thoughts of me from his mind, but to prepare immediately for his departure from home.

"In vain Rinaldi supplicated and expostulated; the count was inexorable, and my lover was therefore compelled to abandon all his efforts to move him to relent, in despair; although there were moments when he was half resolved, at every risk, to disobey the stern commands of his father, which he considered to be so cruel and unjust, and which he had no difficulty in tracing to the right source.

"The wily hypocrite, Rudolphi, affected to sympathise with his deeply injured brother, and even to impart hope and consolation to him; but Rinaldi spurned his condolences with the contempt they merited, and took no pains to conceal from him that he entertained a proper estimate of his real character, and that it was to him that he had to attribute the harsh and unnatural manner with which the count, their father, had ever treated him, while, on the contrary, he had ever lavished on him (Rudolphi), the most unlimited affection and indulgence, being blind to all his faults, and placing the firmest reliance upon everything he thought proper to state to him.

"Rudolphi, however, pretended not to notice the real thoughts and feelings of his brother, though at the same time I need not say that it only added to the hatred he bore him, and increased his determination never to rest until he had fully gratified his revenge against him.

"Alas, signora, how shall I properly describe the agony of the scene at the parting of myself and Rinaldi?—The most dismal forebodings of the future distracted our minds, not the least ray of hope dawned upon our bosoms to console and support us.

"My parents did all they could to comfort us; assured Rinaldi of their everlasting esteem —and urged us to submit to our present fate with patience and fortitude, at the same time seeking to inspire us with the hope that something would yet occur to disperse the dark clouds which obscured our happiness, and to gratify our wishes. But they had a difficult task to perform, and although we were extremely grateful to them for their kind wishes and exertions, they were almost futile.

"At length the melancholy day arrived, and the Count Manfredoni still remaining inflexible, Rinaldi was banished from his home, and I was plunged into the deepest despair, for I never expected to behold him again, and the most torturing anticipations of the troubles that were in store for us both, drove me to a state which I may truly say bordered upon distraction.

"For some days after the departure of my lover, I was confined to my bed, and my parents became seriously alarmed for the consequences. They did all they could to comfort me, and to inspire me with hope, but with very little, or no success; for alas! I could see no other prospect but that of the greatest misery before me. There was only one little consolation left me, and that was the promise which Rinaldi had made to correspond with me at every opportunity, and the solemn and oft-repeated assurances he had made, that let whatever might be the consequences, or in whatever situation fate might place him, he would never cease to remember me with the same ardent affection that had ever glowed in his breast towards me.

"In this manner several weeks passed away, and I became somewhat more calm and reconciled to the cruel destiny that pursued me, though nothing could banish the deep melancholy which had settled upon my mind, and which rendered me insensible to every earthly pleasure.

"The circumstances I have been relating, as you may suppose, signora, interrupted the intimacy which had previously existed between the Count Manfredoni and my parents, and they discontinued their visits to the castle, though they had frequently received invitations to do so, and Rudolphi had often had the boldness to visit their residence, and to affect to regret the circumstances that had taken place, and to express a hope that my parents would in a short time be induced to renew their friendship; but the reception he met with from them was anything but flattering to his vanity and hopes, and I always most sedulously avoided his presence, for it was impossible that I could view the guilty hypocrite with any other feelings than those of disgust and hatred.

"Rinaldi was faithful to his promise, and in a few days one of his most faithful attendants, thoroughly disguised, arrived at the house of my parents, bringing with him the fondly expected letter from Rinaldi.

"He informed me that his master was then at Venice, and in a most distracted and helpless state of mind, and that, in fact, he had for several weeks given himself up entirely to despair and the most violent grief, which would admit of no consolation. All this I was prepared to hear, but I need not say the agony it caused me, and how fervently I prayed to Heaven to interpose in our behalf, or otherwise to release us both from our troubles.

"With what feelings of anguish, yet melancholy joy, did I peruse the contents of this letter, which breathed the most unbounded affection, and in which he implored me not to fail to return him an answer by his messenger, as he should be in a state of the most maddening excitement until he should hear from me again, and was made acquainted with all the particulars which had taken place since his departure from the castle.

"My tears flowed fast as I again and again read this affectionate letter, and it was some time before I could sufficiently compose myself to sit down to write an answer. What that answer was it is impossible for me, after the lapse of so many years, to be able to repeat; but I know, signora, that you will be readily able to imagine the language in which it was couched, and I should only become tedious were I to attempt to particularize it. It may be sufficient for me to say that I felt my mind considerably more at ease after hearing from Rinaldi, and being thus enabled to give vent to my feelings, and I endeavoured to flatter myself with the hope that something would yet occur to render us both happy; but alas! how fallacious was that idea, as you will see by the sequel of my dismal narrative.

"From that time we continued to correspond almost every week, and so well had we arranged everything, that we flattered ourselves that not the least suspicion was entertained by our enemies.

Notwithstanding the coldness with which he was always received by my parents, Rudolphi persisted in visiting our residence, and he watched every opportunity of throwing himself in my way, and of showing me such attentions as it was impossible for me to mistake, and which I need not say did not fail to excite my unmitigated disgust, but every time he accidentally encountered me, he became more bold, and at last was compelled to appeal to my parents to protect me from the annoyance of his hateful advances. They accordingly lost no time in demanding from him an explanation of his conduct, when he at once cast aside the mask, acknowledged that he had long loved me to distraction, that the earl his father was no stranger to his sentiments, but approved of them and he finally concluded by formally re-

questing, or rather demanding, my hand in marriage.

"My father could scarcely hear him out with any degree of patience, but at length, when he had concluded, he firmly and peremptorily, and in my name, rejected his suit, and bitterly reproached him for the treachery and injustice with which it was now evident, if there could have been any doubt before, he had acted towards his unfortunate brother.

"Nothing could exceed the rage of Rudolphi at this scornful rejection of his vows, although he endeavoured to conceal it, and ventured to express a hope that both I and my parents would in a short time think better of it, and that he might still look forward to the day when the sincerity of his passion would be duly appreciated, and that his addresses would be received with favour.

"His effrontery and presumption increased my disgust, while at the same time I could not help feeling the utmost dread as to the lengths to which his rage and disappointment might tempt him to go.

"I almost feared to make Rinaldi acquainted with the particulars, lest he should brave the anger of his father, and returning home, seek satisfaction from Rudolphi for his boldness and treachery. But after mature reflection, I felt convinced that it would be useless to conceal it, as the facts would be sure to reach his ears some time or another, and I therefore wrote a letter to him, stating everything exactly as it had taken place.

"The indignation of Rinaldi was almost insupportable, and it was not without the greatest difficulty that I could dissuade him from immediately returning home and demanding an explanation from his brother. But I entreated him to be calm, to trust to Providence for the result, and, above all, not to write to Rudolphi or Count Manfredoni on the subject, as that would divulge the secret correspondence we had been carrying on together, and might be productive of the most dangerous and fatal consequences. He yielded to my supplications, but implored me not to conceal anything from him, and to give him immediate notice if any danger should threaten me.

"I was somewhat relieved from my apprehensions when Rudolphi discontinued his visits, and more so on hearing that he had left the castle, and was not expected to return for some time. But Rinaldi, in his letters, cautioned me seriously to be upon my guard lest his brother should have some treacherous designs in contemplation.

"Another month elapsed, and Rudolphi did not return, and I was given to understand that he was in England, which intelligence afforded me much satisfaction. The Count Manfredoni kept himself entirely secluded in his castle, and saw little or no company, and the intimacy ᵇetween him and my parents was now entirely broken off, and it did not seem at all likely that it would ever be renewed again.

"In order, if possible, to divert my thoughts in some measure from the gloomy subjects which continually engrossed them, I now ventured to take my accustomed walks among those scenes which had been the favourite haunts of myself and Rinaldi, and there for hours I would remain wrapped in meditation on the past, and in gloomy anticipation of the future.

"I had a miniature likeness of my lover in my possession, and what melancholy delight did it afford me to contemplate that dear resemblance, and how many were the scalding tears I shed upon it, as the painful idea of the distance that separated us, and the dread that we might never meet again, rushed upon my brain.

"One evening, the extreme fineness of the weather had induced me to extend my walk to a later hour than was my usual custom, and indeed I was so deeply wrapped in thought, that I did not notice the lapse of time. The lamp of Heaven beamed brightly on high, and nothing could surpass the lovely serenity of the hour.

"I was seated in the noble ruins of a Roman Temple, which had always been one of the most favourite places of resort for me and Rinaldi, and now the tranquillity of the hour, the silence which reigned around, broken only at intervals by the gentle murmuring of the breeze, recalled to my memory the many blissful moments we had passed together on this very spot; and every observation Rinaldi had at different times breathed in my ear, came as fresh and as vividly upon my recollection as if they had only been uttered the previous moment. I could almost imagine that he stood by my side, and that I again heard the tender accents of his voice. The delusion was a blissful though a melancholy one, and I wished for nothing to break the spell.

"It was here that Rinaldi had first ventured to confess his love, and it was on just such another beautiful evening as the one I have been describing, that those vows were mutually exchanged between us. Alas! we little then anticipated the troubles that were in store for us. Sanguine with hope, we looked only at the sunny side of the prospect, and saw not the heavy clouds that were impending over us, the fearful storm that was about to burst upon our heads. My tears flowed fast at the melancholy retrospection, and convulsive sobs heaved my bosom.

"Again I took forth the treasured resemblance of Rinaldi from my bosom, and gazed upon it with feelings of agony, which it would be a fruitless task for me to seek to describe. The eyes seemed fixed with an earnest and melancholy expression upon my countenance, and I could almost imagine that the lips moved, and that I could hear the tones of his voice addressing me in the same tender strain as on the joyous occasion to which I have alluded.

"I was suddenly aroused by hearing a rustling sound near me, and hastily raising my eyes, you may easily conceive my alarm, signora, when I beheld the dark shadow of a human form on the opposite wall.

"I could not repress a faint scream of terror, and not venturing to look around me, I was about to hurry as fast as my trembling limbs would permit me, when I found my progress suddenly and rudely arrested by a man's hand grasping my wrist, and looking up, my eyes encountered the hated features of Rudolphi.

"Overcome with terror, my limbs tottered beneath me—I made an effort to speak, but could not—my brain turned giddy—my heart sank within me—I was powerless for resistance—a mist floated before my eyes, and with a piercing shriek, I became insensible.

CHAPTER XXI.

THE NARRATIVE OF THE ROBBER'S WIFE CONTINUED.

"How long," continued Theresina, "I had remained in this state, it is impossible for me to say, but I was suddenly aroused to consciousness by feeling the heartless and daring ruffian's odious kisses on my lips, and found that he held me firmly locked in his embrace, and that he was gazing upon me with looks that smote my heart with horror and disgust.

"I struggled hard to release myself from the villain's hold, but in vain, and I made the air resound again with my cries for help.

"'Lovely Theresina,' he exclaimed, 'you call in vain; resistance is all to no purpose. Long have I watched for this opportunity, and now that it is presented to me, I will not fail to take every advantage of it. Oh, what rapture does it afford me to hold you thus in my arms, where there is no one to watch my actions, or to interrupt me in my purpose.'

"'Villain!' I ejaculated, again trying to break from his hold, 'release me, as you value your life and your soul's eternal salvation. What would you have with me? What are your monstrous designs?'

"'To repeat to you my vows of love, of adoration,' he replied. 'Once more to offer you my hand and fortune, and to endeavour to conquer your obstinacy and scorn. Why should the drivelling fool, Rinaldi, possess such powerful influence over your affections? Banish him from your thoughts, Theresina, for he can never be your's, and even ere now he has doubtless transferred his attentions to some other maiden, and laughs at your weakness and folly in being so easily deluded by him.'

"Base calumniator!' I cried, my bosom swelling with indignation, 'were your deeply injured brother here to defend himself, you would not dare to give utterance to these cowardly aspersions. If anything could have been wanting to complete the abhorrence in which I have ever held you, it would have been your present atrocious conduct. Begone, wretch! or most assuredly the vengeance of outraged Heaven will descend upon your head.'

"'Indeed, fair damsel,' he returned, with the utmost coolness and indifference, 'it would be wisdom in you not to venture to try my patience and forbearance too far. I make you a fair, an honourable, and generous offer; by all my hopes, I will not be thwarted in my wishes. If you still refuse to listen with a favourable ear to my vows, though it is far from my wishes to proceed to such extremities, I am fully resolved, if you still continue obstinate, to obtain that by force which you will not yield to my solicitations.'

"Oh, signora, you may judge what my feelings of disgust and horror were at this moment. My situation was fearful, I saw that the villain was desperate, and there was no one at hand to protect me, or to rescue me from his power. What was to be done? how could I help myself? Again I made a desperate effort to release myself from his hold, but it was in vain. What could I do in his powerful grasp? Again he attempted to imprint his hateful kisses on my lips, and once more I made the air resound with my cries for assistance. Suddenly the voices of men replied to my screams, and I could hear footsteps rapidly approaching the ruins! Rudolphi released me from his hold, and started back a few paces confused, and giving utterance to a fearful oath. I took advantage of the moment, and darted towards that part whence the sound of the persons approaching issued, but my strength was exhausted, and I sank inanimate on the earth.

"When I recovered my senses, I found myself reclining on a couch in my own chamber, and my mother hanging affectionately and anxiously over me. Oh! what a relief was this to my mind, and how grateful was I to Heaven for my preservation!

"It appeared that my parents, having felt alarmed at the unusual length of my absence from home, had despatched two or three of their domestics in search of me, and knowing that the ruins of the temple was one of my favourite places of resort, they had fortunately first directed their search there, and, as I have shown, just arrived in time to rescue me from the power of the villain Rudolphi; but before

they had entered the ruins he had contrived to make his escape by another way, and thus they were in entire ignorance as to the cause of my alarm, and the situation in which they found me.

"I need not state to you, signora, the indignation of my parents when I was able to make them acquainted with the facts, and my father was determined to lose no time in demanding satisfaction from the miscreant who had committed so brutal an outrage, though I would fain have persuaded him not to do so at present, nor until his feelings were a little less excited.

"The following morning he repaired to the castle of the Count Manfredoni, and after explaining to him the circumstances which had taken place, demanded to see Rudolphi immediately, and to receive every satisfaction from him for his villanous conduct.

"The count, however, affected the greatest surprise and incredulity; declared that his son had not been to the castle for several weeks, and that he had every reason to believe that he was not in England. My father could obtain no satisfaction from the count, and he was forced to return home in the same state of doubt and apprehension, but with a firm determination to keep a sharp look-out after Rudolphi, who it was evident must be concealed somewhere in the neighbourhood, and whose designs were now made perfectly apparent.

"It was several days before I could recover from the shock which this alarming adventure had occasioned me, and I then hesitated to make Rinaldi acquainted with the circumstances, lest his alarmed resentment should precipitate him into some rash act, and tempt him to brave all consequences by hastening to my protection; but, upon mature consideration, I thought it would be most prudent not to keep it concealed from him, and I therefore despatched a letter to him, in which, after not disguising anything that had taken place, I earnestly requested he would endeavour to calm his feelings, and not to venture to return home for the present, which might only be productive of results which I feared to contemplate.

"The answer which I received was such as I might have expected. Rinaldi was swelling with indignation, and vowed that if his brother persisted in his villanous designs, nothing should prevent him from seeking a terrible revenge, as his conduct had completely broken all ties of nature between them.

"Nothing more particular occurred for several weeks; Rudolphi still remained concealed, and we now all of us began to hope that he had indeed left the country; but still I did not venture to resume my accustomed walks, lest any danger might threaten me; for I could not believe that he would so readily abandon his designs, and I knew not how soon he might attempt to put them into execution.

"But another calamity was awaiting me of a still more awful nature than any I had ever before experienced; and, as I now recall it to my mind, I shudder with horror, and wonder that I could ever find strength to support it."

"My father had occasion to travel some distance from home, in order to receive a considerable sum of money, and when he departed the most dismal forebodings arose to my mind, and that of my mother, which he in vain sought to dissipate. Alas! how fearfully were they realised.

"My poor father had promised faithfully to return at a certain time, and he was always very punctual. The time arrived, but he came not. Another day and a night elapsed, and still he remained absent, and my mother and myself became most seriously alarmed, and we lost no time in despatching a letter to the residence of the gentleman whither he had gone, to know whether he was still remaining with him, or, if not, what time he had departed on his return home.

"Before, however, we could receive any answer to this letter, the melancholy and dreadful intelligence was conveyed to us that my unfortunate father had been found barbarously murdered in a wood only a few miles from home, and there could be no doubt that the hideous crime had been perpetrated by robbers, as he was plundered of every coin of the large sum of money he had had about him.

"Oh, God! how horrible was our anguish on the receipt of this terrible intelligence; we both became insensible, and I remember no more for several days.

"And when I was restored to a state of consciousness, how doubly awful was the suffering that awaited me. The dreadful shock of her husband's untimely death was too much for the strength of my poor mother to undergo. Her senses had entirely fled, and she was lying at the last point of death. What a mercy would it have been for me had I experienced the stroke of death at the same time. Only five short days after the discovery of my murdered father's corpse my mother breathed her last, and thus was I by this terrible blow, left alone in the world."

CHAPTER XXII.

THERESINA'S TALE CONCLUDED.

"Alas! Theresina," said Olympia, compassionately, when the robber's wife arrived at this part of her narrative, "your troubles have indeed been great, and sincerely do I pity you."

"Ah, signora," replied her companion, "those, indeed, are terrible that I have related

already; but I was destined to suffer many, many more."

"For several weeks after the death of my parents, I remained in a frantic state, and it was wonderful how I ever recovered my senses. When I did, and was enabled to inquire into my affairs, I found that by some means or other, which I have never been able to penetrate, my father's circumstances had become so involved that I found myself not only left an orphan in the wide and cheerless world, but also in a condition bordering upon destitution.

"What was now to become of me? I reflected—I had no relations living to whom I could apply for protection or advice. I was driven to madness, and it is wonderful that in such a dreadful situation as that in which I found myself, I was not hurried on to lay violent hands upon myself.

"I made Rinaldi acquainted with my dreadful situation, and implored his advice. I did not attempt to persuade him not to hasten to me, for to whom could I so confidently look for consolation and protection, as he whom I was convinced so ardently loved me. But two days elapsed, and I heard nothing from him, and my heart misgave me. Could he have abandoned me, now that such unparalleled misfortune had overtaken me? Oh, no, to encourage such a thought as that would be worse even, if possible, than all that had happened.

"I had been compelled to dismiss all but one faithful female attendant, and she evinced the same affection for me as if she had been my own sister.

"It happened, however, that on the third evening after I had despatched the letter to Rinaldi, she had occasion to go to a distant village on an errand, and I was left alone.

"I sat for some time in a state of mind of which you may form a proper conception, signora; but my attendant did not return. Still my thoughts were too busily occupied with other subjects to cause me to feel any alarm.

"Suddenly I heard footsteps ascending the stairs, but imagining it was Lauretta, I took no particular notice of it. There was not much time, however, given me for reflection; for the room door was suddenly thrown open, and what was my astonishment and alarm, when I beheld the tall figure of a man enveloped in a dark mantle, and his hat slouched down over his eyes, enter the room.

"I screamed, but he rushed towards me, and seizing me in his arms, exclaimed in the well known voice of the villain Rudolphi—

"'Silence, Theresina, for I am determined; and now, at any rate, you are in my power. Yes, we are alone, and nothing shall now prevent the execution of my purpose.'

"'Inhuman monster!' I cried, 'dare you thus contaminate me by your presence so soon after the dreadful calamities that have befallen me, and now you see me left without a friend or protector in the world? Away, wretch! or I will invoke the sainted spirits of my unfortunate parents, and——'

"' Nay, Theresina,' he interrupted, while the expression of his countenance showed the determination of his purpose, ' I am not to be intimidated from the execution of my designs by any such threats as those you have just held out. On a former occasion, when I offered you my hand, you treated me with scorn, and by a

STORALDI'S PROPOSITION TO RELEASE COUNT ALBERTI D'AMALFI.

mere accident you were rescued from my power; but I need not entertain any such fears now, and I have made up my mind to be far less scrupulous than I have hitherto been. I told you, on the occasion to which I have alluded, that you might have reason to repent of your obduracy, and you will find that my words are true. I came not here to sue, but to demand; so prepare yourself, for this night the triumph I have so long sought shall be complete.'

"' God of Heaven !' I cried, terrified by his looks, 'must this be? Is there no one here to save me from such a monstrous, such a horrible fate? Rudolphi, I beseech you to have mercy on me, and do not attempt to commit a crime which must stamp you ever afterwards as a monster of iniquity of the blackest dye.'

"'You supplicate in vain,' replied the heartless wretch; even now, as I gaze upon you, your transcendant charms inflame my passion still more, and I exult in the opportunity which is thus afforded me. Come then, fair but scornful maiden, let us no longer delay; thus I claim and seize the prize I have long been so anxious to obtain. There is no one here who now can rescue you from my power.'

"He seized me in his arms as he spoke; I uttered a piercing shriek, but my strength was exhausted, and I had no power to resist the monster in his diabolical design, but just at that critical and dreadful moment a voice, which went to my very soul, exclaimed in tones of thunder—

"'Hold! cowardly, atrocious miscreant—hold!'

"At the same instant Rudolphi uttered a cry of agony, and relinquishing his hold of me, sunk bleeding on the floor, for his side had been penetrated by a stiletto. Hastily I turned my gaze towards the person who had come to my rescue, and I uttered an appalling shriek, and became unconscious of everything around me, when I beheld that it was my lover Rinaldi!"

"Good God! is it possible that Rinaldi should thus have become the murderer of his own brother?" said Olympia with a look of astonishment and horror.

"It is true, signora," replied Theresina, "but was he to blame? Was it not in saving me, whom he so fondly loved, from the terrible fate to which Rudolphi would have consigned me, that the deed was committed? And had not that brother, by his cruelty and treachery, forfeited all claim to the ties of kindred blood? But believe me, signora, that dreadful are the years of suffering I have undergone since that awful night."

"I believe it, Theresina," said Olympia, "but most sincerely do I pity you."

"Pity me, signora?" replied the robber's wife; "aye, I am grateful even for that, because it is not the phraseology that many individuals would apply to their less fortunate fellow creatures; but still it is a term that generally appears shallow and contemptible to me. I ask not for pity—unless I have, through absolute viciousness committed myself—but sympathy for my weakness, if I have not done so, and a just appreciation of the motives which guided my conduct."

"Pardon me, Theresina," said Olympia, rather confused by the energy of her manners, "I mean not to insult you, or to wound your feelings."

"I feel assured you did not, lady," returned the robber's wife; "and I must request, in return, that you will pardon me for any apparent hasty language I may have made use of. My brain is sometimes distracted; and can you marvel at it, after the extraordinary troubles I have experienced?"

"No, indeed I cannot," responded Olympia.

"Did not Rudolphi contemplate one of the most cowardly, and at the same time the most atrocious of crimes?"

"Very true."

"Had he not, according to what I have stated, been the sole cause of all the miseries that attended us? Had he not prejudiced the mind of the Count Manfredoni, his father, against my unfortunate husband? Was it not through him that he was rendered a complete outcast from the paternal bosom;—banished from his country, and made to endure all the pangs of blighted hopes, to forward the diabolical plans of his elder brother?"

"Yes, yes, I do indeed believe you," said Olympia. "But still it was most lamentable and unfortunate that his should have been the hand which shed his brother's mortal blood. I can with difficulty, I must admit, Theresina, recognize the amiable and virtuous, the honourable and forbearant neglected son of the Count Manfredoni, in the reckless and daring robber chief, Rinaldi."

"The impression is a natural one, I admit, signora," returned Theresina; "but I pray you take all the circumstances into your most generous consideration. It was no premeditated murder on the part of Rinaldi; while, on the other hand, Rudolphi had not only for a long series of years done all he possibly could to murder his brother's prospect, but likewise to accomplish the basest of purposes against an innocent female. Who was the criminal?—Heaven has answered the question in the terrible retribution it brought upon the head of Rudolphi by the hands of his innocent victim, his own brother. Oh, signora, had you known the virtues of my wretched husband, till trouble and injustice drove him to despair and desperation, you would not feel astonished at the energy with which I advocate his cause."

"I can duly understand your feelings, Theresina," replied the fair prisoner, "and admire them. I only regret that you and your husband should be placed in the degraded situation which you now are, and would feel happy to see you restored to that position in society, it appears to me evident you are formed to ornament."

"It is too late," replied Theresina; "there is a price set upon my husband's head. Could they take him, they would execute him like a dog. Time, as I have before observed to you, has completely changed his nature. He is not the same Rinaldi that he was twenty years ago;

he has become inured to his present perilous course of life—he has learned to love it ; and is it to be marvelled at, when, in what is called the world, he met with nothing but enemies, or shallow pretenders ; sycophants, who, while they wore the mask of friendship, were waiting to take advantage of his credulity and inexperience, whenever they had the opportunity ; whilst those over whom he now holds command, coarse and uncultivated though they may be, have never attempted to deceive him, or injure him by word or deed, are strictly devoted to him, and, I firmly believe, would to a man lay down their lives to serve him. They are outcasts from society, the principal portion of them, but, like himself, been made so through no faults of their own, but by the cruel and unjust acts of those to whom they had an undoubted right to look for everything just, upright, generous, and impartial—upon whom they had every claim ; then, is it surprising that those who have suffered so severely from mankind, should hate and wage war upon mankind ? They have been educated (if so I may term it) in a desperate and villanous school, and no marvel that they should become villains and desperadoes. These may appear harsh and atrocious observations, signora, but they are nevertheless just and appropriate. Time was when, like yourself, I should have shuddered at them, but woful experience has taught me better. Time was when I viewed all mankind through only one medium—when I measured them only by my own thoughts and principles ; but there again, woful experience has taught me better. It is no fault that I and Rinaldi are what we are, but that the vices and injustice of our fellow creatures have precipitated us from the height we formerly occupied in the scale of human beings. We owe mankind no respect, we owe them nothing but hatred ; our natural dispositions have become deformed, degenerated, through their dire agency, and what is left for us but retaliation ?—But pardon me, signora, I am digressing from the subject of my melancholy narrative. Would you wish to have the conclusion of it ?"

"Most undoubtedly, Theresina," replied Olympia, who was struck and astonished by the force and eloquence of her arguments ; " but surely you cannot be so ungenerous as to condemn the whole of mankind for the faults of a few ?"

"Oh, no," returned the robber's wife ; "Heaven forbid that I should do so ; but can you wonder at the feelings and sentiments I have expressed, after the unmerited sufferings it has been my hard lot to. undergo ?—Can you wonder that I should give utterance to those sentiments in language so warm, when you reflect upon what my agony must be on contemplating the dreadful change that has come over the dispositions and the circumstances of

myself and my husband ?—No, I am sure you cannot ; and you will therefore forgive me for the language which my excited feelings have caused me to use."

" But surely your husband cannot have become so callous to every sense of humanity or feeling towards that sex to which you say he was once one of the most devoted slaves, as to pander to the vices of such a heartless miscreant as my betrayer, the Count Alberti, by holding me at his mercy ? He will surely yield to my supplications, and restore me to liberty ?"

Theresina shook her head.

"Rinaldi," she remarked, " is under considerable obligations to the young count ; he is pledged to serve him ; he has tried to forget his former self ; he is now merely the robberchief, and in whatever he has pledged himself, he will not break his word."

" But you," added Olympia emphatically.

" I am his wife—his devoted wife, lady," answered Theresina, " and bound to obey him. I can sympathise with you, but cannot, dare not assist you."

" Alas ! alas ! then," sighed Olympia, " there is no hope for me."

"Say not so, signora ; there is no knowing what may transpire to release you from your present situation. But of this rest assured, that confinement is the only thing that Rinaldi will consent to inflict on you or your innocent offspring. He is no lover of bloodshed, and nothing, I am convinced, would induce him to shed the blood of an innocent woman. But shall I resume my tale ?"

"Yes," answered Olympia, "I feel deeply interested in it, and beg to apologize for having thus interrupted you."

Theresina paused a few seconds to collect her thoughts, and then went on with her narrative in the following words :—

" On awaking again to sensibility from the dreadful scene which I have recorded, I looked anxiously around me, and found myself in a strange apartment, but with Lauretta—my faithful Lauretta, and a prepossessing looking old woman, whom I understood to be her mother—sitting by my bedside.

" For some time I was perfectly unconscious of what had really happened, and only wild and indefinable dreams flitted across my imagination. But suddenly the fearful truth rushed with overwhelming force across my brain, and then I inquired, in frantic tones, what had become of Rinaldi.

" ' He is quite safe, my dear signora,' replied Lauretta, ' pray rest yourself contented upon that point. You will see him, no doubt, before long.'

" ' Thank Heaven !' I exclaimed, fervently, and clasping my hands ; ' then he has not perished ?'

" ' God forbid !' ejaculated Lauretta.

"'But where am I?' I eagerly demanded; 'how came I hither?'

"'This is the residence of my mother, lady,' replied Lauretta, 'and you were brought hither at my suggestion, by the order of Signor Rinaldi.'

"'And you are sure he is quite safe, Lauretta?' I again demanded.

"'Quite, signora,' was the answer; 'rest yourself perfectly satisfied, as I have before said, that he is so.'

"'But Rudolphi?'

"Lauretta shuddered, and my worst surmises were confirmed.

"'Ah, he is dead, then,' I gasped forth, with a look of the most intense horror; 'and Rinaldi, unhappy Rinaldi, is the murderer of his own brother!'

"So powerful and horrible was the effect which this thought had upon me, that my blood seemed congealed in my veins, and I again almost relapsed into a state of insensibility.

"Lauretta and her mother did all that they could to console me, and at length they succeeded sufficiently to communicate the whole of the painful particulars to me.

"It appeared that Rinaldi, on the receipt of my last communication, was plunged into a state of the most absolute despair on finding the dreadful calamities that had befallen me, and determined at all hazards to fly to my protection.

"This he did, and arrived in the neighbourhood on the very eventful evening of which I have been speaking, and made his way immediately towards my residence.

"He had arrived within half a mile of the house I occupied, when, in passing a rather lonely spot, his ears were saluted by the half stifled moans of some human being, apparently in great pain.

"He instantly hurried towards the spot from whence the sounds issued, and there, to his astonishment, by the light of the moon, which was shining brightly at the time, beheld a female form extended upon the earth in a state of insensibility.

"He raised her, and then, to his increased astonishment and alarm, discovered that it was my faithful attendant Lauretta.

"She appeared to be suffering more from fright than from any actual injury she had received, and in a short time she was restored to a state of consciousness, and, as you may imagine, she was not a little surprised to find herself supported in the arms of Rinaldi.

"My lover having tranquillized the poor girl's feelings, eagerly inquired after me, and how it was that he had found her in such a situation.

"The account which Lauretta gave was, that having completed the errand upon which she had been sent, she was on her return home, when, on reaching the spot where Rinaldi had found her, a man enveloped in a dark mantle suddenly sprang from behind an adjacent enclosure and grasped her vehemently by the arm.

"She screamed aloud with terror, which was increased when she discovered that the man who held her was no other than the villain Rudolphi.

"'Hold your cries, girl,' exclaimed the ruffian, pointing a dagger at her breast, 'at the peril of your life I command you to cease this noise.'

"'What would you with me, signor?' asked the terrified Lauretta.

"'You are the principal attendant and confidant of Signor Theresina, are you not?' he demanded.

"Lauretta replied in the affirmative.

"'I must have access to her,' said the ruffian, 'secretly, this very night, and you must be the means of achieving my object.'

"'Never!' boldly returned Lauretta, 'you shall take my life first.'

"'Rash fool!' Rudolphi cried, 'do you know to whom you speak?'

"'Yes,' replied the intrepid girl, 'to Rudolphi, son of the Count Manfredoni, and one who has proved himself a villain, and the Signora Theresina's greatest enemy.'

"She had scarcely given utterance to the words when the brutal and unmanly ruffian felled her to the earth by a violent blow, and she remembered no more until Rinaldi so fortunately discovered her in the manner I have described.

"The rage and alarm of Rinaldi, when he heard the account, you may easily imagine, but that was increased when Lauretta, on searching herself, discovered that she had been robbed of a bunch of keys, by which the villain would be enabled to gain access to my residence, and probably carry his diabolical designs into execution.

"He saw at once that there was not a moment to be lost, and Lauretta having recovered herself, they hastened with all possible speed to my house; Rinaldi being accompanied by one servant alone.

"One key which opened a private door Lauretta discovered had fortunately escaped Rudolphi's observation, and therefore there would be no difficulty in gaining admittance to the house, and taking the miscreant by surprise. What followed, I have already related.

"It was a most remarkable circumstance that Rinaldi should arrive at such a critical time, and that his should be the hand to work the retribution of Heaven against his guilty brother. Would to God that some other hand had been destined to perpetrate the deed; what years of misery and bitter remorse it would have saved me.

" Rudolphi had come wholly unattended upon his diabolical design.

"Rinaldi was completely horrorstruck when he discovered that his guilty brother was no more ; and he was so bewildered, that he scarcely knew how to act.

" The dead body was at length placed upon a couch, and he and Lauretta then applied themselves towards endeavouring to restore me to sensibility, but this they found impossible, and as the danger of remaining where they were was most imminent, they consulted with each other what was best to be done.

"Lauretta at length proposed that I should be removed to the house of her mother, which was about a league distant, with the least possible delay, and undertook to obtain a vehicle to convey me thither.

" Rinaldi could see no other course, and he therefore agreed to it, and Lauretta departed to procure the conveyance.

" During the brief time she was absent, Rinaldi, having in some degree collected his mind, wrote a letter to the Count Manfredoni, describing minutely the whole particulars of the dreadful affair. Lauretta, on her return, found a trustworthy messenger to convey this letter to the count, and then having hastily packed up such moveables and valuable articles as she conveniently could, they bore me from the house, and having placed me in the vehicle, and entered themselves, they departed with all possible expedition to the residence of Lauretta's mother, where, I need not say, I was received with every kindness and attention, and every means were resorted to, to restore me to sensibility.

" I was given to understand that I had remained in the same state of unconsciousness for two days, during which time the agony which Rinaldi endured, it would be impossible for me to convey any adequate idea of. He found that I had received a shock from which I should never recover, or that, if I did, the crime he had committed, although it was to rescue me from a most hideous fate, would cause me to look upon him with feelings of horror and repugnance, and that thus all the hopes he had formed would be entirely annihilated, and there would be nothing left for him but the most unbounded misery and despair.

"Need it be wondered that he was driven to a state almost bordering upon madness, and that, had it not been for the excellent counsel of Lauretta and her amiable mother, who exerted all their energies to console and encourage him, he would have been tempted to lay violent hands upon himself ?

" There were moments even when he was half resolved to resign himself into the hands of the law, and to risk the fate which might be awarded him for the crime he had so accidentally committed, and in the perpetra-

tion of which he was almost justified by the guilty conduct of his brother.

" ' But where is the unhappy Rinaldi concealed ?' was almost my first question on recovering my senses : ' oh, tell me, I beseech you, and do not attempt to deceive me ; is he still at liberty ?—Has he been able to escape detection ?'

" ' Do not alarm yourself, my dear signora," replied Lauretta ; ' as I have before told you, Signor Rinaldi is perfectly secure, although large rewards are offered for his apprehension, and a most vigilant search is being made for him in all parts of the country. There are only a few individuals who are acquainted with the residence of my mother, and on them I know I can depend. Signor Rinaldi, completely disguised, is concealed in a cavern among the mountains, not far from here, where I have been constantly in communication with him, and most anxious is he to meet you, as soon as you feel that you are in a fit condition to see him.'

" 'Oh, God !' I ejaculated, clasping my hands with agony, ' what a trial will that be to us both, and yet I feel that he was not to blame. Alas ! alas ! what is now to become of us both ? We are ruined—irretrievably lost —henceforth rendered outcasts upon society ; and Rinaldi, who is branded with the name of murderer, will be hunted down to inevitable destruction, and consigned to an ignominious fate, like a wild beast. Oh, that I had died at the same time as my unfortunate parents !'

" ' For Heaven's sake, my dear signora,' said the compassionate Lauretta, ' do not give way to these sad thoughts ; you and Signor Rinaldi have little or nothing to reproach yourselves for ; the fate of Rudolphi was caused entirely by his own base conduct, and it is a terrible but just punishment for his crimes.'

" ' But what is to become of me and Rinaldi ?' I again demanded, with a burst of agony ; ' we are left entirely destitute ; we have not a friend in the world, and what is left to us but misery and despair ?'

" ' Say not so, signora,' returned Lauretta, "for gloomy as I must admit your present prospects are, the Almighty, who watches over the good and innocent, will not desert you, depend upon it, in this your time of severe trial.'

. " Thus did the faithful Lauretta and her mother endeavour to console and encourage me, and at length they succeeded much better than could have been at all imagined, and I consented to see Rinaldi at midnight, when he might venture out of the place of his concealment with safety.

" I will not make a futile attempt to describe that meeting, for your imagination, signora, I am certain, can much better depicture it. For some time the agony of our grief almost deprived us of reason, and it was long ere we could regain sufficient tranquillity to talk rationally upon our awful and perilous situation, and to consult what was best to be done.

"Every effort was being made by the Count Manfredoni to discover his unfortunate son, and it was evident that, should he be detected, he would pursue him with his vengeance as far as the law would allow him.

"But was my love for Rinaldi diminished by the dreadful event which had taken place? Oh, no; it was increased, if possible, tenfold. I would willingly have laid down my life to save him, and when I thought of the frightful sacrifice he had made for my sake, my mind was driven to a state bordering upon distraction. Can you wonder at my devotion, signora, when you take all the circumstances into consideration, and you, who have so well known what it is to love with an ardour, an intensity, such as I did?"

"Oh, no," replied Olympia, with a sigh;— "you would have been unworthy of the name of woman had you deserted the man, who had been so faithful to you, in his misery."

"I should, signora," coincided Theresina, "and so I thought, and that made me decide at once upon the course I afterwards pursued. I vowed that, let whatever might be the consequences, I would never abandon him; that henceforth I should consider my fate as linked to his; and that at the first opportunity I would become his wife; and that whatever our future fortunes might be, we would share them together."

"Nobly resolved," said Olympia, "such would have been my determination had I been placed in the same painful circumstances as yourself. But proceed with your narrative, Theresina, for I am deeply interested in it."

"When we had recovered sufficiently to talk calmly," resumed Theresina, "we consulted what was best to be done. Our situation was most desperate. We were surrounded by danger, and apparently the most insurmountable difficulties on every side, and how to escape from them we knew not. We did not imagine that we could remain long where we were without being discovered, for the search that was being made after us was most vigilant; but whither could we go? How make our escape to some distant part of the country, where we might reside unknown, and without suspicion? This was indeed a difficult question to answer, and we bewildered our brains for some time in endeavouring to do so.

"Our pecuniary means were very limited, but sufficient to support us for a year or two, and when they were exhausted, what was to become of us?

"However, at last we determined to trust to Providence, and endeavoured to hope for the best. By degrees we became more calm and reconciled to our fate, but were miserable when we were not in each other's society.

"Lauretta and her mother paid us every possible attention, and indeed they were now the only friends we had in the wide world, and but for them I shudder to think of the fate which must have befallen us.

"I never ventured to stir from the house, and Rinaldi only visited me at night, and was so disguised that it would have been impossible for any one to recognize him, even those who were most intimately acquainted with him. Thus we felt ourselves for the present secure, though we knew not how long it might last, and were consequently in a constant state of dread and anxiety.

"In this manner six weary months passed away, when we were visited by another misfortune which we little anticipated, and from which it was a long time before we could recover. Poor Lauretta was attacked with a sudden illness, which, notwithstanding all the efforts that were made to save her, proved fatal in the short space of three days, and thus were we unfortunately deprived of our best and most faithful friend.

"This was a severe blow to us, and it was some time before we could recover from it. As for poor Lauretta's mother, she was completely inconsolable, and we expected every day to see her sink under the heavy visitation. In the course of time, however, she recovered, and a fresh source of alarm and anguish then awaited us.

"We received information from a friend of Lauretta's mother, who was in our confidence, that those who were in search of us, had obtained some clue to the place of our concealment, and that consequently it would be no longer safe for us to remain where we were.

"This was fearful intelligence for us, and we were completely bewildered how to act. But there was no time for delay; destruction stared us in the face, and flight was inevitable. But whither could we go? How could we avoid the threatened danger? Where could we in future conceal ourselves?

"In this dilemma the old woman at last came to our aid. She remembered a distant relative whom she had residing in a remote part of the country, and whom she had no doubt would receive us kindly on her recommendation, and thither we resolved to go.

"Everything was arranged with the utmost secrecy and expedition, and the following night, disguised in the most careful manner, we started on our weary and hazardous journey

"We parted from Lauretta's mother with the deepest regret, and the poor old woman evinced as much sorrow as if we had been her own children. We, however, promised to correspond with her at every opportunity, and that in some measure reconciled her to our separation.

"I should doubtless become tedious, signora," continued Theresina, "were I to recount the particulars of all that occurred to us on that dreary journey—the fatigue we underwent, and the many hair-breadth escapes we had; but at length we arrived in safety at the place of our destination, and presenting the letter of recommendation and explanation, which Lauretta's mother had written, were received in the most kind and respectful manner.

"The house was admirably adapted for a place of concealment, as it was situated in a most secluded part. It was inhabited by an old man and his wife who were in rather comfortable circumstances, and who were likewise possessed of every excellent quality of heart to recommend them.

"We did not hesitate to make them acquainted with every particular of our melancholy history, and they deeply commiserated with our misfortunes, and endeavoured to comfort us and to reconcile us to our fate. In a few days we felt ourselves quite at home, and our apprehensions of discovery were entirely banished.

"We had not resided here more than a month, when we were privately married, and thus our fates were indissolubly united together.

"We took a small cottage not far from the residence of our friends, and here we hoped to live unmolested and unsuspected. A short time after this we received a letter from Lauretta's mother, informing us of the death of the Count Manfredoni, which had occurred suddenly, and under mysterious and suspicous circumstances, and that he had bequeathed the whole of his large property and estates to a distant relation—thus carrying his hatred and revenge to the tomb.

"We were now compelled to think seriously upon our future prospects, for our means were nearly exhausted, and poverty and destitution stared us in the face. I need not say what hours of anguish and anxiety this reflection cost me, and we racked our brains to no purpose to devise some means for our future support.

"Rinaldi was willing to follow any honest occupation, however humble, if he could have procured it—but that he found to be impossible; and as day after day our pecuniary resources became more limited, he was unable to bear up against the contemplation of the dismal future, and gave himself up to despair.

"I strove to comfort him, and to inspire him with the hope that something would yet turn up to rescue us from the misery with which we were threatened; but all my efforts were of little or no avail, for what advice had I to offer him? Brought up to the different expectations which he had been, how little was he calculated for labour, if even he could have procured it?—and thus it appeared but too evident to him that he was shut out from every hope.

"In this manner our minds were distracted for some time, and as the gloomy aspect of our situation every day—nay, every hour, became the more threatening, and our resources rapidly diminished, it cannot be wondered at that we were reduced to the greatest despair, though I even maintained my fortitude much better than my husband. I never for a moment lost my presence of mind, and although the most dismal forebodings continually haunted my imagination, I never ceased in my efforts to soothe him, and in which our humble but honest friends also joined, although they had no power to assist us.

"While our minds were thus tortured with conflicting thoughts, our friends received the melancholy intelligence of the death of Lauretta's mother; a circumstance which it is quite unnecessary for me to state, signora, caused us all the deepest regret, and made the situation of myself and Rinaldi appear still more wretched and lonely in the world. It seemed as though Providence was about to desert us, and to leave us not a single friend in our destitution to whom we could look up for consolation, commiseration, and advice.

"But even still greater troubles were in store for us: one night, soon after we had retired to rest, we were suddenly aroused from our sleep by a loud alarm of fire, and starting up and hurrying to the window, we beheld the devouring flames and dense clouds of smoke and showers of sparks shooting far up into the heavens.

"'Good God!' I exclaimed in accents of terror, it is in the direction of the dwelling of poor old Ruganto and Nina.'

"It was too true, and so great was our agony, that for a few seconds we were at a loss how to act. Hastily we dressed ourselves, and flew towards the frightful scene of conflagration.

"Numerous persons were gathered together on the spot, and were using all their endeavours to subdue the power of the destructive element, but the flames had gained such a fearful ascendancy, that it was utterly impossible for any one to effect an entrance into the house, for certain death would have been the consequence.

"Distractedly we inquired if any one had seen Ruganto and his wife, but were answered in the negative, and there could not be scarcely any doubt, therefore, of the dreadful fate which had befallen them.

"In a very little more than an hour the

house was reduced to a heap of ruins, and then, being strictly examined the following day, our worst fears were confirmed, for the blackened corpses of old Ruganto and Nina were discovered locked in each other's arms, and burnt in a most shocking manner.

"This frightful catastrophe had a most powerful effect [upon myself and Rinaldi, and we bewailed the loss of our only friends with the most sincere grief.

"The crisis of our fate was now rapidly approaching: Rinaldi was unable to get any employment; we had not a friend in the world from whom we could seek the least assistance, and what was, therefore, to become of us? Nothing but starvation stared us in the face; and there were moments when our feelings of despair so overpowered us, that we were almost driven at once to end our misery, and to rush unbidden into the presence of our Maker; but our fearful purpose was arrested, and we were reserved, for, if possible, still greater trials.

"The long expected dreadful moment arrived, and we had no longer the means of procuring food or shelter. Every article of furniture had been disposed of to procure the common necessaries of life, and now those means were entirely exhausted, and the hardhearted man who belonged to the house we inhabited, drove us forth like dogs.

"Can I ever forget the horrors of that night, when we found ourselves for the first time houseless wanderers in the cheerless world? I am fearful that I shall harrow up your gentle and compassionate feelings, signora, by recounting them.

" was very cold and gloomy, a drizzling rain descended, which quickly penetrated through our scanty clothing, and as we had not tasted food for several hours we were indeed illprepared to struggle against the inclemency of the weather. We felt as if we could have laid ourselves down and died by the way-side, and perhaps it would have been better for us had we done so.

"We wandered on we knew not wither; all places were now alike; there was no beacon light to guide us to hope. Our limbs were so weak that they would scarcely support us, and we were several times compelled to pause on the road to rest ourselves.

"The horrors of the night increased; the moon showed not its bright face in the hemtsphere, and not a single star illumined our dreary way. The wind blew keenly around us, and every object presented an aspect which struck tenfold despair to our hearts.

"We seldom ventured to speak to each other, and then we started aghast at the hollow and almost unearthly sound of our own voices. We shuddered with the cold, and with the utmost difficulty dragged our weary limbs along.

"It is astonishing what the human frame is capable of enduring, and I have often wondered how I and my husband were enabled to bear up against the accumulated, and almost unprecedented horrors of that night, especially reduced as we were by long privation and anxiety of mind.

"At length we reached a shed situated in a lonely part of the country, Our exhausted limbs now failed us; we were unable to proceed further, and we hailed this shed with feelings of gratitude, for at least it would afford us some shelter from the inclemency of the weather, and we might probably be able to obtain a few hours' respite from our misery in sleep.

"The door was broken from its rusty hinges and afforded no obstruction to our entrance but we first cautiously listened, fearing that it might be already occupied; but no sound meeting our ears, we committed ourselves to the care of Providence and entered.

"We secured the door on the inside as well as we could, and then as well as the darkness would perimt, we examined the place more minutely. It was evident that it had not been used for some time, and to what purpose it had originally been appropriated we had no means of ascertaining.

"The roof was broken in several places, but there was one corner which was pretty well sheltered from the weather, and there we were gratified to find a heap of straw, which had probably served as a bed for some poor unfortunate wanderers like ourselves.

"Offering up our prayers to Heaven, we stretched our weary limbs upon it, and Rinaldi wrapping his mantle around us both, to shield us as much as possible from the cold, we endeavoured to compose ourselves to sleep.

"This was for some time a fruitless task, but at last, worn out by complete fatigue and anxiety of mind, it came to our relief, and we forgot our cares till the morning.

"This rest had somewhat refreshed us, and we prepared to resume our dreary journey, though we had yet no idea whither we should direct our footsteps, and we were famishing with hunger.

"Rinaldi had, however, in some measure regained his fortitude, and he endeavoured to encourage me.

"The morning was finer than the previous night, but it was very cold, and the wind seemed to penetrate to our very hearts.

"At length we arrived at a small village, and there, driven by desperate necessity to such a course, Rinaldi appealed to the charity of the humble inhabitants, and fortunately he did not appeal in vain; they supplied us with provisions as their limited means would afford, and expressed the greatest commiseration at our misfortunes.

"Having rested ourselves, we felt much

refreshed, and resumed our journey in better spirits, though Heaven knows that our prospects were as dismal as ever. Throughout the whole of that day we continued to travel, oftentimes appealing to the charity of the persons we met with on the road, but with little success, and another night of horror closed in upon us, and we found ourselves wandering in a dismal part of the country, with lofty mountains frowning upon us from every side. Where we should that night find rest and shelter we knew not, and I was so exhausted with the fatigue I had

PRINCE BIANCHI SURPRISED BY MALVOLIO, A BRAVO, WHOM HE THOUGHT DEAD.

undergone, that had it not been for the support of Rinaldi, I must have dropped on the road. But I am fearful that I tire your patience, signora, by being thus minute, and on such a melancholy theme."

"No, Theresina," replied Olympia, "indeed you do not; pray proceed. Most deeply do I sympathize with you and your husband in the dreadful sufferings it was your hard lot to encounter, and it surprises me how you were enabled to bear up against them."

"Ah, lady!" said the robber's wife, "He -

ven only knows. I cannot recall those sufferings to my memory without shuddering. But to continue,—With slow and faltering footsteps we proceeded on our way, but without the least hope of meeting with a human habitation in that wild part of the country, or any one who would compassionate our miserable condition, or afford us any relief. It would be, we felt, impossible for us to continue in this way much longer, and we saw no other prospect before us than a wretched death. We gazed at each other with ghastly looks of despair, but our tongues refused their office, and every faculty seemed to be enchained and rendered useless.

"At length the red glare of a light which seemed to proceed from a large fire at a distance burst suddenly upon our sight, and for a moment imparted to us some degree of hope. Oh, what a cheerful sight was this to us poor wanderers.

"'Bear up, my Theresina,' said Rinaldi, 'this light probably proceeds from some human habitation, where we may procure a few hours' rest, and permission to warm our weary limbs. Courage, courage, and we shall soon arrive at the spot.'

"His words did encourage me, and we proceeded as fast as our strength would permit us towards the place from whence the light issued, and evidently approached it nearer. But our hopes were, in some measure, diminished when we perceived that the fire blazed from among the mountains.

"'Alas!' I sighed, 'I fear, Rinaldi, that there is no chance of any relief here; who but robbers would infest these mountains?'

"'And if they should be,' replied Rinaldi, 'what have two such wretched and destitute wanderers as ourselves to fear from them? They surely will not be such cowardly ruffians as to ill-use us, but, pitying our forlorn condition, will afford us relief. At any rate, we cannot be worse off than we are at present. Come, Theresina, droop not, nor give way to fruitless apprehensions, but let us hope for the best. If we remain much longer exposed to the night air, after the dreadful fatigue we have undergone, we must perish.'

"Rinaldi's words reanimated me, and without expressing any other objection, I suffered him to lead me towards the place where the fire burnt so cheerfully, and which, as we approached it nearer, seemed to proceed from the mouth of a cavern among the mountains. And now we could hear the indistinct voices of several men, succeeded at intervals by loud laughter, which seemed to confirm my first suspicions, and again inspired me with feelings of dread, which were not diminished when I beheld the dark shadows of men moving about in the glare of the light. I paused, and clung closer to my husband, trembling all over.

"'Oh, do not let us proceed further,' I said, 'they will take us to be spies upon their actions, and may revenge themselves accordingly.'

"'Nay, my Theresina,' answered Rinaldi, 'do not give way to these fears, for, trust me, they are completely erroneous. They can never imagine that two persons like ourselves would venture among them on such an errand. Our appearance must at once convince them of our miserable condition, and lawless and desperate men though they may be, they will surely pity and relieve us. Come, come—let us make the venture.'

"I mustered up all my fortitude, and yielded to my husband's wishes. Again we proceeded towards the spot, and then we discovered that our surmises were correct, for we perceived the entrance to a cavern, and heard several men engaged in conversation. We had not proceeded many paces farther when two of the men suddenly emerged from the place, and by the broad glare of the fire, which blazed within the cavern, they immediately recognised us, and darting hastily towards us, demanded in no very prepossessing accents—

"'Who are you? and how have you dared to wander near our secret haunt?'

"'We are two wretched, destitute wanderers,' replied Rinaldi, 'worn out with fatigue and hunger, and whom accident alone and the cheerful light of your fire has guided hither. For pity's sake do not ill-use us, or refuse us a shelter for a few hours. My poor wife is sinking, and cannot proceed much farther.'

"'Ah!' ejaculated one of the men, 'do you speak the truth? Are you alone?'

"'By all my hopes, signor,' replied my husband, 'I do not attempt to deceive you. We are precisely what I have represented ourselves to be, and of that you can speedily convince yourselves; we are entirely at your mercy.'

"'Advance nearer,' said the robber, 'and let us inspect you; if you have spoken the truth, you will find friends; but if you attempt to deceive us, you will pay for your boldness with your lives.'

"We obeyed, and approached the entrance of the cavern, where we perceived several other men, who surveyed us narrowly, and our wretched and careworn appearance seemed immediately to convince them of the truth of what Rinaldi had stated.

"'Well,' said one of the men who had first addressed us, 'your looks certainly seem to answer the description you gave of yourselves. Wait here a minute or two, and I will quickly return to you. Fear not; we injure not the poor and defenceless.'

"Encouraged by the robber's words, we entered the cavern, and turning round an abrupt angle, he disappeared from our sight. In a few minutes he returned, accompanied by another man, of gigantic stature, and who, from his commanding manners, seemed to be the captain of the band, as indeed he afterwards turned out to be. He surveyed both me and Rinaldi narrowly, and seemed much struck with my miserable appearance.

"'And so you are poor and shelterless?' he said.

"'Yes, signor,' replied my husband; 'the hand of misfortune has fallen heavily upon us; we are two wretched, destitute beings, without a friend in the world, or a place wherein to shelter our heads.'

"'You do indeed appear wretched enough,' said the robber, 'and as we never turn a deaf ear to the truly distressed, although our calling is wild and lawless, I am disposed to grant you the assistance you request.'

"'Thanks—many thanks, signor,' said Rinaldi; 'I can never——'

"'Nay,' interrupted the captain; 'no thanks, I require them not; you are fatigued, and need rest and refreshment. Follow me, and fear not.'

"Leaving two or three of the robbers to guard the entrance to the mountain retreat, the captain led the way, and we followed him with palpitating hearts, but with renewed confidence and hope.

"After traversing several passages, we arrived in what appeared to be the principal cavern, in which a large fire was blazing, and where a number of ferocious looking men were seated round a long table, carousing, and whose looks of scrutiny on our entrance, filled me with alarm.

"'Retire, comrades,' said the captain, addressing himself to the men, 'I would speak to these two strangers alone.'

"The robbers obeyed, and we were left alone with the captain. He invited us to take a seat nearer the fire, and then placed provisions before us, and desired us to eat heartily.

"Notwithstanding the novelty of my situation, I must confess that the manners of the robber-chief reassured me. The warmth of the fire revived me, and I therefore did as he desired, and partook moderately of the provisions which were placed before us, and which served in a great measure to recruit my exhausted strength. The captain did not offer to interrupt us while we proceeded with our meal, but eyed us with much curiosity, and his suspicions seemed to be entirely dissipated.

"When we had concluded, Rinaldi once more thanked him for his hospitality, but he again interrupted him, and observed—

"'I demand no thanks, stranger; those who really need it and deserve it, are always welcome to the assistance of Schedoni, the robberchief. But you and your wife appear to have suffered much, and require rest. We will talk further in the morning.'

"He then opened a door at the farthest extremity of the cavern, and called Inez, and a middle aged woman directly made her appearance, and seemed to eye us with no little surprise, which, however, the captain checked by a look.

"'Inez,' said the robber-chief, 'conduct these persons to one of the sleeping caverns, and see that they have every comfort.'

"Inez curtseyed with as much respect as if the person who issued those commands to her had been a nobleman; and taking up a lamp from a table, motioned us to follow her, which we did, after having bid the captain good night.

"She ushered us into a small arched cavern strewed with rushes, and in which was a bed of remarkably clean appearance, and having lighted a lamp which was suspended from the roof, she bade us good night, and disappeared.

"We secured the door on the inside, and then throwing ourselves into each other's arms, we for some minutes gave ourselves up to the feelings which almost overpowered us. The novelty of our situation was so great, that we could scarcely persuade ourselves of its reality; but we could not sufficiently return thanks to Providence, who had at least afforded us present relief, and brought us friends where we could least have expected to find them. But alas! what was our future prospect?—it was too painful to dwell upon, and we tried to banish it from our minds.

"All was now profoundly still in this cavernous retreat, and being completely exhausted with the extraordinary fatigue we had undergone, we soon fell asleep.

"We did not awake until a late hour the following morning, and we had not long arisen when there was a knock at the door, and giving admittance to the applicant, it proved to be the woman Inez, who informed us that Captain Schedoni wished to see us at the morning repast, if it was convenient for us to do so.

"We immediately arose and followed her to the cavern, or rather saloon (for now we were sufficiently recovered from our confusion and mingled terror, to take a proper survey of it, we found that it was fitted up in a style of elegance that completely astonished us, and rendered it well worthy of that appellation), where we found the robber chief alone, and who received us with true gentlemanly courtesy, and trusted that we had found the accommodation he was able to afford us, all that could have answered our expectation, and that we likewise felt better after the few hours' repose we had enjoyed. We answered him in appropriate terms, and returned our acknowledgments for the kindness we had received.

"'Yourself and the signora, signor,' he observed, 'have, you say, experienced much trouble, and are now reduced to a state of destitution?'"

"'Alas! it is too true, signor,' replied my husband, 'we have met with troubles such as happily seldom fall to the lot of human beings.'

"'And your language and general manners convince me, signor, that you and your wife were born to much higher and happier prospects than those it is now your lot to experience?' remarked Schedoni.

"'True, true,' returned Rinaldi.

"'Pardon me, signor,' said the robber chief, 'for what may sound like an impertinent and unwarrantable question, but has it been from any misconduct of your own that you are brought to this melancholy situation?'

"'By all my hopes, no,' energetically answered my husband,—'cruelty and injustice have worked the melancholy change.'

"Schedoni took two or three strides across the cavern and communed with himself; then he again turned to us, and fixing his eyes upon us earnestly for a minute or two, he asked, addressing himself to Rinaldi—

"'May I inquire your name, signor?'

"'Pardon me,' was the reply, 'my real name, for particular reasons, I wish to conceal. My origin is noble; but the name I have assumed, or rather that cruel and untoward circumstances have compelled me to assume, is Rinaldi.'

"'Rinaldi! be it so; it would ill become me to seek to penetrate your incognito. But you have received injustice from your fellow creatures?'

"'I have, the most atrocious and unmerited.'

"'And you would naturally retaliate?'

"'I seek not revenge.'

"'Pardon me, signor,' returned Schedoni, 'that may be a charitable feeling, but it is a weakness and an injustice to yourself. You will, I think, agree with me when you have lived long enough to experience as much as I have. Signor, I was probably born to as noble and happy prospects as yourself; time was when I would have shuddered at the bare idea of what the world calls dishonesty; and when I believed that all mankind were my friends—my brothers—unmerited oppression aroused me from the delusive dream; I discovered that what most of our fellows call honesty is a mockery and a snare; that he is the most respected who assumes and exercises power to himself, no matter what the form; and from that moment I cast the idle distorted phantom to the winds, and resolved to become a bold, open fronted, dishonest man, but not an hypocritical one; to wage war against that order who had driven me from my natural sphere in society, and to transfer all that I could from their overloaded coffers to the pockets, or rather to the necessities of their less fortunate fellow-creatures; that class whom it is their practice to tyrannize over,

to grind down to the lowest degree; those simple children of toil, the real producers of all wealth, and without whom their aristocratic superiors (as they think proper to call themselves) would be themselves helpless dolts, the veriest nonentities that ever arrogated to themselves the name of man. Since that time I have felt myself a happy and an *honourable* man in the lawless course I have thought proper to adopt, and can laugh to scorn and defiance the most *noble* tyrant that dares to come in contact with me.'

"We were completely astounded by the eloquence and energy of the robber chieftain's speech, and for the moment Rinaldi was unable to return him any answer.

"'Here,' continued Schedoni, after a brief pause, 'in our mountain home, we are as free as the wind that sweeps its lofty summit. No petty jealousies disturb our minds; we fear not the poisonous sting of treachery; we are all brothers, united in one cause; our whole souls devoted to our cause; our purpose each one shares alike in this our principality, one estate is equally that of all, and therefore what incentive have we to quarrelling? But excuse me, signor, I may appear to argue this point rather strangely, and too warmly; you say you have no present prospects in the world?'

"'None, none,' answered Rinaldi.

"Then become one of our gallant band,' said the robber chief, 'and trust me that all the cares which now oppress you will soon be banished from your mind, and you will learn to laugh at the world and all its woes. You are young, and probably enterprizing, then why, since the world has discarded you, why, I say, should you not (if I may be permitted to make use of the term), adopt a world of your own, enter upon a fresh career, and, at any rate, try the experiment?'

"'Oh, no, no, no,' I ejaculated, alarmed at what I then considered the dangerous sophisms which Schedoni put forth; 'what can ever reconcile one dishonourable act to the mind of that man who has ever prided himself upon his strict integrity? Signor, we owe you a lasting debt of gratitude for the kindness which you have so unostentatiously shown to us, but I beseech you do not tempt my husband into a career which I know is so strongly opposed to his nature, to all his principles.'

"'Pardon me, signora,' returned Schedoni, 'I would convince your husband by the means of fair reason and argument. But we will proceed no farther at present. Signor Rinaldi has said that he has no present place of destination; you have suffered much from the fatigue you have undergone—you are in no condition to travel—may I then be permitted to invite you to remain with me for a few days, until you have recruited your strength, and in the meantime, while you are my guests, every hospitality, kindness, and respect shall be shown to you, and you will have an opportunity of reflecting maturely upon that which I have proposed to you?'

"Rinaldi thanked him for the interest which he seemed to take in him, but at the same time assured him that he feared that no reflection he might bestow upon the subject, or any other argument which he (Schedoni) might make use of, would be sufficiently cogent for him to yield to.

"'I am much mistaken, signor,' returned the robber chief, 'and I entertain a wrong estimate of your good sense, if a few days' cool and deliberate consideration of the propositions I have made to you, does not change your opinion. But do you accept of my invitation?'

"Rinaldi looked at me earnestly for an answer; I felt myself too weak and ill to travel, and the thought of encountering the horrors and privations I had already experienced filled me with dread; and although I could not but feel the greatest repugnance at the idea of remaining amongst these lawless men, I could not refuse; to the question of Schedoni, therefore, my husband replied in the affirmative, but requested that we should not be annoyed any more than possible with the presence of the band.

"'Your wishes shall be complied with, signor,' answered Schedoni; 'and as I said before, every attention shall be paid to the comfort of yourself and your wife. But if it may not be considered taking too great a liberty, and may not serve to harrow up your feelings, may I request you to favour me with a few particulars of your history?'

"Rinaldi hesitated, for he knew not how far it might be safe to trust the robber chief with the melancholy facts. However, after some deliberation within himself, and consulting me aside, he assented, and Schedoni listened to him with the most profound attention, interest, and the deepest sympathy.

"'Your wrongs and misfortunes have certainly been very great, Signor Rinaldi,' he observed, when my husband had concluded, 'and they are quite enough to render you thoroughly disgusted with what is called the world; I pity you from my very soul, for my sufferings, and the injustice I have experienced from those where I had the least right to expect them, have been equally as great as yours. I would fain have become your friend. But of this we will speak anon. At present business calls me away, but I shall shortly return, and in the meantime you and the signora your wife will be perfectly safe. No one will dare to disobey the commands I shall issue respecting you, and Inez will attend to all your wishes during my absence. Farewell.'

"Thus saying, the robber chief took his departure, and left us to our own thoughts.

"'You will not feel surprised, signora,' continued Theresina, "that the eloquence of Schedoni should have had a powerful effect on us both, and that his gentlemanly bearing made a great impression on us, and likewise caused us to reflect and consult some time upon the propositions he had made.

"The points he had made in the course of his argument were very persuasive, and notwithstanding I endeavoured to view them in a very far different light, they did away with a great deal of the prejudice which had been created in my mind on entering the cavern.

"And what had we now to do with mankind, that we should so much respect it?—This was the question that me and my husband put to ourselves, and certainly the conclusion we were enabled to arrive at was every way favourable to the argument of Schedoni.

"But the strict integrity and honesty of our principles made us shudder at the idea of entering upon such a course as the one which Schedoni proposed. Such a predatory life was repugnant, most repugnant to all our sense of right and wrong. And yet, when we reflected upon the hopelessness of our prospects, our wretched and destitute condition, the cruelty and injustice we had experienced, I must acknowledge that we wavered and began to look upon the offer which the robber chief had made to us in a far less unfavourable point of view.

"We saw no more of Schedoni that day, and according to the commands which had been issued to her, Inez behaved to us with the utmost civility and attention. She was the wife of one of the band, and it was evident, from her manners, that she had at one time moved in a respectable station of society; in fact, everything that we had observed during the short time we had been in the robbers' cavern was calculated to prepossess us in its favour, and we could scarcely persuade ourselves that we were really amongst men who pursued so lawless and desperate a course.

"The attention that was paid us, and another night's rest, tended to recover us in a great measure from the effects of the sufferings we had undergone; but still when we reflected upon the misery of the future, and were unable to come to a fixed determination as to how we should act, or in what manner we could possibly procure an existence, I need not say that we were truly wretched; and that made us look upon the proposal of Schedoni with far less repugnance than we should otherwise have done.

"And if we entered the world again, should we not be constantly surrounded by danger? Was not a price set upon the life of my husband? and was it likely that he would always be able to escape from detection? He might be taken from me when least expected, and brought to an ignominious death upon the scaffold, and what was then to become of me? Who would throw around me the shield of protection, or guard me against the brutal calumnies of my fellow-creatures! The bare idea of this was sufficient to inspire me with horror, and to cause me to encourage thoughts which under different circumstances I should have recoiled from. But I fear you will deem me too prolix, Signora Olympia, and I will therefore hasten to the conclusion of my narrative.

"The following day we were again introduced into the presence of Schedoni, and he received us with the utmost politeness and kindness.

"After some conversation upon general topics, he turned to my husband and said—

"'Now, Signor Rinaldi, you have seen the manner in which we, lawless robbers as we are, conduct our business here, and I flatter myself that you will be at a loss to censure it. As you have seen us during the short time you have been here, so we always are; we are, in fact, one great family, sworn to fidelity towards each other, living a life of freedom and ease, and scouting gloomy sorrow from our precincts. The cares and anxieties of the world never trouble us; we have a code of laws to govern us, to which we strictly adhere, and never since I have been their captain, have I known one of my band attempt to violate them, for they know full well what the consequences would be. Tell me, Rinaldi, have you thought seriously upon the proposition I have made to you?'

"Rinaldi hesitated for a few moments, and looked to me, and he then replied—

"'I must acknowledge and thank you, Signor Schedoni, for the kindness with which you have treated me and my wife since we have been your guests; I must also candidly own that my prospects in the world are of the gloomiest description, and that I have experienced sufficient to disgust me with the world; but still I have ever been brought up in the paths of rectitude and honour; although goaded on by the most bitter poverty and destitution, I have never yet been guilty or even contemplated one dishonest act, and I cannot therefore look upon the idea of becoming a robber with any other feelings than those of the deepest repugnance.'

"'I am sorry to hear you say so, Signor Rinaldi,' returned Schedoni, with a look of disappointment and regret; 'but still I do not despair of being yet able to prevail with you. You say that you have no other prospects in the world but those of misery and want. Can you make up your mind to see your wife exposed to such severe trials, when the means are offered to you to rescue her from them? I cannot believe that you will. Think of all the horrors to which you will in all probability be exposed, and do not be rash. Do not reject the means of comfort and fortune, of liberty and independence, when they are offered to you. Reason points out to you the course you ought to pursue, and, placed in the desperate situation in which you are, you would be mad to neglect it. Here you shall meet with every attention and respect, and trust me; that time will soon inure you to so different a life to that you have hitherto moved in. Again I urge you to reflect maturely upon all that I have said, and do not come hastily to a conclusion which you may afterwards have bitter cause to regret. What say you, Rinaldi?'

"'I cannot—indeed I cannot make up my mind to become the lawless desperado; to prey upon the property of my fellow men,' replied my husband.

"'Psha!' observed the robber chief, in a tone of vexation, 'this is sheer nonsense, Rinaldi. What have you experienced from society that you should hold it in such respect? Will you then prefer becoming the wretched outcast, the wandering mendicant, to leading a life of liberty, ease, and luxury? Banish such ridiculous prejudice from your mind, and become a man. For fifteen years I have led the life I am now pursuing, and I can safely say that it has been the happiest portion of my existence. The same opportunity is offered to you, and therefore do not rashly reject it.'

"'But you will give me some further time to reflect on it, Signor Schedoni?' said Rinaldi.

"'Undoubtedly,' replied the former; 'but at the expiration of three days I shall expect your final answer.'

"'And should I then reject your offer?' said my husband.

"'Why, there will be an end to the matter,' returned Schedoni. 'I will put no restraint upon your conduct, and having pledged yourself to secresy, you shall be at liberty to depart from this cavern if you think proper.'

"Rinaldi thanked him, and they then changed the subject of their conversation, and entered into a free discussion upon various topics, in the course of which the robber chief showed himself to be a man of extraordinary intelligence, and fully proved the different spheres of life in which he had formerly been accustomed to move.

"We remained in his company during the whole of the day, and separated from him far more prejudiced in favour of him than before.

"Long and seriously did I and my husband argue the proposition Schedoni had made; it was a desperate one, but so were our circumstances; when we reflected upon all that we had suffered, and what was yet probably in store for us, we shuddered with horror, and again our resolution wavered. To be brief, at the expiration of the three days we made up our minds to accept the offer of Schedoni, and Rinaldi was duly initiated into all the rules and secrets of the band, and took the oath of fidelity.

"He soon became a great favourite among the robbers, and was unanimously elected their lieutenant, whilst in Inez I found a most agreeable companion, and soon became reconciled to my new course of life, though my fears were constantly excited for the safety of my husband whenever they were away on any of their predatory expeditions.

"We had been not more than two years with the robbers, when Schedoni, in a mountain skirmish, received a mortal wound, and Rinaldi was elected captain of the band, which situation he has now filled for more than ten years, encountering many vicissitudes and hair-breadth escapes, which have all tended greatly to change his temper, and to render him what you now behold him, signora. Ours has been a chequered life, but I think you will be ready to admit that the misfortunes we have experienced have not been entirely brought on us by any misconduct of our own; and that had it not been for the villany of Rudolphi, and the injustice of Count Manfredoni, we might still have been virtuous and happy. But it is useless to murmur at the decrees of fate, however stern they may be, and I have at last learnt to submit to them in silence."

CHAPTER XXIV.

OLYMPIA'S VAIN APPEAL TO RINALDI, THE ROBBER CHIEF.—THREATENED DANGER.— THERESINA'S HEROIC CONDUCT.—THE ESCAPE.

THUS did Theresina conclude her tale of sorrow, to which we need scarcely say that Olympia had listened with no little interest and sympathy.

"You have indeed had your share of trouble, Theresina," she remarked, "and I pity you from my very soul. But, surely, your husband, who was once so good and honourable, cannot fail to be moved by my supplications; he will not persist in detaining me a prisoner here; I, who have never injured him, and who have so many claims upon his compassion?"

Theresina shook her head.

"Alas! signora," she replied, "I am certain it would be useless to appeal to him. Many years passed in his present desperate course of life have rendered him stern and unbending; he is not the same Rinaldi that he formerly was, though I must ever remain devoted to him, and obey his every will; besides, he is under great obligations to the Count Alberti—he has sworn to aid him in all his designs, and nothing, I am satisfied, will ever induce him to break his word."

"Alas! alas, then," sighed Olympia, "what will become of me and my poor child, placed as we are at the mercy of one who has proved himself to be so heartless a villain?"

"Do not give way to any unnecessary alarm, signora," said Theresina, "for although Rinaldi will persist in holding you his prisoner, he will not be guilty, or even suffer the Count Alberti to be guilty of any other act of violence against you or your offspring. He would scorn to be guilty of any such act of ruffianism; nor do I think that Alberti has any other design in view than to keep you secure in confinement. He has fixed his thoughts, I understand, upon the fair Melina, the niece of the Prince Bianchi, and he is fearful that if you were at liberty you would present an insurmountable obstacle to the gratification of his wishes."

"Signora Melina is good and virtuous," said Olympia; "she loves Signor Florio, and can never place her affections upon such a man as Alberti."

"Probably not," replied Theresina, "but the Prince Bianchi, I am told, approves of his suit, and therefore will probably compel her to become his bride."

"If he loves her with the affection that he has ever professed to do," remarked Olympia, "he will never force her into an alliance that must be so repugnant to her feelings. Surely he can never be so cruel as to force her to become the wife of a man who has so thoroughly disgraced himself—the atrocious seducer of female innocence. But Rinaldi, again I must venture to hope that he will yield to my entreaties, and restore me to that liberty of which I have been so unjustly deprived."

"Indeed, signora," returned Theresina, "I fear it is useless for you to encourage such an idea. Should Rinaldi break his faith with the Count Alberti, it could not fail to be productive of the most fatal consequences to himself. Alberti, you must be aware, is possessed of great power, and he would not fail to exercise it for the gratification of his revenge, should Rinaldi venture to deceive him."

"But you possess great influence over your husband, do you not, Theresina?"

"True," answered the robber's wife.

"And will you not exercise it in my behalf?" eagerly asked Olympia.

"Most readily I will," was the reply, "but I fear it will be with little success."

"Surely he cannot remain unmoved. When he takes into consideration the troubles you have endured, he will pity me."

"I know he pities you, signora," returned Theresina, "but he has no alternative; he dare not offend the Count Alberti, which could scarcely fail to bring destruction upon himself and the band."

"If he would but grant me an interview," remarked Olympia, "I cannot help thinking that, in spite of all those difficulties you have mentioned, my earnest tears and supplications might be able to prevail upon him."

"Would that I could hold out to you any hope, signora, but I cannot."

"But will you not do me the favour to endeavour to persuade him to grant me the interview I request?" asked Olympia.

"I will do so," answered Theresina.

"Thanks, thanks; I feel convinced that I have at least a sympathising friend in you, Theresina."

"You do me no more than justice by that supposition, signora. But, in the meantime, seek to compose yourself, and to hope that everything will yet turn out for the best, and that the time is not far distant when you will be restored to happiness."

"Would to heaven that I could think so," said Olympia; "but alas! what prospect have I at present that such will be the case? Happiness will never again be mine. It would be madness in me to entertain such an idea. Alberti has blighted that for ever, and it would have been mercy in him to have sacrified the lives of me and my offspring at once, rather than to consign us to such a dreadful fate as this."

"Talk not thus, signora, I pray you," said Theresina, compassionately, "for, gloomy as I own your prospects are at present, depend upon it something will yet occur to banish the clouds which now obscure your destiny."

"I thank you sincerely for the sympathy you express, Theresina," said Olympia, "and would fain encourage the hopes with which you seek to inspire me; but alas! I see the utter futility of doing so. But I may depend upon your promise to prevail upon your husband to grant me an interview, may I not?"

"You may," replied Theresina; "and I only hope it may be crowned with better success than I dare venture to anticipate."

Olympia again fervently expressed her thanks, and after some further conversation they separated, and she was left to her own thoughts. Gloomy enough, as the reader may imagine, they were, and it was in vain that she exerted herself to give encouragement to the least ray of hope. The description which Theresina had given of Rinaldi, and which she had no doubt was correct to the very letter, was sufficient of itself to stifle all such feelings in her breast, and she anticipated the troubles that were yet in store for her, with the greatest dread. It was some consolation to her, however, that she had a sympathising friend in the robber's wife, and that circumstance rendered her incarceration the less intolerable; but still she feared that she had but little power to serve her,

however much she might be disposed to do so; and that thought filled her mind with despair. To think that Alberti, to whom she had, in the confidence of her love, sacrificed all that was precious to her in the world, should behave to her with such unparalleled inhumanity, drove her to a state bordering upon distraction; and for some time after Theresina left her she paced the place in which she was confined in the most disordered manner, giving utterance to the anguish of her mind in the most melancholy lamentations. She cursed the hour she was born, and in the frenzy of her feelings, if she had had the fatal means at hand, she would not have hesitated to have put a period to her wretched existence; but Providence mercifully preserved her from the perpetration of such a crime, and by degrees somewhat calmed her feelings. She saw no more of Theresina that day, but the following morning she made her appearance, bringing in the usual repast. Olympia could perceive by her looks that she had something to communicate to her, and she awaited impatiently to hear what it was.

"Tell me, Theresina," she said at length, "have you any good news for me?"

"No, signora," replied the robber's wife, "that which I have to impart is unfortunately not of a very promising description."

"Have you seen your husband?" eagerly demanded the fair prisoner.

"I have," answered Theresina.

"And spoken to him upon the subject we were conversing about yesterday?"

Theresina replied in the affirmative.

"Ah!" eagerly ejaculated Olympia; "and what has been your success?"

"No better than I expected. Rinaldi expresses the deepest sympathy in your misfortunes, signora, but he declares that he has no power to assist you; he dare not offend the Count Alberti."

"But will he not grant me the interview I seek?"

"Yes, he will see you to-morrow."

"Thank God!" exclaimed Olympia, as a ray of hope flashed across her mind. "Then surely he will not be able to withstand the fervent appeal I shall make to him?"

"Indeed, signora," remarked Theresina, "I would not have you flatter yourself with hopes which too probably will only be doomed to be disappointed. Rinaldi may and does pity you, but I have too much reason to believe that nothing will induce him to break his promise to the Count Alberti."

"Alas! alas!" sighed Olympia, "then what will become of me?"

"I exerted all my powers of persuasion, signora," observed Theresina, "but with little or no effect. As I have before told you, my husband is under great obligations to Alberti, and any attempt on his part to deceive him, would be almost certain to be followed by the destruction of himself and his band. But why do you give way to these feelings of agony and despair? 'Tis true you are a prisoner; but you may depend upon it, that beyond that restriction, no harm shall come to you or your child, and that all the comfort that this place can afford shall be at your command."

" Oh, God !" ejaculated Olympia, wringing her hands, " what comfort can I expect to find with these thoughts distracting my brain? Would that myself and my poor little innocent

PIETRO (THE FALSE GUIDE) DELUDES COUNT DI STROZZI.

were at rest in the silent grave—we have no friends in this world."

She hugged her infant frantically to her heart as she gave utterance to these melancholy observations, and her tears of anguish flowed fast upon its face. Theresina again tried to tranquillize her feelings, but with little or no effect, and after a while she left her. When she was gone, Olympia gave herself up entirely to despair; and gave utterance to the most dismal lamentations at the cruel destiny which pursued her, but at length the violence of her grief had almost exhausted itself, and she did become more calm, and sought to divert her thoughts to other subjects, but that was impossible. They would continue to haunt her imagination into some frightful dreams, and to render her one of the most wretched beings in existence. She awaited her interview with Rinaldi with mingled hopes and fears, and, notwithstanding all that Theresina had said to her, she could not help encouraging the idea that he would not be able to resist her fervent supplications, if indeed he had not become entirely insensible to every feeling of humanity; and with these thoughts she tried to console herself, and to look forward to the most favourable results. Theresina returned to her in the course of the day, and they passed several hours together in conversation; and when they separated for the night, Theresina was gratified that she was much more tranquil than she could have anticipated. Olympia, however, slept but little that night, for her mind was too busily occupied in endeavouring to imagine what would be the result of the following day; and she arose at an early hour, and offering up her prayers to Heaven, she prepared herself for that interview upon which her future destiny seemed to depend. Theresina came to her at the usual hour, but Olympia's mind was too much agitated to suffer her to partake but sparingly of the morning meal, and she eagerly inquired at what hour she might expect to see Rinaldi?

"He told me to inform you that he would be here in about an hour, signora," replied Theresina.

"Thank Heaven!" ejaculated Olympia, "and oh, may my efforts be crowned with success."

Theresina shook her head.

"I sincerely hope that they will, signora," she observed, "but still I cannot flatter you with any false hopes. The will of Rinaldi I know is good to promote your wishes, but he dare not offend the Count Alberti."

"And yet you have boasted of the power of your husband," said Olympia.

"Very true," replied her companion, "and there are but few who would venture to question it, but Alberti possesses an influence over him which nothing can destroy, and as he is pledged to aid him in all his plans he will not on any consideration, I am convinced, break his oath."

"Then there is no hope for me," said Olympia, with a look of anguish; "will nothing release me from this terrible and unmerited situation?—Inhumanly as Alberti has even treated me, I am ready to forgive him, and to banish myself to some distant place where he will have no occasion to bear any future annoyance from me, if he will but abandon his cruel designs, and restore me to that liberty of which he has so unjustly deprived me."

"Wait patiently, signora," said Theresina, "and however obstinate he may be at present, he may yet be induced to relent, and of his own free will restore you to freedom, and endeavour to make you all the atonement in his power for the injuries he has done you."

"Alas!" groaned Olympia, "what atonement can he make me?—Can he restore to me my lost honour?—Can he make me again that happy and innocent being that I once was, before I listened to his deceitful vows?—Oh, no, it is impossible!—He has by his villany sealed my doom, and there is nothing but despair and misery left for me in the world. Oh, Alberti, little did I imagine that you could ever become so heartless a villain!"

She covered her face with her hands and wept bitterly, and Theresina did not offer to interrupt her, for she hoped that by thus giving vent to her feelings, it would afford some relief to the agony of her mind. At length Theresina left her, and Olympia awaited with a throbbing heart the appearance of Rinaldi. She was not long kept in suspense; she heard footsteps approaching, then the key was turned in the lock, the door opened, and the robber chief entered. Olympia, notwithstanding what his wife had related of him, could not help trembling in his presence; she averted her looks, and for a moment or two all her fortitude forsook her, and she felt as if she should find it impossible to address herself to him. He, however, smiled encouragingly upon her, and she regained her composure.

"You wished to see me, signora?" he said.

"I did, signor," replied Olympia in a flattering voice, "and your wife has doubtless informed you of the important business I wished to see you upon?"

"True, signora," said Rinaldi, "and believe me, I much regret that it is not in my power to comply with your wishes. I trust that since you have been here you have experienced every comfort and respectful attention; that, I assure you, you shall continue to receive, but, without the command of the Count Alberti, I cannot restore you to liberty."

"Oh, signor," cried Olympia, "you surely cannot be so cruel as to persist in keeping in confinement a poor persecuted female, who never injured you or human being? You will not pander to the vices of my dastardly betrayer, for your wife has told me that you still possess honourable humane feelings, and therefore I cannot bring myself to believe that you will turn a deaf ear to my earnest appeal. Release me from this horrible confinement, and I am ready to bind myself by any oath, that neither you nor the Count Alberti shall ever hear of me again."

"I would willingly do so, signora," returned Rinaldi, "for lawless and desperate though my present course of life be, I have not yet forgotten to sympathise in the misfortunes of the injured and oppressed. But I cannot do so without bringing down certain destruction upon myself and all those who are connected with me. I dare not set at defiance the power of the Count Alberti, to whom I am also under the greatest obligations for many important services which he has rendered me; but this I promise you, and you will find that I will faithfully keep my word, that no farther harm shall come to you; moreover, I am satisfied that the count has no other object in view than to keep you securely confined for the present, and that at some future period, perhaps not far distant, he will himself restore you to liberty."

"For the love of Heaven," supplicated Olympia, with clasped hands, "do not—oh, do not refuse my request."

"It pains me, indeed, to be compelled to do so," replied the robber-chief; "but you have heard my statement, and it is useless for me to repeat it. I have no power to act as my own feelings would prompt me to do in the present instance, or most happy should I be to avail myself of it. All that I can do to contribute to your comfort while you remain here, depend upon it shall be done, and with that assurance you must endeavour to rest your mind content. Besides, signora, even supposing that you were restored to liberty, whither could you go—where seek a refuge, friendless and unprovided for as I understand you are ?"

"Oh! I would willingly brave everything," returned Olympia, "encounter any danger, suffer any privation, rather than remain in my present situation. I would put my trust in that wise and beneficent Providence, who, I am certain, would not desert me in my hour of need. Again I implore you to yield to my supplications, and I will ever bless and revere your name."

"What more can I say, signora," remarked Rinaldi, "than that I have already? You ask me to do that which I dare not, although my will is good, and I deeply sympathise in your misfortunes. This answer to your appeal is decisive, and it is useless to prolong this interview."

Olympia saw plainly enough that all her efforts would be unavailing, and she therefore abandoned them in despair; and Rinaldi, after a few more observations of no particular importance, requested her to make her mind perfectly easy, for that she should meet with every respectful attention while she remained at the cavern, at the same time assuring her that, when he again saw the Count Alberti, he would venture to intercede in her behalf, and that he confidentially hoped that, in a little time, he would be induced to restore her to liberty. Rinaldi then politely took his leave, and departed from the cavern. Olympia threw herself upon a seat, and gave herself up to the most racking thoughts. All her hopes were now entirely annihilated, and she saw nothing

but misery before her. 'Tis true she placed every confidence in the assurances of Rinaldi; but the power which he admitted Alberti had over him, and his inability to disobey his will, caused her the greatest uneasiness, for she felt satisfied that the count would show her no mercy—that he would never consent to restore her to liberty, fearful as he undoubtedly was that she would prove an almost insurmountable obstacle to his presumptuous views regarding the Signora Melina; and to remain a prisoner with her tender offspring in that place, surrounded by such lawless and desperate men, was enough of itself to inspire her with feelings of the greatest horror. Tears came to her relief, and she wept bitterly. In a short time she was rejoined by Theresina, who exerted herself to the utmost to console her, and to reconcile her to her fate, at the same time seeking to inspire her with the hope that something would yet transpire to restore her to liberty, and to cause the Count Alberti to relent when she least expected; but her endeavours were crowned with little or no success.

"Courage, courage, signora," she said;— "you may depend upon my friendship and sympathy, and you may also rest assured that whatever Rinaldi has promised you, he will not fail to perform. Of this I am convinced, that neither the threats nor the gold of Alberti will induce him to act with any other outrage towards you. Rinaldi is no brutal miscreant, although an outlaw and a robber. Let this assurance comfort you and inspire you with hope."

"Hope!" repeated Olympia, with a deep sigh: "alas!" there is none for me. Would that I and my poor innocent offspring were no more. Oh! what have I done that I should be thus cruelly persecuted? Was it not enough that all my youthful hopes should be blighted, that I should be abandoned by that man on whom my very soul was rivetted, to whom I sacrificed my honour, and became hateful, despicable to myself, but that I should be thus brutally incarcerated—shut out from the light of day, and deprived of the means of flying from my own painful thoughts ?"

"Indeed, signora, returned the compassionate Theresina, "your situation is far from being so dreadful as your imagination makes it appear to be. It is true you are a prisoner; but you are the prisoner of those who can and do sympathise in your misfortunes, and who will readily contribute all in their power to your comfort. From them you have nothing to fear; try, then, to reconcile yourself to your fate, and trust in the goodness and mercy of Providence to release you from your present difficulties, and to bring your persecutor to a due sense of the manifold injuries he has most unquestionably inflicted upon you."

"Oh, that will never be," replied Olympia,

"it would be in vain for me to endeavour to encourage such a thought, which could only be followed by a more cruel disappointment. Alberti's conduct has proved that he is stern, cruel, inflexible, and unrelenting, and that from him I can expect no mercy. But still I could forgive him all, if he would release me and my child from our present confinement. I would be content to become a wanderer upon the face of the earth, exposed to every privation, existing on the scanty charity of strangers, even to lie myself down and die, sooner than to submit to such a fate as this."

"But think, signora," observed her companion, "upon the probable horrors that you and your poor child would have to encounter. I need not, I am sure, point out to you that that there is but little pity or charity in the world for the forlorn and destitute. Whither could you go?—How hope to exist?—Where could you look for a friend?—Reflect seriously upon all these facts, and I am convinced that you will be obliged to admit that your present situation, painful though it be, is far more preferable. The Count Alberti, I do firmly believe, will not think of proceeding to any further extremities, and of this I am likewise certain, that notwithstanding the influence which he possesses over Rinaldi, and the obligations which the latter is under to him, nothing whatever will induce him to act with any greater severity towards you than he is doing at present; let this assurance, signora, inspire you with confidence and fortitude, and try to be calm."

"I do believe in the truth and sincerity of what you say, Theresina," answered Olympia, "and I assure you that I am extremely grateful for the kind sympathy you evince in my misfortunes; but oh, how can you expect me to be calm under such trying circumstances? Despair will certainly drive me to madness. The cruelty of that man, who vowed to love me so fondly, to whom my affections were so warmly, so sincerely devoted, is more—much more than I can find fortitude to bear. He would have been more merciful to me and my child had he sacrificed our lives."

"Would that I could banish these dismal —these distracting thoughts from your mind, signora," said Theresina; "again let me point out to you the horrors of what your situation would be, were you to be driven forth a houseless wanderer upon the wide and cheerless world."

"There is no suffering that I should not be prepared to encounter, were I but released from the power of the Count Alberti," remarked the fair prisoner; "Providence would surely raise me up a friend; I should find some one who would sympathise with my misfortunes; oh, yes, I cannot think so harshly of my fellow-creatures as to believe otherwise."

Theresina shook her head.

"I fear, signora," she remarked, "that you would be doomed to woful disappointment. You have not experienced so much of mankind as I have done, or you would not talk thus. Consider again, what could become of you and your child, without money, without friends, or any asylum under which to place your head, and endeavour to think less severely of your present situation. Besides, the Count Alberti may still relent, and releasing you from your present confinement, atone in some measure for the injuries he has inflicted on you by making some future provision for you."

"Oh, no," sighed Olympia, "I dare not encourage such a hope. Nothing, I feel convinced, can now move him to pity, after he has proceeded to such a length as he has done. What a wretched being I am, to be exposed to so cruel a fate as this. It was an unfortunate hour which gave me birth—oh, why did my parents desert me in my infancy?—and why did cruel destiny ever introduce me to that man who afterwards became my betrayer, and now pursues me with the same spirit of revenge as if I had been his deadliest enemy."

"Your sorrows, I admit, have been great, signora," observed Theresina, "and such as it requires the greatest fortitude and patience to support with resignation."

"Resignation!" repeated Olympia, "alas! it is utterly impossible to be resigned under such dreadful, such truly unparalleled circumstances. Thought will drive me to distraction. Would that my heart would break, and thus put an end to my insupportable troubles."

"Put your trust in Providence, signora, and depend upon it, the time will come when you will be restored to happiness."

"Oh, no, no," returned Olympia, "that, I am thoroughly convinced, can never be. I have received a blow from which I can never hope to recover. There will be no future happiness in this world for me, and the sooner I am out of it the better. God help me, for I am one of the most truly miserable of his creatures. Theresina, think you that your husband will indeed continue to remain inexorable?—Can you not hope to succeed in prevailing upon him to yield to my supplications?"

"It would be cruel in me, signora, to hold out to you any such delusive hopes," replied Theresina. "The will of Rinaldi, I know, is good to serve you; but you have heard what he has said—no arguments of mine can move him from his determination; he dare not disobey the commands of the Count Alberti, for should he do so, he would not fail to bring destruction upon himself and his band."

"Then there is no hope for me," sighed

Olympia, wringing her hands, and weeping bitterly.

"Oh, yes, there is—indeed there is, signora," replied the robber's wife.

"Oh, where?—where?"

"In the repentance of the count; wait with patience, and he will surely take pity on you, and restore you and your child to liberty, though he may not be able to restore you to happiness."

"I dare not, must not entertain such a' thought, which can never be realized," said Olympia. "How can I hope to move him to pity, since there is no probability of my seeing him?"

"I have no doubt that he will visit you ere long," said Theresina, "and then your remonstrances and supplications may make a favourable impression on him."

"Would to Heaven I could think so, I might then support my present trials with some degree of fortitude," returned Olympia; "but he seems to have abandoned me to my fate altogether; and I despair of ever beholding him again. He will not dare to meet me, to encounter my reproaches, and, unless I can move your husband to pity and befriend me, here must I remain for the rest of my wretched existence."

Theresina again exerted herself to inspire her with hope and to tranquillize her feelings, but with no better success; despair settled entirely upon her heart—no ray of comfort was permitted to dawn upon her mind, all before her appeared black and gloomy, and Theresina at last gave up her task in despair, and left her to her own dreary thoughts. The anguish of her mind increased every moment, and notwithstanding all the assurances of Rinaldi and Theresina, she could not help encouraging the most dismal apprehensions as to the fate which was in store for her. The day wore drearily away, and at night, when she threw herself upon her couch, she courted sleep in vain. All kinds of frightful thoughts haunted her imagination, and drove her to distraction, and in the frenzy of her feelings she cursed herself and all the human race. Days, weeks, elapsed without any mitigation to her sorrows, and without anything occurring which was at all calculated to impart hope or consolation to her. Theresina was almost constantly her companion, and she tried all that she could to reanimate her spirits, and to render her situation as comfortable as possible, but her efforts were almost completely unsuccessful, and it did not seem likely that anything could have the effect of ameliorating the grief of the unfortunate prisoner. Olympia made frequent inquiries after the Count Alberti, but Theresina assured her that she had heard nothing whatever from him, and that she did not believe that Rinaldi had received any further instructions from him.

"How strange and unaccountable is this," remarked Olympia; "what can be his future designs regarding me?"

"That it is impossible for me to say, signora," replied Theresina, "but I firmly believe that he has no other object in view than to keep you confined while he prosecutes his suit with Signora Melina."

"She will never consent to become the wife of one who has proved himself to be such an unprincipled villain!" said Olympia.

"Not of her own free will, I am convinced," returned her companion! "But the prince, her uncle, favours the addresses of Alberti, and he may compel her into a union that must be so completely repugnant to her feelings."

"He cannot be so cruel—so unjust."

"If all is true that I have heard of the Prince Bianchi," remarked Theresina, "he is imperious and inflexible, and nothing can move him from anything upon which he has fixed his mind."

"Yes," replied Olympia, "that I believe is his character, but he has ever treated his fair niece with the utmost affection and indulgence, and he surely will not thus recklessly consign her to future misery. Poor Melina, I do indeed pity her; but what must be the tenfold horror and disgust she must entertain towards Alberti, did she but know the extent of his atrocious, his inhuman conduct towards me. I know she pitied my misfortunes; she could not but view with abhorrence the heartless betrayer of my unsuspecting innocence. Oh, Theresina, had you but heard the many solemn protestations of love he made to me—how fervently he vowed that I alone should become his bride—that on me depended his future happiness or misery, you would not marvel that he triumphed, and that I, his unfortunate confiding victim, in a moment of weakness fell. God! how terribly am I punished for my offence; but surely the retribution of offended Heaven will overtake him for his cruelty."

"It will, signora," said the robber's wife; "and justice, depend upon it, will be rendered you for the unmerited injuries that have been inflicted upon you. But endeavour to divert your thoughts to some other subject; try to banish him from your mind, and to forget that such a being ever existed."

"Oh, that is impossible!" replied Olympia, "banish Alberti from my memory; the thought is preposterous. I must be mad to encourage it even for a moment. Is he not the father of my child? And whilst I gaze upon its innocent face, can I cease to remember all the vows he uttered, and which he has so cruelly broken? I must despise myself if I could.

Still even now, methinks, if he would but repent, and make me all the atonement in his power, I could forgive him, and become in some measure resigned to my fate."

"And the time will come, I trust, signora, when those wishes will be realized, although your prospects are at present so gloomy."

"Alas! I cannot venture to anticipate any such result," observed Olympia; "it is evident from his conduct that he now views me with hatred and revenge, and that he is anxious to get rid of me and my offspring, and cares not by what means. Nay more, he even dared to insinuate that I was criminally connected with the notorious brigand chief, Allesandro Massaroni."

"Was it not most extraordinary, signora," said Theresina, "that Massaroni should take such an interest in your fate, and that he should also become so well acquainted with your history, and the most secret designs of the Count Alberti?"

"Very true," said Olympia, "and I have often racked my brain to no purpose to imagine how he obtained his knowledge, and what could be his motives. But of this I assure you, that never before that night, or since, have I beheld the brigand. I must admit, however, that his appearance and his extraordinary conduct have made a favourable impression upon me, and I never think of his name without experiencing sensations for which I am totally at a loss to account."

"Allesandro Massaroni is a most remarkable character," observed Theresina, "and it is no easy matter to penetrate his motives; but, at any rate, it is quite evident that he is your friend, and that he will not fail to endeavour to rescue you, if he knows where you are confined. Alberti has run great risk in disobeying his commands. It would be folly to seek to deny his power, and the count may consider himself fortunate if he escape his vengeance."

"I sincerely hope that Massaroni will not attempt anything rash," said Olympia, "for, notwithstanding his cruel behaviour towards me, I should deeply lament any evil that might befall Alberti. God knows I seek not vengeance, but justice."

Another week passed in a similar manner, but the constant arguments of Theresina at last had some effect, and Olympia did become somewhat reconciled to her fate. One morning about this period, Theresina suddenly made her appearance, and the expression of her countenance at once convinced Olympia that she had something particular to impart.

"What is the matter, Theresina?" she demanded eagerly, "you seem agitated. Tell me, has anything particular happened?"

"Compose yourself, signora," replied the former, "I have, indeed, some startling news to communicate."

"Ah! and does it concern me?" asked Olympia."

"It does indeed."

"What is it? Do not keep me in suspense."

"Massaroni has put his threats into execution," answered Theresina, "he and his band made a daring attack upon the castle of the Count Alberti; they burnt it to the ground, and after a desperate combat they succeeded in capturing Alberti, and bearing him away."

"Good God!" exclaimed Olympia, clasping her hands, "is it possible?"

"It is true, signora," answered Theresina, "they were pursued to no purpose; they escaped, and the Count Alberti is, no doubt, a prisoner in one of the secret haunts of Allesandro Massaroni!"

"Alas! alas!" sighed the deeply agitated Olympia, "then my worst fears are realised. Oh, Alberti, guilty even though you have been, and cruel as your conduct has been to me, I should go mad if any harm were to befall you. Massaroni, why should you thus pursue him with your vengeance? How mistaken art thou, if you imagine that by perpetrating such an outrage as this you are rendering me any service, or affording me any gratification. But tell me, Theresina, is not the retreat of this desperate brigand chief known?"

"It is not," replied Theresina, "though it is supposed to be somewhere near the Appenine mountains. It will be no easy task to discover him, and to attack him in his stronghold. His object, no doubt, in capturing the count is to compel him to divulge the place where you are confined."

"This is terrible news," said Olympia, "and I tremble for the fate of Alberti. Massaroni threatened him with his severest vengeance if he dared to disobey his injunctions, and alas! I fear he will not fail to keep his word. What is to be done in this difficulty?"

"Indeed, I know not," returned the robber's wife; "Massaroni is a desperate man, and it is a terrible thing to incur his vengeance. The Prince Bianchi has despatched troops to endeavour to find out the place where the brigands are concealed, and to rescue the count from their power; but I must confess that I have my doubts of their success; the only way that Alberti can save himself, is by confessing the truth and revealing the place where you are confined, and should he do so, I fear that Massaroni will not delay making an attack upon us, and we should find it impossible to resist him and his daring band. I deeply regret that Rinaldi has had anything at all to do with this business."

"This unexpected news distracts me," said Olympia; "and should anything fatal befall the guilty but still beloved Alberti, my doom is sealed, and it will be a matter of indifference what becomes of me."

She wrung her hands in the anguish of her feelings, and it was some time ere Theresina could bring her to any degree of composure.

"But surely," she said at length, "now this has happened, Rinaldi cannot possibly have any pretext for detaining me? Will he not restore me to liberty?"

"Alas, signora," replied Theresina, "I fear I cannot hold out any such hopes to you. Besides, were he to do so, whither could you go? Where find a shelter or protection?"

"Oh," said Olympia, "I would trust to Providence. I am willing to risk anything; but to remain here any longer with the terrible uncertainty upon my mind of the fate which has befallen Alberti, is intolerable."

"And think you, you would be more likely to ascertain his fate were you permitted to leave this cavern?" demanded Theresina.

"I would never rest until I had done so," replied Olympia, "and something assures me that my efforts would be crowned with success. Should I be able to discover the retreat of Massaroni, I could not fail to save the count from his vengeance."

"That I very much doubt, signora, unless Alberti should consent to render you justice, which I fear his pride would not allow him to do. Besides, think of the numerous dangers you would have to encounter, wandering in a strange part of the country, and without a protector."

"I would brave everything with the hope of achieving my object," replied Olympia, resolutely. "There can be nothing more horrible than to be kept in this state of insupportable suspense."

"Bear with it patiently, signora," remarked Theresina, "and the result may be far more fortunate than that you now anticipate."

"Oh, how vainly you advise me," replied Olympia, "how can I be patient in this dreadful state of uncertainty? Will not your husband yield to my earnest solicitations, and thus place me under an eternal obligation to him?"

"It is useless to entertain such a thought, signora, for he has already expressed his determination to me, and that is to retain you in his power at all hazards until the fate of the count is ascertained."

"This, this is indeed most cruel," sighed Olympia, with a burst of anguish; "will nothing prevail upon Rinaldi to render a single act of justice to one who has never injured him?"

"I feel satisfied that Rinaldi acts from the wisest motives, which you will probably be inclined to admit by and by," observed Theresina; "but pray compose your feelings, signora, and probably some satisfactory intelligence will be obtained before long."

"Alas, no!" said Olympia, "I dare not encourage such a hope. The most dismal forebodings distract my mind, for what other fate than a most desperate one can I anticipate will befall Alberti in the power of such a man as Massaroni? Providence, I feel convinced, would guide me to the brigand's retreat, and I might yet be in time to save him. Oh, that Rinaldi would but yield to my wishes, what danger is there that I would not boldly encounter in seeking to accomplish my object."

"It would be madness to make any such attempt, signora," returned Theresina; "you are totally unacquainted with this part of the country, and what clue is it at all likely you could obtain to the brigand's retreat? Here you are safe while under the protection of Rinaldi, and every attention will be paid you that your situation demands. But you will have an opportunity of arguing the point with Rinaldi himself, for he desired me to inform you that he would visit you by and by."

"Ah!" ejaculated Olympia, "then surely if he is not insensible to every feeling of pity and justice, he will yield to my wishes. To remain here any longer will drive me to madness and despair."

Theresina again tried to tranquillize her feelings, and she at last partially succeeded, and she then left her to herself. It would be a vain task to endeavour to describe the emotions of Olympia when she was alone. The most torturing fears crowded upon her mind, and the probable fate which had befallen the count filled her breast with horror. A thousand times she regretted the extraordinary and unaccountable interest which Massaroni had taken in her fate, and which had been productive of such alarming consequences; and then she earnestly invoked the protection of the Supreme for her betrayer. The cruelty of his behaviour towards her was almost forgotten in the thought of his present perilous situation, and she would willingly have sacrificed her own life to save him from the fate with which he was threatened, or which had perhaps already befallen him. The threats which Massaroni had uttered against him, came vividly to her recollection, and her apprehensions increased every moment, for those threats she had not the least doubt the Brigand Chief would not fail to put into execution.

These painful reflections were interrupted by the key being turned in the lock of the door, and Rinaldi once more stood before her. His manner appeared somewhat excited, and Olympia imagined that he looked upon her with an expression of compassion, which inspired her with confidence.

"Theresina has informed you, I presume, signora," he remarked, "of the capture of the

Count Alberti, by the brigand chief, Allesandro Massaroni ?"

"She has, signor," replied Olympia, "and notwithstanding the severe injuries I have experienced at his hand, most deeply do I regret his misfortune, and sincerely hope that no further harm will befall him. But I trust that you will now no longer consider it necessary to detain me in your captivity ?"

"I am sorry, signora," returned Rinaldi, "to be compelled to disappoint your hopes; but, as I have before told you, I am pledged to the count by the most solemn ties, and however painful it may be to yourself and me, to have to keep you under such restraint, I cannot, will not break my promise. All the accommodation that my rough retreat can afford you, you shall receive, but anything more I cannot promise."

"Oh, signor," expostulated Olympia, "consider the anxiety I must be in whilst I remain here, and I implore you to yield to my solicitations. Massaroni has threatened Alberti with his vengeance if he dared to set his power at defiance, and his present conduct fully shows that he is determined to carry such threats into execution, unless some one who has influence over him, should interpose to save Alberti. Your wife has assured me that you have not the power to oppose him, if even you were acquainted with the place where he is concealed, and any attempt of the kind, I feel convinced, would only be followed by the death of the count. If you are sincerely the friend of that misguided young nobleman, you will not hesitate to set me at liberty immediately. Believe me, I will not betray you, but will ever feel grateful for the kindness you have shown me since I have been in your power; but something convinces me that I should be able to discover the retreat of Massaroni; Providence would guide me to it, and my intercession would avert the fate which now impends over the head of my betrayer."

"The idea, signora," observed Rinaldi, "reflects credit on your humanity and courage; but still, allow me to say, that it is a preposterous and impracticable one, and that I fear I should have to reproach myself for the consequences which would in all probability ensue, were I to yield to your request. What could you do, alone and unprotected, in a strange part of the country ? —What means have you of discovering the haunt of the Brigand Chief ?—You will be much more safe by remaining here, under the assurance that I will do all in my power to rescue the Count Alberti, and to adjust the differences between him and Massaroni. The count will probably be compelled to reveal the place where you are confined, and then, and not till then, shall I feel justified in restoring you to liberty."

"And is it just in you to retain me here a prisoner ?—I, who have never injured you?" demanded Olympia.

"I admit that it is not," replied Rinaldi, "but I am so circumstanced that I have no alternative. Signora, it is useless to argue this point any further—strange as it may appear to you, I am sincerely your friend, and will protect you to the best of my power from every danger, but I cannot yield to your request."

"Then I am lost," sighed Olympia, clasping her hands with agony, "and so is he to whom I owe all my misfortunes, but whom I still love with all the ardour which can animate the breast of human being."

"Nay, Signora Olympia," replied Rinaldi, "talk not thus, I beg of you; for, alarming as matters, I confess, appear to be at present, I have strong hope that everything will yet turn out for the best. The Prince Bianchi is using his utmost vigilance to find out the place where the brigand chief is concealed, and I doubt not that his efforts will be ultimately crowned with success."

"Alas !" sighed Olympia, "I dare not entertain any such hope; besides, if even the prince should discover the secret haunt of Massaroni, and should make an attack on him, the latter would not hesitate a moment, in sacrificing Alberti to his vengeance. Oh, again I beseech you to release me from this horrible state of confinement, and suffer me to wander forth on my melancholy expedition. Willingly will I brave every danger that may occur to me, buoyed up in the hope of being enabled to accomplish my object. Massaroni has professed himself to be my friend, to take the deepest interest in my fate, and should fortune guide me to him, he will not fail to yield to my earnest supplications."

"And can you, signora," asked the robber chief, "forgive Alberti for all the injuries he has undoubtedly inflicted upon you ? Will you consent to abandon all your hopes of him, all the claims you have upon him, and leave him to the uninterrupted pursuit of his own future designs and inclinations ?"

"Though my heart should burst in the struggle, I would do so," replied Olympia, energetically; "it is plain he no longer loves me, and I absolve him from his vows. I will resign myself to my fate with as much Christian forbearance as my strength will permit me to do, and together with my poor innocent child will brave all the vicissitudes that may be in store for me."

Rinaldi was evidently moved by the earnestness of her manner, and averting his looks seemed to deliberate within himself for a few moments. Olympia took advantage of his seeming irresolution, and again urged her suit with increased eloquence, but it was of no avail, the robber's stern resolve was fixed, and nothing whatever could move him from it.

"I pity you, signora," he remarked; "and would fain assist you all in my power, but I again assure you that I cannot swerve from the promise I have made to the Count Alberti.

What more can I assure you than that here you shall be protected from every harm, and that no further outrage than the one you have already experienced shall be inflicted upon you? With this rest contented, and live in hopes that something will shortly occur to release you from your

MELINA AND FLORETTA DISGUISED FOR THEIR MEETING WITH FLORIO CLAIRVILLE.

present difficulties, and restore you to much greater happiness than that which you now can anticipate."

"Alas! alas!" groaned Olympia, "how perfectly futile would be any such attempt. My sun of happiness is set for ever, and to talk to

me of hope is a bitter mockery. Signor Rinaldi, I did trust, from the description which Theresina had given me of your character, to move you to yield to my wishes, and that you would not turn a deaf ear to my solicitations; but oh, how cruelly have I deceived myself."

No. 21.

"Do me not an injustice, signora," replied the robber chief, "by supposing me cruel and inflexible; from my very soul I once more repeat, I sincerely pity you, and would fain do all in my power to serve you; but in that which you so earnestly require I have no power. Farewell, signora, and rest assured that every exertion shall be made to rescue the Count Alberti from the fate with which he now appears to be threatened; and should I succeed, I have very little doubt that I shall be able to prevail upon him to render you that justice and reparation for his past conduct which he has so long withheld from you."

With these words, and without waiting for any reply from Olympia, Rinaldi quitted her presence, and she flung herself upon a seat in a state of despair, and her bosom found a temporary relief in a copious flood of tears. It was now evident that any further appeal to the robber chief would be useless— that here she must remain a prisoner, in a state of horrible uncertainty as to the fate which had befallen Alberti, and that there was nothing left for her but to put her trust in the merciful interposition of Providence. For some time she was perfectly inconsolable, and Theresina exerted all her efforts to no purpose in seeking to tranquillize her feelings. In this manner several days elapsed, without anything occurring to inspire her with hope; but at length Theresina imparted to her the news of the dying brigand having given the Prince Bianchi some clew to the retreat of Massaroni, and that troops had been despatched without delay to the rescue of the Count Alberti. With what impatience did Olympia await the result of this expedition, but still the most dismal forebodings continued to distract her mind, and she could not help fearing that the Count Alberti had already fallen a victim to the vengeance of the brigand chief. This anxiety was increased when she received the intelligence of the first defeat of the Prince Bianchi's troops, and her agony of mind became completely insupportable, for she could not but believe that Massaroni would be so exasperated by the attack which had been made on him, that even if he had been disposed to show any mercy to Alberti before, he would no longer delay putting his threats into execution. But when the account of the second defeat of the troops which the Prince Bianchi had sent against the brigand chief reached her, her agony of mind was beyond description, and she at once gave up the fate of the Count Alberti as decided. It was in vain that Theresina sought to persuade her to the contrary; and, in fact, there was so much reason and probability in what the fears of Olympia suggested, that she was completely bewildered for argument. Despair settled upon her heart, and for a few days she was confined to her bed, requiring the constant attendance of Theresina, and creating the utmost fears as to

her ultimate recovery. But youth at last prevailed, and Olympia was again enabled to leave her couch, though her spirits were in that depressed state that Theresina had to exert herself to the utmost to prevent a relapse. All the cruelties which Alberti had inflicted upon her were nearly forgotten by Olympia in the terrible anxiety she felt for his fate; and she would have been willing to have undergone the most terrible destiny that could fall to the lot of human beings, had it only been in her power to rescue him from his present situation. She would even willingly have abandoned all her hopes of atonement from him; nay, more, she thought she could submit to remain his prisoner and to be subjected to any cruelty he might be disposed to inflict upon her, rather than that he should meet with an untimely fate. Such is the strength of woman's pure love, even under the sense of the greatest injustice. At length Olympia acquired, or rather regained somewhat of her usual fortitude and resignation, and in her attention to her tender offspring sought to forget much of her own immediate sorrows. In this praiseworthy effort she succeeded much better than might have been expected under the painful circumstances in which she was placed. But this tranquillity of her feeling was interrupted by Theresina neglecting to attend her as usual, and her place being supplied by one of the robbers, who brought her her meals, and whose vulgar and insolent manners filled her bosom with terror and disgust. Of Rinaldi she could also hear nothing, neither could she gain any information from Dargoni (which was the name of the robber) of what was the reason of Theresina's absence, or when it was likely that she would return. Olympia's mind was filled with the most terrible apprehensions, and it was to no purpose that she racked her brain to imagine what could be the cause of this extraordinary alteration in the arrangements of her imprisonment. Sometimes she imagined that Rinaldi and his wife had entirely deserted her to her fate, and at others that they might have heard of something that would tend towards the liberation of the count, and that they had gone to prosecute their designs; but then, why should they not have made her acquainted with their intentions previously, knowing the anxiety of mind she would be naturally placed under in such an uncertainty? And certainly it did not appear much like keeping to the promises of protection and comfort which they had held out to her, by leaving her to the tender mercies of such a ruffian as Dargoni. The longer she ruminated upon this, the more her mind became bewildered and distracted; and it was wonderful how she was enabled to support herself at all under the terrible trial. Dargoni was certainly a most repulsive looking fellow; a gaunt limbed masculine ruffian, standing upwards of six feet high, and with a cast of features that bespoke the villain capable of any atrocious act. Olympia could not help shuddering with horror in his presence, and the boldness of his looks, and the insolence and confidence of his language whenever he addressed her, were in no way calculated to do away with this unfavourable impression. A dread, of which she could not divest herself, constantly haunted her, and she had not a moment's respite from anxiety and apprehension. She was fearful to address him, and the fellow was not slow to observe her timidity, and did not fail to take advantage of it.

Three more wretched days and nights, the most wretched that poor Olympia ever remembered to have experienced, passed away in this manner, and still she saw nor heard anything of Rinaldi or Theresina. Such a death-like silence also constantly prevailed throughout the cavernous retreat, that it appeared to her as if the whole of the robbers, with the exception of Dargoni, had abandoned it, and that thought of itself was sufficient to inspire her with a feeling of more than usual terror. Sometimes Dargoni would stop and gaze at her with an expression of countenance which called the blushes of offended modesty into her cheeks, and filled her bosom with the most inexpressible feelings of disgust. When he witnessed her confusion, a malignant smile would overspread his repulsive features, and he would retire from the place with a half stifled laugh of triumph. Can it be wonderful that all these circumstances kept Olympia in a constant state of alarm, and that her days should become restless, her nights sleepless? What could she anticipate but the most dreadful consequences from all those threatening preliminaries? She hourly wished herself and her offspring dead, for death even under the most frightful circumstances would have been far more preferable than to be thus constantly kept in such a horrible state of suspense. We have said that three days had thus passed away, and that Olympia had not been able to obtain any information as to the cause of the absence of Rinaldi and Theresina, and it seemed as though they had entirely consigned her to the keeping and the mercy of the ruffian Dargoni. Oh, God! what did she suffer during those three days? Shall we attempt to describe it? No, we are confident that we need not do so, for the reader may very readily imagine what her feelings were. In her despair, it appeared to her as if Heaven had itself entirely deserted her, and in the bitterness of her heart she cursed the hour of her birth and the very authors of her existence. Whilst Theresina had been almost her constant companion, she had been enabled to derive some little degree of consolation from her conversation and friendly advice, but now she felt

herself abandoned to her fate, and that fate she could not help depicturing in the blackest colours that a disordered mind could imagine. As near as she was capable of forming an idea, it was midnight, and she was seated, wrapped in such dismal meditations as those we have described, when she was suddenly aroused by hearing a footstep cautiously approaching the place of her confinement. Her child had been sleeping soundly for several hours; but Olympia's mind was too distracted by racking though, to suffer her to seek repose herself. And now beset by numerous fears, she started to her feet and listened with breathless attention and anxiety for the approaching sounds, her breast filled with emotions as to who it could be that was about to obtrude upon her at that solemn hour of the night.

"God preserve me!" she inwardly ejaculated, "and protect me, I beseech Thee, from any danger which may threaten me."

The footsteps approached nearer, and at length they stopped at the door. Olympia cast a hasty glance around her, but no means of defence presented themselves to her gaze: her heart sunk within her, and she gave herself up to despair. She now heard the bolts of the door being cautiously withdrawn, and the key turned in the lock, the next moment the door flew back on its hinges, and Olympia started and trembled with horror when the gaunt figure of the ruffian Dargoni presented itself to her sight. She could not repress a scream, and retreated to the remotest corner of the cell.

"Silence, signora," said the ruffian; "you do but waste your breath: there is no one to hear you; I have taken good care to steep the senses of my comrades, and, therefore, they are not in a condition to interrupt me in my purpose."

"Villain! what are your designs?" exclaimed the terrified Olympia; "why do you seek my presence at this solemn hour of the night? Is your purpose murder?"

"No, fair signora," replied Dargoni, and an expression of the most revolting description overspread his coarse and repulsive features whilst he spoke; "I come to communicate that to your ears which I have long been anxious to do, but never till now had so excellent an opportunity."

"For the love of Heaven, what mean you?" demanded the terrified Olympia.

"Simply this, beauteous damsel," replied the miscreant, approaching her nearer, and having the effrontery to attempt to take her hand, "that from the first moment I beheld you, your charms have made the most powerful impression upon me, robber and ruffian though I be, and that I made up my mind to possess you at all hazards. By an artful invention of mine, Rinaldi, Theresina, and the principal portion of the band have been induced to quit the cavern for awhile, and there is nothing therefore left to baulk me in my purpose; prepare, then, to yield to my wishes, lovely Signora Olympia, and we will immediately leave this place, and that liberty which you are so anxious so obtain, and which Rinaldi has, and ever will refuse you, shall be yours."

It would be utterly impossible to describe the feelings of shame and horror which pervaded the bosom of Olympia while the robber Dargoni was making this brutal speech. The blood ran boiling hot throughout her veins, and indignation flashed from her fine expressive eyes.

"Monster!" she cried, when she could find power sufficient to reply, "dare you thus insult me? Begone, wretch, or fear the vengeance of offended Heaven, which will most assuredly descend upon your devoted head, and crush you in the midst of all your iniquity!"

The ruffian laughed outright in the derision of his soul, and advanced more boldly towards the horror-struck damsel.

"Of what use is all this opposition?" he said; "have I not already told you that my determination is fixed; that there is nothing whatever to obstruct me in the accomplishment of my wishes; and therefore, what think you resistance will avail you? This night, this very hour you shall be mine, though all the fiends of hell were to rise up to oppose me. Dargoni may be a bandit and a ruffian, but he is nevertheless not yet insensible to the fascinations of female beauty. We are alone; the senses of my comrades are steeped in forgetfulness; this, then, shall be the hour of my triumph!"

As the villain thus spoke, in spite of all her struggles, he encircled her in his embrace, and endeavoured to pollute her lips with his unholy kisses. Wound up to a pitch of the most indescribable horror, Olympia screamed aloud, and again endeavoured to release herself from the cowardly and brutal fellow's hold, but she struggled to no purpose, and her strength every moment became the more exhausted.

"Signora," observed Dargoni, "again I tell you that all resistance to my will is completely useless. For weeks I have watched and waited for this opportunity, and now that it is afforded me, I will not fail to avail myself of it. Yield to my will, and the doors to liberty shall be immediately opened to you."

"All Merciful God help me!" cried Olympia: "oh! protect me in this trying hour!— Help! help!"

Gradually she found herself becoming weaker in the grasp of the miscreant, and her destination seemed to be inevitable. At that critical moment, however, happening to cast her eyes in the direction of the door which Dargoni had not taken the precaution to close after him, she beheld the shadow of a human form upon the floor, and the next instant what was the utter astonishment of Olympia to behold Theresina cautiously

enter? Olympia could scarcely repress a scream, but Theresina placed her finger significantly on her lips, and enjoined her to silence, and she then cautiously approached Dargoni, whose back was most fortunately placed towards her, so that he had no means of observing her, or frustrating her in her purpose, whatever it might be. Determination flashed from Theresina's eyes, and Olympia could perceive that she clutched a stiletto in her hand.

"Release your hold, villain!" cried Olympia, "or be the fate that is at present impending over you upon your own head!"

"Never!" shouted Dargoni; "the triumph is mine, and thus do I avail myself of it. There is no one here to rescue you, and——"

"Liar!" interrupted Theresina, as she rushed suddenly upon him, and plunged the stiletto to the hilt in his side: "such is the reward of thy villany!"

The ruffian turned a ghastly look upon her; his features became frightfully distorted; he tried to speak, but could not, and gradually relaxing his hold of Olympia, he sunk on the earth a corpse!" With a cry of mingled terror and surprise, Olympia rushed to the arms of her preserver, and totally incapable of giving expression to a single syllable, she almost became insensible. Theresina pressed her affectionately to her bosom, and, for a few moments, speech was also denied her.

"Oh, God!" ejaculated Olympia, at length, "how is this? Where have you been, and what brings you here at this critical moment, to save me from a fate, the bare idea of which fills my bosom with horror? Where is Rinaldi?"

"This is not a time for explanation," hastily answered Theresina; "there is not a single moment to be lost. Rinaldi has not yet returned to the cave. My conduct may cost me my life, but nevertheless, I am resolved this night, this very hour, to restore you to liberty, if you are willing to venture alone."

"To liberty!" exclaimed Olympia, in accents of unspeakable delight; "oh! my best, my only friend—my preserver, how can I ever sufficiently thank you? But will you not accompany me? Will you not——"

"No," interrupted Theresina; "I must not —I cannot abandon my husband. Heaven speed you on your dreary way, my poor girl, and bless you with future happiness. At some future time we may meet again, and, let us hope, under more auspicious circumstances. But come, the time wanes apace, and if we any longer delay, my resolution may fail me, or it might be too late to put my designs into execution. Courage, Signora Olympia, courage: the senses of the few robbers who are left in the cavern are at present steeped in forgetfulness, and you may depart without fear of detection; but there is no knowing how soon they may recover, and then all my plans would be rendered abortive."

"Excellent, kind-hearted woman!" ejaculated Olympia; "how shall I find words to express to you my gratitude? I am ready to brave every danger that may present itself, rather than remain here for another hour."

"Enough, then," said Theresina, "let us at once to business; take your child in your arms, signora."

Olympia immediately did so, and the robber's wife then stooped down, and removing the cloak from the body of Dargoni, she enveloped the forms of Olympia and her child in it. She also placed the hat of the deceased ruffian on Olympia's head, and pulled it far over her brows so as to conceal her features, and she then took a lamp from the table, and motioned her to follow silently. Without uttering a word, and her heart at the same time palpitating with expectation, Olympia did so, and after traversing two or three passages, they arrived in the cavern in which Rinaldi and his comrades usually assembled, and where three or four of the robbers were now in a state of insensibility, under the influence of the strong opiate which Dargoni had administered to them. Olympia trembled as she passed by those terrible men, and she scarcely ventured to breathe, but Theresina encouraged her by a look, and in a few moments more they were in the open air.

"Take the path to the right," said the robber's wife, pointing in that direction, "you will have a league and a half to travel before you arrive at any village, but that will be one where you may procure what you require. I need not, I presume, enjoin you not to divulge from whence you have come. Do away with your disguise before you enter the village; here is money, all that it is in my power to give you, and may Heaven prosper you!"

As Theresina thus spoke she fervently grasped the hand of Olympia, and it was quite evident that her bosom underwent the deepest emotion, but as she attempted to depart, Olympia detained her, and in earnest accents ejaculated—

"My best friend, shall we separate thus?— will you not accompany me?"

"I would willingly share all your troubles," replied Theresina, "but I cannot desert my husband. Farewell, signora, and may Heaven send you happier times."

Before Olympia could render any reply, Theresina was gone, and Olympia found herself alone with her child in the cold midnight air, but still at liberty! For a few moments her thoughts were so bewildered that she stood irresolute, and scarcely knew how to act, but at length she took the direction which Theresina had pointed out to her, and as she proceeded she felt the more encouraged. But Heaven knows she had little enough to encourage her, for the night was one of the most miserable and cheerless that the imagination can depicture. The wind blew in awful gusts around, the rain poured down in torrents, and the darkness which clouded the hemisphere was so dense that nothing could penetrate it. And now that Olympia was at liberty the thought of her hopeless situation was presented more vividly to her imagination. All that Theresina had told her was recalled to her memory with tenfold force, and she was compelled to acknowledge its truth. She even almost regretted that she had quitted the cavern, so utterly lonely and miserable did she feel her present situation, and had any one at that moment attempted to return her to it they would have required no force to do so.

"Whither can I go?" she said, "where can I seek a friend or protection? Alas! alas! what a miserable wretch I am. Why was I ever born? Oh, my poor innocent offspring, what a relief to us both would it be, could we lie ourselves down and die."

Thus soliloquizing, the unhappy woman folded the cloak still more closely around her tender offspring, to shield it as much as possible from the inclemency of the weather, and hurried on her way.

CHAPTER XXV.

THE FARTHER PROGRESS OF OLYMPIA.—THE MEETING WITH THE BRIGAND CHIEF.

THE storm increased as Olympia pursued her way, and she and her infant were very soon drenched to the skin. But notwithstanding all these disheartening circumstances, a certain hope inspired her and gave her courage to proceed. Her whole thoughts were fixed on Alberti, and the idea of preserving him from the fate with which he appeared to be threatened, and that gave her strength under all the difficulties which she had to encounter. She forgot at once the injuries she had received from him; every feeling of animosity, if she had ever entertained one towards him, was banished from her mind, and her only hope and anxiety was to save him from the fate which at present appeared to be impending over him. It was indeed a terrible night, seldom had such a one been witnessed in the genial clime of "sunny Italy." The tempest increased every moment, the wind blew a perfect hurricane, and the rain poured down in one complete sheet of water. The darkness which pervaded the face of nature was also nearly impenetrable, and the way which Theresina had pointed out to Olympia to pursue was a devious one, and to a stranger, presented every possible obstacle. But still Olympia maintained her fortitude much better than might have been expected; and through the tempest she hurried, clasping her infant still closer to her breast. She was at liberty, and that thought was sufficient of itself to inspire her with more than ordinary courage. She placed her dependence upon Providence, and felt convinced that it would not forsake her in that hour of trial. Ever and anon she looked timidly around her, apprehending pursuit; but not a human being, as far as she could penetrate through the darkness, met her gaze, and with the exception of the howling of the tempest, all was as silent as the grave. But whither could she go? That was the thought that again occurred to her; where could she hope to find a friend who would commiserate her misfortunes? She was alone with her infant in the world, and all would scoff at and despise her. Such was the most prominent, and at the same time the most reasonable thought which suggested itself to her mind, and that was sufficient to sink her in despair. But still it was remarkable the manner in which she was able to buoy her spirits up, and to brave the many horrors and difficulties which she had to encounter. Almost regardless of the "pitiless pelting of the storm," Olympia proceeded for more than an hour, and at last she arrived in sight of the village which Theresina had mentioned to her, and finally entered it. But there was not a light to be seen in any of the houses; quietness reigned throughout the place, and it was quite evident that the inhabitants had all retired to rest. Despair fell upon Olympia's heart, especially as the storm did not decrease the least in violence, and she paused for a moment or two, undecided in which manner to act. She feared to rouse any of the inhabitants, uncertain of the reception they might give her, and also apprehensive of discovery, and at length resolved upon proceeding on her dreary way and trusting to chance. The tempest again increased in violence; wind and rain vied with each other, and it required the strongest nerve to bear up against it, independent of which there could not be a wilder tract of country than that which presented itself to the eyes of Olympia after she had quitted the village. Again she regretted having quitted the cavern, and liberty, under her present melancholy circumstances, was robbed of nearly all its charms. But at the same time she could never feel enough grateful to Theresina for the service which she had rendered her, and the risk which she had run for her sake. For more than another hour Olympia pursued her dismal way, and with little or no better prospect to cheer her. But at length the tempest abated in its fury, and ultimately entirely ceased, and then indeed, under all her difficulties, she felt encouraged and invigorated.

"Heaven help me!" she cried, "and guide me to some place where I and my infant may obtain at least a few hours' rest and shelter."

And Heaven did hear the poor wanderer's prayers, for scarcely had she given utterance to the words, when she came upon the ruins of an old building, which had evidently been left for many years to neglect and decay. However, she paused at the threshold and hesitated to enter, fearing that it might be the retreat of robbers; but listening attentively, and hearing not the slightest sound, save the wind murmuring through the numerous cavities, she ventured to enter. All within was buried in profound darkness, and it was not without the greatest difficulty that she made her way over the fallen ruins, while at the same time a feeling of care came over her which she found it utterly impossible to dismiss from her mind. The ruins were those of an old castle, and it had evidently formerly been a place of great strength, and as far as the partial light would enable Olympia to see, of much architectural beauty, but dark weeds now invaded every part of its once spacious and magnificent apartments, and unwholesome dews clung upon its black and ivy-mantled walls. At length, after wandering for some time over the ruins, Olympia came to an apartment which had in a great measure escaped the ruthless scythe of time, and here she resolved to take up her abode for the remainder of the night. Supplicating the protection of the Supreme, she spread the mantle which Theresina had taken from the corpse of the villain Dargani in the warmest part of the room, and pressing her infant to her breast, laid herself down upon it, and enveloped herself in it, and endeavoured to gain a short respite from her cares and anxieties in sleep. But notwithstanding the extraordinary fatigue which she had undergone for the last two or three hours, it was some time ere she could do so. At length, however, the refreshing god came to her relief, and she did not awake again until the morning's sun was gleaming in at the broken casement of the ruined apartment in which she had sought a shelter. She arose and fervently returned thanks to Providence for having protected her throughout the perils of the night, and then prepared to resume her dreary journey, which she did in much greater spirits, as a fine morning had succeeded the tempest of the preceding night. The atmosphere was particularly clear; the air mild, and all around was as serene as one of the loveliest days in Italy. Olympia felt invigorated in spirits, and pursued her way with renewed courage and confidence. But we should have stated that previous to her leaving the ruins, she had put aside the robber's cloak and hat, imagining that she was now far beyond the reach of pursuit, and that her own apparel was the least likely to excite suspicion. She met with few persons on the road, and nothing particularly worthy of recording occurred to her on the way. But she avoided the high road as much as possible, and shunned the sight of every human being, lest she should happen to encounter an enemy. She followed the directions which Theresina had hastily given her, and pursued her way towards the Appennines, trusting that Providence would guide her footsteps to the retreat of Massaroni, and that she might yet be in time to rescue the Count Alberti from the fate with which he was threatened. After travelling for an hour or two, she arrived at a small retired village, where she procured refreshment, and further directions, and resumed her journey with renewed spirits, though Heaven knows the prospect before her was dreary enough. She met with no adventure throughout the day, and at night she arrived at a town, where she procured a shelter for herself and child; but with the gloomy certainty that she had still many weary miles to travel before she would be able to reach the place of her destination, and even then she might be as distant from the object she had in view as at present, for she felt too painfully convinced that it would be a most difficult task to discover the secret haunt of Massaroni, and she was fearful to make any inquiry of persons whom she might meet with on the road respecting him, lest it should excite any suspicion, and consequently expose her to danger. The following morning at an early hour, she left the house in which she had sought a temporary lodging, and proceeded on her way. About mid-day she came to another village, and was about to enter a house in order to procure some refreshment, when putting her hand in her pocket to her dismay she discovered that the purse containing the money which Theresina had given her was gone, and she was thus left completely destitute. She must have dropped it on the road, or left it at the house where she had last lodged; but what was now to be done? Her situation was most awful, and she beat her breast in despair. However, it was useless to lament, and she had no other alternative but to continue her route, and to place her trust in the goodness of Providence to assist her in the midst of her terrible difficulty. To add to her misfortunes, the sky became overcast, and soon the storm commenced with as much violence as on the night on which she had quitted the cavern. For hours she travelled through a dreary uncultivated part of the country, without meeting with a human habitation, and she seemed to be as far off the place of her destination as ever. She was fast sinking with fatigue, and perishing with cold, wet, and hunger, for many hours had elapsed since she had partaken of food, and such extraordinary exertions and privations was more than she had strength to bear up against. Notwithstanding the raging of the tempest, she was compelled to pause on the road to rest herself, and bitter indeed was the anguish which corroded her breast.

"Alas!" she sighed, "too painfully do I now feel the truth of the warning which Theresina gave me of the perils I should have to encounter. God help me! I had better have remained where I was, and have trusted to Providence to bring about the accomplishment of my wishes? What is now to become of me and my child, exposed to this fearful tempest, in a strange part of the country, and without the means of procuring food or shelter?"

She smote her breast in despair, and for a few minutes was unable to proceed on her way, and was undecided in what manner to act. At length she again slowly proceeded, though her limbs trembled so much with the cold, and the unusual fatigue she had already undergone, that they would scarcely support her, and she expected every moment that she must sink exhausted to the earth. Night came on, and still the storm was raging with unabated fury, and there was not the remotest prospect of her meeting with any place of shelter, nor had she the smallest idea as to what part of the country she had come. She felt confident that she could not proceed much further, but that she must lie herself down and die; but suddenly a glimmering light at a distance burst upon her sight, and revived her hopes. It seemed most probable to her that it proceeded from a human habitation, and surely if the persons to whom it belonged possessed one spark of humanity, they would not fail to pity her in her deplorable situation, and afford her at least a shelter for the night. This thought inspired her with fresh courage, and she walked as rapidly as her enfeebled limbs would permit her, in the direction from whence the light proceeded. It was, however, at a considerable distance, and the way to it was most gloomy and intricate, therefore it was not without considerable difficulty that she was enabled to bear up against these complicated evils; nevertheless, she surmounted them, and at last arrived at a lonely hut, from one of the windows of which the light proceeded. She hesitated at the door, almost fearful to knock; but at length inspired with courage, she did so, and after a short pause, a female put her head out of the window and demanded who was there, and what they wanted?

"A wretched wanderer," replied Olympia, "worn out with fatigue and the inclemency of the weather;—oh, for the love of Heaven grant a few hours' shelter to her and her helpless child."

"It is a dreadful night, sure enough," remarked the woman, "and awful, indeed, for those who are exposed to its fury. My dwelling is humble, but such as it is you are welcome to; never will I refuse a shelter to any of my fellow-creatures who may require it."

"Oh, thanks, thanks, my good woman," said

Olympia; "but alas, a poor destitute being like myself, has no means of rewarding you for your kindness."

"Do not mention it," said the woman; "it is enough for me to know you are unfortunate and without shelter; I seek no reward. Wait but a moment, and I will admit you."

The woman drew in her head as she spoke. and the light disappeared from the window, Presently Olympia heard her descending the stairs, and immediately afterwards the door was opened, and an elderly woman presented herself, bearing a lamp in her hand. She eyed Olympia with much compassion, mingled with curiosity, but instantly requested her to walk into her humble dwelling; and lighting the fuel on the hearth, placed a seat before it for Olympia, without any further ceremony.

"I am but a lone woman, signora," she said "and my means are limited enough, but such as I have you are heartily welcome to. Poor thing, you must have suffered much, exposed to the fury of such a tempest as this; and your poor child, too; oh, what can have placed you in such a melancholy situation? However, that is no business of mine; all that I have to do is to render you such assistance as is in my power. Have you travelled far, signora?"

"Many, many weary miles," replied Olympia, "and having the misfortune to lose what little money I had, on the road, I am left entirely destitute."

"Your case is indeed a most pitiful one, signora," remarked the kind-hearted woman; "have you much farther to travel?"

"I know not," answered Olympia, "for I am a complete stranger in this part of the country. The Appennines is the place of my destination."

"The Appennines," said the woman; "they are a long way from here, and the journey is a dangerous one. I understood that Massaroni, he brigand, is located in that vicinity, though or the matter of that you have nothing to apprehend from him, for he never commits any outrage upon the poor and helpless, especially a woman."

"Have you ever seen Massaroni?" inquired Olympia, eagerly.

"Oh, yes," replied the old woman, "two or three times, and a handsome gentlemanly signor he is. They say he was born to far better prospects, and his manners fully corroborate that assertion. But you require refreshment, signora, and such humble fare as it lies in my power to offer you, you are extremely welcome to."

Olympia again returned her thanks, and her kind-hearted hostess immediately busied herself in placing before her such humble fare as she had, and invited her to partake of it heartily, at the same time expressing her regret that she had nothing better to offer her. Olympia partook freely of the meal, and having warmed herself and her infant by the fire, she felt much re-lieved; the old woman too seemed much gratified with the beneficent results of the attention she had paid her unfortunate guest, and looked upon her with the utmost sympathy and kindness.

"Ah, signora," she remarked, "this is a fearful night for any person to be without a shelter, let it be ever so humble, and I feel happy to think that Providence guided you to me. Your misfortunes must have been very great to expose you and your poor babe to such perils and vicissitudes."

"Alas! they have, my good woman," replied Olympia, "and Heaven only knows when they will terminate. But for you, myself and my tender offspring must have perished, and perhaps——"

"Say no more, signora, I beseech you," interrupted the good old woman; "I have done no more than my duty towards my fellow creatures, and you are extremely welcome. I only regret that I cannot do more."

"Ah," returned Olympia, "how few, how very few, though placed in far better circumstances, would have done so much. May the blessings of God descend upon your head for it. But the Appennines are still a long way from here?"

"Ah, yes, signora," answered her hostess, "more than a day's journey for those who can walk well, and you appear to be quite exhausted already."

"I am indeed worn out with fatigue," observed Olympia; "but still I trust that I shall find strength to reach the end of my journey. The errand I go upon is one of life and death."

"I pity you, signora, from the very bottom of my soul, and wish you success in the undertaking you are going upon; but I have no desire to pry into your secrets, and I only wish it was in my power to assist you more. But it is late, and you had better retire to rest immediately. I will make you up a bed as well as I can in this room, where the fire will help to keep you warm, and I only regret that it is not in my power to accommodate you better."

"Kind woman," ejaculated Olympia, gratefully, "do not mention it, I pray you; I assure you that I can never cease to remember your unostentatious hospitality and benevolence."

The old woman returned no answer, but bustled about, and in a few minutes had made up a comfortable temporary bed, and having placed some more fuel on the fire, and secured the door, she bade Olympia good night, and retired to her own room. When Olympia, was thus left to himself, she placed her sleeping infant on the bed, and covered it up warmly, and then sinking on her knees, she poured forth her thanks to the Almighty for having protected her thus far on her weary journey, and earnestly supplicated His future aid in the prosecution of her designs; though the distance she had yet to travel before she could reach the Appennines, and the uncertainty of her then being able to discover Massaroni, somewhat diminished her spirits, and excited in her bosom numerous doubts and apprehensions. However, she at length became more composed, and having retired to the humble bed which her kind hostess had prepared for her, the extraordinary fatigue she had undergone soon steeped her senses in sleep, which remained undisturbed till the morning, when she awoke much refreshed, and with renewed

FLORIO CLAIRVILLE IN HIS DUNGEON.

fortitude. The old woman was already in the room and was busying herself in preparing breakfast, and when she perceived that Olympia was awake, she saluted her in the most friendly manner, hoped that she had slept well, and that she felt refreshed. Olympia returned a suitable answer, and again thanked her hostess warmly and sincerely for the kindness she had displayed towards her, an entire and destitute stranger; but the old woman interrupted her, and seemed annoyed at the many acknowledgments Olympia made her.

"But I fear, signora," she added, "that you are in no condition to resume your journey at present; a day's rest would do you a world of good, and if it meets with your approbation, I am sure you are extremely welcome to remain here till to-morrow, or even longer if you think proper."

"Oh no, my good woman," replied Olympia, "indeed I cannot think of so far encroaching upon your hospitality and benevolence. Besides, the errand I am going upon will admit of no delay, and even now I fear that I shall be too late."

"Well, signora, you know best; it is not my business to seek to persuade you, and all that I wish is, that your wishes may be crowned with success, and that happier times are in store for you."

"Thanks, thanks," ejaculated Olympia, "but alas! I fear that happiness is never fated to be mine again."

"Say not so—say not so, signora; it is never too late to hope, and you are young; but come, the breakfast is ready, and that will, I trust, serve to revive you."

Olympia now arose, and having dressed herself, she seated herself at the table by the side of the old woman, and gratefully partook of the plentiful though homely meal she had so generously provided for her. When this was over, she prepared to resume her journey.

"I deeply regret, signora," said the old woman, "that my means are so limited that it is not in my power to assist you with money, but here are provisions for the day, and may God speed you on your way, and bring your journey to a successful termination."

Olympia was so overpowered by the unexampled kindness of this excellent hearted woman, that she could not refrain from tears. She pressed her hand cordially, and for several minutes was unable to give any other expression to her feelings. The old woman now gave her some more instructions as to the route she had better pursue, in order to be able to reach her journey's end in the least possible distance, and Olympia having again poured forth her thanks for the kindness she had received from her, they parted with as much regret as if they had been acquainted for many years, and Olympia resumed her melancholy journey. The storm had ceased, but still the aspect of the heavens was most threatening, and it was perfectly apparent that another and perhaps severer tempest was impending. Olympia wrapped her cloak closely around the tender form of her infant, and pursued her devious way with much better fortitude than it could have been expected for her to muster on such an occasion. The kindness of the hospitable old woman, who had afforded her shelter and relief, had made a lasting impression upon her mind, and many were the mental prayers she offered up to the Throne of Grace for her welfare. Alas! how few individuals in the world, and moving in a far more elevated situation, possessed of every means to assist their less fortunate fellow creatures, would have been the friend to her that that humble individual had. But when she reflected upon the distance she had yet to travel before she could reach the place of her destination, the many dangers and vicissitudes she might have to encounter, and the terrible uncertainty, after all, of achieving her object, her heart sickened, and she could scarcely find strength to proceed on her way. The storm which had threatened now came on, and Olympia found herself at that time in one of the wildest and most uncultivated parts of the country, without the smallest prospect of any place of shelter, and her journey's end appeared to be as far off as ever. And what were her prospects when she had even arrived at the termination of that journey? She had not a fraction of coin; the provisions with which the old woman had supplied her so generously were now almost exhausted; she had not a friend upon the earth to whom to apply for assistance, and what was then to become of her and her child? These dismal thoughts drove her to such a state of despair, that she was several times almost urged to lay violent hands upon herself and her innocent offspring, and thus at once rid themselves of an existence which seemed to be by fate fraught with every misery that could attend the human race. But an inscrutable power maintained and supported her throughout, and saved her from the perpetration of so fatal and awful a crime. The distance she was travelling, notwithstanding the old woman had doubtless given her the clearest and shortest directions, seemed to her to be interminable; her frame was sinking fast with fatigue, and she now regretted that she had not accepted of her hostess's kind offer to remain another day at her humble dwelling, as she might then have been in a better condition to prosecute her dreary journey to the end. Through the raging storm the wretched woman continued to travel, nor did she meet with a single individual from whom she might ask relief, or who would probably commiserate the deplorable situation of herself and her infant. At length, however, she came upon a little hamlet, the inhabitants of which seemed to be in the humblest circumstances, and were incapable of furnishing her with more than a temporary shelter. There seemed no probability of the storm subsiding, and even worn out with fatigue as she was, so anxious was she to reach the end of her journey, and so fearful was she of the fate which might await Alberti, if Providence did not quickly guide her to his rescue, that Olympia, braving the fury of the tempest, and, notwithstanding the day was waning fast, resumed her dreary way. Night came on and found her in the midst of a dismal forest, the very aspect of which, even under far different circumstances, was sufficient to inspire the stoutest heart with feelings of terror and dismay. The thunder roared, and the lightning blazed, rendering the scene one of the most marked for terror and danger; but still the hapless wanderer pursued her way with much greater fortitude than could have been at all anticipated. She had penetrated some distance into the forest, when the tempest fortunately abated in violence, and by degrees it entirely ceased, and the black and ponderous clouds which had before obscured the sky dispersing, the moon showed her silvery face, as if to inspire the weary traveller with hope. But completely exhausted, and drenched to the skin, Olympia could with difficulty drag one limb before the other, and she would have given the world, had it been at her command, to have found a spot where she could have rested herself if it had only been for the shortest time. At length fortune favoured her; she arrived at a spot so over-canopied by thickly foliaged trees, that it had been rendered completely impervious to the recent storm, and by Nature was formed for a place of rest and shelter to those who might need its friendly aid. Olympia hailed it with gratitude and delight, and selecting a spot whereon the moist dew of Heaven had scarcely descended, she seated herself, and enfolding her infant closer to her breast to shield it from the cold, she endeavoured to compose herself to rest. It was no easy task to accomplish, and long she struggled to obtain even a moment's respite from her cares, but at length she was about to fall into a kind of deze, when she was suddenly startled by hearing the sounds of numerous approaching footsteps, interspersed by the voices of men in busy but subdued conversation. She started to her feet, and trembled in every limb, not knowing what course to adopt, and for the moment she was apprehensive that the robbers had been sent in pursuit of her, and had by some means or other tracked out the course she was pursuing. They were evidently approaching in the exact direction of the spot where she was concealed, and to fly was impossible; all that she had to hope was that they might pass by without observing her, and she therefore again crouched down in the smallest compass she possibly could, and awaited the issue in the most trembling state of anxiety. She was not kept many minutes in suspense; for the party approached to within a few paces even of the spot where she was concealed, and she was enabled to distinguish by the light of the moon that there were some dozen of them, and to all appearance they were mere simple rustics. However, fearful that she might be mistaken in her conjectures, she concealed herself from observation as much as she could, in order that, as they passed her, she might be enabled to gather from their conversation what they actually were. They now came so close to her, that she could hear distinctly

all they said, and she listened with the most breathless attention.

"Have we not mistaken our way, do you think?" remarked one of them;—"it strikes me that we had no business to cross this forest, and that we have been misled."

"Oh, no, Aldroni," returned another of the men, "we are right enough, I am certain of that, for I have travelled the same way years ago, and know every inch of the ground. Our captain, I have no doubt, can bear me out in my observations."

"Yes, Carlotz," said a voice, which struck with the power of an electric clock upon the ears of Olympia, "you speak the truth; we are now in the right direction, though we have previously wandered from our way, or we should now have been more advanced on our journey. Nevertheless, there is one fortunate thing, namely, that the tempest has subsided and by the appearance of yon silvery planet, it does not seem likely that it will commence again for some time. Our companions, it seems, have reached the place of assignation in safety, and will be ready to assist us in our plans."

Who shall describe the emotions of Olympia as she recognized in the tones of the voice of the last speaker, those of Massaroni?—She could not repress an exclamation of surprise, which immediately attracted the attention of the brigands, and they directed their notice to the spot from whence it issued.

"Who have we here?" exclaimed Massaroni, advancing first; "speak, stranger—if you need assistance you will find those that are ready to render it you, as far as it lies in their power."

Olympia endeavoured to answer, but utterance was denied her, and the brigand chief approached her nearer.

"It is a female," he exclaimed; "and apparently in the last stage of exhaustion.—Quick, Carlotz—the lantern and the flagon."

Carlotz advanced accordingly, and opening his lantern, threw its full light upon the pale countenance of Olympia; but how Massaroni started, when in a moment he recognized her.

"Signora Olympia!" he exclaimed, "is it possible that fate has so guided us to you whom we were going to rescue? This, this, is indeed fortunate."

"Massaroni," gasped forth Olympia, "you profess yourself, and I believe you to be my friend, and willing to serve me to the utmost of your power."

"Yes, yes," fervently returned the brigand chief, "but what brings you in your present situation? How have you been enabled to effect your escape from the power of those who have so long and so unjustly deprived you of your liberty?"

As he put these questions to her he raised her from the earth with the utmost respect, and awaited her answer with the utmost impatience and curiosity.

"Every explanation I will give you anon, Massaroni," Olympia at last replied, "but the Count Alberti——"

"Your betrayer, your greatest enemy——"

"Most true—most true; you succeeded in getting him into your power, did you not?"

"I did."

"But you have proceeded to no further acts of violence against him, have you, Massaroni?" eagerly questioned Olympia.

"I solemnly declare that I have not, signora," replied Massaroni; "after long obstinately refusing to make me acquainted with the place where he had you confined, he at last thought it prudent to yield, and myself and my comrades were now on our way to liberate you."

"But he is still your prisoner?"

"Yes, and will remain so until you are secure from his further cruelty and oppression," answered Massaroni.

"Thank Heaven!" ejaculated Olympia, "that his life has not fallen a sacrifice. My mind is now relieved of a heavy burthen of care and anxiety, and I care little what may become of me."

"Say not so, signora," said Massaroni, kindly; "believe me, robber though I be, I deeply sympathise in your fate, and will do all I can to serve you and restore you to happiness. You must be aware, from what I have already told you, that I am no stranger to your history, and its similarity to my own has created no ordinary interest in my breast. From the brigand chief you have nothing to fear, but everything to hope. Already he feels towards you, the sentiments of a brother, as he is, at any rate, a brother in misfortune, and by Heaven you shall find him act as those sentiments dictate."

"Thanks, thanks, Massaroni," returned Olympia, for the sympathy you express in my welfare; but alas! there is no hope for him; it seems as though I had no business in the world, and the sooner that I and my poor infant are out of it the better."

"Nay, I beseech you, signora," remarked Massaroni, "do not talk in this melancholy strain, for dismal as your prospects, I admit at present seem to be, depend upon it there are happier days in store for you, and the time will come when you will be enabled to look upon the dreary past as only a frightful dream."

"Would that I could think so," sighed Olympia.

"My predictions will be verified, depend upon it," returned the brigand chief; "set your mind at rest, Signora Olympia, and all will yet turn out much better than your most sanguine anticipations can at present conceive. In my

secret retreat you shall find every respectful attention and protection; and woe to those who shall dare to offer you insult. I am an outlaw, it is true, whom they endeavour to hunt from society, to stigmatize with the title of fiend; but they shall yet find that Allesandro Massaroni, the brigand chief, is a man in every sense of the word, and possessed of all man's noblest attributes and aspirations."

As he expressed himself in these words, the handsome countenance of Massaroni was animated with even more than usual energy and intelligence, and Olympia could not help looking upon him with feelings of the utmost admiration, if not approaching to veneration. Desperate as was his calling, lawless as were his pursuits; terrible as was the name he had acquired in the country, she placed the greatest reliance on his honour, and hailed her extraordinary and unexpected meeting with him at a moment so critical as a most fortunate circumstance, and the observations he had made use of, and which evidently sprung from his very soul, revived her hopes.

"Massaroni," she said at length, "I am a poor, wretched, forlorn creature, without a friend in the world, unless I find one in you, where I had the least right to look for one; but I will place every reliance on your honour and on your promises, seeing that you have no reasonable motive for wishing to deceive me, and convinced of the many risks you have already run in seeking to serve me. I place myself under your protection, and may Heaven reward you as you fulfil the hopes, to the best of your ability, which you have held out to me."

"I thank you for this confidence, signora," replied the brigand chief, "and you shall find that I will not abuse it. Allesandro Massaroni never yet deceived mortal being, whether for good or evil. But this Rinaldi, the bandit, in whose power you have been, and whom, I understand, is entirely the creature of the Count Alberti, and compelled to do his bidding, how has he behaved to you since you have been in his power?"

"Oh, with the utmost respect and forbearance," answered Olympia; "it is true that he is under certain obligations to Alberti, which I am totally unacquainted with, and feels bound to do his bidding; but I solemnly assure you, that during the time I have been in confinement, I have experienced no insult from him, but, on the contrary, he professed to do so, and I sincerely believe he did, sympathise in my misfortunes."

"Now this is well," observed Massaroni; "his character is very different to what it has been represented to me, and by it he may save himself from that severe account, to which I was resolved to call him for misconduct."

"Oh, I implore you, Massaroni," said Olympia, "that whatever designs you may have formed against Rinaldi, now that I am restored to liberty, and you have heard his treatment of me, you will abandon them. It would inflict the greatest anguish on me should any harm befall him through my means."

"Your good feeling does you credit, signora," remarked Massaroni; "but let me ask you whether it was a voluntary act on his part by which you were restored to liberty, or merely by accident?"

"It was not a voluntary act on the part of Rinaldi, I candidly acknowledge," replied Olympia, "though I firmly believe his will was good to do so, could he have shaken himself from the trammels of Alberti; but his wife, an excellent woman, and one devoted to her husband, released me at every risk, and I should be the most ungrateful of human beings did I not wish to save her and her husband from the consequences which might otherwise follow."

Massaroni was evidently affected by these observations, and he communed with himself for a few moments in silence.

"Woman, woman," he said at length, "thou art ever the same—kind, humane, and amiable—whatsoever may be the station in which fate has placed thee, when thy nature has not been corrupted. My dear devoted Maria, methinks in this same bandit's wife I already see a reflection of thy fair self, and I am prepared to honour her in consequence. Signora Olympia, I would fain be put in possession of the name of this amiable though unfortunate woman?"

"Theresina," replied Olympia without hesitation. "She has indeed been the victim of a cruel destiny, but I will make you acquainted with all the particulars at a more fitting opportunity."

"Be it so," returned Massaroni; then addresing himself to Carlotz, he observed, "hasten you without delay to the place where our comrades await our arrival, and bid them return to rejoin us in our secret haunt without delay. Such a fortunate termination to our expedition I little anticipated, and I am glad enough of it, after the recent struggles that we have had with the Prince Bianchi's troops."

Carlotz waited for no further orders, but immediately took his departure, and Massaroni, turning to Olympia, said—

"We delay time, and the hour is getting late; come, signora, resign your infant to the care of one of my band, and lean on me for support. We should not be able to reach the place of my retreat to-night, were we to attempt it, but about a league across this forest, will bring us to a place where I am well known, and where we shall be enabled to procure every accommodation that we may require. Do not fear, lady, for you are now under the protection of one, brigand though he be, who will not deceive you, but will, at the very hazard of his life, guard you from every danger that may assail you."

The words of Massaroni inspired Olympia with the utmost confidence, and she expressed herself accordingly. Accepting the arm of the brigand-chief accordingly, after having first resigned her infant to the care of one of the band, she walked on with renewed hope, and grateful to that Omnipotence who had so mercifully and unexpectedly brought about the gratification of her wishes. They conversed but little on the way, Olympia reserving the questions she was so anxious to put to Massaroni, till a future opportunity, and after walking for more than an hour, they emerged from the forest, and came upon a more open part of the country. They met not a single individual in the way, and at length a light, as if glimmering from the window of a human habitation, met the observation of Olympia.

"It is fortunate," remarked Massaroni, "they have not yet retired to rest; but if they had, we could soon have aroused them. Cheer up, signora, for your journey for to night will soon be at an end."

"And is that the place of our destination from whence the light issues?" asked Olympia.

"It is," answered Massaroni; "I am well known to those who keep it, for they have experienced no little services from me, and there we shall find every accommodation."

A few minutes' more walking brought them to the door of a pretty large house, and of not uninviting appearance, though there was no other building near it, and the spot on which it was situated was not the most agreeable one in the world. Massaroni gave three peculiar knocks on the door with his knuckles, and the light immediately disappeared, a head emerged from the window, and a man's voice demanded in cautious accents, who was there, and what they wanted.

"Friends," answered the brigand-chief; "you know me, Ruberti?"

"Ah!" replied the man, "so soon returned? I was about to retire for the night."

"Be quick, then," said Massaroni, "for I have one with me who requires immediate assistance."

"I will be down with you in an instant," returned the man, and he drew in his head, and Olympia heard him descending the stairs. The next moment the door was opened, and a man habited as a farmer appeared with a lamp in his hand, which he held above his head, and scrutinized Olympia with no little curiosity.

"All right, Ruberti," answered Massaroni, "lead the way; we shall, by your permission, be your guests for to-night. Has your wife retired to bed yet?"

"She has not, signor," replied Ruberti.

"That is well," said Massaroni; "I shall want her to attend upon this lady, and to show her every kindness and attention, for she is my particular friend, and under my protection. Do you mark me, Ruberti?"

"Very good, signor," returned Ruberti, bowing obsequiously; "this way, signora, if you please. Mannetti! Mannetti!"

Thus speaking, Ruberti led the way into an inner room, where a cheerful fire was still blazing on the hearth, and Olympia, taking her child from the arms of the brigand, who had carried it. sunk on a seat, greatly relieved from the weight of care and anxiety which had previously oppressed her mind. Massaroni now drew Ruberti aside, and conversed with him for a few seconds in an under tone, at the termination of which the man bowed in obedience to what Massaroni had said to him, and then made his exit from the room, motioning to the companions of the brigand chief to follow him, which they did, having bid Massaroni good night. They had not been gone many minutes when an elderly woman made her appearance, bringing in refreshments, which she placed before Olympia and Massaroni, at the same time observing that —

"When the signora thought fit to retire, she should be most happy to conduct her to the chamber allotted to her."

Notwithstanding the exhaustion which Olympia had undergone, she felt but little inclined to eat, and only partook of the repast sparingly.

"I will not detain you longer, signora," observed Massaroni, when she had concluded, "for the hour is late, and you must, after the extraordinary fatigue you have undergone for so many hours, require rest. It is also necessary that we should depart by daylight in the morning. Here, I assure you, you may rest yourself perfectly secure, for no harm can possibly befall you. Good night, unfortunate signora, and may your dreams be those of happiness and hope; that is the sincere wish of Allesandro Massaroni, the brigand chief."

Olympia returned her thanks to him with fervour and sincerity. Mannetti was then summoned to attend upon her, and having bade Massaroni good night, and told him she would be ready to attend him at any hour of the morning, she followed Mannetti from the room. Having conducted her up a long winding flight of stairs to the top of the house, Mannetti stopped at an oaken door, which she unlocked, and Olympia was ushered into a very comfortable-looking bed-chamber, in which a fire had been kindled, and everything that the time would permit, prepared for her accommodation.

"You can rest here in safety, signora," remarked Mannetti, "for no one will attempt to disturb you. Under the protection of Massaroni you are more safe than if you were surrounded by all the Prince Bianchi's troops.

Good night, signora, and may the morning find you refreshed after the fatigue you have evidently undergone."

Olympia returned her acknowledgments for Mannetti's good wishes, and the latter then took her leave and left her to herself. For a few minutes after Mannetti had departed, Olympia was so bewildered at the singularity of all that had happened to her, that she sat wholly absorbed in thought, but at length arousing herself from this lethargy, she clasped her hands vehemently together, and fervently returned her thanks to that All-Merciful Power who had preserved her thus far through all her unexampled trials, and humbly but earnestly implored His future protection. She placed the utmost reliance on the promises of Massaroni, and, assured of the safety of Alberti, she felt far lighter of heart than she had done for some months previously. Having secured the door of the chamber by bolting it on the inside, she retired to the bed prepared for her, and it was not long ere sleep descended upon her eyelids. She did not awake until Mannetti aroused her in the morning, and requested to know whether she was prepared to arise, as Massaroni was awaiting her below, and was ready to resume the journey as soon as they had partaken of the morning repast. Olympia immediately arose, feeling invigorated after her night's rest, and returning her thanks to Mannetti for the respect and attention, she had paid her, she prepared to join the brigand chief. Previous, however, to her leaving the chamber, she again returned her thanks to the Almighty for having thus preserved and supported her throughout her many difficulties, and supplicated His further mercy. Having performed this act of duty, she felt inspired with fresh confidence, and pressing her still sleeping child to her breast with all a mother's fondest affection, she descended the stairs and entered the apartment in which Massaroni was awaiting her. He received her with the utmost politeness and respect, inquiring with the affection of a brother after her health, and requesting to know whether she felt herself in a condition to travel for the present.

"Because, if you are not," he observed, "my friends here will afford you every accommodation till you are, and I will also remain to protect you."

Olympia most fervently returned her acknowledgments for his kindness, but at the same time assured him that she felt fully competent to undertake the journey, and that she was most anxious to arrive at its termination in order that she might again see the Count Alberti, and be assured of his safety.

"Be it so, fair signora," remarked Massaroni, "and as you may command, so will I act, always having a due regard for your future happiness and welfare, and insisting that my prisoner renders you all the justice in his power for the injuries he has inflicted on you."

"I thank you, Massaroni, most fervently, for the interest you take in my fate," remarked Olympia, "but I can freely forgive Alberti, notwithstanding his cruel and treacherous conduct towards me. He must have suffered much already, and I regret that you should have been induced to proceed to such lengths, but I earnestly hope that no further harm will come to him."

"And is it possible, signora, that, after all the degradation and misery to which the count has so mercilessly subjected you, you can so easily pardon him and sympathise in his future fate?" asked Massaroni.

"Oh, yes, most willingly," answered Olympia, "for, in spite of all that it has been my hard lot to endure from him, I feel that I can never cease to love him with all the fervour with which he at first inspired me, when I believed him to be the very soul of virtue and honour."

"Unexampled self-devotion," ejaculated the brigand chief, admiringly, "how little worthy is the Count Alberti of such clemency and affectionate regard. But believe me, lady, I will not in any way seek to control your wishes in any respect, though I must insist that your heartless betrayer and persecutor shall render you some adequate atonement for the wrongs and oppressions he has inflicted upon your head, before I can consent to part with him. To this you cannot, I think, raise any reasonable objection in justice to yourself, and for your future protection."

"It is evident that you are my friend, Massaroni," returned Olympia, "and I will therefore be guided entirely by you, certain that you will not abuse the confidence I place in you."

"I thank you, fair signora, for the good opinion you are pleased to entertain of my motives," said the brigand chief, "and believe me, you shall have no cause to repent of the reliance you place upon me. Let whatever may be the consequences, you shall ever find that in Allesandro Massaroni you have at least a sincere friend, as he has always been to the injured and oppressed. Ah! lady, I too have experienced many bitter sorrows and wrongs, wrongs that would have crushed many a weaker spirit, and made him the general enemy of his fellow creatures. Like yourself, the beloved parent who gave me being was the victim of a noble villain, who afterwards abandoned her and her offspring to misery, shame, and want. She died of a broken heart, and left me alone in the world, without a friend or protector."

"Unfortunate woman," ejaculated Olympia, with a tear of sympathy; "and her betrayer's name was——"

"I know not," interrupted Massaroni; "she ever refused to reveal it to me, lest I should pursue him with my vengeance, and the secret perished with her; but the time will yet come, I feel satisfied, when I shall discover him, and then let him tremble, for he shall receive a terrible retribution for his past crimes."

"Not at your hands, Massaroni," said Olympia; "you could not seek to wreak your vengeance on the head of the author of your being?"

"Was he not the seducer, the murderer of my mother?" demanded the brigand;—"did he not abandon us both to every shame and sorrow?—Is it not he who has made me what I am, an outlaw and a robber, hunted from society, with a price set upon my head—the bloodhounds of the law constantly tracking my path, and thirsting for my life?—What mercy can such a miscreant expect at my hands?— But pardon me, signora, for entering upon this subject, and for having thus thrust my melancholy history upon your notice. I have merely done so to convince you how much reason I have to sympathise with you, and to prove to you that cruel destiny alone, and not my own faults, have made me what I am, and that I am not exactly the heartless, reckless villain that by some I am represented to be."

"Indeed I do believe you, Massaroni," remarked Olympia, "and sincerely pity you, and trust that something will yet occur to alter your condition, and to restore you to that sphere of society you were evidently born to adorn."

"I thank you, lady, for your good wishes, but still I cannot flatter myself with the hope that they will ever be realised. Besides, I am now inured to my wild mountain life. I have a wife whose very soul is devoted to me; who has freely, cheerfully shared all my dangers and vicissitudes, and who would gladly lay down her very life to serve me. My comrades are brave and faithful; I rule a little kingdom of my own, and I can have no wish beyond it. No, Allesandro Massaroni feels satisfied that he shall live and die a brigand chief, though the time will yet come when it will be shown that, had it not been for cruelty and injustice, he might have moved amongst the noblest and most honourable."

This conversation took place while Olympia and Massaroni were partaking of the plenteous meal which had been prepared for them; and Olympia became more deeply interested with the brigand chief every word that he uttered. At length, when it was concluded, and Olympia was fully prepared for the journey, Massaroni excused himself to her for a few minutes, and retired from the apartment, to consult, as he informed her, with their host. He was not long gone, and when he returned he informed her that he had arranged with the man to procure a vehicle, for the distance to the place of his retreat was yet considerable, and he was fearful that, after the fatigue she had already undergone, she would not be able to walk it; besides, it would be the best means of conceal-ment. Olympia thanked him for his kind con-sideration, and in a few minutes afterwards the vehicle drove up to the door, and Massaroni taking her arm, handed her into it, and follow-ing himself, they proceeded on their journey at a rapid pace, Olympia's spirits reviving the farther they advanced; for when she reflected on the good fortune which had crowned her wishes in throwing her in the way of Mas-saroni at the very moment when nothing but the gloomiest prospects of despair seemed spread before her, she felt confident that she must have perished with her infant on the road.

————

CHAPTER XXVI.

THE JOURNEY COMPLETED.—A DISCOVERY.—
THE ALARM.

ALL symptoms of the late inclement wea-ther had entirely disappeared, and the sun was now shining with golden majesty upon the face of nature, invigorating the spirits of the tra-vellers, and inspiring Olympia with renewed hope. As they proceeded, Massaroni requested Olympia, in order to while away the tediousness of the journey, to make him acquainted with the particulars that had happened to her while she was confined in the robber's cavern, and how it, was she had succeeded in effecting her escape, with which, of course, she did not hesitate to comply, and Massaroni listened to her with no little degree of interest; and when she had arrived at the conclusion he remarked—

"Your escape was most fortunate, signora, for had it not have been effected until my arrival at the cavern, there might have been much bloodshed, which, believe me, I am al-ways most anxious to avoid ; and I should the more have regretted it as Rinaldi behaved to you with so much respect and forbearance. I must see this robber chief, and personally return my acknowledgments to him for his conduct towards you. From all that you have stated to me respecting him, he too, like myself, appears to have been the victim of misfortune, cruelty, and oppression."

"He has," coincided Olympia, "and I firmly believe that he is sincerely to be pitied. I trust, however, that his wife, Theresina, will not incur his wrath for the service she has rendered me."

"I hope not," observed Massaroni, "for her conduct towards you proves that she is a noble-minded woman, and such a one as must ever meet my warmest admiration and friendship. The retribution she inflicted upon the cowardly ruffian Dargoni was a bold act, and you are greatly indebted to her, signora."

Massaroni now related to Olympia such par-ticulars as had occurred to him since they had last met, and during the time that the Count Alberti had been in his power; the various attempts that had been made by the Prince Bianchi and his other friends to rescue him, and the signal defeat they had experienced at his hands. Olympia could not but listen to these details with feelings of terror; but at the same time she was compelled to admit that the brigand chief had only acted in self-defence, and that, considering the obstinacy of Alberti, and the pertinacity with which he had denied all knowledge of the place of her con-finement, or that she had been forced from her home by his means, Massaroni had behaved with considerable forbearance towards him. But how could he encounter her, she reflected, after the cruelty and injustice with which he had acted towards her ? What could he say in extenuation for his conduct ? What atone-ment could he offer for the irreparable injuries he had done her? Was it at all likely—obstinate, proud, and unfeeling as she knew him to be—that he would be brought to a proper sense of compassion ? That he would acknow-ledge how deeply he had wronged her, and express a wish to make her all the reparation in his power ? She dared not encourage such a hope. And how could she again find courage to meet him ? What could she say to move him to pity and repentance ? She firmly believed he would remain inflexible, and that all that he had suffered from the brigand chief would but serve to incite him at the first oppor-tunity to pursue her with his vengeance. These thoughts she communicated to Massaroni, and he tried all he could to combat them, and to dismiss them from her mind.

"Do not entertain any such apprehensions, signora," he remarked, "for while Alberti knows you are under my protection, he will not dare to attempt anything to your future annoyance. He is by this time, I should think, fully convinced of the power I wield, and will not recklessly brave it. Rest your mind con-tented, and all will terminate anon more satis-factorily than you now anticipate."

"But what are the conditions you mean to try to exact from him, Massaroni ?" asked his companion.

"A future and ample provision for yourself and child," answered the brigand, "and like-wise that he shall abandon his presumptuous designs against the fair Signora Melina, whose heart is irrevocab'y attached to Signor Clair-ville, whose numerous virtues render him every way worthy of her."

"Oh, that he will never submit to," said Olympia; "his proud spirit, I am convinced, will never permit him to do so."

"Then he must take the consequences, for on no other conditions will I consent to restore him to liberty. On that, Olympia, my mind is firmly fixed."

"Nay, Massaroni, for my sake, you will alter your mind. I seek nothing more from him than an acknowledgment of the injustice with which he has behaved towards me, and a solemn promise that he will never again seek to annoy me in any shape. I might be happy, had I the means of hiding my sorrows from the world in the holy walls of some religious asylum."

"Compose yourself, signora," observed Mas-

STORALDI FURNISHES ALBERTI WITH A DISGUISE AND AIDS HIS ESCAPE.

saroni in accents of respect and compassion, "and we will talk further of this anor. I entertain the most sanguine hopes as to your own future destiny, and it shall not be any fault of mine if they are not realised."

Olympia again thanked him for his good intentions towards her, and by a powerful effort her feelings did become more tranquil. Having now travelled for some time, they stopped at a roadside house of entertainment, which was well known to Massaroni, and where he knew they would be secure from every danger; and

No. 23.

having assisted Olympia to alight, they entered a room at the back of the house, where they were quickly joined by the landlord, who received the brigand chief with all due respect and cordiality, but eyed his companion with no inconsiderable degree of curiosity. Massaroni, however, diverted his attention from her by a significant look, and then drawing him aside, conversed with him privately for a few minutes. The man bowed in apparent compliance with the request which Massaroni had made to him, and he then retired from the room. In a short time he returned, bringing in the refreshments which Massaroni had ordered, and he then again retired and left him and Olympia to themselves. Little conversation passed during this meal, and it being despatched, and a change of horses having taken place, they once more took their departure, and proceeded through a romantic part of the country, but which seemed to be, notwithstanding, but little frequented.

"The distance is much greater than I anticipated," said Olympia. "I should never have been able to have accomplished it on foot."

"No, signora," returned Massaroni, "you must have sunk under it, I am afraid, and it was therefore a most providential thing that you encountered me and my companions."

"But have we much farther to go?" asked Olympia.

"We cannot reach the end of our journey before night," answered the brigand, "for the road is a bad one to travel, and we cannot proceed so fast as I could wish; but make your mind easy, for no danger will beset us, and we shall be received with every kindness and respect in the place of my retreat."

Olympia returned no answer, and gave herself up entirely to her own thoughts, which, as the reader may imagine, were of the most conflicting and painful nature. Massaroni did not offer to interrupt her, and they proceeded for some distance farther in silence. If anything could have diverted the thoughts of Olympia from the gloomy subjects which engrossed them, it would have been the extreme beauty of the scenery they were travelling among, now glittering in the broad effulgent rays of the setting sun; but that which at any other time would have excited her utmost enthusiasm, was now viewed by her with feelings of almost perfect indifference, and she became still more anxious than ever to reach the end of the journey. The sun now retired, twilight succeeded, and then the moon burst forth with the greatest splendour, and caused every object to appear as distinct as if it had been noonday. The dark shadows of the majestic Appenines at length burst upon their view, and the spirits of Olympia revived as they approached nearer the place of their destination, but still she could not entirely banish from her mind certain me-

lancholy doubts and forebodings, although Massaroni sought to the best of his ability to inspire her with hope. In about another hour they arrived at the residence of old Montaldi, whom Massaroni had already mentioned to Olympia in the most favourable terms, and where he stopped, resolving to place her under the old man's care until such time as he had prepared his wife for her reception. They found Montaldi alone, but he arose immediately on their entrance, and greeted Olympia with much kindness and respect, though there was an agitation in his manner which immediately attracted the attention of the brigand, and excited his impatient curiosity.

"You see," he remarked, "that I have succeeded in my expedition, and have rescued the signora without having had occasion to have recourse to any act of violence. But how is this, my good friend, you look agitated; has anything occurred to disturb you? How is the Signora Ottavia?"

"Much the same, Massaroni," replied the old man, "and at present in her own room;—but—but—I regret to have to impart bad news to you, and which particularly concerns you and the signora. All is confusion at the cavern, and your return has been most anxiously looked forward to by Maria your wife."

"Ah!" exclaimed Massaroni, hurriedly, "what has happened? Has there been another attack made by the enemy during my absence from the cavern?"

"No," replied Montaldi, "but after what has taken place, it is to be apprehended that there soon will be."

"Remove my doubts at once by telling me the truth exactly as it stands," said Massaroni, impatiently.

"The fact then is," returned Montaldi, "that the Count Alberti has escaped!"

Olympia uttered a shriek of mingled astonishment and pleasure, and she was so overpowered by her feelings that she almost fainted; but it would be impossible to describe the emotions of Massaroni at the unexpected and astounding intelligence of old Montaldi.

"Escaped!" he cried, "the Count Alberti once more at liberty? Is it possible? or do my ears deceive me?"

"It is true," replied Montaldi, "as you will soon ascertain beyond all doubts!"

"Diavolo!" cried the brigand chief, stamping his feet furiously, and his countenance flushed with rage, "how is this? Who are those among my band who have dared to turn traitors to me?——"

"Storaldi!" answered Montaldi, "who was formerly, it appears, in the service of the count's father. He contrived to drug the drink of his companions, and he and Alberti, while they were in a state of insensibility, and your wife was absent from the cave, took their departure, an although they were pursued as soon as their flight was discovered, they succeeded in making their escape."

"May eternal curses light upon the wretch," exclaimed the brigand chief, fiercely, and pacing the room with disordered steps; "is it then come to this, that Massaroni can no longer depend upon his own comrades? Oh, but the dastardly knave shall not escape me, even though he has now placed himself under the protection of the Count Alberti, and terrible is the revenge that I will wreak upon his head. Little did I expect to receive such news as this on my return. But I will lose no time in guarding against the consequences that might otherwise follow this misfortune. Montaldi, to your care I will entrust the Signora Olympia, and I know I need not request you to behave with every kindness and respect towards her. Olympia, endeavour to compose yourself, and fear not—Massaroni has sworn to guard you against every danger, even at the hazard of his life, and he will not fail to keep his word. Montaldi will attend to your wants, and I will shortly return."

Thus saying he abruptly quitted the house, and left Olympia in a most agitated state of mind, from which it did not seem likely that she would quickly recover. The escape of Alberti, although it caused her some satisfaction, could not but create the greatest emotion in her breast, not only on account of Massaroni, who had evinced such a warm feeling of generous and disinterested friendship towards her, but also in consequence of what the result might be to the count himself, whom the brigand chief would now not fail to pursue with his deadliest animosity and revenge, and whose power was so great, that she could not imagine Alberti would long be able to escape from it. These thoughts were sufficient to distract her mind, and she remained, for some time after the departure of Massaroni, unable to utter a syllable. Montaldi looked at her with the deepest kindness and sympathy, and seemed much struck with her appearance and the painful circumstances in which one so young and lovely was placed.

"My dear young signora," he remarked at length, "Massaroni has made me acquainted with the melancholy particulars of your history, and I sincerely assure you that I deeply pity your misfortunes, and entertain a proper feeling of abhorrence towards that man who has heaped such cruel wrongs upon your head. But be comforted; for there is an all-merciful God above who ever watches over the innocent; He will restore you to happiness, and bring your oppressor to a terrible account for the injustice he has done you.

"Indeed, signor," replied Olympia, "I cannot sufficiently thank you for the commiseration you are pleased to express towards me;

but happiness, alas! can never more be mine in this world; and it would be a blessed release should it please the Almighty to take me and my poor child to himself."

"Indeed, my good young lady," said Montaldi, "I cannot bear to hear you talk in this dismal strain. It would be dreadful indeed for one so young to be shut out from every hope in this world. Few are the fortunate mortals who escape the storms of adversity, but religion and a firm reliance on the goodness of Providence should sustain us in the midst of even our severest trials, and we should never give way entirely to despair; the same hand that stretches us low in misery is enabled suddenly to raise us to the very pinnacle of earthly happiness."

The old man then fixed his eyes stedfastly on her countenance for a moment or two, and muttered to himself—

"The resemblance is most extraordinary; the longer I gaze at her the more am I struck with it."

"What mean you, signor?" said Olympia, who, although they had been spoken in so low a tone, had overheard his observations, "why do you look so earnestly at me?"

"Pardon me, signora," returned the old man, "for my apparent rudeness, but the remarkable likeness to one who has long been placed under my protection, and who has drained the cup of sorrow to the very dregs, struck me; but after all it may be but imagination. However, you need refreshment. Excuse me, and I will return to you in a few minutes."

Before Olympia could make any reply, Montaldi quitted the room, and she was left to her own reflections. What the nature of those were we have no occasion to describe, for the reader may easily imagine them, and she felt in a state of the greatest agony and suspense until Massaroni should return. While she was thus occupied, the plaintive voice of a female, which seemed to proceed from a room above, saluted her ears, and rivetted her whole attention. She was singing a melancholy song, and Olympia was enabled to distinguish the following words:—

"Maiden of Florence, oh, listen to me,
    Nor think that I seek thy fond heart to ensnare;
If I deceive thee accurs'd may I be,
    And my bosom be plunged in the darkest despair.

Maiden of Florence, my bosom reviles
    The wretch who'd the innocent damsel betray;
Maiden of Florence, more bright are thy smiles
    To me than the radiant orb of the day!"

Olympia could not distinguish any more, and at that moment old Montaldi returned to the room, bringing with him some refreshments, which he placed before her, and requested her to partake heartily.

"I thank you, signor, for your kindness," replied Olympia, "but indeed I am in no humour to eat; but who is that female I just now heard singing in so melancholy a strain?"

"It is the poor unfortunate I mentioned to you, signora," replied Montaldi; "her mind is a dismal wreck; chance threw her under my protection, and she has been with me now for several years, but I am perfectly ignorant of her history, nor do I even so much as know her name, but call her Ottavia."

"Unhappy lady," said Olympia, "how deeply can I pity her. And are you not aware whether she has any relations or friends living?"

"I am not," answered Montaldi, "though I have made all the inquiries in my power. It is to her whom, in my opinion, you bear so extraordinary a resemblance, signora; and I should say that were she not much older than yourself, you might very well be taken for sisters. Massaroni has several times remarked the same, and takes no little interest in the unfortunate stranger's fate."

"It is strange!" observed Olympia, "I feel a curiosity to see this ill-fated woman."

At that moment her ears were saluted with a wild laugh, and hastily turning her eyes in the direction from whence it came, Olympia beheld standing by the room door the unhappy subject of their conversation. She had entered the room so quietly, that had it not been for the laugh, neither Montaldi nor Olympia would have been aware of her presence, and the whole attention of the latter was immediately rivetted upon her, and the singular likeness which Montaldi had mentioned, most forcibly struck her, and created a feeling in her breast which at the time was to her perfectly incomprehensible. She was standing in an attitude of perfect unconsciousness, playing with her long glossy hair, which hung loosely over her shoulders, and her eyes were fixed on vacancy. Her countenance was ghastly pale, and her bosom seemed to swell with some emotion of the most powerful nature. Montaldi mentioned to Olympia not to interrupt her, and after a pause the wretched maniac said, in tones of wild but melancholy impressiveness—

"Another day—another day, and he has not come, but he will be here to-morrow, and bring with him our little one, the sweet pledge of our mutual love; oh, yes, he will come, he would not deceive me for the world, and we will be so happy, so very, very happy. We will again wander o'er the sunny scenes of our youthful love, and inhale the perfume of the opening flowers, whilst the pretty birds shall carol forth their song of welcome to us. To-morrow, only till to-morrow, and then every earthly bliss shall again be ours. Ah! who is that dares to whisper of deceit? What calumniating fiend can venture to insinuate aught against the honour of he to whom I have sacrificed my heart, my soul, my innocence? 'Tis false; 'tis false!—there is no truth in man if he should attempt to deceive me, after all the vows of constancy he has uttered to me."

There was something so appropriate to her own melancholy circumstances, in the words which the unfortunate Ottavia gave utterance to, that Olympia could no longer control her feelings, but an exclamation of agony escaped her, which immediately caught the ear of the maniac, and fixed the whole of her attention upon her. She advanced hastily towards Olympia, and grasping her vehemently by the wrist, before old Montaldi could interpose to prevent her, she exlaimed in the same wild and impassioned accents as before—

"Who are you that with your superior charms came here to mock me in my decay? Are you some fascinating rival, who seeks to lure him from the solemn vows he has so often plighted to me, by your soft blandishments? Beware, beware—he is mine, wholly mine in the face of high Heaven, and woe to those who try to win him from me. A curse will pursue them, and bring tortures to them in their dying moments more terrible than those of perdition. And yet thou lookest fair and gentle, and so like to what I was when youth and happiness were upon my brow. Do not shrink from me, maiden, I will not harm thee, though they say I am mad. Ah! thou art very beautiful, but beauty is only an inducement to the heartless betrayer. Better to be born ugly, deformed, or not at all. Get thee gone, maiden, I like thee not for thy good looks."

As the unfortunate woman thus spoke, she turned away from Olympia, and seemed to become again deeply immersed in her own melancholy and disordered meditations. But most powerful, as may well be imagined, were the emotions of Olympia during the time the maniac was thus addressing her, and whilst she continued to gaze intently on her countenance. There was something in the expression of her features which created a sensation in her bosom that went to her heart, and tears started to her eyes, which she in vain sought to repress. Montaldi advanced towards Ottavia, and taking her hand, said in kind and gentle accents—

"Ottavia, this is a friend of mine and Massaroni's, and I know you will welcome her kindly, will you not?"

The countenance of the wretched woman brightened up as he spoke, and for the moment some degree of reason seemed to be recalled to her wandering intellect. She once more turned towards Olympia, and in altered accents, taking her hand in her's, she said—

"Montaldi has told me to be kind to you, signora; he says you are his friend, and therefore you must be mine. Yes—yes, I have still some few friends, though man has behaved so cruel to me. But you look sad and pale. although so lovely and so young. Yes, dark clouds frequently obscure the sun of our youth, and they burst in storms that crush the brightest and the lightest hearts. It has been so with me, maiden; ah, me! it has been so. But do not tremble, fair one; again I tell you I will not harm you. No—no.—But you weep! —Dry your tears, they ill become the eyes of youth—it is time enough to weep when you are old, and deserted by those who have vowed to love and cherish you as they would their own life. By such fell means were my youthful days blighted—my fond hopes crushed, annihilated; but you have met with no such fate, therefore should smiles irradiate your brow."

She paused and passed her thin hands across her forehead, as though endeavouring to collect her thoughts. Olympia's heart was full to bursting, so great was the impression which the poor maniac's words had made upon her mind, but she found it impossible to give utterance to a syllable. She felt as if she could at once have thrown herself into Ottavia's arms, and wept forth her whole thoughts and soul upon her bosom. And then the extraordinary likeness she bore to herself, still more interested and astonished her. Montaldi also felt deeply interested in the scene, but still did not offer to interrupt. At length Ottavia seemed to arouse herself from her temporary forgetfulness, and turning again to Olympia, said—

"Ah! you have a child!—I, too, once had one, a sweet, smiling innocent, just such another cherub as that you now press to your bosom with maternal fondness. Hug it closer—closer, or they will tear it from you, and you will never behold it more. 'Twas so they served me, and then all became dark;—black and cheerless as the gloomiest midnight. Closer—closer! you know not how soon the fiend may step in, and, with glistening smiles, tear the tender innocent of your care from your arms, and afterwards revile and scoff at you when you ask for it. But have you, too, been unfortunate?—Is not that the word which man gives to those of our sex whom their guilty arts and false promises have betrayed?—Yes, yes, I know it well. Have you fallen?—Then indeed I pity you, and could weep tears of blood for you. Weep—no, I never weep now;—I have wept so long that I have exhausted the fount from whence all sorrow springs. And he who lured you from the paths of virtue, was he rich, and noble, and handsome?—Were his accents soft and melodious?—Did he vow to love you above all earthly beings?—Mine did so; but he deceived me—he deserted me; went, I know not whither, and left me to die of a broken heart. No—no! I wrong him;—he did not deceive me;—the vows he uttered were too solemn for him to break. He is coming to-morrow, and then we will rejoice; oh, yes, we will have such a gala.

The feast is even now preparing, and I invite you as one of the guests. You shall receive due honours; for who so generous, or so hospitable as my affectionate bridegroom?—You will see him seated by my side.—You will observe his looks of love; and then, oh, then, will we not all be happy—so happy, so very, very happy?"

Again she paused, and laughed wildly to herself. Montaldi again motioned to Olympia not to interrupt her; but he had no occasion to have done so, for Olympia was too deeply moved and concerned by all that the ill-fated Ottavia, in her madness, had uttered, to make any observations, and she experienced, at the same time, sensations which were entirely new to her. The silence of Ottavia, however, was but brief; and at length, again taking the hand of Olympia, and fixing her fine full eyes with an indescribable expression upon her countenance, she said—

"Did he whom you loved, the father of your child, ever sing to you?—Did he ever give expression to his feelings in such words as these? —I have not forgotten them, though they say that my reason has fled. I will sing them to you."

"Maiden of Florence, oh, listen to me,
  Nor think that I seek thy fond heart to ensnare;
If I deceive thee accurs'd may I be,
  And my bosom be sunk in the darkest despair.

Maiden of Florence, my bosom reviles
  The wretch who'd the innocent maiden betray.
Maiden of Florence, more bright are thy smiles
  To me, than the radiant orb of the day.

Maiden of Florence, I liken thine eyes,
  That now with such lustre are beaming on me,
To the stars that so brilliantly shine in the skies,
  And I love them not, dearest, more than I love thee.

Can I deceive thee?—Never! oh, never!
  Let no such thoughts in thy bosom have birth;
May I, if false to thee, curs'd be for ever,
  Wandering, hated, despised, o'er the earth.

Maiden of Florence, oh, listen to me.
  Nor think that I seek thy fond heart to ensnare;
If I ever deceive thee accurs'd may I be,
  And my bosom be sunk in the darkest despair."

"Those were the words, damsel," continued the maniac, "and oh, how sweetly used he to sing them. Can you wonder, then, that he won my heart? or can you believe that he would ever deceive me?—No, no; heed not what the calumniators say;—it is, false, false! he has not deserted me—he would be a monster of the blackest dye could he do so. Another day has gone; but get ready the feast and the revelry; let there be nothing wanting to give him a bridegroom's welcome, for he is coming to-morrow;—he is coming to-morrow! Ha! ha! ha!"

Thus wildly laughing, the unfortunate woman turned suddenly away from Olympia and abruptly quitted the room, leaving her in a state of excitement and agitation which the reader may easily imagine.

"Ill-fated woman!" said Olympia, after a pause, "how sincerely do I pity her; indeed, how can I do otherwise than sympathize with her when her misfortunes are so similar to my own?—And has reason never, for a brief interval, dawned upon her mind, signor, since she has been with you?"

"It has not, signora," replied Montaldi, "or I might have ascertained who she is, and thus have discovered and restored her to her friends or relations, if she has any living. It is quite evident that she has in her youthful days been made the victim of some heartless villain."

"Alas! alas!" sighed Olympia, and a pang shot through her heart, when she likened her own fate to that of Ottavia, which nearly overwhelmed her; while at the same time, she felt another sensation which she did not remember ever before to have experienced.

"But did you not observe the remarkable resemblance which she bears to yourself, signora?" demanded Montaldi, "and which I mentioned to you."

"I did, signor," answered Olympia, "and it has created thoughts in my breast for which I am totally at a loss to account. The words of the song she sung, too, I have heard before, but where I cannot recollect. From them it appears that she is a native of Florence."

"Very true, signora, and that is all that, during the many years she has been with me, I have been enabled to elicit from her."

"It is most strange," remarked Olympia, "most strange indeed, that no inquiries should ever have been made after her."

"It is, signora; and from that circumstance I am inclined to believe that she has no friends or relations in the world, who care at all about her. They probably all deserted her when she unfortunately fell beneath the insidious arts of her betrayer."

"Alas! it is but too probable," said Olympia; "the world, I know from experience, is too apt to condemn the fallen, and to exonerate the author of her degradation. May Heaven pity her, and yet restore her to happiness in this world."

Montaldi heartily responded to this compassionate wish, and then again urged Olympia to partake of the refreshments he had placed before her; but with many thanks she declined, for her heart was too full to suffer her to eat, and she awaited with the most eager impatience the return of Massaroni. The escape of the Count Alberti was so totally unexpected, that she could scarcely believe it true, but mingled with other feelings at such a circumstance was one of gra-

tification, and she mentally prayed to Heaven to protect him from any future danger, and likewise to bring him to a full sense of the errors he had committed, and which had entailed such misery on the innocent, ere it was too late to repent.

The appearance of Ottavia, and the observations she had made use of, had made an impression upon her which nothing could eradicate, and the longer she reflected upon them, the more powerful and inexplicable did it become. In the unhappy maniac she saw a complete reflex of herself, and had she been repeating her own history it could scarcely have come nearer to the facts. And then the extraordinary likeness which existed between her and Ottavia; how was she to account for that? She had also hinted at a child having been taken from her by some surreptitious means, and that added to the interest which she felt to know all the particulars of her unfortunate history, and to ascertain who she actually was; but of this, in her present state of mind, there did not seem to be the slightest chance.

She eagerly inquired of Montaldi the manner in which she had come under his protection, and he gratified her curiosity, which he could not consider was by any means an impertinent one, as concisely as he could. This, however, served to throw little light upon the mystery, and she remained in the same state of perplexity as she had been before.

"It is strange," she again said, "that in the course of all this number of years you should not have been able to ascertain anything satisfactory respecting her, signor, or that any person has made any inquiries after her?"

"It is, signora," coincided Montaldi, "but I can only come to the same conclusion that I have mentioned already, namely, that she has either got no friends or relations living, or that they have abandoned her, and care not whether she be living or dead."

"That does indeed seem to be the most likely conclusion to arrive at, signor," observed Olympia; "for friends or relatives are too apt to forsake those who should be dear to them when misfortune has overtaken them. Too bitterly have I experienced the truth of that."

"I do believe you, signora," returned Montaldi; "but I fervently hope that your troubles will soon be at an end, and that happier days are in store for you."

Olympia shook her head in the most sorrowful and desponding manner, and a deep sigh escaped her bosom, which she found it utterly impossible to repress.

"My hopes of happiness are finished for ever," she said; "there is but one thing that could restore me to joy, and that is the love of Alberti; but that I can never, never hope to obtain. His conduct towards me shows too plainly that I hold no place in his affections."

"He has proved himself a villain, signora," remarked old Montaldi, warmly, "one whom you should endeavour to forget and despise."

"Forget—despise him," repeated Olympia, whilst the tears started to her eyes, and the most painful emotions throbbed in her bosom, "oh, that is impossible. Notwithstanding his cruel conduct towards me, his image is entwined so closely round my heart, that whilst that heart shall continue to beat, nothing whatever can have the power to remove it. I pardon him, but cannot forget or despise him."

"I admire your sentiments, signora," said Montaldi, "your generous devotion to one who has proved himself to be so utterly unworthy of it; and sincerely do I trust that you will yet receive some atonement for the unmerited injuries you have received, and be rewarded by future years of happiness."

"Again I thank you for your good wishes, signor, and the sympathies you express in my fate," replied Olympia; "but let us drop the subject.—Massaroni tarries."

"He does," coincided Montaldi; "but he will be here shortly."

"I hope no danger has befallen him," said Olympia.

"Oh, there is not much fear of that," returned Montaldi; "at present I believe he is safe in his retreat, for although, of course, since the escape of the Count Alberti it has become known, there has not yet been time for any attack upon him, and no doubt, now that he is fully aware of his danger, he will take all necessary precautions, with his usual ability, to guard against it. But, hark, some one knocks; it is he, I dare say."

Montaldi went and opened the door as he spoke, and Massaroni entered the room and approached Olympia, extending his hand in a friendly manner towards her. His appearance was somewhat excited, but not so much so as it had been when he left the residence of Montaldi.

"You have found all that I stated to you to be correct, have you not, Signor Massaroni?" asked Montaldi.

"Unfortunately I have, to the very letter," replied the brigand chief; "and may curses light upon the dastard knave who has betrayed me. But think not that I entertain any fear of the consequences;—no, Allesandro Massaroni is not to be so easily daunted; he will yet find means to elude the vigilance, and to defeat the designs of his enemies, and likewise to wreak his vengeance on their heads.—They may become acquainted with my retreat, but, by the Mass, if they attempt to hunt me from it, they shall pay dearly for their daring. They have already had several tasters of my quality, and I invite them to more if they feel so disposed."

"I regret, Massaroni," remarked Olympia, "that any interference in my behalf should involve you in danger; but I beseech you to abandon any designs of vengeance you may have formed against Count Alberti or his friends. Now that he has regained his liberty, he may not feel disposed to take any farther measures against you."

"Cospetto!" returned Massaroni, with a scornful laugh; "it will be well for him if he does not. But we will talk further upon this subject anon, signora. My wife is prepared to receive you with all proper kindness and respect; you will find every comfort and accommodation in my mountain home, and I will lose my life sooner than any harm shall befall you. So let us depart without any further delay, for you must require rest after the bodily fatigue and anxiety of mind you have undergone for so many hours."

Olympia made no reply to these observations, but rising from her seat, she prepared to follow him, but still most anxiously hoping for another opportunity of seeing Ottavia, who had made so deep and lasting an impression upon her mind.

"I shall see you again to-morrow, Montaldi," said Massaroni, as he prepared to depart: "in the meantime, entertain no fears for my safety, for I have taken every precaution to guard against any danger that may threaten me. Allesandro Massaroni, the brigand chief, must ever be a stranger to fear. Come, Signora Olympia, my wife will be on the tiptoe of expectation till she sees you. Farewell, Montaldi; I thank you for the attention and respect you have paid to this lady, and depend upon it that you shall ever find a sincere friend in me."

Montaldi returned his acknowledgments, and Massaroni, taking the arm of Olympia, proceeded with her from the house, and bent his way by a circuitous, intricate, and unfrequented route towards the place of his secret retreat. On the way thither, Massaroni, perceiving that something seemed to press heavily upon the mind of his companion, questioned her upon the subject, and then she related to him all the particulars of her meeting with Ottavia, and about what had taken place between them.

"Unfortunate woman!" said the brigand chief, "it is evident that she has been the victim of some heartless and designing miscreant, and I sincerely pity her, and trust that she may yet be restored to her senses, and receive ample, though tardy justice for her wrongs."

"Your observations do honour to your heart, signor," replied Olympia: "I confess that Ottavia has made such an impression upon me as I cannot easily forget, and I am anxious to have an opportunity of beholding her again."

"You shall do so, signora," observed Massaroni: "but did not her remarkable likeness to yourself strike you?"

"It did, indeed," returned Olympia; "and I cannot banish the recollection from my mind: her features seem to haunt me now."

"I wonder not at it," said the brigand; "and it is that singular circumstance that makes me the more anxious to become acquainted with the particulars of her history, and who she actually is."

"But since the escape of Alberti, do you feel yourself safe in your retreat?" asked Olympia, eagerly.

"Oh, yes," replied Massaroni; "nature has rendered it impregnable, and should any enemy venture to approach it, it will only be to rush upon almost certain destruction. Besides, my comrades have returned, and you will find that they are a staunch and gallant band, such as it will take no small force to subdue. But see, we approach the narrow pass which leads to it."

In spite of all her efforts to the contrary, and the repeated assurances of Massaroni, Olympia could not but feel a trembling sensation steal over her, as she gazed upon the wild scenery around, dimly lighted by the moon; and she almost repented having placed herself under the protection of the brigand, and wished she had requested and been permitted to remain at the house of Montaldi. But she had very little time for reflection, for they entered upon the devious and difficult way which Massaroni had mentioned, and she thought she could perceive the dark shadows of human forms moving about in the distance. She clung closer to Massaroni, and hesitated to proceed.

"Be not alarmed, signora," he observed; "those you see are only some of my band on the watch. Hark! I will convince you of it."

He gave a shrill whistle as he thus spoke, which was immediately answered by a similar signal, and Olympia felt fresh courage, and suffered Massaroni to lead her on the way without any further hesitation. At length they arrived at the spot where the brigands were standing, and they saluted their chief and his fair companion with the utmost respect. They then removed a large stone concealed behind some brushwood, and revealed the entrance to their secret haunt.

"A light, Gionotti," said Massaroni, addressing himself to one of his band; and the man instantly opened a small lantern, and led the way, followed by Massaroni and Olympia. As they proceeded along the different winding passages, and crossed numerous caverns, well stored with ammunition and different implements of defence, the astonishment of Olympia at the power of the place increased, and she no longer wondered at the contempt which Massaroni had expressed for any force that might be sent to attack him. The voices of men at last assailed her ears, and at length they stopped at an oaken door, which was strongly secured on the inside, and at which Massaroni knocked three times.

It was immediately opened, and Massaroni leading Olympia forward, she beheld herself in the principal cavern, the stronghold of the brigands, who were assembled there in great numbers, and who gazed upon her as she entered with much curiosity.

"Retire!" commanded Massaroni, and the men instantly obeyed, and he led her to a seat, encouraging her by a look which was not lost upon her.

"Thus have we arrived at the end of our journey, signora," he remarked; "and you are now perfectly safe. No harm can come to you in the strong retreat of the brigand chief. But you look dull and spiritless."

"The fatigue I have undergone has been greater than my strength could well endure," answered Olympia, "but I have no doubt that a few hours' rest will restore me."

"Be it so," said Massaroni; "you will find much better accommodation here than you could have expected; but I must first introduce you to Maria Grazie, my wife."

"She is here," replied a voice behind him, and the brigand's wife stood before them.

Olympia started at her appearance, and gazed upon her with timid looks. The handsome figure and countenance of Maria could not fail to excite her admiration, but there was a haughty and suspicious expression in her eyes as she fixed them upon her, which created anything but pleasurable feelings in her breast.

"Maria," said Massaroni, "I recommend the Signora Olympia to your care; you will, I am sure, find her every way worthy of your friendship."

"The signora is unfortunate, I believe," replied Maria; "and she therefore has my sympathy; besides, you take so deep an interest in her fate, Massaroni, that she cannot be otherwise than an object of the greatest solicitude to me."

These latter observations were uttered in a tone, and with an emphasis that did not sound at all gratifying to the ears of Olympia; and Maria, as she spoke, fixed a peculiar look upon Massaroni, which he seemed to understand, for he bit his lips and frowned. However, Olympia soon recovered herself, and addressing herself to the brigand's wife, she said—

"I thank you, signora, for the sympathy you have so generously expressed towards me, and believe me you shall not find me ungrateful for any kindness you may show towards me."

"Maria Grazie requires no thanks for anything she does," answered the brigand's wife. "It is the will of my husband that I should treat you with becoming respect, and his will I never attempt to disobey."

"Well spoken, Maria," said Massaroni, with a more cheerful countenance, "the oppressed and unfortunate should ever claim our utmost care, and you would be unworthy to be the wife of Allesandro Massaroni, did you possess any other sentiments than those you have just expressed. Fear not, for although the Count Alberti has escaped, we shall yet find ourselves secure in this our impregnable retreat."

"I hope you may not be disappointed, Massaroni," replied Maria, with another peculiar look, which seemed to be anything but pleasing to her husband.

"I should deeply regret, signora," said Olympia, "should your husband involve him-

MARIA GRAZIE, WIFE OF THE BRIGAND CHIEF.

self in any danger through his interposition in my behalf."

"Name it not, Signora Olympia," returned Massaroni, "I am fully prepared to set any force that may be sent against me at defiance. But," he added, addressing himself to his wife,

"the signora is tired and requires rest; have you prepared a comfortable place for her to sleep in?"

"I have obeyed your instructions," answered Maria.

"'Tis well," remarked Massaroni; "then

you will be pleased to conduct her to it. Signora, good night, and I hope you will rest in tranquillity."

Olympia again expressed her thanks, and Maria having taken up a lamp, motioned her to follow, which she did with trembling hesitation, not at all prepossessed with the manners of the brigand's wife. After proceeding along a narrow and extensive passage, Maria stopped at a low door, which she unlocked, and Olympia found herself in a cavern, which was fitted up with a much greater degree of comfort than she could have expected, and where every necessary was prepared for her accommodation.

"This is your chamber, signora," said the brigand's wife, lighting a lamp which was standing on the table. "You need not fear any interruption. Good night."

"Good night, signora," repeated Olympia, "and many thanks for the kind attentions you have already shown me."

"Enough, signora," replied Maria, haughtily, and moving towards the door; "I have before told you that I need no thanks for having obeyed the injunctions of my husband."

She said no more, but immediately withdrew, and as she retired towards the cavern in which she had left Massaroni, she muttered to herself—

"She is very handsome, and her manners are gentle and insinuating, but still I like her not. It must be something more than her misfortunes which has so deeply interested Massaroni in her favour, and caused him to brave so many risks for her sake. It will be well for him and for us all if no harm comes of it."

She now re-entered the cavern where her husband was, and she could not conceal the dissatisfaction which inhabited her breast.

"Well, Maria," said the brigand, "have you conducted the unfortunate signora to the place prepared for her accommodation?"

"Of course, I have done as you desired me," was the reply.

"And now tell me, Maria," said Massaroni, "what is your opinion of Olympia? Do you not think her very beautiful?"

"It is not for me to give an opinion of the personal attractions of one of my own sex," said Maria.

"And why not?"

"Because, should not my opinions exactly correspond with your own, you might think that I was prompted by motives of envy or jealousy."

"Jealousy, Maria," returned Massaroni, with a look of displeasure; "nay, now this is unjust and ungenerous of you. Did I ever give you cause for jealousy?"

"I know not that you did."

"Then why throw out such insinuations now? However, I will not be cross with you, although you made use of certain observations in the presence of Olympia which were anything but pleasing or satisfactory to me. You will, I am certain, treat one who is so truly unfortunate with every kindness and respect?"

"You will have no cause to complain of me, Massaroni," replied his wife; "and I only hope that you may not have cause to repent of the interest you have taken in her welfare. The Count Alberti, now that he has escaped, and is perfectly well acquainted with our retreat, will not fail to seek revenge, and, assisted by the Prince Bianchi, may bring such an overwhelming force against us as we may find it impossible to resist."

"Psha!" exclaimed Massaroni, "can this be the once bold and intrepid Maria Grazie, the brigand's wife, who speaks thus?"

"Yes, and it is reason that guides her tongue," she answered.

"Hold!" cried the brigand; "I cannot listen to you with any degree of patience. What care I for the Count Alberti, or the Prince Bianchi? Have I not always shamefully defeated all the bravest of the troops they have sent against me, and think you that fortune will now abandon me? Maria, I tell you again that you cannot mean what you say."

"But indeed I do, Massaroni," replied his wife; "and I much fear that you will yet have cause to acknowledge the truth of my conjectures."

Massaroni looked at her intently for a few seconds, and then said—

"Maria, I am fully aware that you speak from your soul; but, indeed, you wrong me, greatly wrong me, if you can suffer the thought for one moment to enter your mind, that I am actuated in my conduct towards Olympia by any other than the purest and most honourable motives. I know that, as a woman, you feel for her, deeply wronged as she has been, and only as the champion of woman's rights, as the stern but honest redressor of their grievances have I taken up her cause; and, by the saints, I will continue to do so towards her or any other female at any personal risk. But we will talk further upon this subject at a future opportunity. I am certain that from you Olympia will receive every kindness."

"Allesandro Massaroni never yet found his wife disappoint his hopes and wishes," said Maria, proudly, "and she will not do so on this occasion. It is only my anxiety for your welfare that has induced me to speak as I have done. But, come, it is time to retire."

Massaroni embraced the partner of his perils affectionately, and with a look of confidence they then retired for the night. When Olympia was left to herself, she gave way to most racking and conflicting thoughts upon all which had occurred to her, not only previously, but in the last few hours, and one of the most painful of these was the remembrance of the suspicious and haughty behaviour of the brigand's wife towards her, and from which she apprehended the worst results. She felt herself to be a most forlorn and wretched being, despised and persecuted by her fellow creatures, and life was a burthen to her that had now become intolerable. Where could she go to find repose, where seek a friend? In the sincerity of Massaroni's professions she placed every confidence, but what a melancholy and degrading position was it for her to be placed in, to have to depend on the protection of an outlaw and a robber. She shuddered involuntarily as these thoughts flashed upon her brain, and the most dismal forebodings of the future occurred to her imagination, of which she in vain sought to divest herself. We need not say that the escape of Alberti was the source of various thoughts, doubts, hopes, and fears in her breast, and whilst she felt gratified to think that he was once more at liberty, and had thus for the present, at any rate, eluded the vengeance which Massaroni might have been disposed to have inflicted on him, should he have obstinately continued to resist his demands, she could not help feeling the greatest anxiety as to what the ultimate results would be. Then the singular interview which had taken place between her and the unfortunate maniac Ottavia, the dismal history she had related in her wild ravings, and which was in all its particulars so similar to her own; moreover, the very striking and remarkable resemblance which that hapless being bore to herself, rushed with full force, and gave rise in her mind to a variety of conjectures, as bewildering as they were unsatisfactory and torturing. She sought in vain to find a solution to them, but still she felt her heart drawn by no common sympathy in her misfortunes towards her, and she was most anxious to behold her again. And not the least of her most anxious thoughts was the fate of Theresina, the robber's wife, to whom she was indebted for her liberty. By that generous act she had braved the wrath of her husband, upon whom she might bring down the vengeance of the Count Alberti, and she should for ever reproach herself should any evil befall them in consequence of her. All these conflicting thoughts were enough to torture even a much stronger mind than Olympia possessed, especially, worn out and harassed as it had been by such unparalleled misfortunes, and it was no wonder that she gave herself up almost entirely to the dismal thoughts which now oppressed her.

"Why should I continue to drag on this miserable existence?" she soliloquised in the depth of her despair; "whichever way I direct my thoughts, there is no hope for me; no, nothing else but black despair surrounds me on every side, and better would it be that I and my child were no more. I have the certainty of Alberti's hatred, and that of itself is more than sufficient to drive me to distraction. Would that I had the means, I would at once end this career of misery."

She started with horror as these thoughts occurred to her mind, and hugged her infant still closer to her bosom. She fixed her earnest gaze with all a mother's fondness upon its innocent countenance, and at that moment a cherub smile overspread its beauteous features. That smile at once appealed to the fond young mother's heart, and after pressing the most ardent kisses upon its cheeks, she placed it upon the couch, and continued to gaze at it for some moments with the utmost affection.

"God help me!" she cried, with a burst of the most intense agony, "and banish from my mind such terrible thoughts as those which have just occurred to it. My little angel! my unconscious babe! and could I for an instant entertain the monstrous, the unnatural thought of sacrificing thine innocent life? Heaven pardon me, for I scarcely know what I say or do. No, my poor child, we will still brave the world's misfortunes; I will put my trust in Providence, and boldly endeavour to meet all the troubles that may yet be in store for me. Surely it will not permit me to be sacrificed entirely to the villany of my fellow creatures."

She sunk upon her knees, and breathed a prayer to Heaven for its future protection, and then in some measure regaining her composure and confidence, she arose, and securing the door, she prepared herself to retire to rest, for she really felt worn out with fatigue, and the great anxiety of mind she had undergone. In a strange place, however, and with such a multiplicity of painful thoughts as crowded upon her mind, it was no wonder that it was some time before sleep was permitted to descend upon her eyelids, and when it did, strange visions haunted her busy imagination, and rendered her slumbers anything but refreshing. At one time she imagined herself with her infant tossed about on a wild and stormy ocean, lashed to a few spars, the black clouds frowning above them, and nothing but despair and death around. God! how she struggled against the terrible fate which seemed to be inevitable, and called upon the Supreme for mercy: but hideous voices appeared to mock and revile her, and every instant brought with it its accumulated horrors, and the bellowing voice of the tempest howled despair in her ears. How the surging billows dashed, and gurgled, and splashed over her, now raising her almost to the clouds, and anon overwhelming and burying her in their bosom: but when sight was permitted her, there was one form that was ever presented to her gaze—it was that of her betrayer, the Count Alberti. He seemed in his proud galley to ride recklessly over the turbulent waves, and to bid defiance to the frightful fury of the storm. When utterance was allowed her, she imagined that she shrieked to him in frenzied accents to save her and her child, but he only laughed triumphantly at her cries, and in the coarsest accents bade her despair. At length, she imagined, in her fearful dream, that her and her child were cast upon a barren rock, with nothing but the raging ocean around them, dashing at their feet, and rapidly gaining upon them. With difficulty she raised herself on her feet, and clasping her shivering infant to her bosom, gazed around with feelings of the most maddening despair. All was horror and destruction in whatever direction she turned her eyes; but yet only at a short distance from the rock on which she was cast, and standing on the deck of his vessel, his form and features fully revealed to her in the glare of the lightning, she still beheld Alberti, and his eyes were fixed with a malignant expression of satisfaction and exultation upon her countenance. She held forth her infant at arm's length towards him, and shrieked to him for the love of Heaven to have mercy upon them, and so save them from their present horrible situation; but again he laughed aloud at her anguish, and the next moment, as if by the effect of magic, he vanished from her sight. Oh, the agony of that moment! The most eloquent pen would be far too weak to describe it. Faster and faster the waters gurgled and gathered around them. There was scarcely one little space for the wretched mother to stand upon. Faster and faster! She cannot stand against their impetuous violence. Faster and faster! howling! bellowing, splashing,— she sinks down exhausted, but still with all a mother's fond care endeavours to shield her little one from the dreadful fate which seems to be beyond all human power to avert. The waters gather over her; they ascend to her breast; she feels them roaring in her ears with the noise of thunder! they gurgle in her throat; a hundred fires seem to flash before her eyes; her senses leave her, and she awoke? But such was the impression that this frightful dream had made upon Olympia's mind, that for several minutes she could not persuade herself of its non-reality. She gazed earnestly upon the countenance of her child, to convince herself that it still existed, and then a heavy flood of tears came to her relief. She looked fearfully around her, scarcely yet conscious of where she was, and all the horrors of her dream haunted her imagination in the most vivid colours. She felt at that moment as if it would be a happy release for her to die, for she could not but believe that the vision which had occurred to her imagination, augured the most terrible future misfortunes to her. A solemn silence reigned around; there seemed to be no one moving in the retreat of the brigands, and gradually she became inspired with more confidence, and yet she feared to go to sleep again, lest her brain should again be distracted by dreams of a similar description. However, she was so worn out with fatigue, that she found it impossible to resist the drowsy god, and once more did slumber descend upon her eye-lids. Again was busy imagination at work, but the vision that was now conjured up was of a very different description to the one she had beheld before. She fancied herself wandering amid the most halcyon scenes. The choicest flowers luxuriantly sprang up in her path, and impregnated the air with their varied perfumes. Richly mantled trees, loaded with the most delicious fruit of every description, met her gaze in whichever direction she moved her eyes. A silvery rivulet meandered through a verdant valley, and the whole scene was bounded by majestic hills, whose green verdure glistened in the sun's golden rays. To her left was a bower of roses, which invited her to sweet repose, and retiring to it, she threw herself with a feeling of the most indescribable transport upon a seat, and gave herself up to such reflections as the lovely scene and the tranquillity of the hour naturally inspired in her bosom. The innocent lambkins came and fondled at her feet, and the playful fawn indulged in its sportive gambols before her eyes. Her very soul was wrapped in extacy, and she seemed as if suddenly transported to some fairy land. Whilst she was thus seated, the most soft and melodious music floated on the air, which seemed to proceed from no mortal instruments, and had an effect upon the soul which was truly enchanting. More and more distinct became the heavenly sounds, and the next moment Olympia imagined in her dream that she beheld, tripping lightly and gracefully towards her, a troop of the most lovely sylph-like forms that the glowing imagination of the poet could ever depicture. She arose from her seat, and knelt in reverence to them as they surrounded her, holding her infant in her arms, upon whose head they scattered the richest of flowers, which filled the air with their fragrance.

"Come, come," said one who appeared to be the queen of this fairy group, "the betrayer awaits to clasp the betrayed one to his breast. The storms of adversity have subsided—retribution has overtaken the oppressors, and the sun of happiness shall in future illumine thy path. Come, come; why delay the moment of thy bliss?"

Again the most heavenly music floated upon the air, and Olympia felt herself carried, as if by some irresistible impulse, forward, the fairy forms dancing lightly and fantastically before her. Through sylvan scenes, such as the eye of mortal had never before rested on, they bent their way, and as they proceeded fresh flowers every instant seemed to spring up in their path. At length they came in sight of a spot where the light was so intense that Olympia could scarcely bear to gaze upon it, but at length, when she had somewhat recovered from its influence, a magnificent temple formed of precious stones met her gaze, and filled her with awe and amazement at its novelty and dazzling splendour. Still, although she was bound up in confusion and admiration, she felt herself compelled to advance towards it, preceded by her lovely and unearthly conductors, and at length they arrived at its entrance. They entered, and in a gorgeous apartment, and reclining upon a splendid ottoman, was a female form of much elegance of figure. She arose upon their entrance, and what was the astonishment of the dreamer when she recognized Ottavia! But how different was her appearance now to what it had been in Olympia's waking moments. The fire of reason lighted her eyes: the flush of health was again restored to her cheeks; cheerful smiles sported around her lips, and age seemed almost metamorphosed into youth. Olympia imagined that a feeling of awe stole over her, which she could not suppress, whilst the most delightful sensations throbbed within her bosom. She knelt at Ottavia's feet; the fair vision raised her hands above her head as if invoking a blessing; again the seraphic music swelled into one full burst of harmony, and in the midst of the rapture of the moment, Olympia again awoke. As near as she could guess, it must now be morning, and indeed she was convinced it was, for she could hear the brigands moving about in the outer caverns, and the voice of Massaroni giving various instructions to them. She raised herself up in her bed, and gazed around her, but it was impossible that she could easily shake off the influence of her last dream. Alas! how painful was it to be awakened from such a blissful imagination to such a dreary reality.

"But what can be the meaning of this dream?" she said; "is it a harbinger of happier days? Ah! are they ever in store for me? Has the Almighty conjured this up to my imagination to inspire me with hope? And why was Ottavia presented to me in so remarkable a form? Can she in any way be connected with my fate? I am lost in amazement and perplexity. Oh, God! why am I kept in this state of suspense?"

She pressed her hands upon her forehead, and endeavoured to collect her wandering ideas, but the more she reflected upon the singular circumstances of her dream, the deeper she became involved in doubt and bewilderment. But nevertheless she could not but feel inspired with hope after what her imagination had conjured up, and she arose in greater spirits than she had experienced for many months; at the same time that she felt the greatest anxiety to behold Ottavia again. She had scarcely dressed herself, when there was a knock at the door, and having opened it, the brigand's wife presented herself before her. Olympia remembering her conduct on the previous night, could not help shrinking timidly before her, but immediately perceiving a great alteration in her demeanour, she quickly recovered her self-possession. Whatever might have been the real feelings of Maria Grazie at the time, she certainly now seemed to eye Olympia with compassion and respect, and probably she did regret having suffered any feelings of jealousy to have entered for a moment into her breast against the fair unfortunate.

"You are looking better, signora," she remarked, "and I trust that the few hours' rest you have obtained after the fatigue and anxiety you must have undergone, have refreshed you."

"I thank you, signora," replied Olympia, "for your kindness, and do assure you that, with the exception of the effects of one terrible dream, I feel much better."

"Dreams, signora," returned Maria, "are but the offspring of a disturbed mind, and we should not take any serious notice of them."

"I agree with you, signora," said Olympia, "but still one dream that I had, I cannot but think seriously of; and should it only in part be realized, I might yet hope again to be happy."

"Indeed," observed the brigand's wife, "I am glad whenever such visions haunt the pillow of the unfortunate. But come, the morning repast awaits us."

Olympia accompanied her without any further remark, and they entered the cavern where they had parted the previous night, on the table of which the breakfast was spread, and Massaroni was awaiting them. He arose on their entrance, and greeting Olympia with every possible mark of respect, placed her at the table by his side, Maria occupying the other. He then kindly inquired after her health, and how she had slept, and received the same answers that she had given to Maria. Olympia now felt far less restraint in the society of the brigand and his wife, and therefore, while the repast was proceeding, at their request she related the particulars of the singular dreams which had occurred to her, to which they listened with much apparent interest and attention.

"They are most extraordinary, signora," remarked Massaroni, when she had concluded, "particularly the second one; but, no doubt, it is the impression which your interview with the unfortunate Ottavia, at the residence of Montaldi last night, made upon you, which has haunted your imagination, and been the cause of it."

"It may be so," replied Olympia, "but still I am most anxious to behold her again."

"No doubt you will have frequent opportunities of doing so, signora, while you remain under my protection," said Massaroni, "and most happy should I be if your kind exertions would tend towards the recovery of her senses. I confess I feel no common anxiety to know who she is, and what has been the cause of reducing her to her present melancholy situation, though there can be no doubt that it has been caused by the blackest villany."

"Alas!" it is but too evident," sighed Olympia.

"And yet," continued the brigand chief, "these lordly seducers, these devastators of all that is pure and innocent in existence, pride themselves upon their honour and nobility of mind, and hunt, like beasts of prey, those whom misfortune has driven from the path of society. Bah! it makes the very blood boil in my veins with disgust and indignation to think of it. But pardon me, signora, if I appear too excited ; you will soon know Allesandro Massaroni, the brigand chief, to be a very different man to what he has been represented."

"Signor," replied Olympia, "I feel that I should be doing you the greatest injustice, if, after the interest you have taken in my fate, and the many risks you have run to serve me—an entire stranger to you, and a poor friendless unfortunate—I did not feel the utmost respect for, and gratitude towards you."

"Do not mention it, Signora Olympia," returned the brigand, "I take no great credit to myself for what I have done, for he is less than man who would not raise his arm in the defence of the injured and oppressed. That feeling has ever guided my conduct, and it must continue to do so while life remains within me. But in respect to Ottavia, what astonishes and interests me more than all, is the very extraordinary likeness that exists between yourself and her, signora."

"I could not but remark it myself, the moment I beheld her," observed Olympia, "and it is most unaccountable. Would that it would please Providence to restore her to her senses, that we might become acquainted with her history. But what are your intentions, Massaroni, regarding the Count Alberti?"

"I have not yet exactly made up my mind, signora," replied the brigand; "but he must not be permitted to escape with impunity, to triumph in his guilt, and to set my power at defiance."

"Oh, Massaroni," said Olympia, "notwithstanding the great and irreparable injuries he has done me, I can freely forgive him. Surely the upbraidings, the bitter upbraidings of his conscience, some time or other, will be a sufficient punishment for the crimes he has committed."

"I cannot but admire your clemency and forbearance, signora," said Massaroni, "but still one who has acted in the treacherous, the cruel, and heartless manner that Alberti has done, must not be suffered to escape so easily, and to laugh to scorn his unfortunate victim. Justice revolts at the bare idea. He must be compelled to render you all the atonement in his power, and it shall be my task to make him do so. Massaroni never yet made up his mind to anything, without persevering till he accomplished his object; he has not yet, and never will suffer himself to be defeated. Besides, Olympia, can you patiently bear the thought of his becoming the husband of the Signora Melina ?"

"Oh, no, no, no !" returned Olympia, "because he is totally unworthy of one so good and amiable. But that can never be, for I know that Melina must despise and loathe him."

"She does; but the Prince Bianchi, her uncle, favours Alberti's suit, and even at the cost of her future happiness, without some powerful interposition to prevent it, she will be forced into an union with him."

"Heaven forbid !" ejaculated Olympia, fervently, "for deeply should I regret for one so young, so good, and virtuous, to be plunged into so much misery."

"Such will be her fate," observed the brigand, "unless the Count Alberti be curtailed of his power."

"I should never forgive myself if I should be the cause of any evil befalling him. Alas ! I am a most unfortunate being, and can only bring trouble upon any one who may take an interest in my welfare. I fear that what you have already done for my sake, Massaroni, will bring down upon you the vengeance of Alberti and the Prince Bianchi, whose power you will find it impossible to resist."

"Do not, I pray you, signora, make yourself uneasy on my account; I fear them not, nor all the force they can send against me. Here will I remain in my stronghold, and brave the worst ! Fortune, I feel assured, will not yet desert me, and that there are many more triumphs still in store for the brigand chief, Massaroni. I will take every precaution to guard against any sudden surprise, and leave the rest to chance. But, in the meantime, Olympia, rest your mind content, and be assured that while you are under my protection, your comfort shall be the constant study of myself and Maria, my wife."

"Indeed I do not doubt your word, Massaroni," said Olympia, "and I can but repeat my thanks for your kindness, but still I cannot help expressing once more my fears for the danger in which your friendship for me may involve you. The Count Alberti is revengeful, his power is great, and——"

She was interrupted by the abrupt entrance of one of the brigands, who advanced towards Massaroni, evincing by his looks that he had something particular to communicate.

"How now, Spaladro?" demanded the brigand chief, "what brings you here?"

"Your pardon, signor," replied Spaladro, "I would speak to you a few words in private."

"Does any fresh danger threaten us?" hastily asked Massaroni.

"No, signor, none that I am aware of; but I have some intelligence for you which it is necessary you should receive without delay."

Massaroni quitted the cavern with him without any further delay, and Olympia and the brigand's wife were left to themselves.

"Your observations, signora," said Maria, "were partly just; Massaroni has run great risks, but still I have no doubt that Providence will not desert him in the prosecution of his laudable design, therefore, rest your mind contented, and be assured that all that it may be in our power to do for you, will be done with a right good will, and that whatever the consequences may be, we shall never blame you for them."

"How can I sufficiently express my gratitude for this generous feeling towards me?" said Olympia. "Alas! it will never be in my power to reward you for your services, or how willingly would I do so, and——"

"Massaroni and his band seek no reward for doing their duty, signora," interrupted Maria, "they find it in their consciences, and they would despise themselves were they not always ready to stand forward in the defence of the victim or victims of oppression."

Before Olympia could return any answer to these observations, Massaroni re-entered the cavern, and it was plain to be seen from the expression of his countenance, that he had heard something which had excited his uneasiness or displeasure.

"You seem agitated, Allesandro," said his wife; "has Spaladro had any disagreeable news to communicate to you?"

"He has," replied Massaroni; "and my indignation is more than ever excited against the Prince Bianchi."

"Ah! how is that?" eagerly demanded Maria.

"Florio Clairville——"

"The young painter."

"The same," replied the brigand chief.

"What of him?"

"He is at present the inmate of a dungeon, by the orders of the prince."

"Unfortunate man!" ejaculated Olympia, "what will be the anguish of the Signora Melina?—But what has he done that he should incur the vengeance of the Prince Bianchi?"

"Goaded on by despair," answered Massa-

roni, "he ventured to break through the stern decree of the prince, and to seek a private interview with the Signora Melina, which she granted him. One of the prince's servants overheard the assignation, and apprised his master of the same. The lovers met at the hour appointed, when they were suddenly pounced upon by his highness and his attendants; a scuffle ensued; the prince drew his sword and was rushing upon Florio, when he stumbled, and his weapon penetrated the bosom of Melina."

"Gracious Heaven!" exclaimed Olympia, with much emotion, "is it possible? What a dreadful tale is this! Unfortunate Melina!"

"Do not alarm yourself, signora," said the brigand, "the wound which Melina received, although a severe one, is not dangerous, and there is every hope of her speedy recovery."

"Thank Heaven for that," said Olympia "but the unfortunate Florio; what became of him?"

"He was dragged off to prison by the orders of the prince, where he now lingers."

"It is indeed a sad affair," remarked Olympia; "how intense must be the sufferings of Signor Clairville, uncertain, as he probably is, of the fate which has really befallen her to whom he is so devotedly attached."

"He must indeed, signora," coincided Massaroni.

"And how bitterly must the Prince Bianchi reproach himself for the calamity of which he has been the cause."

"If he has one spark of feeling, he must," said the brigand.

"But surely he will not detain Signor Clairville in prison, when he has committed no absolute offence?"

"Should the affection he has ever professed for his fair niece be sincere, he will not," replied Massaroni; "but I know his vindictive character well, though he would fain appear a paragon of virtue and generosity, and therefore I do not believe that Florio can expect much mercy at his hands."

"And what course do you intend to adopt in this affair?" demanded Maria.

"You know I entertain the warmest friendship for Signor Clairville," said her husband.

"True, but what then?"

"Why, I am resolved to try every means to rescue him from confinement."

"That will be a hazardous undertaking," observed Maria.

"It is one that, at any rate, I will not hesitate to undertake."

"You had better consider the matter well before you do so. There is no charge, from all that you have stated, that can at all affect Signor Clairville, and no doubt he will shortly be set at liberty."

"I am of a different opinion," returned Massaroni, "however, I will make further inquiries into the case, and take my measures accordingly; "I am, however, determined that Florio shall not fall a victim to the vengeance of the Prince Bianchi."

"And have you heard any more of the Count Alberti?" eagerly asked Olympia.

"I have not," replied the brigand, "but no doubt he has by this time reached a place of present security. His own noble castle is now a heap of ruins."

"And deeply do I regret that such an outrage was committed," said Olympia.

"It was no outrage, signora," returned Massaroni, "but a pure accident. However, it is only a just punishment for the many villanies of which Alberti has been guilty."

"Well, Massaroni," remarked Olympia, "we will say no more upon that subject at present; the account you have just given of this melancholy catastrophe deeply afflicts me. Unfortunate Signora Melina, so kind and gentle, how sincerely do I pity her. May Heaven watch over her and quickly restore her to health, and surely this alarming event will induce the prince, her uncle, to relent."

"You appear to entertain a much better opinion of him, Signora Olympia," said the brigand chief, "than I can possibly do."

"He surely will never persist in sacrificing her to one whom I know from painful experience is so totally unworthy of her."

"The prince is proud, imperious, and obdurate, and think you he will ever sanction the addresses of the poor but amiable Florio, especially after what has happened? No, it would be worse than folly to encourage such a thought."

At this moment Spaladro again made his appearance, and informed Massaroni that old Montaldi had arrived at the retreat, and requested to see him.

"Show him in, Spaladro," said Massaroni, and the man immediately departed to obey the orders of his chief.

At the mention of the name of Montaldi Olympia started, and a strange sensation shot through her bosom. The old man immediately afterwards entered, and greeted them with the utmost respect.

"You will pardon me, Massaroni," he said, "for the liberty I have taken in obtruding upon you?"

"Do not mention it, my good Montaldi," answered the brigand chief, "I think you must be fully aware that you are always heartily welcome."

"I could not resist the temptation to pay my respects to your fair charge," continued the old man, "and to inquire after her health, knowing the fatigue and anxiety she must have undergone."

Olympia thanked him.

"There is another individual," observed Montaldi, "who ever since last night, when she beheld the Signora Olympia, has been in a state of greater excitement than I have seen her for some time. I need not say that I allude to Ottavia, so, as I was fearful of leaving her by herself, I have taken the liberty of bringing her with me."

At the mention of the unfortunate Ottavia's name, Olympia started, and a feeling of emotion shot through her bosom, for which she was at a loss exactly to account. After the strange circumstances which had taken place at their first interview, it will not be wondered at that she should be anxious to see her again, and she was very well pleased when Massaroni observed—

"The Signora Olympia has made me acquainted with all that took place between her and Ottavia at your house last night, Montaldi, and I assure you that my anxiety and curiosity are not a little excited by it. Signora, have you any objection to see this unfortunate woman again?"

"Oh, no," replied Olympia, eagerly, "on the contrary, I have the strongest wish to do so; for I cannot describe to you the interest which her misfortunes, apparently so similar to my own, have created in my breast."

"She is indeed most worthy of your warmest sympathies, signora," remarked Massaroni, "pr'ythee, good Montaldi, let your hapless charge be ushered into our presence."

Montaldi made no answer to this, but bowing, quitted the cavern, and Olympia awaited the appearance of the poor maniac with much anxiety and expectation.

———

CHAPTER XXVII.

THE MANIAC AND OLYMPIA.—DARK SHADOWS OF THE PAST.—ANOTHER ATTACK.

In a few minutes Montaldi returned, conducting in the wretched object of his care, upon whom all eyes were immediately fixed with the deepest expressions of sympathy, and Olympia felt a sensation at her heart in particular, which she found almost impossible to control. Ottavia was very pale, and her eyes wandered wildly and vacantly around the place for a few moments, and she seemed to have no idea where she was, or to recognise the presence of any one, with the exception of Montaldi.

"Unfortunate woman!" said Olympia, in her tenderest accents, "how awful is the wreck that cruelty and oppression have made here."

The words seemed to strike upon the ear of the maniac immediately, and to arouse her into temporary consciousness.

"Ah!" she exclaimed, "what angelic tones are these so unusual to my ears? I have heard them before! Yes—yes, they have often haunted me, but then it has only been in some sweet, though delusive dream, and I have in vain looked for the fair spirit from whom they could alone have proceeded. Oh, how sweet! how soothing! Speak again, heavenly being, for such thou must be, and impart consolation to the wretched outcast's benighted soul. No, she will not listen to me; it is all a mockery of my poor distracted brain."

She turned away and sighed deeply. Olympia, who was moved by no common feeling of emotion, gently approached her, and kindly took her hand. The maniac started at the touch, and fixed her bright eyes wildly but earnestly upon her.

"What is this that now haunts my imagination?" she cried, "who art thou, so lovely and celestial? Comest thou from Heaven to cheer me by thy presence? What features are those I gaze upon? Do my eyes deceive me?—No —no, it is the same bright vision that has so often haunted my imagination. Speak, tell me who and what art thou? Such was I before I fell; ay, thy very image; art thou my fetch, my shadow, the counterpart of myself, sent hither to remind me of what I once was? But you will not leave me? Oh, 'tis such happiness to gaze upon thee. Speak to me again, fair spirit, for my very soul hangs in transports over the tones of thy voice, and the darkness and obscurity seem gradually to vanish from my bewildered brain."

"Poor victim of oppression," said Olympia, "how my heart bleeds for thee. May Heaven have mercy upon thee, and once more illumine thy dreary path with the rays of reason and happiness."

Ottavia continued to fix her eyes with the most intense earnestness upon Olympia's countenance, and seemed to hang upon every syllable to which she gave utterance, with the most indescribable transport.

"Speak on—speak on!" she said, "I will not interrupt you. And have you too been unfortunate that you can thus pity the wretched outcast? You must have been, for it is only those who have themselves experienced the world's treachery and ingratitude who could speak such words of kindness. Did one of noble form and birth e'er win your virgin heart with vows of love, and then deceive, abandon you? Poor thing!—poor thing!—poor thing!"

She placed her arms around the neck of Olympia as she thus spoke, and pressed her lips upon her cheek. The heart of Olympia was full to bursting, and she found it impossible to give utterance to a syllable. Deeply impressed with the scene, Massaroni, his wife, and Montaldi stood by, and did not offer to interrupt them, for they were in hopes that something might be elicited from Ottavia to throw some light upon the dark mystery of her melancholy history.

" Did he vow that you were fairest of the fair?" continued the maniac, after a pause, "did he declare that you were the idol of his soul, and when he had accomplished your ruin, heartlessly abandon you?—leave you to all the misery of remorse and despair?—But no; I know not what I say. He did not deceive me! He must have been a monster indeed could he have done so, after all the solemn promises he made to me. Do not believe the base traducers of his fair fame, maiden; they only envy me the happiness of his love, and would fain supplant me in his affections. But they cannot do so; oh, no, I know his noble heart too well. He will loathe and despise them. They cannot lower him in my estimation. He will be here to-morrow, for he promised me, faithfully promised me, and I am certain that he will not fail to keep his word."

"Oh, yes," said Olympia, taking advantage of the opportunity, and thinking to obtain some clue to the painful mystery, "and the name of he whom you love is——"

"No—no—no!" hastily interrupted Ottavia, "that shall not pass my lips; I must not utter it; it is a secret that shall remain locked within my bosom, for there are those who would take advantage of the knowledge to suit their own base ends. And yet they could not win his heart from me; oh, no, that would be impossible; for he is pledged to me in the sight of Heaven, and think you he would deceive me? They are liars, calumniators, who would make you believe so, maiden. He is coming to-morrow, he is coming to-morrow."

Again she paused, but continued to hold Olympia in her embrace, and seemed fearful of losing sight of her. Of the other persons present she appeared to take no notice.

"But you will not leave me, fair spirit, or whatever you are?" she resumed at length. "No, no, my heart would break if you were; for you are all so gentle and so lovely, and to gaze upon you, to listen to the soft and seraphic tones of your voice imparts such feelings of transport to my benighted soul. I will be so happy and so very good if you will but remain with me; and we will wander hand in hand together over the green fields, and I will guide your footsteps to the sunniest spots, where only such a creature of light and loveliness should be. You will not leave me, will you?"

"We will be together as often as possible," said Olympia, soothingly, "and oh, how gladly will I do anything in my humble power to contribute to your happiness."

The expression of the unfortunate maniac's eyes became unusually animated, and she again kissed the cheeks of Olympia.

"Oh, thanks, thanks, sweet being," she ejaculated, "for this kind assurance. And we will repeat tales of love and constancy to each other, and I will call you sister;—no—no—not sister, for you are too young for that, daughter!—yes daughter! That will I call you, and you will permit me to do so, will you not?"

Nothing could exceed the emotion of Olympia at the words of the maniac; her heart throbbed quick, and feelings as powerful as they were strange shot through her bosom.

"Yes," she replied, pressing the hand of Ottavia warmly within her own, "you shall call me daughter, and I will bestow upon you all a daughter's love and sympathy."

"Oh, this is indeed happiness," cried Ottavia, smiles of pleasure irradiating her pale features. "Daughter! daughter! what a delightful word, and you will call me mother! Ha! ha! ha!—mother!—But I have no child, though I dreamt that I had one once, but that must have been all a delusion!—She is dead!—Ah! me!—how my poor brain wanders!—I know not what I say!"

Her head sank upon Olympia's bosom, and tears gushed to her eyes. The agitation of Olympia increased, and she was unable to control her feelings. Ottavia at length again looked up, and fixing her eyes upon the countenance of Olympia, said—

"Fear not, fair maiden, that any harm shall come to you while I am with you; although but a woman, I have strength enough to oppose any who would dare to disturb your peace. Fear not the seducer's arts, for Heaven will protect you, and guard you against the honeyed voice of treachery and deceit. Oh, we will be so happy, so very, very happy!"

Again she paused, and seemed to be endeavouring to recall her scattered senses, while the observations she had made use of smote deep into the bosom of Olympia, and inspired her with thoughts such as never occurred to her before.

"It is long ago, very long ago," at last resumed the maiden; "dark clouds have obscured the horizon since that period, and fierce storms have laid waste and desolate what was once so lovely and enchanting; but there was a time when I was so happy, and so innocent; when the bright smiles of affection ever beamed upon me; when the accents of love and tenderness ever saluted my ears! But oh, how changed! —oh, how dreary is all around me. And what has caused this desolation?—why has the fair face of nature become sterile and barren?—why do the flowers no more spring up in my path, and gladden my senses with their fragrant breath?—what have I done that I should become this thing of darkness and of hate?— why do my fellow creatures shun me, as if I were something loathsome, and murmur strange and guilty stories in my ears?—am I not a woman?—why should they pursue and persecute me, as if I were a monster?—there are bright sunny spots still upon the earth; calm resting places for the weary and oppressed; why am I not permitted to seek them?—where is he, the noble lord of my affections?—why does he tarry?—why comes he not to lead me to those scenes of bliss and tranquillity?—the priest awaits at the altar:—shall we longer hesitate to unite our fates together, loving each other as we do so fondly?—the wedding banquet is prepared, the guests assemble; but where are the bride and bridegroom?—villany has been at work! I see it all now, they have traduced my fair fame, they have prejudiced him against me—they keep him from me! The monsters! —what have I done that they should rob me of the idol of my soul?—but they shall not triumph—I will have justice rendered me!—I will seek them out and revenge the wrongs they have done me, though they should seek to hide themselves in the remotest corners of the earth! —justice! justice!—revenge! revenge!"

Overcome by the violence of her emotions, the unfortunate woman sank back on her seat completely exhausted, and Olympia and the others were more deeply affected than before at the sufferings of the poor maniac, and the cruel treatment which had doubtless reduced her to her present wretched state. She seemed to be perfectly unconscious of all around her, and none of them attempted to arouse her from her present state of apathy. But what language could do adequate justice to the feelings which now agitated the bosom of Olympia? Every word that Ottavia had given utterance to, went deep to her heart, and created sensations which were entirely new to her. From what she could glean by her observations of her history, it was so similar to her own, that she could not help but be most forcibly and painfully struck with it, and she would willingly have made any sacrifice in her power to have been enabled to impart comfort to that seared bosom, or to have restored the light of reason to her soul.

"Unfortunate woman," remarked Massaroni, "it is but too clear that she has been made the unhappy victim of some designing and heartless villain. May justice overtake him, if he be still living, and punish him severely for the melancholy wreck he has thus caused."

"Most fervently do I respond to your wishes, Massaroni," returned Montaldi; "and I do not yet despair that justice will some time or other be rendered to her, and that it will please Heaven to restore her to reason and happiness."

"It was by such base and atrocious means as those to which this poor creature in her wild ravings alluded," continued the brigand chief, and indignation and grief the most intense flashed from his fine expressive eyes; "it was by such brutal means as those that my unfortunate, and too confiding mother fell; it was the inhuman miscreant who betrayed her, and afterwards deserted her, and left her to die of a broken heart, while I, the innocent fruit of their unhappy connection, was cast like a dog upon the wide and cheerless world, made an outcast from society, and driven to become what I am. May eternal curses light upon his head, and rack his guilty soul! Can you then wonder, Montaldi, that I should so deeply commiserate with Ottavia in her misfortunes?"

"Indeed I marvel not, Massaroni," remarked the old man; "but try to banish such painful thoughts from your memory, and rest assured that full justice will yet be rendered you."

"Yes," said Massaroni; "I do entertain that hope, although so many years have elapsed, and it is that which has always sustained me throughout the numerous trials and vicissitudes it has been my lot to endure, and which has emboldened me in all my actions. But see, Ottavia recovers; we must try to put an end to this scene, for I am fearful that the excitement of her feelings may be too much for her strength to endure. The fancy she has taken to Signora Olympia is fortunate, and, in the course of time, if they are brought frequently into each other's society, may be productive of the most happy and desirable results."

"Heaven send that it may," ejaculated Olympia, fervently.

Ottavia now raised her head, which for some time she had suffered to drop upon her breast, and gazed eagerly but vacantly around her.

"Whither have they conveyed me?" she said, passing her hands across her forehead; "why have they brought me hither? Oh, I thought I was in the presence of that fair being who has so often haunted my imagination;—that I heard the heavenly tones of her voice, speaking words of pity, hope, and consolation to me! That she fixed upon me looks of affection, such as it has not been my lot to behold for many a weary year. But it could only have been a dream."

"Ottavia!" said Olympia, in a tone of the sweetest tenderness, and again taking her hand. The poor maniac started at the well remembered sound, and fixing her eyes full upon her countenance, she ejaculated—

"Ah! once more that lovely voice salutes mine ears, and penetrates to my very soul with irresistible power. The same beauteous form meets my eyes. It was no delusion then. We will not part, maiden—no, no, we will not part, for Heaven has united our souls, although they say I am mad, and have no longer a mind to think, to love, to admire. But heed not what they say, sweet maiden; they speak falsely, and only seek to prejudice mankind against me. Why do you weep, damsel?—Tears should not dim such youthful eyes as these; there all should be smiles and happiness. Sorrow surely cannot yet have seared your heart, and rendered that desolate which should be so fair and tranquil. You have not yet felt the world's treachery, cruelty, and deceit. No—no—I will not believe it!—Did you ever know what it is to love and to be betrayed, abandoned, by the fond object of your adoration?—Did you ever know what it was to bear the world's contumely and scorn; to be scouted from society as something loathsome?—To have the finger of opprobrium pointed at you, when your heart was bursting? Did you ever know a mother's pangs, and yet to be deprived of a mother's hope? Oh, no, no, no; you cannot have suffered this; but I have done so, and, oh! how much more!—But you still weep. Why is this?—Oh, let me know the cause, and I, yes, even I, wretched being though I am, will soothe your soul to serenity and peace."

How torturing were these observations, and expressed in the tones they were, to the heart of Olympia! Had the unfortunate woman been fully acquainted with all the dismal circumstances of her history, her remarks could not have been more pointed or appropriate, and it was in vain that she sought to the utmost of her power to stifle her emotions. Massaroni saw plainly the anguish she was enduring, and wished the interview, which had now become too painfully interesting, to be brought to a termination. He spoke to old Montaldi in an under tone, aside, to that effect, and approaching Ottavia, kindly said—

"Come, Ottavia, it is time for us to return home, for you see our good friends here have particular business to attend to, and our presence here can only be considered as an intrusion. Come, bid the Signora Olympia, who you know is to be your future companion, farewell, and you shall soon behold each other again."

"No, no, no," cried Ottavia, passionately, and clinging vehemently to her; "you shall not part us—you shall not tear me from her—she has promised that she will not leave me; and one so fair, so good, so innocent, can never break her word. We will wander to scenes where sorrow is unknown, where all is sunshine and bliss, and there will we end our days together in tranquillity and peace. Fair maiden, speak, you will not let them separate us after the promise you have given me?"

"Be calm, my good Ottavia," said Olympia, in her most gentle and persuasive accents, "and yield to the wishes of your kind protector. To-morrow we will meet again, and every day, I trust, while I remain here. Farewell, and may Heaven's blessings light upon you."

"You are not going away?" said Ottavia, eagerly; "tell me that you are not, and oh, I will endeavour to be so happy."

"No, no," replied Olympia, deeply moved, "I once more assure you, please Providence, we shall frequently meet again."

"I will believe you," said the maniac, her eyes brightening as she spoke; "I will believe you, for such a gentle being can never seek to deceive a poor unfortunate."

"God forbid!" replied Olympia, fervently.

"Thank you!—bless you—bless you for that assurance," said Ottavia; "to-morrow, then, to-morrow: yes, and he will be here to-morrow;—I know he will not disappoint me—and we will be so happy. You will not go away, you have promised me you will not; and that you will permit me to call you daughter!—Daughter! oh, what a delightful word!"

With these words the two unfortunates embraced fervently, and then Ottavia, with much reluctance, retired with Montaldi. Olympia threw herself on a seat, and for a few moments gave herself up entirely to the power of her emotions.

"I am afraid, signora," said Massaroni, "that this interview has been a most painful and trying one to your feelings; but I cannot help feeling gratified that Ottavia has taken such a particular fancy to you, which, as I before said, may be productive of the most favourable results, and by your kind exertions, she may happily be restored to reason."

"God grant that she may," ejaculated Olympia: "how thankful should I be, were I to be made the humble instrument of bringing about such a fortunate and desirable change. This interview with Ottavia, and the observations that fell from her, has made an impression upon me, which nothing can eradicate. Terrible, indeed, must have been her misfortunes to cause such a deplorable wreck in her mind."

"No doubt of it, signora," coincided the brigand chief; "and I sincerely hope that retribution will overtake the guilty author of them, if he be still alive."

"Heaven surely will never suffer him to go unpunished," remarked Olympia; "but if he is not entirely destitute of every spark of humanity and proper feeling, his own conscience must prove to him a severe and terrible monitor."

"I fear," returned Massaroni, "that such a man must be insensible to the reproaches of remorse. But probably you may wish to be alone. Should you require anything, my wife will promptly attend to your wishes."

Olympia thanked him for his kindness and attention, and was then re-conducted by Maria to the place in which she had slept the night before, and where everything was prepared for her comfort and accommodation. The second meeting between her and Ottavia continued to occupy Olympia's thoughts, and filled her mind with a variety of painful and perplexing conjectures. Every word that the poor maniac had spoken was as fresh in her memory as if she had only that moment given utterance to them. She felt her heart drawn towards her with feelings of the deepest affection and sympathy, whilst the similarity of her fate to that of her own struck her the more forcibly the longer she reflected upon it. And then the powerful resemblance that existed between them was not the least extraordinary of all the remarkable coincidences; and at times she could scarcely persuade herself that they were not in some manner connected with each other.

"She alluded to a child, too," she said, "which appears, from all that I could make out from her wild wanderings, to have been taken from her in its infancy. That child, too, a daughter!—My God! what strange thoughts and conjectures are those which are crowding on my brain?—Should fate ever prove that I —but no, into what a wild and intricate course am I suffering my mind to wander! I dare not encourage such an idea, which seems too preposterous to be realized."

All the circumstances of her dream now rushed upon her memory, and added to the anxiety and anguish of her mind; but it was utterly impossible for her to come to any satisfactory or reasonable conclusion, and reflection only involved her still further in the perplexity. The escape of Alberti, the imprisonment of Florio Clairville, and the unlucky accident which had befallen the gentle and amiable Signora Melina, [also afforded her ample food for the most serious and torturing reflections, and excited her deepest sympathies. She could not but deprecate the conduct of the Prince Bianchi, but still she could not persuade herself that he would persist in sacrificing his fair niece to such a man as the Count Alberti, especially after what had happened. f

"He is unworthy of her—totally unworthy of her," she ejaculated; "and even if he were, and she could love him, what maddening torture it would be for me to know that he who is the author of my ruin, the father of my child, had become the husband of another. He is lost to me for ever; it would be folly for me to encourage any hope to the contrary; but oh, I dare not entertain such a thought."

For some time she continued in this state of mind, and was unable to look to any side for consolation. She placed the greatest reliance on the friendship and disinterestedness of Massaroni; but still the danger he had involved himself in on her account caused her much uneasiness, and she would fain have been placed under some other protection. But alas! she had not a friend in the world to whom she could apply for assistance; she knew no place where she could fly to, or hope to receive a shelter; and therefore she had no alternative but to remain where she was, and to put her trust in Providence, and even had she had an opportunity she would have hesitated to quit the neighbourhood after her meeting with the unfortunate Ottavia, and the mystery which was connected with her.

Throughout the day she continued immersed in those reflections, only seeing the brigand and his wife when they met at meals, and then their behaviour towards her was characterized by every possible mark of kindness and respectful attention. They sought to divert her thoughts by conversing upon the most cheerful subjects, and they in some measure succeeded; for towards night she became more contented and resigned to her fate, and endeavoured to hope that something would yet occur to restore her to that happiness and serenity to which she had so long been a stranger. She retired at an early hour to rest; but before she sought her pillow she knelt down and returned her fervent thanks to that Omnipotent Power which had preserved her so far, and solicited its future protection. Nor did she forget the wretched Ottavia in her prayers, but earnestly supplicated the Supreme in her behalf, and implored Him to restore her wandering senses, and to suffer her declining days to be those of uninterrupted peace. Having performed this sacred duty, she felt more at ease, and with her infant retired to bed, and in a very short time fell into a sound sleep. How long she had slept she knew not, but she was suddenly aroused by a loud and confused noise that prevailed in the cavern, and she hastily arose, and listened with the most breathless attention and anxiety. The noise every moment increased; Olympia could hear the rushing to and fro of numerous persons, as if in a state of considerable excitement and confusion, mingled with the voices of men, though she could not distinguish a word that any of them uttered. She became more alarmed, and hastily dressed herself, for she knew not what danger might threaten.

"What can have happened?" she ejaculated; "this confusion and excitement cannot proceed from any trifling cause. My heart misgives me."

She had scarcely given utterance to these words, when she heard a loud knocking at the door, which did not serve by any means to diminish her alarm.

"Who's there?" she demanded, tremulously.

"It is I, signora," replied the voice of Maria, "pray open the door."

Olympia did so as readily as her trepidation would permit her, and Maria Grazie, with an agitated countenance and demeanour, entered.

"For Heaven's sake, signora," asked Olympia, "what is the meaning of this disturbance? what has happened?"

"Do not alarm yourself," replied the brigand's wife, "for no danger shall befall you. Some of our band who were on the look-out have discovered the approach of a body of troops, led on by the friends of Alberti and the late Count di Strozzi, doubtless with the hope of taking Massaroni by surprise; but they will find themselves deceived, and that we are in every way prepared to meet them. Massaroni and a chosen portion of his band have just hastened from the cavern in order to obstruct them in their march, and but a short time will decide the conflict, and that in our favour. So secure are we in this our mountain stronghold, that we may safely set almost any force at defiance."

"Alas!" sighed Olympia, "I tremble for the result of this combat, notwithstanding the advantages which you say you possess. Should your husband be defeated, what will become of me and my child?"

"Courage—courage, signora," remarked Maria, "the triumph of Massaroni is all but certain. The enemy little suspect that their approach has been discovered, and, taken by surprise, they will be easily put to the rout. Secure yourself in this place, and I will soon return to you; I must now away to join Massaroni; whatever dangers he may have to en-counter must be equally shared by Maria Grazie."

Thus saying, the brigand's wife abruptly hastened from Olympia's presence, and left her in a state of mind of the greatest agitation.

"Alas!" she sighed, "what a terrible situation is this to be placed in; should the brigands be defeated, I and my poor child are lost. Oh, would that I had never been brought hither."

Notwithstanding her agitation, however, she had still the presence of mind to secure the door as Maria had advised her; and she then awaited the issue of this alarming event, with the most trembling suspense. She listened to catch the slightest sound, but all was profoundly silent, and it would seem as if she was the only person left behind in the cavern. It was indeed a moment of the greatest excitement to Olympia; but committing herself to the care of Providence, she became more calm, and awaited the result of the adventure with some degree of patience. In the meantime Massaroni and his heroic band were bent upon their expedition to frustrate the plans of the approaching enemy, and by the side of the brigand chief, prepared to share in all his dangers, was Maria Grazie, his wife. The persons who had given the information to Massaroni had well watched the route of the troops, and consequently he knew in what particular place it would be best to attack them, and where he could better take them by surprise, and thus bring the combat to a speedy decision. Stealthily the brigands moved on their way amongst the mountain passes, which none but a well accustomed foot could tread, and not a word escaped from any of them. The moon sent forth a clear effulgent light, so that they had a distinct view of the country for some miles around, and the approaching enemy was soon visible to them.

"They come this way," said Massaroni, "and little are the fools aware of the reception they are about to meet with. Secrete yourselves, my brave fellows, and as soon as they come within reach of the contents of your carbines, I need not instruct you how to act."

The brigands immediately concealed themselves in various places, but so that they could take every advantage of the enemy without being exposed to any danger themselves, and Massaroni and his wife took their station behind a butting portion of the mountain, where they could give immediate directions to the band, watch the progress of the troops, and be completely sheltered from observation by those who were advancing to attack them. Nearer and nearer they came, and so bright shone the moon, that Massaroni and his wife had a distinct view of the features even of the officers who led them on.

"Poor wretches!" whispered Massaroni to his

wife, " they do but rush upon their own destruction. I would save the sacrifice of human life as much as possible, but these men afford me no opportunity of doing so. They come ! they come !—Would that Alberti or the Prince Bianchi were among them."

The troops had now reached the foot of the mountain—in the various nooks and corners of which the foes they so little expected were secreted—and commenced ascending it. Massaroni watched them narrowly, but gave the signal to his men not to interfere until a good opportunity offered itself, for they far out-numbered them, and therefore their only chance depended upon stratagem. They came faster on, although they ascended the devious and rugged way with difficulty at first, and at length the officers approached to within a few paces of the spot where Massaroni and his wife were concealed.

" Thus far we have proceeded safely," said one of them, who appeared to be the leader; " our information has been good, and no doubt we shall take the scoundrels by surprise, unprepared to meet us, and hunt them like dogs from their secret lair."

" Ha! ha! ha !" laughed Massaroni aloud.

" Eh! what was that?" demanded the person who had spoken, starting back amazed.

" Why, did you not laugh ?" asked one of his companions.

" I laugh?—certainly not," replied the other.

" Well, I thought you did, and that it might be the echo."

" Diavolo ! the echo !" said the officer.

" Diavolo ! the echo !" repeated Massaroni, closely imitating his voice.

" There," observed the companion of the officer, " is not that a convincing proof ? It was nothing more than the echo of your own voice. The troops lag ; they find it difficult to ascend these mountains, but I am most anxious to take this daring brigand chief; though I think, with all his boasted bravery, he would shrink from encountering us, could he perceive our number."

" Liar !" exclaimed Massaroni ; and the two officers started back in amazement, and looked bewildered around them.

" Did you hear that ?" said the one who had first spoken.

" Yes, I thought somebody called me liar," replied the other, " but of course it could not be you."

" No, it was I, Massaroni, whom you are so easily going to subdue," said the brigand chief, rushing from the place of his concealment accompanied by his wife, and confronting the astonished officers ; " you would take me, would you, most brave and noble signors," he continued, " be it so, but it must be when Allesandro Massaroni is deserted by his brave followers. Would you spare reckless blood-shed ?—If you would, retire, and tell your proud masters that you found discretion the better part of valour !"

" Daring villain !" exclaimed one of the officers ; but scarcely had the words escaped his lips, than the stiletto of Maria was buried in his breast, and he sank back a corpse upon the earth.

The troops now rapidly advanced up the mountain ; Massaroni and his wife retreated to their former place of concealment, and no sooner had the soldiers approached within the reach of their carbines, than the brigands opened such a destructive fire upon them, that fifty were stretched either lifeless or wounded upon the earth. Before they could recover from their confusion, the fire was repeated, with even double effect, and never expecting such an attack, they were thrown into the utmost dismay and confusion, and consequently but ill prepared to retaliate. Massaroni saw this advantage, and availed himself of it ; giving the signal to his band, they rushed from the various places where they had been concealed, and, headed by their chief, made a desperate attack upon their foes, slaughtering all before them, until the troops, without having the power to make scarcely the least resistance, were driven down the mountain, and dispersed themselves in all directions, followed by the exulting shouts of their victors, who, during the whole conflict, had not met with one casualty. A portion of the band pursued the stragglers to some distance, but the rest of them remained with their leader, by his command ; and at length the whole of the brigands assembled round Massaroni, to join with him in hailing another signal defeat of the enemy, so strongly, but so ineffectually opposed to them.

" Well done, my bold comrades," said the brigand chief, when they were all gathered about him ; " once more have we triumphed over that foe who has so often felt the superior force of our arms, and yet, urged on by the dastardly spirit of revenge instilled into them by their lordly masters, they perseveringly continue to annoy us, and would fain bring us all to the scaffold. What say ye, my brothers in peril ? Shall we tamely submit to the hands of the executioner, and leave our enemies to exult over our downfall ?"

Loud shouts of " Never ! Never !—We will die first on the spot where we contest the point."

" Bravely spoken," continued the brigand chief, " and I know that I may depend on ye all, although of late we have found some traitors amongst us. His highness, the Prince Bianchi, and our late prisoner, the Count Alberti, are my bitterest enemies, and it is evident from these secret, cowardly, and frequent attacks that they would pursue us to destruction, that they would exterminate us !

Say, then, shall we not retaliate? Shall we not teach them that even princes and nobles are not to be allowed to insult and persecute the brigand with impunity?"

"Evviva Massaroni!" cried the brigands simultaneously, and in tones that rent the air. "Vengeance on his enemies! Death to all who oppose the mountain brigand chief!"

"Thanks! thanks!" replied Massaroni; "to our mountain home—to our mountain home! See the morn is slowly awaking, dividing the grey veil of night, and, gliding over the face of nature, steals the first light of the new coming day. A few hours' rest, my bold comrades, and then once more to the business of our predatory life. Maria, my wife!"

Maria Grazie returned the fond look of her husband, and locking her arm within his, they led the way to their secret haunt, followed by their courageous adherents singing this, their favourite chorus—

> This, our maxim, wise and bold,
> Naught for naught, and all for gold;
> Banish every weaker feeling,
> Let the bigot prate of crime,
> Time from all is daily stealing;
> We but do as teaches Time.

CHAPTER XXVIII.

THE TERMINATION OF THE COMBAT, AND ITS RESULTS.

WE left Olympia in the greatest state of excitement and agitation, while this brief but desperate conflict was going on between the brigands, and the troops that were sent to oppose them, and need we say that every moment it increased to a pitch almost beyond endurance. She pictured to herself all sorts of horrors, and dreaded to hear the result of it. Notwithstanding all that Maria had said to her, she could not help bringing to her affrighted imagination the idea that Alberti was the leader of the attack, and while at the same time that she frequently prayed for the preservation of her generous and disinterested protector, Massaroni, she feared that some serious harm would befall him whom she still so sincerely, so ardently loved, notwithstanding all the cruelties he had inflicted on her. The reports of the firing reached her ears distinctly, and every volley seemed to go to her heart, and to speak a tale of horror, and she could likewise plainly hear the shouts of the various parties engaged in the combat, and even the agonizing groans of the dying struck upon her vivid and excited imagination.

"My God!" she ejaculated, "what a wretched being I am, to be reduced to such a dreadful situation as this. Heaven preserve me and my child, for without Thy help I fear we are lost! Oh! Alberti—cruel, relentless Alberti, what misery has thy treachery caused!"

She sobbed aloud in the bitterness of her feelings, and wrung her hands in despair. Suddenly, however, the firing ceased, and all was again wrapped in the most profound silence. The expectations, forebodings, and feelings of suspense, were aroused to the utmost, and almost intolerable pitch, in the bosom of Olympia, and the stillness which now reigned around was almost more painful to her imagination than the noise and confusion which had so recently prevailed. It was the awful silence which succeeds death, and the effect it had upon the mind of Olympia was most intense and melancholy. What had been the result of the battle? she reflected. Who were the conquerors? How many lives might have been sacrificed in that fearful contest, and was she not the indirect cause? She almost dreaded the approach of a footstep, lest it should announce the harbinger of her worst apprehensions. At length the sound of some person advancing along the passage which led to the place in which she was confined, did salute her ears, and immediately afterwards there was a knock at her door. Her heart beat high with doubt and expectation, and she tremulously inquired who it was that demanded admission. The voice of Maria Grazie answered her, and she instantly unfastened her door, and the brigand's wife, evidently much excited by the late stirring event, in which she had been so deeply engaged, once more stood before her.

"You are pale, signora," she said, "you tremble; but do not agitate yourself, all is well."

"Thank Heaven!" ejaculated Olympia, fervently; "but Alberti?"

"He was not present at the combat," replied Maria; "I tell you once more that the troops were led on by his friends and those of the Prince Bianchi. They have suffered, as I prognosticated, a most shameful defeat, and those who have been fortunate enough to escape, no doubt think themselves lucky that they have been able to make good their retreat."

"Oh, how horrible are these recitals of slaughter," observed Olympia, with a shudder; "but your husband, is he safe?"

"Perfectly so," answered the brigand's wife, "and fully prepared to set his enemies at defiance. They little suspect the secret means that Massaroni has of discovering their designs. The time will come when he will fully revenge all these outrages."

"God grant that I may not be the cause of bloodshed," said Olympia, clasping her hands; "I would sooner, much sooner endure every suffering and privation, nay, even to perish by the most miserable of deaths, than have such an insupportable weight upon my conscience. Let me, with my poor innocent offspring, become a wanderer upon the earth, but do not let me plunge my fellow creatures, even my bitterest enemies, into additional, and reckless crime."

"Do not torture yourself with these ideas, Signora Olympia," remarked Maria, "for indeed your fears are unfounded. That just Providence, in which you seem to place such firm reliance, will, no doubt, watch over and protect the right, and

RINALDI, CAPTAIN OF THE BRIGANDS, WHEN A YOUTH.

only punish the really guilty. Let those tremble only who have incurred the wrath of the Supreme Ruler of us all. I am a brigand's wife, 'tis true, and considered with him a lawless, abandoned outcast; but you see, signora, that I am not yet quite insensible to the dic-

tates of that which is right and wrong. Judge of myself and Massaroni fairly as you find us; we require no more of you."

"As God is my judge, I will do so," replied Olympia, solemnly.

"Enough," said Maria, "and you will find

that you have no friends who are more sincere, or more fervently devoted to your welfare; none more anxious to see full justice rendered you, and to release you from the persecution of your enemies."

"Thanks, thanks, for the good motives which I feel satisfied actuate you," said Olympia; "but I am fearful that the interest which you and your husband take in my destiny, may involve you in some imminent danger."

"Entertain no apprehensions of the sort, signora, for it is no trifling foe, as has been several times proved, that can defeat Allessandro Massaroni."

"But your retreat is now known, and you will no longer be able to remain with safety here."

"Our retreat is known, 'tis true," answered the brigand's wife; "but the affair of this night has proved that we are always so well upon our guard that we may bid defiance to any attempt to surprise us. I tell you again, signora, that it is impossible for any enemy, however powerful—unless they should be as well acquainted with these mountain passes as we who are inured to all their wilds, intricacies, and perils—to approach us without inevitable destruction; therefore, upon that point, rest your mind perfectly secure and contented."

"But this attack will, I fear, excite a feeling of terrible revenge in the bosom of Massaroni, against Alberti and the Prince Bianchi," observed Olympia.

"And can you feel surprised if it should do so?" demanded Maria.

"And shall I not be the primary cause of anything that may happen?"

"Not so, signora; rest assured that Massaroni will do nothing more than such as prudence and justice dictate. But this event, I am afraid, has greatly disturbed you; endeavour to snatch a few hours' repose, and in the morning my husband will again see you, and probably explain to you more fully what are his future intentions."

"What is the time?" inquired Olympia.

"It is now nearly four hours past midnight," replied her companion.

"And you say that all is safe?"

"Perfectly safe, I repeat."

"The troops sent against you have retired?"

"They were put to the route in the greatest confusion," returned Maria; "the brave band under the command of Massaroni received but little injury; but the enemy must have suffered severely, and the corpse of many a brave fellow now strews the mountain side."

Olympia again shuddered.

"God help me!" she ejaculated: "oh! that I should be mixed up in such terrible scenes of slaughter as these!"

"Compose yourself, signora," said the brigand's wife: "you have nothing whatever to reproach yourself with, and surely we are not at all to blame in defending ourselves in the best manner we could against the cowardly midnight attack of an inveterate enemy. Come—come; this is no time to talk upon the subject, for your feelings are now excited. To rest, signora—to rest."

"Alas!" sighed Olympia, "there is no rest for a wretched being like me!"

"Say not so, Olympia," returned Maria, kindly, "the storms that at present beset your fate will subside, and you will yet be happy."

Olympia returned no answer, and Maria pressing her hand in a most friendly and cordial manner, took her leave, and left her to her own melancholy reflections. Dismal enough they were, and for some time they almost bore her down with their oppressive weight; but at length she somewhat recovered herself, and all remaining quiet in the various caverns, and no symptoms of the late fearful conflict remaining, having committed herself to the care of Omnipotence, she once more ventured to retire to bed, but in vain she courted the drowsy god; he would not come to her relief, and she lay tossing about on her pillow in a restless and anxious manner, until Maria knocked at the door to inform her that the morning meal was ready."

"You look very ill, signora," said the brigand's wife, gazing earnestly upon her; "had you not better rest yourself for an hour or two longer?"

"No," replied Olympia, "I cannot rest; my mind is too disturbed to suffer me to do so."

"Is there anything I can bring you, signora," asked Maria, "that you think might afford you relief?"

Olympia replied in the negative, and after a pause intimated that she would rise and accompany her to the place where she understood Massaroni was awaiting them. Maria assisted her to dress, and she then accompanied her to the cavern in which breakfast was prepared for them, and where she again beheld the brigand chief, who was pacing the cavern on their entrance, apparently absorbed in deep meditation; on beholding Olympia, however, he saluted her with his usual politeness, and handed her a seat.

"I am afraid, signora," he remarked, "that the little affray of last night has alarmed you, for you look much agitated."

"Believe me, Massaroni," she answered, "that it is not not for myself that I fear alone, but for you."

"For me, signora?"

"Yes, Massaroni, my being under your protection may bring the most fatal consequences upon your head, and for which I should ever reproach myself after the disinterested kindness you have shewn towards me"

"Oh, my dear signora," returned the brigand, "I pray you banish such notions from your mind, for I am perfectly safe. These mountains are quite impregnable to all but those who are thoroughly acquainted with them, and keeping a constant and wary look-out, I shall always prove myself and my daring band more than a match for any force that may be sent against me. I presume that Maria has made you acquainted with all the particulars?"

"She has," answered Olympia; "and while I sincerely rejoice that you have come off victorious, I fervently hope that you will not be goaded on to seek revenge against your powerful enemies, which might only recoil upon yourself."

"As for my enemies, Olympia," said Massaroni, proudly, "I utterly despise them; "but think you, after such an outrage as this, I will suffer them to escape unpunished? No—they shall yet learn, to their cost, what it is to defy Massaroni, and to endeavour to hunt him from his lair like a beast of prey."

"But you are not naturally revengeful, Massaroni," observed Olympia, anxiously.

"I am not, lady," replied the brigand chief, "but no man or men did I ever yet suffer to offend me with impunity, and by the dome of St. Peter's, I will not do so on the present occasion. They came upon me like bloodhounds, in the night, when they thought that I should be unprepared to meet or resist them; they would have slaughtered me and my brave comrades in cold blood; even you and your innocent child they would not have spared; then what mercy or forbearance have they any right to expect at my hands? Signora, much as I study your feelings, and value your happiness, I must and will have retaliation."

"But in what way will you seek it, Massaroni," anxiously demanded Olympia.

"That must be for my more serious consideration," replied the brigand.

"But Alberti, you will not visit him with your vengeance?"

"That entirely depends on himself; should he still set me at defiance, and refuse to comply with my demands, which will only be founded in honour and justice, he must take the consequences. But why should you so deeply interest yourself in the behalf of one who has so cruelly treated you, Olympia?"

"Heaven knows he has indeed deeply wronged me," sighed Olympia; "but still I can forgive him—freely forgive him, and——"

"He is a villain, and deserves it not," interrupted Massaroni, vehemently.

"But surely he has been sufficiently punished for his crimes already?"

"He has not, signora; and mark my words, a terrible retribution yet awaits him."

"You forget that he is the father of my child."

"I do not, signora, and it is that which makes me more inveterate against him. It is he who forgets that he is the father of your innocent offspring, and has abandoned it, and you, to misery."

"Heaven help us, my poor babe!" groaned the wretched mother, hugging her innocent infant frantically to her breast; "it would be a blessing for us both were we no more."

"Take comfort, signora," said Massaroni, kindly.

"Comfort!" repeated Olympia; "alas! there is none for me. Massaroni, earnestly—fervently I thank you for all the kindness you have shown me, and must ever remember you with feelings of the most unbounded gratitude; but I beseech you to abandon your designs against the Count Alberti, which can be productive of no good, and may be the cause of the most unspeakable misery. Suffer me no longer to be a burthen to you, involving you in danger; I am ready to commit my destiny to the wide world, and God knows I have little reason now to care what becomes of me."

"Far be it from me, Olympia," replied the brigand, "to wish to put any restraint upon your conduct; but indeed I cannot suffer you to encounter the perils to which, in your friendless and destitute state, you would be exposed in the world were you to become a houseless wanderer. Picture to yourself what they would be, and I am confident you will not blame me for thus opposing your hasty formed wishes."

"The signora is in no condition now to argue the point," interposed Maria, "although I perfectly agree in everything you have said, Massaroni, and will freely act in concert with you in contributing all in my power towards her comfort and consolation."

Olympia's emotions were too powerful to suffer her to speak, but her looks, and the tears which started to her eyes, sufficiently testified her gratitude.

"Let us change the subject," suggested Massaroni, "and by and by, we may all be in a better condition to discuss it. It is only natural that the stirring and painful events of the last few months should cause Signora Olympia considerable excitement; but fear not, the clouds will shortly pass away, and all will terminate much more happily than she now imagines."

Olympia shook her head.

"Alas!" she sighed, "I see no prospect of it. The fates seem to have conspired against me, and nothing but misery, I fear, will be my lot in this world."

"Try to look on the brighter side of the question, signora," remarked Maria, "and depend upon it your hopes will in the end be realized."

"Besides," said the brigand, "if I were even to yield to your desires, Olympia, and suffer you to leave my protection, whither could you go, friendless as you are, and destitute of the bare means of existence?"

"Alas! 'tis too true," sighed Olympia.

"Then why reject the offer of shelter, of friendship, and protection I make you?" demanded Massaroni. "Seek to compose your feelings, to banish all apprehensions from your breast, and to rest yourself contented here until your prospects mend, and happier days may dawn upon you."

"But will you promise me, Massaroni," she said, "that you will do nothing precipitately as regards the Count Alberti?"

"Undoubtedly I will, signora; Massaroni never does anything without due deliberation; let that answer satisfy you."

"I will depend upon your word, Massaroni," returned Olympia, with more confidence, "for I do not think you would break it."

"Never!" replied Massaroni, emphatically, "I should despise myself if I thought myself capable of doing so."

The conversation here dropped, and the remainder of the breakfast passed over in silence. At the conclusion, Olympia, who felt herself quite indisposed for society, requested permission to retire, which of course was granted, and she quitted the presence of the brigand and his wife. When she was alone she recalled to her memory all that had passed in the conversation we have just described, and it gave rise to a variety of conjectures in her mind. She had no reason to doubt the honour of Massaroni's intentions, for what interest could he have in deceiving a poor friendless destitute creature like her? but still she liked not the revengeful feelings he had expressed towards Alberti, and she shuddered to think what the consequences might be should he attempt to put his threats into execution. She earnestly prayed that something would occur to bring about an amicable arrangement between him and the brigand, and the other enemies of the latter, for it would cause her extreme regret should any harm befall Massaroni after the many noble and generous traits of character he had displayed. It was quite evident that the brigand had taken to his present lawless and perilous course of life from no natural vicious propensities of his own, but that he had been driven to it by misfortune, and therefore Olympia could not but feel the most lively interest in his fate. He evinced intrinsic qualities that would adorn the highest station of society, and she deeply deplored the cruel fate which had placed him in his present degrading and dangerous position. Independent of all this, there was another feeling took possession of her bosom whenever Massaroni occurred to her thoughts, for which she was totally at a loss to account, and which she was utterly unable to comprehend. The

brief history he had given of his mother's wrongs was ever fresh in her memory, and excited her deepest sympathy; and how indeed could it do otherwise, so similar as it was to her own? She was interrupted in the midst of these reflections by the entrance of Maria.

"I ask your pardon, signora," she said, "for intruding on you; but Montaldi and Ottavia have just arrived at the cavern, and the latter will not be pacified until she sees you. Do you feel yourself in a condition to meet her?"

"Oh, yes," answered Olympia, hastily arising from her seat; "unfortunate woman, how sincerely do I feel for her deplorable situation. I will attend you immediately, signora."

Her infant had fallen into a sound sleep, and placing it on the bed, Olympia followed Maria out of the place, with a heart beating high with expectation and various strange and powerful sensations. When they arrived at the door of the cavern, they could hear the poor maniac talking in her usual wild manner, and laughing hysterically at intervals. Olympia felt a pang shoot through her bosom, and she paused at the door for a moment or two to recover herself, and thinking it would be as well not to interrupt Ottavia, until the frenzy of the moment had somewhat subsided. At length she became silent, and Maria having gently opened the door, they entered the cavern. Ottavia was seated with her back towards them, playing with her glossy tresses, and muttering incoherent words to herself, so that she did not notice their entrance, and Massaroni motioning them to silence, they paused a moment or two to observe her; but she did not offer to move from her position in the slightest degree, and appeared to be totally unconscious of everything around her. Olympia felt herself still more deeply affected as she gazed upon the wretched woman, and tears started to her eyes unrestrained. Still Ottavia was unconscious of their presence, and continued occupied in the same manner for several minutes, laughing at intervals, but taking no notice of any one near her.

"She has been in a most anxious and unsettled state of mind since she saw you yesterday, signora," Montaldi whispered to Olympia, "and has been constantly talking about you, calling you her daughter, and declaring that no earthly power shall again separate you. I know not how it is, but I cannot help thinking that the remarkable fancy she has taken to you, and your kind attentions towards her, which I feel confident you will freely bestow, will have the most beneficial and desirable effect upon her wandering intellect, and that the painful and perplexing mystery that hangs about her history may yet be elucidated."

"God grant that it may," re; lied Olympia, fervently ; "how happy should I be to become the instrument in the hands of Providence of restoring the unfortunate lady to her senses. But hist ! she speaks."

Ottavia had been singing a few snatches of a pathetic ballad in a low and plaintive voice ; but she now suddenly paused, and passing her hands across her forehead, as if to recall her scattered thoughts, she said, talking to herself, and still taking no notice of any one present—

"To-morrow ! what is to-morrow ? It was the same yesterday, and yet I never see to-morrow ! Is it a mockery, a snare, a wild delusion, to torture the disordered mind of the poor deserted one ? Yes, it must be so ; it is all a blank ! a something glittering at a distance, but never approaching nearer. No ! no ! there is no morrow ; I will not believe them when they tell me so ; they would but deceive me ; for if it were true, would he not be here ? Oh, yes, for did he not promise to meet me on the morrow, and I know he would not break his word ; one so fond, so loving, so faithful and so honourable, could never deceive me ; and yet what a long, long time I have been waiting for to-morrow, it must have been years, and yet it has not come. Ah ! me ! what a sad thing it is to wait for to-morrow. But it will come ! Oh, yes, it will come ; and then I shall see him again. I must prepare myself to meet him with my accustomed smiles of love and gladness, for 'twould break his constant heart to see me sad, and lonely, and wretched. I will twine the roses in my hair, and array myself in my bridal robes ; all white, pure white, and glittering with the choicest brilliants. The banquet waits, and loud shall be the sounds of mirth and revelry that shall re-echo through our princely halls. Oh, it shall be a festive day—to-morrow ! Where are my handmaidens ? Why do they tarry, when they know I have to meet my much-loved lord ? They were not wont to be so tardy, and why are they now on this joyous occasion ? I must chide them well for their unpardonable neglect !"

She now suddenly turned round, and beholding Olympia, with a cry of delight she rushed towards her and enfolded her in her embrace, at the same time pressing the most fervent kisses upon her lips, and laughing with hysterical joy.

"Ah !" she cried, "sweet one, thou hast not then deceived me—thou comest again to glad mine eyes with thy presence—thou hast not gone away, and we will never—never part, will we, dearest ?"

"We will, meet as frequently as possible, dear Ottavia," replied Olympia, greatly affected by the earnestness of the poor maniac's manner, and the touching impressiveness of her words.

"Yes, yes, we will live together, ramble through green fields together," said Ottavia, "and never be apart from each other. And I will call you daughter—yes, daughter ; it is a pretty word, is it not, sweetest ? I will take you to all his favourite haunts—I will show you those fair places where we plighted our mutual vows, and were so happy, so very—very happy. You will delight to see them, for they are dedicated to love and constancy, made sacred by the holiest ties. He is coming to-morrow—he is coming to-morrow, and then you will acknowledge how proud I ought to be that I am sole mistress of so noble a heart."

Olympia could make no reply, for every moment that she remained in the unfortunate maniac's company, her emotions increased, and feelings came over her to which she had hitherto been a stranger, but which she found it impossible to resist.

"I have been dreaming of you again, fair being," resumed Ottavia, gently urging Olympia to a seat by her side, taking her hand within her own, and appearing to take no notice of the other persons present, who retired to the farthest extremity of the cavern, so that they might enjoy their interview without interruption. "Yes," she continued, "thy fair image was present to me all last night, and made the hours of sleep those of bliss, but when the morning came you vanished from my sight, and left me so sad, so very—very sad. But we meet again, and we will not part again. He will be here anon—he promised me he would come, and never did falsehood escape his lips. No, it is only those who have dared to traduce his fair fame, and to accuse him of deserting me. Do not believe them, dearest, they utter naught but the most shameless falsehoods ; when you have learned what it is to live as I do—when the vows of a faithful heart have been breathed in your ear, and you shall have sacrificed everything for the one dear object of your affections, you will know how to appreciate my feelings, and learn to despise the calumny of the cruel and ungenerous world."

She paused, and for a moment or two seemed to be lost in meditation. The anguish of Olympia was almost insupportable ; every word that the hapless woman had uttered went like a dagger to her heart, and she was unable to restrain the tears that rushed copiously to her eyes. Alas ! little did the wretched maniac dream how similar had been Olympia's misfortunes to her own !

"But you weep," said Ottavia, suddenly, and gazing earnestly in her countenance. "Your bright eyes are dimmed with tears, and I can feel your bosom throb with emotion against my own. Why is this ?—Why are you not all smiles and happiness ?—One so young and innocent surely cannot yet have cause for sorrow !—No, no ;—I will not believe it. Had you known what it is to love and be deceived, abandoned, and—ah! me !—my poor brain ! —But no, what cause have I for complaints ? —I was never deceived, deserted, and therefore what cause have I to murmur ?—It was only a frightful dream ; but why does it continue to haunt me ?—Away ! I will no more of it !—He is coming ! the lord of my affections is coming ! —To-morrow he will be here, and then, oh joy ! —joy !—What a Heaven is in store for me ! —Come, fair being ! do not cry—do not cry ! Have I said anything to wound your feelings ? If I have, then indeed shall I be wretched."

Olympia pressed her hand, and endeavoured to compose her feelings, and to divert the wandering mind of her unfortunate companion to some other subject, but that was a task not easy of accomplishment.

"Ah ! now again you look yourself," said Ottavia, "smile on—smile on, dearest, for it wrings my heart to see you sad. Come, let us forth into the bright sunshine, and inhale the balmy fragrance of the morning air. Sweet-scented flowers await our presence, and shady groves invite us to rest and tranquillity. I will show you our favourite trysting place, and there I will repeat to you all the tales of love he has breathed so often in my ears. You will be delighted to hear them, and feel convinced that one who thus could vow could never deceive the confiding object of his affections. And yet they say that man is false, and delight in triumphing over the good and innocent. It is a monstrous calumny ! Heed not what they say, they would but make your young heart wretched, and lay desolate all that should be so fair, so fertile, and so lovely. When they tell you your love is false, spurn them from you, and look upon them with loathing. Do not heed their words, or they will drive you to madness !—Yes, believe my words, maiden, for they are true. I listened to them, I believed them, and all has been darkness and despair in my mind ever since. The wretches !—where are they now ?—They dare not appear before me—they dare not contemplate the awful wreck their poisonous tongues have made. Where are they, I say again?—Let them confront me, and terrible is the vengeance I will leave upon their dastard heads. Vengeance ! vengeance !"

Overcome by the frenzy of her feelings, the wretched Ottavia uttered an hysterical laugh, and sunk back exhausted in her seat. Olympia gazed upon her with the utmost sympathy and emotion, but did not seek to interrupt her. Several minutes elapsed in this manner, and Ottavia continued to mutter incoherent sentences to herself. But at length her countenance brightened up, and once more turning her gaze towards Olympia, she said—

"You are still here, fair being; you will not leave me, and I will be so very happy. Your countenance is bright and smiling again, and why should I be sad? Come—come, let us begone from here, and wander in the light and air. This is not the place for us. Do not shrink from me, maiden, for I will not harm you ; oh, no, I would sooner lose my life than cause you a single pang. And who shall dare to attempt to injure you while I am with you? I would sacrifice such wretches to my deadliest vengeance ! They say I am mad, dearest, but they little know the strength there is in madness. It will be well for them if they do not brave it."

"Dearest Ottavia," said Olympia, in her gentlest accents, "calm your feelings, there is no one here who would seek to injure either of us ; they are all our friends."

"Friends !—friends !" repeated the maniac, wildly, "what is the meaning of that word ? I have heard it often, but never believed in its truth. Friends, as they call themselves, are hollow, treacherous ; I have found them so, and I hate them all. We will not talk of them, dearest ; no, we will speak of the future joys that are in store for us, and talk only of love and happiness. Wait till to-morrow comes, and then—oh, then ; ha—ha—ha !"

She laughed aloud with delirious glee, and still retaining her hold of Olympia's hand, gazed in her face with earnest affection. Olympia humoured her in every way she could, and at length she became calm, and at intervals a dawn of reason seemed to light upon her soul, but it was only for an instant, and all again became darkness and obscurity. Several hours were passed away in this manner, but at length Montaldi thought it was time to depart, and he therefore kindly approached his unfortunate charge, and in the gentlest manner possible endeavoured to withdraw her from Olympia, but clinging still closer to Olympia, the wretched maniac resisted him with all her strength, at the same time exclaiming—

"Off—off ! You shall not separate us ! Cruel man, what would you do ? Why should you seek to tear those asunder who have vowed to love each other with the affection of mother and daughter ? Speak to him, dearest ! He will listen to you, and will suffer us to remain together. Come—come, let us away to the green fields, and wander hand-in-hand beneath the bright blue sky ! There no one shall dare to interrupt us, and we will inhale the sweets of the various flowers that will spring up in our path to welcome us."

"Dear Ottavia," said Olympia, embracing her with the same affection as if she had been her mother, "I pray you yield to the wishes of your kind guardian, and I promise you that every day we will meet again. Indeed I am not going away, and I hope that there are yet many hours of happiness in store for us."

"Happiness!" repeated Ottavia; " oh, yes, we will be so very happy if you will not leave me. But why will you not accompany me? You are not afraid of me, are you?—Oh, you cannot be, for I love you too fondly to do you harm. Come, come, let us away together."

"Ottavia," said Olympia, soothingly, "I must not leave this place; my life most likely depends upon my remaining here. I have enemies, who, should they discover me, might inflict the greatest tortures upon me; do you understand me?"

Ottavia pressed her hands upon her forehead, as if endeavouring to comprehend the meaning of Olympia's words, and gazed steadfastly upon her.

"Oh, yes, I understand you, sweetest," she said at length; "but can it be possible that one so lovely and so innocent can have enemies? It is the wicked and unjust who should alone be annoyed by them. But who are they? Point them out to me; and you shall find that, poor maniac though I be—at least they call me so—I have the power to exterminate them! Death! ay, death, should be the portion of the wretches who should dare to attempt to harm you. Let us begone, fair being, and under my protection you shall be perfectly safe."

"My good Ottavia," said Montaldi, mildly and soothingly, "indeed the very life of the Signora Olympia would be in jeopardy if she were to quit the protection of our kind friends here. Do not, then, resist my wishes, I beg of you, or I may find it necessary not to allow you to see each other again."

"Ah!" ejaculated Ottavia; "you would not be so cruel. Assure me that we shall meet again to-morrow, and I will yield to your wishes."

"You have heard what Signora Olympia has said," replied Montaldi, "and rest satisfied that she will not deceive you."

"Oh, no, indeed I will not," ejaculated Olympia fervently.

"Deceive me!" cried Ottavia; "no, no,— I do not believe that you can have the heart to do so. I will trust you, dearest farewell— farewell, till to-morrow,"

"Till to-morrow," repeated Olympia, returning her embrace; "and in the meantime may all good angels watch over and protect you."

The poor maniac could not find words to return an answer, but there was that in her looks, which told how powerful were the feelings which at that moment held possession of her wandering mind. Again and again she embraced Olympia, and it was not without the greatest difficulty that old Montaldi could tear them apart and prevail upon Ottavia to quit the cavern with him. Olympia felt more deeply

affected and impressed with this interview than she had been before, and every word that Ottavia had spoken was stamped indelibly upon her memory.

"It is most extraordinary, signora," observed Massaroni," that this unfortunate woman should have taken such a remarkable fancy to you."

"It is indeed," coincided Olympia, "and my heart also yearns towards her. Would that it would please Heaven to restore her to her senses, that we might ascertain who she really is, and what has reduced her to her present melancholy and deplorable condition."

"In that wish I most cordially join, signora," remarked the brigand; "and I am not without hopes that our wishes will be ultimately gratified."

"God grant that they may," said Olympia; "there were moments during our interview when I imagined that some dawn of reason had broken in upon her mind."

"Yes, I also noticed that," observed Massaroni, "and I trust, from such symptoms, that with care and attention she will ultimately recover from her present lamentable malady, but the longer I gaze at her, the more forcibly am I struck with the extraordinary likeness that exists between you and her, signora."

"Not more wonderful, I fear, than the resemblance in our history. Oh, how every word she uttered went to my heart!"

"Do not suffer such thoughts to torture your mind, Olympia, or I fear it would be imprudent to suffer you to meet often."

"Ah, indeed I should feel unhappy," said Olympia, "should the meetings of myself and poor Ottavia now be prohibited. She has formed an unaccountable attachment towards me, and should she not be permitted to meet me again, it might be attended with the most fatal consequences. I will seek to subdue my feelings in her presence, and I have no doubt that after a few more interviews she will become more calm, and that she may gradually be restored to reason."

"True," coincided Maria, "and I think it would be highly imprudent, and attended with much danger, should any obstacle be thrown in the way of those meetings."

"Far be it from me to wish to do so," said the brigand; I only spoke for the best, and most cordially do I hope that our wishes and endeavours may be attended with the most fortunate results."

After some farther conversation on the same subject, Olympia retired, and in the solitude of her own apartment gave herself up to such thoughts as her interview with Ottavia had naturally excited in her mind. The more she reflected upon the deplorable situation of the hapless maniac, and the melancholy mystery which hung over her, the more deeply interested did she become, and the greater was her anxiety to penetrate into her history; but of that there seemed to be no chance at present, and she was therefore compelled to wait patiently, or till such time as Providence should please to unravel it.

———

CHAPTER XXIX.

THE ENCOUNTER.—THE RECOGNITION.

IN the meantime old Montaldi, conducting his unfortunate charge, led the way from the cavernous retreat of Massaroni, towards his own residence, and as they proceeded he did all in his power to divert her wandering mind, though with little success. She continued to talk in the wildest accents of Olympia, and expressed frequent apprehensions that she would never be permitted to see her again, and then she would wring her hands and weep bitterly, and Montaldi found it impossible to pacify her.

"She is so good, so fair, so gentle a being!" she ejaculated—"the bright vison that for years has haunted my imagination, rendering that Heaven which was before darkness, horror, and despair. And shall she now be torn from me? Shall she not be permitted to gladden my heart by her presence?—What has poor Ottavia done that she should thus be deprived of every happiness?—But I will see her, though I force my way through stubborn rocks to meet her. Old man, who art thou, that would'st prevent me? Begone, I know thee not, and thou must be very cruel, oh, most cruel, to seek to torture me thus."

"My poor Ottavia," said Montaldi, "do not give way to those paroxysms; come—come, be calm; I am your old friend, your best friend, and Heaven knows that I would do anything to serve you and restore you to happiness. The Signora Olympia is not going away, and I again promise you that you shall see her every day, if it be agreeable to her."

"Ah! you would deceive me, old man," said the maniac, "you think I am mad, and that therefore you can impose upon me, but you shall not, indeed you shall not. No,—no, I defy your power, nothing shall withhold me from that fair bright being who has permitted me to call her daughter. Daughter!—ha! ha! It is a right loving name. But why should I be separated from her? Is it not monstrous and unnatural to tear the mother from her child? Release your hold of me, and let me go to her!"

"To-morrow,—to-morrow," replied the old man, soothingly, "you shall go to her again."

"To-morrow! to-morrow!" repeated Ottavia with a scornful laugh, "what a bitter mockery is that word. I tell you again, old man, that there is no morrow, and wherefore should you seek to deceive me thus?"

"God forbid that I should seek to deceive you, my poor Ottavia," said the old man, "but a few hours will elapse, and then shall you and the Signora Olympia once more meet."

"But do you speak the truth?" said the maniac, her eyes brightening.

"As Heaven is my judge, I do," replied Montaldi solemnly.

"Then, then, I will be calm and patient," said Ottavia, "and I will do everything you wish me, so that you will once more take me to her."

"Enough, Ottavia," returned the old man, "then let us now proceed, and——"

He was interrupted by an exclamation of surprise from some person near him, and looking up he beheld a man enveloped in a dark mantle standing before him, and only a few paces distant, and who was gazing with the most intense earnestness upon the countenance of Ottavia. He was a tall ill looking man, long past the meridian of life, and whose countenance seemed at that time agitated by a variety of evil passions. And Montaldi was so surprised at his sudden appearance that he was rivetted to the spot.

"By the infernal host!" cried the man, in a hoarse voice, "it is the very same, my eyes cannot deceive me!"

The tones of his voice appeared at once to smite the ears of Ottavia, and fixing her wild eyes full upon him, she uttered an exclamation of mingled horror and astonishment as she cried—

"Ah! 'tis he! the villain? The murderer of my innocent, the dark phantom that has haunted my wandering imagination throughout so many dreary years, but who has hitherto avoided justice and retribution. Do you not see him? Do you not mark with what malignant triumph he gazes upon me? Let him not escape! My life depends upon his security!"

Laughing, however, exultingly, the man presented a pistol towards the astonished Montaldi, in a menacing manner, and turning upon his heels, was out of sight in an instant.

"Gone!—gone!" shrieked Ottavia, looking frantically towards the spot where the stranger had stood; "have you then suffered him to escape? Pursue him without delay! I tell you again it is he!"

"He!—whom, Ottavia?" demanded the bewildered Montaldi, eagerly.

"You say you pity me, and ask that question," replied Ottavia, scornfully. "Begone! You mock me, or you would not have suffered the murderer to elude my vengeance. Release me from your hold, old man, and I will follow the cowardly heartless miscreant to the remotest corner of the earth. Oh, my poor innocent little one!—God! God!"

"What mean those strange expressions,

Ottavia ?" cried Montaldi; "answer me, I beseech you, if reason will permit you ?"

"Reason," reiterated Ottavia, fiercely, "why do you talk to me thus? I am not mad, though you would make me appear to be so; but you would pry into my secret, and hold me up to the world as an object of shame and infamy. Ah! old man, I read your object, but will defeat it."

"God knows how much I am wronged by such a thought," said Montaldi, "but if you know this man, who seems to have inspired

OTTAVIA FAINTS IN MONTALDI'S ARMS.

you with so much horror, reveal to me his name."

"No, no, no," said Ottavia, after a pause, and passing her hand across her forehead, "I was deceived, it was all a dream, a phantom of the imagination, such as is constantly haunting it, and torturing my soul with horror. Ask me no questions, old man, I dare not answer them; come, come, let us not tarry here, guide me where thou wilt."

"Unfortunate woman," sighed the compassionate Montaldi, "will nothing ever solve the dreadful mystery which seems connected with thee?"

He looked about him to see whether there was any person at hand, but the coast was perfectly clear, and, filled with amazement and perplexity at the singularity of this adventure, he led forward the now unconscious Ottavia, and in a few minutes arrived at his dwelling. Ottavia threw herself on a seat, on their entrance, and seemed lost to everything around her, and Montaldi was too busily occupied by his own thoughts, to offer to interrupt her. He had such a distinct view of the stranger's forbidding countenance, that he felt confident that he should know it again from a thousand, and there was something so malignant about the expression of it, that he could not recall it to his memory without a feeling approaching to horror. It was evident from the expressions he had made use of, that he recognised in Ottavia one whom he had reason to dread: and there could be no doubt that the unfortunate maniac had also recognised him at the same moment, and that his presence had inspired her with the utmost horror and alarm. He was at a perfect loss how to act under the circumstances, or in what manner to guard against any danger that might threaten. He was most anxious for the arrival of the next day, that he might seek the advice of Massaroni. At length Ottavia seemed to partially arouse herself from her state of unconsciousness, and looking anxiously around the room, she said—

"Where is he? I do not see him here; and yet methought he stood before me with his savage eyes fixed full upon me, and that I heard the harsh tones of his repulsive voice. But no; it could not be; I must have been dreaming. Montaldi!"

"I am here, Ottavia," answered the old man, approaching her, and taking her hand with a look of kindness; "try to collect your thoughts, and to throw some light upon this painful mystery."

"Mystery! what mystery?" said Ottavia, staring vacantly upon him.

"This man," said Montaldi, "whose appearance so alarmed you; tell me who he is?"

"Ah, then!" cried the maniac; "it was no dream; no—no—and you permitted him to escape!—ah, that was cowardice. But do not ask me his name? I dare not repeat it; and if I did, my memory is a wreck, and I cannot think of it. But bar all the doors! let him not come near me, or there will be murder done! Bar the doors, I say, lest he should be lurking near the spot!"

"Do not fear, Ottavia," replied Montaldi, "for no harm shall come to you here. How torturing is this mystery and suspense!" he added to himself.

Ottavia again sunk into a state of apathy, from which it seemed impossible to arouse her, and old Montaldi was once more left to his own reflections, which were of the most perplexing and unsatisfactory description; "nor did it appear probable that he would be enabled to elicit anything in explanation from the unfortunate object of his solicitude and anxiety. At length Ottavia, apparently lost in forgetfulness, slowly arose from her seat, and quitting the room without taking any notice of Montaldi, retired to her own chamber, where he heard her for some time afterwards pacing backwards and forwards in a most agitated manner, and muttering wild and incoherent sentences to herself. At length all became quiet in her chamber, and Montaldi concluded that she had retired to rest, but although it was now nearly eleven o'clock, the thoughts of the old man were too busy to suffer him to seek his bed, and he sat meditating upon the singular event of the day, becoming more involved in perplexity every moment. He was startled by a loud exclamation of horror, proceeding from Ottavia's chamber, and jumping from his seat, he was about to inquire the cause, when he heard her hastily descending the stairs; the next instant the door was burst open, and Ottavia, pale and trembling, with her hair flying loosely over her shoulders—and it was evident that she had not been to rest—rushed into the room, and flying into his arms, clung fearfully to him, gazing with steadfast horror upon the door from which she had just emerged, as though she expected some one to follow.

"For Heaven's sake, my poor Ottavia," said Montaldi, "what is the matter? what has occurred to alarm you thus?"

Ottavia tried to speak, but she could not, and the next moment she sunk in the arms of the old man, perfectly inanimate. Montaldi gently placed her on a couch, and then seizing a loaded pistol, and taking a lamp in the other hand, he cautiously ascended the stairs to Ottavia's chamber, to ascertain what was the cause of her violent alarm; but he could see nothing whatever to excite his suspicions in the least, and more and more amazed and bewildered at the mystery, he again descended the stairs to the room in which he had left Ottavia, and took the readiest means in his power to recover her. But it was some time before the unfortunate woman was restored to any degree of consciousness, and then she stared vacantly around her, and her horror seemed to be so great that Montaldi was fearful she would suffer a relapse.

"Where is he?" she cried, "keep him from me, with his fearful looks; it will chill my blood with horror to gaze upon him."

"Who do you mean, Ottavia?" demanded Montaldi, eagerly.

"Who!" repeated Ottavia; "he—the villain—the assassin who crossed our path to-day? But a few minutes since I beheld his ferocious countenance glaring in at my chamber window from the tree."

"Oh, it is impossible!" said Montaldi:— "you must have been mistaken, Ottavia."

"Mistaken! no—no," she replied; "I know I'm mad, and that sometimes I have fearful dreams; but this was no vision: I tell you again I saw him, and that he peered into my window with such a look as I can never forget; and he menaced me, and pointed to me with a contemptuous finger. Go, go; he is in the garden now, I tell you; in the tree; I saw him look from it; he will do us harm if he is not prevented; I am not afraid of remaining here alone, but go you now."

As she thus spoke she extricated herself from the hold of Montaldi, and pointed towards the door from which she had just emerged. He saw that there was no means of pacifying her than by satisfying her that her imagination had deceived her (for he did not believe that the ruffian had appeared to her as she represented), so, having fastened the outer door, he went to the back of the house, and examined every portion of the garden minutely, but no signs of any individual having been there presented themselves to him. But still the old man felt considerably alarmed by what Ottavia had said, and had his doubts and suspicions upon the subject. He returned to the room where he had left her, and found her pacing it in an uneasy manner.

"Have you seen him?" she demanded, hastily, and gazing fiercely in his countenance, as if she was doubtful of the truth of the answer he would return. "Have you seen him?—Is he not a ferocious-looking miscreant? It was he who murdered my child! If you saw him, why—oh! why did you not secure him? Such blood-thirsty monsters surely ought not to be suffered to escape! I tell you again that he it was who murdered my child, and left me desolate and miserable. But he I loved did not authorize him to commit the atrocious crime. No—no; he was too honourable—too humane —too affectionate to do so. They say, too, that he deserted me; that he left me alone to battle with the world's vicissitudes; believe them not —they are base calumniators. He is coming again — to-morrow; yes, to-morrow! But search for that man who gazed in upon me from the tree. Suffer him not to escape, I say —but do not let him approach me, for there is blood upon his hands—the blood of my innocent offspring. Keep him away from my sight, but deliver him into the hands of justice."

"My good Ottavia," said Montaldi, soothingly, "indeed you have nothing to apprehend. You have suffered your imagination, I say again, to mislead you. I have well searched every part of the house and the premises adjoining, and not a soul have I been able to discover. It must have been a dream that has thus disturbed you."

"A dream!—ha! ha!" laughed Ottavia, in her usual wild manner. "No, no; it was no dream. Think you I am mad? They say I am so; but do not believe them; it is another of their calumnies. They say that those who are mad forget realities, stern facts, and wander into the realms of dream and impossibilities. If so, then, how can I be mad who have such a keen sense of the cruelties and injustice that have been practiced on me? I am not mad!—I am not mad!"

"Tell me, then, the name of the fellow we saw to-day?" said Montaldi, seizing the opportunity of the moment when the unfortunate woman appeared to be a little rational, and hoping to elicit something which might throw a light upon the cloud of mystery which surrounded her. But he was doomed to disappointment. She gazed at him vacantly for a moment or two, and then, after bursting into another wild laugh, she said—

"Tell you his name? No, no—I must not; 'twould freeze the very blood in my veins to do so—turn my heart to stone, and paralyze my every faculty. It was not by the orders of he whom I love that he perpetrated the crime, nor has he deserted me. No, no; he was too good and honourable for that! He has promised to make me his wife, and is not the bridal feast awaiting the arrival of the guests? Do you not hear the melodious strains of minstrelsy that issue from our princely halls? Oh, there will be such revelry there to-day. Smiles shall be seated on every brow; such a thing as sadness shall not be known. Who shall venture to wear the cloud of care when my young lord comes to claim his own one?—Hark! The merry dance!—See, how lightly they trip it! What jocund hearts, what lovely forms are there to do honour to our union! Tra lara! tra lara! tra lara!—Oh, it is a joyful strain!"

Overcome by the excitement of her feelings, the poor maniac gradually sunk in the arms of Montaldi, and again became unconscious to all around her.

"Unfortunate woman!" ejaculated Montaldi, "what a hard destiny is thine. Would to Heaven that the light of reason was restored to thee, that my melancholy history might be revealed, and thy wrongs redressed."

He again placed her on the couch, and continued to watch by her side throughout the night, not feeling it prudent or safe to retire to rest, though he still could not help imagining that Ottavia had been labouring under the delusion of a dream, especially as he had taken such particular care to notice whether any individual had watched them on their way home. At the same time he felt the most burning anxiety to know who the ruffian was they had encountered, and who it was perfectly evident was most closely and importantly connected with his hapless charge. Nothing occurred during the night to create any further alarm, and Ottavia only revived at intervals, and then only to give utterance to the most vague and wild exclamations. When the first streak of day appeared in the eastern horizon, Montaldi persuaded her to retire to her chamber, and endeavour to snatch a few hours' repose, but he continued up watching himself, and reflecting deeply upon all the strange events which the previous day had produced; but it was all to no purpose; for the longer he reflected, the more did he become involved in the maze of perplexity. It was quite evident to him, however, that from their meeting with the unknown, and the dread which Ottavia seemed to entertain of him, that there was some danger to be apprehended from him, and he therefore determined to be on his guard as much as possible.

CHAPTER XXX.

THE PRINCE BIANCHI AND HIS NIECE.—THE FRUITLESS APPEAL.—FLORIO IN HIS DUNGEON.—A MIDNIGHT VISIT.

AND now it becomes necessary that we should return once more to the Villa Rosa, where we left Melina and her noble uncle in so peculiar a situation. For several days Melina remained in a precarious state, more from the excitement of her mind at the melancholy events which had taken place, than from the wound she had received. Her whole thoughts were fixed upon her lover; the fate that in all probability awaited, through the obdurate and revengeful disposition of the Prince Bianchi, which had never been so strongly evinced till latterly, and the excruciating anguish of mind which Florio must be enduring on her account. The prince, too, was racked by a variety of the most torturing thoughts, over which, however, his pride and obstinacy predominated, and he determined that nothing whatever should save Florio from his vengeance, unless Melina renounced him altogether, and consented to become the wife of the Count Alberti, should he ever be restored to liberty, which he could not but hope that he ultimately would. He sent frequently every day to inquire into the progress of his niece, and his mind felt relieved from a ponderous weight, when he was assured that the wound she had unfortunately, but so accidentally, received at his hands, was not dangerous, and that there was every prospect of her speedily recovering; but still he could not at present form the resolution of visiting her himself. He guessed full well the reception he would receive from her, and he shrunk alike from the reproaches it was probable she would heap upon him, and the appeal she would make to him on behalf of Clairville. To yield now to her solicitations, he considered would be

cowardice, and let whatever might be the consequences, he determined not to do so. For two days he did not leave his chamber, and would not be seen by any one, and during that period his reflections were of that torturing nature which may well be imagined. And not the most unimportant subject of his thoughts was the fate which in all probability had befallen the Count Alberti after the death of the Count di Strozzi; but he swore that if Massaroni should proceed to extremities, and sacrifice Alberti's life, he would at all hazards have a terrible revenge. He racked his brain, however, in vain to devise some means of ascertaining what had really become of Alberti, and how to release him from the brigand's power, if he should still be living. The frequent defeats his troops had met with almost intimidated him, and he was perfectly at a loss what course in future to adopt. Massaroni seemed gifted with almost supernatural powers, and to set every force at defiance; and what plan to take to counteract his designs, and bring him to the fate he considered he merited, the prince knew not. He had offered immense rewards — he had tried every stratagem—but all to no purpose; such was the favour in which Massaroni was held by the peasantry, to whom he was so generous a friend, that nothing would induce any of them to betray him: and without their aid he was fearful that his hopes would be long retarded before they would be crowned with success.

"But shall this daring outlaw be permitted to continue to set me at defiance?" he soliloquised; "the thought is degrading—it is maddening; but it shall not be. No, though it cost me half my wealth, I will yet have him in my power, and have him kneeling at my feet for mercy. Shall I, the Prince Bianchi, Governor of Rome, thus be braved by a brigand chief? Never! Some means must be devised to cut short his guilty career of triumph. I can never rest until I see him mount the scaffold. Fool that I was not to recognise him when he was securely in my power. And—ah! a thought strikes me: it was by means of a portrait of himself, taken by Theodore, as well as the knowledge of old Nicolo, that he was recognised on that occasion. How did Theodore obtain the opportunity of taking that likeness? He has since absconded, and that, to say the least of it, looks suspicious. Clairville was his most intimate friend and fellow-student; they were like brothers together, and no doubt were well acquainted with each other's secrets. Florio must know the means by which his friend obtained that likeness, and if he refuses to disclose the truth to me, be the consequences upon his own head. This may lead to the discovery of Massaroni, and he may yet be trepanned in his lair. Happy thought!—I will immediately to the dungeon of my prisoner, and by threats and persuasion elicit from him the truth."

Elated with the thought, the prince instantly departed from the villa, and bent his way towards the prison in which the wretched Florio Clairville was confined. He found him traversing his dungeon in the most excited manner, and on beholding the prince he turned upon him a look of mingled reproach and contempt, though his heart at the same time was yearning to know the condition of Melina. Bianchi shrank beneath his gaze, and for some moments he hesitated to speak. His conscience bitterly reproached him with the injustice of his conduct, and he turned his head away, and pondered in his own mind how he should proceed. When Florio beheld him enter, he paused, and it was evident from the expression of his countenance that his bosom was undergoing the most violent emotions.

"So, my lord," he said at length, "you have at last condescended to visit the victim of your injustice in the dreary dungeon to which you have consigned him. But I will not reproach you; no—your own conscience will do that ere long severely enough; but if you are capable of feeling any pity towards me, I implore you to make me acquainted with the fate of the unfortunate Signora Melina. Tell me, does she still exist?"

"She does," answered the prince, in a faint voice, "and is rapidly approaching to convalescence. Let that suffice you."

"Oh, thank Heaven for that!" said Florio fervently, and clasping his hands; "but for what purpose has your highness visited me?"

"Simply this," answered the prince, "to elicit some information from you which I know you can give me."

"Name it, my lord."

"Your friend, Theodore, executed a portrait of the brigand, Massaroni?"

"True."

"He must, then, have seen him before his appearance at the Villa Rosa?"

"He did."

"And were you in his company on the occasion?"

"I was."

"'Tis well," said the prince, triumphantly, "we shall soon arrive at the truth."

"Do not flatter yourself too prematurely with such a hope, my lord," said Florio, "for you may be doomed to disappointment."

"Ah! say you so?—You had better beware, and remember the danger which hangs over your head. Do you know where you are?"

"These blackened walls, this gloomy cell, will not allow me to be ignorant, your highness," returned Florio.

"And yet you may have the means of regaining your liberty, on the condition that you immediately quit the country."

"Indeed! But how?"

"By being candid."

"What mean you, my lord?"

"Do you know the place of Massaroni's present concealment?"

"I do," answered Clairville, "and have but recently quitted him."

"Ah! and the Count Alberti?"

"He is his prisoner, of that I am satisfied."

"And will you not reveal to me the means by which I may best surprise and secure this daring brigand chief?" demanded the prince, eagerly.

"Never!" replied the prisoner, firmly; "I should despise myself if I could be capable of such a base act."

"Beware, beware, young man; you had better not refuse."

"No threats shall induce me to betray one whom, in spite of all his faults, I believe to be the victim of misfortune and injustice."

"What do I hear?" said the prince, passionately; "do you acknowledge yourself to be the friend of this desperado?"

"I do, for he has proved himself to be mine."

"And know you not what the consequences may be to yourself by such an acknowledgment?"

"I do," answered Florio, "and heed them not; I will never betray Massaroni."

"Not to save your own life; to regain your liberty?"

"No."

"Rash youth; reflect, reflect!"

"There is no necessity for it, my lord, for my mind is already made up."

"Tortures then shall wring the secret from your breast!" said the prince.

"I will brave them," firmly answered Clairville; "you cannot inflict severer tortures upon me than those I now endure."

"That shall be seen; but once more I offer you liberty upon the terms I have proposed."

"And once more, and positively, I reject them, my lord. The brigand chief, Massaroni, shall never fall into your clutches by my means."

"Then you connive at the imprisonment of the Count Alberti by this daring marauder?"

"I do not, but I respect the liberty of Massaroni."

"By Heaven, you shall be made to answer for this!" said the prince.

"Do your best and your worst, my lord," returned Florio; "I am perfectly reckless."

"This daring spirit shall soon be curbed, young stripling."

"I much doubt it, your highness; I act as justice dictates, and am not to be daunted in the right course which it points out for me to pursue."

"What madness is this, Clairville?"

"It may appear so, my lord."

"You cannot mean what you say."

"I am not in the habit of making idle assertions," said Florio.

"Once more I urge you to reveal to me all that you know concerning Massaroni."

"It is perfectly useless, my lord; you have heard my determination."

"But you will think better of this."

"Indeed I shall not."

"Remember that the penalty is death to all those who are known to be connected with or to shield the brigand chief from justice."

"I know it well, your highness; but that shall not intimidate me."

"What headstrong obstinacy!" ejaculated the Prince Bianchi; "what worse than folly!"

"Your highness is at liberty to term it what you please," remarked the prisoner, "but I am fully prepared to abide by the consequences, whatever they may be."

The prince took two or three hasty strides across the cell, and then again turning towards Clairville, and fixing upon him a penetrating look, he said—

"Answer me one question, Florio?"

"Name it, my lord."

"Was you aware of the presence of Massaroni at the Villa Rosa, on the night of the fete, before he was discovered by Nicolo?"

"The question is an unfair one," returned Clairville, "but I will answer it candidly, nevertheless. I was."

"And yet would not betray him?"

"No."

"By Heaven! this is worse and worse. And you call yourself a man of honour and integrity?"

"I do, but should consider myself unworthy of the titles were I to break my solemn promise, merely to gratify the vengeance of the enemy of an injured and unfortunate man."

"Then you acknowledge yourself to be an accomplice of the brigand?"

"I do not."

"But you have said that you were aware of his presence at the Villa Rosa before he was detected by Nicolo?"

"True."

"Then you must have been acquainted with his designs," said his highness.

"Indeed I was not, my lord," answered Florio, "neither was I aware that it was his intention to venture to the Villa."

"And who aided him in his escape? Who pointed out to him the secret passage?"

"That will I also answer candidly, and without any fear of the consequences. It was I who directed him."

"Villain! traitor!" cried the prince, foaming with rage.

"I merit not the epithets, my lord," said Florio, coolly, "and despise them."

"And is this reward for the friendship with which I have honoured you?"

"I never abused your highness's friendship. But is this all you have to say to me; because if it be, I presume that our interview is at an end?"

"So haughty, too; but I am nevertheless prepared to forgive you all, if you will but yield to my demands."

"Your highness has heard my decision," said Clairville, firmly.

"Will nothing tempt you to abandon it?"

"Nothing."

"Rash youth, again I urge you to consider the consequences of your obduracy."

"There needs no consideration, my lord."

"By the saints, I will yet force the secret from you."

"I will suffer death first. My lord, permit me to remind you that you have no wavering coward to deal with, or happily you might succeed in intimidating me. My mind is made up, and all the persuasion or threats in the world shall not move me from my purpose. The Count Alberti is a villain, and richly merits any fate that may befall him."

"Ah! this to me?" exclaimed the prince, with a look of indignation.

"Ay, my lord, I am ever accustomed to speak my mind boldly."

"Mark my words, young man, you shall bitterly repent this."

"Do with me as you like, my lord, I am now quite indifferent as to what may become of me."

"I will give you time to reflect maturely upon what I have said, before I proceed to extremities," remarked the prince, "and it strikes me that you will yet change your mind."

"Do not deceive yourself with such an idea, my lord," replied Florio, "for you will find that what I promise, under any circumstances, I have always the firmness to adhere to."

"The boy must surely be mad," said the prince, looking at him with an expression of astonishment; "liberty is offered to you on the simple condition that you reveal all you know of the rascal Massaroni, and yet you refuse it."

"I do, my lord; again I say that I will not betray him."

"Idiot!" cried Bianchi, furiously, as he stalked from the cell; "then take the consequences, for on no other conditions than those I have offered can you expect any mercy from me."

"I ask it not," replied Clairville, proudly, "I have committed no offence, and am prepared to abide by my fate, whatever it may be."

"The obstinate fool!" muttered the prince to himself, as he departed from the prison, "it is in his power to betray Massaroni into my hands, and to restore the Count Alberti to liberty, and yet he refuses. But no means must be left untried to induce him to yield. I will force the secret from him, or he shall pay for his obduracy with his life."

When the prince had quitted him, Florio gave himself up entirely to those racking thoughts which the interview with him had excited in his breast. But the certainty that Melina still lived, and was out of danger, afforded him the greatest consolation, and he endeavoured to resign himself to his fate, whatever it might be.

"Dear Melina," he cried, "for thy sake I will bear up against my cruel destiny, and meet whatever may be in store for me with fortitude. May the Almighty watch over thee and protect thee from all danger, and defeat the machinations of thine enemies. Thou canst never be mine. I am now convinced, and therefore life has no longer any charms for me; but still something seems to whisper to me that we shall meet again; and there is a melancholy consolation in that hope. But oh, gentle and affectionate girl, how dreadful must be the anguish you are enduring; and you have no one near to sympathize with you in your sorrow. Cruel indeed must be the prince, your uncle, to act in the manner he is now doing towards you. And will nothing move him to relent? —Alas! I fear it will not. And should the Count Alberti succeed in making his escape, in spite of your tears and supplications, he will compel you to become his wife. Horrible thought! Surely Heaven will not permit so monstrous a sacrifice. My heart sickens at the thought, and my imprisonment becomes the more intolerable; but even if I were at liberty I should have no power to save thee."

"He beat his breast, and traversed his dreary cell with disordered steps as these thoughts arose to his mind, and it was some time before he could regain the least composure. He reflected deeply on all the prince had said to him, but nothing could induce him to alter his mind, and he would, as he said, have despised himself could he have done so. Every hour his uneasiness increased, and night came, but he found it utterly impossible to compose himself to sleep, and various were the conjectures that tortured his brain. Melina was now completely out of danger, and was fast approaching to recovery, but most intense was the agony of her mind, when she reflected on the situation of Florio, and most anxious was she again to behold the prince her uncle, that she might intercede with him, in his favour.

"Surely," she said, "he cannot be so cruel as to turn a deaf ear to my supplications, and persist in detaining the unfortunate Clairville a prisoner. He has committed no offence that can merit so severe a punishment, and why, then, should my uncle thus cruelly persecute him? Poor Florio, how terrible must be your sufferings in your gloomy dungeon, ignorant as you probably are of my fate. May God give you fortitude to bear up against it, and once more restore you to liberty and happiness. Happiness!—alas! how vainly I talk; can you ever again, and know that Fate has separated us for ever? I know your faithful heart too well to imagine for a moment that you can; and I am truly wretched."

Her tears flowed fast as she uttered these words, and it was in vain that she sought to find the smallest consolation. How much greater would have been her anguish had she been aware of the interview which had taken place between the prince and Florio, and the imminent danger which threatened the latter. In a few days more Melina was sufficiently recovered to be able to leave her chamber, and the prince then consented to see her, though it was not without considerable reluctance that he did so. Melina approached the apartment in which her uncle was awaiting to receive her, with a trembling step and a palpitating heart, though she had fully determined to make an eloquent appeal to his feelings on behalf of Florio; but at the same time she could not flatter herself with the idea that she would meet with any success. On her entrance the prince advanced towards her and received her kindly, though with evident confusion, and placing her by his side, he contemplated her earnestly for a few moments in silence, and seemed at a loss what to say.

"It affords me infinite pleasure, my dear Melina," he at length remarked in a faltering voice, "to see you again restored to health after your late alarming accident. I can assure you I have suffered much from anxiety; but can you forgive me for the suffering I have so unintentionally caused you?"

"Most sincerely, most willingly, my dear uncle," replied Melina, extending to him her hand.

"Spoken like yourself, my sweet niece," said the prince; "it is Clairville who is alone to blame."

"Not so, my good lord," hastily returned Melina; "and I would fain plead to you for him. He is noble, and virtuous, and is deserving of a far better fate than it has pleased Providence to bestow upon him. It is true he might have been to blame for seeking a clandestine interview with me after you had prohibited our meeting; but surely for this one simple offence your highness will not continue to visit him with your wrath?"

"Melina," said the prince, "I am not vindictive, but Clairville has abused the friendship with which I honoured him, and boldly set my authority at defiance; these are offences that I cannot overlook, and he must take the consequences of his presumption."

"Oh, no, my dear uncle," ejaculated Melina imploringly, "you will relent; I am sure you will, you will forgive him. But tell me, is he still in prison?"

"He is," replied the prince, "and there he is likely to remain. He is obstinate, Melina—he is grossly obstinate; he admits that he has been connected with the rascal Massaroni; that he has been one of his prisoners—that he knows perfectly well the place of his present concealment; nay, more, that he had assisted him to escape from the Villa Rosa, on the night of the fete given to celebrate the anniversary of your birth; and yet he positively refuses to inform me where the daring brigand chief and his desperate band of marauders are located, and acknowledges himself to be friendly disposed towards him."

"Dear, dear Florio," ejaculated Melina, fervently, "how much do I admire you for your noble and generous spirit."

The prince looked at her amazed; he seemed perfectly astounded.

"How now, girl?" he exclaimed, passionately, "can I believe my ears—my senses, altogether? is the world turned topsy-turvy? what great revolution is working? Are you my sister's daughter, and conspired against me? Cospetto! I must be dreaming! It cannot be the gentle Melina, that sweet gentle creature that I have cherished as my heart's core, who is now advocating the cause of robbers and traitors!"

"Dear uncle," interposed Melina, clasping her hands, and looking in his face with an expression of supplication as fervent and as sweetly persuasive as if she had been his own offspring, "how sadly do you mistake my feelings on this occasion; how unjust and cruel is the construction you put upon my motives. Have I not ever returned the goodness I have received from you with gratitude? If I have failed to do so to your wishes, God knows it has been from no want of anxious will on my part; but you mean not what you have said;—no—no—you are excited by some false delusion. I conspire with robbers and traitors! oh, horrible idea! Sooner, my lord, would I perish than do aught that might affect your happiness, or that I should feel ashamed to acknowledge as a woman. Expressing those principles, I admit that not only did Clairville assist in the escape of Allesandro Massaroni on the occasion you mention, but that I also connived at it;—I believed him worthy of a better fate than that to which you would destine him; I perceived, or fancied I perceived, that the brigand chief

possessed all the noble attributes of man, and that misfortune, not his own will, has placed him in his present position; I confess I sympathise with him; I would rescue you from after self-reproach, in having been the means of sacrificing the life of one who, but for the cruelty and injustice of others, might not only be an ornament but a blessing to society. Clairville has done no more; therefore, if he be guilty of the serious offence you seem to imagine him, I—I am equally culpable, and should in justice share the same punishment. Nay, I shrink not from it, but demand it, if it be your will that he whom I confess to love, and towards whom my sentiments must and ever shall remain the same, while I consider him to be worthy of them, shall suffer for the conduct he has thought proper to adopt."

While Melina was giving utterance to this speech, which she did with the greatest energy, and her fine eyes expressing the true index of her noble soul, the Prince Bianchi gazed at her completely amazed and bewildered. He could, in fact, scarcely credit the evidence of his senses, whilst the observations she had made use of were so strictly in accordance with what truth and reason would suggest, that he was quite staggered, and knew not how to answer. He gazed upon her for a few moments with a mingled expression of surprise, regret, confusion, and affection, and then folding his arms across his chest, he paced the room in the most violent state of agitation, muttering indistinct sentences to himself. Melina watched him with the utmost anxiety, but did not offer to interrupt him, for she hoped that his better feelings would predominate, and that he would yet yield to her importunities, and see the injustice and cruelty of his conduct towards her lover. At length the prince paused, and turning towards her, in a voice of greater calmness than he had yet spoken, he said—

"And so, Melina, you acknowledge that you still love Florio Clairville?"

"I do, my lord," replied the blushing Melina, timidly, but with all the innocent sincerity of her nature; "and so must I ever continue to do till I am convinced that he is unworthy of my love, then, with becoming resolution, though not without regret, can I discard him from my heart for ever!"

"And should the Count Alberti be restored to liberty?"

"I can, I will never view him with any other sentiments than than those I do at present."

"You will reject him as your husband?"

"The idea alone of Alberti as my husband is odious to me."

"Rash girl! knew you not that it is my will?"

"Unfortunately, my lord, I do, and sincerely does it grieve me that I am compelled, for the first time, compelled to disobey that will. Sooner would I die a thousand deaths of the most excruciating agony, than become the wife of the seducer of the unfortunate Olympia."

"Then you hold with his present detention by Massaroni?" said the prince, almost bursting with rage.

"No, my dear uncle, I do not," replied Melina; "but I consider the misfortunes he has met with no more than a just punishment for his manifold crimes."

The Prince Bianchi knitted his brows, and traversed the room passionately. His conscience assured him that he was acting an un-

MONTALDI'S VISIT TO FLORIO IN HIS DUNGEON.

just part, and that his fair niece spoke no more than the truth; his heart also still yearned towards her with its wonted affection; but yet so firmly had he fixed his mind upon the unnatural alliance, that he could not form the resolution to yield, much less would his pride

allow him to submit to the suit of Florio Clairville.

"Uncle, dear uncle," supplicated Melina, sinking on her knees at his feet, "you cannot, you will not, persist in your present cruel determination. Clairville never injured you by word or deed; he has committed no absolute offence against any one; why, then, persecute him so mercilessly? Release him then, I beseech you, and I promise, solemnly promise you—although I confess that I can never cease to remember him, never cease to love him with the same fervour I do at present, until he may prove himself to be unworthy of it—without your sanction I will not consent or attempt to meet him again."

"He knows the retreat of Massaroni," replied the prince, "and, consequently, the place where the Count Alberti is confined; he has confessed that he does, and consequently while he refuses to reveal where it is, he proves himself to be one of the partizans of the brigand chief, and must and shall take all the penalties."

"Oh, no—no—no, you will not be so cruel?"

"At any rate, I will be thus just and politic," returned the prince. "I have offered him his liberty on those conditions; if he remains obstinate, he proves not only that he is a fool, but that his professions of love for you are all a farce."

"He has doubtless pledged his word to that unfortunate man, Massaroni, from whom he has received services," said Melina; "and I should despise him were he to break it."

"Then be the consequences of his obstinacy on his own head; for much as I love you, Melina, I swear——"

"No—no," interrupted the agitated Melina, "do not, I implore you, take any rash vows; you will think better of this."

"Melina, my mind is made up," said the prince, determinedly.

"And you will sacrifice Florio to your vengeance?" demanded Melina.

"Vengeance, girl?" replied the Prince Bianchi, somewhat abashed by her manner. "Other lips than your's could not have dared to have given utterance to such assertions. Justice, and not revenge, ever guide the actions of the Prince Bianchi. The daring marauder, Massaroni, must be brought to punishment; Count Alberti must be restored to that liberty of which he has been so unjustly deprived; Clairville has the power to effect both; he refuses, and by so doing proves himself to be an abettor of one of the most lawless pests of the country; and I, as governor of Rome, must see that he pays the penalty. That penalty, I need scarcely say, is death!"

"Oh, horror—horror!" ejaculated Melina; "but you surely could not be so cruel as to consign him to such a fate?"

"I have offered him the means of saving himself, but he has refused," answered the prince; "am I to be made responsible for his obstinacy? And shall the Count Alberti be sacrificed to the vengeance of Massaroni, when a word from Clairville might save him? By all my hopes, it shall not be; and much as I regard you, Melina, you plead to me, and ever will do so under the circumstances, in his behalf in vain."

"Alas—alas!" sighed Melina, clasping her hands in despair; "how cruel, how ungenerous is this. Oh, my uncle, never did I imagine that your heart could become insensible to pity. Remember, I supplicate you, all the noble qualities of Florio, and place his virtues in contrast with the vices of Alberti, and——"

"Girl!" interrupted the prince, passionately, "I will not, must not listen to such an argument as this. Compare the beggar Clairville with the noble Count Alberti?—pshaw!"

"The *noble* count!" repeated Melina, unable to conceal her scorn and disgust; "oh, what a libel it is upon virtuous nobility, the nobility of the mind, not that of mere rank and station in society, to apply the term to one who has so basely committed himself as Alberti!"

"Bah, girl!" returned his highness, impatiently, "you are too severe and uncharitable towards the count. 'Tis true he has been guilty of some youthful indiscretion; but is he for ever to be condemned for these, and to be for ever more looked upon as a monster of iniquity? By the holy St. Peter, I have no patience with you."

"Youthful indiscretions, my lord?" said Melina, looking at him with a mingled expression of astonishment and reproach; "is it possible that you can attempt to extenuate the crimes of Alberti?—for youthful indiscretion is by far too mild a term to apply to them. Can you recall to your memory his base conduct towards the unfortunate Olympia and her innocent offspring, his child, and yet hold him up as not only one who is blameless, but who is likewise deserving of admiration and esteem? I can scarcely believe that you are serious; but of this, rest assured—and I would say it with all deference and respect to your highness—that no power on earth can ever alter my sentiments towards him, and they are those of disgust and abhorrence."

The prince frowned with rage, and stamped his foot.

"Melina," he said, "beware! For although I have hitherto treated you with the utmost affection and indulgence, you may try my patience too much, and this ridiculous obstinacy on your part may induce me to adopt a course I would fain avoid. Again I tell you it is useless for you to attempt to intercede with me for the prisoner, Clairville; on no other conditions will I consent to extend mercy to him than his confessing the place where the brigand chief is concealed, and affording every facility in his power for the restoration of the Count Alberti to liberty. Am I to be dared and defied, insulted, scorned, and persecuted, by this lawless marauder; because, forsooth, he has a few romantic qualities about him, which have turned the brains of many silly girls like yourself? The bare thought is in itself past enduring. Again I command you to renounce all hopes of Florio Clairville for ever, and to prepare yourself to become the wife of the Count Alberti, should he ever be released from the power of Massaroni."

"Forbid it, great Heaven!" ejaculated the damsel, solemnly, and with a shudder of horror.

"Do you, then, exult in the captivity of the count?" demanded Prince Bianchi.

"No, my uncle," answered Melina; "how much you wrong me by such a supposition. Guilty as he has been, I should despise myself could I exult o'er his misfortunes. Still, can I look upon his restoration to liberty with any other feelings than those of dread after what you have said? Oh! my lord, for Heaven's sake take pity on me, and do not consign me to so revolting a fate. Sooner would I perish by the most torturing death than become the bride of the Count Alberti."

"Obdurate girl!" cried the prince, "you seem resolved to arouse my utmost indignation. Again I tell you to beware, for nothing can move me from my purpose; and this obstinate resistance to my will can only recoil upon your own head."

"My lord," returned Melina, firmly, and her bosom swelling with wounded pride, "pardon the boldness of my speech, but justice to myself demands that I should, at such a moment as this, speak out fearlessly and candidly. Allow me to say, then, that it is your highness who has become obstinate, uncharitable, and unjust. Ay, these expressions may sound harsh, but they are, nevertheless, dictated by truth and reason. You have hitherto found me dutiful and subservient to your will, and God knows I am anxious to continue to be so while I can, consistently with my duty to myself; but I can never submit to that by which I must not only sacrifice my future happiness, but become degraded in my own estimation. As the wife of Alberti, I should become one of the most wretched beings in existence; and surely, my uncle, after all the affection you have ever professed and shown towards me, you must shrink from the idea of consigning me to a state of misery, which I am at a loss to find language to describe. Alberti must be aware that not only do I not love him, but that I look upon him with loathing and disgust; and if he really possesses that innate pride of which he boasts, should he again be restored to liberty (which I sincerely hope he may), he will at once abandon his hateful suit."

"Melina," said the prince, frowning, "this language will not tend to move me from my purpose. I have pledged my word to Alberti,

and nothing on earth shall induce me to break it."

"Then," cried Melina, again clasping her hands with agony, "then I am lost! Alas! my lord, you have doomed me to perpetual misery."

"Nay, Melina," replied the prince, assuming as much composure as he could, though he really keenly felt the truth and poignancy of his niece's observations, and could not but secretly condemn his own conduct, "you do me an injustice by such a supposition; and so you will ultimately discover. I have your future happiness studiously at heart, however preposterous such an assertion may at present seem to you."

"If you have, indeed," remarked Melina, eagerly, "you will at once show mercy to Florio, and abandon your designs as regards the Count Alberti and myself. Oh! my good lord, I entreat you to reflect calmly and dispassionately upon this painful subject, and I am satisfied that your goodness, your strict sense of honour and justice, and the love you bear me, will induce you to yield to my supplications. I am ready to admit that perhaps it was wrong in Florio to seek an interview with me after you had forbidden him; but surely every allowance should be made for the fervour of his passion, the anguish of his despair; and am I not as much to blame as himself?"

"Clairville has acknowledged himself to have been connected with the brigand, Massaroni," answered the prince.

"By accident only," said Melina, "but in none of his lawless pursuits."

"He has confessed that it was he who pointed out to him the secret passage on the night of the festival at Villa Rosa. Was it not his duty rather to have consigned him to the hands of justice?"

"His noble spirit would not suffer him to do so," answered Melina; "he took compassion on the unfortunate man, surrounded as he was at that time by the most imminent danger."

"Noble spirit!" repeated his highness passionately; "take compassion on a robber and a murderer! 'Sdeath, girl! I have no patience with you. Such maudlin sentimentality suits not my taste and judgment. Clairville by his conduct has identified himself with the mountain chief. He is aware of the place of his concealment; he refuses to divulge it; he is shielding the daring rascal from the law; and if he persists in doing so, he must take the consequences. The murderer of the Count di Strozzi, the capturer of the noble Alberti, and the reckless and merciless destroyer of a large portion of his property, must not be allowed to escape with impunity. You have heard my determination, and it is no use for you to appeal to me further. The Prince Bianchi, the governor of Rome, swerve from his duty to his country and his own conscience? Bah! the very thought brings degradation with it. I leave you now, Melina, for it is useless to argue this subject further with you at present; reflect maturely upon all I have said, and come to a prompt decision, or the fate of Florio Clairville is sealed."

As he thus spoke, the prince moved towards the door of the apartment, but Melina followed him, and placing her fair hands upon his arm, earnestly supplicated him to stay.

"But for another moment, my lord, hear me," she ejaculated, tears starting to her eyes; "you cannot, you surely will not leave me thus. If I have said anything wrong, oh, pardon me, and make at least some little allowance for the excitement of my feelings. Remember the circumstances under which myself and the unfortunate Clairville met—the pure motives which gave rise to the love which we entertain towards each other, and do not, oh! do not, so hastily, so cruelly, condemn us."

"No more, no more, Melina," replied the prince, forcibly tearing himself away; "you have heard my will, and you must learn to submit to it. If Clairville remains obstinate, and still refuses to reveal the place of Massaroni's concealment, and likewise objects to abandon all his future hopes of you, he dies!"

"Oh, God! oh God!" groaned Melina, shrinking back with horror as her inexorable uncle retired from the apartment; and sinking upon a seat—"what a dreadful fate is mine; can this indeed be he whom I have ever loved with the same affection as if he had been my own father? Florio! dear, unfortunate Florio! what will become of us?—Oh, would to Heaven that we had never met on that fatal night, then this would not have happened. But surely the prince cannot be so entirely lost to all sense of pity as to remain inflexible. He cannot consign the hapless Florio, towards whom he ever evinced such warm friendship, to so awful and cruel a fate; neither can he sacrifice me to so hateful and guilty an individual as the Count Alberti!—No, I will still endeavour to think better of him, than to believe him capable of such refined cruelty and injustice. Rather let me die than that such should be my fate. Oh, my revered parents, never did I feel your loss so severely as in this hour of fearful trial. Had you been living, I should have been saved from the dangers which now threaten me, and there might have been hope both for myself and Florio. But let whatever may be the consequences, I will still endeavour to remain firm, and to put my trust in Providence. They may drag me to the altar, and there will I die, sooner than become the wife of the hated, the abandoned Alberti.—Heaven watch over you, my beloved Florio, and shield you from the designs of your enemies!"

She wept bitterly as she gave utterance to these words; and in this state of anguish Floretta found her when she entered the room to see whether Melina required her services. This faithful attendant having been made acquainted with all the particulars which had taken place at the interview between Malina and her uncle, exerted herself to the utmost to console her as much as was in her power, but with little prospect of success.

"Do not give way to despair, my dear signora," she said, "for although your illustrious uncle at present appears so harsh and inflexible, I am satisfied that he loves you too well, and has too great a regard for your future happiness, long to remain so. He will relent; and should the Count Alberti escape from his confinement, he will at once reject a suit which he finds to be so totally odious to you."

"Alas! alas!" sighed Melina, "I would, but cannot think as you do, after the stern and unfeeling observations which my uncle, the prince, has made to me this morning. Alberti has contrived to ingratiate himself in the favour of his highness in the most extraordinary manner, and I do not think it will be a very easy task to do away with the favourable impression he has made upon him, which is the more remarkable, seeing the numerous vices of which he has been guilty. And Florio! Oh, God! how terrible is his situation; for without he reveals to the prince all he knows respecting the secret haunt of Massaroni, which I feel convinced he will not do, he can expect no mercy from him. How deeply do I regret that I ever consented to that clandestine meeting; Florio would still have been at liberty; and although every obstacle is thrown in the way of our passion, I might still have become somewhat resigned, thought I could never be completely happy."

"I fear, signora," said Floretta, "that I was principally to blame in having consented to become the messenger between you; but, indeed, I could not resist the earnest importunities of Signor Clairville."

"Do not reproach yourself, my good Floretta," replied her mistress, "for you performed no more than your duty to me. Alas! how terrible must be the anguish of poor Florio in his dreary place of confinement, and I have not the means of imparting the least consolation to him. Would that I had an opportunity of conveying only a few lines to him, to make him acquainted with the thoughts which are at present passing in my mind, and how doubly dear his image is now to me."

"That opportunity may present itself, my dear lady," observed Floretta; "but depend upon it, he feels fully aware of the continuance of your love, and it is that assurance which will sustain him under all his severe trials. Courage, signora, and Providence, depend upon it, will yet bring about a happy termination to all your troubles."

Melina shook her head doubtfully; and after some further conversation of no importance, Floretta quitted the room. The most torturing thoughts continued to distract the brain of Melina for several hours; and it was not till after the most painful reflection that she could acquire the least degree of composure. The prince did not visit her again that day, and she was thus left entirely to her own meditations, the nature of which we need not attempt to describe to the reader. Night came; and worn out with the harass of her mind, she retired to bed; but although she speedily sunk off to sleep, it was rendered painful and unrefreshing by the most torturing visions, which left an impression on her mind on awaking which she could not easily eradicate. The Prince Bianchi, after his interview with his beauteous neice, retired to his study, and again locking himself in would not allow himself to be intruded upon by any one, but gave himself up to the varied and conflicting thoughts which naturally held paramount possession of his mind. To say that he could feel satisfied with his own conduct would be to state that which was false. He still loved Melina with the same fondness as if she had been his own daughter, and it grieved him to be the cause of imparting one single pang to her gentle bosom; but so strangely had he fixed his mind upon an union between her and the Count Alberti, that he could not on any account abandon the idea, although he felt satisfied that he was not altogether worthy of her. Besides, he was so accustomed to have implicit obedience paid to his will, that his pride felt mortified at her obstinacy; and he was firmly resolved that he would reduce her spirit, and make her bend to his wishes, let whatever might be the consequences. Then the love which she still entertained for Clairville, and the firmness with which he resisted all his persuasions and threats to make him reveal the place of Massaroni's concealment, added to his annoyance and vexation, and, if possible, exasperated him more than all. Every hour that the Count Alberti remained in the power of the brigand chief increased his alarm, and he knew not what course to adopt, for he had no doubt, that should he (the prince) proceed to any extremites against Florio, Massaroni would wreak his vengeance on the head of his prisoner. He was completely bewildered how to act; and reflection only added to his perplexity. He determined, however, to visit Clairville again in his dungeon, and to try his utmost to extort the truth from him; for all the plans he had adopted to discover Massaroni, and to rescue Alberti, did not appear likely to be crowned with the least success, and there were times when he was fearful that the young count had already fallen a victim to the brigand's vengeance.

"I must use every precaution," he said, "for I am placed in a situation the most critical; and any false or hasty step might be the means of realizing all the apprehensions I entertain. Massaroni, if possible, must be taken by surprise and stratagem, for I have already had sufficient proof of his power, and it will not do to risk the life of Alberti by openly braving it. Could I persuade Clairville to accede to my wishes, all would be well, and the task might be accomplished without much difficulty. He will be worse than an idot if he refuses; for his liberty, nay his very life, depend on his compliance. And yet," he added, after a moment's painful reflection, "dare I venture to proceed to such desperate extremities? Melina could never survive such a dreadful and untimely fate befalling her lover; and what could I then consider myself but her murderer? I shudder at the thought. I know not how to act."

He folded his arms across his chest as he thus spoke, and paced backwards and forwards in a state of the most violent agitation.

"But I must be firm," he said at length, "or I cannot hope to succeed. And yet, am I not acting the part of a tyrant? Can I deny that Count Clairville and Melina are equally worthy of each other, whilst Alberti, on the contrary, has been guilty of vices which should cause him to be shunned and dreaded by every virtuous female? I cannot; and why should I then seek to annihilate all her young hopes, and render two fond hearts miserable for ever? Psha! I am becoming weak! I must arouse myself from these thoughts, and resolve to act with firmness."

But notwithstanding all his efforts to do so, he succeeded but indifferently; the voice of conscience would not be stifled, and that told him that he was acting with the grossest cruelty and injustice. Florio Clairville, in his lonely dungeon, was a prey to the most anxious and painful thoughts; but still religion enabled him to bear up with more confidence and fortitude than might have been expected. Notwithstanding all the threats which the Prince Bianchi had held out to him on their interview, he could not make up his mind to believe that he had become so entirely insensible to pity, shame, and justice as to consign him and his beloved Melina to the fate which he had pointed out; and he still encouraged a latent hope, when he reflected upon all the affection he had shown for Melina, and the warmth of the friendship he had ever evinced toward him, that he would be persuaded to relent, and that all might yet terminate more happily than at present appeared probable. But whatever the consequences might be to himself, he was fully determined to remain firm, and on no account to betray Massaroni.

"I have given him my word," he said, "and I should thoroughly despise myself if I thought I could break it. No, Massaroni, you are perfectly safe for me; but I hope to Heaven that you will not be tempted to lay violent hands upon your prisoner, whom you have so securely in your power, and from whom you have not the least reason to apprehend any danger. Oh, Melina!" he added, after a pause, "willingly, most willingly, would I sacrifice my life, if by so doing, I could save you from your present sufferings, and the dangers which threaten you. Should the Count Alberti obtain his freedom, there appears but little doubt that the prince, notwithstanding your aversion, and the certain destruction it will be to your happiness, will compel you to become his bride, and then your doom will be for ever sealed. I cannot endure the thought, for it is too probable, although so revolting to my feelings."

Such were the thoughts that continued to harass the mind of Clairville; but still he did not in the least regret what he had done. He considered himself bound in honour to keep the secret of Massaroni; and he was determined, in spite of whatever might be the consequences to himself, that nothing should induce him to betray him. As for Alberti, he could not possibly feel any sympathy for him; but he trusted that the brigand would not be exasperated by his obstinacy into laying violent hands on him. In such a state of mind as this, it was not to be supposed that Clairville could obtain much rest, and the want of that wore him out more even than the anguish of his mind. But still he remained firm in his resolution, and constantly prayed to Heaven to watch over the safety of his beloved Melina, and to avert those evils with which she was at present so fearfully threatened. He recalled to his memory all the moments of happiness they had passed together, the mutual vows of affection they had exchanged with each other; and this was a source of mingled pain and pleasure to him, but served in some measure to diminish the tediousness of his confinement. When he reviewed the actions of his past life, it was a great consolation to him that he had nothing to reproach himself with; he had never wilfully injured any of his fellow-creatures either by word or deed, but on the contrary, he had ever been anxious to serve them to the best of his power, and to deserve their good opinion; and he could therefore meet death without a shudder, were it not for the dreadful shock he knew that his fate would cause the hapless Melina.

"Would to Heaven," he said, "that we had never met, since Fate has thrown such insurmountable obstacles in the way of our affection; or had it pleased Heaven not to have made such a disparity in our fortunes; then indeed might we have looked forward to hope, and all the happiness that two fond hearts could wish, might have been ours. But was I not to blame when I found that there was no probability of the prince sanctioning our passion, not to endeavour to stifle the unfortunate sentiment in my breast, and, by tearing myself from her presence, seek to banish her from my memory altogether? But that is impossible, so firm is the hold that dear girl has taken on my heart. Oh, no, let whatever may be the consequences—and I anticipate the worst—my sentiments must ever remain the same while I continue to exist. God preserve her, and give her fortitude to support the heavy trials which I fear are yet in store for her. Bianchi, you could never have felt the affection towards her which you professed to do, or you could not remain so stern and inexorable; nor wish to sacrifice one so gentle, so loving, and so virtuous, to such a villain as the Count Alberti. But I trust that you will yet be brought to relent, or that Heaven will defeat your plans, though it may never be my fate to behold the beauteous Melina again, or to aspire to her hand."

Tortured by alternate hopes and fears, Florio thus continued for several days without being able to learn anything of the prince or Melina, and his suspense and anxiety became almost insupportable. He felt convinced that the anguish of mind Melina must now experience would be more than she could find strength to endure; and when he recalled to his memory the observations which the Prince Bianchi had made use of, he was apprehensive that all her tears and supplications would not have the power to move him from his cruel purpose. This thought drove him almost to distraction, and he paced the narrow confines of his dreary cell in an agony of mind we need not attempt to portray. A week had now elapsed since his interview with the prince, and his patience was quite exhausted, when one day he heard the bolts of his dungeon door being withdrawn, and the prince entered. The aspect of his countenance was stern and inflexible, and his demeanour haughty and commanding; but Florio met him with a firm eye, and the most perfect calmness, for he felt the justice of his cause, and was fully prepared to abide the consequences of his conduct. The prince folded his arms, and with his eyes still fixed earnestly upon him, he remained silent for a few moments.

"So, Signor Clairville," he said at length, "you see I have visited you again, in order that I may ascertain whether you have reflected on my propositions?"

"I have, my lord," answered Florio, calmly

"And what conclusion have you come to?" asked the prince.

"My resolution remains unaltered," said Florio.

"You will not reveal the place of Massaroni's concealment?"

"I will not."

"Rash man!" cried the prince passionately, "know you not what will be the consequences of your obstinacy?"

"You have told me, my lord," answered Clairville, "and I am ready to abide by them. I will never betray that man to whom I have pledged my word."

"Then you acknowledge yourself to be the friend of a robber and a murderer?"

"I do not; but still I sympathize with Massaroni in his misfortunes; I believe him to have been a persecuted man; and I will never be the means of bringing him to that fate to which you would consign him."

"Then you obstinately condemn yourself," said the prince. "Pause, young man, and consider the folly and danger of the proceeding."

"I have considered everything, my lord," said Clairville, "and nothing can make me alter my determination. Pardon me, your highness, if my words may sound bold and harsh; but you pride yourself, I know, upon your strict sense of probity and justice; why, then, do you thus persecute me?—What have I done that I should be visited with the punishment with which you threaten me?—'Tis true, I love your fair niece, and she returns my passion; but surely that is no monstrous crime, though I might be considered presumptuous in aspiring to the love of one so far above me. You commanded me to leave the neighbourhood of Villa Rosa, and to banish Melina from my mind. The first injunction I obeyed, but the second, notwithstanding all my efforts, I found it utterly impossible to comply with. Despair and the violence of my passion induced me to return and seek a clandestine interview; in that, perhaps, I committed myself, but certainly not to such an extent as to deserve to be imprisoned like the vilest criminal, and to be threatened with a criminal's ignominious death."

"And have you not acknowledged," demanded the prince, "that you connived at the escape of the brigand chief, Massaroni; that you know his present haunt, but refuse to reveal it?"

"True," replied Clairville; "but those I consider acts of honour and not of crime."

"'Sdeath!" cried his highness, furiously, "the boy talks like a madman. But by all my hopes, unless you yield to my desires, notwithstanding all the friendship I own I once felt towards you, all that I have threatened shall overtake you."

"My lord," said Florio, firmly, "you disgrace yourself by such observations. Mercy is one of the noblest attributes of our nature, and if we deny it to each other, what mercy can we expect from the Almighty Judge of all? To sacrifice my life for that which you have truly stated, would be a hideous murder, and my blood would be upon your head. Pause ere you proceed to extremities, or fearfully will your cruelty recoil upon your own head. I appeal not for myself, for whatever may be my fate, I feel satisfied that I shall be prepared to meet it as becomes a man; but earnestly I supplicate your mercy towards your niece. If you sincerely love her, as you profess to do, you will cease to persecute her, and abandon all thoughts of sacrificing her to such a villain as the Count Alberti."

"A villain!" cried the prince; "dare you apply such an epithet to the Count Alberti?"

"I dare," replied Florio, coolly; "I repeat that he is a villain; and has not his conduct sufficiently proved it?"

"Beware, beware, or you shall pay dearly for such observations."

"Nothing, my lord, shall prevent me from speaking the truth and the real sentiments of my mind."

"Do you still refuse to betray the brigand chief?" demanded the prince, "and to be the means of restoring the Count Alberti to liberty?"

"I do," answered Clairville, fearlessly.

"Then be the consequences of your obduracy on your own head. Comply with my demands: promise to leave the country, never more to return to it, and I will instantly unbar the doors of your dungeon; refuse, and the certain penalty is death. Once for all I ask you, will you yield?"

"Never!"

"Enough," returned the prince, "then your fate is sealed, and from that fate no earthly power can save you."

"But there is a power above which can," retorted Florio, solemnly, "and to which you, though Prince Bianchi, and Governor of Rome, are as well as the lowliest of its creators, amenable. In that All-merciful Power I will put my trust, and remain firm under all my trials."

"Foolish, headstrong man," remarked the prince, "why will you thus obstinately rush upon an untimely fate?"

"What have I done that you should thus mercilessly precipitate me into it, my lord?" demanded Clairville. "But I see it is useless to expostulate with one who has proved himself to be entirely insensible to reason, mercy, and justice. Oh, Melina, I care not for myself, for without you life would be unendurable; but how my heart bleeds for you. Oh, my lord, if you have no pity for me, at least show some towards that poor innocent girl whom you should regard with the same affection as if she were your own daughter."

"How dare you presume to intercede for her, when at the same time you prove yourself to be one of my greatest enemies?"

"By Heaven it is false! I have never felt the least vindictive feeling towards you; but, on the contrary, my breast has overflowed with gratitude for the friendship with which you once honoured me. Do I prove myself an enemy by seeking to prevent you from committing yourself in the fatal manner you would were you to sacrifice Melina to such a man as the Count Alberti, a man whom she must ever loathe and despise? Oh, my lord, where is that honest noble pride of which I once believed you to be the possessor, when you can for a moment think of compelling your lovely and innocent niece to become the wife of the heartless seducer of the unfortunate Olympia, whom it was his duty to protect?"

"Bah!" exclaimed the prince, impatiently, "shall I tamely submit to be schooled thus by a beardless boy? Clairville, your obstinacy has condemned you. I leave you to your own reflections."

"My lord," said Florio, as the prince was about to retire from the dungeon, "once more I supplicate your mercy for Melina; whatever fate you think proper to inflict on me I care not; but oh, as you hope for mercy hereafter spare her."

The Prince Bianchi did not deign to return any answer to this, but stalked haughtily from the dungeon. Rage and disappointment filled his bosom as he proceeded homeward. The observations of Clairville had made a deep impression on him and cut him to the core; he could not deny their truth and justice, but yet he could not make up his mind to act as justice dictated.

"The obstinate fool," he soliloquized, "he seems determined to rush headlong on his fate. Why does he not, by complying with my demands, save me from that I would so willingly avoid? Shall Massaroni be suffered to triumph with impunity, and Alberti remain at his mercy, when a word from Florio would accomplish all I wish? The thought is more than I can find patience to endure. But I must be determined, and notwithstanding all that my prisoner has said, I do believe that he will ultimately yield. But this delay is torturing; every moment is fraught with danger, and even now it may be too late; Alberti may already have fallen a victim to the vengeance of Massaroni; for I feel certain that he will never confess where he has Olympia concealed."

By this time he had arrived at the villa, and was making his way to his own suite of apartments, when he was met by Melina. In the present ruffled state of his mind he would fain have avoided her, but he could not. She could plainly see by the agitated expression of his countenance that he had met with something to annoy him, and she readily guessed the truth. Seeing that she was determined to speak to him, he hurried her into an apartment, and closed the door.

"My dear uncle," said Melina, "what has occurred to agitate you thus? Tell me, have you again visited him?"

"I have," answered the prince, abruptly; "what then?"

"You have yielded to his supplications, have you not?" demanded Melina, eagerly; "oh, tell me that the unfortunate Florio is again at liberty, and I shall be comparatively happy."

"At liberty, girl!" repeated her uncle; "think you I am mad? He remains obstinate, and he must therefore take the consequences."

"Oh, mercy, mercy, my lord," implored Melina; "you cannot surely pursue the unfortunate Clairville with such cruel and vindictive feelings. He never did you any injury, then why should you seek to inflict upon him a fate which is only due to the most guilty culprit?"

"You plead for him to no purpose," said the prince; "he is the associate of robbers and murderers, my greatest enemies; he has acknowledged himself to be so; he refuses to betray the rascal, Massaroni, to my power; and the punishment for his obstinacy will be death!"

"Oh, no, no, no!" groaned Melina; "you cannot mean what you say; you cannot, will not, be so inhuman!"

"I have given him plenty of time for consideration," returned the prince. "I have made him every fair offer, but he scornfully rejects them, and therefore he seals his own fate."

Melina looked at her uncle with a shudder of horror, and could scarcely believe it was him who spoke.

"If you have no mercy to bestow upon him," she gasped forth, "have you no pity or consideration for me? Remember, I am your only sister's child, whom, on her death-bed, you promised to cherish and protect me with the same affection as if I were your own child; and do not condemn me to a fate which is worse, far worse, than the most lingering death of torture. Oh, relent ere it be too late; and most freely, most gladly, will I forgive you all the misery you have caused me, and bury the past in oblivion."

The prince was indeed somewhat moved by the earnestness of her manner, and remained for several minutes silent, for he was quite at a loss what answer to return. But he soon regained his self-possession, and the previous sternness and inflexibility of his manner as he replied—

"Melina, you have reminded me of the promise I made your mother in her dying moments ; and I now ask you if I have not ever fulfilled that promise to the very letter? Have I not bestowed upon you every affection and indulgence, and ever been most studious of your happiness ?"

"You have, you have," answered Melina, fervently," and Heaven knows how sincerely grateful I have been for it, and how anxious

MELINA REJECTING THE COUNT ALBERTI'S PROPOSAL.

I have ever been to deserve your love, and to obey your every will ; but can I submit to be sacrificed to a man whose very name inspires me with a feeling of the most unconquerable disgust, and to see the unfortunate Clairville punished for only loving me too fondly ? But you will not remain insensible to every feeling of justice and humanity. I know it is quite foreign to your nature ; and it is that which emboldens me thus to appeal to you."

"Nothing that you can say, Melina, can move me from the resolution I have formed," said the prince.

"Oh, this is most cruel," sighed the poor girl; "if you thus remain obstinate and obdurate, what will become of me and Florio! Dear uncle, if you persist in going to the dreadful length which you have threatened, you will break my heart."

"I have offered Clairville his liberty on the most simple conditions. I repeat," said the prince, "on no other terms will I consent to pardon him. Massaroni must not be suffered to escape me, and to keep the whole country in a constant state of alarm and excitement, and Alberti must be restored to liberty; both these Clairville has the means of accomplishing; he refuses, and by so doing, naturally incurs my vengeance. But we are neither of us in any humour to argue this subject at present; retire, Melina, I would be alone."

"For pity's sake hear me, my lord, and do not be guilty of that you will afterwards have such bitter cause to regret."

"Enough," said Bianchi, "I am ready to take every responsibility. Leave me!"

Melina, with the tears trembling in her eyes was again about to speak, but her uncle raised his hand authoritatively; and with a heart almost full to bursting, she slowly quitted the room and retired to her own apartment, where she gave herself up to the most violent grief and despair. She now plainly saw that it was useless to endeavour to move the prince from his cruel and fatal purpose, and that unless Clairville yielded to his demands, which she felt convinced he never would, that his fate was certain. The anguish of her mind at these thoughts was most excruciating, and it was some time ere she could tranquilize her feelings in the slightest degree. She would willingly have laid down her own life to save that of her lover; but, alas! she saw no probable means of saving him; and yet she could scarcely bring her mind to believe that the prince could ever become so cruel and revengeful as he now threatened to be.

"My God!" she ejaculated, "how little did I imagine that it would ever come to this! Alas! how unfortunate it was that we should ever have met; we might both of us now have been happy. Father of Mercy, release him from the hands of his enemies; and then, though we may never be destined to meet each other again, I trust that I should in a great measure be able to resign myself to my fate. How unfortunate it is that he should thus accidentally have become connected with Massaroni; and what can be the meaning of the interest which the brigand chief seems to take in all that concerns us? There is a mystery about the actions of that remarkable man which I cannot unravel; and I never think of his name but a feeling comes over me which I find it impossible to comprehend. What can be the meaning of this?"

She paused and reflected deeply; but so varied and conflicting were the thoughts which crowded upon her brain, that she became completely bewildered. The Prince Bianchi did not leave his room again that day, for he could not endure the presence of Melina. His conscience bitterly reproached him with the unjust severity of his conduct towards her; but still he was unable to form the virtuous resolution to yield to her supplications, to restore her lover to that liberty of which he was so unjustly deprived, and to abandon his designs as regarded the hated marriage between her and the Count Alberti, should the latter ever be rescued from the power of Massaroni, of which at present there did not seem to be any probability.

"I have given him my word," he said, "and by all my hopes I will not break it. The resistance of Melina does but make me the more determined; and yet the fates seem to conspire against me, and to defeat my wishes. Could Alberti but be rescued, the union should take place without delay, and then all my doubts would be set at rest. But will anything conquer the repugnance of Melina towards the count? I fear it will not, for the hatred she bears him is evidently too deeply ingrafted in her heart. It is unfortunate that Alberti should have so committed himself as regards the girl Olympia; for then the prejudice of Melina might not have been so strong against him; however, it cannot be helped, and I must trust to chance. Women are fickle creatures, and who knows but that Melina may yet be brought to bend to my desires?"

Thus did the prince continue to encourage alternative hopes and fears; but remained firm in his cruel and guilty determination. Florio was for some time greatly agitated after his recent meeting with the Prince Bianchi; but his resolution was unshaken, and he was determined to suffer anything rather than betray Massaroni. There were moments, too, when a hope would spring up in his breast that the brigand, when he came to hear of his imprisonment, would adopt some means to release him; but this idea seemed so improbable and impracticable, that he rejected it almost as soon as he had formed it.

"No," he said, "the prince has got me too secure; and daring even though Massaroni is, he would not venture to make any attack on this place where his defeat is certain. I must leave my fate in the hands of Providence, who, knowing my innocence, and the purity of the motives from which I act, will surely not desert me. Oh, God, I beseech you to inspire my beloved Melina with fortitude and patience to support this dreadful trial; and whatever may become of me, oh, protect her from the snares and artifices of her enemies."

He clasped his hands energetically together as he thus spoke, and endeavoured to resign himself to his fate, in which effort he succeeded much better than he had anticipated. But Melina was constantly present to his mind; and he would have given the world, had it been in his possession, to have seen her, and tried to impart some consolation to her heavily-oppressed bosom. He could well imagine the agony of mind she was enduring at his melancholy and dangerous situation, and what little effect her tears and entreaties would have on the obstinate disposition of the prince her uncle; and these thoughts grieved him more than all. Again and again he regretted having sought the fatal interview with her, and which had been productive of so much misery to them both; but it was too late to repent; and after all he could not reproach himself for having done that to which he was prompted by the violence of his love and despair, and from the purest of motives. But how grateful was he to Providence for having preserved her life; and that thought afforded him the greatest consolation in the midst of all his misery. The prince, he imagined, would not again seek an interview with him, since he had received so positive and decided an answer from him; and he sought to prepare himself for that trial, upon which he would doubtless shortly be put. That any mercy would be extended to him, he did not expect; he knew how severe the laws were with respect to the offence with which he was charged, namely, aiding the escape, and shielding from justice, an outlaw and a brigand, one upon whose head a price was set; and he therefore made up his mind for the worst. He could not, under the circumstances, do otherwise than plead guilty; and his immediate condemnation would be sure to follow. The fate that awaited him, unless Providence should interpose to avert it, was death. And yet it was hard to fall so young, to meet with such a cruel and ignominious fate, for having been guilty of nothing for which he considered he should feel ashamed; and what an awful shock it would be to poor Melina. It was impossible that she could ever survive it; and how cruel, how perfectly monstrous, the Prince Bianchi must be to consign two innocent persons, who had never injured him by word or deed, to such an untimely fate.

"Oh, surely he will have bitter cause to repent his brutal tyranny," he said; "such injustice and inhumanity as he is guilty of, will not be suffered to go unpunished. Would that I had never been introduced to him; then would both myself and Melina have been saved this dreadful trial; but let me be firm, and I may yet, with the help of Heaven, be able to set my enemies at defiance."

Inspired with fresh hope, he became more calm, and looked forward to the future with far less dread than he had done before. Days passed away without any change in his situation, and he saw no more of the Prince Bianchi, and was unable to form any conjecture when his fate would be decided. He knew it was useless to put any questions to his jailor, for the man was morose and taciturn, and always entered and quitted his dungeon without giving utterance to a word; so that Clairville was obliged to content himself to remain in the same state of ignorance and suspense. The prince had several interviews with his beauteous niece; but although she exerted all the powers of her eloquence to move him to relent, she was unable to make the least favourable impression on him; and all hope seemed too evidently to be at an end. The constant agony of her mind was more than her strength could bear; and she was again confined to her chamber, and received no other society than that of her faithful attendant Floretta, who waited upon her and attended to all her wants with the utmost solicitude. The prince had adopted every means to discover the secret retreat of Massaroni, and to restore the Count Alberti to liberty, but without success; and as day after day elapsed, and still he could obtain no intelligence that was calculated to flatter his wishes, he gave himself up to despair, and began to fear that Alberti had indeed fallen a victim to the vengeance of Massaroni.

"But should my terrible surmises prove correct," he said, "I will have a fearful revenge. The brigand cannot always escape me, and the numerous other persons who are in search of him; and let me only once get him in my power, and I will have ample satisfaction for all the crimes he has committed."

He clenched his fist and knitted his brows as he spoke, and remained for some time in the greatest excitement, and endeavouring to devise some scheme which might bring about the accomplishment of his wishes, but to no purpose; and that made him the more exasperated against Clairville for refusing to divulge all he knew; but still he was not without some hope that the dread of the punishment that would be inflicted on him, should he remain obstinate, would have a salutary effect; and that he would yet, with the hope of being restored to liberty, be induced to betray the brigand chief into the hands of justice.

"By Heaven, if he does not," exclaimed the prince, "he can expect, and shall receive, no mercy at my hands; though I would fain not have his death upon my conscience. Had it not been for him conniving at, and aiding him, in his escape, Massaroni would long ere this have been in my power, and the Count Alberti would never have been his prisoner. For that alone Florio deserves a severe punishment."

In this inflexible state of mind the Prince Bianchi continued, notwithstanding the alarming effect which the confinement of her lover, and the probable fate which awaited him, had taken upon Melina. It was long past the hour of midnight, and all the inmates of the Villa Rosa had for some time retired to their chambers, when suddenly they were aroused by a loud knocking at the outer door, which was repeated several times, as though the business that the applicant or applicants had come upon was of the most urgent and important nature. The prince started from his bed; and putting on his dressing-gown, was about to ring the bell in order to ascertain what was the matter, when one of his servants entered the chamber, and the expression of his countenance showed that he had some intelligence of an important nature to impart.

"How now, Guiseppe?" demanded the Prince, "what is the meaning of all this?"

"Your highness will be pleased to hear the cause of this nocturnal interruption," replied Guiseppe.

"Indeed?" said the prince; "but quick, tell me what you have to communicate?"

"The Count Alberti has escaped from the power of Massaroni, my lord, and is now below, waiting to see you."

"The count escaped!" exclaimed the prince, joyfully, but incredulously; "is it possible? By Heaven, this is the best news I have heard for some time. But I can scarce believe the evidence of my senses. Let my doubts be immediately removed; usher the count directly into my presence."

Guiseppe quitted the room instantly, leaving the prince in the greatest state of excitement; and the next minute Alberti stood before him, and grasped him cordially by the hand.

"Alberti," ejaculated the prince, "is it possible that I have the pleasure of once more beholding you at liberty?"

"I need not say that it is true, your highness, since I am here *propria personae*;" replied the count, with a smile. "I have indeed escaped the clutches of the daring villain Massaroni; and by the dome of St. Peter's I will not fail to have an ample revenge for the manifold injuries I have received from him. But how fares the coy but lovely Melina?"

"Indifferently as you may expect my lord: the beggar Clairville still holds paramount possession of her heart; however I have him secure in prison. He has confessed he aided Massaroni in his escape from the villa on the memorable night of the festival, and that he has since been connected with him,

and refuses to reveal the place of his concealment; so you have nothing to fear from him."

"Clairville in prison!" exclaimed Alberti joyfully; "this is, indeed, welcome intelligence, and what I little expected to hear."

"But tell me, my lord," asked the prince, eagerly, "how have you been so fortunate as to effect your escape from Massaroni, for I am all impatience to hear. Even now, I can scarcely pursuade myself that I am not labouring under the influence of a dream, so joyful and so unexpected is your escape from the power of the brigand chief, to whose vengeance I began to fear you had fallen a victim."

"The particulars can be told in a few words, my lord," said the Count Alberti; and he then briefly related to the prince that with which the reader is already acquainted, and to which he listened with the deepest interest and satisfaction.

"By the saints!" exclaimed the prince, when Count Alberti had concluded; "the whole affair has been managed well, and the fellow who aided you in your escape deserves a rich reward. No time must be lost in making an attack on Massaroni; and I am much deceived if he will not shortly be in our power."

"He shall be so, at any hazard," said Alberti, "and we will have an ample revenge for all the injuries he has inflicted on us."

"But you say that you yielded to his demands?"

"I was forced to do so, my lord, or he would undoubtedly have sacrificed my life."

"Then the probability is that Olympia is at liberty?" said the prince.

"No doubt of it," answered the count.

"That is awkward," remarked Bianchi; "however, we must devise some plan to prevent her being any annoyance to you for the future."

"Oh, yes," returned Alberti, "I have no fear of that. But tell me, my lord, what has happened since I have been away?"

The prince, in as few words as possible, related to him all that he wanted to know, and did not disguise from him the repugnance which Melina still felt towards him.

"But her obduracy must and shall be conquered, my lord," he added; "she knows that I am determined, and will not dare to set my will at defiance. Should your sentiments remain the same, I pledge you my word that she shall be yours in spite of everything."

"Enough, your highness," said the Count Alberti, "I am perfectly satisfied with your promise. Separation from the fair Melina has but strengthened my love towards her; and could I but overcome her scorn and repugnance, I should be the happiest man in existence. I long to behold her again, and to breathe my vows in her ears."

"That you shall do, my lord, before many hours have elapsed," said the prince ; and I trust that you will not be daunted by the reception she will possibly give you."

"I will not," answered Count Alberti ; "and I do not despair of yet being able to remove the prejudice she entertains against me."

"She must yield," observed the prince, "for the very life of Clairville depends upon it, and if she loves him as she professes to do, she will not hesitate. But you have travelled far, and must need rest. After a few hours repose we will meet again."

Alberti was indeed fatigued both in body and mind, and therefore gladly availed himself of the offer of the prince, who, summoning an attendant, desired him to conduct the count to a chamber, and they then separated.

CHAPTER XXXI.

THE MEETING BETWEEN THE COUNT ALBERTI
AND MELINA.—THE ESCAPE OF FLORIO.

WE need not seek to describe the feelings of exultation which the Prince Bianchi experienced at the escape of Alberti. He could sleep no more that night, and anxiously awaited the time when they should meet again. Melina had been alarmed by the knocking at such an unusual hour, and was unable to conjecture the cause ; but she felt confident that something important had taken place ; and a dismal presentiment of something unpleasant took possession of her mind. She was unable to sleep, such was the state of suspense in which she was placed. At an early hour in the morning Floretta entered her chamber, and Melina immediately saw by her looks that she had something of a disagreeable nature to communicate.

"My dear signora," she said, "compose yourself and hear with firmness the unpleasant news I have to impart to you."

"Ah ! what mean you ?" eagerly demanded Melina ; "your words and your manner make me apprehend the worst. Do not keep me in suspense ; you know the cause of the loud knocking at such an unseasonable hour last night ?"

"I do, signora," replied Floretta, "and sorry I am that I should have such painful intelligence to communicate to you."

"What is it, Floretta ? I am all impatience to hear it."

"The Count Alberti, signora——"

"Ah, what of him ?" interrupted Melina.

"He has escaped, my lady," replied Floretta.

"Escaped !" repeated Melina, turning ghastly pale, and trembling in every limb.

"Yes, signora, and he is at present in the house."

"My God, what alarming news is this," said Melina ; " alas ! what will now become of me ? The prince will remain obstinate, and the count will not fail to persist in his hated suit ; of what use then will be all the resistance I can offer ? I am lost—I am lost, unless Providence interposes to save me."

"And it will do so, signora, depend on it," said Floretta ; "do not give way to despair, but prepare yourself to meet the count with firmness and determination."

"Alas !" sighed Melina, "how vainly you advise me ; how can I meet that man whom my soul abhors with any other feelings than those of horror and disgust ? And must my ears be shocked by the confession of his odious passion ? Oh, Floretta, you may judge what my feelings must be."

" I do, indeed, my dear signora," answered the faithful attendant, "and deeply do I sympathise with you. But be resolute, and you may yet be able to triumph over the count, and to move his highness, your uncle, to abandon his designs ; for he surely can never have the heart so cruelly to sacrifice your happiness.'

"Oh ! would that I could think so," said Melina ; " but after all my uncle has said, and the threats he has held out, have I not sufficient cause to apprehend the worst ? He is so prejudiced in favour of Alberti, that I fear nothing will induce him to relent ; and now that the count is again at liberty, my doom is all but sealed."

"For goodness' sake, my dear signora," remarked Floretta, "banish such dismal thoughts from your mind, and put yuor trust in the goodness of that Providence which will never suffer you to be sacrificed to one who is so totally unworthy of you."

" How can I ever find courage to meet him ?" ejaculated Melina ; "I shall shrink appalled in his presence, and encouraged as he is in his, odious vows by the prince, it will be entirely useless for me to appeal to or remonstrate with him."

" You know not, signora, what firmness and determination may accomplish ; therefore summon up all your resolution, and depend upon i it will meet with a favourable result."

Melina shook her head doubtfully, and sighed deeply ; and Floretta, after having in vain sought to console her, retired and left her to her own reflections. Gloomy and agonizing they were, and she in vain tried to find comfort and resolution. Now that the count was at liberty, what could she expect but that her worst fears would be confirmed, and that her misery would be completed ? She threw herself on her knees, and fervently supplicated the protection of the Supreme, for without His merciful interposition she saw plainly that her destruction was inevitable. She was interrupted by a knock at her door, and the Prince Bianchi immediately afterwards entered. She started and trembled at his appearance, but he approached her with a smile; and taking hear hand, said—

"My dear Melina, you look pale and ill; come, come, cheer up, and endeavour to become yourself again; I have good news for you."

"Oh, my lord," replied Melina, "I know too well what you would say; the Count Alberti has escaped, and is now in the Villa."

"True," remarked the prince, "and surely it must afford your gentle bosom the greatest gratification to know that he has escaped from the power of such a villain as the brigand chief Massaroni."

"I should have been sorry, my lord," said Melina, "had any harm befallen the count; but can I look upon his release from confinement with any other feelings than those of alarm, fearing as I do that he will again urge those vows which are so hateful to me, and that his suit will meet with every encouragement from you?"

"Psha! Melina," said the prince, with a frown of displeasure; "this is ridiculous obstinacy, and you must conquer your ungenerous prejudices. The Count Alberti loves you sincerely, ardently; his rank and character render him worthy of you; and I expect, nay, command you to receive him with the respect that is due to him, and to prepare to return his passion."

"Never," exclaimed Melina, firmly. "Love the Count Alberti, the betrayer of the unfortunate Olympia? the bare thought is revolting to me; and sooner would I perish than be consigned to such a fate. Oh, my lord, you cannot be so lost to pity as to wish it."

"Melina," returned the prince, "you have already heard my determination, and I now again tell you that nothing shall move me from it. Your resistance will but serve to exasperate me; and remember that the life of Florio Clairville depends upon your submission to my will."

"This, oh this, is indeed cruel!" said Melina; "will nothing move you to compassion? —It is impossible that I can ever conquer my feelings of repugnance towards Alberti; and if you compel me to become his wife, you will condemn me to everlasting misery, and will have bitter cause to reproach yourself for an act which I cannot designate otherwise than cruel, tyrannical, and unjust. But you will think better of it, I am sure that you will. If you have ever loved me with that fondness you have professed to do, and which I have so sincerely returned, you will not turn a deaf ear

to my supplications, but release me from the torturing and disgusting importunities of a man whom I must ever despise. He is convinced that I cannot esteem him, much more love him; and why will he persist in making me wretched by his odious advances?"

"Melina," said the prince, angrily, "I cannot listen to observations such as these, nor will they have the effect on me you are so anxious they should do. The Count Alberti is the man of my choice; and should you disobey my will and persist in scornfully rejecting him, you will bring down upon yourself my lasting indignation."

"Oh, say not so, my lord, and thus consign me to complete despair," said Melina; "to all that is just and reasonable you will ever find me submissive; but never will I consent to become the wife of one whom my heart abhors. But if the count has a spark of manliness in his nature he will abandon all thoughts of me, and look out for some other woman on whom he can fix his affections, and who might feel honoured by his hand."

"But indeed you little know the strength of the sentiments Alberti entertains towards you if you entertain such a thought," replied the prince; "he can never love any other woman than you; his whole soul is devoted to you. I have given him my word that you shall become his bride, and I will not suffer his hopes to be disappointed."

"Oh, God! oh, God," groaned Melina in agony, and clasping her hands, "then I am indeed lost. Let me die rather than be united to such a man as the Count Alberti."

"You will do well to banish these thoughts from your mind, Melina, and to compose yourself, for you must prepare for an interview with Alberti immediately, who is waiting most anxiously to see you."

"Oh, I cannot meet him; I implore you, my lord, to spare me this anguish."

"Bah! can his presence be so alarming and so hateful to you, girl?"

"It is, it is; how can I do otherwise than dread an interview with one who entertains such cruel designs against against my future happiness? But you will spare my feelings this severe trial; earnestly, fervently I implore you to do so."

"Ridiculous!" ejaculated the prince, sternly "I should be worse than weak to do so. Melina, remember what I have said, and do not, by your foolish opposition to my will, exasperate me. You must learn, at least, to treat the count with the respect which is due to his rank."

"I have ever done so, my lord," replied Melina; "but must I not shrink from him in dread when I know that he aspires to that heart which is so fervently devoted to another?"

"Then you still love the beggar, Clairville?"

"Yes; no other man can ever possess my affections; though he can never be mine, and we may never meet again."

"Beware! beware!" said the prince, frowning; "the life of Clairville is at my mercy, and should you remain obstinate, you may be the means of sacrificing it."

"And can this indeed be that uncle towards whom I have ever behaved with such dutiful affection?" said Melina, with a look of reproach; "I can scarcely believe the evidence of my ears, or imagine that he can contemplate anything so utterly cruel and unjust. But I will yet think better of you, my lord, and believe that you will not persist in that which must break the heart of her whom you have vowed to protect and cherish."

"That which I have promised I will perform to the very letter," returned her uncle, determinedly; "I must not allow your weakness and obstinacy to crush the hopes of the count, whom I again declare to be fully worthy of you."

"Alas! alas! what have I done to become so degraded in your opinion? Do you then consider a libertine and seducer fully worthy of my love?"

"And is the Count Alberti for ever to be reproached for that one imprudent act?"

"He should be shunned and despised by all who lay any claim to virtue. Did he not promise to make his unfortunate victim, the mother of his child, his wife?"

"And was it likely that he would degrade himself by an alliance with an unknown and friendless girl?" demanded the prince.

"Justice demanded that he should have done so," replied Melina.

"Justice?" repeated Bianchi.

"Yes, my lord, justice; had he not blasted all her prospects? I appeal to your sense of honour and virtue, could you have acted in the manner Alberti has done? could you thus cruelly have deserted your hapless victim and your child?"

These words went to the heart of Bianchi, and he evinced the most powerful emotion.

"Girl," he exclaimed, fiercely, "why do you address such words to me? Dare you accuse me of——"

"Accuse you, my dear uncle!" interrupted the astonished Melina; "oh, why do you put such a wrong construction on my observations? Of what can I accuse you?"

"No more—no more," said the prince, passionately; "beware what you say;—but we have discussed this subject long enough. Are you prepared to accompany me to the room in which the Count Alberti impatiently awaits you?"

"Oh, spare me—spare me, my lord."

"Nonsense! would you thus daringly insult the count? Come, come—do not try my patience too far."

"Not now—not now, my lord," supplicated Melina, "my feelings are too violently excited to suffer me to meet Alberti at present."

"You must subdue them, girl, for the interview must take place, and I shall expect you to give him such a reception as will gratify his most sanguine wishes."

"Oh, that is impossible," replied Melina, with a shudder; "the bare thought inspires me with terror and disgust."

"Obdurate girl! will nothing cure you of this folly."

"Have pity on me, I again beseech you. It is impossible that I can control the sentiments that reign predominant in my breast. If Alberti really feels for me the respect which he pretends to do, he will not put me to this severe, this painful, trial. Excuse me to him, my lord, I beg of you; and at some future time, if it be your will, I will endeavour to meet him with becoming respect, though I cannot listen to vows which are so perfectly repugnant to my feelings."

"However repugnant to your feelings it may be, you must yield to my wishes," replied the prince; "however, for the present I will comply with your request, in order to give you an opportunity of composing yourself; but remember that the interview must take place before the day is out; and you must be prepared to attend me whenever I may think proper to summon you."

"Alas! alas!" sighed Melina, "would that I could prevail upon you to relent."

"I will yield no more than I have just done," replied Bianchi, sternly; "and you must not, therefore, expect it. Remember what I have said, and profit by the advice I have given you."

Melina could return no answer, and the prince quitted the room. She clasped her hands in despair and wept bitterly, and in vain she sought to conquer the feelings of dread which had taken possession of her bosom.

"Oh, my uncle," she sighed, "you to whom I have ever paid the love and duty of a daughter, never did I believe that you could have acted with such cruelty and tyranny towards me. Nothing—nothing, it is evident, will move you to take compassion on me; what a fatal infatuation has taken possession of your reason. My God! look down with pity on me, or my destruction is inevitable. Become the wife of the Count Alberti, and thus sacrifice all my earthly hopes of happiness? Oh, monstrous thought! But it shall never be; Providence will not permit it; and let whatever may be the consequences, they shall never force me to consent. No, I will be firm, and the designs of the prince and Alberti may yet be defeated."

She tried to become more calm, but her

efforts met with little success; and when Floretta returned to the apartment, she found her, as she had expected, in a state of the greatest agitation.

"You have seen the prince, your uncle, signora, have you not?" asked Floretta.

"I have," answered Melina, with a sigh, "he has but just left me."

"And what has he said to agitate you thus, my dear lady?"

"His observations were stern, harsh, and unfeeling," said Melina; "in vain I appealed to him—he still remains inflexible, commands me, on pain of bringing down on me his ever-lasting displeasure, to receive the addresses of the hated Alberti with favour, and has determined that I shall meet him to-day. Oh, Floretta, can you wonder at my agitation when I think of that? How shall I find resolution to support an interview which is so repugnant to me?"

"Be calm, signora," said her attendant, "and all will yet be well, although it appears so alarming at present. The count will surely have too much respect for your feelings to urge his suit at present."

"I dare not entertain such a hope," replied Melina, "encouraged as he is by the prince. Never did I expect that my uncle could behave in so arbitrary and cruel a manner towards me; would that my poor mother was now alive, how soon would she snatch me from the dangers with which I am now surrounded. In a short time the prince will summon me into his presence and that of the count, and I dare not venture to disobey him."

"I trust that Providence will give you fortitude to support the interview, my dear signora," observed Floretta, "and that it may not turn out so painful as you now anticipate. If the prince has any regard for your feelings, he will not suffer them to be put to such a severe trial."

"Alas!" replied her mistress, "my uncle is led away by some blind infatuation, and will not listen to the voice of reason or justice; I fear that I can expect but little from his indulgence."

"Then he will be guilty of that for which he will have to reproach himself ever afterwards."

"He will, Floretta; but so prepossessed is he in the favour of Alberti, that nothing will induce him to alter the resolution he has formed."

"Would to Heaven that Massaroni had him still in his power," said Floretta, fervently; "I cannot imagine how he suffered him to escape. But do not despair, signora, the Almighty will never permit you to be consigned to so cruel a fate; and when Alberti finds that the hatred you bear towards him is implacable,

he will, I am tempted to believe, abandon his designs."

"Ah! no! backed by the prince he will remain obstinate. I cannot encourage any other thought. Besides, the treatment he has experienced from Massaroni on account of Olympia will but urge him on to revenge; and that would be greatly gratified by obtaining possession of me."

"He must be a daring villain," said Floretta, "and I should not mind telling him so, although he is the count Alberti, after his base conduct to the poor signora Olympia, to presume to aspire to your hand, my lady; and I cannot imagine what his highness, the prince, is thinking about to encourage his suit. But never mind, for I still firmly believe that he will not succeed."

Floretta remained with her mistress for some time, and continued to exert herself to the best of her abilities to inspire her with fortitude; and at length she partly succeeded, and she then left her to attend to other business. Melina seated herself, and gave herself up to the most melancholy thoughts, and was in the greatest anxiety and suspense, expecting every moment to receive the dreadful summons from her uncle; but several hours passed away without her receiving any interruption, and she began to hope that the prince had made up his mind to excuse her for that day at any rate. Towards the afternoon, however, Floretta entered the room, and Melina could perceive, from the expression of her countenance, that she had some message to communicate.

"Now, Floretta," she said, eagerly, "what have you to say?"

"His highness has desired me to inform you, signora, that he expects your presence immediately in his study," replied Floretta.

"Ah! the interview I so much dread," said Melina; "and I cannot avoid it."

"Courage, my lady, and it will soon be over."

"But is the count with my uncle?"

"He is, signora."

"Heaven give me strength," ejaculated Melina, solemnly; and she then arose from her seat, and supporting herself on the arm of Floretta, with trembling steps she quitted the room and made her way to the apartment in which her uncle and the Count Alberti were awaiting her.

She paused on the threshhold, and her heart palpitated violently against her side. The door was standing partially open, and her eyes immediately encountered the hated form of Alberti, who was in earnest conversation with the prince. She shuddered, and was half tempted to retreat; but her uncle at that moment beheld her, and advancing hastily towards her, he took her hand, and conducted her into the room, leading her towards the count. Melina cast her eyes towards the ground, and did not venture to raise them lest they should encounter the gaze of him she so much dreaded; but she was quickly aroused by the voice of Alberti, who, without the least confusion in his manners, addressed her in the following words:

"I need not state the great pleasure it affords me to behold the fair Signora Melina again, after so long an absence; but I regret much to see her looking so pale and ill, and trust that the roses of health will shortly be restored to her cheeks. Allow me to salute

PRINCE BIANCHI.

one who has never been absent from my most anxious and fondest thoughts for a single moment."

As he spoke, he bent one knee, and taking her fair hand, which she endeavoured to withhold, he pressed it warmly to his lips. The blood of Melina curdled in her veins with shame and indignation; and it was with the utmost difficulty that she could save herself from fainting. The count, however, led her to a seat; and after a minute or two she partially revived, but was unable to give utterance to a single syllable. The prince, in the meantime, stood aside without offering to make any ob-servation, or to offer to interrupt Alberti in his advances; but at the same time he fixed a penetrating eye upon Melina, and watched her conduct with feelings of jealousy and suspicion. Melina trembled; she knew that her uncle's eyes were fixed on her, and likewise the emo-tions that were passing in his mind; but she dared not to look up, lest by encountering his gaze she should be overpowered altogether. Oh, how anxiously did she wish that the inter-view was at an end, for every moment she felt her repugnance to the count increase, for it was evident that he could entertain not the least respect for her feelings, otherwise he would not have urged a meeting with her at present, at **any rate.**

"Fair Melina," at length said Alberti, taking a seat by her side, and endeavouring once more to take her hand within his own, but which she scornfully withdrew, and at the same time her bosom swelled with disgust and indignation; "fair Melina," he repeated, in accents which were meant to be gently re-proachful and persuasive, "why this coldness? Have you not one word to congratulate me on my escape from the power of the daring villian from whom I have experienced such manifold and unpardonable injuries? What have I done to merit your scorn?"

"The count Alberti," replied Melina, in a voice of timidity, "forms a wrong estimate of the character of her whom he addresses, if he believes her capable of being indifferent to the welfare of any of her fellow-creatures, however circumstances may prevent her from feeling that personal respect for them she would other-wise wish. Pardon me, my lord, if I may ap-pear too bold and uncharitable; but your obser-vations have elicited from me that which I would fain have kept confined to my own breast. My uncle, the prince Bianchi, however, must, in justice to myself, already have made you acquainted with my sentiments; and that will, therefore, save me the pain of having to repeat them to you."

She looked up as she spoke, and to her con-fusion and dismay found that the prince had retired from the room, and that she was left alone with the man she so much dreaded and despised. The emotions which at that moment filled her bosom may be readily imagined; but she mustered sufficient fortitude to arise from her seat; and advancing towards the door, she said—

"My lord, this is taking an advantage that is unfair, indelicate, and unbecoming of you. Our interview is at an end. I wish you good day. I cannot, I will not, consent to see you, only in the presence of my uncle."

"Stay, lovely but scornful Melina," ejacula-ted the count, hastily advancing towards her,

and detaining her as she was about to retreat by the door, "you must not, shall not, leave me thus. What have I done thus to incur your displeasure?—What is there so hateful about me, that you should treat me with this freezing scorn and indifference?"

"Unhand me, my lord," commanded Melina firmly, and her fine eyes flashing with resent-ment. "I will not be detained: I owe you no further explanation than that I have already given, and you shall not force one from me. It is cruel of the prince, my uncle, thus to ex-pose me to these unmerited indignities."

"Indignities! signora Melina?" said Alberti; "surely such observations are as uncalled for as they are unmerited. Sooner would I perish than offer anything approaching an indignity to you."

"If you speak sincerely, my lord," retorted Melina, "you will best prove it by allowing me to retire from your presence."

"By Heaven!" exclaimed the count, passion-ately, "this is too torturing to be endured. But you cannot mean what you say, Melina."

"Your lordship has sadly mistaken my charac-ter," replied the damsel, firmly and pointedly, "if you imagine that I am accustomed to dis-guise my real feelings. Again I desire that you will suffer me to depart."

"By all my hopes," ejaculated Alberti, placing himself between her and the door, "you shall not leave me thus, with these wrong impressions on your mind. I have long panted for this opportunity: his highness, the prince, has granted it to me; and I am deter-mined to avail myself of it."

"Can you expect to gain any advantage by this boldness?" demanded Melina, still seek-ing to force her hand from the hold of the count; "what would you with me, my lord?"

"To confess to you, beauteous Melina," re-plied Alberti, sinking on one knee, and look-ing up into her blushing countenance with an expression that was meant to be impressive, "to confess to you, beauteous Melina," he re-peated, "that which has long been labouring in my bosom, and to which time and absence has but served to add strength, namely, that your numerous and unequalled charms, personal and intrinsic, have inspired me with a passion as ardent as it is sincere and unconquerable. I love you, Melina, even unto madness; you are the constant object of my thoughts, even sleeping or waking; and on you, and you alone, depends my earthly happiness or misery. Nay, do not fix upon me that look of scorn, for it is more painful to me than a thousand daggers to my heart. I would worship you with the same adoration as if you were something unearthly, every moment of my existance would I devote to your service, and to contribute to your hap-piness, and ——"

"Let me go, my lord," interrupted Melina,

with an expression of disgust she could not, had no wish to conceal. "I must not, will not listen to language so repugnant to my feelings as this is. What encouragement have I ever given to your hopes, that you should thus boldly address me? You cannot have been so blind as not to have seen long ere this the real sentiments I entertain towards you; why then provoke me to express them openly to you? It is only by forbearance and justice to others that you can hope even to gain my esteem."

"And why thus despise me?"

"Let your cruel conduct to the unfortunate Olympia, and her innocent offspring, be my answer."

The count Alberti quailed under this retort, and his confusion was so great that he could not reply for a few moments, though he still retained his hold of Melina's hand, notwithstanding all her efforts to withdraw it.

"You reproach me unjustly, Melina," at last he answered; "I am willing to render Olympia all the justice, as you are pleased to designate it, that she has a right to demand; and deeply do I regret the unhappy conection between us. But am I for ever to be upbraided for the follies and indiscretions of youth? Are there no extenuating circumstances in your estimation? However, we will drop that subject which must be so unpleasant to us both. Once more I confess the power of the sentiments I entertain towards you, and declare that it shall be the whole study of my life to deserve your love. Do not then from any mistaken prejudices drive me to utter despair. Your noble uncle approves of my passion; and thus am I emboldened to——"

"I owe the prince, my uncle, obedience in all that is just," interrupted Melina, with increased firmness; "but never will I consent to sacrifice my happiness at the bidding of any mortal being. Let this answer suffice, my lord; and do not again insult my ears by the acknowledgment of a passion which I candidly confess is hateful to me, and can never, by any possibility, meet with a return. Unhand me, I repeat: I will not be detained!"

As she thus spoke, she forcibly withdrew her hand from his hold, and retreated from the room before he had recovered from the astonishment and confusion into which the unexpected firmness of her manner had thrown him. With a swelling bosom she hastened to her own apartment; and locking the door, she flung herself on a seat, and gave free vent to the violent emotions that agitated her breast. Nothing could surpass the rage of the Count Alberti when he found himself left alone; and he reflected upon all the scornful observations which Melina had made use of towards him. With hasty strides he traversed the apartment, and muttered bitter curses between his teeth.

"The proud, disdainful beauty," he exclaimed; "'tis plain she hates me; she has taken no pains to disguise her real feelings; and it will be entirely useless for me to endeavour to banish the unfavourable impression she bears towards me. The beggar, Clairville, holds sole possession of her heart; but what have I to fear from his rivalry—powerless as he is, and backed as I am by the encouragement of the prince? No; I will not entirely despair; some means may yet present themselves to subdue the obstinate spirit of this proud maiden; and, in spite of herself, she will yet be forced to yield to my importunities. Of this I am determined, while the Prince Bianchi remains my friend, I will not abandon my hopes. No, Melina; your scorn does but add strength to the sentiments with which your incomparable charms have inspired me; and at every risk, they must and shall be gratified."

He was interrupted in the midst of his soliloquy by the return of the prince.

"What, alone, my lord?" said his highness; "have you permitted my fair niece to abandon your society?"

"Much against my own will, your highness may be sure," answered the count; "but I did not suffer her to leave me until I had availed myself of your gracious permission to make a full confession of the ardent sentiments with which she has inspired me."

"That is well," observed the prince; "and how did Melina receive them?"

"With the bitterest scorn, my lord: it is evident that she loathes and despises me."

"The obstinate girl!" exclaimed the prince, passionately: "and is this the meek submission she should show to my will? But do not despair, my lord, for notwithstanding her present opposition, she shall be made to yield. I pledge you my word that she shall be yours. This reception that you have met with from her is no more than I anticipated; but if she values the life and liberty of Florio Clairville, she will not much longer remain obdurate."

"I hope not, your highness," remarked Alberti; "for notwithstanding the scorn with which she treats me, my heart is fixed upon her, and I shall find it in vain to banish her from my mind."

"Do not endeavour to do so, my lord," said the prince; "for, indeed, there is no necessity for it. She dare not disobey my will."

"I think you will find her more firm than you seem to expect," said the count: "the feelings of repugnance she bears towards me, I fear, it will be no easy task to conquer. She upbraided me for my conduct towards Olympia, and it is evident that the prejudice she has imbibed against me is deep-rooted and immovable."

"Time will show, my lord; have patience. But I think it would be prudent not to force her to another interview for a few days; in the meantime I will see her, and try what further effect the voice of persuasion will have upon her."

"Be it so, your highness," returned Alberti; "and I will try to hope that the opinions you have expressed will be realized."

The count now related to Prince Bianchi all that had passed between him and Melina at their interview, to which his highness listened with feelings of indignation, though not of disappointment.

"The boldness of Melina annoys me," he observed, when Alberti had concluded; "but I will yet conquer her obstinate feelings, and make her succumb to my will, or I am not the Prince Bianchi."

"I fear you will have a more difficult task to perform, my lord, than you now seem to anticipate," said the count. "Would to Heaven that Olympia and her child were no more; but they are now, doubtless, in the power of Massaroni, and if so, I have everything to fear."

"Nay, my lord, do not fear anything; we must take immediate steps for the destruction of the brigand chief and his daring band, and then we shall have no further danger to apprehend, or any interruption to our future designs."

"Very true, your highness; we must consult together upon that subject anon. I long to have my revenge against Massaroni for the injuries he has done me, and the numerous indignities he has heaped upon me; but we must act with prudence and precaution, or we shall still be foiled in our designs."

"Very true," coincided Bianchi; "but still, we must use no more delay than is possible, for it is not at all improbable that Massaroni, when he finds you have escaped, will fly to some other place of concealment, and thus elude us altogether."

"Oh, no," returned the count; "I do not think it is at all likely, for he would find it difficult to meet with another place of such security as the present mountain fastnesses in which he is located; but until the re-erection of my castle, I must beg to intrude upon the hospitality of your highness."

"Certainly," said the prince, "and all the accommodation I can afford you, I think your lordship must be fully aware you are heartily welcome to."

The count returned his acknowledgments, and the subject dropped. The remainder of the day was occupied by the two friends in concocting their future plans; and when they separated for the night, it was with the most sanguine hopes of their ultimate success. Notwithstanding the scorn with which Melina had treat him, and which he had fully expected, the delight of Count Alberti was most unspeakable at the idea of being under the same roof with her; and that he should have such frequent opportunities of seeing her, and the observations which the prince had made use of to him, encouraged him to hope, in spite of the damsel's opposition, the gratifications of his wishes were yet certain.

"Yes," he said; "it is useless for her to stand out against the determined will of her uncle, her only friend and guardian; and therefore, she will be forced to submit. Only let her become my wife, and if I do not soon conquer her repugnance, it will be strange to me. What is there so repulsive in my person or my manners, that she should view me with such hatred? Other maidens of wealth, and rank, and beauty, would be proud of the alliance, and shall I then tamely yield to her scorn? No, I will persevere; I will not be intimidated; and something seems to whisper to me that my ultimate triumph is certain."

Thus buoyed up with hope, he every moment became more sanguine and resolute, and looked forward to his next interview with Melina with impatience, determined to urge his suit with redoubled energy, though he could not expect that it would meet with any more favourable a result. The emotions which Melina experienced when alone, after her interview with the Count Alberti, may be easily conceived. For some time disgust and indignation swelled her gentle bosom, and she could only give vent to her feelings in tears. But at length, clasping her hands together in agony, she ejaculated:—

"My God, to what heavy trials is it Your will to expose me. Oh, I beseech You to look down with an eye of pity upon me, and avert the terrible evils by which I am threatened. Uncle, whom I have ever loved, and made it my study to obey you in everything which reason and justice demanded, how can you find it in your heart to persecute me in the cruel manner you are now doing? But you will surely yet take compassion on me, and not consign me to a fate, the bare thought of which fills my breast with horror, and for which you must for ever afterwards reproach yourself. The more I behold Alberti, the greater becomes the feeling of hatred with which his cruel conduct towards the friendless and defenceless Olympia has inspired me; and I feel that I could court death, even in its most horrible shape, in preference to becoming his wife. His wife? the thought's madness!—I will remain firm in resisting all his importunities, and the cruel threats of the prince, my uncle, though the consequences that follow to me should be most dreadful! They cannot be half so horrible as an union with so hated a villain."

She was interrupted by a gentle tap at her room-door, and ascertaining that it was her kind-hearted attendant, Floretta, she admitted her.

"In tears, signora?" said Floretta, compasionately; "alas! I fear that your interview with the Count Alberti has been a painful one."

"It has filled my bosom with disgust and anguish, Floretta," replied her mistress; "my uncle left me alone with the count, and I was compelled to listen to his bold and odious addresses, with which, encouraged as he had been by the prince, he did not hesitate to insult my ears."

"Need I say how much I feel for you, my dear signora?" remarked Floretta; "but I hope you found resolution to reply to the count as he deserved."

"I did," answered Melina. "I did not attempt to conceal from him the abhorrence in which I held him; but he was nothing daunted, and I can expect nothing less than that he will persist in torturing me with his suit, and in which he will be warmly and remorselessly aided by my uncle. Thank Heaven that the meeting is over; but it is only the prelude to many others of an equally painful nature."

"Be of good cheer, my lady," said Floretta, "and Heaven will give you fortitude to support them, and to defeat the wishes of the Count Alberti, and his highness, your uncle."

"I would fain think so, if I could, Floretta; but when I weigh maturely all the circumstances, the most fearful misgivings distract my mind."

"Banish them, signora, and be firm."

"Alas! it is impossible! And the Count Alberti, I have every reason to believe, will remain here for some time, so that I shall be constantly exposed to the misery and degradation of his society. My uncle is inexorable, and will compel me to meet him whenever he thinks fit, or he will visit me with his utmost wrath, and poor Florio with his deadly vengeance. He has already told me that his fate depends on me; and after his late conduct, I cannot expect that he will fail to keep his word. Oh, Florio, dear, noble-hearted Florio, what will become of you?"

"Do not despair, dear signora," said Floretta; "the Almighty, who knows his innocence, will watch over and protect him from the fate with which he is threatened, and which at present seems to be almost inevitable."

"Could I but see him, if it were but for one minute," ejaculated Melina, "could I but get a few lines conveyed to him in his solitary dungeon, methinks I could be comparatively happy."

"That is impossible, my lady," answered her attendant; "the prince is not likely to suffer any one, especially yourself, to communicate with Signor Clairville, and there is no possible means of doing so by stealth."

"Oh, no," sighed Melina; "I never anticipated for a moment that there was; I must have been mad to do so, and it is that which adds to my anguish. I shudder at the thought of the fate which awaits him, should I still persist in rejecting the addresses of the count, and yet I could sooner die than yield to such a fate."

"His highness can never be so merciless as to fulfil his terrible threats," remarked Floretta; "he must be aware that such a cruel and desperate step must break your heart."

"Since it appears too evident that there is nothing but misery in store for us, would to Heaven that I and Florio might die together."

"Oh, I pray you, dear signora, to dismiss such sad thoughts from your mind; notwithstanding the dismal prospect which is at present spread before you both, I trust that there are many happy days in store for you."

Floretta remained with her mistress till a late hour of the evening, and sought by every means in her power to impart comfort to her lacerated breast; but her efforts met with very little success, and she left her deeply moved with the misery and anguish of her situation, and greatly incensed at the unfeeling conduct of the prince and Count Alberti. Melina passed a sleepless night, and in the morning she was too ill to leave her chamber, intelligence that greatly annoyed her uncle and the count, and showed them the necessity of acting with caution in their future proceedings. Clairville, in his gloomy dungeon, remained a prey to the most agonizing thoughts, and in vain tried to encourage the least feeling of hope; but he still felt much more for the situation of his beloved Melina than his own, and every moment his anxiety and suspense became the more intense and insupportable. At times he was worked up to almost a pitch of madness, and dashing himself against the damp and blackened wall of his dungeon, gave vent to the anguish of his feelings in the most heart-rending groans. Confinement and constant thought had so impaired his faculties that he was not like the same individual, and his fortitude almost entirely forsook him. How gladly would he have welcomed death, could he have been assured that Melina would be released from the terrible, the disgusting fate with which she was threatened; but of that there was, alas! not the least prospect. In this manner three more dreary days rolled on, and there seemed to be not the least prospect of a change in his situation. His strength was sinking rapidly, and he thought it would be impossible for him to survive much longer in that awful state of confinement. What had he done that he should be thus inhumanly persecuted? Never could he have believed that the Prince Bianchi could have acted with such refined cruelty towards him or any other human being; and there were moments when his brain wandered, and he could scarcely persuade himself that he was not under the influence of some fearful dream; but he was very soon aroused to all the horrors of the dreadful certainty, and then his agony became more intolerable than ever. Such were the thoughts that distracted the mind of the unhappy Clairville, when he was startled by hearing the bolts withdrawn, the key turned in the lock, the door flew back on its hinges, and the Prince Bianchi once more stood before him. He seemed somewhat startled by the alteration in Florio's appearance, and for a moment a feeling of pity and self-reproach entered his breast; but it quickly vanished, and he advanced towards him with his usual and stern demeanour. Florio felt his fortitude revive, and he returned the look of the prince with one of scorn and reproach, as he thus demanded—

"To what may I attribute the honour of this visit, my lord?"

"I came to ask you whether you have thought better of your obstinate and foolish determination?" replied Bianchi.

"No, my lord," said Clairville, firmly; "my resolution is the same that it ever was."

"Then you will not disclose the retreat of Massaroni?"

"I have told you repeatedly that I will not, my lord."

"Fool!" cried the prince, with a scornful laugh, "your obstinacy is now of no avail; I have discovered the retreat of the brigand chief without your aid, and ere many days have elapsed, he will also be an inmate of this prison. The Count Alberti has escaped!"

"Escaped!" repeated Florio, unable to conceal his emotion.

"Ay, escaped!" answered Bianchi, "and he is at present residing beneath my roof, and in daily intercourse with Melina."

"Then God help her!" fervently ejaculated Clairville, clasping his hands; "for without His aid, I fear that her doom is sealed. But, oh, my lord, you surely will abandon your unjust and cruel designs. You cannot—you will not sacrifice that innocent girl, who has ever looked upon you with the same veneration as if you were her parent, to such a villain as the Count Alberti."

"She must—she shall become his wife," said the prince, sternly; "my resolution is fixed—unalterably fixed. If Melina still continues to reject him, force shall make her yield; but if she voluntarily consents, she will be the means of saving your life, and restoring you to liberty."

"By heaven!" exclaimed Florio, resolutely, "I will never consent to purchase my life or my liberty on any such hateful and degrading terms. My lord, pause ere you proceed to the frightful lengths you have threatened; remember, there is a just God above, who ever watches over and protects the innocent, and who never fails to bring a terrible retribution upon the head of its guilty persecutor. You cannot be so entirely lost to every sense of justice and humanity. Again I adjure you to pause, or you will have bitter cause to repent when it will be too late."

"You do but waste your breath in these appeals to me," replied the prince, with a haughty look of scorn; "you have heard what I have promised, and I will not fail to keep my word."

"Monstrous decision!" cried Clairville. "Oh, Melina, how I pity you; I would die a thousand deaths of torture to save you from such a revolting fate."

"Very heroic," said the prince, disdainfully, "but it is all to no purpose; Melina has received my commands, and she must obey them; she has no alternative. I have selected for her a nobleman who is every way worthy of her, and I am not to be persuaded from my purpose by her ridiculous objections."

"Oh, my lord," said Florio, "can you, do you consider, that such a man as the Count Alberti, the heartless betrayer of the unfortunate Olympia, is worthy to become the husband of one so pure and lovely as your affectionate niece? Nature recoils at the thought, and he who is the cause of such an unholy alliance taking place, cannot but bring a heavy curse upon his own head, and all who are connected with him. I ask not mercy for myself; I am reckless what fate may be awarded me; but I supplicate for one who must ever be dearer to me than my own existence, though I abandon all presumptuous thoughts respecting her, and perchance may never behold her again; do not, oh, do not——"

"Daring boy, cease this whining cant!" interrupted the prince, passionately; "think you it will have the least effect on me? But I degrade myself by holding further converse with you, and I leave you to your own reflections."

Florio fixed upon him a look of the most bitter reproach as he quitted the dungeon, but he attempted not to make any reply, and the next moment he was alone. He clasped his forehead in agony, and for some moments he was unable to give expression to the torturing feelings that laboured in his breast.

"This intelligence," he sighed at last, "completes my misery; oh, Melina, unfortunate, persecuted girl, will no friendly arm be stretched forth to save you from the hideous fate which is now impending o'er your head? Will All-Just Heaven permit your inexorable enemies to triumph? It cannot be! It were monstrous to entertain such a thought. And yet what prospect is there at present of your fate being averted?—None, none! The prince, your uncle, seems to have banished every feeling of pity and justice from his breast. If he remains firm to what he has threatened, you can expect no mercy from him. Had the Count Alberti still remained a prisoner, there would have been some hope, but now there is none. Alas, how unfortunate is this! By what means has Alberti been enabled to effect his escape, so secure as I thought he was in the power of Massaroni? There must have been some treachery amongst the band of the brigand. Oh, how terrible must be the anguish of Melina, now that he whom she so thoroughly detests, and whom she has such cause to dread, is residing under the same roof with her; and she is hourly exposed to his odious importunities, backed by the encouragement of her uncle!— The thought will drive me mad; but sooner will I perish ignominiously on the scaffold, than purchase my life and liberty on the infamous terms which the prince has proposed to me. Life cannot longer have any charms for me, and I will gladly resign the insupportable burthen!"

He beat his breast, and tore his hair in the anguish of his feelings, and could find no relief to the fever of his brain, which threatened to drive him to a state bordering upon madness. In this state he continued throughout the whole of the night, and sleep never once descended upon his eyelids. The blackest despair had settled upon his heart, and a thousand times he prayed to Heaven to terminate his wretched existence. It was several days before Melina was sufficiently recovered to leave her bed, and then the prince and Count Alberti did not think it prudent to insist upon an interview with her at present, though Alberti was all impatience to behold her again, and had made up his mind to urge his suit with tenfold energy and boldness. Melina continued a prey to the most distracting thoughts, and had very few moments of tranquillity. How could it be expected that she could have, with such a fearful prospect before her. Floretta was her only companion; and had it not been for her society, she must have been reduced to a state of the most abject despair. That faithful attendant devised every means in her power to divert the thoughts of her mistress from the gloomy subjects which completely engrossed them; but although Melina fully appreciated her humane efforts, she found it impossible that they could have any influence on her. At length, however, the patience of Alberti was exhausted, and he begged of the prince to grant him another interview with Melina, with which request Bianchi complied, and conveyed his commands to his beauteous but unhappy niece through Floretta. Melina was by no means taken by surprise, for it was what she had for several days expected; but it caused her the most acute anguish nevertheless, and she trembled as the moment arrived when she must meet her persecutor. Nothing more particular passed at this interview than there had on the previous occasion, with the exception that the prince remained present during the whole of the time, and backed the hateful suit of the count by every means in his power. But threats and importunities were alike vain; Melina remained firm; and when she was permitted to retire from the presence of her uncle and Alberti, she left them in a state of excitement, which they felt it difficult to govern within the bounds of reason.

"It is entirely hopeless," remarked the count; "neither arguments, threats, or persuasions, will have any effect upon this obstinate girl; it is plain she views me with the most unconquerable hatred."

"She may do so at present, my lord," replied the prince; "but if you are determined not to abandon your suit, I will yet devise some means to break her proud and scornful spirit. I have given you my word, my lord, and you shall find that I will not break it. What, then, have you to fear? My will is imperative—and again I solemnly promise you, in spite of all the consequences that may follow, Melina shall become your wife, and that before many weeks have elapsed; if she does not consent, force shall compel her."

"Enough, my lord," said the count; "I am satisfied. Notwithstanding the feelings of abhorrence which she evidently entertains towards me, and which she takes no pains to conceal, I cannot resign my hopes of her; though could I but win her love, I should, indeed, be one of the happiest men in existence."

"Well spoken, count," said the prince; "we now, then, thoroughly understand each other?"

"We do, your highness."

"Say no more then upon the subject at present, but leave everything to me."

"I will do so, my lord," said Alberti, and they separated.

From that time, there was not a day passed that Melina was not tortured and annoyed by the importunities of Alberti, and the threats and persuasions of her uncle; but although her heart was full almost to bursting, and she saw not the least possible chance of escaping the fate with which she was threatened, she remained firm in her opposition, much to the astonishment and disappointment of her persecutors. There were moments when the prince reminded her that by consenting she would save the life of her lover, and be the means of restoring him to liberty, when she was almost tempted to yield; but something whispered to her that Florio would yet be rescued without any such sacrifice on her part, and she again resolutely rejected the offer, and put the whole of her trust in the goodness and merciful interposition of Providence. The Prince Bianchi and Alberti, being busily occupied in arranging their plans for an attack on Massaroni, Melina was permitted to experience a few days respite ; and that time she occupied in endeavouring to combat her fears, and to gather to her aid all possible fortitude to encounter the future trials that were doubtless in store for her ; and in that task she succeeded much better than the most sanguine expectations could have anticipated, and was greatly assisted by the advice of Floretta. Everything being arranged to the mutual satisfaction of the prince and his friend, the troops were despatched to the secret haunt of the brigand chief, with every prospect of the expedition being crowned with success, and that Massaroni would in a few days be placed in their power. The reader has been shown how those hopes were doomed to be disappointed ; and the rage of Bianchi and the count, on the return of the survivors, with the news of their defeat, was most unbounded, as may very well be imagined.

"Is this fellow man or devil ?" cried the prince, furiously, "that he thus sets every stratagem devised to entrap him — every force that may be sent against him—at defiance ?   Diavolo! are we to be thus constantly defeated—laughed at—mocked at ? I have no patience to endure the repeated insults and outrages.   My lord, cannot you suggest any future plan of operations that may be likely to be crowned with success ?"

"Indeed I cannot, your highness," replied Alberti ; "indeed, the power of this lawless marauder is immense ; and he is so well protected in his mountain retreat, that I fear he may well laugh to scorn every attempt on our part to apprehend him.   It will be advisable to appear to abandon any such design, at the same time using every precaution, and employing secret spies in all parts of the country ; and by such means we may perchance entrap the brigand when he is off his guard, and lacks the protection of his daring band."

"A wise suggestion," said Bianchi ; "it shall be attended to. Diavolo! it would be monstrous to allow such a villain as this Allesandro Massaroni to escape us. Had he a hundred heads, they deserve to be forfeited for the crimes he has committed ; and yet there is something about the appearance and manners of the fellow which have made a most unaccountable impression upon me. I never think of his name but a strange feeling comes over my heart which renders me miserable for several hours afterwards. What can be the meaning of this, when I have had every proof that he is not only my greatest enemy but that of his country ?"

"It is strange," replied the count, " and

I must confess that there is something about the man which to me is inexplicable ; and notwithstanding all the wrongs I have received at his hand, inspires me with a certain feeling of awe, if not respect for him.   He was evidently born to fill a far different position in society than that he now occupies.   His bearing is noble and dignified, his manners and language those of the most polished gentleman, and no wonder that he should have excited a sort of sympathy for himself amongst the fair sex, his daring exploits partaking of all the character of romance.   What surprises me even more than all is, that he should take such an interest in the fate of Olympia, and the destinies of your fair niece, an interest which leads him to encounter any danger to accomplish his designs."

"It is perfectly inexplicable," said the prince ; then, after a pause he added :—

"Have you seen the veiled portrait, my lord, that I have in one of the rooms of this villa ?"

"I have," answered the count ; "and I feel the most anxious curiosity to know its history. The likeness is that of a most beautiful woman."

"It is indeed," said Bianchi, with much emotion ; "but oh, what a faint resemblance of the lovely original."

"Some particular friend, or dear relation, I presume, your highness ?" said Alberti.

"Pardon me, my lord," said the prince, with increased agitation ; "I was wrong in broaching a subject which is ever a source of the deepest anguish to me. The history of that portrait has never yet passed my lips to mortal being. Would to God that I could wash it from my memory altogether ; but it will not be. However, at some future period I may disclose the melancholy secret to you, and then *you* will see the reason why I so deeply sympathise with you in your unfortunate connection with the girl Olympia."

"Whenever it suits your highness, I shall feel most honoured by being made acquainted with it," returned Alberti, who now formed a pretty just conception of the nature of the narrative to which he referred.

"You say you have seen the portrait, my lord ?" again said the prince, after a pause.

"I have, your highness," replied the count.

"Have you examined it minutely ?"

"Most minutely."

"And has it never struck you that the features, and the expression of the eyes, bear a most extraordinary likeness to those of Massaroni ?"

"Now you remind me of it, my lord, I certainly have," answered Alberti. "But that coincidence is most unaccountable."

Bianchi evinced the greatest emotion, and walked two or three time across the room, muttering incoherent sentences to himself.

"I was foolish to have said so much," he observed; "it can only be imagination; but we will drop the subject; at some future period I may feel disposed to return to it, and to make a confidant of you. Think you that Massaroni has succeeded in rescuing Olympia and her child from the confinement in which you had placed them?"

"I can have very little doubt of it, my

MELINA REPULSING THE COUNT ALBERTI'S PROPOSALS.

lord," replied Alberti; "for I fear the power of Massaroni would prove too much for that of Rinaldi and his band; but no doubt I shall soon be made acquainted with the facts."

"It is unfortunate that you did not make your escape before the place of her confinement had been forced from you."

"It is," coincided the count; "but if I had not yielded to the demands of the brigand chief, I can entertain no doubt that he would have sacrificed my life as he threatened to do."

"True," said the prince; "but an opportunity may yet present itself to place her once more in your power, and then, of course, we can adopt some certain means of preventing her being any future annoyance to you."

"Ay, my lord, that shall most assuredly be done."

"And in the meantime rest yourself perfectly satisfied as regards Melina; in spite of all her opposition, a few weeks shall only intervene ere you lead her to the altar.'

"Your highness fills my soul with ecstacy," ejaculated the count; "and I know I can depend upon your word."

"You may, my lord," replied Bianchi; "I never yet broke it with any man. I will not suffer myself to be intimidated from my purpose by the obduracy of one of whom I am the sole guardian. Her scorn and indifference must and shall be conquered."

The conversation then dropped, and the prince and Alberti separated. Melina received the news of the defeat of the troops which had been sent against Massaroni with the most unfeigned satisfaction, for she hoped that it would at least retard the consummation of her fate, although she had but little hope of its being ultimately averted. Many were the wretched hours she passed; and constantly did she offer up her supplications to Heaven to interpose in her favour. Every day she was exposed to the misery of Count Alberti's society; she found it utterly impossible for her to avoid it; and backed by the prince, her uncle, at every interview he became more bold in his advances, and made no scruple of showing her that he felt confident that she must become his wife; and indeed the prince ultimately informed her that at the expiration of one short month only she must either yield to his wishes, or that force should compel her to bestow her hand upon that man whom she now more thoroughly detested and dreaded than ever. The thought was a dreadful, a revolting one, and her reason almost sank beneath it. Notwithstanding all her efforts, she could find no ray of hope or consolation to sustain her, and she looked upon herself as one of the most unfortunate and wretched being in existence. But the threatened fate of her lover Florio, and the agony of mind she felt certain he must now be enduring, wrung her heart more than all. Many were the tears she shed as she thought upon him, and constantly were her prayers offered up to the Supreme to rescue him from the numerous dangers by which he was surrounded; but hope came not to her breast. Her uncle had evidently became insensible to every feeling of pity, and she could expect no mercy or indulgence from him.

"Oh," she would sigh, "what has wrought this fearful change in him? I can scarce believe the evidence of my senses, and would fain believe that I was labouring under the influence of some fearful dream, were not the painful truth but too apparent. Oh, my uncle, can you have forgotten the solemn promises you made to my poor mother in her dying moments? Surely you will at some future period have bitter cause to repent your present cruel and tyrannical conduct; but then it will be too late to recal the terrible fate to which you will so unjustly have assigned me. Become the wife of the libertine Alberti, the destroyer of female innocence?—the bare idea curdles the blood within my veins, and drives me almost to madness. All-Merciful God, take compassion on me, and do not suffer, I beseech you, such a monstrous sacrifice to take place. I am prepared to die, to encounter any fate, let it be ever so dreadful, rather than become the wife of the hated Alberti. But there is no hope of my escaping from it, and my misery is complete."

In such moments as these, the kind-hearted Floretta exerted all her powers of eloquence to console her, and sometimes she succeeded to a certain degree; but it was only transient, and afterwards the anguish of Melina would become, if possible, more intense."

"But a short month," she sighed, "and there is no hope; oh, God! what will become of me? What have I done that I should merit such a fate as this?"

"The prince, your uncle, my dear signora," replied Floretta, "cannot—will not be so insensible to every feeling of humanity and justice as to remain inflexible. He will yield to your tears and supplications, if he really possesses that affection towards you which he has ever professed to do, and the Count Alberti will be commanded to abandon his presumptuous hopes."

"Ah, Floretta," ejaculated her mistress, "why so sanguine? I am certain you cannot feel sincerely that which you have just expressed. You would buoy me up with hopes which never can be realised. Does not the conduct of my uncle altogether bid me despair? Has he not turned a deaf ear to all the earnest and tender appeals I have made to him, and is there is the least reason for me to imagine that he will alter his cruel determination? Oh, no, I cannot, dare not encourage such a thought, which can only end in the bitterest disappointment."

"I cannot, will not, think so badly of his highness, my lady," said Floretta; "he must have become base indeed could he make up his mind to consign you to so revolting a fate. Take courage, signora, and who knows what may take place ere the month has expired? I am much deceived if something does not occur to avert the evils which you now so justly apprehend. I trust that your fears may prove to be entirely groundless."

But all these endeavours on the part of the sympathising Floretta, to banish the dismal apprehensions from the mind of her mistress, had but little, if any effect ; there was too much reason in them to be combatted in such a manner, and as day after day wore away, and Melina was compelled to listen to the odious vows of the Count Alberti, she became most truly miserable, and it was wonderful how she could sustain herself under the painful trial at all. In a few days Alberti received from Rinaldi intelligence of the escape of Olympia and her child, but of course he could not give him the least idea whither she had gone, and the count, therefore, remained in ignorance of her being under the protection of the brigand chief ; Rinaldi also concealed from him the fact of his wife, Theresina, having been the cause of her escape ; and although he at first reproached her for the deed, he soon became reconciled to it, and could not but commend the humane and womanly feeling which had prompted her to such a step, and he earnestly hoped that Olympia would in future be able to elude the power and the cruelty of her betrayer. The rage of the count on the receipt of this intelligence was excessive, and he vowed that if Olympia should ever again fall within his power, he would take especial care to prevent her being of any future annoyance to him. It was midnight, and the Prince Bianchi had but just dropped into a troubled sleep, when he was suddenly aroused by a heavy hand being placed upon his shoulder, and hearing his name pronounced in a coarse but subdued voice. He started up in astonishment and alarm, which was not the least diminished when he beheld the tall figure of a man enveloped in a dark mantle standing by his bedside. He was so confused that for a moment he could not recognise the features of the intruder, and was about to call for assistance when the man prevented him.

"Silence, my lord," he said ; "you have nothing to fear. Do you not know me? It is not so long since we met before."

"Ah! Malvolio!" exclaimed the prince, with increased amazement ; "is it possible that it is you?"

"Ay, even so, your highness," answered the man.

"How have you obtained admittance to my chamber at this hour of the night?"

"By the means of these keys, which I took good care to secure," replied Malvolio, exhibiting a bunch.

"You are a daring scoundrel," said the confounded prince.

"I know it, my lord;" coincided Malvolio, with an ironical smile, "or I should not have been ready to lend you such good service years ago, as I have done."

"Have you been seen by any of the domestics?"

"That is not very likely, as they have all retired to rest, I presume, some hours ago."

"What brings you hither?"

"First, a fresh supply of money, for my finances are quite exhausted."

"And what else?"

"Why, to bring you some news, which I know not whether you will be pleased or not to hear," answered Malvolio.

"What is it?" demanded the prince, eagerly.

"Zitella still lives!"

"D——n!"

"I have seen her ; she accidentally crossed my path accompanied by an old man, and although her senses evidently wandered, she recognised me on the instant."

"Where did you see her?" asked Bianchi, in a state of the greatest agitation.

"That I do not think proper to disclose to your highness for the present," answered Malvolio.

"Why not?"

"I have my reasons ; you have but to reward me handsomely, and you need entertain no apprehensions of her appearing to annoy you."

"Zitella living!" exclaimed the prince ;— "this is unfortunate. Should she discover me, my reputation is blasted for ever."

"It would be so, my lord," said Malvolio, with a look of exultation ; "but again I tell you, that if you pay me handsomely, you need not entertain any such apprehensions."

"You see yonder dressing-case," said the prince, pointing to it ; "the key is in the lock ; you will find money in it ; take what you require. only swear to be faithful to me."

"There is no necessity for my doing so," answered Malvolio ; "my word is my bond."

He then walked to the dressing-case, and, unlocking it, took from it a couple of well filled purses, which he weighed with much apparent satisfaction in his hands.

"These will do at present, I think," he said ; "I am not extravagant in my demands."

"Will you not reveal to me the place where Zitella is at present concealed?" again asked the prince.

"No, my lord," replied Malvolio, "I must, for certain reasons best known to myself, beg leave to decline. However, I will watch her narrowly ; and should any danger threaten, I will take immediate steps to avert it ; of that you may rest satisfied."

"You will not lay violent hands upon her?"

"Not without I receive your instructions to do so," answered the villain.

"Do you think I would become a murderer?" demanded the prince sternly.

"I did not say so," said Malvolio ; "but having thus made you acquainted with these important facts, I suppose you can dispense with my presence?"

"Stay," commanded Bianchi; "why will you leave me in this state of doubt and uncertainty? What necessity is there for so much secrecy?"

"It is of every importance to me," replied Malvolio, with a sinister look.

"You say that you believe Zitella's child is still living?"

"I am certain that she is."

"Where, oh, where?"

"That also must remain a secret for the present, confined to my own breast," replied the ruffian.

"This is most torturing," ejaculated the prince. "If you speak the truth, why should you hesitate to divulge to me the place of her concealment?"

"For my own protection, and because I have other objects in view."

"Malvolio, your mysterious conduct and evasive answers begin to excite my suspicions."

"I cannot help it, my lord," returned Malvolio, "but I can assure you they are groundless. The girl is safe; but did you know who she really is, you would, I think, be truly miserable, though, of course, you can have no wish to acknowledge her; that would not, methinks, agree with the dignity of the Prince Bianchi."

"Agonizing thought," groaned the prince; "oh, that I should ever so have committed myself. But is she lovely?"

"She is the very counterpart of her mother," answered Malvolio.

The prince sighed deeply, and clasped his forehead.

"Is she virtuous?" he demanded eagerly.

"She was," was the reply; "but I have revealed sufficient, and it is useless for you at present to seek to know more. Good night, my lord; you may depend upon my secrecy while you continue to supply my wants; but if once you fail, you must take the consequences."

"Ah! dare you threaten me?" demanded Bianchi, haughtily.

"I have no wish to do so, my lord," retorted Malvolio, coolly; "but I must and will speak my mind, and it is better I should do so, so that we may not misunderstand each other. Good-night."

"Stay, Malvolio; when shall we meet again?"

"When I require a fresh supply of cash," replied the ruffian, dryly, "and I dare say that will be before long. You see that I have ready means of access to you."

"Be cautious, Malvolio," said the prince, "I strictly enjoin you; for should you be seen by any of my domestics, I am ruined."

"You may be satisfied that I will ever be on my guard, my lord," answered Malvolio; "it would not be convenient for me to be seen by any person but yourself. Remember what I have told you, and be sure that it is strictly true; once more, I wish you good-night."

Thus saying, before the prince had time to recover from his astonishment and confusion, or to give utterance to another word, Malvolio quitted the chamber, and the prince heard his footsteps cautiously descending the stairs.

He hastily arose from the bed, for after what had so unexpectedly happened, he found it impossible to compose himself again to rest. He walked to the window, and by the light of the moon beheld Malvolio crossing the garden; and he felt his mind more at ease now that he was gone without having been observed by any one. The intelligence which the ruffian, Malvolio, had imparted to him, filled his breast with mingled feelings of astonishment, compunction, and alarm; and he traversed the room in a state of the most inconceivable emotion.

"Still living!" he ejaculated; "she and her child, although they are unknown to each other? Can this be possible?—May it not be all an invention of the villain Malvolio to extort money from me? What dependence can I place upon such a miscreant? And yet it will not do for me to venture to offend him; he holds me entirely in his power. Oh, Zitella, one so lovely, so accomplished, and so virtuous, what a villain have I been to you; and you, poor, confiding Valentia! but for me, might you not still have been living and happy? Why do these thoughts occur to me? They will drive me mad! Will the voice of conscience never be hushed? But no; I deserve all the torture I am enduring, and oh, how much more! I like not the threats of Malvolio—oh, why have I ever exposed myself to the malignity of such a villain? And I cannot now help myself; no, I feel myself to be entirely powerless; and one false step may plunge me into irretrievable ruin."

Thus he continued to soliloquise until the morning dawned, when he quitted his room, and hastened from the house, with the hope of being able to recruit his spirits by a walk before breakfast; but nothing could banish from his mind the torturing thoughts that had taken possession of it, and all the events of long past years crowded upon his memory in characters as fresh as if they had occurred but yesterday. It was, indeed, a sad retrospect, and the longer he reflected the more painful and insupportable became his emotion. After some time, finding that the walk afforded him no relief, he returned to the house, and locking himself in his chamber, gave himself up entirely to the feelings which agitated his breast until he was summoned to breakfast.

The Count Albert noticed the extreme agitation of his manner, but he did not take the liberty to inquire the cause, and of course the prince did not consider it prudent on his part to make him acquainted with what had happened. Before breakfast was over, however, Bianchi became more composed, and entered more freely into conversation with his companion. The greater portion of the day the prince passed alone in his study, and would see no one, and Melina experienced a short respite from the persecutions of himself and the Count Alberti, whom she most sedulously avoided, notwithstanding he several times requested her to favour him with her society. Thus left to himself the count became restless and impatient, and in order to endeavour to divert his thoughts into some more agreeable channel, he walked from the villa.—To return to Florio Clairville. It need not be said that he remained in the same wretched state of mind, and tried in vain to encourage the hope that it would please Providence to work some favourable change in his prospects, and that the prince, at length awakened to a sense of the cruelty and injustice of his conduct, would relent, and not only restore him to liberty, but would also abandon his harsh and unnatural designs against Melina. For her preservation, his prayers were constantly offered up to Heaven, and many were the curses that he invoked upon the head of Alberti, and could not help now lamenting that he had not fallen a victim to the vengeance of Massaroni. He continued in the greatest suspense and anxiety to imagine what the prince intended to do with him, though after what he had said, he could expect little or nothing from his mercy. He felt at a loss to conceive if it was the intention of Bianchi to sacrifice him, why he was not brought to trial; surely his enemies could not be so monstrous as to condemn him unheard; and yet after the manner in which he had been treated, he had little reason to expect justice from their hands. Another week passed away, when Florio could not help noticing a marked change in the manner of his jailor. His looks were less stern and repulsive; and several times Clairville was half inclined to speak to him, and appeal to his humanity; but whenever he was about to do so, the man, who seemed to understand the thoughts that were passing in his mind, placed his finger upon his lips enjoining him to silence, and then abruptly quitted the dungeon. However, these circumstances inspired Florio with hope, and he endeavoured to wait with patience the result. Two more days passed away, and the favourable demeanour of the jailor increased, but still he evaded all the questions which Clairville naturally was disposed to put to him, and left him

in the same state of doubt and suspense, and anxious expectation. That the jailor was more favourably disposed towards him, and that he had some object in view, Florio could entertain no doubt; but still he found it impossible to solve the mystery of his continued taciturnity, and this perplexity was aided by the non-appearance of the Prince Bianchi. He was not much longer kept in suspense: for one evening when the man had been to bring him his usual rations, just as he was about to quit the dungeon, he beckoned him towards him, and placing a strip of paper in his hand, immediately vanished. With eager impatience, and his heart palpitating with hope, Florio rushed beneath the light which was suspended from the roof of his cell, and read the following lines—

"Do no attempt to speak to me, for the walls may have ears. I am your friend. Courage, prudence, and to-morrow at midnight shall see you safe beyond the walls of this prison. Destroy this as soon as you have perused it."

How shall we describe the feelings which swelled the bosom of the unfortunate Clairville as he read these lines? The intelligence was so good, and came upon him so suddenly and so unexpectedly, that he could scarcely believe the evidence of his senses; but when he had a little recovered from his astonishment and bewilderment, he sank upon his knees, and clasping his hands vehemently together, he ejaculated—

"Great God! for this Thy merciful interposition, I thank Thee. And shall I, indeed, be once more restored to liberty? Shall I again breathe the pure air, and escape from the danger which now threatens me? It appears scarcely possible. What can have influenced this man, whom I have hitherto looked upon with such repugnance and suspicion, to become my friend, and run the risk he must evidently be doing to render me such an inestimable service? It is an inexplicable mystery. There must be some other person in the background. Ah! Massaroni, perhaps!"

This idea every moment gained strength in his mind, and he did not suffer himself to question the probability of it. He well knew the power which the Brigand Chief possessed, and that he had secret agents everywhere, and in every department, and he likewise felt convinced that he would be disposed to render him a service if he had the opportunity; consequently, the idea was by no means a preposterous one. How blissful is the prospect of liberty to the incarcerated victim of persecution; it must be apparent to every reflective mind, and therefore, we need not attempt to portray the feelings of Clairville on this occasion. The anguish and dispair he had previously felt, gradually vanished from his mind, and hope revived in his bosom. The man could surely have no motive in deceiving him: and yet what was it that could have tempted one who appeared so stern and callous, to look upon his situation with feelings of compassion, to run the risks he would undoubtedly be doing in aiding his escape? He was quite lost in bewilderment, but one thing appeared certain, namely, that the jailor was not acting entirely on his own responsibility, but that he was merely the instrument of some individual of greater power and influence: yet who could that be? He racked his brain to no purpose in endeavouring to form a reasonable conjecture; but the longer he weighed the circumstance over in his mind, the deeper did he become involved in doubt and perplexity. But though he should be restored to liberty, he ruminated, could he be happy, when he knew the deplorable, the wretched situation of his beloved Melina, and the disgusting fate to which her inexorable uncle seemed resolved to consign her? Alas! he could not; and that thought made him begin to look upon his promised liberation with a feeling almost approaching to indifference. When the Prince Bianchi should discover his escape, rage and revenge would urge him on to the consummation of the misery of his fair niece; and totally unprotected as she was, she would have not the least power to offer any resistance, and the triumph of the Count Alberti would thus be rendered complete. These reflections caused him the greatest anguish of mind, and he found it quite impossible to tranquilise his spirits, or to gain the smallest repose during the night. Several were the prayers he offered up to the Most High to protect Melina, and to avert the fate with which she was threatened; and the morning found him in the same disturbed state of mind. However, in the course of the following day he struggled with his feelings, and becoming more composed, awaited with impatience the arrival of midnight. The jailor visited him at the usual time to bring him his provisions, but although he exchanged significant looks with him, he offered not the least observation, and Clairville in obedience to the injunctions he had received in the note, did not attempt to speak to him. The day passed tediously away, and as midnight gradually approached, the anxiety and impatience of Florio increased. Sometimes he had his doubts whether or not the man would keep his word; for the risk he would be running appeared to him too great for a stranger voluntarily to undertake; but the prison clock had scarcely tolled the midnight hour when his doubts were removed, by hearing the bolts of his dungeon door being cautiously withdrawn, and the next moment the jailor stood before him. He was enveloped in a large mantle, and his hat was so slouched down over his forehead as partially to conceal his features. He carried a bundle under his arm, which, unfastening, he revealed to the gaze of Florio the disguise of a monk, which, by significant signs, he instructed him to assume without delay. Clairville obeyed, and the jailor then placed a pistol and a stiletto in his hands, and seeing that Florio was about to speak, he again motioned him to silence. Clairville mentally invoked the protection of Heaven, and then prepared to follow his mysterious companion from the dungeon, though it was not without many powerful misgivings that he did so. The jailor closed the dungeon-door silently after them; and then taking the hand of Florio, he proceeded to lead him through the different subterranean passages of the prison, which seemed to be interminable, and were only feebly lighted by the rays of the lamp which the jailor carried with him. For some time all was silent as the grave, and the hopes of Clairville revived, and the prospect of liberty seemed fast opening upon him; but suddenly they were both startled by what appeared to be the closing of a heavy door, at no great distance from them; and then they distinctly heard the hollow echoes of a foot-fall upon the pavement, and which for the moment seemed to be approaching towards them. The jailor hastily shaded his lamp beneath his mantle, and grasping the arm of Florio, drew him into a deep recess in the wall near which they were standing, and here they both stood and listened with the most breathless attention and anxiety.

"Fear not," whispered the jailor in Clairville's ear.

This reassured him; and in a few seconds the sound of the footsteps died away in the distance, and the jailor again taking the hand of Clairville, issued forth from the place of their concealment. After passing through several cells, and ascending different flights of steps, they emerged from the lower part of the building, and at length arriving at a low iron door, which the man unlocked from a large bunch of keys which he had brought with him, they found themselves in an open court-yard. They crept along cautiously by the wall, which was best calculated to conceal them, and at last arrived in sight of the sentinel on duty, whose back being turned towards them, he could not observe them. Before Clairville could have any idea of his design, the jailor sprang upon the unfortunate sentinel, and burying his poniard deep in his side, he sunk on the earth a corpse and without giving utterance to a single groan. Clairville was shocked at the suddenness and inhumanity of this deed; but his conductor did not give him much time for reflection; but unlocking the prison gates, he dragged him forth, and hurried him along beneath the walls of the castle with breathless haste. When they had proceeded a short distance, Clairville was surprised and somewhat startled by hearing a shrill whistle, to which the jailor replied, and urged him on towards the spot from which it seemed to proceed.

"What is the meaning of this?" Florio now ventured to demand.

"It means, signor," answered the man, "that your friends are at hand; that I have faithfully performed my promise; and that you are now safe."

He had scarcely given utterance to these observations, when Clairville beheld the shadows of several men approaching them, and before he had time to recover from his surprise, he heard his own name repeated in a well known voice—

"Good God!" he exclaimed, starting with amazement, "is it possible—Massaroni?"

"Ay, signor," replied the brigand chief, hastily approaching him, and grasping him cordially by the hand; "it is indeed your friend, Allessandro Massaroni, who has the pleasure of congratulating you on your restoration to liberty. Jacomo, you have well performed your duty."

"Oh, Massaroni," said the grateful Florio; "and it is indeed to you that I am indebted for this inestimable service?"

"Yes, signor," replied the brigand. "The weight of my gold, and my influence with this worthy fellow, has effected all. The base designs of the Prince Bianchi against you are defeated, and this will be another source of rage and disappointment to him."

"How can I express to you my thanks for this disinterested kindness?" said Florio, heartily returning his shake of the hand; "the risks you have run, and——"

"Enough, enough," interrupted Massaroni, impatiently; "for what I have done, I require no acknowledgments but those of friendship. But come, there is not a moment to be lost; there is no knowing how soon your escape may be discovered, and there is danger in delay. I have horses waiting yonder, and when we have got some distance from this castle, we can talk further on this subject."

Florio did not attempt to utter another observation, but suffered Massaroni and the other brigands to conduct him away from the spot, and having reached the secluded place where the horses were waiting, they mounted them and were soon proceeding with great speed towards the mountains.

CHAPTER XXXII.

THE FLIGHT OF CLAIRVILLE DISCOVERED.—THE RAGE AND DISAPPOINTMENT OF THE PRINCE BIANCHI AND THE COUNT.—THE CONTINUED PERSECUTION OF MELINA.

THE discovery of the dead body of the sentinal, first gave the alarm at the castle, and a search being immediately made, the surprise and consternation of every one on discovering that the dungeon in which Clairville had been confined was vacated, may be easily conjectured; and Jacomo being also missing, there could be no doubt that it was through his means the prisoner had escaped. The news was quickly conveyed to the Prince Bianchi, who at that time was seated in conversation with Alberti, and busily engaged in discussing their plans for the future. It came like a thunderbolt to them.

"Escaped!" they both exclaimed together, and starting to their feet; "rascals! how is this?"

"Pardon me, your highness," said the man who had first spoken; "but we are none of us to blame; it is Jacomo who has been the author of it all, for he has absconded."

"The treacherous villain," cried the prince, furiously; "a lingering death of torture shall be his portion should he ever be discovered. I would not have had this happen for any money. Is my authority for ever to be despised and set at defiance by such dastard knaves? Let an immediate and strict search be made after the fugitives, and if they are not re-taken speedily, you shall all of you answer dearly for it. Begone!"

The men departed disconsolately, and left the prince and Alberti foaming with rage.

"Curses light on this misfortune," exclaimed the former; "it could not have occurred at a worse time. While I held Clairville a prisoner and at my mercy, I had the means of compelling Melina to yield to my will, by intimidation; but now, when she knows he is at liberty, her obstinacy will increase, and we may find it doubly difficult to subdue her."

"Still, we must not be daunted, my lord," observed Alberti; "but it strikes me there has been more than one engaged in this act of treachery."

"It is a daring deed," said Bianchi; "and is well worthy of the brigand chief, Massaroni."

"True," coincided the count, "and who knows but it is to him we are indebted for the success of this infernal plot? There are few but him who would have undertaken such a hazardous task."

"I will be revenged," ejaculated the prince determinedly, "though it cost me half my fortune to obtain it. As for the beggar Clairville, I have nothing to fear from him; he is powerless to work me any mischief; but I will never rest until I have him once more secure. Oh, how Melina will exult when she hears of his escape."

"But it cannot benefit her, my lord," returned the count, "if you still remain firm in your determination, and the promises you have held out to me."

"And have you any reason to doubt that I will do so, my lord?" demanded Bianchi.

"I have not, your highness."

"In spite of every obstacle that may be thrown in the way, Melina shall become your wife, at the expiration of the time I have allowed her to prepare herself."

"Enough, your highness," returned the count, "I am satisfied; for I know I can depend on your word."

"You may. But to think I should be thus foiled when I thought I had the presumptuous Clairville securely in my power."

"It is indeed most vexatious, my lord; but I trust that he will not long be suffered to escape us; and if he is, he cannot thwart the designs we have in view respecting your beauteous but scornful niece."

"He cannot! he dare not attempt it."

"Let her but once become my bride," added Alberti, "and my most sanguine hopes will be fully realized, and I shall have no apprehension for the future results."

"Come, my lord," said the prince, "we will away to the castle and make further inquiries into the particulars of this unfortunate affair, and give such instructions as may suggest themselves for the recovery of the fugitives."

The count readily assented, and they quitted the villa together. From one of the men who had brought the news to the villa, Floretta learnt the particulars of the escape of Clairville, and knowing the gratification it would afford her, she instantly conveyed it to her mistress. Melina stared at her with an expression of incredulity, and could scarcely trust herself to believe the evidence of her senses.

"Escaped!" she repeated, clasping her hands vehemently together, and tears of gratitude starting to her eyes; "my beloved Florio once more at liberty, and rescued from the cruel and unmerited fate with which he was threatened? Can it be possible?—Oh, God! how fervently do I return my thanks to Thee for this! I beseech Thee to preserve him from all future danger, and to bring his enemies to relent. But to whom is he indebted for his deliverance, Floretta?"

"From all that has appeared at present, to his jailor only, Signora; but I think that there must have been others connected with the plot."

"Yes, it is not improbable," coincided Melina; "but whither can he have directed his steps? And shall I never hear from him again?"

"Oh, yes, my lady," returned Floretta. "depend upon it you will, and that he will contrive some means of communicating with you secretly when he has reached a place of safety."

"Alas!" sighed Melina, "that would be only a melancholy consolation, for my uncle, now that he has escaped, will be certain to be only exasperated to persevere the more resolutely in his cruel designs; and I can see no possibility of abandoning the fate which is in store for me. The Count Alberti is insensible to every feeling of humanity, forbearance, or honour; and can I look upon him in the character of my future husband with any other sentiment than one of the most unmitigated horror?"

"I cannot wonder at your feelings, my dear signora," said her attendant; "but I would yet encourage the hope that something will still occur to prevent the fears you at present, with so much reason, entertain from being realized."

"I hourly seek to do so," replied Melina; "but find that it is impossible. But a month, but one short month, my uncle has given me to make up my mind, and then if I still refuse to yield to his stern and unnatural decree, he has threatened to force me to the altar with the Count Alberti."

"I cannot bring my mind to believe that his highness will persist in acting with such cruelty."

"Alas, have I not, Floretta, exhausted all my powers of eloquence to move him to compassion in vain? I see no hope unless Providence should interpose to save me. But are the prince and Alberti now in the villa?"

"They are not, signora," answered Floretta; "they quitted it together a few moments before I came to you."

"No doubt to give instructions for the pursuit of Florio," observed Melina.

"Probably so, my lady."

"God grant that their efforts may be unsuccessful, and that the unfortunate Clairville will be able to reach some place of security, and that he may be able to find fortitude to endure with patience the cruel fate to which he is exposed. Alas!—alas! I feel too well convinced that we are never destined to meet again; and to what may he not be driven by the intensity of his despair? He is also poor and friendless; and how will he be able to struggle against the vicissitudes and persecutions of the world?"

"Do not encourage these dismal thoughts, signora," remarked Floretta, "which can only have the effect of preventing you from meeting the trials that may yet be in store for you with the firmness they require. It must afford you the greatest consolation to know that Signor Clairville is again at liberty; and I would fain inspire you with the hope that you will, ere long, meet again, and under much more gratifying and happy circumstances than any which you have lately experienced."

Melina shook her head, and sighed deeply;

but it was in vain that she sought to indulge in the same feelings which her attendant had expressed. To know that Florio had escaped from the power of his enemies was a great relief to her mind; but still she was in a state of the most agonizing and insupportable anx-iety and suspense, to imagine what would, in future, become of him, and whither we could direct his steps—where hope to find that consolation which his deeply lacerated bosom so much needed. The prince would be goaded still more on, by a feeling of disappointment and

MELINA READING FLORIO CLAIRVILLE'S LETTER.

revenge, to put the threats he had uttered against her into operation; and situated as she was, she saw no prospect of being able to extricate herself from the cruel and revolting fate which was impending over her. These meditations had occurred to her on Floretta being compelled to leave her to attend to some particular business; but she was suddenly aroused from them by her return, and she could see, in a minute, that she had some message of a disagreeable nature to deliver to her.

"Have my uncle and the count returned?" inquired Melina, eagerly.

"They have, signora," replied Floretta; "and his highness desires to see you immediately."

"Alas! in what an unfit condition of mind am I to meet them!" sighed Melina; "had they the least spark of delicacy or feeling, they would excuse me."

"They would, my lady," coincided her attendant, "but it would only excite their anger should you venture to decline. Take courage, and it will soon be over, and may terminate much more satisfactory than you anticipate."

"Oh, no," returned her mistress; "I cannot expect that; I should only be flattering myself with false hopes, were I to do so. But I will endeavour to muster courage to brave the worst, and may Heaven support me throughout the painful trial."

To this prayer Floretta fervently responded; and Melina, collecting all the firmness she could, leaning on the arm of her attendant, bent her way to the apartment in which the prince and Alberti were seated. They quickly arose on her entrance, and her uncle conducted her to a seat near himself and the count with a great assumption of kindness, which she felt too certain was not sincere. She just ventured to raise her eyes towards him and Alberti, and she noticed, in an instant, the extreme agitation of their manner, which did not at all surprise her, under the circumstances. The count made some observations to her, which she was too bewildered and agitated to understand or reply to; and then her uncle turning to her, said,—

"You are still pale and timid, Melina; why do you persist in this ridiculous weakness, which can have no other effect than to make you miserable? However, I sent for you to make you acquainted with a circumstance which, no doubt, will contribute to your happiness."

As he uttered these words a malicious expression passed over the countenance of the prince, and it was quite evident that the most powerful feelings of rage and disappointment were labouring in his breast.

"My lord," replied Melina, in an agitated voice, "I know all you would communicate; why, then, torture me with those sarcastic observations?"

"Oh, you have heard of the escape of the beggar, Clairville, have you?" said the prince; "'tis well, and no doubt you are exulting at the circumstance. But do not flatter yourself with any false hopes, for, depend upon it, that ere long, perhaps before many hours have elapsed, he shall be again in my power; moreover, his escape will not at all alter the determination I have come to respecting you; the Count Alberti——"

"My lord," interrupted the blushing girl, her fair bosom at the same time swelling with indignation; "this is cruel;—I will not listen to it, in the presence of the Count Alberti, who has frequently heard my sentiments regarding him. You, whom I have always, till now, been accustomed to look up to as my best, my only earthly friend, to take a delight in torturing me thus?—oh, it is unnatural—it is monstrous.—Suffer me to retire, I beseech you!"

"Beauteous Melina," said the Count, in his most insinuating tones, and stifling his rage as well as he could; "you do me a great wrong in entertaining these false and unmerited prejudices against me. The sentiments I experience towards you are of the purest, the most fervent description; they have long been implanted in my breast, and nothing can ever eradicate them. Why, then, treat me with such freezing coldness and disrespect? why—"

"Hold! my lord!" cried Melina, her fine eyes flashing with resentment; "this language is hateful, insulting to me, and I will not listen to it. I have never deceived you, or held out hopes to you, which are so repugnant to my feelings, and, by Heaven, there is no fate, however dreadful, which I am not fully prepared to encounter, rather than submit to an union with you."

Alberti bit his lips, and the prince frowned with rage, as Melina gave utterance to these words.

"Girl," exclaimed the latter, "dare you, in my presence, give expression to language so bold, so insulting, and so disobedient? Beware! Beware!"

"It is your cruelty and injustice, my lord, that compels me to speak my mind boldly as I have done. I am but woman; but by the just God above, I will not tamely submit to be sacrificed to a man who does not, and never can, possess my affections. You may force me to the altar, but I will sooner perish than give utterance to those vows which would bind me to a fate so horrible. Spirit of my sainted mother! I solemnly invoke your protection!"

Overpowered by her feelings, the poor girl sank insensible in her seat. When she recovered, it was a great relief to her to find that she was in her own apartment, and that Floretta was anxiously watching her.

"Where are they?" she demanded, in a voice of extreme agitation; "were are my uncle and the Count Alberti?"

"Do not agitate yourself, my dear signora," replied Floretta; his highness and the count have again quitted the house.

"Oh, thank Heaven for that," ejaculated Melina, fervently, "and may it be long ere they return. Oh, Floretta, you can little imagine the cruelty and insults I have been exposed to at that meeting. These frequent trials are more than I can find fortitude to support; and yet the prince, my uncle, seems to exult in my misery rather than to take pity on me, and to relieve me from the importunities of the count. Alas! alas! what will become of me, when I am thus inhumanly persecuted?——

"Compose your feelings, I pray, signora," replied her attendant; "I need not assure you how deeply I sympathise with you, and how much I abhor the obstinate perseverance of the Count Alberti in his hateful suit."

"Encouraged as he is by the prince," sighed Melina, "can it be wondered that his boldness every day increases?—And what power have I to defend myself from him? Floretta, this is more than my strength can endure; would to Heaven that death might put an end to my sufferings, for I see no other prospect but shame and misery before me."

"For goodness' sake do not talk thus, my lady," said the kind-hearted Floretta; "I trust that, however threatening and cheerless your prospects may now seem to be, you may yet live to experience many years of happiness."

"You are now my only friend, Floretta, with the exception of the unfortunate Clairville," said Melina, affectionately; "to you I make no scruple to confide my whole thoughts, for I know that you ever sympathise with me in all my feelings, and that it is your most anxious wish to see me happy."

"You do me no more than justice, my dear signora," returned Floretta, "and I feel highly honoured and flattered by the good opinion you are pleased to entertain of me. God knows how delighted I should be were it in my power to serve you to the extent of my heart's wish."

"I believe you, my good girl; but you will not leave me to-day? I should go distracted were I to be left to the misery of my own reflections."

"I will remain with you, signora, as is my duty," answered Floretta, "and I hope to Heaven that I may yet be able to tranquillise your feelings."

Melina thanked her, and remained silent for a few moments; but at length the agitation of her bosom was considerably abated, and she then related to her companion all that had taken place at the interview between her and the prince and Alberti, to which the faithful Floretta listened with feelings of disgust and indignation.

"I cannot conceive, my lady," observed her attendant, "how his highness can find the heart to expose you to such insults; and any one who has had an opportunity of observing his previous affectionate conduct towards you, might be lead to imagine that his reason had become disordered."

"They would indeed," said Melina; "but how terrible and alarming is the delusion (if I may use so mild a term) under which he now labours; and to what frightful consequences may it not lead? Heaven knows with what pleasure and solicitude I have ever, and would continue to submit to anything that my duty should demand from me; but I cannot, will not, yield to that from which my very nature recoils with horror!"

"No, my lady," said Floretta, "it would be monstrous for you to do so; and Providence will, I trust, give you strenth to resist it to the last. Had the Count Alberti the least sense of shame, of feeling, or becoming pride about him, he would at once abandon the hopeless contest, and seek some other damsel who might feel disposed to receive his addresses with a favourable eye. But thus obstinately to persist in persecuting you, shows that he is a man in whose breast every principle of right has become extinguished. How the prince, your uncle, can have become so prepossessed in favour of him, is a mystery which I find it utterly impossible to solve. One would have thought that his cruel conduct towards the unfortunate Olympia would have been quite sufficient to prejudice his mind against him."

"Yes," returned Melina, "and what surprises me more than all is, that not only does my uncle treat Alberti's conduct in that respect with perfect levity and indifference, but he attempts to exculpate him from all blame. Surely the count's behaviour towards his hapless victim and her innocent offspring, is sufficient to stamp him with the character of a villain of the most heartless description."

"It is, signora; and all lovers of honour and virtue must shun him with loathing and disgust. The prince can never, when he is once more aroused to reason, think of sacrificing you to a man who has so basely, so grossly, committed himself. His feelings of pride and self-respect can never permit him to do so."

"Ah, Floretta," sighed her mistress, "fain would I endeavour to think as you have now expressed yourself; but after all that has taken place, and the threats which my uncle has held out towards me, I cannot. The count possesses the most extraordinary influence over him, the cause of which I am at a perfect loss to imagine, but which Alberti will not fail to take every advantage of; and thus surrounded by danger, what room have I for hope?"

"Something will take place, my lady, I feel certain of it," answered Floretta, "to avert the dangers you now apprehend. Be of good cheer, and you will yet triumph."

But the day passed away, and when Floretta retired from the presence of her mistress, she left her in a most disconsolate state of mind. If anything had been wanting to convince her that her uncle would show no clemency toward her, but that by some strange infatuation he had determined to sacrifice her 'to the count Alberti, it would have been in the harsh, (and she wished to believe) the unconsidered observations of the prince; but there was no reason for her to suppose anything of the kind; and consequently she gave herself up to the feelings which such unfortunate circumstances naturally engendered in her breast. What would she not have given to have known the present place of her love'r retreat, and to have had the opportunity of communicating with him? She felt that she would have been imbued with new strength and fortitude to encounter the troubles which might be in store for her, and that the knowledge she so much craved would have enabled her more effectually to resist the importunities and the persecutions of the prince and Alberti. The means by which Clairville had effected his escape from the strong prison in which he had been confined, for some time perplexed her brain; but at length she could not help considering that there must have been some powerful influence to induce the jailer to run a risk which not only involved the loss of his situation, but his own life; and when she recalled to her mind how destitute Clairville was of any friends in the world, the idea naturally suggested itself to her from all that she had heard, that Massaroni, the brigand chief, had something to do with the business. In spite of the lawless character of Massaroni's acts, Melina, especially after what she had seen of him on the memorable night of the festival at Villa Rosa, when his wife was placed in so much jeopardy, could not help feeling some degree of respect for him, independent of the deep interest which his romantic exploits, and the mystery in which his history was involved; and his name never occurred to her thoughts but it was coupled with a feeling of the most extraordinary nature, and for which she could not account. Thus harassed by conflicting thoughts, Melina at length sought her pillow, but her rest was disturbed by visions of the most painful nature, and it was a relief to her when she awoke and found the golden beams of the sun streaming in at the casement of her chamber. She arose with a heavy heart, but immediately offered up her prayers to the Supreme to protect her lover from all danger, and to render the harsh and cruel designs of the prince and Alberti abortive. Having thus given vent to her feelings, she was more composed, and sought to await the issue of her destiny with fortitude, patience, and resignation.

CHAPTER XXXIII.

THE ROUTE OF THE BRIGANDS FROM THE PRISON. CLAIRVILLE ONCE MORE IN THE MOUNTAIN RETREAT. OLYMPIA AND OTTAVIA. THE DAWN OF REASON.

"Triumph! triumph! triumph!
    Ever crowns the brigand's career;
He laughs at every danger,
    He's a stranger to all fear!
Triumph! triumph! triumph!
    Must e'er fall to the brigand's share.
        Massaroni! Massaroni!
        Evviva! Massaroni!

Victory! victory! victory!
    Shall ever crown his daring deeds;
Our mountain chief is fearless,
    And no mortal power heeds.
Victory! victory! victory!
    Fortune to him concedes!
        Massaroni! Massaroni!
        Evviva! Massaroni!"

SUCH was the rude chorus, shouted by the brigands, as they pursued their way through a wild tract of country, and where there was nothing but the echoes to reply to them. In such a spot their unstudied notes had a peculiar and impressive effect, and Clairville could not but for the moment feel his mind diverted from the melancholy subjects that had previously engrossed it, and he listened with a sort of melancholy pleasure to the mirth of his unpolished companions. The moon was at intervals completely hidden behind dense clouds, and they proceeded on their devious way in total darkness; but Massaroni kept himself close by Florio's side, and by every means in his power sought to inspire him with hope and cheerfulness.

"We are now more than three leagues from the castle," he observed, "and perfectly safe beyond the reach of pursuit. By the time yon silvery moon shall have retreated from the brighter beams of the golden orb of day, we shall have gained my home in the mountains; and once there, I can set, as I have repeatedly done, every force that may be sent against me at defiance. Courage, my friend Clairville: it shall yet be your turn to triumph over your enemies."

"Massaroni," said Florio, "how much am I indebted to you for the extraordinary interest you take in my fate! Alas! I have no reward to offer for such disinterested kindness."

"Hold, Signor Clairville," remarked the brigand chief; "you much mistake the character of Allesandro Massaroni if you imagine that he requires any reward for performing his duty towards his fellow-creatures. You should know sufficient to judge better of me by this time. I knew you be be the innocent victim of oppression, and that your life would be sacrificed to the malice of your enemies unless some one speedily interposed to save you; I did not forget the service you had rendered me on the night of the festival at Villa Rosa, and I should have been unworthy of the name I bear had I not ventured everything in return, to rescue you from the fate which was impending over you. The Count Alberti, through the treachery of one of my band, had escaped from my power, and I knew, therefore, that there was no time to be lost, not only to save you, but she you love, I firmly believe, far dearer than your own existence; I, therefore, adopted my plans with all the expedition that was possible. How far they have succeeded you have seen; and I now assure you, and you may believe me when I say that Massaroni is no empty boaster, not only shall the fair Signora Melina be released from the hateful importunities of the unprincipled Alberti, and the persecution and tyranny of her uncle, the imbecile Prince Bianchi, but she shall ultimately become your bride. The brigand chief promises you this, and you may rest satisfied that, as sure as yon bright moon now shines down upon us, what he promises he can and will fulfil to the very letter."

"Massaroni," said Clairville, gazing at him with a mingled look of astonishment and admiration, " you are a most remarkable man."

"I am a most unfortunate one," replied the brigand; " but no matter; we will not talk of present sorrows, but of future prospects of happiness and triumph."

"Massaroni," returned Clairville, cordially grasping his hand, " it would be a waste of words, and I am likewise convinced, an insult to your feelings, were I to attempt to express my gratitude for all the inestimable services you have rendered me as a stranger; the promises you have held out, also inspire my bosom with hope; but may I inquire of you how it is that you have been enabled to effect my deliverance?"

"I had no sooner heard of your unjust confinement," replied the brigand, " than I was determined your restoration to liberty should be accomplished at all hazards. Whether I was too sanguine or not in my expectations, I think has been sufficiently proved. The escape of the Count Alberti urged me still further on, for revenge stimulated me, and I was fully determined to carry my plans into effect, emboldened as I was by the success which has hitherto crowned my efforts. The discomfiture of the troops sent against me, by me and my brave band, further encouraged me to proceed, and I resolved to lose no time in putting my designs into operation. To make an attack upon the prison, I knew would be attended with very little chance of success, so I had nothing to do but to use stratagem. I placed spies in the vicinity of your confinement, and at length one of the persons employed by

the authorities of the castle was accosted by my lieutenant, Rubaldo. They instantly recognized each other. It was Jacomo, your jailer, who had formerly received great service from me and my band; in fact, to us he had been indebted for his life. Gratitude, and the promise of reward, quickly had the desired effect; besides, notwithstanding the repulsive manners he may have evinced towards you, he felt disgusted with his situation, and had long been anxious to abandon it, if the opportunity should present itself. Our plans were soon arranged accordingly, and what has followed you are acquainted with. Once more, Signor Clairville, I have to congratulate you on your escape from the power of your enemies; and if you will only place confidence in my friendship, depend upon it that I will ultimately bring about the realization of all you can wish."

"Thanks, thanks, Massaroni," said Florio, grasping once more the brigand's hand, " for the interest you take in my unfortunate destiny; but alas! I fear that my troubles are not yet half at an end; and that, although I have at present escaped from the power of the Prince Bianchi, I shall never be destined to meet my beloved Melina again."

Nonsense, Clairville," returned Massaroni. "Do not entertain such melancholy ideas. Cospetto, man! I promise you, that not only shall you behold the Signora Melina again, but that, in spite of all the designs of the Prince Bianchi and Alberti, she shall ultimately become your bride."

"My bride!" ejaculated Clairville; "transporting thought! I dare not flatter myself by encouraging such a hope; it would be presumptuous in me to do so."

"Indeed it would not," replied the brigand chief; " on the contrary, it would be weakness on your part to give yourself up to despair."

"Alas!" sighed Florio, " how can I do otherwise? Now that I have escaped, the prince, her uncle, will but urge on her union with the detested count; and totally unprotected as she is, what power has she to resist?"

"I tell you again, Signor Clairville, it shall never be," said Massaroni; "I will have my spies constantly in the neighbourhood of the Villa Rosa, who will give me immediate notice of all that takes place; and fear not but I will adopt every means to avert the evil you apprehend. Let that assurance suffice you, for the brigand chief ever performs what he promises."

"Well, Massaroni, I will place every reliance on you; but alas! I fear that it will never be in my power to reward you for the friendship, the disinterested friendship, you have evinced in so disinterested a manner towards me, and the risks you have run for my sake."

"Psha! Clairville," returned his companion, impatiently; "why talk to me thus? Think you that Allesandro Massaroni requires any reward for performing a good action? You do not know him sufficiently yet; but when you become better acquainted with his character, I am convinced that you will not entertain any such ideas."

"Pardon me, my friend, for such I must, indeed, call you, if the agitation of my feelings do not allow me to express myself as I ought to do; I know you to be noble and generous, and I therefore resign myself entirely to your will."

"Enough! enough! You shall find, signor, that I will not abuse your confidence. I deeply regretted your abrupt departure from my mountain abode, though I duly appreciated the cause; and your resolute refusal to reveal the place of my retreat, has proved to me that you are a man of honour in every sense of the word."

"Massaroni," said Florio, "you may believe me when I say that I would have perished first."

"I do believe you," replied the brigand. "I admire you more than ever for it. But come, let us proceed on our journey. I have a surprise for you when we reach the termination of it."

"What mean you?" demanded Clairville, eagerly.

"Signora Olympia and her child——"

"Ah! what of them?"

"They have escaped from the confinement in which the villain Count Alberti had placed them, and are at present under my protection."

"I am much gratified to hear this," said Florio, "for I deeply sympathise in the misfortunes of the much-wronged Olympia, and cannot help thinking that while she continues to exist, she will present a great obstacle to the union between Alberti and Melina."

"It is my determination that she shall do so," replied Massaroni, "and I am also resolved that he shall yet redress her wrongs, as much as is in his power."

The brigand chief then related to him all those particulars of the deliverance of Olympia and her child with which the reader is already acquainted, and to which Clairville paid the most profound attention. They then proceeded to some further distance on their route without entering into any conversation; but the mind of Florio was deeply occupied by his own thoughts, and various and conflicting were the conjectures he formed as to the probable results of the future. On the sincerity of Massaroni, he placed the firmest reliance; and when he took into consideration all that he had observed, he could not help encouraging some degree of hope. What a relief to the mind of Melina would his escape be; but how great would be the rage and disappointment of the Prince Bianchi and the Count Alberti when they dis-

covered it. He could well imagine everything, and the torture to which Melina would be exposed; for the prince, although she was not to blame, would be certain to vent all his spleen upon her; however, he trusted that Heaven would give her fortitude to support it in a becoming manner, and that all the nefarious designs they had against her would yet be defeated.

"You are silent, my young friend," at last observed Massaroni; "but I can find no difficulty in imagining the thoughts that are passing in your mind. Do not despair, signor, for, depend upon it that the time is not far distant when all your doubts and anxieties will be removed, and you will be received as the acknowledged suitor of she to whom your affections are devoted."

"Would to Heaven that I could think so," said Clairville; "but the pride of the Prince Bianchi will never suffer him to permit my addresses to his peerless niece. I am poor and friendless, and how can I aspire to one of her rank and station?"

"Banish such thoughts from your mind," returned the brigand chief, "for trust me that all such difficulties may, and shall, be surmounted."

"You are sanguine, Massaroni."

"I am, and you will find that my ideas will be realized. Courage, man—courage, man—for you have nothing to apprehend."

"Would that I could see Melina, or get a letter conveyed to her," said Clairville.

"That may yet be done," observed Massaroni.

"Ah! your words inspire me with hope; for, oh, how anxious will Melina naturally be to know what has become of me."

"We will take of that anon," said the brigand, "and I dare say we shall find but very little difficulty in accomplishing your wishes."

Clairville, by these assurances, felt lighter at heart, and they proceeded on their way with increased speed.

"Have we much farther to travel?" asked Florio.

"Yes—several leagues," answered his companion; "for, in order to baffle pursuit, I have taken a circuitous and unfrequented route, or we should have arrived at the place of our destination by this time."

The moon was now completely hidden behind black and ponderous clouds; the wind began to bellow in fitful gusts, and a few heavy drops of rain descended.

"We shall have a heavy storm presently," remarked Massaroni; "this is unfortunate, as there is no place of temporary shelter at hand; but we must push on our way."

He had scarcely given utterance to these words, when the storm commenced in earnest; the clouds discharged their contents in overwhelming torrents, and the wind blew a perfect hurricane. The part of the country they were traversing, too, afforded not the smallest means of shelter from the fury of the tempest, and the prospect before them was one of the most dismal description. However, they urged on their steeds as well as they could, and proceeded at a most rapid rate on their journey. They were quickly drenched to the skin, but the storm continued to rage with unabated violence, and Florio, from his long confinement, and the anxiety of mind he had endured, felt it most severely; in fact, he was so much exhausted that he could with difficulty retain his seat in the saddle, although he struggled as much as he could against the horrors of the season, and Massaroni, who was inured to such scenes, tried all in his power to maintain his fortitude.

"If we continue at the rate we are at present travelling," he remarked, "in little more than an hour we shall arrive at the end of our journey, and then we shall soon find the means of counteracting the effects of this tempest."

They had not proceeded much further, when the storm greatly abated; and at length, almost as suddenly as it had commenced, it abruptly ceased altogether, and the moon once more darting from behind the clouds, shed her refulgent beams on all around.

"This is fortunate," said Massaroni. "I thought it was too violent to last long. We have made the best use of our time, and see, the majestic mountains which inclose my retreat, appear in sight. Ride forward with all speed, Rubaldo, and apprise them of our approach. Maria, my wife, will no doubt be most anxious to know the result of our expedition.,'

Rubaldo spurred on his steed, and was soon out of sight. Clairville felt his spirits revive at the near approach to the end of their journey, although he was wet and miserable, and stood much in need of repose after the extraordinary exertions he had undergone. He bore up against everything, however, manfully; and as they rapidly approached nearer the lofty mountains, care and anxiety were in a great measure banished from his mind. So extraordinary and unexpected was all that had happened in the last few hours, that he could scarcely believe in its reality; and he could never feel sufficiently grateful to the brigand chief for the services he had rendered him, and the many and great risks he had run to accomplish them. The observations he had made use of, also inspired him with hope, and by the time they were winding their way among the mountains, Clairville felt that lightness of spirits he had not experienced for many a day. Through the narrow defiles they wended their way; and when they had reached a certain point, Massaroni applied his whistle to his

lips, and gave the usual signal, which was immediately answered, and the next moment they had arrived at the entrance to the cavern, where one of the brigands was awaiting with a flaring torch to light them on their way. Clairville having dismounted from his horse, took the proffered arm of Massaroni, and by him was conducted along the various passages to the spacious cavern where the brigand's wife, and several of the band, were waiting to receive them.

"Husband, Massaroni!" ejaculated Maria Grazie, advancing joyfully towards him, "you have returned, then, and in safety."

"Ay, Maria," replied the brigand, returning her embrace; "kind fortune, you see, has not yet deserted us."

"The saints be praised!" ejaculated Maria, solemnly.

"But have you not one word of welcome for our young friend, Maria?" demanded her husband.

"Signor Clairville," said Maria, "I once more welcome you to our cavernous retreat, and fervently congratulate you on your deliverance from that unjust incarceration you have lately experienced."

Clairville bent one knee to the ground, and pressing the hand of Maria Grazie respectfully to his lips, he replied—

"Signora, I think I need scarcely assure you how duly I appreciate the kind solicitude you express towards me. To you and your husband, the humble Florio Clairville owes a debt of gratitude he feels it impossible he can ever adequately repay; but he will endeavour by his future conduct to prove to you how truly sensible he is of the vast benefits he has received at your hands."

"Enough, signor," said Maria; "neither myself nor Massaroni require more."

"Retire, comrades," commanded Massaroni, addressing himself to the brigands; "the time is advanced, and you need rest after the fatigue you have undergone. See that the entrances to the cavern are perfectly secure."

The brigands obeyed, and departed, singing the first verse of their favourite chorus—

"Triumph! triumph! triumph!
    Ever crowns the brigand's career;
He laughs at every danger,
    He's a stranger to all fear.
Triumph! triumph! triumph!
    Must e'er be the brigand's share.
    Massaroni! Massaroni!
    Evviva! Massaroni!"

"And now, Signor Clairville," said the brigand chief, conducting him to the table, on which ample store of provisions were spread; "after you have partaken of some refreshments, I think it will be as well for us also to separate, for you must be weary, and a few hours repose will probably revive you."

Florio would fain have excused himself, for indeed he felt in no humour to eat ; but Massaroni and his wife pressed him so hard, that he was forced to comply, and he partook but sparingly of that which was placed before him. The repast over, Clairville bade Maria adieu, till they should meet again, and was then conducted by Massaroni to the same place he had occupied when he was there before ; here the brigand chief bade him farewell, and without giving utterance to another word, left him to his repose, and returned to the cavern in which he had left his wife, and to whom he related all that had happened to him while he was absent on the expedition.

"The business has been managed very well, Massaroni, and with your usual skill,", she remarked, when he had concluded ; "and I am glad you did not come into collision with any of the enemy ; for, on such a spot, and unprotected by our mountain barriers, the consequences might have been most disastrous."

"Ah, I feared them not," replied the brigand.

"I know you did not, Massaroni," said his wife ; "but is it not as well, at all times, not to rush madly into danger ?"

"True—true."

"And neither the prince nor Count Alberti can have the least suspicion that Florio Clairville owes his deliverance to you, and that he is now under your protection," said Maria.

"They cannot," answered her husband ; "but I will soon take good care to make them acquainted with it."

"And of what use will that be ?"

"It will gratify my revenge."

"I think it is best avoided."

"Why so ?"

"Because it may enable them to frustrate your future designs."

"Oh, I do not entertain any apprehensions of that sort."

"Is it not more than probable, now that Clairville has escaped, the Prince Bianchi, in a spirit of revenge, may hurry on the union of Signora Melina and the Count Alberti ?" asked Maria.

"Why," replied Massaroni ; "it certainly is not at all unlikely ; but I have my spies in the neighbourhood of Villa Rosa, who will give me timely notice of all that takes place there ; and should he attempt to do so, I will adopt immediate steps not only to prevent him, but also to rescue Melina from his tyrannical power. and to restore her to the arms of her lover."

"Such an attempt would be surrounded by the most imminent danger," observed his wife, with a look of dissatisfaction.

"Such dangers, I am certain, I should be able easily to surmount," returned Massaroni ;

"I have pledged my word to Clairville, and by all my hopes, the fair and gentle Signora Melina shall never be sacrificed to such a heartless villain as the Count Alberti."

"I would warn you, Massaroni, to act with due precaution," said Maria.

"You need not caution me, Maria," he replied ; "do I not ever act with prudence ?"

"True."

"Enough then."

"And yet, Massaroni," said his wife, after a pause, "it appears to me, after all, that you have chosen a hazardous and unprofitable game."

"Do you not sympathise with Signora Melina and her lover, Maria ?"

"I do."

"Do you not detest and despise the Prince Bianchi and his worthy friend, the Count Alberti ?"

"Most heartily."

"How then can you consider the course I have adopted an unprofitable one ?" demanded Massaroni ; "shall I not be serving Melina and her lover, and at the same time, gratifying my revenge against our bitterest enemies, the Prince Bianchi, and Count Alberti."

"I cannot deny that you will," replied Maria, "if you succeed."

"Succeed ?" replied Massaroni, "what is there to prevent me ? I will manage my plans with such nice ingenuity that it will be impossible for them to discover them, until it will be too late to defeat them. I am yet determined to wring the heart of the proud prince, who is so anxious to work my destruction, to distraction ; and by all my hopes, I will not rest till I have done so. But how fares the Signora Olympia ?"

"As well as can be expected," replied Maria.

"That is well ; and Ottavia ?"

"She remains in much the same condition ; and the man who so suddenly crossed the path of her and old Montaldi, still continues to haunt her imagination."

"There is a mystery about that which I find it impossible to solve," observed the brigand chief ; "from what Montaldi has told us, it is evident that the unfortunate Ottavia and this stranger knew each other, and that he is in some way connected with her melancholy history."

"I have not the least doubt of it," coincided Maria ; "but come, had we not better retire to rest ?"

Massaroni replied in the affirmative, and the brigand and his wife departed to that part of their mountain retreat in which they reposed. The feelings of Clarville were of the most varied and intense description, when he found himself alone ; but hope once more sprung up in his breast, and he became comparatively more tranquil. He fervently offered up his supplications to Heaven for its merciful interposition to save Melina from that fate which seemed so alarmingly impending over her; and though it might never be their fate to come together, at least to prevent her from being sacrificed to such a thoroughly-heartless and unprincipled villain as the Count Alberti. He pictured to himself the rage and disappointment the Prince Bianchi and Alberti would experience when they found that he had escaped; and he could not help at times fearing

MALVOLIO BROUGHT BEFORE THE BRIGAND CHIEF.

that in revenge they might be induced to precipitate Melina's fate; and if they did, her destruction would be inevitable. Still he could not believe that the Almighty would desert her in the hour of her need, or that the prince could become so entirely callous to every feeling of humanity and honour as to persist in his cruel designs. There was one promise which Massaroni had made him, which afforded him considerable consolation, and that was to get a letter conveyed from him to Melina; and he had not the least doubt that he would keep his word, but that he would readily hit upon the means of doing so, without running any particular danger. Oh, how anxious he was to have an opportunity of once more communicating to her his thoughts and feelings; and he was the more desirous of doing so, because he thought it might be the means in a great measure of soothing the anguish of her mind, and give her fortitude to support the fresh trials to which she might yet be subjected. At length, quite exhausted, Clairville sought the couch prepared for him, and soon sunk into a calm and refreshing sleep. Early in the morning Olympia was aroused by hearing a knock at her chamber-door, and then the voice of Maria Grazie requesting to be admitted, as she had something to communicate to her. Olympia immediately opened the door, and the brigand's wife entered and inquired kindly after her health, for Olympia had been rather indisposed on the night before. She replied that she felt much better after a night's rest, and desired to know what it was that Maria had to communicate to her.

"You were aware of the expedition which Massaroni had gone upon?" said Maria.

Olympia replied in the affirmative.

"He has returned," observed Maria.

"And what success has he met with?" asked Olympia, eagerly.

"All that could be wished," was the reply. "Signor Clairville is now an inmate of these caverns."

"Oh, I am most gratified to hear that," said Olympia, "for it will serve in a great measure to foil the designs of Alberti and the Prince Bianchi, and, I trust, inspire Signora Melina with fresh courage to resist their importunities."

"It may do so," coincided the brigand's wife; and she then related the means by which Massaroni had effected the escape of Florio, to which Olympia listened with much attention and satisfaction.

"The prince," remarked Olympia, when Maria had concluded, "must have become destitute of every feeling of shame and humanity, if he still remains inexorable and compels his fair and gentle niece to become the wife of one who is so totally unworthy of her as the Count Alberti. Alas! ought not his cruel treatment of me be sufficient to drive him from the pale of all decent society?"

"It should," returned Maria, "and depend upon it that justice will overtake him yet."

"May Heaven pardon him," fervently ejaculated Olympia, "and bring him to a due sense of the crimes he has committed; but God knows, notwithstanding all the injuries he has inflicted on me, I entertain no vindictive feeling towards him."

"Your sentiments do you honour, signora," said the brigand's wife; "Alberti deserves no such clemency at your hands. Even now, I am convinced, if he could once again get you in his power, he would not fail to wreak his vengeance on you and your innocent offspring."

"Alas! I fear," said Olympia, "that your ideas are too correct."

"But come, signora, the morning repast awaits us, and I suppose you have no objection to be introduced to Signor Clairville, who I believe to be sincerely your friend, and that he deeply sympathises with you in your misfortunes."

"I do believe he does," returned Olympia, "and I feel most earnestly grateful to him for his kindness, and hope that something may yet occur to bring about his happiness, and that of the unfortunate lady to whom he is so devotedly attached."

"To that wish I fervently respond," said Maria; and they then retired to the cavern, where the morning meal was prepared, and where Massaroni and Florio were awaiting to receive them.

Clairville greeted his fellow-unfortunate with the utmost solicitude and kindness; and the first ceremony of introduction being over, they sat down and conversed with much greater freedom of manners. Florio had never been in the society of Olympia more than once or twice before, but it was impossible that he should feel otherwise than deeply interested in her fate, lovely as she was, possessed of such rare intrinsic qualities; and when he remembered the unmerited and irremediable injuries she had received at the hands of his most implacable enemy, Count Alberti, he joined Massaroni in doing all in his power to console her, and to inspire her with the hope that the time would come when justice would be rendered her, and she would be restored to happiness and that position in society she was so well formed to embellish; and Olympia did not fail to return every suitable acknowledgment for the kind commiseration he was pleased to profess towards her. The morning meal was scarcely disposed of when Montaldi and Ottavia were announced, and were immediately ushered into their presence, and Montaldi greeted Clairville with the utmost respect, and offered him his warmest congratulations on his deliverance from confinement, and which Florio received and acknowledged in the most becoming manner. Clairville beheld the unfortunate maniac with the deepest pity, and could not help, in a moment, noticing the extraordinary resemblance that existed between her and Olympia, and which Massaroni had mentioned to him before; but Ottavia did not appear to observe him at all, but immediately on her entrance flew to Olympia, whom she embraced evidently with the greatest delight, and seemed to be totally indifferent to the presence of anybody else.

"Oh, how beautiful and gentle you look this morning," she ejaculated, playfully parting the glossy ringlets of Olympia from her brow; "just as you appeared to me in my dreams last night; when there was sweet music in the air, and angel forms flitted around us, and smiled upon us. I am always dreaming of you, dearest; then wild fears will present themselves to my mind, that they are about to separate me from you, and that we shall never meet again. But you will not suffer them to do that, will you, sweet?"

"No, no, my good Ottavia," replied Olympia, "we will not part; so let that assurance content you."

"There is no one wishes or intends to separate you and Signora Olympia, Ottavia," said Montaldi; "so do not torture youself with any such apprehensions."

"Ha! ha!" laughed the poor maniac wildly, "but do not think to deceive me, for I know more than you imagine. Keep away that frightful man, who after so many years again crossed my path, and stood over me in the silence of the night with his glaring eyes. Let him not come near me, or see her; for ruin, crime, and misery are following ever in his train. She is pure and innocent, and he would be sure to fix upon her as his victim. He would deprive me of her, as he did me of my little innocent. I tell you again that he is a monster! a murderer!"

"Then, my good Ottavia," said Massaroni, kindly, and seizing upon the opportunity when a dawn of reason seemed to flash upon her mind, with the hope of being enabled to obtain some clue to the painful mystery; "if he is indeed the villain you represent him to be, and has inflicted such terrible injuries on you as those to which you have alluded, it is necessary that no means shou'd be left untried for the purpose of bringing him to punishment."

"And who are you," demanded Ottavia, fixing an angry look on Massaroni, and still retaining her place by the side of Olympia, "who are you, who seem to doubt my assertions? Think you I am mad?"

"It is our kind friend, Signor Massaroni," said Montaldi, in a coaxing tone; "who merely wishes you to endeavour to recall your scattered recollections, so that justice may be rendered you, and yourself once more restored to happiness."

"Happiness?" repeated the unfortunate Ottavia, with an hysterical laugh; "who talks to me of happiness when he, my soul's idol, is away? You mock me, because you think me powerless; but beware; for you know not who I am! All the sovereigns of the world do homage to me; and he to whom I am betrothed, and for whom the bridal feast now waits, is the Emperor of all Europe! Ha—ha—ha! bow down, slaves, bow down, and grovel in the dust at my feet!"

As the poor maniac gave utterance to these distracted observations, she buried her face in Olympia's bosom, and seemed to be unconscious of the presence of any other individual. Every one was much affected; and fearful of the effect it might have upon her, they did not offer to disturb her.

"Oh, yes, I am happy! I will be happy!" she said at length, "if you do not part us; but you cannot, you will not, be so cruel as to do so. She has permitted me to call her daughter, have you not, sweetest? And who shall dare to interpose to the contrary?"

"Dear Ottavia," said Olympia, who was deeply moved by her observations; "why distress yourself thus? All here are your friends, and would not for the world separate us from each other."

"Would they not?" cried Ottavia, joyfully, "then I will love them all, and be so very— very happy. And I will introduce them to my lover; you shall listen to the fascination of his conversation, and cease to wonder that I love him so fondly—why I place such implicit confidence in his truth. But the wretches said that he had deceived me; that he had deserted me, and I should never see him more! 'Tis false! They only envied me my felicity! He will be here anon, he will be here to-morrow! To-morrow? ah, me! but what a long time to-morrow is in coming. It seems to me as if I had waited ages for its arrival; but that could only have been a dream. No—no, he will be here!—he will be here!"

"Ottavia," remarked Olympia, in her most gentle and persuasive accents; "I feel convinced that you might recall your scattered recollection, if you were to try. Come—come, compose yourself, and——"

"Let me see," interrupted the maniac, and passing her long thin hands accross her forehead; "but—but it is so many years ago, that it seems like some vision of the imagination. It was a frightful night, ah, I recollect that, which first introduced my lover to me; he was benighted, and sought shelter from the rain and cold in the dwelling of my parents."

"Yes—yes," ejaculated Olympia, with breathless impatience, "and his name was, and the name of your parents——"

Ottavia stared at her vacantly for a moment or two; the faint gleam of reason and recollection vanished again, and she exclaimed—

"No—no, it will not be; it is all gone; I know not what I say; it is so long ago, and I have wandered in such strange places, and been haunted by such wild visions since. Do not chide me, sweetest, for my poor brain wanders."

The few observations she had made in allusion to her melancholy history, had excited the deepest interest in the bosoms of her anxious listeners; but they were only doomed to disappointment, which was rendered the more insupportable under the circumstances, and at the very moment when they had hoped that some light was about to be thrown upon the truth. Ottavia again relapsed into silence, keeping close to Olympia, and gazing earnestly into her face; and they did not think it prudent to interrupt her, fearful of the bad effect it might have upon her. Montaldi and she remained for two or three hours longer at the cavern, and nothing more particular occurred; but when he arose to take his departure, he had the same difficulty as upon every previous occasion to persuade his unfortunate charge to separate from Olympia, whom she earnestly implored might be permitted to accompany her.

"I think," said Clairville, in the course of some observations that followed, "that it is no difficult task to read the dismal history of this unfortunate woman. It is evident that she has been made the victim of some designing and unprincipled villain; and if we can place any faith in the insinuations she threw out, murder has also been committed."

"There can be little doubt of it," coincided the brigand chief, "and this man who appeared so suddenly and unexpectedly before Montaldi and Ottavia, it seems but too probable is the guilty man. The unusual horror which she evinced on beholding him, all but confirms the truth of the supposition. I have a full description of his person from Montaldi, however; and should he be lurking anywhere in this neighbourhood, the persons whom I have on the lookout for him will be certain to detect him, and bring him before me."

"The attachment Ottavia has formed for Signora Olympia is most extraordinary," remarked Clairville; "and the very striking resemblance that exists between them, is not the least remarkable portion of the business. They would pass uncommonly well for mother and daughter."

Olympia felt an unusual and powerful sensation come over her as Florio made use of these observations; and feeling too deeply agitated to enter with any spirit into the conversation, she excused herself to Massaroni and Clairville, and made her exit, accompanied by Maria. When the brigand and Florio found themselves alone, they entered freely into a discussion of all that was so deeply interesting to them, and their future prospects; and Massaroni tried to persuade his companion that everything promised well, though Clairville could not avoid encouraging doubts upon the subject.

"What would I give to know the present situation of my beloved Melina!" he said.

"Take my word for it, Signor Clairville, you shall not long be kept in suspense," replied Massaroni. "As I told you before, I have those

in the vicinity of Villa Rosa, who will forward me all the intelligence that may be of use to us."

"Alas! I fear that the prince and Alberti, goaded on by revenge and disappointment, will show Melina no mercy, but will hasten the consummation of their infamous designs."

"Let them attempt to do so at their peril," returned Massaroni, determinedly; "they will find me waking, and fully prepared to frustrate their plans, however secure they may imagine them to be. Be of good heart, and you may set them entirely at defiance."

"But have you forgotten the promise you made me, Massaroni?" asked Florio.

"What mean you?" demanded Massaroni.

"To get a communication forwarded from me to Melina?"

"That shall be done, and I have no doubt I shall accomplish it easily."

"Oh, when?"

"Why, you can write your epistle as soon as you like, my young friend, and I will lose no time about the business."

"Thanks, thanks," replied Clairville, cordially and gratefully shaking him by the hand; "you have removed a weight of care and anxiety from my mind, and I owe you my eternal gratitude. To hear again from that fair being, who shares my undivided affections, will afford me the greatest consolation under my numerous and almost insupportable troubles, and will give me courage to persevere. Dear, dear Melina, may the Almighty parent of us all protect you from the fearful dangers with which you are at present surrounded."

"I feel confident as to what the result will be," observed the brigand chief; "and it is not often that I am wrong in my conjectures. Are you prepared to act with me for the preservation of Signora Melina?"

"Oh, need you ask such a question, Massaroni?" returned Clairville.

"And to run any risk?"

"Unquestionably! What risk is there that I would not willingly encounter to rescue my beloved Melina from so revolting a fate?"

"Enough, then," said the brigand chief; "since it is so, I do not despair of complete success. While they had you in their power, there was far greater danger of their triumphing in their designs."

"Very true; but the letter; when will you be prepared to despatch it?"

"Immediately."

"And by those whom you can safely trust?"

"Undoubtedly so; you do not suppose that I would not be sure to use every prudent precaution upon a matter of such importance? Make your mind easy, Florio; write your epistle to your fair mistress; exert all your eloquence to encourage her to hope; tell her that she has a staunch and faithful friend in

Massaroni, who will rescue her from the power of her enemies, even at the hazard of his life; do all this, Clairville, and trust me, before many hours have elapsed, your letter shall be in the hands of the gentle and deeply persecuted Melina."

Again Clairville thanked the brigand in the most cordial manner; and Massaroni having some business to transact, they separated, and Florio was left alone once more to address himself to his beloved Melina. For some time he pondered over the blank paper, and knew not how to begin. His ideas flowed so quick, and he had so much to say, that he was completely confused, and several times he threw down the pen in despair; fearing that he should never be able to write one half that he wished, or to find language sufficiently fervid to express his feelings. But at length he became more composed, and once more seized the pen, seeming as if inspired, and never ceased until he had completed the letter, which he perused and perused again before he could satisfy himself that it was sufficiently eloquent and tender for the purpose. He then once more sought the presence of Massaroni, and showed him the epistle he had written, of which the brigand expressed the highest approbation, and again sought to inspire Clairville with the hope, that the time was not far distant when he and Melina would be restored to that happiness they so well deserved to experience. Massaroni then called in Rubaldo, to whom he intended to intrust this commission; and having given him every necessary instruction, which the brigand promised scrupulously to obey, he desired him to assume such a disguise as would render it impossible for any one to recognise or suspect him, and to depart to the neighbourhood of Villa Rosa, and execute his mission with all possible despatch.

In a very short time Rubaldo was disguised as a corpulent old friar; and having showed himself again to Massaroni and Clairville, they could not but express their admiration, especially the latter, at the clever manner in which Rubaldo had concealed his person and his real character from the searching eye of curiosity.

"Ay, ay, signor," said Rubaldo, "leave Allesandro Massaroni, or any of his band, alone for stratagem or disguise. Before many days, perhaps hours, have elapsed, you shall hear favourably from me."

"Thanks, thanks; your words encourage me to confidence," said Florio; "but do you know the girl, Floretta, the faithful attendant of Signora Melina?"

"I have seen her often," replied Rubaldo.

"It is to her hands alone you can intrust the letter," remarked Clairville; "unless you are fortunate enough to see her mistress."

"I understand you," said the brigand; "and will attend to you; but of course you require an answer to this?"

"Oh, yes," replied Clairville, hastily, "and I leave it to you to appoint the place to meet Floretta with it."

"Very good, signor," observed Rubaldo; "are these all the instructions you have to give me?"

"They are—only to implore you once more to use all the expedition you can."

Rubaldo bowed and quitted the cavern.

"Now, Clairville," said Massaroni, when he was gone, "is your mind a little more easy?"

"Oh, yes," answered Florio; "Massaroni, you have conferred favours on me that I can never repay."

"Tush, tush! enough of this, man," returned the brigand chief, impatiently.

"This Rubaldo seems to be a shrewd fellow?"

"He is, and an honest one, too; only he is sometimes a little too bold in his manners."

"He will be sure to perform this mission with ability, do you not think so?" demanded Clairville.

"Had I not thought so," answered Massaroni, "of course, I should not have sent him upon it. I am much deceived, if before a couple of days are over he is not here again with the answer you so much desire."

"Joyful assurance!" ejaculated Florio; "how comparatively happy I shall be, if your surmises are verified, Massaroni."

"And you may depend upon it they will be," said the brigand chief; "there is no time to be lost, and when we peruse Signora Melina's answer to your letter, we shall know better how to act."

"Very true," coincided Clairville, "and I wait for it with the utmost possible impatience. Alas! too well I can imagine the cruelty to which she has been subjected, and to which my escape from their clutches will exasperate her inhuman oppressors more than all."

"No doubt Signora Melina has not experienced much mercy from them," remarked the brigand; "but still, after all, I cannot bring my mind to believe that they will go to the lengths you apprehend. When we hear again from Rubaldo, we shall see at once the course it will be most prudent to adopt. But probably the confinement to this cavern may become irksome to you, and I have been thinking of the means by which you may take some recreation without running the risk of being detected."

"Oh! how is that?" eagerly demanded Florio.

"Why," answered Massaroni, "you see that we are rather clever at disguises here; and I think it would be impossible to recognise you."

"Oh! most true."

"Thus disguised," continued Massaroni, "you

might occasionally indulge in a walk in the neighbourhood, always taking care not to wander too far from the cavern, and to be strictly on your guard to make sure that no one is watching you."

"Thank you for the suggestion, my friend," said Clairville; "I am ready to abide by your advice in everything. This will indeed be the means of affording me recreation, and some relief to my mind."

"Of course, you will not abandon me again, as you did on a former occasion?"

"Oh, no," answered Florio; "I should be mad, under all the circumstances, and most ungrateful, to do so. It was only despair, and the determination, at all hazards, to behold Melina once more, that urged me to do so then. I think you will do me the justice to believe what I assert, Massaroni?"

"I do," replied the brigand chief; "but yet the step was fraught with great danger, and you see that you and Melina had to suffer for your temporary imprudence."

"Very true; when I reflect upon all the circumstances which took place, and how narrowly my beloved Melina escaped an untimely death, I cannot help shuddering with horror."

"Well," observed Massaroni, "it is fortunate it was no worse. But come, Florio, I must introduce you to my wardrobe, and there you can select such a disguise as you may think proper."

Clairville again returned his thanks, and then left the place with the brigand, and entered another cavern, which was used as a kind of store-room. The place was hung round with dresses and wigs of various descriptions, and Florio could not but be amused with the great variety, and the ingenuity that was displayed in their construction.

"This peasant's dress," said Massaroni, taking one from a peg, "I think, would effectually conceal your person, and with the addition of a wig and a pair of false whiskers, it would be no easy matter for those who are well acquainted with you to recognise you."

"True," said Clairville; "and I think it is the most appropriate disguise I could assume. I will choose it, Massaroni."

This was agreed upon, and Clairville being equipped, and cautioned by Massaroni to avoid all intercourse with the inhabitants of the vicinity as much as possible, and on no account to wander beyond a certain boundary, was permitted to leave the cavern, and to walk forth into the forest, where he gave himself up to the various and perplexing reflections that crowded upon his mind, and was absent from the cavern more than a couple of hours; but this relaxation afforded him considerable relief, and he could never feel sufficiently grateful to the brigand chief for allowing him the indulgence.

CHAPTER XXXIV.

THE LETTER.—RENEWED HOPE.—THE DAY FIXED FOR THE SACRIFICE.—THE CONTINUED ANGUISH OF MELINA.

ALL chance of getting Florio Clairville again in their power, after the lapse of a few days, during which time the search was continued with unabated zeal, appeared to the prince and the Count Alberti to be at an end, and nothing could exceed the rage which filled their bosoms at the thought. They now entertained but very little doubt that his escape had been effected by Massaroni, and they felt their rage and revenge increase against the daring brigand chief as that thought suggested itself to their minds; but yet, at present, they saw no prospect of their being able to gratify those feelings; and it seemed more than probable that Massaroni would still continue to set them at defiance, and might yet be the source of great annoyance to them.

Melina remained unmoved by all their threats and persuasions, and they were greatly astonished at her firmness, for they had never imagined that one of her gentle nature could find courage to resist them in the manner she had done. However, nothing could move the heart of the Prince Bianchi to relent, and he was fully determined that at the expiration of the time he had fixed upon, if Melina still refused to give her consent, he would force her to the altar with the odious Count Alberti. Melina avoided the presence of her uncle and the count as much as possible; but not a day was permitted to pass over without her being compelled to listen to the hateful importunities of her persecutors; and need we say, therefore, that she felt herself to be one of the most wretched of human beings, and could not avoid giving herself up to abject despair? From the kind-hearted Floretta alone she could receive consolation, but that was only to a limited extent. How anxious was she to know the destination of Florio; but, alas! there was no chance of her doing so, and the longer she reflected upon the subject, the more miserable she became. Whither could he go? Where find a friend? How could he hope to escape for any length of time from the vengeance of the Prince Bianchi, who would pursue him with the most implacable hatred, and never rest until he had destroyed him altogether? These thoughts completely distracted her, and it was some time ere she could discover the least degree of tranquillity. Could she only have been satisfied that Florio was in safety, she could have been, she thought, comparatively happy; but this state of suspense was even more intolerable than the most painful certainty, and various were the fears and conjectures which crossed her mind. And should she never behold him again? Alas! it seemed but too probable that she would not, or if she did, it might be too late to rescue her from the dreadful fate which at that time was impending over her: besides what power had he to attempt to effect her deliverance? Was he not friendless and alone in the world? and any such an effort on his part, could only end in his destruction.

"But my dear signora," said Floretta, on the occasion when her mistress made use of these observations; "may not Signor Clairville find friends to assist him?—Massaroni, for instance, to whom I cannot help thinking he is indebted for his liberty?"

"Ah! no," answered Melina, "I dare not entertain such a thought. Besides, can I contemplate the danger which such a circumstance might involve my uncle in with indifference, notwithstanding the recent cruelty of his conduct towards me? And what would be the opinion of the world, if I should resign myself to the protection of the brigand chief?"

"They dare not question your honour and virtue," replied Floretta; "besides, who would be to blame if such a circumstance took place, but your uncle and the count themselves?—The world would pity, but not condemn you, signora."

"I would that such a step could be avoided," said Melina, "for I cannot think upon it without a feeling of repugnance. How gladly could I forgive them all the anguish they have hitherto caused me, if they would only now abandon their designs, and suffer me to remain at peace, though I might never be permitted to become the wife of the unfortunate Clairville."

"They may yet relent, my good lady."

"Oh, no, there is no prospect of it; they have told me repeatedly that I have nothing to hope; and then how short is the time allowed me. In a few days only it will be here; and then, unless Providence interpose to rescue me, my doom is sealed. Would to God that I were dead."

"Oh, signora," said the affectionate Floretta, "it wrings my heart, indeed it does, to hear you talk thus. Heaven knows that your prospects are dismal enough at present; but I feel assured that you will not be abandoned to such a fate as that with which you are now threatened; moreover, something strikes me that before many days have elapsed, Signor Clairville will adopt some means of making you acquainted with his present locality, and what has occurred to him since he made his escape from prison."

"And what makes you imagine that, Floretta?" asked her mistress.

"I know not how it is, signora," replied the faithful attendant; "but such is the impression on my mind."

"Could I entertain the same idea, Floretta," remarked Melina, "I might become more calm and resigned; but indeed I think it would be preposterous to encourage such a thought."

Notwithstanding all that Melina said on that occasion, the remarks of Floretta made a far more powerful impression upon her than she thought proper to acknowledge, and they continued to haunt her imagination, giving rise to the most remarkable dreams, which she found it in vain to comprehend. She, however, endeavoured to put her full confidence and reliance on the goodness of Omnipotence, and to await the issue of her and her lover's fate with patience and tranquillity. The Prince Bianchi, in the midst of his other cares, frequently reflected upon the observations of Malvolio; and the gloomy retrospection of the past it recalled to his conscience was torturing in the extreme. He in vain tried to rush from it, for the more he did so the more poignant became the impression on his mind.

"Still living," he would mutter to himself when he was alone; "this is most unfortunate;—should the fellow, Malvolio turn traitor to me, all my misdeeds will be exposed to the world, and my reputation will be blasted and destroyed for ever!—Would that he were dead; then, at any rate, I might continue safe. I liked not many of his remarks; there was the lurking devil about them; he seemed to exult in the power he holds over me; and notwithstanding all the promises he made to me, I feel satisfied that it would not take much to cause him to betray me. If he was sincere in what he stated to me, why does he refuse to inform me where the objects of my fear are at present to be found?—To say the least of it, that looks suspicious. Fool that I was to trust to him; and yet how could I avoid it? But the career of my youth was one scene of folly altogether, and severely have I now to pay for it. Valentia! Zitella! had I never known ye, I might now have been happy, and set the voice of calumny at defiance."

Thus was the mind of the Prince Bianchi tortured at intervals; but in spite of it all, let the consequences be whatever they may, he was still determined to put his nefarious designs against his beauteous and innocent niece into effect; and the more firm she became in her resistance to his tyrannical will, the more obstinately resolute did he become to compel her to yield to his desires. Thus it will be seen that the situation of Melina was of the most melancholy and alarming description. About the fourth day after the escape of Clairville from prison, Melina was sitting in her chamber, absorbed in dismal thoughts, when she was aroused from her meditations by a gentle knock at the door, and demanding who was there? Floretta answered, and was immediately admitted. She exhibited much agitation of manner, and cautiously closing the door after her, she advanced towards her mistress, and placing her finger on her lips, enjoined her to silence. Melina looked astonished and impatient, while some strange forebodings, for which she could not account, arose in her mind.

"Compose yourself, my dear lady," she said, in an under tone, "for I have good news to impart to you."

"Good news!" repeated Melina, with a look of incredulity and impatience.

"Yes, signora," answered her attendant; "I have met with a most extraordinary adventure this morning. My ideas are verified; Signor Clairville is safe, under the protection of Massaroni."

"Clairville, safe!" ejaculated Melina, fervently clasping her hands together, and raising her eyes towards Heaven. "Great God! I thank thee for this. But how know you that it is true? Do not keep me in suspense."

"I have the best proof with me of the truth of what I state, signora," returned Floretta; "I bear with me a letter, addressed to you, from Signor Clairville himself."

"A letter!" cried Melina, and her whole frame convulsed with the violence of emotion; "can I believe the evidence of my ears?— Where is it? Dear—dear—unfortunate Florio! Give it me!"

"It is here, signora," said Floretta, placing the letter in Melina's hand, who gazed at it eagerly, recognized the well known characters directly, and pressing it to her lips, bedewed it with her tears. For some moments the power of her emotions would not allow her to break the seal; but at length, with a trembling hand, she did so, and with feelings such as we need not attempt to describe, she perused the contents. Eloquent and affectionate were the sentiments it breathed, and the damsel's heart palpitated so violently against her side, while she read them, that it seemed as if it would burst its tenement. He gave a minute detail of his escape from the prison to which the Prince Bianchi had consigned him, and of his present situation; expressed the most painful anxiety to know all that had happened to her since they had last met; and concluded by assuring her of the continued fervour of the passion he entertained for her, and by seeking to inspire her with the hope that fortune would yet smile upon them, and the clouds of sorrow which at present obscured their sun of happiness would be dispersed; and that the felicity of the future would amply repay them for all the sorrows it had been their hard lot to endure.

"Beloved Florio!" ejaculated Melina, when she had perused these lines again and again, "I will endeavour to think so too; this dear letter has removed a weight of the most insupportable care and anxiety from my bosom. But how did it come into your possession, Floretta?"

"I was walking, signora," answered Floretta, "in the green meadows about a quarter of a mile from the villa, when one who appeared to be a holy father suddenly crossed my path, and much to my amazement, addressed me by my name. 'You are Floretta, the faithful attendant of Signora Melina, if I mistake not?' he said. 'I am, most holy father,' I replied. 'Psha! girl!' he returned; 'I am no holy father, but Rubaldo, the lieutenant of Massaroni, the brigand chief, under whose protection, Signor Clairville at present is. I believe I can depend upon you, and I therefore request you to deliver this letter from Signor Clairville to your mistress, and I will await the answer at nine o'clock this morning on the same spot'.— Having thus spoken, he vanished in a moment, and I was left in a state of astonishment, which you may very well imagine, signora."

"And are you confident that no one was watching you?" demanded her mistress, eagerly.

"Oh, I am quite positive of that, my lady," returned Floretta.

"That is fortunate," observed Melina, "for had you been observed by any of the partizans of the prince, the consequences would have been such as I shudder to think of. Beloved Florio! this, at any rate, will be some consolation to us both to know that we can communicate with each other."

"You will then return an answer to Signor Clairville's letter, signora?"

"Unquestionably I will; think you that I could keep him in such a painful state of suspense? Leave me, Floretta, for I must be alone while I write this dear and important letter. You will be ready to convey it to Rubaldo at the hour appointed?"

"I will, my lady," replied Floretta, ; and she then quitted the apartment.

When Melina was alone, she again perused the letter and bedewed it with her tears. Every syllable it breathed was a treasure to her heart, and was calculated to inspire her with hopes such as she had not for some time before entertained. Fervently she returned her thanks to the Supreme, and implored His future protection, but it was some time ere she could sufficiently tranquilise her feelings to enable her to commence her reply to her lover. At length she locked her door, to guard against any sudden intrusion, and with a heart overflowing with emotions of the most powerful nature, set herself to her important task. Pathetic indeed was the language in which that letter was couched, and Melina's tears almost blinded her while she was writing it; but at length she came to the conclusion, and folding it up and sealing it, she rung the bell, again summoning Floretta into her presence.

"It is done, Floretta," she said; "and to your care I now commit it, not doubting but that you will be cautious in delivering it to Rubaldo; and to make sure that you are not observed by any one, or I am ruined."

"I need not assure you, signora," returned Floretta, "that you may depend on me."

"I know I can, my good girl," said her mistress, kindly, "and I am under the deepest obligations to you for all the numerous services you have rendered me. But beg of Rubaldo

BIANCHI AND THE COUNT IN CONSULTATION.

to let me hear from him again as soon as possible."

"I will, my lady," replied Floretta; "and no doubt it will not be long before you receive another communication from Signor Clairville."

"Heaven send that it may not," said Me-

lina, fervently; "and that something may occur to give us cause to hope."

Floretta now withdrew, and Melina gave herself up to her own reflections, the nature of which we need not seek to pourtray. Not many minutes, however, had elapsed, when she was again interrupted by a gentle tap at the door, and Floretta once more entered.

"What now, Floretta?" demanded her mistress; why have you returned so soon?"

"I am sorry to say, signora," answered her attendant, "that his highness, the prince, desires to see you immediately."

"Oh, this is most painful," sighed Melina; "in the present agitated state of my feelings. Can I not excuse myself?"

"No, my lady, I am afraid you cannot."

"Is my uncle alone?" asked Melina.

"He is, signora," was the reply. "The Count Alberti is at present absent from the villa."

"That, at any rate, is fortunate," remarked Melina; "I must endeavour to support this meeting as well as I can. More importunities, I suppose, and unfeeling reproaches. When will this continual anguish have an end? Floretta, let me have the support of your arm."

Leaning on the arm of her attendant, Melina quitted the chamber, and with faltering footsteps made her way to the apartment, in which her uncle was awaiting her. Floretta left her at the door, and she timidly entered the room, scarcely daring to raise her eyes towards the prince. He advanced towards her, and conducting her to a seat, took a chair by her side, and remained for some moments silent.

"I have not seen you since yesterday morning, Melina," he said, at last; "and I must say, that you seem to have forgotten the respect that is due to me by thus avoiding my presence. However, of this you may rest assured, namely, that I am determined not to be trifled with; you are no stranger to my sentiments."

"Alas! I am not, my lord," sighed Melina, "and it is that knowledge which renders me one of the most miserable of human beings. Oh, why will you persist in urging me to that which is so abhorrent to my feelings?"

"You must submit to my will," said the prince, harshly.

"If you force me to it, you will break my heart," said Melina.

"And think you that I will yield to this wayward and obdurate spirit?"

"Indeed, it is not waywardness or obduracy that prompts me to resistance. But why call upon me so often to repeat the ardent and unconquerable sentiments of my mind. Count Alberti is the object of my detestation, and every day, every hour strengthens that feeling towards him."

"So bold, girl," cried the prince, sternly; "be cautious and do not try my patience too far."

"Uncle, dear uncle," sobbed Melina, with much emotion; "if you no longer love me, which much I fear is the sad case, though what I have done to forfeit your affections I know not, consign me to the sanctuary, banish me for ever from your presence; to such a fate I will endeavour to submit without a murmur, but do not, oh, do not sacrifice me to such a man as the Count Alberti."

"He is your destined husband," returned the prince, with the coldest indifference.

"Then, welcome death, even in its most horrible shape," exclaimed Melina, firmly. "My lord, you will, I fear, have bitter cause to repent this harsh treatment of her who has ever been studious of your happiness, and sought to merit your affection."

"Do you presume to threaten, girl?"

"No, my lord; but can I avoid giving expression to my feelings, when I am thus persecuted? Did the count possess one spark of honour, common decency or humanity, he would at once resign his presumptuous and disgusting pretensions."

"He would be a weak fool, were he to do so," returned Bianchi, passionately, "when he is sanctioned by me. He is now absent from the villa, to make all necessary arrangements for his nuptials."

"Oh, no—no—no," said the terrified Melina; "you cannot be so cruel, so unnatural—you will think better of this."

"You may depend upon it that nothing will induce me to change my mind," replied her uncle; "and, hark ye, Melina, it will be as well for you to prepare yourself for the change in your condition, for the time rapidly approaches; next Monday fortnight is the day I have fixed upon for your nuptials."

"So soon?" sobbed Melina; "my God! what will become of me? Spirit of my mother look down with pity upon me, and protect me!"

"Hold, girl!" cried the prince, with much emotion; "why do you annoy my ears with language such as this?"

"My poor mother," sighed Melina, and her eyes at the same time streaming with tears, "my poor mother on her death-bed, my lord, committed me to your care; alas! she would never have done so, had she had any presentiment that you would at some future period seek to consign me to such a terrible and disgusting fate as that you now contemplate."

"Had your mother been still living," replied the prince, "she would never have been so foolish as to have rejected such a man as the Count Alberti."

"Oh, my lord, say not so; it is a scandal on the memory of you sister."

"Cease, girl;" ejaculated Bianchi, imperiously, "I will listen no longer to language such as this; I am your lawful guardian, and am determined to exercise my authority."

"Then, alas! there is no hope!"

"None, whatever, if you think to dissuade

me from my purpose. I have already suffered myself to be tampered with too long, but I am now heartily sick of any further delay. The count will return to the villa the day after to-morrow, and I shall then expect a very favourable change in your conduct towards him."

"I cannot, will not act the hypocrite, my lord," said Melina, proudly, "I should hate and despise myself if I thought I could; I have already boldly spoken my mind to the count, and I will not now seek to disguise those feelings from him."

"Again I caution you to beware," said the Prince, sternly; "the Count Alberti, your destined lord, must not always be subjected to these degrading insults. You have already tried his patience too far."

"No language of mine can adequately express the feelings of contempt and abhorrence I entertain towards him," retorted Melina. "Those sentiments must gain strength, instead of decreasing, and I should be unworthy of the proud and honourable name I bear, did I encourage any other."

"This haughty spirit must be subdued, Melina," observed the prince, "or you may have bitter cause to repent."

"You would doom me to everlasting misery, my lord," said the damsel, "and I have, therefore, no hope but in the merciful interposition of Omnipotence. He, I trust, will not forsake me, in the hour of trial, and sooner than doom me to such a fate, I earnestly pray that He may deprive me of life."

"Bah!" cried Bianchi, "I have no patience to listen to such ridiculous nonsence as this. Rather say that you will live for the enjoyment of every earthly happiness!"

"Happiness, with such a man as Alberti!" cried Melina, with a shudder of horror; "oh, what a monstrous libel is that upon the name! But, alas, my lord! I see it is still useless to attempt to talk to you, or to seek to move you to compassion."

"It is useless to seek to argue me out of my firm resolution," answered her uncle, "I should prove myself to be as weak as yourself if you could."

"Pardon me, my lord," retorted Melina, with a look of reproach, "but methinks that you would prove yourself to be not yet entirely insensible to every feeling of justice and humanity."

"Girl!" cried Bianchi, furiously, "such language as this, and addressed to me, is not to be borne; if you have forgotten that I am your relative, you will please to remember that I am your guardian, and the Prince Bianchi."

"My lord," returned his fair niece, "I have never forgotten that, but on the contrary, I have made it my constant study to show you every proper respect, but when my peace of mind, and my honour are threatened, and that in the most cruel manner, I must be allowed to protest against it, boldly, fearlessly. Nature, common decency, revolt with the bare idea of an union with the Count Alberti, and not all the arguments or persuasions in the world can alter my sentiments upon that disgusting subject."

"Retire, girl!" commanded the prince, haughtily, "I can endure no more. You have again heard my firm resolution, and perhaps when you are alone, you will reflect seriously upon the folly and obstinacy of your opposition."

Melina did not attempt to speak another word, for she was glad to escape from the presence of her uncle, and retiring from the room she hastened to her own apartment, where she threw herself on a seat in a paroxysm of grief.

"No hope! no hope!" she sobbed forth, "the fates seem to conspire against me. Next Monday fortnight he has commanded me to prepare for the sacrifice, and what chance is there of my escaping? None, none, whatever. Oh, this is most cruel!"

Thus she continued in a state of the greatest agitation and despair, for more than a couple of hours, and, in spite of all her efforts, could find no relief to her agony. The prince seemed determined to destroy her hopes, and to delight in her misery; and the success of Alberti, therefore, appeared to be but too certain. From such a fate as that, she shrank with feelings of the most inconquerable horror, and there were moments when she was half inclined to boldly fly from it, and to commit herself to the mercy of the world. Surely, it would be better to risk everything than to suffer herself to be consigned to such an awful doom. Could she only succeed in finding her way to the retreat of Massaroni, she might be sure of his protection, and that of her lover; but would not the voice of calumny be raised against her if she should adopt such a determined course? And what was to become of her and Florio, friendless and penniless as they were? These thoughts continued to distract her mind beyond all endurance, and she was unable to come to any fixed resolution. It was now past ten o'clock, and she looked with anxiety for the return of Floretta. She was not long kept in suspense, for a knock at her chamber-door, a short time afterwards, announced that it was she, and she immediately gave her admittance.

"You are weeping, signora," said Floretta, compassionately. "Oh, how it afflicts me to behold this."

"Alas! Floretta," replied the damsel, "I have ample cause for grief; the interview I have had with my uncle has been one of the most painful description, and he has commanded me to prepare to become the wife of Count Alberti on Monday fortnight."

"Monday fortnight, my lady?"

"Alas! alas! 'tis too true!"

" But it shall never be," said Floretta ; " nay, dry your tears, my dear signora, for you know not what may occur to rescue you between this and then."

"Ah, no !" sobbed Melina, as if her heart would break ; " I am past all hope ; Alberti has left the villa for a day or two to prepare for the nuptials."

"Which will never take place, signora," returned Floretta, confidently ; " take my word for it. It would be absolutely monstrous to encourage such an idea."

"And it would be equally preposterous to attempt to banish it," said Melina.

"Say not so, my lady," remarked Floretta ; " for, Massaroni, who is your friend, and that of Signor Clairville, will prevent it."

" And should I avail myself of the brigand chief's offer of protection, what would the world say of it ?" demanded her mistress.

" Why, the world must condemn the cruel and tyrannical conduct of his highness, and the count which had driven you to such a course."

" Alas! I know that the world is too ungenerous at times, not to condemn the innocent instead of the guilty," sighed Melina ; " and I shrink from the idea of incurring its aspersions. I see there is no chance for me, but to trust to fortune, which has hitherto been opposed to me."

" You view the question on its darkest side, signora."

" And have I not too much reason to do so ; but have you seen Rubaldo ?"

" I have, my lady."

" And delivered the letter safely, to him ?"

" You may be sure of that, signora."

"That is well," remarked Melina ; " dear Florio, it will, at any rate, be some relief to the anguish of your mind, to hear again from me, and to be assured that my sentiments still remain unchanged towards you."

" Oh, signora," said Floretta, " I am certain that you wrong your lover, if you imagine that he could ever entertain an idea to the contrary."

" No, no," rejoined Melina, eagerly, " I do not believe so ; I knew the heart of Florio too well ; but I scarcely know what I say ; my brain is bewildered and distracted. What said Rubaldo, Floretta ?"

" He is not a man of many words, my lady," answered her attendant, " and I did not like to detain him long in conversation, lest we should happen to be observed by any one."

" That was very prudent ; but did he not say when I might be likely to hear from Florio again ?"

" He said, signora, that he (Rubaldo) should be in this neighbourhood again in the course of a few days, when, no doubt, he should bring another communication from Signor Clairville."

" God grant that he may keep his word," fervently ejaculated Melina ; " but, alas ! how sensible will be the sufferings of poor Florio, when he is made acquainted with the near approach of the consummation of my misery."

" Massaroni will devise some means to save you, signora," said Floretta ; " for, has he not promised to do so ? and he never fails, I believe, to keep his word."

" But, why should he run any risk for my sake ?" demanded Melina.

" Massaroni is brave and gallant, and he has ever proved himself to be the friend of the innocent and oppressed."

" Very true ; but alas ! that I should be driven to the necessity of seeking such aid."

" And who is to blame, but your uncle and Count Alberti ? I am much mistaken if they do not have bitter cause to repent their conduct. But it is late, signora, and you require rest."

" Alas ! I fear, Floretta, there will be but little rest for me."

" Pray endeavour to arouse yourself from this melancholy state of despair, my lady," said her attendant ; " good night !"

" Good night, Floretta ;" responded Melina, and the former quitted the chamber.

When she was gone, Melina threw herself disconsolately in her chair, and once more gave herelf up to the agony of her grief. She then took the letter of Florio from her bosom, and once more devoured the precious contents with eager fondness, whilst she bathed it with tears of mingled sorrow and delight. She could almost imagine that his beloved form stood before her, that she heard him speak, and this delusion served to divert her thoughts from more melancholy subjects, for a brief period. At last she sought her couch, but very little did she sleep during the night, and in the morning she was informed that it was her uncle's commands that in future she should not venture to leave her chamber without his express permission, and that no one was to be allowed to see her except Floretta, and that only at certain hours of the day. This convinced her that the prince had suffered some suspicions to enter his mind, that she might make some attempt to escape from his power ; and such a restraint upon her actions, although it was no more than she had expected, added to her misery, and increased her despair.

CHAPTER XXXV.

THE DAY OF TRIAL ARRIVES.—THE MIDNIGHT NUPTIALS.—THE INTERRUPTION BY MASSARONI AND HIS BAND, AND THE RESULT.

THE hours passed by Florio Clairville during the absence of Rubaldo from the cavern, were of the most tedious and anxious description, and his mind was tormented with the most painful and conflicting doubts and apprehensions. Should Rubaldo fail to meet with Floretta, there was no other means of getting the letter conveyed to Melina. And then again, what might not have happened to her since his escape from prison? to what lengths might not the revenge of the prince and Count Alberti have carried them? Already Melina might have been forced to the altar, and that union effected, the bare thought of which inspired his breast with feelings of horror. At all his attempts to reconcile his mind, and reduce these agonising thoughts to some degree of consistency, he failed, nor could all the efforts of Massaroni succeed in arousing him from this state of melancholy and apprehension.

"Rubaldo tarries," he observed to Massaroni, on the second evening after the departure of that individual with the important letter to Melina; "I fear that he will fail in accomplishing his object."

"You need entertain no such apprehensions," returned the brigand chief; "Rubaldo knows well his business, and, as I have before told you, is to be depended upon. You may feel confident that he will never rest until he has performed his mission to the very letter, and brought you back an answer from the beauteous object of your affections."

"Oh, what transport would it impart to my heart," ejaculated Clairville, rapturously, "to hear again, to gloat over the sentiments coming from that adored, but much persecuted maiden, would impart more transport to my soul, than I can give utterance to in words. But still my heart misgives me."

"Wherefore?" demanded Massaroni.

"You know the power and the arbitrary spirit which the Prince Bianchi possesses," replied Florio.

"True," coincided the brigand.

"His attachment to the Count Alberti?"

"Certainly."

"My escape from confinement must have greatly exasperated them, at the same time created some alarm in their minds as to the consequences which may be likely to follow."

"Unquestionably; and not without reason."

"Then," said Clairville, "is it not also reasonable to suppose that they will precipitate their designs, and force Melina to the altar?"

"You alarm yourself unnecessarily, my young friend," returned Massaroni; "I have given you my word that Signora Melina shall, under no circumstances, become the wife of Alberti; and depend on it, I will not fail to fulfil my promise. The power of the Prince Bianchi and the miscreant Alberti, I admit is great, but it has hitherto been found to be insignificant when opposed to me, and so it shall be now, if they put me to the test. Despair not, Clairville; Melina in spite of all the obstacles which at present appear, shall be yours."

"I dare not aspire to the thought," said Clairville; "the lady Melina is a prize far too rich for me to presume to obtain possession of; though I know full well her heart responds most fervently to the sentiments I entertain towards her. But could I feel assured that she would, at any rate, be rescued from the fate with which she is at this time threatened, I should feel myself the happiest man in existence."

"Then set your mind at rest," observed Massaroni, "for once more I promise you, and without any vain boasting, that Signora Melina shall be saved from the fate to which her haughty and imperious uncle, and the Count Alberti have destined her. My plans are all well preconcerted, and nothing whatever can transpire at Villa Rosa without its reaching my immediate knowledge."

"Your assurances encourage me to hope, Massaroni," said Florio; "but why should you run such risks for one who is almost a stranger to you?"

"It matters not," replied the brigand; "you have kept your word with me, and what Massaroni promises he will perform. No danger ever daunted him, especially when he had justice on his side."

"I owe you a debt of gratitude, Massaroni," said Clairville, which I knew not how properly to acknowledge."

Mention it not, my young friend," answered the brigand chief; "thanks are at all times distasteful to me, especially when I feel that I have done no more than I should wish to be done by. Believe me, Clairville I am no prophet, if the haughty and imperious spirit of the Prince Bianchi be not ultimately subdued—the Count Alberti brought to the shame and degradation he so richly merits—yourself made a happy and prosperous man—and I and my brave comrades not only escape the rather uncomfortable fate to which we are now invited—but have the pleasure of dancing at the wedding of yourself and the lovely Signora Melina."

"You are sanguine in your anticipations, Massaroni," remarked Florio.

"And mark me," returned the brigand, "that which I anticipate will be realized."

"I have often thought," said Clairville, after a brief pause; "I have often thought, Massaroni, and with a feeling of regret, what a pity it is that a man possessing your excellent qualities of mind, should be placed in the questionable possition you now are. Nature has formed you to adorn the first rank of society, how then is it that you are plunged into your present course of life?"

"You question me on a most tender point," replied the brigand chief, with considerable emotion depicted in his handsome countenance;

"But I will answer you. You remember the night of the festival at the Villa Rosa, to celebrate the birth-day of the Signora Melina?"

"Oh, can I ever forget it?"

"You recollect my emotion on accidentally beholding the portrait which the Prince Bianchi has concealed in a certain apartment?"

"I do."

"And you know not the exact history of that portrait?"

"I know no more than what I have elicited from common rumour," replied Florio, "namely, that it is the portrait of a lady to whom the prince was once devotedly attached, but who died in the youth and bloom of her beauty."

"And know you not her name?"

"I do not."

"I think it is said that she was a young Florentine," said Massaroni with considerable agitation in the expression of his countenance, and his whole demeanour.

Clairville replied in the affirmative.

"Examine this miniature," observed Massaroni, taking one from his bosom, and presenting it to Florio; "do you think you have ever seen anything that resembled it before?"

"By Heaven!" exclaimed Clairville, examining it with the deepest interest, "it is the very counterpart of the portrait you have just mentioned. Any person might imagine that it had been copied from it. Whom does this miniature represent?"

"My mother!" repeated Massaroni, solemnly, and his voice faltered.

"Your mother?"

"Yes; such must she have appeared in her youthful days; such were her dear features as I remember them in the days of my childhood, when care and sorrow had set their cankering seal upon her."

"She is no more?"

"Dead, dead!"

"And her name?"

"At present I must not reveal it; for by so doing, I might counteract the ends of justice."

"And is your father still alive?" asked Clairville, with increasing interest.

"I know not, but have every reason to believe that he is," answered the brigand chief.

"And what, may I ask, is his name?"

"I am ignorant of it."

"How?" demanded Florio, with a look of astonishment.

"It is even as I tell you," remarked Massaroni; "I know not the name of him who gave me being; I have heard that he was of noble rank, but his conduct proved him to be a villain at heart; and so far from my feeling any regard towards him, I cherish the most deadly feelings of hatred and revenge."

"Oh, surely these thoughts are dreadful;—

you should endeavour to conquer them," said Clairville.

"Never!" returned Massaroni, vehemently; "they are only natural, and I think you will agree with me in saying so, when I make you acquainted with some of the particulars of his crimes. He found my poor mother an innocent, unsuspecting girl; he won her affections, and promised her marriage; in a fatal hour he robbed her of woman's brightest jewel—her honour; I am the offspring of that guilty connection."

"But did he not fulfil his promise, by making your mother his bride?" asked Clairville.

"He did not, the heartless scoundrel," replied the brigand chief; "from time to time he evaded her solicitations, by every subtle means in his power, and at length he abandoned her and myself to misery, poverty, and shame."

"But knew she not where to find him?"

"She did; but her proud and independent spirit would not suffer her to seek him out, and to hold him up to the opprobrium, the hatred, and shame of the world, as she should have done. Enduring every misery; deserted by her friends, but still cherishing the same affection for her cruel and cold-hearted seducer, she struggled on for years, and until I had become a stout lad, and did my best to contribute towards her happiness and support; but at length nature was exhausted, and she died in my arms of a broken heart, and left me alone and destitute. I became a wandering, friendless outcast: accident at last placed me in the hands of brigands, from whom I received every kindness, and at length, on the death of their chief, I was promoted to the situation I at present occupy."

"And is it possible," said Clairville, "that your mother should never make you acquainted with the name of your father?"

"She did not," answered the brigand chief; "she still loved the destroyer of her innocence and happiness; she well knew the impetuousness and determination of my disposition, and even in her last moments she refused to reveal it."

"Your's has indeed been a cruel fate," observed Clairville, "and I deeply sympathise with you."

"You need, therefore, no longer marvel at the interest I feel in the misfortunes of the Signora Olympia, whose destiny is so similar to that which attended my unfortunate mother," said Massaroni.

"I do not," replied Clairville; "but how many years is it since the death of your mother?"

"More than twenty; but she is as fresh and as dear to my memory as if she now stood before me, and——"

He was interrupted by the abrupt entrance of Maria, and whose countenance showed that she had some intelligence to communicate.

"Ah, Maria!" said Massaroni, "you came in haste. Has anything particular occurred?"

"The man who it is suspected is the same that crossed the path of Montaldi and Ottavia, has been seized whilst lurking in this neighbourhood by some of our band," answered Maria.

"Ah!" ejaculated Massaroni, starting from his seat; "this is well; the mystery which at present hangs over the unfortunate Ottavia may now be unravelled. Let him be immediately brought into my presence. Signor Clairville, perhaps it will be as well for you to retire for a short time."

Clairville obeyed, and Maria quitted the cavern. In a short time the fellow Malvolio was ushered by two or three of the brigands into the presence of their chief. He folded his arms across his chest, and confronted Massaroni with a bold and determined air, and a stern expression of countenance.

"Your servant, signor," said the brigand, with his accustomed politeness. "I trust you will pardon the unceremonious manner in which you have been introduced to me; but I have long been most anxious to have the pleasure of seeing you; and therefore desired my men to escort you hither, if they should be so fortunate as to meet with you."

"I am sure I ought to feel extremely obliged to you for your very kind consideration, signor," replied Malvolio, in tones of equal sarcasm; "but really the honour you have done me was quite uncalled for."

"Pray be seated," said Massaroni.

Malvolio bowed with much politeness, and took a seat opposite to the brigand chief, without the least discomposure of manner.

"May I inquire, Signor Massaroni," he demanded, "what is your pleasure with me?"

"Oh, certainly," answered Massaroni, with the same imperturbable coolness; "but first I must request to be put into possession of the name of my guest?"

"To comply with which I must beg leave most respectfully to decline," returned Malvolio.

"Well, well, I will not be too urgent at present; perhaps you may feel disposed to be more communicative by and by."

"I do not feel quite certain that I may be prevailed upon, deeming the name of so humble and insignificant a being as myself of no importance to such a renowned robber and cut-throat as Allesandro Massaroni."

"You are extremely flattering, my murderous-visaged friend," laughed Massaroni, "and I must beg to return you every suitable acknowledgment. No doubt we shall perfectly understand each other ere long."

"Probably we may," sneered Malvolio, "and the readiest way to do that is for you to explain yourself as soon as possible."

"All in good time, signor, as we shall not part company just yet. Do you take wine?"

"Not any at present, I thank you."

"Very good. I am rather partial to it when it is good. Your health, signor."

Malvolio bowed, but bit his lips with rage.

"You are sojourning in this neighbourhood, signor, I believe?" said the brigand, replenishing his glass.

"No," was the laconic reply.

"Indeed! I thought you were, as you have lately been seen by two or three friends of mine; an old gentleman, and an unfortunate female, for instance, whose path you crossed a few days since, and the latter of whom, whose real name I am anxious to know, in spite of her wandering senses, seemed to recognise you."

"Ah!" exclaimed Malvolio, with a look of alarm; "did she then mention my name?"

"She did not," answered Massaroni.

"That is well."

"However, there can be very little doubt that she has good reason to know you; and from your observations I have every reason to believe that you are thoroughly acquainted with her."

"And what if I should be?" demanded Malvolio sternly,

"Why, then I must request you to impart your knowledge to me," replied Massaroni.

"And I must again beg leave most respectfully to decline," said Malvolio. "Once for all, I tell you that you have a man before you who is not to be trifled or tampered with, and that not a word shall pass his lips but what he considers prudent."

"Very good: and, perhaps, it may be necessary to inform you that Allesandro Massaroni, the brigand chief, is not a man to be trifled or tampered with."

"That is a matter of perfect indifference to me," said Malvolio.

"Indeed! well, you can use your own discretion; but, at the same time, I must beg leave to remind you that you are in my power, and that disobedience to my will is usually attended with rather disagreeable consequences."

"I will brave them all."

"Will you, then, still persist in refusing to tell me who and what you are?"

"I certainly shall," answered Malvolio.

"You had better reflect awhile, before you come to a final decision," said Massaroni.

"It needs no consideration," replied Malvolio; "my mind is already made up."

"And so is mine," returned the brigand.

"And may I ask you what is your determination?"

"Oh, certainly: it is simply this, to compel you to be explicit, and if you remain obstinate

I have the means to punish you for your folly and obduracy. I suppose you can understand that?"

"Perfectly well," returned the ruffian, with the utmost indifference.

"And if you are wise you will not oppose my wishes."

"I should be a weak fool to be threatened into obedience."

"Methinks you will alter your tone by-and-by."

"If you suppose that, I can only assure you that you are doomed to disappointment," said Malvolio.

"Are you mad?"

"If I am, I am not aware of the malady."

"You acknowledge that you know this unfortunate woman?"

"I do."

"And that you have been her enemy?"

"Yes."

"She has hinted as much as to throw the suspicion of murder upon you."

"Then she has spoken that which is false," answered Malvolio.

"Well, you will have an opportunity of again meeting her, face to face, in my presence, and the truth may then be elicited."

"I am fully prepared for everything," said Malvolio; "you will elicit nothing from me."

"We shall soon see that," answered Massaroni. "You will find me resolute."

"And you shall find me equally so."

"Fool! Could I not in a moment stretch you a corpse at my feet?"

"Undoubtedly you could," replied the ruffian, with the greatest sang froid; "and that would be a deed worthy of the brigand chief, Massaroni"

"I would advise you to be more cautious in your language."

"I usually suit it to those I am addressing."

"Dare you?"

"You have heard me," said Malvolio. "By what right do you detain me here? I have never injured you."

"But you have one whom I respect, and am resolved to protect; and it is only by a full confession of everything that you can hope to escape my vengeance."

"Well, I must abide by the consequences, for nothing will move me from my purpose."

"Neither will I be moved from mine. For what purpose have you been lurking in this neighbourhood?"

"That is my business."

"And you will find ere long that it is mine also."

"Your threats will not intimidate me," said Malvolio.

"But perhaps punishment may."

"You are welcome to try the experiment."

"You are a daring knave."

"That is just my character; and it is one that I have ever felt proud to bear."

"You must be a fool to defy me." said Massaroni.

"Well, I am ready to take the consequences of my folly: not all the torments of the damned should wring the truth from me."

Massaroni's patience was completely exhausted, for he had not expected to meet with such obstinate resistance, and he stamped with rage.

"Search the rascal," he commanded, addressing himself to the brigands who were present; "he may have that about him which may prove more communicative than himself."

Malvolio laughed contemptuously, and offered no resistance whilst the brigands proceeded to search his person narrowly. They, however, found nothing of any consequence upon him; and turning to Massaroni, he demanded with a sneer "if he were satisfied?"

"No," returned the brigand chief; "I am not; but I will be before long, or you will have bitter cause to repent it."

"Be it so," answered Malvolio, firmly.

"Do you still refuse to tell me your name—who you are—whence you came—and who the unfortunate woman is whom your appearance before has caused so much alarm?"

"I do,"

"Remember that by tortures I might force the truth from you."

"Try your tortures: you will find they will have no effect on me."

"That daring spirit may yet be crushed."

"I much doubt it."

"A night's meditation may cause you to change your mind."

"A night's meditation will only serve to add to my determination."

"Away with him!" commanded Massaroni; "place him in the gloomiest cell this subterranean retreat contains. In the morning I shall expect to find him in a different humour."

"I regret to think that you will be doomed to disappointment," laughed Malvolio, scornfully. "Lead on, fellows, I am ready to attend you."

The brigands obeyed the command of their chief; and Malvolio, folding his arms across his chest, and fixing a look of defiance on Massaroni, was led out of the cavern.

"What a stubborn rascal is this," said Massaroni, when he was gone. "He is evidently a fellow who is capable of any deed; but he must be mad if he obstinately resists my will. It must be something of a very important nature that he knows about Ottavia, or he would not so resolutely refuse to reveal it; and my curiosity and anxiety are more than ever excited, and I will not rest until I have, by some means or other, elicited the whole truth. When Ottavia again beholds him, she may for a moment be restored to reason and divulge the truth. At any rate, it is most fortunate that I have the rascal secure in my power; and if he still refuses to yield to my demands, he shall never more quit this place alive."

He was interrupted by hearing a knock at the door which secured the entrance to the cavern, and he hastily demanded who was there?

"It is I, captain," answered the voice of Rubaldi; "I have but just returned from my expedition."

"Ah!" exclaimed Massaroni, as he opened

OLYMPIA AND OTTAVIA.

the door, and gave admittance to his lieutenant; "you are welcome, Rubaldi, I have been long expecting you, and Signor Clairville has been on the tiptoe of impatience."

"I have been as expeditious as I could," replied Rubaldo; "and the journey, you know, is a long one."

"True, true," coincided Massaroni; "but have you been successful?"

"Nothing could turn out better."

"You delivered Clairville's note, then?"

"Yes."

"And Floretta conveyed it faithfully to her mistress?"

"She did," answered Rubaldo, "as this reply from Signora Melina will fully justify."

"Then," observed Massaroni, "the mind of Clairville will be set at rest. He must instantly be made acquainted with everything."

He then took Melina's letter from the hand of Rubaldo, and hastened to the cavern, where Clairville was awaiting in the greatest suspense. He arose from his seat on the entrance of Massaroni, and advanced eagerly towards him.

"I have good news for you, Clairville," said the brigand, cheerfully; "Rubaldo has just returned."

"Ah!" exclaimed Clairville, eagerly, "and tell me, I beg, do not keep me in suspense; has he been successful?"

"He has," answered Massaroni; "your fondest wishes are gratified; Rubaldo has performed his task with his usual ability, as this letter will testify."

Florio hastily took the letter from his hand, and no sooner did he behold the well known characters, than he pressed it to his lips in a transport of joy. The brigand retired to another part of the cavern, whilst Clairville proceeded to peruse the contents of the important epistle; and he pondered over every syllable with feelings of the most indescribable emotion and delight. The ardent and affectionate language in which that letter was couched was no more than Florio had anticipated, and, for a short time, he felt as though a heavy weight of care and anxiety was removed from his heart; and as though hope once more began to dawn upon him.

"Beloved Melina," he cried, "your sentiments remain unchanged, and I must in that assurance, feel comparatively happy. But could I, for a moment, doubt the sincerity of your love?—Could I believe that anything could ever induce you to banish me from your memory? Oh, no; I could not wrong you by such a thought. But, alas! how horrible is your situation; and dare I hope that anything will move your uncle, or the presumptuous villain, Alberti, to abandon their perfidious designs? I cannot; and unless the Almighty shall interpose to save you, in a few days your fate is certain; your doom will be sealed for ever, and the most unspeakable misery will be the lot of us both.'

"Again I promise you, Clairville," said the brigand chief, "that Signora Melina shall at all hazards be rescued from the fate with which she is at present threatened, and restored to your arms. Make your mind easy then, and a few days may bring about such a change as you now little anticipate."

"Massaroni," cried Florio, cordially grasping the brigand's hand, "your words convince me that you are sincere, my friend, and that

you will gladly do everything that lies in your power to serve me. I thank you from my very soul, and cannot but feel a latent hope that your wishes may yet be gratified."

"Well said, my young friend," returned Massaroni; "still encourage that feeling, and depend upon it you will not be doomed to disappointment."

"But did not Rubaldo obtain any further particulars?" asked Clairville.

"No more than such as Signora Melina has doubtless furnished you with in her letter. The excitement caused by your escape remains unabated, and the prince and Alberti are straining every nerve to discover you; but they will find that they are doomed to disappointment."

"And Rubaldo promised Floretta to meet her again in the course of a few days, did he not?" asked Florio.

"He did," replied Massaroni; "and on the intelligence we may then receive from Signora Melina, everything will depend, and we shall see what course it may be necessary for us both to adopt. Everything will depend upon promptitude and stratagem, in which respect Massaroni is never at fault. Shoud they persist in their designs, the lady must be rescued from their power, at any risk, and in spite of the consequences that may follow."

"It is a daring idea, and one that Melina may object to."

"Nay, Florio, think you that the maiden will not rather risk any fate, than suffer herself to fall a sacrifice to so hateful an individual as the Count Alberti?'

"Oh, Melina," ejaculated Clairville, "would that Providence would bring your haughty uncle to a proper sense of his duty; I dare not aspire to your hand, but did I know that you were secure from the fate with which you are at present threatened, methinks, though we should never be destined to come together, I could become somewhat resigned, if not comparatively happy."

"Courage, my young friend, and again I promise you that not only shall Signora Melina be protected from the danger which is now impending over her, but that she shall likewise become your bride. 'Tis true that the disparity between your stations in society is great; but love, constancy, and perseverance will conquer everything, and remove every difficulty. Good night!"

Clairville responded to this wish, and the brigand left him to himself. A dozen times did Clairville re-peruse the affectionate letter of his adored Melina, and his bosom was distracted by alternate hopes and fears. But although he placed every confidence in the friendship of Massaroni, the idea of forcing Melina away from the authority of the prince, her uncle, seemed too extravagant and impracticable for him to encourage it; and notwithstanding the dread which Melina entertained of the fate with which she was threatened, he could not imagine that she would ever give her consent to a course which might expose her to the voice of scandal, and would be sure to bring down upon her the vengeance of the prince. In spite of the love which he knew she bore him, she would surely hesitate ere she resigned herself entirely to his protection, knowing the consequences which must follow, and poor and friendless as he was. These thoughts completely bewildered his brain, and he knew not how to act. Massaroni left the cavern at an early hour and made his way to the dwelling of Montaldi, whom he made acquainted with the fact of Malvolio being in his power, but his obstinate refusal to reveal who he was, or to throw the least light upon his connection with Ottavia.

"He is some desperate rascal, I'll be bound," said Massaroni; "but he will find that he has one to deal with in me, who will not be trifled with; and if he is wise, he will not remain obstinate."

"It is a fortunate job you have secured him," said Montaldi, "for notwithstanding his present obduracy, he may in a little time see the prudence of becoming more communicative, and the long hidden mystery which enshrouds the fate of the unfortunate Ottavia may be unravelled. It is quite evident from the terror she evinced on beholding him, and the observations that she made use of, he is well known to her, and that he is her enemy."

"There can be no doubt of that," remarked the brigand; "besides, he has acknowledged it, and seems to exult in the idea. It is necessary that he and Ottavia should be brought into each other's presence, and when they are thus confronted together, the truth may be extorted. Will you bring Ottavia to my retreat in the course of an hour or two?"

Montaldi replied in the affirmative, and Massaroni took his leave. On arriving at the cavern, he ordered Rubaldo and another of the band to bring Malvolia into his presence, and presently afterwards that ruffian made his appearance, with the same stern and dogged expression of countenance, and firmness and indifference of demeanour.

"Now, signor," demanded Massaroni, "has the night's cool reflection worked any change in your mind?"

"No," was the brief reply.

"Humph! You are an obstinate rascal."

"I am not to be intimidated, I assure you, Signor Massaroni," returned Malvolio.

"Then you are still resolved not to render any account of yourself, or to reveal what you know respecting the unfortunate woman whom we call Ottavia?"

"You have heard my answer; you will elicit not a word from me."

"We shall soon see that," said the brigand.

"You are welcome to try your utmost as soon as you like," said Malvolio; "you will find that I will not flinch from that which I have determined upon."

"What obstinate folly is this?"

"It may be so, in your opinion; I care not."

"Are you not in my power, and at my mercy?" asked Massaroni.

"Very true," answered Malvolio, scornfully, "and I am fully prepared to take the consequences of what you are pleased to term my obstinate folly. Not all the tortures that you can inflict shall force the secret from me."

"Beware—beware!"

"I need no warning, Massaroni; my mind is made up: it is determined and inflexible."

"Are you not aware that I never fail to make those dearly pay who dare to set me at defiance?"

"Yes."

"You cannot flatter yourself with the idea that you will be able to escape from me?"

"I have not troubled myself to think anything upon the subject," returned Malvolio, contemptuously.

"Then you had better do so at once; and come to a wise and speedy conclusion."

"You have heard the conclusion I have come to, let that suffice; it is useless for you to waste your time in questioning and importuning me."

"You admit that you are the enemy of Ottavia?"

"I admit that I am the enemy of her you call by that name."

"Well, that is bold and candid enough."

"I am always bold and candid; I do not admire fine figures of speech."

"And what has made her your enemy?"

"Simply because she could not pay for my friendship."

"Then if I understand you rightly, you are the creature of some wealthy villain who has been the persecutor of this hapless female?"

"You are at liberty to form your own conclusions upon the subject," replied Malvolio; "I do not think proper to enlighten you any farther."

"Will you not reveal to me her name?"

"I will not."

"Nor the name of her persecutor?"

"No."

"You had better not try my patience too far."

"I have no wish to do so; but once for all I tell you that nothing you can say or do shall wring the secret from me. Why should I yield to your demands? Who authorised you to become inquisitor? Are you my father confessor?"

Massaroni bit his lips with vexation, and remained for some moments silent, while Malvolio continued as firm and inflexible as before, and seemed to view the danger of his situation with the utmost indifference.

"In a short time," the brigand said at last, "you will have an opportunity of again beholding the object of my solicitude, and you may then be disposed to alter your mind."

"Indeed I shall not," said Malvolio; "but you have heard all I have to say. I have been candid with you, and therefore I do not see the utility of prolonging this interview. I am ready to go back to the agreeable cell you have provided for my accommodation."

"Again I wish to impress upon you the absolute madness of this obduracy."

"And again I answer that I am prepared to abide the consequences, whatever they may be; but mark me, and think not that I make use of any empty threats, great as you may consider your power and your present triumph; there are those who have the means and the will to avenge me."

"Dare you threaten, fellow?"

"You heard me, brigand."

"Well, well," said Massaroni; "I will be calm, and suffer you to indulge in your idle whim for the present. Poor wretch!—Such empty words as those you have just given utterance to are the only means you have of venting your rage and indignation. Now would I wager all that I possess, you are the veriest scoundrel that ever remained unhung."

"With the exception of yourself, Signor Massaroni," retorted Malvolio, with a bitter sneer.

"Away with him!" commanded the brigand, addressing himself to Rubaldo and his companion.

"I am ready, most worthy signor," said the ruffian, laughing;—"good day generous, and noble minded Signor Massaroni."

Thus saying, he fixed a scornful look upon the brigand chief, and followed Rubaldo and the other man from the place.

"What a stubborn rascal is this," said Massaroni, when he was alone; "I am afraid that I shall not be able to prevail upon him either by threats or persuasions to reveal that which I am so anxious to know; but we shall see what the effect will be when he and Ottavia are confronted with one another."

In a short time after this Montaldi and Ottavia arrived, and were shown into the presence of Massaroni, who related to the former what had just taken place between himself and Malvolio, while Ottavia was fully occupied with Olympia, who had entered the cavern, and seemed to take no notice of any body else.

"What a determined ruffian he must be,"

observed old Montaldi; "it is evident that he is a fellow who is capable of perpetrating any crime; and I have no doubt that he is one of the principal authors of Ottavia's misfortunes."

"True," coincided Massaroni; "and the few observation he made use of, has thrown some little light upon the mystery. Ottavia I have no doubt has been the victim of some wealthy libertine, whose base instrument this fellow appears to be."

"No doubt of it," said Montaldi; "but when Ottavia and he again behold each other, the truth may all come out; either the guilty conscience of this ruffian may throw him off his guard; or the light of reason may for a moment dawn upon the disordered brain of Ottavia, and she may be enabled to reveal his name, and likewise that of her betrayer."

"Do you think we may venture to bring him forward at once?" asked Massaroni.

"Yes," replied Montaldi, "for Ottavia is more calm than she has been for the last day or two, and she will not be alarmed as we are all present."

Massaroni summoned Rubaldo into his presence, and desired him to conduct the stranger before them. They waited with no inconsiderable degree of anxiety to see what the result would be. In a few moments the door was thrown open, and the ruffian Malvolio stood before them. He fixed a scornful look upon Massaroni and Montaldi, and then cast a hasty glance around the cavern, and his eyes immediately became rivetted on the countenance of Olympia, who was looking towards. He started with evident amazement and confusion, and the expression of his features exhibited much agitation, as he advanced a few paces nearer towards Olympia, and gazed more earnestly upon her countenance. Massaroni and the others watched his emotions with the deepest interest and attention, and they began to hope that someting was about to be elicited from him which might tend in some measure to unravel the mystery.

"How is this?" he exclaimed, in a horse voice; "is it a phantom, no—no by h—l, it must be the same!"

Olympia felt very much confused and alarmed, but a shriek of terror from poor Ottavia aroused her. She had recognised Malvolio, and was rushing towards him, but she was held back by Montaldi and Massaroni.

"Ah!" she cried, "he is here again! Once more the fiend, the murderer crosses my path, and mocks me with his hideous looks of triumph!—Let me approach him!—I will tear the frightful secret from his breast, and invoke the vengeance of Heaven on his head! Why do you hold me back? Do you not see that there is blood upon his hands? It is the blood of the innocent! Wretch! miscreant! murderer! Where is my child?—Where is its father? The bridal feast awaits; why then does he tarry? You smile!—Oh, villain!—villain!"

"Ha! ha! ha!" laughed Malvolio triumphantly; "you will elicit all the facts, no doubt, from this raving maniac."

"Beware what you say," returned the brigand chief, sternly; "it will be well for you if you do not refuse to reveal the truth."

"Indeed!" sneered Malvalio; "however, I am perfectly willing to take my chance; if you think that I am to be frightened by trifles you will find yourself much mistaken. Pray proceed with your examination of this sensible witness."

"Still he is there!" again exclaimed Ottavia, "still the villain mocks me with his frightful looks! Why do you all stand by inanimate as statues?—Will no one see justice rendered me?—You are cowards, cowards all of ye!"

"Ottavia," said Montaldi, in the gentlest and most persuasive accents; "pray endeavour to be calm and to recollect yourself. Your friends are anxious to see justice rendered you; tell me, who is this man, of whom you evince so much terror, and I fear not without ample cause?—Come, come, you know him, do you not?"

"Know him!" repeated Ottavia, as a sudden thought seemed to flash upon her bewildered brain;—"Oh, yes, yes; too well; too well!"

Malvolio turned pale and his lips quivered, for now indeed he feared that the secret was about to escape the lips of the unfortunate woman.

"His name! his name! my good Ottavia?" asked Montaldi eagerly.

"His name!" repeated Ottavia, and she pressed her hand upon her forehead, as if endeavouring to recall her scattered memory; "his name is—is—no!—no!—it is gone!—I cannot recollect it!"

"But your own name, Ottavia?"

"Ha! ha! ha!" returned the poor woman with a wild laugh; "why, Ottavia, is it not?"

Massaroni and the others could not conceal their disappointment, whilst Malvolio laughed aloud in the exultation of his feelings.

"Whose is the triumph now?" he demanded; "methinks you are likely to gain much satisfaction by this interview. Oh, she is a most intelligent witness."

"Wretch!" exclaimed Massaroni, "let me hear another word like that escape your lips and I will strike you to my feet like a dog!"

"Oh, no doubt you can talk largely to a defenceless man, and surrounded as you are by your myrmidons," sneered Malvolio; "but I heed you not, and am perfectly indifferent as to what you do with me. The secret shall never pass my lips though you inflict upon me all the tortures of perdition."

"We shall put your courage or rather foolhardiness to the test by-and-by, depend on it," returned Massaroni.

"Whenever you please," was the fellows cold and audacious reply.

"Take him from my sight!" again cried Ottavia, "I cannot, dare not gaze upon him; all the fury of the demon is in his eyes, and his hands are reeking with the blood of his fellow creatures. Off! off! Away with him! Do not let him approach her who is so good and innocent, and whom he would contaminate. He would tear her from me! That is the purpose that brings him hither. Oh, God! will no one interpose to save her?"

Massaroni now consulted with Montaldi in an under tone, and considering it would be better, as she was so much excited, that Ottavia should be removed from the presence of the object of her alarm. She and Olympia retired from the cavern, much to the relief of the villain Malvolio, the expression of whose countenance plainly showed the exultation of his feelings. A pause of some minutes ensured, when Massaroni again turning to Malvolio, demanded—

"Do you still persist in refusing to answer my questions?"

"More firmly than ever," answered Malvolio.

"You must be mad," said the brigand.

"I should be a cowardly dolt if I yielded to your peremptory demands. You have no right to question me, nor more has any one present, and I will not suffer myself to be bullied out of the secret. Let this answer once for all suffice; and if it does not satisfy you, you have your remedy; I am in your power, and you can therefore do with me as you please."

"Your unfortunate victim has accused you of murder!" remarked Montaldi.

"She has accused me falsely," retorted Malvolio; "besides, what care I for the ravings of a maniac?"

"The time may come when you will not venture to despise them," observed Massaroni.

"Indeed it will not," said Malvolio; "but have you any further commands for me, Signor Massaroni?"

"I will give you forty-eight hours to make up your mind," replied the brigand; "and if at the end of that time you still remain obstinate, be the consequences on your own head."

"Be it so; you will find me in the same temper, I'll warrant."

"Away with him!" commanded Massaroni, and Malvolio was again conducted to the place of his confinement, apparently quite unmoved at the threats which had been held out to him, and which there was every likelihood of Massaroni putting into execution.

"It seems as if neither threats nor persuasions would move this ruffian," said Montaldi when Malvolio was gone.

"He is indeed an obstinate and daring rascal," said the brigand; "but if he sets me at defiance ne shall pay dearly for it. I was in hopes that Ottavia was about to divulge everything."

"Ay, it was most unfortunate that she could not," said Montaldi; "but I do not despair that the time will yet come when her reason will be restored to her, and the guilty parties be brought to punishment."

"I hope your anticipations may be realised, Montaldi," said Massaroni; "but did you notice the alarm and confusion the fellow exhibited when he beheld Olympia?"

"Certainly; and no doubt it was the extraordinary likeness she bears to Ottavia which struck him; the observations he made use of also, did not escape my ear; they were of a very singular description."

"Yes," returned Massaroni; "and it would seem from them that he recognised in her some individual whom he had not seen for many years, and had not expected to meet with again."

Ottavia and Olympia now returned to the cavern. The former was much more composed, but they did not venture to put any more questions to her, they deeming it not prudent after the unusual excitement she had experienced. She appeared not to have the least recollection of what had taken place, but seating herself by the side of Olympia, with her arm round her waist, she looked up in her face with all the fervour of the most intense affection.

The remainder of the afternoon passed away without anything particular occurring; and towards the evening, Montaldi and his unfortunate charge took their departure.

Olympia felt no little surprise and alarm at the emotion Malvolio had exhibited and the extraordinary observations he had made use of on beholding her; but she was unable to form any reasonable conjecture as to the cause. She racked her brain to no purpose to endeavour to remember whether she had ever seen him before, and under what circumstances; but she could not recollect anything of the kind, and she therefore concluded that he must have mistaken her for some other person.

The repulsive features and savage manners of the ruffian filled her with disgust; at the same time she looked upon him with horror, when she remembered the hints to which the unfortunate Ottavia had given utterance, and the fearful manner in which he seemed to be connected with her melancholy fate.

Every day, every hour, she felt her attachment to the poor maniac increase, and she was restless and unhappy during the time that she was absent from her presence.

Florio, when alone, continued to ponder over the letter of Melina, and to offer up his supplications to Heaven to protect her, and avert those evils with which she was so fearfully threatened. She was never for a moment absent from his thoughts, and his mind wavered between hope and fear. He was most anxious to ascertain her present condition, and endeavour to prevail upon Massaroni to lose no time in forwarding Rubaldo again to the villa, he having already written a second letter to his beloved Melina, in which he earnestly requested her not to conceal anything from him, as his mind was in a state of the most intolerable suspense until he should be made acquainted with the fate that probably awaited her, and whether there was any room for hope.

Massaroni at length complied with the request of Clairville, and Rubaldo was again despatched to the neighbourhood of Villa Rosa, with strict injunctions to return with all possible speed. When we had departed, Florio's mind felt more at ease.

Once more, we will now return to Melina, who, as day after day fled rapidly away, and the fatal time drew nearer which was to decide her fate, became more truly wretched than ever, and gave herself up entirely to despair. Not all the arguments and consolations of Floretta could have any beneficial effect on her; for to hope that the prince would abandon his designs, or that there was any chance of her escaping, now that matters had gone so far, she thought would be little short of madness. She looked out most anxiously every day with the hope of hearing again from Clairville; and it was that hope which alone sustained her.

Floretta did not miss an evening going to the spot where she had before met Rubaldo; but when she every time returned disappointed, Melina began to despair, and to think that either something had happened to her lover, or that Massaroni had declined assisting him any further in his plans. We need not say that many a pang it cost her whilst remaining in this state of suspense.

But this was aggravated by the return of the Count Alberti to the villa, and it was then that Melina felt the real difficulty and emergency of her situation.

On the morning subsequent to the return of the count, himself and the prince Bianchi held a secret council together, the object of which was, as the succeeding dialogue will show, to consummate their oppressive and tyrannical designs against our fair heroine, and also to adopt such measures as might be likely to place Massaroni, the brigand chief, and Florio Clairville (who Alberti had ascertained was under the protection of the former) once more in their power.

It would appear that a spirit of evil and obstinate determination had taken possession of Bianchi's mind; that he had stifled every feeling of nature, and the ties of consanguinity in his breast, and was resolved, at all hazards, to sacrifice his beauteous niece to the man whom she naturally so thoroughly detested.

"You have arranged, my lord," he said, "for your approaching nuptials?"

"I have, your highness," was the reply from the libertine count; "during my brief absence, I have so arranged that nothing whatever can or shall obstruct us in the consummation of our wishes."

"'Tis well, my lord," said the prince, "on me you may depend."

"I feel satisfied of that, your highness," said Alberti, "and in spite of the evident dislike which Melina bears towards me, trusting to your friendship and determination, at the time appointed, I hope to claim her as my bride."

"You shall, count," returned Bianchi; "my mind is so fixed upon achieving that object, that nothing whatever can change it. You say that you have heard of the rascal Massaroni?"

"I have, my lord; he is still in his old retreat, and with him is residing Clairville, whom he was the means of rescuing from captivity."

"The daring villain! But are there no means of crushing him, and by getting him and the presumptuous beggar, Clairville once more in our power, prevent every possible obstacle to the accomplishment of our designs?"

"There are, your highness," replied Alberti, "and I have a design for effecting that object, which I will submit to you by and by. I have so arranged that they cannot possibly escape us."

"Good," said the prince; "it pleases me much to see you have become so vigilant during your temporary absence from the villa."

"The union of myself and your fair, but haughty niece, I propose shall take place at midnight, in the chapel attached to your villa, and I have engaged a trustworthy priest, who is not over scrupulous, to perform the ceremony, *under all circumstances*. Does that meet with your highness's approbation?"

"Entirely so; you have acted prudently, and success must crown our designs. On Monday week, at the hour of midnight, Melina shall become your bride. I have no doubt that you will soon be able to conquer the repugnance she at present evinces towards you. But what of Olympia?"

"I have ascertained beyond all doubt," answered Alberti, "that she also is under the protection of the brigand chief."

"The daring miscreant!" said the prince. "There appears to be no limit to his insolence and presumption."

"True, my lord; but we shall yet be able to subdue him, never fear."

"Ay, ay, and when I have him securely in my power, my mind will be at rest. And yet I know not how it is, whenever his name, as I have before told your lordship, arises to my memory, a sensation of the most powerful nature, and for which I cannot account, comes across my mind."

"What can be the reason of that, your highness?" asked the count.

"As I said before, I cannot tell," replied the Prince Bianchi; "but his features haunt my imagination sleeping or waking, and his extraordinary resemblance to the veiled portrait, which you have doubtless observed, adds to the impression on my mind."

"There is indeed a remarkable likeness between Massaroni and the protrait your highness has mentioned," observed the Count Alberti; "that, however, can only, I should imagine, be one of those freaks which nature sometimes delights to play. But your highness promised to give me the history of that mysterious painting."

"I did," replied Bianchi, with much emotion; "and I will keep my word, though the secret has been for many years locked within my own breast. But I know that in your lordship, I can confide."

"You may."

"No doubt you will sympathize with me."

"Indeed?"

"Yes; for you are no stranger to the *peculiar* facts upon which it bears."

"I do not understand your highness."

"You will do so presently. Listen; and on your word of honour as a nobleman, never to any one let the secret which I am about to divulge to you pass your lips."

"I promise your highness faithfully," replied Alberti. "I am willing to swear never to do so."

"Enough; draw nearer."

The count drew his chair closer to that of the prince, who after a pause, during which he seemed to have undergone a painful struggle with his feelings, thus commenced:

"It is now more than thirty years ago, since gay and wild, I was residing incog at Florence. There I became acquainted with a beautiful maiden, named Valentia Di Cerito; I need not attempt to describe her charms, when I inform you that she is the original of the portrait to which I have alluded."

"She must then have been most lovely," remarked Alberti.

"Oh, far more lovely," said the prince, with a burst of emotion, "than the most skilful limner could ever convey an adequate idea of on canvas. She was a simple peasant girl, unconscious of guile, who had but one parent living at the time, an aged mother."

"Whom you befriended?"

"Yes; to gain my ends; for I need scarcely say that Valentia's surpassing charms soon captivated my heart, and I in return, won her affections."

" Was she aware of your name and rank?"

"Not at first, but accident afterwars disclosed them to her. Her mother died; she was left alone in the world, and it was then that under the pretence of becoming her protector, and a promise of marriage, I triumphed over her innocence. A boy was the fruit of that intercourse. Some time after this, my father recalled me peremptory to Rome, and I was compelled to obey. I made certain provisions for Valentia and her child, and left her with a bursting heart, promising at the earliest opportunity to return and secretly make her my bride."

"A promise," observed the count, with a satirical smile, "which I presume I need scarcely say, your highness had no intention of fulfilling?"

"My rank, my future prospects, and the will of my father rendered that impossible," answered the Prince Bianchi; "and yet I loved her ardently, fondly."

"Oh, no doubt, and so did I Olympia," returned Alberti; "but circumstances, of course, compelled you to abandon her and her offspring?"

"Alas—alas! it is too true. But for some time I continued to correspond with her, and to transmit her large sums of money."

"And she never betrayed you?"

"Never! Oh, she was most sincere in her love, most patient and confiding."

"And what became of her?"

"I know not."

"Indeed?"

"'Tis true. Suddenly she disappeared from Florence with her offspring, and I could never ascertain whither she directed her steps."

"Then your highness knows not whether she be still living or dead?" asked Alberti.

"I do not," replied the prince.

"Your highness's amour was a most fortunate one, and I only wish that Olympia had acted with the same prudence and forbearance. But I presume that was not your only love intrigue?"

"It was not; but, ah! did you not hear a footstep?"

"I did not."

The prince hurried to the door, and opening it looked cautiously into the gallery beyond.

"I could have sworn I heard a retreating footstep," he observed; "but there is no one here."

"Your lordship must have been mistaken," said the count.

"True," coincided the prince; "I would not for the world that any one one should have overheard that which I have just stated."

"Why it would be rather inconvenient," returned Alberti, with a sarcastic smile.

"We will talk no farther upon this subject for the present," said Bianchi, with considerable agitation; "I do not feel in the vein for it."

"Be it so, my lord," said the count; "but the brief history you have given me has deeply interested me."

"No doubt of it; you speak feelingly."

"Certainly."

"I can depend upon your lordship keeping it a secret?"

"Most unquestionably; why should you doubt me?" demanded the count.

"I do not," answered Bianchi; "oh, my lord, had you but seen Valantia as she was when I first beheld her, lovely as the rising day, artless and innocent as a child, you must have been captivated with her."

"No doubt of it," returned Alberti, with another satirical smile, which was unpleasant to look at; "I can fully appreciate the taste of your highness."

"There are times when my conscience bitterly reproaches me for my abandonment of her and her child," said the prince.

"Psha, my lord," returned his companion, "that is a weakness which you should seek to overcome."

"Very true; but I cannot."

"And you could never by any means ascertain what became of her and her child?"

"Never!"

"It is strange."

"It is; and I would give the world to know their fate."

"Oh, it is most likely that they are both no more," remarked the count, carelessly; "at any rate, it is not at all probable, that they will ever trouble you again."

"Sometimes, I have my misgivings in that respect."

"Oh, I see no reason for them. But when shall I have the pleasure of seeing your beauteous neice Melina again?"

"This afternoon," answered the prince; "and we will then make known to her our final determination, and command her to prepare herself for the nuptials. Think you that we shall receive an interruption from Massaroni?"

"Oh, no," replied Alberti, "he will not dare."

"I know not that, observed Bianchi; "we have already had sufficient and frequent proof of his daring."

"I will take every precaution to frustrate any designs the rascal may have in contemplation," said Alberti, "and I have no doubt that I shall succeed. But I am about to take a walk to Rome, and perhaps your highness will do me the honour to accompany me; the walk may refresh you, and serve to banish unpleasant thoughts."

"Ay," answered the prince, "I will attend

you ; and on our return the interview between yourself and Melina shall take place."

They then quitted the villa.

The Prince Bianchi had not been mistaken, when he imagined that he heard a footstep in the gallery. It was that of Floretta, who hap-pening to be passing by the apartment in which he and the count were conversing, was attrac-ted by the sound of their voices, and induced to stop at the door to listen. What she heard, the reader has already been made acquainted with. She was alarmed by hearing the prince

MELINA SUPPLICATING PRINCE BIANCHI TO DEFER HER MARRIAGE WITH ALBERTI.

hastily arise from his seat, and succeeded, as has been seen, in making her escape before she was detected, and immediately repaired to the apartment of her mistress, to whom she related what she had overheard. Melina heard her with the utmost astonishment and emotion.

"Alas!" she ejaculated, when Floretta had concluded, "I can no longer wonder at the fa-vour with which my uncle views the count, and the utter indifference he evinces respecting his heartless treatment of the unfortunate Olympia. Never could I have imagined that he could have been so guilty. But are you certain that you heard correctly, Floretta?"

"Oh, yes, signora," answered Floretta; "it is quite impossible that I could have been deceived."

"And the prince said that he was not aware whether this Valentia and her offspring were living or dead?"

"He did, my lady."

"Unfortunate woman, how deeply do I sympathise in her cruel fate," said Melina. "This now fully accounts for the extreme emotion my uncle has at all times evinced whenever the portrait happened to be alluded to. But the strong likeness which the brigand chief, Massaroni, bears to that portrait astonishes me more than all; and well do I remember the extraordinary emotion he evinced on beholding it, on the night when he so narrowly escaped from the villa."

"It is, indeed, most remarkable, signora," said Floretta.

"My uncle and the count, then, are resolved to persist in their design?"

"From the observations I heard them make use of, and which I have stated to you, it does indeed appear so, my lady. But still I trust that something will yet occur to thwart them, and to rescue you from the cruel fate with which you are threatened."

"Alas!" sighed her mistress, "what chance is there of your wishes being gratified? Oh, would that I could hear again from Florio, although he has it not in his power to assist me."

"Indeed you know not that, signora," re-returned Floretta. "Massaroni is his friend; he has pledged himself to serve him; he has the power, and depend upon it, he will not fail to keep his word."

"Oh, no," ejaculated Melina, disconsolately, "I dare not entertain such a thought;—I could not, must not accept assistance from the brigand chief, were it even in his power to render it."

"Surely no blame could attach to you, signora, for doing so, since it would be the injustice and cruelty of the prince, your uncle, which would have driven you to it."

"And the time is so short," said Melina; "I shudder to think of it."

"Providence will never allow you to be thus sacrificed, my lady," said Floretta, encouragingly. "The prince will yet relent, otherwise he must be destitute of every feeling of humanity."

"Ah, no; after what you have told me, I am more convinced than ever that there is no hope. Oh, my sainted mother, look down with pity on your poor defenceless child, and intercede with the Almighty in her behalf. But a few days, a few short days, and my fate will be sealed, my misery will be complete.

Oh, that I were dead rather than be consigned to so horrible a destiny."

Tears gushed to her eyes, and for a few minutes she was unable to give utterance to a syllable.

"At midnight," she said, at length; "at midnight did they say this hateful and unholy union was to be solemnised?"

'They did, signora."

"Then there is no hope for me. Oh, I can never survive so monstrous a sacrifice. What an inhuman villain must the Count Alberti be, thus to persist in his cruel design. He must be goaded on by a spirit of revenge, for it would be a gross libel on the sacred name of love to say that he entertains such a sentiment towards me. And have I not taken every means to convince him of the disgust and abhorrence with which he has inspired me? Am I so degraded in the estimation of the prince, my uncle, that he should consider the base and profligate betrayer of the hapless Olympia, worthy to become my husband? Oh, how, agonizing is the thought!"

She sobbed aloud in the anguish of her mind, and her faithful attendant in vain sought compose her.

"The prince and Alberti, you say, have both quitted the villa, have they not?"

Floretta replied in the affirmative.

"Would to Heaven that they may remain away from it during the day," remarked Melina, "for I dread to meet them."

Floretta remained in conversation with her mistress for some time longer, when she was compelled to leave her to go upon some other business; and Melina gave herself up to the most racking thoughts. In this manner the morning wore away; and Melina, hearing the sound of horses hoofs approaching the house, went to the window, and saw that it was the prince and Alberti who had returned. In a few minutes afterwards Floretta re-entered her apartment, and informed her that the prince desired to see her immediately. Melina was fully prepared to receive such a command, and struggling with her feelings as well as she could, she accompanied Floretta to the room in which her uncle and the count were seated. It was the first time she had seen Alberti since his recent return to the villa, and when she beheld the boldness of his looks she could not help shuddering with disgust and alarm; the count, however, noticed her emotion with the utmost indifference, and, in spite of all her efforts to the contrary, he took her hand and pressed it to his lips, with an insolent assumption of the greatest devotion. With what emotions of disgust and indignation did the bosom of Melina swell; but Alberti was by no means discountenanced. She looked imploringly at her uncle; but the expression of his countenance was austere and commanding, and it was evident she could expect neither pity nor for-bearance from him. As these thoughts flashed across her brain she struggled violently with her feelings, and determined to act with forti-tude and decision, let the consequences be whatever they might. She, therefore, assumed an air of dignity and insulted modesty, and returned the bold looks of the count with those of scorn and hatred.

"You sent for me, my lord," she said, at length, addressing the prince in a firm voice, "and as I wish not to be subjected to any fur-ther insult from this *nobleman*, I beg that you will communicate your pleasure with me as briefly as possible, and suffer me once more to retire to my chamber."

"My pleasure, Signora Melina," replied her uncle, haughtily, "is that you remain here, and condescend to listen with patience and serious attention, to that which myself and your affianced lord, the count Alberti, have to say to you."

"The beauteous and gentle Melina," said the count, in a half-sarcastic tone, "surely cannot be so cruel as to refuse an audience to the man who is so fondly and ardently devoted to her, and who is ready to become her slave for ever."

Melina turned upon him a look of abhorrence as she replied—

"Knowing the sentiments of the Count Alberti towards me, and the little regard he can have for my feelings, his society cannot be otherwise than painful and disgusting to me."

"Beware! beware!" exclaimed the prince, passionately, "this obstinate boldness instead of benefiting you, will but serve to excite my wrath, and give you bitter cause for future re-pentance."

"My lord," returned Melina, with dignity and unshaken fortitude; "you are my guar-dian I admit, and as such it is your duty to be as studious of my happiness as if I were your own daughter, and to protect my feelings from outrage. You have heard my sentiments as regards the Count Alberti, and in the name of justice, of humanity, and the ties of consen-guinity, I implore you no longer to urge me to that from which my heart revolts. If you have, indeed, any regard for my future peace and welfare; if you would not, indeed, consign me to misery, shame, and degradation, you will abandon your present designs, and suffer me to act as the dictates of conscience and virtue prompt me."

The Count Alberti bit his lips with morti-fied pride, and could scarcely prevent himself from giving utterance to his feelings; whilst the Prince Bianchi frowned, and was so con-founded and abashed by the firmness of his fair niece, and the force and truth of her observa-tions, that for a few moments he could make no reply.

"Signora Melina," at length said Alberti, "treats me with undue severity and scorn. I know not how I have deserved her hatred and indignation. Surely it cannot be in loving her with all the fervour——"

"Hold, my lord," interrupted the blushing damsel, her eyes flashing with shame and resentment; "such protestations are a brutal insult to my ears; Count Alberti can need no further explanation from me; his own con-science should be able to answer him. Suffer me to retire, your highness, I beseech you."

"Obdurate girl!" cried her infuriated uncle, "you supplicate to me in vain; you remain here until it is my will to permit you to retire. The time has gone by for any squeamish oppo-sition; there is nothing on earth will shake my resolution; all the preparations for the nuptials of yourself and his lordship are nearly complete, and on Monday week, by all my hopes, in spite of the consequences, you shall become his bride."

"Never! never!" ejaculated Melina, ve-hemently; "sooner will I meet death in its most awful form, than such a revoltnig, such a detestable fate. The great God above, who knows the justice and purity of my feelings, will not suffer such a monstrous sacrifice to take place; in Him will I put my trust, and still remain firm in the resolution I have formed."

"You shall find that your firmness will not avail you," replied the prince, sternly; "once the resolution of the Prince Bianchi formed, there is nothing can shake his purpose."

"Alas! alas!" sighed Melina, and tears, in spite of all her efforts to restrain them, started to her eyes; "what have I done to merit such a cruel persecution as this? Oh, my uncle, what has become of that affection, that solicitude for my happiness which you once professed towards me?"

She sunk on a seat, and burying her face in her handkerchief, gave unrestrained indul-gence to the violence of her emotions. The Count Alberti approached her with a sem-blance of pity in the expression of his coun-tenance, but she started with horror at his touch, and looking up indignantly, she ex-claimed—

"Stand back, my lord! Do not dare to approach me; the sight of you becomes more odious to me than ever, and every word you utter is poison to my ears."

"Can nothing I say plead for me in your favour, sweet Signora Melina?" said Alberti; "is there no way by which I can prove the sincerity of the love I entertain for you, and induce you to listen to my vows with patience and indulgence? Why should you be so pre-judiced against me? I know not; for by Heaven, there is not another woman on earth whom I am so fully prepared to love, to worship, to obey! To render you happy shall be the constant study of my life; not a thought, not a single wish that you can entertain shall remain ungratified; my whole soul shall be devoted to your service; your welfare shall be my constant aim: should any care beset your gentle bosom, it shall be my sole anxiety to banish it, and to replace it by happiness, and serenity, and——"

"I will hear no more," interrupted our heroine, rising hastily from her chair, and moving towards the door; "my lord," she added, addressing herself to her uncle, "once more I desire you to suffer me to depart, and do not, oh, do not permit me any longer to be subjected to such insolence as this. You cannot surely be quite indifferent to my feelings."

"Stay, Melina," said the prince, determinedly, and laying his hand upon her arm, "you must not go thus; you must learn to conquer this childish weakness which so ill-becomes you. You treat his lordship with undue severity, and I am surprised at you. I have hitherto endured your obstinate resistance with patience and forbearance; but, mark me, you had better not try me too far."

"Oh, this is most cruel," sighed Melina, again sinking on a chair. "My lord, *you* may try my feelings too far. There is a limit to human endurance, and the heart which you thus seem to take such delight to torture might break. How bitterly must you then reproach yourself as the cause. Reflect, reflect, again I earnestly supplicate you, and take pity on me."

She burst into a paroxysm of convulsive sobs and tears, and the prince did indeed seem somewhat moved by the power of her emotions, whilst Alberti paced the room backwards and forwards with mingled feelings of confusion, vexation, and impatience. He was several times about to speak, but a significant look from the prince (who was fearful of the effect it might have upon Melina in her present excited state) prevented him.

"Melina," said her uncle, in more gentle accents, "why will you continue to give way to those feelings, which can only serve to torture your mind?—You do me an injustice if you imagine that I am no longer mindful of your happiness; on the contrary, it is that which urges me to induce you to comply with my desires; and I think on mature consideration you will come to the conclusion that I speak sincerely."

"Oh, my lord," replied Melina, "how can you, after you have so frequently heard my candid assertions, entertain such an idea? I wish not to appear harsh or bold, but indeed nothing whatever can ever alter the sentiments that at present hold possession of my bosom. I would fain obey your will in every respect;

but in this which so completely involves my future happiness, I cannot, indeed I cannot. If the Count Alberti would alter my opinion of him, and gain my future esteem, he will abandon his designs, and seek to place his affections upon some other female whose heart may respond to his sentiments."

"Never! beauteous Melina!" replied the count, energetically; "that is impossible. My heart is indissolubly fixed on you; and all other women I must view with indifference. Whatever may have been my former errors, and I will not attempt to deny them, I will seek to redeem them, and never give you cause for a single pang or a murmur of complaint. Endeavour then, I pray you, to endeavour to conquer the feelings of prejudice you now entertain against me; and by so doing render me one of the most happy and grateful of human beings."

"My lord," replied Melina, in a firm voice, "you have repeatedly heard my determination, and nothing can—I again assure you that nothing shall, move me from it. Why, then, persist in torturing me with your importunities? Dear uncle, I can support this interview no longer; suffer me, again I ask you, to retire."

"Be it so," said the prince, after a pause; "but, again, I strictly enjoin you to reflect maturely upon what I have said, and to do away with the silly prejudices which you have suffered to take such firm possession of your mind."

"Oh, why urge me to that which is so impossible—so unreasonable?" ejaculated the damsel; "it is fruitless for me to endeavour to conquer those feelings which are prompted by justice and virtue."

"What ridiculous nonsense is this," said the prince, impatiently; "it is the mere caprice of a thoughtless and inexperienced girl, which must not be suffered to be indulged in."

"Alas!" sighed Melina, "can you view the natural and honest feelings of my heart so lightly? I cannot, I dare not, believe that you speak the real sentiments of your heart."

"But, indeed, I do," replied the prince, "and I should consider myself swerving from my duty, if I did not adhere to my resolution. However, I will not urge you further at present; you may retire."

"Oh, thanks, thanks, my lord," eagerly returned Melina, hastily arising from her seat, and advancing towards the door; but the Count Alberti interposed to prevent her, and in the most persuasive accents he could assume, he said—

"And will you leave me thus, fair Melina, in anger? Not one word at parting? Surely I cannot have merited such treatment as this."

"Do not seek to detain me, my lord," replied our heroine, with looks of shame and indignation; "the prince, my uncle, has given me permission to retire, and you cannot expect to do away with the unfavourable impressions I entertain towards you, by throwing any obstruction in my way. Not a word, Count Alberti. I have candidly spoken my mind, and I have already listened too long to observations which are every way so repugnant to my feelings."

The Count Alberti bit his lips with vexation, but attempted not to make any reply; and Melina having respectfully kissed the hand of her uncle, with a bursting heart hurried from the apartment to her own chamber, glad to escape from the painful interview.

She found Floretta awaiting in the room her arrival, and throwing herself into her arms she gave vent to her feelings in a copious flood of tears, Floretta inquired kindly into the circumstances that had taken place at the interview, and our heroine in a few words made her acquainted with all the painful particulars, and gave free expression to her feelings of sorrow and despair.

"Alas!" she sighed, "little did I think it would come to this; never did I imagine that that uncle, who from my earliest youth has behaved to me with such uniform kindness and indulgence, and whose every will it has been my constant study to obey, could have become so stern and obdurate. Oh, what a fearful change has come over him in the last few weeks. I can scarcely believe the evidence of my senses; it appears to me like a frightful dream, and yet I am but too well convinced of its fatal reality. But the Prince, my uncle, who prides himself upon his noble qualities of heart and mind, who is so tenacious of the honour of his house, to think of sacrificing me to a man whom I must ever loathe and despise—a notorious libertine, the destroyer of female innocence; oh, the bare thought is monstrous! It maddens, it distracts my brain!"

"Indeed my lady," remarked Floretta, "I cannot make up my mind to believe that the Prince Bianchi will ever be so cruel and unjust. He can never think of plunging you whom he has ever treated with the same affection as if you had been his own daughter, into so much misery and shame. He will relent, rest assured he will."

"Oh, no," replied Melina, and tears of anguish trembled in her eyes; "I dare not encourage such a thought, after what he has said, and the fixed determination he has so frequently expressed. The Count Alberti has obtained a most extraordinary and unaccountable influence over him, and all my tears and supplications have not the least effect upon him. In a few days he will force me to the altar, and the escape of Clairville does but urge him on in his fatal and cruel purpose. Oh! Florio, beloved Florio! shall I never more behold you?

How truly wretched and miserable I am! All my fond hopes are annihilated: my sun of happiness is set for ever. Would that I were dead!"

"For the love of Heaven, my dear signora," said the faithful Floretta, "do not talk thus. I trust that there are yet many years of happiness in store for you. Do not give way entirely to despair, and depend upon it all the fears you at present entertain—and I confess not without reason—will prove to be groundless. The strange infatuation which now possesses the prince, your uncle's, mind will be dissipated, and he will no longer seek to force you into an alliance so repugnant to your feelings, and which must destroy your happiness for ever, and bring shame and misery upon himself. The Count Alberti, presumptuous though his hopes may be, and even flattered as he at present is by the sanction and encouragement of the prince, take my word for it, will never become your husband. The idea of itself is perfectly odious."

"It is, my good Floretta," coincided Melina; "and I cannot reflect upon it without a shudder. But alas! what other prospect is there before me, after the threats which my uncle daily and hourly holds out to me? I could meet any fate but that with fortitude—without a murmur. Oh! that an All-merciful Almighty would interpose in my behalf!"

"And He will, signora," returned her attendant: "put your trust in Him, and the cares and fears which at present beset your mind will be removed, and you will be restored to that peace and happiness you so well deserve to enjoy. It must afford you consolation, at least, to know that Signor Clairville is in safety."

"It does, indeed, Floretta: but oh! how terrible must be the anguish of mind he must be enduring!"

"Calm your thoughts, dear lady, and rest assured that Heaven will give him fortitude to support his troubles as a man. He will find a sincere friend in Massaroni, of that you may be certain; and I have not the least doubt but that the brigand chief will yet interpose in your behalf, and rescue you from the danger with which you are threatened, should the worst come to the worst."

"Ah! Floretta, I must not, I dare not indulge in such a thought. Think you that I could ever consent to avail myself of the assistance of that lawless man, if even he should be disposed to offer it me? Oh, no! that is impossible."

"Indeed, my lady, I do not see why you should object to it, since it would be the injustice and obstinacy of your uncle which would drive you to such an extremity. Massaroni is a noble-minded man, although misfortunes have driven him to his present lawless course of life, and he possesses qualities of heart which would do any person honour."

"True," answered Melina: "I agree with what you say, and cannot help entertaining a certain feeling of respect towards him, and sympathising with him in his misfortunes; but still I could never consent to place myself under his protection. No; if my uncle do not relent, although my heart would surely break, I see no other prospect than to submit to my cruel fate."

"It must not be—it cannot be, signora," ejaculated Floretta. "Providence will never permit so unholy and unnatural a sacrifice. Remain firm, lady, and you will yet be able to triumph over the obstinate determination of the Prince Bianchi."

"Alas!" returned our heroine, "I now find that my uncle is stern and inflexible in anything to which he has made up his mind; and the interview I have just had with him fully confirms my worst fears. Would that I could have an opportunity of once more seeing my unfortunate lover, that I might assure him of my unutterable affection, and bid him farewell for ever!"

"And your hopes will yet be gratified, signora," said Floretta, "or I am much mistaken. But you will not have to bid him farewell for ever. Oh, no! the clouds that at present obscure the horizon of your happiness and your hopes will yet be banished, and there will be no obstruction to the free indulgence of that love you both so fondly entertain for each other."

"Would to Heaven that I dare encourage such hopes, Floretta!" remarked Melina; "but that is impossible; they could never—never be realised."

"Say not so, my lady," returned her attendant, "but look forward to the best, and take my word for it all will yet turn out well, gloomy though your prospects at present seem to be."

"You are a good, kind-hearted girl, Floretta," said her mistress, "and believe me I feel most grateful to you for your endeavours to inspire me with hope and fortitude under the terrible misfortunes which threaten me. But indeed, I find it impossible to think as you suggest. Would to God that my uncle, since he refuses his sanction to the addresses of the only man who can ever possess my affections, would allow me to lead a life of celibacy; would place me in some holy asylum, where, at any rate, I might be permitted to pass the remainder of my days in calm reflection, and in seeking to reconcile myself to the wreck of my youthful hopes; but to become the wife of the reckless debauchee, Count Alberti; he, the destroyer of the innocent and too-confiding Olympia, and the miscreant who abandoned her and her helpless offspring to misery, if not to death,—oh, horrible thought! Let me die, by the

most dreadful and lingerings of deaths, rather than meet with such a fate as that!"

"It will not be, signora, it will not be."

"Will not be, Floretta; what prospect is there of the contrary?"

"Your uncle, as I have before said, signora, will be aroused from the extraordinary delusion which has for the present taken possession of his senses, and will see through the madness, the cruelty, and injustice of his designs. Courage, lady; maintain your resolution, oppose them to the utmost; call upon Heaven for its protection and assistance, and you will yet be able to crush the hopes of the Count Alberti, and to interest the proper sympathies of the Prince Bianchi in your favour. Florio is poor, 'tis true; and so far as rank and station go, is unworthy of your hand; but his intrinsic worth must ultimately, I feel convinced, triumph over the prejudices of your uncle; he will be aroused from the dream which now steeps his senses, and be only too happy to encourage and sanction the affections of two beings so fondly and virtuously devoted to each other. Come, come, dear lady, away, I humbly, but fervently beseech you, with these sad thoughts, and doubt not that the prognostications I have been bold enough to utter will be verified."

"Your words, spoken so sanguinely, but which I know spring sincerely from your heart, Floretta," returned our heroine, "do indeed encourage me, and I will endeavour to indulge in the same hopes that you express, and put my trust in the mercy and goodness of that Supreme Being, who never forsakes the innocent."

"Spoken like yourself, my dear signora," said the faithful Floretta, joyfully; "continue to enjoy those feelings and you will be able to combat with all the trials to which you are now exposed. Even the latter observations of your uncle at this last interview, show that his heart was somewhat touched by your remonstrances, and who knows what effect a few hours calm and dispassionate reflection may have upon him. My word for it, he cannot much longer remain obstinate and inexorable; I know that it is not in his nature to do so, and therefore I auger the most favourable and desirable result."

"I cannot be as sanguine as you, Floretta; but still I will endeavour to encourage hope."

"Do so, signora, and my utmost wishes will be gratified. But I have no doubt that I shall soon again behold the man who brought the former communication from Signor Florio, and I do not fail every evening at the same hour when I before saw him, to go to the same place of appointment."

"To hear again from dear Florio," said Melina, "though it would afford me no hope, would be a sweet relief to the anguish of my feelings. But think you that the brigand will keep his word?"

"When was Allesandro Massaroni known to break it?"

"True—true; but the time is so short."

"Do not give way to despair, signora; act with firmness, decision, and precaution, and all will yet be well. You, surely, if your uncle remains obstinate, will not persist in rejecting any aid which the brigand chief may offer you?"

"Alas! my mind is bewildered; I know not how to decide, in what way to act."

"The laws of God, and every feeling of justice, are opposed to your union with a man who has so far degraded himself, and who is so repugnant to your feelings, as the Count Alberti; is it not so, signora?"

"True, true, Floretta, there is no denying that."

"Then reason ought to teach you how to act. No false scruples of delicacy should bias you in a moment of such infinite peril to your future happiness. What if you seek the protection of Massaroni; he is honourable, notwithstanding the questionable character of his mode of life; and who is there that would be bold enough to impugn the purity of your motives, or to deny that you were not driven to the course you had taken by the injustice of your uncle's conduct? Reflect on all these observations, I beg, signora, and I feel satisfied that you will come to the same conclusion which I have done. The Prince Bianchi will then, doubtlessly, be brought to his senses; he will repent of his conduct, and only be too happy to bring about a reconciliation. It cannot be supposed that a nobleman of his natural good sense, and strict integrity of principle, can long be blinded and influenced by such a man as the Count Alberti."

"If I could think so," observed Melina, "I should, indeed, be comparatively happy."

"Persevere in trying to do so," returned her attendant, "and I have no doubt but that you will succeed."

"I will do so, my good girl," said Melina, "and may Heaven, in its infinite kindness and mercy, aid me in my efforts."

"I have not the least doubt that it will do so, lady," answered Floretta; "but the time approaches at which the brigand told me every evening to await his coming, and I will, therefore, with your permission, sally forth in the hope of meeting with him."

Melina readily gave her consent, and Floretta left her. When she was gone, our heroine sank upon her knees, and fervently implored the protection of the most High; but in spite of all her efforts to the contrary, and the promises which she had made to Floretto, she found it impossible to banish those fears from her mind which the recent interview she had had with her uncle, and the threats he had held out to her, had naturally engendered in her bosom; and many were the torturing reflections that distracted her brain.

"Alas! dear Florio," she ejaculated, "I see too plainly that our doom is sealed, and that in a few days we shall, by an union the bare thoughts of which fill my mind with horror the most insupportable, be for ever separated from each other. Oh, why did we ever meet, since all the hopes we have dared to encourage are doomed thus to be so cruelly annihilated? But my uncle can never be so cruel as to persist!—If he really loves me as he has hitherto professed to do, he will abandon his cruel designs, and although he may never sanction the affections which I and Clairville entertain for each other, he will not, at any rate, force me to become the wife of one who is so totally unworthy of me, and whom I must ever so utterly desert. No, no, I will not think so harshly of him. He will relent, and I may yet be happy."

She arose from her knees, and endeavoured to compose her feelings, and in which effort, after much exertion, she succeeded much better than could have been at all expected.

The thoughts of the Count Alberti, after our heroine had so abruptly quitted him, may be very well imagined. The Prince Bianchi had left him for a short time to his own reflections, and for a few moments he traversed the room with the most hasty and disordered steps, and muttering curses to himself.

"The scornful beauty; the stubborn prude!" he ejaculated, "to dare so openly to avow her repugnance to me. But I will yet tame her stubborn spirit, and give her good cause to repent the opposition she has given to my passion. She must become mine! She cannot help herself, and, therefore, what have I to fear? The prince, however, methinks, was rather too much moved by her supplications just now, and he must be taught to continue firm and resolute, or even at the eleventh hour my hopes may be disappointed. If I could only crush the power of the daring brigand chief, Massaroni, and once more secure the person of the beggar, Clairville, I should feel more at ease; however, I will not despair, and I have no doubt that all my hopes and wishes will be in a short time gratified. Would that Olympia and her offspring were out of the way, however; they are a source of the most infinite annoyance to my mind; and had my amour with Olympia never taken place, Melina might not now have entertained such a powerful prejudice against me. Pshaw! of what use is it giving way to these reflections? I have the sanction and encouragement of the Prince Bianchi; in a few days I shall force his lovely and peerless niece to the altar, and what then have I to fear? Be bold, Alberti, and the prize you have so long covetted will be yours."

He was interrupted in the midst of these meditations by the return of the prince; and he endeavoured to conceal the excitement of his feelings from his observation as much as possible.

"So, my lord," said Bianchi, "how feel you after your interview with my fair niece?"

"Why, your highness," replied Alberti, "you may be sure that I am not altogether gratified with the reception she gave me."

"It was no more than you had a right to expect, count."

"True; but I must acknowledge that her scorn and obduracy annoys me."

"Tush, man, tush," returned the prince; "you should heed them not. I have no doubt that if you only play your cards right, you will soon be able to conquer those feelings."

"I trust I may," said Alberti; "though I have strong doubts as to whether I shall be able to conquer her repugnance to me; at any rate, while Florio Clairville continues to exist."

"Nonsense! what have you to fear from the beggar Clairville? He is powerless to oppose you, and fear not that he will ever venture to cross your path again."

"I know not, aided and befriended as he is by the brigand chief, Allesandro Massaroni."

"I will yet adopt some means to get that daring rascal in my power; and to pay him in full for the many tricks he has for years past played me and the community at large."

"Pardon me, your highness; but it strikes me forcibly that that is much easier said than done; of which, I think, we have had sufficient proof already. Could we only hunt him from his mountain fastnesses, we might stand some chance."

"And that shall be done," returned the prince, "or there is no power or gold in Rome. Cospetto! think you that I am going long to suffer the impudent robber to set me at defiance altogether?"

"Well, I only hope that your highness may succeed in your wishes; and I suppose I need not tell you that you may command all the assistance in my power?"

"True."

"I long for an opportunity to revenge myself upon Massaroni for the outrages he has committed against me," remarked Alberti, "and I will not relax in my efforts till I have succeeded."

"Well spoken, count," said the Prince Bianchi; "and I have no doubt that with prudence and perseverance the brigand chief may yet be entrapped at a time when he least expects it."

"But, my lord," said Alberti, after a pause, "it struck me that the tears and supplications of your beauteous niece this day made too favourable an impression on your mind."

"You were mistaken, count; though I thought it advisable in her excited state of mind not to prolong the interview."

"I am glad to hear your highness say so. Then I am to conclude that you remain firm?"

"Certainly. What reason have you to doubt me?"

"Enough—I am satisfied."

"You ought to be so," said the prince. "I am not a man to be moved from anything on which I have fixed my mind. I have promised you, solemnly promised you, that in a few days my niece shall either by her own consent or force, become your bride; and you may rest assured that I will not fail to keep my promise."

"Your words inspire me with confidence, my lord; and we have agreed that the nuptials shall take place at the hour of midnight."

"Certainly; we could not make a better or more prudent arrangement, I think."

"We could not, and most impatiently shall I await for the arrival of the time at which my hopes shall be consummated."

"Ay, my lord," remarked Bianchi; "and you ought to consider yourself one of the happiest men in christendom."

"Indeed, I do, your highness."

"Melina is a maiden whom an emperor might be proud to possess."

"True," replied Alberti; "and, believe me, I shall know full well how to prize my good fortune, though I would to Heaven I could conquer her scorn and induce her to view me with less repugnance."

"Perseverance will accomplish that, I have no doubt," said the Prince Bianchi. "Melina must learn to submit to a fate which she cannot avoid. But we have said enough upon this subject for the present; you have my word, my lord, and let that satisfy you, and remove all doubts that may you have suffered to enter your mind."

"It does, your highness," answered the Count Alberti; "and I will look forward to the future with the most sanguine expectations."

"You may do so confidently," said Bianchi; "and rest assured that they will not be disappointed."

With these words the Prince Bianchi took his leave, and left Alberti to his own reflections.

"Yes," remarked the count, when Bianchi was gone; "I triumph: Melina is securely mine, and nothing can save her from becoming my bride, in spite of her resistance and the detestation with which she views me. Well might her uncle say that I should be proud of my prize; she is one that any mortal being might envy the possession of. What will be the anguish and despair of the beggar Clairville when he hears of my triumph, and that Melina is lost to him for ever! Presumptuous varlet, to dare to aspire to the hand of one so lovely, and so far elevated above him, and to seek to rival me! But I flatter myself that his hopes are long ere this annihilated, and that he will never more venture to cross my path. Still the sentiments he has succeeded in implanting in the breast of Melina, inspires me with no common feelings of hatred towards him, and I will not rest until I have, by some means or other, wreaked my vengeance on his head. He must

OLYMPIA.

be annihilated, and all those who have proved themselves to be my bitter enemies. Massaroni, notwithstanding his power, shall not for ever be permitted to escape me. No, I will, if Fortune fails me not, fully repay him for all the injuries and insults he has heaped upon me. Olympia and her child, too, I must get them by some means again in my power, and so secure them that they shall never again cross my path, or any one form the least conjecture what has become of them. Would that they had died years ago, then probably Melina might not have viewed me with the feelings of detestation that she does now. But let me away with all tormenting thoughts, and anticipate alone the triumph and the happiness that are in store for me. The Prince Bianchi is firm in his determination, and I have nothing to fear. But a few days only, and the gratification of all my desires will take place."

Thus exulting, the depraved young nobleman continued for some time to give free indulgence to his guilty thoughts, when he rejoined the Prince Bianchi in the banquetting-room, and continued conversing with him until a late hour of the night.

Floretta was absent from the villa for a considerable time, and Melina awaited her return with no small degree of impatience; but at length there was a gentle tap at her chamber door, and opening it, Floretta entered, and advanced eagerly towards her mistress, after having cautiously fastened the door after her, to prevent any one from suddenly intruding upon them. Our heroine could perceive from the expression of her features that she had agreeable news for her, and she eagerly inquired what it was.

"Speak low, signora," cautioned Floretta, "for we know not who might be listening to us, though I am certain that no one saw me enter the house. I have at last got more news for you, which I have no doubt will afford you pleasure and satisfaction."

"Do not keep me in suspense, dear Floretta," said her mistress; "what is it you have now to communicate to me?"

"I have again seen him, signora," said the damsel.

"Him? Whom do you mean?"

"Who should I mean, lady, but the man whom I wanted to see—Rubaldo, the lieutenant of Massaroni?" replied Floretta.

"Ah!" ejaculated Melina; "is it possible?"

"It is true, signora."

"Then does he bring news from Signor Clairville?" demanded our heroine eagerly.

"He does, signora," returned Floretta. "Signor Clairville is still under the protection of Massaroni, and sends you this letter. I promised to meet Rubaldo again in an hour with your answer."

Melina hastily took the letter, which she pressed vehemently to her lips, and then with a trembling and anxious hand, she broke the seal; and as well as her tears would permit her, perused the contents. We will not attempt to describe the language in which it was couched; let it suffice to say that it was all that the peculiar and painful circumstances could dictate, and every word went forcibly to the heart of Melina. It was some time before she could sufficiently subdue her feelings to give utterance to a syllable, but at length she ejaculated—

"Dear, unfortunate Florio, how keenly do I feel for your situation; how terrible must be the anguish and suspense you must be enduring, and alas! I have it not in my power to communicate anything to you that may inspire you with hope. May Heaven watch over you, and give you fortitude to support the dreadful trials to which you are subjected."

"But you will return him an answer, signora, will you not?" asked Floretta.

"Oh, yes," replied Melina; "but alas! how doubly will the fearful news I have to impart to him increase the agony of his mind. Are you certain, Floretta, that you will be able to leave the villa without being observed?"

"Yes, signora," answered her attendant, "and even if I should not, it is not likely that any one will have any suspicion as to whither I am going. Depend on my using every precaution. Rubaldo made me promise faithfully to return to him in an hour with your answer."

"Well," said our heroine, composing her feelings; "he must not be disappointed, though the task that devolves upon me is a most painful one."

Floretta having placed the writing materials before her, Melina sat down, and with a trembling hand commenced her answer to her lover's letter. It breathed the same ardent sentiments of affection as his own; she concealed no circumstance from him, but she earnestly implored him to endeavour to tranquillise the anguish of his mind, and to resign himself to that fate which seemed to be inevitable, assuring him of the continuance of her love, which could cease only with her existence Having completed the lettter, she folded and sealed it, and delivering it to Floretta, desired her to hasten with all speed to Rubaldo. Her faithful attendant immediately departed on her errand; and when she was gone, Melina threw herself upon her knees, and earnestly supplicated the mercy of the Supreme Being. She felt her mind somewhat relieved after having written her answer to Florio, and again she perused his affectionate epistle with mingled feelings of delight and anguish.

"God grant," she sighed, "that he may be able to receive this mournful intelligence with fortitude and resignation, though well convinced I am how bitterly it will wring his heart. Oh, my uncle, how can you thus delight to torture us?—How can you thus persist in consigning me to a fate which must render me so inexpressibly miserable? Will nothing move you to take compassion on me, and arouse you to a full sense of the cruelty and injustice with which you are acting towards me?—I can scarcely believe that you are the same being from whom I have hitherto experienced such unexampled kindness and indulgence, and towards whom I have ever acted with the strictest obedience and affection. What fatal infatuation has come over you ? May Heaven change your sentiments, and avert the terrible fate with which you have threatened me! Dear Florio, I can never love any other man than you ; and if it is the will of Heaven that we shall never come together, oh, may it take me speedily to itself, for life would then become an insupportable burthen to me. But to become the wife of the Count Alberti—oh, horrible thought, my very soul shrinks appalled from it.''

She clasped her hands together, and for a few minutes remained in a state of the greatest agony and despair.

Floretta was not gone long, and re-entered the apartment of our heroine in the same cautious manner that she had done before, and without being observed by any one.

" Now, Floretta," said her mistress, eagerly, " say, have you executed your errand ?''

" Oh, yes, my dear signora," replied her attendant ; " Rubaldo, as I expected, was true to his appointment, and is now on his way back to the retreat of Massaroni.''

"And did he put any questions to you as to how I was situated, and the danger that was impending over my head ?'' interrogated Melina.

" He did,'' answered Floretta ; "and I thought it best not to conceal anything from him, especially as he would be sure to hear all the particulars on his return.''

" And did he make any observations in reply to the information you gave him ?''

" He did, signora.''

" What did he say ?'' demanded Melina.

" 'Tell the signora, your mistress,' he said, ' not to despair, for she has a warm friend in Allesandro Massaroni, who will not fail to take immediate steps to rescue her from the fate with which she is threatened.'

" Alas !'' said Melina, " I fear the interference of the brigand chief ; I cannot accept of his protection, and should my uncle and he encounter each other, how terrible may the consequences be to one or both of them !''

" Do not let such apprehensions torture your mind, signora," observed Floretta, " but depend upon the prudence and honor of Massaroni.— Surely no fate can be half so dreadful as that to which the Prince Bianchi would consign you, and should you be rescued from his power and that of the Count Alberti, he might relent, and only be too happy to receive you again to his arms.''

" Oh, no,'' ejaculated Melina, " I fear, alas, that nothing will ever move him from the cruel determination he has come to. I see no hope, no means of escape, and nothing remains for me to do than to endeavour to resign myself to my fate.''

" It is impossible that you can do so, signora,'' returned Floretta ; "nature and justice revolt from the bare idea ; besides, think you that Signor Clairville can ever make up his mind to resign you thus ? Oh, no, he could not love you so ardently as he has ever professed to do if he could. But try to calm your feelings, my dear lady, and leave everything to the mercy and wisdom of the Almighty, who, depend upon it, will not desert you in the terrible hour of need.''

" I thank you for your advice, my good Floretta, most sincerely I thank you.''

" And I trust, signora,'' returned her attendant, " that I need not assure you that what I say comes from my heart.''

" I know it—I know it well.''

"Come, lady," said Floretta, "seek to hope for the best, and all will yet be well. But it is late ; had you not better retire to rest ?''

" Leave me, Floretta,'' said her mistress ; " I would commune with my own thoughts, and I do not feel inclined to seek repose just yet.''

Floretta returned no answer, but immediately obeyed, and Melina was left to the free and uninterrupted indulgence of her own dismal thoughts. Wretched, indeed, were those thoughts ; and many were the tears she shed in the truly wretchedness and despair of her heart. She seated herself in a recess by the principal window of her chamber, which commanded a full and uninterrupted view of the beautiful country beyond, and all those scenes which were so fondly cherished in her memory as the hallowed and favourite places of resort for her and her lover. How lovely was the night ! what a painful contrast, however, at the same time, did it present to the feelings which at the moment were passing in that gentle but troubled bosom. Never did moon shine more brilliantly even in the light and transparent hemisphere of ever-beauteous Italy. What a rich flood of radiance it shed upon the waters of the Mediterranean ! How all the tranquil beauties of the night seemed to rejoice, to laugh, to dance beneath the refreshing influence of the season !—and yet that fair maid's heart so sad, so lonely ! She could distinctly see their trysting place—that sacred spot where their pure vows of love and eternal constancy had been so often plighted to each other. She could, in fact, almost imagine that she could trace the initials of their names which they had mutually carved upon their favourite tree ; and oh ! how her fair bosom swelled, how her heart palpitated, how fast her tears flowed, as the idea suggested itself to her mind !

" Beloved Florio !'' she ejaculated, in tones of the deepest emotion, " and shall we never more meet on that spot where our tide of affections were permitted to gush forth, and when we little dreamed of the miseries that were in store for us—the fearful blight that was to fall upon our dream of happiness? Alas, no! My foreboding heart tells me that our hopes are annihilated ; that we are doomed to inevitable misery. Oh, God! what a change, what a frightful change has come over that uncle whom I have ever so loved and honoured. Can madness have seized upon his brain, that he thus forgets the affection he has hitherto shown me, and can make up his mind to sacrifice me to such a villain, such an unprincipled villain, as the count Alberti? The name of that man alone, is detestable to me. I could die the most horrible, even the most degrading, of deaths, rather than be forced to the altar with him. But, no, it cannot, must not, shall not be; nature, humanity, justice, everything revolt at the idea, and Providence will not permit the unholy sacrifice. I will not despair—I will not despair. Uncle, still loved uncle, in everything but this will I obey you; but, by Heaven, if you persist in forcing me into an union so repugnant to my feelings, you shall find the now-made bride a lifeless corpse at the altar, the instant the ceremony is performed."

As the hapless maiden thus gave utterance to these words, there came over her beautiful features an expression of terrible determination. She placed her fair hands upon her brow, and for a few moments her thoughts were entirely absorbed in the agony of the feelings which these reflections engendered. But she was suddenly aroused from her meditations by hearing a rustling sound among the foliage of the garden, and directing her attention to the spot from whence it seemed to issue, she thought she beheld the white flowing robes of a female in the moonlight; but in an instant it it was gone, and, however strong the impression might have been upon her mind at the instant, she concluded that she had suffered her imagination to deceive her. But still she could not but feel greatly agitated, and continued to direct her eyes towards the spot. There was nothing to be seen, and again she supposed that she must have been mistaken: but she was not long permitted to remain in doubt, for presently there emerged from a shrubbery in the garden a light, shadowy form, in robes of flowing white—so light and shadowy, indeed, that it seemed not one of mortal coil, and with a wing-like step advanced towards a spot immediately in front of the casement at which our heroine was sitting.

It was the form of a female of the most lovely and graceful proportions; her forehead was encircled by a wreath of white roses, upon which the moonbeams fell full, and gave them all the appearance of silver; but her head being drooping upon her chest, in a melancholy attitude, Melina, for a time, had no opportunity of observing her features, though every feeling was bound up in the greatest interest and agitation, and she watched her every movement with the deepest possible attention. For awhile she appeared to stand buried in deep thought, but at length she raised her head, and the moonbeams falling full upon her countenance, distinctly revealed her features to our heroine, and made her start, and give utterance to an exclamation of surprise at the striking resemblance which they bore to the portrait which her uncle, the Prince Bianchi, so carefully preserved and concealed in one of the apartments of the villa.— Had that painting been instinct with life, and moved from its frame, and taken up its position on the same spot now occupied by its singular and mysterious counterpart, the impression which it now created in Melina's mind could not possibly have been stronger ; and yet, at the same time, a feeling of awe stole over her senses for which she could not account, but which she could not overcome. Yes, there was the same youthful lovely face, the same innocent, melancholy expression; but oh, how pale, how supernaturally pale, the features. It inspired the mind of the gazer with a sentiment of the most uncontrollable awe, and our heroine drew in her breath, and watched the actions of the unknown with the deepest and most breathless anxiety.

She advanced with noiseless steps towards that wing of the villa in which the Prince Bianchi slept, and waving her long thin hands in a singular way for an instant or two above her head, in a voice of the most solemn and sepulchral impressiveness, every syllable of which went to the heart of Melina, and the more strongly persuaded her that she was listening to no mortal being, but that the realms of eternity had permitted one of its celestial inhabitants, for some wise and inscrutable purpose, to revisit the earth, she sang the following words :—

> " Hast thou heart, hast thou feeling,
>   Seducer wake and list to me ;
> Hear that spirit's sad revealing,
>   Of the deeds been wrought by thee !"

The strange being paused, and a violent trembling came over the frame of our heroine, which she found it impossible to subdue; but still she was unable to remove an inch from the spot on which she was seated, or to take her eyes for an instant from the mysterious form on which her attention was rivetted, and in a few moments she sang in the same melancholy, impressive, and plaintive strains, the well known ballad which has so often, and must now again be quoted in the pages of this narrative :—

> " Maiden of Florence, oh, listen to me,
>   Nor think that I seek thy fond heart to
>   ensnare :
> If e'er I deceive thee, accurs'd may I be,
>   And my bosom be plunged in the darkest
>   despair,

' Maiden of Florence, my bosom reviles,
    The wretch who'd the innocent damsel betray ;
Maiden of Florence, more bright are thy smiles
    To me, than the radiant orb of the day.

" Maiden of Florence, I liken thine eyes,
    That now with such lustre are beaming on
        me ;
To the stars that so brilliantly shine in the
        skies,
    And I love them not, dearest, more than I
        love thee !

" Can I deceive thee ?—Never !—oh, never !
    Let no such thought in thy bosom have birth,
May I, if false to thee, curs'd be for ever,
    Wandering, hated, accursed o'er the earth.

" Maiden of Florence, oh, listen to me,
    Nor think that I seek thy fond heart to
        ensnare ;
If I deceive thee, accurs'd may I be,
    And my bosom be plunged in the darkest
        despair !"

The voice of the airy-like form ceased, but it
had scarcely done so, when our herione heard a
wild and delirious cry which seemed to proceed
from the very chamber in which her uncle slept ;
but still the female form moved not, whilst an
expression came over its pale features which
spoke of triumph and melancholy regret. But
a moment, and the loud banging of a closing
door drew the attention of Melina more closely,
and with a wild and disordered demeanour, she
beheld her uncle rush into the garden and dart
towards the spot on which the strange form
stood, but which he no sooner beheld, than his
features became distorted with agony ; his eyes
dilated, and every nerve seemed to be shaken,
and to shrink from the performance of its
natural functions.

" God of Heaven !" he groaned at last ; " is
this some frightful delusion of the distempered
imagination, or am I dreaming ? Can the silent
tomb yield up the dead that has been reposing
in it for years, and restore it to the earth so life-
like, that the soul shrinks appalled at the contemplation ?—What spell is this that steeps
and obscures my senses ?—Valentia !—No, it
cannot be !—Begone !—begone ! and yet mysterious, awful being, who art thou ?"

The lips of the mysterious woman moved,
and she seemed to speak, but Melina was unable to distinguish a single word she uttered,
though the emotion of the Prince Bianchi every
instant became more intense ; his legs tottered
under him, and she expected to see him sink
to the earth. The strange form gradually re-
ceded from him, at the same time waving her
hands in a menacing manner, and he, seemingly
appalled, slowly followed her, but had not the
power to come up to her, By degrees her
form seemed to diminish and to fade, and then
suddenly vanished from the sight, how and
whither our heroine could not form the slightest
conception of. It was all the work of an instant, and Melina was no less appalled than

her uncle appeared to be. For two or three
minutes he stood transfixed to the earth, and
with clasped hands gazed upon the spot where
the phantom had vanished, whilst our heroine
could plainly mark by the clear light of the
moon, the agonized expression of his features,
and the large drops of prespiration which stood
upon his trempling brow ; but at length, in a
voice which vibrated solemnly on her ears,
he exclaimed—

" Spirit of the much wronged Valentia,
whose innocence I destroyed, and then so
cruelly deserted, why do you thus appear to
me ?—Must I ever thus be haunted ?—Will
nothing stifle the voice of conscience, or veil
the imagination in obscurity ?—Why should I
thus live accursed and pursued ?—A demon
urges me on to the continuation of that which I
know to be wrong, and I can only escape his
power by death ! 'Tis but the work of a moment, and all is over ; thus then let me end an
existence which seems but to have been
created to inflict and endure misery. There
is no one by to see me ; there is no one to regret my fatal and untimely end, and thus at
once I consummate the fatal deed.

As he thus spoke, he drew his sword from
its scabbard, and was apparently about to throw
himself upon its point, when the horrified
Melina shrieked aloud, and attracting his attention towards her, arrested him in his deadly
purpose.

" Melina !" he cried, gazing wildly up towards her. She waited to hear no more, but
darting from the room, she rushed precipitately
down the stairs, and the next moment was
standing by her uncle's side, with her fair hand
upon his arm, and gazing earnestly into his pale
and agitated countenance.

" Uncle, dear uncle," she ejaculated, " for
the love of Heaven what would you do ?"

" Melina—girl !" said the prince, shuddering,
and gazing with astonishment upon her ; " you
here ? Not in bed ? Watching my actions ?"

" No—no, by all my hopes," replied our
heroine, " only accidently so. Come, come ;
let me see you to your chamber ; some wild
dream has disorded your imagination ; think
no more about it. Come, dear uncle, come."

" A wild dream !" returned Bianchi, staring
vacantly upon her ; " no, no, it was no vision ;
do not seek to persuade me that it was, Did
I not hear those well known words that are
continually vibrating in my ears ?—Did I not
behold her ?—Did you not yourself behold her ?
Do not tell me a falsehood, girl, for your looks
betray you !"

" Oh, my lord," said Melina, soothingly,
" do not, I beseech you, thus torture yourself.
It is now late, and you need repose, At some
other and more appropriate time, we will talk
farther, if it so please you, on this subject."

" Tell me, girl," said the prince, fixing his

eyes sternly upon her, "and do not attempt to deceive me; how long had you been at your window when I first beheld you?"

"About half an hour, my lord," replied our heroine, falteringly.

"Ah! then you must have seen everything?"

"Say no more about it, my dear uncle."

"Nay, girl! think not to silence me thus! Tell me, did you not behold that female form, which I spoke to?"

"Ye—yes," stammered out Melina; "but it could only have been some one, who in wilfulness of spirit was endeavouring to impose upon your credulity."

"'Tis false!" cried the prince, hastily and passionately; "it was the ghastly shade of her I so deeply wronged and left to misery and death! It will never quit me!—It—but fool! Why do I talk thus? You knew her not—you never heard the history of her wrongs, and therefore dare not, cannot accuse me. Oh, she was most lovely and innocent, and she loved me too—worshiped me, and I vowed to—Pshaw! Leave me, girl, leave me!"

"My dear uncle," said Melina, in the same persuasive accents; "I seek not to penetrate your history, believe me I do not; but let me prevail upon you to retire to your chamber; come, come."

"You will not hate me?—will not despise me?" said the Prince Bianchi, wildly.

"Hate you? despise you?" repeated the maiden. "Oh, Heaven forbid."

"And yet you must do so," said Bianchi, "if you knew all. But why are you here?—Begone, I say; have I not told you that my mind is made up; and who shall dare attempt to move me from my purpose?—Away with you!—Away with you!"

"Oh, my dear uncle, why these harsh words? You are not well;—you have suffered your mind to——"

"Ah!" interrupted the prince, sternly, "dare you seek to penetrate into the hidden secrets of my mind? Would you also upbraid me with cruelty and villany?—"

"My lord, you know not, you cannot know what you say," replied the astonished and agitated Melina; "there is nothing that is in any way connected with you I seek to know; but again let me prevail upon you to quit this spot, and to endeavour to calm your feelings."

"Did you not hear the words of the song she sang?" demanded the Prince Bianchi, imperiously. Melina hesitated for a moment or two, seeing the violent agitation of his manner, and then replied in the affirmative.

"Ah!" he ejaculated, "it was the same ballad that I so often sung to her, and yet deceived her after all. You stare upon me with vacant eyes, girl, and yet with an expression of disgust. Do not seek to deceive me; I see you hate me, despise me, and consider me a villain! But, fool that I am! Why do I talk thus? Girl! I charge you, on your life, to think no more of this—to say nothing of it to mortal being;—do you hear me?—"

"Yes, yes, my lord," replied our heroine, trembling, "can you doubt me?"

"Swear to do as I command you!"

"Oh, what necessity is there for this? You have ever found me obedient, have you not?"

"It will be well for you if I have no occasion to alter my opinion.—There, away with you to your chamber, and think of your speedy union with the Count Alberti."

"The Count Alberti!" repeated Melina, with a shudder of horror and disgust which she could not resist.

"Yes," said the Prince Bianchi, sternly, "dare you still resist my will?"

"Oh, my uncle!"

"Bah! I will not be contradicted."

"I have repeatedly assured you that I cannot love him."

"But you must and shall become his bride, notwithstanding."

"God help me then!" sighed Melina; "for if such is your determination, my misery will be rendered complete."

"Leave me, I say," sternly commanded her uncle, "for this is neither the time nor place to talk upon such a subject."

"But you will retire to your chamber?" said Melina, eagerly.

"Yes, yes;—anon—do not question my conduct, or seek to fathom my secrets, or it will cost you dear."

Poor Melina offered not to make any reply, but pressing the hand of her uncle respectfully to her lips, she slowly withdrew from the garden and retraced her footsteps to her chamber. On her arrival there she immediately extinguished her lamp, so that the prince might imagine she had retired to rest, and then resumed her seat at the window, in such a position that she could not be observed, and watched him anxiously.

The Prince Bianchi continued to pace the garden for some time with the most disordered steps, and seemed to be entirely absorbed in his own gloomy thoughts, frequently striking his forehead and beating his breast in the most agitated manner, but at length he withdrew, and Melina heard him ascending the stairs which led to his chamber. She now fell on her knees and fervently implored the mercy and protection of the Supreme Being. The extraordinary and awful events of the last hour, filled her mind with no less astonishment than awe. Could it be possible that what she had seen was a being of another world?—she was not by any means prone to superstition, and yet all the singular circumstances of the case tended to confirm her in that belief. The extraordinary appearance, and as sudden and unaccountable disappearance of the female; its ghastly countenance and aerial form, and the terror which her uncle had evinced on beholding it, all served to corroborate that opinion, and to increase the feelings of astonishment and dread which had come over her.

"Alas! my uncle," she ejaculated; "you whom I have from the earliest days of my remembrance learnt to look upon with love and reverence, much do I now fear that you have been equally as guilty as him to whom, it seems, you are resolved to sacrifice me. Can I then any longer wonder at your inflexibility?—Dare I any longer entertain a hope that you will relent?—Alas! no! There is nothing left for me but misery and despair. Oh, would to God that I was no more, sooner than be consigned to a fate which makes my blood run cold to reflect upon. Oh, my uncle, how entirely lost to pity, reason, and justice you must have become, to form such a cruel and unnatural determination!"

Her tears flowed fast as she gave utterance to these words, and she beat her breast in a state of the greatest agony; but still, notwithstanding the lateness of the hour, she did not feel the least inclined to retire to rest, but continued seated at the window and to watch the spot where she had seen the mysterious form, expecting, yet fearing, every moment to behold it again. At length the solemn bell of Saint Peter's tolled the hour of midnight; and tired of watching and thinking, she threw herself in her clothes upon the bed, and tried to compose her mind to sleep; but that she found to be impossible, and she continued tossing on her pillow until the morning sun once more peeped in at the window of her chamber. But what were the thoughts and feelings of the Prince Bianchi, when he once more retired to his chamber?—Bearing in mind all the awful circumstances we have related, the reader will be able to form a pretty fair conception of them. That the form he had seen was the phantom of her he had so deeply and so cruelly injured, he could not form the least doubt; and his guilty conscience haunted him to distraction, which was increased by the knowledge that Melina had also been a witness to all that had taken place, and that in the frenzy of his feelings he had divulged more, much more than it was even safe or prudent for her to know.

"Valentia!" he exclaimed; "and will thy spirit never rest?—Will it continue to haunt and distract the unhappy guilty wretch who was the sole cause of all thy misery?—Oh, yes, justice decrees that such should be the terrible punishment of my crimes, and how dare I murmur?—Zittella too!—Where art thou, poor confiding, ruined innocent?—Oh, what a villain have I been, and I would seek to increase my guilt by sacrificing my niece to a man who has been equally guilty as myself!—But it is not yet too late to repent, to abandon those designs, and to set the mind of Melina at rest. Bah! what worse than childish weakness is this? Shall I suffer the obstinacy of a foolish, thoughtless girl to triumph over my reason? Shall I, after all the promises—the solemn promises—I have made to the Count Alberti, deceive him, and disappoint his hopes? No; let whatever may be the consequences, I will not do so. An alliance between him and my fair niece is what I have long coveted, and I will suffer no obstacles to impede my wishes. He is rich and noble, and notwithstanding his liason with the girl, Olympia, he is every way worthy of her. Melina will learn to conquer her aversion of him, and all will yet be well. It is fortunate that I discovered the passion that existed between her and the presumptuous Florio de Clairville, or what disgrace would have been brought upon my noble name. It was a bad job that he escaped though, and that Massaroni has taken him under his protection; however, I must keep a strict eye upon them both, and I have no doubt that I shall be able to frustrate any designs they may have in contemplation. I will not rest until I have the daring brigand chief in my power, and then I will not fail to inflict upon him that punishment which the many impudent outrages he has committed deserve. And yet I cannot get rid of the strange feeling which always comes over me whenever I think of Massaroni; his manners are noble, and there is something in the expression of his features, which makes me feel doubtful and uneasy. I would that I could become better acquainted with the particulars of his history. P'shaw! why do I let such matters disturb me, or to occupy a second thought? What is he to me? And why should I feel any interest in the fortunes of such a lawless rascal?"

Such were the thoughts that continued to occupy and to harass the Prince Bianchi's mind for some time, and although he tried hard, it was not without the greatest difficulty that he was enabled to conquer them. The night wore away, and still he remained up, and the solemn stillness that reigned throughout the villa inspired in his bosom a feeling of the most unconquerable and impressive awe. He almost feared to look around him, lest he should again encounter the phantom which he firmly believed he had seen; and the least breath of wind made him start, as though he expected that something dreadful was about to happen. As soon as the morning dawned, in order to endeavour to recruit his spirits, he walked forth from the house, and rambled thoughtfully amongst the romantic scenery by which it was surrounded.

We will now return to the retreat of Massaroni among the mountains. Nothing particular or worth recording had taken place for some days; the fellow, Malvolio, remained obstinate, and the brigand chief was unable to make up his mind as to what he would do with him, as there seemed to be no probability, at present, at any rate, of being enabled to elicit anything from him. Olympia and her child remained much in the same condition, and no change for the better had come over the unfortunate Ottavia. She daily visited the retreat of the brigands, and seemed to be only comparatively happy alone when in the society of Olympia, as it excited her so much; however, it was thought advisable not to introduce her again to Malvolio for the present, anxious though they were to fathom the mystery connected with them; and she never once alluded to him, but seemed to have forgotten the circumstance of having seen him altogether.

One of the most unhappy of the inmates of the retreat of the brigands, was Florio de Clairville; though Massaroni exerted himself to the utmost to divert his mind and to raise his hopes. He felt far from satisfied with his present situation, and though he could not but admire and feel grateful for the disinterested friendship, attention, and generosity of the brigand chief, he would have felt much more at ease had he been placed in different circumstances. Need we say that his thoughts were constantly fixed on his beloved Melina? and hourly did he offer up his prayers to Heaven for her welfare and safety, though he could not but entertain the most torturing apprehensions as to the fate which was in store for her. He could not for a moment doubt that the Prince Bianchi would put his threats into execution, and unless Providence should be pleased to interpose to rescue her, she would be sure to be sacrificed to the hated Count Alberti. He awaited with the most painful anxiety the return of Rubaldo; and as several days had elapsed since he had departed on his second expedition, he became impatient, and began to fear that some accident had befallen him.

"Oh, fear not, my young friend," said Massaroni to him one day, when he was expressing himself to that effect, "Rubaldo is too cautious to be entrapped, and never yet failed in any errand he went upon. He has doubtless not yet had an opportunity of obtaining any intelligence; but as soon as he has, you may depend upon it that he will use all possible despatch in returning."

"Alas! I fear," said Florio, "there is little hope for me; what can a poor friendless man like myself do? Nothing, absolutely nothing; and I might, therefore, as well make up my mind to the worst."

"Nay, my good fellow," replied the brigand chief, "I must not suffer you to talk thus, nor to give way to such gloomy ideas. My word for it, gloomy though your prospects at present certainly are, all will yet be well, and you and Signora Melina will be rendered happy."

"Oh," remarked Clairville, "I dare not be so sanguine as to entertain any such hope; it would be presumption in me to do so, when I reflect on the lowliness of my station; and could I only be satisfied that her uncle, the Prince Bianchi, would relent, and not seek to sacrifice her to such a man as the Count Alberti, I would endeavour to make my mind content, though fate might ordain that I should never behold my beloved Melina again."

"I tell you, signor," said Massaroni, confidently and impatiently; "that she you love shall never become the wife of the unprincipled villain, Alberti."

"What can save her, should her uncle remain obstinate?"

"I will, at all hazards," replied the brigand chief; "and fear not but I shall succeed.— Allesandro Massaroni has had more difficult tasks than that to accomplish, and he never yet failed to surmount them. I do but wait the return of Rubaldo with the necessary information, and then I will promptly put my plans into execution. Are you not satisfied with my promises?"

"I ought to be so," answered Florio; "and yet I find it impossible to conquer my doubts; besides, pardon me, Massaroni, but I apprehend that Signora Melina would hesitate, and feel the most delicate, and, I must say, reasonable scruples, to place herself under your protection."

"Such objections, should they arise, which it is not unreasonable to suppose they will, may, I think, be speedily overcome," observed Massaroni; "Signora Melina, I am certain, is too generous for a moment to doubt the honour and sincerity of my intentions; and could she once be removed from the power of the prince, her uncle, it might bring him to his senses, and a reconciliation might be effected. Come, Clairville, cheer you; you must become more confident, and not give way to such gloomy thoughts, and you will find that what I have predicted will be verified."

"I would fain encourage the hopes you have expressed, Massaroni," returned Clairville, "but alas, I find that it is impossible to do so; and even if I could, I should only be doomed to disappointment. I can never presume to imagine that Melina will ever become my wife; and it would have been better, much better for us both, had we never met."

"Cospetto, man!" exclaimed Massaroni, "why, what a melancholy, despairing lover you are. I tell you again, that notwithstanding fortune at present frowns upon you, the time will yet come when she will wear her gayest smiles. Signora Melina and you were formed for each other; you love each other sincerely, fervently, and trust me I am no prophet if after all your fates are not united together. I owe the Count Alberti ample revenge for the annoyance he has caused me, for the wrongs he has done to the unfortunate Olympia, in whose fate you know I take so great an interest, and also for the manner in which he has so often and so insolently set my power and authority at defiance; and depend upon it, I will not fail to gratify it, as he will quickly find to his cost. It would be mon-

MELINA WRITING TO FLORIO.

strous for a moment to suppose that the fair and innocent Signora Melina, should ever be sacrificed to such an unprincipled libertine as he."

"True," said Florio, "and the bare idea fills me with shame and disgust; but the Prince Bianchi is inexorable, and therefore what hope is there of her escaping from the fate with which he has threatened her?"

"Signor Clairville," observed Massaroni—"I think I need not tell you that I am a man of determination, and that I never fail to fulfil any promise which I may have made. I have sworn to rescue and protect her whom you so fondly, so devotedly love, and at all hazards I will do so. Let that assurance satisfy you, and trust to fortune for the result."

"I will try to do as you advise, Massaroni," replied Clairville, "for I know you wish me and Signora Melina well; but still I cannot deny to you that I know I shall find the task to be a most difficult one. Could I but rest satisfied that this hated and unnatural union would not be permitted to take place, though I might never dare to hope that I should become the husband of Melina, methinks I could become contented and resigned."

"Then I can tell you again," returned the brigand chief, positively, "that you may rest confident that Signora Melina, even if she does not become your bride (which I predict that she will) shall never be united to such an unprincipled villain as the Count Alberti. On that point I urge you to make your mind perfectly happy, and to put your trust in me."

"I will do so, Massaroni," replied Florio; "for I know you are my friend, and it is quite clear that you must act from the most purely disinterested motives."

"You do me no more than justice by that supposition, signor," remarked Massaroni.

They were now interrupted by the entrance of the brigand's wife, and the conversation for the present ceased. Clairville did try to think as he had advise him, and he became more easy in his mind; but still he awaited most anxiously and impatiently for the return of Rubaldo, and dreaded the intelligence which it was too probable he would have to communicate.

At length Rubaldo did return, and he was immediately ushered into the presence of Florio and Massaroni.

"Now, Rubaldo," said Clairville, eagerly; "tell me what success? Have you anything particular to communicate? Did you deliver my letter?"

"Yes," answered Rubaldo, "I succeeded in doing so at last, and bring you this letter in reply from the Signora Melina: but I am afraid that which it contains is not calculated to raise your hopes."

"Give it me," said the agitated Clairville, eagerly taking the letter, which he pressed with the most fervent emotion to his lips.

He then hastily broke the seal and proceeded to peruse the contents; but he had not read many lines when he turned very pale and trembled violently.

"'Tis all lost!" he ejaculated; "her doom is sealed; the prince is inexorable, and my misery is complete."

"Nay, nay, signor," said the brigand chief; "say not so; you must not give way to such gloomy thoughts and apprehensions as these.

But what is the nature of the intelligence which thus creates your alarm?"

"Read, Massaroni," replied Clairville, giving him the letter, "and judge for yourself."

The brigand chief hastily glanced over the contents, and then said—

"It is a villanous design; but do not give way to despair, Clairville, for I again give you my word that it shall be thwarted."

"Alas! how can that be accomplished?" ejaculated Florio.

"Leave everything to me, and depend upon it the Signora Melina shall yet be rescued from the cruel and unnatural fate with which she is threatened."

"They will force her to the altar, and of what avail will it be for her to offer any resistance? Beloved Melina, thou art lost to me for ever! So young, so innocent to be thus sacrificed: the thought drives me to distraction."

"Calm your feelings, my young friend," said the brigand; "and do not view the prospect before you on the blackest side. There is hope for you, I again tell you, and certain confusion and disappointment for your enemies."

"Oh, how terrible must be the sufferings of that deeply persecuted and innocent girl," observed Florio.

"It shall be but of short duration," returned the brigand, "or my name is not Alessandro Massaroni. Next Monday night, did not Floretta, the faithful attendant of Signora Melina, tell you, Rubaldo, was the time fixed for the secret and midnight nuptials to take place?"

"She did," answered Rubaldo.

"Enough," said Massaroni; "we will be present to prevent the ceremony from taking place, much to the dismay and disappointment of the Count Alberti and the haughty and obstinate old prince."

"How, Massaroni?" exclaimed Florio, with a look of astonishment and incredulity.

"Oh, rest assured, signor," replied the brigand chief, "that I make no empty boast! In a very few days you and Melina shall be far out of the reach of danger."

"Impossible!"

"But you will find it is true. Rubaldo, have you obeyed my instructions, and closely inspected the villa, to ascertain whether or not it would be possible to obtain a secret entrance?"

"I have," answered Rubaldo; "but I have succeeded in other respects far better than could have been anticipated."

"What mean you?"

"Why," returned Rubaldo, "I have discovered that an old acquaintance of mine is living in the service of the Prince Bianchi and I have seen him two or three times, and ventured to sound him on the subject. He is a crafty rascal, and will do anything for money. It would be no difficult task for him to admit us to the villa, privately, and to conceal us till the time should arrive for us to put our designs into execution. The prince and Alberti would be taken by surprise, and able to offer little or no resistance. Success would certainly be ours."

" By the dome of St. Peter's, this is a fortunate circumstance," remaked Massaroni ; "but is this fellow willing to enter into our plot ?"

" Perfectly so," answered Rubaldo.

" And is he to be depended upon?"

" Oh, yes, if he be liberally paid for his services."

" Enough, then; our success is certain," said the brigand chief. "Cheer you, Florio, and in a few days your lover will be rescued from the imminent danger to which she is now exposed, and once more restored to your arms."

" I dare not venture to entertain such a hope," returned Clairville; "and even should you be able to put your wishes into execution, I would much rather that it could be accomplished by other means."

" Then you entertain some doubts of the honour and integrity of my intentions ?" said Massaroni, with a look of reproach.

" Oh, no, Massaroni," replied Florio, " indeed I could not wrong you by such a thought. I am convinced that you have no other motive than such as springs from a disinterested desire to serve me and Signora Melina."

" You judge me rightly," said the brigand chief ; "and you will have no cause to regret if you place the most implicit confidence in my conduct, and follow my advice. Why should you object to my proposals ? Can you tamely make up your mind to suffer the beauteous and innocent Signora Melina to be sacrificed to that man, whom you know she detests, and who is so totally unworthy of her ?"

" Oh, no !" answered Clairville, " I could more calmly and patiently hear of her death, than that such a dreadful and revolting fate had befallen her."

" Then why raise any further objections when there is every chance of rescuing her ?" demanded Allessandro.

" I will not; I will be guided by all that you say and advise, and may an All-merciful Providence aid you in your merciful and charitable designs."

" Spoken like a man, my young friend," said Massaroni ; "and fear not for the result. To-morrow, myself and Rubaldo, disguised in such a manner as it would be impossible for even those who are most familiar with our persons to recognise us, will depart for the Villa Rosa, and see this worthy gentleman

whose assistance we require. A trusty portion of our band can follow in different parties, and depend upon it that our plot is as certain of success as if it were now accomplished."

" Heaven grant that you may not be disappointed in your expectations," said Clairville; "but had I not better accompany you ?"

" Oh, no," answered Massaroni, " you will be much better here ; besides, you could not render us any assistance, and in fact might be more in our way than otherwise."

" Well," remarked Florio, " I will be guided entirely by you."

" Do so, and you will act prudently."

" But are you sure that this man to whom you have spoken, Rubaldo, will not deceive you ?"

" Oh, no," answered Rubaldo ; "gold will always purchase him to fidelity."

" His name ?" asked Florio.

" Guiseppe."

" Ah ! I remember the fellow well, and I always thought him a crafty knave."

" Ah !" observed Massaroni, "I see plainly that he is just the rascal we want for our business."

" You may depend upon that," said Rubaldo; " I have, as I before said, known him for many years, and he would not attempt to deceive me, for he considers me his friend."

" That is fortunate," remarked the brigand chief; " so you may e'en set your mind at rest, Florio, I think, for the success of our expedition is all but certain."

" But should you succeed in getting Melina in your power, what are your future intentions regarding her ?" asked Clairville, eagerly.

" Why, that will be matter for future and deliberate consideration. The signora must be consulted, and you may be sure that I will place no restraint upon her wishes."

" Her abduction will cause the greatest sensation in the country, and I am afraid will raise such an overwhelming force against you, that you will find it impossible to withstand,"

" I will brave all that," returned Allesandro, " and have no doubt that I shall be able, as usual, to come off triumphant. Let no such thoughts disturb your mind ; but rest assured that Allesandro Massaroni will accomplish his wishes, and continue to set his enemies at defiance."

" Massaroni," said Clairville, "I already owe you a debt of gratitude for the many services you have rendered me, which I fear it will never be in my power to repay."

" Enough of that, signor ; what Massaroni does, he does freely, and requires no acknowledgment for it. But we will say no more upon the subject at present. I will now leave you to yourself, and hasten to make my preparations for my departure to-morrow. Be confident, and all will turn out quite as well as you could wish it, and much better than you could anticipate it."

"Your words inspire me with hope," replied Florio, "and ι will place the firmest reliance in you, since you] can have no motive in wishing to deceive me.

"Certainly not," said Massaroni; "the brigand chief never forfeited his word yet, and it is not likely that he is going to do so now."

"I do believe you, Massaroni; and I sincerely hope that the day is not far distant when you will be restored to that station in society you are so well calculated to embellish."

"Oh, no," replied Allesandro; "I do not wish it, or expect it; I am a prescribed man, upon whose head a price is set, and I have no hope beyond revenge against the betrayer of my unfortunate mother, and the wild life of freedom that I at present lead. Something tells me that the day will come when I shall discover the villain, notwithstanding my ignorance of his name and that thought goads me on, and inspires me with fresh courage when my spirits would droop under the weight of wrongs that have been inflicted on me."

"But would you raise your hand against your own father, Massaroni?"

"Did he ever bestow upon me a father's love? Was he not the murderer of my mother, and why should I spare him? No, by all my hopes, should Fate ever throw the heartless seducer in my way, I will not."

"Unfortunate man," said Florio, "I sincerely pity you."

"Rather say that you sympathize with me in the unmerited injuries that have been heaped upon me; Allesandro Massaroni, the brigand chief, likes not pity."

"Pardon me," said Clairville, "I meant not to insult you or to wound your feelings."

"I believe you, signor."

"Your's has indeed been a strange and unfortunate life, Massaroni."

"It has, and so you would say, did you know all the particulars of my history."

"And your mother would never reveal to you the name of your father?"

"I have told you so, signor."

"Then it seems evident to me from that circumstance that she pardoned him, and wished you not to pursue him with a feeling of vengeance."

"It might be so: but although I am not naturally vindictive, think you when I know how that gentle and unfortunate woman who gave me being perished, that I can conquer the feelings of hatred I entertain towards her destroyer?"

"True, true, there is every allowance to be made for the sentiments which have taken possession of your breast; but surely it would be better for you to endeavour to conquer them?"

"It is impossible; I cannot."

"Surely the upbraidings of his own conscience, if he be still living, must be a sufficient punishment to him."

"Such a heartless villain must be insensible to the stings of conscience," answered Massaroni; "but we will talk no more upon this subject, for I am not in the humour. You will remember the advice I have given you, and rest satisfied that all I have promised I will perform to the very letter."

"I do believe you, and will leave everything to your prudence."

"Enough," said the brigand chief; "you will have no cause to regret your confidence. Farewell, for the present. I go to make the necessary arrangement for my expedition."

"Thanks, thanks," said Clairville; "and may every success attend your undertakings."

"There is no fear of that," returned Massaroni; "a very few days will decide all, and I have not the least apprehension as to the result."

They now separated, and Clairville was left to the solitude of his own thoughts, the nature of which we have little occasion to attempt to describe to the reader. Notwithstanding all the promises of the brigand chief, and the urgency of the case, he could not feel exactly satisfied with the determination, and he would much rather that his beloved Melina could have been rescued from the revolting fate that was impending over her by any other means; but that was impossible, and there was nothing left for him to do than to endeavour to reconcile his mind to it. The bare thought of Melina being forced to become the wife of the guilty Count Alberti was insupportable; and he was therefore prepared to encounter anything rather 'than such a revolting sacrifice should take place.

Now he was left alone, again and again he perused the letter of Melina, and it was utterly impossible that anything could exceed the power of his emotions as he did so. But the tone of ardent affection it breathed, was some consolation to his heart, and he endeavoured to hope that providence would yet interpose to avert the misfortunes by which they had so long been surrounded, although all probability of their love ever receiving the sanction of the inflexible Prince Bianchi, was to all appearance entirely at an end. Earnestly he supplicated the mercy and interference of the Supreme, and by degrees he became more calm and confident. He had every reliance on the honour and integrity of Massaroni; though he was at times fearful that his sanguine anticipations were doomed to be disappointed, and that he might by some untoward accident fall into the power of his enemies, and thus fall a victim to his disinterested friendship towards him and his beloved Melina.

During the remainder of the day he saw no more of Massaroni, but in the evening they met again, and entered freely into conversation upon the subject of the intended expedition.

"My preparations are all made," he said, "and to-morrow morning by the fresh blush of day myself and Rubaldo will depart from here, with every prospect of success."

"I trust that your hopes may not be doomed to be disappointed," returned Florio, "but still I cannot reconcile my mind to your running so great a risk for my sake, and that of Signora Melina, who have no claim on your exertions."

"Nonsense, my young friend," replied Massaroni, impatiently; "the ideas you entertain on this subject are far too delicate. I should despise myself, could I for a moment hesitate to render all the assistance in my power in a case of such emergency. Why talk to Allesandro Massaroni of danger? Has he not times and oft encountered far greater perils, and never yet failed to surmount them? Those who know my character well, are perfectly aware that fear is a stranger to me."

"Of that I am certain, Massaroni."

"Then why entertain those doubts?"

"Can I help doing so under all the circumstances?" demanded Clairville.

"Psha, man! there is not the least necessity for them."

"I hope not."

"You will shortly be convinced that there is not. Do not give way to such groundless apprehensions."

"But you will promise me that you will use no more violence than is absolutely necessary?" asked Florio.

"I do," answered the brigand; "and with that assurance seek to rest satisfied."

"You will not inflict any serious injury on the Prince Bianchi, or Count Alberti?"

"Not if I can possibly avoid it."

"That promise is enough, Massaroni, and I will take your word."

"You may safely do so."

"But still I would rather that I might be permitted to accompany you."

"No, Florio," remarked Massaroni, "it would not be safe or prudent for you to do so. Your feelings might overpower you and render you rather an obstruction than an assistance."

"Well, I will place every reliance on you, Massaroni, for I believe that you advise for the best."

"You may be sure of that," answered Allesandro.

"But do you think this man, Guiseppe, can be trusted?"

"Oh, yes, I can depend upon the word of my lieutenant, Rubaldo, who knows him so well. Should I discover anything that may give me cause to suspect him, fear not but that I shall know know how to deal with him. But there is one point on which I must caution you. Florio, during my absence."

"What is that?" demanded the latter.

"It is that you will keep yourself strictly confined to this place," replied the brigand chief, "for there might be danger in going abroad; and you know not who may be lurking in the neighbourhood."

"Very true," coincided Clairville; "I will do as you wish. There are no other instructions you wish to give me?"

"I think not. So now, Florio, we perfectly understand each other?"

"I think we do; but with what impatience and anxiety shall I await your return."

"My absence will be brief, and again I enjoin you to encourage hope, and to rest satisfied that success will be sure to crown my efforts. In less than a week Signora Melina will be an inmate of this retreat, and safe under my protection."

"Dearest Melina," said Florio, fervently, "and shall I indeed again behold you; shall I once more listen to the heavenly music of your voice, and hear you repeat those vows of love which have so often imparted such fond transport to my soul?"

"You will indeed," replied Massaroni; "and when the haughty Prince Bianchi, her uncle, finds that she is released from his power, my word for it, Florio, he will relent, and a reconciliation will be effected."

"Oh, I dare not encourage such a hope," observed Clairville; "it is more likely that his feelings will be more exasperated at her escape from him, and he will be goaded on to revenge."

"If he is wise he will not," returned the brigand; "however, I will take care to use every precaution to prevent that."

"How can you do so?"

"We will discuss that subject on a future occasion. Let us but rescue Melina, and I do not doubt that we shall be able to arrange everything satisfactorily afterwards."

"But think you the prince will ever forgive me; or that the Count Alberti will abandon his intentions?"

"He will have no alternative. I will exact my own terms. He has a sufficient knowledge of my power by this time."

"He should have," answered Clairville, "but I cannot but believe that he will oppose it to the utmost; and the force which he and the prince will be sure to bring against you will be more than you can resist."

"Oh, I fear them not; my usual good fortune, I daresay, will not desert me in any emergency. But away with these thoughts; at present everything goes on as well as we could wish, and it would be useless to anticipate the worst."

"You are most sanguine in your expectations, Massaroni."

"I am, and I see no reason to be otherwise. Come, come, Florio, arouse yourself, and depend upon it all will turn out according to my anticipations."

"God grant that you may not be doomed to disappointment, but I acknowledge that I find it utterly impossible to entirely conquer my misgivings.'

"Pshaw, man! that is a weakness which is unworthy of you. It would be monstrous to abandon the innocent Melina to such a fate as that with which she is threatened."

"No," returned Florio, "I cannot entertain such a thought with any degree of patience. Sooner, much sooner would I that it would please Heaven to take her to itself. Dear Melina, I can never presume to hope that it will be our fate to come together; but were you released from the hated addresses and importunities of Alberti, would your uncle but relent and not force you into an union so revolting and unnatural, methinks I could be content and resign myself to my destiny."

"Cheer you, Signor Clairville," said Massaroni, "and I again predict that the fears and doubts which now beset your mind will never be realized."

After some further conversation to the same effect, Florio and the brigand chief separated for the night, and the former retired to his chamber, promising to meet Massaroni in the morning in order to witness his departure on his important expedition.

Florio slept but little that night, for his mind was two busily occupied with the thoughts that were naturally engendered in his breast, and many were the sad misgivings that still distracted his brain. He frequently offered up his prayers to Heaven for the safety and protection of Melina, and endeavoured to hope that something might yet occur to rescue her from the revolting fate with which she was threatened, and to bring the prince, her uncle, to reason and forbearance; but, alas! there seemed to be but little prospect of that, and in spite of all his efforts to the contrary, Florio could no help giving himself up almost entirely to despair.

At length the morning dawned, and Florio arose, and having again offered up his prayers to the Supreme, he hastened to meet Massaroni, whom he found with Rubaldo, all ready to depart on his journey. They were both so completely disguised that had he not been aware of their intentions, Florio would have found it utterly impossible to recognize them.

"Now, Florio," said the brigand, "how are your spirits this morning? To judge from the appearance of your countenance, you do not seem to have slept much during the night."

"True," answered Clairville, "my thougt were too busily occupied to suffer me to do that."

"Well," said Massaroni, "I do not wonder at that; but you must try to conquer your apprehensions, which I feel positive will be proved ere long to be unfounded. You may trust to me, and you will have no cause to regret your confidence."

"I do not doubt you, Massaroni," said Florio, "for you can have no motive for seeking to deceive me, or to raise in my mind false hopes."

"Certainly not. I should despise myself could I do so."

"Still I should feel more satisfied did you consider it prudent for me to accompany you."

'No," returned Massaroni; "that must not be; I think I have stated sufficient reasons for my objections, and therefore you must try to make your mind contented."

"Well, I will seek to do so," replied Clairville; "although it is a task that will be most difficult to accomplish. The time that you are absent will seem an age to me, and with what torturing anxiety shall I await your return."

"Fear not, I will delay my return no longer than possible; and in the meantime, Maria, my wife, will make all the necessary preparations for the reception of Signora Melina; I have given her the requisite instructions to that effect."

Clairville returned his thanks to the brigand for his attention, and after they had partaken of some refreshment, Massaroni, pressing the hand of Florio cordially, accompanied by Rubaldo, departed on his journey. Clairville then again retired to his chamber, where he could give uninterrupted indulgence to the conflicting thoughts which distracted his mind.

Thus the day wore drearily away, and no sooner had the shadows of evening fallen upon the earth, than a number of the brigands, according to the instructions of Massaroni, departed from the mountain retreat, and followed in detached parties by different routes, towards the neighbourhood of the Villa Rosa. Florio beheld their departure with the same dismal forebodings, and it was sometime before he could tranquilize his feelings in the least degree. He continued to traverse the cavern in which he slept, for several hours, with the most agitated steps, and torturing indeed were the thoughts that distracted his brain. At length he threw himself on the bed without undressing, but it was all to no purpose, for he could not sleep; and the more he endeavoured to do so, the greater became his agitation. Dismally he passed the night, and in the morning he arose with very little relief afforded to his mind. He apprehended all sorts of things from the expidition of Massaroni, notwithstanding he well knew his idomitable bravery, skill, and ingenuity, and felt fully convinced of the fervour, the enthusiastic fervour and integtity of his intentions; but still he could not but fear that the combined power of the Prince Bianchi and the Count Alberti would prove too much for him. In spite of all that Rubaldo had asserted to the contrary, he was extremely doubtful whether or not such an admitted scoundrel as the man Guiseppe could be depended upon, and he looked forward with the most insurmountable apprehensions and misgivings to some act of treachery which would compromise the liberty and safety of the brigand chief, a circumstance he must ever most deeply deplore, from the generous and disinterested part he had always acted in anything that was at all calculated to promote his welfare, and that of his beloved Melina and to frustrate the designs of their enemies; besides, as we have before so frequently stated, he could not at all reconcile to his mind, as Massaroni was situated, his interference in their behalf, and knew well, however much Melina must dread and shrink with horror and repugnance from the fate with which she was threatened, she could not approve of it.

It was with these feelings torturing his mind that he entered the cavern in which Maria Grazie, the brigand's wife, and the fair and unfortunate Signora Olympia, were awaiting him to the morning's repast, although he endeavoured to stifle them as much as possible; but Maria's penetrating eye read his thoughts in a moment, and she observed—

"You seem unusually dull this morning, Signor Clairville. May I make so bold as to ask you what it is that so particularly disturbs your mind?"

"Need you put the question, signora," returned Florio, "when you are aware of the anguish and anxiety which must torture my bosom at the alarming situation of the Signora Melina?"

"True," remarked the brigand's wife; "the situation of the signora is most painful and revolting, and I deeply sympathise with her in her misfortunes and the tyrannical and cruel conduct of the prince, her uncle, and the Count Alberti; but why should you thus give way entirely to despair? Has not Allesandro Massaroni given you his solemn promise that she shall be rescued from the dangers by which she is at present surrounded, and think you that he will break his word?"

"Oh, no; far be it from my thoughts to do so," answered Clairville.

"He never did so yet, and it is not at all likely that he is going to do so now," said the brigand's wife.

"But in spite of all this, signora, I cannot conceal from you or myself, the great danger which Massaroni thus generously rushes into for me who am almost an entire stranger to him."

"Pshaw, signor," replied Maria, proudly and impatiently; "the brigand chief is unacquainted with such a feeling as fear, especially when he has such enemies to encounter with as the Prince Bianchi and the Count Alberti; methinks you should be thoroughly convinced of that ere this. Mark my words; he will return victorious; and that when he does, the fair being who is so dear to your heart will accompany him, and be perfectly secure from the power of her oppressors."

"But will not the vengeance of Bianchi and Alberti be sure to pursue your husband and all in any way connected with him?" demanded Florio.

"Oh, fear not that; we can boldly set them both at defiance. Have we not always done so hitherto, and think you that fortune will now desert us?"

"I fervently hope not."

"She will not, while we have justice on our side. So, set your mind at rest, Signor Clairville, and my word for it, you will have no reason to regret the interference of Allesandro Massaroni, brigand and outlaw though he be. You would be unworthy of the love of Signora Melina, could you object to any course that may be adopted which is at all calculated to rescue her from the revolting fate which is at present impending over her. Here in these caverns she will be secure from insult, and every possible respect will be paid to her; and it strikes me that the Prince Bianchi will only be too ready to come to a proper understanding, and to abandon his present monstrous designs."

"I wish I could think as you express yourself, signora," observed Clairville, in a hesitating tone.

"Persevere, and you will succeed," replied Maria; "you will not be doomed to disappointment, depend on it."

"I feel sincerely obliged to you and your husband for the kind wishes you entertain towards me and she who is far dearer to me than my very existence."

"Name it not, Signor Clairville; I and my husband require not thanks; they are unwelcome to our feelings; what we do springs at all times from the purest and most disinterested of motives."

"I believe you, signora," returned Florio; "I must be most ungrateful and uncharitable did I not do so. But, alas! I fear that it will never be in my power to repay you in the slightest degree for all the manfold services you heap upon me."

"Pardon me, Signora Clairville," replied the brigand's wife, "but you will best do so by saying no more about it, but by placing the utmost reliance in our friendship."

" I do so, signora, and will endeavour as far as is in my power to look forward to the best."

"Well spoken, signor, and I repeat that you will have no cause to regret your confidence, But come, we will, if it pleases you, change the subject for the present."

Florio complied, and in conversation with Maria and Olympia tried to divert his thoughts and to ease the anxiety of his mind; but this, as might be expected, he found to be a task that was most difficult of accomplishment. They were shortly afterwards joined by Montaldi and the unfortunate Ottavia, who was in a less excited state than she had been for some days; and in the conversation that ensued, Clairville did succeed in tranquillizing his feelings far better than could have been, under all the circumstances, expected.

In the meantime, the sufferings and suspense of Melina were almost too much for her fortitude to support, and as day after day wore dismally away, and the time more rapidly approached at which her uncle had so remorselessly threatened to sacrifice her to that man whom she so thoroughly loathed and despised, her agony and despair increased tenfold, and it was as much as all the eloquence and argument of the faithful Floretta could do to impart the least composure or hope to her feelings. How torturing were the thoughts which the receipt of her last letter would inflict upon her lover. The fatal intelligence communicated therein, would certainly, she reflected, drive him to a state of frenzy; and there was no one at hand who could ameliorate the anguish of his mind, or impart the least consolation to him. This thought was sufficient of itself to drive her to despair, and every moment made her feel more keenly the horror of their situation. When she remembered the observations of Rubaldo to Floretta, namely, that Massaroni would not fail to the utmost of his power to interpose towards her rescue, she could not help feeling a sensation of dread, and could not help thinking, that notwithstanding the desperate nature of her situation, she ought not to accept the services or interference of that desperate and prescribed man; for if she did so, what would the ungenerous world think of her afterwards? Would it not be too ready to condemn her?—And Clairville, she felt satisfied, could never reconcile his mind to such a course, notwithstanding that, by rejecting it, he would probably have to resign all his hopes of possessing her for ever. Floretta found the greatest difficulty in combating her arguments, though she exerted herself to the utmost to do so; and, indeed, the scruples of her mistress were so well founded in reason, that it seemed very little better than presumption on her part to do so.

"Alas! my good Floretta," Melina would say, "I see no hope of escaping from the

misery and destruction with which I am threatened, unless my uncle can be moved to forbearance; and, at present, Heaven knows there appears not the slightest chance of that. My heart recoils from the idea of accepting the aid and interference of Massaroni, and I trust that he may be induced to abandon any such design, if ever he should have entertained it."

"Indeed, signora," replied Floretta, "although I must admire the delicacy of the feelings which prompt you, I must say that I consider there would be every excuse to be offered for you. The prince, your uncle, alone would be to blame, in having by his obstinacy driven you to such a desperate and painful emergency. Besides, the honour of Massaroni's intentions on such an occasion as that could never for an instant be questioned; and surely any course would be more prudent and advisable for you to adopt, than to permit yourself to be sacrificed to such a cruel and disgusting fate as that with which you are threatened. Reflect calmly and maturely, my dear signora, on the observations I have presumed to address to you, and I trust that you will yet be able to make up your mind to yield to my advice, should your uncle and the Count Alberti still persist in their cruel and unnatural purpose."

"You are a kind, faithful girl, Floretta," returned our heroine; " and I feel convinced that what you say comes from your heart; but still I cannot, dare not think of such a desperate alternative. May Heaven protect me, for without its merciful interposition, I fear that I am lost for ever."

Sobs choked her further utterance, and it was some time ere Floretta could succeed in consoling her.

" Providence will not desert you, signora, depend on it," she said; " and, therefore, still endeavour to hope. Who knows what may yet occur to prevent the misery you so justly dread?"

"Alas! alas! how short is the time," sighed Melina; "but a few days, and that on which my union with the hated Alberti is appointed to take place will arrive."

"No—no—it cannot be! The prince will surely be moved by your tears and supplications, when he fears that such a fate as that to which he has threatened to consign you, must break your heart."

" What hope is there of that? Has he not hitherto sternly resisted all my earnest entreaties? And think you he will now forfeit his word to the count?"

Floretta scarcely knew how to answer this, and she remained for some time silent; but at length she did partially succeed in tranquillising the feelings of her mistress, and she endeavoured to divert her thoughts to less painful subjects.

Our heroine had not seen her uncle or Alberti for the last two days, and they had been absent a good deal from the villa; but she now received a message from the former to join him in his study, and, with a trembling and palpitating heart, she prepared to obey it. She was lightened considerably of her fears when she found him alone, and she approached him with a faltering step, and downcast eyes; but he handed her gently to a chair

THE APPARITION.

by his side, and took her hand with more kindness and affection than he had been accustomed to do lately, and that somewhat re-assured her.

"Melina," he said, "you look pale, child; you tremble. Nay, why will you persist in giving way to this weakness, when you should be all smiles and happiness?"

"Alas! my lord," replied Melina, timidly, "can you marvel at the alteration in my looks and manners, when——"

"Pshaw, girl!" interrupted the prince,

impatiently; "I know well what you would say, and, therefore, you may as well restrain your observations, lest you should exasperate me."

"Alas!" sobbed our heroine, "I have lost your love, my lord; and can you wonder that I am wretched?"

"You have forgotten your duty," returned Bianchi, sternly.

"Oh, no—no—no!" ejaculated Melina, with the greatest emotion; "why apply such harsh and cruel observations to me, when, Heaven knows, I so little merit them? Dear uncle, I have never forgotten the duty I owe to you, and I should hate and despise myself if I could; but can you expect me to obey you when you would consign me to a fate from which nature revolts."

"But you must, you shall obey me, girl!" exclaimed the prince, passionately. "You know my will, and what obstinate madness it is in you to attempt to resist it! The time, the hour is fixed for your nuptials with the Count Alberti, and nothing whatever can save you."

"Oh, for the love of heaven take compassion on me," implored the distracted maiden. "Consign me to any other fate but that, and I will endeavour to submit to it without a murmur!"

"You supplicate me in vain, Melina," said the inexorable Bianchi, "as I have often told you; why then thus persist in offering a foolish resistance to that which you cannot avoid?"

"Oh, God!" groaned his beauteous niece, "this is most cruel! How have I merited such harshness as this? It cannot surely be the Prince Bianchi, my uncle, whom I have ever honoured and revered, who speaks thus!"

"But you will find that it is," replied Bianchi, sternly. "But away with such folly as this; I have no longer any patience to listen to it. Your words convince me that you still dare to cherish your hateful passion for Florio Cairville. Beware! beware! or you may have bitter cause to repent of your conduct. Do you mark my my words, girl?"

"Alas! too well I do," replied his hapless niece: "but oh, surely you will retract them?"

"Never!" answered Bianchi, determinedly; "do not flatter yourself with any such an idea."

"Then there is no hope for me," sighed Melina, wringing her hands, and weeping bitterly; but the prince remained sternly unmoved; "you doom me to destruction. Would to Heaven that I were dead or had never been born."

"Ridiculous girl! You have suffered these wild and romantic notions to get the better of your good sense; but you must learn to con-

quer them, again I tell you, unless you would bring down my everlasting malediction upon your head. My hopes are entirely fixed upon this alliance, and they must not, shall not, be disappointed."

"Oh, my dear uncle," cried the distracted girl, sinking at his feet in an agony of uncontrolable grief, and clasping his knees; "do not turn an entirely deaf ear to my supplications, lest you drive me mad. Can you for a moment think of uniting my fate with such a man as the Count Alberti? I solemnly declare that I can never look upon him with any other feelings than those of the most unutterable hatred and disgust; and should you persist in your cruel determination, you will drive me to do that which I cannot even contemplate without a shudder of horror, and which might plunge my soul in everlasting perdition."

"What mean you, girl?" demanded Bianchi, with a look of alarm.

"I will never continue to live as the wife of the detested Alberti," replied Melina, solemnly and firmly; "nay, hear me, while I swear——"

"Forbear! rash damsel!" interrupted her uncle, "I will hear no more; these heroics are sickening to me. Have I lived to all these years to be dictated to by a child? Away with you again to your chamber, and there learn reason and submission."

"To anything but this," said Melina; "but from tame submission to such a monstrous and unnatural fate as that to which you would consign me, my lord, my very soul recoils with horror. But oh, bethink yourself, and do not close your heart entirely to justice and mercy. Remember the promise you made to my poor mother, your only sister, on her death-bed, and——"

"Hold! hold!" interrupted her uncle, with quivering lips, and in a voice of the greatest agitation; "why do you repeat that melancholy circumstance to me? Have I not fulfilled that promise to the very letter, and ever cherished you with the same affection, as if you had been my own child?"

"Till now, you have, my dear uncle," answered our heroine; "I should be unjust and ungrateful did I attempt to deny it; and it is therefore that I feel the change, the sudden, the fatal change in your conduct towards me the more keenly. Oh, for the love of Heaven, do not remain inexorable, and I will not only forget all that has recently passed, but, if possible, love you with tenfold more ardent affection than I have hitherto done."

"Obdurate girl, have I not already repeatedly assured you of the utter folly and uselessness of these appeals? Think you I will break the solemn promise I have made to the Count Alberti?"

"And was it just, was it generous, my lord, to enter into any such compact without first consulting my affections?" demanded Melina, with a look and in accents of the deepest reproach.

"I knew well that it was perfectly useless to do so, since your affections were placed upon the beggar Clairville," replied Bianchi, coldly. "But enough of this; you have repeatedly heard my determination, and it is only a waste of time to argue the point any further with you."

"God help me, then," sobbed the unfortunate girl; "for I see plainly that He is my only hope. May you never have cause to repent this harsh conduct, my lord."

"Ah! do you presume to threaten?" said Bianchi, passionately.

"No, my lord," answered our heroine, "Heaven forbid that I should do so; I only venture to remonstrate upon a subject in which my happiness is so deeply involved, and surely I may be permitted to do so?"

"Begone, begone! my patience is exhausted. When next we meet again, I shall expect to find your mind in a different condition."

"Nothing whatever, my lord can alter the sentiment I at present entertain; I should despise myself, could I ever feel anything but the greatest repugnance and contempt for the unmanly and unprincipled Count Alberti!"

"This to my face, Melina?" said Bianchi, fiercely: "again I warn you to be careful what you say, and not to try my patience and forbearance too far."

"Patience! forbearance!" repeated our heroine; "oh, my lord, pardon me, but does your present conduct evince either of these qualities? There was a time when I could not have appealed to you in vain; but I have now lost your love, and I cannot but look upon you as being entirely callous to any misery you may inflict upon me."

"These are bold words, girl," said the prince, biting his lips, "and do not savour much of the meek obedience of which you have boasted."

"Alas!" sighed the damsel; "I scarcely know what I say; your words have quite bewildered my senses; but surely it is innatural to suppose that I can passively give my consent to a union so repugnant to my feelings, and which is opposed to all the laws of God and man."

The prince returned no immediate answer, but paced the room for some moments in a state of the greatest agitation, and muttering incoherent words to himself.

"Melina," he said, at length, "you act madly in opposing my will. It is only by obedience to my desires that you can hope for or expect still to retain my love. Reflect upon the consequences of your obstinacy, and let your mind awaken to reason."

"Oh, my lord, have I not maturely, painfully reflected upon everything? and reason and justice tell me that I have acted rightly, and as virtue ought to dictate to me. Those sentiments can never change, be the consequences whatever they may."

"Then be those consequences upon your head, rash girl," retorted her uncle, sternly; "for notwithstanding all the false hopes you may entertain, at the time I have fixed you shall most assuredly be compelled to become the wife of the Count Alberti."

Poor Melina clasped her hands in despair and wept bitterly, but the prince remained inflexible, and eyed her emotion with an expression fast approaching to indifference.

"You have heard all I have to say on the present occasion," he at last observed;—"and therefore it is useless to prolong this interview. Retire to your chamber, and if you would not be visited by my eternal displeasure, you will abandon these ridiculous and dangerous thoughts."

"Never!" replied Melina, firmly; "they are founded in justice, and I will adhere to them even with my life."

"Foolish, headstrong girl, do you wish to exasperate me?"

"No, my uncle, if I am still permitted to call you by that name; but I cannot, will not act the hypocrite; and, therefore, in spite of all that may follow to myself, I must speak boldly, firmly out."

"By Heaven!" exclaimed the excited Bianchi, "this is too much. I will talk to you no longer, lest I should be tempted to forget myself."

Our heroine covered her face with her hands, and sobbed as though her heart would break. Bianchi then rang the bell violently, and Floretta immediately made her appearance.

"Conduct your mistress to her chamber, girl," he commanded.

Melina turned upon him a gentle but impressive look of expostulation and supplication, but he averted his gaze from her, and motioned her to begone. Taking the arm of her faithful attendant, with a deep sigh she obeyed, and left the prince to himself. The interview with his niece, and the observations she had made use of, and the truth and justice of which he found it impossible to deny, had greatly excited him, and for some time he traversed the apartment with disordered steps, frequently giving utterance to his feelings in language of the most violent description.

"Still obstinate," he soliloquised, "still confirmed in her hatred of Alberti; this is unfortunate; it is bewildering and torturing; but by all my hopes, I am determined it shall not avail her. Shall I be moved from my

Purpose by a thoughtless girl?—No I will not! It would be a disgrace to my dignity and authority; and would not Alberti despise me for my weakness? He would, and justly too. But still, she is young and innocent, and has ever before been submissive to my will, and treated me with the greatest affection and reverence; and it seems cruel to disappoint her young hopes. I would that she had never seen Florio Clairville, or that Alberti had not so committed himself; then might this union have been effected without any repugnance to her feelings, and all my wishes would have been gratified. But it is useless to reflect thus; fate has decreed that it should be otherwise, and I must endeavour to make the best of it."

He was interrupted in the midst of these reflections by a knock at the door, and the Count Alberti, who had been absent for a short time from the villa, entered.

"You seem excited, my lord," he said, noticing the features of the prince narrowly; "may I ask you if anything has occurred to disturb you?"

"Yes," replied Bianchi, "but I know not that it should disturb me so much."

"What is the nature of it, your highness?" asked the count.

"I have again had an interview with Melina."

"Ah! and she still remains obstinate, I suppose?"

"She does," answered the prince; "if possible, she is more determined than ever."

"This is no more than I expected, my lord," said Alberti, "but may I request the particulars of what took place at this meeting?"

"It would enrage you, I fear, count, and you had better remain in ignorance of them."

"No, no, I am fully prepared for everything, especially after all that has taken place at the several interviews between me and Signora Melina."

The prince then complied with his request, and Alberti listened to him with feelings which the imagination of the reader can well depicture. When Bianchi had concluded, he folded his arms across his chest, and paced the room backwards and forwards in a state of considerable excitement, and the prince watched him with anxious looks.

"To be thus despised, hated, abused," he said; "it is almost more than human patience can endure. But still in spite of her opposition to my suit, and the scorn she lavishes upon me, I must ever love her with the most ardent passion, and I would sooner forfeit all the wealth I possess, and become a houseless, friendless wanderer upon the face of the earth, than abandon my hopes of her."

"Well spoken, my lord," said the prince; "but fear not that you will ever be put to such an extremity. I am the lawful guardian of Melina, and notwithstanding her repugnance, it is useless for her to offer any resistance to my will."

"You will not be moved from your present determination, my lord, by any arguments or expostulations which the Signora Melina may make use of?"

"Certainly not," replied the prince; "can you doubt my word, after what has passed between us?"

"I will not, your highness, but will try to make my mind quite easy on the subject."

"You may safely do so," remarked Bianchi; "there is no one who can frustrate our designs."

"I think not, my lord."

"I am sure not; that is impossible."

"Then, at the time appointed, I may expect to lead the fair Melina to the altar?"

"You may; she cannot avoid the fate that is in store for her."

"Enough; I feel all anxiety for the happiness that is preparing for me; and notwithstanding the scorn with which she at present views me, I——"

"Oh, fear not, count," interrupted the prince, "you will yet be able to overcome the antipathy she at present evinces towards you."

"Could I be certain of that," observed Alberti, "I should indeed be a happy man. I should, however, have been much better satisfied had Florio Clairville not escaped from our power."

"It matters little," answered Bianchi;— "he is unable to do us any harm, and it is not likely that he will again venture to cross our path."

"No, he would be mad to do so," said Alberti, "for his own destruction would be sure to follow."

"It would."

"But still I am not so easy as regards the daring brigand chief, Massaroni. Could his power be crushed, I should be more content."

"And it will be so ere long, never fear," returned Bianchi. "Fortune will not always favour him in the manner it has hitherto done, and I am determined not to rest until I have the rascal at my mercy."

"Ay, he has played us some pretty pranks," said the count, "and it is nothing but fair that we should have an opportunity of retaliating."

"Certainly; but most assuredly, as you say, he is a most daring scoundrel; and he still holds Olympia and her child under his protection?"

"He does, and that causes me considerable uneasiness; I was in hopes that I had got rid of them altogether."

"Why, I must say, count," observed Bianchi, "that it was a most unfortunate thing that you ever knew Olympia at all."

"True," coincided Alberti, "and I have always regretted that circumstance ever since; but it was one of the errors of youth, to which the best of us are liable, and why should I be constantly upbraided with it?"

"No," said the prince, with emotion, "but the world is apt to view the errors of the rich and noble with a prejudiced and jaundiced eye; and there are few who will be charitable enough to endeavour to offer any extenuation of their conduct. From sad experience I know—but we will drop this subject, my lord; it is by no means an agreeable one."

"With all my heart," said the count; "though I am afraid it is my connection with Olympia which has been the principal cause of prejudicing the mind of your fair niece against me."

"No doubt of it," answered the prince; "but I do not fear but that in time you will be able to banish that prejudice, strong though at present I admit it is."

"Your highness inspires me with hope."

"Which I trust will be realised."

"It shall be no fault of mine if it is not."

"I believe you."

"I am fully prepared to lavish upon the beauteous Melina the most unbounded affection; and could I only succeed in obtaining her esteem, I should indeed be a happy man. But when shall I be permitted to see her again?"

"Why," answered Bianchi; "I think it would be better for you not to do so for a day or two, until she may in some measure have recovered from the excitement into which her interview with me this day has thrown her."

"Very well, excellenza," remarked Alberti; "I will be guided entirely by you. Then it is finally arranged that the marriage ceremony shall take place in the chapel at midnight?"

"It is, and we cannot entertain the least fear of any interruption."

"I think not."

"From whom should we apprehend it?"

"I know not, unless it be Massaroni."

"Psha, count; he would never be so daring."

"But indeed you well know that he has performed many such bold and reckless deeds as that."

"True; but how is he to know anything about the circumstance?"

"The brigand chef has always his spies lurking about in every neighbourhood, and how he obtains the intelligence he frequently does, is next to miraculous."

"Well, I have no fear of him on this occasion," remarked Bianchi.

"However," said the count, "it will be as well to prepare against any danger that may threaten."

"Exactly so. We will have those at hand who will be prepared to give the rascals a warm reception should any be so daring as to attempt to interrupt us."

"That is enough," said Alberti; "and I am satisfied."

Here the conversation dropped, and a short time afterwards they separated.

We must now follow the beauteous Melina and the faithful Floretta to the chamber of the former, where, when they had arrived, our heroine threw herself on a seat, and for some few moments gave way to a violent paroxysm of grief, which Floretta did not think it prudent to interrupt, as the free indulgence of it, she thought, might serve to lighten the violent anguish of her mind. The last meeting with her uncle served to destroy any faint hopes she might possibly have entertained, and filled her mind with the greatest horror and dread.

"Alas!" she groaned at length, "what an unfortunate being I am; why was I ever born, since I am destined to endure so much misery? Oh, my uncle, why can you, whom I have ever believed so kind and affectionate, so good and so just, thus take delight to torture me?"

"Alas! my dear signora," said Floretta, "does then the prince still remain inexorable?"

"He does," replied her mistress, "and has threatened me with his heaviest malediction should I any longer attempt to oppose his stern will."

"Oh," he cannot, he will not be so cruel. Even far as he has gone, I cannot believe it of him."

"Nay, Floretta," said our heroine, "I cannot any longer entertain a doubt; it would be madness for me to do so. Again he turned a deaf ear to all my tears and entreaties, and even threatened me with his vengeance, if I continued to raise any objection to the hated alliance he has doomed me to. And there is no escape from this revolting, this awful fate."

"Say not so, my lady," remarked Floretta; "there is a just God above who will yet interpose in your behalf, and rescue you from all peril at the very moment when your persecutors think to triumph over you."

"Oh, I dare not entertain such a thought, Floretta," said our heroine; "I shall go distracted. Would that I were dead, for all the bright hopes I had formed are now annihilated!"

Again she sobbed convulsively, and rocked herself backwards and forwards in her chair, in a state of the most insupportable agony. Floretta knew not what to say or do, for she had no consolation to offer; and again she suffered her unfortunate mistress to give free indulgence to her grief. Thus a few minutes of the saddest description passed away; but at length Melina somewhat revived, and looking up with a most melancholy aspect at her attendant, she said—

"Oh, Floretta, this unmerited persecution, and from a source whence I never expected it to spring, is hard to endure. Do you not think me a very wretched being?'

"Truly unfortunate, my dear signora," replied Floretta, "and Heaven knows how sincerely I sympathise with you—would to God that it was in my power to assist you!"

"I know your heart, my good girl," said Melina; "I have ever experienced all the kindness of a sister from you. We were playfellows together; we have been companions from our earliest days of childhood—from that fatal hour when I lost the best of mothers, and——"

She could say no more, for the sad retrospection overpowered her, and again choked her utterance, and once more a dismal silence of some minutes ensued.

"Dear lady," at last said Floretta, "let me beg of you not to distress your mind by recalling these dismal reminiscences to your memory. Have I not also cause to look back upon the past with the saddest reflections? for at the time that benevolence introduced me a child to the family of his highness, your uncle, I was left a friendless orphan, both my parents expiring in one day, and leaving me destitute and unprotected. The Prince Bianchi educated me, treated me with every humanity, and I can never cease to feel towards him the utmost gratitude and veneration. It is for these reasons that I cannot believe that he will persist in his present harsh determination, unless some mad infatuation has for a time seized upon his reason."

"True, Floretta," returned her mistress; "but your latter suggestion is what I unfortunately suppose to be the case, and therefore do I despair of making any favourable impression upon his mind."

"He must have his moments of calm and solemn reflection, signora," said Floretta, "and in one of these he will abandon his present designs, and reproach himself for having ever entertained them."

"It may be so, Floretta," remarked our heroine, "but the time allotted to me prior to this detested, this revolting union taking place, is so short, that it may be too late. The sacrifice will then have been rendered complete, past recal;—I shall consider myself a poor degraded being, and death alone will present itself to me as an escape from my misery."

"Gracious Heaven, signora!" ejaculated Floretta, with a look of alarm, "what awful signification do your observations imply?"

"Would it not be better to die, than to continue to live in a life of dishonour and opprobrium?" asked Melina.

"Oh, signora," observed Floretta with the same expression of alarm upon her countenance, "you will not, do not contemplate to—to—"

"Floretta," interrupted her mistress, "I consider it better to die unsinning, if even by your own hand, than to continue to live a life of degradation with the villain to whom your hopes, your innocence, and happiness is sacrificed. There is, as you observe, a just God above, who will judge of all our acts, but He is too merciful to pass His retributive wrath upon the heads of those who never intentionally or indiscriminately offended His laws.—Should I perish by my own hand——"

"For the love of Heaven!" said the waiting maid with increased looks of horror, "forbear from those terrible thoughts and observations. Would you take away that life which the Almighty has endowed you with as one of His humble creatures, and thus rush unbidden upon His presence."

"Floretta, I have reflected deeply upon the solemn subject; I have no wish to die in all the beautiful spring-time of my life; furthermore is it from my thoughts and wishes to do this desperate and guilty deed; but I have no other alternative (from my pure sense of rectitude) if mortals would plunge me into that vortex of sin which it is my wish to avoid than to voluntarily place myself before the judgment seat of the Almighty judge. From Him, at any rate, I may expect that mercy, which it seems I cannot receive on earth!"

"But, dearest signora, reflect calmly, I implore you," said Floretta.

"Reflect *calmly!*" repeated our heroine, with a look of the wildest expression; "how long have I done so, and what relief has it brought to my tortured mind? Have I not tried all that entreaty, reason, and humanity ought to effect, without avail, and yet you now calmly talk to me of calmness. Did I not know you from long experience, as one of my best earthly friends, Floretta, I should reproach you with an attempt at subterfuge!—But no, I will not do so, for I know your heart too well. I am convinced that you only speak from the best of feelings towards me, and I feel grateful for it. Oh, that I had been born in the same humble sphere as yourself, Floretta, then probably I might not have been subjected to the terrible persecution I am now."

As she spoke, she threw her arms, sobbing as though her heart would break, around her faithful attendant's neck, and neither of them, for the moment, could utter another word, so totally were they absorbed in the conflict of feelings that were passing in their bosoms.

It was now that calm time of evening when all the cares of mankind seem for an interval to be lulled to repose, so tranquil is the spirit that at such moments comes o'er the dream of life. There were such clouds of silvery light dancing in the high arch of Heaven, that could not fail to impart a feeling of joyousness and devotion to the giver of all good, even to the most sceptical. Never did the silvery beams of the chaste queen of night kiss the ripples of the blue waters of the Mediterranean with greater rapture than on the occasion which we are writing. Joyous faces might have been imagined in every moonlit billow that washed the shore, as though to gladden on human beings to that exhaustless banquet of enjoyment and happiness which the supreme power has supplied for us all. And, at the casement which commanded the most extensive view, were placed our heroine and Floretta, her attendant. The breeze came cool and refreshing from its broad surface, and lightened and invigorated their senses. As they viewed the scene, a more tranquil feeling came over them both, and Melina said:—

"Yes, nature is all bountiful! in every aspect it sends us cause for rejoicing, instead of sorrow; then why should its creatures thus tyrannise over each other? Is it the will, Floretta, of that Great, that Almighty Power, whose ways we cannot fathom, that any of His children should suffer? Are we not all the offspring of one Supreme parent? Do we not all possess faculties alike, however neglected we may be in our youthful days, and who shall presume to question us for acts that originate not with the Supreme, but from the tyranny, oppression, and brutality of our fellow clay? Oh! it glads me to witness this lovely scene; such a direct contradiction to the misrepresentations of misguided mortality. Do you not admire it, Floretta?"

"Yes, Signora, it must be an insensible and wicked mind that could do otherwise," replied Floretta, glad to see that mistress to whom she was so fondly attached and so firmly devoted, in such a different train of mind to what she had been for some days past; and at the same time happy to be able to divert her thoughts, if only for a short period, from the melancholy subjects which had before engrossed them.

The casement at which Signora Melina and Floretta were seated, also commanded an extensive view of the most beautiful part of the gardens, and balmy fragrance from the breath of innumerable flowers was wafted to their senses, and was calculated to impart a soothing sensation to their bosoms, of which they both at that period stood so much in need. Suddenly, however, they were both startled by hearing the soft tones of a guitar touched with a skilful and delicate hand, which seemed to proceed from some retired part of the garden; but the minstrel was not to be seen.

"Hist, Floretta!" said our heroine with a look of surprise, "do you not hear that?"

"Yes, yes, signora," answered her attendant in tones of equal astonishment; "this is a most romantic adventure; who can it be? Hark!

—ah! lady, do you not remember that air?"

"Gracious Heaven!" ejaculated Melina, "I do!—It is Massaroni's well known Ritonella. And now, that manly voice. Hark! we can hear the words.—Listen!"

They did, and the well known words of the ballad known as 'Love's Ritonella,' the favourite song of the brigand chief, saluted their ears, and rivetted their most breathless attention.

CHAPTER XXXVI.

THE BRIGAND CHIEF.—THE APPOINTED HOUR ARRIVES.—THE DESPERATE AMD DETERMINED COMBAT IN THE CHAPEL AT MIDNIGHT.

THE voice at length ceased, but Melina and Floretta still continued with their eyes fixed eagerly upon the spot from whence the tones proceeded, with the hope of beholding the minstrel, but no human being met their gaze, and their astonishment and bewilderment increased; but they were soon aroused by observing a human form hastily emerge from behind a shrubbery, and darting into the broad moonlight, they recognized the Prince Bianchi. His demeanour was agitated, and after looking anxiously around him for a moment or two, he hurried towards the spot from whence the sounds which had so rivetted the attention of our heroine and Floretta had come; he was immediately followed by the Count Alberti, and several servants, all armed.

"Ah!" said Melina, "they have overheard the voice of the minstrel, and suspect that there is some danger at hand. Surely the brigand chief can never have been so bold as to venture hither, where, if he should be discovered, his destruction would be certain."

"Indeed, signora," replied Floretta, "I do firmly believe that it is no other than Massaroni we have heard, and that he has adopted this course to assure you that he will not fail to use all his utmost efforts to rescue you from the dangers by which you are at present surrounded."

"Rash, and desperate man," said our heroine, "I can never accept of his interference, let the consequences be whatever they may. It is impossible that Florio could ever have sanctioned such proceedings."

"See, signora," observed Floretta, "they return; they have not discovered him."

"Thank Heaven for that!" said Melina; "and if it should indeed be Massaroni whom we have heard, I trust that he will be induced to abandon his hasty and imprudent designs."

The Prince Bianchi, the Count Alberti and their followers, now entered the house, and

Melina and her attendant retired from the window, and sat for some time conversing on this extraordinary and unexpected adventure before they thought of separating for the night. That it could be no other than the brigand chief whom they had heard, they both, after the most mature deliberation, were perfectly convinced; and they were completely at a loss to imagine by what means he had contrived to obtain admittance to the precincts of the villa.

"I tremble to reflect upon what the consequences of this rash and daring enterprise may be," observed Melina; "I cannot, dare not think of availing myself of the aid of Massaroni, however generous and disinterested his motives may be; and I shudder to reflect on the danger to which my uncle may be exposed. Oh! I was wrong, very wrong in not strictly and solemnly enjoining Florio in the letters I sent to him not to give his consent to any such desperate expedition on the part of the brigand chief. Should Providence not interpose in my behalf, terrible though it will be, I must learn to submit to my cruel fate, though, God knows, it will be impossible for me to survive it long."

"Oh, my dear signora," returned Floretta, "why will you persist in torturing yourself with such ideas?—It would be monstrous to suppose for a moment that you will ever be permitted to fall a victim to such a revolting destiny!"

"Alas! what hope is there of my escaping from it?" sighed her mistress; "is not the determination of the prince, my uncle, immovable? Is not his power absolute? Of what avail will any resistance that I may offer be?"

"Be firm, lady," remarked Floretta, "and notwithstanding the gloominess of your present prospects, you will yet triumph."

"Ah, Floretta, I know full well the kindness of your heart, but Reason tells me that you are far too sanguine in your expectations."

"I trust to heaven that you will not yet find yourself mistaken, signora. As for suffering yourself to be sacrificed to misery and shame, when the means are offered you to escape from them, the thought is monstrous. For whatever may follow, the prince will have to blame himself; but fear not, Massaroni will act with due prudence and precaution."

"Alas! I cannot conquer my apprehensions," replied Melina; "should Massaroni be bold enough to contemplate an attack on the villa, what may not be the dreadful consequences that will be most likely to follow? Oh, I would much rather that he would abandon his designs, and leave me to the will of Providence."

"Indeed, signora, you alarm yourself unnecessarily," observed Floretta.

"Oh, no, that cannot be, when I take all the painful circumstances into consideration," returned Melina; "whichever way I turn my eyes, what hope is there for me?"

"Banish these thoughts. my dear lady, that only serve to distract your mind, and to unfit you for the severe task that is imposed upon you."

"Oh, how is it posible for me to do so?"

"Put your trust in Him, signora, who never fails to protect the-innocent from the designs of the guilty."

"Heaven knows how hard I endeavour to do so," said Melina; "but surely it is more than human fortitude can support to be subjected to such cruel trials. But I cannot now find strength sufficient to converse upon this subject. My heart sickens while I do so. I will seek my couch, my good Floretta, and try in sleep to gain a short respite from my cares."

"And God grant that your efforts may be crowned with success, sweet lady," said Floretta, fervently; "may cheerful dreams attend your sleeping moments. All good angels watch around your pillow, and inspire your soul with consolation and hope."

Thus speaking, Floretta having assisted her mistress to undress, raised her fair hand respectfully to her lips, and with many blessings upon her head, took her leave. Melina remained standing for a few minutes after the departure of her faithful attendant, with her hands pressed upon her temples, and wrapped in the deepest meditation, when she sank on her knees before the portrait of the Virgin, and devoutly offered up her prayers to the Supreme, after which she sought her pillow with a more fortified spirit, and, after a short time, sank into a calm repose.

The Prince Bianchi and Alberti had been seen seated together immersed in conversation, when the tones of the unknown minstrel's voice saluted their ears, and arrested their most profound attention. They both started simultaneously to their feet and gazed from the window of the sala in which they had been sitting towards that part of the gardens from whence the sound seemed to issue, with the most unfounded astonishment; and for an instant or two they were both so confused and astonished as to be unable to speak.

"What is the meaning of this?" at last said the Prince Bianchi, "what insolent dares to intrude himself upon my privacy? Have you not heard that voice and those words before, count?"

"Yes, your highness," replied Alberti, "they are those of the brigand chief, Allesandro Massaroni."

"Allasandro Massaroni! Dare he thus venture?"

"I could swear to the words of the ballad," returned Count Alberti, "and the voice which sung them. Some danger threatens, may lord. We must be upon the alert."

"By all my hopes!" exclaimed Bianchi furiously, "I will penetrate this mystery to its very core. Follow me, Alberti."

Thus saying, the prince rushed hastily from the apartment, and the count having quickly summoned two or three of his most trustworthy attendants, followed, and soon came up with the excited nobleman. They searched every spot of the gardens, and for some distance round the villa, but all to no purpose, as not the least signs of the intruder could be discovered, and they were compelled to return chagrined and disappointed to the house.

"By all the saints!" exclaimed the Prince

MELINA AND THE PRINCE.

Bianchi, throwing himself in a state of the most violent agitation into a chair, "this is too much for human patience to endure. You heard the voice as well I did, count?"

"I did, my lord," replied Alberti. "We could not both have been deceived."

"That is perfectly impossible."

"Some treachery is afloat, which must be immediately discovered."

"Ay, your highness, the more promptly we act, the better. Your domestics should be immediately questioned most strictly, for it is only by the connivance of one of them that this individual, whoever he may be, could have gained admittance to the gardens."

"True," coincided Bianchi, passionately, and ringing the bell violently; "I will have them all before me directly, and should I discover the rascal who has thus dared to set my power and authority at defiance, I will heap upon his head my most terrible vengeance."

At that moment a servant made his appearance, and awaited the commands of his imperious lord.

"Summon hither immediately the whole of your fellows, and return yourself," commanded the prince, sternly.

The man bowed obsequiously, and retired to obey. In a few moments the whole of the domestics, male and female, were in the presence of the prince and the Count Alberti, and were subjected to the strictest examination; but nothing could be elicited from either of them to throw the least light upon the mystery, and the prince dismissed them haughtily, after having given orders that the villa should be surrounded by troops, every avenue strictly guarded, and a most indefatigable search be made in the neighbourhood to discover any suspicious characters, who might be imagined to have some treasonable and nefarious designs in contemplation.

"When they were gone, Bianchi folded his arms across his chest, and for a short time he paced the apartment in the most disordered manner, and muttering imprecations to himself, while the Count Alberti, as may be expected, was in no less a state of excitement.

"This is unbearable," at length said the prince; "I am certain it was the voice of the brigand chief we both heard."

"Of that I am also as thoroughly convinced, my lord," replied Alberti; "those who have once heard it, and the peculiar style in which he sings that Ritornella, can never forget it."

"No," said the prince, "and it is that which convinces me, in spite of the solemn asseverations of these fellows to the contrary, that there are traitors amongst them. Oh, that I could discover them, how terrible would be the vengeance that I would wreak upon their dastard heads."

"Be calm, my lord, I beg of you," said Alberti, "and wait patiently, and doubt not but that we shall yet be able to detect them, and to defeat their plans. I wonder whether the fair Signora Melina also heard the brigand, for that it was he I cannot, for a moment, entertain the least shadow of a doubt."

"We will question her narrowly," returned Bianchi, "and if from her answers our suspicions are confirmed, we may rest assured that she has had some means of corresponding with the presumptuous beggar Cairville, and shall know how to act accordingly."

"Very true, your highness; but we must be cautious how we act."

"We will. But still after all, it is fortunate that we have met with the adventure that we have done to-night, for it will put us on our guard, and enable us to adopt such a course as will effectually frustrate any designs that may be contemplated against us. Fear not, my lord; no power on earth shall prevent my niece from becoming your bride at the time I have appointed."

"I rely upon your highness' word," replied Alberti, "and am perfectly satisfied. Let not the circumstance of this night ruffle your temper, for it proves to us that never were we called upon to act with more coolness, decision, and precaution."

"You are right, count," said Bianchi, "and I will not fail to act in accordance with your suggestion. But is it not astounding that Massaroni should have the daring to contemplate such an outrage as that of which we suspect him?"

"It is, my lord; and yet before now we have been convinced that there is nothing too daring for that desperate ruffian and outlaw to undertake. However, after the warning we have so fortunately received, it will be our own faults, I conceive, if we do not succeed in frustrating his designs."

"It will," coincided the Prince Bianchi, "but you shall find no cause hereafter, count, to complain of me."

"I do not doubt you, my lord, and ere many days have elapsed, I have little doubt that we shall not only succeed in frustrating the designs of the brigand chief, but also have him in our power, and at our mercy."

"Our mercy!" repeated the prince, with a sardonic grin; "what mercy can the lawless scoundrel expect from us?"

"True, excellenza," returned Alberti; "as you must be aware, I have no reason to hold him any good will. Have I not suffered from his daring villany in every shape? Has he not grossly outraged my feelings? Imprisoned me—threatened me with death—secured the persons of Olympia and her child, and destroyed a considerable portion of my property in his deadly revenge? Oh, that I had the rascal in my power, what torture would it not be my delight to inflict upon him! But the time will come—the time will come."

"It will—it shall," answered Bianchi, "and then I will not fail to repay him in full for all the favours he has bestowed upon me. And yet," he added, after a brief pause, "I must confess that there is something about the features and manners of the brigand chief which I can never reflect upon without emotion, though I know not why it is. I would that I could become acquainted with all the particulars of his mysterious history."

"Why should you take so deep an interest in him, my lord?" demanded Alberti.

"I have before told you," answered the prince, "that I knew not how it is; but still I find it impossible to conquer the feeling."

"It is strange."

"True, it is; but he is almost constantly in my thoughts."

"I do not wonder at that, my lord, after all the annoyances you have at different times experienced from him."

"No, it is not that," remarked Bianchi; "it is a stronger and more unaccountable feeling than that. But have you never noticed the extraordinary resemblance that he bears to that portrait which for particular reasons, which I do not think it prudent at present to explain, I always keep concealed from the vulgar gaze?"

"Why, your highness," returned the Count Alberti, "I must confess that it has never very forcibly struck me, though such a resemblance may possibly exist."

"May!" repeated Bianchi, impatiently; "it does! By the mass! I never saw such an extraordinary likeness; and had Massaroni been —but where am I suffering my tongue to ramble? This is no time for explanation,—and it is a secret that must ever remain confined to my own breast; it would by revelation cause the finger of scorn and scandal to be pointed against me!—No more! We will drop the subject. I will seek my chamber, and try to collect my thoughts. Good night, count; at the morning repast we shall meet again, when we will converse further on this important business."

"Good night, my lord," said Alberti; "and let not what has occurred to-night disturb you; if treason is afloat, which I have no doubt it is, we shall find the means to counteract it."

"Ay," agreed the prince, "of that we may be certain; we are, as you say, put upon our guard; we have, therefore, only to use the necessary precautions, and have nothing to fear as to the result."

"True," answered Alberti; and once more pressing the hand of Bianchi, and again wishing him good night, they separated.

Bianchi, on retiring to his chamber, thought not of seeking his couch, for the singular and unexpected adventure of the evening too deeply engrossed his thoughts, and various were the passions that agitated his breast, of which that of rage was most predominant.

"It must have been Massaroni," he muttered to himself; "it could have been no other. The daring, reckless villain! and does he then still seek to thwart me in my plans;—to interpose between me and my authority?— Presumptuous robber!—But he shall yet pay dearly for his insolence!—I will not rest until I have had the gratification of consigning him

to the scaffold, and of exterminating all his desperate and reckless band. But who is the traitorous miscreant that has given him the information he evidently possesses? I will discover him at any cost, and wreak my most terrible vengeance on his head. But can Melina be aware of his intentions? Has she so far forgot her noble station as to accept of the aid of a brigand and a murderer? Psha! it is impossible! I do her an injustice by the bare supposition; but I must question her narrowly, and if I discover anything to confirm my suspicions in the least degree, let her look to it. She hates, she despises the Count Alberti I know, she boldly acknowledges it; but in spite of all I cannot conquer the prejudice I entertain in his favour, and I am determined that nothing whatever shall induce me to break my word with him. She shall be his in spite of all the consequences that may follow.— Shall the obstinate caprices of a foolish girl move me from my purpose? Am I going to be weak enough to suffer my authority to be set at defiance? No, by Heaven I will not, for I should despise myself ever afterwards if I did. Break her heart?—Bah! the sickening talk of giddy inexperienced girls!—The Count Alberti is rich, noble, handsome, accomplished; he is a husband worthy of her, and he shall have her, too, as certain as I am the Prince Bianchi, governor of Rome!"

He paused abruptly and started, for at that moment he imagined he heard a deep and unearthly sigh, and he looked round with a pale aspect and a tremulous demeanour, but nothing met his observation, and he endeavoured, though with difficulty, to re-assure himself.

"Psha!" he ejaculated, "how weak have I become. Why do I suffer my imagination thus to be imposed upon? It was but the whispering of the night breeze. What else should it be?"

But in spite of all his efforts, it was some minutes ere he could completely recover himself, and he then almost feared to look around him. He took a glass of wine, and then felt a little more revived, and sitting himself down, with his elbow resting on the table and his head leaning upon his hand, remained for some time deeply immersed in the most painful and conflicting thoughts; but at length the deep and sonorous bell of Saint Peter's, tolling the hour of eleven, aroused him, and he started suddenly to his feet.

"It is useless to reflect longer," he said; "let me retire to rest, and for a time endeavour to gain a respite from thought in sleep."

Before, however, he did so, he took up his lamp, and left his chamber cautiously in order to see whether those whom he had placed to guard the different entrances to the villa were at their posts; and having satisfied himself that they were, and given them fresh injunctions, he returned to his chamber, and shortly afterwards retired to bed. But sleep was almost an entire stranger to him during the night, and he arose at the earliest dawn of day, and in order to refresh himself walked from the villa into the adjacent country till the time should arrive when he would have to meet the Count Alberti at breakfast.

Melina had scarcely left her couch on the following morning, when there was a knock at her chamber-door, and the voice of Floretta requested admittance, which, of course, was immediately complied with, and our heroine no sooner saw her than she was satisfied she had some intelligence for her.

"I should have returned last night, signora," she observed, "only I was fearful that I might be seen by somebody."

"And what made you wish to return, Floretta?" asked her mistress, eagerly.

"Why, signora," answered her attendant; "on entering my chamber I found the following letter on my dressing-table; it is addressed to you."

"To me!" ejaculated Melina, with a look of astonishment.

Floretta replied in the affirmative, and delivered the letter into the hands of her mistress, who gazed at it with increased amazement.

"The handwriting is unknown to me," said Melina; "this is most extraordinary. Who can have occasion to write to me?"

With trembling impatience she broke the seal, and read the following words:—

"Let not the Signora Melina despair, for there are those at hand who will at all hazards rescue her from the fate with which she is threatened. Be secret; be confident; be resolute, and fear not."

"It is evident enough," remarked Melina, "that this letter is from Massaroni, and that it was he whom we heard in the garden last night. But how has he contrived to place his communication in your apartment, Floretta?"

"I am completely at a loss to imagine," replied the latter, "but it is quite evident he must have some friends in the villa who have resolved to aid him in his designs."

"I cannot, must not, accept of his services," observed Melina. "I find it impossible to reconcile it with any proper sense of delicacy and propriety."

"Indeed, signora," said Floretta, "I see no reason for your scruples. Surely it is better to risk anything rater than to encounter such a revolting and cruel fate as that with which you are threatened. The prince, your uncle, will have himself to blame if he by his own obstinacy and (pardon me, signora,) cruelty urges you to a step which you would otherwise have avoided. Besides, Massaroni is honour-

able, notwithstanding his lawless and predatory life; and I am satisfied that you will, my dear lady, have no cause to regret having availed yourself of his disinterested sympathy and assistance."

Melina hesitated for a few moments, and the most perplexing thoughts seemed to be passing in her mind; but at length she said—

"Yes, my faithful Floretta, I believe him kind and generous; but would that I could see him, that I might the more fully arrive at his intentions, and from them understand how far prudence should guide me to accept of his propositions. Heaven preserve my misguided uncle from any danger that may be impending o'er his head, and bring him to a proper sense of the severity and injustice with which he is acting towards me ere it is too late. But strange thoughts and misgivings beset my mind, Floretta, and I would rather, oh, much rather that the brigand chief had not adopted the course he has."

"Indeed you alarm yourself unnecessarily, I am convinced that you do, my dear signora," remarked Floretta; "but something still seems to assure me that the Prince Bianchi will yet relent, and abandon the harsh and unnatural designs he has against your happiness."

"Oh, no," sighed our heroine, with a look of despair; "I dare not encourage such a hope after it has proceeded so far, and the inexoribility which my uncle has displayed, and that so recently, towards me. The time, too, allowed me is so short, only till Monday next, that it would be little short of madness to entertain such a thought. Oh, Floretta, how can I look otherwise than with a shudder of horror at the terrible prospect which is before me? Dear Florio! Fate is opposed to us, and we can never hope to meet again under any other circumstances than those of agony to us both. Fortunate indeed would it have been for us had we never known each other."

"Be calm, signora," observed Floretta, "for notwithstanding the clouds which at present obscure the horizon of your happiness, they will yet disperse, and the future will, I feel confident, be all that your fondest hopes could wish."

"You are sanguine, Floretta; would to Heaven that reason would allow me to entertain the same thoughts that you (and I believe with all sincerity) profess to do."

"My hopes, dear lady, will not be disappointed," rejoined her attendant; "I feel satisfied that they will not."

"If I could think so," remarked Melina, "I might indeed be able to tranquillise my feelings, and to meet the result of that which threatens me with becoming fortitude. But can I ever make up my mind to resign myself to the protection of Allesandro Massaroni, the brigand chief? Oh, no; my heart revolts at the very idea, however honest his intentions towards me may be; and Clairville could never wish me to do so, or he would have taken the opportunity to forward a communication to that effect. Everything goes to prove that Massaroni acts entirely on his own responsibility, and without the concurrence of Florio."

"Pardon me, signora," returned her attendant, "but there I must be allowed to differ from you."

"And why so, my good girl?"

"It appears to me, lady," replied Floretta, "quite clearly, that Massaroni would never have undertaken to act in the manner he has done, without the full sanction, and at the earnest request of Signor Clairville. Put it to your own reason, and ask yourself whether it is reasonable to suppose that one who loves you so ardently, so sincerely, would not rather avail himself of any opportunity, of almost any means that offered themselves to his mind, in the desperate and alarming situation in which you are both placed, that might avert such a calamity?"

"Then why," again demanded our heroine, "since the means were in his power, did he not forward me a letter to that effect?"

"He might have had his reasons, powerful reasons," said Floretta; "for instance, he might have been fearful that by some accident his letter would fall into the hands of the Prince Bianchi, your uncle, or the Count Alberti, and thus bring additional misery on your head, and in all probability hasten your fate."

"Oh," returned Melina, "he could not suppose that, if he entrusted it to the same safe hands as those which have forwarded the letter which you have just delivered to me."

"Do not give way to these sad thoughts and apprehensions, I implore you, my lady, for Providence is too good and merciful to suffer you to fall a victim to such a man as the Count Alberti. It is monstrous to entertain such a thought for a moment. Signor Clairville and yourself will not only meet again, but take my word for it, the time will come when his highness will deeply regret the misery he has caused you, and be only too happy to render you all the reparation in his power."

"Could I but believe so," observed Melina, "how greatly would my anguish be ameliorated. But, alas! it seems, under existing circumstances, so preposterous to do so, that I find it impossible. But this mysterious letter! How shall I act in respect to it?"

"The best advice I can give you, signora," answered Floretta, "is to destroy it; to bear in mind its brief contents, and to be prepared to act with promptitude and determination as necessity may dictate. Masssaroni, depend on it, will not fail to act with prudence and

precaution; and it will be the prince's fault if everything does not terminate in a way that will be satisfactory to all parties."

"My uncle will never forfeit his word to the detested Count Alberti," said our heroine; "I cannot expect it; and therefore what have I to look forward to but the greatest, the most insupportable misery?"

"Alas! signora, why why will you persist in giving way to these sad thoughts?—You do but torture your mind to no purpose."

"The kindness and sympathy you bear towards me, Floretta, makes you hold out hopes to me which I feel convinced you cannot entertain in your own mind. Has not my uncle threatened me with his heaviest and eternal malediction if I any longer oppose his will? and can I for a moment suppose, after all the numerous and earnest supplications I have at different times made to him, that he will abandon his designs? Oh, no; the disappointment almost certain to attend such hopes, would, if possible, be even more dreadful than the stern reality. I see that there is no possibility of escaping from my hard fate; and dreadful though the task will assuredly be, I must try to resign myself to it. Would to God that I had never been born, since it seems that I am doomed to endure this unparalleled misery."

She sobbed bitterly, and for some minutes was unable to give utterance to a single syllable; and Floretta, who was at a loss for any further argument that might be calculated to console her, or to remove the sad and dismal forebodings that occupied her breast, also remained silent.

"Know you any one amongst the domestics," at length said our heroine, "on whom your suspicions alight, as regards their connivance with the brigand chief?"

"No one, whatever, signora," answered Floretta; "but Massaroni, as you may be aware, has his spies everywhere, and he conducts his plans with so much secrecy, that it is impossible to penetrate them, or to frustrate them."

"True," coincided Melina; "but would that I could but obtain an interview with him, that I might from his own lips ascertain what it is he proposes to do, and to argue with him on the subject."

"That opportunity may be yet afforded you, signora," returned her attendant.

"It is evident that he has the means of ready access to the villa," said Melina.

"After what has taken place, we cannot doubt it."

"But should the prince discover him?"

"Oh, there is no fear of that; Massaroni always plays a sure game, and they must be shrewd and penetrating indeed who could frustrate any schemes upon which he might have fixed his mind. But courage, signora, and take my word for it that all will yet terminate much better than you now anticipate."

The conversation here dropped, and a short time afterwards Floretta retired from the presence of her mistress, and left her to the undisturbed indulgence of her own thoughts.— The nature of these it requires no great stretch of the imagination to conjecture ; and for some time poor Melina continued to pace her apartment in the most distracted state of mind, to which she found it impossible to obtain the smallest relief.

" How can I act for the best ?" she at length ejaculated ; " shall I accept of the services of Massaroni ; or shall I reveal the truth to my uncle, and once more appeal to his sense of justice and mercy ?—No ;—that would be ungrateful and ungenerous to the brigand chief, whom I cannot but be convinced acts from the most disinterested motives. Besides, can the prince for an instant justify his conduct towards me ? Is it not revolting to think even that he should contemplate to force me into a marriage with one so completely unworthy of me, and so odious as the Count Alberti ?— Have I not every right to oppose it by all the means in my power ?—Reason tells me that I have ; and while he remains thus inexorable why should I any longer hesitate to avail myself of every means in my power of escaping from a fate so revolting? Heaven knows that I have never offended by word, or deed, or thought ; but, on the contrary, have always looked upon him with the same regard and veneration as if he had been my own parent, and surely then, I have not merited this persecution, Had he only opposed my love to Florio, I might have found resolution enough to have submitted, though it might ultimately have broken my heart in the struggle ; but to compel me to become the wife of an unprincipled libertine and debauchee as the Count Alberti, —oh, the thought is too monstrous !—too disgusting to be entertained even for a moment. Let whatever may be the consequences, I will not yield to such a fate without compulsion, and even then, Heaven pardon me the thought, I will not long survive the degradation.— Death, even in its most terrible shape, would be far, far preferable. Beloved Florio, did you but know my present feelings what would be the excruciating anguish of your mind. But you must imagine them. Oh, yes ! too well I know you do, and that your brain must be driven to distraction. May Heaven in its bounden mercy give you fortitude to support your heavy trials with firmness."

Again the hapless maiden traversed her chamber in the most distracted manner, and it was in vain that she sought to tranquillise her feelings in the slightest degree, Again and again she perused the note which she had received in so mysterious a manner, and the more she did so the greater became her astonishment and perplexity, though there could not remain the least shadow of a doubt upon her mind that it had emanated from Massaroni, and that he was secreted somewhere in the neighbourhood of the villa, and was fully determined to put his designs, whatever they were, into execution.

About an hour had elapsed in this manner, when Floretta again entered the room, and closing the door cautiously behind her approached her mistress.

" How now, Floretta ?" demanded our heroine, eagerly ; " you look anxious."

" I have more news for you, signora," replied Floretta, in a whisper.

" More news for me ?" repeated Melina, in the same low tones.

" Yes."

" What is it ?"

" I have seen Rubaldo."

" The lieutenant of Massaroni ?" asked our heroine.

" The same," answered Floretta.

" Where ?"

" Only a short distance from the villa ; but he was so disguised that I could not possibly have recognised him had he not spoken to me."

" Ah ! then," ejaculated Melina, " it was from the brigand chief that I received that note ?"

" It was, signora," said her attendant. " Massaroni and some of the most trusty of his band are concealed in the neighbourhood ; and if Rubaldo speaks the truth, which I have no reason to doubt he does, he is determined to rescue you from the danger which is at present impending over your head, at all hazards. They have bribed one of the domestics of the prince, though Rubaldo would not tell me his name, and they can obtain free access to the villa at any hour."

" Ah !" exclaimed Melina ; " what danger may arise from this ?—But I must see Massaroni, and consult with him as to what are his intentions."

" I suggested the same to Rubaldo, signora," returned Floretta ; " but he said it could not be ; for that such a course might be fraught with danger to all parties interested. However, he added, that he was willing to convey to the brigand chief any letter you might think proper to write to him ; and that he would be ready as soon as the shadows of evening had descended upon the earth, to meet me at the usual place of appointment to receive it."

" And said he aught of Clairville ?" asked Melina anxiously.

" Yes, signora," replied Floretta ; " he said that he was still quite safe under the protection of Massaroni, and most anxious for the result of this expedition."

"Does he approve of the course which the brigand chief has adopted?" asked our heroine eagerly.

"From what Rubaldo said in reply to my questions, I should imagine he does," returned Floretta.—"But the letter, signora?"

"I will write to him," said Melina, after a moment's hesitation; "at any rate, there can be no harm in that."

"And if I may presume to advise you, my dear lady," said Floretta, "you will not seek to dissuade him from his purpose; which, you may depend upon it, springs from the best of motives, and will be guided by reason and prudence."

"I scarcely know how to act," said our heroine, after a pause; "at any rate, I must elicit from him, if I possibly can, the full extent of his intentions."

"Very true, signora," coincided her attendant; "and then you will the better be able to judge how it would be most prudent for you to act."

"Heaven guide me for the best!" said Melina, as she seated herself at the table and commenced writing the letter to the brigand chief, while Floretta stood by and awaited its conclusion with some degree of anxiety. Melina addressed herself with the utmost respect to Massaroni; thanked him fervently for the deep interest he took in her fate; and at the same time, while she earnestly requested him to abandon any designs he might have formed in which the safety of himself and those connected with her might be involved, begged that he would no longer keep her in suspense as to what were the resolutions he had come to. The letter completed, she delivered it to Floretta, with instructions to her to convey it to Rubaldo at the time he had appointed to meet her. Evening at length came, and Floretta departed on her errand. In about an hour she returned, and her mistress eagerly questioned her as to what had taken place.

"I saw both Massaroni and his lieutenant, signora," replied Floretta.

"Ah!" said Melina, with a look of surprise; "and did the brigand chief peruse the letter I sent him in your presence?"

"He did, signora."

"And what said he?" demanded our heroine, eagerly.

"'Tell your lady,' he said, 'that my answer shall be found to-morrow morning in the same place where I left the previous note.'"

"Remarkable!" ejaculated Melina. "By what means can he have obtained admission so freely to the villa?"

"I have before told you, signora, by the treachery of one of his highness's domestics. But may I ask you if you are still determined to reject his services?"

"It is impossible for me yet to make up my mind," answered Melina, "until I am fully acquainted with what are his intentions."

"Depend upon it they will be guided by prudence," observed Floretta, "and that he will use no more violence than is absolutely necessary; but of one thing I feel certain, namely—that he will not be easily persuaded to abandon any resolutions he may have formed, and which he considers are for the best; neither do I see that you can reasonably reject his offers to rescue you from a fate which would be the means of blasting your happiness for ever, and of annihilating all the hopes of yourself and Signor Clairville."

"Alas!" sighed our heroine, "those hopes are crushed already; it would be folly—nay, madness, any longer to encourage them. Oh, Florio! what but the bitterest despair and the most poignant anguish is left to us both?"

"Encourage other thoughts, signora," said her attendant, "and depend upon it, Providence is too good to suffer you to be disappointed."

"It is in vain that you urge me to do so, Floretta," returned Melina; "in whatever direction I turn my eyes, I see nothing but the most hopeless misery in store for me."

Floretta saw that it was useless to argue further, and after some time longer passed in conversation, she separated from her mistress for the night.

Melina had but little sleep, for her mind was so fully occupied by care and anxiety; and she felt glad when the morning's sun streamed in at the casement of her chamber, for it seemed to afford her some temporary relief. She had scarcely quitted her couch when Floretta entered the room; and once more the expression of her features convinced her that she had some fresh intelligence for her.

"Has Massaroni kept his word?" asked Melina, anxiously.

"He has," replied Floretta, placing a note in the hand of her mistress. "I found this on my dressing-table on entering my chamber, after leaving you last night."

"Last night?"

"Yes, signora."

"Most extraordinary!" ejaculated Melina.

"Yes, lady, you may say that. You see that the brigand chief is punctual."

Melina made no reply, but unfolding the letter, she found it to contain merely the following few words:—

"Why should the fair Signora Melina encourage these delicate scruples which she has expressed in her letter, when she is threatened with a fate from which her soul must recoil in disgust and horror? Again I beg of her to place every confidence in the friendship and honour of Allesandro Massaroni, and she shall not only be rescued from the power of her enemies and persecutors, but be restored to the arms of her lover, and all the hopes she formerly cherished be fully realised."

Melina having perused this brief epistle, handed it to Floretta, who also read it, and then observed—

"This is evidently dictated by the best of feelings, my dear signora, and I cannot help thinking that you ought to be fully satisfied with it, and be guided alone by the will of Providence."

"Alas!" ejaculated her mistress, "my brain is bewildered; I know not how to act. I do not doubt the humanity, the honesty, and sincerity of Massaroni's intentions, but still I find it impossible to conquer the repugnance I feel to accept of his services."

"I trust, signora, that you will be able to subdue those feelings upon more mature reflection," observed Floretta.

Melina shook her head.

"At any rate," added her attendant, "no fate, I should imagine, can be half so bad as that to which the Prince Bianchi would consign you."

"It is, indeed, horrible," returned our heroine, with a shudder; "but would that I could escape it by any other means."

"Come, signora," said Floretta, "arouse yourself, and endeavour to think more favourably of the proposals of Massaroni. Under his protection, and that of Signor Clairville, who shall dare to offer you the least insult? Who shall presume to blame you for adopting a course into which you will have been forced by the inflexibility of your uncle, and the disgusting importunities of the Count Alberti?"

"Mankind are too ready to condemn, Floretta."

"But your innocence may defy the voice of scandal, my dear lady. Come, come—assume your wonted courage and energy, and when the eventful and important moment arrives, be prepared to act with that firmness and decision which has hitherto marked your character."

"You advise me for the best, Floretta, I know," said our heroine, "and I will endeavour to do as you say, trusting that Heaven will instruct me for the best."

But in spite of all her efforts, Melina found it utterly impossible to reconcile her mind; nor could all the arguments of Floretta prevail with her, or even work but little effect on her. They were both interrupted in the midst of their reflections by another message from the Prince Bianchi, desiring to see Melina immediately, and our heroine, on hearing it, turned ghastly pale, and trembled violently.

"Another interview!" she sighed, wringing her hands; "fresh troubles are in store for me; alas! when will my trials cease?"

"Courage, signora," said Floretta, "and let not your uncle perceive that your firmness is shaken in the least, or he will not fail to take advantage of it."

"Alas! how vain is my resistance; what can I do against his stern determination? I have exhausted argument, expostulation, and entreaty, in vain. He has closed his heart against me, and all my hopes of happiness are at an end."

"Say not so," replied the faithful Floretta, soothinly; "even at the eleventh hour he may relent, and at last be induced to listen to your supplications, and to yield to your wishes."

Melina shook her head despairingly, and then, with trembling footsteps, she proceeded to obey the summons of her uncle. When she arrived at the door of the apartment in which he awaited her, she paused, and a deathly sickness came over her; and her emotion was increased when the voice of the dreaded Count Alberti saluted her ears. It was with difficulty she could recover herself sufficiently to enter the room; and when she did so, she was compelled to cling to the back of a chair for support. The prince and Alberti were engaged in earnest conversation on her entrance, but they immediately turned round, and both advanced towards; but Melina averted her looks with a shudder of dread, and awaited what they had to say in the utmost suspense.

"Melina," said the prince, taking her hand, "I have again sent for you to know in the presence of the Count Alberti, your future husband, whether any change has come over your mind since last we met. You tremble girl; are you still weak and irresolute? Beware! you must remember what I told you at our last interview, and rest assured that the consequences of your obstinacy will be such as I then described them to you."

"Oh, my lord," replied Melina, in faltering accents, and not venturing to look up, "why will you thus persist in torturing me? You already know my sentiments, and nothing whatever can alter them."

"Rash girl!" returned the prince, in a voice of rage, "and you also know my determination, and need I tell you that nothing on earth can move me from it?"

"Beauteous Melina," said Alberti, with difficulty subduing his rage, "why will you thus remain inflexible, and treat with scorn that man who is ready to worship you, and who——"

"Hold, my lord," interrupted Melina, with a look of the utmost indignation;—"let whatever may be the consequences, I will not listen to observations that are so disgusting and insulting to my feelings. I have already frequently told you the sentiments I entertain towards you, and here, in the presence of the prince, my uncle, I repeat them. The Count Alberti can never possess anything but my detestation and scorn, and those feelings every hour does but serve to add strength to."

The count bit his lips, and Bianchi was so

enraged that for a few minutes he could not give utterance to a syllable.

"Girl!" he said at length, "again I caution you as to what you say. Dare you thus insult the Count Alberti in my presence?"

"I have no wish to insult him, my lord," answered Melina, in a firm voice; "but I must not, will not disguise my real feelings; had he the least spark of manly decency about him, he would not continue to urge a suit which he must perceive is so thoroughly hateful to me."

MELINA BEFORE THE VIRGIN.

"And why," demanded Alberti, in a voice of half stifled rage, "am I so odious in the eyes of Signora Melina?"

"Urge me not to answer that question," returned our heroine, "but rather ask your own conscience."

"Forbear, bold girl!" exclaimed Bianchi, fiercely; "this obdurate spirit must and shall be curbed. But heed not what she says, my lord; let the promise I have given suffice you, and rest assured that on Monday next she shall become your bride."

" By Heaven, never!" cried the indignant damsel, determinedly; "sooner shall you stretch me a corpse at your feet than I will suffer myself to be consigned to such a revolting fate. Oh, my uncle, beware what you do, or most assuredly, much as you may now scorn my observations, you will have bitter cause to repent your harsh and unmerited proceedings."

Her uncle looked at her astonished at the boldness of her language, and the Count Alberti was completely astounded. However, in a few moments the Prince Bianchi recovered himself, and turning furiously upon Melina, said—

"Girl, do you thus dare despise my authority?"

"Dear uncle," she replied in the mildest manner possible, " when did I ever attempt to dispute your authority, when it was exercised with a proper feeling of humanity? No, by Heaven! could I ever do so, recollecting that you were the brother of my mother; that beloved mother whose soul is now in Heaven. I have always reverenced you, my uncle, but I cannot, will not, yield to an obstinate and unnatural sacrifice which is opposed to all reason. The Count Alberti—and he is present now—I repeat, I view with feelings of the greatest repugnance; nothing whatever can change those sentiments; you may compel me to become his wife, but by Heaven I swear, that I will not exist as such a single day."

The Count Alberti frowned and bit his lips at the determined tone in which Melina spoke; he could not conceal his rage, while the Prince Bianchi paced the room for a few minutes totally unable to give utterance to the feelings that predominated in his mind. He felt keenly the injustice and cruelty of his own conduct, and was unable to justify it by any observations he might call to his assistance, and consequently that left him in a position of the most embarrassing and humiliating difficulty. But at length he partially recovered himself, and turning round upon his fair niece, he exclaimed fiercely—

"Girl! do you still persist in uttering such remarks, so offensive to myself and the Count Alberti? Have you no fear of the consequences they may bring upon your head? But I will not threaten. You know my will, and my determination, and you must therefore prepare yourself, and make up your mind as to the result."

" And, my lord," replied our heroine, with the same resolute, but respectful demeanour, " you likewise should know *my* determination, and that nothing whatever shall induce me to swerve from it. I once more repeat, that so thoroughly do I detest the Count Alberti, that even the most torturing and lingering death that the human mind could invent and inflict would be preferable to a union with him. I

say again, that I will never, unless I am dragged to the altar, become his wife; and that even if such should be my fate, the same day shall witness me a bride and a corpse. By the beatified spirit of my mother, who in her dying moments committed me to your care and protection, I ~~swore~~ that——"

" Girl! girl!" interrupted the Prince Bianchi, greatly agitated, while Alberti continued to pace the apartment in a state of the most indescribable excitement, and was unable to give utterance to a syllable; " are you resolved to drive me mad?"

"How so, uncle?" demanded our heroine, meekly.

" Why these allusions to your mother?"

"She was your sister, your only sister, my lord, was she not? And surely, if you have lost or forgotten your love for me, you must still entertain some little respect for her dying injunctions."

"D—n!" exclaimed Bianchi, still more enfuriated; " you are resolved to insult me, to torture me! Your—your mother! she——"

"Be calm your excelanzy," interposed the Count Alberti, recovering himself, and fearful that the observations of Melina would have too powerful and dangerous an effect upon the prince, " the fair Signora Melina is somewhat excited, and I believe scarcely knows to what she is giving utterance."

"My lord," retorted the damsel, turning upon him a look of the most superlative contempt, " you either affect to do, or grossly misunderstand me. It is true that I am excited, and how should I be otherwise, persecuted as I am; but nevertheless, if you imagine that I know not what I am saying, you are most grievously mistaken. I told you, and I repeat it now, that I thoroughly detest and despise you, and that, sooner than become your wife, I will be a corpse. Understand you that, my Lord Alberti?"

The Count bit his lips, and resumed his pacing of the chamber, with his arms folded across his chest, while the agitation of the Prince Bianchi was as great as his own; but neither of them for a few moments ventured to make use of any observation. At length the Prince Bianchi turned to his niece, and said in a stern and peremptory tone:

"Retire girl; we will have no more foolery of this description on the present occasion; retire, I say again, but remember well what I have said, namely, that Monday next, in spite of whatever may take place, however your hopes or ideas may flatter you to the contrary, you *shall* become the wife of him you profess so much to hate and despise."

"Good, my lord," returned Melina, with equal resolution; " and allow me to assure you equally, candidly, and determinedly, that nothing whatever on earth shall, or can, alter the resolution I have formed, and change the threats I have held out as regards myself, should you persevere in carrying your harsh decrees into effect. I still revere you, my lord, as my uncle; but nothing whatever shall induce me voluntarily to be sacrificed to a man who I consider, and so does the general world, has grossly, foully degraded, disgraced himself."

The temper of the Count Alberti could endure no more; the taunts, the truths to which Melina gave utterance, wounded his pride and stung him to the heart. His countenance flushed to the highest pitch with the feelings that her observations had called forth, he advanced towards her, and endeavouring to control his rage as well as he could, he said:—

"Signora Melina, the love, the adoration I bear you, has controlled my tongue hitherto; but surely you will not attempt to deny that there are limits to persons remarks, and when they overstep those bounds which prudence or propriety dictate, the patience of the adversary whom they attack, may be exhausted. In that position I at this moment stand; but still, in spite of all, I will treat you with manly forbearance, and trust that you will have the candour and proper feeling to appreciate my conduct on this occasion, at any rate. To resign my hopes of you, I cannot—will not—while they are sanctioned by your august uncle; but to persecute you is, indeed, farthest from my thoughts."

"Then why, my lord," returned our heroine, "persevere in prosecuting a suit which I have so frequently told you is perfectly odious to me? I bear you no ill-will, nor the least animosity, I solemnly assure you; but still, I can never willingly become your wife; and I swear now, in the presence of my uncle, that, should I be forced into a marriage with you, I will take that life which then would have become hateful to me."

The Prince Bianchi became more exasperated than ever at these observations, and advancing towards Melina, he seized he roughly by the arm, and exclaimed—

"Obstinate, stubborn girl! you should feel obliged to me for my patience and forbearance in thus submitting to your observations, that are sufficient to arouse the utmost feelings of excitement in my breast. But, my lord," he added, turning to the count; "I pray you be not irritated by what this obdurate girl has said; we will find they way to quell her proud and scornful spirit yet. Melina, you may retire. We will not prolong this interview; but remember, that all I have threatened shall be fulfilled; that Monday next you become the wife of his lordship, the Count Alberti."

"And that day, my lord," replied our heroine solemnly and firmly, "seals my doom. You understand me, I dare say. I have no occa-sion to enter into a long statement of what I mean; but I wish you well. my lord, cruel though, I must say, this persecution of your towards me is."

"Rash girl!" replied Bianchi, furiously; "but you know not what you say. My lord, I repeat, heed her not. I have pledged my word to you, and by all the saints in Christendom, the Prince Bianchi will not forfeit it."

"My lord," returned the Count Alberti, obsequiously, and not venturing to direct his eyes towards our heroine, "I bow with all due submission to your will. I wish not to prolong this interview."

"You may retire, girl," said the Prince Bianchi authoritatively and imperatively; "you have heard what I said, and it will be well for you if you bear it strictly in your mind."

"It will be impossible that I can forget it, my lord," replied our heroine, with a deep sigh. "Farewell; and may Heaven open your heart, and change your mind towards me, and not compel me to adopt that course to which I shall otherwise, much against my will, be driven."

"What mean you?" demanded her uncle and the count, in a breath.

"No matter," replied Melina. "If you drive me to extremities, sooner than meet with a fate so revolting to my feelings, I will avail myself of the desperate course that is, at any rate, opened to me."

"Explain yourself," exclaimed the prince, fiercely, and alarmed by the determination of her manner. "What is it you contemplate?"

"No matter," replied Melina, with the most perfect calmness. "It all rests with yourself whether or not you force me to do that which, Heaven knows, is so repugnant to my feelings; but again I solemnly declare that I will risk, meet with any fate, sooner than become the wife of a man whom I so thoroughly detest and despise. I mean his lordship, the Count Alberti. You may call me bold, obdurate, if you please, but I am no hypocrite, uncle; and it is thus I speak my mind."

"By Heaven!" exclaimed Bianchi, passionately, "this is almost beyond endurance. Shall I be thus taunted and defied by a foolish, headstrong girl, whom I have ever treated with too much indulgence? Have you no fear of the consequences of your disobedience to my will? Have you no dread of my curse, which will most assuredly descend upon your head, should you still obstinately oppose me."

"Be calm, my lord, I beseech you, and bear with her," said Alberti. "The fair Melina will think better of this in her maturer moments of reflection, and I have no fear of the result."

"Indeed, my lord," replied our heroine,

scornfully, "you may enjoy your opinion, if you think proper—of course, I have no business to question that; but I must be permitted to inform you, that if you flatter yourself with the idea that any change can possibly take place in my sentiments towards you, or that anything can alter my determination, you will find yourself most grievously mistaken. I repeat that the bare idea of becoming your wife is revolting and disgusting to my feelings, and there is no fate that I would not much sooner encounter. I thank you, uncle, for permitting me to retire; and I hope that you will think better of this, and be enabled to see the injustice of the fate you would inflict upon me."

The prince and the count were both too much excited and exasperated to make any reply, and suffered Melina to leave the room without any further observation; and after she was gone, they paced the room together for several moments, without exchanging a word with each other.

"By the mass," observed Bianchi, at last, "she is most perverse. But I will not suffer her to triumph over the determination I have formed. I trust, my lord, that you will not be seriously chagrined with the observations she has made use of."

"Why, your highness," returned Alberti, "you must, I think, yourself admit, that they can be anything but pleasant to me. It is evident, and she takes no pains to disguise it, that she detests me; but still, so powerful is the love I bear her, that nothing can make me forfeit the claim I have to her hand, while I am still honoured and favoured by your sanction."

"Well spoken, count," said Bianchi, grasping his hand cordially, "and you shall find that I will fulfil all the promises I have made to you to the very letter."

"I do not doubt you, my lord," said Alberti, in reply; "but still I have some misgivings on my mind that all will not turn out so happily as we could wish."

"What mean you?" demanded the prince; "can there be any doubt upon the consummation of our wishes? Next Monday, at midnight, I repeat, if you remain in the same mind, Melina shall become your bride."

"I do not doubt for an instant the fulfilment of your promise, my lord," remarked Alberti; "but still the observations that your fair niece made use of, induce me to suspect that she flatters herself with the hope that she will be able to escape us."

"Impossible!" returned Bianchi, "what makes you entertain such an idea?"

"Did you not notice what she said, my lord, which seemed to imply, nay, she even candidly acknowledged it, that she had some means or prospect of rescue."

"Rescue!" reiterated the Prince Bianchi, "impossible! Who is there could, or would dare to assist her?"

"Florio Clairville is under the protection of the brigand chief," replied Alberti; "you know well the hatred, the mortal hatred which they both naturally bear towards me; and the sympathy which they bear in respect to your beauteous niece, will induce Massaroni to interpose to save her if possible."

"No, no," returned Bianchi, "he will never be so daring."

"Ah, my lord," remarked Alberti, "what is there that the brigand chief will not dare to do?"

"He will never venture such a bold attempt as that at which you have hinted," said the Prince Bianchi.

"As I have before observed, your highness," returned the count, "I have very strong suspicions that he will do so; and they are strengthened, if not all but confirmed, by what occurred the other evening."

"What mean you?" demanded Bianchi, eagerly.

"Why," replied the Count Alberti, "the song we both heard in the gardens of the villa, and which, I am certain, proceeded from no other lips than those of Allesandro Massaroni."

"Ah!" ejaculated the prince, "by Heaven! I did not think of that. It must have been him, certainly; and if such is the case, he may be lurking, with his desperate band, in some part of the neighbourhood."

"I think there can be very little doubt of that."

"But still," observed the prince, "he could not become acquainted with our designs, and the time at which we intend to carry them into effect."

"You well know the craftiness of the brigand chief," replied Alberti, "and the means he has of secretly carrying into effect and accomplishing anything upon which he has once fixed his mind."

"Very true," answered Bianchi; "he is a crafty, designing rascal, but he must not be allowed to outwit us in this affair."

"No, it would be most provoking and unfortunate if he should do so," said Alberti, "and therefore it behoves us to use every possible precaution to prevent him."

"Very good; what do you propose?"

"Why, that we should have a sufficient force in the villa on the occasion of this ceremony taking place to oppose any attack that may be made upon us."

"True, I perfectly coincide with the advice you offer," said Bianchi, "and will give my instructions accordingly; but still I cannot help thinking that there will be no necessity for them. Massaroni will never be bold enough to make such an attempt; and think you that Melina could reconcile it with her feelings to throw herself on the protection of the brigand chief?"

"So great is the horror and disgust that she entertains at the idea of a marriage with me," replied Alberti, "that I feel satisfied she is prepared to adopt any course, however naturally repugnant to her feelings, to avoid it."

"By the dome of St. Peter's!" exclaimed the prince, passionately, "if I could bring my mind to think as you suggest, I would take the readiest means to prevent it. But have I traitors about me?"

"Should Allesandro Massaroni be really in possession of the secret of this intended forced marriage, and the time at which it is to take place, there can be little or no doubt that you have, my lord," answered the Count Alberti.

"Could I but discover them," said Prince Bianchi, his face inflamed with indignation, "my utmost vengeance should descend upon their heads."

"It strikes me forcibly, your highness, that one of your domestics has been bribed to play you falsely."

"Ah!" exclaimed Bianchi, "can any one have been so bold?"

"Money will effect much, my lord."

"True; but still I cannot persuade myself that Massaroni would be inclined to part with his money in such a cause."

"We know not what he would do in order to gratify his revenge," said Alberti.

"But we examined all my fellows minutely," remarked the prince, "and we elicited nothing that was calculated to excite the least suspicion."

"Exactly so, my lord; but, of course, they would be on their guard. However, we have only to use the necessary precaution, and we may be enabled to frustrate any designs that may be contemplated against us."

"All that you suggest shall be attended to," said Bianchi, "and I entertain no fear of the result. I trust that the rude observations which Melina has made to you, will have no serious effect upon your mind, but that you will continue in the same state of determination."

"Of that you may be sure, my lord," returned the count; "the charms of your niece have made too powerful an impression upon my heart to suffer me easily to resign her, much as her scorn has wounded my feelings. But I may depend upon you? You will not abandon your determination, and forfeit your word to me, prevailed upon by the tears and supplications of the beauteous Melina?"

"Deceive you!" replied the Prince Bianchi, hastily; "what reason have you to doubt me? Have I not given you my solemn promise, and think you that the Prince Bianchi will ever forfeit his word? Are not all the preparations for the marriage rites made? Have I not fixed my mind upon this union, and resisted all the entreaties and remonstrances of the obstinate girl, my niece; and think you now, at the eleventh hour, that I am going to yield? No, count; you know me not correctly if you imagine such a thing. Next Monday at midnight, and you are willing, my niece, Melina, shall become your lawful bride, and I doubt not but that you will soon be able to subdue the aversion she now evinces towards you. Fear not, man, her proud spirit will be crushed, when she finds that she cannot help herself."

"Enough, my lord," said Alberti, "your words encourage me; but still I should have been more satisfied if Florio Clairville had been in our power, and safely disposed of, instead of being under the protection of the brigand chief, Allesandro Massaroni."

"Why," remarked Bianchi, "that certainly would have been much better, and it was an unfortunate job that he managed to escape, when we had him in prison so conveniently. However, let not that disturb your mind, or raise any apprehensions in your breast; for although he is backed by the protection and friendship of the brigand chief, I still believe him powerless to effect us any annoyance, especially as we are so well prepared against any designs that may be contemplated. Are you not satisfied, count?"

"I am," replied the latter, "and will look forward to Monday next with the most blissful anticipations. By Heaven! in spite of the scorn and aversion with which she views me, I would not resign my hopes of the beauteous Melina, even though by doing so I might purchase the worth of a kingdom."

"Well said, my lord," observed the Prince Bianchi, again grasping his hand cordially; "all then, is arranged to our mutual satisfaction?"

"It is, your highness," coincided the Count Alberti; and after some more conversation of an unimportant character, they separated.

It may, perhaps, now be satisfactory to the reader, and certainly of importance to keep up the chain of events in our narrative, to return to Massaroni, and relate what had taken place, and how his plot progressed previous to the circumstances we have detailed in the previous pages.

On the arrival of the brigand chief and Rubaldo in the vicinity of the Villa Rosa, the latter lost no time in obtaining an interview with Guiseppe, and making an appointment with him where he should meet Massaroni to adjust the important business they had in contemplation, and to make their arrangements accordingly; and the fellow, Guiseppe, was true to his appointment, and met them at a certain place in which they had taken up their temporary residence, the other portion of the band being located in the various habitations of the peasantry just outside the city, amongst whom they were known, and who were their friends, having received so many kindnesses and assistance from them—ready at a moment's summons to fly to the assistance of their chief.

It was on the same evening of the arrival of Allesandro Massaroni and his trustworthy and long-tried companion at the place of their destination, that Guiseppe made his appearance before them, and they were at the time occupied in their usual way under such circumstances, namely, regaling themselves with some of the best wines that the vintages of Italy could produce, and flavouring the beverage by imbibing the smoke of their cigars. But certainly the manner in which they were at that moment disguised, would have rendered it extremely difficult for any one to have recognised in them the dashing and daring characters who for so many years had caused such a sensation in the country, and of whom so many romantic stories were in circulation. Massaroni and his companion wore the garb of the humblest peasants, Rubaldo wearing a sandy wig, and false whiskers of the same hue, and Massaroni assuming the character of a feeble old man, with silvery hair flowing over his shoulders, and a long beard to match.

Guiseppe looked his character well; he was a tall, muscular man, with a peculiar crafty and villanous expression of countenance, dark, and swarthy, with a low forehead, shaggy eye brows, small eyes, sunk deep in their sockets, but bright and restless, and gleaming with cunning and mischief. He fixed them keenly on Massaroni on his being introduced to him by Rubaldo, and waited for him to commence the conversation, the door having first been secured, to prevent the sudden intrusion of any individual, whom it might have been extremely inconvenient to have overheard the particulars of that which was about to be discussed. At length the brigand chief said—

"So, you are Guiseppe, I presume?"

"The same, signor," replied the fellow, "and I presume that you are no other than Allesandro Massaroni, the brigand chief."

"Perfectly correct," said Massaroni, with a smile; "then you had better be seated."

Guiseppe bowed, and took a seat accordingly.

"You know the nature of the business we have come upon?" resumed our hero.

"Certainly," answered Guiseppe. "Rubaldo has told me."

"Are you worthy to be trusted, in an affair of danger?" demanded our hero.

"I suppose that my friend here, Rubaldo, has told you my character," was the reply of Guiseppe; "it needs but gold to bind me to the performance of any act."

"Even to an act of treachery?"

"Exactly so; or else I should not undertake to assist you in your designs against my master, His Highness the Prince Bianchi."

"Well, well," said Massaroni, "we shall understand each other presently. Here is a purse for you to commence with; and if you are faithful to your promise, you will find that Allesandro Massaroni can be generous to those whose services he requires."

"Thank you, signor," returned Guiseppe, first weighing the purse in his hand and then depositing it in his pocket; "now we shall better understand each other."

"We shall, I trust. The Signora Melina is to be compelled to marry the Count Alberti, at a certain fixed period, unless some power interposes to rescue her?"

"True," answered Guiseppe.

"You are aware of my power, I suppose?" said Massaroni.

"I am."

"I would rescue her from such a fate, and you say that you are willing to assist me?"

"Yes, signor."

"Could you admit me and my band at any hour to the villa in order to effect that purpose?"

"Certainly I could; and, if I understand rightly, that is what we have now met upon. Let there be no mistake between us, Signor Massaroni. I tell you again that I am willing to do anything for gold."

"Ah!" replied the brigand chief, with a laugh; "a time-serving knave, I perceive."

"You are inclined to be complimentary, signor," said Guiseppe, with an ironical grin. "However, you shall find that all I have promised I will perform."

"Enough," said our hero, "I like your candour, and you shall also find that I will keep my word. The ceremony is arranged to take place at midnight, is it not?"

"It is," answered Guiseppe.

"Then what I require of you to do is this," remarked Massaroni, "that on the night appointed you be ready to admit me and Rubaldo into the chapel, and conceal us, an hour or two before the time fixed upon, and afterwards to give admission to my band, in case their assistance should be required."

"That shall be done, signor."

"You will not attempt to deceive me?"

"Ask your friend, Rubaldo."

"I will answer for him, as I have told you before," replied Rubaldo.

"I am satisfied," said the brigand chief; "be faithful to the promise you have made me, and you shall find that I know how fully to appreciate any services that may be rendered me by you. The Count Alberti is at present sojourning at the villa, with the Prince Bianchi, is he not?"

Guiseppe replied in the affirmative.

"'Tis well," replied Massaroni; "Rubaldo, I will yet have my revenge of him."

"You shall, captain," returned Rubaldo, "there can be no doubt of that."

"I shall not rest satisfied," said Massaroni, "until I have him once again in my power, and have compelled him to render all the justice he can to the deeply wronged and persecuted Olympia and her child."

"And that shall be accomplished," said Rubaldo.

"But," remarked Massaroni, after a minute or two's reflection; "I must have the means of access to the villa at any hour I please. How is that to be accomplished, Guiseppe?"

"Oh," answered the latter, "very simply, signor. You see this key which I am about to deliver into your hands? It is one that opens a small door at the back of the house, seldom used, and always left unbolted. I secured it some time ago to suit my own purposes, which there is no occasion to explain just now, and I deliver it into your hands."

"That is fortunate," said the brigand, taking the key; "I have a wish to survey the villa, and likewise to make the Signora Melina acquainted with my proximity at my leisure; but again I ask you, Guiseppe, can I depend upon your secrecy?"

"Why should you any longer doubt me?" replied Guiseppe; "am I not willing to render you every satisfactory proof that you wish? Has not Signor Rubaldo, who has known me for so many years, repeatedly assured you of the same? I am willing to be bound by any oath you may think proper to administer to me; or, if that does not satisfy you, as I suppose you do no much value the oath of such a fellow as me, why, I will return you your gold, wish you good-night, and there is an end to the business."

"No, no," returned our hero, "I am perfectly satisfied; but of course, in a matter of such importance, it is necessary that I should use all due precaution. I suppose I need not tell you what the consequences always are of offending Allesandro Massaroni, the brigand chief, and that even should he be betrayed into the hands of the executioner, he would leave those behind him who would terribly avenge his death?"

"I know it well, signor," returned the fellow Guiseppe, "and entertain every respect for you. By the mass, I would sooner serve Allesandro Massaroni, the daring and noble-hearted brigand chief, than all the sovereigns in Europe, even though they offered me additional pay—ay, even tenfold!"

"Well spoken," said our hero; "I do no longer doubt you."

"You have no occasion to do so, signor."

"I believe not," observed Massaroni. "By-the-by, you should become one of my bold band; I think you are the sort of man that would suit me."

"Well, Signor Massaroni," replied Guiseppe, "I have often thought that your wild and romantic course of life would suit me much better than that I am pursuing; and as you entertain that favourable opinion of me that you have expressed, I will avail myself of your offer, after the business we have at present on hand is completed."

"Enough," said the brigand chief; "then we perfectly now understand each other?"

"We do," answered Guiseppe. "Have you any further commands for me?"

"No more than that you will keep as strict a watch as you possibly can upon all that takes place at the villa, and give me timely notice of it."

"I will not fail to do so."

"Only a few days have to elapse ere the ceremony is appointed to take place?"

"Next Monday," was the answer.

"Very good," returned Massaroni; "and there are places in the villa where I and a few of the chosen of my band might conceal ourselves, so that we might rush out at the very instant our services were required, and take the Prince Bianchi and Count Alberti by surprise?"

"There are," answered Guiseppe; "but at midnight, when all the family are at rest, if you think proper, I will be ready to admit you and Rubaldo, and to show you over the place, so that you may be the better able to form your own opinion, and arrange your plans accordingly."

"Good," said Massaroni; "we will be there."

"At midnight?"

"Yes, at midnight."

"You know the door I mean, which the key I have given you opens? if not, Rubaldo does, and there you will find me, at the hour of midnight, waiting to receive you."

"That is satisfactory; we will be punctual. But has the prince many retainers near the spot?"

"No," answered Guiseppe, "there is nothing whatever to apprehend on that point; and I think you have already given him sufficient proof as to what you can do with those under your command whenever he has ventured to oppose you."

"True," returned the brigand chief, with a smile. "I think I have proved to him that Allesandro Massaroni is no child to be played with. But how fares the beauteous Signora Melina?"

"Why," replied Guiseppe, "as badly as can be expected, under the circumstances. She is kept closely confined to her chamber, and sees no one but her waiting-maid, Floretta, except when her uncle and the Count Alberti demand an interview with her. But pardon me, signor, I must begone."

"As you please," answered our hero; "at midnight you may expect me, at any rate."

"You will find me faithful to my promise; I will not deceive you."

"It will be well for you if you do not."

"If you still doubt me, here is your gold again, and an end to the matter."

"No, no, I do not; have I not convinced you of that before?" replied the brigand chief; "but, of course, it is necessary that we should perfectly understand each other, or the important business we have on hand could never be carried out with due effect.

"True," continued Guiseppe, "and when I fail in the promises I have made you, I shall be willing and prepared to take all the consequences that might follow. You will find, as I have stated before, that Guiseppe is ready to do anything for gold, especially against one whom he so throughly detests as the Count Alberti."

"Ah! you hate him?"

"Mortally."

"Has he ever done you any injury?"

"Not he, but his late father was the cause of the ruin and degradation of me and my family, although he knows me not now; but this is not the time to talk upon such a subject, and it would be uninteresting to you. Were you to ask me to secretly plunge a poniard in his heart, I would obey the order promptly and with pleasure."

"No, no, Guiseppe," replied the brigand, "do not misunderstand me; I hate the Count Alberti, and despise him as much as it is possible for you to do; but Allesandro Massaroni delights not in the shedding of human blood, even that of his greatest enemies; and it is only those that oppose him in mortal combat that must take the consequences which fate may ordain. But I can appreciate your feelings, and the warmth with which you express them, if, as you say, you and your family have received wrongs and degradations, for bitterly have I experienced the same; but let me not dwell upon that subject now, or it might drive me to a state of mind that would unfit me for the more pressing business I have in contemplation. I repeat to you once more that, at the hour of midnight, you may expect me at the place we have appointed."

"And you, Signor Massaroni," replied Guiseppe, "will find me waiting to receive you. Adieu!"

"You will drink before you retire, to the success of our projects?" said the brigand chief, filling a bumper, and handing it to him.

"Most willingly, signor," answered Guiseppe; "here's success to the designs you have in contemplation, and confusion to all the enemies of Allesandro Massaroni, the bold Mountain Chief."

"Bravissimo!" ejaculated Rubaldo, filling himself a glass from the beverage before them, and raising it to his lips: "here's success to all our undertakings, and confusion and destruction to all the enemies of the bold brigand chief, Allesandro Massaroni."

"I thank you," said Massaroni, with his accustomed politeness; "but I must propose one more toast ere you depart, Guiseppe. Here's to the health and happiness of the lovely Signora Melina, and may all her hopes be realised!"

This toast was also done due honour to; and some little more conversation having taken place, which it is needless to particularise here, the man Guiseppe took his departure, well pleased with the arrangements he had made, and left the brigand and his companion to their own reflections.

"That certainly is an ill-looking rascal, Rubaldo," returned Massaroni, after a pause; "but if he performs all that he has promised, he will be just the man for our purpose, and it is a lucky thing that you happened to know him. But do you really think that he is to be depended upon?"

"Undoubtedly," replied Rubaldo; "have I not repeatedly told you so? It is not likely that I would recommend any person to you on such important and delicate business, unless I knew him well. Besides, you hear that he has some interest in aiding you in your designs, in consequence of the injuries he has received from the family of the Count Alberti."

"Very true," replied Massaroni. "I think I may trust him, though I believe him to be an arrant scoundrel."

"You may," returned Rubaldo; "and if he deceives you I will be ready to receive, without a murmur, the severest punishment that you can possibly inflict upon me."

"Enough," said Massaroni; "I am perfectly satisfied. I will go alone to the villa, at the hour appointed."

"Had I not better accompany you?"

"No; there is one particular room which contains the veiled portrait of which you have heard me speak, that I have a particular wish to inspect and to commune with my own thoughts; but you can be at hand, and also have our comrades ready to make their appearance at a moment's notice, should their services be required."

"Very good," said Rubaldo, "I will do as you wish."

They continued drinking together till the time arrived; and Massaroni having provided himself with a dark lantern, which he concealed underneath his cloak, quitted the place, and made his way to the Villa Rosa. He was not many minutes in reaching there, and looking up at all the windows, he found the house involved in the most complete darkness. He then walked round to the back, and quickly discovered the door which Guiseppe had mentioned, but stood for a minute or two and hesitated to put the key in the lock. He approached the door and listened, but all was quite still, and he was about to enter, when the door was suddenly and cautiously opened, and Guiseppe presented himself.

"All right, signor," he said, "you are punctual; the prince and all the family have long since retired to rest, and we may now enter with perfect safety. Follow me."

"I have a light, you see," said the brigand chief, showing him the lantern.

"That was unnecessary," answered Guiseppe,

RUBALDO RETURNS WITH A LETTER FOR CLAIRVILLE

"for you might have been sure that I should have been provided; but come."

Massaroni followed him into the house without saying another word, and they proceeded along a passage of considerable extent, till they came to the foot of a flight of stairs.

"Those lead to the apartments of the Signora Melina," observed Guiseppe; "but come, I will conduct you to the chapel where it is intended that the marriage shall take place, and show you where you and your band may conceal yourselves, and rush out at a moment,

No. 42.

to the surprise and confusion of the Prince Bianchi and the Count Alberti."

Massaroni returned no answer, but followed Guiseppe, who led him beneath an archway to the right, and there was then revealed to them a short flight of stone steps, which, having descended, they found themselves in another passage, at the extremity of which was a low door which Guiseppe unlocked from one of a bunch of keys he had brought with him, and laying hold of the arm of Massaroni he led him forward. The brigand chief held up the lantern, and found that they were standing in the chapel.

It was of large dimensions, and a fine specimen of Roman architecture of about the middle ages, and our hero could scarcely have believed that there had been such a place in a house of such simple pretensions as the Villa Rosa.

"This way," said Guiseppe, pointing towards the altar, "and I will soon convince you that there are every means of concealment, and for carrying out the designs you have in contemplation."

Massaroni obeyed without making use of any observation, and Guiseppe led him to the back of the altar, and raising the drapery, discovered to him a low iron-door in the wall.

"Whither does this lead to?" demanded Massaroni, having some suspicions.

"I will show you," answered his conductor; "do not hesitate; do you doubt me?"

"Why, for the matter of that," replied the brigand chief, coolly, showing him a brace of pistols and a poniard, "if you were to play me falsely, you see I have not come unprepared to defend myself."

"Pshaw!" returned Guiseppe, "I thought we had understood each other this evening. You see I am unarmed, and entirely at your mercy; but I tell you again, and I am ready to swear it, that no treachery is intended."

"Well, well," said Massaroni, more satisfied, "I will not doubt you; lead on, and let me see the place of which you have spoken."

Guiseppe again applied to the bunch of keys he had with him, and applying one of them to the lock of the door, it immediately flew open, and revealed a long arched passage, which was capable of containing a number of individuals.

"What think you of this?" asked Guiseppe.

"Nothing could be better," answered the brigand chief, "if even it had been contrived expressly for my purpose. But where does it lead to?—Are there any means of effecting an easy escape by it?"

"You shall see," returned Guiseppe; "this way, signor."

Massaroni followed him in silence; and after proceeding for some distance, they came to the end, where another door presented itself, and Guiseppe having unlocked it, Massaroni saw that they were in the open air.

"Ay," he said, "this is most fortunate; by this passage we may immediately make our escape from the villa, and set pursuit at defiance. But I wish to visit the room in which the portrait about which so much secrecy is maintained, is hung. Have you also a key that will unlock the door of that apartment?"

"I have," answered Guiseppe; "you see that I have not deceived you in regard to what I promised you, and that I have come well provided for your accommodation."

"You have," said Massaroni, "and you have my thanks for it; and depend upon it you shall not go unrewarded. But know you any of the particulars concerning the history of that portrait?"

"I do not," answered Guiseppe, "no more than that it represents a young Florentine damsel of whom the Prince Bianchi, they say, was very fond."

"Did you ever hear her name?" asked the brigand.

"Never!" replied Guiseppe; "but you seem to take a particular interest in that portrait, signor?"

"I do, indeed," said Massaroni; "it so strongly reminds me of one who—but no matter—I——"

"You have seen it, then, signor?" interrupted Guiseppe, whose curiosity was, in turn, excited.

"Oh, yes," answered the brigand chief; "and my thoughts have ever since been fixed upon it. But we will talk no more upon this subject, Guiseppe; it is a painful one to me. Lead the way to the room."

Guiseppe obeyed, without making any remark, and they left the passage, retraced their steps, and having arrived at the place from which they had at first started, they turned into another passage to the right, and ascending a staircase, with noiseless steps, though there was no one in that part of the building, if they had been awake, to overhear them, they quickly stopped at the door of that room in which our hero had been once before, and where was the mysterious portrait he was so anxious to behold again.

Guiseppe opened the door from the bunch of keys, and they both stepped into the room; and Massaroni immediately fixed his eyes upon that part of the room, from the wainscot of which the likeness was suspended, and which was concealed from observation by a blue gauze curtain.

"Leave me for a few minutes, Guiseppe," said Massaroni; "wait outside the door until I summon you again. I wish to contemplate the portrait alone."

"Very good, signor," said Guiseppe, looking

at him with an expression of no little surprise. "I have no wish to interrupt you in your meditations; but you will recollect the lateness of the hour, and I suppose you will not be long?"

"No, no," said Massaroni, in reply; "but leave me."

Guiseppe quitted the room accordingly, and the brigand chief slowly advanced towards the portrait, and, as he did so, a feeling of awe stole over his senses, which he found it utterly impossible to conquer, and he was obliged to pause for a moment or two, in order to recover himself. At length, he became more calm, and placing the lantern on the floor, in such a situation as to throw the best light upon the picture, he, with a trembling hand, drew the curtain aside, but no sooner did his eyes fall upon the lovely features that were represented on the canvas, than his heart palpitated violently against his side, and a kind of giddiness seized upon his brain; but he could not have removed his gaze from it had it even been to save his life.

He clasped his hands fervently together, and a holy feeling of devotion came over him. He took the miniature of his mother from his bosom, and compared it with the portrait, and as he did so, his agitation increased.

"How like!" he ejaculated, in a voice of the deepest emotion; "it must have been done for her; and she was a Florentine, too. How extraordinary is the coincidence. I could swear, by Heaven, that I once more gazed upon the features of that dear mother, whose wrongs were so great, and who met with so untimely a fate."

He knelt down before the portrait, and the brigand chief—he, the lawless and the outcast, —prayed fervently.

"Beauteous resemblance of her who gave me being," he said, "here, as I kneel, I swear never to rest until I have discovered the base author of your misery, if he be still alive, and have wreaked my vengeance upon his head. No power, no rank, no wealth shall save him, even though I lose my own life in avenging the wrongs of my unfortunate parent upon his guilty head!"

He paused and started, for, at that moment, either his imagination deceived him, or he believed—nay, he could almost have sworn—that he saw the lips of the portrait move, and that a melancholy sigh escaped from them.

"God of Heaven!" he exclaimed, "can this be real, or is it only the effects of my disordered imagination? No, no; Allesandro Massaroni, the brigand chief, must not thus give way to superstitious ideas, that are unworthy of him. I must have been labouring under a delusion. I cannot, for the present, gaze any longer at this extraordinary portrait

or I shall go mad. But they say that this is the portrait of a young Florentine female, whom the Prince Bianchi loved. Can it be— No, no, it is impossible! My brain is bewildered, and I know not what I say!"

He drew the curtain once more across the portrait, and after reflecting for a few minutes, and trying to calm his feelings, he again requested Guiseppe to enter.

"Are you satisfied, signor?" asked the latter, when he entered the room.

"Yes, yes," replied Massaroni, hastily; "but shall I, at all times, have free access to this apartment?"

"Until after the accomplishment of your plot," answered Guiseppe. "I have already given you the key that opens the private door of the villa, and I now present you with the key of this apartment; but I trust, signor, that you will not deceive me, and lead me into any error, so willing as I am to serve you?"

"Guiseppe," replied Massaroni, "have I not given you my word, and who ever yet heard of the brigand chief breaking any promise he had made? Moreover, I have made you an offer of becoming one of my brave band, and methinks, if you study well your interest, you will accept of it."

"I will, most readily," answered Guiseppe, "for this tame life suits not me, and the hatred I bear towards the Prince Bianchi, and more especially to the Count Alberti, whose cursed relations have been the cause of my ruin, further urge me to it."

"Enough," said our hero, "I am perfectly satisfied. Here is more gold for you; I see plainly that we shall properly understand each other by and by."

"Signor Massaroni," said Guiseppe, "I perfectly understand you already, and I trust that from what has hitherto taken place between us you have come to the conclusion that you may depend upon my word, and that what I promise I will faithfully fulfil."

"Oh," returned the brigand chief, "I do not doubt you, and for one very good reason, that I have the gold wherewith to reward you for any services you may render me, and that you are likewise aware that should you attempt to deceive me, the most deadly vengeance of Massaroni and his band would pursue you to destruction."

"I admit your power," observed Guiseppe, "and in doing so you have the assurance of my fidelity. Are you satisfied with my conduct to night, and that which I have shown you?"

"I am," replied Massaroni.

"Is there anything more you wish to see?"

"Nothing. We will talk more upon this business anon. Will you meet me again at the place where I am secreted to morrow evening at the hour of seven?"

"I will, signor."

"You will be punctual?"

"I never fail," answered Guiseppe.

"'Tis well," said Massaroni; "I will depend upon you."

"You may do so safely, signor," replied the man Guiseppe.

"The Count Alberti, I know, is at present staying here?"

"He is."

"And in what part of the villa are his chambers situated?"

"On the left wing. I will show you on another occasion," answered Guiseppe. "You could at any hour strike a dagger to his heart, and thus rid the world of a miscreant, and the Signora Melina of her most bitter enemy and persecutor."

"Guiseppe," said the brigand chief, fixing a stern look upon him, "take you Allesandro Massaroni for a cowardly assassin? Think you that he would steal upon those who have excited his wrath when they were unprepared to meet him or defend themselves?"

"No, no, signor," returned Guiseppe, "you misunderstand me. I meant not to put any such construction upon the object of the question you put to me."

"Well, well," said our hero, "I do believe you. By the dome of Saint Peter's, Allesandro Massaroni would sooner die the death of a dog than he would become a secret and midnight assassin. He has been misrepresented, libelled, but who is there that dare to his face accuse him of ever having taken a cowardly advantage of even his bitterest enemy? Persecuted, outraged he has been, but still it was, and ever will be his wish, nay, more, his determination, to meet his enemies boldly face to face, and to trust to justice and to reason to protect the right. But we waste time—the hour is late."

"'Tis true, signor," said Guiseppe, "and as you say I have shown you all that you wish to see on the present occasion, and have satisfied you that there is every facility for carrying your designs into execution, I think it would be as well if you were now to depart."

"I will," said Massaroni; "but first let me again ask you if you know, or have ever heard the name of the female whom that mysterious portrait represents?"

"I solemnly swear that I have not," replied Guiseppe. "Of course I could have no interest in concealing it from you, after what I have stated to you as regards my hatred of the Prince Bianchi. But you appear to take a remarkable interest in that portrait, signor."

"I do, indeed," remarked the brigand, with considerable emotion; "it reminds me of one who suffered the most cruel wrongs, and whose fate remains yet to be avenged whenever I can meet with the villanous author of it. He was great and wealthy; he—but why do I suffer my tongue to ramble thus? The time will come when, if he lives, the deceiver, the libertine, the seducer, the heartless miscreant, will meet with that punishment his offences so richly merit. Lead the way, Guiseppe; it is time, as you say, that I departed."

Guiseppe made no answer, but taking the light from Massaroni, he conducted him in the same silent and cautious manner to the door at which he had been admitted.

"Farewell, signor," he said, when they had arrived there; "I hope you are satisfied with my conduct so far?"

"Perfectly so, Guiseppe," replied the brigand chief; "remain faithful to your promise, and you will have no cause to regret the services you may have rendered to Allesandro Massaroni."

"I do believe you, signor," said Guiseppe, in answer to these observations from our hero, "and you shall find that, although I own myself to be an arrant scoundrel, when my mind is fixed upon any purpose, and I have one whom I respect to serve, I am to be depended upon, ay, even though death and the devil should stare me in the face."

"Well spoken, Guiseppe," returned Massaroni; "I like the observations you have made use of, and will trust to you. Good-night."

"Good-night," responded Guiseppe.

"You will not forget to meet me to-morrow evening at the hour I have appointed?" said the brigand.

"Fear not," answered Guiseppe. "I will be punctual.

"Six o'clock!"

"I remember."

With these words the brigand chief and Guiseppe separated, and the former made his way to the place at which he and Rubaldo were at present staying, fully satisfied with what had at present taken place, and at the prospect there was of the ultimate success of the designs he had in contemplation. But the portrait upon which he had again gazed still engrossed the whole of his thoughts, and dismal and torturing were the reflections it excited in his mind.

"By the saints!" he exclaimed, "the coincidence is most extraordinary; all parties agree in stating that the fair being whom that portrait represents, was a young maiden of Florence, and that she was beloved, or was the mistress of the Prince Bianchi. My unfortunate mother was also a Florentine, and the portrait is the very counterpart of herself, as she must have appeared in the bright season of her youth and beauty. Her seducer was noble and wealthy;—should he prove to be the Prince Bianchi!—The thought maddens me, and sets my brain whirling. But let me not give way to such wild thoughts, but calmly endeavour to await the will of Providence, and suffer myself to be guided by the dictates of prudence alone. Massaroni, you have a solemn duty to perform, which justice demands, and let no rash act of your own mar or frustrate it. My poor deeply-injured mother's untimely fate calls for retribution on the head of the author of her misery, and by Heaven, though I sacrifice my own life in the effort, if he be still in existence, that retribution shall be obtained."

Thus speaking he hurried on his way, and was directly afterwards joined by Rubaldo and the other brigands who had been waiting near the villa, in case their services should be required.

"Well, captain, what success?" inquired Rubaldo.

"All that I could have wished," replied the brigand chief; "there is every facility for the execution of my purpose, and the fellow Guiseppe is just the man I wanted."

"Ay," observed Rubaldo, "I thought you would approve of him; and you have only to continue to reward and encourage him, and you will find him a useful man at all times. You say that he is willing to become one of our band?"

"He is most anxious to do so," answered Massaroni, "and I think I cannot do better than to gratify his wish, since he seems so well calculated for our course of life."

"True," coincided Rubaldo; "I know him for a daring fellow, or I would not have recommended him to you. But you seem agitated, captain; has anything particular occurred to disturb you?"

"No," replied Massaroni, "no more than that I have again beheld that mysterious portrait of which you have so often heard me speak; and am struck more forcibly than ever with the extraordinary likeness it bears to my unfortunate mother. As I gazed upon it, I could almost have believed that she stood before me."

"'Tis strange," said Rubaldo.

"It is," returned the brigand chief; "but I swear never to rest until I have by some means or other penetrated the secret. I have my suspicions, and should they be confirmed, let the guilty tremble, for most assuredly my bitterest, my most deadly vengeance shall descend upon their head. But enough of this, we will talk further on this subject at a future occasion. At present all goes well, and the completion of our plot is all but certain. Signora Melina must be rescued from the fate with which she is threatened, and the Count Alberti must be taught that he will not be permitted to set the power of the brigand chief at defiance with impunity."

"True," replied Rubaldo, "and there can be no fear of your wishes not being gratified to the fullest extent. Who is there that can defeat the designs of Massaroni?"

"They have not been able to do so hitherto," said Massaroni, "though they have sent strong forces against him. But come—we tarry. Let us hasten on our way, for the hour is late, and it is time that we sought some repose."

Rubaldo made no answer, and quickening their pace, he and Massaroni soon arrived at the place where they were at present concealed, while the other brigands also retired to the different places in which they were concealed.

The brigand chief and Rubaldo separated for the night, and Massaroni retired to rest; but still the portrait of the lovely young Florentine maiden was constantly present to his imagination, and it was some time ere he could compose his mind to sleep; and when he did, it again haunted him in his dreams, and seemed to smile upon him benignantly, as though in approval of his conduct; and when he awoke in the morning, the impression upon his mind had become more powerful than ever.

Guiseppe was true to his appointment in the evening, and found the brigand alone.

"You have kept your word faithfully, Guiseppe," said Massaroni, "and I commend you for it. You shall lose nothing by your fidelity to me."

"I do not doubt you, signor," said Guiseppe, "and you shall find that what I have promised I will perform to the very letter."

"I am satisfied. But the Prince Bianchi has no suspicion of my having gained access to the villa last night, has he?"

"Oh, that is impossible, for had not all the family retired to rest? Besides, how can any suspicion be excited in his breast if we only act with secresy and prudence?"

"Very true; but are the preparations for the midnight marriage still going on?"

"They are," answered Guiseppe.

"And how fares the beauteous Signora Melina?" asked Massaroni.

"Sadly enough, you may be sure, signor," answered Guiseppe; "she is still kept confined to her own chamber; but has had another interview with her uncle and the Count Alberti to-day."

"And do they still remain inexorable?" demanded the brigand chief.

"No doubt of it," replied Guiseppe; "it is not at all likely that they will relent."

"The obstinate tyrants," ejaculated our hero; "but they little imagine the plot that is contemplated to frustrate their nefarious designs. However, I am anxious that Melina should become assured that there are those at hand who will rescue her even at the hazard of their lives. Have you no means of communicating it to her, Guiseppe?"

"I know of none at present, signor."

Massaroni paused, and reflected for a few minutes, and he then said—

"I have it; a thought as just suggested itself to me."

"And what may that be pray?" demanded Guiseppe.

"You must admit me to the garden of the villa, as soon as the shadows of evening shall have descended upon the earth, Guiseppe."

"And what would you there?"

"No matter; will you do as I desire?"

"Certainly," answered Guiseppe; "but I must say, signor, that I think it is extremely hazardous for you to venture thus."

"Not at all," said our hero; "the gardens afford plenty of places for concealment, do they not? Besides, I have the means of escape should I be discovered."

"Well, do as you please, signor," observed Guiseppe; "it is not my province to dictate to you."

"Enough," said Massaroni; "then at nine o'clock this evening you will be prepared to admit me?"

"I will, signor."

"This, then, is all I have to say to you, or to require of you for the present," remarked Massaroni; "but come, drink and enjoy yourself, for I already consider you as one of my band, although you have not yet taken the necessary oath required of every one before they are admitted into our confidence."

"I shall be most ready to do so at any time, signor," returned Guiseppe, "and you shall find that I will never disgrace you or those under your command."

"Why, you must be a madman if you dared to do so," replied Massaroni; "for death is always the certain fate of those who turn traitors to us."

"Justly so, signor," said Guiseppe; "so now I presume we understand each other better than ever?"

"Why," answered the brigand chief, "I should think we did. I am satisfied if you are."

"Perfectly so. But if you have no further commands for me at present, I had better depart, lest my absence from the villa might excite some suspicion."

"Be it so. Farewell! but remember the hour, nine o'clock."

"I will not forget, signor," replied Guiseppe; and after bowing to Massaroni and Rubaldo, he took his departure.

"What is your motive for visiting the gardens of the villa this evening, Massaroni?" asked Rubaldo when Guiseppe was gone.

"Simply to make Signora Melina aware of my being near at hand, and thus to inspire her with fresh courage and confidence," replied the brigand.

"And how do you purpose doing that?"

"By singing my favourite ritornella as near under her chamber window as possible."

"It is a hazardous plan, signor."

"How so?"

"Why, should the prince or Count Alberti overhear you, you might find it a difficult matter to effect your escape; besides, it would put them on their guard, and might be the means of frustrating our designs."

"Oh, I have no fear of that," said our hero; "I will use all due precaution; besides, you and your comrades will be close at hand in case of accidents."

"Well, signor," said Rubaldo, "of course you can do as you think proper, though I cannot help thinking that it would have been much better could you have hit upon a different plan of carrying out your wishes."

"Leave everything to me, Rubaldo," said the brigand, "and I feel satisfied that I shall meet with every success. Time presses, and it is indispensably necessary that Signora Melina should be apprised that there are those at hand who are ready and willing to assist her, or her fortitude might forsake her, and she might fall a victim to her terror and despair."

"True," said Rubaldo, "and I leave everything to your judgment."

"Which never failed me yet," returned our hero.

"Never," coincided his lieutenant. The conversation on this subject now dropped, and they discoursed on different topics, and farther arranged their plans for the future.

No sooner had darkness spread its sable curtain o'er the earth, than Massaroni and Rubaldo, having enveloped themselves in large cloaks, which completely concealed their persons from observation, set out for the villa, while the other brigands followed at a short distance, to be in readiness in case they were wanted. They were not long in reaching it, and finding the coast clear they walked round the house and looked up at the different windows, in most of which lights were burning. Massaroni also pointed out to his companion the door by which he had the means of obtaining admission to the villa, and he then proceeded to the gate which led into the garden, and exactly as the bell of St. Peter's tolled the hour of nine, it was slowly opened, and Guiseppe made his appearance, and beckoned them in. They obeyed instantly, and they hurried on by the most secluded part of the garden until they had arrived at a shrubbery, where Guiseppe stopped, and in a half-stifled voice, said—

"You had better conceal yourself here, signor Rubaldo, where you will be handy to render any assistance should it be required. I must leave you. Be cautious, Massaroni; for should you be discovered, your destruction would be almost certain."

"Oh, fear not," said our hero, in the same low accents, "I will be upon my guard. But tell me, is the Prince Bianchi and the Count Alberti in the villa?"

"They are," answered Guiseppe; "the apartment yonder, from the windows of which you perceive so powerful a light streaming, is where they are seated in consultation. You know the chamber of the Signora Melina. It is situated in the other wing."

"Yes—yes," replied Massaroni, hastily, "I know."

"But what is it you intend to do, signor?" demanded Guiseppe.

"No matter" returned Massaroni, "you need be under no apprehensions. Shall I see you again at midnight?"

"If you wish it, and it is your intention to return to the villa."

"Why, I think I had better do so," said the brigand, "for I may have something to consult you upon after the family have retired to rest."

"You will find me at the usual place, should nothing occur to render it prudent for you to change your mind," said Guiseppe: and without saying another word, he hurried from the spot.

"Conceal yourself," said our hero, turning to Rubaldo; "you need no instructions how to act should necessity require?"

"I shall be on the alert, captain," replied Rubaldo; and having concealed himself behind the shrubbery, Massaroni walked slowly away, looking cautiously around to make sure that he was not observed. He paused beneath the windows of the apartment in which the Prince Bianchi and Alberti were at that moment seated in conversation, and concealing himself behind the trunk of a lofty tree, considered within himself how it would be best for him to proceed. However, he did not remain there long, but advanced towards the wing of the building in which the chamber of Melina was situated, and again looked around him to make sure that there was no one near. Not the least signs of any individual was to be seen, and all that broke the stillness of the night was the gentle sighing of the wind amongst the foliage of the trees. Placing himself in such a position where his voice might be heard by Melina without his being seen by any one, he commenced singing the well-known ballad which was the production of his own brain. What followed has already been related.

Massaroni had scarcely concluded, when he noticed, from the confusion which seemed all in an instant to prevail in the house, that he had been overheard by others as well as Melina; and folding his cloak around him, after having first drawn his sword, in order to be prepared for immediate defence, in case of an attack, he hurried towards the spot where his lieutenant, Rubaldo, was concealed. He had not proceeded many paces when he perceived the Prince Bianchi and the Count Alberti, followed by several attendants, issue from the villa and make towards the spot whence, no doubt, they imagined the sounds to proceed; and abruptly turning into another path, he fortunately eluded them, and reached the spot where Rubaldo was secreted in safety.

"Haste—haste, Rubaldo," he said; "the inmates of the villa are alarmed, and we have not, therefore, a moment to lose."

Rubaldo waited to hear no more, but he and the brigand chief hastened towards the gate by which they had entered the garden, and which Guiseppe had fortunately left ajar. They emerged from the place, and closing the gate after them, they hurried precipitately towards the place where their comrades were awaiting them, and were soon far beyond the reach of danger, though not knowing the numbers they might have to oppose should they be discovered; they did not pause or venture to make use of any observations until they had arrived once more at the house where they had taken up their temporary abode.

"Well," said Massaroni, after they had been seated for a short time; "we have escaped them, at any rate, and I have, I feel convinced, succeeded in assuring Signora Melina that she has friends at hand, who, at every risk, are determined to rescue her from the power of her enemies. It is cursed unfortunate that the prince and Alberti overheard me though."

"Ay, it is indeed," coincided Rubaldo, "for they are now put upon their guard, and they may adopt such steps as will render all our plans abortive."

"Well, it cannot be helped," said the brigand; "but we must also be upon our guard, and I have no doubt that we shall yet be able to thwart them in their schemes."

"I hope we may," returned Rubaldo, "though I confess, after what has occurred, I am not so sanguine as you seem to be. But you will not attempt to visit the villa again to-night?"

"And why not?" demanded Massaroni.

"Why," answered his lieutenant, "it is more than probable that Bianchi will now use such precautions as might lead to your detection."

"Oh, I do not much apprehend that," said our hero; "I can enter safely by the secret door which I pointed out to you, without being seen by any one, and I wish to see Guiseppe, in order that I may learn what has taken place since this adventure, and then I shall know better in future how to act."

"Well," said Rubaldo, "of course you can

please yourself, but if you would only take my advice, you would at least delay your visit till to-morrow night, and in the meantime you will probably see something of Guiseppe."

"I do not see the necessity of that," remarked Massaroni; "however, I will consider the matter more maturely between this and midnight,"

They now sat themselves down to partake of some refreshment, and they had not been occupied in that manner many minutes, when they heard a knock at the outer door given in the peculiar manner which they had agreed upon with Guiseppe.

"It is one of our band, I dare say," observed Rubaldo; "shall I admit him?"

"Certainly," answered Massaroni; "but be cautious."

"Never fear me," answered Rubaldo, and he then left the room.

On arriving at the outer door he stopped to listen, and the knock was then repeated.

"Who's there?" demanded Rubaldo.

"Guiseppe," was the answer; "quick! open the door, Rubaldo, I have something to communicate."

The brigand immediately opened the door, and Guiseppe entered.

"Where is Massaroni?" he asked.

"In the house," answered Rubaldo; "follow me."

Guiseppe complied, without saying another word, and was quickly ushered into the presence of the brigand chief.

"Ah! Guiseppe, is it you?" said Massaroni; "I am glad to see you. But what brings you hither?"

"You need scarcely ask that question, I should imagine, after what has happened, signor," replied Guiseppe. "Pardon me, but I think you acted very rashly and imprudently, by adopting the course you did. I contrived to leave the villa that I might apprise you of the state of confusion and excitement in which everything now is there. The place is full of the soldiers of the prince and Alberti, and armed men are sent in every direction in pursuit of you."

"And let them discover me if they can," said the brigand, with a laugh. "Allesandro Massaroni is not so easily caught."

"But you will not venture to the villa tonight?" said Guiseppe.

"And why not?"

"Pardon me, signor, but it would be little better than madness to do so, and you would rush upon almost certain destruction. You had better wait until the excitement has abated."

"Well, well," said the brigand, after a pause, "I do not know but that your advice is reasonable, Guiseppe."

"In my opinion, it is perfectly so," remarked Rubaldo.

"But what of Signora Melina?" asked our hero; "has her uncle or the Count Alberti seen her since this event took place?"

"They have not," answered Guiseppe.

"That is well. But have you nothing more to communicate?"

"I have not, signor. Then I am to understand that you will not venture to the villa again to-night?"

"I will not," answered Massaroni; "but you will not fail to let me see you some time in the course of to-morrow, for I shall be most anxious to hear all that takes place at the villa."

"I will be sure to come, signor," answered Guiseppe.

"Enough," said the brigand; "no doubt this excitement will soon pass away; but at any rate, nothing shall prevent me from carrying my designs into effect."

"And as I have before assured you," said Guiseppe, "you shall find me ready to assist you to the utmost of my power and abilities in your designs."

"I am satisfied with the promises you have made, Guiseppe," said Massaroni, "and I have not the least doubt that you will fulfil them."

"You may depend upon me, signor, for I long to gratify the feelings of hatred and revenge I bear towards the Count Alberti."

"Fear not," returned the brigand, "you shall have a full opportunity of doing so. But you had better return, and mind you do not forget to-morrow, and likewise to bring me all the particulars you can."

"I will be sure to do so, signor," said Guiseppe.

And Rubaldo having once more conducted him to the door, he took his departure.

"This is no more than I expected, Massaroni," remarked Rubaldo, on his return to the room in which he had left the former, "and I am afraid it may lead to the most dangerous results, which will be calculated to retard, if not altogether to prevent the execution of our designs."

"Nonsense, man," replied the brigand chief, impatiently, "you are too ready to encourage apprehensions on the subject, which, take my word for it, will turn out to be entirely groundless. This excitement will shortly be at an end, and all will then go on as well as we could wish."

"Well, it may do so," remarked Rubaldo, "and I hope it will: but after all I cannot help thinking, as I have said before, that you had better have adopted any other course."

"And what would you have suggested as best to be done?" demanded Massaroni.

"Why," answered his lieutenant, "I cannot say at present. But since you have got such secret ingress to the villa, would it not have been possible to have got into communication with the Signor Melina, and to have persuaded her to place herself under your protection, and to elope from the villa before the time appointed for this forced marriage to take place?"

"No," replied the brigand, "I feel certain that the signora's nice sense of delicacy and propriety would have induced her to reject such a proposal. Her rescue can only be effected in the manner we have already planned, and when the moment of desperation will leave

FLORETTA BRINGS THE LETTER TO MELINA.

her no other alternative of escaping from a fate so revolting to her feelings. She is now doubtless fully aware of my being at hand, and likewise of my intentions, and it will inspire her with fresh courage to offer every resistance in her power to the importunities of her persecutors."

"But her uncle, the prince, may now place her under even greater restraint than before," said Rubaldo, "and may so alter his arrangements as to baffle us entirely."

"Oh, no," returned Massaroni, "that is not at all likely; besides, if he did so, it would speedily come to the knowledge of Guiseppe, and he would give me immediate notice of it. I tell you again, Rubaldo, that we have no occasion to fear, and that nothing whatever shall move me from my purpose, the success of which I feel to be as certain as if it were now accomplished."

"Well, I hope it may," returned Rubaldo.

"Do you not know," said the brigand chief, impatiently, "after all the number of years we have been together, that Allesandro Massaroni was seldom, if ever, disappointed in his expectations? and I am much mistaken if he is so on the present occasion."

"I am glad to see you so sanguine, Massaroni," observed his lieutenant; "but I know it is not necessary to remind you that it is proper to use the utmost precaution."

"Of course it is, and you will always find that I shall do so on every occasion. If Guiseppe only remains faithful, we have nothing to fear."

"And I should think you have seen enough of him already to place every confidence in him."

"Well, I do not doubt the rascal," said the brigand, "and it will be well for him if he does not attempt to deceive me. However, we have talked long enough upon this subject; my mind is fully made up, and I am resolved to carry out my projects even at the risk of my life."

"Well, well," said Rubaldo, "I have no further objection to urge, and of course you are certain of my hearty co-operation?"

"Oh, yes," answered Massaroni, "I am fully aware of that. No doubt Florio is in a state of the most painful suspense until our return, and he is made acquainted with the result."

"That he is sure to be," said Rubaldo, "and should we fail in our efforts to rescue her whom he so fondly loves, I verily believe the poor fellow would go mad."

"Yes," coincided Massaroni, "but there is no fear of that. If I am not much mistaken, but a very few days will restore the lovers to each other's arms."

"But they can never hope to be united."

"And why not?"

"The difference of their rank, and the fear of bringing down the everlasting anger of her uncle upon her head, will prevent the Signora Melina from giving her consent to become his wife."

"If she really love him it will not," replied Massaroni, "and it shall be no fault of mine if she reject him. It will be glorious revenge against the Prince Bianchi, who has ever thirsted for my blood, and the unprincipled villain, Count Alberti, whom I so mortally detest and despise."

"It would indeed, captain," observed Rubaldo, "and I only hope it may be accomplished."

"It shall be, or my name is not Allesandro Massaroni. The wrongs of the unfortunate Olympia must be redressed likewise. I have sworn that they shall be, and I will not break my oath, of that you may be certain. I have have often told you how deeply I am interested in the fate of that hapless woman; there is an extraordinary similarity in her history and mine, and I sympathise as deeply in the unmerited sufferings she has endured as if she were my own sister."

"She is indeed," said Rubaldo, "in my opinion, though I do not pride myself upon being much of a judge in such matters, worthy of every respect; and the Count Alberti has proved himself to be a heartless villain by the manner in which he has behaved towards her."

"True," answered the brigand chief, "he is a scoundrel of the blackest dye, and only let me get him once more in my power, which I do not despair of being able to accomplish, and I will make him pay dearly for all his past misdeeds, and for having dared to set the power of Allesandro Massaroni at defiance."

"Well, I think you have already punished him pretty severely in the destruction of his property, and by confining him and subjecting him to such numerous indignities for so long a time in our mountain retreat."

"Not half enough to gratify the feelings of hatred I bear towards him," said Massaroni. "But we will talk no more about him, for he is totally unworthy of wasting any words upon."

The time now getting late, after some further conversation of no importance, they separated for the night, having first ascertained that the house was perfectly secure from intrusion.

Guiseppe did not make his appearance until towards the evening of the following day, and the patience of Massaroni was almost exhausted, for he began to fear that something of a serious nature had happened.

"So you have come at last," said Massaroni. "I began to think you had forgotten your promise."

"I could not find an opportunity of leaving the villa before, signor," answered Guiseppe.

"And have you any fresh intelligence?" asked our hero.

"Nothing of importance," replied Guiseppe.

"Has the excitement at all abated?"

"A little, but not much, signor; the Prince Bianchi has been in a furious rage ever since the event took place, and the servants are all afraid to approach him. From what I myself overheard him say, he firmly believes that it was you he heard in the garden, and he vows the most terrible vengeance against you."

"Ha! ha! ha!" laughed the brigand chief, scornfully; "he must first catch me. The old fool, one would have thought that he had already experienced enough of my character to know that I set both his threats and himself at defiance. But have you heard anything of the situation of the Signora Melina?"

"It has undergone little if any change, I believe," answered Guiseppe; "she was closetted for some time to day with her uncle and Count Alberti, but what took place at the interview, of course I had no means of ascertaining. I am not on very friendly terms with her waiting-maid Floretta, or probably I might have learned all the particulars."

Massaroni paused and reflected for a minute or two, and then turning to Guiseppe, he said—

"I have been thinking that it requires something more to convince the Signora Melina of my being in the neighbourhood and my friendly intentions towards her. Do you not think it possible, Guiseppe, to get a letter secretly conveyed to her?"

"I do not see how it is possible to do that, signor," replied Guiseppe, "since she is so strictly confined, and Floretta is not suffered at present to leave the villa."

"I think it might be done in this manner," observed Massaroni. "Could you contrive to get admittance to the chamber of Floretta when she was out of the way, and leave it in a conspicuous part where she would be sure to see it? What think you of that plan?"

"Why," replied Guiseppe, hesitating, "I do not know but it might be accomplished."

"Are you willing to undertake to try it?" asked Massaroni.

"Why, yes," returned Guiseppe, "I do not see that there can be any harm in that."

"Enough," said Massaroni. "Wait here a few minutes, and I will return to you with the note."

The brigand now left the room, and Rubaldo turning to his companion, said,—

"Well, Guiseppe, what is your opinion of this business?"

"Why, I scarcely know what to think of it, Rubaldo," answered the former, "though I heartily wish that Massaroni may succeed."

"It is but seldom that he has failed in anything in which he has resolved," observed Rubaldo.

"I am aware of it," said Guiseppe. "Who that has heard the name of Allesandro Massaroni, the mountain chief, does not know that? He is a bold man."

"Ay," returned the other, "and as generous as he is bold."

"I believe it, and I long for the time when I shall be admitted one of his band, for I am heartily tired of the inactive and insipid life I have been so long leading."

"Well," said Rubaldo, "only let this important business be disposed of, and your wishes shall at once be complied with."

"The sooner the better," said Guiseppe, "for I shall then feel myself in my native ele-

ment. I was never meant for such a situation in life as that I am at present placed in. It was a lucky job for me when I met with you, Rubaldo."

"Ay," answered the latter, "I am certain you will have no cause to regret it if you only act with fidelity; if you do not, you must take the consequences."

"Oh, you need not fear me," said Guiseppe, "I think I have already proved that I may be depended upon."

"I belive you, Guiseppe," observed his companion; "but I thought it was only right to caution you."

"Very good, and I am obliged to you for it."

At this juncture Massaroni re-entered the room.

"Here is the note, Guiseppe," he said, "and you will remember my instructions concerning it."

"I will not forget them, signor," replied Guiseppe, taking the note. "I will remember all, as I have said before; but I should advise you not to come to-night at the place of appointment."

"And why so?" demanded Massaroni.

"Because," replied Guiseppe, "you must be aware, signor, after what I have explained to you, that there may be plans with which, of course, I am unacquainted to entrap you, and leave you no chance of defence."

"I will go there, and endeavour to carry out my purpose," observed the brigand chief, "though the devil himself should stand to obstruct me. Guiseppe, I perfectly approve of what you say, and what you recommend, but I must use my own discretion. At twelve to-night you may expect me at the villa, to know the result of the note."

"Well, signor," replied Guiseppe, "I will perform your errand faithfully, and, if you are so resolved, you will find me at the place you have thought proper to appoint."

"Adieu!" said the brigand chief, with a smile upon his countenance; "before many hours are over, we shall meet again."

"I will be punctual, signor," repeated Guiseppe, and he then took his departure.

"Well, captain," remarked Rubaldo, "what think you now of our new ally?"

"Why," answered Massaroni, "that he is to be depended upon."

"Of that," returned Rubaldo, "I was perfectly satisfied, otherwise, you may be sure, I should not have recommended him to you. But still you will, perhaps, pardon me, Massaroni, for suggesting to you that it is not only rash but imprudent to venture to the villa until the excitement has in some manner abated. Guiseppe tells you it has not, and I believe him."

"Why now, Rubaldo," said Massaroni, fixing upon him a look of astonishment, "are you really speaking seriously, or do my ears deceive me? Have you turned chicken-hearted, that you should speak as you do now?"

"Allesandro Massaroni," replied Rubaldo, with an expression of countenance that showed plainly he said what he meant, and, at the same time, fully expressed the determination of his feelings; "did you ever yet know Rubaldo Stillonzi to be a coward?"

"No," replied our hero, "but you are getting warm, Rubaldo, and if I have said anything to offend you, I would wish to apologise. We will, I hope, understand each other better anon."

"I accept your apology," said Rubaldo, in rather a sullen tone; "but it is the first time in his existence that Rubaldo was designated chicken-hearted; and if that be your opinion of him, the sooner you get quit of such a one the better."

"No, no," replied the brigand chief, taking his hand; "you still misunderstand me, Rubaldo. I had no wish ro impugn your character. Who has had a better opportunity of witnessing your bravery and fidelity than myself? But a truce with such observations as these; you have heard my determination to visit the villa at midnight, and that ought to be sufficient to convince you that nothing whatever, even though death, yes, certain death stood in the way, should prevent me."

"Well," returned Rubaldo, "I know it perfectly well; but of what use is it your making such ventures, when Guiseppe can bring you all the information you require?"

"I must judge for myself," said Massaroni, "nothing less will satisfy me."

"Very well," replied his lieutenant, "I have no wish to interpose between your will and judgment. I merely ventured to throw out a suggestion. Then it is your determination to venture to the villa to-night?"

"Have I not said so repeatedly," returned our hero, "why so often put those questions to me? What have I to fear? What did Allesandro Massaroni ever fear?"

"True, captain," said Rubaldo. "I wished not, and believe I did not insinuate anything of the kind; who knows your bravery or recklessness of danger better than Rubaldo? Oh, Massaroni, I am surprised that we should thus argue upon subjects that are trifling to us both. But, if it pleases you, we will say no more upon the subject. You are satisfied with Guiseppe?"

"Perfectly so," answered Massaroni, "or else depend on it I should not have entrusted that communication to the Signora Melina to him."

"And he will carry out your wishes, if there be a possibility," remarked Rubaldo.

"I have no doubt of it," returned the brigand chief; "he knows well the consequences should he attempt to deceive me."

"Shall I accompany you to-night?" asked Rubaldo.

"Yes, to the villa," replied our hero, "and so will our men follow, but I must enter alone; and should anything occur to me that may intimate danger, you will know my signal, and be ready to rush to my aid."

"Enough," said Rubaldo, in reply, "I will be prepared. When do you depart?"

"You have heard my appointment with Guiseppe," answered Massaroni.

"True," said Rubaldo, "but let me advise you to do nothing rashly."

"I am obliged to you for your advice, my good Rubaldo," returned Massaroni with a smile, "but I believe you are aware that Allesandro Massaroni, the mountain chief, never does anything rashly. His plans are always thoroughly concocted, his designs matured before he attempts to put them into execution, and consequently his success is certain. But why those doubts upon your mind, man? You seem to have taken some strange fancies into your head for which I cannot account. We will succeed, Rubaldo, in all that I have undertaken to do, though perhaps not on the present occasion, or I will forfeit my reputation, notoriety, or whatever else they may please to term it. Do you hear me, Rubaldo?"

"I do, captain," answered the latter, "and, of course, am ready to abide by your orders. However, I am glad that you seem to place so much confidence in Guiseppe, especially as I recommended him to your notice."

"As I have frequently told you, Rubaldo," replied Massaroni, "I believe Guiseppe to be a trustworthy rascal, as ready to cut a throat as to steal a purse, if he had the opportunity. Am I not correct in my estimation of his character?"

"You are," answered Rubaldo; "but still, I firmly believe that he will become a most useful member of our band, if you accept him."

"I think so, too," remarked the brigand chief, "or you know full well that I should not have accepted him. Rubaldo, I should be wretched had I not an opportunity of again gazing upon that mysterious portrait which has excited all my deepest interest; and, coupled with the anxiety I feel for the fate which threatens the beauteous Signora Melina, nothing could prevent me, but death, from visiting the villa to-night."

"I fully appreciate your feelings, signor," said Rubaldo, "and have no further objection to offer. The Signora Melina is a beautiful damsel; and it would, indeed, be monstrous were she to be sacrificed to such a villain as the Count Alberti."

"He shall never possess her!" exclaimed the brigand chief. "I will sacrifice my life first. The Count Alberti is, as you say, Rubaldo, a most reckless villain. He has dared to set my power at defiance; but there will a time come when we shall be fairly placed in contact with each other, and then will be the time to gratify the feelings of hatred and revenge that I bear towards him. However, we have done with this business for the present, Rubaldo; it is enough for us to know that we have our plans arranged, and have those whom we may depend upon to assist us in carrying them into execution.'

"Exactly so, captain," returned Rubaldo, "and I am only anxious for the affray, certain, as I am, if all is managed prudently previously, that we shall be successful."

"What is to prevent us?" asked Massaroni.

"Nothing," replied his lieutenant; "but at the same time, I would suggest that—"

"What?" demanded Massaroni, impatiently, having been pacing the apartment in which they were talking for several minutes with hasty strides.

"You interrupt me hastily," said Rubaldo, feeling rather indignant at the abrupt manner of Massaroni; "you interrupt me hastily, I repeat; but still, do you not think it would have been much better for you to have heard what I had to say before you made use of any observation?"

"True, true, Rubaldo," said the brigand chief; "I admit I was wrong; but I was excited at the moment, and that must plead my excuse."

"Captain," replied Rubaldo, "you have no excuse to make to me. What I was about to observe is, nothing can prevent our success if we only act with the same prudence that we have hitherto done."

"Pshaw!" exclaimed Massaroni, testily, "that is merely repeating what I have said. Of course, we shall act with prudence. When did you ever know the conduct of Massaroni to be guided by any different rule? To-night, at the hour I stated to Guiseppe, I will be at the villa; and you shall accompany me to see all the places I have pointed out to you, and to prove to you that what I have stated, so far as regards the chance of our success in rescuing the Signora Melina from her persecutors, is not erroneous."

"Very good, captain," remarked Rubaldo; "but might you not as well permit me to enter the house with you?"

"Why, of course, I shall do so," replied the brigand chief; "but you must not attempt to act until I give the word of command."

"Have I ever acted in disobedience to your orders, captain?" asked Rubaldo.

"No," replied our hero; "but still I thought it as well to caution you. However, as I said before, there is enough of

this subject. When the hour of midnight approaches, we must make our departure from this place, and be prepared to meet with any obstructions that may present themselves to us."

"You will find me ready, Massaroni," said his lieutenant; "I suppose I need not assure you of that?"

"No—no," replied the brigand chief, "I have long tried your fidelity, and you ought to know by this time that I do not question it."

"I am satisfied, captain," said Rubaldo.

"And so am I," answered the brigand chief. "But until the hour that I make my departure to the Villa Rosa, we will separate. I will there show you all the curiosities of the place, and you will, I think, then agree with me, that there is every facility for our not only entering but carrying our designs into complete effect."

"I have no doubt of it," observed Rubaldo; "and I am perfectly satisfied with what you say. I have a wish to inspect those parts of the villa, so that I may be placed in a better position to judge how the plans we have in contemplation are likely to have effect. But that portrait, signor, which seems to engross so much of your interest?"

"You say truly there, Rubaldo," said our hero, sighing; "it is that portrait which excites my principal interest. You have not yet seen it?"

"I have not," answered Rubaldo.

"You have often seen this," said the brigand chief, taking the minature from his bosom.

"Yes," replied Rubaldo.

"Know you whose features it represents?"

"I have often heard you say that the likeness was that of your mother."

"True, true," said Massaroni, with much emotion; "this is the faint resemblance of that revered being who brought me into the world. That gentle amiable mother whose kiss of love upon my cheeks—whose tender smiles, like sunshine, are present to my senses at this moment as fresh and vivid as when I received them. Yes, Rubaldo, I say again, this is the faint resemblance of that loved being, whose soul is now in Heaven, and whose wrongs I solemnly swore to avenge. This likeness, Rubaldo, is the very counterpart of the portrait you have so often heard me speak of as being placed in one of the apartments of the Villa Rosa, and concealed by a curtain."

"Most extraordinary," said Rubaldo.

"Extraordinary!" repeated Massaroni, with increased agitation; "yes, and what is more, from all that I have heard, that portrait represents a young Florentine damsel. My mother was a native of Florence, and—but let me not think, or I shall go mad. To-night you shall see the portrait, and then you will have an opportunity of judging for yourself."

"I feel most anxious to do so," remarked Rubaldo, "after what you have said. But have you any suspicions that——"

"Suspicion!" interrupted Massaroni, his fine manly brow displaying the anger and excitement of his feelings; "suspicion that the portrait so carefully covered with the curtain is meant for the likeness of my mother, and that the Prince Bianchi was her seducer and my father?—Yes, I have! and by all the saints I will not rest until I have ascertained that fact, and wreaked my vengeance on her murderer's head."

"What," demanded Rubaldo, "would you revenge yourself in the blood of the author of your being?"

"Yes," replied Massaroni, determinedly; "for was he not the murderer of all that was good and pure, till he by his vile arts seduced her from the paths of innocence and rectitude—my dear mother? And why should I respect him, or show him any mercy?—No, may my soul be plunged into perdition if I do not plunge a dagger to his heart if ever it should be my fate to meet with him."

"You are excited, Massaroni," said Rubaldo.

"Yes, the subject makes me so," replied our hero. "Rubaldo, could you witness a mother's wrongs without feeling a deadly hatred towards the author of them? Could you see that kind and gentle mother sink into a premature grave, knowing that she had been hurried thither by the systematic designs of a consummate villain, without registering an oath in Heaven, that, whenever you had the opportunity, you would hurl destruction upon the head of him who had been the cause of her misery? No, I am satisfied that you could not, and therefore do I feel satisfied that you must and will appreciate my feelings on the present occasion!"

"I do indeed, captain," replied Rubaldo. "However, we will drop the subject, since I see it is so dissonant to your feelings. I trust that your mother's wrongs may yet be avenged."

"It is for that alone I wish to live," observed the brigand chief; "it is that alone which guides my actions. Rubaldo, should I by any accident perish, will you not swear, if you have the opportunity, to avenge yourself to the death upon the head of the seducer of the mother of Allesandro Massaroni?"

"I will," replied Rubaldo; "and if I fail to keep my word may perdition be my fate."

"Enough," said the brigand chief. "I can trust you, Rubaldo, for I know that you will not break your word."

"I never did yet, Massaroni," replied his lieutenant, "and it is not at all likely that I am going to do so now. But are you still determined in the designs you have formed against Bianchi and the Count Alberti?"

"Certainly," replied Massaroni, "what reason have you to doubt that I am not?"

"None, none whatever," returned Massaroni's lieutenant; "still it behoves me to be satisfied upon all those points."

"Undoubtedly," coincided the chief. "Mine has been a strange and melancholy history," he said, after a brief pause, during which time he was wrapped in deep meditation.

"It has, I believe," returned Rubaldo, "although you never acquainted me with all the particulars."

"Rubaldo," said the brigand chief, grasping his arm, "did you ever have a mother that you loved—whom you could almost worship—into whose benevolent eyes you could look and see the reflection of your own soul?"

"Yes, yes," replied Rubaldo, hastily, and with considerable emotion.

"What then," demanded Massaroni, with increased agitation, "would have been your feelings had you known that gentle, that amiable mother, to have been the victim of a villain—to have been betrayed?"

"I would have cursed him from my heart's deepest core," replied Rubaldo.

"Cursed him!" repeated Massaroni, "of what avail would that have been? Would you not also have sworn to have a deadly revenge against the base and cowardly perpetrator of such wrongs?"

"I would," said Rubaldo; "and never would I have rested until my oath had been fulfilled."

"Your hand, Rubaldo," ejaculated Massaroni, "your sentiments are mine own. Then such is my situation, such is my history: I had a mother, young, beautiful, innocent, unsuspecting. In an evil hour, a devil wearing human shape, crossed her path; he professed love for her, and his honied accents won her youthful heart. He was rich and powerful; she, as I before said, humble, young, inexperienced, and unsuspecting. I cannot—dare not dwell upon the revolting tale; suffice it to say, that he by his base arts triumphed o'er her innocence, and she became a poor, wretched and degraded being. By the most specious promises he triumphed over her, and then, when he had completed his work of ruin, he deserted here and her helpless offspring, and left them to perish. I am the fruit of that unhappy connection."

"All this I have heard before, Massaroni," said his lieutenant. "But did not your unfortunate and deeply-injured mother never reveal the name of her seducer?"

"I have told you frequently before that she

did not," answered our hero; "would to Heaven she had, it would have set my mind at rest, and long ere this I would have exacted from him some atonement for the irreparable wrongs he had done her."

"But could you forget that he was your own father?" asked Rubaldo.

"My father!" repeated the brigand, a frown crossing his fine manly brow, "and think you that I can look upon the wretch who has been the author of all these atrocities, Rubaldo, in the character of a father? By all the saints, never! I loathe, I despise him; my mother's mild and beauteous countenance ever arises to my imagination when I reflect on it, and makes me still more determined in the course of vengeance I have adopted. Father! no, no! it would be a gross, a monstrous libel upon humanity to call him by such a name. I say again, Rubaldo, that could I only discover him, I should at once dismiss from my recollection that the same blood flows within both our veins; and the wrongs of my murdered mother being uppermost in my thoughts, I should plunge my poniard to the hilt in his heart!"

"I marvel not at the warmth of your feelings upon the subject, Massaroni," said Rubaldo, "but still the mystery in which all the circumstances connected with your mother's history are involved, are most extraordinary. Can you form any idea why she refused to give you up the name of your father?"

"Oh, yes," replied Massaroni, "because she still loved her betrayer, notwithstanding his brutal treatment towards her; and when I arrived at the age at which I might have had the power, as I had the impulse, to avenge her wrongs, she refused, from her affection to her seducer, as I said before, to reveal his name, lest I should wreak upon his head that vengeance which he so richly merited. Oh, Rubaldo, had you but seen her in her last moments; had you but witnessed that wreck of female beauty and innocence, I am confident you could never have forgotten it, and although in no way connected with her, you must have entertained similar feelings to my own. Whenever I think of the last moments of that revered parent, it unmans me, and I could weep like a child."

The brigand chief covered his fine expressive brow with his hand, and found it impossible to restrain his emotions as these sad reminiscences crossed his mind.

"Nay, Massaroni," said Rubaldo, who was a sincere and devoted friend to the brigand chief; "do not give way to these sad and melancholy reflections, but endeavour to look on the brightest side of the question."

"And have I not always done so?" said Massaroni, suddenly turning round, and with a remarkable change of aspect; "ha, ha, ha!

We will say no more about it, Rubaldo; that subject is for discussion at some future period. What we have now to think of and arrange is the rescue of the Signora Melina, and that must be accomplished at all hazards."

"There can be very little doubt of our success, captain," returned Rubaldo, "while you are in the same humour as you are at present."

"And that my humour will undergo no change you may be certain," said the brigand chief; "my mind is fixed upon the accomplishment of my wishes, and even should my head be placed upon the block the next moment, nothing whatever should stay me in the attempt to consummate my designs."

"Well said, Massaroni," observed his lieutenant; "there you spoke like yourself. The Signora Melina must never become the wife of such a man as the Count Alberti."

"By all my hopes she shall not," said the brigand chief, fervently. "I have sworn it, Rubaldo, and you know full well that Allesandro Massaroni never broke his oath."

"Very true," answered Rubaldo; "but at what hour do you intend to go to the villa?"

"Why," said Massaroni, "did you not hear me tell Guiseppe?"

"Yes, yes," replied Rubaldo. "I had forgotten. But previous to our going there it is necessary that you should in some measure compose your feelings, or you will not be able to act with that degree of caution which the occasion requires."

"Oh, fear not," said Massaroni, smiling. "I am perfectly calm. But come, we will have a glass or two, and then to business."

Rubaldo returned no answer, and Massaroni having filled their glasses, they pledged each other with the greatest cordiality.

"All depends, or at least the principle depends upon Guiseppe," said Massaroni, after some trivial conversation; "should he prove false, all our plans would be rendered abortive."

"Oh, there is not the least fear of him," said Rubaldo; "can you not take my word, Massaroni? Think you I would recommend any one to you that was not to be trusted?"

"No," replied our hero. "I do not for a moment believe that you would; but still you must admit that, in such particular business as that upon which we are at present engaged, we should be extremely cautious."

"I agree with you, Massaroni," replied his lieutenant; "but still I repeat that you have nothing whatever to fear from Guiseppe; at any rate, I would answer for him with my life."

"That is enough," said the brigand chief. "I am perfectly satisfied; in fact, I ought to be confident that no one would attempt to deceive Allesandro Massaroni: for however they might triumph for the moment, the vengeance that would pursue them would be terrible."

"Ay, captain," said Rubaldo. "The penalty of treachery to the brigand chief I believe is pretty well known. That penalty is death."

"Death!" repeated Massaroni: "that is the penalty of all who dare to turn traitor against the brigand chief."

"True," coincided Rubaldo; "and therefore, those who know it will never be bold enough to attempt to play us falsely."

"They must, indeed, be mad, if they did," remarked the brigand chief.

*   *   *   *

Massaroni and his lieutenant remained in conversation for some time after the departure of Guiseppe; but as the hour of midnight rapidly approached, they assumed their usual disguises; and having previously despatched that portion of the band that they had brought with them, they quitted the house, and made their way with all expedition towards the Villa Rosa. They took a circuitous route, however, and watched narrowly to ascertain if there were any suspicious parties lurking about; but they could see nothing whatever to corroborate the statements which the man Guiseppe had made, and they, in consequence, concluded that the excitement had greatly abated, if it had not altogether subsided.

"It is as I anticipated, Rubaldo," said Massaroni; "there is nothing whatever to apprehend. The prince and Count Alberti are, I am satisfied, not so silly as to imagine that the brigand chief is to be entrapped like a rat. My word for it that he will yet be enabled to read them both such a lesson as they will not easily forget. This way, Rubaldo, and I will show you the opportunities, the facilities we have for carrying our designs into execution, and I also wait with the utmost anxiety to know the result of our friend Guiseppe's mission."

"Lead on, captain," replied Rubaldo; "I am ready to follow you."

They now walked round to the back of the villa, having first cautiously looked to see whether or not there were any persons watching them; and having ascertained that all was safe, they stopped at the door by which Massaroni had previously gained admission to the villa. The brigand chief took the key from his pocket, and was about to apply it to the lock, when the door was silently opened, and Guiseppe presented himself, bearing a small lamp in his hand. He motioned them in silence to enter, and they obeyed, and followed him along the passage before described, until they arrived at a small apartment on the left, into which Massaroni had not before been introduced, and which from its appearance was evidently seldom made use of by any of the family. Guiseppe closed the door, and placing the lamp on a table, he turned to Massaroni and said—

"You have then persisted in venturing here, signor, notwithstanding the warning I gave you? I expected you would."

"Ay," returned our hero, "Massaroni is not the sort of man to be daunted at trifles. But how goes the business now?"

"Much the same, signor," answered Guiseppe, "though the excitement has, in some measure, abated."

"Ah!" observed Massaroni, "I thought it would. The Prince Bianchi and his worthy colleague must be fully aware that the brigand chief has the determination and the means also to carry out his plans into execution, and to set all their threats and puny attempts to capture him at defiance. But the letter—have you succeeded according to my wishes?"

"I have, signor," answered Guiseppe; "I found the means of access to the chamber of Floretta when she was out of the way, and placed it on her dressing table."

"That is well," said Massaroni; "then I shall probably receive an answer to it from Signora Melina to-morrow."

"It is not at all unlikely," replied Guiseppe.

"And should you receive it, you will bring it to me immediately?"

"I will, signor; at least, at the earliest opportunity."

"Enough," said our hero, "I am satisfied. Are the prince and the count at present in the villa?"

"They are," replied Guiseppe, "and it is but a short time since they have retired to their chambers. They have been in deep consultation together for several hours."

"Probably concocting some fresh mischief against the peace of the hapless victim of their cowardly and brutal persecution."

"No doubt of it, signor," returned Guiseppe; "and I much fear that they will triumph in their nefarious designs."

"Cospetto!" exclaimed the brigand chief, hastily; "never! Allesandro Massaroni swears it, and if he fails in keeping his promise, why, then, let him die the death of a dog."

"Well," observed Guiseppe, "I presume I need not assure you that I wish you every success."

"Yes, yes," said the brigand, "I believe you, Guiseppe, and on your fidelity I entirely depend."

"I assure you, signor," said Guiseppe, "that in expressing that confidence in me, you do me no more than justice. But I have, I imagine, already said sufficient upon that point."

"You have," returned Massaroni; "but have you been enabled to ascertain anything more respecting the Signora Melina since we last met?"

"No more than that she is in a state of the

utmost excitement, as must be expected, after all the events that have occurred, and the critical situation in which she is placed; but no doubt she still remains determined in opposing to the fullest extent of her power the designs of her uncle and the Count Alberti."

"Yes," coincided Massaroni, "and it is for that reason that I anticipate a favourable answer to the note I have written her. She will surely accept of any aid rather than be sacrificed to such a fate as the revolting one with which she is at this moment threatened."

MELINA DECLARING HER REPUGNANCE OF ALBERTI TO BIANCHI.

"Well, signor," observed Guiseppe, "I should also imagine so. But have you anything more to say to me?"

"No—no more than again to enjoin you, that, should you find an answer to the letter I have addressed to the Signora Melina, you will bring it here to me without the least possible delay."

"I will strictly attend to your wishes, depend upon it," replied Guiseppe.

"I wish to show Rubaldo the means we have of accomplishing the designs we have in contemplation," said our hero; "perhaps you will lead the way, as you are better acquainted with the intricacies of the place than I am at present?"

Guiseppe returned no answer, but once more taking up the lamp, he led the way along the different passages which we have described in the previous pages, until they arrived in the chapel.

Rubaldo gazed around him with astonishment, for even after Massaroni's description, he never expected to find such a place in a building of such comparative unimportance as the Villa Rosa.

"And it is here," he said, "where the ceremony is appointed to take place?"

"Yes," answered Massaroni; "but, of course, I need not assure you, Rubaldo, that it must and shall be prevented?"

"I have no doubt of that, captain," replied Rubaldo, "if the fickle dame Fortune does not desert us."

"She has never done so yet," rejoined the brigand chief, "and I do not anticipate that she will do so now. But you have not yet seen the means of concealment that we have, and so of carrying our projects into full effect. Guiseppe, you will perhaps gratify his curiosity."

Guiseppe immediately unlocked the door that was concealed behind the drapery at the back of the altar, and they entered the extensive passages beyond, Rubaldo becoming still more amazed at every step they took.

"Well," he said, "nothing could possibly be better adapted for our purpose; I could never have imagined that there was such a place as this in the villa. And is there every means of speedy escape from here also?"

"You shall see," replied Guiseppe, "although Signor Massaroni has already been satisfied upon that point, I believe."

"Undoubtedly I have," returned the brigand chief; "however, give Rubaldo an equal opportunity of being so."

Guiseppe, without making use of any farther observations, led the way along the different passages until they arrived at the door at the extremity, which opened upon the country beyond.

"Admirable!" said Rubaldo; "nothing could possibly have proved more favourable to our designs. In those passages our bold band can conceal themselves, and at the very moment when the Prince Bianchi and Alberti flatter themselves that their triumph is complete, and that the fair and innocent Signora Melina must become the victim of their diabolical designs, we can rush out, and taking them by surprise, rescue her from their power."

"Exactly," returned Massaroni, "did I not tell you so?"

"You did."

"Well, you are satisfied with what you have seen already?"

"I am."

"But there is more I wish to show you," said our hero. "I wish you to behold the portrait of which I have so often spoken to you about, and which has excited so deep an interest in my breast."

"And I am no less anxious to view it, captain," observed Rubaldo.

"Lead the way, Guiseppe," said the brigand chief, "for time presses, and there might be danger in remaining here much longer."

"Very true," answered Guiseppe. "This way, signors."

They followed him in silence, and it was not long before they arrived at the door of the apartment which contained the portrait to which we have so often alluded, and of which Massaroni possessed the key. It was opened, and they all three stood within the spacious and elegant apartment.

"Leave us, Guiseppe," said Massaroni, "I can find my way from the villa without your guidance."

"Be it so, signor," replied Guiseppe.

"But you will bear in mind what I have told you," said the brigand, "and will not fail to bring me the answer which signora may think proper to return to my note immediately?"

"I will be prompt and punctual, signor," answered Guiseppe, and he then quitted the room, and left the brigand chief and his companion to themselves. Massaroni felt the same sensation of awe steal over him on entering the room as he had experienced before, and for several moments he paused, and was unable to give utterance to a word, and Rubaldo did not offer to interrupt him. But at length he advanced to that side of the apartment where the portrait was suspended, and Rubaldo followed him. With a trembling hand he withdrew the curtain, and holding the lamp above his head, in order the better to accelerate the view, the light streamed full upon the features of the painting. Rubaldo was much struck by the extraordinary and impressive character of it at the first glance, and his whole attention was rivetted upon it.

"Did you ever behold anything more beautiful, Rubaldo?" at length said Massaroni.

"It certainly represents the countenance of a most lovely female," replied Rubaldo.

"Can you call to mind ever seeing anything that resembled it before?" demanded our hero.

"Yes," answered Rubaldo, promptly: "the portrait, the miniature rather, which you always wear in your bosom."

"The likeness of my much injured mother," rejoined Massaroni.

"The same," said Rubaldo; "any one

might swear that the same fair being sat for both likenesses."

"By all the saints, you are right, Rubaldo," ejaculated the brigand; "and that confirms me in the suspicions I have formed. Look again on the miniature," he continued, taking it from his bosom; "compare it with the portrait, and the resemblance must be more strongly impressed upon your mind."

Rubaldo took the miniature from his hand, and gazed alternately at it and the portrait.

"It is most extraordinary, I repeat," he said; "the eyes, the expression of the features, the half melancholy smile that plays around the lips, are the very same. They must both represent one and the same being."

"And the original of the portrait was a native of Florence," remarked Massaroni.

"The same place, you have often told me, where your mother was born," said Rubaldo.

"Exactly so," answered the brigand chief. "Now, by Heaven, should I discover that she whom this portrait represents was my mother, I shall know on whose head my vengeance ought to fall."

"The Prince Bianchi?"

"The same."

"He would then be your father."

"Father!" replied Massaroni, and his fine eyes flashed fire; "no—no—I should hate, despise myself could I acknowledge him by any such a title."

"But you could not think of wreaking your vengeance on his head?" said Rubaldo.

"Rubaldo," replied the brigand chief, "I have an oath registered in Heaven to destroy the base and heartless betrayer of my unfortunate mother, if ever I should discover him; and let the consequences be whatever they may, even though perdition should the next instant light upon my soul, I will not break it. What other feeling but one of the most implacable hatred, think you, I can bear towards him? No; though every earthly power should interpose to save him, nought should move me from my determination. Hear me bright spirit of my sainted mother, while I swear, that——"

"Hold! hold! Massaroni," interrupted his lieutenant; "utter not anything rashly, and which you may afterwards have cause to repent. I sympathise with you—deeply sympathise with you in the misfortunes it has been your lot to experience; but still I must protest against your giving utterance to any such unnatural vow as that which was at that moment about to escape your lips."

"Rubaldo," replied Massaroni, "it is no rash or hasty vow; it is one that I have for years, for many, many years contemplated and calmly deliberated upon. It is one that nature and justice demand the fulfilment of, and all argument to endeavour to move me from my purpose is useless. Think of all the facts place yourself in my position, and then ask your own conscience whether you would not act the same as I have sworn to do?"

"No, no," answered Rubaldo; "I could not, would not, under any circumstances, become a fratricide. But you will think better of this, Massaroni; and should fate ever bring you in contact with the author of your mother's seduction, you will, I am certain, not forget that he is your father."

"Father!" repeated Massaroni, vehemently, and his countenance plainly indicating the power of the emotions that struggled in his breast; " no, by Heaven, I will never acknowledge him by any such title; the remembrance of my poor, gentle, affectionate, and confiding mother's wrongs must ever be present to my mind, and I must hate him, loathe him, as something unfit to live. Oh, Rubaldo, when I think of that beloved parent's end, her untimely end; when I recal to my recollection all the miseries and privations she so patiently endured, a feeling arises in my breast which I find it impossible to control. It almost drives me mad. It will be well for her heartless betrayer should he never cross my path."

"Come, Massaroni," said Rubaldo, who was much moved by the extraordinary warmth and excitement of his manner, "let us quit this place which excites such dismal thoughts in your mind."

"I could gaze on this portrait for ever," said the brigand, taking but little, if any, notice of the observations of his lieutenant; "and the longer I view it the more confident do I become that it is the resemblance of that beloved being to whom I owe my birth. By the mass! I could almost swear that she again stood before me. Oh, mother, whose soul is now in Heaven, watch over and guide me how to act!"

Devoutly the brigand chief knelt before the portrait, and offered up his prayers and supplications to the Supreme, whilst Rubaldo stood by and gazed at him with the deepest interest, but did not offer to interrupt him. At length he arose from his knees, and once more drawing the curtain across the painting, regained his usual composure with the most extraordinary rapidity.

"You have seen enough to-night to satisfy you as to the practicability of our plans, Rubaldo, I presume?" he said.

"Quite," answered Rubaldo; "I do not see how they can very well fail, if we only act with due precaution."

"They cannot, they must not," said Massaroni, confidently and determinedly. "By all my hopes, I would sooner forfeit all I possess, and become the inmate of a dungeon, at the mercy of my enemies, than I would be doomed to disappointment."

"Well, captain," observed Rubaldo, "I do not think there is much fear of that."

"No," returned the brigand ; "our schemes are too well laid, I think, to fail. But come, we will depart."

Rubaldo nodded assent, and Massaroni led the way towards the door by which they had entered the villa, where, contrary to their expectations, they found Guiseppe awaiting them.

"The coast is quite clear, signor," he said, addressing himself to Massaroni; "the soldiers are at present away from the villa, and you can depart in perfect safety."

"'Tis well," said Massaroni ; "I shall expect to see you to-morrow."

"I will be punctual as I have hitherto been," replied Guiseppe.

"And," added the brigand, "I hope you will then bring me some favourable intelligence."

"I trust I shall," said Guiseppe, "for the Signora Melina will no doubt return an answer to the note you have written her."

"I think she would," observed the brigand chief.

"She is sure to do so," returned Guiseppe.

"And," added Massaroni, "in the meantime you keep a strict watch upon all that takes place at the villa, and give me all the information you can, which is at all likely to guide me in the execution of my plans."

"You may depend upon me," replied Guiseppe. "I feel the deepest interest in the accomplishment of your designs."

"I am glad to hear it," remarked the brigand ; "and as I have repeatedly before told you, if you keep your promise and remain faithful to me, you shall not go unrewarded, but if you act differently, you may expect to be pursued with my most terrible vengeance."

"I am ready to meet it, Signor Massaroni," said Guiseppe in reply, "should I attempt to deceive you; but you will find that I am a man of my word, and that you will have no cause to complain of me."

"With that assurance I am perfectly satisfied," said Massaroni, "and will not again question your fidelity, since we both so perfectly now seem to understand each other."

"I thank you, Signor Massaroni, for this confidence," said Guiseppe, "which you shall find that I will not betray."

"Then," said the brigand chief, "that business is settled; adieu till we meet again."

"Good night, signor," answered Guiseppe, and Massaroni and Rubaldo immediately emerged from the villa, and made their way back to the house in which they were at present secreted. But on the way the brigand chief again evinced the utmost melancholy of feelings, so powerful and painful was the impression which the portrait had made upon his mind, and so many and torturing were the thoughts to which it naturally gave rise. Rubaldo tried to arouse him from them, but he succeeded only indifferently, and he at last abandoned the task in despair. On their arriving at the house, as they neither of them felt inclined for conversation, they quickly separated for the night, and both of them retired to their separate chambers. Massaroni's mind, however, was too much agitated to suffer him to think about retiring to rest, and with folded arms and an aching brain he continued for some time to pace the apartment, and to give himself up to the most dismal and conflicting meditations.

"It must be the likeness of my mother," he soliloquised ; "and if so, in the Prince Bianchi, my implacable foe, I see her betrayer and my own father. How wonderful are the ways of Providence. But I am determined to unravel the mystery at all hazards, or perish in the attempt; and should it really turn out to be as my suspicions suggest, nothing whatever shall withhold my hand from inflicting a terrible revenge upon the head of my unfortunate mother's murderer, and the author of my wrongs and degradation."

His eyes sparkled with determination as he thus gave utterance to these words, and the agitation of his mind increased every moment. It was some time ere he could at all calm his feelings, but at length feeling fatigued, he retired to bed, and shortly afterwards dropped off to sleep.

He arose at an early hour the following morning, and having joined Rubaldo, awaited with no small degree of impatience and anxiety the time when it was likely that Guiseppe would make his appearance at the house. Rubaldo sought to divert his mind in the best manner he could, and he partly succeeded, but still he could not rest easy until he knew what would be the result of the letter he had sent to Melina. His anxiety was at last relieved by the arrival of Guiseppe.

"Ah !" ejaculated Massaroni, "I have been waiting for you most impatiently."

"No doubt of it, signor," replied Guiseppe; "but I came to you at the earliest opportunity."

"I dare say you have," returned our hero, "and you have my thanks for your attention ; but what news do you bring?"

"I bring this answer from the Signora Melina," replied Guiseppe, placing a letter in his hands. Massaroni hastily took it, and breaking open the seal, he attentively perused the contents.

"Ah !" he remarked, "it is no more than I expected."

"Does the Signora Melina then decline your aid?" asked Rubaldo.

"She does," replied Massaroni, "from a false notion of propriety."

"I was certain that she would entertain such scruples, Massaroni," observed Rubaldo.

"They are only erroneous," returned the brigand chief, "and they must be banished from her mind."

"It strikes me that you will have some difficulty in doing that," said Rubaldo.

"No, no," replied Massaroni, "there is no time to be lost, and what I have fixed my mind on must and shall be done. We must contrive some means of seeing her waiting-maid, Floretta."

"And how is that to be done?" demanded Rubaldo.

"We will talk of that anon," answered the brigand; "but have you any further intelligence from the villa, Guiseppe?"

"None, signor," answered Guiseppe.

"I must write another letter to Melina," said Massaroni, after a pause, "which you must get conveyed in the same manner."

"Very good, signor," said Guiseppe; "I am at your service, and will do my best."

Massaroni thanked him, and having hastily written the letter, Guiseppe took his departure. We should, however, become tedious were we to repeat that with which the reader has already been acquainted, and we will now therefore once more return to Melina, who, as the time rapidly approached which was to decide her fate, was worked up to a pitch bordering upon distraction. Notwithstanding the promises of Massaroni, she gave herself up entirely to despair, and it was quite in vain that the faithful Floretta exerted herself to the utmost to console her.

"There is no hope for me, Floretta," she would say, "and it would be madness for me to encourage it. Would to Heaven that I were dead!"

"Oh, my dear signora," replied Floretta, "how it grieves me to hear you talk in that dismal manner. Massaroni has promised you his aid; you know that he is brave and powerful, and he will not fail to keep his word."

"Alas!" sighed our heroine, "that I should ever be driven to such a painful extremity as this. Floretta, let the consequences be whatever they may, I cannot accept of the assistance of the brigand chief."

"Why should you thus hesitate, lady, when it is the only chance you have of saving yourself from so revolting and disgusting a fate?"

"My uncle's curse would descend upon my head were I to do so, Floretta," said her mistress, "and what would the uncharitable world say of me?"

"Oh, who could blame you, signora, for adopting a course into which the cruelty and obstinacy of the prince, your uncle, would have

driven you?" said Floretta. "Pardon me, lady, but I cannot help thinking that you are far too nice and sensitive upon that point."

Melina shook her head.

"Alas!" she said, after a pause, "should I abandon my uncle's roof, whither could I go?"

"Allesandro Massaroni and Signor Clairville would protect you, signora," replied Floretta; "and no doubt a reconciliation could soon be effected with your uncle, when he found that matters had gone to such an extremity."

"Ah, no," exclaimed our heroine, "I know my uncle's temper too well; he would never forgive me. Besides, while the Count Alberti is sanctioned by him, think you that he will abandon his designs, or that he would fail to pursue me with his vengeance, and all those who had befriended me?"

"Massaroni can defy him, you know that full well, signora."

"He might; but Florio?"

"Is he not also under the protection of the brigand chief?" demanded Floretta.

"True," answered Melina; "but why should I involve any one in danger? No, Floretta, I must put my trust in Providence alone, and, if it does not mercifully interpose to save me, there is nothing left for me but to endeavour to resign myself to my fate."

"To such a horrible fate as that, signora?" said the kind-hearted Floretta; "oh, never! I cannot bear to think of it with any degree of patience. Again I say, lady, courage; banish those delicate scruples from your breast; accept of the services of Massaroni, offered to you in such a generous and honourable spirit, and all will yet be well, and the clouds of adversity that now hang over your head will pass away."

"Never! never!" sobbed Melina; "my doom I plainly see is sealed. I fully appreciate the kindness of your feelings towards me, Floretta; but were I to encourage the hopes that you would fain inspire me with, they could only end in the most bitter disappointment."

"I wish I could bring you into a different way of thinking, signora," said her faithful attendant.

"It is impossible," answered our heroine; "for, in whatever direction I turn my gaze, I see nothing but the most absolute despair and misery before me. But a day or two, nay, only a few hours, and my doom will be sealed past recal. Oh, wretched, unfortunate Melina, what a terrible lot is yours; better, far better would it have been for you had you never been born. Cruel uncle, what have I done that you should treat me with this severity; that you should persecute me thus?"

Her tears flowed fast as she gave utterance to these melancholy words, and her attendant, finding that it was useless to attempt to console her, for some time suffered her to indulge her grief without offering to interrupt her.

The prince every day demanded an interview with her, and nothing whatever could shake him in his stern determination, while the firmness with which she opposed his wishes only served to exasperate him the more.

"Remember girl," he said on one of those occasions, "that I am lord and master of your actions, and that any opposition to my will is worse than madness, and will only serve to bring down my everlasting wrath upon your head."

"Oh, my uncle," replied Melina, "how have I ever deserved such harsh treatment from you whom I always looked upon as kind and generous, and treated with every reverence and respect?—You surely cannot wish to make me miserable for ever, to blight all my young hopes, and——"

"Pshaw!" interrupted the prince, impatiently, "can I make you miserable for ever, silly girl, and blight all your young hopes, as your are pleased to call them, by presenting you with a noble and wealthy husband?"

"And are then your motives so mercenary, my lord?" demanded Melina, with a look of reproach; "am I to be sold?—Oh, this is surely a degradation, an insult I do not deserve from you."

"A degradation—an insult!" repeated the prince, passionately; "this to me?—Beware what you say, or I may be tempted to go to such an extremity as I would fain avoid."

"I would not for the world say anything disrespectful or unbecoming to you, my lord," said the poor girl; "but surely you will make same allowance for my feelings."

"Feelings!" repeated the prince, scornfully; "it is a weakness that ill becomes you; however, I tell you again that Monday next decides your fate, and that you must then become the bride of the Count Alberti."

"Oh, my lord," ejaculated Melina, "have you so far forgotten——"

"Forgotten what!" hastily and passionately demanded the prince.

"Pardon me, my lord," calmly replied our heroine, "you did not permit me to continue. When it be your pleasure, I will do so."

The Prince Bianchi knit his brows, and for a few moments he was unprepared to return an answer, but at length he turned to his beauteous niece, and said—

"I am ready to hear you, girl, but at the same time you will remember, as I have before said, that I am your uncle, your guardian, the only individual who holds supreme power over you, and who has a right to command your duty and obedience. Proceed, Signora Melina."

"*Signora* Melina," repeated the maiden, with a sigh; "why not Melina *only*, dear uncle? Such used to be the endearing epithet you ever applied to me ere by some strange fatality.

which I cannot comprehend, I lost my place in your heart. But—but I will not reproach you my lord; I would merely appeal to your better feelings, which I know full well must predominate over the false prejudices you have imbibed from crafty and designing villany, and——"

"False prejudices, imbibed from crafty and designing villany, girl?" again interrupted Prince Bianchi, his countenance still flushed with the excitement of his feelings: "what mean you by that?"

"Will you bear with me, my lord, while I explain calmly?" asked his beauteous niece.

"Yes, yes," replied Bianchi, as patiently as he could; "I again ask you from whom have I received those false prejudices?"

"From the unprincipled nobleman whom you would now sacrifice me to, my lord, the Count Alberti," replied Melina, in a firm tone, and with an air of dignity which quite astounded and abashed her uncle; "but I will proceed; I again ask you, have you so far forgotten your solemn promise to my beloved mother, to your own, your only sister, on her death-bed, as to yield me up to a libertine, a villain, a heartless scoundrel; a wretch (pardon, my lord, the warmth of my language) who it would be degrading in the most degraded of my sex to accept as a husband? I repeat once more, can you have banished from your memory altogether the solemn compact you entered into with the revered being who bore me?"

As our heroine thus spoke her countenance and whole demeanour was most impressive, and the Prince Bianchi was so struck by the force of her words that he was deprived, for several minutes, of the power of giving utterance to a single word; he started back, and stared at her aghast, the same as if he had encountered a spectre; his conscience smote him, and he knew not how to reply to her; but at length he recovered himself in some degree, and said—

"Girl! girl!—why do you persist in reminding me of that which should now be buried in oblivion?"

"Buried in oblivion!" reiterated our heroine; "oh, my lord, should the dying injunctions of an only, an affectionate sister, ever be buried in oblivion?—Did you not make a vow, a solemn vow, only a few minutes before her death, which is registered in heaven, to obey those injunctions; and have you done so? Would you not now consign that child she, in every confidence, entrusted to your care and protection, to a fate far worse than death?—Bethink yourself, my uncle, and I feel satisfied that you will not persist in your present cruel and unnatural course. Remember the last words of my mother, your sister, and——"

"Hold!" cried the Prince Bianchi, interrupting her, and his whole frame convulsed with the violent emotions the pointed observations of his fair niece had aroused; "you seek to intimidate me;—you would make me, by your observations and reminiscences, as imbecile as an infant, but it shall have no effect upon me. I say again, that on Monday next, at midnight, you shall become the wife of the Count Alberti. To that is my mind made up, and nothing whatever shall move me from my purpose. Am I to be bearded, dared, obstructed, opposed, by an obstinate girl? By all the saints I will not. The Prince Bianchi is governor of Rome; his power is despotic, and he will at least teach one who is——"

"Forbear, my lord," interrupted Melina, once more, and assuming as much calmness as she possibly could under the circumstances; "utter no rash vows, which you may afterwards have reason to repent; I fear me, alas! that some fatal infatuation has seized upon your intellect, for certainly I cannot reconcile to my reason that the spirit of my uncle is speaking now. Oh, bethink you, my lord; calmly, dispassionately bethink yourself, and I am satisfied that you will no longer persist in your present designs. I tell you now once more, as I have often times done hitherto, and I do so in all sincerity of heart, and with every respect and reverance to you, that the man to whom you would sacrifice me (for I can use no milder a term) I can never look upon with any other feelings than those of disgust and abhorrence, and why then seek to make her eternally wretched whom you have hitherto professed to love the same as if she had been your daughter? It is unnatural—it is monstrous!"

"You may call it by whatever term you please, Melina," said Bianchi, cooly, in reply, and recovering himself; "but such is my determination, and no words—no arguments—no supplications, will have the effect of moving me from it. The Count Alberti I have fixed upon to become your husband, and at the time I have appointed for the solemnization of your nuptials you shall as assuredly become his bride as you are now in existence."

"Then, mark me, my lord," said our heroine in reply, and an expression of determination animating her lovely features, "and believe me that sincerity and candour guides my tongue; if such be you firm resolve, whatever step I may take to endeavour to avoid the revolting fate to which you would consign me, be the disgrace on your own head, as Heaven knows that I do not voluntarily yield to it."

"What mean you, girl?" demanded the Prince Bianchi, with a look of astonishment.

"No matter, my lord," replied Melina, "time and circumstances will probably explain everything."

"You speak in riddles," said her uncle; "be more explicit."

"Be more generous, just, and reasonable, my lord," retorted Melina, with far more calmness and self-possession than could have been expected under the circumstances; "and you will require no explanation."

"I must hear more of this, obdurate girl," exclaimed Bianchi, passionately, and grasping her by the wrist.

"Unhand me, my lord, I beseech you," replied Melina; "you will know no more than you do at present, till the time arrives. Let your sense of justice guide you in your conduct."

The Prince Bianchi gazed at her with the utmost amazement, and for a few moment she was totally unable, from the confusion in which his mind was, to make any reply; but at length in a half suppressed tone of anger he said—

"Now, by the Saints, Melina, you tire my patience. Are you, I again demand, still determined to resist my authority?"

"Where my future happiness is involved, I repeat I am, my lord," replied Melina. "Act with forbearance; attempt not to force upon me such a man as the Count Alberti, doom me to eternal celibacy, to the gloom and solitude of the sanctuary, and you shall find that I will not even murmur; but by the spirit of my mother which I now invoke——"

"Hold!" interrupted Bianchi, in a hoarse voice, and his features distorted with the emotions that her observations had excited; "what would you say? Why do you thus repeat the name of your mother?"

"She was your sister, my lord," replied our heroine, solemnly, "and you should never hear her name, but with a spirit of reverence and awe."

Bianchi again stared at his fair niece aghast, and his whole frame was convulsed with emotion. His conscience upbraided him with the injustice of his conduct towards the poor girl who had been committed to his charge, but still he had advanced so far that he could not well, he thought, recede, and he therefore mustered all the command he could of his temper, and while fully resolved at any cost to carry out his nefarious designs, he said in mild and persuasive accents—

"Melina, where is the use of our thus wasting words in anger, when I would fain persuade you for your good? Your mother confided you to my care, I admit; to protect, to instruct, to advise, to watch over the same as if you had been my own daughter, and you have often acknowledged that I have fulfilled that task to the best of my ability and natural good will. I would see you settled in life with one whose rank and wealth is worthy of you, and I——"

"And who," added Melina, "should, at any rate, possess virtues to recommend him to my heart. The Count Alberti is noble by birth, he is also wealthy I admit, but have not his actions proved him to be a libertine, a heartless seducer, one who has thought nothing of destroying the innocence and, consequently, the happiness of unsuspecting and confiding woman, and is such the man that you consider worthy to become the husband of your niece, my lord? Is she so fallen in your estimation that you would fain degrade her by so unholy an alliance?"

The prince bit his lips, and again for a few moments remained silent, for, in fact, he knew not how to reply.

"You still love Florio Clairville?" he said at length.

"As I am no hypocrite, my lord," replied Melina, with firmness, "I candidly admit I do so, and must ever continue to do, while the purple current of life continues to circulate throughout my veins."

"Obdurate girl!" exclaimed the Prince Bianchi, passionately; "why persist in indulging in a passion which can never be gratified? The presumptuous beggar Clairville, towards whom my indulgence and forbearance was too great, I swear shall never become your husband."

"Then, my lord, I will never be the wife of any other man."

"But I tell you, girl that you shall; and that on Monday next; the wife of the Count Alberti. To him I have pledged my word, and sooner than I would forfeit it, I would lose all the wealth I at present possess, and become the veriest beggar that ever crawled the earth. Think not to move me from my purpose by your supplications or ridiculous resistance, for I think you should ere this have been convinced that I am inflexible."

"Alas, I have my lord," sighed the poor girl, "and many a wretched hour has that conviction caused me. Oh, my uncle, if such I may still call you, for the present severity of your conduct towards me almost induces me to think that you have discarded me from your breast, why thus persist in torturing one who has ever, the just God above knows, ever looked upon you with such reverence and affection? Doom me to anything—to death, but not to an union with such a villain as the Count Alberti."

"Villain!" repeated Bianchi, passionately, "dare you apply such an epithet to a nobleman whom I respect?"

"I do, my lord," replied Melina, firmly, "for such is the opinion that I entertain of him, and so, I believe, do most of those who know him."

"'Tis false, obstinate girl!" cried the prince, passionately; "who dare cast any such aspersions upon the character of the noble Count Alberti?"

"My lord," returned our heroine, calmly, for she had succeeded in conquering her emo-

tions in a most remarkable manner, "I have always understood true nobility to exist alone in honourable and virtuous deeds. Point out to me any traits of that description in the character of the Count Alberti, and I will be ready to admit that I have done him an injustice in the estimate I have formed of him, that I am in error, and that you are perfectly correct."

"This argument is ridiculous," returned Bianchi, impatiently; "you have heard my decision, Melina, and you must prepare yourself to abide by it. No foolish heroics will have the least effect upon me, and therefore you might as well spare yourself the trouble of displaying them. On Monday next, I once more repeat, you must become the wife of the Count Alberti, and nothing whatever can prevent you."

"But, my lord," answered Melina, determinedly, "I also repeat, that if such is your harsh and unnatural resolve, I will avail myself of one chance that is offered me to escape from the fate to which you would consign me, let the world think of me whatever it may. Of that be certain, uncle, for indeed I make no empty boast."

"Melina," said the prince, looking at her narrowly, "I do not understand you."

"Probably not, my lord; but with all due submission to you, I decline to explain myself any further," replied our heroine.

The prince frowned and bit his lips with rage, but he was incapable of returning any answer for a few minutes.

"Girl," he said at last, in a voice of half-stifled rage, "do you dare to defy my authority?"

"I have never sought to do so, my lord," replied our heroine, meekly.

"Then why refuse to answer the questions I think proper to put to you explicitly?" demanded Bianchi.

"Because," answered Melina, in the same tone of calmness and decision, "they are not put in a spirit of justice and reason."

"Justice and reason, bah!" retorted the Prince Bianchi, testily; "you repudiate my authority, girl—you defy my power, and——"

"No, no," interrupted our heroine, hastily, "by Heaven you misconstrue me; you misrepresent my motives and intentions altogether; you would force me into an alliance with one who is detestable to my mind. You may have some authority over my person, but you cannot, no law, human or divine, gives you the least control over my affections. Nature has implanted in all our breasts certain feelings and prejudices, and when they are dictated by reason, prudence, and virtue, who shall presume to question them? My feelings and prejudices I have taken every pains to reveal to you, and by the just God above, I say again, nothing shall alter them or move me from the resolution I have formed, if you still remain inexorable."

The Prince Bianchi again looked at her completely astounded; he was not prepared to meet with such a spirit of determination in one so naturally gentle and yielding, and he was therefore the more astonished. Melina, however, preserved the calm dignity of her demeanour, and awaited his answer with much more patience than she thought she could have summoned to her command.

PRINCE BIANCHI AND COUNT ALBERTI IN COUNCIL.

"Melina," he said at length, stifling his rage as much as he could, "you seem resolved to try my patience to the utmost limits, and might exasperate me to invoke upon your head my everlasting malediction. But in spite of all, I will be calm, and only treat your observations as such as would emanate from a wayward and thoughtless girl."

"Thoughtless, uncle?" replied Melina, in a tone of reproach; "oh, when did ever you find me giving utterance to a syllable which had not been calmly and dispassionately discussed in my own mind, and which reason and virtue did not dictate? You would consign me to misery and degradation; naturally I oppose it, and wherefore thus persist in urging that which I am satisfied your own conscience must tell you is unjust and tyrannical?"

"Tyrannical!" repeated Bianchi, with a frown.

"Ay, tyrannical, my lord," replied Melina; "I can apply no milder term to it, though I wish not to irritate or offend you."

"By Heaven!" exclaimed Bianchi, stamping his foot; "this is almost too much. Have you forgotten all the proper respect that is due to me, Melina?"

"No, my lord," answered the latter, "but alas! it appears too painfully plain to me that you have forgotten I am the orphan daughter of your only sister."

"Girl!" cried the prince, fiercely, and grasping her arm; "you seem determined to insult and excite me! Why continue to allude to your mother, towards whom I ever acted a brother's part? What have I to reproach myself with? In loving you too well?—In treating you with too much indulgence?"

"No, my lord," replied Melina, solemnly and fervently, "but in forgetting the promise you made to that beloved mother in her last moments."

"'Tis false!" exclaimed the Prince Bianchi, in accents of the greatest excitement; "have I not protected you with a father's care?—Have I not lavished upon you every affection?"

"True, my lord," answered Melina.

"Then of what have you now to complain?" demanded her uncle.

"Simply this, my lord," replied our heroine, "that you would sacrifice me to a man whom I despise and loathe; whose dishonourable deeds have made him notorious in the world. Oh, bethink yourself, I beseech you; think of the misery and shame you would bring upon my head by this unholy alliance, and the remorse it must afterwards cause you, and I am satisfied in my own mind that you will not persist in your present determination. I acknowledge all the love you have bestowed upon me; the attention you have ever paid to my happiness, the leniency with which you have always viewed those errors to which we are all prone; I am grateful for it—Heaven knows that no one can feel more grateful; then why seek to undo all that you have so nobly, so generously, and affectionately done? Why thus at one fell swoop blight the golden prospects that your kindness made me indulge in? But you will not, my dear uncle, I am convinced you will not, if you will only calmly reflect upon every point. Say that you will not, and though I may never be permitted to become the wife of the man who possesses my heart's warmest affections, and who I admit to be the humble Florio Clairville, I can still be comparatively happy. Let me implore, my dear uncle, to turn not a deaf ear to that which I urge, and my prayers, as they have hitherto done, shall ever ascend to Heaven for your happiness and welfare."

The Prince Bianchi was indeed somewhat moved by this earnest appeal, and he averted his looks from his lovely niece, and remained for some minutes after she had spoken silent, and meditating with himself. To deny the justice, the truth, and reason of her observations, it was impossible, but still he could not bring his proud and obstinate spirit to yield; he could not make up his mind to abandon the designs he had in contemplation, and therefore he once more turned sternly towards his niece, and said—

"Melina, I have listened with patience to all the arguments you have made use of, but still, after mature consideration, I cannot suffer them to make any impression upon my mind. I act entirely for your welfare, and——"

"For my welfare, my lord?" replied Melina, interrupting him, and with a look of the bitterest reproach; "oh, what a cruel mockery it is to say so, when you would consign me to a fate so wretched, so revolting and disgraceful. Believe me, I wish not to give utterance to a single word that might savour the least of disrespect towards you, but I cannot refrain from saying that if you persist in sacrificing me to such a man as the Count Alberti, you will be guilty of an act which must, in your more rational moments, ever be a reproach upon your conscience."

"Melina," exclaimed the prince, passionately, for the truth of her remarks had touched him keenly, "you seem resolved to insult me."

"Oh, no, my lord," replied our heroine, "why thus harshly misconstrue my sentiments and intentions? I would merely appeal to your sense of justice and humanity, if you can for a moment forget that we are connected by the ties of consanguinity."

"I do not forget," retorted the prince, in the same harsh and determined tone, "I do not forget that you are my niece, that you are under my jurisdiction, and as such bound to obey my will. That will you have heard repeatedly, and it is uselss to resist it."

"Alas, alas, then!" sobbed the hapless maiden, pressing her delicate hands upon her burning temples, "you will break my heart; my death will lie at your door."

"Pshaw!" replied Bianchi, assuming as much indifference as he could; "what romantic nonsense is this? Broken hearts indeed! it is perfectly sickening. But I find that I waste argument upon you in vain. Get you back to your chamber, girl, and endeavour to learn reason and obedience."

Melina saw plainly that it was useless to endeavour to make any reply, or to seek to move her uncle from his stern purpose, and with a heavy and desponding heart, therefore, she retired from the room, and sought her own apartment, and the consoling influence of her faithful attendant, Floretta.

The Prince Bianchi after her departure, remained in deep meditation for some time, and paced the room in a most uneasy state of mind. The remarks she had given utterance to ; the pathetic and tender appeals she had made to his feelings, had caused the greatest sensation in his mind, and he in vain tried to justify his own conduct towards her ; but still he could not bring himself to yield to her supplications. Proud, haughty, and arrogant, he would not suffer any one to interpose between himself and any determination he might have formed, and thus it was that he often committed acts, which in his more sober and rational moments he bitterly regretted, and reproached himself with. But this union between his niece and the Count Alberti was one of his pet ideas; he had taken a singular fancy to that young nobleman, for what reason we are at a loss to conjecture; probably from a coincidence in some of the circumstances of their lives ; and nothing whatever could have prejudiced him against him, or have tempted him to forfeit the promise he had made to him. The determined hatred and disgust, then, which our heroine so openly evinced towards him greatly exasperated him, and only served to render him the more determined in his harsh designs.

"Nothing shall move me," he said at length ; "all her supplications are useless. I should be weaker than a child if I were to yield to them, and what would the Count Alberti think of me if I were to forfeit my word to him ? Why, that I was a pusillanimous old idiot, and very justly too. No, she shall become his bride, and at the time I have fixed, next Monday. But still I am at a loss to penetrate what she meant when she spoke of availing herself of the chances of escape that were offered to her. Humph! what may they be ? I must have a strict eye to this, for it signifies some mischief."

He was interrupted at this point of his soliloquy by the entrance of the Count Alberti, who had just returned from a walk he had been taking in the neighbourhood of the villa.

"Your highness seems somewhat excited," observed Alberti, noticing the expression of his countenance ; "has anything particular occurred during my absence ?"

"Nothing more," answered the Prince Bianchi, "than that I have had an interview with Melina."

"And if I may judge from your manner,"

remarked the Count Alberti, "it has not been altogether an agreeable one."

"You are right, count," returned Bianchi. "My niece has vexed me, ruffled my temper much ; she still remains obdurate."

"That is no more than I expected," remarked the count ; "may I trouble your highness for the particulars of the interview ? Be not afraid, but relate them to me, if it so please you, just as they occurred."

"I will do so," answered the prince, "for I am certain that you have too much good sense to feel offended."

"Oh, no," remarked Alberti, "I am fully prepared for everything."

The prince then complied with his request, and related all with which the reader is already acquainted, to which the Count Alberti listened with much more patience and forbearance than could have been anticipated, though, of course, he was inwardly deeply chagrined.

"Well, I must say," he observed, when Bianchi had concluded, "that the Signora Melina does not flatter me much, and I am afraid that nothing will ever do away with the prejudice she entertains towards me."

"Oh," replied Bianchi, "obstinate though she at present appears to be, I do not doubt that it will be in your power, my lord, yet to subdue her proud spirit. You are still determined to become her husband ?"

"If your highness will permit me," answered Alberti. "I would not resign her, in spite of the evident hatred she bears towards me and the scorn with which she treats me, for all the wealth I possess."

"Enough," observed the prince, "then that point is decided, I presume ?"

"It is, so far as I am concerned," said Alberti. "On Monday next then, at midnight, the nuptials without fail will take place ?"

"They will," answered Bianchi, "and it will be entirely useless for her to offer any resistance to them."

"But there is one point on which we ought to use every precaution," observed the Count.

"And what is that ?" demanded Bianchi, though he guessed what he meant.

"The hint which Melina threw out of her having assistance to rescue her, should she think proper to avail herself of it," answered Alberti.

"Yes," returned the prince, "that has not escaped me, though I am half inclined to believe that it was a mere idle boast, if possible to intimidate me and cause me to relent,"

"I am not disposed to think so lightly of it, your highness," said the count.

"Who think you, then, would be bold enough to attempt to obstruct us in our designs, and to rescue Melina from our power ?" asked the Prince Bianchi.

"Allesandro Massaroni, the brigand chief,"

replied his companion; "he is bold enough for anything, and it strikes me forcibly that he is somewhere lurking in the neighbourhood, from what we heard the other night."

"Think you then that the minstrel was him?"

"I feel confident it was: I could swear to the tones of his voice, and the ballad is well known to be peculiarly his own," said the Count Alberti.

"Ah!" returned the prince, "what you have just now said, count, convinces me that you are perfectly right in your conjectures. It could have been no other than Massaroni that we heard on that occasion, I am now, the same as yourself, thoroughly satisfied. The daring scoundrel! and thinks he to obstruct me in my determinations?"

"Depend upon it, your highness, he not only means to obstruct us but to frustrate our plans, if he possibly can," said Alberti, "and, therefore, I repeat that it behoves us to be on our guard, and to adopt speedily every means of precaution in our power."

"True," coincided Bianchi, "but what do you propose?"

"Why, that we should have a strong force around the villa, on the night of the nuptials; such a force as we may consider sufficient to repel any attack that may be made upon us by the brigands," replied the Count Alberti.

"That shall be done," observed the prince, "and I think it would likewise be as well to have also a sufficient guard in the chapel at the time."

"No, my lord," replied the Count Alberti, "I do not think there will be any necessity for that, as the brigand chief, finding such an array outside the villa, will not probably deem it prudent to proceed in any designs he may have contemplated, and certainly, before he could reach the chapel, we should find means to place the Signora Melina in security until a more fitting opportunity arrived for completing the ceremony. I think that he might possibly be put to the rout in a short time, when he saw the force he had to contend with, and I believe him to be too good a general to do anything rashly. Before he could again muster his forces, and re-arrange his plans, Melina, with your sanction, would have become my bride, and thus all his hopes and all his wishes rendered abortive."

"You are right, count," observed Bianchi, after a pause; "I perfectly agree with your ideas upon the subject, and will adopt your suggestions. This daring brigand chief, who has for so many years held all the authorities of the country at defiance, must be defeated at any cost."

"True, your highness."

"By all the saints," exclaimed Bianchi, "I would give a fortune to any one who could place him in my power, so that he might be brought to justice; for while he continues to exist, though there is so much said of the generosity and nobility of his character—bah! I do not consider that society at large is safe."

"That is also my firm opinion," said the Count Alberti, "and your highness knows full well that I have no reason to bear him any good will, or to wish that any mercy should be extended to him, if once he were trepanned, from the various outrages he has committed against me."

"You have not," answered the Prince Bianchi, "and I trust that you will ere long have the opportunity of avenging yourself upon him for all the wrongs he has done you."

"I do not entertain the least doubt that I shall," returned the Count Alberti. "But now I believe all our plans are arranged?"

"They are," answered Bianchi.

"And as regards the marriage ceremony?"

"That is all settled, I hope to your satisfaction; you know that I am determined nothing that my niece can say will have the power to move me from my purpose. All the preparations, as you perceive, are in readiness; you have also made your arrangements, I believe, for her reception at your palace in Florence immediately after the solemnization of the nuptials?"

"I have, your highness," replied the Count Alberti.

"Enough, then," remarked the Prince Bianchi, "on Monday next at midnight, I will forfeit my title and dignity if the marriage does not take place."

"I am satisfied, my lord," said the count, "for I know full well that nothing whatever will induce you to break your word."

"You do me more than justice, count, by that supposition," said the Prince Bianchi, "I do not seek to flatter you when I say that I have long looked anxiously for an alliance between you and my fair niece; your parents and myself were always on terms of the greatest friendship; in fact, we are related to each other, the same noble blood flows within our veins; it is an alliance which reason and policy dictate; and, you willing, which I know you to be, nothing whatever on earth shall prevent the consummation of our wishes."

"Your highness's words inspire me with renewed courage," said the Count Alberti, "notwithstanding I have have had sufficient to daunt me in my suit from the scorn and insult which the beauteous Signora Melina (who, in spite of all, I love with a fervour and sincerity that a few men have ever before experienced) has heaped upon me."

"Fear not, my lord," returned the Prince Bianchi, "her conduct towards you hitherto has alone been dictated by the caprices of a thoughtless and inexperienced girl, and not, I firmly believe, from any natural antipithics or prejudices she entertains towards you. Those whims and caprices, I have no doubt, you will soon after marriage be able to overcome, and I predict many years of happiness for yourself and my niece."

"The observations your highness are pleased to make use of, are most satsfatory and gratifying to my feelings," said Alberti, "and I trust that the predictions you have so sanguinely expressed, will be realized. I can only repeat that all the attention and affection that man can bestow upon a woman, shall be lavished by me upon your beauteous niece."

"I do not doubt you, count, and therefore I believe that point is settled," said the Prince Bianchi.

"It is," answered his companion; "but still, could Florio Clairville be secured, and it were possible to estrange him from the Signora Melina's heart, I must confess that I should feel more satisfied."

"As I have frequently told you, my lord," returned Bianchi, "you have nothing whatever to fear from him. He is perfectly powerless to do harm; and even should he not again fall into our hands, when he finds that my niece has become your wife, without recal, he will abandon all the presumptuous hopes he has entertained, depend on it, and never again venture to cross our path."

"Why, he would be little better than a madman if he were to do so."

"He would," coincided the prince, "No, my lord, again I tell you to rest satisfied and all will turn out exactly as your most sanguine wishes could suggest."

"Enough," said the Count Alberti; "I will no longer encourage any such doubts as those I have just expessed to you, but look forward with the most joyful anticipations to the bliss which is in store for me."

"You may do so with safety, my lord, and rest assured that your hopes will not be doomed to be disappointed."

"And yet," said the count, after a brief pause; "may not the excitement under which the Signora Melina is at present labouring prove too much for her strength to endure, and even short as the interval is that will occur previous to the time fixed upon for our nuptials to take place, may she not be reduced to such a state of anguish and despair as to render it dangerous for us to persist in the accomplishment of our wishes?"

"By all my hopes," replied the Prince Bianchi, determinedly, "she shall become your bride at the hour I have appointed, let the consequences be whatever they may. Anguish, despair? Bah! are you such a novice in the world, my lord, as not to know, that such feelings are only assumed by obstinate females of strong passions like Melina, merely to answer

their purposes, and to endeavour to counteract the wishes of those who possess authority over them? When she finds that all hope of her escaping from the fate to which I have consigned her is at an end, believe me, she will resign herself to it, and we shall find none of the difficulties which you now seem to anticipate."

"Well, your highness," observed the Count Alberti, "I will be guided entirely by what you say, because I believe that you speak the truth."

"Why," replied Bianchi, "it is not likely that I should attempt to deceive you."

"Oh, no, my lord," said Alberti, "I never for a moment suspected anything of the kind. I am perfectly satisfied with all that you have said and promised, and the arrangements we have come to."

"I am glad to hear you say so," said the Prince Bianchi; "as for the brigand chief, Allesandro Massaroni, I fear him not; the rascal will not venture to attempt to obstruct us in our plans, for he knows full well, and I believe he is not fool enough to neglect, to avail himself of his knowledge, that he would only be rushing upon certain destruction by doing so."

At this moment a loud laugh of derision saluted their ears, and which seemed to proceed from immediately outside the door of the apartment in which they were sitting. They both started involuntarily to their feet, and gazed at each other with astonishment.

"By the Saints!" exclaimed the Prince Bianchi, his countenance flashed with indignation; "that was no delusion; who has been so bold as ——"

He rushed to the room door before he finished the sentence, and threw it open, but there was not a soul to be seen, nor were there any traces of any one having been.

"It is most extraordinary," observed the Count Alberti; "I could have sworn that I heard some person laugh outside this door."

"Sworn it?" returned the Prince Bianchi, hastily; "yes, and with safety too. There is some treachery in this which we must penetrate."

He immediately rang the bell for the attendance of his servant, and he quickly made his appearance, no doubt wondering at the hastiness of the summons.

"Jiacomo," said the Prince.

"Yes, your highness," returned the former, "what may be your pleasure?"

"Are there any strangers in the house?" demanded Bianchi, sternly.

"None that I am aware of, your highness," answered his attendant.

"Have you seen no one pass the gates?"

"I have not observed any person, my lord, but those connected with your highness's establishment," answered Jiacomo.

" You are certain that you are speaking the truth ?" said the Prince Bianchi, and fixing upon the old man, at the same time, a keen and penetrating look.

" I have had the honour of being in your highness's service for nearly thirty years," replied old Jiacomo, calmly; but at the same time with a look of reproach, which his feelings would not allow him to repress ; "and have you ever had reason to doubt my truth or fidelity yet ?"

" No, no, ' returned the prince, after a pause, and somewhat confused; "I—I did not mean to insinuate anything of that kind :—you have —however, you may retire, Jiacomo."

Jiacomo bowed, and made his exit accordingly, and Bianchi having again closed the door, turned to the Count Alberti, and said—

" Well, this is most extraordinarily remarkable and unaccountable."

" It is, your highness," coincided Alberti, " You heard the laugh as well as myself ?"

" I did."

" Then we could not both of us have been deceived ?"

" No," replied the Count Alberti, " that is totally impossible."

" I cannot rest satisfied," remarked the Prince Bianchi ; "some treachery, it strikes me, is afloat, though I do not for a moment suspect my old and faithful servant, Jiacomo. I have thought this ever since the night when we heard the ballad in the gardens of the villa, and which you say you are satisfied could proceed from no other individual than Massaroni."

" I feel perfectly convinced in my own mind, my lord," returned Alberti, "that Allesandro Massaroni, the brigand chief, was the minstrel we heard on that occasion."

" Then, there must be traitors amongst my own domestics," said the Prince Bianchi, decidedly; "and I will not rest until I have discovered them, and inflicted upon them that punishment which they deserve. If my suspicions are correct, notwithstanding all the precautions we may make use of, and the plans we may adopt, those who oppose our designs may yet triumph, and defeat all our well-formed designs at the very moment when we the least expect it."

" By Heaven !" exclaimed the Count Alberti, vehemently, " that shall never be."

" Come then, my lord," said Bianchi, taking the lamp in his hand ; " let us at once take a silent and secret survey of the premises, and see whether or not there is anything to authorize our suspicions."

Alberti assented, and they emerged from the room, quietly closing the door after them, and with cautious steps proceeded over every part of the villa where it was at all likely that any person might be concealed, at the same time listening attentively at the doors of the different servants' apartments in order to find whether they could elicit anything from their conversation to throw a light upon the subject. But nothing did they either see or hear to unravel the mystery or to excite their suspicions, and they returned once more to the room they had just before quitted, the Prince Bianchi in particular, being in a state of the greatest excitement. He threw himself on a seat, and for a few moments was unable to give utterance to a single syllable, while the Count Alberti traversed the apartment with hasty strides, communing with himself, and at times giving utterance, in under tones, to the most bitter oaths.

" This is most torturing," said the prince, at length starting to his feet ; " it seems as if the fates had conspired against us to mock us, and excite our feelings to the utmost degree."

" It does, indeed, your highness," coincided Alberti ; " some strange fatuity appears to hang over us."

" True," said the prince; " but, by all my hopes, we will not be disappointed in the resolutions we have formed."

" We should be weaker than children did we suffer ourselves to be so, my lord," returned the Count Alberti.

" You heard the ironical laugh as well as myself ?"

" Of course I did; I have said so, repeatedly," answered the count.

" Then," remarked the Prince Bianchi, "it is evident, perfectly evident, that we must have some secret enemy or enemies concealed in some part of the villa."

" Well, it certainly appears like it."

" And if we do not discover them in time," added the prince, " even with all the prospect of success that our designs at present bear, they may be defeated. I will immediately summons the whole of my domestics into our presence, and question them minutely ; and mark you, count, you observe well their answers, and notice the expression of their countenances; for, it is probably by that means we may be enabled to detect the truth, and to avoid the danger we apprehend ere it come too suddenly upon us."

" I will do as your highness advises," answered Alberti, "and I hope that we may yet be enabled to unravel the mystery, for this present state of suspicion and uncertainty is indeed most torturing."

" It is," agreed the Prince Bianchi, " and I can no longer endure it with the least degree of patience."

Thus saying, he rang the bell violently, and old Jiacomo again made his appearance, in considerable alarm, for he could not at all form the least conjecture as to the cause of his master's extraordinary excitement, and being old and feeble, he stood trembling to await his orders.

"Order the whole of the domestics, male and female, into my presence immediately," commanded the Prince Bianchi, peremptorily, "and see that all the doors of the villa are secured, so that no one can pass either in or out."

"Yes, your highness," replied old Jiacomo, bowing obsequiously, and retiring from the room to execute his orders.

"We will arrive at the truth of this, if it be possible," observed Bianchi, when he was gone. "I do not suspect old Jiacomo in the least, for I have always found him faithful to me; but unless our imagination led us both astray, which does not seem to be very probable, there is evidently one traitor, if not more in the house."

"I am precisely of the same opinion, my lord," remarked the Count Alberti, "and no more time than possible should be lost in endeavouring to detect him."

"By the mass!" exclaimed the prince, passionately, "should I succeed in discovering him, I will inflict such a punishment upon him as I think will be quite sufficient to deter others from following his example."

He was interrupted by the entrance of the domestics, who, having arranged themselves before their master and the Count Alberti, the former proceeded to question and cross-question them sternly and minutely; but he elicited nothing whatever of a satisfactory nature from them, and after the lapse of some time he again dismissed them from his presence, and folding his arms across his chest, he walked the apartment backwards and forwards, buried in deep meditation, and without saying a word to the Count Alberti, whose agitation was equal to his own.

"This mystery is most torturing," he said at length, "and it seems, the more we endeavour to fathom it, the deeper we become involved in perplexity. My domestics appeared to speak the truth."

"They did, my lord," returned Alberti; "I can, from their manner, scarcely believe that there is any treachery amongst them."

"Then, how are we to account for what we heard?" demanded the Prince Bianchi.

"Indeed I know not," answered the count; "it is a mystery which is altogether unfathomable to me."

"I will penetrate it," said Bianchi, in a determined tone, "if there be a possibility.— Can Massaroni have got any of his emissaries into the villa?"

"I do not see, your highness, how it is possible they can be secreted here, if, as you say, you believe your domestics to be faithful."

"True, true; no, no, daring even as we know Allesandro Massaroni to be, I do not believe him to be mad enough thus to rush at once into the lion's den, and where his destruction must be inevitable. The brigand chief, notwithstanding his boast, knows the power of the Prince Bianchi, the governor of Rome, too well to make such a venture."

Another laugh, louder than the one they had heard before, and which seemed to proceed from the same direction as before, at that moment again smote their ears, and completely paralysed them with astonishment. They looked at each other quite stupified and astounded, and neither of them for a moment or two had the power to utter a word, or to move from the spot on which they were standing.

"Are we to be tortured, defied thus?" at last exclaimed the Prince Bianchi, drawing his sword, and rushing towards the door, which he threw furiously open, the Count Alberti closely following him. The result was the same as before; there was no one to be seen. Bianchi hastily snatched up the lamp from the table, and, sword in hand, hurried precipitately along the gallery, followed closely by Alberti, but not a single individual could they see. They descended the various staircases, and entered several apartments with no better success, and at length made their way to the servants' hall, whom they found all congregated together, and busily discussing the circumstance upon which their master had so closely examined them; their astonishment and consternation at the abrupt entrance of himself and the Count Alberti, and at their excited appearance, may readily be imagined. But they started to their feet immediately, and bowed respectfully and obsequiously.

"Have any of you left this room since you retired from my presence?" demanded the Prince Bianchi, peremptorily.

They all replied solemnly in the negative.

"And did you obey my orders, Jiacomo, and see that all the doors were fastened?" asked Bianchi.

"I did, excellenza," replied the old man.

"'Tis strange; 'tis most unaccountable," muttered the prince, aside to Alberti.

"It is indeed," returned the latter; "it is a mystery which I cannot at all penetrate, and which the more I reflect on it involves me the deeper in perplexity."

"Are you certain you have heard no one in the house?" again demanded the Prince Bianchi of Jiacomo.

"Oh, quite, your highness," answered the old man; "your highness may be certain that I would not attempt to deceive you. Santa Maria! Who could enter here without our knowledge? And think you that we would be bold enough to admit strangers without the knowledge and authority of your highness?"

The prince paused and reflected for a

minute or two, but he was unable to come to any satisfactory conclusion, otherwise than he was satisfied that old Jiacomo was speaking the truth.

"By all the saints!" he said, at last, addressing himself to the Count Alberti, "this is most bewildering; and it seems as if some infernal spell had alighted upon us." He then turned to Jiacomo, and said, "You will be careful to see that every door in the house is secured; and let you and all your fellows keep watch during the night. Do you hear me?"

"I do, your highness," replied Jiacomo; "and will punctually obey your instructions."

"'Tis well," observed the prince. "Know you whether the Signora Melina is secure in her chamber?"

"She is, my lord," answered the old man; "at least, she was so only a few minutes since, according to the account of her waiting maid, Floretta."

The Prince Bianchi made use of no further observation, but taking the arm of the Count Alberti, they walked from the servants' hall in an agitated manner, and returned to the apartment they had so recently quitted. When they had entered the room, the prince closed the door, and turning to his companion, said—

"This adventure bewilders me more than any I have recently met with, count."

"And so it does me, your highness," returned Alberti; "indeed, I know not what to make of it."

"There's one thing is certain," remarked the Prince Bianchi, "it shows the absolute necessity of our being upon our guard."

"Very true," said the count; "but after all, I am inclined to believe that we were mistaken."

"What, twice!" said Bianchi, impatiently; "that is impossible: if it were not a human voice we heard, I will be ready to forfeit my existence."

"Well," returned the count, "if it was, the mystery is the most extraordinary and impenetrable I ever heard of."

"You may say that, my lord," replied the Prince Bianchi, "and I perfectly agree with you; but I shall not rest until I have fathomed it."

"I am fearful, your highness, that you will find a difficulty in doing that," said the Count Alberti. "Are there any secret means of access to the villa?"

"There are," answered Bianchi; "but I have the keys of them all in my possession, and it is utterly impossible that any one could avail themselves of them."

"And is there no one among your numerous domestics whom you particulary suspect of having betrayed you?" asked the Count Alberti."

"Not one," replied Bianchi; "they have all been in my service for many years, and I believe them all faithful."

"Well, then," observed Alberti, "I confess myself to be completely at a loss what to say upon the subject. That I twice heard a laugh of derision which interrupted our conversation, I could almost swear; but from whom it could emanate it is impossible for me to form even the most remote conjecture."

"I would give a handsome sum in gold to know," remarked Bianchi.

"No doubt of it, your highness," said the count; "and so would I. Think you it would be likely to lead to any beneficial results if we were to offer a reward?"

"No," answered the prince; "but in my simple opinion, on the contrary it would be much more likely to endanger the success of plans were we to give publicity to it, and put our enemies on their guard."

"True," coincided the Count Alberti. "I did not think of that."

"All that we can do," resumed Bianchi, "is to watch cautiously, and then if we see anything to excite our suspicions, we shall know how to act. The time is short which I have appointed for the nuptials to take place, and they once over, there is nothing else to fear."

"Except from the vengeance of Massaroni," rejoined the Count Alberti.

"Pshaw!" returned the prince impatiently; "you entertain too much fear of that lawless marauder, count.

"And forsooth, have I not very good reason to do so, your highness?" demanded the Count Alberti, "after all that I have experienced from the spirit of hatred and revenge he bears towards me? Indeed, powerful even as your highness is, and also taking into consideration the forces you have at your command, I think you will be ready to admit that he is no mean enemy to cope with. In his mountain fastness, and surrounded by his daring band, who, each of them, if engaged in a better cause, would be worthy of the name of a hero, he has for many years proved himself to be unconquerable, and I fear that it will be some time longer ere his power will be subdued, if indeed, he ever suffers himself to be taken alive, which I do not believe he ever will. Pardon me, your highness, but I have seen more, and had better means of judging of the character of the brigand chief, to my cost, than yourself; and it is only due to him to say that he is no ordinary individual; that he is not one of your common thieves and cut-throats, and that had fate cast him into a different sphere of action, he is by nature calculated to embellish and do honour to society instead of degrading it."

"By the mass, my lord," said the prince with a half smile, "you are most eloquent in your praises of this mountain robber. One might almost imagine that he had sat to you for his portrait. However, I am ready to admit, as you observe, from all I have seen of him, that Allesandro Massaroni, the brigand chief, is no common character, and that although I feel anxious to rid society at large of such an abominable pest, and have exerted myself to the utmost to do so, which yourself and everybody else know full well, I never think of him without some unaccountable feeling of emotion. Whether it be pity or regret I know not, but when I recall his features to my recollection,

THE PRINCE BIANCHI IN MEDITATION.

there is something in their expression that reminds me of one—But, pshaw! What am I talking about? My mind is wandering. Why should the brigand chief, from whom I have experienced so much annoyance, and who has ever proved himself to be one of my most bitter enemies, interest me? We will change the subject, my lord, for I must confess that this accords not with my feelings, especially at the present moment."

The Count Alberti returned no answer, and Bianchi took several rapid and disorded strides across the room, and seemed to be greatly excited, although he strove to stifle the expression of his feelings as much as possible. At length he turned to the Count Alberti and said—

"My lord, the events of this night have somewhat discomposed me, I confess, and I wish to commune with my own thoughts. If it please you we will separate, and meet again early in the morning."

"As your highness pleases," replied the Count Alberti, with an insinuating smile, "but I trust that nothing that has taken place will induce you to alter your determination?"

"Impossible!" said Bianchi, "you must deem me weak indeed if you thought it could. Have I not pledged to you my solemn word?"

"True, you have, my lord," replied Alberti.

"And think you that anything would induce me to break it?" demanded the Prince Bianchi, hastily.

"No, no, your highness," returned the Count; "pardon me for what I said, which arose from an over anxiety upon the subject; I am satisfied."

"It is no fault of mine if you are not," remarked the Prince Bianchi. "But good night, we will converse further on this in the morning."

"Good night, your highness," said Alberti, and he then retired from the room and sought his own apartment in a frame of mind which, in spite of the asseverations of the Prince Bianchi, and the confidence he placed in the perfect sincerity of them, he could not by any means bring to a degree of composure.

"I feel satisfied," he soliloquised to himself, "that, notwithstanding the strict examination we have made against the domestics, some treachery is at the present time going on in the villa, and unless we can discover it in time, we may yet be foiled in our designs. I would fain persuade myself that we were both labouring under a false delusion when we imagined that we heard the laugh of derision outside the door of the apartment in which the Prince Bianchi and myself were consulting together; but I find that to be perfectly impossible, and therefore it appears evident that our enemies are upon the alert, and will, unless we use the most prompt and efficacious measures, defeat us yet in our deep-laid schemes. Allesandro Massaroni, I am satisfied, will do his utmost, will exert all his energies to effect that object, and in spite of all the Prince Bianchi may say, I know his power and determination too well to treat them with indifference. Would that he were no more, and that the presumptuous beggar, Florio Clairville, to whom Melina is so devotedly attached, and whose sentiments I am satisfied nothing whatever can alter, was in our power, then indeed I might be somewhat sanguine in my hopes; but as it is I cannot but anticipate a painful disappointment. The scorn and hatred with which the Signora Melina treats me is perfect wormwood to my soul; but still I am determined to persevere, let the consequences be whatever they may. The Prince Bianchi seems firm; I cannot doubt the sincerity of his promises, and therefore it will only be by some cursed accident, if his fair but proud and disdainful niece escape me."

Thus he continued to give utterance to the conflicting feelings which were passing in his breast for some time, and unable to arrive at any satisfactory conclusion, still apprehensive that something would occur to disappoint him in his hopes and guilty wishes, the Count Alberti at length sought his couch, and sleep for a short interval served to banish his anxieties.

The Prince Bianchi, as may be imagined, was in no better frame of mind after Alberti had quitted him, and he long pondered o'er the events of the evening, and in vain endeavoured to treat them with indifference. It was quite evident to him that they could not both have been mistaken in the sounds they had heard, and if so, it was equally clear that some danger was afloat, and unless they used the utmost precaution they would not be able to avoid it or to counteract the designs of their secret enemies. That they had everything to fear from the brigand chief, he perfectly agreed with the Count Alberti, and that conviction rendered him the more anxious and determined to use every precaution in his power to counteract any designs which Massaroni might have in contemplation. It is strange, however, that the private entrance to the villa, and the secret passages behind the altar in the chapel, never for a moment occurred to his recollection, and while he determined to place a strong guard in the other parts of the building, that portion was forgotten and neglected.

Melina, after retiring from the presence of her uncle, again sought her chamber and the society of the faithful Floretta, completely heart-broken and despairing. Floretta had been for some time waiting her return in a state of the utmost anxiety and impatience; and when she entered the room, she advanced kindly towards her and conducted her to a seat, on to which Melina sank and burst into tears, which her waiting maid did not offer to interrupt, as she was in hopes it would relieve her mind. She needed no information as to what had taken place at the interview, as she was well convinced that it was of the same painful nature as usual; and deeply were her sympathies aroused for that unfortunate mistress to whom she was so affectionately attached, and for whom she would most willingly have made any sacrifice in her power to serve.

"Dear signora," she said at length, "do not take on so, I implore of you. I know full well what must be the nature of your feelings, cruelly persecuted as you are, and would to

Heaven that it was in my power to serve you; but for Heaven's sake do endeavour to be firm and to compose yourself."

"Oh, Floretta," sighed her mistress, and her eyes were still humid with tears; "I duly appreciate your kindness, believe me, and the good feelings you entertain towards me; but can I be otherwise than wretched and despairing, when I contemplate the fate that is impending over me, and from which it now appears too certain there is no escape?"

"Nay, signora," remarked Floretta, in her most soothing accents, "do not say so; for although the time allowed you is short, I cannot help feeling convinced that something will occur to rescue you, and to defeat the plans of your enemies. Does your uncle, his highness, the Prince Bianchi, still remain inexorable?"

"He does," replied our heroine, "and nothing whatever, I am now convinced, will move him to relent."

"What strange infatuation can have seized him?" said Florretta; "it is so unlike his usual conduct towards you, signora."

"True," coincided Melina; "but the Count Alberti has obtained complete mastery over him, and seems to have stiffled all his better feelings. On Monday next, unless Providence interferes to save me, I shall be consigned to a fate than which death would be far, far preferable."

"Oh, never, sweet lady," returned Floretta, "I cannot, will not believe that such will be the case; and therefore I beg of you to endeavour to set your mind easy upon that point."

"Oh, Floretta, how can I do so? Where can I look to for hope?"

"Massaroni will keep his word, signora, depend on it, and I do not fear that he will fail in the accomplishment of his wishes."

"Alas, Floretta," said her mistress, "I cannot conquer the repugnance I feel at accepting of his services, although I entertain the highest opinion of the honesty and purity of his motives."

"Indeed, signora," replied Floretta; "you will pardon me I hope, but I cannot help thinking that the scruples you entertain are erroneous, and that they ought to be immediately banished from your mind. Massaroni would save you from destruction, and notwithstanding his unfortunate and questionable situation in the world, I do not think you ought to reject his offers. But you will reflect better on this, I am certain you will."

"I will try to do so," said Melina, "but I much doubt whether I shall ever be able to reconcile it with my feelings."

"Can you then, in preference, make up your mind to become the victim of the Count Alberti?" asked Floretta.

"Oh, never!" replied our heroine, with a shudder; "the bare thought is horrible, it is insupportable."

"Yet such will unquestionably be your fate, signora;" observed Floretta, "unless you comply with the wishes of the brigand chief. Under his protection, and that of Signor Clairville, you will be perfectly safe, and fear not but the Prince Bianchi will then be as anxious as yourself for a reconciliation. Come, my dear signora, time presses, and it is absolutely necessary that you should make up your mind without delay."

"I will endeavour to do so," answered Melina; "but indeed I fear that I sha'l not be able to overcome my repugnance."

"Oh, yes," said Floretta, fervently, "I trust that you will, and who shall venture to blame you for adopting a course to which you will have been driven by hard necessity?"

"The world is most uncharitable, Floretta," said Melina.

"I know it is, my lady," answered Floretta, "but in this instance all that are acquainted with the business must acknowledge that the prince your uncle is alone to blame."

"Would to Heaven that the time were over which is to decide my fate," said our heroine; "for this terrible state of agony and suspense is insupportable. Would to God that I were no more, or that I had not been born."

"It grieves me, signora, indeed it does," replied her attendant, "to hear you talk in this melancholy strain. The clouds of adversity, that now obscure the horizon of your hopes, will be dispersed: I feel convinced that they will; and you will again be restored to happiness."

"Oh, no," ejaculated the hapless damsel, "I dare not flatter myself with any such hopes, which I feel convinced could only end in disappointment. All the preparations for my dreaded nuptials with the hated Count Alberti are made, and nothing, I fear, will save me from the cruel fate to which my inexorable uncle has consigned me."

"If you will only follow the advice I have so often given you, signora," said Floretta, "I feel satisfied, perfectly satisfied, that you will have nothing to fear."

"If your wishes could be realised, my good Floretta," returned Melina, "I feel certain that I should not. But under the present existing circumstances, it would be madness for me to entertain any such thoughts. No, I must try to make my mind up to the worst, and I fervently hope that Providence will give me fortitude to support my misfortunes."

"To which wish I believe I need not tell you I most heartily respond," said the faithful Floretta.

"I know you do, my kind-hearted girl," replied our heroine, "and most grateful do I feel to you for your wishes. But we have already conversed long enough upon this subject, and, as I feel anxious to commune with my own thoughts, I must request you to retire."

Not wishing to appear intrusive, Floretta obeyed, and the Signora Melina was left to herself, and for hours she continued in the same agitated state of mind; but at length, worn out with fatigue and thinking, she retired to rest, and slept more calmly and soundly than, under existing circumstances, might have been expected.

Little did the Prince Bianchi, and Count Alberti, however, imagine that the whole of the conversation which had taken place between them, as related in the previous pages, had been overheard by any person in the villa; but it had, and that individual was no other than Guiseppe, and it was he whom they had twice heard give utterance to the laugh of derision which had so startled and surprised them. He had the means of concealing himself in an adjoining apartment, of which he possessed the key, and thus he escaped discovery, and added to their astonishment and confusion. As soon as the excitement had a little abated, he watched an opportunity to leave the villa unobserved, and immediately made his way to the place where the brigand chief was concealed, in order to communicate to him what he had overheard, and who received him with his usual air of satisfaction and welcome, and eagerly inquired what had brought him there at that late hour.

"Has anything particular occurred, Guiseppe?" he said.

"Nothing particular, signor," replied Guiseppe, "with the exception of a conversation which I have overheard between the Prince Bianchi and the Count Alberti, and which, no doubt, you will be glad to be made acquainted with, as it fully discloses all their plans, and will therefore the better teach you how to act."

"Ah!" said Massaroni, with a look of satisfaction; "this is fortunate, for we need all the information we can obtain for our guidance. You are performing you part well, Guiseppe, and I commend you for it. I do not entertain the least doubt that I shall succeed."

"Why, signor," returned Guiseppe, "I do not entertain any fear of your failing if you only act with the same caution that you have hitherto done."

"And that you may be sure I will not fail to do," remarked the brigand; "but what is this conversation you have overheard?—Tell it to me, for I am all impatience to hear it."

Guiseppe immediately complied with his request, and Massaroni listened to him with the deepest interest and much evident satisfaction.

"'Tis well," he said, when Guiseppe had concluded; "this information will be of much use to us. The prince and the villain Alberti will find themselves greatly disappointed in the hopes they have formed, or my name is not Allesandro Massaroni. So they are still determined to force the fair Signora Melina to the altar on Monday next at midnight?"

"Yes, signor," answered Guiseppe, "and they will succeed too, without a doubt, if you do not interfere to save her, for what can all the resistance of Signora Melina avail her."

"Fear not but I will be determined," said the brigand chief; "and if Fortune does not desert me on this occasion, which I do not apprehend that she will, I shall be as successful as I have hitherto been in all my undertakings. So they still flatter themselves with the idea that they will get Massaroni in their power, and be enabled to sacrifice him to their cowardly vengeance, do they?'

"You see they do, signor, and they will leave no means, no stratagem untried to effect their object," replied Guiseppe.

"Ha! ha! ha!" laughed our hero, scornfully; "the fools; they forget that they have no boy or cowardly churl to deal with. By the dome of St. Peter's, I will yet teach them such a lesson that they little expect."

"But you say that it is their intention to have a strong force at hand in order to repel any attack which may be made upon them, Guiseppe?" said Rubaldo.

"True," answered the former.

"That will be awkward," observed Rubaldo; "for, notwithstanding the superior and indomitable courage of our band, they might overpower us by numbers."

"Pshaw!" exclaimed Massaroni impatiently, "I do not entertain any such apprehensions, Have we not always proved more than a match for any force that we have encountered?"

"True," answered Rubaldo.

"Then, think you Fortune will desert us now, when we shall be engaged in so good a cause?" demanded the brigand chief.

"Well, I should not think she would," returned Rubaldo.

"Oh, I feel confident of success," said Massaroni, "and feel anxious for the time to arrive when I can put my plans into execution. You say, Guiseppe, that it is not their intention to have any of the troops in the chapel on the night appointed for the nuptials to take place?

"It is not," replied Guiseppe.

"Why, what strange neglect is that," remarked the brigand chief; "but it is most fortunate, nevertheless; for we can secure the Signora Melina and carry her away before any alarm can be given to the soldiers outside the villa, and we can safely make our escape by the secret passages which you have pointed out to us, Guiseppe?"

"You can," returned the latter; "you know it leads to the back part of the villa, and if you only act with due precaution, you can make good you retreat without any fear of detection."

"True," coincided Massaroni.

"But have you well considered your plans?" asked Rubaldo.

"I have," answered Massaroni, "you may be very well assured of that, and need not ask me such a question."

"And what are they?" inquired his lieutenant.

"Why," returned the brigand chief, "our band must be secreted in the passages behind the altar, the night before the one appointed for the marriage ceremony, after the family have retired to rest, and they will then be in readiness to act on the moment. They can easily be admitted by the secret door without any danger of discovery, I think, Guiseppe?"

"They can, signor," answered the latter.

"That is well; then our plot will be accomplished, I flatter myself, without much difficulty."

"I have no doubt of it," said Guiseppe.

"I will provide a vehicle to convey the Signora Melina to our mountain retreat, which must be in waiting in some convenient and secluded spot. Have you seen anything of Floretta, Guiseppe?"

"I have, signor."

"And did you venture to put any questions to her respecting her mistress?"

"I did, which she answered cautiously, for, as I before told you, she is not much prepossessed in my favour, and I am certain has always looked upon me with eyes of suspicion. However, I managed to elicit from her that the Signora Melina is in a state of the greatest excitement, as might be expected under the circumstances, and is undecided how to act."

"She surely cannot think of rejecting the offer of my aid to rescue her, and to resign herself to the revolting fate with which she is threatened?" said the brigand chief.

"I should think not," returned Guiseppe; "but, of course, it would not have been prudent for me to appear to know anything about that business."

"True," coincided Massaroni, "you have acted with the greatest discretion, Guiseppe, and have my best thanks for it."

"Why, as for that, signor," said Guiseppe, "I have done no more than what I considered to be my duty, and merely to convince you also that I know how to keep my word."

"I am perfectly satisfied with you," said Massaroni, "and you shall find that I also know how to keep my word to those who are faithful to me; but that my vengeance never fails to overtake those who should attempt to deceive me."

"You need not remind me of that, signor," returned Guiseppe, "for I think, although I have never before now been connected with you, I think I know your character well."

"Ay," said our hero, "who does not know the character of Allesandro Massaroni, the brigand chief? But a truce with this, for it is not to the purpose. You will still continue on the watch, Guiseppe, and give me timely notice if anything should occur which it may be important for me to know?"

"I will not fail to attend to your wishes, signor," answered Guiseppe; and after some further conversation of no importance, he took his departure, and made his way back to the villa.

"The rascal does his work well," said our hero, when he was gone, and addressing himself to Rubaldo.

"Yes," replied the latter, "I told you you would find him a useful fellow, did I not?"

"You did," answered Massaroni; "and you did not deceive me."

"It was not likely that I should attempt to do so," remarked Rubaldo; "but I must confess that I do not feel quite so sanguine as to the success of our plot as you seem to be."

"Why so?" demanded the brigand chief, impatiently.

"In the first place," returned Rubaldo, "it is quite evident that Signora Melina is most reluctant to accept of your aid; and, secondly, notwithstanding all that Guiseppe has said, it does not seem likely to me that the Prince Bianchi and the Count Alberti will fail to have plenty of troops in the chapel, where it is proposed that the ceremony is to be preformed, in case of any attack being made upon them; for it is evident that they now suspect that you are concealed somewhere in the neighbourhood, and that you have some designs against them."

"Bah!" exclaimed the brigand chief, with a frown, "what absurd fears are these. I have no patience with them. I am surprised at you, Rubaldo."

"Well," observed the latter, "there is no harm in being on our guard, I should imagine, for when we have such a desperate game to play, it is as well to use every precaution."

"True," agreed Massaroni, "and I will take good care to do so. As for the forces of the Prince and Count Alberti, I fear them not, for I have not the least doubt that our men will do their duty as they have hitherto done."

"Oh, there is not the least fear of that," said Rubaldo, "they never shrank from danger yet."

"No," said Massaroni "and their courage has been sufficiently tested in many a desperate engagement. But enough of this; the time fast approaches, and we must prepare ourselves for action."

" I need not tell you, I believe, that you will find me ready and willing at any moment ?" said Rubaldo.

" I am very well convinced of that," replied Massaroni ; " oh, how I long to have my revenge on those who so long have thirsted for my blood."

" Fear not," returned Rubaldo, " they will not escape you."

" I will take good care that they shall not," said the brigand chief. " The fools! they dare to threaten Massaroni ? They little suspect that he is so near at hand, and that he is fully aware of all their actions. As for the Count Alberti, I have a long account to settle with him, and I will not rest until I have received ample satisfaction for the manner in which he has dared to set my power at defiance, and he has made full atonement to the unfortunate Olympia for the wrongs he has done her."

" Ay," said Rubaldo, "it is time that he was made to answer for his villany."

" It is," said Massaroni ; " but retribution will overtake him, perhaps sooner than he expets."

They now changed the subject, and continued in conversation till the lateness of the hour warned them that it was time to retire to rest.

The time passed swiftly away, and it now wanted but two short days to the time on which it was fixed the unholy marriage of the Count Alberti and Melina was to take place. The anguish of her feelings increased every moment, and it was in vain that she endeavoured to encourage the least ray of hope ; there was not the least prospect of escape, and her fate appeared to be irrevocably sealed. Floretta was constantly with her ; and had it not been for her soothing conversation, she must have sunk under the weight of grief and despair.

On the Saturday morning the Prince Bianchi again demanded to see her, and when she entered the apartment where he was awaiting her, with a trembling step, and a palpitating heart, she found the hated Count Alberti seated by his side, and he had evidently taken more than usual pains to set off his fine manly person to the best advantage. He arose on her entrance, and was advancing towards her, but she shrunk back with a feeling of abhorrence which she found it impossible to conceal, and the prince coming forward took her hand, and to her confusion and dismay led her to a seat which was placed between himself and the count, and for a few moments he watched the expression of her countenance, which so plainly revealed the violent and torturing emotions which were passing in her breast, in silence, whilst Alberti fixed upon her the most bold looks of admiration, which brought the blushes of shame and indignation in her cheeks.

" Melina," said her uncle, at length," I sent for you, that yourself, the Count Alberti, and myself might have one decided interview ere the time arrives which finally decides your fate, and which you are aware will be on Monday next at the hour of midnight. Nay, do not shudder, girl, and avert your eyes ; it is too late to trifle now, and you will find that I am still determined to fulfil that which I have so frequently promised."

" Then, my lord," said our heroine, in a firm and solemn voice, at the same time she fixed a reproachful glance upon him, which, however, he beheld unmoved, " then, my lord," she repeated, in still firmer accents than before, " you cruelly doom me to misery and shame, and would be far more merciful were you to take my life."

The Count Alberti could not conceal his mortification and indignation as she gave utterance to these words, and he arose hastily from his chair, and walking to the other side of the room, he folded his arms across his chest, and listened to the discussion that ensued between our heroine and the Prince Bianchi, with the greatest impatience.

" Melina," said the Prince, " you are a silly, headstrong girl, and try my patience too far. What mean you by saying that I doom you to misery and shame, and that too in presence of the Count Alberti, your future husband ?"

" My husband !" repeated Melina, with a look of increased disgust ; " oh, never! never! Though you may force me to the altar with him, I will never own allegiance to him, I will never acknowledge him for my husband. I have never, my lord, sought for an instant to conceal from the Count Alberti the feelings of repugnance, to call it by no harsher name, that I entertain towards him, for I am no hypocrite ; those feelings must ever remain the same, and here in his presence I repeat my sentiments."

" Girl !" cried her uncle, sternly, and stamping his foot with passion, " the boldness of this language and to me, your uncle, andr your guardian, is unbearable. Recall you words, or you may have bitter cause to repent it when too late."

" I have nothing to recall, my lord," replied our heroine, firmly, and with the most perfect calmness ; " I speak the language of truth, and if it sound harsh and ungrateful to your ears, you have no one but yourself to blame, since it is your severe conduct towards me which calls it forth, when I would fain speak nothing but the language of duty and of reverence to you. Oh, my uncle, I venture to make one more, one final, one earnest appeal to you for pity and forbearance. I cannot love the man whom you would force me to wed ; my soul shudders at the bare idea. Think then what bitter cause you will have to reproach yourself ever afterwards for having consigned me to such unspeakable misery, for having doomed me to a fate more abhorrent to my feelings than any other I can imagine."

The Count Alberti could contain himself no longer, and advancing hastily towards her, while his face was flushed with rage, he exclaimed—

"Signora Melina, you treat me most harshly, most severely, most ungenerously; were I even the greatest villain in existence you could not apply more insulting, more scornful language to me. What has been my conduct that I should deserve such treatment as this?"

"My lord," replied Melina, in the same firm, calm tone, "it is not my province to canvass your conduct, since I have no control, neither do I wish to do, over your actions. It is sufficient for me to state the sentiments I entertain towards you, since my happiness is at stake; them I have candidly expressed; and if you possess a spark of manly pride or honour, you will at once abandon your hopes, and cease to persecute me with a suit which, I repeat, is so odious to me."

"Signora Melina," ejaculated Alberti, in a voice half choked with resentment; "you cannot mean what you say. I will never believe that one so lovely and so gentle——"

"Hold, my lord," interrupted Melina, with a look of scorn; "I will not listen to any fulsome flattery from your lips. I am not in the habit of giving utterance to that which I do not mean. Let that answer suffice you. I wish to say no more."

"Forbear, my lord, to argue with her," said the Prince Bianchi, "but leave me to combat with that stubborn spirit until the bonds of matrimony shall have placed her under your authority, which, by all the saints, I swear shall take place at the time I have appointed on Monday next. Melina, this heroic display is useless, and you ought long ere this to have been convinced of it, and obediently resign yourself to your fate, for it is unavoidable. I tell you, girl, that there is no hope for you, and the continuance of such conduct as that which you have all along displayed, will not fail to bring down my everlasting indignation on your head. You should be grateful to the Count Alberti, for bearing so patiently with you, when the observations you have made use of were sufficient to arouse his utmost resentment."

"My lord," returned Melina, "I have no wish to insult or wound the feelings of his lordship, but surely I must be permitted boldly, openly to speak my mind on a subject in which my happiness and all my future hopes are involved. Why subject me to the torture of this meeting? Suffer me to retire, and indulge in the anguish of my feelings alone."

The Prince Bianchi frowned upon her, and

for a few seconds so excited and confounded was he by the determination of her manner that he could not give utterance to a single word.

"Of what avail is all this obduracy and stubbornness of spirit?" he at length said; "it can do you no possible good; it will not release you from the doom to which I have consigned you, and for which you will at some future time have ample cause to be grateful to me."

"Oh, my lord," sighed Melina, at the same time bursting into a copious flood of tears, which she could no longer restrain; "how different was the language you formerly used to me that you now address to me. I can scarcely believe the evidence of my senses; I can with difficulty persuade myself that it is my uncle who is speaking to me. Then affection, and the fondest indulgence dictated all your observations and conduct towards me, and Heaven knows full well that I never wilfully abused that generous kindness, but on the contrary, made it my constant study to see how I could adequately evince my full sense of the affection and attention so lavishly bestowed upon me. What then has caused this deplorable change to come over your sentiments regarding me? What have I done to turn the current of your affections? If I have in any way committed myself and rendered myself deserving of your censure and ill will, I solemnly swear that it has been done in perfect unconsciousness. Acquaint me then, my lord, with the head and front of my offending, I most humbly but earnestly beseech you, and God knows how readily I will make to you all the atonement in my power."

The Prince Bianchi was indeed staggered by the earnestness of her manner, and seemed at a loss for two or three minutes to return any answer; but at length conquering his feelings as well as he could, and re-assuming his former tone of sternness and decision, he said—

"It is no province of mine, girl, nor will I condescend to reply to your interrogatories. It is quite sufficient for me that you have revolted against my authority, and opposed my will, and I should be degrading myself were I to yield to your silly caprices. You have presumed to insult his lordship, the Count Alberti, in my presence, and think you that I will thus suffer myself to be defeated, and held up to public ridicule? No, by all the saints, I swear that that which I have promised shall be fulfilled to the very letter."

"Oh, what a fatal infatuation is this which has taken possession of your reason, my lord," said our heroine. "Can you so heartlessly consign me to a fate than which there is not one I look upon with so much horror and repugnance? But you will not do so, notwithstanding all that you have said; I cannot believe that you will ever become insensible to the dictates of reason, humanity, and justice, as to do so."

"What folly it is, Melina," said her uncle, impatiently, " to encourage any such fallacious hopes. Do you look upon me as some weak and undecided fool, that you should flatter yourself with the erroneous idea you have just expressed ? If you do, I pity you, for how painful will be your disappointment, of which you will be thoroughly convinced, before many hours have elapsed."

"Then, my lord," replied Melina, resolutely, and fixing upon him a look which ought to have penetrated to his heart and made the deepest impression upon his feelings, " my fate be upon your head, for again I solemnly swear that I will never survive the cruel degradation to which you would sacrifice me."

"Signora Melina," ejaculated the Count Alberti, totally unable to conceal the indignation which her observations had created in his breast ; "how have I deserved this ?—You treat me unjustly, uncharitably, and had you—"

"Hold, my lord," interrupted Melina, proudly ; "I will not listen to any explanations on your part, which can make not the least impression on my mind, and which can only lead to a discussion which would be painful and unsatisfactory to us both. You know the sentiments I entertain towards you ; I have taken no pains to disguise them from you, and if you possess the slightest particle of that manly honour and dignity to which you lay claim, you will urge me no further, but on the contrary, will at once abandon your designs, which are so obnoxious to my feelings, and release me from that persecution, which I must say his cruel and unnatural in the extreme. Of this, however, be assured that, should my uncle persist in forcing me to the altar with you, I will not survive the sacrifice many days, and that my fate will rest upon your head, and pursue you with torture and disgrace to the end of your existence."

"Obstinate girl !" exclaimed the Prince Bianchi, in a state of the greatest excitement, " will nothing arouse you to reason and obedience ?"

"Will nothing, my lord," returned Melina with calm dignity, " will nothing arouse you to a sense of justice and humanity ?—I wish to speak to you with every respect, but when I find you are determined to act with so much severity, that nothing whatever will excite you to forbearance, my patience becomes exhausted, and I perhaps speak more unguardedly than my feelings might otherwise dictate."

The prince again frowned upon her, but was unable to return any immediate answer, and took two or three hasty strides across the room. At length he turned to her, and said, in the same stern and unbending accents—

"My patience is exhausted; it will not suffer me to listen to you any longer, girl ; get you gone to your own room, and there prepare yourself for the ceremony, which shall, in spite of all resistance, take place on Monday next at midnight."

"My mind is made up, my lord," said our heroine in the same resolute tones that she had assumed all along ; " if you persist in dooming me to become the wife of the Count Alberti, you sentence me to a certain and untimely death."

"We shall see all about that," replied the Prince Bianchi with an air of the utmost indifference, but which he was, nevertheless, far from experiencing. " My lord," he continued, turning to Alberti, who was standing with his arms folded across his chest at the farther end of the room, and unable to conceal the extreme agitation and excitement of his feelings ; " I trust to your good sense and forbearance to take no heed of the bold and insolent observations of this silly and thoughtless girl. It may be enough for you to know the understanding that exists between us, and to rest assured likewise that every promise I have made I will fulfil to the very letter."

"I am satisfied, your highness," returned the Count Alberti, disguising his chagrin as well as he could ; " and I trust that the Signora Melina will be induced to think better of this, and to change the sentiments she is now pleased to express towards me, and of which I believe myself to be so totally unworthy."

Melina fixed upon him a look of the most unmitigated scorn and hatred, but did not condescend to reply, and Floretta having been summoned to attend her, she courtesied to her uncle, and was permitted to retire from the apartment.

CHAPTER XXXVII.

THE CRISIS.

THE racking thoughts which disturbed the mind of the hapless Melina during the brief period which was to elapse ere her fate was to be decided, needs no description from us, and it required all the eloquent exertions of the faithful Floretta to be put into full play to keep her like anything within the bounds of reason. To become the wife of such a man as the Count Alberti, was so perfectly monstrous in the bare thought, that she could scarcely contemplate it with the least degree of patience, and the longer she reflected upon the conduct of her uncle, the more harsh and unnatural did it appear to be. Her mind now wavered as regarded her rejection of the offered aid of the brigand chief, and she almost wished that she could have some communication with him, though she did not believe, knowing his character so well, that, in spite of her objections, he would readily be induced to abandon his designs; and she had very little doubt that he and his daring band were still concealed somewhere in the neighbourhood, and only awaiting the opportunity to carry his plans into effect.

In that opinion, Floretta, as might have been expected, fully coincided, and she continued to express herself warmly upon the subject.

"Massaroni," she observed, "is a bold and honourable man, notwithstanding the questionable character of his callings, and I am sure,

MASSARONI AND RUBALDO IN THEIR MOUNTAIN RETREAT.

signora, if I were placed in your situation, I should not hesitate a moment to accept of his generous and disinterested offer. Signor Colville no doubt approves of his designs, and would be greatly disappointed should you suffer any false scruples to interpose between you and escape from the cruel and unnatural fate with which you are threatened; and I am sure, for my own part, I consider it would be little short of madness for you to reject the offers which are held out to you."

"Alas, Floretta," replied Melina, "I

scarcely know how to act—my mind is distracted."

"Surely you cannot deem anything half so terrible, my lady," remarked Floretta, "as to become the wife of a man whom you so thoroughly detest and despise as the Count Alberti?"

"Oh, no, no, no," said our heroine, with a shudder; "a thousand deaths would be even far more preferable."

"And think of the anguish and despair to which Signor Clairville would be subjected when he knew that you were lost to him for ever, and that you were sacrificed to such a man as Alberti."

"Alas!" sighed our heroine, "I cannot bear to think of it with any degree of patience or fortitude. Oh, Florio, beloved Florio, what a cruel destiny is ours. Shall we never behold each other again?"

"Oh, yes," replied Floretta, "I feel convinced that you will, and that you will yet be happy, if you will only follow my advice."

"Indeed, I fear," returned Melina, "that happiness, real happiness, is never fated to be my lot in this world,"

"Do not say so, dear signora," remarked her faithful attendant; "for it would be arraigning the mercy and justice of the Supreme to imagine for a moment that He would ever doom one so good and innocent as yourself to perpetual misery. Ah, no, signora, I cannot think it, indeed I cannot."

"I thank you, Floretta, most sincerely," said her mistress, "for your praise-worthy exertions in endeavouring to inspire me with hope; but, indeed, I cannot entertain it, especially when I review all the dark circumstances of my melancholy case. My uncle has become quite insensible to all those feelings of pity and humanity for which his character was at one time so pre-eminent; he has turned a deaf ear to all my expostulations, and seems to feel an unnatural spirit of exultation at my misery and despair. It is useless to appeal to him again, and but a few hours, only a few brief hours, will elapse ere my fate will be decided, and I shall be rendered one of the most wretched and degraded of beings in existence."

"It cannot be, signora," said her attendant confidently and soothingly, "Providence will never permit it. Courage, dear lady, courage, and I do not despair of yet seeing you enabled to defeat the designs of those who prove themselves to be your enemies; nay, more, to see you the happy wife of Signor Florio Clairville, who is every way so worthy of you"

"Alas! alas!" sighed our heroine, "I dare not flatter myself with any such sanguine hopes, for the disappointment would be much greater than I could find strength to support. Even

though I should be rescued from the revolting fate which is at present impending over me, the prince my uncle would never, I am certain, give his consent to my nuptials with one who is so far beneath me in rank and fortune, though he is my equal in intrinsic qualifications."

Floretta could not but inwardly admit the reason and justice of these observations, and she was at a loss to return any answer, and after some further conversation, she left her to attend to some particular business, and our heroine abandoned herself to those dismal thoughts, to which the danger and misery of her situation naturally gave rise.

Time flew swiftly away, and at length the fatal and much dreaded Monday arrived, and Melina was informed by Floretta that all the preparations in the chapel for the marriage ceremony were completed, and that the Prince Bianchi and the Count Alberti were closetted together. It would be quite impossible to do adequate justice to the sufferings which our unfortunate heroine endured that day; it was only surprising that her strength did not sink under the poignant anguish of her feelings altogether. Floretta never left her for a moment, and she did all that was in her power to console her, and inspire her with the hope that Providence would yet interpose to save her; but it was all to no purpose, and the poor girl counted the few short hours that must intervene between her and the consummation of her so much dreaded fate, with feelings of the greatest anguish, suspense, and despair. She felt surprised that neither the prince or Alberti desired to see her during the day; but as the evening approached, Floretta received a summons to attend Bianchi, and she had no doubt that it was something relating to the intended nocturnal marriage between her mistress and the Count Alberti. After she had quitted the room, Melina sank on her knees and offered up her fervent supplications to Heaven for its mercy and protection in her critical situation. Floretta was not absent long, and her mistress saw plainly from the expression of her countenance on her return that the intelligence she had to communicate was not of the most pleasant description.

"Now, Floretta," she demanded, "you have seen the prince, my uncle, have you not?"

"I have, signora," answered her attendant, "and the Count Alberti also."

"Ah! and what did they say to you?"

"They inquired particularly as to the state of your mind, signora," said Floretta, "and commanded me to tell you to prepare yourself for the ceremony, which is to take place precisely at the hour of midnight."

"Oh, this is most cruel—'tis monstrous!"

ejaculated Melina; "will nothing move them to relent?"

"I fear not, signora," replied Floretta. "But I have something more to communicate, which probably may be of the utmost importance to you."

"Ah!" exclaimed our heroine eagerly; "what is that? what do you mean?"

"We had better speak low, my dear lady," observed Floretta, "for we do not know who might be listening to us, and any discovery of that which I am about to impart to you, might be fraught with the greatest danger."

"Do not keep me in suspense, my good girl, I beg of you," said Melina. "What is the intelligence you have to communicate?"

"On leaving the prince and the Count Alberti," answered Floretta, "I accidentally encountered Guiseppe, whom, by-the-by, I never entertained a very high opinion of, and he seemed as if he wished to speak to me, but was afraid. He placed his finger on his lips significantly, as if to enjoin me to silence, and then hastily putting this note into my hand, he hurriedly made his exit, without giving me time to say a word."

Floretta now produced the note to which she had just alluded, which Melina took hastily from her, and glanced eagerly at the superscription, at the same time exclaiming—

"This is the hand-writing of Massaroni; did you not recognise it, Floretta?"

"I did, signora," answered Floretta.

"What can he now have to communicate?" said our heroine in a faltering voice.

"Good news, I trust, my dear signora," answered her attendant; "he is evidently close at hand, and has not forgotten his promise. Courage, my lady, and depend upon it you will yet be rescued from the fate with which you are threatened, if you will but accept of those services so generously and disinterestedly offered."

Melina made no reply, and hastily opening the note, read the following few lines:—

"Let not the Signora Melina give way to despair; Massaroni is still her faithful friend, and will rescue her from the fate with which she is threatened, at the hazard of his life, if she will but put her trust in him. Courage, lady, and the clouds which now obscure the horizon of your happiness, shall quickly be dispersed, and you shall be restored to the arms of one who so fondly loves you, and to whom I believe you are so devotedly attached. My plans are all matured and ripe for action, and their success is all but certain. At the hour of midnight you may expect me. Prepare yourself to act with resolution and decision, and trust to the honour of ALLESANDRO MASSARONI."

"Daring man!" ejaculated Melina, when she had perused the note, "what would he do? Whither has he concealed himself, and by what means does he think to carry his designs into execution?"

"No doubt, signora, as he says," replied her attendant, "that his plans are all well matured, and that he is confident of their success. Be firm, and all will yet be well."

"But I cannot, indeed, I cannot avail myself of his offers, notwithstanding the feeling of generosity and honour in which they are made," said Melina. "There is something repugnant to me in the thought, and I cannot divest it from my mind."

"Pardon me, signora," remarked Floretta; "but this is no time for hesitation, and the Prince Bianchi and the Count Alberti will have themselves to blame entirely for the course you will be thus driven to adopt. You must be rescued from the revolting fate with which you are threatened, at all hazards."

"Alas! alas!" sighed our heroine; "how painful, how torturing is the alternative. I tremble as the hour approaches, for it seems to my imagination as if something terrible was about to happen; and should any resistance be offered to the brigand chief, which doubtless there will be, the consequences to my uncle may be of the most fatal description. Heaven direct me how to act. Oh, Florio, would that I had been able to see you ere this, that I might have consulted with you, and considered in what manner it was best to act.'

"Fear not, signora," said Floretta, "Providence will protect you, and counteract the dangers and evils which you now apprehend. Unless you accept of the aid of Massaroni your doom is sealed, and surely nothing can be more horrible or revolting than even the bare contemplation of that."

Melina reflected deeply for a few minutes, and then fresh courage seemed to animate her.

"Yes," she said, as a sudden thought seemed to flash upon her brain; "it must be so; I have no other alternative but misery and degradation.—Heaven knows how gladly I would avoid this desperate course to which I am advised; but the prince, my uncle, is inexorable, and he therefore leaves me no choice."

"True, signora," said her attendant; "you have then made up your mind to throw yourself upon the protection of Allesandro Massaroni?"

"Yes," replied Melina, "I see that there is nothing else left for me, and I hope that the Almighty will pardon me for a step to which I am driven by hard necessity alone."

"Oh, fear not, my dear lady," said Floretta; "who shall dare to blame you, or to question the purity of your motives? You may depend upon the strict honour of the brigand chief, I am confident; besides, will you not be under the protection of Signor Clairville? and the very idea of your beholding him again ought to inspire you with fresh courage.''

"It does!'' returned Melina; "I will be firm, and endeavour to await the result of my fate with patience and resignation.''

"Well spoken, signora,'' said Floretta; "and take my word for it, all will yet turn out far better, than you now anticipate.''

"God grant that it may,'' ejaculated our heroine, fervently, "and that I may soon be able to bring about a reconciliation with my misguided uncle.''

"Oh, I entertain the most sanguine hopes that you will be able to do so, signora,'' observed Floretta. "The loss of you will no doubt soon bring him to his senses, and he will only be too happy to abandon his designs and to release you from the odious addresses of the Count Alberti.''

"Could I but feel certain that such would be the case I might even now be comparatively happy,'' said Melina; "but should the brigand chief fail, how terrible would doubtless be the consequences to us all.''

"Do not give way to any such apprehensions,'' said Floretta, "for depend upon it they will not be realised. Massaroni, no doubt, has well laid his plans, and you know full well that it is not often he has suffered defeat.''

"Very true,'' coincided Melina; "and so it appears that the man, Guiseppe, who has been for some time in the service of my uncle, is in the plot?''

"Certainly,'' said Floretta. "Massaroni could not very well accomplish his designs without the assistance of one or more of the domestics. It strikes me that he is even now concealed somewhere in the villa.''

"Do you indeed think so?'' said Melina. "He surely would not venture so much.''

"I do not doubt it for a moment, signora,'' returned Floretta; "nay, more, that he has a trusty portion of his daring band close at hand, ready to fly to his assistance at a moment's notice.''

"But how could they gain admittance to the villa without being discovered?'' asked our heroine.

"Oh, I have no doubt that Guiseppe would be able to manage that part of the business,'' replied Floretta. "But is your mind made up, signora?''

"It is,'' replied her mistress; "for though I would gladly have adopted any other means to escape from the cruel and revolting fate which is at present impending over me, I see no prospect of my being enabled to do so. Would that the time on which so much depends had arrived, and that I might no longer be kept in suspense. Oh, my uncle, what misery and anxiety has your obstinate determination been productive of!''

In this manner another hour passed away, and the anxiety of our heroine's mind increased every moment; it requiring the exertion of all the energies of Floretta to keep up her fortitude to meet the severe trial to which she was so shortly to be subjected. The hour of midnight fast approached; but all was silent in the villa; and no one could imagine for a moment that such an important event was on the eve of taking place.

In the meantime, lights were burning on the altar, and several of the domestics had already assembled, and awaited the arrival of the expected bride and bridegroom with the utmost impatience. The priest, who was in the pay of the Prince Bianchi, was also present.

Bianchi and the Count Alberti had been seated together all the afternoon, and awaited the arrival of the time they had fixed on for the unnatural ceremony to take place with the greatest impatience; but as the hour approached, the prince could not help feeling some strange and unaccountable misgivings, and, notwithstanding all his efforts to the contrary, the Count Alberti was far from easy or confident.

"I think all our arrangements are complete, your highness?'' he said.

"Quite so,'' answered Bianchi.

"And yet,'' said his companion, "I heartily wish that the ceremony was over, and that there was no longer any fear of interruption.''

"And what reason is there now to fear any?'' demanded the prince; "there is no one but ourselves and our domestics in the villa—and it is not likely that they will venture to interrupt us—and what motive could they have in doing so?''

"Oh, it is not them I fear or suspect,'' said the Count Alberti.

"Who, then?'' asked his companion, hastily.

"Alessandro Massaroni!'' replied Alberti. "I cannot banish the idea from my mind that he is somewhere lurking in the neighbourhood.''

"And if he should be, do you think he would be bold enough to make an attack upon us, when he sees the precautions we have adopted, and which must lead to his certain defeat?'' demanded Bianchi.

"I know not,'' answered the count, "for the brigand chief, as we have often enough experienced, is bold and daring enough for anything.''

"Your fears are groundless, count, depend upon it,'' remarked Bianchi. "But come, time presses—it is now nearly eleven o'clock, and it will be as well to summon Melina into our presence previous to our repairing to the chapel. Are you prepared to meet her, my lord?''

"I am," answered the latter, "though I have no doubt she will meet me with her usual scorn and expressions of hatred. I would make any sacrifice, could I but obtain merely her esteem."

"Have patience, my lord, and no doubt, obdurate though she at present be, when she finds that her fate is sealed, she will endeavour to resign herself to it, and that you will soon be enabled to win her to your wishes."

"I trust that your highness' predictions will be verified," said the count, "for then indeed should I be one of the happiest men in existence. But had you not better summon your fair niece into our presence?"

"I will do so immediately," replied the prince, and ringing the bell, Floretta shortly made her appearance, and awaited to receive his commands which were promptly delivered to her.

The Signora Melina in the meantime, in her chamber, awaited with a palpitating heart, and the greatest anxiety, the arrival of the important hour which was to decide her fate; and as it rapidly approached, she felt animated with much more fortitude and hope than could have been expected. When the bell rang for the attendance of her faithful maid, Floretta, in the apartment where the Prince Bianchi and the Count Alberti were seated, she felt very well convinced what it was for, and now it required the exercise of all her energies to maintain her fortitude for the severe trial to which she was about to be put. She sank on her knees, and once more most earnestly supplicated the protection of the Supreme.

"The fearful moment I have so long looked forward to with so much dread, has at last arrived!" she ejaculated; "and but a short time will decide my fate, and I shall either be consigned to the most insupportable misery, shame, and despair, or once more restored to hope, if not complete happiness. Father of Mercy, guide me how to act, and avert, I humbly beseech Thee, the evils which are now impending over my head. Oh, my uncle, can you still remain inflexible, and will the Count Alberti persist in forcing one to the altar, whom he is fully convinced, views him with such utter feelings of abhorrence and disgust? I can scarcely believe that they will be so cruel; and yet, after what has taken place, what right have I to expect that they will show any mercy towards me?—And will Massaroni keep his word to me?—I cannot doubt that he will, if he has the power, though I should have been much more satisfied had he been more explicit in the note he sent to me, and made me better acquainted with his plans."

She was now interrupted by the return of Floretta, of whom she eagerly inquired the purport of the message she had for her.

"Courage, my dear signora," replied her faithful attendant; "and I trust, with the blessing of Omnipotence, that all will yet terminate much more favourably than you now apprehend. The prince, your uncle, has commanded me to conduct you into his presence without delay. Do not let your fortitude forsake you, and depend upon it the time is not far distant when you will be able to look back upon the stirring events of this night without a pang of regret."

"And is all ready in the chapel?" asked the damsel eagerly.

"It is," answered Floretta, "and the priest who is engaged to perform the ceremony, is already at the altar."

"Alas!" sighed Melina, "my heart again misgives me. But is the count Alberti with the prince."

Floretta replied in the affirmative; and in spite of all her efforts, our heroine could not help trembling violently.

"Oh," she ejaculated, "how can I meet that odious man; how find courage to listen to his bold, disgusting observations? Floretta, this is a trial too much for human nature to bear up against with any degree of patience."

"Providence will sustain you, signora," said Floretta; "but come, the patience of his highness will be exhausted. Courage, courage, I again say, my dear lady, and all will soon be over. I will not forsake you, but will follow your footsteps through whatever fortunes it may be your lot to experience."

"Thanks, thanks, my kind and faithful Floretta," said her mistress; "without your advice and consolation I should indeed be a wretched lost being. Come; I will brave my fate let it be whatever it may."

She felt inspired with fresh courage as she gave utterance to these words, and supporting herself on the arm of Floretta, she quitted her room, and made her way to the apartment in which her uncle and the Count Albert were impatiently waiting to receive her. She paused when they arrived at the door, and made a powerful effort to summon to her aid all the firmness she could, and in which she succeeded to a marvellous extent. On entering she found the Prince Bianchi, her uncle, and the Count Alberti in deep conversation, but they arose immediately on her entrance, and fixing upon her the most earnest look, in which confusion was not unmingled, Bianchi advanced towards her, and taking her hand endeavoured to place it in that of the Count Alberti, but Melina hastily, and indignantly withdrew it, and averted her gaze with a feeling of disgust. The prince frowned, and Alberti could with difficulty control the feelings of rage and wounded pride that struggled in his haughty breast. Floretta stood by, and watched all that took place with feelings of the deepest interest and anxiety, and sincerely did her heart beat for the situation of that mistress for whom she would almost have sacrificed her very existence. At length, the Prince Bianchi, who for a few minutes had endeavoured to subdue the passion with which the contemptuous treatment of the Count Alberti by his fair and deeply persecuted niece had excited him, once more advanced towards her, and again trying to place her hand in his, which she, as before, as promptly withdrew, said—

"Melina, the hour has arrived that decides your fate; the bridegroom is present; the priest who is to join your hands awaits our arrival at the altar, and, therefore, since you see that there now is no escaping from the alliance to which my prudence and experience of the world and mankind has destined you, it is time you threw away those airs of diffidence and repugnance; it is time, I say, that——"

"My lord," interrupted Melina, in a voice, and with an air of determination; "hear me, whilst I solemnly, and in the face of High Heaven, and all that is just and reasonable, protest against this monstrous, this unholy, this unnatural sacrifice. I am but a poor, weak, and unprotected girl, since I have been deprived of that affection and consideration which the ties of consanguinity ought to have urged you to bestow upon me; still I again boldly tell you, that, if you compel me to become the wife of that man whom I so thoroughly detest, that I cannot find language sufficiently powerful to express my aversion, you doom me to infamy, to misery, to death, and my fate will be upon your head. To you, Count Alberti," she continued, fixing upon him such a look of scorn and abhorrence, that made him quail and feel his own insignificance, "I do not condescend to make any appeal, well concinced that you are totally insensible to every feeling of honour or manly pride, or you would never persist in following up a suit, which I have so frequently and candidly assured you is so revolting to my feelings; but of this I will assure you, and think not that I speak idly, if I am forced to become your wife, *in name*, it will be but to bring a curse upon your head, it will be but to——"

"Cease! rash, obdurate girl!" interrupted the Prince Bianchi, in the greatest possible state of excitement, "of what use are these observations now? Of what avail, think you, are your threats? My lord, I beseech you not to notice them."

"Beauteous Melina, my destined bride," said the Count Alberti, with the greatest difficultly subduing the chagrin under which he was smarting from the severity of her observations, "although I would not for a moment attempt to impugn your truth, I cannot bring my mind to believe that you entertain the cruel sentiments you have expressed toward me. But I will not reproach you, on the contrary, it shall be my future study, when you have become my bride, which you shortly will, to convince you of the injustice you have done me by the opinion you have formed of my character and principles."

"Your character, your principles!" retorted our heroine with a look of the most superlative contempt and disgust; "you do well to boast of them, my Lord Alberti; they are well known to the world. Your conduct towards the unfortunate Signora Olympia, and her tender offspring, your child, has stamped you in the eyes of every virtuous individual as——"

"As what?" demanded the Prince Bianchi, furiously.

"As a villain!" replied Melina, firmly, and at the same time fixing upon her uncle and the Count Alberti such a look as completely abashed them; they could neither of them help feeling the full force of the truth of her assertions.

"A villain!" at length repeated the Count Alberti, and his lips quivered while he spoke, and he could scarcely help giving full expression to the feelings of rage that struggled within his breast.

"Yes, my lord," returned Melina, "I do not recal the word, and I see plainly that your conscience acknowledges it is not misapplied. Such a term, if I am compelled to become your wife, let the consequences be whatever they may to myself, I will not fail to apply to you; and you may now therefore form a pretty correct judgment of the happiness that is in store for you from this forced, this unholy, this unnatural marriage. The actions of your highness, whom I dare no longer venture to call my uncle and my guardian, and this *nobleman*, the shameless seducer of female innocence, speak for themselves, and shun the broad glare of open day."

"Mad girl," cried the infuriated prince, "what do you mean?"

"I speak explicitly enough, my lord, I should imagine," replied our heroine, firmly. "If your consciences did not tell you you were acting wrong, why this secret, this midnight marriage? Is it thus that so solemn a ceremony should be performed in which the niece of the Prince Bianchi, the governor of Rome, is concerned?"

"Bah!" exclaimed Bianchi, passionately, "I have no longer patience with this. Time presses. Are you prepared, my lord?"

"I am, your highness," answered the Count Alberti, mustering all the firmness and indifference to the observations of Melina that he could command.

"Enough," said Bianchi, grasping the wrist of Melina with a vehemence that almost made her scream; "then from my hands receive your future bride. Let us at once proceed to the altar."

"Hold, Prince Bianchi—uncle or guardian I will not now attempt, or even condescend to call you," vehemently ejaculated Melina, extricating herself from his hold, and shrinking back, at the same time fixing upon them both a look which could not fail to inspire them with feelings of shame and awe. "Count Alberti, dare not to approach me; your very touch is contamination. My lord," she added, turning to Bianchi, while the expression of her features were even more fixed and resolute than before, "I ask you now for the last time, is it your determination to sacrifice me to this man, whom I so utterly loathe that I cannot give adequate expression to my feelings of abhorrence?"

"It is," replied the Prince Bianchi, sternly; "what necessity is there for you to repeat the question?"

"Then," exclaimed our heroine, and an expression came over her features so suddenly and so powerfully, that it completely appalled Bianchi and the Count Alberti, and took them by surprise; "my determination is also fixed; may God forgive me for that act to which I am driven by desperation and injustice."

As she spoke, she suddenly drew forth a poniard, which she had had concealed under her mantle, and was about to plunge it into her bosom, when the prince and Alberti rushed simultaneously forward, and wresting it from her hand, she sank overpowered by the strength of her feelings in the arms of the faithful and terrified Floretta.

"Rash girl!" exclaimed her uncle, "what would you do?"

"Rid myself of a life which with such a man as the Count Alberti, must become hateful and insupportable to me," replied Melina; "you have failed me this time, but mark my words, I will never continue to live as the wife of one whom I detest. I told you, my lord, that, by an union so obnoxious, so hateful, so revolting to my feelings, you doomed me to a premature and violent death, and you will find, when too late, that I spoke not erroneously. My fate will rest upon your head."

The prince could return no answer, but with the Count Alberti (who was greatly excited) walked to the farther end of the room, and consulted together for a few minutes, during which brief interval, Melina was supported in the arms of Floretta, who, in whispers, sought to impart to her all the consolation that was in her power. At length the bell of Saint Peter's tolled forth a quarter to the hour of midnight, and to the ears of our unfortunate and distracted heroine it sounded like a death knell. The Prince Bianchi and his companion then turned round, and the former said—

"The time has arrived, my lord; we must not let trifles deter us from the execution of our purpose; the priest has long been waiting, and will marvel at our delay; Floretta, girl, conduct your mistress to the chapel; we will follow anon."

"I will be firm," said our heroine, looking with proud disdain and confidence upon her uncle and Alberti; "you shall not find a nerve of me shaken, since my determination is fixed. Perform your hateful and unholy ceremony, and be the consequences which will assuredly follow, upon your own heads. Come, my faithful Floretta, lead me to the sacrifice."

Thus saying, Melina took the arm of her attendant, and without so much as deigning another glance towards Bianchi or his companion, preceded by a domestic bearing a light, she quitted the room. A strange bridal procession!

"Come, my lord," said Bianchi, after a brief pause; "we tarry; in a short time all will be over, and you will have your bride secure. You look sad, count."

"I must acknowledge, your highness,' answered Alberti, "that the observations and general conduct of the Signora Melina, has greatly disconcerted me. The hatred she bears towards me is evidently most inveterate."

"Pshaw, my lord," returned the Prince Bianchi, "why let the observations of a forward and obstinate girl disturb your mind at all? When she finds that she is yours past recall, I am positive she will change her tone, and endeavour to reconcile herself to her fate."

"I would fain try to persuade myself that she would," said Alberti, in reply "but, indeed I cannot. She seems determined, and this attempt upon her life, and the threats she has subsequently held out, I confess, alarm me, and ——"

"Nonsense!" interrupted the prince, impatiently; "all will yet be well, or I will forfeit my princely dignity. To the chapel—to the chapel, my lord, and let us at once terminate this business in a manner that must be satisfactory to us both. What ho, there, fellows! lead the way! Come, my lord, your arm; I conduct you to your beauteous, though at present obdurate, bride."

The count suffered Bianchi to take his arm, though he could not banish from his mind the misgivings that had taken possession of it; and six of the male domestics, each of them bearing a torch in his hand, preceding them, they quitted the apartment, and proceeded to the chapel, where Melina, supported by Floretta, was seated in the most retired part and a number of domestics, male and female were in attendance.

The priest who was to perform the ceremony was standing behind the altar, but the cowl was drawn over his face and concealed his features, and as the Count Alberti beheld it, he could not help feeling his misgivings increase. The Prince Bianchi also felt rather surprised for the moment, but he said nothing, and advancing towards his niece, he took her arm gently and with much apparent kindness, and she suffered him without a murmur to lead her to the altar, and place her by the side of the Count Alberti, but she never once raised her eyes towards that nobleman, but stood as inanimate as a statue. A dead pause for a moment or two ensued, and all was breathless anxiety. At length Bianchi spoke—

"Holy father, how is this?" he said; "why do you not remove the cowl from your features?"

"Pardon me, your highness," replied the monk, who had to perform the ceremony, "but it is in accordance with a solemn vow I have made, and I cannot deviate from it."

"Well," said the prince, "e'en take your whim. All here present can bear witness and testify that I give my niece, the Signora Melina, whose lawful guardian I am, in marriage with his lordship, the Count Alberti. Proceed with the ceremony."

"Hold! holy father, as you would save yourself from the curse of God!" exclaimed our heroine, in a voice of most remarkable firmness, and her fine form assuming an air of dignity that was sufficient to make an impression, and to strike awe into the most insensible breast; "here before the holy altar I solemnly protest against this monstrous, this sacrilegious outrage. The man to whom the Prince Bianchi would sacrifice me, I detest, they both know it well, for I have frequently told them so; the laws of Heaven denounce such an union. Proceed then at your peril."

"Girl!" cried the prince, furiously; "do you then to the last persist in opposing my authority?"

"You have no authority over my soul's affections, my soul's welfare, my lord," answered our heroine, resolutely; "you would make me the victim of your caprice, and your own private views; I do not hesitate to tell you so, for this is no time to speak in problems; and if this holy man lends himself a willing instrument to your designs, be the consequences, as assuredly they will, upon his own head. Here stands the Count Alberti, whom you would force upon me as my husband, and I here publicly denounce him as a villain, a seducer, a libertine, a purjurer, and——"

"Melina," interrupted the Count Alberti, almost choked with rage, and covered with shame from the consciousness of guilt.

"Nay, my Lord Alberti," said Melina, "you may writhe under what I say, but you know full well I speak the truth. Where is the unfortunate and confiding Olympia, whose innocence you betrayed, and then deserted? Where is the hapless offspring of that illicit intercourse? Can you answer those questions without proclaiming yourself as I have accused you of being—a villain?"

"By Heaven!" said the excited Alberti, "this is too much for human patience to endure. The Signora Melina raves, she knows not to what she gives utterance. Are you still willing, my lord, that I should become her husband?"

"I swear by all the saints that she shall," replied the Prince Bianchi, "and who is there that dare dispute my authority? Again I command you, holy father, to proceed with the ceremony."

"Pardon me, your highness," replied the monk, "but——"

"What!" interrupted Bianchi, passionately; "do you dare to raise any objections, after the solemn compact you have entered into with me?"

"I never entered into any compact with your highness," returned the monk, in the same calm tone of voice.

"How!" ejaculated the astonished Bianchi, "can a man of your holy order and functions give utterance to so atrocious a falsehood."

"I speak the truth, Prince Bianchi," replied the monk; "I entered into no compact with you, and I will never be a party in sacrificing an innocent maiden to one who is unworthy of her, and whom it is evident she hates and despises."

"Can I hear aright?" said the enraged Bianchi; "have you then deceived me?"

"I have, indeed, my lord," answered the monk, in the same composed and quiet manner.

"There is treason afloat," cried the Count Alberti; "we are betrayed!"

"Reveal your features!" commanded the Prince Bianchi, "or——"

"Do not irritate yourself, Prince Bianchi," said the supposed monk, in a very different tone of voice to that which he had hitherto assumed; "you wish to see my features; behold! Allesandro Massaroni was never afraid of exposing them to a villain yet!"

As he spoke, he threw aside his monkish garb, and the brigand chief stood revealed to the astonished eyes of all present. Melina uttered a faint scream, and staggered back into the arms of Floretta, while the Prince Bianchi and the Count Alberti were so completely taken by surprise that they stood as inanimate as statues. Massaroni laughed ironically and triumphantly, and springing forward from the place where he had been standing, he was advancing towards our heroine, when Bianchi and the count intercepted him.

"It is the mountain chief, the brigand, the lawless thief, the cutthroat," said the former, furiously; "he has acknowledged himself to be so; a price is set upon the rascal's head;—seize him!"

"Be not too hasty, Excellenza," said the brigand chief with the most consummate coolness, and at the same time drawing his sword; "there are two words to be said to that bargain; Massaroni never comes unprovided, you may depend upon it;—stand back, knaves! I command you, for the first that stirs an inch, or

MASSARONI SHOWING RUBALDO THE PORTRAIT OF HIS MOTHER.

offers to raise the least alarm, is a dead man. The plain and simple fact is this, Prince Bianchi, you would sacrifice your fair and innocent niece to yon trembling scoundrel, and that I am determined to prevent, at all hazards; since it seems that you have forgotten your duty towards her, I must e'en take her under my protection until you have learnt justice and humanity."

"Summon the troops outside!" exclaimed

frightful in the extreme, the brigands being prepared to encounter anything while their chief led the way, and the troops being completely daunted by the indomitable courage of those desperate men against whom they were opposed. Many a lifeless corse strewed the ground, while the loss which the brigands sustained was small indeed compared with that of their opponents. At last the soldiers were compelled to give way, notwithstanding the superiority of their numbers, and retired with precipitation to the place from whence they had come.

"Now, by the dome of Saint Peters," said Massaroni, turning to Rubaldo, "I have as good a mind as ever I had in my life, to make another and more bold attack upon the villa, and to wreak my vengeance upon the heads of all who have dared to foil me in my designs."

"Nay, captain," observed Rubaldo, "pardon me, but I cannot help giving it as my opinion that that would be rash and impolitic in the extreme, under the present circumstances."

"Tut, man," returned the brigand chief, impatiently, "is not the main object of our expedition, which has cost us so much trouble, thwarted? Has not the Signora Melina been prevented from being placed under my protection?"

"Very true," answered Rubaldo, "but another opportunity may speedily present itself; besides, the wound you have inflicted upon the Count Alberti, and which I think is not unlikely to prove mortal, will prevent the marriage taking place, and thus, at any rate one of your principal objects will be attained."

"To be thus defeated," said Massaroni, biting his lips, and exhibiting other signs of the greatest impatience. "Cospetto! I can scarcely endure the thought with any degree of patience. I have now as good a mind as ever I possessed in my life to——"

"Nay nay," interrupted Rubaldo; "do not anything rash. Come, let us leave this spot, for we know not what danger may threaten us by loitering here,"

"Danger!" repeated our hero, "have you known Allesandro Massaroni all these years, Rubaldo, and yet imagine him to be acquainted with fear, or to tremble at the idea of danger? P'sha! it is but a waste of breath and time to talk to me thus. Besides, what think you that Clairville, that my Maria, that all of those who are left behind in our mountain retreat, will say to us on our return?"

"That we have acted as well as circumstances would permit us," replied Rubaldo. "Our plans were well laid, and well conducted, and had not fortune, over which we have no control, frowned upon us, nothing could possibly have prevented them from being successful. Come, come, captain, do not excite yourself unnecessarily in this manner; although we have now failed, I do not for a moment doubt that another time we shall be more successful, and that your wishes as regards the fair Signora Melina will be gratified to the fullest extent."

"That Melina should escape me, after all my plans were so well laid for her rescue from the fate with which she was threatened, vexes me more than all," remarked the brigand chief; "but I swear that I will never rest until I have fully accomplished my object, and restored her to the arms of the man who, from all that I have seen of him, I believe to be so worthy of her."

"In that determination I agree with you, captain," said Rubaldo, "and I think I need not assure you that, in any future designs you may form, you shall have my most willing and ablest co-operation."

"I am convinced of that, Rubaldo," returned our hero; "but the Count Alberti;—think you the wound I inflicted upon him is likely to prove mortal?"

"It seems to me very probable," answered Rubaldo, "and thus, at any rate, you will have the satisfaction of knowing that from this expedition you have at least gratified your revenge."

"Very true," said Massaroni, "but still I must confess that I would much rather have got him in my power. Villain even though he has been to the Signora Olympia, I fear that she will much regret what has befallen him. But you are satisfied, Rubaldo, that it was no fault of mine?"

"Certainly," replied his lieutenant; "he rushed madly upon his own fate, and he must pay the penalty of his rashness. But come, let us proceed, for it is perfectly useless remaining here."

The brigand chief cast another anxious look towards the villa, and then without saying another word to Rubaldo, he moved from the spot, and the band following, taking the most unfrequented route, they were soon far away from the neighbourhood of the Villa Rosa.

CHAPTER XXXVIII.

THE RAGE OF THE PRINCE BIANCHI.—THE CRITICAL SITUATION OF THE COUNT ALBERTI, SIGNORA MELINA, AND FLORETTA.

THE consternation which prevailed in the villa after the startling and unexpected events which we have related in the previous chapter, was of the most intense description, and it was some time before any of the principal actors in it could at all recover themselves. Our heroine, perfectly insensible, was removed to her own apartment, and the Count Alberti being conveyed to a chamber, a surgeon was called in without the least delay, in order to see to the injury he had received, and to apply such remedies as his skill might suggest. He found that he had received a wound of the most dangerous nature, and although he was not very explicit in the answers he gave to the questions that were put to him, it was quite evident that he considered his life to be placed in the most imminent danger. For more than an hour he remained in a state of perfect unconsciousness; and when he did recover, it was plain that he was labouring under the most excruciating agony. However, he seemed to be but little aware of what had absolutely taken place, and the surgeon who attended him strictly prohibited all persons from holding any conversation with him. But how shall we describe the state of the Prince Bianchi's mind? For some minutes after the scene which we have described to have taken place in the chapel, and the retreat of Massaroni and his determined band, he stood in a complete state of stupefaction and it was not till after he had been aroused, that he could form any lucid idea of what had absolutely taken place; then, suddenly starting round, he exclaimed to those who were in attendance—

" Where is my niece? Where is the Count Alberti?"

" Your niece, my lord," answered one of the principal attendants, " is just removed in an insensible state to her chamber; and his lordship, the Count Alberti, who is badly wounded, is also conveyed to his own apartment, and is under the care of the surgeon."

" Ah!" exclaimed the prince, starting, and exhibiting considerable emotion; " I remember all now. Dastards! Knaves! Why did you suffer the villain, Massaroni, to escape? My hopes to be thus annihilated; my designs frustrated; (by Heaven, I shall go mad!— What are you all standing here for, staring at me like idiots?—Why do you not go in pursuit of the brigand chief, the murderer and robber?"

" Pardon me, your highness," said the domestic who had before spoken, " but an overwhelming body of troops are now attacking the brigands outside the villa, and I should imagine that there can be but little doubt on which side victory will determine."

" Ah!" cried Bianchi, with a look of satisfaction, " that is well; if they can only succeed in securing the brigand chief alive, so that I may have the full gratification to my revenge, I shall be satisfied. I can never rest until I have seen him expire in the most lingering and excruciating tortures, for all the miseries that he has caused me. Ah! I hear they are at it. The reports of their pistols, and the shouts of those engaged in the deadly conflict, smite my ears. By the mass, I cannot remain inactive here. I must mingle amongst them, and—"

" Nay, my good lord, your Excellenza," said the domestic, venturing to lay his hand upon his arm; " pardon me for my boldness in advising you to remain where you are, or to retire to your own room; the danger that is abroad you should not enter into."

" Danger!" repeated Bianchi, passionately, " who dare venture to talk to the Prince Bianchi of danger, especially when he has so much at stake?"

He was about to proceed when he was interrupted by the entrance of several of the soldiers who had been engaged with the brigands outside, and the officer who had been in command of them, and who was wounded, advanced towards him.

" How now, Signor Geronimo?" demanded the Prince Bianchi, hastily; " you are bleeding, what success?"

" I am sorry to inform your highness," replied Geronimo, " that the brigands have defeated us, and that we thought it prudent to retreat, in order that we might save any further sacrifice of human life."

" Retreat! cowards, dastards!" cried the Prince Bianchi, furiously, " and have you then suffered the brigand chief, Allésandro Massaroni, to escape?"

Geronimo returned no answer, but his looks sufficiently replied in the affirmative.

" Now, by all my hopes," ejaculated Bianchi, in a hoarse voice; " I would sooner, much sooner, have sacrificed a fortune, than that this should have occurred. You far outnumbered them, and it must have been through either want of skill, or what is worse, arrant cowardice, that you suffered yourselves to be thus shamefully defeated."

" Your highness is rather too warm upon this subject," remarked Geronimo, with a look of offended pride, " and come too soon to hasty conclusions. There is not a man who was engaged in this combat that did not do his duty, but fortune was against us, and the consequence was that the brigands were enabled to make good their retreat."

The Prince Bianchi muttered a curse between his teeth, and folding his arms strode several times across the chapel in a most disordered manner.

" The fates have conspired against me!" he said at length; " some infernal spell is upon me, and my enemies are enabled to laugh me to scorn. By this time I had fully expected that Melina would have been the wife of the Count Alberti, and that any further opposition to my will would have been useless; but what is the difference? I cannot bear the thought! I shall go mad! Get ye gone, fellows, and leave me to my own thoughts."

Geronimo and the soldiers under his command retired, and the Prince Bianchi continued to pace the chapel for a few minutes longer; communing with himself, and giving utterance at intervals to the most passionate exclamations.

"Had not your highness better retire to your own apartment?" ventured to suggest the domestic who had before spoken to him.

"Presumptuous fool!" returned Bianchi, in a stern voice; "who are you that dare thus dictate to me?"

"Pardon me, my lord, but I——"

"Begone, fellow!" interrupted Bianchi, "and in future learn your proper distance."

The man did not venture to make any reply, but retired, according to the command he had received, and the Prince Bianchi was left alone in the chapel. How different was the scene it now presented to that it did but so short a time before. In every part of it was some striking evidence of the desperate struggle which had so recently taken place within it, and as the prince gazed upon them his excitement, and the disappointment of his feelings increased.

"To be thus foiled," he exclaimed, "when I had every prospect of the accomplishment of my designs being effected, is almost more than human patience can endure. And the Count Alberti, too, to be wounded by this daring ruffian! Should the injury he has received prove fatal, all chance of the gratification of my wishes will be at an end. But no, I must not encourage such an idea. Fortunately Melina did not fall into the power of Massaroni, or I have no doubt that a very few days would have seen her the wife of the beggar Clairville. This must and shall be prevented at all hazards. But I must see Alberti, and judge for myself as to his condition."

Thus saying, the Prince Bianchi stalked from the chapel, and made his way to the chamber in which the wounded count was lying. On his entrance, he found him in a state of utter unconsciousness, and the paleness of his countenance, and the distortion of his features from evident pain, filled him with the utmost alarm. He drew the surgeon aside, and questioned him narrowly.

"Think you there is any danger?" he demanded; "tell me candidly, and do not attempt to deceive me."

"He is wounded very severely, your highness," answered the surgeon, "but I cannot undertake to give any decided opinion at present; however, he must on no account whatever be disturbed, as the least excitement might prove fatal. I would advise your highness to retire before he recovers his sensibility, as the sight of you might be productive of the most unfortunate consequences."

"Well, I will do so," returned the prince, "but I charge you to pay him all the attention in your power, and to try everything for his recovery that your skill and experience may suggest."

"Your highness may depend on me," replied the doctor, and the Prince Bianch then retired to his own room, where he immediately summoned the attendance of Floretta, and of whom he most anxiously inquired after the condition of our heroine. Floretta informed him that she was in a very exhausted state, and that she feared it would be many days before she entirely recovered from the extraordinary excitement to which she had been exposed.

"Obstinate girl!" exclaimed the prince, passionately, "it is all her own conduct that has caused this, and has brought all those accumulated troubles upon us. She shall find, however, that I am not to be thwarted in my determination. But away, girl, and see that you pay every attention to her."

Floretta courtesied and withdrew, very glad to escape, and the Prince Bianchi then continued to pace his apartment for some time, deeply wrapped in thought. In spite of the feelings of prejudice he entertained towards the brigand chief, there was something in his appearance and manners which greatly interested him, and his features, so handsome, and intelligent, were stamped upon his memory with a force for which he was totally at a loss to account. He felt a burning curiosity to know the full particulars of his history.

"And yet," he said, as a feeling of pride came over him, "why should I feel this interest in one whom I know to be my most bitter enemy, and who for so many years has been the terror of the whole country? Psha! this is a weakness which it becomes me not to indulge in, and I should feel ashamed to find myself giving way to it. Rather let me exert all my energies to get him in my power that I may gratify my revenge against him."

Thus he continued to soliloquise for some time longer, and it was not until the first streak of day appeared in the eastern horizon that he thought about endeavouring to snatch an hour or two's repose, and then his imagination was disturbed by the most torturing dreams. Frequently he started up in his bed, and gazed vacantly in the dim light of the lamp, as some wild phantasy of his disordered brain presented itself to his mind's eye; conscience, with all its most torturing, its most goading influences, was busy at work, and drove him almost to distraction. The deeds of his past life, which he would fain have designated by the mild term of mere youthful indiscretions, started before him in appalling array, rendered doubly so by the solemnity of the hour and the awful silence which reigned around; his limbs trembled convulsively; every nerve, for the time being, was unstrung, and large drops of perspiration stood upon his quivering temples, while he almost feared to look around him, lest his eyes should encounter the ghastly objects that his affrighted imagination had conjured up. How he longed for the appearance of daylight; but at last, unable any longer to compose his mind to sleep, he left his couch, and for some time continued to pace his chamber in a state of excitement which we have no occasion to attempt to describe, as the imagination of the reader will probably be enabled to form a more correct idea of it. The startling events of the night filled him with dismay and despair; it seemed as if the fates had conspired against him, that some irresistible spell had descended upon him, and that the plans which he had so long concocted, and which he had flattered himself were on the eve of being accomplished, were now frustrated for ever. The wound which the Count Alberti had received might prove mortal; and although the brigand chief had failed, for the present, in getting Melina into his power, still, if Alberti should die, where would be the hopes that he, the Prince Bianchi, had formed? The thought was perfectly distracting, and he could not endure it with any degree of patience. And Melina too; what might not be the effect which this shock might have upon her feelings? It might render her mind a future wreck, and however much he might endeavour to quiet the voice of conscience, he could not conceal from himself the solemn and awful fact, that he should ever afterwards have to reproach himself with being the destroyer of her happiness, her prospects, her hopes, if not of her life, and this was a thought that pressed like molten lead upon his brain, and filled his mind with the greatest terror.

But did the Prince Bianchi repent sincerely of his harsh and tyrannical conduct towards his gentle niece? Did he hope for her restoration to health that he might have the opportunity of convincing her that he had abandoned his most unjust designs, and was anxious to make her all the atonement in his power for the manifold sufferings he had caused her? Oh, no, disappointment and rage were the predominant passions that held their sway at that time in his breast, and could he but have been satisfied that the Count Alberti would recover from the injuries he had received, his determination was as strong as ever to compel her to become his wife, even though he felt assured that by so doing he should condemn her to the most insupportable misery. Haughty, proud, obdurate, arrogant, and overbearing, he could not endure the least opposition to his will, and the frequent disappointments he had lately received, served but to add to the acerbity of his disposition, and to render him the more anxious to gratify his despotic will. The character of the Prince Bianchi presented many remarkable anomalies, as must have been perceived from his recent conduct, as depicured in the pages of this narrative; in fact, it was a problem it would be rather difficult to attempt to solve, though it is quite evident that two of the principal ingredients in his nature were obstinacy and arrogance.

At length, weary of remaining any longer in the solitude of his chamber, and to the torturing influence of his thoughts, Bianchi silently retired from the room, and descending the stairs with stealthy footsteps, he quitted the house, and wandered on he scarcely knew whither. Change of scene, however, did not serve to alleviate the anxiety and anguish of mind, or to quiet the voice of conscience, and every moment that anxiety and anguish, if possible, increased. The dark shadows of night were now fast dispersing, and yielding to the coming day. Gradually the gray mists that hung upon the summits of the hills faded away, and the first golden streak that heralded in the resplendent monarch of the day, appeared in the eastern horizon. Wider and wider still became the flood of light, until Sol burst forth in all his majestic glory; dispersing the dew drops that had hung upon the silken petals of the various flowers, and the green foliage of the trees, and giving new birth and vigour to the wondrous works of nature; waking up the song-birds to their sweetest melody, and shedding a bright halo of happiness on all around. But with perfect indifference did Prince Bianchi gaze upon the various beauties that were spread in such rich luxuriance before him; cold and apathetic was he to all but the troubled sea of thoughts that were raging in his mind. He continued to ramble on, and took not the least notice of anything that was passing around him. However, in this mood of mind, we will leave him to his own meditations, and return once more to our hapless heroine.

It was not until towards the morning that she awoke from the disturbed slumber into which she had fallen, and found her faithful attendant, Floretta, watching anxiously by her bed-side. She passed her fair hand across her aching forehead, but still she had but a confused idea of what had happened; and, notwithstanding she immediately recognised Floretta, so bewildered and distracted was she that for a few minutes she could not recollect where she was.

"Dear signora," said Floretta in her most gentle accents; "how do you feel now?"

"Ah! Floretta, my faithful, Floretta, you here?" ejaculated Melina; "what is the meaning of all this? How confused is my brain—where am I?"

"In the Villa Rosa, signora," replied her attendant, "and in your own chamber."

"Is it indeed so?" said our heroine, gazing

incredulously around her; " methought I was wandering through dismal charnel houses, and mingling with the festering and ghastly remains of the dead. Methought that a sea of human blood was spread wide before my seared eyes, and prevented me from quitting those frightful receptacles for mortality. Oh, the agony of that moment! and I imagined that my uncle and the Count Alberti stood by, and laughed at and mocked at my sufferings. I——"

" Oh, for Heaven's sake, my dear signora," interrupted Floretta, " calm your feelings, and do not give way to such fearful thoughts. It was but a frightful dream."

" A dream!" repeated the unfortunate damsel, " a dream! Can it be so? Is not my fate sealed for ever, past recall? Am I not a bride, the bride of the man whom my soul abhors, and the bare thought of whom congeals the very blood in my veins with horror and disgust? The bride of the detested Count Alberti?"

" No, my lady," replied Floretta, " let not such a fearful, such a revolting idea, disturb your mind. Recall your scattered thoughts; the unholy ceremony was prevented from taking place by the interference of the brigand chief, Allesandro Massaroni, and——"

" Ah!" interrupted Signora Melina, hastily " the whole truth now flashes upon my recollection; there was a dreadful combat in the chapel, was there not, and Count Alberti fell beneath the sword of Massaroni?"

" True, signora," returned Floretta.

" But did he die?" eagerly demanded our heroine.

" He did not, signora," answered her attendant, " but he now lies badly wounded, and in a state of insensibility, in his own chamber."

" But, my uncle; did he escape unhurt?"

" He did, my dear lady."

" And the brigand chief?"

" He defeated the numbers that were sent to oppose him, and with his daring band, succeeded in making good his retreat," answered Floretta.

" Thank Heaven for that," fervently ejaculated her mistress, " for I could never have forgiven myself had he fallen in his generous and disinterested efforts to serve me. But, oh, what will be the agony of Florio when he hears the particulars of what has happened, and the critical situation in which I am placed."

" Do not agonize your feelings, my dear signora, I beg of you," said Floretta; " there is yet hope for you."

" Hope for me?"

" Yes; Signor Clairville will, I trust, be enabled to endure this disappointment with fortitude, and something will yet occur to restore you to each other and to dissipate the dark clouds which at present are impending over you."

" Alas, no!" sighed our heroine, " you are by far too sanguine in your expectations, Floretta; I dare not, cannot think that that will ever be; the Count Alberti may soon recover, and should he do so, my fate is irrevocably sealed."

" Say not so, signora," returned Floretta, " for however inflexible his highness, your uncle, has hitherto been, I cannot but believe that this last event will arouse him to reason and justice, and that he will relent."

Melina shook her head despairingly, as she replied—

" Ah, no, Floretta, I know my uncle's disposition too well; this last disappointment will but serve to exasperate him the more, and render him the more determined, at the earliest opportunity, to put his cruel designs into execution. I dread the moment when I must see him again, and should Alberti die, what may I not expect from him, goaded on as he will be by a feeling of revenge?"

" I cannot believe, signora," remarked her attendant, " notwithstanding his recent harsh conduct towards you, that the Prince Bianchi can ever become so insensible to the feelings of humanity, justice, and nature, as, under such circumstances, to continue to persecute you. Surely he can feel no gratification in seeing you miserable."

" Alas! painful as the idea is," said Melina, " have I not had too much reason for months past to believe that my happiness is scarcely of secondary consideration with him, when he has his own stern will to gratify? Would to Heaven, that he would permit me to retire into a convent, where, in the holy and sacred duties of religion, I might at least learn to reconcile myself to my fate."

" Oh, my lady," said Floretta, " and could you for a moment think of immuring yourself within the dreary walls of a convent, while there is so much of light, and life, and happiness in the world?"

" What other hope is there for me, Floretta, since I have lost my uncle's love, and he to whom my heart is so fondly, so fervently devoted, can never be mine, and will never be permitted to see me again? What is all the light, and life, and happiness of the world you speak of, now to me? A dreary blank is before me, ponderous clouds, which threaten every moment to burst with tenfold fury upon my devoted head, hang over the horizon of my hopes, and despair points the finger of bitter mockery and exultation at me at every turn. I am a poor wretched being, a miserable outcast from every joy that should animate the bosom of youth; the flowers that once profusely strewed my path are crushed and trodden under foot, and there is no hope of tranquillity for me but in the silent grave! Would that my cold remains now rested by the side of those of my sainted mother, or that I had never been born."

Convulsive sobs choked her utterance, and the faithful Floretta, who was deeply affected, stood by and watched her in silence, in fact, for a few moments not knowing what to say.

"My dear signora," she at last observed, "how it afflicts me to see you give way to this excessive violence of grief and despair. I

BIANCHI AND THE COUNT INTERRUPTED IN THEIR SECRET MEETING.

am ready to admit that your prospects at present are dismal enough, but Providence is good, and never fails to watch over and protect the innocent in the hour of adversity. Once more I urge you to put your trust in him, and he will enable you to bear up against the heavy trials and afflictions to which you are exposed, and to pass triumphant through the painful ordeal."

"You seek to raise in me thoughts and expectations which I fear you cannot sincerely indulge in yourself, Floretta," said her mistress.

"Heaven forbid that I should do so, honoured lady," replied Floretta ; "indeed you do me an injustice if you n imagine for an instant that I would presume to attempt to deceive you."

"No, Floretta," said the Signora Melina, "it is not thus I judge you; for many year have I tried your fidelity and devoted attachment to me, and I must therefore crave your indulgence and forgiveness if the observations I have made use of should sound harsh and ungenerous to your ears. But, alas ! my mind is so destracted that I scarcely know what I say. Have you seen the prince, my uncle, since the startling events in the chapel ?"

Floretta replied in the affirmative, and her mistress eagerly inquired what state of mind he appeared to be in, though her mind apprehended the worst.

"It is useless to attempt to conceal from you, signora," answered her attendant, "that his highness is in a state of the greatest excitement ; but I trust that when reason resumes her sway, that will soon subside."

"Ah, no," returned our heroine, "I cannot expect it, especially after the violence of temper he has exhibited of late. I tremble to anticipate the time when he will demand to see me again, more particularly should the wound which the Count Alberti has received prove fatal."

"Do not unnecessarily alarm yourself, signora," said Floretta.

"And have I not ample cause to do so ?" demanded Melina ; "would to Heaven that Massareni had never made the desperate attempt he did to rescue me, which he must have felt certain would have been useless."

"And if he had not done so, my lady, you would at this time have been the wife of the Count Alberti," returned Floretta.

Melina shuddered with a sensation of horror and disgust at the revolting thought, and a silence of several minutes ensued, during which interval the most racking thoughts passed through the mind of our heroine, especially when she now more rividly recalled to her memory all that had taken place in the chapel. Devoutly she supplicated the mercy and protection of the Almighty, and then by dint of great exertion, and the persuasive eloquence of the faithful and affectionate Floretta, she became more calm, and sought to await the issue with patience and fortitude. She sincerely rejoiced in the escape of the brigand chief ; but when she reflected upon the despair and anguish her lover would endure when he should become acquainted with the result of the expedition, she could scarcely contain herself.

" But I am not at all disappointed, Floretta," she said ; "I never expected that Massaroni would succeed in his designs, and you know full well that I never approved of them."

" True, signora," replied Floretta ; " but you will pardon me, if I repeat what I have often said before, namely, that I think you were urged to do so from a mistaken notion of delicacy and propriety. The brigand chief is honourable in principle, notwithstanding his lawless and questionable calling, and I feel convinced that he would have scorned to take any unmanly advantage of the confidence you might have reposed in him."

" True," said Melina ; " that opinion of the character of Allesandro Massaroni, I also entertain : but still I must always feel the same reluctance to accept of his services, notwithstanding the danger of the situation in which I may be placed."

" Ah! my lady," said her attendant, " I trust that on more mature consideration, you will be induced to come to a different determination."

" No, Floretta," returned our heroine, " I am certain that I shall not. I feel grateful to Massaroni for his good wishes towards me, but I cannot accept of his aid."

" Do not say so, signora, for who knows the dreadful extremity in which you may yet be placed ?"

" Very true, my good girl," answered Melina, "but still I can never alter my mind."

" Not if the Count Alberti should recover, and the Prince Bianchi should again force you to the altar with him ?"

" No, Floretta; I must endeavour to resign myself to the will of Providence, which surely in its infinite mercy will rescue me from such a revolting and terrible fate."

" In that hope, signora," replied Floretta, " I think I need not assure you that I most heartily and sincerely participate. In fact, it would be monstrous to encourage any other idea ; but although Massaroni has in this instance been defeated, depend upon it that he will not abandon his designs."

" I hope that he will," said Melina.

" But the Signor Clairville, lady ?"

" Alas ! alas !" sighed our heroine.

" Can you make up your mind to abandon him to despair ?"

" And think you, Floretta," said her mistress, "that the noble and honourable spirit of Florio Clairville, would ever permit him to accept of my hand, even if I were to offer it, without the consent of my uncle ?"

" If he loves you sincerely, signora," replied Floretta, "as I believe he does, he would ; and who would his highness, your uncle, have but himself to blame ?"

" Oh, no," returned Melina, " I know my Florio's heart too well, to think that he would ever give his consent to such a clandestine union, which, under all the circumstances, could only be productive of the greatest misery to us both. Painful and arduous though the task would be, he would rather struggle against his feelings with manly fortitude, and endeavour to resign himself to his fate. Oh, Florio, what a sad—what a cruel destiny is ours; why did Providence ever suffer us to meet, since it had ordained that we should suffer all these overwhelming trials and bitter disappointments?"

She pressed her hands upon her temples in the greatest anguish of mind, and the tears streamed rapidly down her cheeks.

"Well, my dear signora," said Floretta, soothingly, after a pause; "you must endeavour to hope for the best, and to keep up your spirits all that you can."

"I do seek to do so," answered our heroine, "but, alas! what can be expected of me, painfully situated as I am? But I will arise, Floretta, and try to await the issue of this day with all the firmness I can. Leave me for awhile, my good girl, to my own reflections, and I hope the Almighty will give me strength to tranquillise my feelings, and to meet the fate which I fear is still in store for me with patience and resignation."

"Heaven send that your prayers may not be unheard, my sweet lady," said Floretta; "is there anything I can do for you before I retire?"

"No, Floretta," answered Melina, "I repeat that for a short time I wish to be alone, that I may commune with my own sad thoughts."

Floretta made no answer, and curtseying, was about to retire, when Melina motioned her back.

"During you absence, Floretta," she said, "I must request you to ascertain all the particulars you can respecting the Count Alberti and my uncle. I shall be all anxiety until I know."

Floretta promised obedience and then retired from the room, and left her unfortunate mistress to her own meditations. For some minutes after she was gone our heroine continued seated in her chair, in a state of complete abstraction; in fact, her mind was so distracted and bewildered, that she knew not how to arrange her thoughts. She stood on the extreme verge of a frightful precipice, from which there seemed no possibility of escaping, and every moment appeared to precipitate her fate, and to bring her nearer to that destruction, which, unless by some wonderful and merciful interposition of Providence, seemed inevitably to await her. Oh, the terrible, the insupportable anguish of her feelings as that idea flashed upon her brain! But at length the poor girl arose from the seat, and traversed the room in the most agitated manner, convulsive sobs for some minutes choking her utterance.

"My God!—my God!" she ejaculated at last, "that I should ever have been born to undergo such terrible sufferings as these. Why did not death stretch me in the same peaceful grave with my poor mother, in my days of childhood, and before I knew what sorrow was? Alas! my uncle, if not now, surely your conscience will, at some future period, bitterly reproach you for your present harsh and unnatural conduct towards me. Heaven knows how little I have merited it; with what holy reverence I have ever looked upon you, and how anxious I have always been to evince towards you the fervent gratitude I felt for the kindness you formerly lavished upon me. Alas! what a fearful change has come over you; I can scarcely believe it is the same indulgent guardian who seemed to derive pleasure alone from witnessing my happiness. And what is the cause of this? What can have wrought so terrible a revolution in your nature? Where are now the solemn promises you made to my mother, your only sister, on her death-bed? Oh, if her beautified spirit is permitted to look down upon you from the realms of bliss, how bitterly must it reproach you for your cruel conduct to the poor orphan child committed to your care."

She paused again for a few minutes, for the violence of her emotion once more deprived her of the power of speech, and the tears almost blinded her.

"And there is no escape from my fate," she at length resumed; "it would be only flattering myself with false hopes to seek to persuade myself that there was. Dismal fate enshrouds my form like a funeral pall, and grim despair encounters my gaze on every side. Even should Alberti not recover, though I shall thus be spared the horror of becoming his wife, will my uncle cease to persecute me? I feel a dread conviction that he will not, but on the contrary, that he will be goaded on by disappointment to fresh acts of severity, and will render my life, if possible, a still greater burthen to me than it is at present. Florio, my beloved, but unfortunate Florio, we are parted for ever; never on earth destined to meet again."

She was interrupted in the midst of this melancholy soliloquy by a gentle tap at the door, and Floretta re-entered the room.

"My faithful Floretta," said our heroine, eagerly, "tell me, what news of my uncle?"

"I have heard from the other servants, that he is still in a state of the utmost excitement," answered Floretta; "it seems that he wandered from the villa before daylight this morning, and that he is at present, and has been ever since his return, in the chamber of the Count Alberti."

"Ah!" ejaculated Melina; "and the latter, how is he?"

"He is, I understand, restored to consciousness, but the surgeon has pronounced him to be in a state of considerable danger," replied Floretta.

"May Heaven pardon him for the many sins he has committed, should it not be his fate to recover," said Melina, fervently ; "and should be, on the contrary, be restored to convalescence may he be brought to repentance, and seek to make all the atonement in his power to those whom he has so deeply wronged."

"Ay, signora," observed her attendant, "he has indeed much to answer for ; but should he recover, I sincerely trust that he will abandon his designs against you."

Signora Melina shook her head, despairingly.

"Alas, Floretta!" she said, "I much fear that he will not ; especially encouraged as he will doubtless be in his odious suit by my uncle."

"Pardon me, signora," remarked Floretta, "but if the prince should still persist in forcing you to the altar with a man whom you so utterly despise, he must have become entirely insensible to every feeling of humanity. But I cannot bring my mind to think that he will do so, indeed I cannot."

"Ah, Floretta," ejaculated Melina, "what else can I expect, after the threats he has held out to me, and the deaf ear he has constantly turned to my earnest supplications. I should only be deceiving myself were I to think otherwise. Fate is against me, and there are no means of avoiding my doom."

"Oh, yes, signora, there may be yet," said Floretta ; "if you will only follow the advice I have so frequently give you."

"What," demanded our heroine, impatiently ; "accept of the services of Massaroni?"

"Exactly so, my lady."

"Oh, no, Floretta, that is impossible. To place myself under the protection of the brigand chief in his wild mountain retreat, and surrounded by his daring and lawless band, my my heart revolts at the idea. There is nothing left for me but to remain here, and to brave the worst."

"It might appear presumption in me to attempt to advise you, signora," said Floretta ; "but I could sincerely wish that you would change your mind, and try to divest it of this false prejudice."

"Prejudice, Floretta!"

"Yes, signora, for indeed I cannot call it by any other name Your uncle has forgotten the duty he owes towards you, and the anxiety he should feel for your future happiness and welfare ; he would sacrifice you to a man who is totally unworthy of you, who is notorious as a libertine, an unprincipled libertine, the betrayer of female innocence (pardon my warmth, signora) ; nature, reason, and justice revolt at the idea, and yet you would hesitate to avail yourself of the only means of avoiding such a fate. Oh, I cannot believe

that you will persist in rejecting those offers made to you in so generous and honourable a spirit. Signor Clairville must have sanctioned the designs of Massaroni, I am certain, or he would never have attempted to put them into execution. His whole hopes doubtless rest on your deliverance from the revolting fate with which you are threatened, and would you drive him to despair ?"

"I admit the force of your arguments, Floretta," replied her mistress, "and I know full well the generous spirit that dictates them ; but still I cannot change my mind ; there is a feeling of repugnance comes over me when I think of it, which I find it is impossible to conquer. Why should Massaroni run such risks for me ?"

"Because he pities your situation, signora, entertains a warm friendship for Signor Clairville, and a feeling of natural aversion against one so dishonourable as the Count Alberti," answered Floretta ; "those can be his only motives, for what has he to gain by your abduction ?"

"True," returned our heroine ; "but let us drop the subject, I am in no frame of mind to argue further at present. Alas ! I have indeed already sufficient to distract my brain."

"'Tis too true, signora," said her attendant, "and would to Heaven that it was in my power to render you any relief or consolation."

"But have you heard anything to lead you to suppose that my uncle will demand to see me to day ?" eagerly asked Melina.

"No, signora," replied Floretta, "but I should think he would have a more decent regard for your feelings than to seek to obtrude himself upon your presence for a day or two, at any rate."

"I tremble to meet him," said our heroine, "for doubtless the utmost venom of his wrath will be lavished on me."

"Oh, why so, signora?" inquired Floretta, "Will he not imagine that I connived at the interference of the brigand chief ?"

"But he can have no proof that you did so."

"No matter," said Melina ; "I know the obstinate disposition of the prince, my uncle, too well (alas ! I have lately too bitterly experienced it) to imagine for a moment that he will be persuaded to the contrary. Would to Heaven that this had never occurred."

"And if it had not, signora," said Floretta, "you would now, as I before observed, have been the wife of the Count Alberti."

"No," returned Melina, solemnly, whilst an expression of awful determination flashed from her eyes, "I swear by Heaven, that though I might have been forced to the altar with the detested Count Alberti, I would not now have been his bride."

"What mean you, my dear lady?" said the faithful attendant, with a feeling of awe, when she noticed the remarkable demeanour of her mistress.

"Floretta," returned our heroine, in the same impressive accents, "think you that I could have continued to live in such misery and degradation? Think you that life would any longer have been valuable to me, when all my hopes were annihilated? Think you that I would have consented to drag out a wretched existence with the brand of shame upon my brow? No, by the just God that reigns above us, who, I hope, will pardon us all our sins, I would not; my hand would at any time be firm to destroy that life, which must, under such circumstances, become hateful and a burthen to me!"

"Oh, my unfortunate signora," said the trembling Floretta, "with what feelings of horror do your words inspire me. For the love of Heaven, banish such dreadful thoughts from your mind, and live to hope, and——"

"Hope!" interrupted Melina, her whole frame agitated with the most indescribable emotion, "hope! Too long did I indulge in the idle dream, but I am now aroused from it; all the bright visions of the past have evaporated into thin air, and I see the utter misery of the fate which is spread before me in all its hideous colours! Hope! To one who is situated like myself, it is a bitter mockery, a delusion, and I scout it with scorn."

There was a wildness in the hapless damsel's demeanour, and the expression of her eyes, as she gave utterance to these words, that filled the bosom of Floretta with alarm, and for a moment or two she could only stare at her mistress aghast, and was unable to return any answer; but she strongly feared that the manifold sorrows she had for the last few months experienced had at length taken a fatal effect upon her intellect; and as this idea struck the kind-hearted girl, she felt a far keener pang of anguish than any she ever remembered to have experienced before.

"Why do you gaze at me with such vacant looks?" demanded Melina, in the same wild strain; "think you that I am mad, or that I speak erroneously! Think you that I should not have the courage to perform what I say? Floretta, you have never known what it was to suffer persecution and misery; to have your brightest prospects blighted, or you would judge me differently. Did I not tell the prince, my uncle, what he might expect, if he should dare to sacrifice me to the odious Count Alberti? and think you I would fail to keep my word? No, by Heaven, again I swear——"

"Oh, hold! hold!" interrupted the horror-stricken Floretta; "for mercy's sake forbear; do not take an oath to perpetrate that which,

although innocent as you now are, would doom your soul to perdition. But sorrow has distracted your brain; you cannot know the dreadful words to which you give utterance. Come, my dear signora, calm your feelings, and——"

"Calm my feelings!" exclaimed Melina. "Can you stand there, Floretta, knowing what I have suffered, and yet talk to me of calmness?"

"Alas, my lady," said her attendant; "who knows better than myself the unmerited wrongs you have suffered, and who more deeply can sympathise in your misfortunes! But I cannot listen to the dreadful threats to which you have given utterance without endeavouring to arouse you to reason, and to pacify your anguish. Come, my dear signora, you will not turn a deaf ear to the advice of your humble, but faithful attendant, who has your interest deeply at heart, I feel convinced that you will not."

"My good girl," said Melina, bursting into tears, and the excitement of her feelings greatly subdued; "pardon me, if the distraction of my mind, and the frenzy of my dark despair, have caused me to make use of one harsh or ungenerous word to you."

"Oh, signora," replied Floretta, who was deeply affected; "why should you thus humble yourself to me? The gentle signora, could never, I am certain, make use of one angry word towards Floretta, who has served her from the days of her earliest childhood, and Heaven knows with what fidelity and sincerity of heart."

"True, Floretta," said her mistress, "you have ever been faithful, kind, and affectionate, to me, and God is my judge that I always duly appreciated your numerous good qualities, and have ever been anxious to acknowledge how much I feel I am indebted to you. If it had not been for your gentle and affectionate consolation and advice, what would have become of me under the many cruel sufferings it has been my hard lot to endure? Oh, Floretta, I prythee bear with me when the power of my emotions overcome my reason; I owe you a debt of gratitude which I feel that I can never repay."

"Nay, my dear lady," answered Floretta, "say not so; what have I done any more than was my duty?"

"Ah! Floretta," returned her mistress, as she fervently pressed her hand; "how few are there of our fellow-creatures who sincerely do their duty? And can we help—must we not be most ungrateful, were we not to duly appreciate those who do? Floretta, I may be considered wrong, extremely rash in what I have stated as to my intentions should I be plunged into the abyss of misery I anticipate; but, alas! have I not full cause for coming to that fearful determination? However, I will say no more at the present time : in fact, my mind is too distracted to do so ; leave me again, my faithful girl."

"Leave you, signora?" said her attendant, looking at her with an expression of alarm ; "not in your present state of mind. Pardon me, but allow me to remain with you, and to dissipate the melancholy thoughts that now haunt your imagination like a night-mare.

"No, Floretta," returned her mistress, "I shall be much better able to collect my ideas, and regain my fortitude [of mind, if left alone, at the present time. Heaven send that my uncle will at least have the forbearance not to insist upon an interview with me just now ; God alone knows how I should endure such a trial."

"He will not so so, dear lady," said Floretta ; "depend upon it, he will not attempt anything so harsh and cruel and unjust as to urge the odious advances of the Count Alberti at this time ; he will, at least wait until the shock which your feelings have received has in some measure subsided. It would indeed be monstrous to suppose otherwise. Again let me beg of you, signora, not to despair ; to muster all the fortitude you can, and with Heaven's will, all will yet be well, and happiness will once more be your lot. Farewell, my beloved mistress, for the present. Should anything reach my ears that may give me the least cause to apprehend danger, I will give you timely notice of it."

Our heroine, completely overpowered by the disinterested kindness of Floretta, once more embraced her, and they separated.

The Prince Bianchi on his return from his early ramble, as we have described in the foregoing pages, was in the same excited state of mind as he had been on his going out, and walking immediately to his study, he there for some time gave himself up to the same distracting train of thoughts which had bewildered his brain for so many hours. He locked his door, so that no one should intrude upon him, and to and fro he hurriedly paced the apartment, with his arms folded across his chest, and muttering curses at intervals between his teeth.

"That I should be so foiled, beset on every side," he observed,—"disappointed in all my most darling projects ; thwarted by the rascal against whom my principal hatred is excited ; it is more than human nature can tamely endure. And should the Count Alberti die, or recovering, abandon his former resolutions, and resign the hand of my niece, how shall I be laughed at, scoffed at, in the world ! The name of the Prince Bianchi will be used as a bitter mockery, a by-word ; a vulgar jest for every idle ribaldrer in Italy. Bah! I must not indulge in such cowardly specu-

lations! Who dare insult the governor of Rome thus? No, no, I will be firm, and likewise let them see I can be determined. Melina, you shall yet be the wife of the Count Alberti, though it break your heart, or my name is not Bianchi."

He unlocked the door of his apartment, and hastily rang his bell, and a servant made his appearance, promptly, at the summons.

"Has his lordship, the Count Alberti, recovered to a state of consciousness ?" demanded Bianchi.

"He has, your highness," replied the domestic.

"'Tis well," observed the prince ; "desire Signor Giachomo, the chirurgeon, to attend me."

The servant bowed and took his departure immediately, to execute his master's orders ; and shortly afterwards, Signor Giachomo entered the apartment.

"Now, signer," said Bianchi, eagerly, "what of your patient?"

"He is sensible, your highness," replied the doctor.

"Ah! I am glad to hear that," observed the prince.

"Still, excellenza," added Signor Giachomo, "he is in that excited state, that I think it would be advisable for you to defer an interview with him for the present. In a day or two, he may be more calm."

"In a day or two?" returned Bianchi, impatiently ; "pshaw! I can no longer procrastinate my visit ; we have much to converse about, and any longer delay might be attended with the most important and fatal results to us both. Signor Giachomo, I will this moment attend him in his own chamber."

"Your highness, of course, will suit your own pleasure," said the doctor ; "I have stated my opinion, and you will have an opportunity of judging whether or not it is a correct one."

Thus saying, Signor Giachomo bowed, and retired from the room, and the Prince Bianchi made his way to the chamber of the wounded nobleman.

On entering the chamber, he found the Count Alberti sitting almost upright, supported by pillows ; his eyes staring wildly around the room, and giving utterance to the most extravagant and partly incoherent exclamations, while the servants who were deputed to attend upon him, stood aside, staring at him in stupified amazement, and fearful of venturing to utter a syllable.

"D—n him !" the prince heard him exclaim as he entered the room ; "he knew it well ;—he, the robber, the murderer ;—Allesandro Massaroni, I mean, knew full well—he knew full well, I repeat, that my soul was not now fit to appear before the judgment-seat of

God!—and, therefore, in his savage vengeance he has sent it before the tribunal of hell! Oh, the triumph is indeed his; would that I had him now within my grasp, that I———."

"My lord," interrupted the Prince Bianchi.

"Ah!" said Alberti, gazing at him vacantly, "you here?—Where is your daughter?—Where is the wife you promised me?—Where———."

"Retire!" said the Prince Bianchi, addressing himself to the domestics. They obeyed in an instant, and the Count Alberti and himself were left alone.

"Now, my Lord Alberti" said Bianchi, after a brief pause, "I must beg of you to be as calm as you possibly can under the circumstances, for we both have had enough to excite us, and it would be sheer madness to aggravate our feelings. The wife I promised you is still in my power;—my determination remains unchanged, it therefore behoves you not to irritate your feelings too much, especially in your present condition, and———."

"Is the Signora Melina still an inmate of this villa?" hastily interrupted the count.

"I repeat that she is," answered Bianchi. "But your wound, count?"

"Oh! it is nothing," returned the patient, with a forced smile, "now that you have assured me of the security of her upon whom my very soul is fixed. A mere scratch, prince;—a—a—ah!"

"Do not exert, do not excite yourself, I once more request of you," said the Prince Bianchi, alarmed by the symptoms he betrayed; "when you have approached something nearer to convalescence, which I flatter myself you shortly will, I shall have something important to reveal to you."

"I—I am well," faltered out Alberti, his eyes still wandering in a strange manner around the chamber, without being fixed upon any particular object; "but, have you seen her? Does she still entertain the feelings of abhorrence she has hitherto expressed towards me? Does she feel any sort of sympathy with me in the misfortune, the—the—the *accident* which has befallen me?"

The Prince Bianchi would rather have had any other question put to him at that time, and he was bewildered for the moment how to answer it, and at length he said—

"I have not seen my niece since your accident, Count Alberti, and therefore you must be perfectly aware that I am unable to answer the questions you put to me. Of this, however, you may rest assured, that my determinations remain unaltered;—whatever I have promised to you, if you are willing to adhere to the compact we have both entered into, I will fulfil, let the consequences be whatever they may. Let that assurance calm and satisfy your feelings; though every earthly power should stand forth to oppose me, be you willing, the Signora Melina, my niece, shall become your wife!"

"Blessed words!" said the Count Alberti, with much more energy than could be expected from a man in his situation; "your hand, my lord; I feel already another man; —this wound is—But the rascal Massaroni, what of him?"

"He defeated the troops that were sent against him, and managed to effect his escape," answered Bianchi.

"Curses light on him!" ejaculated Alberti; "had he been secured, and brought to justice, I might have been more satisfied; but now—"

"Oh, fear him not, my lord," interrupted Bianchi, "we shall yet entrap him when he least expects it, and be able to wreak our vengeance on his head."

"Could I be certain of that," returned the wounded man, biting his lips, and the expression of his pale features plainly showing the feelings of hatred, revenge, and disappointment which at that moment inhabited his breast, "I should be satisfied. But in spite of all the arguments we may adduce to the contrary, Prince Bianchi, I feel thoroughly convinced of his power, and that he is enabled to laugh us both to scorn."

"To scorn!" repeated Bianchi, with a look of offended dignity.

"Ay," returned Alberti, "it is useless to attempt to deny it, however we may be disposed to do so. Allesandro Massaroni possesses a certain tact in his designs; a consummate skill; a surpassing supremacy over all other adventurers, which nothing has yet been proof against; and, although he has failed in his present object, namely, to carry off the Signora Melina, and restore her to the arms of Clairville, I fear much that, unless we are, as I before observed, on the alert, he will ultimately achieve his object."

"By the saints, I swear," said Bianchi, determinedly, "that he shall not, even though I sacrifice my fortune in frustrating his designs. But fear not, ounte; after the defeat he has at present sustained, I do not think he will feel disposed to make another attempt, for the present, at any rate. But in order to baffle the rascal, should he have such a design in contemplation, I have bethought me of a plan."

"And what is that, your highness?" inquired Alberti, eagerly.

"In a few days," answered Bianchi, "I will remove Melina to an estate of mine, some distance from here, and which I believe is unknown to the brigand chief; there I will place her under the strict surveillance of those whom I know I can trust, until you are enabled to accompany me thither, and then the marriage ceremony shall take place without delay, and without any fear of obstruction."

"An excellent plan, my lord," remarked

Alberti, his pale features animated with hope and satisfaction; "it has my entire approval; and I think it cannot fail to succeed."

"It is impossible that it can do so," replied the Prince Bianchi; "my niece shall be held in the strictest confinement till the time arrives, and it will be utterly useless for her to attempt to offer any resistance. Let this assurance content you, count, and fear not as to the results. By the mass, are we to suffer ourselves to be foiled in our designs by an obstinate, froward girl, over whom I hold supreme authority, and this daring robber and cutthroat, Allesandro Massaroni?"

"It is not meet that we should do so," said the Count Alberti; "but we must keep our plans secret till the time arrives to put them into execution, for it is my opinion that your fair niece has some means of holding communication with the brigand chief, and that at times when we the least expect it."

"I will adopt every means to prevent that," said the Prince Bianchi, "should your suspicions be correct. The strictest watch shall be kept over Melina and her attendant Floretta, and neither of them shall be permitted to leave the villa, on any pretext whatever."

"That resolution is wise and judicious, your highness— But— oh !— that pang !—Curses light upon the villain who inflicted upon me this deadly injury."

"Ah!" exclaimed Bianchi, alarmed; "you have turned more ghastly pale; your features are distorted, and you appear to be suffering great pain ; curses, I say again, light upon the head of the miscreant Massaroni."

"I feel faint," observed Alberti, in a low and tremulous voice; "but—but it will soon pass over."

"You have exerted yourself too much in this conversation," said the prince; "I had better summon the attendance of Doctor Giachomo."

The Count Alberti returned no answer, for he seemed incapable of doing so, and was evidently suffering the most excruciating bodily agony; and the prince immediately rang the bell, and ordered the servant to desire the instant attendance of the medical man, who promptly made his appearance.

"This is no more than I expected, your highness," he remarked; "his lordship, the Count Alberti, is at present in too weak and precarious a state to be able to bear the excitemet of conversation. Should you persist in it, I will not be answerable for the consequences."

"Is there any immediate danger?" demanded Bianchi, with a look of increased alarm.

"Probably there may not be, with prompt attention," replied Doctor Giachomo; "but I must desire your highness to retire, and leave the patient to me."

"I will do so," said the prince. "My lord," he added, taking the count's hands; "farewell for the present; we shall shortly meet again."

Alberti made no reply, for he was deprived of speech, and the wild and vacant look which he turned upon the Prince Bianchi, convinced the latter that his mind was wandering, and that he did not know him.

"For God's sake," said Bianchi, addressing himself to Doctor Giachomo; "pay him all the attention you can; and exercise the utmost of your skill."

"Your highness may depend upon me," replied the doctor.

"There is no pecuniary demand that you can make which shall not be acceded to, if you restore him to convalescence," observed the prince.

"I know that, your highness," returned Doctor Giachomo, "and all that mortal man can do for the Count Alberti shall be done by me ; but he must be kept quiet, he must not be excited in the least degree, or, as I said before, I will not, cannot be answerable for the consequences."

"Enough," said Bianchi, "I will obey you, Signor Giachomo, and will not again venture to intrude upon the count until I have your express permission."

With these words, and casting an anxious look upon the suffering Count Alberti, the Prince Bianchi retired from the room, and once more sought his own apartment, in a frame of mind which we have no occasion to describe. The danger of the count was quite apparent to him, and the rage and excitement under which he laboured were almost insupportable.

"And must all my hopes be thus annihilated," he exclaimed, as he paced his room with the most disordered steps, "and that by the rascal Massaroni? By Heaven this is more than human patience can endure. May the deadliest curses light upon the head of the brigand chief ! May all the tortures of perdition overtake him in this world ! Would that I had him now in my power, would I not have an ample and deadly revenge ! But he mocks my power, and sets all my efforts to capture him, and to bring him to that condign punishment which he deserves, at defiance. The time, however, must and shall come when I will triumph ; and then how exquisite is the vengeance that I will wreak upon his head. And that I should have traitors in my own establishment; those who would assist the brigand chief in his designs against me. But so it is, there can no longer be any doubt upon it; the fellow Guiseppe has disappeared from the villa, and it is quite evident that he is the treacherous scoundrel who enabled Massaroni and his daring band to gain a secret entrance into the chapel, and thus to frustrate my designs at the very moment when I thought them certain of accomplishment. Oh, that I had suspected the villain; most terrible is the punishment I would have inflicted upon him. Melina, too, she must have been aware of, and sanctioned the designs of Massaroni, and that after all her pretended modesty and delicacy of feeling, to receive the aid of a desperate outlaw, robber, and murderer. Bah! I have no patience to think of it. But I will retaliate upon her,

GUISEPPE'S SECRET INTERVIEW WITH MASSARONI.

even though I consign her to future misery. The Prince Bianchi, the Governor of Rome, will never suffer his authority to be set at defiance, by an obstinate, foolish girl! She may flatter herself with the idea that since the Count Alberti is so dangerously wounded, that she will escape from the fate with which I have threatened her altogether; that I will relent, and ultimately give my consent to her becoming the wife of the presumptuous beggar, on whom she has fixed her affections, Florio Clairville; but she will find herself most woefully mistaken; for even should the Count Alberti not recover, to punish her, I will select some other nobleman who I know will be obnoxious to her wishes, to possess her hand. Her tears, her supplications, her remonstrances and entreaties, shall have no effect upon me. When the determination of the Prince Bianchi is once formed, nothing on earth can alter it, he will endure no opposition to his will."

He paused; for in spite of all his efforts to the contrary, his conscience could not help upbraiding him for the cruelty and injustice of his designs. The solemn promises he had made her mother on her death-bed, rushed upon his memory with overwhelming force, and for a moment or two he shrank back within himself. He could almost imagine that he saw the pale face of his sister fixed reproachfully upon him, and that he heard her hollow and solemn voice breathing curses in his ears.

"But why should I give way to such weak and distracting thoughts as these?" he said; "have I not fulfilled the promise I made to the best of my abilities? Have I not ever done my duty towards her? Have I not always been a protector to her? Behaved to her with all the affection of a father, treated her with every possible indulgence? And now, forsooth, because I will not give my consent to her becoming the wife of a beggar, but would bestow her hand upon a nobleman of wealth and rank, and who is every way worthy of her, I am to be stigmatized as cruel and unjust. Pshaw! I have no patience with such folly. I will be firm to my purpose, let the consequences that shall follow be whatever they may. I must see Melina, and undeceive her, if she has flattered herself with any such false hope."

He immediately rang the bell, and ordered the servant who made his appearance to desire Floretta to come to him directly. Floretta quickly obeyed the summons, and the Prince Bianchi said—

"Now, damsel, how is your mistress, the Signora Melina?"

"In a very weak and desponding state, your highness," answered Floretta.

"Humph!" said Bianchi; "indulging in her usual heroics, I suppose. Is she up?"

Floretta replied in the affirmative.

"'Tis well," observed the prince; "tell her that she may expect to see me in a few minutes in her apartment."

"Oh, your highness," Floretta ventured to say, "I would humbly beg of you to defer the interview for the present; the signora is in an agitated state of mind, and the excitement—"

"Obey my orders," interrupted the Prince Bianchi, sternly, and Floretta not daring to make use of another observation, left the room, and hastened to the chamber of her mistress, who had been waiting her return in the greatest anxiety.

"What was it that the Prince Bianchi required of you, Floretta?" she demanded, eagerly.

"He commanded me to tell you that you might expect to see him in a few minutes, signora," answered Floretta.

Our heroine turned ghastly pale, and trembled violently.

"Alas! alas!" she sighed, "how cruel is this of him; but it is no more than I expected. Can nothing induce him to act with the least forbearance towards me?"

"Unfortunately, my dear signora," returned Floretta; "it seems not; but muster all the fortitude you can, and who knows but that in this interview you will be able to make some impression upon him?"

"Oh, no!" ejaculated Melina, "I cannot encourage any such a hope, for I am certain that it would only be doomed to be disappointed. I tremble at the thoughts of the interview, for too well can I guess what the character of it will be. My uncle is exasperated at the critical situation in which the Count Alberti has been placed by Massaroni, and will listen to no remonstrance. Would to Heaven that such a catastrophe had not occurred, though I should indeed have been consigned to the dreadful and revolt fate with which I have been so long threatened."

"Oh, my lady," said her attendant, "how can you talk so? Surely no fate could be half so awful as that to which you have alluded."

"True, Floretta," said our heroine, "but still—hark! Some one is ascending the stairs; it must be the prince. God help me!"

"Courage, courage, signora," said Floretta, and she had scarcely given utterance to the words when the room door was opened, and the Prince Bianchi stood before them. Melina shrunk back alarmed, and did not venture to look towards her uncle, who eyed her sternly for a minute or two, and then turning to Floretta, he said—

"Leave the room, girl."

Floretta cast a look of pity towards her mistress, who had sank in a chair and covered her face with her hands, and then with some hesitation, she obeyed.

Prince Bianchi remained silent for a short time, and then advancing towards his fair and unfortunate niece, he said, in accents which sufficiently expressed the exasperation and excitement of his feelings—

"So, Melina, I suppose you are now satisfied with what your obstinacy and deception have been the means of producing. The Count Alberti lies dangerously wounded by the hand of you friend the notorious brigand chief, and should he die, his fate will rest at your door."

"My lord!" said Melina, starting, and fixing upon him a look of the most keen reproach, which, however, he beheld totally unmoved; "can you talk to me thus?"

"I can, I do," answered Bianchi, in the same stern and determined voice; "and I mean what I say, girl. You must have secretly connived with Massaroni, or he would never have ventured so much to rescue you."

"Oh, how cruelly you wrong me, my lord, by such a supposition," returned his niece, the tears at the same time trembling in her eyes. "I never, I solemnly swear, in the sight of Heaven, sanctioned the interference of the brigand chief."

"But you knew of his intentions?" said the Prince Bianchi, hastily. Our heroine returned no answer, and her heart palpitated violently against her side with emotion.

"Ah!" exclaimed Bianchi, passionately; "your silence is an acknowledgment of the truth."

"My lord," returned Melina, firmly; "I am no hypocrite, and therefore I will not attempt to deny that I knew of the designs of Massaroni."

"And encouraged them!" cried the prince, frowning fearfully.

"By the just God above, I did not!" replied our heroine, solemnly.

"'Tis false!" exclaimed her uncle, "in vain you may attempt to deceive me. And so this is the fair, and gentle, and imaculate Signora Melina, who entertains such horror at becoming the wife of a worthy nobleman, and yet does not blush at colleaguing with a robber and a murderer with the hope of being able to set my authority at defiance."

"My lord," said the agitated damsel, rising from her chair, "this is monstrous! You wrong me, deeply wrong me, by such cruel accusations. I accepted not of the aid of Massaroni; but he was determined. No one can more deeply regret the accident which has befallen the Count Alberti, than myself."

"Oh, doubtless so," returned Bianchi, with a satirical and disagreeable grin; "your respectful conduct towards him is a sufficient proof of the truth of your asseverations."

"The behaviour of the Count Alberti towards me, my lord," said Melina, "was ever such as to excite my utmost abhorrence and disgust; and you know, full well, that I never endeavoured to conceal my real sentiments from yourself or him."

"True," said Bianchi, bitterly; "and no doubt you now exult in his dangerous situation, and flatter yourself with the most sanguine hopes that he will not recover."

"My lord," said our heroine, with increased firmness, and fixing upon him a look which ought to have penetrated to his very soul, "if I were one of the vilest wretches that ever disgraced the earth, you could not but thus express yourself towards me. What has there ever been in my conduct to cause you to entertain such an opinion of me?—Could I prevent the accident which befel the Count Alberti?—Did I direct the hand of Massaroni? No, it was his own rashness and impetuosity that caused it all; and he was himself to blame alone for all that has happened. Had he abandoned his odious designs against me—had you not, my lord, remained inexorable, he would now have remained in safety."

"Ah!" said the prince, in the same passionate strain, "you do well to brave it out thus boldly. But think you that your words will make any impression on me? No, by all my hopes they shall not. You have acknowledged that you knew of the designs of Massaroni?"

"I have, my lord."

"And yet, although you pretended not to sanction them, you took no means to prevent his putting them into execution? You did not seek to make me acquainted with his intentions?"

"I did not, my lord, and for this reason," replied our heroine, "notwithstanding the prejudices you entertain towards him, I feel convinced that the brigand chief acted from the most generous and disinterested motives; and it would have been the basest and most brutal ingratitude in me, to have betrayed him, and thus probably consigned him to an ignominious death."

"What!" exclaimed Bianchi; "and do you dare to advocate the cause of that villain who has ever proved himself to be my most bitter enemy? By Heaven! you had better not try my patience too far, or you may tempt me to do that which I would fain avoid. But I will yet have a most terrible revenge. The villain shall not escape me, and I will never rest until I have seen him pay the full penalty of his crimes upon the public scaffold."

"Oh, my lord," said the terrified Melina; "entertain not such cruel thoughts, but extend mercy to Massaroni, as you would hope for mercy yourself hereafter."

"Mercy to Massaroni!" cried the prince, fiercely; "mercy to him from whom I have experienced so many insults and injuries? By the Just God that made me, I would not spare him though it were to save my life. A short time will, I trust, place the daring ruffian in my power, and then ——"

"Oh, God forbid!" interrupted our heroine, earnestly, "since such is your determination."

"Hold, girl!" commanded her uncle, in a hoarse voice; "beware of what you say. But answer me one question, I command you, and that truly:—Who admitted Massaroni and his band into the chapel?"

"I know not, my lord," answered Melina, "unless it was Guiseppe."

"Ah! the villain!" said Bianchi, "it is as I thought. And you knew of this?"

"I solemnly declare that I did not, my lord, though I confess that I suspected it."

"By all the saints!" ejaculated the prince, "this is insupportable. And do you, girl, still entertain the same sentiments you have always expressed towards the Count Alberti?"

"Nothing on earth can ever alter them, my lord," replied the damsel, firmly.

"Again I tell you to beware! Consider well what you say."

"I have considered it maturely, my lord."

"And if the Count Alberti should recover, will you still persist in refusing to become his wife?"

"I would sooner endure the most torturing and lingering death," answered our heroine, resolutely.

"Rash! obstinate girl!" cried her uncle; "think you that any opposition you could offer would prevent me from putting my designs into execution?"

"Alas! I fear not," sighed Melina; "God help me!"

"Do you still love the beggar Clairville?" demanded the Prince Bianchi, sternly.

"I do," replied his niece, "and must ever continue to do so with unabated fervour, until my heart shall cease to beat. Oh, Florio!—

"Dare not repeat his hated name," interrupted Bianchi, "unless you would bring down upon your head my deadliest wrath! Hear me, Melina, while I declare to you my fixed, my unalterable determination: Even should the Count Alberti not recover, I will take care to compel you to become the wife of some other nobleman, whom I will select, and whom you may view with equal feelings of aversion."

"Oh, monstrous!" gasped forth the agonised Melina! "how have I deserved this cruelty? Can this be my uncle who speaks? —Have you no feeling of pity and humanity towards me?"

"You have heard my determination," replied Bianchi, in the same inflexible tone.

"Oh, recall your words," implored Melina; "you cannot thus have become so totally insensible to every feeling of justice and nature. Consider, I earnestly supplicate you, what it is you would do; and if you would not break my heart, and bring eternal misery upon your own head, you will no longer remain obstinate. What a fearful change has come over you, my lord, in the course of a few short months. I can scarcely believe it is the same being who was once so studious of my happiness, but who now seems only anxious to consign me to the most insupportable shame and misery."

"You have tried my patience too long, Melina," said her uncle; "but I am resolved to let you see that I must and will have my authority obeyed."

"Oh, in everything but that, my lord," returned our heroine, the tears starting rapidly from her eyes and bedewing her pale cheeks; Heaven knows how willingly I will obey you; but how can you expect me calmly, passively resign myself to a fate so revolting, that the bare idea of it makes me shudder with horror? But you will think better of this, when your mind is divested of the wrath which at present disfigures it, and you reflect dispassionately upon the cruelty and injustice of that which you contemplate. I ask you not to sanction my love for Clairville, for I know you will not; and as I can never hope to possess his hand, I faithfully promise you that I will endeavour to forget that such a being ever existed; though, alas! too well I know that I shall find it a most painful and difficult task to accomplish, and my heart may break in the struggle."

"Bah!" exclaimed the stern and inflexible prince; "I have no patience to listen to such folly as this. Think you girl, that I have become old and imbecile, that I am so easily to be persuaded from anything upon which I have once fixed my mind?"

"Heaven help me then," groaned Melina, "for that is my sole dependance. Oh! that I should ever live to endure such misery as this! Would that I had died in my infancy, and now rested in the same peaceful grave with my poor mother,"

The Prince Bianchi's countenance underwent a great change as Melina gave utterance to these words; his lips quivered; the expression of his eyes were wild and wandering, and grasping the arm of the poor girl, he fiercely exclaimed—

"Hold, girl! lest you would hear me curse you!— Why do you give utterance to such words as those you have just now spoken?"

"My lord!" said the astonished damsel, "why does the bare mention of that revered name thus violently agitate you?"

"Question me not!" cried Bianchi, with the same excessive emotion; "but dare not to repeat it again in my presence But why do I thus torture myself? Girl, you have heard my decree, and you must prepare yourself to resign yourself to it, for it is irrevocable!"

Our heroine clasped her hands together with agony, and raised her eyes towards heaven, as she ejaculated, in a voice broken by convulsive sobs—

"Father of mercy, I humbly supplicate Thee to look down upon me!"

"Hear me, Melina," remarked the Prince Bianchi, after a brief pause, "until you know my further will and pleasure, I command you to keep yourself closely confined to your chamber, and at your peril not to venture to leave it without my permission, or to hold any communication with any person except your maid Floretta. Do you hear me, girl?"

"Alas! I do," sighed our heroine in reply.

"Then mind you do not attempt to disobey my injunctions," said her uncle.

"It would be useless for me to do so," said Melina.

"It would," remarked Bianchi; "for a strict watch will be set upon your actions, depend upon it. Your fate depends upon that of the Count Alberti."

"Alas! then, I know too well it is sealed," said Bianchi. "Oh, my lord, you surely will have reason to repent this unnatural severity when it may be too late."

"I care not," returned the prince; "your words make no impression on me; I will risk the consequences. I have been trifled with too long, and had I not have treated you with so much indulgence, this might not have happened."

"Indulgence!" repeated our heroine, looking at him with an expression of the most bitter reproach.

"Yes," returned Bianchi, "indulgence and forbearance. Had I forced you to the altar before, you would now have been the wife of the Count Alberti, and all my doubts would have been set at rest."

"The wife of Count Alberti," said Melina, vehemently; "oh, horrible, revolting thought! Oh, my lord! how can you thus delight to torture me?"

"And what is there," returned the Prince Bianchi, sarcastically, "so horrible and revolting in hearing the name of your future husband mentioned?"

"My future husband!" repeated the damsel. "Oh, never! Heaven will not permit it."

"Pshaw!" replied her uncle; "what is the use of flattering yourself with such false hopes? Take my word for it, that you will be mistaken. But I waste time with you; remember my injunctions, and again I command you to obey them."

Having thus spoken, and without waiting for any reply from his hapless niece, the Prince Bianchi quitted the room. Melina sunk into a chair, when he was gone, and gave herself up to all the agony of her grief; and in this condition the faithful Floretta found her on her return to the room, and for a few minutes did not offer to interrupt her.

"Oh, Floretta," sobbed her mistress, at length, sinking in her arms and weeping hysterically on her bosom—"it is all settled; my fate is decided; I see plainly that there is no possibility of escaping from it, and I am one of the most wretched and unfortunate of beings in existence."

"Be firm, signora," said Floretta, "for,

after all it may not turn out so bad as you now anticipate. The Count Alberti is in a most dangerous condition; and should he not recover——"

"Still there would be no hope for me, Floretta," interrupted our heroine.

"No hope!" repeated Floretta, with a look of utter amazement; "what mean you, signora?"

"Even what I say," answered her mistress; "this interview with my uncle has fully convinced me of that. Should the Count Alberti die, he has threatened to compel me to become the wife of another nobleman selected by himself, and whom I might have equal cause to hate."

"Oh, impossible!" ejaculated Floretta.

"Alas it is too true," replied Melina.

"It can only be an idle threat," observed the faithful attendant; "the prince, your uncle, signora, can never become so completely insensible to every feeling of shame and humanity as to put it into execution."

"I have nothing to hope from him, Floretta; his nature is completely changed, and I am convinced that he no longer views me with the least affection. Oh, my faithful friend, what have I suffered during this interview!"

"Banish the remembrance of it from your mind, signora," remarked Floretta.

"It is impossible that I can do so," said our heroine; "but listen, and you shall know all."

Floretta drew a chair close to her, and Melina, as well as her agitation would permit, and in as few words as possible, related to her all those particulars with which the reader is already acquainted. Floretta listened to her with the most profound attention and sympathy, and when Melina had concluded, she could scarcely conceal the disgust which the brutal conduct of the Prince Bianchi had excited in her breast.

"Now, Floretta," demanded her mistress, "what think you of my situation and the dismal prospect before me? Have I not reason to give myself up to despair, and to wish that I were dead?"

"Alas! signora," replied Floretta, "yours is indeed a cruel, a melancholy fate, and I know not how to attempt to offer consolation to you. Never could I have believed that the prince would go to such fearful and disgusting extremes as this. But Heaven will never permit him to accomplish his unnatural wishes; something will yet occur to frustrate them, and to restore you to that serenity and peace of mind you once so deservedly enjoyed."

"Oh, no, Floretta," returned our heroine, shaking her head, sorrowfully, "serenity and peace of mind are never more fated to be my lot. My days of happiness are fled, never more to return."

"Would that I could persuade you to entertain a different opinion, my dear lady," said her companion; "the Almighty will never suffer one so good and innocent to be doomed to perpetual misery."

"Alas! it would seem that unavoidable fatality is attached to me," remarked Melina; "and that I may in vain try to avoid my cruel destiny."

"Endeavour to think different, and you may still find consolation."

"Consolation!—oh, where?—How fruitless would be the task, were even I to set about it."

"Depend upon it, signora," observed her attendant, "that Massaroni will make another attempt to rescue you, before the Count Alberti may possibly be restored to convalescence."

"Oh, I hope not," replied Melina.

"And why so, my lady?"

"Because it might only end in his own destruction, and could scarcely fail to bring misery and disgrace upon me."

"I do not, cannot believe so," said Floretta. "Reason dictates to you to adopt any course to effect your escape from the disgusting fate which is at present impending o'er your head; but still you will persist in entertaining those delicate scruples."

"It is no use, Floretta," said her mistress, in reply, "I cannot conquer them. Besides, my uncle will be sure now to use every precaution to resist any attack that may be made upon him, and the brigand chief's success will be much more doubtful than the last. Unless an All-merciful Providence should interpose to save me, there is no hope for me."

"It will, signora, depend upon it," said Floretta, "and the plans of the Prince Bianchi will be defeated. It seems scarcely possible that so fearful a change should come over him in so short a time, and I am inclined to think that he does not mean all he says, but that he wishes to intimidate you, so that he may the more readily induce you to accede to his will."

"Means not what he says, Floretta?" repeated our heroine; "oh, what reason have I to think to the contrary!—I am certain from the sternness and decision of his manner that he his determined."

"Then, pardon me, signora," returned the waiting maid, "if such is indeed the case, I must say that the Prince Bianchi has disgraced himself as a man, and that he is no longer worthy of your esteem. But I will not credit it; I cannot believe it, for it would be to suppose your uncle one of the greatest villains in existennce."

t "It would be encouraging a vain hope to think otherwise," said Melina; "but I do not; the clouds which have so long hung over the horizon of my happiness are about to burst, and I feel it is impossible to resist its fury."

"Do not abandon yourself altogether to despair, my dear signora," remarked Floretta; "for I feel satisfied that something will occur to rescue you from the threatened danger."

Our heroine shook her head despairingly, and the conversation for the present dropped, and they remained silent for a short time, and Melina gave herself up to the violence of the emotions which filled her bosom.

CHAPTER XXXIX.

MASSARONI IN HIS MOUNTAIN RETREAT.— THE DESPAIR OF FLORIO CLAIRVILLE.— THE ATTEMPTED ESCAPE OF MALVOLIO.— HE IS SHOT —DYING CONFESSION—EXTRAORDINARY DISCOVERY, AND HIS DEATH.

WE must again pursue the footsteps of the brigand chief, who, vexed and disappointed, at length arrived at his secret haunt among the mountains, followed by his daring and dauntless band.

We imagine it is unnecessary to describe to the reader the anxiety of mind which Florio Clairville had experienced during the absence of Massaroni on his expedition, and the fears and misgivings which continually disturbed his imagination; but he never even for a moment scarcely flattered himself with the hope that they would be successful, and consequently he was the better prepared for the result which had taken place. When alone, which he was ever most anxious to be when the brigand chief had taken his departure, he constantly, in the most fervent terms, supplicated the mercy and protection of the Supreme for that beloved being in whose happiness and deliverance from the fate with which she was threatened, his whole hopes were centred; but as day after day elapsed, and he heard nothing from Massaroni, his patience was almost exhausted, and his apprehensions increased as to the result of the expedition.

The brigand's wife also awaited the return of Massaroni with the utmost impatience and anxiety, and she had her doubts excited in no small degree as to whether or not his designs would be crowned with success, though she well knew that it would not be through any fault of his if he should fail. These doubts, however, she endeavoured to conceal from Clairville, and when she found him sad and desponding, she sought to the utmost of her power to buoy him up with hope, though, in truth, she succeeded but very indifferently.

"It is but seldom that Massaroni has failed in any designs upon which he may have fixed his mind," she would say, "and so confident is he of his present success, that I can scarcely make up my mind to believe he will be doomed to be disappointed. Be of good cheer, therefore, Signor Clairville, and take my word for it that a very short time will set your doubts at rest, and that the Signora Melina will be released from the power of her enemies, and once more restored to your arms."

"But knowing the delicate sensitiveness of Signora Melina," replied Florio, "notwithstanding the gratitude she will be sure to feel for the generous and disinterested interference of Massaroni, I cannot help thinking that she will have the greatest repugnance at accepting of his services, when she reflects upon the wrong construction which the world is not at all unlikely to put upon her motives."

"If she sincerely love you," rejoined Maria, "and would not become the victim of a fate so revolting to every feeling of nature and of justice, she will not hesitate to waive all such delicate scruples. The Prince Bianchi and the Count Alberti will be alone to blame for all that may happen."

"But will they not be sure to pursue her with their deadliest vengeance?" said Clairville.

"She will be under the protection of Allesandro Massaroni," answered the brigand's wife, "and he may safely set their power at defiance."

"But think you," said Florio, "that, if even the signora should be willing, I can ever consent to accept her hand under such circumstances? Oh, no, that would be dooming her to poverty and misery of the most abject description."

"Nay, Clairville," returned Maria, "you unnecessarily alarm yourself—you view the darkest side of the question."

"How so, signora?"

"When the Prince Bianchi finds that his designs are defeated, he will repent him of his harsh and tyrannical conduct," replied the brigand's wife, "and I am much mistaken if he will not be glad to effect a reconciliation upon any terms."

"You know not the stern and inflexible disposition of the prince so well as I do," observed Floria, "or you would not entertain any such ideas. He would never forgive his fair niece for having fled from his power and frustrated his plans, much less would he consent to bestow her hand upon one against whom he entertains so many prejudices, and who is so far, so very far beneath her in point of station. And should I not be acting a selfish part were I, merely to gratify my own wishes, consent to plunge her into so much, and such irremediable misery? No, signora, let whatever may be the consequences to myself, I can never consent to become the husband of Signora Melina, without the free consent of her uncle, which it would be absolute madness in me to expect to obtain."

"You will change your mind, Signor Clairville," remarked the brigand's wife, "or I am much deceived."

"Never," answered Florio, resolutely "that is impossible."

"Stop till you behold the Signora Melina again, which I anticipate will be before many days, probably many hours, have elapsed," returned Maria, "and then it strikes me that you will change your mind. In this retreat, rude though it be, the delicacy, the happiness, and feelings of the Signora Melina will be held most sacred."

"Of that I entertain not the least doubt," replied Clairville.

"You have no occasion to do so," added the brigand's wife; "Allesandro Massaroni entertains too high a feeling of reverence for the whole sex, to suffer them to be outraged while he has the power to protect them. But calm yourself, Signor Clairville; reflect maturely upon the subject, and I flatter myself that you will yet be induced to come to the same conclusion that I have done."

"Well," replied Clairville, "I will try to do so, though I much doubt whether it will be with any success; though I thank you heartily for the good wishes you have been pleased to express towards me and the Signora Melina, and at the same time to assure you that I shall ever entertain the highest sense of the kindness of your husband, in espousing the cause of one who is already under so many lasting obligations to him, and which he much fears it will never be in his power to repay."

"Mention it not, Signor Clairville," said Maria: "whatever Massaroni the brigand chief does, springs spontaneously from his heart, and he needs no other reward than his own self-approving conscience."

"I am satisfied that he does not, signora," replied Florio, "and it is therefore that I feel the more grateful towards him, and should feel the greatest regret, in fact, I should never be able to forgive myself, should any accident befal him in his generous efforts to serve me."

"Fear not," returned Maria; "Massaroni has braved far greater dangers than this, times and oft, and has always escaped unscathed; besides, has he not well concerted his plans?"

"I firmly believe that he has," answered Clairville; "but should fortune abandon him at the very moment when he stands most in need of her aid?"

"Psha!" exclaimed the brigand's wife, impatiently and confidently, "I do not entertain any such apprehensions. He would not have entered into the undertaking had he not well considered what the results were likely to be. Let that assurance satisfy you, and look forward to the future with hope."

"Your words would almost induce me to do so, and yet——"

"Nay, nay, banish all doubts from your mind; seek to conquer your present objections, and take my word for it that you will find that your hopes will not be destined to be disappointed."

With these words Maria retired from the place where this conversation had taken place, and left Clairville to his own reflections, which, as the reader may easily imagine, were of the most multifarious and conflicting description. In spite of all that Maria had said, he could not but entertain the most serious apprehensions as to the result of the expedition; and notwithstanding the great anxiety he felt to behold his beloved Melina again, he was unable to bring his mind to believe that she would ever willingly agree to accept of the aid of Massaroni; nor could he hope that by even so doing she could ever become his wife.

"Oh, no," he said, "I know her gentle and delicate spirit too well to believe that she would be tempted to adopt a course which might bring scandal upon her fair and spotless name, and excite the everlasting wrath of the Prince Bianchi, her uncle, against her. It would be madness and presumption in me, were I to give encouragement to any such wishes. Dear Melina! the Fates conspire against us, and there is nothing left for us to do but to endeavour to resign ourselves to our unfortunate destinies. And yet 'tis hard that hearts so fondly united, should be thus doomed to be disappointed of all their hopes, and that to gratify the haughty caprice of he who should have studied the happiness of one so pure and innocent and who is so closely allied to him. It would have been much better had Fate never introduced us to each other, then we might have been spared the pangs we are both enduring."

He made a powerful effort to calm his feelings, but he found that to be a task that was most difficult to accomplish, and he remained in the same feverish state of excitement, with very few and brief intervals of relief.

Olympia also experienced the greatest anxiety of mind during the absence of Massaroni; she entertained the strongest fears that some calamity was was about to take place, and notwithstanding all the cruelty and injustice she had suffered from the Count Alberti, she could not stifle the feelings of love he had inspired in her breast altogether; and consequently she dreaded what might in all probability befal him when he and the brigand chief should encounter each other. She sincerely felt for the melancholy and dangerous situation of Melina, and she could never sufficiently deprecate the cruel persecution to which she was exposed by the count and the Prince Bianchi; and how much greater would be her agony and regret, should that innocent and beauteous damsel be sacrificed to the former, who, in every respect, she knew to be so totally unworthy of her.

"Oh, Alberti," she sighed, "would to Heaven that conscience could bring you to a full sense of the monstrous injustic with which you have acted towards me and our helpless and innocent offspring, ere it be too late; then indeed, great even as have been the sorrows you have inflicted on me, methinks I could pardon you all, though I could not now ever expect or consent to become your wife. But no, I fear that there is no hope for that; you are plunged too deep in iniquity to repent; and it is that thought which drives me to state almost bordering upon distraction."

The greater portion of Olympia's time was passed in the chamber of the unfortunate Ottavia, who was very ill, and had been ever since her meeting with Malvolio; and Olympia watched by the side of her couch with the greatest anxiety, and hourly felt the interest she experienced in the poor maniac's fate increase. Ottavia's mind remained in the same deplorable state; she continued to give utterance to the most wild and unintelligible sentences, but was never happy or the least calm when Olympia was absent from her.

Thus stood matters when Massaroni and his daring band returned to their mountain retreat, and Maria, his wife, no sooner heard his well known signal than she rushed eagerly to meet him; but her countenance fell when she saw that he was unaccompanied by the Signora Melina, and the disorder of his air convinced her that he had been disappointed.

"So, Massaroni," she observed; "you have returned; but how is this? Where is the Signora Melina?"

"At the Villa Rosa, more's the pity," answered her husband.

"Ah, then," ejaculated Maria, "your designs have been frustrated?"

"They have," replied the brigand chief.

"It is no more than I expected," observed Maria; "it was a rash and mad undertaking."

"No reproaches, Maria," said our hero, angrily; "fortune has for once deceived me, but the jade shall not do so again. Send Signor Clairville hither, and then I will relate the whole particulars."

Maria obeyed without making use of any further observation, but it was quite evident that she felt far from satisfied. Massaroni walked backwards and forwards for a minute or two in some disorder, but he struggled with his feelings, and by the time that his wife had returned accompanied by the anxious Clairville, he had quite regained his composure. Massaroni advanced eagerly towards him and grasped his hand.

"Ah!" exclaimed Clairville, "the Signora Maria informs me that you have failed, Massaroni?"

"True," answered the latter; "but do not

let that disturb you, Clairville ; fortune will yet smile upon my efforts."

"Alas!" sighed Florio, " that can never be, for doubtless my beloved Melina ere this has been compelled to become the wife of the detested Count Alberti."

"No," returned the brigand chief, " there is no fear of that at present, at any rate."

"How so?" demanded Clairville.

"Because," replied our hero, " the Count Alberti is wounded severely, if not mortally, and that by my hand."

MELINA IN HER BRIDAL DRESS.—IN TEARS.

"Ah!" ejaculated Florio, "I thought you assured me that you would use no more violence than was necessary, and that moreover you would avoid bloodshed, if possible?"

"True, and it was no fault of mine that this occurred. Alberti rushed like a mad beast upon me, and I only inflicted the wound in self-defence. But your patience, signor, and I will briefly relate all the particulars, and I think you will then be inclined to acquit me of all blame."

Florio Clairville and Maria listened attentively and eagerly, and then the brigand chief made them acquainted with that which has been detailed at length in the foregoing chapters.

"By Heaven!" said Clairville, when he had concluded, "this is the annihilation of my hopes. Massaroni, this failure is no more than I apprehended from the first. Poor, deeply wronged, and persecuted Melina!"

"Nay," observed Massaroni, "do not agitate yourself thus, Signor Clairville, for she to whom your heart is devoted shall yet be rescued from the power of her enemies, or I will lose my life in the attempt."

"Oh, no," said Florio, "I dare not entertain any such futile hopes."

"At any rate," remarked the brigand, "the wound which the Count Alberti has received, if even it does not prove mortal, will prevent the revolting ceremony from taking place for the present and for some time to come, and in the meantime there is no knowing what may take place."

"But to what additional misery will she not be sure to be subjected from the rage and revenge of the Prince Bianchi," observed Florio, "I shudder to think of it. Oh, Melina, that I should be the principal cause of bringing you into this sea of trouble!"

"Pshaw!" ejaculated the brigand chief, impatiently, "I tell you that you reproach yourself unjustly. It is the villany of Prince Bianchi and the Count Alberti, which is the cause of all, and on their heads be the consequences. This accident to the count will give us breathing time, and I do not doubt that I shall be able to concoct some other plan to rescue the Signora Melina, and which will be attended with success."

"You are much more sanguine in your expectations than I am, Massaroni," observed his wife.

"Indeed?"

"Yes," replied Maria. "Do you not think that the Prince Bianchi will now be sure to adopt such precautions as will render all your schemes abortive, and may bring down upon your head, when you least expect it, his utmost vengeance?"

"His vengeance!" repeated Massaroni, with a look of scorn; "I defy it. I tell you again, Maria, that I am resolved to persevere, and I have no doubt that the next attempt I make will be crowned with all the success that I could wish. Signor Clairville, do not let this one failure disturb your mind, nor banish from your thoughts all hope of possessing Melina; fortune for a time may frown upon you, but anon she will wear her gayest of smiles, and then you will learn to look back upon the past, I trust, without one feeling of regret. Do you not remember what I once told you, namely, that I should dance at your wedding?—And if

that prediction be not ultimately fulfilled, say that I am no prophet."

"I thank you from my heart, Massaroni, for the hopes with which you seek to inspire me," returned Florio Clairville, "and the good wishes you express towards me; but I find it impossible under all the circumstances to conquer my apprehensions, or to banish from my mind the dismal misgivings that have taken possession of me. It is no use, I must abandon all my hopes of ever possessing the fair and gentle Melina; it would be madness for me to encourage them."

"And it would be the height of madness for you entirely to discard them," returned the brigand chief; "what opinion do you think the Signora Melina could possibly form of the sincerity of your love, if you could thus so readily forsake her? Come, man, arouse yourself; you must not give way to such thoughts as these. If I am not deceived, even the Prince Bianchi will yet be brought to his senses, and will see the necessity of abandoning his harsh and cruel designs, if he would not break the heart of his fair and deeply injured niece."

"Ah, no!" said Florio, "the Prince is quite inexorable; his conduct has hitherto shown it; and even should the Count Alberti die, he will be sure to adopt some fresh course in order to gratify his revenge."

"If he values his own safety, he will not," remarked the brigand chief.

"He knows his own power," returned Clairville, "and will therefore set all consequences at defiance."

"But he may find himself powerless when he least anticipates it," said the brigand.

"Would to heaven that I could once more behold Melina," observed Clairville, "that I might consult with her upon the subject."

"And yet you object to any attempt being made to further that object, and to rescue her from the danger with which she is at present surrounded," returned Massaroni.

"Alas!" ejaculated Clairville, clasping his forehead; "I am completely bewildered and distracted; I know not how to act."

"Be guided entirely by me," said the brigand chief, "and all will yet be well."

"I would fain do so, Massaroni,—but—but—oh, how terrible must be the anguish which Melina is now enduring; and how great is the sufferings she must yet expect to experience from the cruelty of her unnatural uncle."

"He must be foiled in his designs," remarked Massaroni, "and if possible be brought to a full sense of the enormity of his conduct."

"I fear there is little or no chance of that," said Clairville.

"That is also my opinion," said the brigand's wife, "especially after what has taken place."

"Nay," said Massaroni, hastily, "I have no patience with such fears. Clairville, bear well in mind what I have said to you, and keep up your spirits. Bad as your prospects at present appear to be, a change may come over them for the better when you least anticipate it. Retire, and endeavour to compose your feelings. Maria, follow me; I must a word with you alone."

Thus saying, the brigand chief retired from the cavern, attended by his wife, and left Clairville alone. It was in vain that he attempted to follow the advice of Massaroni, and to tranquillize his feelings; the longer he reflected upon all the stirring events that had taken place, the more did his anguish and despair increase, and his feelings at last became so greatly excited that they were almost insupportable. He paced the cavern with disordered steps, and the anguish of his mind found vent in the most piteous groans.

"Fate is against us, dear Melina," he sighed, "and there is no hope for us. Oh, how heartless must be the Prince Bianchi, your uncle, have become, thus to delight to torture you; surely he will have bitter cause, when it is too late, to repent his unnatural conduct towards you. This attempt of the brigand chief, and the accident which has occurred to the Count Alberti, will but serve to exasperate him the more, and to goad him on to vengeance. Would that it had never occurred; and if it had not, would not the innocent Melina at this very moment have been the wife of the odious Count Alberti? She would! There can be no doubt of it; and, oh, how I shudder at the thought. Alas! Melina, had it been the will of Providence that we should both have been born in a humble sphere of life, we might both now have been happy in each other's love; but as it is, oh, how different is our doom. But what presumption was it in me to aspire to the hand and love of that peerless maiden. How was it that I did not feel my own utter unworthiness, and abandon such ambitious hopes ere I had won her innocent heart, and thus plunged her into such irremediable misery and despair? I feel that I have acted wrong—very, very wrong; but it is too late to recall the past—and, in spite of all my efforts to the contrary, I must ever most bitterly reproach myself."

He paused, for his feelings overpowered him, and the more he attempted to compose them, the greater, if possible, became his anguish. He recalled all the incidents that had taken place in the chapel to his mind's eye as vividly as if he had himself witnessed them; and he pictured to himself, in the most painful characters, all the sufferings which our beauteous and unfortunate heroine was at present enduring, until his brain was driven to distraction, and it required all the fortitude he could muster to be able to support his anguished feelings with the least degree of fortitude.

He found it impossible to entertain the same sanguine expectations as the brigand chief had professed to do, as to the success of any future attempts to rescue Melina, for it was very certain that the Prince Bianchi would now use every possible precaution to prevent them; and even if Massaroni were to triumph, and should succeed in bearing Melina away to his mountain retreat, what would be the consequences?—Was it at all likely that the damsel's strict sense of propriety would suffer her to yield to a clandestine marriage; or that he could ever give his consent?—He could not encourage the idea for a moment, and yet he was unable to abandon his hopes of her altogether. Thus was he tossed about on a wild sea of doubts and fears, and was totally unable to come to any satisfactory conclusion.

But no one was more violently agitated than Olympia, when she was made acquainted with the remarkable and exciting events which had taken place in the chapel of the Villa Rosa, and the alarming and dangerous situation of the Count Alberti. Her worst fears were now realised, and she gave vent to her feelings in the most melancholy lamentations.

"Wretched, guilty Alberti!" she ejaculated, "this is surely a terrible judgment upon you for the many and cruel wrongs which you have done to me and others. But must he die with all his sins upon his head, unrepented, and unatoned for?—Fearful thought! Forbid it, Heaven; and rather let him live to become a different being to what he has hitherto been. Manifold are the sins he has to answer for, and what would become of his soul if he should now be summoned before the awful judgment seat of the Supreme? Rather let him live, I say again, that he may by his future conduct make full reparation, as far as is in his power, for the past. Oh, Alberti!—how sincerely do I pity you, notwithstanding your crimes, and how freely could I forgive you all the wrongs you have done me, could I but rest assured that you were brought to a full sense of the cruelty and injustice of your conduct."

Thus Olympia continued to soliloquise for hours together, and her tears fell fast upon the cheeks of the innocent and unconscious offspring, affording a little but transitory relief to her overcharged heart.

The next day, Massaroni received a communication from the brigand whom he had left behind in the neighbourhood of the Villa Rosa, in order that he might gather all the information he could as to what took place there, and from that he learnt that the Count Alberti was considered to be in a very dangerous state; that Signora Melina was strictly confined to her chamber, and was said to be suffering from great anxiety of mind, as might naturally be expected; while the Prince Bianchi was in a state of the greatest excitement, and had sent numerous troops in every direction in search of the brigand chief and his band, and had given utterance to the most dreadful threats of vengeance, should they happen to fall in his power.

"Ha! ha! ha!" laughed Massaroni, scornfully, "he does well to threaten, but that is all he will be enabled to do. Allesandro Massaroni defies his power, and will yet make him quail beneath his authority."

"You talk boldly, Massaroni," said the brigand's wife, who was present; "but methinks it would be as well for you not to be too sanguine on the subject, lest you should be doomed to be disappointed."

"Why, how now, Maria?" demanded our hero, with a look of astonishment, ;—"what mean you by those observations?—Can this be Maria Grazie, the brigand's wife, who gave utterance to those words?"

"'Twas even so, Massaroni," she replied; "Maria Grazie always speaks what she thinks."

"And why these misgivings, Maria?"

"They are not misgivings, Massaroni, but rather forebodings," answered his wife. "Fortune has not seemed to smile upon you much of late, and I therefore think it would only be right for you to act with due precaution."

"And do I not always act with precaution?" demanded the brigand chief impatiently; "when did ever you find me do anything rashly? When did you ever find me attempt that which I had not previously well considered?"

"That may be," returned Maria, "and I do not attempt to deny it; but sometimes success is apt to make us careless, and the enemy never fails to take advantage of such a circumstance."

"Maria," remarked Massaroni, "you were not wont to speak in such doubtful tones."

"It was haply because I had no cause," she replied, "but as your wife, and the sharer in all your vicissitudes and dangers, I feel that I have an undoubted right to offer an opinion on every subject which involves your interest. I do but speak for your good."

"Maria," said her husband, "you do not approve of my designs against Bianchi and the Count Alberti?"

"I would that you could crush them, for you cannot more thoroughly hate and despise them than I do," answered Maria. "Most deeply do I also sympathise in the misfortunes of Signora Melina, and glad should I be could she be delivered from her present captivity, and restored to happiness; but the means to accomplish that are so surrounded by danger, that I must be again allowed to caution you how to proceed."

"Pshaw!" exclaimed the brigand chief, "I need no such caution. Cespetto! Maria,

do you think that I have became weak and childish, that my wits have forsook me, that you offer me such sage advise? You speak to me as though a sudden qualm had come over me, and that I were to be intimidated by the name of danger. I am surprised at you, Maria, and I cannot think upon what you have said with any degree of patience."

"Well," said Maria, "I hope the time will not come, Massaroni, when you may have reason to acknowledge that what I have said is not to be despised."

"Nonsense!" said the brigand, "what strange notions are these you have got into your head? Banish them, Maria, and trust to me for the safety and success of my designs."

Maria returned no answer, and the conversation then for the present dropped, and the brigand and his wife separated.

We must now direct the attention of the reader to the situation of the imprisoned ruffian Malvolio, who, in the late stirring events, has been almost lost sight of. He still remained firmly resolved not to divulge who he was, or the secret connected with the unfortunate Ottavia, even though he should be put to the most excruciating tortures that cruelty could suggest to induce him to confess, and he maintained the most dogged silence to all who came near him, appearing to exult in the anxiety they seemed to feel to learn all the particulars which were locked within his own breast. He did not, however, give up all hope of being some time or the other enabled to effect his escape, though at present there seemed not to be the remotest prospect of his having an opportunity to do so.

It was on the second day after the return of Massaroni and the other brigands that, as Malvolio was sitting disconsolately in his gloomy dungeon, with his chin resting on his hands, that a sudden thought flashed across his brain, which he wondered had never occurred to him before; and he arose hastily and walked to the farther end of the dungeon, where was collected a heap of filthy rubbish in one corner, apparently the remains of a mattress which had rotted away with time and the dampness of the place. Curiosity prompted Malvolio to remove it, and in doing so his hand came in contact with some hard substance, which he eagerly grasped and surveyed it as well as he could by the faint light which was admitted to the dungeon, through a narrow opening in the wall. It was part of a rusty iron-bar, about a foot long, but for what purpose it had been used Malvolio could not form the least conjecture, nor why it had been left there.

As the ruffian's eye surveyed it, a look of fiendish triumph overspread his repulsive features, and he could scarcely repress a laugh.

" Now, by the infernal host !" he ejaculated, " this is fortunate : this shall work my way to liberty, or I am much mistaken. Now Malvolio, let your hand be firm, and you may set your enemies at defiance, and will yet live to have a terrible revenge."

He concealed it in his bosom, and then anxiously awaited the arrival of night, when one of the brigands usually visited him, and whose keys the miscreant determined to secure at all hazards.

At length the time arrived ; and Malvolio with a palpitating heart, but a fixed determination, heard the bolts of the door of the dungeon in which he was confined being withdrawn, and the next instant the brigand entered, bringing with him a pitcher of water, some coarse bread, and light, which having placed on the ground, he prepared to retire without speaking a word. Malvolio suffered him to reach the door ; and then, when his back was turned towards him, he rushed suddenly upon him, and dealing him a tremendous blow with the iron-bar upon the head, he felled him to the earth, perfectly insensible and weltering in his blood !

"Ha! ha! ha!" laughed the murderer to himself, " that job was managed cleverly, at any rate. Now, Allesandro Massaroni, we shall see whether you will any longer keep Malvolio caged like a wild beast. The time is not far distant when I will repay you in full for all the insults and degradations I have received from you !"

He now removed a bunch of keys and a stiletto from the belt of the murdered brigand, and having wrapped his cloak around him, and placed his hat upon his head, he determined to make the attempt to effect his escape without delay.

He first listened at the door, in order to endeavour to ascertain whether or not there was any person at hand ; but all being perfectly silent, he imagined it was safe ; and issuing from the dungeon, he locked the door cautiously after him, and partially shading the lamp with his hand, he threaded his way as well as he could along the narrow passage, which he imagined led distinctly from that part of the mountain retreat in which Massaroni and the principal brigands were accustomed to congregate, and to a ready means of egress. He found a door at the extremity, however, impede his further progress, and there he again paused and listened attentively ; but there were no sounds to excite his apprehensions, and applying another key from the bunch to the lock, it yielded to him, and Malvolio found himself in a long range of vaults, filled with various stores, but which seemed at no very distant period to have been used as places of confinement. He wandered through these, scarce knowing what course to take ;

and at length ascending a rude flight of steps, he entered another passage, winding and very low, and which, gradually rising, he was inclined to believe that it led to the upper part of one of the mountains, from which there might be the secret means of emerging.

He had continued to grope his way along this passage for some distance, when he thought he suddenly heard footsteps approaching ; and crouching into a corner, he awaited the result with the greatest anxiety, and with the stiletto in his hand, determined to pounce upon the person, whoever it was, and plunge it to his heart.

The footsteps now became more distinct, and it was evident they were approaching rapidly towards the spot on which Malvolio was standing. All was, however, involved in complete darkness, and he could see nobody. He scarcely ventured to breathe ; but, as ill-luck would have it, just as the person seemed to have got within a few paces of him, Malvolio was seized with a loud cough, which he found it impossible to restrain, and, of course, he was immediately betrayed.

"Ah! who's there ?" demanded the man. "Speak ! the watchword, or I fire !"

The sound of the man's voice now directed the ruffian Malvolio, and, with a terrible oath, he darted forward, stiletto in hand, and endeavoured to plunge it into the body of the brigand , but before he could do so, he received the contents of a pistol in his head, and with an exclamation of mingled rage and agony, he sank upon the earth.

"Ah! by h—l!" he cried, " I am caught at last!—Curses light upon he who has dealt me this blow ! Oh, that my dagger's point could yet penetrate his heart !"

"What ho! lights there !" shouted the brigand ; " there is treason afloat ! Lights, I say again !"

He had no occasion to shout, however, for the report of the pistol had reached the ears of Massaroni and those who were in his company at the time, and the brigand chief and Rubaldo, together with several others of the band, quickly arrived at the spot with lights, and their astonishment may be readily conceived when they beheld the miscreant Malvolio weltering in his blood and writhing in agony.

"Ah !" exclaimed our hero, " what is the meaning of this?—How has this villain managed to escape from the dungeon in which he was confined ?—Where is Andrea, who had to attend upon him ?"

A malicious grin of triumph passed over the ghastly features of Malvolio, now distorted with agony, as he replied—

" He is stretched a lifeless, mangled corpse in the dungeon where you lately had me confined!—But to think that I should be thus foiled, when I was so near accomplishing my object, and the prospect of revenge was before me. May all the torments of perdition pursue the wretch who has done this!"

"Away with the villain to some place of security," commanded the brigand chief, "and let his wound be attended to; his life must be saved for the present, if possible."

"His life must be preserved," gasped forth the wretch, struggling with the agony of his bodily feelings, and with an energy that no one could have expected him to evince at that moment; "his life must be preserved, *for the present*," he repeated, fixing upon our hero a look of the most fiendish description; "and why for the present, Signor Massaroni? Think you that, by so protracting my death, you will be enabled to elicit anything from me that might be to your advantage? Ha! h— Oh! that pang—d——n! But I will still deceive ye all! I know much—ay, all that you wish to know, but you shall never learn it from my lips. Oh, that—that this cursed wound——"

As Malvolio thus spoke, he grappled with the empty air in a vain effort to recover his stiletto, and endeavoured to rise from the ground, but completely exhausted with the loss of blood and the excitement of his feelings, he once more sank back insensible, and in that state was conveyed to one of the principal caverns, where a brigand, who acted in the capacity of surgeon to the band, and who was likewise skilful, was immediately in attendance upon him, and dressed his wound, which he at once pronounced to be mortal.

"By the mass," said Massaroni, "that is unfortunate. But think you, Riberi, that there is any immediate danger? think you that he will not again recover, if it be only for a short time?"

"Why, captain," replied Riberi, "if he be kept quiet, it is not unlikely that he may. But even when restored to consciousness, you must be very cautious in the manner in which you proceed, if you wish to elicit any information from him."

"Good," said the brigand chief, "I will follow your advice, Riberi. There is much that I would have him confess before he dies. It is evident that he is connected with the history of the unfortunate Ottavia, and acquainted with all its dark secrets. The certain conviction of the approach of death might induce him to divulge, and——"

"He appears to be a most hardened and desperate miscreant, captain," interrupted Riberi, "and I much fear, if you flatter yourself with that hope, you will only be fated to disappointment. However, I will do my best to revive him, and, if you act with your usual

prudence, the best results may ensue, and all your wishes be gratified."

"Enough," said the brigand chief; "I leave everything to you, Riberi, and will act according to your advice. The villain! so much, too, depending upon him; by what means did he contrive to escape from his dungeon?"

"By the means, he said, captain," replied one of the brigands, who at that moment entered the cavern; "poor Andrea lies there a frightful corpse, and this iron bar, no doubt, is the instrument with which the murder was effected. You see that the assassin has possessed himself of Andrea's keys, and by that means escaped from his dungeon. He has also assumed the hat and cloak of Andrea, and but for the timely arrival of our comrade, Sangrado, would doubtless have obtained his liberty altogether."

"Very true—very true," replied our hero. "But away, comrades; let us leave the villain to the care of Riberi. You will give me immediate notice," he added, addressing himself to Riberi, "should any sudden change take place?"

"I will do so, captain," answered Riberi, and our hero immediately retired.

The event we have just been recording, caused the greatest excitement amongst the brigands, and the females especially were most anxious as to the result, and none more so than Olympia, who anxiously hoped that the miscreant Malvolio would make a confession as to who he was, but more than all, the connexion there was between himself and poor Ottavia, with whose secret and melancholy history, it was quite evident he was perfectly well acquainted, and in the unravelment of which she felt such a remarkable interest. There were certain circumstances in the fate of the unfortunate maniac, which so strangely corresponded with her own, that the longer she reflected upon them, the more deeply did she become interested, while at the same time a certain feeling came over her for which she was unable satisfactorily to account. For hours as she had watched by the side of the couch of the poor afflicted one, and gazed intently upon her pale and expressive features, a sensation, amounting to far more than sympathy had swelled her bosom, and she felt as if she could love her with all the dutiful affection of a daughter, as if she could willingly lay down her life to save hers, or to restore her poor wandering, demented brain, to its reasoning faculties. There was a sort of magic in the wild light of the unfortunate maniac's eyes, that imparted a magnetic influence to the soul of Olympia; and many a time when the former, after some melancholy ravings, had sank exhausted into a tranquil sleep, she would press warm kisses upon her careworn cheeks, weep like a child, in all the uncontrollable fulness of her heart, and then kneel down, and fervently offer up her prayers to the Almighty to restore her to her reason, that she might be enabled to reveal the many wrongs which it was too evident she had sustained, and happily, to bring the perpetrators of them (if they still existed) to that punishment which she firmly believed they so richly merited. She pictured to herself in the most glowing and painful characters that the imagination can conceive, what her feelings must have been, had she had a mother who was placed in the same deplorable situation as the unfortunate being for whom her sympathies were so deeply excited, and then her tears would flow afresh, and her feelings would gain such a powerful ascendancy, that she knew not how to subdue them.

"Mother!" she would sob forth, "oh! what a blessed, what a sacred, what a loved name is that; how deeply is it entwined round the fondest emotions of my heart! what an invigorating, a blissful sensation does it thrill throughout the purple current of my veins! and yet I never was sensible to a mother's love. Alas! mine has been an unfortunate fate, and perhaps it would have been better had I never been born. My poor child—child of sorrow, my innocent, helpless boy! what will be thy future fate, should Providence ordain that thou shouldst live? Who will look with respect upon the unfortunate offspring of shame? Perhaps, with all the noblest feelings instinct within thy breast, taunted, hunted, scandalised, by the unfeeling world, thy nature may become perverted, and you will sink to crime and degradation! Oh, wilt thou not then have reason to curse thy mother's memory, when the remains of that hapless, betrayed parent have long since mouldered into dust? Horrible thought! Oh, God, I most humbly beseech Thee, that sooner than such a——"

She was suddenly interrupted by the entrance of Maria Grazie, the brigand's wife.

"What! on your knees, Olympia?" said the former, in the gentlest and most sympathising accents; "come, come, you must not give way to this violence of grief; there is one above who never fails to render justice to His suffering creatures, whatever may be the trials it shall be His wise will to subject them to; patience, Olympia, resignation, and you will yet be rewarded by that ultimate happiness which your virtues deserve."

"Oh, Signora Maria," returned Olympia, "the constant and unfeigned words of kindness and consolation you administer to me in so generous a spirit, go to my heart. Woman you are, in all the purest, the brightest essence of the term; I could love you as a sister; but even with all a sister's overflowing affection, could never sufficiently express the boundless feelings of gratitue I do and must ever entertain towards you!"

"Enough! enough, my good girl," said Maria, "I can read the sentiments of your mind as distinctly and as truly as if they were presented to my sight in a book; but compose your feelings, for something may shortly transpire, which will change your prospects altogether, and——"

"Oh, what do you mean?" interrupted Olympia, eagerly; "and what brings you so suddenly here?"

"The wretch Malvolio, for such he has acknowledged to be his name," replied the brigand's wife, "is struck with remorse, and finding he is dying, he has expressed a wish to make a confession of his past crimes, to listen to which he earnestly desires you will be present, as what he has to divulge particularly concerns you and the unfortunate Signora Ottavia."

"Myself and the Signora Ottavia!" repeated Olympia, and at the same time feelings of the most indescribable nature rushing to her heart.

"Yes, yes," answered Maria; "but let us not delay, for every moment is precious; should the villain expire before he has made the confession he wishes——"

"Ah!" again interrupted Olympia, "I see. I feel at once the importance of your suggestion. Lead the way, signora, I am ready to attend you."

The brigand's wife made use of no further observation, but taking the child of Olympia in her arms, she led the way, and the latter followed her to the cavern in which the dying Malvolio was lying, with the brigand chief anxiously watching over him at one side of his pallet, and a monk on the other, whom Massaroni had sent for expressly to attend on the solemn and important occasion.

The features of the dying wretch were frightfully distorted by his mental sufferings, but the more ferocious passions of his nature were calmed down into an expression of remorse and a strong determination to render all the atonement in his power for the many crimes he had perpetrated, during the short time he believed he had to live; but Olympia approached towards the couch on which he was reclining with a feeling of the most unaccountable awe and trepidation, whilst her heart beat at double its wonted or natural pace.

No sooner did Malvolio behold her, than the expression which came over his features was ghastly in the extreme, and he hastily and convulsively buried his countenance in the bed-clothes, and groaned aloud.

"Courage, my son," said the monk, solemnly, "Heaven is All-Merciful, even to the most guilty of its erring children, and there is hope for you, if you freely confess your sins, and feel the spirit of true penitence within you which can alone be done by acknowledging the truth to those whom you have injured and——"

"Hope for me!" interrupted the poor wretch, raising his cadaverous countenance, and looking into the holy man's face with an expression that was truly awful and electrifying; "hope for a monster like myself, one who has waded through oceans of blood to achieve his guilty ends? 'Tis false, old man! Perdition now is before me; my guilty soul is about to be plunged into endless torment, and yet you mock we with these wild delusions! No—no—I feel you trifle with me, and will say no more. Let me die! let me die, and meet the everlasting doom that is in store for me!"

"Son, son," interposed the holy father, meekly; "I speak but the words of the Supreme, and would pour the balm of consolation into your guilty soul; there is mercy for all from on High, even at the eleventh hour!—Son, thine hours, thy moments are numbered; let me, then, implore you not to waste that precious time, but repent, confess, and with the will and mercy of Almighty God receive salvation!"

"Yes, yes," replied Malvolio, after a struggle; "your words, holy man, inspire me with a confidence which I never thought I should experience in my dying moments. I will confess; I—I—draw closer round me all.'

At this moment his eye, for the first time, fell upon Olympia, and the agitation of his countenance was increased tenfold.

"Ah!" he ejaculated; "you here!—Oh, 'tis well!—Give me one sup of wine, to moisten my parched lips, and stay the struggling breath while I acknowledge the dreadful truth."

The brigand chief, who was waiting in a state of the utmost anxiety to hear what he had to reveal, placed the glass to his lips, and Malvolio, having just sipped of the contents, after a brief pause thus commenced his short and guilty recital, during which he was frequently compelled to stop for an instant or two, owing to exhaustion, or the agony of his feelings—

"Many years ago, there was a maiden, humble, but happy in her humble sphere, the idol of her parents, and the pride of all who knew her. That maiden's name was Zitella!"

"Zitella!" repeated the brigand chief, eagerly.

"Ay, even so," replied Malvolio, with much more calmness than could have been expected. "The name seems to agitate you, Massaroni, and I marvel not that it does so, for your history is deeply connected with that poor unfortunate, deeply wronged individual."

Olympia felt a most extraordinary sensation came over her as the dying Malvolio uttered these words, and more especially at the peculiar and impressive look which he fixed upon her, and she could not, without considerable difficulty, restrain her feelings.

"Young she was, innocent, and beautiful," resumed Malvolio, "one of noble birth, possesssed of boundless wealth; but a villain at heart, by accident crossed her path; fatal, accursed was the hour—She knew not his rank at the time;—he rendered her parent's a service;—he had an oily tongue, a fair exterior, and he won the poor, inexperienced, confiding Zitella's affections. An awful calamity deprived her of both her parents in one day, and it was then that the villain to whom she had devoted her young and innocent heart, took a cowardly advantage of the influence he had gained over her affections, and under the mask of a protector and a friend, succeeded in working her destruction. A child—a girl—was the offspring of this unfortunate and illicit intercourse; and a few weeks after its birth, the seducer brutally deserted it and his unfortunate victim. Zitella, however, discovered his rank, and appealed to him for pity for herself and child. She was repulsed, and it was then that the demon thought entered his mind to rid himself of them both. He employed a desperate ruffian whom he knew he could entrust to perpetrate the fiendish deed—to murder them!"

"Oh, horrible!" gasped forth Olympia.

"Ay, horrible you may well say," returned Malvolio; "but it is nevertheless true. The miscreant he employed was myself."

"And did you perform his bidding?" demanded Massaroni, hastily.

"No," answered Malvolio; "heartless wretch though I was, I could not do that deed. I tore the infant from its mother's breast, and sent her forth upon the world a wandering maniac. It were better, perhaps, and far more merciful had my dagger's point penetrated her heart."

"And that much wronged female is——" said the brigand chief.

"Her whom you know as Ottavia," answered Malvolio.

"And the villain, her betrayer?"

"The Prince Bianchi!"

"Ah! by the saints——"

"'Tis true!" interrupted Malvolio; "the Prince Bianchi was the vile seducer of her whom you know by the name of Ottavia, and the father of her child."

"But that child?" demanded Olympia and Massaroni in a breath.

"Unable to take its innocent life," replied Malvolio, "I left it at the door of the Palazzo of the late Count Alberti!—Signora Olympia, you are that child, and Zitella, and the Prince Bianchi, the proud Governor of Rome, are your parents!"

"Oh, God!" shrieked the astonished Olympia, and she immediately sank insensible in the arms of the brigand's wife, and was conveyed without delay to her own apartment.

"Is it possible, Malvolio," said our hero, after a pause, "that you have spoken the truth?"

"Massaroni," replied Malvolio, "the

hand of death is upon me, and here in the presence of this holy man, and you all, I swear, as I hope for forgiveness for my manifold and heinous offences, that I have spoken nothing but the truth. Olympia is the daughter of the Prince Bianchi, and you——"

"Ah!" interrupted the brigand chief, in

THE FIGHT IN THE CHAPEL.—MASSARONI WOUNDS COUNT ALBERTI.

a state of the greatest possible emotion, "who am I?"

Malvolio tried to answer, but he could not; the exertion he had already undergone had overpowered him; two or three desperate struggles he made, but without the least effect;

his features suddenly became frightfully distorted; his form convulsed—his eyes glared for a moment, with an expression upon vacancy, and with one awful groan of agony, the wretched, guilty man, sunk back on his pillow a corpse!

CHAPTER XL.

THE EMOTION OF OLYMPIA.— THE ILLNESS OF OTTAVIA.— HER SUDDEN AND MIRACULOUS RESTORATION TO REASON, AND THE AFFECTED MEETING BETWEEN THE MOTHER AND DAUGHTER.

WE will hastily pass over the feelings of astonishment which the confession of Malvolio excited in the bosom of the brigand chief and his wife.

"By the mass!" exclaimed our hero; "this is more, much more than I expected to hear, and but serves to convince me in the opinion I had formed, that the Prince Bianchi, my bitterest enemy, is a villain of the blackest dye, and stimulates me to fresh acts of vengeance upon his head. Olympia, and the unfortunate Ottavia, whom we have so long befriended, related by the closest ties of consanguinity? It seems scarcely possible, and yet I have no reason to doubt the accuracy of the statement of this wretched man. Holy father, you have heard all that he stated, and have taken good note of it?"

"I have, Massaroni," answered the monk, "and am ready at any time to testify to the same."

"Would to Heaven that his life could have been prolonged for a few moments," said the brigand chief; "for it is evident he had something more to reveal, and which, from the observations he made use of, deeply interested me."

"True," returned the monk, "but you must leave it to time and providence to reveal all."

"Ay," replied Massaroni, "I must e'en do so; but I must acknowledge that my patience is nearly exhausted. But see to Olympia, Maria."

The brigand's wife obeyed, and retired to the cavernous apartment to which Olympia had been conveyed, accompanied by Riberi, who had been present during the closing scene of Malvolio's guilty life.

They found her just restored to consciousness, and on their entrance she burst into tears, which somewhat relieved her heart. Maria approached her couch, and kindly inquired how she felt.

"Oh, better! much better!" replied Olympia; "the painful mystery which has so long enveloped my fate is at length unravelled, and a world of anxiety is removed from my mind. But to discover that the Prince Bianchi is my father, and that the unfortunate Ottavia is that mother whom I never expected to know, is surely enough to overpower me."

"It is," coincided the brigand's wife; "but still you must endeavour to compose your feelings."

"But Malvolio?"

"He is no more," answered Maria.

"Wretched man!" observed Olympia; "but think you that which he has stated is to be depended upon as truth?"

"Oh, yes," returned Maria, "there can be no doubt of it."

"My mother! my poor afflicted, deeply injured mother!" sobbed Olympia, with an indescribable burst of emotion, "I must see her, and strain her beloved form to my bosom, without a moment's delay. Oh, God! that we should meet thus! May Heaven in its infinite mercy help her, and restore her wandering mind to reason."

Thus saying, she arose hastily from the couch on which she had been declining, and prepared to leave the place hastily.

"Stay, stay!" said Maria; "do not unnecessarily excite yourself, before that unfortunate and revered being to whom you are now about to pay so important a visit, for, in her present delicate and precarious situation, it might be attended with the worst consequences."

"True, true," answered Olympia; "God help her, I again say. I thank you, Signora Maria, for your kind consideration, I owe you a debt of gratitude, and also your husband, which I fear it will never be in my power to repay. You will accompany me, will you not?"

"I will," replied the brigand's wife, "if you wish it."

"Oh, yes," said Olympia, "it is fit that I should have some confidential friend present with me at the trying interview. Come, come; let us not delay."

Olympia and Maria hastily slipped on their cloaks, and emerging from the cavernous retreat of Massaroni, bent their steps in the direction of the residence of old Montaldi, Olympia's heart fluttering as she went with a sensation which the reader may easily imagine.

Ottavia was asleep when they entered the apartment in which she was lying, but no sooner did Olympia behold her, than her feelings overpowered her, and uttering the name of mother in a voice of the most inexpressible emotion, she attempted to embrace her, but sank insensible in the arms of her companion. She soon, however, recovered; and in the meantime, Maria having made old Montaldi acquainted with the extraordinary circumstances that had taken place, he was fully prepared to assist her in the scene which was about to take place.

"Mother! beloved mother!" exclaimed Olympia, throwing herself on her knees by the side of the bed, and taking her pale, thin hand in her own, pressing it frantically to her lips, and bathing it with her tears; "mother! it is that wretched, betrayed child, so long estranged from you, who thus addresses you. Oh. God of Heaven! grant that she may look up and address me with the light of returning reason."

"My dear signora," observed Montaldi, "let me beseech you to calm your feelings, for on your fortitude and prudence everything depends. Believe me there is no one who can more duly appreciate and sympathise with the emotions that naturally throb within your breast than myself, and I trust that Providence will bring about a speedy termination of the sorrows that yourself and your much wronged mother have so unjustly experienced; but, as I said before, much, nay, everything depends upon the manner in which you act upon this trying occasion. With care and attention, the Signora Zitella, your mother may be restored to her senses, and then I trust that that justice will be rendered you which has been so long denied, and that you will be repaid for the many years of suffering you have both endured, by an adequate return of happiness for the future."

"Oh, Signor Montaldi," remarked Olympia, "how can I do otherwise than acknowledge the truth, the force, and justice of your observations? You have been the kind, the humane, and disinterested protector of my poor mother in the midst of her adversity. Without you, what would have become of her, and——"

"No more, Signora Olympia," interrupted the kind hearted old man, "you completely overwhelm me with your thanks, and I scarcely know what to say in reply. I have but performed my duty towards my fellow creature, and thank God, there is no one who can conscientiously accuse old Montaldi of not having done so yet."

"May Heaven reward you, good old man," ejaculated Olympia, fervently, "for it will never be in my power to do so as I ought."

"Let me but see your unfortunate parent restored to her senses," said Montaldi, "and I trust the time is not far distant when she will be so, and my utmost wishes will be gratified. But see, your mother awakes. Be cautious, I once more beg of you."

The unfortunate maniac now opened her eyes, and gazed vacantly around the apartment.

"Mother! beloved mother!" cried the deeply agitated Olympia, throwing her fair arms around the sufferer's neck, and unable, in spite of all that old Montaldi had said, and the promises she had made to him, to control her feelings; "mother! do you not know me? Does not the powerful voice of nature whisper to you who I am?"

"Mother!" repeated the maniac, wildly, and forcibly disengaging herself from the embrace of Olympia, "mother! who dared to call me by that name? It is a bitter mockery! I have no child now, though once I had a sweet smiling innocent; but the wretches tore her from me, and left me alone to misery and despair. Come, come, walk with me, and I will take you to her grave. It is a pretty spot, on which the rose, the lily, and the violet ever bloom. Come, come, will you not go with me?"

"Mother! beloved mother!" again gasped forth Olympia, "oh, arouse yourself from this fearful delusion which has so long enfettered your reason. Your child was preserved from the murderer's knife; she still lives, to bless, to honour, to worship you, till the latest moment of her existence. Look on my features; recall your scattered senses. I am that daughter whom you have so long mourned as dead!"

The poor maniac fixed upon her a vacant look, and laughed aloud as she replied—

"You her! you my little innocent? No—no—no, she would be an infant now, were she living, and you to dare to boast of being her! Ha! ha! ha! Oh! the cruel world does well to laugh at and deride me. Go—go; he will be here to-morrow, for he promised he would, and he possesses too much the soul of honour to fail to keep his word. But no! stay, stay, do not leave me yet. I know you now! you are that gentle spirit that has ever appeared to me in my dreams. You will stay with me and talk to me, will you not? for there is such Heavenly music in the tone of your voice, that it enraptures my very soul."

"Oh, I will never leave you," said Olympia, in a voice of the deepest emotion.

"You will not, you will not?" said the unfortunate woman, eagerly. and her eyes sparkling with pleasure; "oh, that is kind very kind of you; and we will be so happy, together. We will talk of days gone by. I will allow you to call me mother; you shall be my daughter—in name only—mind that, for I have no daughter now; and I will tell you all the fond things he used to say to me; the many promises he made to me, and which he never can forget; but—but, he will be here to-morrow, and then——"

"Who do you mean?" hastily interrupted Olympia, eagerly catching at the opportunity which presented itself; "the Prince Bianchi?"

"The Prince Bianchi," cried Ottavia, staring wildly around her; "who mentioned that name?"

"The Prince Bianchi," repeated Olympia, and her heart almost seemed to rise to her lips as she spoke, "the father of your child!"

The maniac started at the words, and clasped her burning temples, as she exclaimed—

"The father of my child! The Prince Bianchi! Yes, 'twas he! The whole truth now flashes upon my disordered memory like an electric shock! I seem as though I were awakening from some fearful dream, which has endured for so many years. The Prince Bianchi! that name so familiar to me! He—he deserted me, at the very time he vowed to love me the most. But my child! Ah! the monster Malvolio, that was his name, I remember it all now; he whom I thought I saw, or dreamt I saw, the other day—he robbed me of my child."

"Oh! thank God!" exclaimed Olympia, in a voice of the most extreme agitation. "Reason is resuming its seat. Beloved being, I implore you to arouse yourself! You were not deceived! it was the villain Malvolio whom you beheld, when you was accompanied by your kind friend and protector, Montaldi. He is now no more, but previous to his death, he confessed all. It is true he bore your child away, but he had not the courage to take its innocent life; your daughter still lives!"

"Still lives!" repeated Zitella (for by that name we must in future call her) fixing upon Olympia a look which penetrated to her very soul; "who are you that tell me so, and would thus flatter my broken spirit with such fallacious hopes? Still lives! where! oh, where?"

"Here! here! beloved mother!" cried Olympia in a frantic voice, and her heart almost ready to burst; "I am that child, who has been so long and so cruelly separated from you! I am your daughter! and I call on high Heaven to bear witness to the truth of what I say!"

"My daughter! blessed name!" ejaculated Zitella, fixing her eyes with the most intense earnestness upon her countenance. "Ah! the mist evaporates before me—a new light flashes upon my brain—'tis no longer darkness! Those features! I cannot be deceived! God of Heaven! my child! my long lost child!"

"Mother! mother!" cried Olympia, and they sunk convulsively into each other's arms.

———

CHAPTER XLI.

THE NARRATIVE OF ZITELLA.

WHAT a scene was that which followed this affecting meeting, and miraculous restoration of Zitella so suddenly to her senses. Language must fail in attempting to describe it. For some time the unfortunate mother and daughter could do nothing but embrace and weep upon each other's bosom, while Montaldi and the brigand's wife stood by deeply affected, but did not offer to interrupt them.

"Oh, God!" at length exclaimed Zitella, "and as it at length pleased Thee, in Thine infinite mercy, to recall my scattered reason, and to restore that beloved child whom I thought lost to me for ever to my arms?—I can scarce believe in this, the extent of my happiness. Daughter, daughter! beloved daughter! yes; the instinct of nature tells me that you are so! Oh, let me again press you to my swelling heart with all a mother's fondness, and weep my tears of joy upon your bosom."

"Mother! mother!" cried Olympia, again returning her fond embrace with increased fervour. "Oh, that endearing name; Heaven has indeed been merciful to us, after all our troubles, in restoring us to each other; and never shall our voices cease in its praise; we will never, never more part until death shall separate us!"

"We will not, my beloved child," said Zitella, "and may the time when death shall part us be far distant. Oh, what a frightful dream has been that which I have so long experienced; but thank Heaven, I am at last aroused from it, and may I hope that happiness may be the portion of my declining years."

"Amen!" said Olympia, solemnly, "and may my misguided parent yet live to repent of the errors he has committed, and to make you all the atonement he can, for the brutal (for I cannot call it by any milder term) treatment you have experienced from him."

"Ah!" replied her mother, "thus spoke the feelings that have always, when reason was not shifted from her throne, held possession of my breast, and which convince me still more, if Nature did not speak to me in undeniable tones, that you are my daughter; and sincerely, fervently do I respond to the sentiments you have expressed towards the princely author of your being. Freely do I pardon him, and may the just God of heaven do the same. But what a fearful dream has mine been—and yet, I have some slight recollection of seeing a smiling little innocent in your arms, Mira (for such is your name), such a one as you were when you were so mercilessly torn from me. Your husband, for you are united—where is he?"

What an agonising question was this to put to poor Mira, (for such we must in future call that unfortunate being who has hitherto been known to the reader as Olympia); she averted her gaze from that of her mother, drooped her head, and sobbed as though her heart would break, the tears at the same time streaming down in torrents from between her fair and taper fingers. The Signora Zitella watched her with the utmost anxiety, and throwing her arms around her neck, she drew her towards her with tenderness, at the same time that she observed—

"You weep, my child;—what is the meaning of this?—Have my words distressed you?

Ah!—a light dawns upon me!—Good God! have you——"

"Mother! mother! dear unfortunate mother!" gasped forth the distracted Mira;—" I —I should blush to look you in the face! And yet—oh! I cannot say more than to confess to you that the same cruel fate has attended us both!—I am, like yourself, the victim of a confiding love, as pure as ever reigned within the breast of woman; and—and with my helpless offspring have been deserted by he who worked my destruction!"

"My poor daughter," ejaculated her mother, straining her at the same time frantically to her bosom; " and have you indeed suffered thus?—This—this indeed makes you, if possible, doubly dear to me. Alas! the ways of Providence seem severe, but who shall presume to arraign their justice?—My child! my child! you are restored to me, and in sympathising with each other's misfortunes, and looking forward with hope to the future, we will seek to derive our consolation and happiness. The father of your child—"

"Is the Count Alberti D'Almafi, at whose parents door, the villain Malvolio has confessed he left me, after having so brutally torn me from your maternal bosom," replied Mira.

"Ah! the Count Alberti D'Almafi!" repeated Zitella, "methinks I have heard that name before, though it now appears to me only as one of the indistinct visions of the past— one of those troubled dreams which have so long flitted before my wandering senses. He has deserted you?"

"Alas! alas!"

"And does he still live?"

"He does: but he has within these last few days received such injuries as are not at all unlikely to prove fatal," replied Mira.

"But your child! your little innocent," said Zitella, eagerly, " why have you not brought it with you, that it might receive the fond caresses of its unfortunate relative, and—"

"Pardon me, Signora Zitella," interposed Montaldi, "but, as your friend, and the humble instrument, in the hands of Providence, for many years your protector, may I be allowed to suggest that yourself and your amiable daughter should now separate for a short time, and that you should both of you endeavour to tranquillise your feelings; for the excitement which these extraordinary events have naturally created might be productive of the most fatal and melancholy consequences."

"No, no, no!" returned Zitella, hastily, and still infolding her daughter in her arms, "after so many years of estrangement, we must not—shall not, now be parted. What say you, my beloved Mira, in whose eyes I read my own soul: in whose features I read all the fond expression of administering angels;

we will not part?—Now that we are restored to each other, we will live and die together. Pardon me, good old man, to whom I owe a debt of gratitude, which alas! I feel it will never be in my power to repay, for words which may to your ears sound harsh and ungenerous; but Providence has restored to my seared heart that dear child whom I thought lost to me for ever, and can you marvel that I should now cling to her as the ivy to the tree? No, no—we must not part, my Mira, my sweet Mira, the angel of my wandering dreams:— you will not leave me, will you, love?"

"No, no, my adored mother!" replied Mira, with an hysterical burst of sobs:—" we will never again part till it be the will of Heaven to separate us by death, and then let us trust that we shall finally be re-united in those realms of eternal bliss, where sorrow never enters. But let us endeavour to follow the advice of our excellent friend, Signor Montaldi, my mother, and to calm our feelings; the Almighty looks down with mercy upon us, and after the terrible tempest it has been the lot of us both to encounter, I trust that the time is not far distant when we shall be fully compensated for all in the most unbounded happiness. Signora Maria, may I request you to communicate to your husband what has so fortunately occurred, and to request his attendance here to-morrow morning, accompanied by yourself and my poor child, when, no doubt, myself and my revered parent will both be in a better condition to enter into mutual explanations.

"I will do so, signora," replied the brigand's wife, " and rest assured that there is no one who feels a more lively interest in the welfare of you both, than Maria Grazie, the wife of Allesandro Massaroni, the mountain chief."

"I know it, my kind, my noble-hearted, my disinterested friend!" returned Maria, at the same time warmly pressing her hand. "Oh, dear mother, to this excellent woman and her husband, we are indebted for all the happiness we at present enjoy in this miraculous and providential discovery. Without them we might ever have remained unknown to each other, and might have sank with sorrowing and bereaved hearts into the silent grave, and our memories have been despised and stigmatized by the ungenerous world. They have befriended, protected us both, and——"

"May the great God above," interrupted Zitella, solemnly, and raising her clasped hands and her eyes devoutly towards Heaven, " bless them, and shower upon their heads all the happiness that can attend His creatures upon this earth. Oh! where shall I find words to express the feelings that overflow my heart towards them?"

"Signora," replied Maria, " the life of myself and my husband, the brigand chief, is one of peril ; but thank Heaven, scandalized as we have been and still are, it has always been our aim to redress the wrongs of our suffering and oppressed fellow-creatures, and to bring a just, though sometimes a terrible retribution upon their heads. In what we have been so fortunately enabled to do for you and the Signora Mira, your daughter, we have performed no more than our duty, and we seek no acknowledgments. Farewell, till we meet again, which, with your permission and that of your daughter, shall be to-morrow morning. Montaldi, adieu!"

Thus saying, without waiting to receive any reply from them, the brigand's wife hastily took her departure, and made her way with all possible speed to the mountain retreat, in order that she might make her husband acquainted with the fortunate and extraordinary restoration of Zitella to her senses.

The reader may be able to form an adequate idea of the astonishment and satisfaction of Massaroni, when he heard of those remarkable particulars.

"By the saints!" he ejaculated; "Providence has favoured us all all at once; this is far more fortunate than I ever, in my most sanguine moments, anticipated. Zitella restored to reason, she will be enabled to explain everything, and to bring confusion and dismay upon the haughty tyrant, Prince Bianchi. Allesandro Massaroni has achieved a triumph which he never expected, and it shall now be his study to bring that proud spirit to its due submission, and to make him tremble at the bare mention of my name. Maria, you find that I was not mistaken when I espoused the cause of the Signora Melina and Olympia. The Prince Bianchi—the mighty governor of Rome, consign the brigand chief to a scaffold! Ha, ha, ha! 'tis not a bad joke! Verily, 'tis not a bad joke!"

"We appear to triumph now, it is true," remarked Maria ; "but still, I would advise you, Massaroni, not to be too sanguine."

"And why so?" demanded the brigand.

"Because, there are many dangers, I am convinced, which you do not yet foresee," answered his wife, "and, which, without due precaution, may be the means of turning the tide of fortune against us."

"Pshaw! I entertain no such apprehensions," said Massaroni ; "the discovery of the existence of his victim Zitella, and her daughter, will strike confusion into the guilty breast of Prince Bianchi, and fearful of exposure, he will be glad to yield to any demands which I may make of him. I wait with impatience until to-morrow arrives, that I may learn all the melancholy particulars of the history of Signora Zitella, from her own lips, so that I may be the better enable to encounter his highness."

"But do you intend to venture upon his presence again?" asked Maria.

"Do I?" repeated the brigand; "yes, I will face him boldly, and ring in his ears such a tale as shall make his guilty soul quail with horror. The interview, I anticipate, will be such a one as will be anything but agreeable to his feelings. The confession of the rascal Malvolio will be enough for him, but I must confess that I had much rather he had lived, that he might personally have accused Bianchi of the crimes that are laid to his charge, and which there can be no doubt have their foundation in truth."

"Again I must urge upon you, Massaroni," remarked his wife, "the necessity of using due caution."

"There is no occasion for such advice, Maria, for you know full well that Massaroni is never off his guard. As for the power of the Prince Bianchi, I repeat that I utterly despise it; I am armed tenfold against him, with the information I have already obtained, and that which I have no doubt I shall yet receive, and I feel confident in the confusion and remorse which I shall bring upon his guilty soul. Oh! what a glorious hour of exultation will that be to me, when I shall see the haughty tyrant who has ever pursued me with such unprovoked and deadly feelings of vindictiveness, humbled and levelled with the dust at my feet, and suing to me, ay, to me, the outcast, the proscribed brigand chief, whose blood he has so long panted for, thirsted after, suing to me, I say, for mercy! No wonder that he should so deeply sympathise with the villain Alberti, when he himself has been guilty of the same atrocities! No marvel that he, the vile seducer, the betrayer of confiding woman, should be deaf to all the supplications and remonstrances of his innocent niece! Oh! I will ring in his ears such a tale of horror and shame, that shall sink him into his native insignificance, and brand him in the eyes of the world as a villain of the blackest dye. It will be in vain for him to look to his rank to shield him from the odium and abhorrence which will justly attach themselves to his character. The Almighty in His just retribution, knows no distinction among any of his erring creatures."

"Massaroni!" said Maria, laying her hand gently upon his arm, and looking up with a mild expression of reproof in his face, "you are warm; you are unnaturally excited."

"No, not unnaturally, Maria," replied our hero. "When I recall to my memory a mother's wrongs, and recollect that it was by such means, and by such a heartless miscreant, her happiness was destroyed—her life was sacrificed—Maria, wife, when I reflect upon all the melancholy circumstances of my mother's life, and compare them with those of the Signora Zitella and her unfortunate daughter, certain feelings arise in my breast which I find it impossible to control ; and methinks I could, if the Prince Bianchi were now standing before me, plunge a dagger to his heart without the least repugnance !"

"Oh, Massaroni," said his wife, with a shudder of horror, "I beseech you to banish such dreadful thoughts from your mind. You never yet thirsted for human blood, and——"

"Yes, I did," interrupted the brigand chief, and an expression of determination flashed from his fine intelligent eyes, which was quite awful to look upon; "the blood of the brutal seducer—the murderer of one of the best of mothers !"

"Your own father, Alessandro ?"

"Even so, Maria ; and I should feel far less reluctance in taking his life than I would that of a dog !"

"Oh, horrible !"

"Nay, it is not so, revolting though it may seem. Justice demands the perpetration of the deed. I have registered a solemn vow in Heaven, and I now again swear, that should I ever discover the guilty object of my vengeance, even though perdition should be my fate, I will keep my oath! He dies !"

"Forbear—forbear !" exclaimed the horror-struck Maria ; "you know not what you say !"

"You may deem me mad," replied the brigand, "or labouring under the influence of momentary excited feelings ; but, by all my hopes, I mean what I have said. Would to Heaven that I could discover him whom I scorn to call father, that I might at once, in his blood, wash out all the wrongs that my poor mother and myself have received from him."

"Massaroni," said his wife, "I cannot listen to language such as that to which you have just now given utterance ; it freezes my very blood with horror, and I can scarcely persuade myself that it is my husband whom I am addressing. For the love of Heaven, calm your feelings, and endeavour to think with mercy towards the guilty man who has been the cause of so much misery."

"Mercy !" repeated the brigand chief ; "mercy to a wretch like him, the murderer of my mother ? Never !"

"That mother, whose fate you so justly and sincerely deplore," rejoined Maria, "could never have wished you to pursue her betrayer with your vengeance, or she would not have refused, even upon her death-bed, to reveal to you his name."

"But shall my hatred and revenge sleep the more for that ?" hastily demanded our hero "No, I feel convinced in my own mind that he still lives, and I can never rest satisfied until I have discovered him, and made him pay the full penalty of the unpardonable crimes he has committed. Maria, you talk to me in vain. You well know that my feelings are not naturally sanguinary ; but think you, when I recall to my memory all the injuries that have been inflicted on myself and her who gave me birth, that I can entertain any other feelings but those of hatred and disgust towards the brutal perpetrator of them? No—no, I cannot ; my mind is made up, and nothing whatever can move me from my purpose.'

"It is, I fear, useless to expostulate with you, at present," said Maria ; "but I trust that you will yet be able to conquer the fearful and dangerous passions which now predominate in your breast, and that, should it be the will of Heaven that the misguided author of your being should be revealed to you, your hand may be stayed in its deadly purpose, and that a reconciliation may be effected between you."

"A reconciliation !" repeated the brigand chief, impatiently, "a reconciliation with the betrayer, the murderer of my sainted mother; he from whom I have to date the origin of all my misfortunes —who has made me what I am ? What madness is it to talk thus! Maria, retire, for your arguments are not in accordance with my present feelings, and I would not say a word that might sound harsh and uncharitable to your ears. Leave me to myself."

"I obey, Massaroni," returned his wife, with a sigh ; "but I hope that the arguments which in my affection and anxiety I have made use of towards you, may yet not be lost upon you. Retribution is Heaven's alone, and woe to the presumptuous mortal who dares to arrogate to himself the power."

"Enough, enough," said Massaroni, testily, "I am in no humour to listen to language such as this. My thoughts are worked up to a pitch of desperation. But leave me, I once more command you."

Maria fixed upon him an expressive look, but returned no answer, and she then retired from the cavern in which they had held their conversation, and left him to his own reflections.

"Yes," he said, when she was gone, and still pacing the cavernous apartment backwards and forwards with the most disordered steps ; "the similarity of the fates of Signora Zitella and her daughter to that of my poor mother, excites my warmest feelings, and raises the strangest ideas in my mind. Should that man whom I blush to call father, be still living and I should discover him, in spite of all that Maria has said, I feel that my hatred is so strong for the abominable crimes he has committed, that nothing would have the power to withhold my hand, but that I should wreak a terrible retribution upon his head, though perdition should be my fate the next moment. And something tells me he still lives, and that we shall yet meet; oh, that it may be so; though it would be a fearful and fatal moment for him whenever I cross his path. The last words of the villain Malvolio have made a strong impression upon my mind. Would that he had lived to finish the sentence. I cannot but imagine from what he said, that he knew my guilty parent, and was about to reveal his name, when death sealed his tongue. Oh, it was an unfortunate job. But, patience, Massaroni, and all your wishes shall be gratified."

He was now interrupted in the midst of his soliloquy, by the sudden entrance of Rubaldo.

"You seem excited, Massaroni," said the former.

"Ay, ay, Rubaldo," replied the brigand chief, "I confess I am somewhat excited by painful thoughts."

"Indeed!" said his lieutenant, "may I presume to inquire what those particular thoughts are, that thus unusually ruffle the temper of Allesandro Massaroni?"

"I have been thinking of the probable gratification of revenge, Rubaldo, of long smothered revenge," replied our hero, "but only become more fierce and determined because the object that has excited it has hitherto escaped my detection."

"Whom do you mean, captain?" inquired Rubaldo.

"He of whom you have often heard me speak; the betrayer, the destroyer of my mother."

"Your father?"

"No, no," returned the brigand; "call him not by such a name, Rubaldo, but rather that of villain, murderer!"

"And you have never yet been enabled to discover him?"

"I have not."

"You were given to understand by your unfortunate mother that he was a man of wealth and rank, were you not?"

"I was; but that should not protect him," returned the brigand chief. "My dagger's point should pierce his heart, though thousands stood round to defend him, and should wreak their vengeance immediately upon my head."

"What has re-kindled those thoughts in your breast?" asked Rubaldo.

"The events that have lately taken place," answered Massaroni, "and the discovery of the relationship between those two unfortunate beings whom we have hitherto known as Ottavia and Olympia. The similarity of their fate to that of my poor mother is most remarkable."

"True," coincided Rubaldo, "but it is most fortunate that the villain Malvolio was seized with remorse in his dying moments, or the secret might never have been disclosed. Have you heard anything more upon the subject?"

"Yes," answered our hero. "The Signora Zitella is restored in the most miraculous way to her reason."

"Is it possible?" said Rubaldo.

"It is even so," replied the brigand chief, "and she and Olympia, or more correctly speaking, Mira, for that is her right name, are now together."

"Ah!" said Rubaldo, "that is fortunate. And does she corroborate all that Malvolio has stated?"

"She does," answered the brigand.

"Then," observed Rubaldo, "the discomfiture of the Prince Bianchi is certain, and so far you have triumphed, and the Signora Melina may yet be saved from the fate with which he has so long threatened her."

"She shall be, Rubaldo," returned our hero, determinedly, "and I am, as I have all along said, prepared to run any risk to secure such a result. But I am urged on still more in my purpose by discovering him to be the heartless betrayer of the much injured Signora Zitella."

"Ay," remarked Rubaldo, "I wonder not at your feelings. The portrait then, of which I have so often heard you speak, I presume is that of this unfortunate woman?"

"No," replied Massaroni, with much emotion, "and that arouses fresh thoughts of agony in my breast. That portrait, Rubaldo, is the likeness of my unfortunate mother, or my name is not Allesandro Massaroni."

"Then," said Rubaldo, "if such be the fact, and you are convinced of it, the mystery you have been so long seeking to unravel is at once solved, and the Prince Bianchi must be the betrayer of your mother as well as the Signora Zitella."

"Ah!" exclaimed Massaroni, starting, and laying his hand upon the hilt of his poniard instinctively; "that thought!—Can that be the cause of the deadly hatred I feel towards him?—Were I satisfied that such was the case, the proud and haughty Prince Bianchi, surrounded even as he is by all his myrmidons, should not have many hours to live!—But no; it cannot be; and yet the coincidence is so remarkable, that—I must be calm, and seek to discover the truth or fallacy of my surmises before I proceed to do anything rash and precipitate, and which I may afterwards have reason to repent."

"Your mother was a native of Florence, was she not?" asked Rubaldo.

"She was—she was!" hastily replied the brigand chief.

"And that mysterious portrait is said to

"And that mysterious portrait is said to represent a young Florentine maid?" said Rubaldo.

"Yes, yes!"

"The favourite mistress of Prince Bianchi, to whom it is stated he professed to be most fondly attached?"

"True—true—Oh, those thoughts!—they are most torturing."

"It is strange," remarked Rubaldo; "I should almost be inclined to think that——"

"No, no," interrupted Massareni; "I must not allow myself to give way to such ideas for the present. I must use caution and judgment,

FLORETTA TRYING TO CONSOLE MELINA.

and not permit myself to do anything rash, however suspicious the circumstances may appear to be. By Heaven! should it prove to be that the Prince Bianchi, he who has so long thirsted for my blood, is—But no. I must not trust myself with such a thought, or it will drive me to madness. I will endeavour to wait patiently until I hear the narrative of the Signora Zitella, and that may throw some light upon the painful and mysterious subject."

No. 53.

"And how do you propose to act with respect to this discovery of the secret connected with Signora Zitella?" asked Rubaldo.

"I have not yet decided," answered our hero, "and shall not be able to do so until I have consulted with Signora Zitella herself."

"The Prince Bianchi, no doubt, believes both her and her offspring dead," observed Rubaldo.

"True," returned the brigand chief. "How great then will be his confusion and dismay when he finds that they are both living, and that the unfortunate victim of his favourite, Count Alberti, is his own daughter."

"Ay," said Massaroni, "if anything can make the least impression upon his inflexible nature, one would think that that discovery would wring his guilty soul to madness."

"Yes," said Rubaldo, "and my word for it, if even the Count Alberti should recover, it will be the means of saving the Signora Melina from the fate to which her uncle had destined her."

"How so?"

"How so? Why, do you for a moment imagine that he could ever be so heartless and unnatural as to think of compelling his fair and innocent niece to become the wife of the seducer of his own daughter?"

"I should scarcely believe it possible that he could become so insensible to every feeling of honour and shame, as to commit such an outrage against nature and humanity," answered the brigand chief "but he may attempt to deny the claims which Zitella and her daughter have upon him."

"One would think it would be almost impossible that he could do so, when he meets that deeply-wronged woman face to face, like an accusing spirit come from eternity."

"I believe him to be almost villain enough for anything, notwithstanding his hypocritical assumption of every virtue," said Massaroni; "but time will show, and I am fully resolved to put him to the test."

"Yes," said Rubaldo, "that is no more than just. But I cannot conquer the surprise I feel at the sudden restoration of Signora Zitella to her senses."

"It is indeed miraculous."

"The meeting between her and her daughter must have been a most affecting one."

"So my wife has described it to have been," returned Massaroni. "But leave me, Rubaldo, I would be alone. It is probable I shall wish to consult with you, on what is best to be done, after I have had an interview with the Signoras Zitella and Mira."

"Very good, captain," replied Rubaldo, "you will always find me ready at your command at any time."

With these words Rubaldo retired, and the brigand chief again paced the cavern, wrapped in the deepest meditation. Some of the observations which Rubaldo had made use of had made the greatest impression upon him, and he found it difficult to come to any satisfactory conclusion upon them. His mind was tortured with mingled doubts and apprehensions; but a burning desire to have an ample revenge against the destroyer of his mother, predominated over every other feeling, and not all that his wife had said could move him from his purpose.

"That mysterious portrait!" he ejaculated, "it haunts my imagination like a spectre. The features so like, and then the history connected with it so similar, by Heaven! it must be the same, and if so, the Prince Bianchi is the villain whom I seek. But is it possible that the father of Mira is my parent also? Oh! how torturing is that thought! It drives me almost to distraction! Let me banish it for the present from my mind. I know not how to act. But by all my hopes, should I discover that the Prince Bianchi is my father, nothing shall move me from my purpose. Nothing shall save him from my vengeance. Father! I repudiate the title. The destroyer of that gentle creature who gave me being has never proved himself a father to me. He abandoned me in my infancy, left me to become an outcast upon society, and wherefore should I not despise and hate him? Can I recall to my memory the last moments of my unfortunate mother without breathing a curse upon his name? No, I cannot, and justice sanctions me in the feeling. I have taken an oath, a solemn oath, to retain my feelings of deadly hatred till I have washed out the injuries he has done to me and my hapless parent in his blood, and be the consequences whatever they may be to myself, I will not break my oath! Spirit of my sainted mother, you know the feelings of justice that prompt me to this desperate course, and I humbly implore thee to look down upon me, and approve of my conduct."

Overpowered by the intensity of his feelings, he was compelled to pause for a minute or two, and folding his arms across his chest, he again traversed the cavern in the most disordered state of mind. But at length he threw himself on a seat, and gave himself up entirely to silent and gloomy meditation; and in that wretched frame of mind we will leave him, and return once more to Zitella and her daughter.

We left them in a state of the greatest excitement, consequent upon the extraordinary discovery they had made of their consanguinity; but even the feelings created by that remarkable circumstance were completely superseded in Mira's breast, by the inexpressible delight and gratitude which she felt for the restoration of that beloved and unfortunate woman who had given her being. However, she endeavoured to control her emotions as much as

possible, fearful that in the present delicate
state of her mother's health, it might be productive of the most fatal consequences. She
persuaded her to recline once more upon her
couch, and try to soothe her mind by an hour
or two's repose ; and when she did so, Mira
knelt down by the bedside, and in the most
eloquent and fervent language returned her
thanks to the Almighty for the discovery which
in his infinite mercy, He had so miraculously
brought about.

"All bountiful Creator !" she ejaculated,
clasping her hands, and raising her eyes, humid
with tears, but tears of the heart's overflowing,
towards heaven, " oh, how can I ever sufficiently evince my gratitude to Thee for thus
restoring to me that revered being to whose
affectionate and maternal bosom I never expected again to be pressed, or to feel the
impression of her fond kiss upon my cheek. Oh,
how amply does this repay me for all the manifold
and poignant sorrows it has been my hard lot
to endure. I humbly beseech Thee, Almighty
God, to suffer her not to relapse into her former
state of mind, so deplorable, so melancholy, so
unmerited, but let her future days be those of
peace and tranquillity. And oh, may my misguided father be brought to a full sense of the
cruelty and injustice he has inflicted, and
endeavour to make all the atonement in his
power for the guilty past."

At this moment the unfortunate Zitella, who
had only slightly slumbered, awoke, and, looking
up, and observing her daughter hanging affectionately over her, a sweet smile overspread
her melancholy features, as she ejaculated—

" Ah ! you are still here, my sweet one ;
you will not leave me ?"

" No, no, my beloved mother," replied Mira,
fervently ; " we will never part again, with
the blessing of Heaven. But do not excite
yourself, for, in your present weak state, consequent upon the many years of unprecedented suffering it has been your lot to experience, God
only knows what might be the consequences."

" No, no, my child," returned her mother
eagerly, " I am now calm, perfectly calm, you
see I am. Now that you are restored to my arms,
the dismal past seems gradually to fade from
my recollection, and I feel as though I could
again be happy. But you look pale, and
careworn. Alas! I fear that you have suffered
much. And now I remember me, you had a
child, a sweet little cherub, such as you were
when the wretch Malvolio tore you from my
bosom. That—that child was yours?"

" Oh, yes, my mother," replied Mira in a
voice of the deepest emotion.

" And your husband ?"

" Alas! alas! my mother, you must know
the dreadful truth, it would be cruel and sinful
to conceal it from you. Mother I have never
yet been a wife !"

" Ah !" gasped forth Zitella, " is it even
so ? And have you then also fallen a victim
to the deceptive arts of some designing villain ?"

" It is too true," answered Mira ; " the same
cruel fate has pursued us both."

" My poor child," said Zitella, throwing her
arms around her neck, and sobbing bitterly.
" But who is the villain who has done you this
irreparable wrong ?"

" The son of the nobleman at the door of whose
palazzo Malvolio left me," replied Mira : " the
Count Alberti."

" May eternal curses for ever light upon his
guilty soul !" exclaimed Zitella, vehemently ;
" may——"

" Oh, forbear, my dear mother," interrupted
Mira, with a shudder ; " I forgive him, most
freely forgive him, and——"

" But has he not brutally deserted you and
your tender offspring ?"

" Alas ! it is too true ; but still from my
very soul I pardon him, and may Heaven do so
likewise."

" Gentle being," ejaculated Zitella, looking
with all a mother's fondness in her lovely
countenance ; " there spoke the true spirit of
my child. But does he still live ?"

" I trust he does," answered Mira, " and
that he may yet live to repent, though at present he lies dangerously wounded at the villa
of the Prince Bianchi."

" The Prince Bianchi !" repeated her mother,
in an agitated voice, and her countenance at
once revealing the conflicting emotions that
predominated in her mind, at the mention of
that name she had such good cause to shudder at.

" Yes, my dear mother," returned Mira,
" the Prince Bianchi, whose friend he is."

" My God !" exclaimed Zitella, clasping her
hands fervently together ; " how wonderful and
inscrutable are Thy ways! My child, my beloved child ! that fate should have ordained
that our darkened path of life should have to
be pursued the same—But he—your betrayer—
who gained advantage by all your confiding
innocence, does he still live ?"

" He does, my mother," replied Mira, " but,
as I have previously stated to you, he now lies
dangerously wounded, and it is doubtful whether
he will recover."

" Heaven pardon him," ejaculated Zitella,
solemnly.

" Amen !" responded Mira, devoutly ; " as
it knows that I fervently forgive him. Oh, my
mother, it has been the will of the Supreme to
inflict upon and to visit us with these severe
trials, but at the same time He has in His bounden
mercy, enabled us to meet them with fortitude,
patience, and resignation ; and with the same
merciful blessing extending over us, I trust
that we shall still be empowered to meet that

which may still be in store for us. This restoration to each other's arms is a sufficient guarantee for all the beneficent blessings that it is His Almighty will to extend towards us. Let us return Him thanks for His manifold kindnesses to us under all our afflictions."

"Most devoutly will I join with you, my charming Mira, in doing so," said her mother; and uniting their hands together, they poured forth the heart-felt overflowings of their grateful hearts to the fountain of all good.

"May Thou, Almighty God!" continued Zitella, "in Thine All-Merciful decrees, blot out from Thine awful book of judgment, the sins of those, our bitter enemies, from whom we have experienced so many and such cruel wrongs, and pardon them as freely as we Thine humble creatures now do. May they be brought to a sincere conviction of the crimes they have committed, and not be snatched from the world until they have enabled themselves to the best of their power and their will to render every possible atonement to those whom they have injured."

"Blessed words!" said Mira, fervently. "They will be received by that All-Merciful parent to whom they are addressed. Oh, my beloved mother, I feel as if invigorated with new life, with a fresh existence! Your words have imparted that bright halo of consolation to my breast which I never thought it would be my happiness to receive, and I seem as if I were fully prepared, clothed in armour to resist any future troubles that it may be written in the book of fate I should encounter. Oh! what are all the sorrows of the past, manifold and terrible even as they have been, when placed in juxta-position with the indescribable happiness of this moment? They vanish like the shadows upon the wall, like the scarcely created phantoms of a dream. Mother! we are restored to each other! Death alone shall again separate us; and in that blessed assurance, I reap more—ay, even far more than the full reward, for the years, the many years of suffering, the agony of mind, the personal indignities, the world's scorn and contumely, I have experienced. Mother! mother! I have been, by the mercy of Heaven, permitted to utter that blessed word upon your neck, and I am happy!"

She threw her arms around her parent's neck, and for a few moments they were both of them too overpowered by their feelings to give utterance to a syllable. At length Zitella recovered herself, and looking up with an intensity of feeling in her daughter's face, which no language could possibly do adequate justice to, she said—

"My dear Mira, in the mad moments of my wandering reason, I have pictured to myself that, if at any time that child whom I imagined had fallen beneath the murderer's knife, should ever be restored to me by some miraculous and merciful dispensation and interposition of Providence, how bright, how fair, how gentle and angel-like she would be; what a bright halo would she shed around the gloom and solitude of my declining days; how would her sweet voice ever awaken me to comfort and hope; and God be praised that vision is realised; I see my child all that my fondest wishes could portray, when reason for a brief period held her dominion o'er my distracted senses. I see her all that I could hope; o'erflowing with every generous feeling, rich in all that is virtuous and good: and God, Thou knowest how greatful I feel towards Thee, and how amply I feel myself repaid for all the sorrows and sufferings it has been Thy will to impose upon me. My child! my beloved Mira!"

Again the mother and daughter embraced fervently, and mingled their tears, tears of unspeakable joy they were, together; a pause ensued, in which they gave free indulgence to the feelings that throbbed so tumultuously in their bosoms; but at length the Signora Zitella said—

"My, Mira, if it will pain you not, give me a brief history of your wrongs from the parent of your child; the—the Count Alberti, the friend of your father, the prince Bianchi—oh, God!"

"No, no, my dear mother," replied Mira; "not now—another time; you seem to be too much excited, and——"

"Nay, my child," hastily interrupted Zitella, "I am now fully nerved and prepared for everything you can relate; let me hear the whole, the worst; do not conceal anything from me. Come, child, to a mother's sympathising bosom, confide the tale of guilt."

Mira did so, and her mother was frequently from the excitement of her feelings compelled to interrupt her to give expression to the emotions which it naturally created in her breast.

"My Mira," she said at length, in a tone of calmness which could scarcely have been expected; "what a similarity there is in our fates, and leaving alone the ties o' consanguinity that bind us to each other, how deeply ought we to sympathise with one another's misfortunes. The Count Alberti is—but I will call him by no more opprobrious a name than that—oh, God! let me not mention that name, lest it should send me into that darkness which for so many years has obscured my reason. Mira, where is your child? Why do I not have the felicity of embracing the second child of my misfortune, my indiscretion?"

"The Signora Maria and her husband will be here anon, dear mother," replied Mira, "and they will bring my little innocent with them."

"The Signora Maria and her husband?" repeated Zitella; "who are they?"

"They have proved themselves to be both your and my particular friends, mother," replied Mira; "they have been our protectors when all others would probably have treated us with scorn—it is they who have enabled the good Signor Montaldi, under whose humble roof you have for so many years existed, to carry out the wishes of his benevolent heart to their fullest extent. Allessandro Massaroni, the brigand chief, ever had his feelings alive to the cause of humanity and justice!"

"Allesandro Massaroni, the brigand chief!" repeated Zitella. "Ah! a light now seems to break upon my so long slumbering intellect. It is he who has preserved you, my fond one, to be a blessing and a solace to me in my declining days—it is he who has enabled the good man, the excellent man, to protect me when I was friendless, in intellect as well as purse—the Signor Montaldi, in whose dwelling I am now. May the most manifold blessings of Heaven light upon them both, for that is all I have now to offer them; and that I do with all sincerity."

At that moment old Montaldi knocked at the door, and, of course, was immediately admitted.

The Signora Zitella, who had arisen from her couch, dropped at his feet, and clasping his knees with a feeling of gratitude which no language could express, she said—

"Signor Montaldi!—protector in the darkness of my sorrow—benefactor, more than parent!—how can I give utterance to the feelings that fill my grateful bosom towards you?—how find language sufficiently strong to convey to yourself the emotions with which your unprecedented goodness have inspired me? May all-bounteous Heaven reward you, for I cannot!"

"Signora," replied the old man, "let me beg of you not to excite yourself in your present delicate situation. I am more than sufficiently rewarded for any services I may have been so happy as to have rendered, or any difficulties to which they have exposed me, in seeing you restored to reason and the arms of that daughter whom you thought lost to you for ever. Be calm as possible, I again beg of you, and I trust to God that all will yet be well, and that you will be amply repaid for all the troubles it has been your hard lot to experience."

As old Montaldi thus spoke, he raised Zitella from her knees, and having embraced her with the same affection as if she had been his own daughter, he ejaculated—

"This is one of the happiest moments that I have experienced for many a day throughout my lengthened life; and I thank Heaven sincerely for having made me the humble instrument in its hands of performing so much good. Signora Zitella, when I recall to my memory the fearful night which guided your footsteps to my humble dwelling, I cannot help feeling a shuddering of horror, to think what might otherwise have been your fate on that dreadful night; and I feel the still more grateful to Providence for having deputed me to be the means of rescuing a fellow-creature from it. Signora Zitella, I wish not to harrow up your feelings by what I am about to describe, or to take especial credit to myself for what I have done, but it is merely to show in more prominent characters, if possible, the boundless mercy of that Almighty God to us all, His humble and insignificant creatures, in the midst of our adversity, and when all hope seems to have abandoned us altogether. It was, indeed, a fearful night, and I was sitting wrapped in melancholy thought (for only some three months prior I had lost my wife). My niece, who then was my sole companion, and attended to my domestic affairs—Heaven rest her gentle soul, for she is now, I trust, in Heaven—was seated opposite to me, busily employed in perusing the pages of one of her favourite authors. It was indeed a cold, cheerless, and fearful night. The snow descended in heavy flakes, like a funeral shroud, spreading itself over one vast field of desolation, while the thick and hazy clouds that hung above, seemed like a pale hanging over the departure of hope to the children of the earth. The blazing and cracking wood upon the hearth rendered the contrast still more striking and painful, and my feelings rose to that pitch from meditation that I could scarcely control them within the bounds of reason. My niece, no doubt experiencing the same emotions, as the dismal howling of the night wind drew her attention from the subject she had been perusing, suddenly threw aside her book, and looking up in my face with an expression of the utmost anxiety, observed—

"'Dear uncle, what an awful night is this! Oh, may the Almighty extend His mercy to those unfortunate beings who are at this moment exposed to all the inclemencies of the season, and know not where to rest their head, or where to seek a shelter.'

'Amen, my dear Celina,' I replied, fervently and devoutly; 'but God is good; and terrible and unjust as His judgments may at times appear to us living mortals, His mercy is ever extended, in the hour of extremity, even to the most guilty of His creatures.'

"The words had scarcely escaped my lips, when the faint, plaintive cry of a person apparently in its last extremities saluted both our ears, and made us start involuntarily to our feet. The cry was so faint, yet withal so melancholy and so piercing, that although it seemed to be at some distance from our habitation, it struck with electrical effect upon our senses, and convinced us that immediate assistance was required to rescue one of our suffering fellow-creatures from an awful and premature death. I hastily clapped on my hat, my niece throwing her cloak around her shoulders at the same time, and taking up a lantern which I had burning at the same time upon the table, and a stout staff to assist my steps in wading through the snow, which the wind had drifted into immense heaps near my cottage, we issued forth, and made towards the spot from whence we imagined the sound to have issued, I calling aloud upon the sufferer to direct us; but for some time we proceeded in uncertainty, and a difficult task we had to perform. The snow was almost up to our knees, and the wind was so high and so piercing, that it required a good resolution, and the stimulus of the most philanthropic feelings, to stand against it. But at length the same wailing, mournful cry that we had at first heard, once more saluted our ears, but very faint, and which proved to us that the unfortunate being was in his or her last extremity, and that we must redouble our energies with any probability of rescuing life.

"A most difficult task it was for us to wade our way through the snow; but the moans of the unfortunate being, every moment getting lower and lower, and becoming more indistinct, guided us, and encouraged us; and at length, after much difficulty, which I have no occasion to attempt to describe to you, we reached the foot of a hill, in which was a small excavation, almost blocked up by the drifting snow, and from which we could still hear the indistinct wailings, now almost hushed to whispers, of the poor creature of whom we were in search. Almost hopeless as the case then appeared to be, I felt a weight like that of lead removed from my heart, and I immediately set about removing with my staff, in the best manner I could, the snow from the mouth of the small aperture in the side of the hill, and no sooner had I succeeded in doing so than I beheld the form of a woman, cramped up, and apparently lifeless. You may judge of my feelings and those of my excellent niece at that moment; but we allowed ourselves not a moment to give vent to our emotions; we extricated the unfortunate from that, which but for our timely arrival, must assuredly have proved her grave, and with all the difficulty you may imagine, conveyed her in an insensible state to our dwelling. That female, I suppose I need scarcely inform you, Signora Zitella, was yourself."

"Excellent old man!" ejaculated Mira; "how can I ever sufficiently express to you my gratitude for this act of christian benevolence, which has preserved to me a mother?"

"Name it not, signora," said Montaldi. "I am more than repaid in having the happiness to witness the restoration."

"May the great God above heap upon your venerable head His choicest blessings," ejaculated Signora Zitella, deeply affected; "alas! alas! what a poor miserable, bereaved, abandoned outcast I was, and you——"

"Enough—enough, signora," hastily interrupted Montaldi; "and allow me to proceed. Myself and my niece, as I have before observed, with much difficulty conveyed you to our dwelling, and there we watched and attended upon you night and day, having the best advice that my limited means could engage; but for some weeks you remained in a most precarious state, and with scarcely any intervals of consciousness; and when you did recover, we found, to our extreme sorrow and regret, that your intellect had fled, apparently for ever, and we were unable to elicit from you who you were, your name, or what had brought you into the awful situation in which we had found you. At times you seemed to have a consciousness of the kindness that was bestowed upon you, and some dreamy recollection of the past; but it quickly vanished, and we could never gather sufficient from you to furnish us with the least idea as to whom you belonged, or the circumstance connected with your melancholy history, though we gathered enough in the ravings of your frenzy to convince us that you had been the victim of villany, and——"

"The victim of villany," interrupted Zitella hastily; "oh, yes, and that of the blackest dye. Oh, Montaldi, imagine to yourself a poor unsuspecting confiding girl deprived of the brightest jewel that her sex is possessed of, by the vilest and most insidious arts that man can employ to achieve his guilty object. Picture to yourself that poor betrayed one a mother, an alien from the world, fearful again to enter into it lest she should meet with its scorn and oppression, and buoyed with the hopes of justice being rendered to her, held out to her by her vile seducer. Picture to yourself, I say, that young mother abandoned by him to whom she had been taught to look up to for protection and consolation, to all the misery and despair of degradation, and marvel, if you can, that her reason forsook her. Wonder, if you can, that for so many years she has been the wretched, wandering one that you have known her. But if the picture of horror be not yet complete, imagine what that mother's feelings must have been, when the innocent offspring of her guilty intercourse was ruthlessly torn from her breast and consigned, as she had every reason to suppose at the time, to a monstrous death! Was not this more than sufficient to turn the most ordinary brain?—I now wonder that the blow did not strike me dead!"

"Mother! dear mother! ejaculated Mira,

"terrible indeed are the injuries you have received, and the trials to which you have been put; but we are now restored to each other, and let the gloomy past be forgotten."

"Ay, Signora Mira," remarked old Montaldi, "you say well; Heaven has vouchsafed that brighter days and prospects should dawn upon you and your mother, and the past should only be remembered as a fearful dream, from which you may draw a lesson for the future. —But to conclude my brief explanation, which I considered was necessary, and I thought you might be anxious to hear. Signora Zitella had not been more than eighteen months under my protection, during which time I had made every possible inquiry which might lead to a discovery of her connexions, without the least success, when my poor niece was seized with a sudden illness which baffled all the skill it was in my humble power to employ, and she expired, leaving me alone with the object of my sympathy and anxiety, who thus, if it were possible, became doubly more precious to me."

"Ah!" said Zitella, passing her hand across her forehead, as if endeavouring to recall her scattered memory; "I have now some faint recollection of a fair and gentle being—such as my beloved Mira has ever been to me, since Providence in its boundless mercy restored us to each other—watching over me, attending to my wants, humouring my wild fancies, and singing to me in a voice of heavenly melody, which has haunted my wandering imagination long after sleep had closed my eyelids. That must have been your Celina, my benefactor?"

"It was, it was indeed," replied Montaldi, in a voice of the deepest emotion. "Heaven knows that you have not drawn an exaggerated picture of her. Oh! she was indeed most beautiful, most amiable, but it was the will of Heaven to take her from me, and why should I, presumptuous mortal as I am, dare to murmur?—Some years after this, accident introduced me to Allesandro Massaroni, the brigand chief, to whom you and your daughter have been subsequently, principally, indebted for protection. The rest you know."

Montaldi ceased, and Signora Zitella and her daughter were both of them too much overpowered by their feelings for some moments to allow them to speak, but at length they both fervently grasped his hands, and with looks that sufficiently expressed the feelings that were passing in her mind, Mira said—

"Signor Montaldi, it would be an insult to your good sense to say that I can ever give utterance in words, however eloquent they might be, to the feelings which your unexampled and disinterested conduct have inspired in my breast; it is a debt of gratitude which neither time nor circumstance can ever repay; it must rest with the Almighty to reward you as you deserve, and I trust he will do so, and render your future days those of happiness and serenity. From the bottom of a grateful heart, I can but thank you for myself and my dear mother."

"May all the blessings that can attend you be your lot, excellent old man," said Signora Zitella; "may——"

"Stay, stay, I beseech you," interrupted Montaldi; "you overwhelm me with thanks that are so little my due; if I have performed my duty, and my conscience assures me that I have, I am satisfied. Oh! where can be a greater consolation to a well formed mind than to witness the happiness of our fellow-creatures? But some one knocks below; doubtless it is Massaroni and his wife, with your child, Mira. Are you prepared to receive them?"

"Oh, yes, yes, yes," eagerly replied Zitella; "ready to receive those who have proved themselves to be such inestimable friends to me and my daughter! ready to receive, and enfold to my bosom the innocent offspring of my child! Oh, blissful thought! For the love of Heaven, good Montaldi, instantly admit them. Oh, my heart! surely it will break under this unexpected trial of its affections."

"Calm your feelings, my beloved mother," said Mira; "and think only of future happiness and peace!"

Signora Zitella returned no answer, but threw herself sobbing on the bosom of her daughter, and old Montaldi retired from the room to give admittance to those whom he expected; and soon afterwards he returned escorting in Massaroni and his wife, the latter of whom carried in her arms the child of Mira, which the fond but unfortunate mother no sooner beheld, than she snatched it frantically from her and clasping it convulsively to her bosom, devoured it with her kisses. She then placed it in the arms of her mother, who had for the last few seconds stood bewildered and transfixed as a statue; but as soon as she beheld the little innocent, and gazed intently on its features, she burst into a paroxysm of sobs and tears, and with difficulty exclaimed—

"Now Heaven be praised since it has enabled me to behold and press to my heart my child, and the child, the innocent child, of my daughter. Almighty God! may thy choicest blessings descend in mercy upon this tender one, and mayest thou, in thine infinite mercy, shield it from all the manifold and almost insupportable troubles it has been the hard lot of its parent to experience!"

As she thus spoke she solemnly knelt down, Mira following her example, and they both remained in silent but fervent prayer for several minutes; Montaldi and the brigand and his wife, looking on with the deepest respect and emotion.

At length Signora Zitella arose from her knees, and having pressed the warmest and most affectionate kisses upon the smiling features of her grandchild, she restored it to the arms of her daughter.

"Alas!" she said, "how fruitless is the task to endeavour to express the feelings that animate my breast on this important and unexpected occasion. It seems to me like a delusive dream; it is almost too joyful for me to persuade myself that it is reality. But let me not appear ungrateful; oh, pardon me, Signor Massaroni, and you my good signora, if this sudden tumult of joy bewilders me and for the moment renders me unmindful of the obligations I owe you, obligations of which I can never enough evince my due appreciation, and which I fear it will never be in my power to repay. To you myself and my daughter are indebted for—"

"I pray you, signora," interrupted the brigand chief; "I pray you cease; you owe neither myself nor my wife any more than friendship, and that I hope we shall never prove ourselves unworthy of."

"Noble-minded man," said Zitella, raising his hand to her lips, "my future conduct must evince the feelings of gratitude I bear towards you, for words are far inadequate to describe them. May that power which reigns above and watches all our actions, reward you as you deserve, for I can never do so."

"Signora," returned Massaroni, "I seek no other reward than the consciousness of having done that which honour and virtue dictated, I am but a plain spoken man, one who is an alien from society, an outlaw, an outcast—one whom the world has first injured, and then stigmatizes with the name of villain and of robber! But e'en let the world say what it pleases of me, I care not; I am happy in the consciousness that no misconduct of my own brought me to my present position; that it was all the work of black-hearted villany, and I live in hope that the day will yet come when I shall have retribution on the heads of my enemies, for the wrongs that have been inflicted on me. Thank Heaven that Allesandro Massaroni, the brigand chief, is not insensible to the feelings of honour and virtue. Most cordially he congratulates you, signora, on your restoration to reason, and the miraculous and providential discovery of that daughter whom you believed to be lost to you for ever."

"Noble-minded man!" said Signora Zitella, almost overpowered by her feelings; "it is to you that I am indebted for all; it is to you that I owe the restoration of my poor child. She has told me all; and where shall I ever find words sufficiently strong to convey to you the feelings that throb in my bosom at the thought?"

"I must again beg of you, signora," returned Massaroni, "not to overwhelm me with thanks, which I sensibly feel are so little merited. I am more than rewarded for any trouble to which I may have been put, by winessing the consummation which has been so happily brought about; and any services that I can in future render you, you may most readily command."

Again Zitella and Mira returned their thanks to the brigand and his wife, and it was some time before they could sufficiently compose their feelings to converse calmly, but at length they did so, and for a few minutes they discoursed freely, and Zitella, at length having collected her thoughts, and conquered her feelings for the occasion, commenced the narrative of her wrongs and sufferings in the following words:—

THE NARRATIVE OF SIGNORA ZITELLA.

"When I take a retrospect of my past life, what melancholy feelings of regret, what bitter self reproaches, yet, withal, what joyous reminiscences, does it recall to my memory! Oh! the halcyon days of childhood and of youth! when the hopes are fresh, and vigorous, and buoyant, when all around is fairy-land to the mind's perception—what a pity it is that we should ever be awakened from the blissful dream, by the stern realities of destiny! I have often thought that what a blissful, what a merciful dispensation of Providence it would be to take us again to the bosom of our Creator, in those happy moments of unconsciousness of evil, and ere our minds had become sullied and contaminated by guilt. But the thought is sinful; it is arraigning the wisdom of the Supreme who does all things for the best, and perhaps I should consider myself justly punished for having ever indulged in it. But you will doubtless consider me prolix and tedious, and I will therefore proceed at once to the recital of the melancholy fact of my history.

"I was born not far from the Abbruzzi Mountains, my parents being persons in the humblest sphere of life, but from their intrinsic virtues gaining the esteem of all who knew them, and the respect of those who were placed in a far more elevated situation of society above them. So much were they respected indeed, that even the proud and wealthy lord of the extensive domains on which they resided, showed them the most marked favour, and condescended to converse with them whenever they met, with the same freedom and familiarity as they would have done to their equals. Dear parents, as I recall your numerous and transcendent virtues to my memory, my heart overflows, and I could weep again, like a very child!"

The feelings of Signora Zitella overpowered her, and she was compelled to pause, and those who listened to her had too great a respect and veneration for the sentiment which called them forth, to offer to interrupt them; but at length she was enabled to resume in the following words—

"Myself and a brother, two years my senior, were the only children of my parents, and with what fond remembrance do I look back upon that dear brother, so kind, so affectionate, so studious of my happiness; so ready to form any excuse for me, when I had committed some childish foiable; so ready to take the blame on

THE PRINCE BIANCHI AT THE BED-SIDE OF COUNT ALBERTI.

himself, and to impart to me the words of sweet consolation, if our parents had expressed one angry sentiment towards me—that dear brother, with whom in the joyousness of my childhood's innocence, I used to ramble the green fields, and climb the mountain sides, or descending into the peaceful vallies, he would gather the wild flowers that grew there in such luxuriance, to form a garland for my hair. Oh, those were days of bliss that have never since been realised to me. Dear brother, beloved Alfonse, can I ever cease to revere your memory?

"But the first misfortune of my life—the first time when I was destined to taste of the bitter cup of sorrow, was about to overtake me. Alas! with what feelings of horror and bitter regret do I look back upon that fatal day!

"Alfonso was two years my senior, and, on the anniversary of his fourteenth birth-day, my parents celebrated it with all the *eclat* that their humble means would allow them to do; and they, as I have before stated, being universally respected, their more wealthy neighbours contributed their assistance to render the festival complete, and, moreover many of them honoured it with their presence. Oh, it was a joyous day; all was mirth and hilarity; but, alas! how melancholy was the termination. The sports had been kept up with unabated vivacity, and evening approached, the chaste moon appearing with unusual brilliancy in the heavens, as if to smile upon and approve our innocent enjoyments. There was a lad present, about the same age as my brother, with his parents. His father was a ranger, and had thoughtlessly brought his gun with him, which, when he joined one of the old-fashioned dances on the lawn, he placed by the trunk of an old tree that grew beside my father's dwelling. In boyish sport, the lad that I have mentioned, not knowing that it was loaded, and his father's attention being attracted another way, took up the dangerous weapon, and presented it towards my brother. I was terrified and started in between them, just at the moment when the lad was about to discharge it; at that instant a young man, of noble exterior, but who was a stranger to any of the company, dashed forward, and seizing me by the arm, drew me aside! Oh, God! I heard a report! the terrified shrieks of all assembled! I saw my poor brother sink to the earth deluged in blood, and my senses immediately left me!

"When I was restored to consciousness, it was to hear that my unfortunate brother, the companion of my childhood, was no more; the gun had been loaded, and thus in a childish frolic, he met with an untimely death!

"How shall I attempt to describe my own agony, or that of my parents? It would be a fruitless task, and therefore I will not intrude upon your time by seeking to delineate it. But where was the preserver of my life? He who had snatched me from the fatal instrument of destruction? No one knew him—no one acknowledged to having introduced him to the company, and he had vanished, like a phantom. Although his dress was humble, his bearing—his general demeanour—showed him to be a person of superior rank to that of the humble individuals he thought proper to mingle with on that melancholy and fatal occasion; but it was utterly impossible to form even the slightest conjecture as to who he was. Child, however,

as I was, I retained a vivid recollection of his features; they had made an impression upon me that I could never eradicate, and, young even as I was, in my heart of hearts I loved him. He haunted my thoughts, either sleeping or waking, and I longed for the time when fate might allow me to see him again. My young imagination pictured him all that was good and excellent, and I longed for the opportunity to express to him the feelings of gratitude I experienced towards him, although in saving my life, that of my brother had been sacrificed.

"It was long—very long ere my parents could recover from the dreadful shock which they had received on the calamitous death of their son; and strange to say, and I cannot otherwise account for it than that they could not have loved me as well as my brother, the affection that they had formerly bestowed upon me, seemed to evaporate, and they appeared to view me with feelings almost amounting to aversion. You may judge of the agony of my young mind when I experienced this melancholy change. I redoubled my dutiful attentions to them; I studied night and day how it was likely I should conciliate their favour, and bring back that love which my conscience assured me no act of my own had entitled me to lose; many were the bitter tears I shed when I was alone; many were the sleepless and racking nights I passed; innumerable were the prayers I offered up to the Almighty; but all was of no avail; their behaviour was cold, and even morose towards me, and it at last became too painfully evident to me that they regretted the interference of the stranger, and would rather that my life should have been sacrificed than that of their son. It is a horrible, a repugnant, and unnatural conclusion to arrive at, but alas! I had too much reason to do so, and thus you see that misfortunes of the most insupportable kind came upon me in the days of my earliest youth—misfortunes which were not my own seeking, or caused from any errors of my own, but as if a terrible fatality had presided over my birth, which it was impossible for me to avoid."

"Oh! my beloved and unfortunate mother," said the gentle Mira, throwing her fair arms around her neck, and looking in her face with an expression of the utmost affection, "how deeply do I sympathise with you; how can I ever sufficiently express the power of the feelings which throb within my bosom? Terrible indeed has been your lot, and oh, how unmerited!"

"My Mira," replied her mother, most fervently returning her embrace, "full well do I feel the force of what you say, but Heaven forbid that I should reproach the memory of my parents. Some strange and unfortunate infatuation must have come over them which they were unable to resist, and for which I feel it impossible to account. But to resume my narrative. No change came over the behaviour of my parents towards me, and, if possible, they became every day still more harsh and indifferent towards me, until at last they seemed to view me with—for I can apply no other term to it—absolute hatred, and every little simple error I committed was magnified almost to a crime, and punished accordingly. You may guess what I suffered, child as I was, from this dreadful and unexpected change; but I stifled my feelings as well as I could when in their presence, and it was only in the solitude of my own chamber, and when they had retired to rest, that I ventured to give free vent to the indulgence of my own sorrows. And, oh, the agony of those moments! I must fail were I to attempt to pourtray it. I knew of nothing that I had done, or even for a moment conceived that should entitle me to such harsh and cruel treatment, and consequently my despair and anguish were the greater. But amidst all these cares and anxieties, the image of the handsome stranger who had rescued me from sudden death was constantly before my mind's eye, and still I hoped that the time would arrive when I should behold him again and become better acquainted with him. Fatal hope! how fearfully for my own peace of mind, and for my future honour, was it gratified.

"My poor brother had been dead little more than eighteen months, when my mother was seized with a sudden illness, which baffled all the medical skill which was called in to her aid, and she expired, evincing not the least change in her feelings towards me. I then redoubled my affectionate attentions towards my father, but it elicited no responsive feelings in return, but, on the contrary, he only seemed to be happy (from what I could learn from others) when I was not in his presence, and to all my tender advances, he returned the most repulsive answers. What a wretched and lonely being was I now! Where was the companion of my childhood? Where the smiles and endearments of my parents? It seemed as though I had become an outcast upon the world; a thing to hate and despise; and many a time, and with the greatest sincerity too, have I solemnly wished that I had never been born, or that it would now please Heaven to take me to itself, since it seemed that I was destined to experience such manifold misfortunes.

"My father (who had saved enough from his industry to retire from his labours, and to pass the rest of his days in a state of independence) seldom quitted his residence; but he did not permit me to approach him more than he could possibly help, kept himself almost constantly secluded in his own room, and, in fact, became a perfect misanthrope. He took

no heed of what I did; indeed he seemed almost to have forgotten that there was such a person in existence, and I might therefore say that I was almost left alone and friendless in the word. To endeavour to drown the horrors of my thoughts, I would ramble for hours amongst the beautiful and romantic scenery at the foot of the Apennines, and for which Florence, that city of flowers, is so celebrated. There I would recall to my memory the happy days that were gone, and contrast them with the dismal present, and need I attempt to describe to you the pangs which those reflections cost me; how many were the tears I shed; how fervent were the prayers I constantly offered up to the Supreme, to work an alteration in my fate, or to take me to himself? Oh, no! I am confident I need not, for I am satisfied that hearts like those which I know full well you possess, can duly appreciate my feelings. A poor little wandering, lonely creature I was then, and it was but the foreshadowing of the misfortunes that were in future destined to attend me. But again I fear that I am becoming tedious, and that I shall tire your patience too far."

"Pray proceed, in the way that you think proper, and that best suits your feelings, signora," said Massaroni, "for I am convinced that every one here is most deeply interested in your melancholy narrative."

The Signora Zitella returned no answer to these observations, but she paused a few moments to collect her thoughts, and she then resumed, in the following words—

"My favourite haunts were those that my poor brother and myself used to resort to; and in pondering over the scenes which he used to admire, I have passed many of the most melancholy hours of enjoyment and calm contemplation in my existence. There was the grassy and rugged hill which he used to assist my footsteps to climb; there was the purling brook into whose lucid waters we used to cast the pebbles that we had gathered on the sand; there was the stately tree under whose cool shade we had so often sat, when we were fatigued with our youthful and jocund sports; the peaceful valley, luxuriant in flowers, from which he had delighted to cull me a beautiful bouquet; all, everything that I gazed upon reminded me of the dear and affectionate brother I had lost; and when I compared those days of happiness with my present situation, the contrast was almost too painful for contemplation. Oh! how bitterly did I lament the loss of that dear brother, whom I had now learnt, from woeful experience, was my only true earthly friend, and at the same time, how deeply and sincerely I regretted that it had not been my fate to die instead of him. How many sufferings would it not have saved me afterwards! What errors, what fatal errors might I have been spared! And I should have been called before the judgment seat of my Maker, as pure and innocent as when I first was born.

"I was a great favourite with most of the persons in the village where I resided; they appreciated the melancholy life to which my young days were subjected; and while they reproached my father for the unnatural and unaccountable way in which he treated me, and for which they were satisfied he had no reason, they ever endeavoured to reconcile me to my fate; to inspire me with hope; and, at the same time, never sought to prejudice my mind against the author of my being; but, on the contrary, tried to persuade me that sorrow alone for the untimely loss of his son had soured his temper, and made him appear what he was absolutely not. I endeavoured to believe them; I affected to do so, for I knew well the kindness of their motives; but, alas! I had had too painful experience how erroneous were the arguments they sought to impress upon my mind. I knew full well that I no longer possessed the love of my father; that, in fact, he now viewed me as if I were a curse upon him—as though I had blighted all his hopes. I remembered the death-bed of my mother; the looks of absolute aversion she had fixed upon me; and, therefore, can you wonder that I was wretched?

"With these good people I was always a welcome guest; and had it not been for their kind sympathies, Heaven only knews how I should ever have been enabled to support the heavy trials to which I was subjected when so very young. Days and days have I passed in their society, and my father knew not where I was, and I firmly believe, cared not what became of me, or if he should ever behold me again. These are harsh words to say of a parent; but God knows they are dictated by nothing but the truth.

"Thus four years from the death of my brother passed away, and I was now sixteen years of age. I had heard that I was considered handsome, but the flattering compliment could have no effect upon my mind, tutored as it had been in the school of adversity, and the future presented to me no prospect to inspire me with hope. Still the stranger who had rescued my life, and who disappeared so mysteriously, constantly was present to my mind. Would to Heaven that he had not been so! for I might then have been spared all the miseries and degradations it was afterwards my hard lot to encounter. I longed to behold him again, as I then thought, in my innocence, merely to thank him for the service he had rendered me, and I flattered myself with the idea that the time would sometime arrive when my wishes would be gratified. Alas! fataly for myself, it arrived too soon!

"One evening when I had returned home, after my customary rambles, and I had in vain endeavoured to draw my father (who was seated in his arm-chair, by the side of the fire) from his solitude; I took up a book in order to occupy my my mind, and to divert my thoughts from the misery which at that time enthralled them.

"It had been a particularly fine day, but towards the evening it had lowered in, and the distant murmuring of the thunder now portended a coming storm. Louder and louder the voice of the Heavenly lion became, until at last it burst over the roof of our dwelling with deafening fury; the lightning blazed in at the casements, and the rain descended in expansive sheets, almost threatening a second deluge. Still my father remained unmoved, and seemed to take not the least notice of the horrors that were raging around him. I must confess that I was terrified, and endeavoured to arouse him into conversation, but it was all of no avail, for he took no more notice of me than as if I had not been present at all, and I was left to the gloom and misery of my own thoughts. They were strange and conflicting, nor could I divest my mind of the impression that there was something of an important nature that was about to happen. I walked to the window, scarcely knowing what I did, and looked out upon the storm. It was truly terrific; the flashes of blue lightning and the peals of thunder (which seemed to shake the earth to its very centre,) followed each other in rapid succession; and horrified, and alarmed, I retreated again to my chair, and once more sought to arouse my father to conversation, but he either did not, or affected not to hear me, and continued with his arm resting upon the elbow of his chair, and his chin leaning upon his hand, seemingly wrapped in gloomy meditation.

"The storm momentarily increased in fury, until it had swelled to such an height that it seemed to threaten universal destruction; but still it made not the least impression, apparently, upon the mind of my father. I did not dare to venture to leave him, and was afraid to retire to my chamber, for I knew full well that I could not rest in such a furious and dreadful battling of the elements; and still the same strange presentiments of some approaching extraordinary event haunted my imagination, nor could I, by any means whatever, remove it from my mind.

"Suddenly, between the pauses of the tempest, I imagined that I heard the voice of a human being, as if in distress, and I started to my feet, and again approached the window; but the darkness which prevailed prevented me from seeing anything beyond, and the loud voice of the raging storm drowned any further cries, if they were even at that moment repeated. I returned to my seat in a state of the greatest anxiety, for I could not do away with the impression that I had heard cries of distress, which I imagined had proceeded from the voice of some benighted traveller, who was anxious to seek a shelter from the storm.

"Two or three minutes elapsed, when the cries were repeated, more distinct and nearer than before, and I was certain this time that I had not been mistaken.

"'Father, dear father,' I ejaculated, nudging his elbow; 'do you not hear?'

"'Hear, girl!' he repeated morosely; 'hear what?—Why do you disturb me?—I hear nothing but a little thunder. I believe it is a slight storm.'

"'A storm, father!' I returned; 'oh, yes, a terrific one, and it has been for some time raging with the greatest violence.'

"'Then, if you are frightened,' he said, in the same harsh and indifferent tones, 'go to bed, and forget all about it; do not disturb me; I have something else to think about. Storms!—Bah!'

"Again the voice of the person, whoever he was, sounded more loudly than before, and my father now evidently heard it.

"'It is there again, father,' I said; 'it is quite evident that some person is exposed to the fury of this dreadful night.'

"'Then, why does he not seek a proper inn?' returned my father, in the same surly tones; 'my house is no place for the accommodation of travellers.'

"'But, my father,' I ventured to say, 'you know there is no place of accommodation for travellers for upwards of a mile from this place, and surely you would not refuse a shelter to any one on such a night as this?'

"'Go to bed, girl,' replied my father, sternly, 'and do not make yourself officious.

"He had scarcely given utterance to the words, when there was a loud knock at the door, and the next instant the voice of a man requested admittance. My heart palpitated violently against my side with emotion, for I thought that the voice was familiar to my ears, though where I had before heard it, I could not, for the moment, conjecture. My father arose from his seat, looking very much displeased, and advancing to the door, he demanded—

"'Who's there? and why do you knock so loud at this unseasonable hour of the night?'

"'I am a traveller, who has lost my way in the dark, and have also missed my attendants,' replied the stranger. 'I, therefore, request a shelter for the night, or, at any rate till the storm has abated.'

"'I cannot accommodate you,' said my father, in the same disagreeable tones; 'there his no one here but myself and my daughter,

so you had better travel on till you meet with a proper place of reception.'

"'I am drenched to the skin,' remarked the traveller, 'and you surely will not refuse me the hospitality of a simple shelter.'

"'I do not like intruders,' said my father.

"'I will put you to no more trouble than I can possibly help,' remarked the stranger, 'and I will liberally reward you.'

"'Oh, as for reward,' muttered my father, 'that is a matter of secondary consideration; for, perhaps, I am not quite so poor as I may appear to be. But who are you? and what's your name?'

"The stranger seemed to hesitate for a minute, and then he replied—

"'I am a gentleman, travelling to Rome, and my name is Signor Carlotti!'

"'For goodness sake, my dear father,' I now ventured to urge, 'do not keep the signor any longer exposed to the tempest; his request is most reasonable; and surely you cannot doubt the truth of what he says?'

"'I have a right to doubt every one whom I do not know,' replied my father. 'However, I will venture to open the door to him and satisfy myself; I can but turn him adrift afterwards!'

"As he made use of these surly expressions, he opened the door, and the traveller, enveloped in a large cloak and drenched to the skin, as he had described himself to be, entered the room. My father took the lamp from the table, and thrust it rudely in his face; and he had no sooner beheld it, than he started back with an expression of amazement and emotion, as he exclaimed—

"'Ah! we have met before, signor!'

"I now directed my attention more particularly towards him; and I could scarcely repress a scream when I recognised in his features those of the man who had been the constant subject of my thoughts for the last four years, and whom I had been so anxious to behold again — the stranger who had interposed between me and destruction on the fatal and melancholy occasion when my poor brother met his untimely death!"

"Is it possible?" said Mira, interrupting her.

"It is true," replied her mother; "it was the same man—and can you wonder at the emotions, taking all the circumstances into consideration, that were excited in my breast? But I feel myself exhausted for the present, and overpowered with the recollection of the past; I must claim your indulgence while I rest for a few minutes."

To this request, of course, no one present could raise any objection; and the unfortunate Signora Zitella paused, and was allowed for a few minutes to give free vent to her feelings without interruption. At length she resumed her narrative in the following words:—

CHAPTER XLII.

THE NARRATIVE OF SIGNORA ZITELLA CONCLUDED.

"THE agitation of Signor Carlotti, as he called himself, was, as you may imagine, equal to our own, and for a few moments we were neither of us enabled to break the silence; but at length he said—

"'What strange fortune has guided my footsteps hither? That beauteous girl, whom it was my good fortune to rescue from an untimely death, and to whom my thoughts have ever since been devoted! Yes, it is the same; there cannot be another countenance half so lovely or—Yes, signor, you say aright, we have, indeed, before met, and under most peculiar and fortunate circumstances.'

"'Fortunate circumstances?' repeated my father, with a frown; 'call you those fortunate circumstances, signor, which deprived me of an only son?'

"'And preserved to you a daughter, signor, of whom you should be proud, and whom, I am certain, must prove a blessing to you in your declining days,' replied Signor Carlotti.

"'Bah!' exclaimed my father, impatiently; 'such observations are out of place.'

"'Out of place, signor?' said Carlotti, with a look of astonishment; 'pardon me, but I must say that you are mistaken. Beauteous signora, allow me to express the pleasure I feel at again beholding you, and to congratulate you on your appearing in such good health.'

"I find it a most difficult task to describe the feelings that agitated my bosom, as the pretended Signor Carlotti gave utterance to these observations. I felt myself blush to the eyes, and that I must have looked very much confused; but in spite of all my efforts I could not remove my eyes from his countenance, and I thought that I had never beheld a more interesting, or amiable-looking object. He evidently read the thoughts that were passing in my mind at the moment, and felt satisfied and delighted with the impression he had made. Fatal meeting was that to me, for from that I have to date the origin of all my principal misfortunes!

"'Signor,' I said at last, in a tremulous voice; 'to you I feel I owe a debt of gratitude which I can never repay, and you will pardon me if I cannot express to you in adequate terms the sentiments that are passing in my mind, but——'

"'There girl,' interrupted my father, impatiently, and in his usual disagreeable tones; 'there is quite enough of that nonsense; Signor Carlotti requires no flattery or compliments, I dare say. You are wet, signor, so you had better throw your cloak aside, and dry yourself by the fire; I suppose I must endeavour to find you accomodation till the morning; but do you think your servants will be able to find out where you are?'

"'No,' answered Signor Carlotti; 'I do not think it is very probable; I lost them in the wood about two miles from hence, and I think it is most likely that they will endeavour to find out the nearest inn till the morning.'

"'So much the better,' said my father, 'for I should be puzzled to find any convenience for them here; and one guest is quite enough at a time.'

"Signor Carlotti looked at him with some surprise and disgust, but returned no answer, whilst I felt still more confused and vexed, especially as the signor never for a moment scarcely removed his eyes from my countenance, and I could penetrate the feelings that were passing in his mind as readily as he could mine.

"'I suppose you need some refreshment?' said my parent.

"'A glass of wine will be sufficient, signor,' replied Carlotti, 'if it will not be putting you to any inconvenience.'

"'Zitella, bring refreshments,' commanded my father; 'and after Signor Carlotti has partaken of them, I will show him to his chamber at once, for doubtless he requires rest.'

"I immediately left the room to obey the orders of my father, and on my return in a few minutes with the refreshments, I found him and Signor Carlotti engaged in earnest conversation.

"'Tis true,' Carlotti was saying when I first came in, 'that my birth is noble, but my fortune is at present limited. I have been travelling on various parts of the continent since we last met, and am I now on my return home.'

"'You reside at Rome, then, signor?' said my father inquisitively.

"Carlotti hesitated for a moment or two and did not seem to like the question, but at length he replied in the affirmative.

"'Have you been much to Rome, signor?' inquired Carlotti.

"'Frequently,' answered my father; 'but I never remember hear mention of the name of Carlotti.'

"'Probably not,' returned the latter, 'for we have always kept ourselves very secluded.'

"'Oh, indeed?' said my father, with a half smile.

"'It is even so, signor,' replied Carlotti, appearing to take no notice of the expression of my father's countenance.

"'The most wealthy and influential family in Rome, if I have heard aright,' observed my parent; 'is that of the Prince Bianchi.'

"'Ah!' exclaimed Carlotti, with some expression of confusion; 'have you any particular knowledge of the prince or any of the members of his family?'

"'No,' answered my father,' 'a man in my humble circumstances cannot be supposed to be on very intimate terms with such high personages.'

"'True, true,' coincided Carlotti; 'have you ever seen any of them?'

"'Not to my knowledge; but if report speaks true the son of the Prince Bianchi is no better than he should be, but on the contrary is one of the most profligate and unprincipled nobleman in Rome.'

"'Report is a common liar!' said Carlotti, with considerable warmth; 'and such aspersions on the character of the young nobleman are as cowardly as they are unjust. I know him well, and I pledge my honour that a better man, or one who would sooner shrink from the performance of a guilty action does not exist. Were he present, you would I'm sure speedily be convinced of the truth of what I say.'

"'Well, well,' returned my father, carelessly, 'I will allow you to know best, signor, and it is a matter of perfect indifference to me. I do not suppose that he will ever trouble me, and I cannot blame you for espousing the cause of your friend, and attempting to vindicate his character; I can only repeat that what I have stated is the current report.'

"'It is false, basely false, I say again,' remarked Carlotti, with increased warmth; 'and probably you will some time have an opportunity of convincing yourself that what I have stated is correct!'

"'I do not expect that I shall,' answered my father, 'but, however, it matters not to me. I do not expect that any of the family will ever trouble me.'

"'Probably not,' remarked Signor Carlotti, with a peculiar expression of countenance which I could not help observing; 'but still it would be as well to do away with those prejudices which scandal has instilled into your mind. If you were ever to become acquainted with this profligate and unprincipled son of the Prince Bianchi, I will answer for it, that you would find he took a remarkable interest in yourself and your fair daughter.'

"'Ha! ha! ha!' laughed my father, 'that is not a bad joke, certainly; the son of the Prince Bianchi, the present Governor of Rome, the wealthiest and most powerful nobleman in all Italy, take an interest in the humble Martino Serranzi and his daughter. Ha! ha!— yes, yes; his *daughter*, he might, but by my soul's welfare, if he dared to attempt anything wrong to me or mine, not all the rank or wealth that has fallen to his lot, should shield him from my vengeance. I would have his life's blood, even though I mounted the scaffold for the justifiable deed the next moment.'

"'Pardon me, Signor Martino,' said Carlotti, after a pause; 'but you seem somewhat too much excited.'

"'No, Signor,' replied my father, regaining his wonted coolness and indifference; 'I merely expressed my mind; and if the son of the Prince Bianchi were now before me, I should not hesitate to tell him the same.'

"'Well, well,' returned Carlotti, endeavouring to laugh it off, though I could perceive plainly enough that he was much confused and abashed, though for why I could not conceive. 'Every person to their humour, though I still strongly imagine if you should ever become personally acquainted with the young nobleman of whom you have been speaking, you will entertain a very different opinion of him than that which you have just now expressed.'

"'Probably I may,' said my father, 'when I have that honour. But, may I ask you, signor, why it was you left so abruptly on that important day when you preserved the life of—of—my daughter?'

"Signor Carlotti hesitated for a few moments, and appeared to be at a loss for an answer; but at length he said—

"'Important business called me to the neighbourhood in which you were residing, Signor Martino, and being young and full of life and spirits, I could not resist the temptation to be present at the festivities got up on the anniversary of your unfortunate son's birth-day, though I wished to be there incog, and consequently did not introduce myself to you. The very moment after I had preserved the life of your daughter, my confidential servant made his appearance, in a state of great trepidation, and calling me aside, thrust a note into my hand, at the same time informing me that a messenger had just delivered it into his hands, informing him that my father was lying in a most dangerous state of illness and was not expected to recover. I hastily tore the note open, and the contents confirmed all that he had said. It was from my mother, and she earnestly requested me to return home with all possible expedition. Agitated as I was by this melancholy intelligence, you may naturally suppose that I was anxious to comply with the request with all the alacrity I could; and that accounts for the abrupt departure I made, and of which you have spoken.'

"'True, signor,' said my father; 'but did your father die on the occasion?'

"'He did not,' answered Carlotti; 'he still lies, though his health has grately declined, and it is that which has urged me to abandon my continental tours, and to return home, so that I may be near him, when it may please Heaven to summon him into its presence.'

"'And a very pious feeling too,' observed my father. 'It is a strange coincidence, but it strikes me, if my memory be correct, that the

Prince Bianchi was seriously ill, and not expected to recover, exactly at the same period.'

"'Indeed?' said Signor Carlotti, in a hesitating voice, and fixing a particular look upon my father; 'it may be so. I—I think it was so; but—but still I do not remember.'

"'That is strange too, as you resided in the same city. And the Prince Bianchi is now so old and so feeble, that I believe it is expected he cannot possibly long survive?"

"'Yes, yes,' replied Signora Carlotti, hastily. 'I believe you have spoken the truth. But, I feel tired, signor, and with your permission I will avail myself of the use of the chamber you have so hospitably offered for my accommodation.'

"'Very good, signor," said my father, lighting another lamp from the one that was burning on the table. 'This way, if you please.'

"Signor Carlotti arose from his chair and prepared to follow him, but first turning round to me with an air of the utmost politeness, and saying—

"'Fair Signora Zitella, I wish you good night, and may happy dreams attend your slumbers.'

"I blushed, curtseyed, but could make no reply, and Signor Carlotti, fixing upon me a look which I found it impossible to efface from my mind, followed my father out of the room, and left me to my own reflections, the nature of which you may very readily imagine. But I was not long left to the indulgence of them, for in a few seconds afterwards my father returned, and after looking at me with a peculiar expression of countenance for a moment or two, he said—

"'Well, Zitella, what think you of our guest?'

"I felt extremely confused at the question, and scarcely knew what answer to return; but at last I said—

"'Why, my dear father, he appears to be a noble gentleman, and—and I should indeed be ungrateful did I not remember that he is the preserver of my life.'

"'The preserver of your life!' repeated my father, sternly; 'and I know not that he may be any the better for that.'

"'How, father?' I said with a felling of astonishment, and the crimson blood mounting to my cheeks as I spoke.

"It is even as I say, girl,' he returned. "I do believe this Signor Carlotti, as he calls himself, to be a wily hypocrite and a villain!'

"How can I express the emotions of astonishment and disgust with which those observations inspired me, couched in the spirit of uncharitableness and injustice as they seemed to me to be!

"'Oh, my father,' I said at length, 'surely you wrong our noble guest by such a supposition; he cannot——'

"'Girl,' interrupted my father, impatiently. 'I have had sufficient experience in the world to enable me to read human nature, and I repeat my opinion of the character of the Signor Carlotti. There is a lurking devil in his eye, which could not escape my penetration. Mark my words, he is a libertine, a debauchee, a villain!'

"'Oh, no, no, impossible!' I exclaimed, warmly. 'Impossible!'

"'I tel you it is so,' repeated my parent; 'marked you the energy with which he defended the character of that notoriously abandoned young nobleman, the son of the Prince Bianchi?"

"'But are you certain that the reports circulated concerning the son of his highness are correct?' I demanded.

"'Certain!' he replied, 'yes, I am positive. I have had proof of it. Zitella, I perceive that this fascinating young stranger has made too powerful an impression upon you, and you must banish him from your thoughts.'

"'I must ever remember him with gratitude,' I returned; 'it would be monstrous in me to do otherwise.'

"'Remember what I have enjoined you,' said my father, sternly, 'and be prepared to obey it. This Signor Carlotti, I feel convinced, is not what he pretends to be; but in the morning he will take his departure, and I trust that we shall never behold him again. But you turn pale, and sigh, girl; what is the meaning of this?'

"I did indeed turn pale, and I felt a trembling sensation come over me which I found it was impossible to control; but I was unable to return any immediate reply to my father, and after looking at me sternly for a minute or two, he said—

"'Away to your chamber, girl; we must discuss this subject another time.'

"I was compelled to obey, and I was glad to escape from his presence; but when in the solitude of my own chamber, and left to the free indulgence of my thoughts, how shall I attempt to describe my feelings? In spite of all the prejudices which my father had expressed against the character of the Signor Carlotti, I found it utterly impossible to do away with the favourable impression with which he had inspired me, and my heart overflowed with a felling far more powerful than that of gratitude towards him for the service he had rendered me. I considered the opinion which my father had expressed of him to be most ungenerous and unjust, and, coupled with the strange behaviour he had evinced towards me for some years past, I was unable to account for it. That Carlotti was so soon to leave us, and the probability that we might never meet again, filled my mind with the most melancholy thoughts, and yet I could not help reproaching myself for entertaining them when I considered the disparity of our situations in life, and the danger which might ensue from my entertaining hopes which could never be realised.   The looks which Carlotti had bestowed upon me, were vividly impressed upon my recollection, and I could not help thinking that he was one of the most interesting and gallant individuals I had ever seen.   Alas! how fatal to my future happiness was the impression I had allowed him

MALVOLIO KILLS HIS JAILOR.

to make upon my mind! Would to Heaven that I could recall the past; how different would be my conduct. But it is useless now to murmur, or express a felling of regret.

"Sleep scarcely ever descended upon my eyelids during the night, and I was glad when the morning dawned, and I was enabled to leave my chamber, and wander in the neighbourhood until the hour for breakfast should arrive; but still, in spite of all my efforts to the contrary, the form of Signor Carlotti was constantly present to my thoughts, and completely superseded every other feeling. There were no traces of the storm which had raged the previous night, but, on the contrary, the weather was beautiful and serene, and the fair face of nature never wore a more lovely and smiling aspect; but all its beauties were entirely lost upon me in my present state of mind, and the most dismal forebodings of what was destined to take place in future came over me. At length I returned to the house, and found my father and the Signor Carlotti already seated together in the parlour, and engaged in conversation, which, to judge from the expression of their countenances, did not seem to be of a very agreeable description to either of them.

"Carlotti arose on my entrance, and greeted me politely, but I was so confused that I scarcely knew what answer I returned; and the looks which my father bestowed upon me, were calculated still more to disconcert me. I seated myself timidly at the table, scarcely daring to raise my eyes, and the meal passed off in comparative silence. It was scarcely over, when there was a knock at the door, and on my father opening it, the servants of Signor Carlotti, whom he had lost the night before, and who had succeeded in discovering where he was, made their appearance.

"'Signor Martino,' said Carlotti, 'I must no longer intrude upon your hospitality, and allow me to return you my sincere thanks for the kindness I have experienced at your hands.'

"'I require no thanks, Signor Carlotti,' returned my father coldly; 'I am but a plain-spoken man, and I detest flattery. The object of a night's lodging is not much; you have had it; I suppose you are satisfied, and there is an end to the matter.'

"'I hope that we shall meet again, signor,' said Carlotti, at the same time casting a glance towards me which I could not misunderstand, and which added greatly to my agitation and confusion.

"'I do not think it is very likely, considering the difference of our stations, unless it is by accident,' returned my father, in the same disagreeable and repulsive tones.

"'I must ever retain a lively sense of your kindness,' said Signor Carlotti; 'and depend upon it I shall not fail to take the liberty of calling upon you again the first time I pass this way.'

"'It is an honour I do not seek or expect, Signor Carlotti,' replied my father.

"Carlotti seemed somewhat abashed by the manner in which my father treated him, and returned no immediate answer, and I must own that I felt both vexed and surprised, and my looks must fully have expressed what I felt; but I saw the displeasure which was expressed in my father's countenance, and I endeavoured to conceal the feelings that were passing in my mind, and heartily wished that the scene were over.

"'Farewell, Signora Zitella,' said Carlotti at length; 'I do hope that we shall meet again; and in the meantime, I most heartily and respectfully wish you all the happiness that can befal you, and to which your manifold virtues so justly entitle you.'

"'I thank you, signor,' I replied, in a faint voice; 'Signor Carlotti must ever hold the highest place in my esteem for the service he has rendered me.'

"I noticed the pleasure which animated his countenance as I gave utterance to these words, and I cast my eyes towards the floor and concealed the crimson blushes which mantled in my cheeks as well as I could from the observation of my father.

"'Pardon me, signor,' said the latter, 'but there has, in my opinion, been quite enough said upon this trifling subject, and there is nothing I dislike more than compliments or fulsome flattery. I wish you farewell, as I have no doubt, considering the precarious state in which you say your father is at present lying, you are in a hurry to proceed on your journey.'

"I saw the vexation of Carlotti at the coldness, and almost insolence with which my father treated him, and my agitation and confusion increased.

"'Well, Signor Martino,' remarked Carlotti at length, 'I see that my presence here is no longer welcome, and I will not therefore detain you. Adieu! adieu! Signora Zitella!'

"I found it impossible to return any reply, and Signor Carlotti having fixed upon me a look which made a lasting impression upon my mind, took his departure. I sank in a chair, overpowered by my feelings, and covered my face with my hands, for it seemed as if at that moment all hope had gone from me altogether; and I almost forgot where I was.

"'Why, how now, girl?' demanded my father, abruptly, and in angry tones; 'what is the meaning of this agitation?'

"'Pardon me, dear father,' I replied, in a faltering voice, and not venturing to look up, 'it was only a faint and sickly sensation that came over me; it is gone now.'

"'Zitella,' returned my father, in the same accents of displeasure, and laying his hand upon my arm, 'forbear; do not attempt to deceive me, for I can read your thoughts. You have suffered this young nobleman, with his smiling exterior, and flowery accents, to captivate you, and——'

"'Father!' I interrupted, blushing deeply; 'you judge me too hastily; I——'

"'Nay,' he observed, sternly, 'it is even as I say; you cannot conceal anything from me; but I again warn you, as you fear my wrath, to banish him from your thoughts, for there is danger in encouraging any hopes towards him, which it would be preposterous to imagine could ever be realised.'

"'Oh, my father,' I ejaculated, 'what hopes can I ever entertain towards the Signor Carlotti, though it is impossible I can help feeling towards him a sentiment of the most unbounded gratitude as the preserver of my life?'

"'You attach too much importance to that simple circumstance,' observed my father.

"'Too much importance?' I repeated, with a look of astonishment; 'oh, surely you cannot think the preservation of my life a circumstance of so trifling a nature as to require no serious thought. What can have thus prejudiced your mind against Signor Carlotti?'

"'Believe me, girl, I have my reasons,' he answered; 'I am convinced that Signor Carlotti, in spite of his plausible exterior and honeyed accents, possesses a depraved heart.'

"'Oh, it is impossible! How deeply you wrong him by such uncharitable surmises.'

"'Indeed I do not; and time will prove that I am right, or I am much mistaken. It will be fortunate for yourself if you never behold him again. I see libertine and villain plainly imprinted in the lineaments of his features. Beware of him! forget that there is such a being in existence, as you value your honour and your future peace of mind.'

"Thus saying, without waiting to give me an opportunity of making any reply, he quitted the room, and left me overwhelmed with emotion. Left alone, I gave free indulgence to the anguish of mind, and it was a considerable time ere I could succeed in obtaining the least composure; but at last a copious flood of tears came to my relief, and in that state I remained for several minutes. To banish the interesting Signor Carlotti from my thoughts I felt would be a fruitless task; and the more I endeavoured to do so, the stronger became the impression. The conduct of my father I considered to be most ungenerous and unjust, and in vain I tried to imagine the cause of the prejudices which had been so strangely excited in his mind against him.

"'He knows him not,' I said, 'and therefore what cause has he to suspect him to be the unprincipled character he takes him for?—The idea is perfectly preposterous and monstrous, and is unworthy of a serious thought. And yet Signor Carlotti, it would perhaps have been better for us both had we never met. I feel that my bosom must ever overflow with gratitude towards you for the inestimable service you have rendered me, under any circumstances.'

"As my father had quitted the house to take his customary rambles, I experienced no interruption to my thoughts, and dismal and desponding enough were the feelings that agitated my breast. At length, however, tired of the house, and hoping by change of scene to obtain some relief, I walked forth, and sauntered slowly along towards those favourite haunts I was accustomed to frequent. I had not proceeded far, however, when I was startled by hearing a hasty footstep behind me, and looking back, you may imagine my astonishment and agitation, when I beheld one of the Signor Carlotti's servants hastening towards me and beckoning me to stop. I did so, and he shortly came up to.

"'Pardon me, signora,' said the man, 'for thus appearing before you; but my master desired me to endeavour to see you alone, that I might deliver to you this letter.'

"'You master, the Signor Carlotti?' I said, in a faltering voice; 'a letter for me? What can he possibly have to communicate to me in so secret a manner?—It would not be proper for me to receive it.'

"'I trust you will not decline to do so, signora,' replied the man, 'for my master is most anxious that you should receive it.'

"'And where is your master at present?' I demanded.

"'He is proceeding on his journey to Rome, where I am to follow him, signora,' replied the domestic; 'he bade me tell you that you would find something in the letter which you might desire to hear.'

"''Tis strange,' I remarked; 'I hardly know how to act.'

"'There can be no harm in your perusing the contents of the letter, signora,' said the man.

"'I know not,' said I; 'however, I will e'en risk it; give it me.'

"With many thanks for my condescension, the man put the letter in my hand, and then abruptly took his departure. I trembled violently, and for several moments I gazed earnestly at the letter, without mustering resolution enough to break the seal. I seated myself beneath the umbrageous foliage of a tree, and at length unfolding the letter, I perused the following words, written in an elegant hand.

"'Beauteous signora, I cannot resist the temptation I have to communicate to you the glowing sentiments of admiration and esteem, (to call it by the weakest name) with which you have inspired me. May I trust that he whom you have hitherto known as Carlotti only, may sometimes hold a place in your thoughts and regards, and then, indeed, shall I be happy. Oh, Zitella, I dare not venture to give utterance to all my thoughts, but may I hope that Providence will permit us soon to meet again; and that then you may not look altogether with coldness and indifference upon—BIANCHI?'

" You may readily imagine the agitation of my feelings on reading this epistle, and the discovery it made to me.

" 'Ah !' I ejaculated, 'is it possible that the preserver of my life is the son of the Prince Bianchi? I can scarcely believe the evidence of my senses. Alas! alas! what hope is there for me, prejudiced as my father is against him, and when I take into consideration the immense disparity of our stations? He can never become mine, even though I love him with all the strength of woman's most ardent passion, and he returns my sentiments with equal sincerity and fervour. Oh, no, it would be the height of madness to encourage such a hope. Oh, better, far better would it have been for the peace of mind of us both, had we never known each other. And can that which is reported to the prejudice of the character of this young nobleman, be true? It is impossible. I cannot believe it. No, Bianchi, so noble a form can never cover the heart of a villain and a hypocrite.'

" Having given utterance to those words, I pressed the letter to my lips, and then refolding it, I placed it carefully in my bosom, and resumed my walk, buried in profound meditation, and trying to imagine what was the fate which Providence had in store for me.

" From that moment Bianchi, as you may suppose, was the constant subject of my thoughts ; and the longer I reflected on him, the more ardent became the feelings of regard I entertained towards him, and the more anxious did I feel to behold him again or to hear from him. I tried all in my power to conceal the agitation of my feelings from the observation of my father, whenever I was in his presence ; but he watched me with a jealous eye ; and he seemed to have a pretty ready knowledge of what was passing in my mind, and frequently reproached me for it.

" In this manner about a month passed away after the departure of Bianchi, and I heard no more after him ; but one day my father returned rather unexpectedly from one of his accustomed walks, and the expression of his features showed that he had something of a particular description to communicate.

" 'The old Prince Bianchi is no more,' he said.

" 'Ah !' I exclaimed, starting on hearing this, 'dead ?'

" 'Yes,' said my father, looking at me with an expression of surprise ; 'but why does the news startle you in such a manner? The death of the prince must be a matter of indifference to you.'

" 'Yes—no,' I returned, with no little confusion ; 'but his son ?'

" 'Has now succeeded his father in his rank and title, of course,' replied my father ; 'and mark me girl, that son is no other than the constant subject of your thoughts, the pretended Signor Carlotti.'

" 'Ah !' I exclaimed with affected astonishment, 'is it possible ?'

" 'It is true,' he returned, 'and is no more than I suspected. Now have I not proved him to be a consummate hyprocrite ? No wonder that he should so eloquently espouse his own cause. But report, I am convinced, has given a fair estimate of his character, and I feel certain that he is a villain, who ought not to be tolerated in virtuous society.'

" 'Oh, it is impossible !' I ejaculated, warmly. 'I cannot believe it.'

" 'And do you dare to stand up in his defence, girl ?' demanded my father with a frown, and in tones of the greatest anger.

" 'Have I not a right to respect him, after what he has done for me ?' I returned. 'And why should I thus rashly condemn a man whom I know so little about ?'

" 'I see how it is, Zitella, you still cherish the form of Bianchi in your memory ; but beware ! for shame and misery follow in his path ; and should you not obey my injunctions, my heaviest wrath will descend upon your head.'

" 'Alas! my father,' I sighed, 'what cruel words are these ! how have I deserved this treatment ?'

" 'It is nothing to what you will experience if you do not banish the Prince Bianchi from your memory altogether. Dare you, a humble peasant girl, dare to aspire to the hand of one of the most wealthy and powerful noblemen in all Italy ? And think you that he would ever seek anything else than your dishonour ? Bah ! such presumption is intolerable !'

" 'And what reason have you to imagine that I entertain such presumptuous thoughts ?' I demanded, my bosom swelling with emotion and indignation.

" 'I am convinced you do,' he replied. 'I tell you again, girl, that there is not a thought which passes in your mind which I cannot penetrate. Remember my injunctions, and prepare yourself to obey them. The libertine Bianchi must never more pass the threshold of our dwelling.'

" With these words he retired from the room and left me to my meditations, the nature of which it is needless for me to attempt to portray, as you will be enabled to form a just conception of them. Notwithstanding all the injunctions of my father, I felt that it would be utterly impossible for me to obey them, and that though I might never presume to become the wife of one in the exalted station of the Prince Bianchi, I was very certain that I could never banish him from my memory. Would to Heaven that I had tried to obey the commands of my father, for harsh and arbitrary though they at that time appeared to be, they were just, and the suspicions he entertained against the Prince Bianchi were, alas! too correct. What years of shame and misery it would have saved me! When alone, I gave free vent to the poignant anguish of my mind, and again and again I perused the brief epistle I had received from Bianchi; pondered deeply over every syllable, and wept the bitterest tears upon it; but when in the presence of my father (which I avoided as much as I could), I was forced to assume an appearance of composure I was far from experiencing; though I had the greatest difficulty in deceiving him. I was a great deal absent from home; and took solitary walks where I was least likely to be interrupted or to be observed by any one. Another month had now passed away since my father had announced to me the death of the old Prince Bianchi, and not the slightest change for the better had come over my feelings. In fact I became more miserable than before, as the probability arose to my mind that Bianchi had forgotten me, and that I must never hope to see or hear from him again. It was no longer any use attempting to deny to myself that the sentiments of esteem and gratitude I had at first entertained towards him had ripened into love, and that passion increased in strength every hour. And yet what madness was it for me to encourage a passion which there was not the slightest possibility or prospect in the world of ever being gratified.

"One afternoon I had taken my favourite seat under the wide spreading branches of a lofty tree, and was immersed in meditation, when I was suddenly aroused from my lethargy by hearing an approaching footstep in the grass, and looking round, you may judge of my astonishment and delight on beholding the very object of my thoughts; he who possessed my most ardent love, the Prince Bianchi! Taken so suddenly by surprise, you will not wonder that I should not be able to control my feelings; I uttered a faint scream and immediately became insensible.

"When I recovered I found myself in the arms of the prince, who was gazing with looks of the most earnest love and admiration upon my blushing face. Confused and abashed, I tried to withdraw myself, but he still held me in his arms, and continued to look upon me with the same animated and delighted expression of countenance.

"'Beauteous Zitella,' he said, 'and have I at last the felicity to behold you again? Believe me fair being, my thoughts have been constantly fixed upon you since we last parted, and I have taken the earliest opportunity to return to this neighbourhood, in order that I might have an interview with you, and reveal to you the unconquerable sentiments with which your numerous charms have inspired within me.'

"'Oh, my lord,' I faltered out, blushing, 'indeed I must not listen to such words as these. I am but a poor humble girl, and you——'

"'By Heaven!' exclaimed the prince, rapturously, 'you are more valuable to me than the mightiest empress of the earth! What are riches compared to the wealth of the mind? Zitella, it is no use disguising my feelings; I love you to distraction, and nothing whatever can stifle the passion within my breast. Hither have I hastened to breath my vows at your feet and to implore your mercy.'

"It would be impossible for me to describe as they merit the varied feelings that agitated my breast, as the Prince Bianchi thus eloquently breathed his deceptive vows in my ears; but trembling with confusion, I extricated myself from his arms, and in a voice of emotion ejaculated—

"'Forbear, my lord, I beseech you; you cannot mean what you say, or let whatever may be your feelings, I must not encourage them. I owe you a debt of gratitude, and you must ever possess my respect and esteem; but more I must not presume to. The Prince Bianchi and the peasant girl, are separated by stations too far apart ever to come together. Leave me, your highness.'

"'Leave you, Zitella?' repeated Bianchi, 'and without one word of comfort and of hope? Oh, that is impossible. Beauteous girl, think not that the difference of our stations can make any change in the sentiments I entertain towards you; no, I love you, and you alone; and by all my hopes I would not resign you for all the world.'

"'Again I implore you to cease, my lord, I said, though every word to which he gave utterance went to my heart with the most pleasurable sensations; 'should my father discover us together——'

"'And what if he should, my sweet?' he interrupted.

"'Oh, I tremble, your highness, to think what the consequences might be,' I replied; 'my father entertains some fatal prejudices against you, which——'

"'And do you believe the calumnious tales, fair Zitella?' he asked eagerly.

"No, my lord, I cannot do so, after what I have experienced from you,' I replied.

"'Thanks, thanks, Zitella,' said the prince; 'you do me no more than justice. I know well the scandalous reports that are circulated respecting me, but they are base and cowardly fabrications, and I can well afford to treat them with contempt.'

"'My father, however, unfortunately believes them,' I remarked; 'and I do not think that anything will persuade him to the contrary.'

" 'This is most provoking,' observed Bianchi, ' and very uncharitable of your father, Zitella; —surely I have done nothing to excite such an ill feeling in him.'

" ' Very true, your highness,' I returned, ' but on the contrary, he is under an obligation to you, which should excite feelings of the utmost respect towards you in his breast. But—but I almost blush to acknowledge it, my lord, he has peremptorily commanded me, on the pain of his future wrath, to banish you from my thoughts.'

" ' Ah! say you so ?' said Bianchi, with a look of indignation; ' but tell me, Zitella, have your thoughts ever been fixed on me since last we met ?'

" ' My lord,' replied I, blushing still more deeply; ' I must not answer such a question. Suffer me to retire, and rest assured that I shall ever entertain a lively recollection of the services you have rendered me.'

" ' Oh, Zitella,' he observed with a melancholy look, ' and must we thus part ? Will you not impart to my mind one ray of hope ?'

" ' You torture me, my lord,' I ejaculated ; ' oh, consider my embarrassing situation, and do not any longer detain me.'

" ' By Heaven,' he exclaimed with great energy, ' it is impossible that I can separate from you in this manner.'

" ' Bold intruder !' exclaimed a voice at that moment behind him, and I uttered a cry of alarm when I beheld my father, his features distorted with passion, as he gazed upon the confused and disconcerted Bianchi. ' Insolent intruder, what brings you here? Do you seek to add another, in the person of my daughter, to the long dark list of your unfortunate victims ?'

" ' Signor Martino,' replied Bianchi, suppressing his wrath as well as he could, ' you are too warm, methinks, and do me an injustice by what you have just given utterance to ; but it is impossible that you can know what you say.'

" ' Indeed ?' said my father, with a sarcastic smile, ' but you will find that I do. I speak the truth, and though you are the powerful Prince Bianchi, you see I do not hesitate to tell you so to your face.'

" ' Father, dear father !' I ventured to interpose, seeing the gathering storm.

" ' Silence, girl !' he interrupted sternly, ' and away home.—The Prince Bianchi must content himself in the society of some other damsel ; I have other business for you to do than listening to the fulsome flattery of every empty and unprincipled coxcomb that may think proper to address himself to you.'

" ' Signor Martino,' said Bianchi, ' these gratuitous insults are almost insupportable ; however, I will not get out of temper with you, for I think that you will yet be ready to

acknowledge the injustice you have done me. Fair Zitella, adieu, since it is the will of Fate that we should part thus ; but I trust that the time is not far distant when we shall meet again, and under far different circumstances.'

" I could not return any answer, but my looks must have told what I felt, and my father, having rudely taken my arm within his, abruptly led me from the place. Once I ventured to look back, when I imagined my father was not observing me, and I saw that the Prince Bianchi was remaining on the same spot and the same attitude in which we had left him. His gaze was earnestly fixed on me, and I could imagine that I could read every thought which at that moment was passing in his mind ; but oh, had I been enabled to do so, how I should have shuddered with terror and disgust, and how different would have been the feelings I should have entertained towards him. I should have been snatched from that destruction upon the brink of which I was at that moment standing, and how many years of bitter suffering would have been saved me !—Bianchi waved his hand to me with an expression of the utmost affection, and the next instant he was hidden from my sight ; and I feared that I should never behold him again.

" I trembled at the idea of the treatment I might now expect from my father, but he said not a word to me on our way home, and seemed to be entirely wrapped in his own gloomy meditations. On arriving at our residence I would have retired immediately to my own apartment in order that I might give free indulgence to my feelings, but my father detained me, and looking sternly in my countenance, he said—

" ' Stay, girl ! you and I must have a few words together ere we separate. So, you have dared to disobey my injunctions, and have not only retained this libertine nobleman in your thoughts, but held secret assignations with him ?'

" ' Oh, father,' I replied, with much emotion, ' how cruelly you wrong me. Indeed I knew not of the Prince Bianchi being in the neighbourhood, and it was only by accident that we met !'

" ' 'Tis false, girl !' he returned, passionately ; ' do not think to deceive me !'

" ' When did I ever seek to deceive you, father ?' I demanded, with a look of reproach.

" ' You would do so now, but I am not to be imposed upon,' replied my father.

" ' Oh, this is most cruel ; it is unjust !' I ejaculated.

" ' Do you not love him?' he demanded sternly, and at the same time fixing upon me a look which penetrated to my very soul, and I could not reply for a moment or two.

" ' Why do you not answer my question ?' he said.

" ' Oh, my father !' I at length replied, in

a tremulous voice, and blushing deeply; 'candour and truth have ever been two of the principle characteristics that I have prided myself upon, and I will not deviate from them now; I do, therefore, acknowledge that the Prince Bianchi has made an impression on my heart, which I find it impossible to conquer, though I know, alas! too well, the utter hopelessness of my passion!'

"'Ah!' exclaimed my father, with rising wrath; 'say you so?—Is it not even as I said?—And you have suffered an unprincipled libertine, an hypocritical villain, to take possession of your heart?'

"'Oh, no, no, no!' I returned; 'you shamefully wrong the Prince Bianchi, I feel confident that you do; you are prejudiced against him, but for why I know not, , and have suffered yourself to believe in the scandalous reports which I believe are falsely circulated about him!'

"'But I am convinced of their truth, girl,' he answered; 'and, as I told him to his face, he would add you to the list of the numerous victims he has made. No doubt he has professed a desperate and ardent passion for you, and you, in your simplicity and ignorance, are ready enough to believe him. Bah! it is the snare he always lays to entrap his destined dupes. Are you mad?—You must be so, or you could never persuade yourself that the Prince Bianchi could ever for an instant entertain serious thoughts of making an humble peasant-girl like yourself his wife.'

"'Oh, no, I could never encourage such a presumptuous thought,' I replied; 'but still I find it is impossible for me to conquer the sentiments which he has excited in my bosom.'

"'He seeks your destruction, Zitella, I repeat, and you, with the infatuation of madness, seem determined to rush upon it. You must forget him; or remember him only as a villain.'

"'Never! never! that is impossible; is he not the preserver of my life?'

"'Pshaw! this is sickening sentimentality. You must banish him from your memory, I say again.'

"'No, no, I cannot.'

"'Beware what you say,' returned my father, with a frown; 'if you would not bring down upon your head my heaviest malediction, you will this moment swear, and that without hesitation, to forget that there is such a being in existence as the Prince Bianchi.'

"'I dare not, father,' I replied; 'you would exact from me an oath which I know it is impossible for me to fulfil.'

"'Ah!' he cried, passionately; 'dare you so boldly defy my wrath?'

"'Oh, no, for on the contrary, I tremble at the thought of it. But you cannot be so cruel and unjust. It is not probable that myself and the prince will ever see each other again, and

therefore what have you to apprehend? Would to Heaven that we had never met!'

"'You will find me determined, Zitella,' remarked my father, 'and resistance to my will is in vain. By all my hopes, I would sooner see you a corpse at my feet, than the degraded victim of the heartless libertine, Prince Bianchi. But I have selected a husband for you, one in your own station of life, who loves you fondly, and is every way worthy of you.'

"I trembled and turned very pale at those observations, and with difficulty faltered out—

"'A husband, father? Oh, whom do you mean?'

"'Matteo Falconi, the son of our worthy neighbour,' he replied.

"'Matteo Falconi!' I repeated, with a look of disgust and repugnance which I found it was impossible to conceal at the mention of the name of one whom I had always looked upon with feelings of indifferance, if not absolute aversion. 'Alas! alas! how can I ever consent to become the wife of a man whom I cannot love?'

"'But you must, you shall,' said my father, resolutely; 'Matteo has acknowledged to me the love he bears towards you, his father approves of his passion, and I have given my consent to his paying his addresses to you.'

"'And that without consulting my feelings upon the subject? Oh, this is surely most cruel.'

"'Pshaw! you are a foolish, obstinate girl, Zitella,' he returned; 'but all opposition to my wishes are useless, and I tell you again that you must be prepared to receive Matteo Falconi as your future husband.'

"'By Heaven! I would sooner perish,' I exclaimed, with unwonted energy; 'and that too, by a death of the most excruciating torture. But you will think better of this.'

"'Indeed I shall not,' he answered; 'my mind is made up, and nothing whatever can alter it.'

"'Oh, say not so,' I ejaculated in the most earnest tones, and tears starting to my eyes; 'you can never surely resolve to doom me to a life of such insupportable misery.'

"'A life of misery! what, in making you the wife of a worthy and honourable man?'

"'You cannot doom me to greater sorrow and despair than in compelling me to accept of Matteo Falconi as my husband.'

"'Do you attempt to deny his merits?' demanded my father.

"'No,' I replied, 'I admit that he is honest and honourable, at least so he has ever appeared to be to me, so far as I have been able to penetrate his character; but I cannot love him, and surely he will not persist in seeking to obtain possession of my hand when he knows that it cannot possibly be accompanied by my heart?'

" ' If he be not weak and foolish, he will,' said my father.

" ' And you will sacrifice me to him ?'

" ' I will not fail to keep the promise I have made to him and his father.'

" ' Then my doom is sealed, and there is nothing but misery and despair before me. Would to God that I were dead !'

" ' Tut, tut, girl,' said my father, hastily; ' I have no patience with such nonsense. The Prince Bianchi has got into your thoughts, and I verily believe has turned your intellect. However, you have heard my determination, and you must prepare yourself to abide the consequences.'

" ' Will nothing induce you to abandon your harsh and cruel determination ?'

" ' Nothing whatever !'

" ' Then there is no hope for me,' I sighed, and at the same time wringing my hands in a state of the greatest agony. ' Oh, my father, you surely will have bitter cause to repent this conduct !'

" ' Enough, girl !' he returned sternly; ' I am heartily sick of this foolery. Get yourself to your chamber; reflect maturely and seriously upon what I have said ; and mark my injunciton, and disobey them at your peril— do not again attempt to leave the house without my express permission. If the Prince Bianchi thinks to hold his secret meetings with you, and to contaminate your mind, in order that he may win you to his purpose,' he will find himself mistaken.'

" ' May Heaven turn your mind,' I ejaculated, earnestly and seriously; ' for if it does not, all my future prospects will be at once annihilated !'

" ' To your chamber, girl !' said my father, in a peremptory voice, ' and do as I have commanded you !'

"Without venturing to make any reply, and glad to escape to the solitude of my own apartment, I retired from the room; and when I was alone, my feelings overpowered me, and and I burst into a copious flood of tears. I saw at once that my doom was sealed ; that my father had made up his mind, and that he would remain stern and inflexible ; and the longer I reflected upon the misery and hopelessness of my fate, the more my anguish increased. I was convinced that in spite of whatever might befall me, I could never cease to love the Prince Bianchi with a passion as ardent as it was sincere; and that though I might never hope to become his wife, and it would be presumption in me to do so, to banish him from my memory would be a task that it would be utterly impossible for me to accomplish. I treasured every word that he had uttered at our accidental and unexpected meeting in my recollection, and they excited in my breast mingled sensations of pleasure and of pain. To think that I possessed his love was a source of the greatest gratification to me; but could what my father had said of him be true?—Oh, no, that I thought was utterly impossible; he seemed the very soul of honour and of truth, and to entertain any other opinion of him I considered would be monstrous and unjust. But should we ever meet again?— There did not seem to be the least probability our doing so, and that was sufficient to add to my despair and agony of mind. But the bare thought of my being compelled to become the wife of Matteo Falconi, (and I could have no doubt my father would adhere to the resolution which he had formed), filled me with horror and disgust; and I earnestly prayed to Heaven to take me to itself, rather then that I should be consigned to such a fate. Matteo Falconi was a simple, good-natured rustic, and I was aware that he was possessed of some very excellent qualifications ; but still nothing could be more dissimilar than our tastes and inclinations, and I could not look upon him with any other feeling than one of respect ; but think of him as my future husband, was what I could not find patience to do, and I was determined to oppose the hated alliance with all the means in my power. But limited indeed were they, and what could I do in opposition to the stern will of my father ? I saw at once, that unless Providence should mercifully interpose in my behalf, my fate was inevitable, and my misery every moment increased, until at length it became insupportable.

"The Prince Bianchi, I felt satisfied, would remain in the neighbourhood for the present, and notwithstanding the stern injunctions, and the insulting observations of my father, would watch every opportunity to see me again, or communicate with me; though I could not imagine by what means he could continue to do so.

"My father did not attempt to interrupt me again throughout the day, and I was left to the indulgence of my own reflections, the painful nature of which, I presume, it is needless for me to attempt to describe to you. I slept but little that night, and I arose at an early hour the following morning; but though it was extremely fine, and a walk would have served to have refreshed me, and done me good, I did not dare to quit the house after the peremptory commands I had received from my father. I waited in a state of great anguish and suspense, until the hour of breakfast had arrived, when, with a faltering step, I ventured to descend to the parlour, where I found my father awaiting me. He received me with his usual coldness and indifference, and he fixed upon me a keen and penetrating look, and frowned.

" ' You look pale, girl,' he said, ' and have been weeping. Your eyes are heavy, and it is evident you have slept but little. Thinking of the Prince Bianchi, I presume, and how you can best oppose my will? Come, come, girl, there has been enough of this, and I am heartily sick of it; you had better be careful that you do not try my patience too far.'

"'Alas! my father,' I sighed, 'how can I help my feelings after what took place at our interview yesterday? Why do you persist in torturing me thus? There was a time when I thought I possessed your love, and I was happy; but that feeling, I fear, is now banished from your mind, and I am wretched.'

"'And there was a time, too,' he returned,

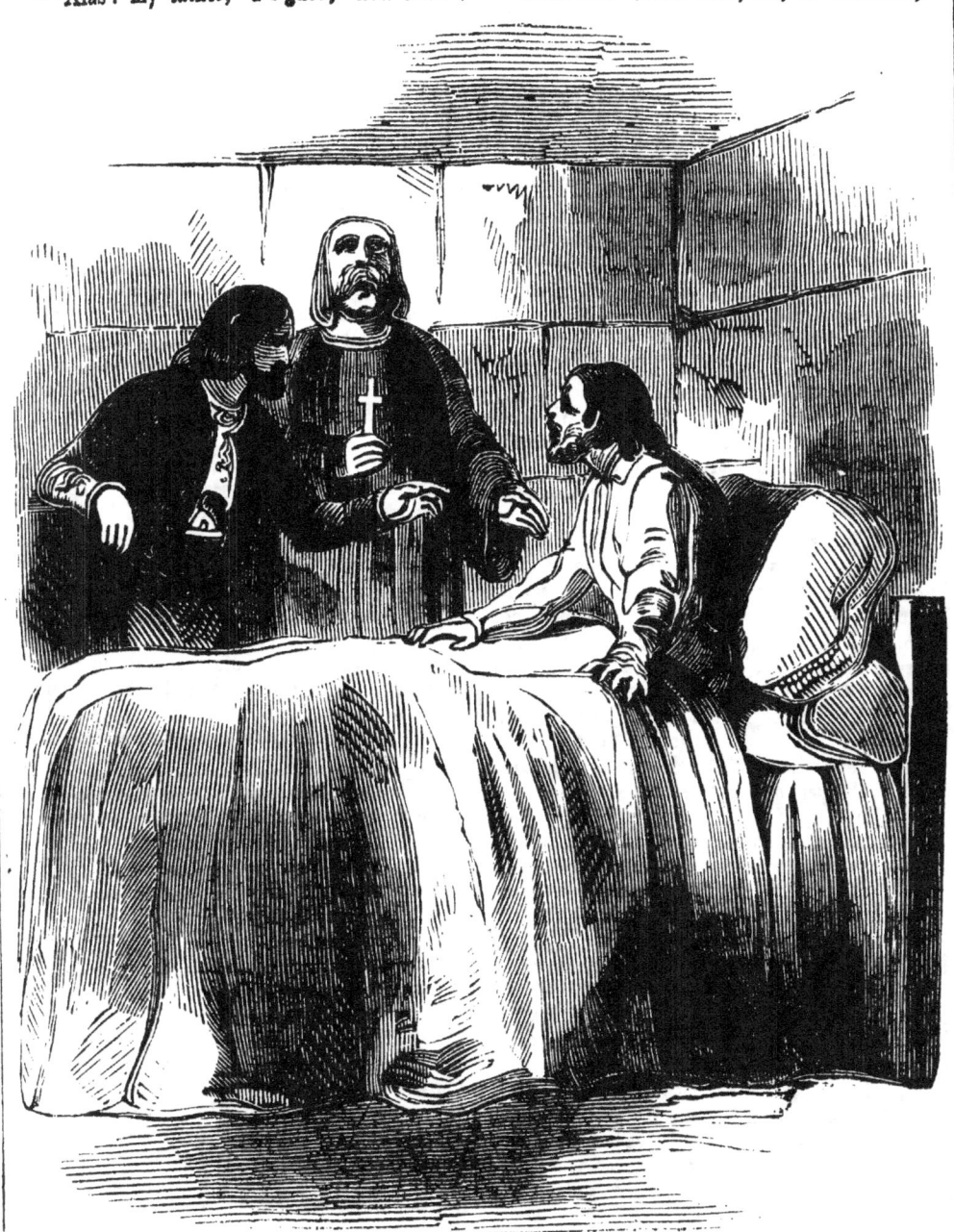

MALVOLIO ATTENDED BY A MONK.

'when Zitella was obedient to my will, and did not dare to encourage a thought of which I could not approve; but her nature is changed, and——'

"'Oh, no, no,' I hastily interrupted, 'it has not; you greatly wrong me by such a supposition; but you would exact promises from me that are cruel and unjust, and how can I conscientiously obey them?'

"'But you must,' said my father, in a stern and determined tone; 'or you will be visited with my bitterest wrath. You must cease to remember the Prince Bianchi in any other character than that which I have truly represented him to be, namely, that of an abandoned and unprincipled villain.'

"'Never!' I replied, firmly; 'the Prince Bianchi, I am certain, is totally unworthy of the guilty character you have given him, and will yet be able to vindicate himself to the satisfaction of every one, and the confusion of his enemies.'

"'Girl!' exclaimed my father, passionately, 'dare you attempt to dispute my assertions? This boldness is unbearable, and if you persist in them, you will excite my utmost indignation, and will have good cause to repent it when it is too late. The Prince Bianchi and yourself must never meet again, and it will be well for you if you dismiss his image from your mind altogether. To think of one who only seeks for an opportunity to effect your ruin, is sinful and disgusting.'

"'I cannot, I will not believe that the Prince Bianchi can ever entertain such guilty thoughts towards me,' I replied, with increased warmth; 'and I can never cease to remember that, but for him, I should in all probability have met with a sudden and untimely death.'

"'Bah! you have already sufficiently acknowledged the service he has rendered you, and it is time that there was an end to the matter. But you will have to talk on other subjects before long, for Matteo Falconi will be here to-day, and I command you to give him such a reception as his merits deserve.'

"'The respect which is his due, he shall receive from me,' I answered; 'but more I cannot bestow upon him, unless you would have me act the part of a hypocrite.'

"'Beware, Zitella, what you say, if you would not excite my wrath,' said my father; 'I again command you to treat Matteo not only with respect, but that warmth of regard which is due to the man who is destined to become your future husband.'

"'You enjoin me to do that, father, at which my feelings revolt, and which I cannot perform. Oh, if you have one spark of feeling and affection left in your breast for me; I implore you to spare me this painful meeting, which can only be productive of regret and misery to us all.'

"'Think you that I am mad?' he demanded, in a stern and inflexible voice; 'or that I have become weak and irresolute as a boy?— My determination is fixed, and unless you receive Matteo's addresses with every favour, my utmost indignation will descend upon your head.'

"'Alas! alas! then,' I sighed, in the most melancholy accents, 'there is no hope for me. Surely Matteo, when he finds that I have no love to bestow upon him, out of pity and justice to me, will at once abandon his suit.'

"'Indeed he will not, girl,' replied my father; 'Matteo loves you too ardently to be repulsed, and think you I will be worse than my word, when I have already promised him your hand?'

"'Ah, this is most cruel; and it seem as if you were resolved to annihilate all my hopes, and to doom me to the most insupportable wretchedness.'

"'If bestowing upon a husband, who loves you so fervently and sincerely, and who is in every way worthy of you, be dooming you to wretchedness, why then I am,' he returned. 'But come, away with this ridiculous weakness, and learn to submit to my will, for it is useless to seek to oppose it.'

"'In everything that is reasonable and just, Heaven knows how readily I will,' I replied, 'but nature revolts at the bare idea of this hateful alliance, and there is no fate I would not dare to encounter, rather than that with which you have threatened me.'

"'But how can you avoid it?' he demanded. 'Do you not see the utter impossibility of your doing so?'

"'Unless you relent, and take pity on me, too painfully I do,' answered I. 'Oh, my father, you surely cannot have stifled all the feelings of nature in your breast, as thus to remain inexorable?'

"'I can remain firm to anything to which I have made up my mind, as you will shortly discover. You cannot offer any reasonable objections to Matteo Falconi; you have admitted that he is good and honourable, and——'

"'And if he be really so,' I eagerly interrupted, 'he will, even at the sacrifice of his own feelings, not hesitate a moment in abandoning his suit, and leaving me at liberty, when he finds that he can never hope to possess my love; and that consequently a union between us could only be productive of the greatest misery to us both.'

"'And if he be as wise as I take him to be, he will do nothing of the kind,' returned my father, 'especially when he knows he has my sanction and especial approbation. Matteo has loved you from childhood; he has by all his actions proved himself deserving of you, and, let the consequences be whatever they may, I am determined that he shall possess you. As for your loving him, I do not doubt that you will do so before long.'

"'Alas! and can you thus treat the affections of my heart so lightly?' I demanded, with a look of reproach. 'Oh, I can scarcely believe it is my father who speaks to me.'

"'All the arguments you may make use of cannot alter my mind,' he said; 'but retire to your chamber, banish those tears and pale looks, and be prepared to meet Matteo Falconi on his arrival, as I have commanded you.'

" ' How shall I ever be able to accomplish a task which is so difficult ?' I ejaculated ; ' it is impossible !'

" ' It is not only possible, but it must be done,' said my father. ' Away to your chamber until I summon you again into my presence, and do as I have ordered you.'

" I saw that it was useless to remonstrate with him, or to endeavour to excuse myself from the meeting, though I anticipated it with feelings of the utmost dread and repugnance ; and with a heavy heart, therefore, I quitted the room.

" On reaching my own room, I sunk on my knees, and supplicated the merciful interposition of Heaven to rescue me from the fate which seemed to be impending over me, and to give me strength to support the coming interview with Matteo Falconi with firmness ; but, in spite of what the consequences might be, I was determined not to disguise my real feelings towards him, and to throw myself upon his mercy. Finding that there were no means of avoiding it, I sought all that was in my power to compose my feelings, so that neither my father nor Matteo might be enabled to obtain any undue advantage over me, and I succeeded far better in doing so than I had any reason to hope. At the end of about half an hour, my room door was opened, and my father entered, and fixed upon me a keen and penetrating look, which I met with much more firmness than he had doubtless expected.

" ' Now, Zitella, are you ready ?' he said. ' Matteo Falconi has arrived, and is awaiting most anxiously to see you below.'

" ' I would fain avoid this interview. my father,' I replied ; ' but since I find that it is useless to appeal to you, I am ready to attend you ; though I promise you before-hand that I cannot and will not attempt to act the hypocrite—I will reveal the true sentiments of my mind, let the consequences to myself be whatever they may.'

" My father frowned as he said—

" ' Beware, Zitella, how you carry your threats into execution, lest you bring down my heaviest malediction upon your head !'

" ' Oh, my father ! will you not act with some pity and forbearance ?' I ejaculated.

" ' Pity and forbearance ?' he repeated ; ' pshaw ! I can suffer no opposition to my will. My conduct towards you depends entirely upon the manner in which you behave yourself at this interview. Follow me !'

" I offered no observation, but obeyed and followed him, though it was with trembling footsteps that I did so ; and descending to the parlour, my father opened the door, and Matteo Falconi hastened to meet me, his countenance animated with love and admiration ; he received no responsive glance, however, from me, but on the contrary, I cast my eyes to the ground, though I suffered him to take my hand, and press it respectfully to his lips, scarcely knowing for the moment what I did, though I quickly recovered my firmness and composure.

" ' Fair Zitella,' said Matteo, ' I trust that you will pardon this intrusion, which I should not have ventured had I not been authorised by your father. I have much to say to you, and I hope that what I have to disclose will be received with favour in your eyes, and if so, Matteo Falconi will consider himself one of the happiest and most fortunate men in existence.'

" ' Well spoken, Signor Matteo,' observed my father ; ' my daughter is fully prepared to listen to the subject you have to converse with her upon ; and as two is company, and three is none, I will leave you to discuss the matter together.'

" ' Oh, you will not surely leave me in this embarrassing and painful situation ?' I said. ' Signor Matteo, whatever you have to say, I request you do it in the presence of my father, and to be as brief as possible.'

" ' No,' said my father, walking towards the door ; ' I will leave you to yourselves, for perhaps my presence might mar the effect of the conversation. I will return when I think it is at an end. Zitella, I warn you to remember my injunctions ; this is no time for trifling.

" Thus saying, and fixing upon me a peculiar look which I could not fail to understand, and which made me shudder, he retired from the room, and left me and Matteo Falconi to ourselves. I need not attempt to describe the agitation of my feelings, and for a few moments Matteo seemed to be almost as confused as myself, and did not appear to know exactly how to begin. At length, however, he aroused himself, and I recovered my firmness and presence of mind, and was fully prepared to reply to what he might think proper to say.

" ' Beauteous Zitella,' he began, ' I have long anxiously panted for this opportunity to reveal to you the sentiments that are passing in my mind, and to receive the decision of my fate from your lips. Your father has at length kindly granted it to me, and with a throbbing heart I now hasten to unfold to you——"

" ' Signor Falconi,' I interrupted, at this point, in a firm voice, ' hold ! I know all that you would say, and may therefore as well save time and much pain and embarrassment to us both, by returning you my answer in as few words as possible. You would acknowledge to me a passion which I candidly confess I cannot return ; therefore I trust that you will at once abandon your suit, and rest assured that you shall ever possess my respect, though you cannot receive my love.

" Matteo looked greatly abashed, disappointed, and agitated, as I uttered these words, and I must confess that I could not help pitying him, though it had removed a great weight of care and anxiety from my mind.

"'Alas!' he sighed at last, 'and all the hopes which I had formed, and in which Signor Martino, your father, encouraged me, thus doomed to be disappointed? Oh Zitella, did you but know the strength and sincerity of the passion which glows within my breast towards you, you would pity me. But you will retract your words; you will not leave me thus entirely to despair.'

"'Signor Falconi,' I returned, 'you have heard my decision, and nothing whatever, depend upon it, can induce me to alter it. If my father has buoyed you up with false hopes, it was without my sanction, and is, therefore, no fault of mine. He knows my mind, and should, therefore, have spared us both the pain of this interview. I am fully sensible of your merits, and thank you for the kind feelings that you express towards me. If my friendship be of any value to you, rest assured that you possess it; but a warmer feeling you can never hope to excite in my breast. I wish you every prosperity in life and that you may meet with some other damsel that is far more worthy of you than myself, who can return your love, and will render your future days happy.'

"'Alas!' he replied, in melancholy accents, 'that can never be; I can never see any other woman whom I can love except the beauteous Signora Zitella; and since fate has so ordained it that I cannot possess her love, life will no longer possess any charms for me. But indeed I cannot resign my hopes altogether; you will even yet think better of what you have said, and—"

"'No, signor,' I interrupted; 'it would be most cruel and unjust in me to encourage any such wishes. You must learn to forget me, for I can never become your wife, even though my father would urge me to it, nay force me to bestow upon you a hand which could never be accompanied by my heart.'

"'You tell me to forget you, Zitella,' said Matteo; 'but oh, fruitless would be the attempt to do so; your image is so deeply enshrined in my heart of hearts that nothing whatever can eradicate it.'

"'Pardon me, Matteo,' I returned, 'but I cannot longer listen to language such as this. I possess too good an opinion of you to imagine for a moment that you will continue to press your suit when you know that it is so repugnant to my feelings.'

"'You do me but justice, fair signora,' he replied, 'by entertaining that opinion of me. Heaven forbid that I should by any conduct of mine cause you one moment's uneasiness. No, Zitella, you say you cannot love me, and since it is so, I must resign myself to my fate; though God know that that will be a task that I shall find it almost impossible to accomplish.

From this moment you shall never hear me breathe a sentence of my unfortunate passion in your presence; I will keep my sorrows confined to my own breast, and endeavour to prove to you that I am at least entitled to your friendship and esteem.'

"'Thanks, many thanks, Signor Falconi, for that assurance,' I said; 'your conduct fully justifies the opinion I had formed of you. My father, however, has threatened me with his heaviest wrath if I should dare to reject your vows, and I have too much reason to fear that he will not fail to keep his word.'

"'Oh, no, signora,' returned Matteo, 'I cannot believe that Signor Martino will be so cruel and unjust; he would not surely wish you to become the wife a man whom you cannot love.'

"'Such a wish, nay determination, he has expressed, notwithstanding my remonstrances and expostulations,' I replied.

"'But can he imagine that I would ever consent to accept the hand of any woman under such circumstances?' said Matteo; 'no, I should hate and despise myself, Zitella, could I be guilty of any such conduct. Do not alarm yourself unnecessarily; I will remonstrate with your father, and perhaps my arguments may work some influence on his feelings.'

"I again thanked for his friendly offers, and allowed him to raise my hand respectfully to his lips; overcome by the power of his emotions, he was then about to retire, when the room-door opened and my father entered.

"'How, now, Signor Matteo,' said my father, seeing that he had been in the act of leaving the apartment; 'are you so soon tired of the presence of my fair daughter that you were about to retire without so much as exchanging a word with me at parting? Come, tell me, for I am most anxious to know—how has this interview terminated? To your satisfaction, of course?'

"'Pardon me, Signor Martino,' returned Matteo, while I trembled with anxiety; 'but I must claim your patience for a few minutes, and especially towards Signora Zitella, while I explain.'

"'Proceed, proceed!' said my father, impatiently, and casting a suspicious look at me.

"'I find, signor,' continued Falconi, after a brief pause, 'that though I possess the friendship of your fair daughter, she has no heart to bestow upon me, and has, with a candour and delicacy which does her honour, rejected my love.'

"'Ah!' exclaimed my father, in a passionate voice, and looking fiercely at me; 'is it even so, and has she dared to——'

"'Be calm my dear signor,' interposed Matteo, 'and do not reproach Zitella for that for which she is not to blame. Who shall seek to control the affections of the youthful and innocent heart?—I would never consent to receive the hand of any woman unless I was certain also I possessed her love; and though it will cost me a severe struggle with my feelings, I have resigned my suit.'

"'Obstinate girl!' cried my father, turning fiercely towards me, 'and so you have dared to set my authority and will at defiance? Oh, by the mass, you shall have bitter cause to rue this! And you, Signor Matteo, so this is the strength of the passion and determination you boasted of!—Bah!—I have no patience with such drivelling cowards!'

"'Signor Martino,' returned Matteo, colouring with indignation, 'methinks that milder and better words would best become you on such an occasion as this. I have nothing to reproach myself with, or Signora Zitella. I should have considered myself a villain had I persisted in urging my suit when I know it was so repugnant to her feelings. But, again I beg of you not to visit her with your unmerited wrath, since, surely, she is not to blame for the manner in which she has acted, and which has probably saved us both from future misery.'

"'By Heaven, I will be revenged!' exclaimed my father; 'this obdurate girl shall yet learn what it is to disobey my injunctions. Signor Matteo, you have deceived me, and held me up to ridicule. From this moment our friendship is at an end. You can retire, for your presence is no longer agreeable to me.'

"'Be it so, Signor Martino,' replied Falconi, proudly. 'I can brook your insults for the sake of your daughter. Farewell, Signora Zitella, and may every happiness attend you.' I was too much agitated to attempt to make any reply, and Matteo quitted the house.

"For some minutes after he had taken his departure, my father traversed the room with haste and uneven footsteps, and uttering incoherent sentences to himself, whilst the agitated state of my mind you may readily form a conception of, and I trembled with apprehensions which I had too much reason to believe were not ill-founded. At length, he turned towards me, and gazed silently upon me, with his arms folded across his chest, but with a stern expression of countenance, which plainly convinced me of the storm which was about to burst upon my devoted head, and quite unnerved me. I waited to hear the result with the most trembling anxiety. Nor had I to wait long.

"'So,' he exclaimed, in a voice half choked with passion, 'this is your dutiful humility, and submissive obedience to my will!—This is the reward I receive for all the many years of care, anxiety, and affection, I have bestowed upon you. Weak fool that I have been, it is fit that I should be thus rewarded. But, mark you, rash girl, you shall not go unpunished for the daring defiance with which you have treated

my authority. I will yet find a way to crush your proud and obdurate spirit, and give you bitter cause to repent your conduct all the days of your life. In future, I will rule you with a rod of iron, and although the idiot Matteo has thought proper to resign his pretensions to you, and thus to heap an unpardonable insult upon my head, I will find some other man, who is less scrupulous and squeamish, to become your husband; and should you refuse, force shall drag you to the altar, be the consequences afterwards whatever they may!'

"'Oh, God!' I ejaculated, with a feeling of horror, which I could not repress; 'can this be my father who thus speaks?—Alas! alas! you could never have loved me, or you would find it impossible to act with such unmerited cruelty and injustice towards me. For the love of Heaven I beseech you to bethink yourself, and, surely, nature will prompt you to forbear, ere it be too late.'

"'My resolution is fixed,' he replied, 'and not all the arguments you can make use of, not all your tears or supplications, can have the least effect to move me from my purpose!'

"'And you can bear to contemplate, with feelings of satisfaction, my future misery?' I observed. 'Oh, how have I merited this?— In all things that are just and reasonable, you always have, and ever shall find me most willing to obey you; but God alone, and my own sense of right and wrong, have any authority to control my heart's affections, or to compel me to do that which must involve my future happiness.'

"'Girl!' he cried, with increased rage; 'dare you thus boldly to address me?—Do you set my authority entirely at nought?'

"'Oh, no,' I answered; 'how much you wrong me by that supposition! Have I not, from the days of my earliest childhood, always endeavoured to show the love and veneration I entertained for you? But, of late years, you have repulsed all my advances, and for why, I know not, unless it be that I have become hateful to you. Alas! I am most unfortunate, and, perhaps, it would have been better for me had the Prince Bianchi not succeeded in rescuing me from the untimely fate with which I was threatened.'

"'Oh!' exclaimed my father, with a look of rage; 'that dissipated nobleman, I see, still holds dominion in your thoughts, and you are willing to rush headlong to destruction. But, mark my words, I will take good care to disappoint you in any guilty wishes you may have formed!'

"'Guilty wishes, father?' I replied, with an expression of indignation and reproach; 'and have I indeed then sunk so low in your estimation, as to cause you to look upon me with such degrading feelings as those you have just expressed? Oh, I am indeed truly wretched

if such be the unmerited thoughts you entertain of me !'

" ' Have I not fully revealed to you the real
character of the Prince Bianchi ?' he demanded ;
' and yet you persist in retaining him in your
thoughts, against my express command, and
have even dared to acknowledge the favourable
impression he has made upon your heart.'

" ' True,' I returned calmly, ' it was gratitude first prompted the feeling, and I should
be unjust and uncharitable were I upon mere
idle report to believe anything to his prejudice.'

" ' Girl !' cried my father, fiercely ; ' and do
you then presume to doubt my word, and to
accuse me of scandal and falsehood ?'

" ' Oh, no,' I answered, ' Heaven forbid ; but
I am firmly of opinion that you have been misinformed, and that ere long you will be as well
convinced as I am that the Prince Bianchi is
totally unworthy of the opprobrium which is
so basely heaped upon his name.'

" ' Cease, girl !' he exclaimed, ' to seek to
champion the cause of one whom I now so
thoroughly hate and despise. Already you
have sufficiently excited my wrath and resentment by the conduct of which you have been
guilty, and I am determined to punish you for
it, and to bring you to your senses, if possible.'

" ' Oh, mercy ! mercy !' I earnestly supplicated, tears starting to my eyes ; ' if I have
become so hateful to you, cast me from you,
immure me in a convent, and——'

" ' No, no,' interrupted my father, in the
same unfeeling tones ; ' I will not thus gratify
your wishes. I have another fate in store for
you ; and by all my hopes, nothing whatever
shall move me from my settled purpose,'

" ' All-Merciful Father !' I solemnly cried,
clasping my hands vehemently together, and
raising my eyes towards Heaven. ' All-Merciful Father, then look down with pity upon me,
and do not suffer me thus to be cruelly sacrificed.
Father, you cannot mean what you say. I will
not believe that you do ; for it would be monstrous and unnatural to do so.'

" ' Enough !' he returned, impatiently ; ' I
will not listen any longer, at present, to what
you have to say. You shall find that I will
keep my word. Away to your own apartment,
and reflect upon the rashness and folly of your
conduct. There you must consider yourself a
prisoner until such time as I may think proper
to release you. Trust me, I will yet learn the
way to subdue this obdurate spirit, and to teach
you obedience to my will. No more, girl ; I
am now in no mood to listen to you.'

" I sighed deeply, and fixing upon him a look
of the bitterest reproach, which ought to have
penetrated to his heart and moved him to compassion and forbearance, I slowly quitted the
room, and once more sought the solitude of my
chamber, where I threw myself on to a seat, and
sank into a paroxysm of sobs and tears. I

could not reproach myself for anything I had
done, for I had acted only as reason and nature
dictated ; but the unparalleled cruelty of my
father surprised and distracted me, and I
trembled when I reflected upon the threats he
had held out to me, and imagined the length
to which he might suffer his indignation to go.
It was painfully evident to me, that if ever he
had felt for me that affection which should
animate the breast of a parent towards his only
child, that sentiment was now entirely extinguished ; and that thought could not fail to
excite in my bosom the utmost anguish and
despair. I could never sufficiently admire the
manly generosity, and nobleness of feeling, which
Matteo Falconi had evinced ; and I heartily
prayed to Heaven for his happiness and welfare,
and that he might soon be able to banish from
his breast the unfortunate passion he had conceived for me. The revengeful spirit with
which my father pursued him inspired me with
disgust ; but I sincerely hoped that no danger
would arise to either of them in consequence
of it.

" My thoughts were constantly fixed upon
the Prince Bianchi, and nothing whatever could
alter the opinion I had formed of him, or change
the sentiments with which my heart throbbed
towards him, although it would have been the
height of presumption in me to hope that I
could ever become the wife of a nobleman who
was placed by fortune in such an exalted station
above me ; still I could not think of his becoming the husband of any other woman than
myself with any other feelings than those of the
utmost distraction. And were we never again
destined to meet ? I feared not ; and if we
were, it would be but to increase my despair.
But it would be a fruitless task for me to attempt to describe the whole of the torturing
reflections which continued to haunt my imagination, in this, my solitude. I was attended
upon by a young girl who had been hired a
short time previously by my father, but she
was extremely simple and illiterate, and I
could have derived but little or no consolation
from her conversation, if even I had ventured
to make a confident of her, which I would not,
for I felt certain that she was placed by my
father more as a spy upon my actions than for
anything else ; and consequently I was always
most guarded in what I said and did whenever
she was present.

" My father did not intrude upon me again
that day, but the next morning he did, and the
interview which then took place between us
was, if possible, of a still more painful description than the previous one. He was deaf to
all my remonstrances and supplications, and
remained stern and inflexible. From him,
however, I managed to elicit that Matteo Falconi had abruptly quitted the neighbourhood,
and my best wishes went with him to what-

ever part of the world he might direct his footsteps.

"In this manner more than a week passed away, without any change taking place in my situation, or the behaviour of my unnatural parent towards me, and my misery and despair every moment increased. Death, I considered, would have been a happy release to my sufferings, for nothing but the most dismal prospects of the future presented themselves to my tortured imagination. I would sit for hours together, buried in the most gloomy meditation, and sometimes to such a pitch of insupportable excitement was I worked, that my reason almost forsook me, and I nearly sunk under the dreadful trial it was my hard lot to endure.

"Thus it was one night that I was seated wrapped in thought, for my mind was too violently agitated to allow me to retire to rest, when I was suddenly aroused and alarmed, by hearing a rattling sound against the window of my chamber, and, at the same instant, I heard something fall rather heavily on the floor. I looked towards the spot, and my agitation and astonishment were not a little increased when I beheld a stone, to which was attached a slip of paper, on which I perceived writing. With a trembling hand I picked it up, and I no sooner glanced my eye over the characters, than I recognised the well-known hand-writing of the Prince Bianchi.

"My emotion was, as you may imagine, so great, that I could scarcely support myself; but at length I recovered sufficiently to peruse the following lines:—

"Adored Zitella, he, 'of whose heart you are the sole empress, and upon whom his future happiness or misery depend, has once more ventured within the forbidden precincts of your dwelling. He waits in the garden, and fervently implores that you will venture to grant him an interview, if you would not drive him altogether to distraction and despair. Oh, beloved girl, could you but imagine the poignant anguish of mind he has been enduring since the last meeting, I am confident that you would not refuse the request of he who adores you, your slave—BIANCHI!'

"How shall I express my feelings?—I am convinced that I must fail to do adequate justice to them, and I will, therefore, not attempt it. I approached the window which looked into the garden. The night was clear, and the moon shone forth with unusual effulgence, and objects might have been seen distinctly, at a considerable distance. I saw the form of a man enveloped in a large mantle, pacing backwards and forwards, with agitated and impatient footsteps, immediately beneath my window. He raised his head, and I instantly recognised the features of the Prince Bianchi. I could scarcely repress a cry of mingled joy and astonishment. He saw me at

the same moment, and waved his hand towards me with an expression of the most unbounded affection and supplication. How could I act? —could I refuse him his request, when, probably, this might be the last meeting that was ever destined to take place between us?—And was it not most imprudent, if not actually criminal to do so?—My father, and the girl who attended upon me, I knew, had retired to rest, and I might easily gain the place where Bianchi was awaiting me, without any fear of discovery.—Yes;—my mind was in a moment made up; and motioning to my lover my determination, I moved with silent steps towards the door. Here, my heart palpitated violently against my side, and I again hesitated. I listened with breathless attention, but all was still, and once more mustering resolution, I silently, but fervently, committed myself to the care and protection of Providence, and issued from the room. In passing the door of my father's chamber, which I was compelled to do, I was obliged to pause, and I trembled violently; but all being silent in the room, I regained my firmness, and passed on; and having reached the door which opened into the garden, I withdrew the bolts without the least noise, and the next instant I was clasped in the arms of the Prince Bianchi.

"For a few minutes we were too much overpowered by our feelings to speak, and could only sob and sigh upon each others bosom. But at length the prince, gazing with the most indescribable transport and adoration in my blushing face, said:—

"'Beauteous, adorable Zitella, oh, how can I ever sufficiently testify my gratitude for this affectionate act of condescension?—Oh, my love, what have been the tortures of my mind since last we met, and on reflecting on the cruel sufferings to which you were subjected, the full particulars of which I heard from the lips of Matteo Falconi, who so nobly resigned a suit which he found to be so repugnant to your feelings! But we meet again; I hold you once more to my heart—that heart which throbs for you alone, and for the moment I am comparatively happy.'

"'Alas! my lord,' I sighed, in a faint voice, 'I fear that I have acted wrong in thus yielding to your wishes, in direct disobedience to the injunctions of my father. What would you with me? Tell me, I implore you, and——

"'What would I?' interrupted Bianchi; 'oh, can you doubt, sweet girl?—To again assure you that I love you beyond all earthly beings; that I cannot live without you, and——'

"'Oh, forbear, my lord,' I ejaculated, 'you torture me; it is not meet that I, a poor humble girl, should listen to language such as this from the lips of one of your exalted birth and station. Fate has placed an insuperable barrier between us; painful though the task may be to us both, we must endeavour to forget that we have ever met!'

"'Forget!' repeated the prince, with the greatest warmth and apparent equal sincerity; 'oh, that is impossible; and why should we do so?—Here I swear that I am ready to lay my heart and fortune at your feet, and if you reject them, you will render me the most wretched being in existence, which I am convinced is not in your gentle nature to do.'

"'Prince Bianchi,' I said, with as much firmness as I could gather; 'I should have myself as one of the most selfish and presumptuous of my sex, could I wish you to make any such a sacrifice. Oh, no, it must not be, and the sooner we make up our minds to part, the better.'

"'What cruel words are these, Zitella!' he remarked, with a look of gentle reproach. 'I had flattered myself with the hope that I had made a favourable impression upon your heart, but I now perceive that I cruelly deceived myself, and that Zitella views me only with the cold sentiment of respect; and my happiness is at an end.'

"'Oh, my lord,' I faltered out, at the same time the crimson blushes mantled in my cheeks, 'how can I, a poor simple girl, and placed in the delicate situation I am, answer you? Heaven knows, and I speak it with all the candour of innocence and sincerity, that had our stations in life been equal, and my father had given his sanction, there is no man on earth towards whom my heart would throb with more strength of feeling than the Prince Bianchi!'

"'Blessed words!' he exclaimed rapturously. 'Ah, most angelic of women, what can I say in reply?'

"'My lord,' I said, 'you have elicited from my lips that which, perhaps, aught never to have been uttered, and let that satisfy you. Fate ordains that we should encourage a hopeless passion for each other; but the confession once made, prudence demands that we should now separate and never meet again.'

"'By Heaven, never!' exclaimed Bianchi, again straining me to his bosom; 'Zitella, if you love me sincerely, we will part no more!'

"'How, my lord,' I ejaculated, starting back, and looking at him with an expression of astonishment and alarm, 'what mean you?'

"'All that is honourable, I swear, fair being,' he replied; 'consent to elope with me this night, and by all my hopes I promise you, and that most solemnly, that by the time the sun shall rise upon the summits of the eastern hills, to-morrow morn a priest shall have secretly joined our hands in the bonds of holy matrimony, and the most unbounded happiness that mortals can possess will then be ours!'

"All the tales that I had heard to the prejudice of the Prince Bianchi, now rushed with overwhelming force upon my memory, and for the first time a dark and fearful suspicion entered my mind.

"'And does the Prince Bianchi,' I said, proudly, 'think so little of the honour and virtue of Zitella, as to imagine that she would ever yield to such a proposal as that he has just now dared to insult her ears with?—Go, my lord, you have mistaken me, and I have been deceived, oh, most cruelly deceived, in you. We meet no more!'

"As I gave utterance to these words, with an almost bursting heart, I was moving hastily from the spot, when he rushed forward, and detaining me, said:—

"'Oh, hold, Zitella, do not drive me to madness and despair! How cruelly have you misunderstood me! I could not harbour an evil thought against thy beauteous self were it to save me from death. You have confessed you love me; I am anxious to make you my wife; situated as we both are, the proposal I have made is the only practicable one that presents itself; I repeat that, by the first dawn of day I will have led you to the altar, and who shall then dare to question the honour and integrity of our conduct? Come, beauteous maiden, time presses, and such an opportunity as that which now presents itself may never again be afforded us.'

"'No, no,' I returned, 'I cannot—I dare not—my heart misgives me.'

"'Cruel Zitella,' he said, in the most melancholy tones, and striking his forehead in apparent despair, 'then you doom me to immediate death. Farewell, all my bright hopes; farewell, too lovely but indifferent maiden; welcome the cold silent grave as the only resting place from my sorrows!'

"As he thus spoke, he hurried from me a few paces, and I saw him take something from beneath his mantle. A feeling of the most deadly horror came over me, and I darted forward with a shriek, and saw him with the muzzle of a pistol presented towards his head, and apparently just in the horrible act of discharging the contents.

"'Hold!—hold! rash man!' I cried; 'would you rush unbidden into the presence of your maker? Heaven guide me for the best: I am yours—I yield, Bianchi!'

"I could say no more; but completely exhausted, I sunk insensible into the arms of my betrayer.'

Here the unfortunate Signora Zitella, overpowered by her feelings, was again compelled to pause in her melancholy narrative; and her auditors, particularly her daughter, were deeply affected by what they had heard.

"Alas! my dear mother," said Mira, "how terrible have been the misfortunes it has been your cruel lot to undergo—and how similar is the fate I have also had to experience!

Heaven pardon the author of my being, for certain it is that he has much to repent of.''

" What a heartless villain he must be,'' remarked Massaroni.

"Alas !'' sighed Signora Zitella, " it is too true; but you have not heard half of his villany yet. Oh, that I should have placed no reliance in the reports that were circulated respecting him ; for had I done so, what shame —what misery—what indescribable anguish should I have been spared. But to resume my dismal story, which, as I fear

THE BRIGAND COMMANDING HIS WIFE TO LEAVE HIS PRESENCE

that I have tired your patience too much already, I will conclude in as few words as possible.

. "When I recovered from the fainting fit into which I had fallen, I found myself reclining in a vehicle, which was proceeding at a rapid rate, and I perceived that the Prince Bianchi was leaning affectionately and anxiously over me.

"' Oh, God !' I exclaimed, passing my hands across my aching temples, and looking with a searching glance into his countenance, ' what have I done?—where am I? and whither are we going?'

"'To where the greatest bliss awaits us, my adored one,' he answered, throwing his arms around my waist, and pressing the most ardent kisses upon my lips. 'Compose yourself, dear Zitella, you have nothing to fear, for are you not with your Bianchi, your future husband?'

"'My husband!' I repeated; 'and can this be reality, or only some flattering delusion? Bianchi, you cannot be so cruel as to deceive me?'

"'Deceive you, Zitella?' answered my betrayer; 'oh, how can you be so uncharitable as to entertain so unjust a thought? All that I have promised I will perform. But let us devote these precious moments to love, and in the bliss of the present and the future, forget all the sorrows of the past.'

"'Alas!' I sighed, 'what must be the excitement of my poor father, should he by this time have discovered my flight? Oh, surely, notwithstanding his harsh treatment of me, it was most unnatural of me to abandon him thus. He threatened me with his everlasting wrath, too, and his heaviest malediction will descend upon my head. Oh, Bianchi, why did you persuade me to this desperate course?'

"'Nay, my, sweet one,' he replied, 'do not give way to these feelings of regret, when we are on the high road to happiness! Your father, when he finds that I have honourably made you my wife, will gladly forgive us both for a step to which we were alone driven by himself.'

"These observations did somewhat reconcile me; but still I had my misgivings, and notwithstanding all the efforts of Bianchi, he could not entirely remove them from my mind. I learnt from the Prince Bianchi that we were some leagues from the dwelling of my father, and that we were proceeding towards a small village not far from Rome, which we should, no doubt, reach by daylight, and where it was his intention that our secret nuptials should be solemnized. Shortly after this we stopped at an inn to change horses, and the prince persuaded me to alight in order to partake of some refreshment; an offer which I very gladly availed myself of, as I felt faint and exhausted. I partook of a slight repast, and sipped the contents of a small glass of wine which Bianchi handed to me, and the horses having been put-to, we once more resumed our journey. We had not proceeded far, however, when I felt an irresistible drowsiness or stupor come over me, and falling back on my seat, I again sunk into a state of utter unconsciousness.

"How long I had remained in this state, I had no means of ascertaining, but on recovering my senses, how different was the situation in which I found myself. I was lying upon a couch, in a handsomely furnished chamber, and two females were in attendance upon me. A strange foreboding of what had happened, and a shuddering of horror, came over me, as looking anxiously in the faces of the females, I demanded where I was.

"'You are in a villa not far from Rome, signora,' answered one of the females.

"'In a villa near Rome!' I repeated. 'Where is the Prince Bianchi?'

"'He is in the house, signora,' answered the woman, 'and will be here anon.'

"'And how long have I been here?' I again demanded, in the most breathless state of anxiety.

"'Several hours,' was the answer.

"'Ah!' I exclaimed, 'what terrible thoughts are those that came over my mind? Tell me, has the Prince Bianchi been with me?'

"'All the time that you have been here, signora,' replied the person whom I had questioned; 'till about half an hour ago.'

"'My worst fears then are realised!' I cried with a burst of the most indescribable agony. 'Oh, monster!—miscreant!—deceiver!'

"I could say no more; my brain swam round; the most hideous phantoms seemed to flit before my disordered imagination, and to mock at my sufferings; and once more insensibility came to my relief.

"When I reflect upon the horrors of that fatal period, the blood freezes in my veins, and I wonder how I could ever survive; for all that my worst apprehensions had suggested had taken place; my betrayer had triumphed over his unfortunate victim, and I was now a wretched and degraded being."

Once more Signora Zitella was obliged to pause in order to recover herself, and she and her daughter wept scalding tears of anguish on each other's bosom.

"For several days," continued Zitella, "as it afterwards appeared, I remained in a delirious state, raving wildly, and invoking curses on the head of my destroyer; and when I was restored to recollection, I found myself in the same chamber, with the Prince Bianchi sitting by my bed-side. How bitter were the reproaches that I heaped upon his head; he did not attempt to deny his guilt, but affected to be stung with remorse, and declared that it was still his intention to make me all the atonement in his power by making me his wife, although particular circumstances, over which he had no control, would not permit him for the present to do so. Alas! the influence he possessed over me, was too great for resistance, and at length the violent anguish of my mind became somewhat abated, and in a moment of weakness, of which he did not fail to take advantage, I forgave him the crime he had committed, and endeavoured to resign myself to my fate. Every luxury and amusement was supplied to me, and the prince was seldom absent from the place of my concealment for more than a day or two together, and lavished upon me every attention and kindness, the more especially when he ascertained from me that I was in a likely way to become a mother. But many a bitter pang of anguish did it cost me, when I reflected that the little innocent I was about to bring into the world would be the offspring of guilt and shame; and there were moments when I wished that it might never be destined to see the light of day.'

"But your father, signora?" said the brigand's wife; "what became of him?"

"Alas! I never knew his fate," replied Zitella.

"Indeed!" said Mira, with a look of astonishment.

"No," returned her mother; "a short time after my elopement, I wrote a letter to him, confessing everything; stating the solemn promises that my seducer had made to me, and requesting him in the most earnest and affecting terms to grant me his forgiveness. A few days afterwards it was returned to me unopened, with a note from one of the neighbours, in which he informed me that my father had disposed of his house, and all that it contained, and abruptly quitted the neighbourhood, no one knowing whither he had gone; and from that day to this I have never been able to ascertain what became of him."

"Most strange and unfortunate," remarked Mira.

"True," coincided her unfortunate parent; "and many a pang of anguish did it cost me, when I reflected that it was too probable he had invoked the curses of Heaven upon my head, though I little merited the cruelty and severity with which he treated me.

"At length you, my my unfortunate child, were born; and many were the mingled tears of sorrow and maternal love I shed upon your innocent cheeks. Bianchi appeared to be very fond of you, and he redoubled his attentions towards me. And now I again renewed my supplications to him to fulfil the promises he had so solemnly made to me; but he contrived to pacify my feelings by various excuses, though I own my mind was frequently haunted by doubts and suspicions, to which I almost dreaded to give encouragement, though I found it equally impossible to conquer them.

"In this manner several more months passed away, and then I noticed a most remarkable and melancholy change in the conduct of Bianchi towards me. He no longer treated me with the marked attention he had formerly done; was frequently gloomy and abstracted, and very often I saw nothing of him for more than a week. He seldom or never took any notice of you my poor child, but on the contrary seemed to view you with as great aversion as he formerly evinced fondness for you. Whenever I questioned him upon this painful change, as I sometimes ventured to do, and begged him to inform me whether anything in my conduct had displeased him, he always returned me some morose or evasive answer, and would immediately quit the room. Oh, the agony of mind that I now endured! I saw plainly that I had lost his love, if, in fact, I had ever possessed it; and the full horrors of my situation burst upon me in the most vivid and overwhelming characters. It was then that I reproached myself, and that most bitterly too, for having been so sceptical in regard to the rumours afloat of the dissipated and unprincipled character of my betrayer, and I considered that I was justly punished for the errors of which I had been guilty.

"The dreadful anxiety of mind which I now constantly endured, made sad inroads upon my constitution, and I was at length confined to my bed, but Bianchi, so far from pitying me, was less frequent in his visits to me than before, and, in fact, almost abandoned me altogether. One day he entered my chamber abruptly, and I was much surprised to see him accompanied by a man; a coarse-featured, ruffianly-looking fellow; but I need not trouble myself to describe him to you when I inform you that it was Malvolio. The sight of this man made me shudder, and I was certain from the particular sinister expression of Bianchi's countenance, that some evil was intended. Involuntarily I pressed my sleeping babe still closer to my breast, and awaited the result with the most painful and trembling anxiety. I had not to wait long.

"'Zitella,' said the prince, 'I am about to relieve you from a great deal of care and trouble, and you ought to feel much obliged to me for it.'

"'Oh, my lord,' I demanded, in a tremulous voice; 'what do you mean? For Heaven's sake explain yourself, and do not keep me in suspense.'

"That can be done in a few words," he said. "In the present state of your health, you are not able to pay the child the necessary attention it requires, so I intend to put it out to nurse, and have selected the wife of this good man for that purpose."

"'Deprive me of my child! my little innocent one! oh, monstrous thought!' I shrieked; 'she—she who is now my only comfort! But no, my lord, you surely cannot be guilty of so cruel and unnatural a deed!'

"'Bah!' he returned, impatiently, 'is there anything cruel or unnatural in providing for her that care and attention it is not in your power to bestow upon her?'

"'You shall not rob me of my innocent

offspring !' I cried, in delirious accents; 'who so fit to have the care of her infant years as her unfortunate mother, who, but for you, might now have been as pure and innocent as she is? You shall take my life—you shall tear the heart from my bosom, but you shall not deprive me of my child !'

"'This wild raving is useless,' said Bianchi; 'Malvolio, you have my commands?'

"'I have, your highness,' replied the ruffian.

"'Then see that they are obeyed; take the child with you, and never heed the observations of this mad woman.' "

"Brutal savage !" observed the brigand chief; "these manifold crimes call for a terrible retribution, and it will most assuredly overtake him. But proceed, Signora Zitella, and pardon me for interrupting you."

"In vain were my frantic shrieks, my supplications for mercy," continued Zitella. "You were torn from my breast, my poor Mira, and consigned to the care of the villain Malvolio, and I sunk back on my pillow, quite exhausted with my exertions, and became insensible.

"It was some time, it must have been some days, it might have been weeks, ere I was again restored to consciousness, and I then found myself in a wretched hovel, scantily furnished, and Malvolio and a shrivelled, hagish-looking old woman were sitting in the room, over a miserable fire. The first question I asked, was in wild accents, for my infant.

"'Oh, the brat is safe enough,' replied the villain Malvolio.

"'Monster ! fiend in human shape!' I cried, 'you have murdered her.'

"'Not quite so bad as that,' said Malvolio, with a frightful grin ; 'she is better taken care of than you could provide for her; but she is where you will never behold her again, I dare say.'

"'Oh, God !' I exclaimed, wringing my hands, 'this is surely too much for human fortitude to endure. But where is he, the miscreant, my betrayer ?'

"'Far enough away from here at present, you may depend upon it,' answered Malvolio. 'It is useless for you to make any further inquiries after him, for he has abandoned you altogether.'

"'Now Heaven help me !' I solemnly ejaculated, 'for the cup of my sorrows is full to the brim. Oh, villain! villain! heartless villain ; may the curse of that Almighty Power, whose sacred laws he has so basely outraged, pursue him. My child ! my child ! my helpless innocent ! where art thou? My brain is turning ! I shall go mad ! Ha ! ha! ha!'

"I remember no more after this ; the rest, up to the time of my restoration to my senses, is all a dream to me. A dark void. You have received from the good Signor Montaldi the account how I came under his protection, and that, together with the confession of Malvolio, will furnish you with all those additional particulars I am unable to supply."

In these words the unfortunate Signora Zitella concluded her melancholy history.

CHAPTER XLIII.

THE PROGRESS OF THE COUNT ALBERTI. —THE MIDNIGHT REMOVAL OF MELINA FROM THE VILLA ROSA.—HER NEW ABODE. —TROUBLES SEEM TO MULTIPLY.

FOR some time after the much-wronged Signora Zitella had concluded her remarkable and important narrative, the whole of her auditors were so deeply affected by what they had heard, that they were unable to speak, and no one had been more deeply interested than the brigand chief, for the dismal history bore so close a similitude to that of his unfortunate mother and his own, that it re-aroused with tenfold force all the sorrows of the past within his breast, and, for a short time, made him so truly wretched, that he withdrew to a retired corner of the room, and leaning against the moulding of the wainscot, he was incapable of uttering a single observation, but became completely lost in meditation. The last words of the guilty man, Malvolio, filled his mind with conflicting thoughts, doubts, and suspicions ; it was quite evident to him that he had something more of importance (and particularly to himself) had not death deprived him of the opportunity ; and Massaroni the more deeply regretted that, as the tenour of his observations went to show that he could have revealed the real name of the betrayer of his unfortunate mother, and thus at once have solved the mystery he had for many years been so anxious to unravel.

Mira and her mother remained locked in each other's arms, and old Montaldi and the brigand's wife gazed on the affecting scene in silence, and with the deepest sympathy.

At length, Mira was the first to regain the use of speech, and gently disengaging herself from the arms of her mother, she said—

"Oh, my beloved parent, to what a painful tale of sorrow is that to which we have been listening; how terrible have been the sufferings, the unmerited sufferings it has been your hard lot to endure ; no wonder that your reason sunk beneath their overwhelming influence. But Providence has not entirely deserted you under all your difficulties, and with the blessing of God, your future days shall be passed in serenity and peace."

"Alas, my dear child, my long lost one," replied the Signora Zitella, in melancholy accents, "I would hope so, now that you are restored to me; but oh, what prospect is there for us, friendless, destitute as we are in the world?"

"Nay, signora," interposed Montaldi; "you cannot be friendless or destitute while you have such warm and sincere friends as myself and Signor Massaroni."

"Pardon me," returned Zitella; "the strange events that have occurred within the last few hours, the remarkable discoveries, the extraordinary change from darkness to light, have bewildered me: it is no wonder that I scarcely know what I say. I should indeed be most ungrateful, and unworthy of your smallest sympathy, could I be unmindful of the generous, the unprecedented kindness and services that yourself and Signor Massaroni have rendered to me and mine. We owe you both a debt of gratitude, which, I fear, it will never be in our power to repay."

"Mention it not, signora," observed our hero, arousing himself from his lethargy; "to all that Allesandro Massaroni, the brigand chief, whose melancholy history of wrongs inflicted, approximates so closely to your own, you are, believe me, most cordially welcome, and you may depend upon his future protection for yourself and your fair daughter. He will not rest until full justice has been rendered you by your heartless betrayer, the proud and tyrannical Prince Bianchi, who is also my most bitter enemy."

"Oh, no," hastily interrupted Zitella, "greatly as Bianchi has wronged me, I would not pursue him with a spirit of revenge:—I would not for the world that a hair of his head should be injured. He is the father of my chi d, whom heaven has so miraculously and mercifully restored to me."

"And did he not brutally desert you both?" demanded Massaroni; "and would he not have consigned your daughter to the murderer's knife?"

"The miscreant Malvolio has said so, in his dying moments," replied Signora Zitella, with an involuntary shudder of horror; "but I cannot, I cannot credit the awful assertion; I cannot believe that Bianchi, even with all his faults, could ever for a moment entertain so hideous and unnatural a thought."

"I have seen enough of Bianchi," returned the brigand chief, "to make me believe him capable of anything to answer his own base and private ends. His conduct towards yourself, and his own fair niece, the innocent Signora Melina, whom he would sacrifice to the unprincipled seducer of your daughter, the Count Alberti, are sufficient proofs of the truth of what I say. Besides, I have wrongs of my own that must, and shall be redressed."

"Oh, spare him, Massaroni, I beseech you," earnestly supplicated Zitella; "I would bring him to a full sense of the crimes he has committed, the wrongs he has inflicted;—I would bring him to sincere repentance, but Heaven knows that, notwithstanding all that I have suffered from him, I would not harm him."

"Well, well, lady," remarked our hero, after a pause, "we will talk farther upon this subject at some future period, when we have become more composed. But one thing strikes me as most remarkable."

"And what is that, signor?" asked Zitella.

"Why," replied the brigand, "that the name of Zitella should have suggested itself to me when I composed the simple little ritornella which I am in the habit of singing occasionally."

"It is indeed singular that it should have done so," said Zitella.

"And," said Massaroni, "there is a disagreement in certain portions of the dying confessions of the villain Malvolio, and your melancholy narrative of wrongs, which somewhat surprises me."

"How so, signor?"

"Why, in the first place, he declared you to have been the idol of your parents," replied Massaroni.

"And I firmly believe myself to have been so once," sighed Signora Zitella; "and how it was that I lost their affections, I know not."

"Then again he says, that death deprived you of both your parents in one day. How do you account for such a statement as that, so utterly at variance with your own, signora?"

"That is indeed most strange," replied the latter, "and I can account for it in no other way than that the recollection of Malvolio must slightly have failed him in his last moments."

"That may have been the case, certainly," observed the brigand chief; "but is is to be regretted that Malvolio did not live to confront the Prince Bianchi, together with yourself, and thus to corroborate his assertions."

"Oh, it is impossible for Bianchi to deny the truth of them."

"I consider him capable of denying anything when his own interest is at stake," answered our hero; "but he considers you long since dead, signora."

"Doubtless he does," returned Zitella; "but surely, when he finds that I am not so, and learns what I have suffered, together with his child, for so many years, he will be stung with remorse, and take pity on us?"

"I know the Prince Bianchi well," returned Massaroni, "and am certain that he is totally incapable of entertaining any such feeling."

"Alas! alas!" sighed Signora Zitella, "you judge him too harshly, Signor Massaroni, and I fear that you are prejudiced against him."

"Indeed I am not, signora," replied the brigand, "any more than the bitter animosity and unmerited vindictive feelings with which he has ever pursued me, have naturally excited in my breast towards him."

"It can only be from a sense of the duty he owes to society (pardon me for the observation) that he seeks to withdraw you from the unfortunate course of life in which a cruel fate has placed you."

"Allesandro Massaroni never injured him, lady," remarked Maria Grazie, proudly; "he would have scorned to do so; but yet he persists in endeavouring to hunt him down like some wild beast, and would exult in the opportunity of shedding his blood upon a public scaffold."

"Which opportunity, I flatter myself," rejoined the brigand chief, "will never be afforded him. If Massaroni is to fall, I trust it will never be by his hands; and I will yet find the opportunity to make him crouch and quail before me, and sue to me for mercy!"

"Oh, Massaroni," said Mira, "you surely cannot forget that, with all his faults, he is still my father?"

"True, lady," returned our hero, "and I also remember that he is the inhuman betrayer of your mother, and that he would also have consigned you, his own offspring, to death."

"Oh, horrible thought!" gasped forth Mira.

"Alas! alas!" sighed her mother, "are there no means of bringing these painful matters amicably about, without resorting to any desperate measures?"

"None whatever that I can perceive at present, signora," replied Massaroni; "but we are none of us in a proper mood of mind to discuss this important subject at present, and with your own permission, we will defer it to another time. We will now leave you and your daughter to yourselves, with every good wish for your future happiness and prosperity."

"Oh, thanks, thanks, signor," returned Zitella, "and may Heaven reward you for all your kindness to me and mine."

"Enough, lady," said the brigand chief. "To what I have hitherto been able to do for yourself and the Signora Mira, your daughter, you are heartily welcome, and I hope that the time is not far distant when in the happiness of the present, you will be enabled to look back upon the sufferings of the dismal past with indifference, and without regret."

Thus saying, Massaroni, his wife, and Montaldi quitted the room, and retired below, leaving Zitella and her daughter locked affectionately in each other's embrace.

"How wonderful are the events that have taken place within the last few short hours," said old Montaldi, when they were alone.

"True," coincided the brigand; "but I firmly believe that they are only the precursors to something still more extraordinary."

"It is evident, in my opinion," observed Montaldi, "that both Signora Zitella and the villain Malvolio have spoken the truth."

"There cannot be the least doubt of it," returned Massaroni; "their statements perfectly agree, except upon one or two immaterial points. What a villain has the Prince Bianchi been proved to be."

"He has," coincided Montaldi; "and a fitting retribution will, no doubt, shortly overtake him."

"I will take good care that it does," rejoined Massaroni, determinedly.

"What course do you mean to pursue towards him?" interrogated his wife.

"Your question is premature, Maria," he answered; "I have not yet made up my mind."

"Are you still determined to venture into his presence?"

"I am: when I will ring in his ears such a tale as will smite him to the earth, if he has any conscience."

"And alone, Massaroni?" asked his wife.

"Yes," answered the brigand chief; "I will seek his presence alone; but I will have those close at hand, who at a signal may instantly fly to my assistance, should their services be required."

"I consider it a rash and perilous undertaking, Massaroni," observed Maria.

"Pshaw! you talk erroneously, Maria," said her husband.

"Pardon me, signor," remarked Montaldi, "but I consider that there is sound reason and prudence in that which Signora Maria has just now suggested, and I would advise you to think maturely and coolly upon it."

"It does not require Massaroni long to deliberate, Signor Montaldi," answered our hero, "and he is seldom far out in his judgment. But we shall be enabled to say more upon the subject when the Signora Zitella and her daughter have recovered from their excitement."

"Very true," remarked Montaldi; "but still I cannot help agreeing with the arguments which your wife has advanced. I think that the course you propose to adopt would be fraught with the most imminent danger, without being at all calculated to be productive of any good."

"There you and I entirely differ, Montaldi."

"Well, it may be so," replied the latter, "but I am certain that I only speak for the best, and as far as my judgment dictates."

"Of that I am thoroughly convinced, Montaldi," coincided our hero, "and I thank you for your suggestions. But come, Maria, we must return to our retreat, where we may probably further discuss this matter. You will pay every attention to the comfort of Signora Zitella and her daughter, Montaldi."

"You may depend upon me," answered the latter; "there shall be nothing wanting on my part."

"Enough," said Massaroni; "I am perfectly satisfied; come, wife, let us depart; we will see you again to-morrow, Montaldi."

Montaldi bowed, and the brigand chief and his wife retired from the residence of the old man, and bent their way to their retreat among the mountains.

On their arrival there, after some conversation between them which is of no importance to the reader, Massaroni sought the presence of Florio, in order to make him acquainted with what had taken place at the cottage of old Montaldi, and Clairville listened to him with the deepest interest and attention, notwithstanding his thoughts were so busily occupied with his own painful affairs, and he expressed the deepest sympathy with the cruel and unmerited sufferings to which the Signora Zitella had been subjected, and his gratification at the restoration of the mother and daughter to each other's arms.

"Who could have imagined some time since," he ejaculated, "that the Prince Bianchi possessed so depraved a heart?"

"I always believed him to do so," replied the brigand; "and therefore I am not at all disappointed in what I have heard. His conduct towards his unfortunate victim and her daughter alone, prove him to be a villain of the blackest dye."

"And after hearing this," said Florio, "can I wonder at his treatment of the beauteous Melina? Can I for a moment hope that he will be induced to extend any mercy or forbearance towards her? And he would sacrifice that fair and innocent being to the base seducer of his own child!"

"Courage, Clairville, courage," said our hero, "I will take good care that he does not; besides, even should the Count Alberti recover, which it seems is extremely doubtful, it does not appear at all likely that when he discovers who the supposed Olympia really is, he will be so entirely lost to shame as to do any such thing."

"But will his behaviour to Melina relax in its severity?" said Florio; "will she not be still in his power, and at his mercy?"

"I tell you again," replied the mountain chief, "as I have repeatedly told you before, that the Signora Melina shall be rescued, at all hazards. Let that satisfy you."

"But still there is no hope for me; she can never become mine."

"But my word for it she shall," answered Massaroni; "that is, if you will only follow my advice, and do not act with a weakness which does not become you."

"Oh, I must be presumptuous indeed to encourage such a thought," said Florio, "and I should have stifled my unfortunate passion in its infancy; what misery would it have saved us both. Oh, I have acted very wrong."

"What, in encouraging an honest and virtuous love for one who returns it with equal sincerity and ardour? Nonsense, man; you must get rid of such thoughts as these."

"Even if I were willing," said Clairville, "my beloved Melina, I am confident, would never consent to become my bride without the sanction of her guardian and protector."

"Call him not by such names," remarked Massaroni, "he has proved himself by his conduct unworthy of the titles."

"He has indeed done so," coincided Florio, "but still I am certain that Melina entertains some respect for his authority, and fears to encounter his indignation."

"It is a foolish scruple," said the brigand; "he has, by being so grossly neglectful of his duty, and by breaking the solemn promise he made to the Signora Melina's mother on her death-bed, forfeited all claims to her esteem; and what, think you, will be her feelings when she hears of the crimes he has committed under the hypocritical mask of virtue?"

"Oh, how will the disgusting tale shock her ears," replied Clairville.

"Do you not think," continued Massaroni, "that any feelings of respect and honour she may have entertained towards him, will be changed to those of disgust and indignation? Will she not be most ready and anxious to fly from the power of one in whose path contamination and destruction follow? Mark my word, Signor Clairville, and it is not often Massaroni is wrong in his conjectures, she will; and then indeed the moment of your triumph will be at hand."

"You would buoy me up with sanguine hopes, Massaroni," remarked Florio, "that I feel all but convinced will never be realised."

"But I pledge you my word that they shall," returned the brigand; "and let that satisfy you."

"But what course do you mean to adopt?"

"I have not yet decided."

"Melina is held in strict confinement?"

"Very true."

"And the villa no doubt is as strictly guarded," remarked Clairville.

"I dare say it is," returned Massaroni.

"Then if even you should form the desperate resolution to do so, how could you hope to obtain access to the house without detection?"

"Leave that to me," answered our hero, "and I will not fail to accomplish my purpose. Of this I am determined, that I will meet the Prince Bianchi face to face, and tell him boldly of his villany, before many nights have elapsed."

"Oh, desperate resolution!" said Florio. "Beware what you do, Massaroni; you would but rush upon your own destruction without being able to effect any good to those whom I know you have a wish to serve."

"Nonsense, Clairville," said the brigand chief, with a smile, "you have suffered your thoughts to run riot; I entertain no such foolish apprehensions. I will take good care to render Bianchi powerless, and I will have those at hand who will be ready and able to assist me in case of any emergency."

"You will not do the prince any harm, Massaroni?" asked Clairville, hastily.

"No," replied our hero, "not unless he compels me to it by any rash conduct of his own."

"Indeed I wish you would abandon this design, which seems to me to be headstrong, useless, and preposterous."

"You may deem it so, Signor Clairville," returned Massaroni, "but I have my ideas to the contrary. At any rate, I am determined to run the risk. It strikes me that I shall so be able to play upon the conscience of Bianchi, as to make it productive of the best results."

"I sincerely hope that you may not be disappointed," said Florio; "but I cannot help having my doubts to the contrary. Could he be moved to relax in his harsh and cruel conduct towards my beloved Melina, and to relinquish his designs against her, though I might never hope to make her mine, which appears to be a thing that is utterly impossible, I might, I believe, be comparatively happy."

"Keep up your spirits," remarked the brigand, "and I promise you that all shall yet be as you desire. The Signora Melina loves you, and if you only remain firm, I promise you that she shall yet become your bride."

"Oh, of what use is it holding out to me any such hopes as these?" said Clairville.

"And of what use is it for you to give yourself up entirely to despair?" demanded Massaroni, "and thus rendering yourself more miserable than there is any occasion for you to be? Come, arouse yourself man; this weakness is quite unworthy of you."

"I would fain do so, Massaroni," said Clairville, "but notwithstanding all my efforts, I cannot. Dear Melina, how deeply do I regret that fate ever introduced us to each other."

"What nonsense is this!" said the brigand; "although fate has hitherto appeared to be against you, does it follow that it always should? My word for it there are days of bliss in store for you, if you do not reject the means of obtaining them, and you will have sufficient reason at some future time to thank me for the advice I now give you."

"And think you, Massaroni, that I am unmindful of the good wishes you entertain towards me, or the services you have rendered me?" demanded Florio. "No, whatever may be the ultimate fate of myself and Melina, I must feel a grateful sense of the many acts of disinterested friendship for which I am indebted to you. But I should be sorry if you were to plunge yourself into any danger on my account."

"And what danger is there, think you, that Allesandro Massaroni is afraid to encounter!" said the latter.

"The Prince Bianch would only be too much gratified to get you in his power," observed Clairville.

"I know it," replied the brigand chief, with a laugh: "but he has got to do so, and he will have to exercise all the ingenuity and stratagy he possesses to accomplish that task. I tell you, Clairville that I set the hoary-headed libertine at complete defiance. If Massaroni be destined to perish on a scaffold (which I do not think he is) it shall not be by his means. But this is a subject which does not exactly suit my humour to converse upon. I will leave you to yourself, and let me once more advise you to exert yourself to endeavour to dissipate the gloomy thoughts which you have so long suffered to occupy your mind, and to look forward with the best anticipations to the future."

"I will try to do so," replied Floria, "but I much doubt whether or not I shall succeed."

Massaroni made use of no further observations, but quitted the place, and Clairville, pacing backwards and forwards, with his arms folded across his chest, continued for some time wrapped in meditation.

"In vain, Massaroni," he soliloquised, "do you seek to inspire me with hope. What is there to authorise me to encourage it? Are not my prospects as black as ever? Melina is still the prisoner of her unnatural relative, and notwithstanding all the brigand chief may say to the contrary, such is the obstinacy and inflexibility of his spirit, that I do not believe anything will induce him to relax in the severity and cruelty of his conduct towards her. What if the Count Alberti should not recover? has he not threatened that she shall still become the wife of the man of his choice? and after what has happened, one may well imagine upon what sort of character that choice will fall. As for the discovery which has been made, I do not expect that it will have much effect upon him. His power is too great for him to fear exposure. Who dare asperse the character of the proud Prince Bianchi, the Governor of Rome? Who dare have the boldness to call his conduct into question? He will give the lie to them direct, and disclaim all knowledge of the much wronged Signora Zitella and her daughter. Nay more, he will visit them with his vengeance should they persist in prosecuting their claims upon him, and demanding justice at his hands; and what could they do, powerless, friendless as they are? Nothing! But can I for a moment doubt the truth of Zitella's statement? Oh, no, that is impossible. Such a tale of wrongs could not have been invented; besides, the dying confession of the miscreant, Malvolio, confirmed it. Oh, Melina! and must you indeed be sacrificed to the base and heartless seducer of your uncle's daughter?—Forbid it,

ZITELLA AND MIRA.

Heaven!—Nature revolts at the idea; but without its merciful interposition, I see no chance of your escape! My poor Melina, could I but be assured of your safety, could I but once more behold you, and pressing you to my heart, bid you a last adieu, methinks I could be comparatively happy. But no;—it will not be, and nothing but the blackest despair meets my eyes whichever way I turn. But I have been to blame, oh, much to blame, in encouraging a passion which I might be certain could never be gratified, and which would be certain to plunge one so good and so innocent into the greatest misery. Would that Melina could banish me from her memory, as one unworthy of her; but that I feel convinced, so well do I know the fervour and sincerity of her love, she can never do. And should I not be miserable, oh, ten times more miserable than I am at present, did I think she could forget or despise me? I should. Oh, God! my fate is indeed wretched!"

He paused, and clasped his forehead in despair, but in the midst of this he was again interrupted by the sudden and unexpected return of Massaroni.

"Ah, my good friend," said Clairville, eagerly, "what brings you here again so soon?"

"Let me beg of you to be firm," said the brigand chief; "for I have sad news for you, which I thought it would be better to communicate to you without delay."

"Ah!" ejaculated Floria, "what now? what fresh troubles are in store for me? Tell me, I beg of you; do not keep me in suspense."

"The Signora Melina—" began Massaroni.

"Ah! what of her?" anxiously interrupted Florio Clairville; "has her strength at length sank beneath the weight of the manifold and unexampled sufferings to which she has been so cruelly subjected? Is she no more?"

"Patience, Signor Florio," returned the brigand chief. "Heaven be praised, it is not so bad as that. The brigand whom I left in the vicinity of the Villa Rosa, to watch what might take place, has just forwarded to me the melancholly intelligence, that the Signora Melina has been secretly conveyed away from the Villa Rosa, by the Prince Bianchi's orders, and no one at present knows where she is now confined."

Florio clasped his forehead in an agony of despair, as he exclaimed:—

"'Tis no more than I expected! This, no doubt, is done to baffle any future attempt which you might make to rescue her, Massaroni. Poor Melina, what insidious designs are at work against her peace. Oh, God—oh, God————

"————————" said our hero, "all ———————— as you now anticipate. ———————— use all my exertions ———————— little doubt that I shall shortly ———————— over the place of Signora Melina's present confinement; that once accomplished, it shall go hard with me if I do not immediately and triumphantly release her from the power of her enemies."

"Oh, no," sighed Clairville, "it is quite useless to try to flatter me with any such delusive hopes; they have taken care to remove her to some place of sufficient security, and will place such a guard over her as may safely defy any attempts you may make to restore her from their power. She is lost to me

for ever, and the cup of my misery is full to the brim."

"Nonsense, Florio," returned the brigand chief, impatiently; "say not so; for the fears you express, take my word for it, will not be realised."

"Alas!" ejaculated Clairville, "how can I imagine anything to the contrary. But are the Prince Bianchi and Count Alberti still at the villa?"

"I am given to understand that they are," replied our her.

"And the faithful Floretta?"

"She is supposed to have accompanied her unfortunate mistress. The Count Alberti is still too dangerously ill to be removed."

"This completes my wretchedness and despair," said Clairville; "I care not now what becomes of me."

"Exert yourself, and become a man, Signor Clairville," remonstrated the brigand chief; "it behoves you not to give yourself thus up entirely to despair."

"And is not this dreadful intelligence more than sufficient to unman me?" demanded Florio.

"No," answered Massaroni, "and if we suffer ourselves to sink under it, and fail to exert ourselves, nothing can be accomplished, and the worst may be apprehended. I will instantly set about the task of discovering the place where Signora Melina is confined, and I feel convinced I shall meet with success."

"I cannot remain here," said Clairville, "and know the danger with which my beloved and unfortunate Melina is surrounded. I will hasten forth, and wander to the remotest corner of the earth till I have succeeded in discovering her, and ascertained the fate that has befallen her."

"Nay," remarked Massaroni, "that would be madness, and would only expose you to danger, and perhaps destruction. What could you singly do?"

"And what danger is there that I should fear to encounter, for the sake of that fair being to whom my soul is devoted?" demanded Clairville, impatiently; "I should be worse than a coward to remain inactive here."

"And you would be worse than a madman to venture forth alone on such an expedition, when you have friends who have the power and the will to serve you," retorted the brigand chief. "The spies of the Prince Bianchi and Count Alberti are doubtless lurking in different parts of the country, and should you be discovered, you may guess the fate that would await you."

"I care not," returned Clairville, "I am reckless of what may befall me; without Melina, life is no longer endurable, and the sooner I am rid of it the better."

"What absurdity is this, Clairville," said

our hero; "I did not imagine that you could have given way to such weakness. Tired of life! Pshaw! I have no patience with you. If you will only follow my advice, and you know I would offer none but for the best, I prognosticate to you many years of happiness to come. I will to-morrow, at the latest, accompanied by several of the most trustworthy of my band, and disguised in such a manner that no one can have the least suspicion of us, set out upon my expedition, and I have very little doubt that, in the course of a few days, I shall be able to forward you good news."

"But may I not at least be permitted to accompany you, and to take part in the proceedings?" interrogated Clairville eagerly.

"No, it would be imprudent to suffer you to do so," answered Massaroni.

"Why so?" demanded Florio.

"Because your feelings might overpower you when caution was most necessary, and thus betray us all. Remain here in security, and patiently await the result with confidence and hope."

"Ah! how easy it is to advise," said Florio, "but did you know the anguish of my feelings you would not wonder at my anxiety."

"And think you that I cannot fully understand your feelings, and duly appreciate them?" said the brigand. "But this is all a waste of time and words; can you trust to my friendship and honour?"

"Oh, yes," answered Clairville; "have I ever for a moment expressed a doubt of them?"

"Enough," said Massaroni; "then you will follow my advice, without any further hesitation, and fear not for the results. Are you satisfied?"

"Since it is your will," replied Clairville, "I have no alternative. But oh, Massaroni, let me earnestly implore of you to leave no means untried to accomplish the important object of your expedition; and not to keep me in suspense any longer than you can help, but to forward me intelligence as soon as you can."

"You may depend on me," answered our hero. "Massaroni never yet fail to keep his word, especially with those on whom he had bestowed his friendship; as I said before, you may expect to hear from me in the course of a few days, and that with favourable intelligence."

"God grant that it may be so," said Florio Clairville, fervently. "Oh, how terrible will be the anxiety of my mind, until my doubts are in some measure dispelled."

"You must struggle against your feelings as well as you can," said Massaroni; "I again pledge my word that your anxiety shall be removed in a few days."

"I yield myself entirely to your discretion, and will endeavour to follow the advice which you have given, I know, in the purest spirit of friendship and humanity," returned Clairville. "Heaven speed you on your way, Signor Massaroni, my disinterested friend and benefactor, and may all the blessings that can attend mortals be your portion, for——"

"Stay, stay, my enthusiastic, and liberal-minded young friend," interrupted the brigand chief, with a good-humoured smile; "I pray you be not so prolific in your compliments to the gentlemanly robber, or cut-throat, as his excellenza, the Prince Bianchi, would probably designate me, or you might overwhelm me. It is sufficient for me that I act as justice prompts me in performing my duty towards my fellow-creatures, and in endeavouring to thwart the evil designs of their oppressors. It is a duty incumbent on us all, Signor Clairville; and let the enemies of the outlaw, Allesandro Massaroni, however high may be their position in the world, at whatever price they be able to purchase the homage of sycophants and serfs, let them ask their consciences, I repeat, whether they have performed that sacred duty, ere they attempt to stigmatize the name of the brigand chief. Oh, Florio!—what insects, mere insects, we mortals are! How we sneak, and crouch, and grovel in the dust, when we imagine we have some interest at stake. Why the veriest worm that ever crawled, if he happens to possess dross and name, and what they call standing in society, can become a demigod in the estimation of those whom he condescends to rob; whilst I, who only plunder from the robbers, to relieve the robbed, am set down by many individuals as little better than a devil incarnate. Cospetto!—Ha, ha, ha!—So the world jogs, and I suppose will continue to do so till men learn wisdom, the ultimation of which will not be obtained in either your time or mine I suspect. But, a truce with this; for the present, Signor Clairville, farewell; and rest assured that you have not a more sincere friend, or one who is more ready to serve you, than Allesandro Massaroni."

"Of that I am satisfied, Massaroni," said the young man, pressing the hand that was extended to him cordially within his own; "your many acts of disenterested kindness towards me, have shown it in a most remarkable degree, and I should indeed be most ungrateful, nay, even despicable, did I not feel and acknowledge the debt of obligation I owe to you. Henceforth, I will no more presume to question, for an instant, the advice you give to me, but will follow it to the utmost of my humble abilities. Go forth then, my best earthly friend and protector, on your mission of humanity, in which, I say again, God speed you; and I will struggle in the meantime with those feelings that were natural to arise in my breast, and wait with confidence and hope till I hear from you, or see you again.''

"Well spoken, Florio," said the brigand chief; "now indeed you are yourself again, and it rejoices me to see it. You shall hear from me, in a very few days, perhaps only, comparatively speaking, in a very few hours; and there is something which convinces me that the intelligence I shall then have to communicate will be of the most agreeable nature; moreover, I will almost venture to promise you, that before many weeks have elapsed, the fair Signora Melina shall not only be safe out of the power of her enemies, but that those enemies will be glad to offer the most advantageous and desirable terms to yourselves, for her restoration and a reconciliation. I can take your word that, during my absence, you will not ramble further from this retreat than the residence of that good old man, Signor Montaldi?"

"You may trust to me, Massaroni," replied Clairville; "as I before observed, your advice and injunctions shall be my future law. But, have you no means of obtaining a clue to the place where Melina and her faithful attendant, Floretta, are conveyed, without going forth in search of it yourself? If you had so, it would save a great loss of time and trouble."

"That is not a bad suggestion, Signor Clairville," returned our hero; "it never occurred to me: and, by the mass! how could I have been so thoughtless? There is Guiseppe, who had been so many years in the service of Bianchi, previous to his joining me and my band, and must be acquainted with all the possessions of the prince; doubtless he can give us all the information that will furnish us with the clue which we require."

"Ah, true!" concided Clairville, eagerly.

"I will bring him into our presence immediately, and hear what he has to say," observed the brigand, and he retired at once from the cavern or appartment (for it was more worthy of the latter designation) and left Florio to his own reflections.

"Excellent, noble-hearted man," said Clairville, when he was gone, "I feel every confidence in him, and will not despair. Oh, how greatly do I feel myself indebted to him. What a pity it is that fate should have cast one of the noblest of nature's children into such a position. Dear Melina, a bright halo of hope now encircles itself round my heart! Something seems to whisper to me that you will be released from the dangers by which you are at present surrounded, and that we shall meet again, though it may never be our fate to be united. That thought inspires me, raises me, elevates me, and——"

He was interrupted by the return of Massaroni, accompanied by Guiseppe.

"Well, Signor Clairville," observed the brigand chief, "our friend, Guiseppe, informs me that he is acquainted with sufficient to afford us some clue to the place where the Signora Melina is at present confined. But I thought it might be much more satisfactory to yourself to bring him here to hear what he has to impart, before I questioned him further."

"I thank you, Massaroni," returned Clairville, "for this kind consideration."

"Proceed, Guiseppe," commanded the brigand. "You know something of the affairs of the Prince Bianchi?"

"Methinks I should do so, captain," replied Guiseppe, "seeing that I was in the service of the prince for a period of some twelve years.''

"Ah! I remember you now," remarked Florio.

"Yes," said Guiseppe, "and so do I you, Signor Clairville, when the Prince Bianchi was supposed to be the friend and patron of the humble artist. You once did me a service which I have never forgotten, but of which I will not now remind you, for I know you would not like to hear it, and I will now serve you in this instance, as far as lies in my power,"

"I thank you, from my heart," replied Clairville; "but pray proceed."

"The Prince Bianchi," observed Guiseppe, "has estates in various parts of the country, of which, no doubt, you must be aware."

"Yes—yes," replied Massaroni, hastily, "and every one of which, I daresay, you are acquainted with?"

"I am," answered Guiseppe; "but there is one, a little retired place, where his excellenza has been accustomed to carry on his private peccadiloes (as some persons might probably term them) which I believe is known only to a few, and thither, I think, it is most likely that the Signora Melina is conveyed."

"Ah!" said our hero, "and where is that?"

"It is situated amongst the mountains of the Abbuzzi," answered Guiseppe.

"And you know the place well?" interrogated Clairville, anxiously.

"Ay, signor," replied Guiseppe, "that I do, and not only do I know the place, but it strikes me that I shall find very little difficulty in gaining private access to it, and of quickly ascertaining whether the Signora Melina be confined there or not."

"Fortunate, by the saints!" ejaculated Massaroni—"Guiseppe, you are a most invaluable fellow."

"You will find me a faithful one, signor," returned Guiseppe, "though I could not *conscientiously* be so to the tyrant Bianchi."

"And it strikes you that my beloved Melina is there confined?" said Clairville, anxiously.

"It does, signor," returned Guiseppe, "and if Massaroni will entrust me, I guarantee to ascertain all the information on the subject that it is possible to attain, in a very few days."

"I will leave everything to your discretion, Guiseppe," remarked the brigand chief; "yourself, and a few of the most trusty of our band, shall depart immediately on this expedition, and I will await here the earliest communication you can forward, to know how it will be advisable for me to act."

"Enough, captain," observed Guiseppe; "I have, then, your commands to that effect?"

"You have," replied our hero.

"And let me implore you," said Florio Clairville, eagerly, "to perform your mission with fidelity, and with all the expedition you can."

"You may depend upon me, signor," replied Guiseppe; "anything that is at all calculated to thwart the schemes of the Prince Bianchi, and to gratify the feelings of revenge I bear towards the Count Alberti, I am sure to perform with fidelity and determination."

"I am satisfied," said Clairville.

"And so am I," responded Massaroni. "Guiseppe knows well his business, without any further instructions from either of us, and he will do it, too, I have no doubt, with the greatest skill."

"I thank you, Signor Massaroni," said Guiseppe, "for the confidence you place in me, and the compliment you have been pleased to bestow upon me. You shall find that I am not unworthy of them both."

"I do not doubt you," said our hero; "you can retire—I will give you further instructions anon."

"Well, Florio, what think you now? Do not your prospects wear a brighter aspect, think you?"

"They do," replied Clairville; "if all be true that Guiseppe has stated, and he is sincere in his professions. Can you depend on him?"

"I can," answered the brigand chief;—"what he has hitherto done convinces me of that. But for him, I should never have been able to gain secret access to the Villa Rosa, and have foiled the designs of Bianchi and Alberti, if I could not, at any rate, at the time, succeed in rescuing Melina from their power. Without the aid of Guiseppe, I could never have obtained the useful information that I did, or been enabled to ascertain the exact situation of your mistress. Oh, take my word for it, he is a trustworthy, and a most invaluable fellow."

"Very true," returned Clairville, "I perfectly coincide with you, and feel more satisfied after hearing the information which Guiseppe possesses, and that you will remain here while he is gone on this expedition of inquiry."

"Nay," observed the brigand chief; "I know not that I shall do so."

"What mean you?" asked Florio Clairville, anxiously.

"Why," answered our hero, "I cannot resist the wish that I have to visit his excellenza, the Prince Bianchi, at the Villa Rosa."

"It would be a rash and dangerous act."

"I think not, but that, on the contrary, it might be productive of the most beneficial and desirable results."

"How so?"

"Because," replied the brigand chief, "I should not fail on that occasion to ring in his ears such a tale as would be likely to startle him, and arouse his slumbering conscience, and probably awaken him to such a proper feeling of remorse, as would induce him to render that justice to those whom he has injured, which he has so long denied."

"Well," remarked Clairville, "there is some reason in that; but will you not wait until you hear something from Guiseppe?"

"Unquestionably I shall," answered Massaroni, "and upon the tenor of that communication will, in a great measure, depend my future plans. Oh, believe me, the brigand chief never does anything rashly, or which he has not well deliberated."

"I do believe you, Massaroni," said Florio; "but still, in such important matters, and where so much is at stake, it needs every precaution."

"True," returned our hero; "and that due and necessary precaution, Massaroni never for a moment loses sight of. If he fail in this instance, dub him a bungler, and never place any further faith in him."

"And how will you gain access to the villa?"

"By the same means I did before."

"But you hear that the villa is surrounded by the troops of Bianchi and Alberti?"

"And what of that?"

"Why, that everything is opposed against you."

"Nonsense."

"Nonsense?" repeated Clairville. "Is it at all possible, signor, under such circumstances, that you and your companions could escape detection?"

"Yes," replied the brigand chief.

"In what way?" asked Clairville.

"In the first instance," replied the brigand chief, "I and my companions will be so disguised, that it would be next to an impossibility for even those who were intimately acquainted with our persons, to recognise us; and, in the next place, I will watch my opportunity, and doubt not that it will be afforded me, to enter the villa by the secret way, which, thanks to Guiseppe, I am acquainted with, when the troops are not on the alert. I know the chamber of Bianchi, and once there, all danger will be at an end."

"How so?" demanded Florio; "he will naturally call for assistance."

"If he attempt to do so, he dies," answered Massaroni.

"Oh, I hope that no such desperate act will take place," remarked Florio; "indeed, even after all that you have said, Massaroni, I cannot perceive that any good can arise from the course you purpose to pursue."

"That may be your opinion, Signor Clairville," said the former, coolly, "but I candidly tell you it is not mine. No, I am determined in my purpose. I will thunder in the hoary libertine's ears the fearful story of his wrongs to the unfortunate and too-confiding Zitella; I will tell him of the contemplated murder of herself and their innocent offspring; I will tell, him that, to his shame and utter confusion, they both live, and are ready to confront him in the broad light of day, and before the face of Heaven; and how will the villain then quail and tremble before the outlawed, the proscribed man, whom he wanted to consign to an ignominious death, and whom he has ever pursued with such bitter, such unwarrantable animosity. Oh, Clairville, will not that be a glorious moment of revenge? And what is more, I may by so doing unravel a mystery which lies heavily upon my mind, and causes me ceaseless hours of anxiety, which it has done for years."

"What mean you?" asked Clairville, feeling the greatest interest in the observations of the brigand chief, and his mind being for the moment diverted from his own immediate troubles.

"Why," answered Massaroni, "simply this, —you have heard that my mother's fate was similar to that of Signora Zitella and her unfortunate daughter?"

"I have."

"And that her betrayer was of noble birth, and exalted station in society?"

"Yes."

"I have also told you," said Massaroni, "that my poor mother, even up to the last moments of her existence, refused to make me acquainted with the villain's name who had inflicted upon her such irreparable wrong."

"True."

"There is an impression upon my mind, that by the interview I propose to take place between myself and the Prince Bianchi, something may transpire which will throw a light upon this mystery."

"The idea," remarked Clairville, "I must confess, appears to me to be a most preposterous one. But even supposing you should discover the author of your being, what would you do then?"

"Why," answered Massaroni, his fine eyes flashing with the power of his feelings, "seek and obtain revenge—a terrible but just revenge."

"What would you do?"

"Tell him that I was the son of that unfortunate being whom he had so brutally betrayed and afterwards deserted, and bury my dagger to the hilt in his black heart."

"Horrible!" ejaculated Clairville. "Would no feelings of nature restrain you from the perpetration of so frightful a crime?"

"Feelings of nature?" repeated the brigand chief, impatiently. "Bah! where were his feelings of nature when he abandoned to want; to misery, to shame, those whom he should have protected and cherished? My determination may appear harsh, brutal, savage;—but it is sanctioned by justice, and let the consequences to myself be whatever they may, I will adhere to it. Would that the villain Malvolio had lived but a short time longer, for I am certain that he had something more of importance to reveal, and his last words satisfy me that he knew the name of the miscreant whom I will not honour by the name of father. But enough of this; my mind will grow sad if I talk much longer upon this painful and revolting subject. You are satisfied, Signor Clairville, with all the arrangements I have made with Guiseppe to endeavour to find out the place to which Signora Melina and her faithful attendant have been conveyed."

"I am," answered Clairville, "and Heaven send that they may be crowned will success."

"I have not the least doubt that they will," answered Massaroni; "I see nothing to prevent them. Keep up your spirits, Florio, and depend upon it there are yet many joyous days in store for you."

"I will endeavour to hope so," returned Clairville, though it was indeed with a sad heart that he said so.

"Well spoken, my young friend," observed Massaroni; "it affords me pleasure to hear you talk thus, and I trust that you believe sincerely in what you say. Take my word for it, and it is not often that I am out in the conjectures I form, whatever hopes you may have been induced to form, you will not be doomed to be disappointed in. But I go to arrange further with Guiseppe."

"Be it so, Massaroni," said Florio. "I leave everything to you."

"And in doing so you act wisely," said the brigand chief; "he shall depart before the day is out on his expedition."

"That is well," said Clairville; "the less delay the better."

"True."

"But I shall see you again shortly, shall I not?" asked Clairville.

"You will," replied the brigand; "and then

we will talk further upon the matters that interest us, and which are of such importance to us."

Having thus spoken, Massaroni left him, and for a short time afterwards he remained wrapped in meditation.

"So," he said, at last, "my dear Melina, there is at last some probability of discovering the place in which your cruel and unnatural persecutor has confined you; but alas! hope is still as far away from me as ever; for even should the brigand chief and his band succeed in rescuing you, can I ever flatter myself with the presumptuous idea that you will consent to become my bride, under the painful and peculiar circumstances in which we are both of us placed? No, it would be ungenerous, it would be madness, it would be preposterous, to encourage such a thought. Oh, Melina, ours is indeed a strange, an untoward fate, and which, it appears, nothing at all will alter. But we may meet again, and in weeping o'er our sorrows together, at least find some slight degree of consolation: Oh, my heart's adored! how terrible must be the pangs you are now enduring; what would I not give could I but alleviate them! But I fear it is not reserved for me to do so. But we may meet again! there is bliss in that simple idea; bliss unutterable, coupled even as it is by so many sorrows. And oh, what will be the emotions that will throb within both our bosoms at that anticipated meeting! what tales of misery and hopeless love shall we have to recapitulate to each other! Methinks it would be almost a mercy to us both did we not meet again. And yet those words, 'not meet again,' seem to freeze the hot blood within my veins, and to palsy every nerve. No, no, kind Heaven, let us, I humbly beseech, meet once more, if it be but to part for ever! I would conquer my love, but it is too strongly ingrafted in my heart to be removed, and there is something tells me that, in spite of all that is opposed to it, and much as fate seems to wage war against it, it is natural, and should be cherished. Then, why should I cast it away from my breast, and leave my mind a desert? No; she, the idol of my very soul, loves me! There is a magic influence in that blessed assurance which counteracts every other opposing feeling, and strengthens my determination. Love on, Florio; encourage hope, though you should ultimately be overwhelmed by despair; you will still have the consolation of knowing that you were faithful to the honest, the virtuous dictates of your heart, and that you never injured the beauteous object of your idolatry by one unholy thought or deed."

He paused for a short time, and reflected, and various were the conflicting thoughts which passed in rapid succession over his mind.

"Dear girl," he said, at length, "methinks I see you now, in your present lonely prison shut out from every hope and comfort, and with the dreadful prospect of a cruel and revolting fate before you. Methinks I see your pale and careworn countenance; that I hear your bitter sighs, and listen to your melancholy expressions of despair. Alas! alas! how terrible must be your sufferings; it quite unnerves me to think of them! Why then, should I longer object to your being rescued from the cruel power which now holds you on any terms, and by any means? I will no longer do so, for it is a fallacy—an erroneous idea, though, Heaven knows, springing from the best and purest of motives. Under the protection of the brigand chief and myself, you will at least be secure from the revolting fate with which you are at present threatened, and even the Prince, your uncle, may then be brought to a sense of the cruelty and injustice of the conduct he has so long pursued towards you, and endeavour to make some atonement for the past. Yes, Melina, I will encourage these hopes, and trust that an All-merciful Providence will not suffer them to be disappointed."

Having arrived at these conclusions, he became somewhat more composed than he had been for several hours previously, and was about to walk from his apartment in order that he might endeavour in some measure to divert his thoughts by visiting Signora Zitella and her daughter, and in congratulating them on their restoration to each other, when, to his surprise, the brigand chief once more made his appearance.

"So soon here again, Massaroni?" he said; "have you anything more of importance to communicate?"

"No," replied the brigand, "nothing particular, any more than that Guiseppe, accompanied by two or three of the most trustworthy of my band, has just now departed on his expedition."

"Ah! that is well," remarked Clairville, approvingly.

"Yes," said the brigand. "You see, my young friend, that I have kept my word, and lost no time."

"I thank you most cordially and sincerely, Massaroni," said Florio; "and may success crown their undertakings."

"Oh, I have not much fear of that," returned our hero; "Guiseppe is shrewd, and I feel satisfied that I can depend upon his fidelity. I thought, perhaps, you might be anxious to hear of his departure, and that was my reason for intruding again so soon upon you."

"I can but repeat my thanks, Massaroni, for your generous and disinterested conduct," observed Clairville.

"Oh, Signor Florio," observed the brigand, "you know full well that I require no acknowledgments. I am only too happy in being enabled to serve you, for I consider you deserving of it; and perhaps you will do Allesandro Massaroni the justice, at some future period, of showing that he is not altogether the unprincipled ruffian he has been represented, or rather misrepresented, to be by some parties?"

"You may depend upon me, Massaroni," replied Clairville; "I should indeed be an ungrateful and despicable wretch, did I not do the best in my humble power to remove the foul and unjust scandal which has attached itself to your name."

"Thanks, signor," returned our hero, "for I am convinced that what you have said came from your heart."

"It did indeed, Massaroni," observed Clairville, cordially pressing the hand of the brigand chief.

"Not that I value what the voice of scandal and malice thinks proper to utter against me, a straw," said Massaroni; "words are but wind, and a man's real character is best pourtrayed in his actions. But I am glad to see you looking so much more cheerful than when I left you a short time since."

"Yes, Massaroni," replied Clairville, "the advice you gave me, and the arguments you made use of, have encouraged and inspired me with hope."

"Bravely spoken, my young friend," said the brigand, taking his hand; "bravely spoken. Now you are in a humour just to suit me, and you will find that there is wisdom, ay, sound wisdom, and prudence too, in always looking on the brightest side of the question. It is that which has enabled me to struggle and wage war with difficulties and misfortunes that would entirely have crushed the spirits of many men. Let not hope desert you, and you are armed to the teeth against any misfortune or calamity that may overtake you."

"I believe you, Massaroni," returned Florio, "and, as I said before, I will endeavour to follow the excellent advice you have given me to the very letter."

"If you do so," remarked our hero, "I promise you that, whatever hopes you may form shall not be disappointed."

"I place confidence in your assertions, Massaroni," said Clairville, "gloomy and cheerless though my prospects certainly are."

"You may do so, for they are dictated by reason and truth," said the brigand chief.

"But are you still determined to pay your secret visit to the Prince Bianchi?" asked Florio.

"I am," replied our hero.

"Had you not better consider the danger of so doing before you undertake it?" said Clairville.

"Pshaw!" returned Massaroni, impa-

tiently, "what a mockery and a waste of time it is to talk to me of danger. Have I not been cradled in the midst of danger—schooled to it, practised in it; and think you that I am going to flinch from encountering it now? By all my hopes, I would not relinquish the gratification I anticipate from this meeting with the proud and tyrannical, and guilty Prince Bianchi, were I by so doing to become the possessor of a kingdom. Some rare truths will be wrung from his overburthened conscience, or I am much mistaken, and perhaps it will form one of the most remarkable and important epochs in my extraordinary career."

"I do not see how it can possibly do so," remarked Clairville.

"You may not, probably," replied Massaroni; "but my opinion holds good, notwithstanding. But if it be nothing more, oh, how it will gratify me to behold the agony of my implacable enemy when I recount to him his numerous crimes, and tell him that his victims still live to denounce him and to hold him up to shame and confusion. Is it fit, think you that such a heartless miscreant as he has proved himself to be, should escape without some tortures of the mind, Florio?"

"I must agree with all that you have said, my excellent and disinterested friend," replied Clairville; "but still I am satisfied that you will be one of the first to make all due allowances for any unreasonable or impatient observations I may make use of, considering the painful and peculiar circumstances under which I am placed."

"And I daresay, I need not assure you that I do so, Florio. and that most sincerely," returned Massaroni. "But fear not,—we shall soon receive a good account from my lieutenant, Rubaldo, and Güiseppe, whose knowledge of all connected with the Prince Bianchi, there cannot be the least doubt of; in the meantime, I shall gratify my own feelings of revenge, and, no doubt, accelerate both your views, by paying my proposed visit to his excellenza, and in pouring into his ears such facts as will strike terror into his guilty soul. Methinks the dying confession of his creature, Malvolio, will somewhat shake his scepticism, and, if that be not enough, why, he shall e'en have the proof of the injured victim of his brutality and deception, the Signora Zitella herself."

"Would it not be dangerous of venture the unfortunate signora in his power?" suggested Clairville.

"She will not be in his power, while Allesandro Massaroni, and his trusty followers, are at hand to protect her," said the brigand chief in reply; "oh, no, believe me, my young friend, I never do anything without having fully matured my plans, and duly deliberated upon them. But I am convinced that the Prince will be so confounded by the tale of truth and of guilt which I shall have to pour into his ears that he will rather be disposed to offer terms of conciliation with me, than to venture any factious opposition to my will. Do you not perceive, Florio, that this plan is calculated in a great measure to bring the prince to reason and forbearance in respect to his fair niece, the Signora Melina?"

"Heaven grant that it may do so," replied Clairville, "though I must confess that I have my doubts upon the subject."

"Nonsense, man," said the brigand chief,

PRINCE BIANCHI TAKING LEAVE OF ZITELLA AND HER FATHER.

"there is every hope for you; only keep up your spirits, and I promise you that all shall yet go as well as your fondest hopes can anticipate."

"I thank you, Massaroni, again sincerely from my heart, for your kind wishes towards me," said Florio; "but indeed, when I take all the dismal circumstances of the situation of my beloved and much persecuted Melina and myself into consideration, I dare not, I cannot, encourage the hope that they will ever be realised."

"Young man," returned Massaroni, seriously, "you ought by this time to know that I never make idle professions; that I never promise anything which I do not think I shall be fully capable to perform. It is so in this instance, and with such assurance rest you satisfied; moreover, that I am not so disinterested in these proceedings as you seem to imagine. I have my own private views to gratify, as I have intimated to you before; let that suffice you. But I will leave you now, still impressing upon your mind the almost certainty of a few days only, perhaps but as many hours, of the place of Signora Melina's present confinement being discovered."

"I am satisfied, Massaroni," said Florio, "and will endeavour to act up to the advice which you have so kindly given me; I will place the fate of my Melina and myself in the hands of Providence, and on its mercy confidently place the issue."

"Well spoken, Signor Clairville," remarked the brigand chief; "continue in this state of mind, and depend upon it you will not be doomed to be disappointed. Farewell, till we meet again."

"And that will be before you depart on your expedition to the Villa Rosa, if you are still determined to do so, will it not?" asked Clairville.

"It will," answered our hero; "and, therefore, shortly, for I shall lose no time in paying my *respects* to his excellenza, the Prince Bianchi; ha! ha! ha!—Oh, how I long for the interview; and should the suspicions which have arisen in my mind be realised, how terrible is the revenge that I will have!—how great will be the satisfaction that I shall obtain!"

Florio Clairville made no reply to the brigand chief, though his mind entirely dissented from the plan which he had formed to visit the Prince Bianchi, since he could not clearly see that it was at all likely to be productive of any good, and might be fraught with much danger; and Massaroni quitted him.

"Dear Melina," said Clairville, after being for a few moments wrapped in meditation; "how painful, how tedious, how harassing is the fate to which we are both at this moment exposed; and whichever way I direct my thoughts, I see little or no prospect of our being released from it. The will of the brigand chief, I know, is good; his motives, I am convinced, are pure and honest; but when I take into consideration the circumstances, the power he has to contend against, the situation of myself and her that I love even more than my own soul, can it be marvelled at that I shall give myself up to despair? Poor girl!—what must be the bitter anguish of mind which you are at the present time enduring? My heart sinks within me at the thought. Oh! that we had never known each other!"

He sighed deeply as he gave utterance to these words, and sinking on a seat, gave himself up to the most melancholy thoughts.

Massaroni, after quitting him, hastened to the apartment in which he had left his wife, whom he found immersed in deep reflection, so much so, that she did not notice his entrance till he addressed her.

"What, Maria, wife," he said, placing his hand affectionately on her shoulder; "so deeply wrapped in meditation; looking so serious, love; may I ask you what is the subject of your profound reflections?"

"Ay, Massaroni," replied the brigand's wife, seriously, "for there needs no disguise from you. I have been thinking, then, that after all the many years of mingled successes and adverse fortunes, it has been our lot to experience, by the determinations you have of late come to, you are about to rush madly upon destruction."

"How so?" demanded Massaroni hastily.

"I will endeavour to explain," replied Maria; "but mark me, Massaroni—I blame you not for the sympathy which you evince in the fate of the Signora Melina, Signor Clairville, and others, with which I also coincide; but this is not, in my opinion, the moment to act."

"What!" said our hero, impatiently, "not when Signora Melina is every moment threatened with a fate so revolting; after the disclosure we have had from the unfortunate Zitella, and the suspicions that have been excited in my breast against her villanous and heartless betrayer, the Prince Bianchi? Maria, you speak erroneously."

"I may do so, Massaroni, in your estimation," replied his wife, "but still I must adhere to my original opinion. Better wait till the excitement caused by the late events have in some measure abated; if you remain passive for a time, the prince will be thrown off his guard, will imagine that you have abandoned your designs, will use less precaution, and then will be the moment that you may carry out your project, with some probability of success."

"And think you, then, that I can thus patiently delay, when such danger threatens?" demanded the brigand chief.—"No: Alessandro Massaroni always acts with promptitude, and he will do so on this occasion, let the consequences be whatever they may; I do not fear them."

"And do you mean to persist in your design to visit the Prince Bianchi, at the Villa Rosa?"

"Most assuredly I do; and why should I not?" asked our hero.

"Because," replied Maria, "from all that

you have heard, the villa is at present surrounded by the troops of Bianchi and Count Alberti, and you are almost certain to be detected in attempting to gain admission."

"No such thing, Maria: your fears are perfectly groundless. Do I not possess the ready means of access? and shall I not be so disguised that it will be next to a matter of impossibility for any one to recognise me?"

"But when Bianchi beholds you he will raise an alarm, and then——"

"And then," rejoined the brigand chief, with a look of determination, "if he does he dies; mark my words, for you know full well that I am not apt to hold out any idle threats."

"I do, indeed, know that full well," answered Maria Grazie; "but let me ask you, Massaroni, what will be the gratification which you expect will reward you for running so much risk?"

"The gratification," returned our hero, "of witnessing the horror and agony of mind of the conscience-stricken man, when I pour into his astonished ears the history of his guilt, and prove to him, to his utter confusion, that his victims are still living. Oh, it will be a glorious moment for the brigand chief, whose blood he has so long thirsted for; and I cannot divest my mind of the impression that I shall likewise elicit something of the utmost importance to myself, and which will throw a light upon the dark mystery which has so long enshrouded my fate."

"Strange idea!" said Maria; "to me it seems perfectly preposterous."

"It may do so," answered her husband; "but nevertheless, your opinion, much even as I value it, will not alter my determination."

"I speak only for your good, Massaroni; and as reason, duty, and affection prompt me to do."

"I know it, my faithful Maria;—you have shared with me too many years in my chequered fortunes for me now for a moment to doubt the purity of your motives. But we will drop this subject; to-morrow I depart."

"So soon?"

"Yes; why should I delay? When my mind is made up, the sooner I act upon my determination the better; is it not so?"

"Well, well, e'en be it so," observed Maria. "I know it will be useless of me to attempt further to dissuade you; my best wishes go with you, though I approve not of your designs."

"Thanks, my faithful wife," said the brigand chief; "you will see to the comfort of Signora Zitella and her daughter, likewise the Signor Clairville, during my absence?"

"You may depend upon me, Massaroni," replied Maria.

"I know it," answered our hero; and they then separated, he to prepare himself for his daring expedition, and Maria Grazie to resume her reflections. Although she struggled hard to do so, she could not divest her mind of the impressions which had gained such strong hold of it; and notwithstanding she was not by any means prone to such feelings, she could not resist the force of the gloomy forebodings that arose so powerfully to her imagination that something would arise from this adventure which would be productive of considerable misery to them, if it did not end in their entire destruction.

"Massaroni," she soliloquised, "we have buffetted the cruel world together, and have equally shared in many vicissitudes, under which many a proud and courageous spirit would have fallen; and Heaven knows that I have never murmured at the lot to which I have been exposed; but now, should you by one rash act fall into the power of your remorseless foes, and suffer an ignominious death——Oh! how terrible is the thought! Let me not encourage it. Father of Mercy! Thou knowest the wrongs he has received;—Thou knowest full well the natural goodness of his heart, and the purity of his motives, notwithstanding the questionable course of life he is pursuing; and I confidently venture to supplicate Your protection for him."

The brigand's wife solemnly knelt down as she gave utterance to these words, and with hands clasped vehemently together, and eyes raised towards the seat of that Almighty Power, whose mercy and protection she invoked, she repeated the prayer. Her mind felt relieved from an almost insupportable weight after she had done so, and she arose from her knees inspired with renewed confidence and hope. But the reader will now be anxious that we should return to Melina, and relate the manner in which she was removed from the Villa Rosa, and accordingly we hasten to do so.

We left the signora in a state of the utmost grief and despair after her last painful and cruel interview with the Prince Bianchi, her uncle, and the threats which he had then held out to her, and which she well knew, from woful experience, he was so capable of performing, and every hour did but serve to increase her misery and to convince her of the utter hopelessness of her situation, unless by some merciful and almost miraculous interposition of Providence she should be rescued from the awful fate which seemed to be inevitably impending over her. Her faithful Floretta, as usual, exerted herself to the utmost to console her, and inspire her with hope, but her efforts were crowned with but very little, if any, success; and having exhausted all her arguments, she was obliged to leave it to the will of Providence to bring about that termination to her sorrows and cruel persecutions which she was so anxious should take place.

Count Alberti continued in a very precarious state, and at times he was perfectly delirious. Signor Giachomo, his medical attendant, prohibited, as much as he possibly could, the visits of the Prince Bianchi to his chamber, endeavouring to impress upon his mind with all the eloquence he could, the danger there was in exciting him by conversation; but in spite of everything the impatience of Bianchi could not be restrained, and he passed many hours in the wounded nobleman's chamber, watching by his couch with the utmost anxiety, when Alberti was totally unconscious of his presence.

Again and again did the Prince Bianchi invoke the most bitter curses upon the head of the brigand chief, and vow a terrible revenge should he by any chance ever fall into his power.

"And shall the daring rascal ever escape me?" he would soliloquise, when he was alone; "are there no means by which I may entrap him, and bring him to that punishment which is so justly his due? I cannot persuade myself that there are not. Hitherto he has mocked me—he has triumphed over me in every shape, and set all my power at complete defiance; but the time must and shall come when the triumph shall be mine, and then will he indeed have cause to tremble. But what is the reason that he pursues me with such implacable hatred, and glories in frustrating all my designs, of which he becomes aware in a manner which I cannot divine? and how is it with all the repugnance of the feelings I bear towards him, there is coupled with those feelings a sensation of awe, almost amounting to dread, whenever I think upon his name and recall his features to my memory? I cannot account for it—and yet, in spite of all my efforts, I cannot conquer it. Pshaw; what a weakness is this—totally unworthy of me; I will not give way to it. Let me continue to exert myself to get him in my power, and then I will have a terrible revenge upon his head, and thus at once rid myself of all my fears, and do away with the annoyances to which he has constantly, and with so much success subjected me."

He endeavoured to become more calm as he gave utterance to these words, but it was not without considerable difficulty that he succeeded in accomplishing that task.

"Melina's tears and supplications shall not conquer my determination," he observed, after a pause; "obdurate girl! dares she thus to oppose my will and authority? She whom I ever believed to be all humility and submission? But of what use is her resistance? She shall find me resolute, though the execution of my designs should break her heart. The Prince Bianchi is not easily to be thwarted in anything

upon which he has fixed his mind. But should Alberti not recover! No, no—I will not encourage any such apprehensions. And then the dying words of her mother, of which she has so often reminded me—I cannot banish them from my memory—they will constantly arise to my imagination, in spite of all my efforts to the contrary, and the promise I then made, and which I have now broken, convicts me of cruelty and villany. But away with such ideas! Why should I heed the words that sprang from a disordered and wandering mind? Such thoughts—such doubts and misgivings are unworthy of me. Arouse yourself, Bianchi, and all will yet terminate as well as you could wish."

He hastily quaffed off the contents of a glass of wine as he gave utterance to these words, and his mind became more composed, and his resolution the more fixed.

Thus two more days passed away, and a more favourable change came over the Count Alberti, and he again became conscious of what was passing around him. He saw the Prince Bianchi sitting in the chamber, and he eagerly called him by his name, and extended his hand towards him.

"My dear count," said Bianchi, "how do you feel yourself now?"

"Oh, better, much better," answered the wounded nobleman; "have my senses been long wandering?"

"For two or three days," said the prince; "but your words and your looks convince me that you are now as you say, much better, and that you will soon recover."

"I trust that I shall," returned Alberti, in a faint voice; "though I have had a severe trial of it. The villain, Massaroni—tell me, is he still at liberty?"

"He is," answered the Prince Bianchi; "but it shall be no fault of mine if he long escapes us."

"Curses light upon him!" exclaimed the Count Alberti, vehemently.

"Ay, you have reason to invoke your heaviest maledictions upon his head," remarked Bianchi; "but do not excite yourself; our day of complete triumph, depend upon it, is not far distant."

"I would fain think so," returned the count; "and yet I must confess that, at times, I have my misgivings."

"And why so?"

"I know not," answered the patient; "but always when our success seemed to be the most certain, we have been doomed to disappointment."

"Do not encourage any such apprehensions, count," remarked Bianchi; "for it will indeed be most strange to me if we are doomed to disappointment now. The very hour that witnesses your restoration to convalescence, shall also make you the husband of my niece ; the fair, though cold and haughty Signora Melina."

"Ay, your highness," remarked Alberti, " it is her coldness that wounds my pride, and dampens the ardour of my hopes; could I but inspire her but with the smallest portion of the love which she entertains for Florio Clairville, I should indeed fancy myself to be one of the happiest and most fortunate men in existence."

"And why do you mention the presumptuous beggar's name, my lord?" demanded the Prince Bianchi; " he should, indeed, be beneath even your contempt. Indeed, when I know the influence he possesses over the affections of the beauteous Signora Melina, I cannot treat him with such contempt, your highness," returned Alberti.

"Ridiculous, my lord," said Bianchi; " I am surprised to hear you talk so; what have you to fear from him?"

"Not much that I am aware of; insignificant as he is, and possessing, as I do, the favour of your highness."

"Exactly so."

"But is he also still at liberty?"

"He is."

"And under the protection of the brigand chief?"

"No doubt of it," answered the prince; " but I trust that he will at length fall in our power, and then he shall pay dearly for his insolent presumption."

"But the Signora Melina?" anxiously inquired the Count Alberti.

"Oh, you may be sure that I have her still confined a close prisoner in her chamber."

"And does she still remain in the same obdurate state of mind?" asked Alberti.

"She does," answered Bianchi; " but she will find that any resistance on her part is sheer madness, and no doubt, after all, she will see the prudence as well as the necessity of resigning herself to her fate."

"Your observations inspire me with hope," observed the count.

"I am glad to hear it," replied his companion ; " you have everything to hope, and nothing to fear, while I am your friend ; you may depend upon it that every promise I have made to you I will fulfil to the very letter."

"Believe me, my lord, I do not doubt you," said Alberti.

"You have no reason to do so; and let that conviction console and encourage you."

"But I remember now, your highness, that you proposed removing Melina from the villa to some residence which is known to few persons but yourself, and which would probably be the means of baffling any designs which Massaroni might have in contemplation ; are you still so determined ?"

"I am," replied the Prince Bianchi.

"You have not yet intimated to you niece your intention of so doing."

"I have not, and shall not do so, until the very evening on which I intend to have her conveyed away."

"And when do you propose that that shall take place ?"

"Now that so favourable and promising a change has taken in you, I care not how soon, my lord," answered Bianchi.

"Will you accompany her yourself ?"

"No ; I do not think it would be prudent for me to do so, for my presence will be required here, until you are restored to convalescence, and her departure must be conducted with as much secrecy as possible."

"Very true; but have you those whom you can trust ?" demanded the Count Alberti.

"I have," returned the prince; " and once there, I think it will puzzle Allesandro Massaroni to discover the place of her confinement. Make your mind easy, my lord, for our prospects were never half so promising as they are at the present time."

"Your words, excellenza, indeed make me most sanguine," said Alberti; " and I feel that they will tend more than anything towards my speedy recovery."

"I am glad to hear you say so, count, and the very day on which you are restored to health, as I before said, shall witness the consummation of your wishes."

"Oh, joyous assurance!" ejaculated Alberti, his countenance brightening up; " they inspire me with new life, and I feel as if nothing had ever happened to me. And shall I indeed become the husband of the all-lovely Melina?"

"Have I not given you my word, my lord?" returned the Prince Bianchi, " and think you I will break my promise? I am as anxious for the union to take place as you can possibly be yourself."

"Enough, your highness," said Alberti. " I am satisfied ; and you have by your kind assurances raised me from the very depths of despair to the pinnacle of hope. Surely I shall in time be able to conquer the aversion which Melina now evinces towards me ?"

"No doubt of it, my lord," replied Bianchi, " if you only persevere ; let not that disturb you ; women are strange, fickle beings, and when Melina knows that she is indissolubly yours, and that nothing can alter her fate, she will melt, depend upon it."

"And Massaroni will probably then abandon his designs?"

"Yes : or more likely, he will, ere that time arrives, have paid the penalty of his crimes upon the scaffold. It shall not be for the want of any vigilance on my part. if he has not."

"And Florio Clairville ?"

"Oh, he is too contemptible for consideration; the poor devil will probably die in despair, or will think it prudent to quit the country altogether, and hide himself in that obscurity from which he should never have ventured to thrust himself."

"True, true; your words, my lord, every one that you utter, convince me of their force and your sincerity."

"Why, count, I should think that you had never any reason to doubt that," said the prince.

"I have not, your highness," replied Count Alberti; "I must have been very unreasonable and unjust had I done so. All then is settled?"

"It is, and I trust to your satisfaction?"

"Entirely so; it is impossible for me to object to it."

"Well, I should think it would," observed Bianchi.

"And have you made all your arrangements, my lord?" asked the count.

"I have, and it needs but my order to put my plans into immediate execution."

"That is well; such promptitude is deserving of all praise, and promises every success."

"Oh, there can be no doubt of that."

"And when do you propose the Signora Melina shall be conveyed away from the villa?"

"To-morrow night," replied Bianchi; "I do not see the necessity to delay it any longer."

"That assurance satisfies me still more. And the place where you intend to convey her, you say, is secure?"

"Certainly it is," replied the prince, "or you may be certain that I should not have chosen it."

"Very true, my lord; and is it far distant from hence?"

"The journey will occupy about three hours."

"And at what time do you propose removing her?"

"At midnight, when there will be no fear of there being any one about."

"Well chosen," remarked the Count Alberti, approvingly; "but have you given the Signora Melina any intimation of your designs?"

"I have informed you before that I have not," answered Bianchi.

"Then she is totally unprepared for the change which is so shortly to take place in her situation?"

"She is; and I shall not apprise her of it till the very last minute."

"How dreadfully agitated she will be when she is made acquainted with it."

"Why, we must expect that."

"And do you intend that her maid, Floretta, shall accompany her?"

"Certainly," answered the prince; "it would not do to deprive her of all attendance altogether; besides it might be fraught with some danger were I to suffer Floretta to remain here."

"Very true," coincided the count; "but do you not think it is likely that the brigand chief may have some of his spies lurking about the neighbourhood?"

"He may," returned Bianchi, "but if he has, we shall be able to buffle him, and it would be madness for them to attempt to rescue her, so well guarded as she will be."

"Yes, I do not see that there is much fear of that, as you say," remarked the Count Alberti.

"None at all," replied his companion, confidently; "our design is as certain of success as if it were now accomplished."

At that moment, Signor Giachomo entered the chamber, and intimated to his highness that there would be danger in prolonging the interview.

"Very well, signor," replied Bianchi, reluctantly; "of course, I yield to your advice; but, tell me, can you pronounce the Count Alberti out of danger?"

"Yes, your highness," returned Signor Giachomo; "I think, from the symptoms I perceive, I can do so with confidence."

"That is well," said Bianchi, in tones of satisfaction; "I commend you, good Signor Giachomo, for your skill. And when do you imagine he will be restored to convalescence?"

"Why, that is almost impossible for me to predict with any degree of certainty," replied Giachomo; "but I should imagine, with care and quiet, it may be in a fortnight, at the latest."

"No sooner?" said Alberti, impatiently, and in a tone of disappointment.

"It is impossible for me to promise that it will be sooner," said Giachomo; "and, as I said before, it will require the greatest care and attention, and, above all, the utmost quiet, to effect it even in that time."

"Very well," observed Alberti; "it is no use murmuring; I suppose I must submit, though it is a severe trial to my patience."

"Never mind it, my dear count," said the Prince Bianchi; "the time will soon pass away, and you will have the satisfaction of knowing that all is going on as well as you could wish in other respects."

"I understand your highness," said Alberti, "and depend upon you."

"You have not the slightest reason to doubt me in the least," replied Bianchi. "Farewell!"

"Farewell, my lord. I shall see you again to-morrow?"

"Certainly you will; and in the meantime, I would advise you not to disturb or harass your mind any more than possible."

"I will follow your advice, my lord," replied Alberti, "to the best of my ability;" and the Prince Bianchi then quitted the chamber. But it was in vain that the count, notwithstanding all that he had promised Bianchi, sought to bring his mind to wait with patience the long, tardy period which, according to Signor Giachomo's opinion, would probably restore him to a state of convalescence. His irritable temperament could brook no delay in the gratification of his designs against the gentle and innocent Melina, and he was worked up and goaded on by a spirit of revenge against her in consequence of the determined opposition she had made towards his suit, and the undisguised feelings of abhorrence she had at all times evinced towards him.

"Oh, that this accursed accident had never befallen me," he soliloquised, when he was alone, (Signor Giachomo having left him for a short time at his own request, and under the impression that he would settle himself down to a few hours repose, which he so much required, to bring about his restoration to health,) "she would now have been my bride, and all my doubts would have been set at rest. May eternal curses light upon the head of the brigand chief, Massaroni, who has thus foiled me in my wishes! But the Prince Bianchi will not fail to keep the many solemn promises he has made to me; he seems to feel it is to his interest to do so, and therefore why should I encourage those misgivings which at times come across my mind? Melina must become mine; she cannot help herself; and then, oh, then will I not retaliate upon her all the insults she has offered to me—all the indignities she has heaped upon my head—all the repugnance she has so lavishly evinced towards me!—Oh, yes, my hour of triumph, of complete triumph, is shortly destined to arrive, and I will not fail to take full and ample advantage of it. No tears, no supplications, no reproaches, will avail her then, when I am her supreme lord and master. And shall I not be enabled to subdue her proud spirit? and if I cannot awaken in her breast the strong passion of love, at least to make her humble and submissive to my will and authority, and to treat me with that respect and deference which she now denies me? These thoughts revive me, and I feel prepared and eager for the struggle. But," he added, after a pause, and his conscience disturbed by the thoughts which started upon it—"what of Olympia and her offspring?—how are they to be disposed of, while they are still under the protection of Massaroni?—That is a difficulty which I know not how to overcome, and, in spite of all my assertions to the contrary, I dread his power and the deadly feeling of animosity he bears towards me. Would that he and his desperate band were exterminated, then, indeed, I might reckon myself safe, and I should have little or nothing to fear from Olympia and her brat. I would soon find some way of ridding myself of them altogether, and without any fear of a stigma being cast upon my character. Would that they were dead!"

He paused, and the expression of his features to any person who could have witnessed it at the time, would plainly have shown the terrible feelings that were passing in his guilty mind, and what little effect his late precarious situation had had in subduing the brutal propensities of his nature. But we will leave the misguided and abandoned nobleman for a while to his own conflicting and distracting meditations, and once more devote our attention to the unfortunate and deeply-persecuted Melina.

Her feelings had undergone little or no change since the last time we referred to her, and certainly, there had nothing whatever taken place to ameliorate the anguish and anxiety of her mind, or to inspire her with hope. It was quite evident that unless Providence interposed to save her, her doom was sealed, and all that Floretta could say could not persuade her to the contrary. How drearily, how dismally, the hours passed away; and every succeeding moment seemed to bring with it more vividly to her imagination the certainty of her fate. To add to her agony and despair, if it were possible to do so, Floretta brought her the information that Signor Giachomo had pronounced his patient to be completely out of danger, and that he had likewise expressed an opinion that, in the course of a few days he would be restored entirely to a state of convalescence.

"That is enough, Floretta," sighed the fair prisoner, wringing her hands, and tears gushing to her eyes; "that announcement is like sounding my funeral knell; it is my death warrant;—for as the bride of the detested Count Alberti, I cannot, will not survive. Farewell, my noble-hearted, my beloved Florio; a long farewell till we meet again in Heaven; farewell to all my hopes!—Oh, what a wretched, unfortunate being am I!—Would to God that I had perished in my infancy, ere I was conscious of sorrow, or the cruelty and wickedness of my fellow-creatures."

Violent and convulsive sobs choked her further utterance, and throwing herself back in her chair, and covering her face with her hands, she wept as if her heart would break.

"My dear and unfortunate signora," said the compassionate Floretta, in her most soothing and gentle accents, "what can I say to you; how endeavour to console you under this dreadful trial? Alas! it is but too plain that you have no other dependance but in the mercy of the Almighty, and in Him I beseech you to endeavour to put your trust."

"You speak truly, Floretta," sobbed her mistress, "and I feel the full force of your observations. But can you wonder at the state of my mind, after the manifold sufferings to which I have been subjected, and the dismal, the truly frightful prospects which are at present before me?"

"Indeed I do not, lady;" answered her

attendant; "but Providence has given you sufficient strength to combat all the weary and terrible persecutions to which you have hitherto been exposed, and I sincerely hope that you may be able to gather fortitude enough to encounter all the future trials that may be in store for you. Dismal as your prospects even are, I cannot help still encouraging the hope that you will be rescued from your dangerous position, and also that you will be enabled to bring your persecutors to a due sense of the cruelty and injustice of their conduct towards you."

"Oh, Floretta," ejaculated her mistress, "what ground is there for my entertaining such an idea? Is there anything in the conduct of the prince, my uncle, to sanction it? But no, on the contrary, his treatment to me of late has been more stern and inexorable than ever; and now that the Count Alberti is expected so soon to recover, he will be urged on towards the completion of his cruel and unnatural designs, and thus my fate will be sealed for ever. But," she added, after a brief pause, and terrible determination flashing from her expressive eyes, "by all my heavenly hopes I swear that the day which I am thus remorselessly sacrificed to the hated Alberti, shall also be the termination of my wretched existence!"

"Oh, forbear, my dear signora," said the horrorstruck Floretta; "forbear, I entreat you; recall that frightful oath, and try to become calm."

"Calm! calm!" repeated Melina, in the same wild accents, "oh, how easy it is for those to talk and advise who know nothing of sorrow but the name! Floretta, I am distracted; I feel those emotions working within my breast and burning my brain, which I never before experienced; I tell you I am determined; I I will never live degraded as the wife of such a villain as the Count Alberti."

"Would you rush unbidden upon the presence of your maker?" demanded her faithful attendant, breathlessly.

"Yes," replied Melina, firmly, "for I feel convinced that the same Almighty Being who knows the innocence of my heart, will forgive me the deed, to which I shall have been urged not by my own free will, but the cruelty and injustice of others. Floretta, think you that I can endure to live to loathe and despise myself?—to be pointed at as thing of scorn?— No, by Heaven, I will not, but I will rather brave all consequences to escape from such a fate."

Overpowered by her emotions the poor girl once more sank exhausted in her chair, and hysterical sobs choked her further utterance, and Floretta, who was completely at a loss what answer to make, remained perfectly silent. At length, the violence of Melina's grief having somewhat exhausted itself, she became more tranquil.

"I am a poor wretched, hopeless, helpless creature!" she sighed, in the most melancholy accents; "abandoned by him who should have watched over me, cherished, and protected me with the same anxious care and affection as if I had been his own child, but whose only study and delight seems now to be to render me miserable. Oh, my uncle, what can thus have changed thy feelings towards me? What fatal influence can have induced thee to forget the solemn and sacred promises you made to my dying mother?—Have you no fear that her sainted spirit should look down upon you, and curse you?—Have you no dread of the terrible retribution of offended Heaven overtaking you for the cruel injustice you are now practising towards an innocent and defenceless girl—the orphan child of your own sister? By the just God, it seems impossible that you should act thus! May Heaven pardon you, and bring you to a due sense of the enormity of your present conduct, ere it be too late."

"And to that wish, signora," observed Floretta, "I most fervently and sincerely respond; and that I trust it will be realised. But again let me beg of you no longer to encourage such fearful thoughts as those to which you have just now given utterance. Heaven will never permit you to be driven to such a dreadful extremity."

"Oh, Floretta," sighed her mistress; "how can I think as you, in your generous sympathy, advise me, when I reflect upon all the circumstances of my situation, and the threats which have been held out to me so often? Indeed, every fresh interview I have with my uncle, but serves to convince me of his cruel determination, and consequently to increase my despair. What motive can guide him in his extraordinary and unnatural conduct I know not; but certainly the Count Alberti seems to have obtained an influence over him which nothing can weaken. God! is it not monstrous to think that he should make up his mind to sacrifice me to a man so notorious for his licentious and abandoned habits as the betrayer of the unfortunate Olympia?"

"It is strange, it is unaccountable, signora; but he will yet abandon his designs, depend upon it."

"No, returned our heroine, "there is not the least hope of that, I see it clearly enough; I have made up my mind to it, and have also fixed my determination as to the course I will pursue. Dear Florio, cherished of my soul! could I but behold you once again, to assure you of my unutterable love, and to bid you a final adieu, then methinks I could resign myself to my fate without a murmur."

"What mean you, signora?" said Floretta, in a timid voice, and looking into the countenance of her mistress, which bore so fearful an expression, with the greatest anxiety.

"No, matter," replied Melina, solemnly, but evasively; "time will show—time will show!"

"Oh, my beloved mistress," ejaculated Floretta; "how sincerely it grieves me to see you in this state of mind. May Heaven watch over you, and avert the evils which you apprehend."

Melina shook her head mournfully, sighed deeply, but returned no answer, but walked to the casement, seated herself by the side of it, and appeared to be engaged in contemplating the

ZITELLA THINKING OF THE PRINCE BIANCHI.

romantic scenery of which it commanded so extensive a view, though her mind was too much occupied by her own distracting thoughts to suffer her to do so.

It was a lovely evening, the moon rising magnificently through oceans of silvery clouds, and imparting a hue of the most impressive grandeur to the beauties of nature around. It was an evening indeed to lull the weary thoughts of the child of sorrow to rest, but it had no effect upon the mind of Melina; her cares and anxieties were too great and overpowering to admit of any relief, and still she continued to sit immersed in meditation, and completely lost to everything else.

Floretta did not offer to interrupt her for some time, for she thought that probably the silent indulgence of her own reflections might tend to afford her some relief, but at length she said——

"What a lovely night it is, signora; oh, what a bright world is this we live in."

"Ah, Floretta," replied our heroine, "the world is indeed bright and beautiful; but how dark and sinful are the beings who dwell in it; how ungrateful for the numerous blessings which all-bounteous Heaven has bestowed upon them. Their only study is to torture, to tyrannize over, and oppress each other. The strong exert their power to persecute the weak, and to gain an advantage over those whom God has made their equals. Would that I had never been born to experience the miseries and the wrongs which I have attempted so faintly to describe."

"Still, my dear signora," remarked her companion, "you will suffer those dismal thoughts to harass and distract your mind; banish them, lady, banish them."

"I cannot, Floretta," returned Melina, "it is in vain for me to try; the more I do so, the more hopeless and gloomy does my fate appear to be."

"Would to Heaven I could persuade you to think to the contrary, signora," said Floretta.

"I know your goodness of heart, Floretta, and your devoted attachment to me, but your efforts are all in vain; I see my fate as clearly as if it were reflected in a mirror, and at the same time I feel convinced that no earthly power can avert it."

"Oh, yes, lady, there is one who I am certain can, and will, save you from it, at all hazards."

"And who is he?" demanded our heroine, hastily.

"Allesandro Massaroni," replied Floretta.

"Ah, no," said Melina; "after the precautions which the prince, my uncle, has taken to guard against him, I place no further confidence in his power, if even I were willing to avail myself of it, which I am not."

"And is it possible, signora, that you still encourage those delicate scruples which you formerly expressed, after what has taken place?"

"I do, Floretta, and nothing can remove them from my mind."

"Pardon me, lady, but I cannot help thinking that you are in the wrong. Surrounded as you are by so many difficulties, and threatened by the prince with a fate so revolting, I am satisfied that no blame can attach to you for adopting any means to avoid it. Besides, the brigand chief is honest and honourable in his motives."

"I firmly believe him to be so."

"Then why object to receive his proffered aid?" asked Floretta.

"Because the world is censorious, Floretta," replied her mistress.

"But, my dear signora," remarked her attendant, "the reasonable and generous portion of mankind, and those about whose good opinion you should care the most, would not venture to censure you for flying from a fate so revolting to nature and humanity, but would rather cast upon his highness, your uncle, and the Count Alberti, all the odium of driving you to such a painful necessity. Come my lady, reflect more seriously upon this subject, and I am satisfied that you will conquer your objections. Had Massaroni succeeded in bearing you away at the time he made the attempt in the chapel, I cannot but persuade myself that a reconciliation would have been effected ere this between yourself and your uncle."

"Oh, no," returned Melina, shaking her head, "I have now had two painful experience of his temper to believe that he would rather have pursued me with his deadliest hatred and vengeance. Besides, what would have become of me, friendless and unprotected in the world as I should then have been?"

"You would never have wanted a friend and protector, lady, while Allesandro Massaroni lived."

"And think you, Floretta," demanded our heroine, proudly, "that I could ever so far forget my proper dignity as to become beholden to the bounty of him, a stranger, and an outlaw?"

"Pardon me, signora, but I am certain you will not do Massaroni the injustice to say that he is cruel and depraved; it is not his will that he is the brigand chief, but that untoward fate and unavoidable circumstances that have made him so. He is noble, generous, and humane, and would adorn any station in society."

"I believe him to be all you say, Floretta, I am grateful to him for the good feelings he entertains towards me; but still I cannot consent to become dependant on his bounty."

"You must not forget, signora," replied the waiting-maid, "that to Massaroni, the Signor Clairville is at present indebted for his safety."

"Forget it?" returned her mistress, warmly. "Oh, no, indeed I do not; and for that I owe him a debt of gratitude which I fear it will never be in my power to repay. Dear Florio, how I shudder when I think upon what your fate might have been, so exasperated as my uncle was against you at the time, had you not have been rescued from prison."

"That single act of Massaroni's, my lady," observed Floretta, "permit me to say, ought to induce you to place every confidence in his honour and disinterestedness."

"You misunderstand me, my good girl," replied our heroine ;; "I never for a moment doubted the honour and disinterestedness of Massaroni's motives ; but still I have the strongest objection, considering his position in society, to place myself under his protection. But even if I had not, I have my doubts as to whether he could succeed in delivering me from the power of the Prince Bianchi and Alberti, now that they are so well upon their guard ; and any such attempt might only bring destruction on himself, which would be a source of never failing regret and reproach to me. Ah, no, Floretta, I see no chance, no hope of escaping the fate with which my uncle has threatened me at present. The Count Alberti, it seems likely, soon will be restored to convalescence, and then there will be no more delay ; I shall be forced to the altar, and that ceremony will be performed which will decide my fate at once. And even if the count had not recovered, did not the prince assure me that he would sacrifice me to some other man who might be equally as repulsive to my feelings ? Oh, God! what a terrible lot is mine !"

The unfortunate damsel clasped her hands vehemently together, and her tears almost blinded her.

"My sweet signora," said the kind-hearted Floretta, soothingly ; "I pray you, do try to keep up your spirits as much as you can, and still to look forward with the most sanguine hopes for the best. But see !"

"What are you gazing so eagerly at, Floretta ?" asked Melina, aroused by her exclamation.

"Do you not see the Prince Bianchi walking yonder in earnest conversation with that strange and ruffianly-looking man ?" asked Floretta, pointing in the direction of a grove of tall trees to which they were advancing, plainly distinguishable in the moonlight.

"Yes, yes," replied our heroine, in a faint voice ; "I like not the appearance of that man. What can my uncle and he do together at such an hour ?"

Floretta returned no answer, and they both watched the Prince Bianchi and his companion with anxious eyes, until they were hidden from their sight.

"There is some evil afloat, I am convinced of it," remarked our heroine ; "my heart misgives me."

"Nay, signora," returned her attendant, "I do not think we ought to view it in so serious a light. What evil can it threaten to you ?"

"I know not," answered her mistress, "but some strange forebodings came across my mind."

"Think no more about it, signora," said her companion ; "for after all it is a circumstance that is too trifling to call for any serious consideration. Let us retire from the window."

Melina did so, and resumed her former seat, and she and Floretta remained in silence for a considerable time ; but at length the deep and sonorous bell of St. Peter's warned them of the lateness of the hour, and they prepared themselves to retire to rest ; but before doing so Melina knelt down and offered up her prayers to Heaven, and solemnly invoked the spirit of her mother, and besought her protection from the evil designs that were contemplated against her. She arose, somewhat tranquillised, and Floretta having assisted her to undress, she sought her pillow, hoping in sleep to gain a temporary forgetfulness of her sorrows.

The morning found her in the same dispirited state, and it required all the exertions of Floretta to at all compose her. Her fears were increased, when as soon as they had finished the morning meal, Floretta received a summons from the Prince Bianchi to attend him immediately below. Melina turned pale, and she felt a deadly sickness come over her.

"Some more mischief is brooding, some more misery is in store for me," she ejaculated. "Heaven help me."

"Be firm, signora," said Floretta, "and your fears may yet prove to be groundless. I will quickly return, and banish your suspense."

The faithful attendant then quitted the room, and Melina awaited her return with the most painful impatience. She was not long kept in suspense, for, in a few minutes, Floretta came back, and her mistress saw by the first glance at her countenance, that she had something of a painful nature to communicate.

"Tell me, Floretta," she said ; "what was it that my uncle wanted with you ?"

"To desire me to tell you that he intends to visit you in about half an hour, signora," replied Floretta.

"It is no more than I expected," said our heroine, in an agitated voice ; "he will again distract and torture my mind, by picturing to me in the most repulsive characters, his intentions towards me. Alas! alas! he seems to exult in my misery."

"Be firm, my dear lady," remarked Floretta, "for, after all, it may not be so bad as you expect."

"Oh, my heart forebodes the worst ; I feel that my fate is fast approaching to a crisis. There was a time when the presence of my uncle was always a source of the most unfeigned delight to me, but now I cannot behold him without a shudder, for his conduct of late has too fatally convinced me that instead of the affectionate relative I once knew and revered, he is now my bitterest enemy."

"Nay, signora," said her attendant, "your apprehensions are premature; who knows but his highness may have relented, and that he seeks this interview to inform you that he has abandoned his designs?"

"Oh, no," returned our heroine, "I dare not encourage any such a hope. His proud and haughty spirit, I am confident, will never yield to my expostulations and entreaties. All that he has threatened he will perform to the very letter."

"I trust not, signora; however, suffer me to advise you to endeavour to await the result of this interview with all the patience and fortitude you can."

"God knows," ejaculated Melina, "that it is a painful task, and I know not how I shall accomplish it. But did you hear anything of the Count Alberti?"

"Yes, signora," answered Floretta; "from what I could gather from the other domestics, he is still progressing favourably."

"Ah!" sighed our heroine, "there is no hope for me; he will soon recover, and probably a few days only will decide my fate. My God! my God! what will become of me?"

The poor girl wrung her hands in despair as she uttered these words, and Floretta tried, but in vain, to soothe her anguish.

"Would that I had but the means in my power," she at length said, in a fearful voice, and with an expression of countenance which fully showed the sate of frenzy and despair to which her feelings were worked up—"I would at once end this misery, disappoint the hopes of my cruel persecutors, and terminate an existence which has now become hateful to me."

"Signora Melina," said Floretta, with a look of horror, "what fearful words are those to which you have just now given utterance? You cannot know what you say; your mind must be distracted."

"My mind distracted!" repeated our heroine, "and can it be wondered at if it be, after all the unparalleled trials to which I have been subject?—I am but woman, and can it be expected that I can endure every misery without complaining?—Oh, Floretta, may you never have to undergo the cruel wrongs which I have experienced."

"Thank you, signora," replied Floretta; "but again I would humbly endeavour to impress upon your mind, the awful nature of the ideas which your despair has suggested to your mind, and to struggle against them. As I before said, (and indeed the manners of the Prince Bianchi fully authorise me in holding out the hope), I cannot help imagining that this interview between yourself and your uncle, Signora Melina, will be productive of the most favourable results to yourself. His highness must be indeed hard of heart if he can turn a deaf ear entirely to your repeated supplications."

Melina was about to make a reply, when there was a knock at the room door, and turning ghastly pale, and trembling violently, she ejaculated—

"He is here!—oh, God, support me!"

As she thus spoke, she threw herself on the neck of Floretta, and hid her face in her bosom. The door was opened, and, as had been expected, the Prince Bianchi entered the room. He gazed for a moment or two at the evident agitation of his beauteous niece, and it might have been supposed by any superficial observer, who was not thoroughly acquainted with his character, if they judged from the expression of his features on the occasion, that he felt some remorse for his past conduct; but that delusion would have been quickly dispelled by the harsh and peremptory tones in which he addressed himself to her attendant.

"Retire from the room, girl, and wait till you are again summoned," he said.

Poor Melina's heart sunk within her, but Floretta having affectionately pressed her hand and whispered to her to be firm and of good cheer, gently disengaged herself from her embrace, and curtseying to the prince, retired from the apartment. Melina was so overpowered by the mingled feelings that struggled within her breast, that she was compelled to lean against the back of a chair with one hand, to support herself, while with the other she covered her eyes that were overflowing with tears, and awaited in a state of the most agonising suspense to hear the purport of her uncle's visit. She had not to wait long.

"Melina," said the prince, "it is quite time that you divested yourself of this nonsense, and learnt that disobedience to my fixed determination can avail you nothing whatever, but, on the contrary, that any further opposition to my will and authority will only be the means of bringing on your head my everlasting wrath, and expose you to such miseries as you can now form but a limited conception of. Come, girl, arouse yourself to reason, if it has not entirely deserted you; and meet with the firmness and resignation of a woman the fate which is inevitable—which is unavoidable!"

"My lord," replied our heroine, hastily dashing the tears from her eyes, and looking up proudly at her stern and inexorable uncle, "I am a woman in all that is pure, just, and reasonable; so much the woman, that my heart rejects with scorn and indignation those base, those degrading overtures, that, if I were to accept them, would not only render me unwor-

...thy of the name, but a thing of scorn to the rest of my sex, a being hateful to myself, and repulsive to others. Ask me to do that which is in strict accordance with virtue, honour, and duty, and you will find no one more ready to submit to your will than the humble and unfortunate girl who has been thrown under your protection; but, by Heaven, I will continue to resist with all the courage and energy that nature has endowed me with, while life remains, that oppressive coercion of my feelings which is calculated to bring upon me shame and dishonour."

The Prince Bianchi was completely astounded by the heroic firmness of Melina, for which he had been so little prepared, and for a second or two gazed upon her in astonishment, and without being able to give utterance to a word.

"Girl," he said at length, "know you to whom you address this language?"

"Yes, my lord!" replied the damsel, in the same accents as those which she had spoken before; "to the Prince Bianchi, whom I was once entitled to call uncle, guardian, parent, but who has painfully taught me since, that I was labouring under a delusion, and that I have no claims upon his affections, his consideration, or forbearance. Oh, my lord! I again humbly, but earnestly and emphatically, urge upon you to consider what it is you would do;—you would, to gratify some private feeling which I cannot fathom, sacrifice me to a man who is notorious as one of the most abandoned of his sex; you would blight at one fell swoop, all my fondest hopes, and consign me to a fate so revolting, that my very blood chills with horror at the thought, and a lingering death of the most excruciating agony would be bliss in comparison with it. Ask yourself, my lord, put it to your reason, to the best feelings of your nature, whether this is the treatment that should be bestowed upon a poor unoffending girl by her only relative?"

The Prince Bianchi was still more confused by the forcible observations of his fair niece, and for a few minutes he walked backwards and forwards across her room, muttering incoherent observations to himself.

"Melina," he at length said; "all these ridiculous arguments you have adduced before, and they are only a waste of time and words. You are prejudiced against the character of the noble Count Alberti, because, forsooth, he has been guilty of a few youthful indiscretions, and——"

"My lord," interrupted Melina, with a look of astonishment and disgust, "and can you in your conscience treat the destruction of female innocence so lightly as to give the crime the mild title of a youthful indiscretion? Is systematic villany of the blackest dye worthy of no more severe a name?—Oh, my lord, pardon me, but I blush for you. The man who would thus betray and abandon innocent, unsuspecting, confiding woman, is worse than the open assassin."

"Girl! girl!" ejaculated the Prince Bianchi, in a state of the greatest excitement, and his lips quivering; "dare you apply such epithets to me?"

"To you, my uncle?" said the damsel, with a look of the most unfeigned astonishment.

"Ay," returned Bianchi, in a hoarse voice 'who told you that I——But, bah!—I do orget myself, and should be ashamed to be thus bearded by a froward, obstinate, and silly girl. Melina, I pardon the Count Alberti for the little peccadillo which took place between him and Olympia, (I suppose it is that to which you allude,) for I know him to be truly repentant, and that he possesses other virtues which entitles him to your most unlimited regard; he has borne patiently with all your insults, and endured much trouble and pain for your sake; but I will suffer no more of it. My resolution remains as firm as ever it was;—I have selected him for your husband, and such he shall become, or my name is not the Prince Bianchi."

"Be it so, my lord," said Melina, solemnly and firmly; "then my fate be upon your head, for you have sealed it."

"What mean you?" demanded the prince, in a tremulous voice.

"That you have consigned me to death."

"To death!"

"Yes," returned our heroine, "for never will I continue to live as the wife of a man I so thoroughly despise and detest as the Count Alberti. Mark my words, my lord, and rest assured that they shall be fulfilled."

"Pshaw!" ejaculated Bianchi, conquering his emotion in the best way he could, "this is mere idle talk."

"Nay, my lord, deem it not so, for, as there is a just God in Heaven who judges all our actions, you will find that it is not so."

"Ridiculous, girl; think you I am to be moved from my purpose by any such threats as these?"

"You may not be so, but you will repent the cruel obstinacy with which you have pursued me when it is too late. Hear me, great Heaven, while I swear——"

"Forbear, girl!" interrupted the prince, hastily, and grasping her arm, "take no irreverant oaths; but rather yield that to duty which obstinacy and madness would induce you to withhold. I see plainly that you still cherish your ill-placed, and unsanctioned love for the presumptuous beggar, Clairville."

"I do," replied our heroine; "his image is enshrined still more firmly in my heart from the opposition I have experienced, and the unmerited wrongs he has received; and I glory in, I feel proud of the feeling. While this heart shall continue to beat, Florio, the much injured Florio, is its lord and master, and no other will it acknowledge."

"Melina," exclaimed her uncle, passionately; "are you determined to excite my utmost wrath?"

"If a candid acknowledgment of the state of my feelings, be to do so, my lord," answered the damsel, in the same firm accents, "why then I am ready to take the consequences. You have demanded the truth from me, and I have given it to you. To Florio Clairville my very soul is devoted, and my latest breath shall be offered up in prayers and blessings for him."

"By the mass!" ejaculated Bianchi, pacing the room backwards and forwards with disordered footsteps, and frowning dreadfully; "this is too much for human patience to endure. But why should I agitate myself thus?—You may love Clairville, girl, but he can never, he shall never be yours. Sooner would I see you perish at my feet than you should both of you thus triumph. But I waste time; no doubt you are anxious to know what made me seek this interview with you."

"Oh, yes, yes," returned Melina, eagerly; "what fresh misery have you in store for me?"

"I merely came to inform you," answered the Prince Bianchi, coolly, "that, to-morrow night you will, accompanied by your maid, Floretta, leave this villa."

"Leave this villa?" repeated our heroine, with a look of astonishment and agitation.

"Yes," said her uncle; "to-morrow night; so you may as well, if you think proper, prepare yourself for the journey."

"Oh, what is the motive for this arrangement?—Whither are you about to remove me?"

"That you will know when you arrive at the place of your destination," replied the prince, "but, if it will afford you any gratification to know, I can inform you that you are going where it is not likely that the brigand chief or any of your friends can discover you."

"My God!" cried the distracted girl, "what unprovoked cruelty is this? Oh, my uncle, if you have still any feeling for me left within your breast, you will abandon the unnatural designs you seem too evidently to have formed against my peace, and——"

"You have heard my determination, girl," interrupted the Prince Bianchi, sternly; "and, perhaps, it is needless to inform you that it is useless to appeal against my decision. The Count Alberti is fast approaching towards convalescence, and then you must be prepared to receive him at your new residence as your husband, for I swear that no sooner shall he have recovered than he shall lead you to the altar, let the after consequences be whatever they may."

"Alas! alas!" sobbed our heroine, wringing he fair hands in an indescribable agony of feeling; "is there no hope for me? Am I to be thus brutally sacrificed? My lord, by all your future hopes I, on my knees, implore you to relent, and not to recklessly consign me to a fate which freezes the very life-blood within my veins at the thought."

"Girl," replied her uncle, harshly, "I have before told you that I am not to be moved from my purpose. I will not suffer my authority to be called into question; so I once more tell you to prepare yourself, for to-morrow, at midnight, you quit this villa. It shows sufficient consideration on my part that I suffer your maid to accompany you. Adieu, I have nothing more to say to you."

"But one word, my lord," supplicated our heroine, in earnest tones.

"Enough," replied the prince, "you have heard my decision, and must abide by it."

With these words he quitted the room, and left the poor girl to her own distracting reflections. She sunk in a chair, and burying her face in her hands, she burst into a paroxysm of hysterical sobs, and in this condition the faithful and affectionate Floretta found her on her return. She advanced towards her, and tenderly taking her hand, said—

"My dear mistress, what has happened to agitate you thus?"

"Oh, Floretta," sighed our heroine, looking up in the countenance of her attendant with a most melancholy expression, "I have heard that which has completed my despair, and convinces me that I am lost for ever."

"Oh, signora," observed the sympathising Floretta, "say not so, I beg of you."

"Alas! I speak but the fatal truth, as you will find when a few hours only have elapsed."

"What mean you, signora?"

"To-morrow at midnight I am to be removed from the villa."

"Removed from the villa? Impossible!"

"Alas! it is too true."

"You astonish me, signora," said Floretta.

"Such is the determination of the Prince Bianchi," returned Melina.

"But whither are you to be conveyed?"

"That I knew not."

"And are you to go alone?" asked her attendant, eagerly.

"No," replied our heroine, "you are to accompany me, my faithful Floretta."

"Oh, that is well," said Floretta; "then do not, my dear lady, give way entirely to despair, since we are not to be separated."

"Alas!" ejaculated her mistress; "what hope is there for me?"

"What can be the motives of his highness for adopting this course?"

"He took no pains to conceal them from me," answered Melina. "It is that I shall be concealed where no one who migh be disposed to interfere in my behalf, shall discover me, until the hated and unnatural union with the Count Alberti shall be accomplished."

"And is indeed the cruel determination of the Prince Bianchi still unshaken?" said Floretta.

"It is," replied Melina; "nothing whatever can move him from it; and there is no alternative left to me but to make up my mind to the worst. Oh, Floretta, when you shall hear the particulars of this interview, you will be able to judge of my feelings."

"If it will not cause you too much pain, my dear mistress," said her companion, "let me hear them."

Signora Melina paused for a minute or two to conquer her emotions, and then complied with Floretta's request, the latter listening to her with the deepest attention and the most heartfelt sympathy.

"And now, Floretta," said our heroine, when she had concluded; "what think you of my situation? Are not my prospects most dismal and cheerless?"

"They are indeed, signora," answered her attendant; "who could have thought that the Prince Bianchi could ever have been so inexorable and cruel?"

"Alas, no," returned her mistress; "oh, what a fearful change have a few short months only wrought in his character."

"But still, lady," remarked Floretta, "I cannot make up my mind to believe that the prince will persist in consigning you to the arms of such a man as the Count Alberti."

"Oh, it would be madness to entertain any hopes to the contrary," returned Melina; "you have heard what he has said, and after his harsh and unnatural behaviour to me, what else can I expect but that he will fulfil his threats to the very letter? My brain is bewildered, and I shall go distracted at the thought."

"Courage, signora," said Floretta, "for something may yet occur before the recovery of the Count Alberti, to frustrate their designs."

"I have too long sought to encourage such ideas," replied our heroine "but to no purpose. My fate is sealed, and there are no means of avoiding it. All that I hope is, that I may perish before the time can arrive for the celebration of a union so hateful to me, and which must consign me to the most insupportable and unmitigated misery."

"It grieves me to the heart, signora," said Floretta, "to hear you talk in this melancholy strain; I trust that you will live for many, many years yet, my dear mistress, to experience every happiness which can be lavished upon mortal being, and which your innumerable virtues so richly merit."

"I know well your kind wishes towards me, my faithful Floretta," remarked the Signora Melina; "for have I not from childhood experienced them? But it is useless to seek to flatter me with false hopes; I must be blind indeed could I not read the destiny which is in store for me. Oh, when I look back upon the happy and tranquil past, and compare it with the terrible present, how does it harrow up my feelings. Alas! why did I not die, ere I was awakened from that blissful dream?"

"Such days of bliss will return to you again, my lady, I feel convinced that they will," said Floretta. "But whither can the Prince Bianchi intend to remove us?"

"I am unable to form the least conjecture," said our heroine; "and, as I have told you, he refused to give me any information on the subject. It will be seen from this determination, how well he has arranged his plans, and how perfectly useless it would be for the brigand chief to attempt to frustrate them."

"I think not that, signora," replied her attendant, "for the skill and discernment of Massaroni in such matters, are too well known. Depend upon it, as soon as he hears of our removal from here, (which I dare say he will shortly do, for doubtless he has his spies in the neighbourhood) he will lose not a moment in endeavouring to discover you."

"Again I say that I consider it a fruitless task," observed Melina, "and I wish him not to undertake it."

"What, my dear lady," said Floretta, "not when you consider the desperate situation in which you are placed? Surely you would be justified in availing yourself of any means of escaping from the fate with which you are threatened; and, under the protection of Massaroni and Signor Clairville, you would be safe, until the Prince Bianchi should have seen the justice and necessity of abandoning his cruel designs, and making you all the reparation in his power for the misery he has caused you."

"Oh, no," returned our heroine, "nothing, I am satisfied, will induce him to forfeit the promise he has made to the Count Alberti."

"But how could he help himself, signora," asked Floretta, "when you had escaped from him?"

"He would speedily devise some means of regaining me," answered her mistress, "and would not fail to wreak his most deadly vengeance on the head of Massaroni and all those who had had any hand in rescuing me."

"You form but a poor estimate of the power of the brigand chief, signora," observed Floretto, "if you imagine that he is to be so easily defeated. In his mountain fastnesses he is invulnerable, as many who have been bold enough to attack him have found to their cost."

"Oh, Floretta," ejaculated Melina, "I shudder at the thought of the dreadful consequences that would probably ensue should Massaroni get me in his power. Could I ever forgive myself if I were the cause of bloodshed?—perhaps the blood of the Prince Bianchi. No—no. I cannot entertain a wish that the brigand chief may attempt to rescue me;—I will place my fate in the hands of Providence, and endeavour calmly and patiently to await the issue."

"Well said, signora," returned Floretta, "and that All-merciful Providence will most assuredly watch over your safety, and frustrate the designs of those from whom you have already experienced so many injuries. To-morrow night, did your uncle say, that you were to be removed?"

"Yes," answered our heroine, "and he will not fail to keep his word. Alas! where can be the place of my destination? I tremble as the time approaches."

"Oh, fear not, my lady," said Floretta; "for the Prince Bianchi will surely not place any more restrictions upon your comfort than he thinks absolutely necessary; besides, shall I not be with you?"

"Oh, yes," returned Melina, "that assurance affords my mind some relief, for had I been placed under the care of strangers, who could not enter into or sympathise with my feelings, I must indeed have given myself up entirely to despair; but in your friendly advice I may at least find some degree of consolation. But how it grieves me to think, Floretta, that you should likewise be exposed to the gloom and misery of my sad and monotonous life."

"Oh, signora, I pray you do not let that trouble you for a moment, for think you that I could be happy if I were separated from you?—Oh, no, I have been your constant companion for so many years, that, pardon me for the liberty, I look upon you with the same feelings of affection as if you were my own sister."

"My kind, my faithful Floretta," ejaculated her mistress, throwing herself into her arms, "how can I ever find words to express my gratitude to you for this warm, and I know, sincere expression of your feelings towards me? May Heaven reward you as your transcendent merits deserve."

"You overwhelm me, signora," returned the kind-hearted attendant, "with the encomiums you bestow upon my humble merits. I should, indeed, be unworthy of so excellent a mistress could I act differently to what I endeavour to do. But try to banish all gloomy thoughts at present from your mind, and to look forward with confidence for the best. The patience and resignation with which you have borne the troubles that have been mercilessly heaped upon you will not go unrewarded; and I firmly believe that the time is not far distant when the Prince Bianchi will be brought to a due sense of the injuries he has inflicted upon you, and will be only too happy to make you all the atonement he can."

"God grant that it may be as you predict, my good girl," replied Signora Melina; "oh, how willing and happy should I be to forget the past, and never by a single word to offer the least reproach towards my at present misguided uncle."

"Oh, no, I am fully satisfied that you would not, signora," returned her attendant; "but that on the contrary, you would only feel too happy and grateful to find such a desirable and fortunate a change come over him."

"You judge truly of my feelings, Floretta," said our heroine; "but, alas! I have too much to fear that there is no such happiness in store for me."

"Do not say so, my dear mistress, for indeed there is yet hope for you."

"Oh, no," returned Melina; "it is too late; I feel convinced in my own mind that it is; the prince, my uncle, has proceeded too far to think now of retracing his steps. I ought to rest fully assured of that after what he has so repeatedly said to me. My removal from the villa is a proof of his determination to carry his designs into effect to the very letter. But it is useless to murmur and repine; I must endeavour to make up my mind to the worst. To the mercy and protection of the Almighty I resign myself, and will seek to meet whatever fate may be in store for me with fortitude."

"And depend upon it, signora," remarked Floretta, "that that all-merciful power to whom you have appealed, will not desert you in the hour of need. As for your removal from the villa, I view it not in so serious a light as you seem to do. I do not see that the change can make much difference to you."

"Probably not," replied her mistress; "for here my unfortunate case is as hopeless as it can possibly be. Unless Providence in its unbounded mercy should interfere to save me, in a very few days I shall be at rest for ever."

"Heaven forbid!"

"Oh! Floretta, it is a terrible thing to think of, and my heart sinks within me as I dwell upon it; but it is useless for me to seek to encourage the least ray of comfort; all the bright prospects which my imagination presented in my early days are now annihilated, and whichever way I turn my eyes, gaunt despair and misery frown upon me. And what will be the sufferings, the fate of him to whom my soul is so fondly devoted, when he knows that I am lost to him for ever?—Where can he then look for happiness and consolation? He cannot expect, neither would his proud and noble spirit accept to be dependant on the bounty of Massaroni for ever; and what will become of him, since the enmity of the prince and Count Alberti have ruined his prospects in this world?"

"Surely the Prince Bianchi will not continue to pursue him with the same vindictive feelings that he now entertains towards him?" said Floretta.

"Oh, yes," answered Melina; the ardent passion that he knows we both entertain to-

ZITELLA RELATING HER LIFE.

wards each other, has excited in his breast a feeling of hatred towards the unfortunate Florio, which nothing, I am convinced, can conquer. He will now brand him with the name of robber, since he has so long resided among the brigands; and, although Heaven knows that I

am most heartily grateful for his preservation from his enemies, it is that which makes me regret that he should not have been indebted for protection to any one else rather than Allesandro Massaroni."

"Indeed, signora," remarked Floretta, "I

cannot help thinking that your apprehensions upon that point are too keenly perceptible. Who dare malign the character of Signor Clairville thus? My word for it, that the time will come, and that perhaps before long, when he will be restored to society, and will be enabled to set all the malice of his enemies at defiance."

"Alas?" sighed our heroine, "and what consolation, think you, he can ever find—what happiness can he ever again experience, when he knows that I am not only entirely lost to him, but that I am likewise sacrificed to a fate, the bare contemplation of which is so revolting that it freezes the very blood in my veins?—Oh, Floretta, with my fate, his will most surely be sealed, and it is that thought which, if possible, tortures me more than all. But let me, oh, let me endeavour to cease to think, or I shall go mad!"

Floretta made no reply, and they remained silent for some time. In this sad and melancholy manner the hours wore tediously away, and at a late hour of the night, Melina sought her couch—the last night, probably, that she would ever again sleep in that villa, which had been the principal place of her abode from the earliest days of childhood, and to which she was, consequently, naturally so much attached. In but a very few short hours, where would she be? To what tenfold miseries might she not be exposed? These dismal thoughts continued to occupy her mind for some time after she had rested her head upon her pillow; and it was not till the hour of two had tolled from the solemn deep-toned bell of St. Peter's, that she could compose herself to sleep; and then her busy imagination was disturbed by the most torturing dreams.

The Prince Bianchi, on leaving his fair and gentle niece, hastened to the chamber of the Count Alberti, whom he was gratified to find much better, and was most anxiously waiting to see him. On his entrance, he raised himself up in the bed, and extended his hand towards him with a look of eagerness.

"Now, my lord," he said, anxiously, "have you seen the Signora Melina, and made her acquainted with your intentions?"

"I have," answered Bianchi.

"Then she is fully prepared for what is so shortly to take place?" said Alberti.

"She was apprised of what I intend to do, count," replied the Prince Bianchi; "what she is prepared to do, is a matter for her own serious consideration. You know the compact that has been entered into between us; I can also believe that you will place every reliance upon me for fulfilling that compact to the very letter. But I am glad to see you looking so much better than when I visited you last. You——"

"Yes—yes," interrupted the Count Alberti hastily and impatiently; "but my fair yet scornful betrothed, how did she receive the announcement? Nay, it is useless for me to put such a question, when I know the feelings of abhorrence with which she views me. I presume she lavished, as usual, plenty of invectives on my head, rated me as a villain of the blackest dye, and, in fact, remains in the same state of feeling which she has ever evinced towards me, namely, that of the most implacable, the most unconquerable and determined detestation?"

"You irritate yourself too much, my lord," replied Bianchi, "by allowing such thoughts to hold possession of your mind. Melina, it is true, possesses a proud and stubborn spirit; but, mark my words, it is yet to be subdued, and if you exert yourself to exercise the powers and the eloquence which you possess, you will be able triumphantly to accomplish the object we have both so dear at heart."

"Not while Clairville lives, and her soul's most ardent affections are devoted to him," replied Alberti.

"Pshaw! count," said the prince, hastily, "let not that disturb your mind. Florio Clairville is but a poor helpless, friendless insect, who——"

"Not while he is aided by the brigand chief, and supported by the knowledge that he possesses the undivided affections of your beauteous niece, my lord," interrupted the Count Alberti; "while assured of that, he is clothed in a suit of mail that can resist all the difficulties and obstructions which we may place in his path to prevent the realization of his hopes. I say again, your highness, while the presumptuous beggar, Florio Clairville, still continues to exist, and especially while he has such friends as the brigand chief, we have much to fear."

"Nothing whatever," replied Bianchi, "when a few days only will make Melina your bride, count."

"Ah! my lord," returned the Count Alberti, still doubtfully, "I know the cunning, stratagem, and facilities of Allesandro Massaroni too well not to apprehend that, notwithstanding all the precautions you have made use of, he will quickly discover the place where you have confined Melina, and at all hazards attempt her rescue."

"Nonsense, my lord, banish such ideas from your mind."

"I cannot."

"And why not?" demanded the Prince Bianchi.

"Because," answered Alberti, "there is too much, in my opinion, to authorise them."

"Ridiculous!" said Bianchi, impatiently, "I wonder that you can encourage such preposterous thoughts, and can only attribute them to the weakness consequent upon your recent illness. Even surrounded as she is with present difficulties, and threatened with a fate which she avows to be so obnoxious to her feelings, think you that the proud spirit of my niece, Signora Melina, would ever permit her to accept of the aid and protection of such a desperate robber and rascal as Massaroni?"

"I knew not," replied the count.

"Why, her conduct on the night when the brigand chief made the attack on us in the chapel of the villa, ought to have satisfied you that she would not," remarked the Prince Bianchi.

"I still have my doubts, and cannot help entertaining them. You say that this place to which you are about to convey your fair niece, is unknown to your domestics?"

"It is."

"And are you certain that the fellow Guiseppe, who has abandoned your service, and there can be little doubt has joined the band of Massaroni, is not acquainted with it?"

"Ah!" replied Bianchi, "there certainly may be something in that; that idea never occurred to me. The villain! But still it may not for some time occur to him that such is the place to which I have conveyed Melina, and in the meanwhile she will in all probability have become your wife, and the interference of the brigand chief, if he should be bold enough to make any such attempt, would then be useless."

"Goaded on by the implacable feeling of hatred and revenge, which he entertains towards us, depend upon it he would do so," observed Alberti.

"And let him make the attempt," said Bianchi, "he would meet with such a reception as, I dare say, he little now calculates upon. Nay, my lord, the apprehensions which you suffer to annoy and harass your mind so much, depend upon it, are perfectly groundless. Let the fellow come; we will be prepared to meet him at every point, and by doing so, he will but only rush upon his more immediate destruction. By the saints! think you that we are always to be defeated and held at defiance by this reckless and daring marauder?"

"Certainly," replied the Count Alberti, "there must be a remarkable change in the fortunes that have hitherto attended the career of Allesandro Massaroni, if he should thus fall into the power of his enemies. No, your highness, after all that I have experienced of him, I can indeed entertain no such hopes. Even at this moment, extravagant as the idea may appear to be, it is not at all improbable that he is thoroughly acquainted with all the designs we have in contemplation, and will thus be enabled to arrange his plans to defeat us, accordingly."

"What absurdity is this," said the prince, impatiently.

"Indeed it is not so; Massaroni has his spies located in every quarter, when he has any particular point to achieve, and indeed there is no knowing what secret means of information he has."

"You suffer your extravagant apprehensions to mislead you, my lord."

"Indeed I do not," answered Alberti; "we have had daily proofs for many years, that they are not without foundation. The brigand chief has all the humbler classes of the community on his side, for he is to them one of their best benefactors and friends, and is it then to be marvelled at that he should, through their means, be enabled to obtain so much important information, unsuspected as they are sure to be in the means that they adopt to obtain it?"

"The daring scoundrel!" said the Prince Bianchi, biting his lips, "would to Heaven that he and his rascally band were exterminated."

"Ay, my lord," returned Alberti, "in that wish I need not, I presume, tell you, I most heartily coincide; but I have my doubts, and very strongly, too, as to whether it will be accomplished, at present, at any rate."

"Nay, Alberti; we must not suffer ourselves to give way to despair; accident and stratagem may yet place Massaroni and his desperadoes in our power, sooner than we at present anticipate. However, enough of this just now; let it satisfy you that to-morrow, at midnight, Melina will be removed from hence to a place of security."

"Would that I were well enough to accompany her," said the Count Alberti, "and that the marriage ceremony could at once take place; this tardy recovery tires my patience, and fills my mind with doubts and fears, which it is useless for me to attempt to dissipate."

"But you must endeavour to do so, count; for while you continue to excite yourself in this manner, I say again, your restoration to convalesence must necessarily be procrastinated. Keep yourself as quiet as you can, and I have not the least doubt from all that Signor Giachome tells me, you will be sufficiently recovered to accompany me to the place of Melina's confinement, where the important ceremony you are naturally so anxious should be accomplished, shall be performed without a moment's delay; and when once the husband of her on whom your affections are fixed, what more have you to fear? The brigand chief will then doubtless abandon any designs he may have had in contemplation as futile and chimerical, and even Melina will feel herself constrained to yield that to duty which she would not previously do to love."

"Your observations do indeed inspire me with hope, my lord," said the Count Alberti, after a pause; "I shall await most anxiously the result of to-morrow night."

"And rest assured that the result will be

all that your fondest wishes could anticipate," returned Bianchi.

"And did the Signora Melina receive the announcement of her intended removal from the Villa Rosa, in the same spirit of firmness, determination, and opposition that she has ever evinced?" inquired the Count Alberti.

"She did," replied the prince; "but I am not without hope that we shall yet be enabled to subdue her proud and obdurate spirit, and make her as obedient and submissive as we could wish."

"I trust, your highness," remarked Alberti, "that in these sanguine expectations we may not be doomed to disappointment."

"Oh, there is no fear of that," returned Bianchi; "I flatter myself, that I am too good a judge of the nature of woman to be deceived. But this interview has lasted long enough, and it might be fraught with danger to you, my lord, were it longer protracted. I will leave you for the present, and let me advise you once more to keep up your spirits, for, depend upon it, the hour of our complete triumph is close at hand."

"Your words encourage me, my lord," replied the invalid; "and I will exert myself to the utmost to do and feel as you advise."

"Well spoken, my lord," said the Prince Bianchi, "and in this happy vein I will leave you."

"I shall see you again before long?"

"Oh, yes," answered the prince; "to-morrow night before or after the removal of Melina, at any rate."

"Enough, your highness," said Alberti, pressing his hand; "I am satisfied, I place every confidence in you. Farewell."

"Farewell," responded Bianchi, and he then quitted the chamber.

"So," said the count, when Bianchi had left him; "all the wishes that I have so long entertained bid fair to be shortly consummated, and in spite of the scorn, the opposition, and hatred which the beauteous Melina has ever displayed towards me; notwithstanding all the many, and apparently insurmountable obstacles that have been placed in my way, she must become mine. Oh, what exquisite bliss is there in that assurance! how my heart exults at the thoughts of it! what a glorious triumph will it be for me! How enraged and despairing will it make my beggarly rival, Florio Clairville, and his friend the brigand chief! As for Olympia—ah! there I must admit that I feel some qualms of conscience; that I am not at all satisfied; I should be so completely, were she and her offspring in the grave. But she will not dare to annoy me, and the knowledge that I am the husband of another, and consequently lost to her for ever, will probably break her heart."

Thus could the villain dare to meditate upon the final destruction of the fair and unfortunate being whom he had by his base artifices destroyed, and not one feeling of remorse did he scarcely for an instant suffer to enter within his breast.

After leaving Alberti, the Prince Bianchi entered his study, where, locking himself in to prevent the intrusion or interruption of any one, he remained wrapped in sullen meditation upon the cruel designs which he had formed against the happiness of his fair niece for the rest of the day.

"Yes," he soliloquised, "I have acted wisely and promptly; I should have been weak had I suffered myself to be conquered by her foolish caprices, and obstinate resistance to my will. Had I done so, and encouraged the love that she and the beggar Clairville have presumed to entertain for each other, what inevitable dishonour should I have brought upon my name and rank! The Prince Bianchi, the governor of Rome, the noblest and the wealthiest man in Italy, wed his peerless niece to a poor painter; a mere adventurer! Pshaw! the very idea is preposterous and monstrous!—The Count Alberti is a nobleman of rank, wealth, of personal attractions, and mental accomplishments, and why should the silly girl object to him?—Merely because of his thoughtless and youthful amour with Olympia?—Cospetto!—I have no patience with it! But the business will now soon be brought to a termination, and then all my cares and anxieties, and annoyances will be brought to an end. To-morrow night Melina will be placed in security, far beyond the reach of discovery by those who might think proper, and be bold enough to attempt to befriend her, and then all my doubts and apprehensions will be set at rest. The Count Alberti is fast approaching to convalescence, and then the ceremony shall at once be celebrated, let the future consequences be whatever they may. The Prince Bianchi will prove that he is not to be shaken from the execution of any purpose upon which he may have fixed his mind. Melina will also perceive the futility of her any longer maintaining an obstinate resistance, and though she may not return the love of her husband (which I do not believe that she ever will) she will at least conquer her feelings of prejudice sufficiently to treat him with proper respect and submission. As for Massaroni and Clairville, they must be crushed at all hazards; and, notwithstanding the various successes they have met with, I do not doubt but that desideratum may yet be achieved."

Thus did the Prince Bianchi continue to reflect, and to endeavour to reconcile his cruel and tyrannical proceedings to his own mind throughout the day; but notwithstanding all his efforts, his conscience would at intervals, in the most unmistakable terms, reproach him with doing wrong; and the solemn promise he had made to his sister in her dying moments would rush upon his memory with overwhelming force, and render him doubtful, dissatisfied, and hesitating.

"But," he said, after some minutes of deep reflection, "had she been still alive, would she ever have consented to the union of her daughter with a man of the lowly station and humble pretensions of Florio Clairville, when wealth and nobility were at her command? Would she thus have consented to have brought disgrace upon our proud house?—No, I am satisfied that she could not, and therefore do I maintain that I am only doing my duty, and fulfilling the promise I made, in pursuing the course I have hitherto done, and in remaining firm to my determination, notwithstanding the oppositions, the objections, and the remonstrances of Melina to the contrary. Away, then, with all idle doubts and hesitation; I am but performing the offices of a faithful guardian in doing that which I have done."

Thus he tried to reconcile his proceedings to his conscience; but he found it impossible entirely to do so, and he continued in the same restless and unsettled state of mind throughout the day.

The evening now set in, and being remarkably fine, with the hope of tranquillising his feelings, Bianchi quitted the apartment, and strolled into the beautiful gardens that surrounded the villa. He sauntered backwards and forwards for some time wrapped in deep meditation upon the same important and perplexing subjects as those we have been describing, but at length feeling somewhat fatigued, he seated himself in an alcove upon which the moon shone brilliantly. Still the same torturing thoughts continued to haunt his imagination, and completely resisted all his efforts to escape from them.

"But why is my mind thus disturbed?" he said. "Am I not acting as prudence and justice, and reason dictate? and am I to be intimidated from the execution of my purpose by the ridiculous fancies of an obstinate girl? No, I will not; it would render me contemptible in my own estimation and that of others, were I to be so. And what are the objections which are raised by Melina against the Count Alberti as a husband?—Merely his liason with the girl Olympia, who doubtless threw every temptation in his way, and took advantage of his ardent disposition. Could she, an unknown girl, the humble dependent upon the benevolence of his noble father, ever presume to think that he would so far forget the lofty station to which he was born as to make her his wife?—Pshaw! the very idea is preposterous; I have no patience with it. And if all men were to be despised and persecuted for acts of indiscretion committed in the giddy and thoughtless days of youth, what would become of my fame and reputation?

Ah! Valentia!—Zitella! why do such thoughts continually flash upon my brain, at the very moment that I most need them to be buried in oblivion? Away! away with them! Years should have banished them from my memory altogether."

He was startled from this soliloquy by hearing a melancholy and plaintive voice break upon the stillness of the night, and singing such tones as penetrated to his very soul. He gazed fearfully around him; but he could not perceive any human being from whom the sound could have proceeded, and he was so overpowered by astonishment and awe that he was completely paralyzed to the spot. Could it be imagination only, working upon a guilty conscience? Oh, no, that was impossible! and while he listened in the most breathless state of agitation, he again heard the well-known words of the song which aroused with such overwhelming force all the guilty recollections of the past in his mind.

"Maiden of Florence, oh, listen to me,
  Nor think that I seek thy fond heart to ensnare;
If e'er I deceive thee, accurs'd may I be,
  And my bosom be plunged in the darkest
    despair.

"Maiden of Florence, my soul most reviles
  The wretch who'd the innocent damsel betray;
Maiden of Florence, more bright are thy smiles
  To me, than the radiant orb of the day.

"Maiden of Florence, I liken thine eyes,
  That now with such lustre are beaming on me,
To the stars that so brilliantly shine in the skies,
  And I love them not, dearest, more than I love
    thee.

"Can I deceive thee? Never,—oh, never!
  Let no such thoughts in thy bosom have birth;
May I, if false to thee, curs'd be for ever,
  Wandering hated, despised o'er the earth!"

"Gracious Heaven!" exclaimed the agitated Bianchi, starting to his feet, and the perspiration pouring in torrents from his brow;—"it's her voice!—it vibrates with horror upon my very soul!—But, no, it must be some wild delusion of the brain!—what fearful, what maddening spell is this that is upon me?—Valentia!—Hark! again!"

Once more the solemn tones of the voice of the invisible being smote his ear, and he could plainly distinguish the following words:—

"Traitor to love, deceiver, beware!—
  Heaven's dread wrath is o'er thee impending;
Shame yet awaits thee, confusion, despair,
  And the madness of conscience thy brain shall
    be rending!"

"God! God!" cried the distracted nobleman, "can I endure this?—Fearful monitor, whoever thou art, let me behold thee! appear, I say!"

As he spoke, he tried to move towards the spot from whence the sounds had proceeded but his limbs refused their office, and he stood transfixed as a statue. A brief pause ensued, and the dread silence that reigned around, rendererd doubly awful the solemnity of the moment. Bianchi strained his eyes in the direction from whence the sounds had issued, and, as he did so, he beheld the tall form of a female, attired in long flowing robes of the purest white, in the distance, and advancing with slow, solemn footsteps towards him. She approached to within a few feet of him, and the light of the moon falling full upon her, he beheld a countenance which froze the blood in his veins, and smote his breast with horror.

"Powers of mercy!" he exclaimed, in a hoarse voice; "am I mad?—Do my eyes deceive me?—Can the dead arise again to torture and appal me?—Valentia!—Valentia!"

He stretched forth his arms as he spoke, and tried to move towards her; but every limb was stiffened and powerless, and while he still gazed the form seemed gradually to become more and more indistinct, to fade into thin air, and then disappeared from his sight.

"Spirit of the much wronged Valentia!—Oh, horror!—horror!" he gasped forth, and completely overpowered by the agony of his feelings, he sunk inanimate and insensible on the earth.

When the Prince Bianchi again recovered, he found himself supported in the arms of two of his domestics, whom accident had led to the spot. He gazed wildly and tremblingly around him, and releasing himself from their hold, he exclaimed—

Where is she?—You have not suffered her to escape me?—Where is she, I say?"

"Who, my lord?" said the astonished servants; "we have seen no one but your highness near this spot."

"Liars!" cried Bianchi, fiercely; "but a moment since she confronted me!—I heard the melancholy tones of her voice, and—but, no; it was some base and presumptuous impostor, who has thus sought to work upon my feelings; and you would aid her in her designs!"

"Pardon me, your highness," replied one of the domestics; "but you accuse us wrongfully, indeed you do. We have seen no one in the gardens; the gates are all secured, and have been for some hours; therefore, it is impossible that any one could have succeeded in obtaining admittance without the knowledge of your lordship's servants. Indeed you must have been mistaken."

"Mistaken!" repeated Bianchi, passionately, "presumptuous varlet!—I tell you that I saw her plainly; that I heard the solemn sounds of her voice; and yet you would persuade me that I have lost my senses!—Oh, Valentia! Valentia!"

He covered his face with his hands as he thus spoke, and the convulsive heaving of his bosom showed the agony he was enduring. The domestics gazed at each other bewildered and astonished, but they ventured not to say a word, and the Prince Bianchi suddenly arousing himself, exclaimed—

"But why do I stand here?—Let me to my chamber and to reflection!—And, mark me, fellows, as you value your lives, dare not to mention a word of this to any one! Away with you; and remember my injunctions!"

The servants bowed and obeyed, lost in amazement at the strange conduct and observations of their master.

For a few moments after they had departed, the Prince Bianchi stood transfixed to the spot, with his hands pressed upon his burning and aching temples, and buried in the most agonizing thought.

"God!" he ejaculated at length; "I could not have been deceived!—I was not dreaming! —no! no!—it was no earthly form that my appalled eyes gazed upon; they were no earthly tones which vibrated in mine ears, and bound up every faculty in herror! Am I, then, doomed thus to be haunted by the phantoms of the victims of my guilt? By all my hopes, this is more, much more than I can endure. But why do I remain here?—Let me to my chamber, before any one further can witness my agitation, and reflect calmly, if I can, upon this strange, this awful, and alarming event!"

Having cast one more anxious look around him, and especially in the direction whence the ghastly form had vanished so suddenly from his sight, the Prince Bianchi, in a state of mind we need not take the trouble to attempt to describe, hurried from the spot, and entering the villa, by a private door, so that he might not encounter any one, he made his way to his own apartment, on entering which he threw himself hastily on a seat, and for sometime gave himself up entirely to the agony of his feelings, and the dreadful and torturing thoughts which crowded in such rapid succession upon his distracted brain. A cold tremor came over him; he felt afraid to be alone, and almost feared to look around him lest he should encounter the ghastly form which he imagined he had beheld in the garden. The silence which reigned throughout the villa tended to add to the terror and solemnity of his feelings, and it was utterly in vain that he tried his utmost to rid himself of the powerful emotions that had taken possession of all his faculties. At length he partially aroused himself, and started to his feet.

"Valentia!" he ejaculated, in a hollow voice, "it must have been thy ghastly shade that I beheld, and which uttered those dreadful words of warning to me. Imagination could not have conjured them up; no, no; they are stamped upon my recollection in characters that nothing whatever can erase. God! how my soul quails with horror and the consciousness of guilt when I recall them to my memory! And can I, when I reflect upon the past, deny my guilt? Am I not the base betrayer of two innocent, beauteous, and confiding women? These whom I vowed to love with my latest breath, and to cherish and protect? Years, many years have elasped since those guilty transactions took place, but can I flatter myself with the hope to escape the just retribution of offended Heaven? No—no—it will overtake me, I feel, and that with an overwhelming force that must crush me beneath its influence. Hark! what sound was that? Surely it was the hollow cry of——This trembling! what dreadful spell is upon me, and paralyses all my senses? There again! Oh, how fearful it is to be alone! I shall go mad! What, ho, there! Quick! quick! villains, do you not hear me call you? And dare you disregard and disobey my summons? Within there, I say!"

Thus shouting at the top of his voice, and ringing the bell violently, the frantic nobleman at length sunk exhausted in a seat, and the next moment several of the servants, alarmed by his cries, rushed into the chamber, and found him in such a fearful state that they considered it necessary to summon the attendance of Signor Giachomo immediately.

"The Prince Bianchi taken suddenly ill?" said Alberti, when Signor Giachomo had quitted the chamber; "by Heaven this is most unfortunate, and may retard, if it does not ultimately frustrate our designs. What can be the cause of this? Am I always to be doomed to disappointment? There is something seems to tell me that Melina will yet escape me; and if so where will be the reward for all the trouble, anxiety, and suffering which I have experienced? Curses light on this misfortune! And to happen too, at such a time!"

He continued in this state of excitement and impatience, until Signor Giachomo returned to his chamber, which was not for upwards of an hour after he had been summoned.

"Now, signor," said Alberti, anxiously; "the Prince Bianchi?"

"Do not alarm yourself, my lord," replied the doctor, "he is merely suffering from fright, and I have persuaded him at last to retire to bed."

"Suffering from fright!" repeated the count; "how so?"

"From all that I could gather from him, he is labouring under a delusion," said Signor Giachomo, "and imagines that he has seen the phantom of some one with whom he was connected when alive."

"A phantom!" said the Count Alberti, "and is it possible that the Prince Bianchi can give way to such a childish weakness as

this? I thought him a very different man. But, tell me, is he seriously ill?"

"No—no," answered the doctor, "do not alarm yourself uncessarily; the sickly delusion, will doubtless soon vanish, and by the morning, I daresay, he will be completely recovered and be himself again."

"Do you really think so, signor?"

"That is my opinion," answered Giachomo, "such delusions of the imagination do not usually continue long; a night's rest will, in all probability, restore him."

"But certainly it must have been something very extraordinary to make such a powerful impression upon him," remarked Alberti; "but have you not been enabled to elicit from him any of the particulars?"

"No more than those I have told you, my lord," replied Signor Giachomo; "it is, as I said before, a mere phantasy of the brain, which will soon pass away."

"I trust it will," observed the Count Alberti, "for I have much depending on it, and should not your ideas be realised, the consequences to me would be of the most painful and fatal description."

"You must not excite yourself, my lord," said Signor Giachomo, "or it may retard your own recovery."

"I will attend to your advice, signor," returned the count; "but is the Signora Melina aware of the sudden illness of the Prince Bianchi, her uncle?"

"I believe not," answered the doctor.

"That is well," observed Alberti; "I must request of you not to permit it to reach her ears; the Prince Bianchi would be displeased should it do so."

"It shall not do so if I can help it, my lord," said Giachomo, and he then quitted him, promising to let him know in a short time the state which the Prince Bianchi was in.

Alberti, however, notwithstanding all that the doctor had said, could not help feeling considerable apprehension respecting the prince, and he awaited with the greatest impatience till he should see him again.

"What foolery is this which has taken such a strong hold of the mind of Bianchi, and at such a particular time?" he said. "Imagine that he has beheld a phantom? Pshaw! the idea is so totally absurd that I can scarcely believe he has been childish enough to encourage it. I cannot brook the least delay in the removal of Melina from the villa; and should this alarm have a more serious effect upon the prince, than Signor Giachomo seems to anticipate, our designs may be altogether frustrated. That idea is torturing, and I can scarcely endure it with any degree of patience."

He was interrupted by the return of Signor Giachomo, of whom he eagerly inquired after the health of Bianchi.

"Why, my lord," answered the doctor, "he is quite as well as I expected; he is now wrapped in a comfortable and sound repose, from which when he awakens, he will doubtless have fully recovered from the late fright he has received."

"I am glad to hear you say that, signor," observed Alberti, "it has removed a weight of anxiety from my mind."

The Prince Bianchi slept soundly till the morning, and on awaking, the fears and delusions which had haunted his imagination on the night before were almost wholly banished from his mind, and he was enabled to leave his couch, without suffering any visible effects from the circumstances of the previous evening, and the shock which they had at the time upon his feelings.

"How could I suffer such absurd and idle phantasies to disturb my mind?" he said. "What a weak fool I must have made myself appear in the eyes of every one! and should I, in the delirium which seized upon my senses, have divulged anything—Pshaw! it must have been all imagination; I will endeavour to think no more of it."

Having partaken of the morning repast, and succeeded in composing his feelings, which had lately been so violently agitated, the Prince Bianchi made his way to the chamber of Alberti, whom he had no doubt would be most anxious to behold him, and he found himself sitting up in his bed, and evidently expecting him with much impatience.

"Indeed, your highness," he observed, "it rejoices me to see you again; your sudden and extraordinary illness much alarmed me."

"No doubt of it, my lord," answered Bianchi; "however, it is all over now, and I feel completely restored."

"I am glad to hear it, my lord," said the Count Alberti, "for this is a most important day to us, and should anything have happened to prevent the removal of the Signora Melina from the villa at the time we have fixed, it is not at all unlikely that our plans might have been frustrated altogether."

"Very true, count," coincided Bianchi, "but there is nothing now to fear; Melina shall be conveyed from the villa most assuredly to-night."

"I am satisfied, your highness," said Alberti. "But what was the cause of your sudden alarm?"

"Oh," answered the Prince, "it was merely the effect of a disordered imagination at the moment. I am ashamed of myself for suffering such a childish feeling to gain such influence over me."

"If it will not trouble you too much, my lord," said the count, "I should be glad to hear you relate the particulars."

"Oh, my lord, you would only laugh at me for a superstitious old idiot, and deservedly so."

"Nay, your highness, not so," replied the Count Alberti; "for such feelings will take possession of the strongest of minds at times, and there is no accounting for it. Will you favour me, my lord?"

"Well, well," returned Bianchi, "I do not mind, for I can now talk of it with indifference, though I must confess that it seriously alarmed me at the time."

"Well, my lord," remarked the Count Alberti, "I am glad to see that you have been enabled to conquer the nervous feeling which you say came over you at the time, and to rid yourself of the delusion altogether. Such phantasies of the brain will at times overcome us, spite of all our efforts to the contrary. I —I myself have experienced the truth of what I advance, though afterwards I have laughed in sheer ridicule of my folly. You are then, I say again, fully prepared to carry out all that you have promised me?"

"Most unquestionably so," replied the Prince Bianchi; "what reason have you to doubt me?"

"I do not, your highness," said Alberti; "and I trust you will believe me when I say as much."

"I do, count," returned Bianchi; "I am no child, to be moved from any purpose upon which I may have fixed my mind, by trifles."

"Enough, my lord," said the Count Alberti; "I place every reliance on you. I, too, have had my dreams."

"Dreams?"

"Ay, you will probably smile at me for that which I am about to relate."

"Proceed, Alberti," said the prince, curiously.

"Last night, then," continued the Count Alberti, "I dreamt that all my fondest hopes and wishes were just on the eve of realisation. Methought that I stood at the altar with my fair betrothed: her delicate hand clasped in mine — the priest proceeding, and half through the solemn ceremony; yourself smiling approbation, and everything propitious to my fondest wishes; suddenly a loud peal of thunder shook the sacred edifice to its very foundation; the holy man started back aghast; your beauteous niece for an instant vanished from my sight;—and when I once more seemed to recover my senses, she was triumphantly supported in the arms of Florio Clairville, protected by Allesandro Massaroni's daring band, and your highness and myself stretched bleeding upon the earth, and rendered powerless. I tried to move, but it was useless; adamantine fetters seemed to bind every limb, and I gasped for breath. You also struggled to raise yourself, but could not; our enemies bore the Signora Melina triumphantly away; and, in the imaginary excitement of my feelings, at that moment I awoke."

"'Twas indeed, a strange dream, Alberti," said Bianchi; "but—but after all—is only worthy of a smile. Massaroni and Clairville frustrate our plans, and convey Melina from our power?—Oh, that is impossible!—We have her securely now; at least she will be so when she is removed from the villa; and with all the ingenuity that the brigand chief possesses, and which he so much prides himself upon, it strikes me forcibly that he will be

ZITELLA A CAPTIVE OF THE PRINCE BIANCHI'S.

rather puzzled to discover her future place of concealment, at any rate, till after the ceremony is accomplished: and then it will be too late for himself and Clairville to proceed with any designs they may have had in contemplation. But come, we waste time in even conversing upon such subjects as these. Despair not, my lord; you will shortly be restored to convalescence; and then, all the preparations in the meantime having been made, not the least delay shall take place in the accomplishment of your fondest wishes."

"The observations of your highness," said the Count Alberti, "inspire me with more hope than ever, and I look forward to the realisation of all my fondest wishes with the most unfeigned and rapturous anticipations. Ah, what a treasure is your lovely niece for any man to possess! It were worth a world of trouble and anxiety to obtain her; and as for her present scorn, and the repugnance with which she either does, or affects to view me——"

"Heed it not, my lord," interrupted Bianchi: "trust me, after your marriage, you will be able to subdue it; it will speedily evaporate, and she will become all that your fondest wishes could desire."

"I do, indeed, hope so," returned Alberti; "and it glads me much, I say again, to see you so completely recovered from the delusion which you so lately suffered to take possession of your imagination, and to find that you are determined to fulfil to the very letter, the promises you have so frequently made to me."

"You could expect no less, count, for you should by this time know my character well."

"True, my lord; and believe me, I never for a moment doubted you; but the bliss of possessing Melina appeared to me too great for one of my humble merits, and, consequently, rendered me anxious and fearful."

"Indeed you think too lightly of your merits, my lord," said the Prince Bianchi, in flattering accents;—"had I not have considered you every way worthy of the hand of my niece, you may depend upon it that I should not have encouraged your addresses, or have been indifferent to her resistance."

"Your highness honours me greatly by the flattering opinion you are pleased to entertain of me," replied Alberti, obsequiously. "Then at midnight, the Signora Melina will be removed from the villa?"

"She will."

"Would that I were in a condition to accompany her," said the count.

"Patience, my lord," said Bianchi, "and fear not you will soon be in a condition to follow her."

"I trust I shall," replied Alberti, "if there is any dependance to be placed upon the opinion of Signor Giachomo, and the condition in which I feel myself."

"Oh, fear not," remarked the Prince Bianchi; "depend upon it, all will progress as well as we could wish. But I must now leave you, for I have some business to arrange before the removal to-night, and I have, consequently, no time to lose. Farewell."

"Farewell, my lord," responded Alberti; and the Prince Bianchi then quitted the chamber.

"Yes," soliloquised Alberti, when he was gone, "Melina, with all thy scorn and repugnance, notwithstanding all the opposition you have hitherto offered to my suit, there is not the least chance of your now escaping me. You are securely mine, and that blissful thought sufficiently repays me for all the insults you have heaped upon my head, and the many difficulties and annoyances I have had to encounter in endeavouring to obtain you. Where are now the opposition and fruitless attempts of Clairville and the brigand chief to rescue you?—I may, indeed, laugh them to scorn; and the time, too, shall come, when I may have it in my power to avenge myself for the injuries I have experienced from them. Oh, these thoughts are as balsam to my soul, and I feel myself endowed with fresh courage and resolution. Would to Heaven that I were in a fit condition to accompany Melina to the place of her destination, for I am all impatience until the whole of my wishes are consummated, and I can say with confidence, 'The fair Melina is now my bride, and who dare interpose between me and happiness!'—What bliss do those words convey to my soul! Shall I not be the envy of all who have seen the peerless beauty?—Ah, Alberti! after all the struggles and difficulties you have had to contend against, you are indeed, at least you should now consider yourself, one of the happiest of human beings!"

He was interrupted by the entrance of Signor Giachomo.

"Ah, my worthy friend," said the Count Alberti, taking his hand; "what think you of me now? Do you not consider that I am progressing fast towards recovery?"

"You are going on as favourably as could have been expected, my lord," answered Giachomo; "but all depends upon yourself; should you give way to excitement, you might suffer a relapse, and then, as I have before frequently told you, I would not be answerable for the consequences."

"Yes, yes," said Alberti, impatiently, "I know that full well; but how can I help being excited, overjoyed, when I think of the bliss that is in store for me? How long, think you, is it probable it will be before I shall be in a fit condition to leave my chamber?"

"If no change for the worse takes place, my lord," answered Signor Giachomo, "most likely in a few days."

"Joyful assurance!" ejaculated Alberti.— "Oh, how I thank you for it, Signor Giachomo. By Heaven! if your anticipations are verified, I will heap riches unbounded upon you, and ever afterwards esteem you as my dearest friend."

"Enough, my lord," returned Giachomo; "I am satisfied; and I do not for a moment doubt that if you follow my advice, all that I have stated to you *will* be verified."

"Depend upon it, signor," replied the

count, "that I will act in strict accordance with all that you advise."

Signor Giachomo bowed, and then left him to himself.

Notwithstanding all that the Prince Bianchi had said to Alberti, and the aspect of indifference he had attempted to assume, he could not entirely rid himself of the impression which the extraordinary adventure of the preceding evening had made upon his mind; nor could he persuade himself that he had been labouring under a delusion. Everything appeared too palpable for him to flatter himself with the idea that he had been deceived, and that he was labouring under the effects of a sickly or disordered imagination. Had he have retired to rest, he might have concluded that he had only been labouring under the delusion of some fearful dream. But under all the circumstances, he could not possibly persuade himself otherwise than that it was the phantom of that unfortunate woman whom he had so cruelly injured in her lifetime, and whose troubled spirit was thus permitted to haunt him, and to torture his conscience, with the view of bringing him to repentance, and inducing him to make all the atonement in his power for the many errors he had committed. This thought appalled his very soul, and in spite of all his efforts, it was some time after he had quitted the Count Alberti, ere he could so far conquer his feelings as to become in the least degree composed.

"But, psha!" he ejaculated, after quaffing the contents of a glass of wine; "let me not give way to this childish—this worse than childish weakness—or it will so far unman me as to render me unfit to accomplish the designs I have in contemplation. My mind must have been disordered at the time I imagined I beheld this ghastly vision. The Prince Bianchi is not so foolish or so superstitious as to believe that the spirits of the dead are ever permitted to revisit this earth. That were, indeed, an idea totally unworthy of him. And yet the features so like: and the words of that song!—It could not have been mere imagination!—Bah!—away with the thought! I am surprised and ashamed of myself! Nothing whatever shall move me from the purpose I have in view."

Thus did the Prince Bianchi waver between doubt and fear for some time, and although he endeavoured to the utmost to persuade himself that he had been mistaken, or that it was a trick which had been played off upon him by some of his domestics, he found it utterly impossible to do so entirely. However, by dint of exertion he at last did succeed in somewhat composing his feelings, and he then set about completing his arrangements for the removal of our heroine at midnight.

In the meantime Melina remained in much the same condition as when we last met her, alternately encouraging a ray of hope, and placing her reliance on the merciful interposition of Providence, and then again sinking as suddenly into a state of the most absolute and abject despair. As the hour approached at which she was to be removed from the villa, her anguish of mind, as may be expected, increased, and at last it became almost insupportable, and defied all the efforts of Floretta to compose her.

In spite of the injunctions which the Prince Bianchi had given his servants, Floretta contrived to learn the particulars of the extraordinary and alarming adventure which we have recorded in the previous pages, and the state of excitement into which it had thrown the prince; and at first it inspired her with a hope that it would be the means of delaying her removal from the villa, and that in the meantime something would occur to rescue her from the fate with which she was threatened; but these thoughts were soon dissipated, when she heard that her uncle had recovered from the shock which he had received, and was again in the chamber of the Count Alberti.

"Alas my uncle," she ejaculated, "too much I fear that some heavy crime, committed in former days, presses heavily upon your conscience, or why should such fearful thoughts enter your imagination? Can I then marvel at the cruel severity of your conduct towards me? Can I wonder that you should sanction the hated addresses of such a man as the Count Alberti, when there is too much reason to believe that you have been guilty of the same vices as himself in your youthful days? I see plain enough now that it would be next to madness for me to expect any mercy or forbearance from you, and there is nothing left me but to endeavour to make up my mind to the worst."

"And yet, signora," observed Floretta, "agreeing with all that you have said respecting the prince, your uncle, I can never believe that Providence will desert you or suffer you to fall a victim to the designs which he and the Count Alberti have against you. Something will yet occur, when least expected, to rescue you from your present critical situation; and to restore you to the arms of him you love."

"Ah! Floretta," returned our heroine; "well do I know the goodness of your heart, but how vain is it for you to seek to flatter me with such false hopes! It is now too late to entertain them; my mind is convinced, and I see plain enough that my fate is sealed. Alas! alas! I am indeed a most wretched being."

"Cheer up, signora," said her faithful attendant; "for it is only by fortitude and resolution that you can hope to pass triumphant through this painful trial."

"I feel full well the force and truth of all

you say, Floretta ; but can you wonder at the anguish of my feelings ?''

"Indeed I do not, my dear lady, and I'm sure I need not again assure you how deeply I sympathise with you. But in spite of all that you have said, I cannot banish from my mind the impression which has taken possession of it, namely, that however gloomy and hopeless your prospects at present appear to be, you will yet be saved from that fate of which you naturally entertain such a horror.''

"Alas! alas! useless would it be for me to indulge in such anticipations, which could only end in disappointment, and would, if possible, render my misery the more complete. Had there been any delay in my removal from the villa, there might have been some slight chance of my being rescued from the fate with which I am threatened ; but as it is, I can see none. The prince, you say, has quite recovered from the shock he received last night ?''

"I should imagine he had, signora, by his seeking the presence of the Count Alberti so early this morning,'' answered Floretta.

"That is enough,'' remarked Melina, " it is evident that they are now completing their plans together, and that at the time fixed I shall be removed from this place, and taken Heaven only knows where.''

"Your situation cannot well be worse than it is at present, signora,'' observed Floretta ; "besides, I shall be your companion, and I will doubly exert myself to arouse yourself from this state of despair, and to inspire you with hope.''

"My good girl,'' returned her mistress, "I feel most sincerely your kindness, and only regret that it is in my power to make but such a poor return for it.''

"Pray do not mention it, dear lady ; am I performing more than my duty to one who has ever been to me the best of mistresses ? I should indeed hate and despise myself could I act otherwise. But I know the time will come when I shall see your face once more clothed in the smile of happiness and content, and when you will be able to look back upon the gloomy past as only a troublesome dream, and without one pang of regret. I shall see you again the beloved of your uncle, and Signor Clairville——''

"Oh, hold, Floretta!'' interrupted Melina, "you overwhelm me by the fond and flattering picture you have drawn, and which nature tells me can never be realised. The prince has shut his heart against me for ever ; he loves me no longer, or, it is evident, he could never have made up his mind to sacrifice me to such a man as the Count Alberti ; he will persist in his cruel designs, and poor Florio is lost to me for ever. Oh, that the pride of rank and fortune should thus have such fatal sway in the human breast ! Would that I were the hum-

blest peasant, that I might without fear encourage my Clairville's love! What is rank? what is wealth ? I never prized them, and now they are rendered doubly hateful to me.''

"I can fully appreciate your feelings, signora,'' replied Floretta, "and Heaven knows what heartfelt pleasure it would give me, could I but afford you any relief. But do not droop, —fortune will change, and then all that it has been your lot to suffer will be forgotten.''

"But a few hours,'' sighed Melina, "but a few short hours, and I shall be torn from this place which is endeared to me by the fondest remembrances of my childhood. Alas! where shall I be when the bright sun ushers in another day ?''

"Do not let such a thought agitate your mind, my dear mistress ; the prince will surely not convey you to any place—where any un- necessary restraint is likely to be placed upon your conduct.''

"Is it not enough for me to know that I shall be held a prisoner ?'' said our heroine, "and that the time is fixed when I am to be sacrificed to the detested Count Alberti ?—Is not that thought enough of itself to make me miserable ?''

"Alas!'' replied Floretta ; "it is too true. But there is no knowing what may yet take place in your favour. The Count Alberti may suffer a relapse, and that circumstance would, in all probability, be the means of frustrating your uncles designs.''

"Ah, Floretta !'' sighed her mistress; "how slender—how very slender is such a hope. Even if Alberti were to die, would my prospects be much better ? for has not my uncle threatened me if such should happen, that he would compel me to become the wife of some other man of his own selecting, and who would be equally abhorrent to my feelings.''

"That threat must have been uttered in a moment of passion, signora,'' said our heroine, "for his highness must surely be lost to all sense of feeling or humanity if ever he could be guilty of so unnatural a deed.''

"The Prince Bianchi,'' returned Melina, "as I too well know from woful experience, is not accustomed to utter threats which he is not prepared and determined to perform ; and in that respect I am confident that he would not fail to keep his word. Floretta, it is in vain for me to think differently, or as you suggest, and in whatever direction I turn my eyes, I see nothing but misery before me.''

"What shall I say ? how endeavour to con- sole you, my dear signora ?'' said Floretta.

"It is a fruitless task, my good girl, though I know full well the sincerity of your wishes,'' replied our heroine.

"Pray endeavour to be firm, signora, for if you do not, it will give the Prince Bianchi that advantage over you which he seeks.''

"I will try to be so," answered Melina; "but much, I fear, that I shall fail, and can it be wondered at, when the horrors of my situation are taken into consideration?"

"Most true, signora; but still I beseech you make the effort. Even at the eleventh hour you may prevail upon your uncle to abandon his designs."

"Oh, no; there is not the least chance of that, stern and inflexible as he is," returned her mistress; "have I not again and again supplicated him to no purpose? My tears and remonstrances do but seem to strengthen him in his cruel resolutions."

It was utterly impossible for Floretta to deny the truth of this, and she therefore returned no answer, but suffered her mistress for awhile to indulge in the feelings which agitated her breast.

In this manner the time passed dismally away; hour after hour winged its rapid flight, and at length sombre night approached, and darkness reigned over all around.

"The time approaches," said Melina, as she listened to the clock, which at that moment was striking the hour of ten, "support me Heaven!"

"Place you dependance on that, signora," remarked her companion, "and believe me, you have nothing to fear. Let not the prince see you agitated and despairing, but rather firm and resigned, and he might feel abashed, and yield that to your fortitude, which he would not do to your remonstrances and expostulations."

"I can look for no forbearance from one who has forgotten the solemn promise he made to his only sister in her last moments," replied Melina.

"Then," observed the faithful Floretta, warmly; "pardon me, signora, but, if he can act thus, he must have become insensible to every feeling of shame and honour!"

"And have I not too much reason to believe that he has done so?" demanded her mistress; "reflect upon his conduct; think of the unfeeling observations he has made to me at all our interviews, and then I am certain you must and will be of the same opinion as that which I have expressed."

"'Tis true, signora," answered Floretta, "that his conduct has hitherto given you but little cause to hope; but still one more appeal to his humanity may have the desired effect, and he may take further time to consider the course he is about to pursue."

"I would fain hope so," returned Melina. "but dare not encourage it, so confident do I feel that it would be doomed to be disappointed. Oh, Floretta, the Prince Bianchi, whom from the earliest period of my childhood it has been my constant study to please, he whom I have ever reverenced as a parent, and to whose every

will I have always been so dutiful and submissive, has become insensible to pity, and in place of that affection which I have a right to expect from him, and which I have never, Heaven knows, justly forfeited, seems to triumph in my misery, and turns a deaf ear to all my supplications. What can I expect from a man like this?"

Floretta knew not what reply to make, and Signora Melina throwing herself on a seat by the side of the window, gave herself up to the agonising thoughts which agitated her breast.

The night was particularly dark; there was no moon, and not a star to be seen, and even nature itself seemed to frown despair upon the poor girl. Another hour passed away, and the emotion of Melina became more powerful and insupportable every moment. Floretta again tried her best efforts to raise her spirits, but with little effect, and she at length gave up the task as fruitless, and set about making such little preparations as were necessary for their melancholy journey. Half-past eleven now struck, and it had scarcely died away on the still night air when footsteps were heard ascending the stairs, and Melina started from her seat, and turned pale.

"He comes!" she ejaculated, "he has not wavered in his resolution. Oh, God! what will become of me? Sainted spirit of my mother, watch over and protect me!"

"Be calm, signora;" said Floretta, "and no harm shall yet befal you."

She had scarcely time to give utterance to these words, when there was a knock at the door. Floretta opened it, and the Prince Bianchi entered. Melina averted her face from him, and trembled violently.

"Retire into another room, Floretta," he commanded; "in a few minutes I shall recall you."

Floretta, casting an anxious look towards her unfortunate mistress, obeyed, and Bianchi gazed at his fair niece for a second or two, but was evidently quite unmoved by the agitation of her manner.

"Come, Melina," he said at length; "arouse yourself, the time is come, and those whom I have employed are awaiting to escort you to the place of your destination."

"Oh, my lord!" ejaculated our heroine, looking up imploringly in his face; "is it yet too late to supplicate your mercy and forbearance?"

"What a fruitless waste of time is this, Melina," returned the prince, "have I not frequently before told you what was my determination, and do you flatter yourself with the hope that anything you can now say can dissuade me from my purpose? Are you ready?"

"Whither am I about to be conveyed?" asked Melina, eagerly.

"What matters it for you to know?" returned the prince ;—"let it satisfy you that it is to a place of security, where you are not likely to be discovered by those who might be daring enough, as they have been before, to attempt to rescue you, but where you will be treated with all the respect that is due to your rank, and have every comfort you can require."

"Oh, pity me! Do not thus cruelly tear me from the home of my childhood."

"Nonsense!" replied Bianchi, impatiently. "What is there so melancholy in your case that requires my pity?"

"Oh, God!" cried the damsel, looking reproachfully at him; can this be my uncle who thus unfeelingly addresses me? I can scarce believe the evidence of my ears! Why am I thus torn at the hour of midnight from my home?—what is your purpose with me?"

"I have told you, girl, and have no time to stand parleying here. It should satisfy you that I allow your attendant to accompany you."

"Oh, my lord," ejaculated our heroine; "depend upon it you will have cause to regret this unjust and cruel treatment. Is it thus that you should behave towards the orphan child of your only sister?"

"Hold! Melina!" said the Prince Bianchi with much emotion visible in his countenance, "I will not listen to language such as this!—The carriage which is to convey you away from hence awaits, and those to whose care you will be entrusted, are also ready; so delay not, for my patience is already quite exhausted."

"Alas! alas!" sighed the poor girl; "is there no hope?"

"None whatever," was the stern reply of her uncle.

"Then I am lost!"

"Bah!"

"Oh, this is most cruel!—My lord, once more I venture to implore you to relent, and not to do that which may afterwards cause you so many hours of bitter remorse."

"I have well considered everything," replied Bianchi, "and am fully prepared to abide by all the consequences that may result from my conduct."

"Alas, then!" said his beauteous niece; "I do indeed see that it is useless to appeal to you further. You have resolved to sacrifice me to a fate from the bare contemplation of which my soul recoils with horror."

"A terrible fate, truly!" returned the prince, with an ironical grin, "to make you the wife of a man of rank and fortune, and by whose love any damsel of sense should feel herself honoured."

"He is a villain, my lord, and you know it, though you do not think prudent to acknowledge it," retorted Melina, firmly.

"These are bold words, Melina," observed her uncle; "but I heed them not. Come, the time has arrived;—I can can brook no more delay."

"And must I indeed be dragged forth at this solemn hour?" said our heroine, and looking piteously in his face.

"It matters not," he replied; "you will have those with you who will protect you from every harm."

"And do you not accompany me, my lord?"

"No," answered Bianchi, "but I shall follow you in a few days I dare say, accompanied by your future husband; and I would have you be prepared to give us a proper reception."

"Alas! alas!" groaned Melina, and wringing her hands in despair, "what can I say? how shall I act?"

"As I have commanded you," answered the prince. "You must by this time, Melina, surely see the folly of any resistance to my will, and consequently, yield with submission."

"And can you expect me quietly to yield to a fate so revolting that the bare thoughts of it freezes the blood in my veins with horror?—Oh, my lord, you do but mock my sufferings, and seems to take an unnatural delight in torturing me."

"Enough, girl!" returned the prince, in the same harsh and unfeeling accents; "you tire my patience."

Melina could offer no further observation, for her feelings overpowered her, and her uncle then recalled Floretta into the room, and having ordered her to assist her mistress on with her cloak, said :—

"Follow me down stairs!"

Melina was now again about to speak, but he interrupted her.

"No more, Melina; we have discussed this business enough already, and I know all that you would say. This way."

Our heroine took the arm of her faithful attendant, without uttering another word, and with trembling footsteps, and a heart almost ready to burst, followed her remorseless and inflexible uncle down the stairs into the parlour, from the window of which she could perceive a vehicle waiting, and several men standing near.

"Now Melina," said the prince, after a pause, "I have but to bid you farewell for a short time, and then you must at once commence your journey. Remember my injunctions, and endeavour to conquer the obstinate and unruly feelings you have so long suffered to hold dominion in your breast."

"My lord," ejaculated Melina, in a voice almost choked with sobs; "again in this solemn moment I earnestly supplicate you to reflect upon what it is you are about to do, and to suffer me to remain where I am till—"

"Girl!" interrupted Bianchi, impatiently, "know you what you ask?—Think you I am mad to abandon my designs after having arranged all my plans ?—Once for all I tell you that I am immovable !"

"Then be the consequences upon your head," said the poor girl, solemnly ; "and rest assured that they will be terrible ! The destested Count Alberti shall never become the husband of Melina ! My lord, you are my uncle, you should be my protector ; but since your breast is insensible to pity, I will no longer condescend to sue to you !"

"Be it so," replied Bianchi, sternly ; "these heroics will have not the least effect on me. This way !"

He walked towards the door as he spoke, and Melina, leaning on the arm of Floretta, attempted to follow him, but her feelings overpowered her and she fainted.

"Confusion !" cried the prince, in accents of vexation ;—"this delay !—See to her recovery, girl !"

Floretta obeyed, and Bianchi traversed the room impatiently. In a few minutes our heroine recovered, and she and Floretta then followed Bianchi from the villa, and the steps of the vehicle being let down, he handed them in, closed the door, and without saying another word, he awaited until it departed, and watched its progress until it was completely hidden from his sight by the darkness beyond. He then made his way to the chamber of the Count Alberti, who had been most anxiously waiting to see him.

"Well, my lord," he asked, eagerly, "what success ?"

"All that could be expected," answered the prince ; "Melina is on her journey."

"Ah, that is well," said the count ; "would that I were in a condition to follow her immediately."

"Be not impatient," remarked Bianchi ; "in a few days I have no doubt your wishes will be gratified."

"But how did she appear on leaving the villa ?"

"Why, you may be sure that she was violently agitated ; but now she finds that there is not the least hope for her, no doubt she will endeavour to resign herself to her fate."

"I owe your highness a debt of gratitude for the interest you have taken in promoting my happiness, which I can never repay," said the Count Alberti.

"Nay, my lord," returned the prince, "thanks are superfluous ; we have both an equal interest in what has been done, so there let the matter rest ; before a fortnight has elapsed, I hope to have the honour of presenting to you the hand of my fair niece."

"Blissful assurance !" cried the count ; "it seems to impart new life into me ; but, could I be equally sure that I could succeed in conquering the aversion which Melina entertains towards me, and in inspiring in her breast towards me a sentiment of esteem, if not of love, I should indeed be happy."

"Fear not, my lord," answered Bianchi ; "for it strikes me, notwithstanding the present scornful behaviour of Melina, you will yet be able to accomplish that desideratum."

"I will endeavour to think so," said Alberti ; "and in the thought luxuriate in imagination in the transport that is in store for me."

"Well said," returned Bianchi ; "and, believe me, I am no prophet, or that I am perfectly ignorant of the nature of woman, if you are doomed to be disappointed."

"You say that it will not take more than three hours to accomplish the journey?"

"It will not."

"And one of the men in whose charge she is, will return to the villa as soon as he can to make us acquainted whether or not she arrived safe ?"

"Yes ; but there is no fear of that, for the road they will travel I have never heard to be infested by Massaroni and his band."

"That is fortunate," remarked the count : "for if he were to see the vehicle, he would be sure to attack it in the hope of plunder, and Melina would at once fall into his power."

"Again, I tell you, count," said the prince, "that you have no occasion to entertain any apprehensions of the sort, so let that satisfy you."

"It does, your highness. And none of your domestics witnessed the departure ?"

"No," answered the prince ; "I took good care to pack them all out of the way ; though it would have been of very little consequence had they witnessed the departure, for they would not have dared to excite my wrath by disclosing the fact to any one."

"True," returned Alberti ; "I am quite satisfied, and shall only wait with impatience for the time to arrive when I shall once more behold the lovely being in whom my very soul is rivetted, and to possess whom there is no sacrifice, however great, that I would hesitate to make."

"The time will soon arrive, my lord," observed the Prince Bianchi ; "and I would, therefore, advise you to hold yourself in readiness for it."

"I will do so, your highness may depend," answered Alberti ; "but still, when I think of the reception I am sure to meet with from Melina, I must acknowlege it somewhat dampens the ardour of my hopes."

"Let no such thoughts as these trouble your mind, count," returned Bianchi ; "my word for it, calm reflection will subdue the turbulent spirit she has hitherto displayed, and she will see the necessity of receiving you with more favour than you now anticipate."

"But you have given orders to those in whose care she will be placed at her new residence to treat her with every indulgence and respect, have you not, my lord?" asked Alberti.

"Certainly I have; her security is all that we require."

"True," returned the count; "but I must confess, in spite of all my efforts to the contrary, there is one thing that annoys me greatly."

"And what is that, my lord?"

"Olympia; she and her child still exist; and goaded on and aided by the brigand chief, especially when she finds that the Signora Melina is my wife, and that all her ambitious hopes are consequently annihilated, she will be aroused to a spirit of revenge against me which nothing will be able to conquer until it is gratified."

"Pshaw! my lord, what have you to fear from her? She is too weak and gentle, I do believe, to entertain any such ideas. As for Massaroni, some means must be adopted to secure him, and to crush that power by which the daring rascal has been enabled for so many years to hold all Italy in a state of terror."

"Ay," observed Alberti, "it would be a fortunate thing if we could do so; but I am inclined to think that will be found to be rather a difficult task."

"Well, we must leave that to time and fortune," said Bianchi; "at present we have much more important matters to occupy our mind. But I must leave you, count, the time is late, and I need rest; good night, my lord, and let your dreams be of Melina and future happiness."

"Good night, Excellenza," replied Alberti, "your observations have indeed made me one of the happiest of human beings."

The Prince Bianchi then left him, and he remained for some time so busily wrapped in thought that he was unable to compose his mind to sleep.

CHAPTER XLIV.

THE MIDNIGHT JOURNEY.—THE ANGUISH OF THE SIGNORA MELINA.—ARRIVAL, AND THE RECEPTION.—THE SINGULAR DISCOVERY.—THE MANUSCRIPT.

THE vehicle drove away at a rapid rate, after the men who conducted it had received a few private instructions from the Prince Bianchi, and they were soon far beyond the Villa Rosa, and as they distanced it more and more every minute, the heart of poor Melina sank within her; the most dismal forebodings and apprehensions crossed her mind, and she wrung her hands in despair. It was a considerable time before she was enabled to give vent to the anguish of her feelings in words, and Floretta did not offer to interrupt her, for

she hoped that the indulgence of her own thoughts for a short time might tend to alleviate her anguish, and prepare her to meet with fortitude the many severe trials she had too much reason to fear were yet in store for her.

The night, as we before observed, had been particularly dark and cheerless, but it now cleared up considerably; the moon burst forth from behind the dense clouds which had previously obscured it, and the aspect of nature became gladdened by its silvery beams. The windows of the vehicle being down, our heroine was enabled to distinguish objects clearly; they were travelling along an unfrequented and lonely road, with no signs of a dwelling, or a human being, and Melina, although it could be at no great distance from the villa, had not the slightest recollection of it.

"Oh, beloved home of my childhood, beneath whose venerated roof a beloved mother died," she sighed; "shall I never be permitted to behold you again? Shall I no more ramble among these romantic scenes which are endeared to me by so many fond associations? Oh, uncle—cruel uncle, what have I ever done to merit such treatment as this? Would to God that this hour were my last, for I am now completely tired of my existence."

She covered her face with her hands, and sobbed convulsively.

"For Heaven's sake do not give way to this excessive grief, signora," said Floretta; "God is good, and will watch over your safety; and depend upon it, you will yet be restored to those scenes which are so dear to you."

"But what shall I be then?" ejaculated the unfortunate damsel, with a shudder of horror; "the wife of the villain Alberti; a poor degraded, wretched, broken-hearted being. Floretta, you talk to me of calmness; oh, how fruitless are such words! They sound like the bitterest mockery in mine ears. Is it possible that I can be calm with such dreadful thoughts upon my mind? with such a terrible prospect before me? As well might you try to calm the battling elements when, in their greatest fury, they spread desolation around. But a few days, and I feel convinced that my fate will be sealed, and to entertain the slightest hope of rescue would be madness. Oh, that my heart would break, and thus at once end my misery. Florio, beloved Florio, farewell for ever, for on this earth we shall never meet again."

"Say not so, my dear mistress, the time will come, when——"

"Hold, Floretta, as you value my favour," hastily interrupted our heroine; "give not utterance to the words; think you that I could ever dare to meet the noble and generous-hearted Clairville again, after I had become the bride of so loathed a wretch as Alberti? Think you that I could bear his agony at witnessing my shame and misery? Heaven forbid! I must perish at his feet! And yet that would be a mercy."

"Alas! signora," ejaculated Floretta, "what can I say to console you? God knows how happy I should be could I but impart one

ray of comfort to you under these numerous and trying difficulties!"

"I know it, my faithful girl, my warmly attached friend, whose feelings towards me neither time nor circumstances have had the power to change," said Melina, pressing her

FLORIO CLAIRVILLE.

hand vehemently within her own. "Oh, would that all possessed the same heart as you; how little misery would there then be in this world of ours; how little of guilt would be known. But why should you thus sacrifice all your happiness, and the natural enjoyments of

youth, to one who is able only to make so poor a return for it as myself? Why should you also become a prisoner, and subjected to such painful restrictions?"

"Oh, signora," said Floretta, "I entreat you not to mention any poor sacrifice I am able to make for your sake. Heaven knows how willingly I would do more, if I could. Think you, my dear mistress, that I could ever be happy if I were separated from you? Oh, no! That I am permitted to be with you, and to render you all the assistance in my power, is my greatest consolation; and were I compelled to resign it, I should be one of the most miserable beings in existence."

"I believe you, Floretta," said her mistress, "and would fain express to you my gratitude, but I cannot; God grant that the time may yet come when I shall be able to reward you as your transcendent merits deserve."

"You overwhelm me, signora, by your observations," returned her companion; "my own feelings are more than a sufficient reward for anything I can possibly do to serve you. Come, come, be of good cheer; shake off the gloom that at present weighs down your spirits, and leave the result to the merciful dispensation of an All-Wise Providence!"

"I will try to do so, Floretta," replied the unfortunate Signora Melina, "but alas! how difficult is the task."

"I own it is, my dear lady," said her attendant; "but exert yourself to the utmost, and I am confident you will succeed."

"But whither can they be conveying us?"

"We shall probably not long be kept in ignorance, signora," answered Floretta.

"This is a wild part of the country," said our heroine, "and I have not the least knowledge of it."

"Neither do I remember to have seen it before, my lady," observed Floretta.

"I wish we were at our journey's end," said Melina, "for that would greatly relieve the anxiety which at present oppresses my mind."

They now relapsed into silence for a short time, and watched the cheerless scene as they travelled throught it.

Barren and dismal enough it certainly was, lofty mountains on either side, and scarcely any signs of vegetation. Melina and her attendant could almost imagine to themselves, from the wildness of the aspect of everything around them, that they were the only human beings who had ever intruded upon its solitude; and that thought, if possible, added to the melancholy feelings which, under the circumstances, naturally came over them.

Looking from the window of the vehicle, they now perceived that they were guarded by many more men than they had expected. Although the same persons whom they had seen on their first emerging from the villa were there, in addition to them, there was a large body of the Prince Bianchi's troops, who surrounded the carriage, and followed in the rear, and that display struck an additional terror to the heart of our heroine, which she tried, but found it in vain, to overcome.

"Alas!" she sighed, "I am indeed a prisoner, and every step that we proceed convinces me that I am on the road to misery and destruction. Oh, my uncle, surely this is a refinement upon cruelty, and shows how little of the natural feelings that should operate within your bosom towards me, remain within you."

"Dear signora," returned her companion, "do not suffer such feelings, such sad thoughts to agitate your breast. The troops that you see around us were necessary for your protection, doubtless, to guard against the numerous bands of brigands which probably infest these parts; and, in that respect, the Prince Bianchi, your uncle, has only performed his duty in protecting you from violence and outrage."

"And yet you strenuously espouse the cause of Allesandro Massaroni and his band?" said her mistress.

"True, signora," replied Floretta; "but Massaroni never commits cruel outrages; and from all I have heard of his character, he would despise himself if he could ever be guilty of anything that could cause a pang in the bosom of a female. Would that he and his brave followers were now here."

"And why so, Floretta?"

"Because then, signora, we might calculate upon almost certain deliverance from our present difficulties; and once under his protection, the Prince Bianchi would be ready enough to come to terms of reconciliation. You would no more be annoyed with the hated addresses of the Count Alberti; you would once more behold Signor Clairville, and——"

"Ah!" ejaculated Melina, a sensation of the most unspeakable delight passing through her bosom at the mention of that much-loved name; "dear Florio, what would I not encounter to have the felicity of once more beholding you, and listening to those vows we have so often plighted to one another? But, no, the thought is futile; it were madness to entertain it. We shall never meet again but in Heaven!"

"Say not so, lady," observed Floretta; "encourage more joyous, more sanguine expectations, and depend upon it they will not be doomed to be disappointed. Would that Massaroni and his gallant band would now appear, I say again."

"Oh, no," returned Melina, "not for worlds would I have it, notwithstanding the terrors and the dangers of my present situation. The slaughter that would be almost certain to ensue, fills my mind with horror to reflect upon, and I cannot conquer the repugnance I feel to avail myself of the aid and protection of the brigand chief, and thus appear to give a sanction to what must, after all, be called his nefarious practices."

"Pardon me, signora," said Floretta, "but shall I never be able to banish that erroneous opinion from your mind?—Massaroni, I am certain, from all that I have heard of him, would scorn to use the power he might obtain to any mean or dishonourable purposes; his sole aim and object would be to effect a reconciliation between yourself and your uncle, if possible, and to disappoint the presumptuous hopes of the Count Alberti; with every respect would he treat you whilst under his protection, and his object once obtained, he would feel himself sufficiently rewarded in possessing your gratitude and esteem."

"You certainly espouse the brigand's cause somewhat warmly, Floretta," said our heroine, looking at her with an expression of surprise.

"True, my lady," replied Floretta, "and for no other reason than because I believe from my heart that he is all he has ever been represented to me. Think of the many noble and generous acts he has performed, which forms the romance of all Italy;—'tis true, he is an outlaw and a robber; he plunders from the overstocked purses of the proud and wealthy to contribute to the wants of the necessitous, and many are the forlorn hearts that he has made cheerful: but is his path ever stained with reckless bloodshed?—Does he not exhibit a mercy and forbearance in all his transactions which those placed in a far different station would do well to copy?—Oh, believe me, Allesandro Massaroni, the brigand chief, is a noble-minded man: he was never born to fill the situation he now occupies; and something strikes me that the time will yet come when the mystery that enshrouds his origin will be unravelled — when justice will be rendered him, and he will be restored to that society he was evidently born to ornament."

"Granting you all this, my good Floretta," said our heroine, "but knowing the rigour with which my uncle has ever pursued him, do you not think it probable that he must feel a spirit of revenge and animosity towards him, and having me once in his power, he would avail himself of the opportunity to gratify it?"

"Oh, no, signora," answered her attendant, "I cannot believe Massaroni capable of being guilty of any such conduct. It is justice and forbearance from the Prince Bianchi that he alone seeks; and that once obtained, his highness, depend upon it, will have nothing more to fear from him."

Melina made no reply, but relapsed into thought, still keeping her eyes steadily fixed upon the country they were travelling through, which presented little diversity of aspect; nor did they once encounter a human being, or the least signs of human dwelling. An uneven and difficult road they were now journeying over, and the vehicle could only proceed at a very slow rate, which rendered it doubly tedious, for Melina was most anxious to arrive at the place of her destination, so that she might know the worst. Now they travelled amidst long ranges of stupendous mountains, whose summits seemed hidden in the clouds, and anon they emerged upon a barren waste, which seemed as though it had never been trodden by the foot of man; but all was desolate and drear, and in strict accordance with the feelings that predominated in the bosom of the hapless Melina.

Thus passed away more than a couple of hours, and still their journey was not terminated, and there was no change for the better in the aspect of the country through which they passed, and the patience of our heroine was quite exhausted, whilst the spirits of the poor girl were so much depressed, that Floretta found it a most difficult matter to sustain her.

The moon continued to shine brightly, and everything was as distinct as in the broad light of day; the air was also calm and tranquil—not a sound disturbed the solitude around, save the tramping of the horses hoofs upon which the soldiers rode who followed the vehicle; and Melina seemed so deeply engrossed by her own meditations, that Floretta did not attempt to interrupt her, knowing that she had exhausted all the arguments she had at her command which were at all calculated to console her.

Again they entered upon a dismal way that was bounded on either side by lofty mountains, and the extent of which seemed to be almost interminable; and, as our heroine gazed upon the prospect before her, the melancholy of her feelings gained strength, and she sighed deeply. It seemed as if this were but the prelude to the sad fate that was in store for her, and the hopes which she had sought to encourage were entirely banished from her mind, nor was it in the power of the faithful Floretta to raise her spirits in the least degree; indeed, as we have before said, she was now completely at a loss for argument, and thought, therefore, to remain as silent as possible was, under all the circumstances, the best policy.

Nothing worthy of recording took place during the remainder of the journey, which occupied about four hours; and just as the first blush of dawn appeared in the eastern horizon, they came to in sight of a pretty large villa, which was situated in a lonely, but still rather romantic, spot, not more than a quarter of a mile off, and was backed by the tall mountains of the Apennines in the distance. This they quickly understood, from some observations which they heard pass between one or two of the men who guarded them, was the place of their destination, and Melina's heart beat high, and her whole frame trembled with the agitation of her feelings.

"This, then," she sighed, "is destined to be my future prison, until by the harsh and cruel decree of my uncle, I am made the victim of the odious and guilty Count Alberti! —Oh, heaven grant that before that hated ceremony can take place I may be no more, and thus all my earthly troubles be brought to a close."

"I beseech you, my dear signora," replied Floretta, "do not talk in such a melancholy strain, for it grieves me to hear you. Courage, courage, I say again, and you will yet be able to surmount the difficulties and dangers by which you are at present surrounded."

The Signora Melina shook her head disconsolately, but returned no answer, and at length the vehicle, after passing through a long avenue of stately trees, stopped in front of the building, the exterior of which presented a much more prepossessing aspect than they had anticipated.

Their arrival had evidently been looked forward to, for no sooner had the carriage stopped at the door than it was opened by a hoary-headed and venerable man, of rather benevolent aspect, and the steps of the vehicle being let down, they were assisted to alight, and were conducted through a spacious hall to an elegantly furnished apartment at the end, where a delicate repast was already spread upon the table for them. A middle-aged woman was also in attendance, and in her demeanour showed the utmost respect and deference to our heroine.

"You may retire, my good woman," said Melina, "for the present we would be alone."

The woman curtseyed, and retired accordingly, and our heroine threw herself into a chair, and for a few moments, overpowered by her feelings, she gave vent to a copious flood of tears, which her attendant was glad to see, for she thought it would serve to relieve her mind.

"Here then," she ejaculated, "at last I am placed in my new prison-house, and shut out from every hope of relief. This place is to witness the consummation of my fate, and here, in a few short days, I shall be rendered wretched and degraded for ever!"

"By the merciful interposition of Heaven I trust not, my lady," returned her companion; "short as the time appears to be on which your fate is to be decided, many things may yet occur to prevent the completion of it taking place, and to restore you to that liberty and happiness which you are so well entitled to enjoy."

"Alas!" sighed Melina, "what prospect is there of such a result?—Am I not securely in the power of those whom I have so much reason to dread, and who it is not likely will readily abandon their cruel designs, now that they have proceeded thus far?—Oh, Floretta, what folly would it be for me to give indulgence to any such expectations, which can only end in disappointment, and must thus render my misery the more complete."

"Well, signora," observed Floretta, "for the present, at any rate, let me beg of you to banish such melancholy thoughts from your mind, and to try and await with patience and confidence the result of this adventure. It is evident that here his highness, the Prince Bianchi, has ordered you to be treated with every respect and indulgence, and therefore you have nothing to apprehend upon that score."

"Respect! indulgence!" repeated Melina. "Alas! can they compensate me for the loss of all my hopes?—Can they rid my mind of the certainty of the terrible fate that is in store for me?"

"But at any rate, my lady, they will serve to ameliorate the horrors of confinement. Come, come, pray be tranquil, and the termination of all will not be so fatal as you now apprehend. Partake of some refreshment, and that will serve to revive your spirits and invigorate your mind."

"Ah! no; think you I can eat whilst my feelings are thus excited?" replied our heroine. "I feel a sickly foreboding at my heart which is almost insupportable."

She arose slowly from her seat as she thus spoke, and advanced towards the window of the apartment, and Floretta followed her. The view commanded from this window was of an extensive, wild, but yet romantic description, and served for a short time to divert the thoughts of our heroine from the melancholy subjects that had before engrossed them. It consisted of a vast tract of land, in some parts in a rich state of cultivation, and in others quite barren and cheerless; but as far as the eye could penetrate, there was not the least signs of a human habitation, and although the hour was too early for any person to be abroad, it had all the appearance of a place that was little frequented. The whole was closed in by the lofty Apennines, which imparted an air of solemn grandeur to the scene.

"The prince has well selected the place for the execution of his cruel and unnatural purpose," observed Melina; "here it is not likely that any one can discover me, if even I had those who were willing to render me any assistance, and nothing therefore can happen to counteract his designs."

"Something, however, may happen, signora," replied Floretta, "when you least expect it. But had you no knowledge that his highness possessed this place before?"

"None, whatever," answered her mistress.

"It seems to be rather an ancient building."

"It does; and the prince could not have selected a place better adapted for his purpose. Oh, Florio! how tenfold more terrible would be the anguish of your mind did you but know my present situation."

"I wish from my heart that Massaroni were acquainted with it," remarked Floretta; "for then I am certain he would adopt some means of rescuing you from it without delay."

" Still, Floretta," said our heroine, " you will persist in fixing your hopes upon the brigand chief, notwithstanding you know the objection I have to his interference."

" Pardon me, signora, if I may seem too bold and officious, but I cannot but believe that to Massaroni alone you have reason to look for your deliverance from the dangers by which you are at present surrounded, nor can I see that you have any just cause to object to receive his aid, taking all the circumstances of your situation into consideration. You are justified in resisting the cruel and unnatural persecution to which you are subjected by every means in your power."

Melina was about to make a reply, when she was interrupted by a knock at the door, and the woman whom they had first seen on their entering the house, returned to the apartment.

" I must request you to follow me, signora," she said, civilly, " and I will conduct you to those apartments which are fitted up for the accommodation of yourself and your attendant."

" Have you been in the service of the Prince Bianchi long ?" asked our heroine.

" Many years," answered the woman, " and my parents before me."

" And have always resided here ?"

" Yes, lady."

" And know you the reason that my uncle keeps this place so secret ?"

" Pardon me, signora, but I am not permitted to answer such questions," said the woman. " Will you be pleased to attend me ?"

" Tell me," said our heroine, eagerly, " is there no place of habitation near this house ?"

" Not for more than a league; it is lonely enough to be sure, and it is but seldom that any person is seen near the spot."

" And will the men who brought me hither remain ?"

" Most of them will, I believe, and await the arrival of his highness and the count Alberti, whom I understand, signora, is to be your future husband."

" Alas! alas!" sighed Melina, in accents of despair; " but lead the way, I am ready to attend you. Floretta, my faithful girl, your arm."

Floretta took her arm, and they followed the woman out of the room, and having ascended two or three flights of stairs, they entered a gallery, the walls of which were decorated with ancient paintings by the most eminent masters, and where several doors presented themselves, which seemed to open upon different suites of apartments. The woman stopped before one of these, and applying a key from a bunch which she had brought with her, to the lock, they entered a spacious and elegant apartment, which presented every means of comfort and accommo-

dation, and had evidently been arranged with great care for their reception.

" There are two more rooms beyond this, signora, to which you may have free access," remarked Viola, (which was the name of the woman,) " and in which you will find everything that you can require for yourself and your attendant. As you must be fatigued after your long journey, I would advise you to seek an hour or two's repose, and you need not fear that any one will disturb you."

" Tell me," said our heroine, " where is this house situated ?"

" Why, signora," answered Viola, " as you may perceive near the foot of the Apennine mountains."

" And it is called——"

" The Villa Civetta !" replied Viola.

" And has the Prince Bianchi often visited it ?" asked Melina.

" Not of late years, signora, but there was a time, when——"

" When—what ?" demanded our heroine, eagerly.

" No matter," returned Viola; " pardon me, signora, but I am not permitted to tell all that I know. Good morning; should you require anything, I will attend you immediately on your ringing the bell."

Thus saying, without giving Melina time to interrogate her further, Viola quitted the room, and they heard her lock and bolt the door after her.

Melina threw herself on a seat, and for a short time remained silent, and totally absorbed in her own dismal thoughts, whilst Floretta watched her with the deepest sympathy and commiseration.

" Alas !" ejaculated our heroine, at length, " thus am I shut out from all hope; here far away from all who know me, or even from any human being but those who are in the employ-ment of my uncle, what is there left for me to do but to endeavour to resign myself to my fate, which I now perceive more than ever is inevitable ? Nay, Floretta, it is useless, good though I know your intentions to be, to attempt to argue against my opinions; I know well what you would say, but my mind is too much agitated to suffer me to listen to them with any degree of patience."

" Pardon me, signora," replied Floretta, " if I may in my zeal to serve you appear too bold and importunate; but I would fain arouse you from these sad thoughts, and inspire you with that fortitude which at present you so much require."

" Oh, Floretta," returned the poor girl; " how can I acquire fortitude when I reflect upon all the horrors of my situation ?"

" It is indeed most painful, lady," said her faithful companion : " but still it might have been worse; the prince has evidently been most studious of your comfort and accommodation, and——''

"My comfort and accommodation!" interrupted her mistress, impatiently; "oh what a bitter mockery is there conveyed in those words when I reflect upon the cruel designs he has in contemplation against me.''

"He may yet be induced to abandon them," said Floretta.

"Never! his conduct in having me conveyed hither is a proof of it, if I had not before been sufficiently convinced by the stern observations he has made to me at our frequent interviews. Floretta, you must be satisfied as well as myself, that he is inexorable, and that he only awaits the restoration of the Count Alberti to convalescence to put his threats into execution.''

"Then let us hope, signora, that the count's recovery will be retarded, and then in the meantime something may occur to rescue you.''

"What can occur?" demanded Melina, "what can possibly take place on which I can rest the least shadow of a hope ?"

"Well, signora," remarked her attendant, "let us waive this subject until your mind is in a more fit state to discuss it. You much need repose, and an hour or two will serve greatly to refresh you.''

"And think you, Floretta, that I can rest with such thoughts distracting my brain ? Oh, no, that is impossible.''

Floretta made no reply, and they both walked to the window, which they found was secured, and which commanded the same prospect, only to a greater extent, as they had seen from the room below. The golden monarch of the day had now arisen in full majesty in the east, and the sides of the distant mountains, and all the scenery around, glittered in his cheerful and genial beams. The prospect lost much of its rude and wild aspect beneath his influence, and the hour was so calm and tranquil, that even our heroine could not help for a moment feeling somewhat soothed.

"Oh, that I were as free and happy as the birds who now wing their flight to the sky," she ejaculated; "would that I were permitted to inhale the pure fresh air of Heaven, and wander wither my fancy might direct me, but to where I might probably find a resting-place from the manifold cares and sorrows that now beset my breast! How have I deserved such a fate as this? and to experience it, too, from my own, my only relation; he who should have been my kindest friend and protector, and have been so studious of my happiness! God!—it will scarcely bear a thought; and but for the stern reality of everything around me, I could scarcely believe but that I was labouring under the influence of some frightful dream. Grant me patience kind heaven; for this is surely almost too much to endure!''

She clasped her hands together, and for a few minutes her anguish could only find vent in convulsive sobs and tears, while Floretta was in a state of mind that was very little better than her own; and what rendered the poor kind-hearted girl more wretched, was that she had no consolation to offer her, and that all that she said was fully justified by the circumstances in which she was placed. At length she persuaded her mistress to leave the window, and they now proceeded to examine the other apartments which Viola had mentioned.

They found them very commodious and cheerful, and filled up as chambers, with everything necessary for use. The furniture was very old-fashioned, and was probably of the same age as the building, and imparted to the rooms a strange and romantic aspect, which could not fail to make some impression upon their minds. One thing, however, which more particularly attracted their attention, was a dingy damask curtain which was drawn across one corner of the room, and which, it struck them, concealed a window. Melina drew it aside, and the oaken doors of a closet then met their observation. A rusty key was in the lock, which after some difficulty they turned, and the door flew open, giving escape to a thick cloud of dust which seemed to have been for many years pent up there. This having dispersed, they were enabled to perceive the contents of the closet, which, however, presented nothing to gratify their curiosty, and consisted only of an heterogeneous mass of old lumber, apparently of no consequence whatever. Melina felt disappointed, and closed the door again.

"This is strange," she remarked; "what could have been the object in concealing this door so carefully, when the contents of the closet are so completely worthless ?''

"I am at a loss to imagine, signora,' replied Floretta, who was equally as disappointed as her mistress; "this door, however, has evidently not been opened for many years before, and it is singular that being so careful to conceal it, they should have left the key in the lock.''

"True," coincided our heroine, "but it strikes me there is more in this than appears at first sight. We will examine the contents more minutely at another time.''

"Yes, signora," returned her attendant, "and in the meanwhile we must be careful to conceal from Viola that we have discovered the closet at all; I am quite of your opinion that there is something more in this than we can at present comprehend, But come, my lady, do endeavour to snatch an hour or two's repose, of which you stand so much in need.''

"I will do so, Floretta," replied our heroine; "though I am afraid it will be to no purpose while my mind is in this state of agitation."

"Struggle with your feelings, signora, and I am convinced that you will be able to overcome them. There is yet time to rescue you from the dangers by which you are now surrounded, and I trust that Providence, in its infinite mercy, will interpose to do so."

"I will seek to entertain the same hopes," said Melina; "for surely I have done nothing to deserve to be deserted by it."

"Oh, no, signora," replied Floretta; "indeed you have not, and you can, therefore, look with confidence for its protection."

Melina made no reply, but sinking on her knees, she earnestly and devoutly offered up her prayers and supplications to the Supreme, and in which Floretta joined her with equal sincerity and fervour. Having secured the door of the chamber, they then both sought the same couch, and Floretta, who was overcome with fatigue, soon sunk off to sleep. But it was some time before our heroine could compose her mind to rest, so busily were her thoughts occupied; and when she did, her sleep was disturbed by painful dreams. When she awoke a few hours afterwards, however, she felt considerably refreshed, and the anguish of her mind was greatly relieved. She arose, and she and Floretta sat for a short time by the window, and gazed upon the scenery of which it commanded so extensive a view, and which was now lighted up by the full rays of the meridian sun. They were interrupted in a few minutes by the entrance of Viola, who brought the morning repast, and likewise several volumes of books, which, as she had said, she thought Melina would like to peruse, in order to while away the tediousness of her confinement.

"I am sure, signora," said Viola, who was not a bad-hearted woman, "I shall be most happy to do anything that lies in my power to contribute to your comfort, and indeed I have his highness's strict orders to do so."

"I thank you, Viola," returned our heroine, "but alas! there is little that any one can do to contribute to my comfort, hopelessly situated as I am. Nothing but a release from the fate with which I am threatened, can restore me to happiness."

"Dear me, signora," said the simple Viola; "and is it possible that you can be unhappy, when you are so shortly to be united to so handsome and wealthy a young nobleman as I understand the Count Alberti to be?"

Melina only sighed in reply to those observations, and Viola quitted the room.

Persuaded by Floretta, Melina partook slightly of the repast, and they then directed their attention to the closet, and opening the door, they proceeded to examine the contents. They met with nothing to gratify their

curiosity for some time, and were about to give up the task, when they perceived something tumble from a small shelf in one corner, and our heroine picking it up, saw that it was a bundle of papers, tied together with tape, and thickly covered with dust. She brought it nearer to the light, and examined it most minutely, and having cleared the dust from it, she perceived some characters written in a female hand on the back of one of the packets, but which was so worn away by time and damp, that for a few moments she had a difficulty in deciphering it; but at length she was enabled to distinguish the name of "Valentia."

"Valentia!" she said, starting, and endeavouring to recal her recollection; "surely I have heard that name before?"

"Oh, yes, signora," replied Floretta, "do you not remember, that is said to have been the name of the original of the mysterious portrait at the Villa Rosa?"

"True, true," said Melina, whose interest and curiosity were excited to the utmost degree; "the young Florentine damsel whom it is supposed my uncle loved?"

"The same."

"How remarkable!" said Melina; "and that these papers which appeared to have been written by her should have fallen into my hands. There is something more in this than I can at present imagine; and probably the secret which the Prince Bianchi has so long kept concealed may now be disclosed, and may prove of importance to me."

"But is it not extraordinary that the papers should have been suffered to remain here?" said Floretta.

"It is," replied her mistress; "and it is evident from their appearance that they must have been deposited in the closet many years."

"True, signora."

"It must have been unknown to any one."

"And yet why has such precaution been used in concealing the door?" asked Floretta.

"That is more than I can understand," answered Melina; "but something tells me that the papers will be productive of some important discovery. Alas! I fear the tale which these manuscripts will probably unfold will not redound much to the honour of the Prince Bianchi, my uncle; and yet why I should think so I know not;—I ask forgiveness of Heaven if I do him wrong. But come, let us no longer delay the gratification of our curiosity. There is no fear of our interruption."

They now replaced the old lumber in the closet exactly as they had found it, and having drawn the curtain again across the door, they seated themselves at the window, and Melina untying the packet, unfolded the papers in regular order, and proceeded to endeavour to decipher the contents. This was task, however, which was not to be effected without considerable trouble, for the papers were so worn with time and damp, as we stated before, that the writing was in many parts rendered almost illegible; but at length, after much difficulty, Melina was enabled to make out the following lines :—

"THE HISTORY OF THE UNFORTUNATE VALENTIA DI VALORI!

"It is a tale of sorrow, then," said our heroine, "and from it I may learn a useful lesson, though I do not see how the writer can have any connection with me."

"Should it be as we suspect, the original of the portrait," remarked Floretta, "the connection between her and the Prince Bianchi your uncle, must render her narrative of the deepest interest to you, signora."

"True," answered our heroine; "but is it possible that this unfortunate Valentia, like myself, can have been a prisoner here?"

"The manuscript will probably explain everything," returned Floretta; "but pray proceed, my dear signora, for I am all anxiety to become acquainted with its contents."

Melina again looked earnestly at the documents which had so singularly fallen into her hands, and after a short time she was enable to read as what will be found in the following chapter.

CHAPTER XLV.

THE MANUSCRIPT.

"IT is night: the wind howls mournfully around; the night-bird shrieks its doleful cry; impenetrable darkness has spread its mantle upon the earth; all is silent in this, my prison-house; my poor innocent is wrapped in unconscious sleep, and now with a trembling hand the unfortunate Valentia sits down to the melancholy and painful task she has long been so anxious to perform, namely, to trace the history of her wrongs and sorrows, though probably these lines may never meet the eye of human being, or, if they should, probably the form of the author of them will long since have mouldered to ashes in the silent grave, and there may be no one who can remember that there was ever such a wretched being in existence.

"But why should the secret of my wrongs and errors, my sufferings, and my degradation, and the villany of one whom I have loved, alas! too fondly, for ever remain locked in this seared bosom? Oh, Bianchi!—Bianchi, why——"

Here several lines of the manuscript were so defaced that our heroine could not make them out.

"Ah!" she exclaimed, "it is then as I suspected; my uncle is the hero of this tale of sorrow, and the errors of his past life, and which I am certain have so heavily pressed upon his conscience, are about to be revealed to me."

"My curiosity is excited more than ever," observed Floretta. "I pray you continue signora."

"Here, then," said Melina reflecting for a moment, and then looking timidly around her, as though she expected to behold the ghastly phantom of the ill-fated woman; "here, then, was the unhappy Valentia confined a prisoner, like myself, many years ago, and probably by the will of that same being from whom I am now suffering such cruel wrongs. Oh, my uncle, and hast thou indeed been guilty of such enormities? No wonder that the hated Count Alberti should find favour in thine eyes, if such be the case."

"True, my lady," said her companion, "but let us hope that it is not so bad as you imagine; the Prince Bianchi must surely have loved this unfortunate Valentia Di Valori, or he would never have preserved her portrait with such jealous care."

"Very true," replied her mistress, "he might at one time have loved her, but much I fear, from the tenour of what I have already read, that he deceived, betrayed her, and then probably left her to perish of a broken heart."

"Do not judge his highness too hastily, signora," said Floretta, "but wait until you have perused all the particulars which the manuscript will doubtless disclose."

"Yes," returned Melina, "you say rightly, my good girl, and Heaven forbid that I should attribute that to my misguided uncle, notwithstanding his conduct to me, which he may prove to have been entirely innocent of. But let me resume."

After the lapse of a few minutes our heroine again proceeded with the manuscript, in the following words—

"Still the horrors of the night increase, but they are in strict accordance with the tempestuous feelings that hold dominion in my breast; the maddening thoughts that rack and scorch my brain! How this poor broken heart throbs within its frail tenement—how my hand trembles, and almost refuses to perform its melancholy office; whilst the scalding tears of anguish and remorse almost blind me, and render me unable to distinguish the characters I am tracing. Oh, thought!—oh, bitter agonizing thought!

"And thou, Bianchi, the idol of my soul, although my betrayer and my persecutor; what are the thoughts that occupy your mind in this solemn hour? Does not one ray of pity dawn upon thy mind towards the wretched being whom thou has destroyed? Does not one feeling of compunction arise in thy breast for the wrongs thou hast committed? Have you no love for your innocent, hapless boy? Has all become sterility within thy bosom? Alas! alas! I fear it has, and all the hopes that once occupied my sanguine imagination are now annihilated. But still I cannot curse thee! No, Bianchi, with all the cruel wrongs you have heaped upon my head, notwithstanding the misery you are hourly adding to my weight of sorrows, I call great Heaven to witness that I love you with all the ardour that animated my breast when I believed that you were all that was honourable, good, and virtuous; and even

PRINCE BIANCHI IN THE CHAMBER OF THE SICK ALBERTI.

with my latest breath will I breathe a blessing upon thy name; that name thy son shall never know unless thou revealest it to him, lest the instinct feeling of revenge should be within him, and should urge him to do that which nature must revolt from in horror."

*   *   *   *

Another vacuum here occurred in the manuscript, and it was some time ere our heroine could decipher what followed.

"Unfortunate woman," she said, "this language bespeaks a noble and generous mind;

alas! my uncle, I fear you have indeed been most guilty, to lay such a fair structure as this appears to have been in ruins."

"True, signora," replied Floretta; "but does not one thing strike you most remarkably, as it certainly does me?"

"What mean you, Floretta?" asked her mistress.

"The allusion to her son?"

"Ah! what of that?"

"Have you not heard that the brigand chief, Massaroni, is supposed to be the illegitimate son of some wealthy nobleman who had deserted himself and his mother in his infancy?"

"True," replied Melina, "the coincidence is most extraordinary."

"And you, doubtless, also remember the agitation he evinced on one occasion, when he accidentally saw the portrait of the young Florentine, at the Villa Rosa?"

"I remember it well," replied our heroine; "can it be?—Should that prove to be the portrait of his mother, there can be very little doubt that Allesandro Massaroni is no other than the Prince Bianchi's son."

"It does, indeed, seem but too probable, signora," said Floretta; "but proceed, and probably the narrative of the unfortunate Valentia will soon throw a light upon the important subject."

"Oh, should it be as we suspect," said our heroine, "how much has my misguided uncle got to answer for."

"Nay, my dear lady, we must not come to too hasty a conclusion, when we have the means of immediately setting all our doubts at rest."

"Very true," agreed her mistress; and she here again took up the manuscript and went on with the narrative as follows:—

"Should these lines ever meet the eye of mortal being, of the young, the lovely, and the innocent, oh, take warning by the fate of the unhappy Valentia di Valori, and shun the paths that lead to misery, ruin, and shame; beware of the seducer's arts, lest in loving too fondly, and confiding too sincerely, you are plunged into that abyss of horror and degradation from which there is no escaping.'

"When I look back upon all the horrors and vicissitudes it has been my lot to encounter in this world; when I recall to mind all the painful and trying circumstances of my past life, I marvel that I still exist, that my heart has not broken years ago; but let me not become tedious in my sorrows; let me rather point a moral to those into whose hands these papers may haply fall, when the hand that writes these lines shall long since have been palsied by the icy grasp of death, than seek to expatiate upon my own errors and misfortunes.

"The parents of Valentia di Valori were born in the lap of fortune and luxury; the time had been when they were amongst the most affluent and influential in the country, and their society was eagerly sought after not only for the wealth they possessed, and the elevated position they occupied, but their noble and generous virtues. The poor looked up to them with reverence, and the wealthy with respect and admiration. Their benevolence was unostentatious, and their whole conduct unassuming, yet dignified. Their greatest pride was to soothe the heart worn down by affliction; their principal maxim to live in peace and good fellowship with all mankind. Beloved parents! when I recall to my memory all the noble qualities you possessed; when I retrace the various scenes of my happy childhood, how does my heart expand; what powerful and uncontrolable feelings throb within my bosom; I could weep like a very child. God! had ye lived to have witnessed the shame, the misery, and degradation, of your unhappy Valentia, how maddening would have been the anguish of your souls! Thank Heaven, that dreadful trial was spared ye; though, when I think upon the frightful and untimely fate which befell you, the blood freezes in my veins, and my pen refuses its office."

The manuscript here again abruptly broke off, and it was evident from the appearance of the paper on which it was written, notwithstanding the lapse of years, that the tears of the writer had flowed fast as she recalled those reminiscences to her memory. It is needless to say that both our heroine and her attendant felt deeply interested in the misfortunes of Valentia, but it was several minutes ere Melina could sufficiently recover herself to resume.

"How painful is the picture that this unhappy woman draws," she said; "is it possible that the Prince Bianchi, my uncle, can have been the guilty cause of so much misery? Alas! when I take into consideration all the circumstances of his late conduct towards me, and the friendship he bestows upon such a man as the Count Alberti, it is impossible for me any longer to doubt it, and I blush to think that I should be related to one who has so greatly committed himself."

"But surely, signora," replied Floretta, "he must repent, and stung with remorse, especially when you make him acquainted with these melancholy facts, which no doubt you will do, he will at once abandon the designs he has now in contemplation against you, and only be too happy to render you all the atonement he can for the misery and anguish he has hitherto caused you."

"I fear not, Floretta," returned her mistress, "he has proceeded too far to retract; his proud spirit will not allow him to do so, and he has pledged himself too strongly to Alberti to break his word. Unfortunate Valentia, I must believe in the truth of all you here may assert, when I know the sympathy which the Prince

Bianchi possesses for that guilty man. But let me proceed."

Floretta made no observation in reply, and Melina went on with the manuscript of Valentia in the following words :—

"No child could ever have been treated with more affection and indulgence than that which I experienced from my parents; their whole study was to make me happy and virtuous, and to instil into my mind all those excellent, those transcendent qualities which they themselves possessed. The days of my childhood were indeed those of uninterrupted happiness and serenity; no care ever beset my mind; light, volatile, sportive and innocent, I was esteemed by all, and my parents looked upon me as the greatest blessing that Heaven could possibly have bestowed upon them. As I have before said, the utmost pains were bestowed upon my education; and when I had only attained the age of twelve years, I was considered to be far more accomplished than most individuals of far maturer age. But it was just at this period, that misfortune for the first time overtook the beloved authors of my being. By some unforeseen and unavoidable calamity, the particulars of which I never became acquainted with, my parents were suddenly reduced from affluence to comparative poverty; their princely establishment was broken up;—those who had eagerly sought their society in the time of prosperity, forsook them in the hour of their adversity, and they were compelled to retire upon a very limited income to a humble dwelling in a village near the fair city of Florence, and to reside for the future in comparative obscurity. But still they bore up with fortitude against the decrees of fate, and never once murmured at the sudden and cruel change which had taken place in their fortunes. If possible, they redoubled their affectionate attentions towards me; and, in fact, I seemed to be the only consolation they had under their afflictions, and Heaven knows that I endeavoured to return it as well as my humble abilities would allow me, and although I knew well the great and melancholy change which had taken place in our circumstances, I never once murmured, but tried by my conduct to convince them that I was as happy as I had always been.

"Thus passed away four years more of my life, without anything taking place which is worthy of recording, and we continued to live happy and contented, although very differently to what we had formerly done; but such were the more tranquil enjoyments we now experienced, that we had no cause to regret the loss of that superabundance which we formerly possessed, except that my excellent parents had not now the power to carry out their benevolent and philanthropic wishes to the same extent.

"Amongst the numerous persons who had honoured my parents with their friendship in the time of their prosperity, was the late Prince Bianchi, the father of that man who is the cruel destroyer of my happiness, the ruthless betrayer and devastator of my innocence.—Oh, Bianchi! Bianchi! Bianchi! thou to whom my heart was so ardently and sincerely devoted; in whose truth I placed such unlimited confidence; that I should ever have to write of thee thus! Father of yon sleeping innocent, Heaven knows full well the bitter anguish it causes me to do so;—how my heart is torn and racked whilst I thus relate the guilty tale! May compunction, ere it be too late, light upon your conscience, and arouse you to a full sense of the cruelty and injustice with which you have—and are now—acting towards one whose only crime, if crime it be, is in loving you too fondly; in trusting too much to the supposed truth and nobleness of your character.

"The intimacy that existed between our families, and the similarity, apparently, of our dispositions and propensities, caused a youthful but mutual affection to spring up between the son of the Prince Bianchi and myself, which was encouraged by our parents, and, no doubt, they looked forward to the time when the friendship would be still more strongly cemented by a union between us. Little, however, did they imagine the real sentiments of the young nobleman; the base and wicked thoughts he even at that early age dared to encourage within his breast, or how quickly would they have taken steps to thwart him, and to have prevented the misery which has now taken place. But who could suspect for a moment that beneath so specious and alluring an exterior rested so base a mind? Oh, Bianchi! thou wert indeed formed to deceive and betray, and evil destiny assisted you in the nefarious, the diabolical plans, I must now believe you from the first must have formed within your own breast. Heaven pardon you for the sake of your innocent boy, who, alas! I fear is never destined to know a father's care or affection."

"Unfortunate woman," said our heroine, again, for a moment or two laying down the manuscript; "terrible indeed must have been your sufferings!—Alas! my uncle, if all is true which is herein stated, and of which I cannot entertain a doubt, how much hast thou to answer for. But you must be aware of the cruelty and injustice of your conduct, or you would not so carefully have preserved the portrait of your victim, and evince so much emotion whenever it is alluded to."

"True, signora," replied her companion, "and it is therefore that I trust he will relax in his conduct towards you when he finds that you have become acquainted with those particulars.'

"I would fain think so, Floretta, but cannot," returned Melina; "but the child—can he still be in existence?"

"That is at present a matter of extreme doubt and uncertainty," answered the former; "but probably time may unravel the secret. I cannot, however, help thinking of the strange coincidence that exists between the history of this child and that of Allesandro Massaroni, the brigand chief."

"It is indeed most extraordinary," observed Melina;—"should Massaroni really prove to be the son of the Prince Bianchi—But for the present I cannot trust myself with such an idea;—it bewilders my brain, and engenders thoughts which I fain would not encourage. The mutual hatred towards each other that exists between them; the—Oh, if such is indeed the case, Heaven grant that they may never know each other."

Once more she took up the manuscript, and after having pondered over it for a few moments, in order to endeavour to decipher the lines, she went on with its perusal.

"The son of the Prince Bianchi and myself were about the same age, and the graces of his person were in every degree equal to the accomplishments of his mind. From the earliest period we were never happy unless we were in each other's society; our tastes, our amusements were the same, and it seemed, indeed, as though nature had formed us to come together; but, alas! how cruelly have my hopes been doomed to be disappointed.

"The first severe shock my feelings sustained was a few months after the great and unexpected change which had taken place in the fortunes of my beloved and unfortunate parents. The Prince Bianchi gradually became more cool and distant in his behaviour towards us; his visits were less frequent than usual; he was seldom accompanied by his son; always avoided as much as possible making any allusion to his name, and there was a certain hauteur in his demeanour towards us which seemed to convey the notion he now entertained of his superiority, and likewise that he wished to break off the intimacy which subsisted between himself and my parents as soon as he conveniently could. It was impossible that the penetrating eye of my father could not immediately perceive this; and while it vexed and hurt him, it mortified his pride, and rendered him uneasy and dissatisfied whenever the prince was present. As for myself, I became truly miserable now that I was deprived of the society of my old companion; I lost all that vivacity of spirit, that innocent hilarity which had before characterized me, and my former haunts no longer possessed the least attraction for me. It was then for the first time that I discovered the powerful influence which my lover possessed over my heart. My parents endeavoured to arouse me from this

melancholy state of mind as much as possible, but with little or no effect; and many a pang, no doubt, it must have cost them to see what I suffered.

"'Why does the Prince Bianchi visit us so seldom, father?' I inquired of him, one day; 'and when he does, Antonio never accompanies him.—How is this?—I'm sure I know not that I have offended him, and——'

"'My dear child,' interrupted my father, 'it is impossible that you or any of us can have given cause for offence to the Prince Bianchi or Antonio; but of course, he must act in accordance with the will of his father, and that will we have no right to question.'

"'But why should he object to our friendship?' I inquired.

"'Valentia,' said my father, solemnly, 'I know your feelings; it is impossible that any one can better appreciate them than myself, and I deeply regret that I should have encouraged hopes which I now perceive can never be realised.'

"'What mean you, my dear father?' I inquired, in a timid voice.

"'Young even as you are, Valentia," he replied, 'I know full well that you love Antonio.'

"I blushed and trembled, but the violent palpitation of my heart convinced me, if it had required anything to do so, that he spoke the truth, and I was incapable of returning any answer.

"'My Valentia,' he continued, after a brief pause, 'painful as the struggle may be, you must endeavour to stifle that passion in your breast, and to forget Antonio in any other character but as the friend and companion of your youth. I need not remind you of the change that has now taken place in the circumstances of the Prince Bianchi and myself; he is wealthy and of elevated rank and station, whilst I am comparatively poor and obscure; such are the reverses of fortune to which I must endeavour to submit as becomes a man. I cannot expect that any alliance can now take place between our families,—bear this in mind, and I know my Valentia will be able to muster fortitude sufficient to do as I desire her.'

"I could make no reply to these observations, but threw myself sobbing into his arms, and after he had exerted himself all that was in his power to console me, our interview terminated, and with a heavier heart than I ever remembered to have experienced, I retired to my chamber, where I gave myself up to the feelings of agony which agitated my bosom.

"'Dear Antonio!' I sighed, 'and must I indeed endeavour to forget you?—Must all the fond hopes which I have dared to encourage be for ever annihilated in my bosom? Alas! alas! I never knew the real power you possessed over me till now. Cruel Fate! why do you thus frown upon us?—But does Antonio now view me with indifference?—Can he cease to remember me?—or have I only deceived myself by imagining that he entertained the same warm feelings of regard for me that I have ever entertained towards him? Oh, no, I cannot think so unkindly of him;—no doubt his sufferings at this moment are as great as mine are; but if the stern will of the Prince Bianchi is such as my father has represented it to be, and there is too much reason to believe that it is, he dare not disobey it. Alas! I see plainly now as if it were reflected in a mirror, that there is nothing but misery before us.'

"Thus did I continue to soliloquise for some time, and in vain I endeavoured to obtain the least degree of hope or consolation. Such was the effect it had upon my spirits that I was taken seriously ill, and for several days I was unable to leave my chamber. A short time fully confirmed all that my father had said; the Prince Bianchi's visits gradually became less frequent than before, and at length he discontinued them altogether, and it was quite evident that he had resolved to bring the intimacy to an end, and that the hopes I had entertained were now entirely crushed.

"How lonely and desolate was now my heart; I did not appear like the same being; solitude was all I sought after, and the efforts of my parents were exerted in vain to arouse me, and to calm the bitter anguish of my mind. Could I but have seen Antonio, and have heard from his lips the true state of his feelings, I thought I could have been content; but, oh! how much better would it have been for me had I never more beheld him; and could I have banished his image from my memory altogether, what shame, what misery would it have saved me. I might now have been innocent, though I could not have been happy. Alas! little at that time did I dream of the terrible calamities that were impending o'er my head, or in the anticipation of them I must surely have sank.

"Several months passed away without any change in my circumstances taking place, and years seemed to have accumulated on my head, and I gave myself up entirely to despair. I heard nothing whatever of Antonio, nor did I indeed venture to mention his name, or to make any inquiries after him. I seldom or ever quitted the house, and when I did, I most carefully avoided those scenes, among which it had formerly been my delight to wander, for the reminiscences they would recall to my mind would have been too painful for endurance. But why should I trouble the individual into whose hands these papers may probably fall by thus minutely detailing the many sad thoughts which constantly tortured my mind?

* * * * *

"It is again night—dark and dismal night; and once more my poor child sleeps in unconscious innocence! Surely it would be a mercy for him if it were the sleep of death!

"Again I take up the pen while all is still around me, and there is no one to interrupt me; and once more with a trembling hand and a heavy heart I resume my narrative of misfortune. Shall I ever be allowed to complete it? For what am I reserved?

"I had returned one afternoon from one of my solitary rambles, when on entering the little parlour in which my parents were seated, I perceived that they were engaged in deep conversation, and I could tell from the expression of their features that it was something of importance. On my entrance, however, they ceased, and both gazed at me earnestly for a moment or two.

"'Valentia, child,' observed my father, at length, handing me a chair, 'be seated, for you look fatigued after your walk.'

"I obeyed him, but my heart palpitated with impatience to know what he had to communicate.

"'We have just heard some news, Valentia,' he continued at last, 'which I have no doubt will afflict you.'

"I trembled, for my heart foreboded that something of a serious nature had happened to Antonio, his image being always uppermost in my thoughts.

"'Do not unnecessarily alarm yourself, child,' said my father;—'but not to keep you in suspense, the Prince Bianchi——'

"'Ah! what of him?' I inquired eagerly.

"'He is no more,' he answered.

"'Dead!' I ejaculated.

"'Yes, Valentia, my former friend and intimate companion, is no longer an inhabitant of this world,' observed my father; 'he had been for some time in a declining state, but his death was rather sudden and unexpected at the last. I lament that our intimacy did not last throughout life, but—but when fortune frowns upon us —However, I will say no more upon that subject; perhaps he only acted as prudence should dictate, and I cannot but believe that to the last hour of his life he continued to entertain the same feelings of respect for me that I have always done for him. But you tremble, Valentia, and turn pale. Ah! my child, too well do I read the thoughts that are fluttering around your heart, and which I am ready to own are no more than natural; but I pray you, if you would save yourself many a pang, seek to banish them from your mind, and to forget the past only as a happy dream. 'Tis true that Antonio is now master of his own actions, he is the Prince Bianchi; and as such, remember, whatever may be his sentiments towards you, he can never think of allying himself to the portionless Valentia di Valori; nor could I, were he so disposed, give my consent, which, by the uncharitable portion of mankind, would be almost certain to be misconstrued into mercenary motives on my part.'

" ' Oh, spare me, father !' I exclaimed ;—
' Antonio—I—I—'

"Agony of the most intense description stifled the conclusion of the sentence in my throat, and I sank inanimate in the arms of my father."

Just as Melina had arrived at this portion of the narrative of Valentia, she was interrupted by hearing a footstep ascending the stairs, and hastily concealing the manuscript, the room-door was immediately afterwards opened, and Viola made her appearance, bringing with her a repast, which she spread upon a table before our heroine and her attendant, and after having exchanged a few observations with them, she again retired, and Melina and Floretta having partaken of the meal, the former went on with the interesting, but melancholy, history of Valentia.

CHAPTER XLVI.

THE MANUSCRIPT CONTINUED AND CONCLUDED.

" WHAT I suffered after receiving this intelligence, and the observations of my father, although I could not deny the reason and justice of them, I must leave the reader of these lines to imagine. It was some time before I recovered my senses, and when I did, I found myself reclining upon my couch in my own chamber, with my mother watching anxiously and attentively by my side. My mind was bewildered and distracted by the thoughts that crowded upon it, and for a short time I had only a dreamy recollection of what had taken place; but at length the whole rushed vividly upon my memory, and I burst into a paroxysm of convulsive sobs and tears. My poor mother exerted herself to the utmost to impart consolation to me, but she met with little success, and was at length compelled to leave it to time and mature reflection to work that happy effect in my mind which herself and my excellent father were so anxious to see realised. My energies were all prostrated, and for several days I was so ill, mentally and bodily, that I was unable to leave my chamber. Would to God ! that my sufferings had terminated there, I should not now have such bitter cause to regret. Oh, that I had never again beheld Antonio; that I could have banished his image from my recollection, only as the friend and companion of my youth, I might now have been innocent and respected, if not happy. But what am I now ? A thing of scorn and degradation ! hateful to myself, despised by him whom I fondly flattered myself had felt the warmest, the most ardent, and virtuous affection that could possibly glow within the human breast; with my helpless offspring a wretched prisoner, with nothing to commune with but my own dismal thoughts ; with nought but black despair and misery around me ! Oh, Antonio, surely the love I bore thee, the fond confidence I reposed in thine integrity and honour, deserved a better reward than this! Thou couldst never have loved me, though thou didst oft so solemnly vow to do so, or thou couldst never have acted in the cruel manner you are now doing towards me. I must again pause, for the intensity of grief unnerves my hand, and my poor brain is so distracted that I scarcely know what it is I write. God help me, I——

* * * * *

" It would have been kind of him, in comparison with his present treatment, had he, when he had effected the destruction of my innocence stretched me a corpse at his feet. Surely this is a refinement upon cruelty. But let me proceed.

" For several days I continued confined to my room, and need I say that my whole thoughts were constantly fixed upon Antonio? I found it utterly impossible to follow the advice of my father ; hope would spring up in the midst of my darkest despair, notwithstanding all the melancholy circumstances of my case, and the love which had been engendered in my breast towards Antonio from the earliest period of my childhood gained strength the longer I reflected upon him.

" ' He is now his own master,' I would soliloquise, when I was alone ; ' he has no one whatever to control his actions or his inclinations, and I can never believe that he can so soon forget the many tender and solemn vows he has so frequently uttered to me as to abandon me altogether, when he must be fully aware of the anguish and anxiety I must at present be enduring for his sake. He will seize the earliest opportunity of seeing me again, and once more we shall be happy. Oh, can the disparity of rank and fortune have any influence where hearts are united ? On such a mind as that which I know my Antonio to possess, it is impossible ! And yet he must act in obedience to the stern and solemn injunctions which he has probably received from his father in his dying moments, and those injunctions were, no doubt, to forget me, and never to marry any one whose wealth and station in society are not equal to his own. Oh, that thought, 'tis madness. Oh, Antonio! I feel too certain that thou art lost to me for ever !'

" Thus did I continue wavering between hope and fear for several days longer, but at length I was enabled to leave my chamber, and when in the society of my parents, they renewed all their affectionate efforts to console me, but with very little or no better effect than before. As I regained strength, I resumed my walks in the neighbourhood of our residence, but always declined the society of any one, for I wished to receive no interruption to the melancholy thoughts which wholly engrossed my mind, and, in fact, in traversing those scenes which had once been the favourite haunts of myself and Antonio, I found the only temporary relief to my anguish, and but for that melancholy indulgence, I must certainly have sunk under the excessive sorrows which beset my bosom.

"Two months more elapsed in this manner, and I heard nothing of Antonio, and I began to think that he had indeed forgotten me, and wished me no longer to remember the love he had at one time so ardently professed towards me, and which in my innocence and affectionate confidence I had flattered myself that neither time nor circumstance could change. The agony which this idea caused me it would be impossible for even the most eloquent pen to do adequate justice to in description.

"'He has seen some more wealthy and fairer maiden to whom he has transferred his affections,' I would sigh to myself, 'and how futile and presumptuous are the hopes I dared to encourage. But can he ever meet with one who can love him half so fondly, so devotedly, as poor Valentia has done? Oh, no, that is impossible! Break, then, my heart, and let me get rid of this wretched existence, if Antonio no longer loves me! Can I live to see him the husband of another? The thought is distraction! Death in any form, however terrible, would be a blessing in comparison with that. But if he ever sincerely loved me, he cannot abandon me because cruel fate has so changed the circumstances under which we were first introduced to each other. Oh, no; I can never believe that my Antonio can ever possess so selfish and sordid a mind.'

"This idea for the time being consoled me, and revived my hopes. Slowly I retraced my steps towards home, and was about to retire to my own apartment, when I was met by my mother, who affectionately took my hand, and after looking earnestly in my face, said—

"'Valentia, child, I do not wish you to retire until you have seen your father; he has something to communicate to you.'

"'Something to communicate to me, my dear mother?' I repeated anxiously, and my heart throbbing with expectation.

"'Yes, Valentia,' returned my mother, 'but do not agitate yourself.'

"I followed her with trembling impatience into the parlour, but without making use of another observation, and I there found my father deeply engaged in the perusal of a letter, which he hastily laid aside on my entrance, and advanced to meet me, handing me to a chair placed between him and my mother, and after a pause he said—

"'Valentia, I must request you to call all the composure you can to your aid, while I impart what I have to communicate to you. The letter which you saw me perusing on your entrance is from Antonio, now Prince Bianchi.'

"'From Antonio!' I said in breathless haste, and my heart fluttering with the violence of my agitation.

"'Yes, Valentia,' he returned, 'from Antonio, and in which he breathes the same tone of friendship he everevinced towards us, though with what sincerity I will not undertake to say, and states his intention of visiting us shortly.'

"'Oh, joy! joy!' I ejaculated, unable to control my feelings;—'and is he well? Does he mention me, and—'

"'Yes,' interrupted my father; 'but let me caution you to bear in mind what I have before said to you; there may be the most imminent danger in encouraging hopes, which circumstances may now render it impossible can ever be realised.'

"'Danger in encouraging hopes with which Antonio is associated, my father?' I replied hastily; 'oh, no, that is impossible.'

"'Remember child, that Antonio is rich, and you are now poor and almost friendless, and it is not likely that he can so far conquer the pride of his station as to think seriously of making you his wife. It is for that reason that I may consider it prudent and imperatively necessary to decline his visits here.'

"'Decline his visits, my dear father?' I repeated, in a voice of the utmost agitation; 'oh, no, you surely cannot think seriously of doing any such a thing? Antonio, I am convinced, is too good and honourable to attempt for a moment to abuse the friendship and confidence you may repose in him.'

"'Ah, Valentia,' he returned, 'you are as yet too inexperienced in the world to be able to form a reasonable opinion of its inmates. But I know that my child will think seriously of what I have said to her, and act accordingly, and as future circumstances may show the necessity of. I have also a letter from the Prince Bianchi, addressed to yourself!'

"'A letter from Antonio and addressed to me?' I ejaculated; 'oh, this is far beyond even my most sanguine expectations.'

"'Yes,' observed my father, 'but I know not whether I shall be acting right in giving it you.'

"'Oh, father,' I exclaimed eagerly, 'what harm can it possibly occasion? I can have no wish to conceal the contents from you.'

"'Well, be it so, Valentia,' he returned;—'but let me caution you not to be too much influenced by anything you may read therein.'

"'You may trust me, my beloved parent,'

I replied; 'you know full well that it is always my most anxious wish to follow your advice to the very letter.'

"'Enough, my child,' said my father; 'I will depend upon you. Here is the letter.'

"I took it eagerly from his hand, and glancing hastily at the characters of the superscription, I pressed it with a feeling of the most unutterable transport to my lips. It was several minutes before I could regain my composure, and I then requested the permission of my parents to retire for a short time, which they having agreed to, with a palpitating heart I hastened to my chamber. Here the power of my feelings found vent in a copious flood of tears, and pressing the letter vehemently to my bosom, it was some minutes ere I could sufficiently regain my composure to unfold it or attempt to peruse the contents which I was so anxious to see. At length I broke the seal and pondered over every precious line with the most eager attention. I will not attempt to describe the language in which it was couched; it is sufficient to say that every word expressed the most unbounded affection, and was written in a tone, the sincerity of which I could not doubt. He stated also that in a few days he hoped to have the felicity of once more beholding me, and of repeating those sentiments which he solemnly declared had undergone no change in his breast.

"Again and again I pressed this welcome epistle to my lips, and bedewed it with my tears, but they were now tears of joy.

"'He is faithful to me then,' I ejaculated; 'the vows he so often uttered to me were those of sincerity, and he still loves me! Blessed assurance!—how could I ever doubt him?—I should have known his noble heart too well to imagine for an instant that the mere change of fortune could alter the sentiments that have ever glowed in his bosom towards me. My father, can you longer doubt his honour?'

"But notwithstanding that I endeavoured to encourage these hopes, powerful and agonising misgivings came over me, and for some time I was unable to conquer them or to venture into the presence of my parents. Alas! could I but at the time have penetrated the real thoughts and designs of Antonio, though the struggle would have cost me dear, and my heart might have broken in the effort, I should doubtlessly have endeavoured to conquer the sentiments he had, unfortunately, excited in my breast, and tried to forget that there was ever such a being in existence. But alas! who could suspect, especially an innocent and inexperienced girl like myself, that any man could act with the cruel duplicity that Antonio has done towards me? Who could imagine that beneath so specious and prepossessing an exterior, could beat so dis-

honourable a heart?—Who could for a moment suspect the unholy and diabolical designs he had, at the very time when he was vowing the fondest, the most unbounded admiration for me, in contemplation against me? Even now, with all the horrors that surround me, I can scarcely believe in the terrible reality! Oh, Antonio! how cruelly hast thou abused the confidence I reposed in thee!—But I will not reproach thee!—for notwithstanding the misery I have experienced from thee, my heart is still fondly thine, and must ever continue to be so till it shall cease to beat; I forgive thee all, as God is my judge!"

"'Unfortunate woman!" said Melina; "what a noble and generous mind you evidently possessed;—how worthy of a far different fate!—Oh, my uncle! and couldst thou heartlessly and brutally deceive and betray such a woman as this? I can scarcely believe the evidence of my senses while I peruse the records of thy guilt."

"The Signora Valentia is, indeed, much to be pitied, my dear lady," observed Floretta; "but let us hope that the Prince Bianchi, your uncle, has repented of his past deeds, and that——"

"Ah, no, Floretta," interrupted her mistress; "there is little hope of that, when his unfeeling conduct towards me, and the friendship he entertains for the detested Count Alberti, are taken into consideration. The melancholy facts here recorded, convince me more than ever that I have nothing whatever to hope from his mercy and forbearance."

"The Prince Bianchi must surely be lost to every sense of feeling, humanity and nature, if he can obstinately persist in sacrificing his own niece to such a man as the Count Alberti," observed Floretta.

"And has not woeful experience shown me that I no longer possess his love, and that such considerations as those you have mentioned will have no effect on him?" said Melina. "I see plain enough that the fate with which I am threatened is inevitable, unless Providence should interpose to save me."

"And it will do so, signora, depend upon it," returned her attendant; "for it never forsakes the innocent, and those who put their trust in it."

Our heroine said nothing in answer to this, and after a brief pause, she again took up the narrative at the part where she had broken off.

"At length after much exertion, I sufficiently regained my tranquillity to repair to the room in which I had left my parents, and who were anxiously awaiting my return, and they both advanced towards me, with the utmost sympathy and affection depicted in their looks. I trembled, for doubts still oppressed my mind, but my father by a look re-assured me, and I placed the letter of Antonio in his hand. He rotired to the farther end of the room, and perused it carefully and attentively, and I watched the expression of his countenance while he did so, and awaited the conclusion of it with the utmost anxiety.

"'Valentia,' he said, at length, folding the letter, and returning it to me, 'I need not ask you what effect this epistle has had upon your mind, for I can read it in the agitated expression of your countenance. Certainly nothing can be more affectionate and apparently sincere than the language in which it is couched; but

FLORETTA.

I would caution you not to place too much reliance in it, lest you should be doomed to disappointment.'

"'Oh, my father,' I ejaculated, warmly, 'can you any longer doubt the honour and sincerity of Antonio? Can you believe him to possess so base a heart as to play the hypocrite in so shameless a manner? If it be possible that you entertain such a suspicion against him, well convinced am I that you do him infinite and unmerited wrong.'

"'Mark me, child,' he repled, 'I am not

so ungenerous or uncharitable as to entertain any such suspicions; but a parent should ever be jealous of his daughter's happiness; and you may believe me when I declare that all I have said is with a fond anxiety for your welfare.'

" 'My dear father,' I returned, 'full well do I know the unbounded affection you bear towards your child, and that it would break your heart should any misfortune happen to her; but surely you can have nothing to fear from the Prince Bianchi; he is the very soul of honour and virtue, and would despise himself could he be guilty of a single act which could call the blush of shame into his cheek. Ought not the number of years that we have known him, and had such opportunities of penetrating his character, to have convinced us of that?'

" 'True, Valentia,' agreed my father; 'but there is one thing that he has omitted in this letter, and the one he has addressed to me, which does not satisfy me, and raises some doubts in my mind.'

" 'And what is that, my father?' I inquired eagerly, and again trembling with apprehension.

" 'Why,' he answered, 'in speaking of the death of the Prince Bianchi, he makes no allusion to any injunctions he has given him in his last moments.'

" 'From which,' I timidly remarked, 'I infer that he gave none of any particular importance.'

" 'Ah! my child,' said my father, 'I construe it very differently; the abrupt manner in which the late Prince Bianchi broke off the intimacy which had for so many years existed between our families is a convincing proof of the change which the alterations in our circumstances must have wrought in his sentiments towards us. The prince was proud; he would never have condescended to consent to his son's becoming the husband of a portionless girl, and I am certain that he would therefore strictly enjoin Antonio when on his death-bed, to abandon all thoughts that he might have entertained towards you.'

" 'Oh, no, if he were studious of his son's happiness,' I replied, 'he could never have exacted such a promise.'

" 'Nay, my child,' answered my father, 'it is not so easy a task as you seem to imagine, to conquer the prejudices of pride.'

" 'But after all this is only a surmise.'

" 'It is one that is too well founded in truth, Valentia.'

" 'But, at any rate, my father,' I remarked, 'I pray you to waive your opinion till we have seen Antonio, when I trust that he will be able to explain everything satisfactorily.'

" 'I will do so, Valentia,' he said, 'and for your sake I sincerely hope that my suspicions may prove to be unfounded; but let me again earnestly advise you not to be too sanguine. Even if Antonio should be willing, I could never consent to your receiving him as your husband, if his father had prohibited him from forming such an alliance.'

" I could not reply, for my heart was full to bursting, for in spite of all I had said to the contrary, I could not help entertaining a melancholy and dismal foreboding that the suspicions which my father had expressed were correct, and I almost dreaded the arrival of Antonio lest he should confirm them.

" I was glad when my parents again permitted me to retire from their presence, that I might alone give free indulgence to the feelings which struggled in my breast; and when I had reached my own chamber, I threw myself in a chair, and for a few moments gave myself up entirely to the most agonizing thoughts. The sanguine hopes I had encouraged on the receipt of the note from my lover, now gradually faded from my mind, and I could not help apprehending that there was yet much misery in store for me. But, no! why should I doubt the honour of Antonio?—Had his father exacted any such a promise from him as that which my parent suspected, would he not have revealed to me the painful truth rather than by such a letter as the one he had sent to me have induced me to encourage fresh hopes?—Away, then, with dismal forebodings; let me rather view everything on the brightest side, and a heavenly prospect of bliss opens upon my mental vision!—Antonio will be mine!—Oh, blissful assurance! to realise which, what are all the anxieties which I at present endure?

" With these flattering ideas did I seek to console myself; alas! would that I had never encouraged them, for they mainly contributed towards my ruin. Had I given any heed to the doubts which my excellent father expressed, most of the evils that have since befallen me might have been avoided; but it was my fate to act differently, and bitter cause have I since had to repent of it. To me, at that time, the conclusions to which my father had arrived seemed not only unreasonable but unjust, and, Heaven pardon me for the thought, I inwardly accused him of entertaining uncharitable prejudices, which I know full well could never have entered his mind. Fearful is the penalty I have had to pay for so doing. Oh, could I but for a moment have imagined the terrible calamities that were impending o'er my head; the awful afflictions and sufferings I was destined to experience, my soul must have shrank appalled, and death would assuredly have at once terminated my career; and fortunate for me would it have been had it done so. But again I become tedious. Let me at once hasten to the more important facts of my melancholy history.

" Every succeeding day I looked anxiously forward to expecting the arrival of Antonio at the house of my parents, and yet, as I before said, I could not help feeling some degree of dread, nor could I entirely dismiss from my mind these suspicions and misgivings which the observations of my father had excited, and which, when I considered the proud and haughty disposition of the late Prince Bianchi, and the abrupt manner, on the ruin of my father's fortunes, he had broken off their former intercourse, I could not but entertain. If, indeed, my father's suspicions should unfortunately prove to be correct, all the fond hopes I had formed and encouraged from the days of earliest childhood would be at once annihilated, and my prospects would be for ever blighted. I shuddered even to think of such a result, and yet when I took all the circumstances into consideration, was it not too probable? Alas! it was; and I found it impossible to conquer the nervous state of excitement into which these too-well founded apprehensions had thrown me.

"'Oh, Antonio,' I would soliloquise when alone, 'if I am not destined to become thine, if, indeed, by the stern and cruel decree of thy father, thou art commanded to forget me, a command which thou dare not disobey, of what value will life in future be to me?—I shudder to anticipate the misery I must then experience, and which I am confident I could never find fortitude sufficient to support with any degree of patience. Oh, God! I humbly beseech thee not to subject me to such a terrible, such an insupportable trial, but rather end at once my misery by terminating an existence which must under such circumstances become wretched and hateful to me. Oh, cruel fate that reduced my unfortunate parents to poverty, and thus at one fell swoop blighted all those happy prospects which were opened to my sanguine imagination.'

"It was in vain that I endeavoured to banish these dismal thoughs from my imagination; they gained strength the longer I reflected on them, until they assumed the shape of reality, and I gave myself almost up to absolute despair. Severe and painful as was the determination which my father had expressed, I could not but admit the reason and justice of it, and there was no alternative for me left but to seek to submit to it. But to forget Antonio, to tear him from my heart altogether, and to transfer my affections to another man, oh, that I felt would be utterly impossible, and my heart must break in the effort. Where could I hope to meet with another man who possessed the noble qualities which adorned his mind? where could I find another whom I could love with the devoted ardour that I did him? It would, I considered, be the height of madness to entertain such an idea.— Alas! little did I at that time suspect the real character of him to whom I had devoted my affections, or I might have found resolution sufficient to conquer the passion with which

he had inspired me, and in time have saved myself from that shame and misery into which I am now unhappily plunged, and from which I have not the slightest means of extricating myself. But who could for a moment suppose, especially so young and inexperienced a girl as myself, that any man could act the hypocrite with such consummate skill? Who could have believed that Antonio, the friend and companion of my youth, could harbour one thought to my injury? My God! when I look back upon the past, and compare it with the horrors of the present, my soul sinks within me, and I can scarcely persuade myself that I am not suffering under the influence of some sickly and painful delusion. But let me not think, or I shall go mad.

"A fortnight had passed away since we had heard from Antonio, and I began to think that he had abandoned the intention he had expressed in his letters, and that he would not visit us, and that idea rendered me restless, impatient, and miserable.

"'Ah, no!' I sighed: 'he is now the Prince Bianchi, he has succeeded to his father's honours, and will no more condescend to notice the humble companion of his youth; her whom he vowed to love. Why should I ever have encouraged such presumptuous hopes?—How could I expect that one of his wealth and lofty station, could ever think of uniting himself to so poor and lowly an individual as I am? The idea is preposterous, and I am properly punished for having dared to encourage it. Antonio will find some other maiden, his equal in wealth and rank, on whom he can place his affections, and poor Valentia will be banished from his memory for ever.'

"'Even so, my child,' said my father, who had entered the room while I was giving utterance to these words; 'even so, Valentia. I am glad to see you at length come to so reasonable a conclusion, and hope that you may be able to encourage it, and to bear the disappointment to your hopes (which I admit is painful) with that fortitude and resignation which become you. The superiority of Antonio's position in society to your own prevents the possibility of his ever making you his wife, and therefore, as I have before urged you, if you are as studious of your own happiness and peace of mind as I am, you will endeavour to banish him from your memory in any other character than that of a former friend.'

"'Alas! my dear father,' I replied, 'how difficult is the task you would impose upon me.'

"'True,' he returned—'it is so; but it is one that circumstances render imperative, and I am confident that my Valentia, if she persevere, and exert all her reasoning faculties, will be able to accomplish it. Do not despair, my child: you are yet young, and there are many worthy men in the world who would be proud to become' the husband of one so amiable and lovely as Valentia di Valori.'

"'Oh, my father!' I ejaculated, 'I pray you do not talk thus, for my heart sinks within me when I think of such a thing. The Prince Bianchi may forget me—he may dismiss from his recollection all the fond and solemn vows he has so often made to me, but no other man can ever have a place in my affections. His image must I continue to cherish to the latest moment of my existence; and, God knows, since all my hopes are thus annihilated, I feel that I cannot long survive.'

"Hysterical sobs choked my further utterance, and I sunk, weeping bitterly, in a chair. My father took my hand tenderly in his, and looking up affectionately in my face, he said—

"'My dear child, do not give way to these sad thoughts, but put your trust in the goodness of the Almighty, who will give you strength to support this cruel disappointment of your young hopes. Come, come—cheer thee, cheer thee, and depend upon it there are yet many years of happiness in store for you.'

"'Alas, no!' I replied, 'I dare not hope for them; deprived of the love of Antonio, life must become hateful and a burthen to me.'

"'My poor child,' observed my father, 'what can I say?—how advise you? Would to Heaven that you and Antonio had never known each other, then you might have fixed your affections upon some other youth of your own station in society, and who might have been equally worthy of becoming your husband. Try to think of the past only as a dream, and to look forward to the future with cheerfulness and hope.'

"'Ah! no,' I ejaculated, 'that is impossible. The image of Antonio is too closely enshrined in my heart, for me ever to eradicate it. But let me not do him an injustice by believing him false and treacherous. He never could have addressed me in such language as that in which his letter was couched if he did not continue to love me with the same fervour he has ever professed to do; he must be base indeed could he thus seek to deceive me, and to raise thoughts in my breast, which he knew full well he never intended to realise.'

"'Believe me, Valentia,' observed my father, 'that I should despise myself could I entertain a thought to the prejudice of Antonio, which he was undeserving of;—I do not doubt that he still continues to love you, but still at the same time I feel equally confident that his father has enjoined him to forget you; that he has in his last moments exacted a solemn promise from him never to make you his bride, and his commands, and given at such a time, reason must convince you he dare not disobey. It is little better than madness to encourage a thought to the contrary. Come, Valentia, arouse yourself

from this dismal mood, and since Fate ordains that you shall never become the wife of the young and wealthy Prince Bianchi, try to hope that you may never meet again.'

"'Oh, how can I do that?' I replied, impatiently; 'my heart must break in the effort. Antonio will keep his word;—he will visit us anon, and surely, my father, you will receive him as——'

"'As becomes the rank of the Prince Bianchi, the Governor of Rome,' interrupted my father; 'but I can no longer permit him to pay his addresses to you, if I learn that he was commanded by his father not to do so, and without I am thoroughly convinced of the honour of his intentions.'

"'Oh, my dear father, surely you cannot doubt him,' I returned. 'Antonio would never dare to entertain a thought which he should be ashamed to acknowledge.'

"'I would fain believe so,' he said, 'but I have seen too much of the world and of the treachery of mankind, Valentia, not to entertain my doubts.'

"'Oh, how much you wrong him,' I cried, 'Antonio act the villain's part, and towards me! Oh, it is impossible! I will not entertain the base and ungenerous thought. Father, you torture me by giving utterance to such cruel suspicions.'

"'I am sorry for it, my child,' he answered; 'and sincerely hope that I may find myself mistaken, for I need not, I think, assure you that Antonio has always possessed my warmest esteem, and no one would more deeply regret it than myself, did I find that he was unworthy of it.'

"'That you will never do,' I remarked, fervently, 'the soul of Antonio is too noble ever to become so degraded, and even though fate should never permit him to become mine, nothing whatever can alter the sentiments with which my heart now beats towards him.'

"'How sincerely do I pity you, my poor girl,' he observed, 'and would to Heaven that I could afford you some relief and consolation. I should not be performing my duty towards you, however, did I not by every means in my power, and by all the force of argument I have at my command, seek to discourage any hopes which, as I before said, I feel satisfied can only end in disappointment. Fate has thrown an insurmountable barrier in the way of your union with the man on whom you have bestowed your heart, and it is therefore that I hope Antonio will fail to keep the promise he has made in the letters he has addressed to us, and that you may not meet again.'

"'Oh, Heaven forbid that we should not,' I ejaculated; 'for that would indeed drive me to distraction. Behold Antonio no more! the bare idea freezes the blood in my veins, and makes me one of the most wretched beings in existence. But he will come, my father, and then, I feel fondly certain, that he will be able to explain everything to your satisfaction.'

" ' Could he do so, he would have been more explicit in his letter. But he never mentions the name of his father, except in announcing his death, and that convinces me that my surmises are correct. Think you, Valentia, that Antonio would dare to disobey the dying injunctions of his father ?'

" ' No, no,' I replied, in a faint voice, ' if the late Prince Bianchi could have been so cruel and unjust as to fetter the will and inclinations of his son with any such injunctions, which I cannot persuade myself that he has ; and recollecting the solemn vows he has so often uttered to me, Antonio could never, I am confident, make such a promise.'

" ' Think you then that he would venture to despise and disregard the commands of his father in his last moments ? The thought is preposterous, and I wonder that you, Valentia, with your good sense, should even for an instant encourage it. Would that I could banish such futile ideas from your mind, and persuade you to meet with calmness and resignation the fate which is in store for you.'

" ' Calmness ! resignation !' I repeated, in a melancholy voice ; ' alas ! how can I do so, placed in the painful circumstances in which I am ? But Antonio will keep his word ; he would not have sent me the letter he did, had he not resolved to do so, for that would then indeed have been a cruel mockery. Something has detained him longer than he anticipated, or he would have been here ere now, for well assured do I feel that his anxiety is equal to my own till we meet again.'

" ' Well, Heaven watch over you, my poor child,' said my father, fervently, ' and grant that the sanguine wishes you still entertain may not be disappointed. I never before felt the loss of riches so severely as I do now, since it has thrown an obstacle in the way of your happiness, which I have too much reason to fear nothing can surmount.'

" ' And think you that Antonio can be so sordid and so mercenary as to suffer the disparity of our fortunes to change the sentiments he has so long professed towards me ?' I demanded. ' Oh, no, no, I will not wrong his noble and generous nature by encouraging such a supposition.'

" ' Well, Valentia,' returned my father, ' I trust that you will reflect maturely and dispassionately upon this painful subject, and be able to make up your mind to the worst. Retire, my child, and in the solitude of your own chamber endeavour to obtain that firmness and composure of which you so much stand in need.'

" With these words, the good old man embraced me affectionately, and invoking a blessing upon my head, I retired from his presence, and once more sought the quiet of my own apartment, where I could give indulgence to my feelings without any fear of interruption.

" The nature of my thoughts may be imagined. It was all to no purpose that I attempted to disregard the observations and opinions of my father ; they were too forcible and reasonable to be disregarded, and I became doubly miserable as a variety of melancholy forebodings crowded upon my imagination.

" ' But he loves me still, though fate may decree that he never shall be mine,' I reflected, ' and in that blissful assurance I must find sweet consolation. Antonio, could I for a moment believe that I no longer held a place in your heart, what could equal the horrors of my despair ? Life would become hateful to me, and I would not hesitate to rid myself of it, and to rush unbidden into the presence of my maker ! Horrible, guilty thought ! Let me banish it, ere it gains too powerful an influence over me. Have I no regard for the feelings of my aged parents that I should contemplate such a deed, that must bring their gray hairs with sorrows to the grave ? Pardon me, Heaven ! for my brain is so distracted with conflicting thoughts that I know not what I say. Antonio will be here anon, and then all these fearful doubts that torture my bosom will be set at rest, and once more I shall be restored to that happiness and contentment which I once enjoyed. My father, in his solicitude for my welfare, judges him too harshly, and I feel convinced that he will find himself mistaken, and that Antonio will prove to be all that my fondest wishes can anticipate.'

" Thus did I continue to alternate between hope and fear, and I was unable to tranquillise my feelings in the least degree. Two more days elapsed, and still Antonio came not, and my anguish and suspense now became insupportable.

" ' Alas !' I sighed, ' can he indeed have deceived me ?—Can he have sent the letter merely to mock me—to sport with my feelings, and to inspire me with false hopes ? Oh, no, that is impossible ; Antonio could never act with such heartless and gratuitous cruelty to one who loves him so ardently, so fondly as I do ; how could I ever suffer such an idea to occur to my imagination ? Antonio would hate and despise himself did he think himself capable of such brutal and unmanly conduct. Something must have detained him beyond the time he expected ; perhaps he is ill ! Oh, Heaven forbid !'

" I trembled as this thought occurred to me, and for some time my emotion was so excessive that I could scarcely contain myself. Thus I continued throughout that day, and my parents exerted themselves to console me, and tran_ quillise my feelings with little or no success. That night when I sought my couch, I lay for hours in a state of mind which it is needless for me to attempt to describe, and before I could compose myself to sleep, and when I did so my rest was disturbed by the most frightful dreams, which presented to my disordered imagination the form of Antonio in every possible position of terror. I felt relieved when the morning sun, streaming in at my chamber window, awoke me; and I immediately arose and tried to compose my feelings ere I entered the presence of my parents. In a few minutes I was summoned to the room in which we took our morning meal, and my parents instantly perceived from the paleness of my countenance and the agitation of my demeanour that I had passed a troublesome night.

"'How it grieves me, Valentia,' said my father, 'to see you give way to those sad thoughts which are making such inroads upon your constitution, and which, if not conquered in time, may be productive of the most serious results. Exert yourself, my poor child, I beseech you; and though dismal your present prospects may be, endeavour to look forward with hope to the future.'

"'Alas! my dear father,' I replied, 'I fear there is no hope for me; Providence seems to have deserted me, and fate to have marked me for its victim.'

"'Talk not thus, child,' observed my mother, 'for it is sinful. Providence never forsakes the good and innocent, and those who put their trust in it. Would that you could vanish the image of the Prince Bianchi from your memory, for it is too evident that you must henceforth be as strangers to each other.'

"'Oh, my dear mother,' I returned, 'and can you think for a moment that I can ever cease to remember Antonio while the purple current of life continues to circulate throughout my veins?—The more I seek to do so, the firmer becomes the hold which he has obtained of my heart; and I feel that unless we shortly meet again, and I receive from his own lips an assurance of the continuance of his love, that my heart must break, and death put a speedy termination to my sufferings.'

"'Forbear, Valentia!' exclaimed my father, solemnly; 'talk not thus wildly; know you what you say?—Have you lost all that religious fortitude and resignation which once characterised you?'

"'Alas! of what use is it to talk of fortitude and resignation to an unfortunate individual situated like myself?—I do try, indeed I do, but it is all in vain; and every day my despair and misery becomes the more intense. Oh, Antonio, why do you not come according to your promise, and banish the doubts and suspense which distract my mind?'

"'His neglecting to do so confirms my suspicions,' replied my father. 'He has thought better of his promise since he sent the letters, and abandoned the intentions he there expressed. Unless it is by accident, depend upon it, you will never behold him again.'

"'No more behold him!' I repeated with a look of agony; 'oh, say not so, or reason will forsake me! Antonio could never deceive me and sport with my feelings thus! You wrong him, father, by such a supposition.'

"'Most unwillingly would I do so,' he replied; 'but have I not reason on my side? Consider the time that has elapsed since he wrote to us, and then you must, I think, feel convinced that if he ever intended to keep his word, he has now banished such a thought from his mind altogether. He loves you not, Valentia, depend upon it, and therefore self-respect and womanly pride should induce you to cease to remember that there is such a being in existence.'

"'Loves me not!' I cried, clasping my hands together, and fixing a look of mingled anguish and reproach upon the countenance of my father. "Oh, horrible thought! I will not suffer it to enter my breast, for Antonio is unworthy of such base suspicion! He will shortly prove to your face how much you wrong him by entertaining such an estimate of his character.'

"'Alas! I see too plainly that Antonio has gained too powerful an ascendancy over your feelings and your confidence for me to persuade you; though my Valentia must be aware that I only do so in my anxiety for her welfare,' remarked my father. 'You greatly mistake me, child, if you imagine that I entertain a single prejudice against the Prince Bianchi; I only speak as reason and circumstances dictate. I would guard you against the danger which may result from your any longer encouraging a passion which it is now evident can meet with no return. There was a time when I looked forward to your union with Antonio as certain and with the fondest anticipations; but a painful change has taken place in our circumstances since then, and it would be madness any longer to indulge in those hopes which I formerly did. Come, Valentia, let me again persuade you to arouse yourself, and you may yet be happy, and learn to look back upon the past without regret.'

"'Never!' I exclaimed vehemently; 'the love of Antonio is my only hope of happiness; deprived of that, I care not what becomes of me.'

"My father was about to make some reply to these observations, when he was interrupted by the sound of a horse's hoofs which seemed to be approaching the house, and going to the window, I beheld a man riding towards our residence, and whom I imagined I had seen before. My heart fluttered, and I awaited his arrival with the greatest anxiety and impatience. He approached nearer, and I then had a distinct view of his features, and with an exclamation of joy I recognised them in a moment.

"'Ah!' I exclaimed, 'it is one of the principal domestics of Antonio; he brings a message from him, no doubt.'

'Be calm, Valentia,' said my father, 'and let us hope at any rate that he brings us good news.'

"The man now arrived at the door, and dismounting from his horse, he was admitted.

"'How now, signor,' I hastily demanded; 'your master, his highness, the Prince Bianchi, he is—"

"'His highness is quite well, signora,' replied the man; 'he has sent me hither to convey to yourself and your father these letters, which will account for his absence, and inform you of his future intentions. He requests that you will favour him with an answer, if it be only a line.'

"I cannot do adequate justice to the feelings which agitated my bosom as I took the letter from his hand; and retiring to another part of the room, with a trembling hand I broke the seal, and unfolding the letter, with eyes bedimmed with tears proceeded to read the contents. It was couched in the same ardent, eloquent, and affectionate language as the one I had before received from him, assured me of the continuance of his unbounded love, and apologised for his having kept me so long in suspense, he having been unavoidably detained at the villa by important business, but that I might depend upon seeing him at the residence of my parents in five or six days at the latest.

"What a tumult of joy swelled my bosom as I perused these welcome lines! All the doubts and apprehensions that had before disturbed me were immediately removed; Antonio was still faithful; he was coming to visit me in a few short days, and I was happy. Having received the permission of my father, I retired to my own apartment to write the answer which Antonio had requested. What the contents of that epistle were I cannot now recall to my memory; but you may be sure that they were all that the peculiar circumstances of the case could dictate, and many were the tears of joy I shed during the time that I was engaged in writing it. Having accomplished this task, I returned to the room, and placed it in the hand of my father for his perusal. He made no remarks when he had done so, but his looks as he returned it to me convinced me that he approved of it; and having sealed it, I delivered it to the care of the messenger, who only stopped to partake of some refreshment, and then took his departure on his return to the Villa Rosa.

"For some minutes after he was gone, my emotions were so great, and so mingled were the thoughts that crowded upon my brain, that I could not give utterance to a word, and my parents conversed in whispers together with each other.

"'Oh, my father,' I said at length, 'what an insupportable weight of doubt and anxiety has this letter removed from my mind. Antonio has not forgotten me—his love has suffered no abatement—in a few days he will be here without fail, and I am now one of the happiest of human beings.'

"'Be not too sanguine, Valentia,' he replied, 'lest you should still be doomed to disappointment. I must confess that I still have my doubts of the Prince Bianchi's sincerity.'

"'Oh, surely this is most unjust and ungenerous,' I remarked; 'what is there in the tenor of his letter that should raise any doubt as to his sincerity? I fear, my father, that, notwithstanding all you have asserted to the contrary, you are most fatally prejudiced against him, and that you are now too ready to attribute to him motives which have never entered his mind.'

"'Indeed I am not, Valentia,' he replied; 'you should know your father's disposition different to that.'

"'Is it likely that he would have taken the trouble to send a messenger hither, unless he intended keeping his word?' I demanded.

"'I do not doubt that he will visit us,' observed my father, 'but at the same time I am still of the opinion I have before expressed, namely, that he has not the sanction of his father for the continuance of his addresses to you; and if such be the case, however painful it may be to your feelings, I shall feel it my duty to break off all further correspondence between you.'

"I trembled and turned pale as he gave utterance to these words, and I was compelled to support myself against the back of a chair.

"'Alas, my father!' I ejaculated, 'recall those hasty words; would you condemn me to lasting misery and despair?'

"'Heaven forbid that I should do so, my child,' he answered; 'it is to save you from misery and despair that I would act in the manner I have stated.'

"'You would banish Antonio from my presence for ever,' I returned, 'and, therefore, you had far better deprive me at once of that life which, under such circumstances, must become insupportable to me.'

"'Would Valentia have Antonio break the solemn promise he has probably made to his father on his death-bed?' he interrogated; 'would she consent to continue to receive his addresses under such circumstances?—Beware, child, and reflect maturely;—you know not what it is you would do;—Antonio could never make you his wife; and, therefore, any correspondence between you must be dishonourable to you both.'

" ' Oh, father, how cruel are the conclusions you arrive at,' I remarked; ' think you that a dishonourable thought against me could for a moment enter the mind of Antonio ?—What has there ever been in his conduct to give rise to such suspicions ?'

" ' Nothing, I admit,' he replied; ' but nevertheless the caution that I would use is prompted by the strictest prudence, and the duty which I owe to you. Believe me, Valentia, harsh as I may seem at present, you will have reason to acknowledge the propriety of the course I have determined to pursue.'

" ' Determine nothing, I beseech you, till you have seen Antonio, and heard his explanation, and I feel convinced that you will then be satisfied that your suspicions are groundless.'

" ' And most happy shall I be, Valentia, to find that they are so,' he returned.

" ' Oh, indeed you will do so,' I ejaculated eagerly; ' I will stake my very existence on the result. Does not every line that Antonio writes bespeak his sincerity and the ardour of his love ?'

" ' They certainly agree with his former professions,' answered my father; ' still all depends upon the injunctions he has received from his father, and which, after the conduct of the late Prince Bianchi towards us, I cannot help thinking are opposed to your wishes; and, if so, I must not, cannot sanction the passion that exists between you,'

" ' Alas! alas! fatal words. What anguish do they impart to my breast !'

" ' Valentia,' said my father, ' I am now comparatively poor, but no change of fortune has been enabled to destroy the innate and proper pride which I naturally possess ; and never will I give the world reason to say that I was guided by sordid and selfish motives in disposing of the hand of my daughter."

" ' Not though the future happiness of your daughter depended on your consent ?' I said, breathlessly.

" ' I could not submit, Valentia; but you are in no fit state of mind to argue this delicate subject further at present. Retire to your chamber, and reflect serious ly upon all that my affection and anxious solicitude for your welfare has prompted me to say to you; and may wisdom guide you in the decision you must at last come to. Would to heaven that this meeting were over, or that it might never take place.'

" ' My whole hopes of happiness or future misery depend upon it,' I said. ' Of what use is my reflecting when I am convinced that I can come to no other conclusion or decision than that which I have already ?'

" ' You will think better of this, Valentia,' observed my father. ' I do not yet despair of you. Come, child, dry your tears ; put your dependance on the gooodness of the Supreme, and you will yet be released from the cares and anxieties by which you are at present surrounded.

" ' God grant that I may !' I cried fervently, ' although at present there appears but little hope for me.'

" I said no more, but with a heavy heart I slowly retired from the room, and with melancholy footsteps I made my way to my own room. Here the power of my accumulated feelings found vent in a copious flood of tears, and for some time my heart was too full to suffer me to give utterance to a syllable. I pondered over every word my father had spoken, and the more I did so, the greater became the anguish of my heart, and the more vividly was my misery presented to my disordered imagination. It seemed quite evident to me that he had made up his mind not to give his consent to Antonio continuing his addresses to me, if the explanation he had to give should not prove satisfactory, and I was also convinced that no arguments or supplications that myself and Antonio might offer would be able to move him from his purpose. I had likewise too much reason to believe that the surmises of my father were correct as regarded the dying injunctions of the late Prince Bianchi; and if such were the case, Antonio durst not disobey them, and all hope would be at an end.

" ' Alas !' I ejaculated, ' why did cruel Fate ever interfere to disturb the happiness and tranquillity we once experienced ? Why did Fortune not continue to smile upon us ? Had she done so, there could have deen no objection to the love which I and Antonio entertain for each other, and we might have quickly looked forward to the consummation of our earthly bliss, and to a long series of the greatest blessings that it is possible for human beings to experience. But as it is, how different is the prospect that opens upon our vision ; so dark and dismal, that the heart shudders at the contemplation.'

" In this manner I continued to reflect for some time longer, and although I exerted all the means in my power, I could not find the least degree of consolation. I threw myself on my knees, and in fervent accents I supplicated the mercy and the guidance of the Almighty, without whose interposition I saw plain enough there was no hope for me, but that my fate, on the contrary was sealed. I did feel a little more confidence after this prayer, and I endeavoured to hope that when Antonio arrived he would be able to explain everything to the satisfaction of my father. Had he known that he could not do so, he would surely not have written, but would rather have been anxious to avoid seeing me again, since an interview under such circumstances must naturally be productive of so much anguish to us both.

"'Oh, yes, my beloved Antonio,' I said, 'I will not despair, but await patiently your arrival, when it will be in your power at once to remove all the painful doubts which at present distract my breast. Your father could never have been so cruel and unjust as to exact a promise from you in his dying moments which he knew must annihilate all your hopes, and render you miserable for ever. The very idea is unnatural and improbable. I will not

THE PRINCE BIANCHI ALARMED AT THE VISION IN THE GARDEN.

give way to it. Dear Antonio, in a few days then I shall behold you again, and once more hear you repeat those vows of love and constancy you have so often uttered in my ears. Blissful assurance! that is enough to banish the dismal ideas that have taken possession of my mind, and to inspire me once more with cheerfulness and hope.'

"I felt more calm and resigned as these thoughts flashed upon my brain; and after a short time longer passed in meditation, I retired to rest, and soon sunk to sleep, reposing more tranquilly than I had done for many nights before.

"How anxiously did I now look forward to the day on which my lover was expected to arrive, and how tediously the hours seemed to wear away. But I trembled at the thought of the reception my father might give him, and in endeavouring to think what would be the result of the explanation which he would demand of him, and on which my future happiness, nay, my very life in all probability depended. I alternated between hope and fear; and sometimes my apprehensions reached to such a pitch as almost to overwhelm me. My father treated me with every kindness and consideration; and seeing how painful it was to me, he did not again offer to broach the subject until the day before that on which Antonio was expected to arrive at our dwelling. As may be expected, I was in a state of the greatest excitement and agitation as the important period approached, and it was not likely that I should be able to conceal my feelings from the observation of my parents, if I had even been so inclined. The tenderness of their looks showed how deeply they sympathised with me, and how anxious they were to mitigate my anguish.

"'The hour of trial rapidly approaches, Valentia,' said my father; 'to-morrow, according to what he stated in his letter, we may expect to behold the Prince Bianchi, when those doubts which at present occupy our minds, I trust, will be removed. Be firm, my child, and endeavour to hope that all will terminate as happily as your fondest wishes can anticipate.'

"'Oh, my dear father,' I replied, 'could I think so, there would not, indeed, be a happier being in existence than your poor Valentia; but should Antonio not be able to satisfy your doubts, my fate will be sealed, and the sooner my wretched existence shall be an end the better.'

"'What melancholy thoughts are these, child?' he observed; 'why do you not endeavour to conquer them, for they are unworthy of you. It is our duty to submit to the will of Heaven, which ordains everything for the best, with patience and resignation. It is sinful to murmur at the decrees (however severe they may appear to be) of that Almighty Being, of whom we are only the humblest of His creatures.'

"'I do not murmur, my father; but when I see the fatality that attends me and those so dearly connected with me,' I replied, 'how can I be content?—I am ready and willing to follow all the dictates of prudence; but prudence is but a cold and unseemly thing when placed in juxtaposition with virtuous love. Antonio bears that love towards me which I honour; our hearts beats in unison,—he, I am certain, would die to save me one little moment's pang, and I, God knows, would freely give up life, if by so doing I could secure his earthly happiness;—

so are our hearts united, and yet you would have us forget each other! Oh, father, I marvel much if ever you knew much of love, unless in its mere superficial acceptation, if it be thus you argue.'

"'Valentia,' replied my father, 'you form altogether a wrong opinion of that which I would endeavour to instil into your mind; but a few hours will bring Antonio hither, and on his explanation you may probably rest satisfied that the advice which I have thrown out and which I would impress upon your mind is not uncalled for. Till then, I shall say no more upon the subject; I see you are melancholy,—sad at heart, and need to-day a little calm reflection in the solitude of your own room; retire, therefore, my dear girl, and may Heaven guide you in its wisdom how to act at this momentous and critical period of your life.'

"With these words he embraced me with his usual ardour of affection; and after a few words of kindness and consolation from my mother, I did retire to my own apartment, glad to escape to the free indulgence of my own thoughts.

"The anxiety of mind which I suffered that day I need not attempt to describe; the various doubts, and hopes, and fears, created quite a tumult in my breast; and it was some time ere I could sufficiently collect myself so as to direct my thoughts into one regular channel. I saw plainly that there was nothing but disappointment, misery, and anxiety in store for me; and as the time drew near at which we expected Antonio to arrive, my fortitude and confidence almost entirely deserted me; and although so anxious once more to behold my lover, I could not divest my mind of a feeling of apprehension as to what would be the result of that meeting. My father would not fail to keep his word, nor could I in my reasonable moments deny that he would be perfectly justified in adopting such a course, should it turn out that his surmises were correct, and that Antonio had been bound by a solemn oath by the Prince Bianchi, his father, in his dying moments, to discontinue his addresses to me; in fact, duty and proper pride demanded imperatively that he should act so, and although the trial would be a severe one to bear, I had no other alternative than to learn to submit without a murmur.

"I slept but little that night, and the same fears that had tortured my mind in my waking moments, haunted my imagination in my dreams. I arose in the morning with a sad heart, and after having offered up my prayers to the Fountain of all good, I left my chamber, and found my parents at the breakfast table. Very little conversation took place during the meal, for they saw plainly that I was not in a fit state of mind to enter into it, and they probably thought it would be much better and more prudent to leave me for a short time to the free indulgence of my own meditations. What the nature of the meditations were I will leave to the imagination of the reader of these lines, and hasten as quickly as I can to the conclusion of this melancholy history, while the opportunity is afforded me: Ah! I am interrupted. Some one is ascending the stairs. It is doubtless he, and I must hasten to conceal these sad memorials. Heaven only knows what would be my melancholy fate should they meet his sight.

* * * * *

"Yes, he has visited me again, and his manners were more stern and unrelenting than before. He has turned a deaf ear to all my remonstrances and supplications, and has refused to satisfy me as to what are his future intentions with regard to myself, and my poor infant boy. Oh, Antonio, who could have thought that you could act with such unprovoked and systematic cruelty towards that unfortunate being whom you fondly led to suppose you loved with all the ardour of affection that man can feel towards woman?—May Heaven pardon you, and bring you to a full sense of the injustice of your conduct. This suspense is dreadful; but it is quite evident that he wishes to rid himself of me and my tender offspring, and will have no scruples as to the plan he shall adopt to do so. Would to God that both myself and my child were no more! But to resume my melancholy narrative.

"The morning repast was scarcely over when we were interrupted in the conversation that was about to ensue between us by hearing the tramp of horses' hoofs advancing rapidly towards the house; and looking from the window, my heart palpitated violently against my side, and my bosom throbbed with emotion and expectation when I beheld the confidential servant of Antonio who had before been dispatched to us riding rapidly towards our dwelling, and the next moment he stopped before the door, and was speedily in the presence of myself and my parents, by whom he was received with every politeness and cordiality, and I awaited with the most anxious impatience to hear the message he had to deliver, though I well guessed the purport of it.

"'His Highness, the Prince Bianchi,' said the messenger, 'desires me to present his compliments to you, Signor Valori, and your fair daughter the Signora Valentia, and to inform you that he is now on his way from the Villa Rosa to your residence, and hopes to have the honour and the pleasure of seeing you in an hour or two.'

"How my heart fluttered with mingled feelings of pleasure and apprehension at this announcement, and I turned ghastly pale and blushed alternately. My parents well read the emotions that agitated my breast, from the expression of my features, and they encouraged

and reassured me by a smile, which I could not misunderstand.

"'His highness does us honour,' said my father, in reply to the domestic of Antonio, 'and rest assured he will receive as cordial and sincere a welcome as our humble means will allow us to give him. Valentia, my love, retire with your mother; I have a few words to say in private to our good friend here.'

"I made no reply, for my bosom was at the time too full with mingled feelings; and my mother taking my arm, we quitted the room and retired to another apartment, where my beloved parent allowed me for a few minutes to give free and uninterrupted vent to my feelings.

"'My dear child,' she at length said, 'let me beg of you to calm the emotions which naturally spring up in your breast at the thought of so soon again beholding the object upon whom you have placed your affections; I would not damp the ardour of your spirits, but I would wish you to be prepared for all that may take place, so that you may the better be enabled to support any disappointment to your hopes which may arise.'

"'Oh, my dear mother,' I returned, 'and are you then of the opinion which my father has so frequently expressed, namely, that Antonio has been commanded by his father on his death-bed to forget me, and that there is, consequently, an end to the fond hopes I had formed of becoming his wife?'

"'Alas, my child,' she answered; 'there is too much reason in the supposition for me easily to reject it; and I cannot but approve of and admire the prudent precaution of your father in seeking to prepare you for the worst that may take place. You well knew the proud spirit of the late Prince Bianchi; and if anything might be wanting to show the feelings which predominated in his breast, surely it would be found in his conduct towards us in so abruptly breaking off the intimacy that had existed between us for so many years on the change which took place in our circumstances. Your father could never consent to Antonio's breaking any solemn promise he may have made under such peculiar circumstances, even if he were willing to do so; and surely my Valentia would find fortitude and womanly pride sufficient to submit to her fate without a murmur?'

"'I trust, my mother,' I returned, with a sigh, 'that you will never find your child unworthy of the name which she possesses; but can Antonio so readily erase from his memory all the tender vows and asseverations he has so frequently made to me? Can he cease to love me, and to discard me from his bosom altogether?'

"'No,' she replied, 'and it is there, Valentia, that the danger may arise to you both, and which it will requires all your energies and self-perseverance to counteract.'

"'Ah, how arduous is the task!' I ejaculated; 'how shall I ever be able to accomplish it! Antonio was the companion of my childhood; mutual love found dominion in our breasts from the earliest period; nature seemed to have formed us for each other; our thoughts and wishes are all in strict harmony and unison, and think you then that it is possible we can so easily forget each other, and look upon ourselves in future with no other but the cold sentiments of friendship and esteem? Oh, it is impossible! But Antonio is under no such restrictions—I am certain he is not, notwithstanding all that yourself and my revered father have said, or would he have written to us as he has done? Would he have so anxiously sought this meeting? Would he not rather have dreaded it, have shrunk from it, rather than have witnessed the anguish of my disappointment and despair? Oh, yes, something seems to satisfy me and assure me that I am right in my surmises, and I cannot, dare not relinquish my hopes.'

"'Well, my dear child,' remarked my mother, in accents which bespoke her sincerity, 'heaven send that your fondest and most sanguine wishes may be realised, for what could possibly afford me greater gratification than to see them consummated? But still let me advise you to calm your emotions, and to bear the result of this meeting, and the explanation which the young Prince Bianchi may have to give, with firmness and self-possession. But, see, Geraldi is about again to take his departure, no doubt to meet his master on his way hither, and to deliver to him the answer of your father.'

"I looked from the window of the room in which we were, and saw Geraldi shaking hands with my father, and about to remount his horse, and directly afterwards he rode off at full speed, and was soon out of sight. My mother then took my arm and we returned to the parlour in which we had left my father.

"'My dear Valentia,' he said, taking my hand affectionately, 'the time now rapidly approaches in which all your energies and fortitude will be put to the test, and I sincerely trust that you will be able to act as becomes you, and that everything will terminate according to your wishes, and most sanguine expectations. But still, my child, I must request you to consult your own dignity of feeling, and not to yield that to your affection, which honour and prudence should deny.'

"'My father, I replied, and feelings of the most powerful description swelled my bosom, 'shall never have cause to blush for or reproach his child. But, tell me, have you been enabled to elicit from Geraldi any more particulars of his master that may serve to dissipate the doubts and suspicions that have gained possession of your mind?'

"'I have not,' he replied, 'but he will shortly be here to answer for himself; and in the meantime I would advise you to retire for a little while to your own apartment, so that you may be able to collect your thoughts, and to prepare yourself for all that may take place at the interview. Believe me, that I have every consideration for your feelings, and that no one is more anxious than myself that the result of it may be the forerunner of future and uninterrupted happiness to you both.'

"I embraced him without making any reply, and then hastened from the room in order that I might commune with my own thoughts, which I need scarcely say were of the most painful and conflicting description.

"How tediously did the time seem to me to wear away until the arrival of my lover! I awaited with the utmost impatience, and my agitation increased every moment. Many were the prayers which I offered up to the Supreme that the doubts and suspicions my father had expressed might prove to be unfounded, for on that alone rested all my future hopes; and if they should by cruel fate be doomed to be disappointed, life would become hateful and a burthen to me, and the sooner I was rid of it the better.

"'But Providence surely has not such misery in store for us both,' I ejaculated; 'hearts so fondly united as ours are, will not, must not be doomed to be severed. No, Antonio, I feel re-assured and inspired with fresh confidence, and I will endeavour to discard from my breast altogether the thoughts, the gloomy thoughts and forebodings which have lately taken possession of it. But a short time will decide all, and dissipate the fearful forebodings that have so long harassed and distracted my mind.'

"I now seated myself by the window, from which was commanded an extensive view of the high road, and anxiously and eagerly watched for the appearance of my lover. In this manner more than an hour and a half passed away, and still I could behold no signs of the object of my anxiety, and I began to fear that some accident had occurred to him, and which would prevent him from arriving at the time he had promised; but at length, I beheld the forms of approaching horsemen at a distance, and my heart leapt within my breast, for something told me it could be no other than he whom I was so anxious to behold; and as they advanced nearer I was convinced that I was not mistaken, for I speedily recognised the well-known form of Antonio, followed by a retinue of servants, and making with all possible speed towards the house. I clasped my hands together in a paroxysm of joy, and my heart palpitated against my side with double its wonted pace. Nearer and nearer they came, and I now had a distinct view of the features of my beloved Antonio. Never had he appeared half so handsome and noble in my imagination as he did on that occasion. I felt as if I could have leaped from the window and sprang into his arms in the transport of my feelings. In a few minutes he arrived to within a few yards of the house, and he then looked anxiously up at the window where I was standing; but I was convinced that he did not see me, for he made no acknowledgment, and the next moment my father came forth, and after greeting him apparently with the greatest cordiality and respect, he escorted him into the house.

"I immediately sank on my knees, and fervently returned my thanks to Providence for conducting him in safety to my dwelling, and earnestly supplicated it to give me strength sufficient to support this important meeting with becoming firmness and composure. I now anxiously awaited the time when I should be summoned into his presence and that of my parents; but nearly half an hour elapsed, and I heard nothing from them, and I began to think that they had either forgotten me, or that something had occurred to cause them to change their minds, and not to suffer the interview between myself and Antonio to take place; but that idea was almost immediately afterwards banished, when the room-door opened, and my mother made her appearance.

"'Now, my dear Valentia,' she observed, 'the important moment has arrived, and I trust you have sufficiently composed your feelings to meet it as becomes you. The Prince Bianchi awaits most anxiously to see you.'

"'Blessed words!' I exclaimed, 'with what feelings of hope and joy do they inspire me. But tell me, my dear mother, has my father had his doubts and suspicions removed; and may I again encourage the hope of peace and happiness?'

"'Your father and Antonio have not yet entered into mutual explanations,' she replied, 'for they probably thought that would be better deferred until the first excitement of your meeting had passed over. But, come, Valentia, be calm, and hope for the best.'

"'Your words encourage me, my dear mother,' I returned, 'and I will endeavour to be so; come, I am ready to attend, and to learn at once the fate that is in store for me.'

"I took her arm, and with a trembling step, and a heart fluttering with emotion, suffered her to lead me down the stairs. At the door of the room in which my father and Antonio were I paused, and sought to collect myself; but I had not much time given me for reflection, for it was speedily opened, and the next instant I found myself clasped frantically in the arms of my lover. I will pass hastily

over the scene which followed, for it was more, much more powerful than I could do adequate justice to, even though my pen were most eloquent. I experienced a few moments of far greater bliss than I had ever before known in my life. Alas! by what painful, what insupportable misery was it too soon to be followed. Even while I now reflect on it, I shudder with horror.

"For a few minutes myself and Antonio were too violently agitated by our feelings to be able to give utterance to a syllable, and my parents did not offer to interrupt us, but retired to the farther end of the room, and watched us in silence and with feelings of the deepest interest.

"'My adored Valentia,' at length exclaimed the prince, still straining me rapturously to his bosom, and gazing in my blushing face with looks which seemed to bespeak the most ardent passion, 'and do we at last meet again? Do I once more press you to that heart which so fondly and sincerely beats for you alone? Oh, moment of extatic bliss! almost too great for human being to experience! And your eyes beam kindness and welcome upon me; may I then indeed hope that those sentiments you formerly expressed towards me remain unchanged? That absence and apparent neglect have not obliterated my image from your heart?'

'My lord!' I faltered out, scarce knowing what reply to make, and that in the presence of my parents, though my lips would fain have given utterance to the words which my heart dictated.

"'My lord?' repeated Bianchi, with a look of gentle reproach and regret. 'Valentia, why that cold and formal word? It chills my very heart, and seems to fill my breast with sad and dismal forebodings. Am I not still your Antonio? your devoted, your most humble slave, ready to worship you, and to resign all the world for your sake? Oh, little can you imagine the many pangs, the hours of misery, and torturing anxiety I have endured since I have been separated from you, how I have prayed to behold you again; tell me then, I beseech you, have such been the feelings that have also animated your breast towards me, or has some more favoured youth supplanted me in your love, and——"

"'Antonio!' I interrupted, in a voice of the greatest agitation and confusion; 'what cruel and ungenerous words are these, and how little, oh, how very little do I deserve them! The sentiments that I have before so frequently expressed towards you remain unchanged, but alas!——'

"'Alas, what?' he eagerly demanded, 'what do your fears portend?'

"'Fate has raised a barrier between us which I fear can never be surmounted,' I replied, in a faint voice.

" ' What mean you?' he ejaculated, looking at me earnestly, and with the greatest anxiety and suspense depicted in his countenance.

" ' The disparity in our stations and circumstances,' I answered; ' the wealthy and noble Prince Bianchi can never condescend to become the husband of the poor and humble Valentia Di Valori!'

" ' Valentia!' he cried, ' how have I deserved this? Can you think so meanly of me as to imagine that such sordid considerations can work any influence upon my heart? Of what value would wealth, and rank, and title, be to me if Valentia were not permitted to share them with me?'

" My father now advanced towards us, and I trembled and turned pale, for too well I guessed what he was about to say.

" ' Pardon me, my lord,' he remarked; ' but before I can suffer this scene to proceed further, I must a word with you.'

" ' I am ready to listen to you, Signor Valori,' replied Antonio, with a doubtful and hesitating look; ' and I trust that I shall be able to answer to your satisfaction.'

" ' For your sake, my lord,' observed my father, ' and that of my dear child, I sincerely hope that you may. Valentia, be seated, and tranquillise your feelings.'

" I suffered myself to be led to a chair, scarcely knowing what I did, and awaited with the most breathless anxiety to hear what my father had to say, and the answer which Antonio should return to it; for on that my future happiness or misery entirely depended, and the prince seemed to experience equal suspense and impatience.

" ' My lord,' at length began my father, ' you have ever professed to love my daughter.'

" ' Love her, Signor Valori!' he answered; ' by Heaven! I speak not bombastically or hypocritically when I declare that she is the very idol of my soul! Can you doubt the truth and sincerity of what I say, signor?'

" ' Well,' returned my father, ' we will e'en waive that point. I do believe you. Valentia, I am also convinced, returns your passion; but there is one point which, if you cannot answer me satisfactorily, will render it necessary that all future correspondence between you shall cease.'

" ' Cease, signor?' exclaimed Antonio, with an expression of astonishment and agitation.

" ' Ay, my lord,' answered my father, ' even so, however painful it may be to you both.'

" ' For Heaven's sake, what do you mean, signor?' demanded Bianchi; ' your observations torture me: do not keep me in suspense.'

" ' Be calm, Prince Bianchi, for it will require all your patience and firmness to listen to what I have to say, and to reply to me with candour and as becomes a man of honour. I need not inform you what a change has come over my fortunes and the future prospects of Valentia. I was once in affluence, but I am now comparatively poor; you are rich, noble, and, in a pecuniary point of view, my daughter is no longer a fitting match for the Prince Bianchi.'

" ' Signor Valori,' returned Antonio, impatiently, ' you deeply wrong me if you imagine that such selfish considerations as those you have mentioned can ever influence my conduct. I should hate and despise myself if I thought they could. I love your daughter for her numerous and transcendent virtues alone, and——'

" ' But are you at liberty to act from your own unbiassed will?' interrupted my father.

" The prince hesitated, and my heart misgave me.

" ' Why do you put such a question to me, signor?' interrogated my lover in a faltering voice.

" ' My lord,' replied my father, ' pardon me, but I must candidly speak my mind, for this is a subject that will not admit of any equivocation or false delicacy. From the many years of intimacy, and I will say friendship, that existed between us, there were few individuals who had so good an opportunity of knowing the character of your late lamented father as myself. Jealous of his great wealth and elevated position in society, he was accustomed to look upon those who were placed in less fortunate circumstances with a haughty feeling of contempt; it was his principal weakness; and think not that by thus reminding you of it I wish to cast any scandal or reproach upon his memory. Fortune frowned upon me, and he then knew me not, and his subsequent conduct has proved to me that he wished to forget that he had ever, at any period, honoured me with his friendship.'

" ' I pray you, signor,' observed Antonio ' dismiss such ideas from your mind, for you wrong the late prince, my honoured father, by entertaining them. He ever spoke of you with the utmost respect.'

" ' For that I owe him my gratitude,' remarked my father; ' but that is not exactly the point at which I wish to arrive. I am satisfied that had he been living, he would never have sanctioned your union with my daughter.'

" Antonio looked more confused than before; and my agitation increased to an insupportable degree.

" ' You do not answer me, my lord,' said my father; ' you look confounded, and that all but confirms me in the suspicions which I have formed.'

" ' Suspicions, signor?' repeated my lover, with a look of surprise; ' what suspicions can you have formed?'

" ' Answer me one question, Prince Bianchi.'

" ' Name it, signor.'

" ' Did you not make any promise to your father in his dying moments in reference to what I have alluded to? In other words, did not the late prince enjoin you never to marry any maiden who was not your equal in rank and fortune?'

" ' Oh, why do you put so painful a question to me, Signor Valori?' demanded Antonio, his confusion and agitation increasing every instant.

" ' Answer me, my lord,' said my father, impatiently.

" ' Alas!' replied Bianchi, after a pause, during which he seemed to suffer very much; ' unfortunately he did.'

" ' And you promised him?'

" ' 'Tis too true! how could I help myself?'

" ' Then, my lord,' returned my father, resolutely, and rising from his chair, ' that decides all; all further correspondence between my daughter and yourself must from this moment cease. You are prohibited from becoming her husband, you dare not disobey the dying commands of your father, and—'

" ' Hear me, signor, I beseech you,' interrupted Antonio, in a state of the greatest excitement.

" ' Enough, Prince Bianchi,' replied my father; ' you can urge nothing that can move me from my determination. Pardon me, my lord, I would not appear rude; but under such circumstances I must decline the honour of your future visits here, and I must also insist that you do not again attempt to communicate with Valentia, who must henceforth be a stranger to you.'

" I heard no more, but uttering a cry of the most indescribable anguish, I became insensible. Happy would it have been for me had I never awoke to consciousness again. I had heard my doom pronounced, and better, far better would it have been for me had death at once have put a period to my sufferings. But I have been reserved to endure such miseries as have seldom fallen to the lot of human being.

" When I was restored to sensibility, I found myself in my own chamber, stretched upon the bed, and my mother anxiously and affectionately attending upon me. All that had taken place, every word that had been uttered at that important and painful interview, rushed upon my memory as vividly as if they had occurred only the instant before, and the anguish of my mind was so intense that I knew not how to contain myself. My amiable mother in her most tender and soothing accents sought to impart consolation to me; but for the time her words were lost upon me, and, if anything, they only served to increase my agony and impatience.

" ' Where is Antonio? Where is the Prince Bianchi?' I demanded.

" ' Be calm, child,' expostulated my mother; ' your father has only acted as stern duty and necessity demanded.'

" ' Duty! necessity!' I repeated; ' cold formal words; was it the duty of my father to sever two hearts so fondly united as mine and Antonio's?—Oh, 'tis most cruel, thus at one fell blow to annihilate all the hopes I had so fondly formed.'

" ' Valentia,' said my mother, ' you surely cannot thus close your mind to reason. Has not the Prince Bianchi acknowledged that his father had exacted an oath from him in his last moments; and think you that he dare break that solemn promise?'

" ' Oh, I cannot, dare not believe it,' I ejaculated, clasping my aching and burning temples; ' the late Prince Bianchi could never have been so cruel and unreasonable, knowing the fervent passion which had existed between us from our earliest days. It must be a bitter mockery altogether, a monstrous invention, fabricated only to torture me, to drive me to madness and despair.'

" ' Valentia,' said my mother, ' I am surprised at you; you cannot know what you say. Think you that the happiness and welfare of our child is not dearer to your father and myself than our very existence? and could we for a moment think of doing that towards you which reason, prudence, and affection did not dictate?—Had circumstances permitted it, Heaven knows how gladly would we have seen you united to the man to whom you have unfortunately devoted your heart; but fate wills it otherwise, and painful though the task may be, there is no other alternative for you left than to endeavour to submit to it.'

" ' Oh, how easy is it to give advice!' I replied, impatiently; ' but had you ever loved like me, you would know how utterly futile would be the task to attempt to follow it. All the bright prospects I had formed, and in which I was encouraged, are crushed, and it matters not now what becomes of me. Would that death would terminate my sufferings; for life has become a curse to me.'

" ' Oh, forbear, Valentia,' she remonstrated, ' such observations as those to which you have just now given utterance are sinful, and I must not, cannot listen to them. It is our bounden duty to bear with patience and resignation all those trials to which it may be the will of Providence to subject us; and if we put our trust in its goodness and mercy, it never fails to raise us up from the despair into which we may have been plunged, at the moment when, probably, we least expect it.'

" I shook my head mournfully, burst into tears, and for some minutes was unable to give utterance to a word, my excellent mother still exerting herself to the utmost to tranquillise my feelings.

" ' But where is Antonio ?' I at length demanded, in a frantic voice ;—' what has become of him. ?'

" ' He has retired from the house, my child,' replied my mother ; ' but do not harass yourself with questions for the present, but rather try to obtain that firmness, which you now, under all the circumstances so much require.'

" ' He is banished from the house, then,' I cried ; ' banished, discarded, insulted, like the veriest wretch that ever crawled the face of the earth. Oh, it is fit treatment for one who possesses the noble mind and soul of honour of my Antonio !—And was I not allowed one single word at parting from one who is so precious to me, and for the preservation of whose happiness I would willingly have laid down my very life ?—Oh, this is indeed most cruel : the thought will drive me to madness ! Alas ! and shall I never more be permitted to behold him? —Must we indeed henceforth become as strangers to each other ?—But, no ! they may tear us asunder ; they may prohibit our meetings ; but what can ever stifle the warm, the ardent, the virtuous passion that glows within our breasts towards each other ?—What can ever have the power to banish us from each other's memory ?—Nothing, while the warm life's-blood shall continue to circulate throughout our veins.'

" I threw myself back on my bed, and gave myself up entirely to the agony of my feelings. Such was the shock I had received that I found it was utterly impossible for me to leave my couch, and my mother continued to watch by me with the most anxious solicitude for some time ; but at length, as I earnestly requested to be left alone that I might commune with my own thoughts, she complied, and retired from the chamber. It was totally in vain that I endeavoured again to obtain the least alleviation of my anguish ; and the more I did so, the greater became its intensity. The acknowledgment of Antonio, which I sought to persuade myself was nothing more than a frightful dream, showed me the utter hopelessness of my fate, and nearly drove my brain to madness. All the worst surmises of my father were verified ; Antonio dare not break the solemn oath his father had so unjustly extorted from him, and he was, therefore, lost to me for ever. Nor could I in the sincerity of my heart blame the course which my father had adopted, though at first it seemed harsh and premature ; no, it was prompted by reason and honour, and I knew full well also that it was my duty to submit without repining, whatever anguish it might cost me. But could Antonio ever banish me from his memory ? I reflected ; notwithstanding the promise he had given to his father ; and could he ever forget those vows of love which he had so often uttered to me, and which I believed to be sincere ?—Oh, no ; I

felt thoroughly convinced that was impossible ; and in that assurance I felt a degree of melancholy consolation. But what must be the sufferings and despair of Bianchi now that he was driven from my presence altogether ? and bound as he was by the injunctions of his father, he had no just ground for urging his suit and combating the arguments of my parent. That idea tortured me more than all ; and yet there were moments when I could not help encouraging a faint hope that we should not only meet again, but that something would also occur to set aside the difficulties by which we were at present surrounded, and to remove the obstacles to our union. Weak fool that I must have been to encourage such an idea for a moment ! and how little did I then know of the real character of the man in whom I placed such fond and implicit confidence ! But I have learnt it since from bitter and terrible experience.

" For three or four days I was in such a weak and melancholy state that I was unable to leave my chamber, and my mother was almost in constant attendance upon me, unless when I expressed a wish to be alone, and tried by every argument which reason, humanity, and maternal love could suggest to her to reconcile me to my fate ; but she met with little or no success ; indeed, grief was so heavy at my heart that it would admit of no amelioration. At length I was persuaded to leave my room, and to grant my father an interview, and indeed I was most anxious to see him, though I never for a moment expected or entertained the idea that he would be induced to change his mind as regarded Bianchi, who indeed had by his oath rendered the determination he had come to imperative and irrevocable.

" My father received me with much kindness and commiseration, and expressed his regret at the illness I had undergone, and at the still delicate state of my appearance. To this I only replied by sighs and tears, and he suffered me for some time to give vent to them undisturbed, or without attempting to make use of a single observation. At length I partially regained my tranquillity, and I then eagerly inquired of him the circumstances which had taken place after I became insensible on the day of my interview with Antonio. He informed me, in as few words as possible, that Bianchi, as might be expected, was very much affected, but he had no argument to offer against my father's decision ; and after about an hour's conversation, he took his leave, begging that my father would assure me of the continuance of his love though fate might never suffer us to meet again, and requesting that I would sometimes bestow a thought upon him, if it were only as the friend and companion of my childhood.

" ' Remember him !' I ejaculated ; ' can I ever tear his image from my heart ? No ; it is impossible! Dear Antonio, surely we have both deserved a far different fate to this. May Heaven watch o'er thee, and give thee strength to meet these misfortunes with fortitude and resignation.'

"'Well said, my dear Valentia,' observed my father; 'that is what you must both exert yourselves to do, since you see the utter impossibility of avoiding the fate that is ordained for you; and, therefore, the sooner you endeavour to conquer the sentiments you now entertain towards each other, the better. Fear not

MELINA CONSOLED BY FLORETTA.

but in time you will both be able to fix your affections upon two other beings, who may be equally calculated to make you happy.'

"'Oh, no,' I replied, emphatically, 'that can never be. I am certain that we are both so fondly and so sincerely devoted to each other, that nothing can ever alter our sentiments, no persons can have the power of supplanting us in each other's love. The bright prospects we once indulged in the anticipation of are now for ever overclouded, and, therefore, all chance of happiness for us is at an end.'

" ' Why thus give way to despair, Valentia?' said my father; ' 'tis true, I am ready to admit, that both of you are subjected to a severe trial, and that you have much cause to complain of the disappointment of your hopes and wishes, and the cruel fate which has overtaken you: but you must struggle against it, and no doubt in time you will be enabled to find that consolation of which you stand so much in need. There is one thing, however, for which I cannot help severely blaming the young Prince Bianchi.'

" ' And what is that?' I eagerly demanded.

" ' For not having explained the whole truth,' he replied; ' that would have spared all the pain of this meeting, and I cannot help thinking likewise, that it would have looked much more honourable on his part.'

" ' What mean you, father?' I asked; ' in what manner has Antonio acted that should bring down the least stain upon his honour?'

" ' He knew well that the injunctions of the late Prince Bianchi would render it impossible for him to make you his wife,' answered my father, ' and he ought not, therefore, thus have sported with your feelings by holding out to you false hopes that could never be realised.'

" ' Oh, blame him not,' I returned, ' it was the intensity of his love which caused him to act as he did; he could not find sufficient fortitude to break the spell which bound him to me, and to make me acquainted with the full extent of my misery.'

" ' Well, my dear child,' he said, ' there may be some truth in what you say; but still it would have been much better, as I said before, had he candidly admitted the truth at once. But we will say no more upon that subject; as circumstances have unfortunately turned out, it is indispensably necessary that you should not see each other, and that all correspondence should cease between you; at any rate, until time may have conquered the ardour of your affections, and you may be able to look upon one another only as friends. I need not tell you that both myself and your mother have always felt the highest respect for the character of Antonio, and that we shall ever esteem him as the friend of your youth, unless, by his future conduct, he should forfeit that claim on our regard.'

" ' Antonio become unworthy of the esteem and friendship of those who have known him from his earliest days?' I said. ' Oh, how utterly impossible is that. He is the true soul of honour, and never did a single thought enter his breast which he should not be proud to own. Alas! I feel deprived of his society, and with the dismal prospect that is now spread before me, one of the most wretched beings in existence. Father, you may argue as you may, but indeed you cannot persuade me that I should cease to love one who possesses so many noble qualities, such glowing virtues as Bianchi; it cannot be; my soul revolts at the thought, and I must still cherish him in my memory, let the consequences be whatever they may.'

" ' Valentia!' said my father, in a solemn voice, ' beware what you say; make no rash vows, lest you should have painful cause to repent them; resolutions such as those you have just now expressed might lead to your destruction. But time will, I trust, alter your mind; and by persevering in the right and prudent course, be enabled to look back upon the past with calmness and without regret.'

" The conversation here dropped, and I was glad when my father allowed me again to retire from his presence, for the observations he made use of respecting Antonio went to my heart, and rendered me truly miserable. When I had gained my own room I again threw myself in a chair, and for a considerable time became lost to everything else but my own dismal reflections, and which seemed by their intense agony to lay prostrate every faculty I possessed. Tears, at length, came to my relief, and then I endeavoured to divert my mind from the heavy sorrows which occupied it by reading. But that was indeed a fruitless task; my brain seemed to swim round, my eyes were dim, I could not distinguish a syllable, and I threw the book aside with impatience and disgust.

" Thus day after day winged its dreary flight, and I became, if possible, still more restless and wretched. I would sit for hours together at the window of my chamber (which I seldom quitted) and gaze eagerly at the country beyond, with the hope of seeing the form of him I so fondly loved; but, alas! how futile was that idea; what little prospect was there of its ever being realised. Never should I behold Antonio again; and even if I should, was I not forbidden to speak to him? Had not my father commanded me to forget him? and unable as I was to deny the prudence or justice of his conduct, could I dare to murmur at his decree, severe and torturing to me though it was? But there were other thoughts in connection with this dismal subject that distracted my brain; driven to despair (for I still flattered myself that he loved me with all the ardour that man could experience for woman), feeling assured that nothing could remove the obstacle to our union, might not the wretched Antonio, I reflected, be tempted to some desperate deed in order to rid himself of his misery? Little did I imagine at that time how different were the thoughts which held possession of his breast, or that he had already formed the most nefarious plans in his own breast for my destruction. How after the solemn protestation, he had so frequently uttered to me, and the apparant sincerity of his demeanour, could I suspect him? I should have reproached myself as one of the most ungenerous and unjust of human beings could I have given encouragement to such a thought, or any idea that might be prejudicial to the character of Antonio, whom I looked upon as one of the most perfect of human beings. Fatal delusion! into what a vortex of misery and shame has it not plunged me! and now can I ever find the power to extricate myself? Oh, Bianchi, shouldst thou continue to live when the hand which traces these lines shall be stiffened in death, may repentance light upon your soul, and may you, by your future conduct, seek and obtain forgiveness from the Almighty for the many errors of which you have been guilty, and the cruel wrongs you have heaped upon me."

"Unfortunate woman," ejaculated our heroine; "much do I fear that your prayers have hitherto been unavailing, and the conduct of my misguided and guilty uncle towards me too plainly proves it. Were he indeed penitent, could he for a moment think of consigning me, his own relation, the orphan daughter of his only sister, to a fate similar to your own? Would he not rather have rejected at once the hated overtures of a man so totally unworthy of me as the Count Alberti, and not have seemed to take a cruel delight in consigning me to shame and misery? The bare thought is monstrous and revolting."

"But surely, signora," said her attendant, "the Prince Bianchi will be awakened to compunction when you inform him that the history of his errors and the wrongs he has heaped upon the unfortunate Valentia have come to your knowledge."

"I am afraid, Floretta," answered her mistress, "that my uncle is too stern and inexorable to be moved by anything to remorse; and he has proceeded too far to retrace his steps. It is evident from his conduct that his determination is fixed. I see no chance of my escaping from the fate with which he has threatened me, unless it is by some miraculous and merciful interposition of Providence."

"And on the mercy and protection of that All-bountiful Providence you may with confidence and safety depend, my dear lady," remarked Floretta; "He will never abandon you to a fate so widely different to that which your numerous virtues deserve."

"I would fain think so," said Melina; "but when I take all the circumstances by which I am surrounded into consideration, can you wonder that my mind should be distracted with doubts and apprehensions?"

"Very true, signora," returned Floretta; "but still I trust that a short time will serve to remove them, and that you will be restored to that happiness from which you have so long and so unjustly been estranged. But, proceed, my lady, for indeed I am most anxious to hear the remainder of this melancholy recital which has so strangely fallen into our hands."

Melina returned no answer, and after a short pause, during which she endeavoured to regain her composure, she resumed the narrative of the unfortunate Signora Valentia in the following words:

"Several weeks passed away without any particular change taking place in my circumstances, and I now gave myself up entirely to despair, and was careless as to what came of me, for I felt satisfied that Antonio was lost to me for ever, and that I should never behold him again. But little did I imagine the terrible calamity which was so shortly about to befall me, and which was about to plunge me into greater, far greater misery than any which I had hitherto experienced. Even now, when I reflect upon it, the blood freezes in my veins with horror, and madness almost seizes upon my brain. How shall I find fortitude to relate it? For a brief period I must lay down my pen to endeavour to compose my feelings sufficiently for the painful task.

* * * * *

"I had hitherto not quitted the house, and had kept myself almost entirely secluded in my own chamber, for even the consolation of my amiable parents was irksome and tedious to me; but at length, with the hope of being able in some measure to divert my thoughts from the melancholy subject which engrossed them, I resumed my customary walks in the neighbourhood, always taking care to be alone, though my father and mother frequently wished to accompany me. I rambled again and again over those scenes which were so endeared to me as having been the favourite haunts of myself and Antonio, and I pondered over every well-known and cherished spot, and recalled the reminiscences of the past to my memory, with feelings such as it will be needless for me to attempt to describe. For hours I would sit beneath the umbrageous foliage of the favourite trysting tree, on whose sturdy trunk we had carved the initials of our names. Oh, what moments of rapture had been those, never fated to return! How fast would fall my tears, and how poignant, how bitter was the anguish of my mind, when I reflected on them. I must acknowledge that I was not without the hope that in one of these rambles I might encounter Antonio, for it seemed probable to me that he would also be tempted to see those scenes which must be endeared to him by so many fond recollections, and where he might hope again to behold me, though fate had placed such an insurmountable barrier to the consummation of my happiness; but my wishes were doomed to be disappointed, and I began to think that Antonio had indeed forgotten me, and had made up his mind to resign himself to his fate. This idea was most torturing and insupportable, for although it was too evident that he could now never become mine, still it would have afforded me some consolation to know that I was still cherished in his memory, and that the ardent love he had ever professed towards me had undergone no change. Could I believe that any other woman had supplanted me in his affections I should have been one of the most wretched of human beings, and life would have become hateful to me. But, no, that was impossible! Nothing could ever alter the sentiments of Bianchi towards me, and I endeavoured to banish such an idea from my brain, and to persuade myself that I was still, and ever must remain dear to the heart of Antonio, and that no other maiden could ever cause him to forget or treat with indifference her who had been the companion of his youth, and whose whole soul he must feel convinced was devoted to him.

"It was thus that I wavered between doubt and hope; but, as day after day wore away, and still nothing occurred to offer the least ray of consolation to my mind, my strength almost sank beneath the continual anxiety to which I was subjected, and my patience was quite exhausted. I discontinued my walks, and once more secluded myself in my chamber, and it was impossible that all the efforts of my parents, notwithstanding the exertions they made, could arouse me from the lethargy and despair into which I had sunk.

"But let me now come to the recital of that dreadful catastrophe to which I have before alluded, and which at once completed the fate that had been so long impending o'er my head. And yet my heart shudders at and revolts from the task, and my hand seems palsied and almost refuses to perform its office.

"Several months had elapsed since the interview between myself and Antonio, and which decided our fate; the winter had now set in, and a most inclement one it was, such a one as had not been experienced for many years before. All was heavy, gloomy, and wretched around me, in strict accordance with the melancholy thoughts which beset my mind, and from which my parents in vain sought to arouse me. Could I have heard anything from Antonio, I might probably have been somewhat reconciled, but I knew not what had become of him, whether he were alive or dead, and my father and mother were, or they otherwise affected to be, in an utter state of ignorance with myself, although they sedulously avoided as much as possible from mentioning his name in my presence, no doubt acting from the purest and best of motives. But it had the contrary effect to that which they desired, and I became more restless and miserable every day. Continual agony of mind at length so preyed upon my constitution, that I became as weak as an infant, and was unable to leave my chamber altogether, and declined the society of my parents, seeking to divert my thoughts by reading, though with little or no beneficial results.

"One evening, worn out with thinking, I stretched my limbs without undressing upon a couch, and had gradually sunk into a half lethargic slumber, when I was suddenly aroused by a loud cracking noise, and the cries of distress, and hastily starting up, I found the room full of smoke and almost suffocating, whilst the lurid glare that shot in at the windows, convinced me at once that the house was on fire. I was unable to scream, and scarcely knowing what I did, I rushed to the door and threw it open, and the flames then rushed in a torrent up the staircase, and into the room, and compelled me to retreat to the farther end of it, all hope of escaping from a horrible death seeming to be at an end; but still my whole thoughts were for the preservation of the lives of my beloved parents, and not of my own. I darted to the windows and dashed them open, and never shall I forget the scene of horror which then presented itself. The whole house was in flames from top to bottom, and to escape from the fury of the desolating element appeared to be a matter of utter impossibility. I threw my arms in agony above my head, and shrieked in despair; I would have thrown myself from one of the windows, but had not strength to do so, and faster and faster the flames were gathering around me, whilst the smoke was so dense that my senses tottered, and I was almost suffocated. The danger every instant became greater, and yet in the confusion and horror of my thoughts I could not perceive that there was any assistance at hand; and the roaring of the flames, as they hurried on in their frightful work of destruction, and the noise of the crackling timber, completely drowned the voices of the numerous persons who were doubtless assembled without.

"'Father! mother!' I frantically shrieked, 'oh, God! where are ye?—Must ye perish by such an awful fate as this?—Oh, mercy, mercy! —save them! save them!'

"At that moment the flames reached to within a foot of me. I could already feel their scorching influence upon my face. Again I shrieked with all the strength of my voice, and clasping my hands together, my senses left me, and I remember no more!—Let me pause, for the dreadful retrospect of that hideous catastrophe overpowers me, and I scarcely know what I write. *   *   *

"Once more I venture to resume the pen, and to proceed with my narrative of misfortune.

"When I recovered my senses (which I was given to understand was not for several hours) I found myself in a strange apartment and with two females watching by the side of the couch on which I was reclining. My thoughts were in a state of confusion, and I scarcely knew what had happened, but the whole fearful truth flashed upon my recollection with tenfold force, and I eagerly inquired where I was. The females informed me that I was in the house of a friend, and that my life had been providentially preserved by the Prince Bianchi, who was at the time in the same house with me, and waiting for my restoration to sensibility in a state of the utmost anxiety and suspense.

"'Oh! I ejaculated, starting hastily up in the bed, and gazing upon the woman with a look of half incredulity; 'Antonio, my preserver! Antonio here!—Good God! is it possible?—But my parents!—Where are they?—Why do I not see them near me?'

"The women shook their heads mournfully, and tried to evade the question.

"'Ah!' I exclaimed; 'I read the whole dreadful truth! They have perished, perished in the devouring flames, and why, oh, why was I preserved to endure this misery?—Heaven help me, for I am now one of the most wretched of human beings.'

"I could say no more, but again sunk into a state of insensibility, and happy would it have been for me had I never recovered from it. Yes, my unfortunate parents had both perished in the flames, and I was now left alone in the world. Is it then to be wondered at that I should so easily be led into the snare that I afterwards was?—that I should be made the victim of one of the basest of plots that ever emanated from the mind of man?—Is there not every excuse to be offered for me, for the manner in which I fell? Oh, how horrible are these reflections! Antonio, what hast thou not got to answer for!

"For several days, as I afterwards learned, I remained in this state of unconsciousness, when, on recovering, I received a note from Antonio commiserating with me on the frightful calamity which had befallen me, and requesting permission to see me, as soon as I felt in a condition to see him. The thoughts of Antonio aroused me from my lethargy of despair; and conquering the agony of my mind to a far greater degree than could have been expected, I gathered sufficient strength to leave my couch, and to undertake to grant him the interview which he requested immediately. The reader of this narrative, should it ever meet the eye of human being, I have no doubt can imagine the scene which took place at this meeting, and under such peculiar and painful circumstances. We rushed frantically into each other's arms, and for some moments our emotions were too powerful for us to give utterance to a syllable.

"'Antonio!' I ejaculated at last, 'and do we then meet again, but under such awful circumstances? Oh, God! my beloved parents, and are you then, indeed, taken from me, and by so horrible a fate? Oh, why did I not perish with you in the devouring flames, for of what value is life now to me, since I am left alone and friendless in the world?'

"'My adored Valentia!' replied my lover, still pressing me to his heart, with every expression of fondness and devotion; 'for the love of Heaven endeavour to calm the anguish of your feelings, and to bear with fortitude and resignation the dreadful calamity with which it has pleased the Almighty to afflict you. Alone and friendless in the world? Oh, how can that be while your Antonio still exists?—exists and for you alone!'

"'For me, Antonio?' I replied, 'oh, no, that is impossible; cruel fate has placed an insupportable barrier between us; the dying injunction of the prince, your father, has decided all, and we must henceforth be strangers to each other.'

"'Strangers to each other, Valentia?' he returned; 'oh, cruel words; no—no, my beloved one, it must not be; reason and Heaven forbid it. I feel that without you life would become an insupportable burthen to me, and the Almighty will pardon me the breaking of a promise extorted from me under such peculiar and unprecedented circumstances. Valentia, do you still love me?'

"'Love you, Antonio?' I answered, in a faint voice, and looking with an expression of gentle reproach in his countenance. 'Oh, why ask me such a question as that? Can you doubt me? Do you believe that any man but Antonio can ever gain a place in this heart? But I am a poor, friendless, portionless girl—a destitute orphan, and why should I presume to aspire to that band which only those of wealth and station can be deserving of?'

"'By Heaven, you do me wrong by supposing that I can suffer such selfish considerations to have any influence upon my mind,' he cried. 'Valentia is in herself a treasure that monarchs might envy the possession of; and wealth and station sink into comparative insignificance when placed in contrast with her own superlative and intrinsic merits. Let me but prove myself worthy of so bright a gem, and where is there a man in existence who will be so happy as Antonio? Come, my love, dry those tears, and look forward to the bliss alone that may be yet in store for us. From this moment I will become your only earthly friend and protector. We will never part again; I will have you constantly under my watchful eye, and endeavour by my assiduous attention to make up in some measure for the serious and melancholy less you have just sustained.'

"'Oh, God!' I exclaimed, 'my unfortunate parents, to live to all those years and then to perish thus! But where there no means of preserving them?'

"'Alas! none whatever,' he replied, 'accident drew me to the spot soon after the terrible conflagration broke out, and with the assistance of my own attendants and numerous other individuals, I exerted myself to the utmost to rescue you all from the inevitable and awful fate which seemed to await you. With great difficulty I succeeded in preserving you at the very moment when the flames were fast encircling your form ; but I lament to say that, ere we could reach the room in which your father and mother were, the burning ruins fell and buried them beneath them.'

" ' Oh, horrible !' I groaned, clasping my aching temples ; ' what can ever banish the recollection of their frightful fate from my memory? Again I say, it would have been a mercy to me had I also perished with them.'

" ' Heaven be praised that you did not,' said Bianchi, shuddering. ' Come, my dear Valentia, struggle with your feelings, and God will, I trust, give you strength to support this calamity with fortitude.'

" There was so much apparent sincerity in all he uttered, that I could no longer doubt him, and I resigned myself entirely to his care. Fatal confidence for me ! it was the forerunner of all the misery which subsequently befel me.

" Antonio having informed me that the house I was then in was that of a kind neighbour who had been on the most intimate terms with my parents, I felt more composed; and he then made me acquainted with all that had happened to him since we had been separated. For several weeks, he stated, he had retired to a distant part of the country, to endeavour by change of scene to drown the agony of his thoughts, but all to no purpose; my image haunted him everywhere ; he could obtain no alleviation to the anguish of his mind, and sometimes he was driven to such a state of despair, that he was almost tempted to lay violent hands upon himself. At last he returned home, but there he could not rest, and he finally made up his mind, notwithstanding the prohibition of my father, to revisit the neighbourhood in which we resided, with the hope that accident might lead him to behold me again, and that he might have an opportunity of assuring me of the constancy of his love, and to inspire me with the hope that something would yet occur to unite our fates together. How it was that we had never before met did not occur, nor did Antonio very satisfactorily explain why he did not seek those haunts where he was, of all others, the most likely to encounter me. After we had passed about a couple of hours in each other's society, Antonio retired and left me to my own reflections; and what the nature of those were the reader will find no difficulty in imagining. The terrible fate which had befallen my unfortunate parents tortured my brain to madness, and for some time I was completely inconsolable. What a terrible situation was I placed in, without any other friend in the wide world, with the exception of Antonio—parent-

less, houseless, moneyless ! I have often marvelled since that my strength did not sink completely under it. And it would have been a fortunate thing for me had I perished at that time, for then should I have been spared the shame and suffering I am now enduring. Can it be wondered that I, young and inexperienced as I was, should so easily be led astray ; or that my betrayer gained so easy a triumph over me ? Alas ! What a base mind must he possess to take so cruel an advantage of the difficulties and misfortunes in which I had become involved.

" It was some days before I had sufficiently recovered from the severe shock which my feelings had sustained by the melancholy bereavement I had so suddenly and unexpectedly experienced, to be in a condition to leave the house, and during that time Antonio was almost my constant companion, and tried all that was in his power to tranquillise my feelings, and to lead me to look forward to the future with brighter prospects, and he succeeded much better than could very well have been anticipated. Hourly he assured me of the fervour and sincerity of his passion, and declared that his only hope of happiness was centred in my becoming his wife ; and he tried by all the arguments he could make use of to do away with the repugnance I felt in consequence of the promise which his father had exacted from him. Alas ! for my own future peace of mind, I lent too willing an ear, and I must ever bitterly reproach myself for so doing. Surely it was most culpable in me to listen to any such propositions; I should have respected the dying injunctions of the late Prince Bianchi, and struggled with my own feelings: what could I expect but that a curse would pursue me ?—and terribly has it done so ever since.

" Antonio proposed that, when I was sufficiently recovered, I should be removed to a villa which he had in a retired part of the country ; and after a due time had expired for me to pay the proper respect to the memory of my parents, I should then, if I found no change in his sentiments towards me, consent to become his wife, and then he hoped that all our troubles would be at an end, and that Heaven would crown our union with future happiness. For some time I hesitated how to act ; but how was it possible to struggle against passion so strong as mine ? How could I for a moment doubt the honour and sincerity of Antonio ? I did, in a fatal moment, give my consent, and I looked forward to the future with the greatest impatience and the most sanguine anticipations. Oh, that I had had some friendly hand to snatch me from that gulf of destruction upon the brink of which I was then standing !

" In another week I was sufficiently restored

to undertake the journey; and accompanied by Antonio (who seemed delighted at the prospect before him) I departed from the house in which I had found a temporary shelter, and in due course we arrived at the villa, which was situated in a secluded and romantic spot well-suited to the state of mind in which I then was; and there I took up my residence, Antonio desiring that I would consider myself its mistress, and not to stand in want of anything that I might wish for, and which was calculated to contribute to my comfort and happiness. He did not take up his residence in the house, to prevent the scandal of the world; but there was seldom a day passed that he did not visit me, and the ardour of his attachment seemed to increase every minute that he was in my society. Nothing could be more respectful and considerate than the attention he paid me, and there was not a wish that I could entertain that remained ungratified; but when I reflected on the dreadful fate that had befallen my beloved parents, it was impossible that I could be completely happy. It was indeed a terrible calamity for me; a greater could not surely befall any human being; for had I not have been deprived of their protection just at such a critical period of my life, the ruin which subsequently befel me could never have taken place. They would have watched me with a jealous eye, and prevented the triumph of my betrayer. But fate had ordained it otherwise, and useless is it now to murmur at its stern decrees.

"For several months I continued in my new residence, Bianchi being unremitting in his attentions towards me, and never by a single act or observation giving me occasion to doubt the honour and integrity of his intentions. In fact, his love seemed to have gained additional strength every time we met; and so powerful was the influence he had obtained over me—so great was the confidence I reposed in him, that I knew no will but his; and had any one ventured to question the purity of his motives in my presence, I should have considered them the basest of calumniators, and the greatest enemies that I could possibly possess. Independent of the agonizing thoughts which the untimely death of my father and mother naturally excited in my breast, I became comparatively happy, and looked forward to the time when I anticipated I should become the wife of the man I so ardently loved with feelings of the most indescribable transport. And Antonio seemed no less anxious for the time to arrive than myself, and pictured to me in the most glaring colours the happiness that must accrue to us both, and to which I listened with an eager and gratified ear. He took great pains, however, to impress upon my mind the necessity and pru-

dence, under all the circumstances, of our nuptials taking place in private, and suggested that they should be solemnised at the villa where I was residing, and in the presence of the principal domestics and a few private friends of his own only; and I, unsuspicious as I was, readily acceded to the suggestion, and could not help thinking that it was in accordance with the strictest propriety, and to prevent the scandal and animadversions that were almost certain to be passed upon the inequality of the match.

"Thus we allowed a twelvemonth to elapse, and at the expiration of that time, my feelings had become settled down into the calm of resignation to the fate with which it had pleased the Divine Ruler of events to visit me, and I sought to look forward to the future with the most sanguine hopes. So constant and powerful had been the arguments which Antonio had made use of, that he had completely done away with the objections I had raised to our union, after the promise he had given to his father in his last moments; and when he at length proposed the day on which the solemn ceremony should take place, I yielded my consent with all the willingness and confidence which the love I bore him, and the strict reliance I placed in his honour, dictated; and the necessary arrangements for our private marriage were accordingly made. But still at times I was not without my misgivings; but I struggled hard to banish them from my bosom, and I succeeded so well that Antonio had me entirely at his will, and I left everything to his management and discretion. He had frequently assured me that only a short time after our union, he would openly introduce me to the world as his wife, and I was too anxious for present retirement to raise the least objection to such an arrangement. Alas! what an infatuation was I labouring under; and what fatal consequences has it not been productive! But not to become unnecessarily prolix.

"All the arrangements being completed, the day was finally fixed, and I endeavoured to muster all the fortitude I possibly could to meet the important change I was about to undergo. And Antonio sought to encourage me by all the fond endearments he could possibly make use of; repeated his vows of eternal constancy, and pictured to me in the most captivating colours, the scenes of bliss that were in store for us; unfortunately for me, I lent but too ready an ear to him, and my mind became contented and happy. I left everything to him and suffered not the slightest doubt to enter my mind. How could I ever imagine that he to whom I had been so devotedly attached from the earliest days of childhood, and who seemed to live alone in my presence, could have the heart to seek to deceive me, especially left as I was, alone and destitute in the world?

At that time I was not in a condition, inexperienced as I was in the world, to form the least idea of the treachery of mankind; and surely, under these circumstances, there was every excuse to be offered for me.

"The day passed over, the ceremony was completed in the presence of the domestics at the villa, and a few individuals, male and female, whom Bianchi introduced to me as his friends, and I considered myself his wife by all the ties sacred to God and man! Unhappy wretch, why did I not die at the altar, ere I had become a poor lost, degraded being, hateful to myself, and an object of scorn and opprobrium to all my fellow creatures? Antonio, it is thou who hast wrought this misery and disgrace, and surely upon thine head alone should fall the vengeance of outraged Heaven, and not upon mine and our innocent, our unconscious offspring! But notwithstanding all the treachery thou hast practised towards me, and the cruelty thou hast and art still inflicting upon me, I could freely forgive thee, wouldst thou permit me to leave this horrible place of confinement, this insupportable state of suspense, and to retire with my poor boy into that obscurity which is all I can now seek after, and to end the few days which may be allotted me, in penitence and peace.

* * * *

"Once more I take up the pen in the silence of night, and the dreary solitude of the chamber in which I am a heartbroken prisoner, with the hope of resuming and being enabled to bring my sad story to a conclusion—at least, as far as it is permitted me to be the narrator of the sorrows and sufferings that have befallen me. Bianchi but an hour since sought an interview with me; he refused to satisfy me as to what are his intentions towards me; he was insensible to all my tears and supplications; his heart has become adamant. God! can this be the same Antonio whom I thought perfection; whose sole happiness appeared to be centred in mine, and to whom my whole soul was devoted?—It seems scarcely possible! It must be some bitter mockery;—some frightful dream!—a wandering of the imagination! And yet the observations he has just made use of convince me that he now detests me, and that there is nothing whatever he will hesitate to do to rid himself of me. Oh, Heaven! his poniard would be far more welcome to my heart than this cruel treatment. I have no wish to live, for life is now a dreary blank to me; an insupportable burthen, that it would be a mercy to me to be rid of."

"My God!" ejaculated Melina, again pausing at this part of the manuscript; 'what horrible thoughts are these that now take possession of my mind?—Surely my uncle cannot have stained his hands in human blood, the blood of his hapless and too confiding victim?"

"Oh, no, signora," replied Floretta; "do not entertain such a dreadful thought; the Prince Bianchi, no doubt, has been guilty, very guilty; but he could never have been the heartless monster (for, pardon me, dear lady, he would deserve no milder title)—as to become an assassin."

"Alas!" remarked our heroine, "when we become steeped in crime, to what fearful lengths may not the tempter induce us to go with the hope of escaping the infamy of the world?—I shudder at the thought, and my heart yearns to become fully acquainted with the fate of the unfortunate and much injured Valentia and her offspring."

"Proceed with the narrative, signora," said her companion, "and probably the anxiety which you naturally feel will be removed. But one thing appears evident to me, namely, that your fears are groundless, or your uncle would not so carefully have preserved the portrait of his victim, which must constantly remind him of his crime."

"True!" coincided her mistress, "and I will seek to think as you do, Floretta. Heaven forbid that such a terrible weight of guilt should rest upon his conscience."

With these thoughts she endeavoured to tranquillise her feelings, and again continued the story.

"For several months we passed our time in the most uninterrupted happiness, and Antonio was never absent from me only for a few hours together, informing me that it was supposed by his friends in the neighbourhood of the Villa Rosa, and his domestics, that business of an important and private nature would detain him from home for some time, and he promised me that, at the expiration of a certain period, he would at once throw aside the veil of mystery, and introduce me to the world as his wife. With these assurances I was perfectly satisfied, and in the confidence of possessing his unbounded love, for I could entertain no suspicion of his truth; and had any one intimated such a thing to me, I should have set them down as the basest of calumniators that could possibly exist, and despised them accordingly. I was the happiest of human beings, believing myself to be the honourable wife of the man I worshipped. His society was all that I cared for, and I possessed no anxiety to be taken from the retirement in which I lived while he was near me. To strengthen, if possible, the love I bore him, I found myself in a condition soon to become a mother, and that interesting circumstance seemed to afford him no less delight than myself, and he redoubled his affectionate attentions towards me. At length the important event took place, and I was delivered of a beautiful boy. My poor child, as I now gaze upon your innocent features, and picture to myself the troubles to which you are probably destined in this world, how sincerely do I wish that heaven in its infinite mercy had never permitted you to see the light of day; and though you are the only comfort which is left to me in my misery, methinks I could be more contented and resigned were I now gazing upon your lifeless corpse. These are awful thoughts for a mother to entertain, but God knows that they are prompted by humanity and maternal affection alone.

"As I have before stated, Antonio seemed to view this addition to our happiness with

THE DISCOVERY OF THE MANUSCRIPT OF VALENTIA DI VALORI.

the most unbounded delight, and for several weeks he scarcely absented himself from my presence for an hour; but at length he intimated to me that it would be necessary for him to depart for the Villa Rosa for a short time, in order that he might make arrangements for my immediate introduction there as his wife.

"Of course, I could raise no objections to what appeared to be so reasonable and imperative, although I felt the anguish of a separation from him, notwithstanding I anticipated it would only be for a brief period, most acutely; and the following day he took his departure accordingly, he appearing to feel equally as much emotion as I did myself, and repeating those vows of affection he had so often given utterance to. When he had gone I felt lonely and wretched, and nothing could banish the dismal thoughts that crowded upon my mind; but still I never for a moment imagined that he could entertain a single idea but what was calculated to contribute to my happiness. I felt some relief to my anxiety when a day or two afterwards I received a letter from him, couched in the fondest and most eloquent language, and informing me that he was losing no time in completing his arrangements, and that in a few days he hoped to clasp me to his bosom again, and with pride to escort me to that home of which I was destined to be the future mistress and the ornament. Heartless deceiver, how terrible and guilty were the plans you were at that moment concocting. How soon and how fatally was I to be aroused from that dream of happiness I had fondly indulged in!

"After the receipt of this letter my mind was easy and expectant, and I devoted my whole attention to my smiling infant, dwelling for hours upon his innocent countenance, and picturing in his features the likeness of his father. Heaven forbid that you should resemble him in heart, my poor boy; if I thought thou could'st, how heartily would I pray for thy death; with what patient indifference, and even gratification, could I gaze upon thy breathless corpse.

"But when more than a fortnight elapsed, and Antonio returned not, and I heard nothing of him, the anguish and anxiety of my mind may be conceived. I imagined all kinds of things; that he was ill, or that something of an important nature had befallen him; and at length unable to support this terrible suspense any longer, I addressed a letter to him, requesting him to explain the cause of his silence, and to give me some idea when it would be likely he would return to me, as, of course, he must be aware of the anguish of mind I was enduring while he was away.

"To this letter I received an answer the following day, breathing the same tone of affection, and apologising for his continued absence, by stating that some trifling obstacles had arisen in the way of the completion of his wishes, which he had, however, at length surmounted, and that I might expect to see him without fail in three days at the farthest. This reply satisfied me, and I endeavoured to await patiently the arrival of the time when I should behold him again. He was punctual to the very hour, the very moment, and the meeting between us was all that could have been expected.

"'All is now arranged, my beloved Valentia, my wife,' he observed, 'and to-morrow we will depart from hence, as privately as possible, to the Villa Rosa, and in a very few days I shall have the pride and the pleasure of introducing you to my friends and relations as my lovely bride, the Princess Bianchi.'

"My heart leapt with delight in my bosom at the thought, and for a few minutes my emotions were too powerful to suffer me to give utterance to a word in reply, and I returned his affectionate embrace with equal ardour and sincerity.

"'Oh, my gracious lord, my husband,' I at length ejaculated; 'what feelings of rapture do your words impart to my breast. May Heaven give me the power, as I have the anxious will to do honour to the elevated position to which you have been pleased to raise me.'

"'Mention it not, my adored Valentia,' he returned; 'it is I who am honoured by becoming the possessor of the hand and heart of one of the most lovely beings in creation; and by Heaven I would not resign the blessing for all the treasures which the universe contains.'

"The hypocrite! how could he find the heart to give utterance to such words as these, when he knew at the same time that he had already accomplished my ruin, and that he had doomed me to a fate more horrible than the imagination can bear to contemplate? My brain is distracted when I reflect upon it! But away with torturing thought, and let me at once come to the conclusion of my dismal history, while I have the strength to do so.

"The next morning, at an early hour, we commenced our journey, in a private vehicle, and accompanied only by two domestics, a male and female, whom Antonio said he had brought with him from the Villa Rosa. During the early part of the journey Bianchi conversed freely, and drew a glowing picture of the happiness that was in store for us; but I noticed, with no little surprise and anxiety, that he gradually became abstracted, and from which, notwithstanding all my efforts, I failed to arouse him. The sanguine feelings I had previously entertained, and which had imparted such vivacity to my spirits, gradually evaporated, and at the same time a strange foreboding of something that was about to happen to me, and which would bring about the crisis of that fate which Omnipotence had in store for me, impressed itself so strongly on my mind, that I found it utterly impossible to banish it.

"I had no knowledge of the road to the Villa Rosa, the reader of these lines may be sure, when they remember that this was the first time that I had been out of the immediate locality of the neighbourhood in which I was born; but I could not help noticing with a melancholy depression of spirits, the wild and even frightful way through which we were journeying; the several leagues we had already accomplished, having presented to me no signs of a human being or habitation, and looking indeed as though it were a spot that had scarcely ever been trodden by the foot of man. "By degrees these melancholy ideas gained such influence over me, that I could scarcely support the various feelings which crowded upon my brain; and as the aspect of the country every moment became more dreary, I was compelled at last to interrupt Antonio from a lethargy of thought into which he had fallen, by communicating to him the dismal thoughts that had taken possesion of my mind. He seemed rather confused, and at a loss what to answer for a moment or two; but at last he observed—

"'My dearest Valentia, I admit that the route I have chosen is none of the most cheerful, but it is the nearest to the place of our destination; and as privacy is what we both most particularly require, I certainly could not have selected a better one. But fear not, my love; we are on the road to permanent happiness.'

"'And yet, Antonio,' I observed, looking narrowly and anxiously into his countenance, 'for some time past you have been dull and abstracted; tell me, are there any cares and anxieties that beset your mind, which it would not be prudent to make your Valentia acquainted with? Any secrets which——'

"'Secrets!' he reiterated, and at the same time his confusion seemed to increase, 'what secrets can Antonio possess with which it is proper that his wife should not be made acquainted? But—but this is all idle talk; I know my Valentia too well to suppose for a moment that she could doubt me. I plead guilty to the charge of having been abstracted, but my thoughts were bound up in the anticipation of the bliss that is in store for us; the pride I shall have in withdrawing you from the seclusion and obscurity in which you have hitherto resided, and in presenting you to the world as the treasure of my soul, my bride, my peerless bride, the Princess Bianchi.'

"I threw myself into his arms, and sobbed forth those emotions to which I could not give utterance, on his bosom. Oh, God! the remembrance of that moment distracts me. Cruel, cruel man, how could he thus pretend such unbounded affection over the ruin of that unfortunate being whom he was at the same time conveying to final destruction?

"It was some time ere I recovered from the state of excitement and emotion into which this brief conversation had thrown me; but at length I recovered, and the observations of Antonio for awhile reassured me, and entirely withdrew my attention from every other subject. He seemed to exert himself to the utmost, and with so much vivacity pictured to me the happy change of life upon which we were about to enter, that all my former impressions were banished from my mind, and I could not help inwardly reproaching myself for having ever entertained them.

"In spite, however, of all the efforts he had made, and the remarks he had given utterance to in such eloquent language, he once more relapsed into the same state of abstraction from which I had recently aroused him, and seemed pained or almost unconscious, whenever I addressed him. Again the same dismal forebodings took possession of my breast, and I regretted that I had been removed from the place in which I had for so many months resided, for it seemed to me that some misfortune, of which I could not at present form the least idea, was about to overtake me, though I could not, for an instant, form the least conception that Antonio had any design against my happiness.

"Through the most rugged and intricate roads (if such they might be termed) the vehicle which conveyed us pursued its way, and more dismal and disheartening became the aspect of everything around us. Still no signs of human dwelling—nothing whatever to cheer me on, or to encourage the hopes that Antonio had sought to inspire within my breast. Through narrow passes, with deep ravines on either side—up almost inaccessible steeps, over wild and moor, barren and cheerless, on we toiled for several hours, and I at last ventured to inquire of Bianchi how much further we had to travel before we should reach the place of our destination. He returned some evasive and, as I could not help thinking at the time, abrupt answer, and then relapsed into his former state of meditation. A heavy weight descended upon my heart, which I found it utterly impossible to remove, and pressing my poor infant still closer to my breast, I gave myself up to the most dismal thoughts. Alas! how could I reconcile it to my feelings that I was about to be introduced to the world as the honoured bride of the man on whom I had placed my soul's affections? The very idea seemed to convey a bitter mockery, and added to the misgivings that had taken such a strong hold upon my senses, and which Antonio had so energetically pretended to endeavour to remove.

"What added to the melancholy tenour of my thoughts, and rendered me doubly wretched, was the aspect of the weather, which was now in strict accordance with the wild district through which we were travelling, and threatened a coming storm. Nor was it long ere it commenced with threatening violence; rain rushing down from the heavily surcharged clouds in a perfect deluge; and the wind howling with the devastating fury of a hurricane. The horses that drew the vehicle which contained us were frightened, and dashed away at a fearful speed, seeming to set all control at defiance, and threatening every instant some dreadful accident to us. I sank back in the carriage, nestling my child to my bosom, and averting my face, for I was afraid to contemplate the horrors that raged around, and even Bianchi seemed somewhat alarmed, and uttered a few words to me which I did not understand, but I suppose were meant to console and encourage me.

"Thus we continued to travel on for more than an hour, without any change taking place, when, at last aroused from the trance of horror, (if I may so term it) that the furious battlement of the elements had steeped my senses in, I observed to Bianchi,—

"'Dear Antonio, how frightful are the horrors that rage around us; how wretched and desolate is the road we are travelling;—this looks not like the journey of a young wife to her future home. Why have you selected this route?'

"'Have I not stated to you before,' replied Antonio, in such harsh accents, that, had he not been alone with me in the vehicle, I could not have believed that it was he who spoke; 'have I not stated before,' he repeated, 'because I knew it to be the shortest?'

"'Then, how much farther is it to the Villa Rosa?' I inquired, in a tremulous voice.

"'Well,' he answered, in the same coarse and abrupt way, 'I cannot say exactly; you are too impatient, Valentia; as for the storm, it will harm us not, I dare say. If I am not mistaken, there is a town only a short distance from hence, where we may put up till it has abated.'

"'Antonio,' I said, looking at him earnestly, and my heart palpitating so violently with the emotion of my feelings, that it seemed as though it were ready to leap out of my breast, and all the dreadful forebodings that I had previously endeavoured to banish from my mind, rushing upon my brain with overwhelming force; 'your tone is harsh, it is not the same Antonio who spoke to me a short time since that addresses me now.'

"He seemed staggered by my observations;—averted his gaze from me, and for a few moments did not make any reply; at last, he said, in a subdued tone:

"'You wrong me, dearest Valentia, by permitting such thoughts to my prejudice to enter your mind. I admit that my words, and the tone in which I spoke then, might sound abrupt; but, believe me, I meant them not to convey any such meaning. Troublesome thoughts engrossed my brain at the moment,—aggravated by the unpropitious state of the weather, when I should have wished it to have been so different, all so lovely, to encourage my sweet bride on the way to her new house, and I scarcely knew what I said. Valentia, can you for an instant doubt me?'

"The only reply I could make was by throw-ing myself into his arms, and sobbing upon his bosom. Alas! alas! how weak I must have been to believe him. But greater villain he to take advantage of my confiding innocence!

"The carriage was driven at as rapid a rate, as the road would permit, the storm raging at the same time with unabated violence, and at length a small town, situated between a range of lofty mountains, appeared in sight, and my spirits somewhat revived; for, indeed, as it was approaching night, and we had travelled many leagues, it was a most welcome sight to me, for I much needed refreshment and rest. Immediately on entering the town, a comfortable inn presented itself, at the door of which we stopped, and were escorted by the host into the best apartments it contained, and a welcome repast was as expeditiously placed before us.

"My spirits were revived; I took no heed of the storm which was still raging without, and Antonio redoubled the affectionate attentions he had displayed on our first starting on our journey.

"'My dearest Valentia,' he said, encircling my waist with his arms, in the most affectionate manner; 'I hope that all your fears and doubts are now removed; though I admit you have had sufficient to try you patience and your fortitude during our journey. The delay, too, is most unfortunate, for anxious am I to introduce my lovely bride to my expectant friends; but here we must remain for the night, for it would not only be imprudent, but perfect madness to attempt to proceed in such a storm as this, and which seems quite unlikely to subside for some time. Come, my love, cheer up, and look forward with the most sanguine hopes to the consummation of that happiness to which we are so rapidly approaching. Do you doubt me, Valentia?—Do you imagine for one moment that your Antonio would seek to deceive you?'

"'Deceive me, Antonio?' I replied, and Heaven knows that my lips gave utterance only to the feelings that sprung from my soul. 'Oh, could love like that which I bear my husband harbour such a thought?—Pardon me, if in the excitement of the feelings which were naturally engendered by the horrors that were raging around us, should have caused me to say anything that might have sounded harsh in your ears. Yes, dear Antonio, *I am* happy; how can I be otherwise, when I have you by my side, and our dear little innocent nestled to my breast? To-morrow, then, I may anticipate that I shall reach my new and final home?'

"'Ay, I trust so,' he replied, in a tone of voice, which I could not help noticing at the time was somewhat singular, and the expression of his features as he gave utterance to the words, corresponded with it, though I was at a loss to understand them; 'that home, I have no doubt, Valentia, will be a final one *to you.*'

"He laid such emphasis on the last few words, that I could not help noticing them, and again a sad and terrible foreboding came across my mind; but, oh God! little could I imagine the dark and villanous meaning his observations were meant to convey. Infatuated fool that I was! I must have been mad at the time, or I should have been able at once to read the diabolical thoughts that were passing in his mind, and denounced, abandoned, loathed, and despised him accordingly. But, alas! even had I done so, what would it have availed me? Only have made my shame and misery the more immediately apparent, without the means of redress. Alas!—what could redress wrongs like mine?—Was I not already unconsciously ruined?—was I not degraded and completely in the power and at the mercy of Antonio? Oh, Heaven! how horrible is the thought! I cannot bear to dwell upon it. Let it suffice that in a short time, by his altered behaviour, he succeeded in quieting my doubts and suspicions; and when we retired for the night my mind was completely tranquillised, and I looked forward to the future with the brightest and most sanguine anticipations.

"We resumed our journey at an early hour on the following morning, and travelled through a country as wild and barren, as gloomy and cheerless as we had previously done, and I could not help making frequent inquiries as to how far we were from the Villa Rosa, and whether it was situated in so wild and dismal a spot as the country we were traversing. To all these questions Bianchi returned the most evasive answers, and I could see plain enough that he became more and more confused every time I put them to him, though he affected to treat me with the utmost tenderness and consideration, and I at length abstained from questioning him further, and reproached myself for having for a moment entertained a doubt of the honour and rectitude of his intentions.

"The aspect of the country at length became more cheerful and my spirits in consequence revived. But to be brief: towards the afternoon our journey was completed, and I arrived at the house in which I am now a miserable prisoner, and wherein my feeble hand relates this melancholy history of woe. I must confess that the appearance of it struck a chill into my heart, and my fears and suspicions were re-kindled with re-doubled force.

"'Antonio,' I said, when the vehicle stopped before the door, 'can it be possible that this is the Villa Rosa of which I have heard so much talk as one of the most splendid of edifices, and situated in the city of Rome? Surely you must be mistaken, all around so gloomy and retired; there appears not to be another house near it, and——'

"'Be satisfied, Valentia,' he interrupted abruptly, 'that, Villa Rosa or not, this is the place I intend to be your residence for the present. Methought you said that you could be contented and happy anywhere, if I were only with you?'

"'And so I can, Heaven knows, Antonio,' I replied, in a trembling voice, 'but indeed it looks not well to deceive me thus. Am I not your wife? and why then should you longer hesitate to introduce me to the world in my real character?'

"'This is not the time to discuss the subject, Valentia,' he returned; 'we will talk further upon it anon. Dismiss your doubts, for they anger me.'

"I returned no answer, and he having descended from the vehicle as the hall door was opened by a gray-headed old man, I suffered him to assist me to alight, and to lead me into the house without making use of a single observation. We were ushered into a parlour, where Bianchi almost immediately afterwards left me, promising to return in a few minutes.

"The depression of my spirits increased, and the gloom and silence that reigned throughout the house tended only to strengthen my fears and suspicions, and they arose to such a pitch that it was not without the greatest difficulty I could contain myself. It was evident from the observations of Antonio that this was not the Villa Rosa, and that he had so far deceived me, and for what purpose had he brought me hither?—Had he not better have suffered me to remain at the house where I had been so long residing?

"'But away with these gloomy and torturing thoughts,' I ejaculated, after a pause; 'why should I doubt the truth and sincerity of Antonio?—He loves me too fondly to intend any harm towards me, and doubtless he has acted for the best, and as prudence dictated. Let me not murmur, or accuse him wrongfully.'

"But in spite of all my efforts to the contrary, my uneasiness increased, when more than half an hour elapsed and he returned not to the room in which he had left me, and from the silence which reigned around, I could almost imagine that there was no one in the house but myself. I arose, and was approaching the door, when it was suddenly opened, and a young woman entered, who eyed me with much curiosity and evident interest.

"'You will be pleased to follow me, signora,' she said, with much civility.

"'Where is the Prince Bianchi?' I inquired eagerly.

"'In the house, signora,' replied the female.

"'Any why has he not returned to me?' I demanded, and my heart sinking within me.

"'Pardon me, signora,' returned the young woman, 'but that is a question I cannot answer.'

"'And this house, what is the name of it?'

"'The Villa Civetti.'

" ' And is it near Rome ?'

" ' Oh, no, signora, it is many leagues distant from there,' replied the young woman, whose name I afterwards ascertained to be Viola.

" ' But come, will you be pleased to attend me ?'

" I saw that it would be useless to question her further, and with a faint heart and a faltering footstep, I followed her out of the room, and leading the way up a wide flight of stairs, she ushered me into the suite of rooms I now occupy, and from which I fear I shall never be removed alive. Alas ! alas ! how fearful is the fate to which I am subjected, and to experience it from that man to whom I have devoted my whole soul, and whom I had flattered myself loved me with all the ardour and sincerity that man could feel towards woman. Oh, that I had died rather than to be awakened from this delusive dream !

" Refreshments were prepared upon the table, of which Viola invited me to partake, but my heart sickened with the painful thoughts that crowded so rapidly upon me, and I eagerly demanded :

" ' Where is the Prince Bianchi ?—How is it that he is not here ?'

" ' I know not, signora,' replied Viola, ' but he commanded me to escort you here, and to inform you if you made any inquiry, that he would be with you anon.'

" ' So cold, so formal !' I ejaculated ; ' what can this mean ? And what domestics besides yourself are in this house ?'

" ' My father and mother only,' was the answer.

" ' Does the Prince Bianchi often visit here ?'

" ' No, signora, he has been here but once before this for some time,' returned Viola.

" ' And to bring me hither,' I observed, ' to a place which has more the aspect of a prison than the dwelling-place of the wife of the Prince Bianchi.'

" ' His wife, signora ?' said Viola, with a look of surprise and incredulity.

" ' Ay,' I replied ; ' do you not know me in that character ?'

" ' Pardon me, signora,' returned Viola, ' if I answer in the negative.'

" Her words increased my doubts and apprehensions, and a trembling sensation came over me which I had the greatest difficulty in conquering ; but when I reflected that it was not likely that Antonio would make his domestics acquainted with that circumstance until he had formally introduced me to his relations and friends, I subdued my emotion, and regretted that I had revealed the secret to her. However, I could not help noticing that Viola viewed me with an expression of pity, and that again aroused the most terrible suspicions within my breast. Viola again urged me to partake of the refreshments.

" ' Oh, no, my good girl,' I replied ; ' I cannot think of doing so, until my lord, the prince, again joins me. He will not be long before he does so, surely ?'

" ' I know not, signora,' answered Viola ; ' I have delivered to you the message you commanded me, and that is all I am acquainted with. I must now leave you.'

" I made no reply, and Viola immediately quitted the room, and to my astonishment and alarm, I heard her lock the door after her. I rushed hastily towards it, and called after her, but I received no answer, and I staggered back and sank in a chair, overcome by the power of my emotions. A veil seemed to be removed from before my eyes, and the whole dreadful truth to be at once revealed to me with overwhelming force.

" ' Gracious Heaven !' I ejaculated, ' am I then a prisoner ?—Antonio, is this the treatment I had a right to expect from you ?—You have deceived me, cruelly deceived me, and I now see plainly when it is too late that there is nought but misery before me.'

" It would be impossible for me to describe the anguish of my feelings as these thoughts occurred to me ; I wrung my hands in despair, and my tears flowed fast.

" ' But am I not his wife,' I cried, after a pause, ' and surely after all the professions of affection he has so frequently made to me, he cannot have the heart to treat me in this manner. It is impossible ; Antonio is the very soul of truth and honour, and oh, how deeply I wrong him for entertaining for a moment these suspicions against him. But am I indeed his wife, or only his victim ?—Was the ceremony only a cruel mockery, got up to entrap me, and the better to accomplish my ruin ? Dreadful thought ! my blood freezes in my veins as it occurs to me. Oh, that my unfortunate parents had not perished, never should I then have been placed in the situation I now am. But it cannot be. Antonio must indeed be a villain of the blackest dye if he could be guilty of such an act of cruel treachery and atrocious baseness. He must have some prudent motive for the course he has adopted, and he will shortly explain all, and remove the doubts and fears which have naturally taken possession of my mind.'

" Thus I endeavoured to compose the excitement of my feelings, and I awaited with the utmost anxiety and impatience to behold Bianchi again ; but when hour after hour passed away and still he came not, my anguish of mind became insupportable, and I gave myself up to the worst fears, for which indeed there seemed to be every foundation.

" ' He will not come,' I sighed ; ' cruel Antonio, thou hast deceived the poor confiding girl who loves thee so fondly, and you now dare not meet the reproaches which you may be certain I shall heap upon your head.—And am I then indeed a poor degraded being?—My little one the offspring of shame? The thought is monstrous and will drive me to distraction!—Antonio, in mercy to me, relieve me from this terrible state of suspense, and let me at once know the worst. Oh, God! should it really prove as I suspect, may death at once put a period to my sufferings, and hide my shame from the world.'

"I clasped my hands together with the intensity of my agony, and I traversed the room in a state of mind bordering upon distraction; then I pressed my unconscious infant to my breast, and my scalding tears fell fast upon his beauteous face. But still Antonio came not, and a dreadful suspicion crossed my mind that he had quitted the house, and left me to my fate and to all the horrors of my own thoughts. Then I went to the door and tried it, thinking that I might have been mistaken; but no, it was fast, and there could no longer be any doubt that I was a prisoner. What a terrible conviction was this!—It is a wonder that my fortitude did not forsake me altogether. I listened with breathless attention, but I could not hear the slightest sound; then I went to the windows and tried them, but they were fast and resisted all my efforts to open them, and showed too plainly that every precaution had been used to secure me, and complete my despair.

"It was now night, and still was Antonio absent, and it was therefore evident that he did not intend to visit me, but having accomplished his designs, he had resolved to abandon me altogether. My heart was full to bursting, and my brain was distracted.

"'My God!' I groaned, 'and is this the reward for my devoted affection?—Can this be the treatment I experience from that man whom I expected was my husband, and with whom I thought to pass so many years of uninterrupted happiness and love?—I can scarcely persuade myself that I am not labouring under the delusion of some frightful dream!—Antonio deceive me; betray me to destruction, and then to desert me in the midst of my misery? It seems too fearful to be true. Oh, if he has indeed acted in this manner, what a heartless hypocrite and villain he must be.'

"But I should become tedious were I to particularize all the thoughts that tortured my mind; the reader of these lines will no doubt be better enabled to imagine what my feelings were than I could describe them; when all the horrors of my situation are taken into consideration. But I was suddenly aroused from my reflections by hearing footsteps ascending the stairs, and my heart palpitated violently against my side, for I thought it was Bianchi, and that all my doubts and apprehensions would be immediately removed; but, alas! I was

doomed to be terribly disappointed, for the door of my apartment being unlocked, Viola again made her appearance. I sank back in my chair, and a deadly sickness came over me.

"'Why am I made a prisoner?' I at last demanded.

"'Pardon me, signora,' replied Viola, 'but I have only acted in obedience to the orders of his highness.'

"'Ah!' I ejaculated; 'say you so? Can the prince have acted in so cruel and unmerited a manner towards me? But why does he not visit me, according to his promise, and explain the meaning of his conduct?'

"'The prince, signora, desired me to inform you, that he feels under the necessity of postponing his visit till to-morrow,' answered Viola.

"'It is too true, then,' I exclaimed, in a voice which told the intense agony of my feelings; 'he has deceived me, and my misery and despair are complete. Oh, Antonio, how terrible is the ruin you have effected, and by means the most heartless and diabolical. But I am his wife; in the face of Heaven he made me so; and I will resist the monstrous injustice with which he is treating me.'

"'Calm your feelings, Signora Valentia,' said Viola, 'and endeavour to await with patience the explanation which his highness will doubtless give to you. I must not listen to observations such as those you have just now made use of. Had you not better retire to rest?'

"'Rest!' I repeated; 'oh, no, there is none for me, while I am in this terrible state of mind. Alas! alas! little did I anticipate such a fate as this. Had my beloved parents been living, what would have been their misery? But I deserve it all for having disobeyed the injunctions of my father; had I not done so, though I might have been friendless, destitute, my conscience would at any rate have been unburthened. Antonio, if thou hast indeed made me the degraded being I suspect thou hast, the course of Heaven will most assuredly pursue thee.'

"'I pity you, signora, from my heart,' remarked Viola, 'and I earnestly hope that your apprehensions may prove to be groundless. But perhaps you will consider me too bold in making use of these observations; I have delivered the message the Prince Bianchi commanded me to do, and I must wish you good night.'

"'But is the prince at present in the house?' I inquired.

"'Yes, signora,' answered Viola, 'and he has just retired to his chamber. Good night, and I trust that to-morrow the anxiety and the fears you now endure will be removed.'

"I could not but thank Viola for the kindness of her observations, and she then quitted the room, again locking the door after her. But in what a state of agony did she leave me! For some time my brain was so distracted with the numerous and torturing thoughts that crowded upon it, that I knew not what I was about.

"When I did recover the use of speech, numerous and bitter were the lamentations to which I gave utterance, and again and again did I curse the hard and melancholy fate which had overtaken me, and which I had so little deserved. Then again I bitterly reproached Antonio, and mourned the loss of that love which I could not help still thinking I had once possessed.

"'Oh, Heaven!' I at last exclaimed, unable to support my feelings any longer, 'it is too true; I have become the wretched victim of the man for whom I was ready and willing to sacrifice my very life, and, in the consciousness of his guilt, he is now ashamed to meet me and to listen to my severe and well-merited reproaches. Weak fool that I was to place such implicit confidence in him, and far greater villain he to take advantage of my innocence and unsuspecting nature. But I see it all now; to hide his guilt from the world, he is now anxious to get rid of me and my child, and——but no; I will not judge him too hastily; he cannot be such a monster. I will endeavour to wait with calmness and patience until I again behold him, and elicit the whole truth from him. Better at once to know the full extent of my misery and shame than to remain in this terrible state of suspense, of doubt and fear.'

"In the same state of agony my mind continued, without my being enabled to obtain the least relief; and as to think of retiring to bed, I could not, for I felt it was totally impossible I could obtain the least respite from its sorrows in sleep. My poor child was wrapped in a calm slumber, and seating myself by his side, I wept abundance of tears upon his innocent face, and breathed a mental prayer to Heaven for its mercy and protection to us both. Thus hour after hour wore tediously and drearily away, and I felt my mind greatly relieved when I beheld from the window of my chamber the first streak of day appear in the eastern horizon. I gazed upon the prospect beyond, but its wild and sombre character was far from being calculated to divert my thoughts from the sad and painful subjects that engrossed them, and my mind was restless and distracted. The refreshments of which Viola had invited me to partake, remained on the table untouched, for although I was faint with long fasting, I could find no appetite to eat. Anxiously I watched the lapse of time, looking forward every moment to the appearance of Antonio, and wondering within myself what explanation of his singular and alarming con-

duct he would be prepared to give, though I was determined, if possible, to know the worst at once.

"'But surely,' I reflected, 'it cannot be his intention to keep me here a prisoner, and to break all the solemn vows he has so often made to me, and upon which he gained my unbounded confidence? Oh, no, it must have been stern necessity that has compelled him to act as he has done, and he will be able to explain everything to my satisfaction, and to remove the terrible doubts and suspicions that at present naturally beset my mind.'

"Thus did I continue to waver between hope and fear, for more than a couple of hours, and my patience was nearly exhausted, when I again heard some one ascending the stairs, and this time I was convinced that they were not the footsteps of Viola. My agitation was excessive, and I now dreaded that interview for which I had hitherto been waiting with so much anxiety.

"I had not to wait long; the door of my apartment was unlocked, and Antonio stood before me. I uttered a cry of mingled joy and agony, and sank almost insensible at his feet, and clasping his knees, looked up imploringly in his face. He seemed somewhat moved and confused by the emotion I displayed, and for a minute or two averted his looks; but at length he raised me from my humble and supplicating posture, and said—

"'Be calm, Valentia, and listen patiently to what I have to say; it will require all your fortitude to hear that I have to communicate!'

"'Oh, Antonio,' I replied, fixing upon him a look that was sufficient to penetrate his very soul; 'what dreadful fact do your words imply? Why am I made a prisoner in this strange place, when you led me to believe that you were about to introduce me to happiness and love?'

"'It may appear harsh, Valentia,' he replied, 'but prudence and necessity render the course I have adopted unavoidable.'

"'Prudence! necessity!' I repeated; 'can this be the Antonio whom I have ever loved so fondly, so truly, and of whose heart I was led to believe that I was the supreme mistress?'

"'And so you are, Valentia,' he said; 'but circumstances, over which I have no control, have rendered it compulsory in me to act as I have done!'

"'Explain yourself,' I commanded, my heart palpitating with redoubled violence against my side, and my whole frame dreadfully agitated; 'you speak in problems; as you value my life, do not equivocate. Am I not your wife?'

"'In all but the name, Valentia!' he answered.

"'In all but the name!' I ejaculated, with

a look of horror. 'Oh, Heaven! Antonio, what do you mean?'

"'Valentia,' he returned, assuming as much firmness as he could, 'it is time that all should be explained, and I am determined that it shall be so, let the consequences be whatever they may, and though by so doing I bring down your bitterest curses and reproaches on myself. I do then at once acknowledge I have deceived you.'

"' Deceived me? Oh, Heaven!'

"'Hear me out,' he continued. 'That I

VALENTIA DI VALORI.

have loved you fervently, I must admit, and it is that alone which urged me to act as I have done, for I could not, with any degree of patience, endure the thought of resigning you altogether. It was wrong—very wrong of me, and deeply do I now regret it; but you knew the barrier that was placed between us, and that the dying injunctions of my father, which I durst not disobey, had prohibited me from making you my wife. It would have been better for the happiness and honour of us both, could we have forgotten each other; but fate willed it otherwise, and it is now too late to recall the past.'

"'Proceed—proceed,' I said, in a hoarse voice, and with my eyes still fixed earnestly upon his countenance.

"'The dreadful calamity that befell your parents rendered you friendless and without protection, and it was then that I determined to——'

"'And I am not your wife?' I interrupted with breathless agony.

"'No, Valentia,' he replied; 'it was no priest that joined our hands; you are still Valentia di Valori!'

"I heard no more, but with a frantic shriek I sank totally insensible upon the floor."

"Oh, Heaven!" ejaculated our heroine, when she had come to this part of the narrative; "what a heartless villain (for I can call him nothing less) does this prove my uncle to have been, nor can I any longer wonder at his treatment of me. Unfortunate Valentia, how sincerely do I pity you, and deprecate the infamous conduct of your betrayer!"

"Yes, my dear signora," said Floretta, "she is indeed worthy of every sympathy; but surely his highness could not be proof altogether against her entreaties and reproaches, and must after all have made her all the atonement in his power for the injuries he had done her by making her his wife."

"Ah! no, Floretta," returned her mistress, "is there not every proof that he did not do so? On the contrary, there is too much reason to fear that he has a still heavier crime upon his conscience. What finally became of Valentia and her child? I shudder to think!"

"Oh, signora," ejaculated her companion, "what is it you suspect?"

"I dare not give utterance to my thoughts," replied Melina; "but Heaven send that my suspicions may prove to be unfounded, and that the prince, my uncle, may yet be brought to repentance for the numerous crimes it is too evident he has committed."

"I trust he will, my dear lady," remarked Floretta; "but let us hear the conclusion of the manuscript, and then we shall probably be better able to form our conjectures upon the subject."

Melina complied, and went on with the manuscript in the following words—

"It was a considerable time before I was restored to sensibility, and I then found myself in bed with Viola leaning over me, with much apparent kindness and commiseration. The whole of the dreadful truth rushed upon my recollection like an electric shock, and raising myself up in the bed, and gazing wildly around me, I exclaimed—

"Not his wife! deceived! betrayed! made a thing of scorn and degradation! Oh, villain, monster! And is this the return for that de-

voted love which I bore towards you? Antonio! the curses of outraged Heaven will too surely pursue you for this inhuman conduct.'

"'Tranquillise your feelings, signora,' said Viola, 'and all may yet be well.'

"'All may yet be well!' I repeated impatiently; 'oh, what madness is it to talk to a poor unfortunate wretch like myself thus! Has he not told me, has he not acknowledged to me that he has deceived me, that I am not his wife, but a poor fallen wretch whom the world will now look upon with scorn? But where is he? Dare he not meet the reproachful eye of that too confiding being whom he has so irreparably wronged? The monster! could nothing move him from his diabolical purpose? And he loved me, he said. Oh, bitter mockery; brutal hypocrisy! I wonder that he was not afraid that the lie would blister his tongue. But where is he, I say again?'

"'He left the house last night, signora,' replied Viola.

"'Ah!' I exclaimed, 'then he has entirely deserted me and our innocent offspring, and thus our fate is sealed for ever. But left he no message?'

"'He did not, signora,' replied my attendant, 'no more than that he commanded me and my parents to pay you every attention.'

"'Let me arise then,' I cried, 'and immediately follow him; I cannot, will not longer remain here.'

"'Pardon me, signora,' said Viola, 'but you are in no condition to leave your bed, if even you were permitted to quit this house, and the Prince Bianchi strictly enjoined myself and my parents on no account to suffer you to leave these apartments.'

"'But you surely cannot act with such cruelty and injustice to one who never injured you?'

"'We dare not disobey his highness's orders, signora,' answered Viola.

"'Oh, God!' I cried, clasping my hands together with the most insupportable agony, 'then there is no hope for me!'

"'Fear not, signora,' observed Viola, 'you shall receive every kindness and attention from myself and my parents.'

"'Kindness, attention!' I repeated; 'alas, what kindness and attention can reconcile me to such a fate as this!'

"'The Prince Bianchi will probably soon return to the villa, signora,' said Viola, 'and then I have no doubt that you will be able to move him to relax in the apparent severity of his conduct towards you.'

"'Oh, no, no, no,' I returned, again clasping my hands vehemently together in despair; 'I can expect nothing from his mercy. He is only now too anxious to rid himself of me and my poor child. Oh, he would have acted much more mercifully towards us both, had he at once sacrificed our lives, and thus have terminated the misery that is now too surely in store for us! Oh, Antonio, who could ever have suspected you of being such a villain at heart? But I shall go mad! Let me go! you shall not detain me here; let me with my child wander the wide world wretched outcasts as we are! Hold me not, I say; am I not my own mistress? and who shall dare to seek to control my actions? Off, off, I am determined!'

"Thus wildly raving, I struggled hard with Viola to arise from the bed, and it was as much as her strength could do to hold me down in the bed.

"'Pray, signora,' she said, soothingly, 'do not excite yourself thus violently. I again assure you that you will experience every kindness and attention from myself and my parents, and——'

"'Alas!' I interrupted, impatiently, 'what kindness can ever compensate me for the loss of Antonio's love?—what atonement can he possibly make, for the base, the cruel treachery with which he has treated me?—Am I not a poor, fallen, and degraded being, and the sooner I am, therefore, out of the world, the better. But by what right do you detain me here?—Once more I command you to suffer me to depart, or you may (friendless though I am) you may have cause, I say, to repent of your conduct when it is too late.'

"'Indeed, my dear lady,' said Viola, 'I am not to blame;—I sincerely pity you, and wish it were in my power to serve you, but I dare not disobey the commands of his highness.'

"I could return no answer, for my feelings overpowered me; I wrung my hands in agony, my brain became more giddy, and again my senses left me.

"In this condition I remained, so I was informed, for several days; and when I was once more restored to consciousness, I found Viola and her mother were in attendance upon me. My first inquiry was for Bianchi; and, after some hesitation, they informed me that he had not yet returned to the villa, though he had sent orders that I should be treated with every mark of respect, and prudent indulgence.

"'The villain! the shameless hypocrite!' I exclaimed, at the same time clasping my poor child frantically to my bosom; 'and it is thus that he triumphs in the ruin he has effected, and mocks my sufferings. Antonio, father of my innocent child, I deserve not this, and—But no, I cannot, will not curse him, notwithstanding all the cruel injuries I have experienced from him.'

"Viola and her mother did all they could to tranquillise my feelings, but they succeeded but very indifferently, and throughout that day and the next I continued in much the same excited state of mind.

"Antonio still continued absent from the villa, and it seemed but too evident to me that he had now abandoned me altogether. It would be utterly impossible for me to describe the anguish of my feelings—the intensity of my despair. I prayed for death, and had I had the means at hand, I am certain that I should not have hesitated to commit suicide, and at the same time have sacrificed the life of my innocent offspring.—When I recall all the circumstances to my memory, I shudder at the horrible thought which took possession of my brain; but, surely, when the dreadful fate to which I was subjected, and the dismal prospects before me, are taken into consideration, there must be every excuse to be offered for me.

"At length, at the end of another week, I received a letter from Antonio, which I hastily perused; it was couched in language the most cold and formal, and it was quite evident from the tenor of it, if indeed I could any longer entertain the least doubt upon the subject, that the love which he had formerly so ardently professed to entertain towards me had evaporated, and that he was only too anxious to get rid of myself and my infant, or to conceal us from the world, so that his own shame and guilt might not be discovered. In the letter he stated that motives of prudence would compel him to keep me confined where I was; that he regretted the unfortunate intercourse that had taken place between us, but, although he had deprived me of liberty, still I should possess every comfort, and that probably in a few days I might see him again, though he intimated at the same time that if I consulted my own welfare and that of my child, I would refrain from giving utterance to any useless reproaches.

"Need I say what disgust and indignation filled my mind as I perused these unfeeling lines?—I could scarcely believe the evidence of my senses, or that one whom I had imagined to be a very paragon of perfection, should turn out to be such a heartless villain.

"'Oh, what a delusion have I been labouring under,' I exclaimed;—'how cruelly have I been deceived. But will Antonio go unpunished for this? And must I be fated to suffer for that over which I had no control? I believed myself to be his wife; how could I have suspected differently, after all his solemn protestations? and if I have fallen into the snare of the betrayer, and become degraded, fallen, surely I am not to blame. And yet ought I to have trusted him when I knew that he had received the dying injunctions of his father to abandon all thoughts of me? Ought I to have suffered him to break his oath? Oh, no, I have been wrong—very wrong; God help me and you, my poor child: for without His merciful interposition, what will become of us?'

"Again I wrung my hands in all the frenzy of my feelings, and it was some time ere I could gain the least degree of composure. I requested that I might be left alone, for the society of any one was now irksome and insupportable to me, and Viola and her mother complied, and I was left to the free indulgence of my own painful reflections.

"Immediately on their leaving me, I arose from the bed, and with my infant clasped to my bosom, I paced the room backwards and forwards in a state of the most violent agitation that could possibly be conceived. But still, in spite of his cruel treatment of me, I found it utterly impossible to subdue the passion with which he had inspired me; and had he showed the least signs of compunction, methinks I could even have forgiven him all that had taken place; but to make a prisoner of me, to abandon me altogether now that he had achieved his object, was surely monstrous in the extreme, and I racked my brain to madness when I reflected upon it. How it tortured my soul when I ruminated upon the past; surely it was a terrible judgment upon me that which I was now enduring, for having disobeyed the wishes and commands of my unfortunate father. Then the terrible fate which had overtaken my beloved and amiable parents rushed upon my memory with tenfold force, and it was a wonder that madness did not seize upon my brain altogether. But still was there not every excuse to be offered for me? Had I not been left alone, destitute, friendless, in the world? Had I not every reason to depend upon the honour and sincerity of Antonio? How could I for a moment suspect that he could ever have the heart to act with such cruel treachery towards me? How could I imagine that, while he was pretending the most unbounded love for me, he was contemplating my destruction? Bianchi, it is thou who art alone to blame, and surely my misfortunes are deserving of pity and commiseration.

*   *   *   *

"He came at last, and oh, how painful was the meeting that took place between us! But that interview convinced me that all my hopes were at an end, and all the expostulations I could make use of would have no effect on him; in fact, he seemed to be quite indifferent to my emotions, and to have made up his mind that this interview should be a final one.

"'It is useless to conceal the truth, Valentia,' he said; 'circumstances will cause me to be away from this villa, and to devote my attention to other objects. This, however, for the present will be the residence of yourself and your child, and if you are wise, you will see the necessity of submitting to your fate, and endeavouring to make yourself as comfortable as possible; the world must know nothing of what has taken place between us.'

"'My God!' I exclaimed, in accents of horror and disgust. 'can this be the man who has so often declared that he was ready to sacrifice his very life for my sake? To talk thus to that unfortunate girl whose happiness he has destroyed for ever? Antonio, can you ever have sincerely loved me?'

"'Pshaw!' he replied, impatiently; 'it is only a waste of time to discuss that subject now; it is enough that fate has chosen to place an insurmountable barrier between us, and henceforth we must cease to look upon each other except as friends.'

"'Heartless man,' I could not help ejaculating, 'you have thrown by all disguise, and I see you in your true character, that of an unprincipled libertine, a shameless hypocrite.'

"'Hold, Valentia!' he cried, and his face colouring up; 'violent language such as that you have just now made use of, will but serve to exasperate me, and urge me to do that which I have no wish to do.'

"'Ah!' I returned, fixing upon him a look of reproach, 'do you then threaten also? Alas, then I see that I have too much reason to dread the past; too true were the suspicions of my poor father: oh, had I but listened to his advice, I should have been spared all the misery and disgrace I am now enduring. Antonio, can you meet my severe but just reproaches without flinching? Have you become totally insensible to every feeling of honour or humanity? Beware—beware, or you will most assuredly have cause to repent this when it is too late.'

"'Valentia,' he returned, 'I am in no mood to listen to observations such as those you have just now made use of. You have heard the determination which necessity has compelled me to come to, and you must abide by it; it is complete folly for you to murmur, or to attempt to offer any resistance to my will.'

"'Must I then, with my child, become a prisoner?' I demanded. 'Oh, my, lord, it would be far more merciful of you at once to take our lives.'

"'Valentia,' he answered, 'I am no assassin.'

"'Yes, you are,' I retorted, warmly, 'an assassin of the worst description.'

"'How?' he demanded, passionately.

"'Nay, you may frown, my lord,' I said, firmly; 'but I speak the truth, and you cannot deny it. Are you not the murderer of female innocence; the destroyer of her hopes?—and what murder can surpass that in atrocity, and cowardly heartlessness?'

"'By the saints!' he exclaimed, 'you try my patience too far, Valentia, and again I caution you to beware what you say.'

"And shall I be afraid to speak?' I demanded, 'when I am thus tyrannised over and oppressed? I command you, my lord, to release me immediately, since from your own admission, you have no authority over me.'

"'I am sorry I cannot comply with your request, Valentia,' he replied; 'it is not likely that I will risk my reputation by such a course.'

"'Your reputation!' I repeated, with a look of scorn; 'and did you study *my* reputation when you lured me to destruction?' Oh, Antonio, how can you have the heart to talk thus? Does not your conscience bitterly upbraid you when you contemplate the unfortunate being whose hopes and prospects you have blighted altogether? But let me away from hence, and in future, with my poor child, wander over the wide and cheerless world a wretched outcast, until death shall put a period to our sufferings.'

"'Enough, enough of this, Valentine,' said Antonio, in the same impatient accents; 'you have heard my resolution, and all that you can say will not move me from it.'

"'Then, beware!' I cried, firmly and solemnly, 'for as sure as there is a just God in Heaven, a terrible punishment will sooner or later overtake you for this. Spirits of my sainted parents! look down with pity upon your unfortunate daughter, and protect her and her offspring from the further dangers with which they are threatened.'

"Antonio affected not to be moved the least in the world by my observations, but notwithstanding, I saw that he had the greatest difficulty in the world to conceal his real feelings, and he averted his face for a minute or two from my looks, and seemed at first considerably at a loss what to answer.

"'This interview has lasted long enough,' he said at length; 'I have no doubt that after a time you will be able to conquer these feelings, and you will then be ready to admit, I presume, that I act only as prudence dictates. Farewell! we may meet again, but the more seldom the better, and, at any rate, it will not be for some time to come.'

"'Alas, Antonio, and will you leave me thus?' I sighed; 'surely I am worthy of different treatment to this.'

"'I have no wish to treat you with any degree of severity,' he answered; 'here you will find every attention paid you; but beyond these walls you must not go.'

"'Oh, this is most cruel!' I ejaculated. 'Could I ever have thought Antonio possessed a mind capable of such inhumanity as this, and towards one whose heart from the earliest period of childhood has been so fondly devoted to him?

"'What a waste of time and words is this,' remarked Bianchi; 'my conduct may appear severe and unjust, but you judge me too hastily, and calm reflection will, I trust, make you think differently.'

"'Oh, no, that is impossible!' I answered; 'how can I think differently, when I recall all the circumstances of the past and present to my memory? Remember the solemn vows you have so often given utterance to, Antonio, and then——

"'Again I say I will hear no more!' interrupted the prince; 'already have I listened with too much patience. Farewell!'

"'Stay, stay! Antonio, but one word,' I cried.

"'I will hear no more,' he repeated; and without giving me time to utter another word, he quitted the room, and left me to myself. I threw myself on a seat, and gave myself up entirely to despair. I was now again reduced to the most melancholy condition, and I found myself totally incapable of leaving my bed for several days, during which time I was waited upon by Viola with the utmost attention, and by her was given to understand that Bianchi had quitted the villa soon after the interview had taken place between us.

"Alas! it seemed too evident to me that I had never possessed his love; or if at any time I had done so, some other damsel had supplanted me in his affections; and that thought was madness to me. In whichever way I directed my thoughts, I could find not one ray of comfort; and although Viola was very kind and attentive to me and my child, I found it impossible to reconcile my mind to the painful and singular fate by which I was surrounded, and from which I knew not how to extricate myself.

* * * * *

"He has been here again, and oh, how stern and ambiguous are his manners. I feel certain that he has some deeper and more cruel design in contemplation. When I appealed to him, he turned a deaf ear to me, and frowning, muttered something between his teeth, which I did not understand, but which sounded to me like a curse. Good God! what can be his intentions towards me and my child? I can scarcely believe that it is the Prince Bianchi I am speaking to, so fearful is the change that has come over him. Oh, that this anxiety, suspense were over, and that I knew the worst; for even death itself could not be more terrible even in its most hideous shape.

"To Viola I am indebted for the materials by which I am enabled to write my melancholy history, although I have not thought it prudent to make her acquainted with what is the nature of the subject that occupies my mind. It affords some melancholy relaxation to my anguished feelings, although I know not whether it will ever meet the eye of mortal.

* * * *

"He vists me more frequently than he used to do; but his manners have now become perfectly savage towards me, and it is quite plain that he would gladly be rid of me and my tender offspring. What will be the result of this Heaven only knows. I am very ill; I become more weak every day; Antoine, fear not; I shall not trouble you long!

* * * *

"How fiercely the tempest rages without! —Hark! to the howling wind, and the pattering rain as it beats against the windows of the apartment in which I am confined. But the fury of the battleing elements can have no terrors for me. They are in strict accordance with my own feelings. Rage on then! rage on! and be your rude voice the music to my soul!—Hark! some one comes! Let me conceal what I am doing, lest—"

Here the manuscript abruptly concluded, and left our heroine and her companion far from satisfied.

CHAPPER XLVII.

THE MYSTERY.—HOPES REVIVED.

"Alas!" said Melina, when she had concluded, "what can have been the ultimate fate of this unfortunate woman and her child?"

"I cannot form a conjecture," answered Floretta; "it is a pity that the manuscript should leave off so abruptly; something particular must have occurred to her at the time, or she would most likely have continued her narrative. Probably his highness discovered how she was engaged."

"Oh, no," returned our heroine; "I do not think that is likely, for had he done so he would have been sure to have secured it, and we should not have had an opportunity of seeing it at all."

"Very true, signora," said Floretta.

"A fearful idea flashes across my mind," said Melina, in a faint voice.

"And what is that, my lady?" asked Floretta eagerly.

"Surely my uncle could not have been so cruel as to sacrifice the life of—"

"Your uncle stain his hands in human blood?" ejaculated Floretta, "especially that of those who ought to have been so dear to him? Oh, my lady, that seems to me impossible."

"You say well, Floretta," returned her mistress, "when you observe those *who ought* to have been so dear to him; but did not his inhuman and unnatural conduct fully prove that they possessed no place in his regard, and indeed that he was only too anxious to rid himself of them? I shudder with horror when I reflect on it, and much I fear, though Heaven forbid that I should judge him wrongfully, that my uncle has many more weighty crimes to answer for than we are at present aware of. Valentia I fear has long since been

the inmate of the grave; and if so, the exact mystery attached to her fate may never be unravelled. Her child, too—I wonder whether that is living or dead?"

"Ah!" said Floretta, "I feel the greatest anxiety about both of them, and would give anything to know what became of them. There is a strange coincidence in the history of the brigand chief and these unfortunates, and what if it should ever turn out that Allesandro Massaroni is the son of the Prince Bianchi and Signora Valentia?"

"It is a romantic idea, Floretta," remarked Melina, "and one that I do not think is very likely to be realised; but should it be so, and Massaroni should prove to be the son of my uncle, by that unfortunate woman whom he so deeply injured, will it not seem like a judgment upon him?"

"True, signora."

"The Prince Bianchi is the brigand chief's most bitter enemy, and he has long been most anxious to get him in his power."

"As for that, signora," returned her attendant, "it strikes me that there is not much love lost between them. The brigand has always appeared to take a delight to annoy him, and many are the tricks he has played upon him, as you are aware. You remember what emotion Massaroni evinced when he accidentally beheld the portrait at the Villa Rosa?"

"Yes," replied her mistress: "I have mentioned that before. Can that be the portrait of the unfortunate and much-wronged Valentia?"

"I have a strong suspicion that it is, though there is no allusion to it in the manuscript."

"The writer, probably, did not think it of sufficient importance," remarked the Signora Melina. "But it certainly seems far from improbable. Florio, who knows more about that portrait than any other person, except my uncle, has always stated it to be that of a young Florentine damsel; and, indeed, the costume sufficiently proves that."

"Exactly so, my lady," returned Floretta. "The mother of the brigand, too, it is supposed, was also a native of Florence."

"So I have always heard."

"That coincidence is still more striking," said Melina. "I confess that I feel the greatest anxiety upon the subject."

"And so do I, signora. Poor Valentia! She must have suffered a good deal."

"Alas! she must, Floretta; and the Prince Bianchi has much to answer for. No wonder that his conscience should at times haunt him, and that he should evince so much excitement."

"But this discovery may be of the most infinite service to you, signora."

"How so?"

"Why, I presume that you intend to convince his highness that you are aware of the errors of his youth?"

"Yes."

"If he has not become totally insensible to every proper feeling," remarked the attendant, "that must awaken him to a sense of remorse, and he will be induced to abandon his harsh and unnatural designs against you."

"Heaven grant that it might turn out as you predict," observed her mistress; "though after the inflexibility of temper he has evinced for some time past, I must acknowledge I can entertain no such sanguine expectations."

"Why, as for that, signora," said Fleretta, in reply, "I do not see that you have any particular reason to give way altogether to despair. But do you intend to say anything to the prince about the manuscript?"

"Oh, no—it would not be prudent to do so, for then he would get them into his possession, and he would set me at defiance. While I retain possession of them, I do hold some little power over him."

"Very true," coincided Floretta; "and shall you inform Viola, who seems to have acted with great kindness towards Valentia, of the singular discovery we have made?"

"No; I do not see that there is any necessity for that," answered Melina; "but hark! she comes."

Melina hastily concealed the manuscript, and Viola then entered the room, bringing with her a comfortable repast, which she placed upon the table before them, and having inquired after their health, was about to retire, when Melina interrupted her.

"Stay, my good woman," she ejaculated, "I would have a word or two with you."

Viola curtseyed.

"You say you have lived several years in this villa?"

"Oh, yes, signora," answered Viola, "from childhood."

"And tell me," said Melina, "in your recollection, has any other female besides myself been brought hither in a clandestine manner in your remembrance?"

Viola hesitated.

"Pardon me, signora," she said, at length, "but I have before told you that I would rather decline answering any such questions as that; for should his highness, the prince, discover that I had done so, I don't know what the consequences might be."

"You need be under no apprehensions whatever in that respect," said our heroine; "for I will hold you harmless. Now tell me, do you ever remember a lady being held a prisoner here by his highness?"

"Ah, signora," replied Viola, taken off her guard, "but that is many years ago."

"Ah, then you do remember such a circumstance?" said Melina, eagerly.

"Dear me, what have I done?" said Viola, with a look of alarm.

"You have nothing to fear," said our heroine, with a smile.

"Well, then, signora," answered Viola, "since it has gone so far, I will tell you all about it, if you will promise not to reveal it to any one."

"You may depend upon me."

"Well, then, it is a great many years since she was brought here by the prince," continued Viola, "for I was quite a young girl at the time."

"And she had an infant with her?" said Melina.

"Yes, a fine infant boy."

"And her name was the Signora Valentia?"

"Dear me! how do you know that?"

"Why," replied our heroine, again faintly smiling, "you see I do know something of the business, so you need not fear to become more communicative. Was the signora very beautiful?"

"Beautiful! oh, I never saw a more lovely creature," replied Viola; "but I have heard that the Prince Bianchi has a portrait of her at the Villa Rosa, which, no doubt, you have seen."

"Ah!" said Melina, looking eagerly at Floretta; "it is then as we suspected. Tell me, Viola, does the unfortunate Signora Valentia and her son still live?"

"That I know not, signora," returned Viola; "but I should not think it at all likely. Ah! poor lady, she did suffer greatly, and it used to pain me much to see her, and I showed her every little kindness and attention that was in my power, though, to be sure, that was not much. But you say you know her history, lady, and——"

"The early part of it I do," said Melina. "But what became of her?"

"Ah! that I could never ascertain," said Viola; "she and her child were removed by the prince at night, when I and my parents had retired to bed, and I never saw them from that day to this."

"And you have never been able to learn whither they were removed?"

"Oh, no, signora; it is not likely that a simple domestic like myself would be entrusted with the secret. But I have my suspicions."

"Suspicions! What are they?" asked our heroine with eager curiosity.

"Pardon me, signora," remarked the loquacious servant; "but I don't know that I ought to be so bold as to venture to give utterance to them."

"You have nothing to apprehend," said Melina; "what are your suspicions?"

"Why, lady, I think it is not at all unlikely that the Prince Bianchi would put the child out to nurse, and get the lady into some religious house."

"Ay, certainly," remarked our heroine; "a reasonable idea enough."

"But to tell the truth, signora, if I may make so bold," continued Viola, "I don't think his highness would have cared much what became of either of them, for he behaved very harshly towards them, and ———"

"Hush!" said Melina, placing her finger on her lips, though she had too much reason to fear that her surmises were correct, 'I must not listen to this.'

"True, signora, it was very bold of me to do so; but I hope you will forgive me. Ah! how she used to weep, and wring her hands for hours together, and complain that she had been shamefully deceived; and from what I could make out, though she never told me, by a false marriage. Well, if she should happen to be still living, I am sure that nothing would afford me more pleasure and satisfaction than to see her, and to find that she had got over all her troubles. As for her son, why, he must be a man of thirty years of age, if he should happen to be living now. For the last few days that she was here, I procured her the materials, unknown to the prince or my parents, and she was constantly writing; but what it was all about I don't know, though I guess that she was writing a narrative of her life; but as I saw nothing of it after she left here, I have no doubt that it fell into the hands of his highness. But I suppose that's all you want to know, signora; and as I have got business to attend to, I must leave you."

"Have you heard anything from Villa Rosa?" asked Melina.

"No, signora," answered Viola; "there has scarcely been time yet, but I have no doubt that the Prince Bianchi will be here in the course of a few days, and I am told by one of the men who escorted you hither, that the Count Alberti is to accompany him; so I declare that we shall be more in style here than we have been for many a day."

Our heroine sighed, but she returned no answer to the simple Viola, and the latter quitted the room,

"Floretta," said Melina, when she was gone, " a number of dark suspicions cross my mind from what Viola has said.'

"What mean you, signora?" asked Floretta.

"Alas!" returned her mistress, "I scarcely dare to give utterance to them; but is not the secret manner in which Valentia and her child were conveyed away at midnight from the villa enough to give rise to painful thoughts and surmises?"

"Why, signora," replied her attendant, "to tell the truth, I do not see anything remarkably suspicious in that circumstance; I think it is very probable that it was as Viola surmised—namely, that the prince placed his son in the charge of some competent and trustworthy person, and obtained admittance for Valentia into some religious house, If so, they may both be living now."

"True," said Melina, "and I hope that it may be so, and that my uncle may be brought to a proper feeling of remorse, and will endeavour to make them all the atonement in his power. You find, there can no longer be any doubt that the portrait at the Villa Rosa is the likeness of the Signora Valentia."

"No," said Floretta, "nor that Massaroni, when he saw it, took it to be the resemblance of his mother."

"Ah!" remarked Melina, "what strange ideas does that give rise to."

"Yes, signora," returned her companion; "and something strikes me that there are many extraordinary things that we little expect to come out yet."

"Should Massaroni really prove to be the son of the Prince Bianchi, what a strange revolution will it effect in our family altogether. But would my uncle ever acknowledge him?"

"Oh, yes; he surely could not be so unnatural as to deny his own offspring."

"But when that offspring is a robber—"

"And whose fault is it that he is so?" said Floretta; "who were the first cause of his taking to the lawless life he has so long pursued? Those who deserted him in his childhood, and left him to struggle with the world as he could."

"Very true," said Melina; "but Bianchi and the brigand chief are mortal enemies, and when Massaroni, taking the wrongs that his mother had experienced, and the neglect with which he himself had been treated, might be goaded on by a feeling of revenge."

"No, signora," remarked her attendant; "I do trust that a reconciliation might be effected, and all be settled amicably."

"Oh, what satisfaction it would afford me, could it be so," said our heroine; "but alas! I fear before anything of that kind can be effected, my fate will be sealed."

"Say not so, signora," returned Floretta; "but look forward to the future with the brightest hopes."

"I have struggled hard to do that," returned her mistress; "but I find all my efforts to accomplish it ineffectual. In a day or two, probably in a very few hours, my uncle and the Count Alberti will be here, and then the hated and unholy ceremony, which I so much dread, will take place without delay, and my peace of mind destroyed for ever."

Floretta sought to comfort her, and by dint of great exertion, she partially succeeded, and having partaken of the meal which Viola had brought, they took their seats by the window, and in conversation, and watching the prospect beyond, which was of a most gloomy description, as we have before stated, they passed the tedious hours away. Evening was approaching, and they were still seated by the window, when Floretta suddenly uttered an exclamation of surprise, and Melina, looking in the same direction as she was gazing, beheld a couple of men advancing cautiously towards the villa, and seeming to reconnoitre about them. But Floretta seemed to know them, and the curiosity of Melina was excited.

"What are you gazing so earnestly at those men for, Floretta?" asked Melina.

"By Heaven! they are two of the band of Massaroni," replied her attendant.

"Ah!" exclaimed our heroine, "what can bring them here?"

"Why, signora," replied Floretta, "doubt-

MELINA READING THE MANUSCRIPT TO FLORETTA.

less Massaroni has, as I have before frequently suggested to you, from the extent of the peculiar resources he has at his command, discovered a clue to the place of your confinement, and has sent those men, one of whom I recognise to be his lieutenant, Rubaldo, to reconnoitre, to ascertain whether the information is correct, previous to his making an attempt to rescue you."

The men now approached nearer the villa,

and Floretta had a more distinct view of their features.

"It is Rubaldo," she said, "and his companion; do you not recognise him, signora? your uncle's former domestic, who absconded so suddenly from the Villa Rosa, and who doubtless was the party who gave the brigand chief the means of entering the house at any time, and of making the bold attempt he did to save you in the chapel on the night when you would otherwise have been sacrificed to the Count Alberti: Guiseppe, I mean."

"Yes, yes," answered Melina, "I recognise him now."

"Then there is at any rate hope for you, lady," observed Floretta, "for could we discover ourselves to them, Massaroni would immediately fly to your rescue."

"Oh, no!" replied our heroine, "not for the world would I avail myself of the services of Massaroni, prejudiced as the world would be against me for doing so."

"Could the world blame you, signora, for availing yourself of. the opportunity of flying from a fate so unnatural, so revolting, so disgusting, so repugnant to your feelings?" asked Floretta; "to your uncle all the blame must attach for having driven you to such a painful extremity by the cruelty and injustice of his conduct. Indeed, my dear lady, you should not hesitate. But see, they come nearer. Could we but make ourselves seen by them!"

"Alas! what would that avail?" said Melina, still hesitating. But Floretta returned no answer; her whole attention was absorbed in watching Rubaldo and Guiseppe, who now advanced nearer, looking cautiously around them, until they stood almost immediately under the window of the room in which our heroine and Floretta were.

"How unfortunate it is that those windows are fast," remarked Floretta; "if they were not, we might easily communicate with them, and they might probably adopt immediate means to aid us in our escape."

"How rashly you talk, Floretta," said her mistress; "I tell you again that I cannot for a moment entertain such a thought. Should the brigands be seen by any of the men that brought us hither, and who are still at the villa, their destruction would be almost sure to follow."

"Oh, no, signora," returned her companion; "doubtless Massaroni, with a number of his daring band, are not far off, and would soon fly to their rescue. Would that they could see us! But it is evident they do not, or they would make some signal to convince us that they did. The foliage of this tree that grows before our window, conceals us from their view."

It was evident that it did so, for after they had reconnoitred for a few minutes, and consulted together, Rubaldo and his companion,

Guiseppe, departed by the same way they had come, and were soon out of sight.

"My hopes are strengthened, signora," remarked Floretta; "for although they did not observe us, they will take good care, depend upon it, to ascertain by some means or other whether or not we are here, and then our deliverance is all but certain."

"Of course, Floretta," said our heroine, "I need not assure you how anxious I am to escape from the revolting fate with which I am threatened; but still I cannot reconcile it to my feelings to owe my deliverance to the brigand chief, not that I for a moment doubt the sincerity of the motives that would prompt him so to act, and the anxiety I feel to behold my beloved Florio again."

"Pardon me, signora," replied her faithful attendant, "but I cannot help still expressing it as my opinion that your scruples are unreasonable, when the desperate situation in which you are placed is taken into consideration."

"They may appear to be so," remarked Melina, "but they are such as I cannot very well divest my mind of. How could the suspicions of Massaroni have been aroused that I was here confined, so secretly as my removal from the Villa Rosa was conducted?"

"To me it seems no matter of astonishment," replied Floretta, "after seeing Guiseppe, who was so long in the service of the Prince Bianchi, and was doubtless acquainted with many of his secrets. Oh, signora, think upon the horrible fate to which you will in a few days be consigned, unless some one who has the power, should interpose to save you, and I am sure you must conquer all the objections you at present entertain to the interference of Massaroni."

"But think you, if he feels satisfied that I am here confined, he will be bold enough to make an attack upon this place?" asked our heroine.

"Certainly." answered Floretta; "what is to prevent him, powerful as he is, and badly as the villa is at present defended. It would be madness for the mere handful of individuals who are here to attempt to oppose him, and there is no doubt he will act with promptitude as soon as he feels convinced that his suspicions are correct. In a day or two, if not in a very few hours, I entertain the most sanguine hopes that we shall be at liberty and far from the power of the Prince Bianchi, who will then, I trust, be brought to his senses, and will render you that justice which he now denies you."

"Heaven protect me and guide me how to act," said Melina, solemnly; "oh, my uncle, how can you persist in acting with such unmerited cruelty towards me? Why will you thus by your own unjust and severe conduct towards me, compel me to act in a manner so repugnant to my feelings? But, alas! I can expect but little clemency from you after what I have read respecting the unmitigated cruelty with which you behaved to your too confiding victim, the unfortunate Valentia. I shudder when I reflect upon the probable fate to which you ultimately consigned her."

"Nay, signora," returned Floretta, "let us hope that the prince, your uncle, is not so guilty as you suspect; he could never be so inhuman as to imbrue his hands in the blood of the unfortunate being he had betrayed. The opinion of Viola seems to me to be founded in reason, and Valentia and her offspring may still be in existence. Had he consigned her to an untimely death, it is not at all probable that he would have preserved her portrait with so much care, when it must constantly remind him of the frightful crime he had committed."

"True, Floretta," observed our heroine, "perhaps I am wrong and too hasty in my conclusions; but surely the treatment I have myself received from him, his only relative, to protect and cherish whom he solemnly pledged himself to my poor mother in her last moments, must offer some excuse for the misgivings that cross my mind. Hard though it would have been for me to have discarded Florio from my breast, still, in obedience to my uncle's will, I would have endeavoured to have submitted; but for him to seek to sacrifice me to such a man as the Count Alberti, one who is notorious as an unprincipled libertine, the thought is monstrous, and fills my very soul with disgust."

"Your observations are perfectly just, signora," returned her companion; "and since you are placed in that extremity by the cruelty and injustice of your uncle, you have an undoubted right to resist it to the best of your ability. He has broken the solemn vow he made to your mother on her death-bed—he has shown, from his conduct to you, that he wishes to gratify his own private feelings—he cares not, even though it be at the sacrifice of your happiness, and all you hold most dear in the world; and, consequently, it behoves you to try to defeat his plans, even though, in doing so, you may have to act in direct opposition to your own feelings. As I before said, since he has broken that solemn pledge he made to your mother, you have no longer any right to acknowledge his authority, but to maintain your own independence to the very letter."

Melina, who was partly convinced by the shrewd and forcible arguments of her attendant, was about to return some answer, when she was prevented from doing so by the sudden entrance of Viola, who, by the expression on her countenance, showed that she had something of importance to communicate.

"Well, Viola," said our heroine, "what brings you here so unexpectedly? Have you any fresh intelligence from the Villa Rosa?"

"No, signora," replied Viola; "but I have something so communicate which I dare say will interest you."

"Indeed!" said Melina, eagerly: "what is it?"

"Why, signora," returned Viola, in an under tone, "I must speak low, for I would not have my parents hear it for the world. I had been on an errand a short time since, and was returning home, when within a short distance of the villa I encountered two men—not very respectable-looking individuals, certainly—who seemed to be coming from here."

"Ah!" ejaculated our heroine and her attendant, in a breath. "Well, what of them? Was there anything remarkable in such a circumstance?"

"Why, no, I don't know that there was," replied the simple Valentia; "but still, as I said before, they were not two of the most prepossessing looking beings in the world; they would indeed make two excellent brigands; and so I endeavoured to avoid them; but it seems they had seen me, and my attempt was therefore of no avail, and they approached me, and one of them, who it strikes me I have seen before, but where I can't call to mind, addressing me, said: 'Your name is Viola, is it not?'—I don't know whether I acted right, but he took me so by surprise, that in the confusion of the moment I answered in the affirmative, and requested to know how he had become acquainted with my name. 'Oh,' said he, 'I have seen you often before, Viola, many years ago, though I daresay you do not recollect me now. You are in the service of the Prince Bianchi, and that is one of his villas yonder.'—'God bless my soul,' I returned, 'how do you know that?'—'No matter,' he answered, 'I see I am correct. You must lead rather a dull life here, you and your parents, Viola; his highness does not often visit here.'—'True,' I replied; 'but still we are happy enough, for we have been used to it for so many years.'—'Exactly so,' he observed; 'but still, if I am not misinformed, you have visitors now, the Signora Melina, and her attendant Floretta, and that pleasure is in a few days about to be augmented by the arrival of the Prince Bianchi, and the Count Alberti, is it not so?' Well, signora, the man took me so by surprise by the knowledge he evidently possessed, that I could not help again replying in the affirmative, though I am afraid I have acted very imprudently and incautiously; and I would not have my parents know it for all the money in the universe."

"Well," said our heroine, "after you had satisfied his interrogatories in the manner you have described, what further did he say?"

"Why, signora," answered Viola, "he merely thanked me for my civility; said I was a very prudent and intelligent woman, wished me good evening, and he and his companion went away, and I saw no more of them. After they were gone, I reproached myself for what I had done without a thought; but I could not rest until I had made you acquainted with it; I hope no harm will come of it."

"Oh, no," said Floretta, "you have no occasion to alarm yourself, I'm sure. The man only had a little idle curiosity; though, by-the-by, he seemed to possess as much knowledge as yourself."

"Yes," returned Viola, "and that's what surprises and bewilders me more than all. How he can have obtained his information I cannot imagine, for I thought that no person was acquainted with your being here except myself and my parents, and the Prince Bianchi and Count Alberti, unless indeed it be the men who brought you here, and who are the most unlikely persons in the world to divulge anything."

"But you did not mention this circumstance to any persons but ourselves?" said Floretta.

"Oh, no," replied Viola; "you may be sure I did not, for I knew I should receive the blame of every one for having divulged that to strangers which was meant to be kept a profound secret. But do you think that any harm will arise from what I have told to these strangers, signora?"

"What harm should arise?" replied our heroine, feeling somewhat confused, and evading the question as much as possible.

"Well, signora," remarked Viola, "I am glad to hear you say that; I thought it were best to tell you, for I wanted to ease my mind to some one. But I have been thinking——"

"What, Viola, what have you been thinking?" demanded Melina, eagerly.

"What could have made the man so inquisitive?"

"Oh, it was merely to suit his whim at the moment, depend upon it," said Floretta; "in fact, it was not inquisitiveness at all, since, according to your own showing, he seemed to be well acquainted with all that you could tell him."

"Exactly so," coincided Viola; "but still it strikes me that the man must have had some motive in ascertaining whether or not his conjectures, or the information he had received, was correct. Now, I'm sure there is no one who would be more sorry than myself to see the good signora here united to a man whom she dislikes, and I mean to say that it is very cruel and unjust of any one to try to force her into such a marriage, and I should be one of the first to rejoice in seeing her escape from it; but then if it should become known that I was in any way instrumental in bringing that about, what would become of me?"

"Do not alarm yourself, Viola," said our heroine; "even if it should so happen that I should be released from the fate with which I am threatened, who is to accuse you of being at all instrumental in it?"

"I am satisfied, signora," returned Viola, "and I wish you well with all my heart, though it is not in my power to serve you."

"I thank you, Viola, for your kind wishes," said our heroine, "and let whatever may be my fate, depend upon it, I shall not blame you for having had any hand in bringing it about."

Viola thanked her, and then, after some more conversation of no importance, she withdrew.

"Now Floretta," said Melina, when she was gone, "what think you of that which Viola has stated?"

"Why, my dear lady," answered the former, "it strengthens my hopes that before many hours have elapsed you will be rescued from the revolting fate which is at present impending o'er your head, and be restored to the arms of Signor Clairville. Rubaldo and Guiseppe have ascertained from the thoughtless Viola all they wished to know, and when they have made Massaroni acquainted with it, he will not fail to act with promptitude, and attempt your rescue before the villa is put in a proper condition to resist him. My word for it, that all will yet be well."

"Would to Heaven that my uncle could be brought to relent without the necessity of going to those extremities," ejaculated Melina. "I dread the idea of being obliged to avail myself of the services of Massaroni."

"And yet it is only by his means that you can hope to escape from the power of your uncle, and save yourself from becoming the wife of that man whom you so naturally and so thoroughly despise and detest," replied Floretta.

"True," coincided our heroine, "any fate is preferable to that which is so repugnant to my feelings, and Heaven knows full well the integrity of my motives, and how anxious I am to avoid anything that can cast the least shade of obloquy on my character."

"No one can dare to blame you for that to which you will have been compelled by persecution the most unnatural and tyrannical," remarked Floretta; "but hark! what noise is that outside?"

The voices of men, as if in loud altercation, and the clashing of swords, now smote their ears, and convinced them that something desperate was going on, and hurrying to the window, they beheld, as well as the twilight would permit them, Rubaldo and Guiseppe engaged in fierce combat with four of the men who had been left to guard them, a short distance from the house. It was quite evident that such an unequal combat could not last long, though the brigands fought determinedly, and seemed to have made up their minds to yield only with their lives. We need not attempt to describe the interest and anxiety with which our heroine and her attendant watched this combat; but it was quite clear that the two brigands must ultimately be overpowered, and they had scarcely come to this conclusion, when Guiseppe sank wounded to the earth, and Rubaldo immediately took to flight, and the men being too busily occupied in securing their wounded prisoner, to pursue him, he speedily effected his escape among the intricacies of the adjacent mountains. Guiseppe was lifted up in the arms of two of the men, and conveyed into the house, and then our heroine and Floretta retired from the window.

"This at once defeats any designs which the brigand chief may have had in contemplation," remarked Melina.

"It is indeed unfortunate," said Floretta; "but still not so bad as you anticipate, signora. Rubaldo has escaped, and will quickly make Massaroni acquainted with what has happened, and he will be sure not to lose any time in bringing a sufficient force to avenge himself and to rescue you."

"Alas! I fear the effusion of blood that will be almost certain to take place," remarked our heroine.

"There is not much fear of that," replied Floretta, "for it is not likely that the few persons here will be rash enough to attempt to oppose the force which Massaroni will be sure to bring against them. Take courage, signora, and rest assured that in a very short time you will be restored to liberty."

"Would to God that it might be by any other means," said Melina.

Before Floretta could make any reply, the door was opened, and Viola entered the room in a state of great trepidation.

"Oh, signora," she ejaculated when she entered, "such an adventure! The two men whom I encountered this evening were met by four of the men who are left to guard the house, and their suspicions being excited at seeing them lurking about, they questioned them, and the answers they gave being far from satisfactory, they endeavoured to secure them, but they resisted valiently; a desperate combat ensued, one of the ruffians was wounded and secured, but the other effected his escape."

"Indeed!" ejaculated Melina and Floretta, affecting not to know anything at all about it.

"Yes," returned Viola, "and what do you think? They say that they are two of the band of Massaroni, the daring brigand chief; the prisoner has been recognised as Guiseppe, formerly a domestic of the Prince Bianchi; so no wonder he should know me or that I should have some recollection of his features."

"Indeed!" said Floretta; "this is most extraordinary; but what could be their motives for lurking about the house? To rob it, think you?"

"Oh, no," replied Viola, "I do not think that; but I have a pretty shrewd guess as to what were their intentions."

"And what may you suspect?" asked Floretta.

"Why," replied Viola, "if I am informed rightly, Massaroni is a mortal enemy of his highness, the prince, and he once attempted to rescue the Siguora Melina, in which the Count Alberti received the wound from which he is now suffering. Is it not so, signora?"

"True," replied our heroine; "but what do you infer from that?"

"Simply this," answered Viola; "that these two men were sent by him to ascertain whether or not you were confined here, signora, preparatory to Massaroni's making a second attempt to rescue you. Indeed, I expect that we shall have a terrible struggle here before long, for as one of the brigands has escaped, he will lose no time in communicating all that has occurred to his captain, and unless the Prince Bianchi sends a sufficient force in time to repel him, I don't know what will become of us all. I only wish that I and my parents were well out of it, that's all."

"Do not unnecessarily alarm yourself, my good Viola," observed Melina, "for depend upon it no harm will come to you. From all I have heard of his character, the brigand chief is always the first to protect a female, instead of injuring her. But I suppose they will make the prince, my uncle, acquainted with what has happened as quickly as possible?"

"Yes, signora," replied Viola; "they have already despatched a messenger to the Villa Rosa; but I doubt much whether the prince will be able to send the troops in time, before we have Massaroni upon us; not but that I should be very happy to see you released from that fate which you seem to dread so much, indeed I should."

"I thank you, Viola," said our heroine; "but believe me that I would much rather it could be accomplished by any other means; that my uncle would relent, for instance, and not compel me to become the wife of a man so totally unworthy of me as the Count Alberti."

"Well, so I wish, with all my heart," returned Viola; "for it is a pity that any one should be compelled to marry a person whom they dislike."

"But is Guiseppe very badly wounded?" asked Melina, thinking it prudent to change the subject.

"I believe not," answered Viola; "but it would have been quite as well for him if he had, for he is sure to suffer death upon the scaffold."

"He has not revealed anything of the designs of Massaroni, has he?" inquired Floretta.

"I have not heard that he has," replied Viola; "and it is not likely that he will. But I must be going, for my parents require my services. Good night, signora, and I hope that all will terminate in your favour."

Melina again thanked her, and Viola then quitted the room.

"This affair causes me the greatest anxiety and uneasiness," observed Melina, when she was gone; "and I tremble for what the result may be."

"Depend upon it, it will be all in your favour, signora," replied Floretta; "Massaroni is probably close at hand, and Rubaldo having escaped, the brigand chief will quickly be here with his trusty followers. It is almost impossible that the prince can despatch his troops in time to resist him. You ought to congratulate yourself on the prospect that is before you."

"Indeed, I see no such grounds for congratulation as you seem to imagine," said Melina.

"What! not in the prospect of a restoration to liberty, and the arms of your lover?" said Floretta.

"To behold Florio again will afford me a melancholy delight," returned our heroine; "but, alas! how transient must be my pleasure when I reflect that he never can be mine."

"Say not so, signora," observed Floretta; "for, notwithstanding your prospects are at present cheerless enough, I admit, I cannot help thinking that providence has destined you for each other."

"Oh, how can I encourage such an idea, situated as Clairville is, and prejudiced as my uncle is against him?"

"But the prince will not always remain inexorable, I am convinced he will not," said Floretta.

"And what room have I to hope that anything will change him in his determination?" said Melina. "No, Floretta, I see the utter hopelessness of my ever becoming the wife of Clairville, with the sanction of the Prince Bianchi; and never could either I or Florio consent to a clandestine union. Perhaps it would be much better for us both if we were never to behold each other again; it will only be strengthening that passion which fate, too surely, appears to have destined shall never be gratified. Would to Heaven that we had never become acquainted, what indescribable misery would it have saved us both!"

"My dear signora," said her attendant, "let not such thoughts distress your mind. There is happiness yet in store for you and the man on whom your affections are placed, and who is every way so deserving of you."

Melina had sunk into meditation, and heard not what she said; and thus she continued for some time, and Floretta did not offer to inter-

rupt her; but at length the lateness of the hour warned them that it was time to rest, and Melina having offer up her prayers to heaven, she and her faithful attendant sought their couch, and for a few hours gained a respite from anxiety.

CHAPTER XLVIII.

THE POWER OF CONSCIENCE.—MASSARONI's MIDNIGHT VISIT TO BIANCHI.—THE ALARM, AND THE DEPARTURE OF TROOPS TO THE VILLA CIVETTI.—THE RAGE AND EXCITEMENT OF THE COUNT ALBERTI.

RUBALDO, enraged at the discomfiture of himself and Guiseppe, just at the very moment they had ascertained all the particulars they wished, but more especially at the capture of his companion, made his way with all the precipitation he could through the various intricate windings of the mountains which sheltered his retreat, until he thought he had got far beyond the reach of danger, when he paused to take breath, and to give vent to his feelings.

"What a cursed unfortunate job is this," he said; "to think that we should encounter those fellows at the very time when we most needed to avoid them. Had it been a little further from the villa, we should have had the aid of our comrades, and not a man of them could possibly have escaped. Poor Guiseppe, too! I fear it is all over with him;—but there is one consolation, that we have yet the power of revenge in our own hands. If Massaroni has not left the cavern on the fool's errand he talked about to the Villa Rosa, we may return to the place where the Signora Melina is confined, and rescue her, before any troops can arrive from the Villa Rosa. Let me hasten to meet my comrades, and then to make my way with all possible expedition to our mountain retreat."

Thus saying, the brigand Rubaldo, having looked cautiously around him to see that no one was pursuing, struck into another track, and in a short time reached the place where his comrades were awaiting him, to whom he hastily related what had happened, and they then departed with all the speed they could make to their retreat. Such was the rapidity with which they travelled that by the time that the first blush of day appeared in the eastern horizon they came in sight of the place of their destination. Rubaldo instantly made his way into the cavern, and shortly after encountered Maria Grazie, who was seated at a table, wrapped in sullen meditation on his entrance. She started up on beholding him, and looking at him earnestly she hastily demanded—

"You return in haste, Rubaldo; how is this?"

"Where is Massaroni?" demanded the brigand, hastily.

"Oh," replied Maria with a look of dissatisfaction, "he has been absent these three days on his rash and useless mission to the Villa Rosa."

"Diavolo!" exclaimed Rubaldo, "it is no more than I expected, and at the very moment when he is so urgently wanted; I think he might better have employed his time than in going upon such a fruitless errand as that."

"Ay, Rubaldo," said the brigand's wife; "I quite agree with you there. But have you discovered the place where the Signora Melina is confined?"

"I have."

"So far then you have been successful. But you seem agitated; has anything occurred to alarm you? Where is your companion, Guiseppe?"

"Ah!" returned Rubaldo, "that's where it is; Guiseppe is wounded, and a prisoner in the Villa Civetti."

"Wounded, and a prisoner!" repeated Maria.

"Yes," answered the brigand, "and I may think myself fortunate that I escaped."

"Confusion! Why, how is this?"

Rubaldo briefly informed her.

"This is most unfortunate," observed Maria, "and Massaroni to be away; what is to be done?"

"Why," answered Rubaldo, "just let me partake of some refreshment, and take half an hour's rest, and then I will immediately depart to meet him. Let a sufficient number of the band repair in detached parties, and by different routes, to the Villa Civetti, and await our coming, which shall be as quickly as possible; there is not a moment to be lost; our comrade, Guiseppe, must be released, if he be still alive, and the Signora Melina restored to liberty, before the Prince Bianchi can have time to despatch any assistance."

"True," coincided Maria; "but still I like not the game which Massaroni is at present playing; it is entirely unprofitable, and is likewise fraught with the most imminent danger."

"Well," observed Rubaldo, "I do not know but that you are right in some respects, but still the situation of the Signora Melina calls for our sympathies, and Massaroni has a just feeling of revenge to gratify against the Prince Bianchi and Count Alberti; they have both ever proved themselves to be our most inveterate and implacable enemies."

"They have so," returned Maria, "but still, Massaroni might have adopted a less dangerous and tedious course to gratify his revenge."

"Perhaps he might. But we waste time; let me have some refreshments, and then to business."

The brigand's wife departed, and in a few minutes returned with a repast, which she spread before Rubaldo, and then hastened to meet Clairville, in order to make him acquainted with what had taken place.

She found him pacing the cave in a melancholy manner, and wrapt in deep meditation; but he aroused himself on her entrance, and received her with his usual friendship and politeness.

"How now, my good friend," he said, eagerly; "what brings you to me so early? Have you any fresh news?"

"Ay, Signor Clairville," she replied; "and none of the best, I can assure you."

"Ah!" he ejaculated, with eager impatience, "anything of Melina?"

"Yes; Rubaldo has ascertained for a fact that she is a prisoner in the place that Guiseppe imagined; but they were discovered by four of the prince's men and——"

"Have they fallen into his power?"

"Guiseppe unfortunately has," answered Maria; "but Rubaldo managed to effect his escape, and is at present in the cavern."

"This is indeed most unfortunate and alarming," remarked Florio; "and is Massaroni still absent?"

"He is," replied the brigand's wife.

"It is no more than my worst fears anticipated," said Clairville. "The Prince Bianchi, informed of what has happened, which he will be sure to be immediately, will be sure to take such precautions as will render all the plans of Massaroni abortive, and my beloved Melina's fate will be hastened. Oh, this is surely too much for human endurance!"

"Nay," returned Maria, "you must not give way to despair: Massaroni and our band will be at the Villa Civetti (if fortune does not frown upon them) long before any assistance can reach those from Bianchi, and then her restoration to liberty and your arms is certain."

"Alas!" ejaculated Clairville, "though her restoration to liberty, I need not say, will afford me the most unspeakable gratification, it can inspire me with not the least hope that she can ever become mine. The Prince Bianchi will remain inexorable, and the rescue of Melina from his power will but the more exasperate him, and goad him on to revenge. Melina can never consent to become my wife under such circumstances, and I should be unworthy of her love were I to seek to persuade her to do so. It would indeed be the height of presumption in me, a poor dependant on the bounty of strangers, to encourage such a thought."

"Keep up your spirits, Signor Clairville,"

said Maria, " and there is no knowing what may yet happen to realise your hopes. Of one thing you may be certain, namely, the unabated friendship and assistance of Massaroni."

" I owe him now a debt of gratitude which I can never repay," observed Clairville, " and why should he run such risks for my sake?"

" Oh, there are no risks that the brigand chief would not run to serve one whom he considers worthy of his friendship," replied Maria. " But I must leave you and see to the departure of Rubaldo and his comrades."

Clairville again returned his thanks to the brigand's wife, and she quitted the cave, and left him to his own reflections.

" Melina," he ejaculated, " Fate frowns upon us, and fresh troubles every hour accumulate upon us. In spite of all that the brigand's wife has said, I cannot help thinking that this circumstance will but hasten your destiny. The prince your uncle, enraged at the designs of Massaroni to rescue you, will lose no time in sacrificing you to the villain, Count Alberti, and then you will indeed be one of the most wretched beings in existence. I shudder at the thought, and sooner would I hear of your death than that you should be consigned to a fate so revolting. But even if you should escape from the power of Bianchi, what would become of you, friendless and destitute as you would then be?—Your proud spirit would not suffer you to become like me a dependant on the bounty of Massaroni, and is it fit that one so lovely and so innocent should be immured within the contaminating precincts of a robber's cave? Oh, no; whichever way I view it, I see nothing in the prospects now spread before us to encourage hope, but everything to apprehend. Melina, it would indeed have been most fortunate for us had we ever been strangers to each other."

In this manner Florio Clairville continued to soliloquise for some time, until he was at length interrupted by the return of the brigand's wife, who informed him that Rubaldo had just taken his departure to endeavour to meet Massaroni, and that a strong party of the most daring and trustworthy of the band had been despatched, in various disguises, by different routes, to the neighbourhood of the place where our heroine was imprisoned, which they would reach in a very few hours, doubtless before the Prince Bianchi could receive intelligence of what had taken place, and adopt means for the defensive.

" So that you see, signor," continued Maria, " that everything so far promises well for the deliverance of the Signora Melina from the fate with which she is threatened, if no accident should have befallen Allesandro, and he is almost certain to keep himself out of the way of danger; therefore, on that score you may, at any rate rest your mind contented, and flatter yourself

with the hope, that in a short time you will have the pleasure of beholding her you love again."

" But with that hope, my kind friend," replied Clairville, " is mingled the most painful doubts and fears."

" And why so, signor?"

" What is to become of Melina, friendless and destitute as she will then be?"

" Friendless, signor?" returned the brigand's wife, in a tone of gentle rebuke; " can she be friendless and destitute with such friends as yourself and Allesandro Massaroni, and will she not be under our protection? Who shall dare attempt to harm her, while the brigand chief holds the shield of protection before her? But I see plainly what your words imply; you think that the fair fame of the maiden will be likely to suffer by her becoming in any way associated with those who are termed robbers, and the outcasts, the refuse of society. It is a natural feeling, I admit, so far as the wealthy, oppressive, and tyrannical, are prejudiced against persons of our calling, and to which course of life they have brought us by their own acts of villany and injustice; but Massaroni is a man of honour; he acts from motives of the strictest purity and disinterestedness in his conduct towards the Signora Melina; and here her person and feelings will be held more sacred than they probably would be in the palaces of the wealthy and miscalled noble."

" Believe me, Signora Maria," replied Florio, " I do not doubt you; but still it is a difficult thing to battle with the prejudices of mankind, who are oftentimes too prone to scandal. Another thing I fear is, that it will bring down upon you the vengeance of the Prince Bianchi and Count Alberti, and—"

" Oh," interrupted Maria, " their vengeance we can afford to treat with the most superlative contempt; trust me, it will be their necessity to succumb."

" But think you that Bianchi and Alberti will ever be induced to abandon their designs, or to yield to the wishes of myself and Melina?" demanded Clairville.

" Time will show," answered Maria; " but I do not despair even of that being the ultimate result, if yourself and Melina act with firmness and resolution. What is more likely than all, in my opinion, to bring that about, is the circumstance of the Signora Zitella being still living, and when it is proved to the Prince Bianchi that Olympia, or rather Mira, the unfortunate being whom the Count Alberti has so cruelly betrayed and deserted, is his own daughter."

" Ah!" ejaculated Clairville, " strange that that idea should never have occurred to me before."

" If the prince can be awakened to remorse," continued the brigand's wife, " or has one spark of nature or humanity remaining within his breast, he can no longer resist in compelling his fair niece to become the wife of the man she so thoroughly hates and despises, and the seducer of his own daughter. Notwithstanding his elevated position, he must tremble at the just opprobrium of the world, and be only too happy to effect a reconciliation, and make all the atonement in his power, in order that the past may be buried in oblivion."

VALENTIA IN THE BURNING DWELLING OF HER PARENTS.

"There is force and reason in your arguments, signora," said Clairville, "Heaven grant that it may turn out as you anticipate."

"I feel very little doubt that it will," returned Maria; "and it is with that idea, at least with the idea of awaking the Prince Bianchi to compunction, that Massaroni has resolved to pay him a secret visit, and to recount to him such facts as have come to his knowledge from the narrative of Zitella, which it will be impossible for him to deny. The tale he has to tell must wring the proud nobleman's heart to the core, if he has not become insensible to every feeling of shame and remorse. That tale published to the world, which most assuredly it shall be if he still remains obstinate and inflexible, would blast his reputation for ever. Come, Signor Clairville, you must cheer up, and live in hopes that there are better days in store for you and the Signora Melina."

"I cannot adequately express to you my gratitude for your kind feelings toward me, and one who is far dearer to me than my very existence," returned Clairville; "I will try to encourage the thoughts you seek to inspire me with, and to look forward with sanguine hopes to a happy termination of all our present troubles and anxieties."

"Well spoken, Signor Florio," remarked the brigand's wife; "such feelings as those you have just now expressed are indispensably necessary to you to enable you to await with calmness and resignation the issue of the events that are now on the tapis."

"But think you that Rubaldo will be able to meet with Massaroni?"

"Oh, there is very little doubt of that," replied Maria; "he knows well the place where he is putting up, while on this secret mission to the Villa Rosa."

"And it is their intention immediately to depart to the place where Melina is confined, and being joined by the band, to make an instant attack upon the house?" asked Clairville.

"Certainly," answered Maria; "they will be sure to act with promptitude, for on that principally depends their success; the few individuals whom Rubaldo ascertained to be left to guard the Villa Civetti, would not be mad enough to attempt to offer any resistance, and, therefore, there is nothing to prevent them from releasing Melina and bearing her safely away."

"Alas!" ejaculated Clairville, "how I feel for the anguish and anxiety which that poor girl must at the present time be enduring."

"True, at the prospect of the revolting fate with which the Prince Bianchi has threatened her," said the brigand's wife; "but surely her mind will be relieved of half its cares when she finds herself at liberty, and, if she loves you so sincerely and so ardently as I believe she does, at the prospect of being so shortly restored to you. Prepare yourself, signor, to meet her with a proper spirit, for everything now depends upon you. She will find here all the kindness, respect, and accommodation that our rude retreat can afford, and when the Prince Bianchi finds himself defeated, as assuredly he will, fear not but that we shall be able to bring him to our own terms."

"But think you that his proud and haughty spirit can ever suffer him to consent to the union of his fair niece with one of such lowly pretensions as myself?" interrogated Florio.

"Prouder spirits than his have been subdued ere now," answered Maria, "and that by the power of Allesandro Massaroni, the brigand chief."

"Oh, no," remarked Clairville, "I dare not be presumptuous enough to entertain such a thought, and yet to know that Melina is rescued from the disgusting and revolting fate which is now impending over her, will indeed afford me the most unspeakable consolation."

"I am glad to hear you say so, signor," said his companion, "and take my word for it, you will not be doomed to be disappointed. Massaroni has seldom failed in any ultimate object he has had in view."

"I place the utmost confidence in his skill, his determination, and the integrity of his motives," remarked Clairville.

"You would do him an injustice, signor, were you to think differently," returned Maria.

"But why should he thus sacrifice his time, and run so many risks for one who can never have it in his power to repay him?" demanded Florio.

"Let not such thoughts trouble your mind, signor; whatever Massaroni does is with a free good will, and he seeks no other reward than gratitude."

"Noble hearted, generous minded man!" said Clairville; "how much worthy of a better fate is he than that which has befallen him."

"You say truly, signor," coincided Maria, "the brigand chief is worthy of the most elevated situation in life that can honour human beings. It is no innate guilt of his own that has placed him in his present position, but the crimes, the cruelties, and the oppression of those to whom he had a right to look up with confidence for protection and love. It is only against such curses to their fellow creatures—such black-hearted miscreants as those that he wages war, and he will continue to do so to the death."

"He has been wronged?"

"Wronged!" repeated Maria, and her fine dark eyes at the same time flashing looks of indignation; "oh, that is far too mild a term to give it, signor; you see the cases of Signora Zitella and her daughter, together with their innocent offspring, and there you have the history of Massaroni and his unfortunate mother. Can you wonder then that he should take such an interest in the wrongs inflicted upon confiding, defenceless woman, or that he should visit with his utmost hatred and vengeance their heartless oppressors?"

"No, signora," replied Clairville, "the feeling is natural, and I cannot but commend him for the just indignation which he feels against those who may have been guilty of the heartless crimes which you have mentioned. I hope the time is not far distant when justice, that justice which he merits will be rendered him."

"Ample justice can never be rendered him," replied Maria; "the wrongs he has received are of too deep a nature to be atoned for. What can compensate him for the loss of that unfortunate mother whom he saw perish of a broken-heart; and yet withal so devoted in affection to her base betrayer that she refused to reveal his name to her own son, fearing, no doubt, that he would never rest until he had had revenge."

"But surely Massaroni could not have sought revenge against his own father?" said Clairville, his thoughts for a brief period diverted from his own troubles.

"His father!" repeated the brigand's wife, with a look of scorn; "had not his brutal conduct rendered him unworthy of the name? and think you that any of the feelings of nature could animate the breast of Massaroni towards him? No, there only a deadly feeling of unconquerable hatred predominates, and it must continue to do so whilst he still exists. But he will yet discover him should he be living, and then let the hoary libertine beware."

"I think I have heard Massaroni say that he was of noble rank?" said Clairville.

"True" answered Maria; "from all that he had ever been able to elicit from his mother, he occupied one of the most elevated positions in society; but that would not screen him from his vengeance."

"But I never believe that your husband could possess such vindictive and deadly feelings," said Florio, looking at her with no small degree of surprise.

"And you judged but rightly of him," returned Maria. "Reckless cruelty never marked the character of the brigand chief; but there are wrongs that inflict so deep a wound upon the human heart, that they goad men on to do that which, on ordinary occasions, they would shrink from in horror. Such are the wrongs that Massaroni has experienced, and such the feelings that are naturally engendered in his breast."

"But should he prove penitent?" said Florio.

"The better for his soul's welfare," replied Maria. "He could expect no mercy from Massaroni. But we have talked long enough upon this subject: I must to my duties in the cavern, and see to making the necessary arrangements for the reception of the Signora Melina, who will doubtless be here in a day or two."

"You seem most sanguine upon the subject, Maria," remarked Clairville.

"I am," she answered, "and I would have you be the same, signor; for I feel convinced that you will not be disappointed, though everything depends upon the promptitude of Massaroni, with which I have not the least doubt

he will act, as he never fails to do on such important occasions; so good morning, Signor Clairville, and rest assured that the time is not far distant when the Prince Bianchi will be awakened to a full sense of the injustice and cruelty of his present conduct, and yourself and the Signora Melina will be rewarded for all you have been so long enduring by being restored to future happiness."

"God grant that your prognostications may be fulfilled," returned Clairville, "though I must confess that I have my doubts upon the subject, which are not, I think, unreasonable, when all the circumstances of my situation and that of my beloved Melina are taken into consideration."

"Very true," coincided Maria; "but still I would advise you too keep up your spirits, for much depends upon your firmness."

"Yes," said Clairville; "I perfectly agree with what you say, and will endeavour to act as you advise. I cannot but again return my thanks to you for the interest you take in the welfare of myself and the Signora Melina, and sincerely hope that it may some day be in my power to convince you of my gratitude."

"Nay, signor," observed the brigand's wife; "myself and Massaroni are satisfied, and shall only be too well pleased should it be in our power to serve you to the full extent of our wishes. You must, I think, by this time, be aware that we are not in the habit of making any idle boasts."

"Oh, yes," returned Clairville. "I should, indeed, be ungrateful and ungenerous, did I not place the utmost reliance upon the sincerity and disinterestedness of your motives. You have nothing to gain, but everything to lose, by serving us."

"Well, signor—be it so," replied Maria: "but do not suffer any undue sense of obligation to disturb your mind."

With these words, Maria quitted his presence, and again left him to his own reflections.

Although Florio felt convinced that there was a good deal of truth and reason in the arguments which Maria had made use of, he still could not close his eyes to the uncertainty there was of the hopes she had expressed ever being realised; and, therefore, he could not become so sanguine as she wished him to be. For some time after she had retired, he paced the cave, which was appropriated to him as his apartment, and carefully digested in his own mind the various arguments that had been adduced for his consolation; but although he admitted the force and reason of most of them, at the same time, he could not encourage the sanguine hopes they were meant to inspire in his breast, nor could he divest himself of the apprehensions — the doubts — the misgivings which it was only natural to suppose would hold a place in his mind. But we must leave him for awhile, and once more return to the Villa Rosa, the Prince Bianchi, and the Count Alberti.

During the short time we have digressed from the circumstances taking place there, the Prince Bianchi had exerted himself to complete the arrangements for the clandestine marriage of his fair and innocent niece to the Count Alberti, and the latter, in spite of all the advice which Signor Giachomo, his medical attendant, had given him, not to excite himself, became so impatient at the delay caused to the gratification and accomplishment of his wishes, that Giachomo was fearful of a relapse, which he told him accordingly, and added, in the presence of Bianchi—

"Pardon me, my lord, but what folly is this to protract that which you are so anxious to accomplish, and which I must candidly premise, is calculated to destroy yourself, and to counteract all that my humble ability and experience have been enabled to do towards your recovery. Unless you persevere to conquer this irritability, much I value your lordship's welfare, and anxious as I am to restore you to a state of convalescence, I must, in justice to myself, decline my future services, which, under such circumstances, are likely to compromise my professional character. I am confident, that his highness, the prince, will agree with me in the truth and reason of that which I have advanced."

"Most unquestionably I do, Signor Giachomo," replied Bianchi, "the truth and force of that which you have just stated, no reasonable person can attempt to contravert, and I know that my young friend here, upon mature reflection, will be one of the first to acknowledge it. Your pardon, signor, but will you favour me with a few minutes' private conversation with the count?"

"Most assuredly, excellenza," replied Signor Giachomo, bowing, and retiring from the chamber.

"Now, Alberti," observed the Prince Bianchi, when he and the patient were alone, "what madness is this, when all is progressing so propitiously; what have you to fear? What doubts or misgivings, I have to ask you, ought you to entertain, when Melina is secure in the Villa Civetti, far away from any hope of rescue, and, unless you by your own folly cause the delay, in a few days she must become yours? Have you any reason to doubt the sincerity of the determination I have all along expressed to you?"

"No, your highness," replied Alberti, "you are a man of honour and the strictest integrity, one whose word is his bond."

"True," remarked Bianchi, "I flatter myself that I can conscientiously take full credit to myself for the compliment you have just now been pleased to bestow upon me."

"But still your highness, I know, will be most ready to make every allowance for the impatience of a man placed in the peculiar circumstances that I am," returned the Count Alberti.

"I do so," said Bianchi; "but are you not protracting the gratification of your hopes, by indulging in the groundless fears you do? What is to prevent Melina from becoming your bride, when I, her uncle and guardian, am determined that she shall be so? Pshaw, count! this is nothing better than sheer folly, and I am really surprised to see you give way to it."

"You may reproach me, my lord," said the Count Alberti, "and perhaps I am deserving of it; but for the last night or two I have had some troublesome dreams, which——"

"Dreams, count!" interrupted the prince; "and is it possible you can be so superstitious as to place any confidence in dreams?"

"Pardon me, your highness," replied Alberti, "but there are times when they present themselves in such a plausible and palpable shape before our imagination, that we find it a most difficult task to get rid of the impression they leave behind upon our mind. Such dreams have occurred to me, and I do not seek to deny the effect they have had upon me; and which have given rise to the fears and suspicions I have but just now expressed to you."

"Fears and suspicions, count?" demanded the Prince Bianchi; "and may I inquire what the nature of those said fears and suspicions are?"

"Briefly, my lord, that, notwithstanding all her present apparent security, the Signora Melina will yet escape us."

"Ridiculous! That is utterly impossible!"

"You may believe so, excellenza, but I do not."

"And why?"

"The brigand chief, Allesandro Massaroni, takes an interest in her fate."

"And what if he does? He has not the power to assist her."

"Pardon me, my lord, but it strikes me that you ought not to come to any such hasty conclusion as that," said Alberti. "Myself and your highness have had occasion to acknowledge his power ere now."

"But he is not acquainted with the place of her present confinement," returned the Prince Bianchi.

"There are few things that escape the knowledge of Massarino," replied Alberti; "and is not Guiseppe, formerly your domestic, and acquainted with many of your secrets, now one of his daring band?"

"True," coincided Prince Bianchi; "that circumstance is certainly unfortunate."

"Guiseppe," rejoined the count, "I dare

say is acquainted with all your possessions, and likewise that of the Villa Civetti."

"No, I think not."

"Should he happen to be so, his suspicions will probably be aroused that it is there the Signora Melina has been conveyed, and Massaroni will not fail to take advantage of the information he will thus be enabled to give him. I think that a sufficient force ought previously to have been despatched to the Villa Civetti, in order to be enabled to repel any sudden and unexpected attack that might be made upon it."

"Pshaw!" replied Bianchi; "these fears, I firmly believe, are utterly groundless, and I consider that the course you suggest would have been highly impolitic, as the appearance of a strange body of men in the neighbourhood of the villa would naturally have created suspicion, and done away with that secrecy which it was our grand object to maintain. But banish such ridiculous and torturing thoughts from your breast, my lord, and fear not all will terminate as well as your most sanguine hopes could anticipate. Still you must, as I have before said, not abandon yourself to the misgivings which you now acknowledge having encouraged. Do not excite yourself, and in the course of a very few days, take my word for it, you will be restored to convalescence; and then the consummation of those hopes which you so fondly entertain will be accomplished, and Melina, my fair niece, become your bride."

"That thought is ecstasy," replied the Count Alberti, "and urges me on to exert myself. I will endeavour to do as you advise."

"Well said, count," observed Bianchi; "and in that disposition I will now leave you, confident that you will profit by the counsel I have given you, when you take into proper consideration the necessity and the policy of so doing.'

"Your observations encourage me, my lord," remarked Alberti; "and I will endeavour to dissipate the gloomy and restless apprehensions I have allowed to take possession of my mind. You are still proceeding with you arrangements for the secret union?"

"I am, my lord," answered Bianchi, "and they fast draw towards completion."

"But still I must confess that there is another thing which troubles me," said the count.

"And what is that?" demanded Bianchi.

"Olympia and her child," answered his companion; "I would to Heaven that the unfortunate liaison had never taken place between us, or that she and her offspring were now no more."

"Why," returned the Prince Bianchi, with some qualms of conscience which he found it impossible to struggle against, "that certainly was an unfortunate affair, and it would be as well if they were safely disposed of; but still, taking all the circumstances into consideration, I do not think it is very probable that they will annoy you again."

"The disposition of Olympia, mild, submissive, and confiding, as I know it to be," answered Alberti, "I should know perfectly well how to deal with, and I have not the least doubt that I should be able to persuade her, by making a proper provision for her, to retire into private life, and never more to advance her claims upon me; but since she is under the protection of the brigand chief, who takes such an extraordinary interest in her fate, have I not everything to apprehend? He has pledged himself to avenge her wrongs, and to compel me to make her all the reparation in my power, and have I not sufficient reason to believe he will not fail to keep his word?"

"Pshaw!" replied Bianchi, "let not such thoughts trouble your mind; the rascal Massaroni, should he even be bold enough to attempt to carry his threats into execution, will be foiled, as he has hitherto been; and, if I am not much mistaken, before many weeks, nay, perhaps many days have expired, he will be in my power, and I need not inform you, I should think, that a speedy termination will then be brought to his guilty career."

"Yes, my lord," said Alberti, "I have not the least doubt that the brigand will meet with summary justice at your hands whenever he may chance to fall into them; but you will pardon me if I have my doubts as to whether that will happen at a very early period, or until he has been enabled to effect a considerable deal more mischief than that he has hitherto done."

"Well, well," observed the Prince Bianchi, after reflecting for a minute or two; "time will show;—however, for the present reflect seriously upon what I have said, and let your good sense guide you to act accordingly; the speedy consummation of your hopes depends entirely upon the prudence of your own conduct; all delay will be caused by your acting contrarily. Do you mark my words, my lord?"

"I do," answered the count, "and admit the truth and force of them, and hope that I may be enabled to act as your wishes dictate."

"Enough," remarked the Prince Bianchi; "after what you have just now said, I have every confidence in you, and will leave you. To morrow I hope to see you, by calm reflection, in a much improved state of health; and in the meantime you may rest assured that I will not fail to use every precaution that may appear necessary for the security of my niece and the completion of our designs. Are you satisfied with that assurance, count?"

"Certainly," answered the latter; "how can I be otherwise?"

"Well, then, I have nothing more to say at present," returned Bianchi, "and I therefore wish you good-day."

"Good-day, excellenza," replied Alberti, and the prince then retired from the chamber.

"But notwithstanding all that the Prince Bianchi has said, and the promises I have made him," observed Alberti, when the former was gone, "I cannot still help entertaining the apprehensions which have taken such powerful hold on my mind; and the impression still holds its influence over me that Melina will by some means or other be rescued from the fate with which she is at present threatened, and be enabled to set the prince, her uncle, and myself at defiance. Massaroni will leave no means untried to save her; and should he be enabled to discover the place where she is at present confined, it will be no difficult task, undefended as it is, to surround it with his daring band, and at once to restore her to liberty and the arms of Forio Clairville. That thought is madness! I cannot exactly see the policy of the Prince Bianchi in the course he has thought proper to adopt, and from it I have a right to augur danger. Would that I were recovered that I might take a more active part in this important business; and it is that which exhausts my patience, notwithstanding all the arguments which the prince has and can make use of. Olympia, too; she and her offspring remain, and while they do so, can I consider myself safe? No, I cannot! Then I know full well that Massaroni will not rest until he has fully gratified the feelings of revenge he has imbibed towards me. Then do I find myself surrounded by innumerable dangers and obstacles to the gratification of my hopes, and under such circumstances, how can I be otherwise than excited? Oh, Melina! would that I had never been the guilty wretch that I must admit myself to have been, then might I have wooed thee with honour and confidence, and have entertained the most sanguine hopes of obtaining a return of that passion which I entertain for thee. But now, is it not presumption?—is it not even madness on my part to entertain such a thought? Yes, it is; I know full well that you view me with feelings of disgust and abhorrence, and it is not by conduct such as that I am now pursuing towards you, that I can hope to effect any change in your sentiments towards me. Self-pride and honour should induce me to abandon all thoughts of you; but still I cannot relinquish the wishes with which your superlative charms and intrinsic qualities have inspired me, and I must continue to prosecute my suit, whatever the consequences may be, or however odious my addresses may be to you."

Thus did the Count Alberti continue to soliloquise at intervals, and it was in vain that he sought to obtain that tranquillity which the Prince Bianchi had advised, or to banish those apprehensions which had taken such powerful possession of his breast.

In spite of all he had said to Alberti to the contrary, the Prince Bianchi was far from feeling in the easy and satisfied state of mind that he wished it to appearhe was; and when he was alone, he gave himself up to the most conflicting and torturing reflections. His conscience keenly reproached him for the cruel manner in which he was acting towards Melina, in compelling her into a marriage so repugnant to her feelings, and every way so unworthy of her; and when he remembered the solemn promise he had given to her mother, his only sister, in her dying moments, he could not but acknowledge to himself that he was acting the part of a villain. Then again there were moments when all the errors of his past life would rush upon his memory with the most overwhelming force, and the pale and ghastly faces of his unfortunate victims would arise before his terrified imagination, and drive him almost to a state of frenzy. And yet he was now about to sacrifice his innocent and unoffending niece to a man who had been equally as guilty as himself, and upon whom the world looked with feelings of scorn and abhorrence. What a strange perversity there is often in our nature, and how obstinately do we rush into the vortex of guilt, which is naturally so repulsive to our better feelings. So it was with the Prince Bianchi; he knew full well, none could know better than himself, the cruelty and injustice of the conduct he was practising, and yet he had not the virtuous resolution to abandon his guilty designs, and to make Melina all the reparation in his power for the injuries he had done her. Nor could he help acknowledging to himself that the apprehensions which the Count Alberti had expressed were not altogether groundless, and he was impatient for him to be restored to a state of convalescence so that they might at once put their designs into execution. The brigand chief's power he had too much reason to know, and notwitstanding the contempt he had expressed towards him before Alberti, he could not help entertaining a feeling of dread towards him, and, likewise, a sensation of a peculiar nature, for which he was at a loss to account, whenever he reflected upon his name. There was something in the expression of his features which had stamped itself indelibly upon his memory; and the longer he reflected on it, the more did his mind become bewildered and distracted.

"And yet," he would say to himself, "why should I suffer this daring outlaw and robber to cause me one anxious thought? What is he to me more than my bitterest enemy? and ought I not to despise and hate him accordingly? Pshaw! it is worse than childish weakness to gave way to such thoughts as these. Away with them, I say; let me banish them from my mind as totally unworthy of me."

He was in the apartment which contained the portrait of Valentia when he gave way to these reflections, and scarcely knowing what he did, he drew aside the curtain which concealed it, and gazed upon it; he started back, trembling, as if he had encountered a spectre, and could almost imagine that he beheld it move, and that its eyes were fixed reproachfully upon him; then the features seemed to change and to assume all the expression of those of the brigand chief.

"Powers of mercy!" he ejaculated in a hoarse voice, and trembling still more convulsively; "what strange and awful delusion is this? I could almost swear that Allessandro Massaroni had taken possession of the frame, and gazed upon me, so powerful is the resemblance! And yet, it is the portrait of Valentia—her whom I betrayed to destruction, and then, with the heart of a demon, deserted—that I gaze upon! Oh, Valentia! what can ever wash out the stain of my guilty conduct towards you? Let me hide thy likeness from my sight, or the contemplation of it will drive me to madness!"

He hastily drew the curtain again across the painting, and rushed in a state of the greatest agony of mind from the room to his own chamber; but the impression of what he had seen, or imagined he had seen, pursued him thither, and throwing himself into a chair, he gave himself up to the most racking thoughts.

"'Tis strange, 'tis most unaccountable," he soliloquised; "and yet I could not have been deceived, though I never noticed it before, how powerful is the likeness which Massaroni bears to the portrait, or else it is my disordered imagination that has led me astray. For a few moments I could almost have believed that the brigand chief stood before me. But no, I have suffered my senses to deceive me; what connection can Massaroni possibly have with the late unfortunate and deeply-injured Valentia? Away with such weak thoughts as those: they are totally unworthy of me."

He tried to banish them, but in vain; they would pursue him and haunt his imagination in spite of all his efforts to the contrary, and he became more restless every moment. In this state of mind the Prince Bianchi continued for some time, until the hour of midnight fast approached, and warned him that it was time to seek his couch, though he doubted much whether he should be enabled to sleep in the state of excitement he then was. A death-like silence reigned throughout the villa, which added to the solemnity of the occasion, and by

degrees, the fears of Bianchi gained such powerful ascendancy over him, that he was almost afraid to be alone or to look around him, lest he should encounter some ghastly phantom. However, at length, worn out with racking thought, he hastily undressed himself and retired to bed, and endeavoured to compose himself to sleep, though for some time to no purpose, such was the restlessness and agitation of his feelings. At length, however, nature was exhausted, and he did drop off into a disturbed slumber, imagination presenting to him a variety of visions of the most painful character, and from one of which he suddenly started, the perspiration standing upon his temples in large drops. He gazed fearfully around the chamber for a few moments scarcely conscious as to where he was. The lamp was still burning upon the table where he had left it, and cast a sickly glare upon the room and the furniture it contained. Suddenly he imagined that he heard some one moving stealthily in the apartment, and he drew his breath short and quick, but was unable to give utterance to a single word. He felt as though something of a fearful nature was about to happen to him, and yet he had not the least power to help himself or to summon that assistance which he might require. He listened attentively, and could again almost swear that he heard footsteps in the room, and which seemed to be moving towards the bed on which he was lying; but he was afraid to draw aside the curtains lest his eyes should encounter the unseen object of his terrors. Then he pinched himself and rubbed his eyes, scarcely able to convince himself that he was awake; and now the footsteps were more distinct, and he was fully satisfied that he was not mistaken, but that there was some one in the room. It would be almost impossible to describe the fears under which the Prince Bianchi laboured, but his tongue clove to the roof of his mouth; every faculty was suspended, and he was unable to call for assistance. And suddenly—could he be mistaken? Oh, no, it was too palpable!—on the wainscot opposite the end of his bed, he beheld the dark shadow of a human form, which seemed to be moving cautiously about; and before he had time to recover himself in the least degree, the curtains of his bed were drawn hastily aside, and the tall figure of a man, enveloped in a huge cloak, presented itself.

Completely thunderstruck by the appearance of this unexpected vision, the Prince Bianchi could not repress a cry of horror; but the stranger presented a poniard at his breast, and in a deep and commanding voice, which showed that he was determined to be obeyed, said—

"Silence, old man, for you have no child to deal with."

"Who are you?" demanded Bianchi, in a tremulous voice.

"Behold!" replied the man, raising his hat from his brows, and then throwing back his cloak.

"Massaroni!" gasped forth the prince, as he recognised the brigand chief, who had so lately occupied his thoughts.

"Ay, Allesandro Massaroni," replied the latter; "your *friend*, and whom, I believe, you have been so anxious to see."

"Villain!"

"Better language, old man, as you value your life; you have to fight against fearful odds, and it would be well for you to be calm and submissive."

"What brings you hither at this solemn hour?" asked Bianchi, "and what would you with me?"

"That you shall quickly know," replied our hero.

"I will raise an alarm, and have you instantly secured," said the agitated prince, raising himself in the bed, and looking around him in terror.

"If you raise your voice beyond a whisper, it shall be the last word you shall utter in this world," said Massaroni, determinedly, and still pointing the weapon towards his breast.

"Would you murder me in cold blood?" gasped forth Bianchi.

"No," replied the brigand. "Massaroni is no midnight assassin, and if he were, your life is not worth the taking."

"How gained you admittance, here?" demand the prince.

"That is my business," was the answer; "there are few things that are impossible to Massaroni, when he has made up his mind to accomplish them."

"Why keep me in suspense?" said Bianchi; "what is your business with me?"

"To try whether it is possible to awaken your guilty conscience to remorse," said our hero; "and to repeat to you a tale of the past, which probably you never expected to hear again. Does not the hoary seducer of female innocence feel no upbraidings of conscience?"

"The seducer of female innocence?" repeated the Prince Bianchi, in a faint voice, and staring at him earnestly and fearfully; "dare you thus accuse me?"

"Dare I!" retorted the brigand, with a laugh of scorn; "dare you deny your guilt?"

"What mean you?"

"Oh, shameless hypocrite! But since your memory seems to fail you, I will be more explicit. Did you, in your youthful days, ever know a damsel, amiable and beautiful, named Zitella?"

The prince turned ghastly pale, and his lips quivered.

"Ah!" ejaculated Massaroni, "the name seems to be familiar to you, old man. Can you deny that you were acquainted with the unfortunate female, whose name I have just now mentioned?"

"How know you that?" demanded Bianchi, in a breathless voice; "and why do you question me thus?"

"Did you know her, I ask?" said our hero, impatiently.

The prince still hesitated, confused by the question, and then replied in the affirmative, in a faint voice.

"Oh, you acknowledge it?" said the brigand chief, with a look of triumph; "so far that is well. She was young, innocent, and most beautiful too, was she not?"

"Yes, yes; but spare me, Massaroni."

"Nay, nay—I must e'en finish the tale I have commenced. Zitella was the idol of her parents when a child, and knew not what sorrow was, till accident deprived her of an only and beloved brother, and introduced her to one who called himself Carlotti. He was young and prepossessing, and having been the means of saving her life, no wonder that he made an impression upon her youthful and susceptible heart. Was it not so, Prince Bianchi?"

"Oh, God! this is most torturing!" ejaculated Bianchi; "how came these painful facts to your knowledge, Massaroni?"

"No matter," answered our hero, "but you shall know that anon. But to proceed with my narrative, which seems so deeply interesting to you. This Signor Carlotti, as he called himself, won the fair Zitella's heart, and he vowed to return her passion with equal ardour; but her father was strongly opposed to his paying his addresses to her, and prohibited his visits; for he suspected him of being a villain, and future circumstances fully proved how well those suspicions were founded."

"By Heaven! I cannot endure this," said Bianchi, impatiently, and in an agitated voice.

"Nay," said Massaroni, coolly, "your highness must hear me out, for I have not half done yet. Carlotti, by his flattering tongue, had gained too firm a hold on the affections of the confiding and inexperienced Zitella for her to be able to banish him from her heart, and in secret, and in spite of all the opposition of her father, she continued to cherish and encourage the fatal passion with which he had inspired her. She was kept closely confined to her room, but at length the real name of her lover reached her ears—that name was the Prince Bianchi!"

"Spare me, Massaroni!" again cried the prince.

"Let me proceed," returned the brigand, "for the narrative deepens in interest. Prince Bianchi persuaded poor Zitella to grant him a secret interview, at which he professed the most ardent love for her; and when she told him that she dared not disobey the commands of her father, and that he must endeavour to forget her, he pretended to be driven to despair, and make an attempt upon his life. It was then that his hour of triumph had arrived; she dashed the pistol from his hand, vowed herself his for ever, and overpowered by her feelings, became insensible. Is this true or not, my lord?"

"Yes, yes, 'tis too true," gasped forth Bianchi; "but never did I expect to hear the tale repeated by lips like thine."

"I dare say not, my lord," returned the brigand chief, with an ironical smile. "And so this is the Prince Bianchi, the immaculate governor of Rome! No wonder that he shoul

VALENTIA'S FIRST MISGIVINGS OF BIANCHI'S LOVE.

acknowledge for his friend, the libertine, Count Alberti."

"Massaroni, beware what you says," ejaculated the prince. "By Heaven, I will not tamely submit to be thus taunted."

"But you must, my lord," replied Massaroni, in a resolute voice; "you have no power to help yourself, and it delights me to torture the conscience of the guilty. However, my tale is not ended yet, as you must be aware."

No. 72.

"Cease—cease, and leave me," cried Bianchi, worked up to a pitch of the most insupportable agitation. Massaroni, however, walked deliberately to the other side of the room, and bringing a chair close to the bed, he seated himself and said—

"Nay, nay, excellenza, Massaroni does not things that way. He has come expressly to visit you, and to explain a few matters of fact, and it, therefore, is not likely that he will but half complete his errand. You have admitted that the tale I have told is anything but an exaggerated one, and, therefore, do you acknowledge yourself a heartless scoundrel."

"Liar! dog! robber!" exclaimed the prince, furiously.

"Beware, old man," said our hero, pointing significantly to his poniard; "one blow, and I send you before the judgment seat of Heaven, with all your heinous sins upon your head. But to the sequel of my narrative: You had triumphed in your guilty designs—Zitella was your victim—she had abandoned her parents and her home, and had no other alternative left but to place herself under your *protection*. You promised to make her your wife when circumstances would permit you—pretended the most unbounded affection for her, and she, poor credulous girl, too readily believed you. A child, a lovely girl, was the fruit of this guilty and unfortunate connexion; and for some time you affected to strengthen in your love, all the time you were plotting the most heartless villany, and seeking to devise some plan by which you might rid yourself of those whom you now considered a burthen to you. At length you cast aside the mask, and appeared in your real character. Need I attempt to describe the horror, the anguish, and despair of Zitella, when she discovered how brutally she had been deceived? Such was the effect it had upon her, that she was confined to her bed, and for some time her senses wandered—her mind was a wreck. It was then that, determined to complete your infamous designs, you introduced one of your creatures, a wretch ready to commit any crime for money, upon the scene. Malvolio I mean."

"Ha! know you him?" ejaculated the Prince Bianchi.

"You will find that I did, your highness," replied the brigand chief; "but you must hear me out without interruption. You employed this wretch to tear the infant from its hapless mother's breast, and left him to dispose of it as he thought proper, so long as it did not trouble you again. This trial was too much for your wretched victim; her senses again fled, and in that state she was conveyed to a distant part of the country, where, on awaking to consciousness, she found herself the prisoner of the miscreant Malvolio."

"Must I, indeed, still listen to this tale of past errors?" interrupted the Prince Bianchi, still more agitated than ever.

"Yes," replied Massaroni, in the same determined accents in which he had at first spoken; "for it is meet that the long slumbering conscience of the guilty should be aroused to a sense of the enormities they have inflicted upon the innocent and unsuspecting. But pardon me, my lord," he added, sarcastically, "for applying so harsh a term to what you have been pleased to designate as mere simple errors; I wonder that you did not style them *youthful indiscretions*, that being, I believe, the light in which noblemen of such peculiar eccentricities as those which I have alluded to, view such unimportant matters."

The bitterness of the sarcasm in which our hero gave utterance to these observations, stung the haughty nobleman to the quick, and he bit his lips, though, from the determined manner of the brigand chief, and knowing that he was entirely in his power, he was afraid to give utterance to his feelings, and remained silent, averting his face from the keen penetrating glance of mingled triumph and scorn that was fixed upon him, while the expression of Massaroni's features awoke sensations in his breast which he could not conquer, and which he would fain should have slumbered for ever.

"The unfortunate Signora Zitella," continued the brigand, after a pause, "as I have said before, on being restored to sensibility, found herself the prisoner of your guilty myrmidon, Malvolio, in a wretched hovel, and robbed of her innocent offspring, that poor child whom you flattered yourself you had got rid of for ever."

"Oh, God!" groaned the prince, in his agony, and at the same time covering his face with his hands.

"Ah!" ejaculated Massaroni, with looks of increased triumph; "does then your conscience feel the force of that which I have challenged it with? 'Tis well—'tis well, indeed; but, mark me, Prince Bianchi, the time has come for retribution, and as sure as you are Governor of Rome, it will descend with overwhelming violence upon your head, unless you seek to make all the atonement you can for the monstrous iniquities of which you have been guilty. I, Allesandro Massaroni, the brigand chief, he whom you are so anxious to consign to the scaffold, tell you so; and rest assured that my predictions will be fulfilled. But I digress; Zitella demanded her child; and the murderous ruffian in whose power she was, informed her that it was where she would never behold it again, and—"

"Mysterious, fearful man!" interrupted Bianchi, in a faint voice; "by what means have you, I once more ask you, become acquainted with these fatal particulars?"

"In the first instance," replied our hero;

"from the dying confession of the villain, Malvolio himself."

"From Malvolio!" exclaimed the prince; "impossible!"

"Possible or not," returned Massaroni, with the utmost coolness; "it is true. Accident made him my prisoner; but he has now paid the penalty of his crimes. In his dying moments, remorse seized upon his guilty soul, and, in the presence of witnesses, whose corroborative evidence cannot be doubted, he divulged that which I have just now repeated, and added, that, fearful to take the life of that unfortunate woman you had so deeply injured, yet anxious to banish her from his sight for ever, and 'save himself from her bitter reproaches, he thrust her from his miserable hovel, while in a state of madness, and left her to her fate."

"Oh, cowardly, treacherous miscreant!" cried Bianchi, in a hoarse voice.

"What!" demanded the brigand chief, fixing upon the guilty nobleman a look which made him tremble; "and do you regret that your blood-thirsty myrmidon did not fulfil the whole of the hellish instructions you gave him? Oh, beware, old man, and repent ere it be too late. Should those guilty transactions be published to the world, how then would the character of the proud and haughty Prince Bianchi stand, think you?"

"And think you that any one would be foolish or credulous enough to believe them, unsubstantiated as they must now ever remain?" demanded the prince.

"Indeed!" returned Massaroni, with a triumphant laugh; "place not such flattering unction to your guilty soul, excellenza, lest you should be doomed to be disappointed."

"Bah!" ejaculated Bianchi, mustering all his fortitude, "think not to intimidate me, for I treat all that you have threatened with the most supreme contempt."

"What if your victim should still be living?" demanded the brigand.

"Living!" repeated the prince, in a faltering voice; "it is impossible!"

"Probably for your own sake you would wish it to be so; but 'tis true; the Signora Zitella still lives, to your own confusion and dismay!"

"Zitella living!" exclaimed Bianchi, fixing his eyes full upon our hero's countenance, and his features plainly exhibiting the powerful emotions of fear and conscious guilt that were struggling in his bosom; "liar!—bold, shameful liar!"

"Be calm—be calm, old man," replied Massaroni; "for these bursts of frenzied passion and despair can have no effect on me. I tell you again, that not only is the Signora Zitella still alive, but her daughter too, and restored to her arms!"

"Living—living!" gasped forth the distracted nobleman, clasping his forehead, and staring vacantly upon Massaroni; "what demon is at work to torture me?—Do my senses wander?—or is this only some frightful dream?"

"It is no dream, Prince Bianchi," answered our hero, "as you will shortly be convinced of to your cost."

"Living!—living!" again ejaculated Bianchi, in wandering accents; "and the child, too?"

"Ay," returned the brigand chief; "that child preserved from the cruel fate to which you had consigned her, and now with her deeply injured mother, safe under the protection of one who will not rest until full and ample justice has been rendered them."

"And who is he who has dared to protect them?" demanded Bianchi, mustering all the resolution he could.

"Even he who stands before you, excellenza," answered our hero, in the same cool accents which had characterised him throughout the interview; "Allesandro Massaroni, the mountain chief."

"You!" cried the prince, trembling convulsively in every limb; "Zitella and her child still living and under your protection? Away! impostor!—miscreant!—robber! 'tis false as hell!"

"Your highness, however, shall soon be convinced to the contrary," said the brigand; "but I have not yet told you all, and no doubt the sequel of my story will afford you infinite satisfaction; the ruffian Malvolio, fearing to take the life of the poor, unconscious innocent you had consigned to his mercy, left her at the door of the palazzo of one of your most intimate friends, by whom she was brought up and educated."

"Ah!" cried Bianchi, a dreadful thought flashing across his brain, "and that nobleman was ——"

"The late Count Alberti di Almafi."

"The late Count Alberti!" groaned the wretched prince; "oh, God!"

"'Tis true," replied Massaroni; "that child, your own daughter, is no other than Olympia, the victim of the present Count Alberti, and to whom you would sacrifice your innocent niece."

Bianchi stared at him for a moment or two in stupified amazement, and was unable to give utterance to a syllable, while, at the same time, it was evident that the emotions which held dominion in his breast were of the most powerful description; but at length he struggled with his feelings, and exclaimed—

"It is all a mockery!—'tis all a scheme, a most villanous scheme, to entrap me, and to make me commit myself. Olympia my daughter? 'Tis a lie!—a base subterfuge!—a —— a ——"

The finish of the sentence was stifled in his

throat, and Massaroni gazed at him with mingled feelings of pity and contempt; but at length he observed in solemn accents :—

"Old man, how terrible is it to witness the workings of conscience upon one whose venerable years should entitle him to respect and honour. Your tongue may deny, but your craven heart must admit the truth of all that which I have said. Why longer then refuse that claim which justice has upon you? Why refuse to acknowledge the too confiding victim of your lust, and the unoffending offspring of that illicit intercourse? And, more, why persist in compelling your niece to become the wife of the base and dastardly seducer of your own daughter?"

"Olympia my daughter!" almost shrieked the Prince Bianchi; "no, no; it is impossible! Fiend!—Devil!—who art thou, that comest thus to torture me?—Avaunt!—I will have nothing to do with thee!—I—I—oh, God!"

Thus saying, the wretched nobleman sunk back upon his pillow in a state of utter insensibility

Massaroni gazed at him attentively for a few minutes; and in spite of the cause he had to hate and despise him from the manner in which he had at all times persecuted him, he could not help entertaining a feeling of pity towards him for his abject misery at that moment.

"Oh," he soliloquised, as he still continued to gaze at him, "how soon is the proudest spirit reduced to that of the merest worm that ever crawled the earth, when the conscience is justly appealed to! Truth and right must ultimately predominate over every other earthly power or passion. Thou liest there, old man, my greatest acknowledged earthly foe, one who has so long thirsted for my blood, and used every endeavour to shed it; thou liest at my mercy; I could plunge my poniard into thy breast, and make thy sleep of unconsciousness one of eternity, thus ridding myself of thy annoyance, whilst no one could possibly accuse me of having perpetrated the deed; but my soul abhors the thought!—How melancholy pitiable does the poor guilty old man appear!—and there is something in his features that, notwithstanding the feelings of animosity and detestation I have a right to entertain towards him, almost excites my veneration. But why these thoughts?—Let me dismiss them, and since I have thus aroused him to a consciousness of his guilt, and left him food for sober reflection, let me retire, lest I allow my more fevered passions to obtain the mastery of me."

He moved towards the door as he spoke, but felt constrained to return and once more gazed upon the countenance of the insensible Bianchi. As he did so, the most strange and unaccountable feelings came over him, and he became, as it were, transfixed by the side of the bed. His brain turned giddy — singular objects appeared to flit before his eyes — the face of his mother was before his vision, as palpable as he had witnessed it when that dear, but unfortunate mother, in all her heart's fondest love, had enfolded him to her breast, and the glance of her melancholy, unearthly eye was fixed upon the countenance of the Prince Bianchi, with an expression of appeal and intercession, which it was impossible to mistake. Labouring under the delusion of the moment, wrought, doubtless, by the power of his own excited imagination, Massaroni clasped his forehead, and hastily left the chamber, as silently as he had entered it. The object he had intended was not entirely accomplished; it was true, he had made Bianchi acquainted with the knowledge he had acquired, and aroused the dormant feelings of his conscience; but still he had elicited nothing whatever to elucidate the facts connected with his own history, and which he had suspected it was not at all improbable he would have done; consequently, he felt somewhat disappointed. More than that, he could not do away with the impression that he had seen the vision of his mother; and the looks which she had, he imagined, fixed upon the Prince Bianchi, bewildered and distracted him. For almost the first time in his life, the brigand chief felt unnerved, and, as he tracked his way along the various passages of the villa, in that solemn hour, he scarcely knew whither he was going, or what had been the object which had called him to it. At length, however, he gained the exterior of the house, and, deeply wrapped in meditation, arrived at the place where he had temporarily taken up his abode, while on his mission to the Prince Bianchi. He immediately retired to the room wherein he was accommodated, and throwing himself into a chair, for a short time gave himself up to the conflicting thoughts which crowded upon his mind.

"It is strange," he soliloquised; "why should my mind be thus harassed and perplexed?—Have I become weak and childish? Has superstition taken possession of my senses?—This is not the temperament that Allesandro Massaroni has been wont to be in; and yet, in spite of all my efforts to the contrary, I cannot shake off the impression which has now obtained such wonderful influence over me. 'Twas surely my mother's face that gazed upon me, and directed my attention so appealingly towards the wretched, guilty Prince Bianchi! But why should her spirit intercede for him?—Ah! strange and powerful thoughts crowd upon my imagination, and all but confirm my suspicions. Can he have been the heartless betrayer of her who gave me being, as well as the Signora Zitella?

There is madness in the thought!—Could I be convinced that my surmises are correct, I would immediately return, and my dagger's blade should pierce his guilty heart!"

He paused, for at that moment, solemn strains of music seemed to float upon the air which enwrapt his senses. More plaintive and impressive it became every moment; it might have been a delusion, but he was worked up to a pitch of excitement which was more than he could find strength to combat with, and gradually sinking upon his knees, he clasped his burning temples, and became totally unconscious of everything moving about him. How long he had remained so, he had no means of calculating, but he was suddenly aroused by a loud knocking at the room door, and starting to his feet he regained his composure in a moment, and opening the door gave admittance to the man who belonged to the house at which he was staying.

"How now, Orsini?" he demanded; "what brings you here in such haste?"

"Rubaldo, your lieutenant, is below, signor," replied Orsini, "fatigued with hasty travelling, and desires to see you immediately."

"Rubaldo here!" ejaculated our hero; "it must indeed be something of importance that brings him hither in such haste. I will immediately attend upon him."

Orsini retired from the room, and the brigand chief, collecting himself, hastily followed, and found Rubaldo anxiously awaiting to see him.

"Rubaldo," said Massaroni, "what brings you hither when I expected you far away?"

"Business of importance, you may depend, captain," answered Rubaldo; "and 'tis well we have met; you must prepare yourself to depart from hence without delay."

"Is there then any danger?"

"Yes, unless every expedition is used," replied Rubaldo.

"Have you discovered the place of the Signora Melina's confinement?" asked our hero.

"I have," answered the lieutenant; "and it is there you must accompany me without delay; I have already given instructions to the principal portion of our band to meet us there and——"

"How! then you have been to our retreat?"

"I have."

"What is the meaning of all this?"

"Simply that I and my companions have been discovered by the retainers of the Prince Bianchi," replied Rubaldo, "that Guiseppe is wounded and taken prisoner; that it was by a complete miracle I effected my escape; and that——"

"Guiseppe wounded and a prisoner!" repeated Massaroni.

"Yes," returned Rubaldo; "it is even as I have said; but, if we use all proper expedition, we can reach the Villa Civetti before the Prince Bianchi can be apprised of the circumstance, or send troops to repel us. Not more than forty hours have elapsed since the affair took place, and our band, I have little doubt, have already nearly arrived there—they await but our command to proceed at once to the rescue of Signora Melina, and revenge."

"By the saints, Rubaldo, you have acted well in this unfortunate affair," remarked Massaroni; "and you deserve my warmest thanks. I am ready to attend you immediately. My worthy host, Orsini, can supply us with mules for the occasion."

"I have brought them with me," replied Rubaldo. "But have you seen the Prince Bianchi?"

"I have not long since returned from the presence of the Prince Bianchi," answered Massaroni; "and I have rung in his ears such a tale, that I question much if he will easily forget. But more of this anon; at present, our whole thoughts and energies must be directed to the rescue of Melina, and the gratification of our revenge; and if we fail, never trust the word of Massaroni again. Before the break of day we shall be far on our journey. Now, Prince Bianchi, there is that in store for thee which will foil all thy guilty designs, and drive thy soul to madness, if the facts I have stated to you have not already done so. Come—Cospetto! we tarry! There are disguises below, such as no one will be able to recognise us under, and my heart feels fired with redoubled energy at the thoughts of the expedition upon which we are going. You have been to our haunt, you say, previous to coming here?"

"Certainly," answered Rubaldo; "or how could I have given the necessary instructions to our band?"

"True, true," said Massaroni, hastily; "but I am so confused that I scarcely know to what it is I give utterance. And is everything secure?"

"Perfectly so."

"And Maria, my wife?"

"She is most anxious for you to hasten to the rescue of our comrade Guiseppe, and the Signora Melina," answered Rubaldo.

"Is the Signor Clairville made acquainted with what has taken place?" asked our hero.

"I believe he is," said Rubaldo. "But come, Massaroni; this is a waste of time, and every moment, you know, is precious; let us be on our journey."

"Ay, ay," returned the brigand chief, impatiently. "I am ready—perfectly ready."

But in spite of all he said, and the affected composure of his demeanour, Massaroni felt ill at ease, nor could he do away with the impressions which had taken possession of him in the chamber of the Prince Bianchi. However, he conquered it as well as he could; and having summoned the attendance of Orsini, he desired him to bring his disguise, and having assumed it, himself and Rubaldo, having all the appearance of a couple of rustics, mounted their mules and departed on their journey; and leaving them to pursue it, we will return to the Prince Bianchi.

It was not long that he remained in the state of unconsciousness we have described in the foregoing pages, nor did his mind receive any respite from its anxieties during that time of comparative apathy; fresh and vivid was everything presented to it; and when he again started into sensibility, his whole frame was frightfully convulsed with the intense power of his emotions; his features were distorted, his face ghastly pale, and his eyes glared wildly in their sockets, as if they expected to encounter some ghastly phantom.

"Zitella living! Olympia, the victim of the Count Alberti, my daughter!" he exclaimed; "impossible! it is false! I will not believe it! But where is he? But now he was standing by my side, and glaring triumphantly and reproachfully upon me. The dreadful tale he repeated to me, and the guilty facts of which I cannot, dare not deny, make my very soul shudder with horror. Oh, conscience—conscience, thy voice cannot be hushed! But should the assertions of the brigand chief prove to be correct, and the unfortunate Zitella should be still in existence, and under the protection of the brigand, have I not everything to fear? My crimes will be bruited to the world, and no atonement I may make will have the power to remove the stigma from my character that will naturally and deservedly attach to it. Oh, guilt, how terrible and certain is the punishment thou never failest to entail upon thy votaries!"

He groaned aloud in the agony of his feelings, and then, covering his face with his hands, remained for some time wrapped in the most torturing thought.

"But how gained the rascal admittance here?" he at length ejaculated, "and whither has he gone? Shall I suffer him to mock and brave me thus? If he can thus enter my presence at the solemn midnight hour or any time he thinks proper, I am not safe a moment! Where are all my servants? I must still have traitors like the scoundrel Guiseppe about me! What, ho! there!—rascals!—slaves!" he vociferated, springing out of bed, shouting at the top of his voice, and pulling the bell violently; "do you not hear me? or are ye all dead? What, no! I say!"

Thus the distracted nobleman continued shouting as loud as he could and ringing the bell for several minutes, till the whole of the inmates of the villa were aroused, and several male domestics immediately hastened to his chamber in a state of the utmost astonishment, wondering what could be the meaning of the most extraordinary excitement of their master.

"Where is he? the villain, the robber!" he exclaimed, hastily.

"Who, my lord?" inquired one of the astonished domestics.

"Oh, you plead ignorance, rascals?" replied the prince, in a voice half choked with rage; "you have deceived me! you would betray me to the vengeance of one of the most daring miscreants that ever existed; but you shall pay dearly for it, all of you!"

"My lord!" said the still more astonished domestics in a breath.

"Nay, said Bianchi, "you cannot deceive me; think you I am mad that I cannot believe the evidence of my senses? There must be a traitor amongst ye, or how did the daring brigand chief Massaroni gain admittance to my chamber?"

"Massaroni?" repeated the servants, staring at him incredulously, and thinking, and with very good reason, that his mind was wandering.

"Ay, Massaroni," ejaculated Bianchi; "but a few minutes since he was in this chamber, and threatened my life, if I ventured to raise an alarm."

"Impossible, your highness!" said the man who had ventured to speak first; "the doors were all secured at the usual hour of the night, and no one, therefore, could obtain admittance to the villa without our knowledge. Pardon me, your lordship, but I humbly conceive you must have been dreaming."

"Dreaming, varlet!" ejaculated Bianchi, passionately, "dare you presume to tell me so? I saw him plainly as I see you now, and held converse with him for more than half an hour."

The servants stared at each other with increased astonishment, and in a state of utter bewilderment.

"This is most strange and mysterious," remarked one of the domestics; "his excellenza could not have been deceived."

"Deceived!" repeated the prince, hastily; "nor will I be deceived by you. Again I say that there must be traitors among ye, and should I discover them, my utmost vengeance shall descend upon their heads. But why do you all stand there staring at me like fools? If ye are sincere in your assertions, search every part of the villa immediately, for probably the villain is still somewhere concealed about the premises. Begone, I say!"

The servants obeyed, and quitted the room; and the prince, having hastily dressed himself, paced the room with disordered steps, and impatiently awaited their return.

"Deceived!" he soliloquised; "it is impossible that I could have been so. The time he old me in conversation—the fearful facts he repeated, and the threats he held out to me, is a proof that I was not. This mystery must be fathomed, and the brigand chief placed in my power, and at my mercy, for I shall not be safe for a moment until he is so. And should his assertions prove true, which I have too much reason to fear they will, and he should publish the guilty secret to the world, my ruin will be accomplished, for I can never more venture to show my face in society. And Zitella, too, if she should venture to confront me, how can I bear the meeting? How endure her keen and bitter reproaches? The thought distracts me! Oh, I am now severely punished for the crimes I have committed."

He was interrupted by the return of one of the servants.

"Now, fellow," he demanded, hastily, "what intelligence do you bring."

"My lord," replied the man, "we have narrowly examined every part of the villa, and have not discovered anything to excite our suspicions; the doors also remain secured the same as we left them at the usual hour before retiring to rest."

"Then, one of you must have betrayed me," returned Bianchi, "or how did the villain Massaroni find his way to my chamber?"

"Pardon me, your highness," replied the man, "but indeed you do us wrong by supposing for an instant that any one of your present servants would act the treacherous part of Guiseppe towards you; indeed I cannot still help thinking that you must have been mistaken, and——"

"Bold fool!" interrupted the prince, passionately, "dare you question my veracity, or presume to think that I have taken leave of my senses? This is more than human patience can endure! But begone, and see that a sufficient number of troops are immediately despatched to scour the country in all directions in search of this daring robber. I will richly reward any one who may be so fortunate as to apprehend him."

The man departed, glad to escape from the presence of his master, excited as he was, and in a state of mind which we have no occasion to seek to describe when all the circumstances are taken into consideration by the reader.

"There is a mystery in this which I cannot solve," he reflected; "my servants appear to speak the truth, and yet it is evident that Massaroni has some means of gaining access to this villa at any hour he thinks proper, and of departing again without any fear of discovery. He is certainly a most extraordinary character, and while he lives he possesses that knowledge of my secrets and that power over me, which render him most dangerous. Would to Heaven that he were now secure within the walls of a prison, then my mind would be a

little more at rest, and I might set everything else at defiance. And yet there is something in his features and demeanour which excites my deepest interest, and, in spite of his lawless conduct, and his hatred of me, command my respect. How is this?—I cannot account for it, and the longer I endeavour to do so, the more I am involved in mystery. But this last adventure with him surpasses all, and fills my mind with the utmost alarm. Zitella alive, and under his protection! Olympia my daughter! If it be so, he does indeed hold me in his power. And I cannot doubt the truth of his assertions after the tale he has repeated to me, and which no other individuals but Zitella and the ruffian Malvolio could have imparted to him! What shall I do? How can I act under these circumstances? Every moment is fraught with danger to me. Had I not better have endeavoured to conciliate the friendship of the brigand chief than to brave him in the manner I did? But no, I am too well acquainted with the determined character of the brigand chief to believe that he could be entrapped or subdued that way. The only plan I can adopt is to exert myself to the utmost of my power to secure him, and rid myself of him in the most summary manner, or it is certain, with all the feelings of hatred he possesses towards me, he will not rest until he has worked my destruction."

He still continued to traverse the room, giving way to these meditations, for some time longer, in a state of the greatest excitement, and perfectly bewildered how to act. Day, however, was now beginning to dawn, and he was aroused into action. Hastily he quitted the room, with the intention of going to the chamber of the Count Alberti to consult him upon the painful subject, and he had no doubt that he would be as much surprised, confused, and alarmed as himself when he became acquainted with what had happened. As he went to the chamber of the Count Alberti, he had occasion to pass through the apartment in which the portrait of his other victim was suspended, and the curtain having, either by design or accident, been withdrawn, the features of that unfortunate individual were presented fully before him, and completely paralyzed him in every sense. His limbs tottered beneath him, as if he had met with some sudden electric shock, and he staggered to the nearest seat; but still could not remove his gaze from that countenance, or rather, the resemblance of that countenance which had excited so vast a sensation in his breast.

"By all my hopes!" he exclaimed, "they have conspired against me! The slaves I employ, incited by those who possess the means—I see it all now; it is a trick to entrap me, and to make me convict myself. And yet those features; they rush thus accidentally before my gaze to withdraw me from the paths I have hitherto pursued, and—Oh, Valentia! beauteous and confiding girl, as thy fellow victim, Zitella, how can I gaze upon the resemblance of thy features without acknowledging myself as a heartless villain? 'Tis all true that Massaroni has said of me. I am a villain, and here stands the conviction before me, if not in mine own conscience. Valentia—and those features, so like! By the mass! if the apparel was that of a male, I could almost swear that Massaroni, the brigand chief, stood before me. What strange and frowning ideas are those that force themselves upon my imagination? Let me begone, or the contemplation of this portrait will drive me to madness."

He hastily drew the curtain once more across the painting; and then, full of the most racking thoughts, he quitted the room, and made his way to the chamber of the Count Alberti.

That young nobleman had already been made acquainted with what had taken place, and he was, therefore, the better prepared to meet the Prince Bianchi under the excited state in which he was, although he was not, of course, furnished with the particulars, which he could only receive from his lips, and was, consequently, most anxious to do so. Bianchi hastily drew a chair by the side of his bed, and looking steadily into the face, of the patient he said—

"Count Alberti, I have something of importance to impart to you."

"I am aware you have, your highness," replied Alberti, "and that accounts, I presume, for your excited demeanour. Tell me, what is the nature of the information you have to communicate to me?"

"Massaroni, the brigand, but an hour or two since, was in my chamber," replied the Prince Bianchi, "and held me in such converse as I would not listen to again for all my fortune."

"That also have I been told, my lord," returned Alberti; "but you will pardon me if I say I cannot credit it; it is very improbable; your highness must have been labouring under some delusion."

"Delusion, Alberti!" returned the prince, "what, when for more than one half hour he was in deep converse with me, and he told me such truths as I cannot deny?—You must suppose me bereft of reason altogether, if I could labour under a delusion such as this."

"But how could the brigand have gained admittance to the villa?" asked Alberti.

"That is what I am most anxious to know," answered Bianchi.

"And what did he tell you?" anxiously interrogated the Count Alberti; "anything that may place an obstacle in my union with your beauteous niece?"

"Yes if all be true that he has asserted; and a portion of it I know too well to be so," answered Bianchi.

"Curses light upon him!" ejaculated the excited Alberti; "but keep me not in suspense, my lord; let me know upon what ground my hopes are to be thus blighted."

"Your patience, then, for a few minutes, my lord," returned Bianchi; "I think I have before told you that, in my youthful days, I have been guilty of similar liaison as yourself?"

"Yes, yes," answered the count, impatiently; "proceed, your highness. Once let me know the worst, and—"

"Patience, my lord," interrupted Bianchi, "you will require it all, I assure you. One of my victims ('or I cannot in conscience apply any other term to it), you may be aware, was called Zitella?"

"Yes, yes."

"I thought her long since dead."

"And is she not so?"

"Not if I am to believe Massaroni," replied the Prince Bianchi, "but preserved in a most miraculous manner, and at present under his protection."

"Oh, it is a base fabrication of the brigand's, merely to intimidate you into a compliance with his wishes and designs," observed the Count Alberti.

"No, I do not believe it to be so," returned Bianchi; "especially after the facts which he stated to me. But to be brief; this Zitella had a child."

"Yes, that you have before told me, my lord."

"A daughter."

"True, true; that I likewise recollect."

"That daughter, if I have heard aright, is also living, and being under the protection of Massaroni, is restored to the arms of her mother."

"Oh, impossible, my lord," said Alberti; "you have permitted too strong an impression to be made upon your mind by some troubled dream or other."

"Count Alberti," returned Bianchi, seriously, "you are too incredulous, and pay me but a very bad compliment in supposing me weak enough to encourage delusions such as these you have described. That daughter, as well as her mother, I employed a man of the name of Malvolio to rid me of; this same Malvolio fell into the power of Massaroni, and in his dying moments confessed everything, and saw and recognised them both. Zitella he drove forth from his hovel, when she became a burthen to him, a wandering maniac."

"And what became of the daughter?" anxiously inquired Alberti.

"He left her at the door of a nobleman's mansion of my intimate acquaintance," replied the Prince Bianchi; "that nobleman brought her up with every care and attention, but confiding in the professed love of the nobleman's son, she, like her mother, fell."

"Ah!' ejaculated the Count Alberti, much excited; "and the name of that girl?"

"The name her benefactor gave to her was OLYMPIA!"

"Olympia!" repeated Alberti, breathlessly, "my—my—and your daughter?"

INTERVIEW BETWEEN BIANCHI AND MELINA.

"Such are the facts I have been obliged to hear from Massaroni," answered Bianchi, "and which I am compelled to believe are too correct."

"Olympia, the victim of my indiscretion, and the mother of my child, your daughter, my lord? Oh, it is impossible!" said the Count Alberti. "Can you believe in the truth of the statement?"

"I would fain not," replied Bianchi; "but there is, at present, nothing whatever to contradict it."

"An infernal spell is upon me!" cried the Count Alberti, clasping his forehead in a state of the greatest excitement; "but you have been deceived, my lord," he added after a pause; "it is a mere trial of your patience and credulity. It is a mere plan of the daring scoundrel Massaroni to intimidate you into a compliance with his wishes. You are surely not going to be deceived and misled this way, my lord?"

"Alas!" replied Bianchi, "there is too much reason for me to believe in the truth of what the brigand chief has asserted. Would to Heaven I could think and prove otherwise."

"Then," said Alberti, "I see at once the complete annihilation of all my hopes. May eternal curses light upon the head of Massaroni!"

"Nay, my lord," said Bianchi, "compose your feelings, and let us discuss this painful business calmly together."

"Should it be proved that Olympia is really the daughter of your highness," remarked Alberti, "there is an end at once to all the hopes I have formed of becoming the husband of your fair niece."

"Not so," answered Bianchi; "could we for instance get this brigand chief in our power, and thus destroy all the evidence that can be adduced against us."

"Ah, my lord," returned the Count Alberti, "the words you have just now given utterance to inspire me with new hope—you still, then, have no objection to my becoming the husband of the beauteous Signora Melina, your niece?"

"The Prince Bianchi never yet was known to forfeit his word," answered the latter; "and it is not likely that he will do so on the present occasion, after it has been so solemnly given. But still, there is great difficulty in the way; should Zitella be really living, and Olympia proved to be her daughter——"

"My tardy recovery is a curse upon me," interrupted Alberti; "had it not been for this cursed accident, I should now, in all probability, have been the husband of Melina. I cannot but regret that she has been removed from the villa."

"And why so?" asked the prince.

"Because the ceremony might have been solemnized in private, (as well as travelling many leagues to perform it," replied Alberti. "It would have been no such difficult matter for me, even in my present condition, to have quitted my chamber, but——"

He was interrupted by a knock at the room-door, and a servant entered.

"How now?" demanded the prince, hastily, "what is the meaning of this intrusion?"

"Pardon me, your highness," replied the man, "but there is a person who has just arrived here in great haste, from the Villa Civetti, and he desires to see you immediately."

"Ah! from the Villa Civetti!" ejaculated the Count Alberti; "can anything have happened to the signora?"

"Silence, my lord," said Bianchi, "I wonder at your want of due precaution. Lead the way, Paolo. I will be with you again in as short a time as possible, count."

Thus, saying, Bianchi quitted the chamber, preceded by the servant.

When he was gone, Alberti gave way to all the excited feelings which his interview with the prince had given rise to.

"There is a spell upon me," he said, "and I see plain enough, notwithstanding all that the prince has said, that there is an insuperable barrier placed between me and an union with his niece. Olympia his daughter!—There is too much in all that Massaroni has stated to leave room to impugn its truth. By Heaven! I could curse myself for having been the author of the insurmountable obstacle which is now placed in the way of my happiness. The prince, with all his professions and pretended convictions, is a weak-minded, superstitious, and credulous man; and, should he be allowed time to reflect, will never, I feel satisfied, bestow the hand of his niece upon the seducer of his own daughter, though that daughter is the offspring of a similar unfortunate amour as my own. No, I feel satisfied that all my hopes are by this cursed misadventure annihilated, and that Melina, after all, will never become mine."

In this state of mind we must for the present leave the Count Alberti, and return to Bianchi, who had, as we have before stated, remained in the same excited condition after his interview with the brigand chief, and his explanation with the count, till he was summoned into the presence of one of the men who had arrived in such haste from the Villa Civetti, and who informed him of what had taken place, and of the capture of Guiseppe.

"And the rascal is not dead?" said the prince; "the wound he received was not mortal?"

"No, my lord," answered Paolo; "but he refuses to divulge anything."

"By the mass!" exclaimed Bianchi, "it shall be extorted from him, by some means or other, though it is quite evident that the brigands have discovered the place of Melina's confinement through his means."

"Yes, my lord," replied Paolo, "and one of the ruffians having escaped, he will lose no time in apprising his captain of all that has taken place, and unless some prompt means are adopted, and troops dispatched without delay to the Villa Civetti, the brigands must succeed in rescuing the signora."

"True," said the prince; "let troops be immediately dispatched; and yet the delay that has already taken place may have enabled the fellows to execute their purpose; though it is but a few hours since Massaroni was in my presence and—But, away, knave! Why do you stand here gaping at me like an idiot? I have nothing but traitors and villains around me. Begone, I say!"

The man waited for no further mandate, but was glad to escape from the presence of the enfuriated nobleman, and Bianchi being once more left to his own reflections, gave himself up entirely to those feelings of excitement which recent events had engendered in his breast. Folding his arms across his chest, he paced the room in the most disordered manner, and for a few minutes could only utter incoherent sentences and oaths to himself. In spite of all his efforts to the contrary, his recent midnight interview with the brigand, and the tale of guilt he had then recounted, and which he had never expected to hear repeated by mortal lips, had still left an impression behind it on his mind, which he found it impossible to efface, and filled him with the utmost consternation.

"The fates conspire against me," he exclaimed; "and all the guilty deeds of my past life seem about to be published to the world, to my shame and confusion. But to think that Massaroni, the brigand chief, whom I so mortally hate, should be made the instrument to effect my ruin—for my ruin it must be should all that he has stated be true, and he should denounce me to the world in my true character! By all the infernal host, that thought is enough to drive me to madness! And shall the proud spirit of the Prince Bianchi be thus subdued? Zitella and her daughter living, and under the protection of the daring robber from whom I have experienced so many annoyances? By all my hopes, it seems impossible; and yet I cannot doubt it, after all that Massaroni has stated! Olympia—the humble dependent on the bounty of the late Count Alberti, and the degraded victim of that man whom I would make the husband of my niece—my daughter!—Oh, this is indeed most torturing! Curses light upon the soul of the villain Malvolio, who thus deceived me, when I flattered myself that he had rid me of her and her mother altogether. But why do I stand thus, when the desperate nature of the dangers which threaten me call for prompt action? Should Massaroni and his band reach the Villa Civetti before the place is put in a proper state of defence, he cannot fail in rescuing Melina and foiling my designs, and then his triumph would indeed be complete. I will immediately dispatch such a number of troops as will be sufficient to overwhelm any force that the brigand may be able to have at his command. I have acted with the most blind stupidity and imprudence in not having done so in the first instance, and now it may

be too late. But every moment of delay is fraught with danger, and may be attended with the most serious consequences. In spite of all, Melina shall become the bride of Alberti, though the sacrifice should break her heart. But come, let me not delay. I would myself accompany this expedition, only that I fear to leave the count in his present excited state, and when there is no knowing what might be the consequences here during my absence. The rascal, Guiseppe, too; had it not been for him, the traitor, villain, Massaroni would never have been able to discover the place of Melina's imprisonment, and all might have proceeded well; but he has fallen into my power, if all that has been stated to me be true, and I will not fail to wreak my most terrible vengeance upon his head. But let me begone!"

He conquered his agitation as much as he could, as he gave utterance to these words, and quitted the room, in order to put his designs into execution. He had again occasion to pass through the apartment which contained the portrait of the unfortunate Valentia, and it being still uncovered, his eyes became rivetted upon it, and he was transfixed to the spot, trembling convulsively in every limb, with the most powerful emotion. Again the painting seemed to be endowed with life; the eyes appeared to be fixed with a melancholy expression of mingled reproach and supplication upon him, he could almost imagine that the lips moved as if in the act of addressing him, and the bosom seemed to heave and throb with life!

"Do my senses wander?" he cried, clasping his aching temples, and straining his eyes to their utmost stretch; "what fearful delusion is this? Valentia, if thou be indeed living, speak to me; even heap thy curses and reproaches on my devoted head, but do not torture me thus! But no; I have become a very child again! Madness must have seized upon my senses, and I know not what I say. Away with these sickly thoughts and ideas, and let me once more become firm. Am I thus to be startled by a mere painting? Let me hide it from my sight, and hasten from the presence of that which my cowardly soul now fears to contemplate."

Hastily, but with a trembling hand, the Prince Bianchi drew the curtain across the painting, and then hurried from the room, his mind so bewildered that strange and dismal noises seemed to sound in his ears, and ghastly objects to flit before his disordered imagination. When he had got outside the room, he was compelled to pause in order to try to recover himself, and it was two or three minutes before he was able to proceed; but at length he did so, and having summoned one of his principal officers in to his presence, he gave him the necessary instructions to depart imme-diately with a large body of troops for the Villa Civetti, enjoining him to use all possible expedition, and to leave no means untried, not only to defeat the designs of the brigand chief, but to secure him either dead or alive. The officer having promised to obey his instructions to the very letter, hurried away, and the Prince Bianchi once more hastened to the chamber of the Count Alberti.

CHAPTER XLIX.

THE PRINCE BIANCHI AND COUNT ALBERTI CONSULT TOGETHER.— THE VISION OF BIANCHI.— A MYSTERIOUS VISITOR, AND THE CONSEQUENCES.

ON entering the chamber of the Count Alberti, the Prince Bianchi found that he had arisen from his bed, and was in a state of the utmost excitement, Signor Giachomo remon-strating with him, and endeavouring by every means at his command to tranquillise his feel-ings; and on beholding Bianchi, his excite-ment, if possible, increased, and thrusting the doctor abruptly away from him, he advanced towards his friend, and said,—

"Now, my lord, have you come to any de-cision? The Signora Melina——"

"Compose yourself, count," interrupted Bianchi; "you and I must consult calmly together for a short time in private. Pardon me, Signor Giachomo, but myself and his lord-ship must be alone for a brief space."

Giachomo bowed and immediately retired from the room.

"Now, Count Alberti," said Bianchi, after a short pause, "you must not excite yourself, though we have both cause enough for it heaven knows; let us discuss this business dispassionately. My fair niece——"

"Ah!" ejaculated Alberti, hastily; "that is the point at which I want to arrive, and your answer will remove all the doubts and anxieties which at present distract my mind. Do you still adhere to your promise, namely, that she shall become my wife?"

"I do," answered the prince.

"And yet you believe in that which the brigand chief has stated to you, that Olympia is your daughter?"

"Ay, even so, my lord," returned Bianchi, "I have too much reason to believe that he has spoken the truth. But I will, neverthe-less, not be foiled ¦in the designs upon which I have fixed my determination. Cursed fate has brought that about which I never anticipated, and by a most extraordinary coincidence, has made you the seducer of the offspring of my illicit intercourse with the Signora Zitella, and consequently, guilty and unnatural though the

world may, perhaps, and justly consider it to be, I feel a sort of sympathy with you, and will, in spite of all consequences, go to the full extent of the promises I have made to you. My niece, Melina, I repeat, shall be your bride."

"That assurance reanimates all my hopes," said Alberti; "but should she be rescued from our power?"

"I do not think there is much danger of that."

"Have you despatched troops to the Villa Civetti, your highness?"

"I have," answered the Prince Bianchi, "and there is now such an overwhelming force gone thither, that Massaroni and the rascals under his command will find it utterly impos-sible to stand against."

"That is well," observed Alberti; "if they only arrive there in time. That is what you should have done before, especially when you knew that the dastard knave who so shamefully betrayed you was well acquainted with most of your secrets."

"Well," replied Bianchi; "I must admit that I am to blame for not doing so; but it was an oversight, and it is useless to regret it now."

"And have you intrusted the command of the troops to one on whom you think you can depend?" interrogated the Count Alberti.

"You may be sure of that," answered his companion.

"This cursed wound," exclaimed Alberti, "it seems to me as though I should never be restored to convalescence."

"Patience, my lord, patience; this excite-ment will but retard your recovery."

"May destruction light upon the head of Massaroni!" exclaimed the count; "he ap-pears to be the fiend who is fated ever to ob-struct my path to happiness; but for him, Melina would, ere now, have been mine. And to think that I must now remain inactive when so much danger threatens. Oh, it is more than human patience can well endure! But do you still firmly believe, my lord, that you saw him in your chamber, and conversed with him last night?"

"Believe so!" repeated Bianchi: "think you I am mad, Alberti?"

"It might have been a dream, your high-ness."

"A dream! What superlative folly it is to throw out such a suggestion as that," returned the Prince Bianchi, impatiently. "Could I be dreaming when he recounted so minutely some of the most unfortunate errors of my past life?"

"And you admit that all which he stated was true?"

"Alas! too true."

"That the Signora Zitella was deceived, betrayed by you?"

"Yes, yes."

"That a daughter was the fruit of that amour, and afterwards, that you deserted them both, and consigned them to the tender mercies of the fellow Malvolio ?"

"Too true! too true!" replied the wretched, guilty nobleman, in a state of the greatest agitation; "but you torture me by such questions, Alberti."

"I have no wish to do so, my lord," replied the count, though in fact he secretly exulted at the acknowledgment, as it rendered his power over the Prince Bianchi the greater, and was a stronger guarantee of his keeping faith with him in regard to Melina. "And you believe them both to be living, as Massaroni has represented, and under his protection?"

"I do, and it is that belief which renders me wretched and makes me still more anxious to get the brigand chief in my power, for I have now reason to believe him one of my most dangerous enemies."

"Even so, your highness," remarked Alberti, "it would be extremely awkward were Massaroni to publish those facts to the world, and to bring forward the individuals themselves to corroborate his assertions,"

"There is madness in the thought," said Bianchi, striking his forehead. "Could Massaroni be secured, I might find means to prevent that exposure."

"True—true," returned the count; "Zitella and Olympia, by the offer of a proper provision, might be persuaded to retire into obscurity, and not to annoy either of us again. But," he continued after a brief pause, "how annoying—how torturing is this, to have such difficulties placed in our way. Much better would it have been for us both, my lord, had we never been guilty of the errors we have."

"Alas!" returned Bianchi, "it would indeed; but this is sheer moralising, and can do neither of us any good; let it satisfy you that I am determined Melina, my fair niece, shall become your bride."

"I am satisfied with your promises, my lord," answered the Count Alberti; "for I am convinced that you will not break your word, unless it is caused by some untoward fortune; but fate seems to frown upon us, and in spite of all my efforts to the contrary, I cannot help fearing that something will yet occur to prevent the accomplishment of my wishes. This delay in my recovery, and——"

"And," interrupted Bianchi, "you cannot expect that you will ever be restored to convalescence while you continue to excite yourself in the manner you are now doing. Why have you left your bed?"

"How think you, my lord, I could remain patiently in it, and know the danger that threatens?" demanded Alberti. "Oh, it is a source of the bitterest anguish to me to know

that all I love is surrounded with the most imminent peril, likely to be snatched from me every moment, and I am rendered powerless to resist the miscreants who would plunder me of my prize. In good truth, Allesandro Massaroni is a most extraordinary individual, and one to be dreaded, likewise, as yourself and I have experienced, excellenza."

"Very true," answered Bianchi; "and I know not how it is, but whenever his name is mentioned to me, or I think upon him there is a feeling comes over me, which I find it impossible to resist, and for which I cannot account. I would fain respect him; and yet I hate and dread him."

"It is strange," remarked the Count Alberti, "but he is evidently a man of superior mind, accomplished, and enterprising, handsome and fascinating, with a grace of deportment that might win and deceive an angel, and yet with a heart and determination that could subdue a devil. He is a singular anomaly, an heterogeneous mass of inconsistences."

"And yet consistent withal," rejoined Bianchi. "My lord, I think I have before intimated to you the impression which his features have made upon me—the remarkable resemblance they bear to——"

"The portrait of the Signora Valentia?" said Alberti.

"Yes—yes," answered the prince, in a state of the greatest emotion.

"True, your highness," said the Count Alberti. "I have frequently gazed upon that portrait, and had it been attired in male costume I could almost have persuaded myself that the brigand chief stood before me, so extraordinary is the resemblance. Pardon me, my lord, but if I have understood you rightly, the history of Signora Valentia and Zitella, as regards yourself, greatly resemble each other?"

"They do—they do; precisely the same," ejaculated the prince, striking his forehead with his clenched fist. "Oh, Valentia! what can ever wash out the stigma which attaches itself to my character for my conduct towards you! What can ever remove that tardy load of guilt from my conscience!"

"But she, at any rate, you are convinced, is no more?" interrogated the count.

"Yes, yes," replied the wretched nobleman beating his breast, and writhing under all the excruciating pangs of remorse; "my cruelty caused her to die of a broken heart."

"And she was good and innocent when you first became acquainted with her?"

"Pure and lovely as mortal being could be from the hands of its Almighty Creator!" replied Bianchi; "more heartless miscreant must I be by the blackest and most systematic course of villany and deception to draw her from those paths of virtue in which she had hitherto trod, and make her a thing of scorn and degradation. And then, too, like my other victim, Zitella, to abandon her to misery, shame, and want.

"And the Signora Valentia was also the mother of a child?" said Alberti.

"Yes; oh God! a beautious boy!"

"A boy?"

"I have said so."

"And did he also die?"

"I believe not."

"What became of him?"

"That I could never ascertain," replied the Prince Bianchi in a faint voice.

"And this likeness—this remarkable resemblance that Allesandro Massaroni bears to the portrait of the Signora Valentia?" said Alberti. "His accomplished manners and noble bearing—his romantic history too—all these are singular coincidences, your highness. What if the brigand chief should, after all, prove to be your own son?"

"My son!—my son a robber, a murderer, an outcast of society!" reiterated Bianchi, his eyes distended, his features absolutely distorted, and at the same time fixing upon Alberti a look in which was blended all the agonizing feelings that were at that moment holding such fearful tumult in his breast. "Would you mock me, count? Or do you take delight in adding to the present torture of my mind? The brigand chief, he who has hitherto shown himself to be my most implacable foe, who has ever crossed my path to frustrate me in any designs I may have had in contemplation; he who now mocks and despises my power, and steals like a midnight assassin into my presence to taunt me with my past transgressions, and to threaten me with his vengeance; he, who holds me now at defiance, and would deprive me of that over which I possess every just and earthly authority, to bestow it on a beggar, a serpent whom I so long nurtured in my breast; he my son!—It is a base lie!—a monstrous delusion!—a scheme to entrap me! to ruin me in the estimation of mankind, and you are at the head of the foul plot to crush me! The world is going mad! There are nothing but designing knaves or fools in it, and—"

"My lord!" interrupted Alberti, completely astounded by the extraordinary language the Prince Bianchi made use of and the excitement of his manner, and at the same time he laid his hand upon his arm; "you surely know not what you say."

"Hold me not! detain me not!" cried Bianchi, in the same frenzied accents; "you take me for an idiot; you conspire with all my other enemies to ruin me, and fiend-like, laugh at the anguish you inflict. The son of the Prince Bianchi, the Governor of Rome, a robber! the proscribed ruffian, Massaroni; I tell you again it is a hideous lie! and those who propagate it will have to pay dearly for so doing. The son of the Prince Bianchi must be all that is noble and good, but not the base thing you would represent him to be; you are my enemy, Count Alberti; I have been deceived in you; were you sincerely my friend, you could never have made use of the observations you have just done."

The prince stared wildly about him, as he made use of these observations, and, it was quite evident that his mind was wandering. The Count Alberti was bewildered, and scarcely knew how to act.

"My lord," he said, at last, "let me beg of you to calm these paroxysms. But now you remonstrated with me for exhibiting what you were pleased to consider some unnecessary excitement; but surely such language as this is uncalled for and totally irrelevant to the important business we have to occupy our present attention. You suggested the idea of the singular resemblance which the features of Massaroni bear to the portrait of Signora Valentia, and—"

"Ah!" interrupted Bianchi, in a tone of wildness which quite startled the count; "there it is again! Those two names coupled together; it is like fiends piping in my ears, and mocking, deriding me on to madness. Let me begone, and in the privacy of my own thoughts seek that consolation which all others deny me! Valentia! Zitella!—Oh, agony!"

Thus saying, the distracted Prince Bianchi, clasping his temples, rushed from the room, before the astounded Alberti could offer to prevent him.

For a few moments the young nobleman stood, as it were, completely paralysed to the spot, and could not conceal his thoughts; but when he did partially recover himself, he rang the bell, and a servant appearing, he desired him to request the Signor Giachomo to attend him immediately. The doctor entered the chamber without delay, and was surprised to behold the excitement under which his patient evidently laboured, and to find that the prince had quitted the room.

"My lord," he said, "what is the meaning of this? Why do you still remain out of bed, and what has become of the Prince Bianchi? You summoned me very abruptly."

"True, signor," replied Alberti; "I would have you attend upon his highness immediately; his mind seems to be affected from the tenour of the conversation upon which we entered, and I fear, without proper attention and advice, some fatal consequences may arise."

"I will attend his excellenza immediately, my lord," replied Signor Giachomo; "but at the same time allow me to advise your lordship to retire to your couch without delay, and to endeavour to calm your feelings."

"Enough, good signor," said Alberti, with a

faint smile ; " I will try to follow your counsel, though I much fear, after the various facts that have come to my knowledge, if I shall be able to succeed. Am I likely to recover shortly ?"

"Pardon me, my lord," replied Signor Giachomo ; " but it is quite impossible I can hold out any such hopes to you, while you obstinately refuse to follow the advice which my humble abilities have hitherto prompted me to offer you ; and I will say more—you will suffer a relapse, which may be attended with the most serious consequences, if you do not confirm to the rules I have felt it my duty to set down to you ; you are endangering your life every moment that you disregard them."

"I thank you, signor, for the trouble you have taken with me," said the Count Alberti, "and the anxiety which you evidently feel in my case ; but pray attend upon his highness with all possible expedition, and exercise all your skill, for I am fearful that madness has seized upon his brain."

The Signor Giachomo bowed, and without making use of another observation, he retired from the room.

Although the count had tried to appear as calm as he possibly could in his presence, when he was gone he gave full vent to the powerful emotions which struggled in his breast, and the ultimate hopes and fears that crowded upon and distracted his brain. He threw himself exhausted upon the bed, and for a few minutes was completely absorbed in torturing thought.

" Mad as he is," he soliloquised, " and with all the horror and remorse upon his conscience from the errors of the past—with the recollection of his victims, and the offspring of one of his victims also the victim of my deceit and villany, vividly stamped upon his distempered brain—what have I to hope ? Can I expect that he will adhere to the promises he has made to me, notwithstanding all his solemn and oft repeated asseverations ? Will he, I say again, ever have the hardihood, or rather the heartless villany, to compel his niece to become the wife of the seducer of his own daughter ? No ; the idea is preposterous, and I cannot entertain it. I feel that all my hopes are annihilated, and that Massaroni is triumphant in his revenge against myself and the Prince Bianchi ! May eternal curses light upon this accident which renders me helpless as an infant ! Had it not been for that, long ere this the beauteous, but proud and scornful Melina, would have been mine, and I might have laughed to scorn the threats of the brigand chief, and all others who are opposed to me. But as it is, I feel assured that he will triumph—that before the troops despatched by Bianchi can reach the Villa Civetti, Melina will have been released and restored to the arms of my beggar rival, Florio Clairville, and then indeed she will be lost to me for ever. That thought alone is

enough to drive me to frenzy, and yet it is too reasonable to be rejected. And will not the world condemn both myself and the Prince Bianchi, and hold us up to scorn and opprobrium ? Massaroni has us entirely in his clutches ; we are completely at his mercy ; and what mercy have we any right to expect from him ? Zitella, Olympia, Clairville, all are under his protection, and can at any moment he thinks proper be brought forward to our utter confusion, dismay, and degradation. The danger thickens around us, and what means have we of averting the coming storm which is about to burst over our heads to our annihilation ? None whatever ! Brave it as we may, disregard it as we may attempt to do, we cannot avoid it. By all my hopes, I never more felt my own powerlessness and insignificance, than I do at this present moment ; and to add to my dismay and utter confusion, Bianchi has become a perfect imbecile ; nothing better than a raving maniac. Oh ! I could myself go mad at the thought !"

He paused, exhausted by the power of his excited feelings, and rolled upon the bed, striking his forehead with his clenched fists, in a state of the greatest agony. He was, however, suddenly aroused from this lethargy of despair, by a knock at his chamber-door, and hastily demanding who was there, his servant entered, in order to assist him to undress, and to attend upon him until the return of Signor Giachomo. It required, however, all the arguments that the servant could make use of to persuade him to retire to rest ; and when he at last did so, he continued in the same excited state of mind, raving at intervals more like a madman than any person in his sane moments, and his attendant was beginning to become alarmed, and thought of calling for assistance, when Signor Giachomo most opportunely entered the chamber. He noticed the extreme agitation of the count's manner with the deepest regret, and having desired the servant to retire from the room, was about to address some observations to him, when Alberti interrupted him.

" I know all that you would say," he remarked, impatiently ; " but you may as well spare yourself the trouble. The Prince Bianchi—how is he ?"

" I found him, as you expected, in a most excited state, my lord," answered the doctor ; " but at length I succeeded in reducing him to some degree of calmness, and he has now retired to bed and sunk off to sleep. These are strange events, my lord, and——"

" No matter—no matter," interrupted Alberti, hastily—" do you think that his highness is likely soon to recover ?"

" Why," answered Signor Giachomo ; " in all probability he will, if nothing again occurs to excite him in the interim. But you will pardon me if I say that you are both acting imprudently, in thus irritating each other's feelings ; and in respect to yourself, I say again, my lord, that if you do not act with more prudence, you will suffer a relapse, and then I will not be answerable for the consequences.''

"Enough, enough," said the Count Alberti ; "I am obliged to you for your anxious care and attention, and will endeavour to follow your advice. But this delay in my recovery, and when the Signora Melina is surrounded with so much danger, is surely enough to try my patience. And now to add to my anxiety, the Prince Bianchi is seized with a malady which probably may be attended with the most serious consequences.''

"Oh, no," returned Signor Giachomo ; "I do not apprehend any such danger ; he is merely suffering from the effects of some shock his feelings have received, and will, no doubt, after a little rest, be entirely restored. As for yourself, my lord, you have heard my opinion, and I can say no more ; your speedy restoration to convalescence depends entirely upon your own conduct ; and if you act contrary to my advice, you will entirely counteract all my efforts to restore you to health."

"Well, well, my good signor," answered the count, "I will not fail to pay due attention to what you have said ; but leave me for the present, for I can better collect my thoughts and compose my feelings alone.''

The doctor bowed and immediately retired, and the Count Alberti was once more left to his own reflections. It was in vain, however, that he for some time could bring his mind to the least degree of tranquillity, such were the dismal and torturing misgivings and apprehensions that continued to haunt it.

"Dangers accumulate upon me every day and hour," he remarked ; "and the more I reflect upon all the circumstances which have recently taken place, the stronger becomes my conviction that the sanguine hopes I have so long formed within my own mind are doomed to be disappointed. Even ere this, Melina may have been rescued by the brigands, and if so, she is lost to me for ever. True to the powerful love she has ever borne towards Florio Clairville, she will let no considerations of the disparity of their rank, no fear of the future indignation of her uncle, prevent her from becoming his wife ; and thus will the humble painter, the subject of my contempt and hatred, obtain a signal triumph over me, and be able in his turn to laugh me to scorn. How that thought, so reasonable, and so likely to be realised, maddens me! The Prince Bianchi has acted with imprudence and tardiness throughout the whole affair. What necessity was there for the removal of Melina from the villa at all ? Why could not the marriage ceremony have been performed here in private, when I was so far recovered from the effects of the wound I had received? Then she would have been securely mine, and I would have adopted such means as would have enabled me to set the power of the brigand chief at defiance, should he in future have sought to annoy me. But then, Olympia and her mother ; what is to be done with them? While they live, myself and the Prince Bianchi have everything to dread from them. How could we brave the scandal and infamy of the world, which would be sure to be heaped upon our heads, after the exposure it is in their power to make of our iniquity? Whichever way I turn my thoughts, nought but despair presents itself to my imagination. Fool that I was, when I knew so well Bianchi's weakness, to make the allusions and throw out the suggestions I did. I might be sure of the effect they would have upon his mind. But still I have frequently remarked the extraordinary resemblance there is between Massaroni's features and those of the portrait of Valentia. The history of the brigand, too, from all I have heard of it, is of the most romantic description. It is said that his father was of noble rank and station, though he knows not his name, and indeed his accomplished manners and general deportment, and many of the acts he has performed, seem to prove that there is noble blood flowing within his veins. What if it should after all be proved that this daring outlaw—this mountain chief, from whom we have experienced so many annoyances, and whom we have so much reason to dread, is the son of this same Valentia whom Bianchi so deceived? That would bring shame and confusion upon us both, and entirely frustrate all the plans we have so long had in contemplation. And there is nothing at all improbable in the idea. It distracts my brain ; I am bewildered, and know not what to think or how to act.''

Such were the thoughts which continued to crowd upon the mind of the Count Alberti throughout the day, and he obtained only a brief respite at intervals from his fears and anxiety. But we must again leave him and return to the Prince Bianchi, who immediately on leaving Alberti, in the dreadful state of excitement we have described, hastened to his own chamber, where, pacing backwards and forwards across the room, he gave himself up to the most maddening reflections. The idea which Alberti had expressed of the probability of Massaroni being the offspring of the much wronged Valentia, and consequently his own son, had made an impression upon his mind which it would be a difficult task to efface; and the longer he reflected on it, the more powerful became the effect it had on him. To his disordered imagination, the forms of Massaroni and Valentia seemed to stand before him, to frown reproaches upon him, and to mock at the sufferings he was at that time enduring from the stern upbraidings of his guilty conscience; and at length the picture assumed so powerful a character, that it became actually insupportable, and he glared wildly around the apartment, being scarcely able to persuade himself that that which his imagination had conjured up was not reality.

"Massaroni, the brigand chief, he who has ever pursued me with such bitter hatred, and who would not hesitate to imbrue his hands in my blood, whenever it should answer his

MELINA AND FLORETTA GAZING FROM THE VILLA CIVETTI.

purpose to do so—be my son! Oh, impossible! there is contamination in the very thought! Who dare attempt to impose him upon me as such? And yet, is there anything at all improbable in the supposition? Alas! no; my conscience too well assures me that there is not. Did I not desert Valentia and her child, a boy? She died of a broken heart; but what became of her son I could never ascertain! Friendless, destitute as he was thus left, might he not have been driven into a career of crime? And upon whom would the blame and stigma rest for his having done so? Why justly upon the head of his unnatural father! And then the extraordinary resemblance that exists between Massaroni and Valentia; by Heaven, the expression of the eyes, the features, are exactly the same! Oh, how torturing are these thougts! The fates conspire against me, and I feel a foreboding that some terrible retribution is about to overtake me. Would that I could recall the past, how different should be the conduct I would pursue! Zitella and her daughter living too, and under the protection of the brigand chief, who, at any time, can produce them, to my utter shame and confusion!—Oh, misery most unutterable! I shall go mad! But away with these childish thoughts, and let me become myself again. It is useless now to fregret what is done and cannot be undone! What have I to apprehend? Who dare accuse the Prince Bianchi? and who would believe their assertions? My power and influence in the world protects me. And after all, it may be false! It may be but an invention of the brigand chief to torture me, and to gratify his revenge. But no—how could he have become so well acquainted with her melancholy history, unless it had been from her own lips? Curses light upon the unfortunate accident which placed her under his protection, and ten thousand curses light upon the soul of the miscreant Malvelio who deceived me, and——"

He was interrupted by the sudden entrance of Signor Giachomo.

"Ah, signor!" he abruptly exclaimed, "what means this intrusion? what brings you here?"

"Pardon me, your highness," answered Giachomo; "but I heard that you were labouring under some powerful excitement, and I thought that my attendance upon your lordship might be required."

"No, no," answered Bianchi, sternly; "no doctors can cure the malady that afflicts me—begone!"

"Excuse me, excellenza," remarked Signor Giachomo, "for my apparent boldness, but surely your highness had much better endeavour to calm your feelings,—you are endangering your health by giving way to these violent fits of excitement."

"Excitement!" reiterated Bianchi; "have I not had enough to excite me, to madden me, after what I have heard? But fool that I am, why should I unburthen my thoughts to you? Leave me: I do not require your attendance!"

"My lord," said the doctor, "believe me, I have no wish to pry into your secrets; but let me advise you to retire to bed, and doubtless a few hours' rest will remove the anxiety which at present troubles your mind."

"Rest!" repeated the prince; "what rest think you is there for me, with all these terrible thoughts upon my mind? But you have all conspired against me, to torture me, and to mock my anguish."

"Your highness," observed Signor Giachomo, "you must be labouring under some singular delusion,—you cannot know what you say,—there is no one here, I am convinced, who would presume to mock you, but, on the contrary, are most anxious for your welfare."

"Pardon me, Signor Giachomo," replied Bianchi, more calmly, "if I have spoken somewhat harshly; but my mind is indeed so bewildered, that I scarcely know what I say. You say I am excited, and indeed if you knew all, you must be ready to admit [that I have had enough to make me so. Every day something fresh occurs to annoy me. Last night, the rascal Massaroni forced himself into my chamber at midnight, by what means I know not, and taunted and threatened me; now I hear that the place where my niece is confined has been discovered, and probably before the troops I have despatched to prevent it can arrive at the place of their destination, she will be in the power of the brigands and lost to me for ever. Independent of this, I have heard that which fills my soul with alarm. But no matter—that is a secret which it behoves me to keep confined to my own breast. Now tell me, Signor Giachomo, is not what I have told you quite sufficient to excite me?"

"True, your highness," returned the doctor, "but still not to such on extraordinary and painful degree as that which you exhibit. As regards the brigand chief having been in your chamber, pardon me, my lord, but I cannot help thinking you must have been mistaken."

"Mistaken!" repeated Bianchi, impatiently, "what nonsense is this? Do you think I am mad, or that I cannot believe my eyes or ears? I tell you again, that Massaroni was in my chamber for more than half-an-hour, and during that time he repeated to me a tale which I never expected to hear again, and which made my very soul tremble to listen to."

"It is most extraordinary," remarked Giachomo,; "but why did you not raise an alarm, so that he might have been secured?"

"Because," answered the prince, "the villain had me completely in his power and at his mercy; and he threatened me if I dared to give utterance to a word which might alarm any of the inmates of the villa, he would instantly plunge his poniard in my heart."

"Most daring outrage!" observed Signor Giachomo.

"Most daring outrage," reiterated Bianchi, "ah, you may well say that; and yet you affect to wonder that I am excited. By all my hopes, these constant annoyances drive me to distraction."

"Pray endeavour to be calm, my lord," said Giachomo; "and let me again persuade you to retire to rest for awhile; your brain seems fevered and needs repose."

"My brain fevered!" cried the wretched nobleman staring at him wildly; "I tell you, Giachome, it is distracted; how can it be otherwise with all the racking thoughts I have upon my mind? There is an infernal spell upon me, and insiduous fiends are at work to destroy my peace and to hold me up to shame and ridicule."

"Oh, forbear, your highness," said the doctor, "do not give way to such feelings as these. All whom you have about you are your friends, sincerely devoted to your welfare."

"'Tis false!" replied Bianchi, passionately. "I am not to be deceived by any such assurances as that. I have traitors, villains about me, or that which has happened could never have occurred; but I will discover them, and terrible is the vengeance that I will then wreak upon their heads."

As he thus spoke he again paced the room with hasty and disordered steps, and muttered the most bitter curses between his teeth.

"Could your highness but persevere, and conquer these agonising feelings," at length Giachomo ventured to observe, "how much better would it be for you."

"Oh, how coolly you can talk and advise, Signor Giachomo," returned Bianchi, with a bitter smile; "but could you imagine the tumult of conflicting passions that are raging in my breast, you would not do so. But leave me, I say again; I am in no vein to listen to you; the Count Alberti probably requires your attendance more than I do; a short time passed in communion with my own thoughts, most likely, will restore me to composure."

"Be it so, your highness," replied the signor; "far be it from my wishes to seek to intrude upon your privacy. I have ventured to offer such advice as I thought it was my duty to do, and I trust that I have not offended by so doing."

"No, no," said the prince, hastily; "but I need no counsel or advice: I am in no humour to listen to it, I say again. I must be alone."

Signor Giachomo made use of no further observation, for he saw it was al to no purpose, and bowing to Bianchi, he quitted the apartment.

For some minutes after he was gone, the prince remained wrapped in painful and silent thought; but at length, after looking around him to make sure that no one was near him, he said,—

"This Signor Giachomo makes himself by far too officious, and seems anxious to pry too much into my secrets. I must get rid of him as soon as I can. Be calm!—bah! what a bitter mockery it is to talk thus to a man with all the anxieties upon his mind that at present torture me. Something whispers to me that the crisis of my fate is approaching, and that all the darling projects I have formed are doomed to be frustrated, and to recoil upon myself. Should Massaroni succeed in rescuing Melina, his triumph will indeed be complete, and I shall be compelled to yield to his demands, however extravagant they may be. I cannot expect that he will long forbear from completing his vengeance by bringing forward Zitella and her daughter to confront me, and thus to denounce me to the world as a villain. Yes, I feel assured that my fate is in the hands of Massaroni, and something seems to convince me, that the time is not far distant when that fate will be decided, and I shall be brought to disgrace and infamy. And must I, the Prince Bianchi, Governor of Rome, fall thus? Must I be so degraded, and all through the means of one whom I endeavour to look upon with contempt?—a robber!—an outcast, whose life has long since been forfeited to the offended laws of his country? The thought of itself is sufficient to drive one to distraction, and yet it is too reasonable and too probable to reject. And yet they marvel that I should be excited. Oh, what human patience can endure this? And then the suggestion which Alberti threw out is so probable that it has made an impression on my mind, which I find it utterly impossible to conquer. Should the brigand chief really prove to be the son of Valentia, the offspring of the illicit intercourse between her and myself, and he should discover that fatal fact, what may I not expect from his vengeance? —But no, it cannot be. What fiends of hell have conjured up such thoughts within my mind? Away with them—I will no longer think."

The guilty nobleman struck his breast and became more violently agitated as he thus spoke; and still he continued to pace the room, his mind labouring under the same torturing tumult of passions, and scarcely knowing what he did, though he was keenly sensible to all the miseries of his position. He dreaded the dangers which threatened him; he shrank appalled from the fate that seemed to be impending over him, and yet he knew not how to avert it; he could see no means by which he could escape. Strange perversity of guilt! Yet he was fully determined not to abandon his designs against Melina; and all that he principally feared was, that Massaroni would succeed in rescuing her from his power, and by that means, frustrate his unnatural and cruel plans.

"He is my curse, my evil destiny!" he ejaculated, after a pause; "I feel him to be so, however I may seek to scout the idea, and while he lives I have everything to fear. And must I fall through the means of one whom it has ever been my object to crush? Shall he, a robber and an outlaw, thus hold me at defiance, and laugh me to scorn? Are there no means of triumphing over him, and making him glad to succumb to me? By the mass! such a thought is degrading and most insupportable. Oh, that I had him in my power at this moment, how soon would I rid myself of my terrors, and satiate my vengeance in his blood. Ah! what hollow voice was that?"

He started, and stared wildly around him, whilst his limbs trembled convulsively, and the perspiration started in large drops upon his forehead.

"I could have sworn that I heard the hollow tones of a supernatural voice breathing in my ear at that moment," he said; "but no—there is no one near me: I am alone. It must have been some wild delusion of my fevered senses. How weak I am to give way to such ideas as these. But, alas! how can I fly from thought? Conscience will pursue me with overwhelming force, however I may seek to fly from it. There is a curse upon my head, and I feel that I richly merit all I suffer. Oh, Valentia!"

Again he paused abruptly; for has he mentioned the name of that deeply-wronged woman, he could almost have sworn that he heard a dismal and mournful sigh, and to such a pitch was his terrified imagination wrought, that he trembled more violently than ever; ghastly faces seemed to frown upon him, and to mock his anguish, and he was almost induced to ring his bell, and to summon his attendants into his presence.

"But no; cowardly idiot that I am," he exclaimed, "shall I thus expose myself, and hold myself up to the ridicule of my menials? Have my senses entirely forsook me? I must and will persevere to conquer this outrageous feeling which thus unnerves me, and makes me unconscious of what I am doing."

He threw himself into a chair as he thus spoke, and gave himself up entirely to the most torturing thoughts. Although it was yet broad daylight, everything around him to his disordered imagination presented the gloom and solitude of night, and so greatly were his fears aroused that he almost trembled to be alone. In this state of mind he continued for some time longer, and terrible indeed were the thoughts that racked his brain. For some time he scarcely knew where he was: then he conjured up all sorts of fearful images, and in the terror of his excited feelings was several times upon the point of calling for assistance. The brigand chief and the unfortunate Valentia were uppermost in his thoughts: he found it utterly impossible to disconnect them, and he marvelled more and more why he should not be able to do so.

"Would to Heaven that Alberti had never spoken to me on the subject," he said; "these torturing thoughts would then never have haunted my imagination. And yet, what he said was true; and, however I may struggle to do so, I cannot deny it. The likeness that exists between the brigand, Massaroni, and my late unfortunate victim, Valentia, is most extraordinary, and gives rise to the most agonising doubts and suspicions in my breast. Should he prove to be that unfortunate offspring, whom, with his mother, I abandoned, and he should discover the fact, what have I not to fear from his vengeance? No thoughts of the relationship in which we stood together, would, I feel convinced, stay his hand. What could I expect from his mercy and forbearance? Would he not have a right to hate and despise that unnatural parent who had been the cause of all his misfortunes, and had brought his mother to a premature grave? He would; and my conscience assures me that he would be justified in any course, however desperate, which he might adopt. I could not sue to him for mercy, for he would remind me of his broken-hearted mother—he would refer me to his own degraded position, and point out to me the hatred with which I had ever pursued him, and sought to bring him to destruction. And what reply could I make to him?—how seek to extenuate my conduct? It would be impossible for me to do so. But me sue for mercy from the brigand, Massaroni, even if he should prove to be my own son!—Perish the thought! The Prince Bianchi could never so descend. And yet, if all be true that he has told me—if it be correct that Zitella still lives, and is under his protection, and that she whom I have hitherto known as Olympia is her daughter, have I not everything to dread? Does he not hold me completely in his power, and can at any time bring me to shame and degradation by denouncing me to the world? It would be worse than madness for me to seek to deny this; and how, then, is it possible for me to conquer the apprehensions which have taken such a strong hold upon my mind? Alas—alas! whichever way I direct my thoughts despair surrounds me. Oh, guilt—guilt! how terrible is the punishment which never fails to follow ye! Would that I could recall the past, how differently, methinks, would I act to what I have done. But that is impossible; and I have now advanced too far to recede. But why should I thus tremble at shadows—mere ephemeral creations of the distempered imagination? Let me again become a man, and I may set all the world at defiance. Should the troops which I have despatched to the Villa Civetti arrive in time, they will be sufficient to defeat any force which Massaroni may muster. He will be secured, and thus the source of all my fears will be at once destroyed. That thought inspires me with fresh courage. I will be firm, and endeavour to await with patience the result of this adventure. The brigand chief once in my power, what have I to fear ? Zitella and Olympia may then be secured, and prevented from offering me any future annoyance. Would that I had accompanied the troops myself. But such an expedition would ill have accorded with one of my advanced years, and might have been fraught with the most imminent danger. Besides, the officer who is entrusted with the command is a man on whom I can depend ; and I know it will be no fault of his if he should fail to accomplish that which I desire. I will endeavour to rest my mind content, and not to give way to these fits of excitement, which only serve to expose me to the impertinent observations of those about me."

Thus, for some time longer, did the Prince Bianchi continue to alternate between hope, and doubt, and fear ; but the latter, in spite of all his efforts to the contrary, would predominate, and it was in vain that he struggled against the agitation of his mind. At length, exhausted with thinking, he threw himself upon the bed, though it was not much more than mid-day, and sleep insensibly stole upon him. The same racking thought, however, pursued him in his slumbers, and presented the most torturing visions to his heated imagination. He fancied himself wandering through a wild and dismal part of the country, between chains of lofty mountains, whose summits were hidden in the clouds : sometimes upon the verge of a lofty precipice, where the least faltering step would have plunged him into a fathomless abyss, and to contemplate which was sufficient to turn the brain giddy, and to make the senses reel. Then the mountain cataract roared and gurgled above him, and seemed to threaten to overwhelm him at every turn. Again, when he emerged from those scenes, he entered upon another equally wild and fearful—an interminable forest, the widespreading foliage of whose tall trees completely shut out the light of Heaven.

He imagined that it was midnight, and the darkness that prevailed was impenetrable ; a fierce storm also raged ; the peals of thunder were deafening ; and the flashes of lightning that shot across the sky, in rapid succession, were perfectly terrific. He was alone, but he could form no idea upon what errand he was bent, or whither he was wandering ; still he was impelled forward by some irresistible power. And now strange and hideous forms seemed to dance around him, and to mock and threaten him, and it was in vain that he endeavoured to avoid them ; they would pursue him whichever way he turned, and grinned at him with their ghastly looks, and spat upon him.

Suddenly he found himself engaged in fierce combat with a tall and powerful man. The lightning's flash revealed his features to him ; it was Massaroni. He thought that he was

endowed with more than double his wonted strength, and that he repelled the attack of the brigand chief desperately, and at length his sword passed through his body, and stretched him bleeding at his feet. Scarcely had he done so, when the thunder roared more fiercely, and the lightning blazed around him in a manner that was truly awful, while the ghastly expression of the brigand's face struck terror to his soul; and as he gazed upon his features he felt a sensation come over him which he had never experienced before. Suddenly a pale, shadowy form, in robes of flowing white, seemed to arise from the earth, and bent over the bleeding form of the brigand, who raised his eyes towards it with an expression of the most indescribable reverence and supplication, and then made a significant motion with his hand towards Bianchi, who imagined in his dream that he was paralysed with awe and terror to the spot. The phantom raised his face towards him, and the prince then recognised the ghastly features of the ill-fated Valentia, which were fixed upon him with a stern expression of reproach that appalled his guilty soul, and froze the blood within his veins. He tried to speak, but could not ; neither could he move from the spot, or avoid the fearful glances of the phantom and the dying brigand.

" Monster !" at length he imagined the hollow voice of Valentia exclaimed ; " the measure of thy crimes is full, and perdition now awaits thee ! Behold the bloody work of thine hands; betrayer of the mother—thou art now the murderer of thy son !"

As the phantom thus spoke, it pointed mournfully and reproachfully towards Massaroni, whose countenance now became more distorted with his dying agonies; again Bianchi imagined in his dream that he endeavoured to speak and to sue for mercy and forgiveness ; but his tongue refused to perform its office, and the shade of Valentia seemed to mock his anguish. Louder roared the thunder; more terrifically the lightning flashed across the sky ; and hideous forms appeared to dance around him, and to exult over him ;—a stream of liquid fire burst forth at his feet—the most awful noises rent the air, and still the hollow eyes of the phantom, and the ghastly looks of the dying Massaroni were fixed upon him. His brain whirled round—the earth seemed to totter beneath his feet—sepulchral voices from every side shouted " Murderer !" in his ears, and in the terror of the moment, the spell of sleep was broken, and, the perspiration starting from every pore, the wretched nobleman awoke. Such was the impression that this fearful dream had made upon him, that for a few moments he could not persuade himself that it had not in reality taken place, and he still imagined that he beheld the dying features of the brigand chief, and that the ghastly phantom of Valentia stood before him, and that he heard her again call him murderer! It would be impossible to describe the agony of his feelings. His limbs trembled violently; his bosom heaved with the power of his emotions; and his brain was distracted. He must have been asleep some time; for it was now dusk, and the objects in his chamber were but indistinct; but at length wound up to a pitch of horror the most insupportable, he sprang from the bed, and staggered towards the door, with the determination at first to rush from the room; but his limbs failed him, and he sunk exhausted and almost powerless in a chair, and gazed vacantly around him, as though he expected again to behold the objects of his dream.

"Where am I?" he at length exclaimed; "whither have my wandering footsteps led me; and what fresh horrors have I became associated with? Am I, indeed, a murderer, and that of my own son? Ah! is it then, true? Is the brigand chief the offspring of the ill-fated Valentia, and my son? Dreadful thought!—But, hold! madman that I am, it was but a dream; but oh, so fearful a dream that the remembrance of it even now shakes my soul with horror. Good God!—and should it be realised, how terrible is the fate that is in store for me! But no; it is impossible! Let me not encourage such a thought! It was but the effect of my disordered imagination wrought upon by my guilty conscience. I am becoming weak as an infant. Oh, that I had never sinned, I should not now experience this fearful agony of mind!"

He covered his face with his hands, and for a few moments he became completely absorbed in the violence of his anguish. But at length, with a powerful effort, he did become somewhat more composed; and fearful of remaining alone in his present state of mind, and with the horrors of his dream stamped so vividly upon his memory, he hastened from the room, and scarcely knowing what he did, made his way towards the chamber of the Count Alberti, whom he found alone and wide awake. The pale countenance and agitated demeanour of the Prince Bianchi immediately struck his observation, and he felt convinced that he had something particular to communicate, or he would never have left his chamber at that advanced hour of the evening.

"How now, your highness," he interrogated, "you look alarmed; has anything particular happened to you that you thus so unexpectedly appear before me?"

"Alberti," replied Bianchi, in a faint voice, and glancing fearfully around him; "I have seen that which has smote my soul with horror!"

"Ah! what mean you, my lord?" said the astonished Count Alberti, with eager curiosity depicted in his countenance.

"Yes, I have," said the prince; "oh, it was most appalling; and yet, after all, it was but a dream."

"A dream, your highness?" observed Alberti; "and is it possible that you have suffered a mere dream to agitate you thus?"

"Yes, Alberti," answered the prince. "nor can you wonder at the agitation of my feelings when I shall have related to you the particulars of the vision which occurred to my imagination. By heaven, it seems to me as if there were some cursed spell upon me, and that the crisis of my fate is approaching."

"My lord," observed the count, "I am surprised to hear you talk thus; indeed you must not give way to such thoughts as these."

"I cannot help them," said Bianchi, in the same agitated accents; "it is impossible for me to do so."

"Persevere, your highness," said Alberti, "and no doubt you will be able to succeed. But what is this painful dream, which has so much alarmed you?"

"I almost shudder to relate it," replied Bianchi, "so fearful is the character of it. Alberti, I have beheld the phantom of the unfortunate and much wronged Valentia."

"It was only your disordered imagination that conjured it up, excellenza."

"True, it was only a dream; but it was so like reality that it has left an impression upon my mind which I shall find it a difficult task to banish."

"And is it possible that a mere dream should have taken such an effect upon you, my lord?" said the Count Alberti.

"Even so," replied the Prince Bianchi; "you may deem me weak, but I think that you must be ready to admit that the emotion I evince is not without cause, when you have heard all that I have to relate."

"Well, your highness," returned Alberti, "that may be; but I must request that you will not keep me in suspense, for what you have said has excited my curiosity."

Bianchi composed his feelings as well as he could, and he then related to the Count Alberti the dream which had occurred to his imagination, and to which the young nobleman listened with the most breathless attention and eager curiosity.

"It was an extraordinary vision, certainly," he observed, when Bianchi had concluded; "but still it is easily accounted for when the agitated and excited state of your mind is taken into consideration. Banish it from your recollection, my lord."

"Indeed," said Bianchi, "that is a task which I shall not be able easily to accomplish."

"Nay, your highness, I wonder that you should suffer it to make such an impression upon you. It is not at all probable that it will ever be realised.'

"Ah! Alberti, you may fancy me weak and credulous, but indeed I have my doubts. Should Massaroni really prove to be my son!—the thought tortures me."

"Do not give way to it." said the count.

"Can I help it, when I reflect upon all the circumstances connected with the brigand chief, and the powerful likeness which exists between him ,and Valentia ?" demanded the Prince Bianchi. "Oh, my lord, my heart misgives me, and I feel convinced that there is some fresh trouble impending o'er my head. Should Massaroni succeed in rescuing Melina, he will not fail to take every advantage of his triumph, and will stop at nothing to gratify his vengeance."

"By all my hopes that must not be," said the Count Alberti, much excited ; "Melina in the brigand's power, and restored to the arms of Clairville ;—the thought is more than I can find patience to endure. But the troops will surely arrive in time to repel any attack which he may make on the Villa Civetti ?"

"I would fain hope that they will do so, my lord," remarked Bianchi ; "but the brigands have the advantage of probably receiving the first intelligence of what had happened, and their retreat is not so far distant from the Villa Civetti as we are."

"That is most unfortunate," ejaculated Alberti, in an excited manner. "The chances are all against us, for Massaroni always acts with the greatest promptitude, and he has also every means at his ready command for carrying his designs into effect. And, when all this danger threatens, I must remain inactive here. Oh, the thought is too much for my patience to endure. May eternal curses light upon the head of Massaroni !"

"Nay, my lord," remarked Bianchi, who within the last few minutes had succeeded, much better than could have been anticipated, in subduing the violent emotion which had previously agitated him; "but just now you lectured me on my excitement, though you yourself would now do well, methinks, to calm your feelings. It is true that the danger which threatens us is most torturing to bear, but still we must hope for the best, and a few hours will, in all probability, relieve us from this state of suspense,"

"After all, my lord," said the Count Alberti, "I cannot help thinking that it would have been much better had Melina not have been removed from this villa, but had remained under your protection."

"Why, count," returned his companion, "your observations are surely very inconsistent."

"How so ?" demanded the young nobleman.

"Why, did you not formerly approve of the plan? Besides, it is evident from the ready means which Massaroni had of entering the villa at any time he thought proper, that Melina was every day in danger of falling into his power while she remained here."

"Nay, with the house properly guarded, what was there to fear? But to send her to the Villa Civetti, and to leave her under the protection of two or three individuals only, appears to me the height of imprudence."

"Well, perhaps it would have been better had I used other precautions," returned the Prince Bianchi; "but so secretly as she was borne away, and situated as the Villa Civetti is, who would have thought that she would ever have been discovered till the ceremony had been accomplished that should make her yours ? '

"Surely your suspicions should have fallen on the rascal Guiseppe, when he had betrayed you before. You were also aware that he was well acquainted with all your estates, and that his suspicions would be almost sure to fall upon the Villa Civetti."

"What would you have had me done' then ?" demanded Bianchi, impatiently.

"Why," replied Alberti, "what was to have prevented my being privately united to the beauteous Melina here, even though I was at the time in so precarious a situation ?"

"You talk preposterously, Count Alberti," replied the prince; "surely you would not that we should have outraged common decency altogether ?"

"And such delicate scruples, if I am not much mistaken, will be the cause of frustrating our designs, if they are not so already," said the Count Alberti. "I should not be at all surprised or disappointed if the Signora Melina is already restored to the arms of Florio Clairville, and that himself and Massaroni are exulting in the triumph of their designs, and forming fresh schemes for our future annoyance."

"You torture me and yourself, too, my lord," said the Prince Bianchi, " by encouraging such apprehensions and suspicions as those you have just now expressed. By all my hopes, if I thought that Melina had indeed fallen into the power of the brigand chief, I should go mad. Everything of late seems to go wrong with me ; and now all seem to conspire to vex and torture me."

"Pardon me, your highness," said Alberti, who began to fear that he had proceeded almost too far; "but far be it from my wishes to seek to torture you, or to excite any unnecessary alarm in your breast. The anxiety and suspense, however, which we both experience, is surely excusable, when all the circumstances of our situation are taken into consideration. However, let us endeavour to tranquillise our feelings, and to await with patience the result of this adventure."

"But that mysterious and awful dream," said the Prince Bianchi, after a pause, and striking his forehead; "as it rushes upon my recollection, I shudder with horror."

"Banish it from your thoughts altogether, my lord," returned the Count Alberti; "surely you are not weak enough to place any faith in dreams, which are the mere creations of the distempered imagination?"

"I try, but in vain, to treat it with indifference," remarked Bianchi; "there is something so peculiar in its character that I find it quite impossible to banish it from my memory; and should it be realised, how great is the misery that is in store for me!"

"Come, come, your highness," remonstrated the count, "you must not give way to such extravagant ideas as those."

"Extravagant!" repeated Bianchi; "have you not acknowledged yourself the resemblance which the features of the brigand chief bear to those of the portrait of Valentia?—Have you not also ventured to throw out a hint of the probability that Massaroni might chance to be her son?"

"True, I did so," acknowledged Alberti, "but my mind was agitated and bewildered at the time, and I knew not what I uttered. The most extraordinary likenesses often exist between persons who are in no way related to each other; for my own part, I do not wonder that such dreams as that you have just described should haunt your imagination under such circumstances, and in your present disordered state of mind, think no more about it."

"Ah, Alberti," returned the prince, "it it is easy for you to advise, but I find it utterly impossible to follow it; something seems to convince me that some misfortune is in store for me which will bring misery and disgrace upon me, and that it will be brought about by the power and the secret machinations of Massaroni. Would to heaven that I could come to some amicable arrangement with him."

"What!" exclaimed the Count Alberti, with a look of astonishment, "and could the noble Prince Bianchi so far degrade himself as to seek to come to terms with a daring robber—who has ever proved himself to be one of his most bitter enemies, and who is at present, no doubt, working fresh schemes for his annoyance?—But you will think better of this, when you come calmly to reflect upon the subject."

The Prince Bianchi returned no immediate answer to this; and after some further conversation of no particular importance, he once more retired to his own chamber. Notwithstanding the indifference with which Alberti had affected to treat the dream of Bianchi, it had made a far more serious impression upon him than he had thought proper to acknowledge; and when he was left alone, he passed some time in ruminating upon it. The count was not superstitious; still, there was something so prophetic in the vision that had occurred to the prince, that he could not help dwelling upon it with the greatest degree of interest.

"The resemblance between the features of Allesandro Massaroni and Valentia, is all but perfect," he remarked; "the expression of the eyes is the same, and in fact, the whole cast of features is so alike that it is impossible to help being powerfully struck with the remarkable coincidence. And then such of the facts as I have heard of the brigand chief's history are sufficient to excite suspicion, and to strengthen the probability of his being the son of the unfortunate Valentia. Should this prove to be the case, and Massaroni should by any means discover it, what a revolution will it effect in my hopes and prospects! The Prince Bianchi, stung with remorse, would tremble at the power of his son, and abandoning his designs against Melina, I should be left to the shame and contempt of the world. But no, though I might be degraded, he also should fall with me; would he not be denounced to the world as a heartless villain?—the diabolical betrayer of Zitella and Valentia? And what is more, oh! far more torturing it must be to him, he would be known as the father of that Allesandro Massaroni, whom he has so long sought to destroy. Zitella would come forward to confront him and to heap upon him her reproaches, whilst in the person of my hapless victim, Olympia, would appear another of the offsprings of his guilt and black-hearted treachery. But why do I thus torture myself with such ideas? Fate surely will never suffer them to be realised! I should go mad if I thought it would. How terrible it is to be kept in this continual state of excitement and suspense. Melina, thou must be mine, though every earthly power should conspire to prevent you. The beggar Clairville must not be suffered to triumph, and to succeed in the gratification of his presumptuous passion; and yet, should Massaroni obtain possession of Melina, which he will not fail to do, unless the troops of the Prince Bianchi arrive at the Villa Civetti before him, it is but too probable that Melina, notwithstanding her delicate scruples, will yield everything to love, and bearing the indignation of her uncle, whom she must now despise, consent to become at once the bride of him to whom her heart is so ardently devoted. That thought distracts my brain; but, alas! it is too reasonable for me to reject it. Curses light upon the hour which first introduced Florio and the beauteous Signora Melina to each other, and when the Prince Bianchi treated him with so much friendship and attention, which gave encouragement to the presumptuous hopes he had suffered to take possession of his mind! Had it not been for that, and I had never known Olympia, I might have won her affections, and long ere this have been a happy man; but as it is, even should I succeed in making her my wife, I can never possess anything but her utmost disgust and abhorrence, and our days must be passed in the utmost misery together.

THE COUNT ALBERTI ATTENDED BY SIGNOR GIACHOMO.

No matter, I will not relinquish my designs while I am still sanctioned by Bianchi, let the consequences be whatever they may."

He remained in this state of mind for a considerable time after the prince had quitted him, and tossed about on the bed, unable for several hours to compose his mind; whilst doubt, fear, and suspicion haunted his imagination alternately, and rendered him truly wretched. But at length he became exhausted, and by degrees he sank into a disturbed slumber.

Bianchi, on reaching his chamber, after his recent interview with Alberti, felt too much agitated to think of retiring to rest, but throwing himself on a seat he gave free indulgence to the painful and conflicting reflections that harassed his brain; and to combat which, or to afford him any relief, he was unable to find the least argument. He had every reason to dread the result of the expedition which he had sent to the defence of the Villa Civetti, notwithstanding he had endeavoured to think otherwise;—and the longer he reflected upon all the circumstances connected with the brigand chief—the interview he had with him at midnight, and the torturing facts he then recounted to him, the more reason did he believe he had to fear him. Then all the circumstances of his dream were stamped upon his memory in characters so vivid that nothing whatever could efface them; and the anguish, and doubt, and suspense of his mind became almost unendurable. The awful words of the spectre still seemed to ring in his ears, and smote his soul with horror; and still in imagination he gazed upon the dying features of Massaroni, and beheld his filmy and fast closing eyes gazing reproachfully upon him. In vain he sought to divert his thoughts to some other subject; it would pursue him, and his mind became wild and distracted.

"But do I not deserve to be punished thus for the many crimes of which I have been guilty?" he muttered to himself; "have I not been a villain of the blackest dye—the destroyer of female innocence, and can I expect that conscience will not sleep for ever? Oh, Valentia—Zitella, would that I had never known ye, or that I had never been tempted to act the infamous and cruel part I did towards ye! And can I hope to find rest while all this weight of guilt remains upon my mind?—And do I not seek to increase my infamy in my monstrous and unnatural persecution of my innocent niece; she whom an only and affectionate sister entrusted to my care, and whom I promised to protect and cherish with the same affectionate care as if she were my own child? Alas! how cruelly have I broken my word, and even now I would fain sacrifice Melina to the man she hates and despises;—the betrayer of one whom I have been told is my own daughter. Pshaw! it cannot be! Let me no longer torture myself with any such ideas; it is all a bitter mockery; a pure invention of the brigand chief, to torture me and gratify his revenge, and also that he may the better lure and trepan me into his plans. And am I thus to be duped, intimidated, treated with contempt?—No, by all my hopes, I will not; let me arouse myself and become firm; I must not permit my enemies to triumph over me altogether. The Prince Bianchi has hitherto been a stranger to fear, and shall he now suffer himself to be reduced in mind and fortitude to worse than a very child?—Never! I feel myself a man again, fresh confidence takes possession of my breast, and notwithstanding the gloomy aspect which my affairs may seem to wear at present, I will live in hopes of the final accomplishment of all my wishes. But a few hours will probably remove my doubts and suspense as regards Melina, and if fortune does not frown upon me, I shall shortly not only hear that the brigand chief is defeated but that he is also taken prisoner. The person of this daring man, whom I have so much reason to dread, once secured, I shall be secure from any annoyance; for I have not the least doubt that I should be able to persuade Zitella and her daughter to retire to some distant and secluded part of the country, where they might live unknown, and for which purpose I would willingly allow them sufficient to keep themselves in comfort, if not in absolute affluence."

In this manner the guilty nobleman sought to console himself, and to stifle the voice of conscience; but it was all to no purpose; its voice would be heard, and he continued restless and apprehensive.

Although the hour of midnight was past, the Prince Bianchi did not feel inclined to retire to bed, but sat buried in moody thought, and almost unconscious of where he was, or what was passing around him. The hour was solemn, and sufficient of itself to inspire the mind with awe, and to create the most dismal and painful thoughts; and this was added to by the profound silence which reigned throughout the house, all the inhabitants, probably, having retired to bed; and at length the effect on the senses of the Prince Bianchi became so powerful, that he found it utterly impossible to conquer his fears, and the most extraordinary ideas took possession of his brain. He almost feared to look around him; for his disordered imagination pictured to him all kinds of frightful forms and countenances, nor could he rid himself of the delusion. He trembled to be alone, and felt as if something dreadful were about to happen to him. He wished that he had not left the chamber of the Count Alberti; but he had not the courage to return to it, and did not like to expose the weakness under which he was labouring to the young nobleman; who, he felt satisfied, would only look upon his fears with scorn and derision. Then all the horrors of his dream rushed with tenfold force upon his memory, and he could almost swear that the wounded brigand and the ghastly phantom of Valentia were again before him.

"But away with these torturing ideas and idle phantasies," he at length ejaculated, in a faint, hoarse voice, and trying to arouse himself; "surely my senses must be fast failing me, or

I should not give way to such idle and extravagant fancies as these. I am alone; there is no one here to disturb me, or to give me the least occasion for apprehension; why, then, should I thus take such pains to disturb myself by encouraging such ridiculous and superstitious notions? I—Ah! what sound was that?"

He started and trembled, for at the moment he spoke, he imagined he heard a deep sigh which seemed to proceed from some individual close to him; and he looked round, almost fearing to encounter some ghastly object sufficient to inspire his soul with horror; but he saw nothing, and he then made a powerful effort to recover 'himself, though his heart palpitated against his side with the most violent emotion, and a strange giddiness seized upon his brain as though his senses were about to forsake him.

"It could only have been the whispering of the night-wind," he remarked, at last; "and why should I give way to such useless apprehensions? No! 'tis there again. This time I could not have been deceived; and, powers of mercy!—hark!"

He listened with breathless attention, and his whole frame was dreadfully agitated. He was not mistaken; this, at any rate, was no dream! Again that melancholy and unearthly voice which he had so often heard before saluted his ears, and once more he distinguished the following words, which went to his heart, and bound every faculty up in the most indescribable horror:

" Traitor to love—deceiver, beware—
  Heaven's dread wrath is o'er thee impending;
Shame yet awaits thee, confusion, despair—
  And the madness of conscience thy brain
      shall be rending!"

"Merciful powers!" exclaimed the agitated nobleman, "it is the voice of Valentia! Oh, God!—I do acknowledge my guilt; but do not punish me so severely as this. Valentia, I——"

The finish of the sentence was stifled in his throat, and he sank overpowered by his emotions, and scarcely knowing what he did, upon his knees. It would be impossible to do adequate justice to the variety of conflicting and tumultuous feelings that raged fiercely in his bosom at that awful moment. Although the voice had ceased, still the unearthly strains of music seemed to reverberate throughout the chamber, and transfixed the soul of the trembling Bianchi in the most mute attention; suddenly the lamp which he had left burning on the table became extinguished, and a supernatural light illumined the apartment! What language shall pourtray the awe and agony of the prince? The blood seemed to be frozen within his veins, and the perspiration streamed

from every pore in torrents. Gradually a vapoury cloud arose before his eyes, which having slowly dispersed, once more to his unspeakable awe and consternation the ghastly shade of the ill-fated Valentia stood gazing, with an expression that went to his very soul, upon him.

"Spirit of the much-wronged Valentia!" he cried, "why dost thou again appear before me?—Oh, avaunt! for I cannot, dare not gaze upon thee!"

The phantom spoke not; but fixing upon the wretched nobleman a solemn and impressive look, she moved with noiseless steps towards the door of the chamber, and motioned him to follow. Wound up to a pitch of agony and horror as he naturally was, Bianchi felt that he had no power to disobey, and with faltering footsteps he followed his unearthly visitor from the room, the door seeming to open of its own accord. The spectre, for such the unhappy Bianchi could not but conclude it was, seemed rather to glide than to walk, and ever and anon it turned its pale and solemn looks upon his countenance, and seemed to reproach him for the wrongs she had sustained, when living, from him. His tongue clove to the roof of his mouth, and he was unable to articulate a single syllable, and it was indeed wonderful how he could find strength or fortitude sufficient to follow his awful guide.

At length they reached the room which contained the portrait of Valentia, before which the phantom paused, and pointed solemnly and significantly towards it.

"Shade of the unfortunate Valentia," at length Bianchi found power to ejaculate, "I do acknowledge my guilt, and now my soul is stung with remorse—Oh, spare me!—spare me!"

He sank upon his knees with clasped hands as he thus spoke, then drooped his head in horror before the countenance of the spirit. Solemn strains of music again resounded through that apartment, which gradually died away until they were heard no more, and Bianchi looking up, beheld himself alone, and in utter darkness. His fears overpowered him, and uttering a groan of horror, he sank insensible on the floor. How long he had been in that state he knew not; but when he partially recovered, he found himself supported in the arms of two or three of his domestics, who were about to convey him to his chamber. Day was just dawning, so it was evident that the prince must have been in a state of unconsciousness for some time before they had discovered him.

"Where is it?" he exclaimed, releasing himself from the hold of his servants; "and why do you seek to hold me? Where is it, I again demand?"

"What mean you, your highness?" asked

one of the domestics; "we saw nothing more than usual in this apartment when we discovered you; you seem alarmed my lord; suffer us to conduct you to your chamber."

"Did you not see it?" once more demanded the Prince Bianchi, staring vacantly and wildly around him; "why do you not answer me, rascals—knaves?"

"Indeed, excellenza," replied another of the attendants, "we do not understand what you mean; to what does your highness allude?"

"The spirit, fellow!" answered Bianchi, fiercely, "the ghastly phantom of the deeply-injured Valentia! Why do you stand there staring at me like idiots? Do you not believe me, or do you think me mad? I tell you again that it was the shade of Valentia I followed from my chamber to this apartment. But where is it now? Why does it not again appear before me to convince the minds of these sceptics?"

The men looked at each other significantly, thinking, no doubt, that the senses of their master wandered, but for a moment or two they did not venture to make use of any observation; however, at length one of them said,

"I crave the pardon of your highness for my boldness, but to me it appears most probable that you have been suddenly awakened out of some troublesome dream, and have wandered unconsciously hither."

"Presumptuous fool!" cried Bianchi, passionately, and frowning frightfully upon the man; "presumptuous fool to dare to doubt the truth of my assertions, think you that I have neither eyes nor ears, nor that I am always dreaming? But why do I stand here wasting my time with you? Retire! and leave me to myself!"

The domestics did not venture to disobey, and retired from the room. For some minutes after they were gone, the unhappy nobleman was transfixed to the spot on which he had been standing, with his pale face buried in his hands—his brain burning and his heart palpitating at double its natural pace. For some time he could not collect his thoughts, nor recall to his memory any distinct reminiscence of what had passed; but at length he raised his eyes timidly towards the portrait, and started trembling back, for he could almost imagine that he again beheld the phantom of Valentia standing before him.

"It was no delusion!" he ejaculated; "oh, no; it was indeed the spirit of my unfortunate victim that I saw; she is permitted to revisit this earth to torture me, and to bring me to a sense of remorse and compunction. Oh, God! and am I to be continually haunted by her grim shade? Am I never to be allowed one moment's respite from anguish and thought? No, what rest is there for the guilty? But why do I add to the torment of my soul by continuing to gaze upon the resemblance of her I so cruelly wronged? Let me away and seek to banish these dismal thoughts from my mind. Let me but be firm and I may yet be able to triumph over the dangers which surround me."

With these words, Bianchi hurried from the room, his hands clasped to his burning temples, and totally unconscious of what he was doing, or what was the ultimate object he had in view. His brain was bewildered, and, in fact, at that moment any person who knew him, and could have seen him, would have been alarmed from the wildness of his demeanour, the vacancy of his eye, and the total absence of all proper control over the feelings which at that time held predominance in his breast.

The Prince Bianchi, we need scarcely inform the reader, after the various traits of his character which we have endeavoured to delineate in the course of our narrative, was one of the weakest of human beings, and from that imbecility of mind, had originated the errors of his past life, which prompted and held control over all his present actions, more than from any natural viciousness of disposition. Nursed in the lap of luxury—accustomed, from his parents, to look upon all his fellow creatures, to whom fortune had not been so lavish in her gifts as himself, as beings of an inferior grade, who were merely created to labour for his enjoyment, inexperienced in the word (in the true essence of the word) as an infant, the haughty, arrogant, and tyrannical spirit he evinced may reasonably be accounted for. In fact, he was a strange anomaly of a man altogether; one of the most decrepid in intellect, though his ignorant vanity led him to suppose that he was something almost supreme. To this gross stupidity of mind, superstitious notions, imbibed from the false precepts instilled by his parents, and the dictates of his own conscience, may be attributed the delusion under which he at present laboured; had he been differently constituted, he would at once have perceived that the supernatural adventure which he thought he had met with, could only have been the phantom of his own disordered imagination, and he would have exerted all his energies to arouse himself, and by a virtuous reformation in his future conduct have sought to redeem the past. In the state of mind we have described, the guilty nobleman, suddenly looking up, found himself in the open air, and that he had unconsciously rambled to some distance from the villa. In the confusion of the moment, he did not recognise the place, and he was looking around him in a bewildered manner, when suddenly a man of muscular and gigantic proportions, and clad in rude garments of a nondescript character, emerged from a thicket near which the Prince Bianchi was standing, and hurrying forward, stopped abruptly before him.

CHAPTER L.

WHAT TOOK PLACE BETWEEN BIANCHI AND THE STRANGER.—FRESH CAUSE FOR ALARM.—UNWELCOME NEWS. — THE ALARMING ACCIDENT OF THE COUNT ALBERTI.

THE Prince Bianchi started, and indeed the uncouth appearance of the individual before him, was sufficient to cause him to entertain no very high opinion of his character. The dress he wore was old and very much tattered, a rusty cloak depended from his shoulders, and his arms, which were completely bare, were browned by exposure to the sun. A couple of poniards and a brace of pistols were stuck in the broad leathern belt that encircled his waist, and by no means served to remove the unfavourable opinion which Bianchi had formed of him, especially as he himself was quite unarmed; and no one being at hand at that early hour of the morning, and in such a lonely spot, he was completely at his mercy, should he intend any harm. The features of the stranger were large, coarse, repulsive, and ferocious, and his fierce black eyes were expressive of desperate villany.

For a moment or two the prince was so surprised and startled by this unexpected and unwelcome appearance, that he could not utter a word, and the man, folding his arms across his chest, earnestly contemplated him in silence, while a malicious grin overspread his repulsive features.

"The Prince Bianchi, governor of Rome," at length said the fellow in the most disgusting and vulgar accents; "I greet you well, my lord, though I did not expect to have the pleasure of meeting you alone, and at so early an hour of the morning."

"Who are you?" demanded Bianchi, in a timid voice.

"One who has good cause to know you well, though it is now some years since we before met, and I doubt much whether you will be much inclined to renew the acquaintance," answered the man.

"What is your business with me?" asked the prince, his alarm increasing from the observations, and the bold and vulgar demeanour of the stranger.

"Compensation for injuries received from you," replied the ruffian.

"Injuries received from me?" replied Bianchi.

"Ay," returned the man; "but I will explain everything before we part, depend upon it; at present I demand money, and I must have it, too; therefore, if you have it not about you, I will accompany you back to the villa, where, of course, you can readily procure it."

"Ah! a robber!" ejaculated Bianchi, looking upon the fellow with the utmost terror.

"Even so," he answered; "I do not disown the character. I am a desperate man; one who will not suffer himself to be disappointed in his designs, and, therefore, excellenza, you will at once, I should think, perceive that I am not to be trifled with. My exchequer is quite exhausted; you can perceive that my wardrobe is not in any of the best conditions—I knew you to be a very charitable nobleman, (at least, that is the character I have heard of you), and, to sum it up in a few words, as you have been the principal cause of my present unfortunate situation, and, as I have the means to expose a few of the little foibles of your youthful days to the world in no very flattering colours, I thought that I might as well pay you a visit. So your highness will just have the kindness to hand me over one hundred ducats, which I will endeavour to make do for the present, and will call upon you for a fresh supply when they are exhausted."

"Insolent ruffian!" exclaimed the excited Prince Bianchi; "and think you that I am thus to be intimidated into a compliance with your extortionate demands? Begone! or in an instant I will raise an alarm which——"

"Which," interrupted the man, with a fiendish grin of triumph, drawing forth one of the poniards, and pointing significantly to the other weapons of destruction in his belt, "would be the signal for your own immediate death. Fool! think you that I would hesitate for a moment to perform that which I threaten? You may frown: I heed it not. You tremble also, and that convinces me, that you fear the wretch, the ruffian, the villain, who stands before you, and boldly tells you that not only are you yourself worthy of all those titles, but that unless you immediately comply with my demands, I will tear the mask from your face, and expose you—you, the mighty Prince Bianchi, the governor of Rome—to the world, in your true character, and bring forward such proofs to corroborate my statements as will sink you into shame and confusion. Miscreant, betrayer of female innocence! perjured scoundrel! have you the hardihood to deny the truth of all the charges I have brought against (you? Knew you ever the names of Zitella, and of the unfortunate Signora Valentia Di Valori?"

The Prince Bianchi turned ghastly pale, and trembled convulsively in every limb, as the unknown gave utterance to these words; for a few moments he was unable to make any reply, but again he looked anxiously around him with the hope of beholding some persons who might come to his assistance; but not an individual met his gaze, and the stranger, who evidently quickly read the thoughts that were passing in his mind, laughed ironically and triumphantly, as he observed—

"Oh, my lord, no doubt it would be a great

relief to your fears and gratify you amazingly, had you the power to hand me over to some of your myrmidons; but you see that fortune favours me, and that even if assistance were to appear in sight, before it could possibly reach you, I could, and would, stretch you a corpse at my feet. You may, therefore, as well be calm, and prolong your life for a short time, by at once listening to me, and acceding to my demands."

"Fearful man," said Bianchi, looking at him more narrowly, and endeavouring, but in vain, to recall his recollection; "who are you?"

"A wretch, a villain, as you have called me, and as I now appear before you!" answered the man; "but one whose name you have just cause to tremble at; one whom you have basely wronged, and made him the wretch he now is. You have no recollection of my features, my lord? No, I should, indeed, marvel if you had, altered as they now are by years of suffering, and reckless dissipation; and in this wretched garb, were I to mention my name, conscience would strike you dumb!"

"Let me hear it," cried the distracted nobleman, "though the mention of it blast me!"

"Be it so, my lord," returned the unknown placing his hand upon his arm, and drawing him closer towards him; "do you remember such a name as that of Francisco Malietevera?"

The Prince Bianchi started as if he had been struck by a thunderbold, and stared at the man who stood before him aghast.

"Franscisco Malietevera!" he ejaculated, "impossible! He was condemned to perpetual banishment for a base attempt upon my life; he must have been dead many years ago!"

"Franscisco Malietevera was unjustly condemned to the fate you have mentioned, for seeking to avenge the injuries inflicted upon his sister, by the son of the late Prince Bianchi," replied the man; "but he escaped, and he now lives to the confusion of the villain who has been the cause of all his miseries and his subsequent crimes."

"Lives!" repeated Bianchi in a hoarse voice; "'tis false! Where? where?"

"He stands before you!"

"You he!" returned the prince, with a look of scorn, though his heart at the same time misgave him; "oh, infamous impostor!"

"Well, my lord," replied the man, "methinks I shall presently be able to convince you that I speak the truth, though probably it may be against your will; and I imagine, I cannot adopt a better course to do so than by recounting to you some of the facts connected with yourself and the unfortunate sister of whom I speak. It is now some two-and-thirty years ago since there resided some leagues from hence, an aged and

respected nobleman of ancient and noble pedigree, but reduced in circumstances, the Count Geraldo Malietevera. He was a widower, and had been so for some years, but he was happy in the possession of one son named Francisco, and a daughter two years younger, Florentia, a maiden whose surpassing loveliness and whose innumerable virtues gained her the esteem and admiration of all who knew her. Francisco was absent abroad, finishing his education, and in the meantime, you, my lord, were accidentally introduced to her, and wooed and won her affections, and the approbation of her father. You promised her marriage, and she and her parent had every reason to place the utmost reliance in your honour; how could they suspect for a moment that such atrocious villany and deception could exist under so specious a guise?"

"How?" exclaimed the exasperated and deeply agitated Bianchi.

"Nay, your highness," returned the man, coolly; "you may as well be calm, though the excitement you evince satisfies me that you know I am speaking the truth. The failure of some foreign affairs brought the count to the verge of complete ruin; and to save himself, he submitted to apply to you, and you advanced him a large sum of money, sufficient to redeem his broken fortunes. All this time, Francisco was kept in a state of complete ignorance. Well, what was the advantage that you took of all these unfortunate circumstances I have just mentioned? Such an one as could only have entered the mind of the blackest-hearted scoundrel. While Florentia's father was confined to his bed with a serious fit of illness that had attacked him suddenly, you endavoured to persuade her to yield to your base passions, and to sacrifice her virtue at the shrine of your lust. She rejected your proposals with indignant scorn; but alas! for her, poor girl, you had her in your power, and knowing that, was not to be abashed or withheld from the accomplishment of your monstrous designs at all hazards. Finding that artifice or persuasion were not likely to have any effect, you adopted a more desperate and determined course, threatening that unless she consented to your diabolical proposals you would immediately proceed against her father for the amount of the large sum of money he was indebted to you, and place him, even ill as he was, in a prison. Terrified, horrorstruck at such a prospect, the poor girl yielded; and you, monster that you were, triumphed. Franscisco returned suddenly and unexpectedly to his home: and what were the horrors that greeted him? His father's corpse—his sister ruined and abandoned by her inhuman betrayer, and himself a beggar!"

"Hold! hold!" ejaculated the Prince Bianchi, covering his face with his hands. "I can listen to no more of this."

"Ah!" cried his companion, with a look of triumph and revenge; "then your conscience does reproach you;—you cannot, you dare not deny the truth of that which I have stated; this then affords me some satisfaction. But my tale is not finished yet, as you are well aware. Only two days after the return of her brother, Florentia expired of a broken heart, and was buried in the same grave as her father. It was then that Francisco swore a deadly revenge against the base perpetrator, the black-hearted author of all these miseries, and can you marvel that he should do so? He sought you out; reproached you with your crimes, and called upon you to defend yourself; coward-like, you shrank from his challenge, and it was then that he attempted to chastise you as you deserved; but at the moment when his avenging sword was about to penetrate your body, and to redress the heavy wrongs of his father and his sister in your blood, some of your creatures flew to your rescue, disarmed and secured him. He was conveyed to prison, brought to a mock trial, but powerless as he was, what could he expect?—He was convicted; condemned to death; but which was afterwards mercifully commuted to banishment and slavery for life. Several years he passed in that wretched and degraded situation; but at length he contrived to effect his escape; but what course had he then to pursue? friendless, moneyless, destitute as he was, and with the felon's brand upon his name? For some weeks he wandered about remote parts of the country, obtaining a wretched subsistence on the precarious charity of strangers, insulted, and often threatened; but at length human patience could endure it no longer, and he resolved to obtain that by force which charity denied him; he turned robber, and for many years he carried on a successful career of villany, and depredation; frequently was he half resolved to make a bold attack upon you (especially when he heard of your monstrous conduct towards the unfortunate Signoras Zitella and Valentia), and at once to gratify his vengeance and his cupidity; but the fear of detection prevented him; however, his affairs have for some time past been in a desperate state; Fortune has not smiled upon him so favourably as she was wont to do, and he now appears before you, as he said before, to demand justice, relief, and compensation. Do you any longer doubt that it is the injured Francisco Malietevera who stands before you?"

"Can it be?" gasped forth the agitated Prince Bianchi, again gazing earnestly upon the wretched and repulsive-looking being before him; "but no, it is impossible: I will not be intimidated or imposed upon. Begone, fellow!"

"Begone!" repeated the ruffian, with an ironical laugh; "oh, you do well to command, Prince Bianchi, to command one who has it in his power to strike you this moment dead at his feet, and who is there to fly to your assistance? But I waste time: you cannot, you dare not deny the truth of the tale I have just repeated to you, and how would you like the world to be made acquainted with it, as well as your other crimes? But time has changed my character, and stifled the feelings and wishes which once held such paramount sway in my breast; I am a proscribed villain, driven to desperation; you have the means to help me, and to enable me to make once more something like an appearance in the world; upon those conditions, I consent to remain silent, but no other. Come, we delay; you have heard what I have said, and it surely cannot take you long to decide upon that which is so fair and reasonable."

"Francisco," returned Bianchi, "if he, indeed, you be, though I have still my doubts, you cannot reasonably expect me to accede to your demands, extravagant as they are."

"Extravagant!" said Francisco, in reply; "what, a mere paltry living from a man of your enormous wealth, to one whom you have so deeply injured, and who has it in his power to denounce you to the world in your true character? Pshaw! you must be dreaming, my lord."

"And who would believe the assertions of a desperate ruffian such as yourself?" said the exasperated nobleman; "a convicted felon, who, to be discovered, would be immediately consigned to death."

"Ha, ha, ha!" laughed the man, ironically and contemptuously; "and can the Prince Bianchi have the courage to talk thus to one who holds him so completely in his power; and who this instant could take his life? But my patience is exhausted: Are you ready to comply with my demands, and to hand over to me the one hundred ducats?"

"And upon my doing so, you will promise me that I shall receive no further annoyance from you?" said Bianchi.

"The one hundred ducats," replied his termentor, peremptorily; "we will talk of the other part of our business anon."

The prince was bewildered and agitated, and scarcely knew what to do; once more he looked anxiously around him to ascertain whether or not any individuals were at hand whom he might call to his assistance, but he saw no one, and feeling convinced that Francisco, as he called himself, and whom he began to fear was really so, was determined, he reluctantly pulled out a well-filled purse, which he presented to him, and the man having weighed it in his hand, and deposited it in his pocket, said—

"'Tis well, your highness, that you have come to this wise resolution, for you may rest assured that it is useless to oppose one who is so determined as myself; I will endeavour to manage to make this installment of the debt which you owe me, do for the present."

"For the present?" repeated Bianchi, with a look of alarm.

"Ay," answered the ruffian, ironically; "for as I intend to lead a different life to that which I have for some time past been compelled to do, no doubt it will soon be exhausted, and then, of course, I shall need it to be replenished."

"Insolent villain!"

"Nay, my lord, I would advise you to make use of better language to one who has you in his power, and the blood that flows in whose veins is at least as noble as your own. The next time you see me, will be in a different character to that in which I now appear before you."

"Wretched man," said Bianchi; "you will not surely venture to annoy me with your presence again?"

"Indeed, but I shall," replied Francisco, triumphantly, "and that before many days have elapsed, I dare say."

"Where—where? and at what time?" asked Bianchi, eagerly.

"That is my business," answered the ruffian; "think not to entrap me, my lord, lest you should yourself be entrapped, for all depends upon your keeping faith with me. Remember what I have said, and if you are wise you will not disregard my injunctions. Depend upon it, I have the ready means of ascertaining all your designs and transactions, and if I find that you intend to play me false, I will have such a revenge that will give you ample cause to regret having deceived me. Remember the murdered Florentia, indirectly murdered by your accursed villany; remember her injured, outcast brother, and thank my mercy that I let you off so leniently."

"Francisco, if such indeed you be," said the agitated and alarmed Bianchi, "will nothing induce you to listen to the voice of remonstrance and persuasion?"

"You have heard my determination, my lord," returned Francisco; "and rest assured that I am a man of my word; let that suffice you; and until we meet again, farewell."

Before Bianchi could make use of any other observation, the ruffian turned hastily away and departed from his presence as suddenly, and by the same means as he had entered it.

For some minutes after he had departed, the Prince Bianchi stood in a state of complete stupefaction, and for some time he could with difficulty persuade himself that he had not been labouring under the influence of some painful dream, although the recollection of all that had taken place was most vivid and torturing. At length he started, and looking around him, exclaimed—

"What fresh misery is this that is in store for me? Have the fates altogether conspired against me? I had entirely banished from my memory the wrongs I had inflicted upon Florentia Malietevera as well as my other victims, and had hoped that all evidence of my guilt had ceased to exist many years ago; and now at the very moment when my excited mind is the least prepared for the shock, her own brother appears before me, to mock at and upbraid me, and set my power at defiance. By Heaven! these accummulated facts, all tending towards my disgrace and confusion, will drive me mad. But can it really be Francisco whom I have just seen? His features and his demeanour are strangely altered, and it is almost impossible to recognise that once noble youth, in the heartless and repulsive ruffian who has just quitted my presence; and yet he cannot be an impostor; for who else could have been so well acquainted with the particulars he related to me? Disgrace and misery have overtaken me at once. Oh, that any of my servants had been at hand to secure him, and thus, at any rate, have enabled me to rid myself of one whom I have so much reason to dread. By all my hopes, an infernal spell is upon me, and I feel convinced that my career of guilt is rapidly drawing towards a close. Shall there be no future rest for me, night or day? It seems not, and when I reflect upon all the errors of my past life, and the many wrongs I have inflicted upon others, what right have I to expect it? The horrors of last night, too, can they ever be effaced from my memory? It is impossible! They were no idle illusions of the disordered imagination. No; it was the ghastly phantom of the unfortunate and ill-fated Valentia that I beheld, and which I followed. In vain would I seek to persuade myself that it was a dream, for the more that I endeavour to do so, the stronger becomes the impressions of the awful truth upon my mind. And how shall I escape from these continual horrors?—I know not!"

The wretched misguided nobleman was too blind to see that the only way he could hope to do so, was by repentance, and in seeking by his future conduct to make all the atonement in his power. He could not for an instant form the resolution to abandon his guilty and cruel designs against his innocent niece, Melina, and the principal of his fears were, even amidst all the other thoughts and circumstances that distracted his brain, lest she should be rescued from his power, and falling under the protection of Massaroni, thus render all those designs abortive; and not the least of his anxieties was to hear what had taken place at the Villa Civetti since he had despatched the troops thither. He, however, entertained the most dismal forebodings; and the events which we have just been describing following each other in such rapid succession, added to the gloom, the doubt, and perturbation of his mind.

"But why do I remain here," he said, after a brief pause, "when all around is cal-culated to add to the melancholy tenor of my thoughts? Let me arouse myself, and endea-vour to consider what is best to be done. No one must become acquainted with this last adventure if I can help it, for already the pain-ful and guilty secrets connected with me are too

THE PRINCE BIANCHI SHOWING THE MINIATURE TO ALBERTI.

well known, and even my domestics begin to look upon me with suspicion. I must and will be firm."

He was about to move from the spot and return to the villa, when the heavy and hasty clatter-ing of horses' hoofs saluted his ears, and looking in the direction from whence they seemed to proceed, he beheld a man galloping at full speed towards him, and whom he recognised immediately as one of the soldiers whom he had despatched to the Villa Civetti, and of course he instantly guessed that he had something of importance to communicate to him.

The man not having at first perceived him, was about to turn his steed in a different direction, which was a nearer cut to the villa, when Bianchi shouted to him, and the next moment he was by his side, and dismounted from his horse, evidently in a breathless and excited state.

"How, now, Marco?" exclaimed the prince; "why this haste? What news have you from the Villa Civetti?"

"Alas, your highness," replied Marco, "the worst that could be feared; the Signora Melina ——"

"Ah! what of her?" demanded Bianchi, in impatient accents.

"She is rescued."

"Rescued!" reiterated Bianchi, fiercely; "liar!"

"Pardon me, my lord," said Marco, "it is too true; the Signora Melina has been delivered from your power;—the troops, although they used all possible expedition, arrived too late."

It would be impossible to describe the excitement of the Prince Bianchi on receiving this intelligence, and for a moment or two he could not give utterance to his feelings.

"Powers of hell!" he at length exclaimed, furiously, and glaring at Marco; "can this be true, or is it only a plot to deceive and torture me?—Melina rescued!—by whom?—when?—how?"

"By Massaroni, my lord," answered Marco. "On our arriving near the villa, we met one of the men who had been sent there in charge of the signora, who, with great difficulty, had effected his escape; and all his companions having perished, he informed us that the brigand-chief, at the head of a vast number of his daring band, had made an attack upon the villa not more than an hour before, and of course meeting with little resistance, he found no difficulty in accomplishing his purpose, in rescuing the Signora Melina, and her attendant Floretta, together with Guiseppe; and leaving Viola and her parents behind him, instantly took his departure."

"Melina gone, and in the power of Massaroni? My worst fears are realised," ejaculated Bianchi, in a hoarse voice; "may infernal curses pursue him to destruction! But my tardy troops; it is all their fault, or this never could have happened."

"Pardon me, your highness," Marco ventured to observe; "but, indeed, you blame them wrongfully, for certainly they must have used all the expedition that was possible, or they could not have arrived at the Villa Civetti so soon after the unfortunate affair had taken place."

"All my misfortunes have come upon me at once," ejaculated Bianchi, striking his forehead in a state of the utmost distraction. "Where are my troops?"

"They went in pursuit of the brigands, immediately on hearing what had taken place, my lord," replied Marco; "and should they be fortunate enough to overtake them, they may yet be able to rescue the Signora Melina from their power, and likewise to secure Allesandro Massaroni."

"Ah, no!" cried Bianchi, "there is no chance of that; the brigand-chief has, doubtless, too well arranged his plans to stand in fear of defeat. She is lost to me for ever, and the beggar Clairville will at last be triumphant! How maddening is that thought!—Oh, that I had Massaroni in my power, how terrible is the vengeance that I would wreak upon his head. But am I awake? or is this only some base scheme to mock and torture me?"

"Unfortunately, your highness," returned Marco, "it is too true; and according to your orders, as soon as I heard of what had taken place, I lost no time in hastening hither to make you acquainted with the particulars."

"And may Heaven curse you for being the bearer of such ill news," said the Prince Bianchi, passionately. "Oh, Melina, and is this thy patient submission to my will?—wilt thou thus willingly place thyself under the protection of my bitterest foe, and a robber and a murderer? For this thou deservest that my heaviest maledictions should descend upon thy head."

Again he clasped his forehead, and for a moment or two his senses tottered upon their seat, and he knew not where he was, or what he was doing; but at length, with a groan of anguish and the most bitter disappointment, he darted hastily from the spot, and entering the villa, made his way towards the chamber of Alberti.

The count had been informed of the peculiar circumstances under which the servants of Bianchi had found him in the apartment which contained the portrait of Valentia, and the extraordinary declaration he had made, and that circumstance had added to the alarm and excitement under which he had himself previously laboured. He felt satisfied that these frequent fits of insanity (for he could consider them as nothing else) must all serve to procrastinate, if not ultimately frustrate, the accomplishment of his wishes; and every moment his hopes of the possession of the Signora Melina became less sanguine, and his impatience and uneasiness consequently increased.

"The Prince Bianchi has become weak as a child," he muttered to himself when he was alone; "such imbecility is calculated to produce the most dangerous consequences, and to prove the annihilation of my hopes. He must be mad, or he never could indulge in such wild ideas and superstitions. Spectres crossing his path, indeed! Bah! the idea is monstrously absurd, and it is worthy only of some weak-minded old woman. It is all the effect of a guilty conscience, and certainly his is heavily laden. But has not he the means to mock at its upbraidings, and to set the consequences of his guilt at defiance? The powerful Prince Bianchi has little to fear from the scandal of the world. But he has solemnly sworn that nothing shall prevent Melina becoming my wife, and I place too much confidence in him to believe for a moment that he will break his word. But this tardy delay in my recovery, and the anxiety I feel to know whether the Signora Melina is still safe at the Villa Civetti, is almost insupportable. Should the brigand chief have seen Rubaldo in time, and acted with his usual promptitude, it is all but certain that before the troops could possibly arrive to oppose him, he must have succeeded in rescuing Melina; and once under his protection, and restored to the man of her heart, Florio Clairville, she is lost to me for ever. We have had sufficient proofs, times and oft, that Massaroni, in his mountain retreat, and surrounded by his courageous and desperate band, may set any force that may be sent against him at defiance, and that it is only by some deep-laid stratagem we can hope to entrap him, and thus put an end to his power. But who can accomplish such a task as that? —who can hope to baffle the ingenuity of the brigand? The thought is hopeless, and I dare not encourage it. Oh, I owe him a terrible debt of vengeance for the many injuries I have experienced from him! and I have too much reason to fear that I shall never have an opportunity of repaying it."

Thus the Count Alberti continued to soliloquise for a considerable time, and his fears every moment became the more powerful and insupportable; but at length he was aroused by hearing a hasty footstep approaching his chamber, and he started up in his bed, fully expecting some fresh intelligence to annoy and distract his mind. He was not long kept in suspense, for the room door was the next instant burst open, and the Prince Bianchi, wild, pale, and trembling, rushed in and sank into a chair by his bed-side, panting for breath, and unable to utter a word.

"My lord!" said Alberti eagerly; "what means this violent agitation? Speak, speak, and do not keep me in suspense."

Bianchi stared at him wildly and vacantly for a moment or so, and was still unable to return any answer, and the fears and impatience of Alberti increased.

"I see plainly enough, my lord," he said, "that you have some painful news to impart, but to be kept in this state of doubt and uncertainty is intolerable; let me at once know the worst!"

"The fiends of hell conspire against us!" ejaculated Bianchi, in a hoarse voice; "we are ruined!—all is lost!"

"Ah!" cried the distracted count, "are then my worst fears realised?—The Signora Melina——"

"Yes, yes," interrupted the Prince Bianchi, with increased agitation; "it is of her I have to speak. The brigand chief has triumphed. Melina has escaped from the villa, and she is at this moment, I have every reason to believe, under his protection."

"Confusion!" exclaimed Alberti, furiously. "Can it be? Melina in the power of Massaroni? It is impossible! You must have been misinformed, my lord."

"Oh, no!" replied the wretched nobleman, "I am too well convinced of the fatal truth. Marco has just arrived in great haste here, and communicated the torturing fact to me."

"Now, may every curse pursue the daring villain!" cried the Count Alberti, his eyes flashing with rage and disappointment. "The girl is lost to me for ever. But where were the cowardly troops you sent to oppose the ruffians?"

"Alas!" sighed the Prince Bianchi, "they did not arrive at the Villa Civetti for about an hour after the rescue of my niece; but as soon as they heard of the daring outrage, they went in pursuit of the ruffians, and should they overtake them, they may yet be able to regain possession of Melina, and to secure the person of our powerful and implacable enemy."

"Oh, no!" returned Alberti, and his whole frame was convulsed with the violence of his emotions; "in vain you seek to flatter me with false and delusive hopes. The brigand chief is unconquerable, and having succeeded in rescuing Melina, no force that we might send against him can wrest her from his power. Thus, then, are all the hopes that I had entertained, crushed. Fool that I was ever to encourage them. In a few hours Signora Melina will, in all human probability, have become the wife of the presumptuous beggar, Florio Clairville, and——"

"The wife of Clairville!" repeated Bianchi, fiercely; "no—no, she will not dare thus to brave my eternal wrath. The thought is sufficient to drive me to distraction."

"Ay, my lord," said Alberti, with a bitter half-malignant look; "and what is the use of regret, now that the evil is effected? Had there been proper precaution used, this would never have happened; but you were not sincere in the promises you made to me, and I must have been an idiot to place any confidence in them."

"Count Alberti," said Bianchi, with a look

of indignation ; "do you dare to accuse me of insincerity ?—You know not what you say, or if you do, you wrong me greatly, and I am surprised to hear you make use of such observations."

"Well—well," replied Alberti, in somewhat subdued tones; "perhaps I was wrong and hasty in what I said. But pardon me, my lord; you must make every allowance for the bitter disappointment I have experienced; the annihilation of all my hopes. Oh, Melina, proud and scornful beauty, and shall I be thus deprived of you, after all that I have suffered to obtain possession of you? I shall go mad! But why do I remain here inactive? Let me arise, and go in pursuit of the villain Massaroni! I will rescue Melina from his power, and wreak my vengeance on his head, or perish in the attempt!"

"Hold, Alberti!" exclaimed the prince; "of what use is this violence! Do you forget the situation you are placed in, and the danger which you run by thus giving way to these feelings of extraordinary excitement? Forbear! forbear! for this conduct is only calculated to increase the evil of which we have to complain."

"Oh, how coolly can you talk, my lord," said Albert, with a look of the utmost impatience. "But if you entertained the same feelings that agitate my breast and drive me to distraction you would act far differently : think you I can remain here, and know that Massaroni and Clairville are at this moment exulting in their triumph, and at my misery and disappointment? I will not—cannot tarry here with such thoughts as these upon my mind. I will instantly away; gather all the forces I can around me, and at their head seek at once the retreat of the brigand, and——"

"Are you mad ?" demanded Bianchi.

"Mad! mad!" cried the distracted count; "yes, I am—and can you marvel at it ?"

"Know you not that any attempt to leave your chamber in your present state of health, would probably be attended with the most fatal consequences ?" said Bianchi.

"It matters not," replied the bewildered and agitated Alberti; "I will brave them all; it is impossible for me to remain here; sudden death would be better than this terrible, this torturing state of suspense."

"Be calm," said the prince, "and rest assured that I will leave no means untried to obtain the restoration of Melina, and to crush the future power of the brigand. I will immediately dispatch fresh troops to the assistance of those who have gone before them, and if fortune does not continue to frown upon us, their joint efforts will be crowned with success."

"Oh, how futile is that hope," returned the Count Alberti; "I see plainly enough that all chance is at an end, and that Melina is never destined to become mine. May the heaviest curses pursue Massaroni and all those who are connected with him for this; may he——"

He was interrupted by the entrance of Signor Giachomo, who, hearing what had taken place, thought that his presence might be required.

"'Tis well, signor, that you have come," remarked Bianchi, "for probably your counsel and advice may serve to abate the excitement under which his lordship labours, and which is fraught with so much danger."

"Signor Giachomo," said Alberti, impatiently "your skill is useless when applied to the malady under which I now labour through disappointment. The Signora Melina has fallen into the power of the brigand chief, Massaroni, and thus are all my hopes crushed, and all the plans I had formed are frustrated."

"It is an unfortunate affair, my lord," said Giachomo, "and I can duly appreciate your feelings ; but probably she will be again shortly rescued, and——"

"No, no," interrupted Alberti, "I cannot entertain such a hope while I lie helpless and inactive here. I must instantly arise, and adopt some means to defeat Massaroni, and force the Signora Melina from his power. Shall I allow him to triumph thus ?"

"What headstrong folly is this, Count Alberti ?" said the Prince Bianchi, impatiently, "are you bent to rush upon your own destruction ?"

"Anything," answered the young nobleman "rather than wait here the issue of events."

"My lord," interposed Signor Giachomo, "you will excuse me, but I cannot help observing, that this is sheer madness, in the delicate state of your health at present. Everything depends upon your keeping yourself as calm and quiet as possible ; if you do not do so, I cannot be answerable for the consequences."

"Oh, how easy is it for you to talk thus!" remarked the count. "Calm and quiet for a man placed in the trying and excitable circumstances that I am ? It is impossible; you might as well talk to the idle winds."

"I am responsible for anything that may happen to your lordship while I have the honour to be in attendance upon you," said the doctor ; "and I should not be performing my duty did I not at once peremptorily prohibit you from leaving your couch, which in all probability would be attended with immediate death."

"D——n !" cried Alberti, passionately, "what human patience can endure this ?"

"Had you not so frequently excited yourself beyond the bounds of reason, my lord," said Giachomo, "you would most likely have been restored to convalescence ere this; and I again assure you that while you persist in rejecting my advice, there is not the least chance of your recovery."

The agitation of the count became so violent that he could not speak; he threw himself back on his pillow quite exhausted, and groaned aloud. The Prince Bianchi, as may be expected, felt equally as much excited as himself, but he stifled his feelings as well as he could, and rising from his seat, and addressing the doctor, he said,—

"To your care, Signor Giachomo, I leave his lordship, and I need not, I am sure, suggest to you in what manner to act towards him."

Signor Giachomo bowed, and Bianchi quitted the room without the Count Alberti being aware of his departure.

The prince lost no time in dispatching some more troops to the assistance of their comrades; though it was with a sad and hopeless heart that he did so, for he could not but imagine that Massaroni had succeeded in conveying Melina in safety to his retreat, and if so, all his efforts to recover her would be in vain.

When the prince was alone, he gave way to all those feelings of agony, despair and apprehension, which were naturally excited in his breast at the painful and stirring misfortunes that had followed each other in such rapid succession; and many were the curses that he lavished upon the hard destiny which seemed to pursue him, though he could not in his conscience but acknowledge that he was deserving of all the troubles and annoyances he met with. He found it impossible to banish from his mind the impression which the supposed appearance of the spectre of Valentia to him had made upon it, and the longer he reflected upon it, the more it appalled his soul with horror. Then his unexpected meeting with Fransisco; the dreadful tale he had recapitulated to him, and the threats he had held out to him, and which he had no doubt he would put into execution, if he did not at all times comply with his extortionate and insolent demands, filled him with consternation and dismay. Would that he only knew the place where he concealed himself, that he might take him by surprise, secure him, and thus rid himself of one whom he had so much reason to dread; but there was no chance of that, at present at any rate, and in the meantime what might not be the mischief he might work him? His conscience bitterly reproached him for the cruel manner in which he had acted towards the unfortunate Florentia, and he felt severely how richly he merited the retribution that was now so rapidly overtaking him, and which seemed likely ultimately to overwhelm him.

"I have been a villain of the blackest dye," he muttered to himself, in a voice of the most extreme agitation, "and I am justly punished.

Florentio, Zitella, Valentia—the monstrous wrongs I inflicted on ye all could only have been suggested by the most abandoned and guilty mind. And what atonement is it in my power now to make, if even I had the will? Florentia and Valentia have long since mouldered to dust in their silent and premature graves; but Zitella and her daughter still exist; and it is in my power to convince them and the world of my sincere repentance by making them all the reparation I can for the injuries I have inflicted on them, and the many miseries to which I have subjected them. But no, my proud and obstinate spirit will not allow me to submit, and I shrink appalled from the very idea of encountering their reproaches. But now, to fill the measure of my despair and anguish to the very brim, my niece, Melina, is taken from me, and by the very man whom I have the most cause to detest. She will be restored to the arms of the beggar Clairville, who, no doubt, will find no great difficulty in persuading her to yield to his ambitious wishes, and thus all my plans will be frustrated, and I shall be laughed at, upbraided, and despised. That idea of itself is sufficient to distract my brain."

He pressed his hands upon his burning and aching temples, and traversed the apartment, wrapped in the most bewildering thought. He was suddenly aroused by hearing a knock at the door, and a servant immediately afterwards entered.

"What is the meaning of this intrusion?" demanded Bianchi, sternly.

"Signor Giachomo requests the attendance of your highness immediately in the chamber of the Count Alberti," answered the servant; "his lordship is taken much worse, and the signor is fearful that he is dying."

"Dying!" repeated the Prince Bianchi, looking at the servant incredulously; "what fresh troubles are in store for me? When will these vexations and annoyances have an end? Away, sirrah—I will attend directly."

The servant made his exit, and again for a short time after he was gone the Prince Bianchi was compelled to pace his apartment, and to meditate within himself, ere he could become sufficiently composed to visit the young nobleman.

"Headstrong, misguided youth," he said, "I fear that your career, owing to the violence of your passions, is doomed to be but a short one upon this earth; and this last shock—But why should I condemn Alberti for his weakness more than myself? Have I not been equally as imprudent and guilty as himself? Can I look back upon my past life without reproach? Have my deeds at all times been so pure and immaculate? Florentia, Zitella, and Valentia—But, pshaw! let me not encourage such useless and torturing thoughts! Rather let me put the boldest determination I can upon the matter; for it is only by so doing that I can hope or expect to overcome the difficulties by which I am at present surrounded, and to come unscathed out of the trials to which my courage and integrity are put. I must see the Count Alberti immediately."

With these words, the Prince Bianchi, assuming all the composure he possibly could, hastily quitted his apartment, and repaired to the chamber of Alberti. A solemn stillness reigned within it on his entrance; Signor Giachomo was seated by the bedside, the Count was stretched inanimate upon it, and one of the window curtains only being half withdrawn, the partial light that fell upon his features, gave such a sickly and ghastly hue to them, that Bianchi started back a few paces on beholding them, thinking he was a corpse; but Giachomo beckoned him forward, and in a whisper, observed——

"He still lives, your highness, though he is at present unconscious, and I entertain the most serious apprehensions as to the result."

"Good God!" ejaculated Bianchi, still more shocked as he gazed upon him, "what can be the cause of this sudden and awful change?"

"Why, your highness," replied the doctor, "soon after you quitted the chamber, his excitement reached to a pitch which I found it impossible to control: in fact, it amounted to perfect delirium. He raved wildly of your fair niece—declared that all near him were his bitterest enemies; and had it not been for the aid of two or three of your lordship's domestics, he could not have been detained in bed; and, alas! I grieve to have to add that, in the extraordinary exertions he made, straining every muscle, so much weakened by his long illness, he ruptured a blood-vessel, and——"

"Ruptured a blood-vessel?" interrupted the prince.

"It is too true, your highness," answered Giachomo.

"Unfortunate man!" ejaculated Bianchi; "then I fear there are now but little hopes of his recovery."

Signor Giachomo shook his head.

"It will require the greatest skill, care, and attention to effect it," he observed, after a pause. "He has, certainly, youth on his side; and if he should remain for awhile in his present state of unconsciousness and quiet, it may be productive of the most happy results."

The prince fixed one more earnest look upon the ghastly countenance of Alberti, and then, arising from his seat, he paced the room for a few moments in a state of the greatest disorder.

"What an unfortunate affair is this," he said at last, turning to Giachomo, and his countenance fully showing the agony of his mind; "and to occur at such a time, too. All our troubles seem to come at once: my brain is bewildered and distracted."

"Pardon me, your highness," observed the doctor, "but you must not give way to these powerful feelings of emotion, or I will not be answerable what the consequences may also be to yourself. The Count Alberti is certainly in a most dangerous state—it would be folly to attempt to deny that; but still, as I before said, I will exercise all the abilities I possess, and I trust, as he has youth on his side, they will not fail."

"Thanks, my good signor," said Bianchi: "I place the most implicit confidence in you, for I well know the skill you possess."

"Your lordship flatters me," returned Giachomo, who was not without his full share of vanity, like all human beings; "but still you may depend on me. I will do my best; and if I do not succeed according to my wishes, it shall be from no want of exertion on my part; I can assure you".

"Enough," said the prince: "I am satisfied, and will now leave you. Poor Alberti! Of course, I need not desire you, Signor Giachomo, to let me know immediately, should any unfavourable or more alarming change take place?"

"Certainly, your highness," replied the doctor; and Bianchi, having once more gazed with commiseration upon the pale and inanimate countenance of the unfortunate Count Alberti, retired from the room, to indulge in the gloomy and painful thoughts which oppressed his mind alone. But he did not return to his own room, but quitted the house, and wandered, wrapped in silent meditation, among the romantic scenery by which he was surrounded, thinking that the fresh air might serve more than anything to revive him; for his brain was heated and oppressed, and a burning fever, from the powerful excitement of his feelings, seemed to scorch his brain.

It was a beautiful Italian day; not a cloud obscured the horizon; the sun shone forth with all his full meridian splendour, and the air was light, balmy, and refreshing. It was the loveliness of the season that induced the prince to extend his walk, almost unconsciously, much farther than he had intended; and when at last he aroused himself, and looked up, he found to his surprise that he had rambled to some distance from the city, and was now in a wild and rather mountainous part of the country, with no signs of a human habitation near him.

"How foolish of me to wander to such a place as this," he said; "but still, its gloomy character well accords with the present aspect of my mind. Unfortunate Alberti! The present accident must, I fear, prove fatal to him, and——"

He paused, for at that moment the voice of a man, singing a song in tones rather more rollicksome than harmonious, saluted his ears,

...d he started with astonishment and some ...egree of alarm.

What is the use of sadness or sorrow?
Tira la lara; tira la lara!
Though to-day it is gloomy, 'twill bright be to-
morrow,
Tira la lara; tira la lara!
Can man expect to have nothing but gladness?
Tira la lara; tira la lara!
We must travel the road, though 'tis darken'd
by sadness,
Tira la lara; tira la lara!"

Such were some of the words of the song with which the man was amusing himself, and Bianchi looked eagerly towards the spot from which the sounds proceeded, with the hope of discovering the character of the unknown minstrel; nor was he long kept in suspense, for presently the tall figure of a man, fashionably dressed, appeared in sight, and advanced towards him.

The stranger had not advanced near enough for him to distinguish his features, but it struck Bianchi that he had seen his form before, and the man having seen him, appeared to recognise him in a moment, and hastened his steps towards him. The astonishment, confusion, and alarm of the prince may be readily imagined, when, as he approached nearer, he recognised the features of the man whom, of all others, he the least wished or expected to see — Fransisco Malietevera, though he was so completely metamorphosed from what he had been only a few hours before, that it was almost impossible to know him. Bianchi, somewhat recovering from his surprise, was about to fly from the spot, but Fransisco called peremptorily upon him to stop, and in a moment or two afterwards came up with him.

"What, my lord," he said, in tones of sarcastic familiarity, "would you thus shy an old acquaintance?—Nay, this is most uncivil of you, indeed it is."

"Fransisco!" ejaculated Bianchi, in a faint voice.

"Ay, Fransisco Malietevera," replied the latter, "though somewhat changed in personal appearance since you saw him this morning. You see I have lost no time in putting the money you advanced me on account to a good purpose. How like you this new dress?— You perceive it is one of the first style of fashion, and I think it becomes me remarkably."

"Hold this raillery, man," said the indignant Bianchi; "what brings you here?"

"Why," answered Fransisco, "mere accident, nothing more; I was rambling I scarcely knew whither; but since I have met with you, it affords me the most infinite pleasure."

"Leave me," said Bianchi, sternly.

"Nay, nay, not so soon, my lord," replied his companion; "I must have a few more words with you."

"With me?"

"Yes."

"I am in no humour to hold conversation with you: begone."

"Not till I have arranged my business with your highness," returned Fransisco, with the most provoking coolness.

"What would you?" demanded Bianchi.

"Money," answered Fransisco.

"Money, daring scoundrel?"

"Come, come, old man," said Fransisco, fixing upon the Prince Bianchi a look that made him quail, "be a little more choice in your language when you are addressing your equal, or you may have bitter cause to repent it. You forget yourself, Prince Bianchi; it is you who are the scoundrel, the hoary-headed villain; the miscreant, the murderer, the—"

"How?—dare you?"

"Dare I!" retorted Fransisco, with a look of contempt, "when I address such a thing as you?—Bah!—it is only pity for your infirmities that prevents me from taking that revenge which your monstrous injuries towards myself, my poor sister, and my aged parent, would justify; and because I see that you are racked in conscience, which will prove a greater punishment to you than any vengeance I could take. You have dared to call me scoundrel, villain, miscreant; but if I have even now become all these, who has made me so?—You, who, by your brutality and injustice, have made me lose all self respect. But, at any rate, I have you now in my power, and I will not fail to avail myself of the opportunity that is afforded me to take advantage of you. I will wring your heart to madness! I——"

"Oh, forbear! forbear! fearful man!" said the wretched Prince Bianchi, terrified by his observations, and the threats which he held out.

"Well, well," replied Fransisco, with a triumphant smile, "I have no wish to persist in such language for the present, neither should I have adopted it, if you had not compelled me to do so; in fact, it would, perhaps, be as well for us to be on rather amicable terms just now; and therefore it is that I act with that forbearance towards you, which, I am sure, in your reasonable moments, you must duly approve and appreciate."

"Again I ask you, what it is you demand?" said Bianchi.

"And once more I inform you, that it is simply, money," returned Fransisco.

"Give you money?" said the prince; "why, it is only a few hours since you extorted from me one hundred ducats!"

"Very true; but a great portion of that has been exhausted in the embellishment of my person, which you must be ready to admit, I think, much needed it," replied Fransisco, in the most ironical tones; "and as that outlay has considerably reduced my funds, and I have a wish to act up to the character which my present appearance conveys, I must request you to accommodate me with the instalment of another hundred ducats."

"Confusion!" cried Bianchi, "am I to be thus braved?—Wretch!—know you not that one word of mine would consign you to a prison?"

"Fool!" answered Fransisco, drawing a poniard from his breast; "and know you not that ere you could give utterance to that word, I could consign *you* to death?"

The Prince Bianchi trembled, and turned pale, for he saw that he had a desperate and determined man to deal with, and it would be to no purpose his opposing him, especially situated as he at present was; he, therefore, conquered his feelings of indignation as well as he possibly could, and addressing Fransisco in more subdued accents, he said—

"It is folly for us to hold altercation in this manner; since fate has thus unfortunately connected us with each other, let us endeavour to come to some amicable arrangement."

"Ah!" answered Fransisco, with a triumphant grin, "there your highness does, indeed, speak a little reasonable. You must feel convinced upon more serious reflection, that it would not be altogether convenient for you and me to quarrel with each other; and to make use of an old English adage, which I have frequently heard, 'Short reckonings make the longest friends;' so a hundred more ducats, and I will not trouble you again till——"

"Till what?" hastily demanded Bianchi.

"Not until they are nearly exhausted," replied Fransisco, laughing; "and, in good truth, I do not know how soon that may be, for, do you know, that I have made up my mind, since I have been so fortunate in meeting with you, and this metamorphose in my personal appearance, to follow the genuine pursuits of a gentleman: dice, women, cards, wine, and all the etceteras; you understand me, excellenza, eh?"

The Prince Bianchi could scarcely confine his rage within the bounds of reason at the consummate coolness and impudence of the man before him; but Fransisco folded his arms across his chest, and fixed upon him at the same time a look of the most bitter irony and malignant triumph, and was evidently gratified at the mental torture he was inflicting upon the wretched and guilty nobleman.

"As these little and necessary enjoyments," he added, after a brief pause, "will, of course, render a moderate supply of cash absolutely requisite, and as your coffers, I know, are amply filled, an occasional draw upon them cannot, I presume, put you to any serious inconvenience."

"Good God!" cried the excited Prince Bianchi, "surely, this is not to be borne; am I to be thus made the victim of a convicted thief and extortioner?"

"Beware, Prince Bianchi," said Fransisco, seriously, and once more pointing his dagger to his breast—"beware what you say, lest you try my temper too far, and arouse all the demon feelings of revenge within my breast. It is madness, I tell you again, for you to seek to resist my demands; experience has given me more than common power over my fellow creatures, wretched outcast and wanderer though I have been; I play a desperate game; it is one of life or death, knowing that I am hunted to the death, and it is dangerous, therefore, to exasperate me, especially you who have been the cause of all my miseries and my degradation; therefore, if you value yourself, and all who are in any way connected with you, you will at once quietly yield to my demands. One hundred ducats more, and I am gone."

"What if I have not the money about me?" demanded the terrified Bianchi.

"Why," answered Fransisco, with the utmost degree of coolness, "then I must e'en walk with you to the Villa Rosa, where you can, of course, immediately obtain it."

"What!" said the prince; "would you dare do that? where I could at once have you secured, and——"

"Idiot!" interrupted Fransisco, with an ironical and triumphant laugh; "and think you that I would be entrapped ere my dagger's point had pierced your guilty heart? You might consign me to the hands, to the tender mercies of your myrmidons; but ere a hand could be stretched forth to save you, your own life should pay the forfeit of your treachery. Lead on to the villa, and see whether or not I am prepared to keep my word."

The Prince Bianchi stared at him for a minute or two completely appalled, and knew not what to answer. He saw plainly, however, that Fransisco was not to be trifled with; that he was a man fully competent to perform all he threatened, and, therefore, he again felt the policy, however aggravating and degrading it might be to his feelings, to comply with his demands, anxious, too, as he was to rid himself of his presence.

"Fransisco," he remarked, after a brief pause, "I acknowledge I have wronged you, but many—many years have elapsed since then. I have truly repented, and am willing to make you all the compensation in my power."

"Compensation!" replied Fransisco, with a look of the most superlative hatred and contempt. "Oh, it is a mild word, a marvellously plausible and pretty word; one that suits the fornicating hypocrite to make use of when danger threatens him, and terror seizes upon his guilty soul. But you are much mistaken, Prince Bianchi, if you imagine that I am to be deceived or cajoled by it. Compensation!—Bah! What!—compensate me for a father and a sister murdered? What can compensate me for years of slavery and degradation, brought about by your accursed means? You tremble and turn pale; well you may—it

FRANSISCO MALIETEVERA EXTORTS MONEY FROM THE PRINCE BIANCHI.

is your black and guilty conscience that upbraids you. You know I speak the truth, for it is he who, by right, is the Count Malietevera, the brother of Florentia, who addresses you, and the mere presence of whom should strike you dead. Compensation!—Oh, bitter mockery added to injuries unparalleled!"

"Fransisco," remarked Bianchi, in subdued accents, "it is useless to talk in this manner; I am ready to admit that all you have accused me of is unfortunately too true—would to Heaven that I could recall the past; but as far as lies within my power, as I before observed, I am willing to make you compensation; for instance, were I to give you a sufficient sum of money to keep you in respectability and independence for the rest of your days, would you retire to some distant part of the country and never trouble me again?"

"No," answered Fransisco, with another malicious and triumphant grin; "for your injustice has made me and respectability henceforth strangers; and however large the sum of money I might receive, my only study would be to squander it away as fast as I possibly could in dissipation, in order that I might drown thought. Besides, the principal gratification to my revenge will be in appearing before you, as I do at present, at times and seasons when you least expect to see me, to remind you of your crimes, and to exult over your misery."

The Prince Bianchi groaned in the intense agony of his feelings, and for a few moments covered his face with his hands to shut out the reproachful and vindictive glances of Fransisco; but at length, once more venturing to raise his head, he said—

"What, then, am I to do? How can I come to terms with you?"

"In no other way than that which I have proposed," replied Fransisco; "one hundred more ducats, and then, for the present, I leave you."

The prince drew forth another purse and placed it in his hands, at the same time observing in a faint voice—

"There—there is your demand, and more to it; now leave me, and let me not be again annoyed with you for some time to come."

"I take the ducats," replied his tormentor, "as another instalment of the unlimited debt you owe me; but as for the time when you may see me again, as I am a man of my word, I never make any hasty promises. However, you take the wisest means, my lord, of securing my silence and saving your own credit, and I cannot but compliment you on the wise determination you have arrived at. No doubt we shall perfectly understand each other by and by. What a singular thing that we should meet again to-day, and at the very moment when I so much needed the replenishing of my purse! Oh, my lord, I will make good use of the various sums of money it is my intention from time to time to extort from you; I will take you, in your youthful days, as my pattern; there is not a scene of gaiety and reckless dissipation into which I will not enter with a proper spirit, and such as shall gain me the applause and admiration of all accomplished libertines and debauchees. Cospetto! but I will have a merry life of it; for what is the

use of men muddling their brains, and wasting their time over the idle dogmas of straight-haired novelists, and canting philosophers? Life is a road of ups and downs which we must travel over in the best way we can — what say you, your highness?

"What is the use of sadness or soorrw?
  Tira la lara! tira la lara!
Though to-day it is gloomy, 'twill bright be to-morrow,
  Tira la lara! tira la lara!
Can man expect to have nothing but gladness?
  Tira la lara! tira la lara!
We must travel the road, though it be darken'd by sorrow,
  Tira la lara! tira la lara!"

You see, my lord, that I am fully prepared to enter with becoming spirit into the scenes in which you so eminently distinguished yourself when a young man, and, I dare say, when we meet again, I shall be able to render you a good account of my proceedings; never mind about innocence destroyed, or broken-hearted parents, they all serve to make up the round of amusements of a man of fashion, eh, your highness?"

"Demon of hell!" cried the Prince Bianchi, hoarsely, "sent here to torture me! I will no longer listen to your brutal taunts. Begone!"

"Ha! ha! ha!" laughed Fransisco triumphantly; "my observations do not seem to agree with you, Prince Bianchi; well, I am sorry for it, and hope they will be more in unison with your feelings the next time we meet, which I promise you faithfully shall be before many days have elapsed, for my cash, no doubt, will soon be exhausted, and I shall need a fresh supply. It is very convenient, too, to have such a banker as yourself. Ha! ha! ha!—One thing, however, I must take the liberty of intimating to you before I leave you."

"And what is that, tormenter?" demanded the Prince Bianchi, eagerly, and with a look of terror.

"Why, merely that I have the means of entering into your presence, in the villa, unperceived, and at any time I think proper," answered Fransisco.

"You—you!"

"Yes, I, I," returned his companion; "you seem to doubt my word, my lord, but you shall soon be convinced of the truth of what I state if at any time I should find any difficulty in meeting with you at the time I want you."

"You will not venture there?"

"You will not dare to try me."

"And where do you at present reside?"

"Everywhere and nowhere," laughed Fransisco. "Oh, no doubt, my lord, you would like to know the place of my concealment, that you might pounce upon me with your myrmidons and secure me in your power; but if such are the hopes you entertain, you will be doomed to be disappointed, and I would advise you, if you value your own life, not to make the attempt.'

" Mysterious, fearful man, how can I understand you ?"

" Methinks I have taken great pains to make you understand me," replied Fransisco; " it is no fault of mine if you still remain dull of comprehension. But it seems that our interview has already been prolonged to a greater extent than is agreeable to your lordship, and, thanking you for all favours, I will take my departure."

" Stay!" said Bianchi; " one word with you."

" What is it, your highness?"

" You will not reveal any of the facts you have mentioned to me to any person?" said the prince.

" Not while your lordship keeps faith with me," answered Fransisco; " or till it suits my purpose to do so."

" Ah! suits your purpose to do so! What mean you by that?"

" No matter; it does not please me to explain at present," returned Fransisco; " but this you may depend upon, that the least symptoms you evince of acting treacherously towards me, or of forfeiting your word, shall be the signal for your disgrace and destruction. Bear these remarks in mind, Prince Bianchi, and rest assured that they are no idle threats, but emanating from one who has not only the will but the power to put them into execution, if he should be aggravated to do so. I wish you adieu, excellenza, and pleasant reflections to you; I go to enjoy myself with the few odd ducats you have given me in part payment. Tira la lara! tira la lara! tira la lara! lara la, la!"

And thus singing and dancing, the now abandoned Fransisco Malietevera took his departure, leaving the Prince Bianchi, as may be expected, in a state of the utmost confusion and consternation.

It was some time ere he could at all recover his composure, and when he did do so in some measure, he looked around him vacantly, scarcely conscious for the time being of what had taken place; but soon the whole of the observations of Fransisco darted upon his recollection with overwhelming force, and in a voice of the deepest emotion he exclaimed:—

" A fresh enemy has sprung up where I least expected to find one, and one of the most implacable character, and which I know not how to deal with. How I tremble at his threats! I know not in what way to escape from him. It seems impossible. And yet I must acknowledge the justice of the revenge with which he pursues me. The wrongs I have

heaped upon his head, and those of the other members of his family, are monstrous, and it is in vain that I seek to find any excuse for myself. Oh! I have been a villain of the blackest dye! But to be thus held in constant terror by one whom I have so much cause to dread, and who sets my power and authority at defiance, and can at any time denounce me to the world!—that conviction of itself is enough to hurl my reason from its seat, and to plunge me into the darkest despair. Could I but secure him! Ah! the apparent impossibility of doing that is what tortures me more than all. My punishment has come upon me all at once, and nothing but despair and misery stare me in the face. Oh! who would be guilty if they could perceive the retribution, the terrible retribution, which must ultimately overtake them? And he asserted that he can enter my presence at any time he thinks proper! Massaroni has proved that he can do so—how is this? It is evident that I must have traitors about me, and that I am not safe from the knife of the secret assassin a moment. How terrible is it to live in this constant state of fear; but such is the penalty that guilt imposes upon itself. Were I even to fly from my present place of residence—but that is impossible while I remain Governor of Rome —my enemies would pursue me, and still, doubtless, from the powerful means which they seem to have at their command, would contrive to obtain access to me, and to gratify their feelings of revenge against me. I see no chance of escaping from the fate which seems to be inevitably impending o'er my head. But why do I remain here? Let me away, and endeavour to compose my thoughts."

He once more looked around him, almost fearful that some fresh danger threatened him; and then, with disordered steps, and a mind, the state of which we need not attempt to describe, he retraced his way to the villa, where, on arriving, he despatched a servant to Signor Giachomo to ascertain the condition of Alberti. He quickly returned and informed his master that the count remained in the same unconscious state as when he had seen him, and with an intimation that the Signor Giachomo would wait upon him in a few minutes, if it were his pleasure. Bianchi sent word that he should be glad to see him as soon as it was convenient, for he was most anxious to ascertain from his own lips the actual condition of Alberti, which his fears assured him was of the most dangerous description. In a very few minutes afterwards the doctor entered the room, and Bianchi could perceive from his countenance, that he had intelligence of the most unpleasant and unfavourable character to communicate.

" Well, signor," said Bianchi, on his entrance, " you state in your message to me that the unfortunate Count Alberti remains in the same state of lethargy as when I last saw him?"

"He does, your highness," answered Signor Giachomo; "he has never for an instant revived to consciousness."

"And are you of opinion that that is any favourable sign?" asked Bianchi.

"I was so at first, my lord," answered the doctor; "but from its long continuance, I am inclined to think differently now. Should he revive to sensibility, I would advise your highness to urge upon him to settle his earthly affairs, for there is no knowing what fatal consequences even an hour or two might produce."

"Ah!" ejaculated Bianchi, starting from his seat in a state of the greatest agitation, "has it then come to this? But you surely cannot mean what you say, signor?"

"I have expressed my firm conviction, my lord," answered Giachomo, "though I most sincerely hope that it may prove to be erroneous."

"Unfortunate Alberti!" exclaimed the prince, his agitation increasing to an almost insupportable degree, "and must you thus be cut off in the prime of life, and with so many splendid prospects before you? Oh, this is indeed hard; and Massaroni has been the cause of all this;—may my heaviest curses light upon him."

"Pardon me, your highness," said Giachomo, "but suffer not such thoughts at these to agitate you thus; now is the time that you require all the exertion of your greatest energy and fortitude."

"Energy and fortitude!" returned the prince, impatiently. "Oh, how ridiculous and vain is it to talk thus to a man so beset and surrounded with difficulties and troubles as I am! Signor Giachomo, you know not half that I have upon my mind, or you would entertain very different thoughts from those which you seem to do at present."

"I wish not to pry into the private affairs of your highness," answered Giachomo; "though I am fully aware that you have lately had enough to vex and distress you."

"Vex and distress me!" repeated Bianchi; "say, rather, enough to drive me mad. And now the loss of my niece, the perilous situation of the Count Alberti, and other matters of similar importance, press heavily upon my mind, and are almost too much for my fortitude to endure."

"Struggle against it, my lord," said Signor Giachomo, "for your own sake and all that is dear to you. Should you be confined to your bed, which is not at all unlikely if you give way to this anxiety of mind, what might not be the consequences?"

"I know the force of all that you say, signor, well," returned Bianchi; "but do you think that I am more than man that I can bear all these accumulated misfortunes and disappointments without a murmur?"

"No, your highness," replied the doctor, "I do not expect anything of the kind; but you must admit the necessity there is for your exerting yourself to the utmost to conquer your feelings as much as possible."

"True, true, Giachomo," coincided the prince, "I acknowledge the truth of your observations, and take the advice that you are pleased to give me in the same spirit in which it is meant; but your unfortunate patient—how deeply do I feel for his melancholy situation; I am greatly afraid that I was much to blame in communicating the news of the loss of Melina too abruptly."

"Well, perhaps it would have been better had the painful fact been imparted to him by degrees," returned Giachomo; "but his anxiety and impatience would have been sure to have discovered it."

"The daring scoundrel, Massaroni," observed the prince, his countenance flushed with indignation; "the implacable spirit of revenge he entertains towards myself and the Count Alberti has been the cause of all these calamities; why should he otherwise so interest himself in the fate of my niece and Florio Clairville, the serpent whom I harboured in my breast to sting me?"

"The determination with which the brigand chief has ever pursued his designs against your lordship, is certainly most extraordinary," remarked Giachomo; "he is a desperate man, and one whose enmity it is dangerous to encounter; but I trust that you will yet be able to defeat him."

"By the mass!" exclaimed Bianchi, "I will leave no means untried to do so; and should I ever be fortunate enough to get him in my power, I will have such a terrible revenge that shall gratify me for the many injuries I have received from him. But you must not remain longer away from your patient, Signor Giachomo, in the dangerous situation in which he is placed; I will accompany you to his chamber, and——"

"No, my lord," interrupted the doctor, "you had better not do so; your presence there can do no possible good; and should the count be restored to consciousness, the sight of you might excite him to such a degree as would probably be attended with immediate and fatal consequences."

"Well—well," answered Bianchi, "I will take your advice, confident that you will do your best to restore him, and will give me immediate notice if any unfavourable change should take place."

"Your highness may depend upon that," replied Giachomo; and bowing to the prince, he left him to his own reflections.

CHAPTER LI.

THE ESCAPE OF MELINA BY THE MEANS OF MASSARONI.—THE DESPERATE COMBAT BETWEEN THE BRIGANDS AND THE TROOPS. —DEFEAT OF THE LATTER.—OUR HEROINE ESCORTED TO THE MOUNTAIN RETREAT. —THE MEETING BETWEEN HER AND CLAIRVILLE.

WE must now return to the Signora Melina and her faithful Floretta at the Villa Civetti. We left them in a state of great excitement in consequence of the capture of Guiseppe, and the probable consequences that were likely to result from it, Rubalde having escaped, and who no doubt would lose no time in apprising Massaroni of what had happened, in which event the brigands would be sure to make an immediate attack upon the villa, and unless assistance arrived in time from the Prince Bianchi, (which seemed very doubtful, if not impossible,) their success was certain.

As hour after hour wore away, the anxiety and impatience of our heroine increased, and the prospect of her deliverance from the revolting fate with which she had been so long threatened, and the unfeeling and inexorable conduct of her uncle towards her, entirely conquered those delicate scruples she had previously entertained as to the means by which that deliverance might be effected. The arguments of Floretta had also tended in a great measure to bring about this change in her mind.

"I do believe that Massaroni is sincere and honourable in his intentions," observed Melina, "and that he is entirely prompted to act as he has done towards me, by the friendship he entertains for Florio, his abhorrence of the tyrannical and unnatural manner in which my uncle has persecuted me, and the feeling of hatred he bears towards the guilty Count Alberti. Why, then, should I hesitate to accept of his voluntary and generous aid, since I can expect no mercy from my haughty relative, but who, on the contrary, can so far forget the solemn promise he made to my poor mother on her death-bed, as to resolve to sacrifice me to one, the very mention of whose name fills my bosom with horror and disgust? No, I will be firm and resolute, and trust to providence for the result."

"Well spoken, my dear signora," said Floretta; "it glads me much to see you at last come to so reasonable a determination. The brigand chief is all that you have represented him to be, depend upon it; and under his protection and that of the Signor Clairville, you will be perfectly safe from all harm."

"Dear Florio!" ejaculated our heroine, with much emotion, "and shall I indeed behold you again? Oh, what a meeting will be ours, after the long and painful separation we have had to endure! But, alas! can we ever hope to be united? Will my misguided uncle relent, when he finds that I am delivered from his power, and waiving the disparity of our rank and fortune, make some atonement for the misery he has caused us, by giving his consent to our nuptials? Oh, what transport does that idea convey to my breast! But I can scarcely dare to hope that it will be realised."

"It will, signora, depend upon it," returned her companion; "the prince, your uncle, when he finds himself foiled in his designs by your escape from his power, will only be too ready to bring about a reconciliation, and will render you happy by bestowing your hand upon that man who is so worthy of you, and to whom your heart is so fondly attached."

"But the Count Alberti?" said Melina.

"Oh, what have you to fear from him, signora?" replied Floretta; "however great his rage and disappointment, which it is sure to be, he must submit to the will of the Prince Bianchi."

"But should my uncle receive immediate intelligence of what has happened, which he is sure to do," remarked her mistress, "he will dispatch troops here without delay, and have me conveyed to some other place of security."

"The Villa Rosa, you are aware, is a considerable distance from this place," replied Floretta, "and ere he can receive intelligence, and forward troops hither, Massaroni and his bold band will have accomplished their object; for they are probably secreted not far from the neighbourhood. For my own part, I look for an attack upon the villa every hour. But there is one thing I wish to ask you, my dear lady."

"And what is that, Floretta?"

"The manuscript of Valentia?"

"Ah!" said our heroine, "I must take good care to secure that important but melancholy document. There is no knowing what extraordinary results it may be productive of."

"True, signora," remarked Floretta; "but should you be taken under the protection of Massoroni, is it your intention to make him acquainted with it?"

"Why," answered Melina, after a moment's hesitation, "I scarcely know; the strange resemblance which the features of the brigand chief bear to those of the portrait at the Villa Rosa, and the singular facts recorded in Valentia's narrative, lead me to suspect that Massaroni is no other than that unfortunate woman's son."

"Very true, signora," coincided Floretta; "and the history of Massaroni himself, from all that we have heard of it, goes far to corroborate that opinion."

"Should he indeed prove to be the son of the Prince Bianchi," said our heroine, "there might be danger in communicating that fact to him: his feelings of revenge might be aroused, and I tremble to think what the consequences might be to my uncle."

"Oh, signora," said Floretta, "surely you cannot suppose that Massaroni, if he discovered that the Prince Bianchi were his father, could be so unnatural as to seek to avenge himself upon him ?"

"I know not," answered Melina; "he would have little cause to entertain any feelings of respect or forbearance towards him, and the recollection of his mother's wrongs might goad him on to do that which in his more sober moments his heart would revolt from. Should the brigand succeed in rescuing me, I will first take the advice Clairville upon the subject."

"Ay, signora," said Floretta; "it would, indeed, perhaps be as well to do so."

Melina was about to make use of some observation, when she was prevented from doing so by the sudden entrance of Viola, who was still in a state of great excitement and alarm.

"Oh, signora," she ejaculated; "what will become of us ?"

"What is the matter, my good woman ?" demanded our heroine; "has anything else happened to alarm you ?"

"No, signora," answered Viola, "not yet, and I think there has been enough already. Not but I should be most happy to see you rescued from a fate that is so repugnant to your feelings, but then I wish it could be done by any other means than those which I anticipate."

"Do not alarm yourself, Viola," said Floretta, "for let what may take place, no harm can possibly come to you."

"I know not that," returned Viola; "these brigands, I have heard, are terrible fellows, and as myself and my parents are the servants of the Prince Bianchi, I fear they will show no mercy towards us."

"Massaroni never wages war against defenceless women," remarked Melina; "so you may make your mind perfectly easy on that point, Viola. But Guiseppe ?"

"Oh, he is in no danger, signora," replied Viola; "what a daring rascal he is, to be sure ! He completely laughs at the threats which are held out to him, and when he heard that Rubaldo had escaped, he expressed his utmost satisfaction, for he said that before many hours had elapsed Massaroni and his daring band would be at the villa, and would amply revenge himself for the attack which had been made upon his men. I shudder at the thought, and

would give anything if I were fairly out of the danger which threatens."

"Calm your apprehensions, Viola," said our heroine, "for they are groundless. But you say that a messenger was despatched to the Villa Rosa immediately after the capture of Guiseppe ?"

"Yes, signora," answered Viola; "but the distance is so great from here to the Villa Rosa, that Massaroni, I fear, will be enabled to accomplish his designs before any assistance can arrive. I wonder that his highness did not take the precaution to have this place better guarded; though, to be sure, it is a fortunate job for you, signora, that he did not, and I am glad of it."

"I thank you, Viola," said Melina, "for the good wishes you express towards me, and I hope that some time or other I may be able to reward you for the kindness you have evinced towards me since I have been confined here."

"As for my reward, signora, I do not seek it, and I only wish it had been in my power to do more for you. But when you have left this place, which I know you shortly will, perhaps you will sometimes bestow a thought upon the humble Viola ?"

"You may depend upon it, I will," replied our heroine; "and should you feel inclined to leave this solitary villa, I will take good care to make such arrangements as will enable you to do so."

"Oh, thank you, signora," said Viola, "I am sure that myself and my parents would be heartily glad to leave this place, where we pass such a dull and melancholy life. I wish we had never seen it. But I have known no other home from my childhood."

"And I fear that you have witnessed many strange and painful scenes in it," observed our heroine.

"Ah! signora, you may say that," returned Viola; "I am afraid to mention all that I have seen, and perhaps it is not my business to do so. I am afraid the prince, your uncle, has much to answer for."

Melina sighed, and returned no answer, but she was fully convinced of the truth of Viola's surmises, and she shuddered to think of the numerous crimes the Prince Bianchi had been guilty of.

"How many men are there in the villa ?" she inquired, after a pause.

"Why, not more than half a dozen, signora," replied Viola, "and what resistance could they make against the brigands? They are all in a dreadful state of alarm, and I verily believe are half inclined to take to flight, for they seem to consider, and very justly too, I think, that unless some assistance arrives from the Villa Rosa before the brigands make their attack, their destruction is inevitable."

"Should such be the case," observed Melina,

"it would be madness for them to offer any resistance, and Massaroni is not so sanguinary as to take their lives in cold blood."

"Do you think that, signora?" asked the timid Viola, eagerly, " and that myself and my parents are safe."

"I am confident of it, Viola," returned our heroine, "for I know the character of the brigand chief too well, to believe him capable of being guilty of so wanton and cruel an outrage."

"Thanks, dear signora; that assurance from your lips, has quieted my fears, and Massaroni and his bold band may come as soon as they like—the sooner the better. But I must leave you, and see what is going on down stairs. Keep up your spirits, lady, for I feel satisfied that before many hours have elapsed you will be restored to liberty, and I only hope that circumstance may have the effect of bringing the Prince Bianchi to a full sense of the cruelty and injustice with which he has acted towards you."

With these words Viola quitted the room, and left Melina and her faithful companion to themselves.

"Fortune smiles upon you, signora," said Floretta; "the hopes of Viola will be realised, I have no doubt; and before any assistance can arrive from the Villa Rosa, you will be safe under the protection of Massaroni, and on your way to the Signor Clairville."

"Blissful thought!" ejaculated her mistress; "that will more than reward me for the many months of misery to which I have been subjected. And should my misguided uncle be brought to relent, my happiness will be completed, and all the guilty hopes of the abandoned Count Alberti will be annihilated for ever."

"And, depend upon it, they will be so, signora," returned Floretta; "the Prince Bianchi will no longer remain obdurate when he finds you are released from his power—it would be madness for him to do so; and he will be happy to make you all the reparation he can, by sanctioning the union of yourself and Signor Clairville."

"God grant that your predictions may be verified," said our heroine; "my every hope will then be accomplished, and I can freely forgive my uncle for all the many wrongs he has inflicted on me. Oh, with what anxiety do I await the arrival of Massaroni! and I sincerely hope that it may be before any assistance arrives from the Villa Rosa, to save the effusion of blood that would otherwise take place."

Thus did our heroine and her faithful attendant continue to converse together, alternately between hope and fear; but the whole of the day passed away without anything occurring to realise their expectations, and when

night approached, and still all remained undisturbed, their anxiety and impatience naturally gained strength, and Melina, in particular, began to fear that some accident had befallen Rubaldo on the road to the retreat of the brigands, and that Massaroni being in consequence ignorant of what had happened, would not be able to reach the Villa Cevetti in time to rescue them.

The Signora Melina and her attendant had seated themselves by the window, it being a fine moonlight night, and for some time they watched anxiously in order to ascertain whether there was any prospect of approaching relief; but not the least signs of anything to gratify their hopes met their gaze; no human being appeared near the spot, and the heart of our heroine gradually sickened with despair and disappointment.

"Oh," she ejaculated, "it was madness for me to encourage for a moment the sanguine and futile hopes I did: Massaroni is unacquainted with what has taken place; by this time, doubtless, my uncle has received full intelligence of everything, and has adopted plans accordingly to remove me to some other place of security, and will lose no time in accomplishing his unnatural designs against me, and sealing my fate. How terrible is this state of constant doubt and suspense. But to be sacrificed to one whom I so thoroughly detest as the Count Alberti, is sufficient of itself to drive me to madness. God! God! must I be consigned to a fate so revolting? Must all my fond hopes thus be annihilated at one fell swoop, and all my prospects be overclouded in a manner that freezes the very blood within my veins to think of? Florio! Florio! we shall never meet again!—Something tells me that we shall not, and life becomes hateful to me in that dread conviction. Would to Heaven that I had breathed my last on the bosom of my dying mother, what years of misery, and perpetual anguish and disappointment of mind would it have spared me."

"My dear signora," remarked Floretta, "how does it torture my mind to behold you give way to this excessive grief. For your own sake, and that of him whom you so fondly love, and whose whole happiness depends upon your welfare, do endeavour to muster all the fortitude and confidence you can, and to look forward with the most sanguine expectations to the future. Providence is too good and merciful to permit one so amiable and innocent to fall a sacrifice to the cruel and inexorable feelings of that man who ought to be her protector, and to be even more studious of her happiness than his own. The brigand chief and his bold band will be here anon, depend upon it, and in time to save you from the revolting fate with which you are at present threatened. The Count Alberti, too, has probably not yet recovered from the effects of his wounds, and, therefore, it will be impossible for the Prince Bianchi to put his designs into execution, for the present, at any rate."

"But should fresh troops arrive from the Villa Rosa," remarked Melina, "I should doubtless be removed, with all possible expedition, to some other place of confinement, where it will be impossible for any one to discover me; and I shall be left to the mercy of my uncle, who will not fail to put his designs into operation at the earliest opportunity, and thus my future degradation and misery will be consummated past recall. Floretta, I fully appreciate the kindness of your motives, in thus encouraging me to hope differently, but I cannot close my eyes to the fate that seems to be inevitably awaiting me."

"What can I say?—how seek to banish from your mind those dismal forebodings, my beloved mistress?" said Floretta.

Melina returned no answer, for her thoughts were completely absorbed in the anguish of her own feelings, and she continued to gaze vacantly upon the wild and cheerless prospect that was commanded from the window at which she and her companion were seated.

Suddenly the bright face of the moon became obscured by dense and murky clouds, and all was now involved in complete darkness, adding still greater intensity to the melancholy feelings which held predominant sway in our heroine's breast. But she seemed to be rivetted to the spot, although the sombre aspect of all around was so well calculated to increase the anguish of her thoughts. The storm, of which this had been the harbinger, now burst forth with the utmost violence, and aroused the unfortunate damsel from the deep lethargy of painful meditation into which she had fallen; and soon the elemental strife that commenced so threateningly, became quite terrific to contemplate. Floretta drew the casement down, and placing her hand upon the arm of her mistress, she said—

"Come, my dear signora, this is indeed no fitting place for you in such a terrible season as this, and at such an hour. It is now near midnight, and it would be much better for you were you to seek your couch, and by a few hours' repose, to endeavour to compose the feelings and the apprehensions which at present beset your mind."

"Alas! my faithful Floretta," replied her mistress, "I feel assured that I can find no rest whilst left in this dreadful state of doubt and suspense. The most certain misery would be even preferable to this torturing anxiety. I had flattered myself with the hope that Massaroni would exert himself to save me from the horrible and disgusting fate which has so long

been impending o'er my head, but now I see too plainly how completely fallacious and delusive were all such ideas, and that he will not run any further risk to serve one who is entirely unconnected with him."

"Indeed, signora!" observed Floretta, "you wrong the brigand chief, by encouraging such ideas. He has pledged his word to release you from the power of your enemies; to see justice rendered you; and depend upon it he will not fail to do so. What can intimidate Allesandro Massaroni, especially when he has justice on his side, and the cause of woman is the stimulas? My word for it—he will be here anon, and before any force can be sent by the Prince Bianchi to oppose him. You may deem me sanguine, but, indeed, that which I predict emanates from my heart, and is prompted by reason. All is now still in the villa; the inmates have doubtless retired to their chambers, and, therefore, let me once more advise you to seek an hour or two's repose, which will enable you to meet with greater composure and fortitude, anything that may shortly take place to call your energies into action. I do not feel tired or inclined for sleep, and I will therefore remain up and on the watch, and give you timely notice should anything of a particular nature occur."

The Signora Melina still hesitated, and looked anxiously towards the window, but at length she said—

"Well, well, my good Floretta, I will be guided by your advice, for I know it springs from the best and purest of motives, though I much doubt in my present anxiety of mind whether I shall be able to compose myself to rest."

Supporting herself on the arm of her attendant, our heroine now retired to her chamber, where, having first invoked the mercy and protection of the Almighty, she stretched her limbs, without undressing, upon the couch, and notwitstanding her apprehensions to the contrary, fatigue of mind quickly overcame her, and she sunk off to sleep.

Floretta continued to watch by the side of her bed for some time, and to listen to the howling and raging of the tempest, which seemed to increase in violence every moment, but at length she was drawn once more, instinctively as it were, to the window, and there she gazed with mingled feelings of awe and anxiety upon the horrors of the night, and to which the death-like silence which prevailed throughout the house presented a remarkable and solemn contrast. The flashes of lightning that shot across the sky were frequent and most vivid; and suddenly, by their sickly glare, Floretta imagined that she could catch an outline of some indistinct and shadowy objects moving towards the villa. The lightning ceased to play for a few seconds, and all was again darkness and obscurity; but still did Floretta strain her eyes to their utmost extent, for she felt persuaded that she could not have been mistaken. Again the electric fluid assisted her observation, and now she was convinced that a number of individuals were advancing stealthily towards the house, and her heart palpitated violently against her side with hope and expectation. Nearer and nearer they came, and she was then enabled to distinguish, beyond a doubt, that they were the forms of men, and that there was also a con-

THE PRINCE BIANCHI AFTER BEHOLDING THE VISION.

siderable number of them. That they were not the troops of the Prince Bianchi, she felt satisfied from the cautious manner in which they approached, and she could, therefore, come to no other conclusion but that they were the brigands, and if so, their deliverance was at hand.

With eager eyes and a throbbing bosom, did Floretta continue to watch them, until they turned abruptly an angle of the building, and they were lost to her view. The next instant she heard a confused noise from below, followed by a loud crashing sound, as if proceeding from the battering in of doors; and

Melina, aroused from her sleep by the unusual disturbance, started from the bed, and rushing hastily towards Floretta, demanded, in a a tremulous voice, what was the matter.

"Be calm and firm, my dear signora," replied her domestic; "for I feel certain that the assistance we have been so anxiously looking for and anticipating, has arrived. A large body of men has arrived at the villa, and it is evident that they are now engaged in forcing an entrance. They must be the brigands."

"Good God!" said the agitated Melina, "can it be possible? Oh, how my heart palpitates! Should it, indeed, be Massaroni and his courageous band!—But hark!"

The men, whoever they were, had now evidently forced their way into the house, and the confusion which prevailed below became more intense. There was the shouting of numerous voices, mingled with oaths and execrations, and the clashing of swords, and the heart of our heroine sunk within her with terror and dismay, and she was compelled to cling breathlessly to the form of her faithful attendant for support. Another moment, and the room-door was burst violently open, and Viola, pale and trembling, and dreadfully excited, rushed in.

"They are here, signora!" she gasped forth; "the brigands! with Massaroni at their head!—Holy Virgin! what will become of us? —Three of the men, who were mad enough to oppose them, are already slain, and—but they come this way! Jesu Maria, protect us— I——"

Before the terrified woman could finish the sentence, the room was filled with armed men, and Melina, immediately on recognising our hero, overpowered by the tumult of feelings that crowded upon her brain, fainted.

"Fortune once more smiles upon the brigand chief," exclaimed Massaroni; "we triumph! Woman, you have nothing to fear; remain you here, and no harm shall come to you and your parents. Now, Prince Bianchi, and Count Alberti, will you any longer despise the threats of Allesandro Massaroni? But we waste time," he added, raising the insensible form of Melina in his arms; "there is not a single moment to be lost. Follow us, Floretta; your mistress is now secure from every danger and insult. This way, Rubaldo!"

As the brigand thus spoke, he rushed hastily from the room, bearing our heroine with him, and followed by his band; and Rubaldo taking the arm of Floretta, who was too confused and agitated to give utterance to a syllable, led her from the apartment.

They soon reached the open air, and having quickly traversed the grounds attached to the villa, they entered upon a wild and woody glade, where a carriage and several horses were in waiting, guarded by a number of the brigands. Massaroni handed our heroine and Floretta into the vehicle, and then mounting a horse by the side of Rubaldo, they were all soon departing at a rapid rate from the neighbourhood of the villa, heedless of the storm, which still raged with unabated violence.

"This is a night of triumph, Rubaldo," said Massaroni, as they proceeded; "thanks to the promptitude and expedition with which you acted. By the time that the morning's sun appears in the eastern horizon, the Signora Melina will be safe in our mountain retreat, and all the base and revolting designs of the Prince Bianchi and Count Alberti will be thwarted. Nothing could possibly have been managed better than this affair throughout."

"Very true, captain," coincided Rubaldo, "and how great will be the rage and disappointment of Bianchi and the count, when they discover that the Signora Melina is rescued from their power."

"Ay," said our hero, "this is a gratification to my revenge that I have long been most anxious for; justice, too, will now be rendered to Signor Clairville, Zitella, and all under my protection. But, cospetto! it is no pleasant thing to have to travel in such a tempest as this, and it does not seem as if it were likely to abate in a hurry. We must push on our way."

They increased their speed, and had soon got a considerable distance from the Villa Civetti. But the storm was now perfectly terrific, and the brigands were soon completely drenched to the skin, while their horses were so frightened by the repeated and awful flashes of lightning, that they had the greatest difficulty to control them.

The jolting of the vehicle over the rough road they were pursuing, and the loud voice of the tempest, at length aroused Melina to sensibility, and she looked up with feelings of amazement and bewilderment, and could scarcely for a moment or two bring her mind to conceive what had taken place.

"Gracious Heaven!" she exclaimed, after a brief pause; "what is the meaning of all this? Where am I? Ah! you here, my faithful Floretta? For the love of Heaven do not keep me in suspense, but explain to me what has happened."

"Compose yourself, signora," answered her domestic; "you are now surrounded by those who will protect you from all danger; you are now once more restored to liberty, and——"

"To liberty!" interrupted Melina, her brain still bewildered, and staring at her incredulously and confusedly.

"Yes, my dear signora," returned Floretta, "do you not remember that you were released from the Villa Civetti but a short time since, by Allesandro Massaroni, and that you are now on your way to the place of his retreat, where you will again behold the Signor Clairville?"

"Behold my beloved Floria again!" ejaculated our heroine ; "restored to liberty ! Can it be possible ? or is it only a dream ?"

"It is true," answered Floretta, "and the brigand chief is here to corroborate all that I have stated."

At this moment the vehicle was suddenly stopped, and the brigand riding up to the side of it, presented himself to Melina.

"Signora," he said, "allow me to congratulate you on your restoration to liberty. To think that I have at last succeeded in what I have been so long anxious to accomplish, affords me the highest possible gratification. Under the protection of Allesandro Massaroni, you will be safe from every danger ; and I do not doubt that ere many weeks, perhaps days, have elapsed, you will be completely restored to happiness."

"Oh, signor," replied our heroine, "what can I say, how reply to you, under the peculiar circumstances in which I am placed ? Why should you take such an interest in my fate, in the fate of one who is almost an entire stranger to you ? And will not the world blame me for having consented to avail myself of your services ?"

"The fair Signora Melina, I am convinced," replied Massaroni, "is too generous to be prejudiced against me, because of my peculiar and questionable position. Of this rest assured, that I am prompted in my conduct towards you by motives of the strictest honour. I would save you from that cruel persecution to which you have been so long subjected—I would rescue you from that revolting fate with which your unnatural relative has threatened you, and, if I possible, place you in that state of happiness to which your numerous virtues so justly entitle you."

"Your kind wishes towards me, Signor Massaroni," said our heroine, "merit my warmest thanks and gratitude. But my uncle ! Oh, what will be his feelings when he learns that I am in your power, at least, under your protection ; one whom he has, I know, ever been accustomed to look upon as his bitterest enemy ? Will he not visit me with his everlasting indignation ?"

"No, signora," returned the brigand chief ; "the Prince Bianchi, if he be not insensible to every feeling of shame, will be awakened to a full conviction of the cruelty and injustice of the conduct he has hitherto so unrelentingly pursued towards you, and will be anxious to make you all the atonement in his power. I do not despair of being enabled to bring about a speedy reconciliation between you. But pardon me ; every moment that we delay the prosecution of our journey is fraught with danger."

"And whither are you about to convey me, Massaroni ?" asked Melina.

"To my secret haunt among the mountains," answered the brigand, "where you will be perfectly safe from every danger, and the utmost attention and respect will be paid to you. You will there find those of your own sex, who can fully commiserate with you, and who are not unworthy of your confidence and friendship, and, moreover, one to whom, if I mistake not, your heart is fondly attached, and who loves you with equal devotion."

Our heroine blushed deeply as Massaroni made use of these observations, and her heart palpitated violently against her side.

"The Signor Clairville," continued the brigand chief, after a pause, "has endured the most painful and unceasing anxiety, since he has been separated from you, signora ; and I need not attempt to describe to you what will be his feelings of transport when he again beholds you. But pardon me, Signora Melina, for the apparent boldness of my speech ; it is necessary that we should proceed on our journey without delay ; but let me again advise you to compose your feelings, and to rest satisfied and confident as to the result of this adventure."

Thus saying, and bowing politely to our heroine, Massaroni withdrew himself from the carriage, and they once more resumed their journey.

For some moments, Melina was so confused by the novelty of her situation, that she could not collect her thoughts, and throwing herself back in the vehicle, she became silent and abstracted, and Floretta did not offer to interrupt her ; but at length she said—

"How wonderful and incredible is all this ! Alas ! my uncle, what a delicate and painful situation has the severity and injustice of your conduct placed me in, to be compelled to avail myself of the protection of one who is proscribed by the laws of his country."

"Nay, signora," remarked Floretta, "you do Massaroni an injustice by speaking thus of him. It is true that the laws of his country have proscribed him, but has he not evidently been led to the infringement of those laws by the grossest oppression and the heaviest wrongs ? He is no heartless ruffian, worthy of every reprobation, but one who possesses all the noble qualities that can adorn mankind ; and he is urged in his present conduct towards you, by the most honourable, generous, and friendly motives."

"I do believe you, Floretta," said her mistress, "and Heaven forbid that I should wrong him by entertaining one unworthy thought to his prejudice ; but can I help feeling some repugnance at entering a place which is the haunt of such desperate men as those who compose the band of Massaroni ?"

"And who amongst them would dare to insult you, while under the protection of the mountain chief ?" demanded Floretta. "Besides, will not the Signor Clairville be near you, and——"

"Ah, Florio! dearest Florio!" interrupted our heroine, "and shall we indeed meet again? Shall we once more be permitted the happiness of each other's society? That thought alone is sufficient to inspire me with confidence. Yes, I will be firm, and look forward to the future with hope and blissful anticipation."

"It glads my heart to hear you talk thus, my dear signora," said Floretta; "persevere in encouraging such hopes as those you have just now expressed, and depend upon it you will not be doomed to be disappointed. The Prince Bianchi, your uncle, will be compelled to yield when he finds that you are entirely removed from his power, and all your wishes will at length be gratified."

"Your observations, my kind Floretta," said her mistress, "impart consolation to me; but this journey—what a tedious and a dismal one it is at this solemn hour of the night, and in such a frightful storm as this. Would that we had arrived at the place of our destination, for my heart sickens when I gaze at the horrors around me."

The scene and the season were, indeed, awful; the thunder shook the vault of heaven, and echoed in deafening echoes along the mountain passes they were traversing; the rain came down in one broad sheet, and the lightning blazed in at the windows of the carriage in which our heroine and her attendant were seated, seeming to threaten them every moment with a frightful and untimely death. Melina shuddered, and it was with the greatest difficulty that Floretta could at all succeed in tranquillising her feelings.

At length, between the pauses of the tempest, they heard a confused noise among the brigands who followed behind the vehicle, and they felt certain that something serious had happened, and that some fresh danger threatened. The carriage was stopped for an instant, and several of the band surrounding it, Massaroni rode up to the window.

"For Heaven's sake, what is the matter?" interrogated our heroine, eagerly.

"Do not alarm yourself, signora," replied the brigand; "you are secure from every danger. Drive on with all the rapidity you can towards our secret haunt, and doubtless we shall soon overtake you, when we have given these fellows a taste of our quailty. I see there is nothing left but for myself and my brave comrades to give them battle, and, perhaps, it will be better for us to do so, in order that we may cool their courage. Ah! see! they gain upon us! There is not one moment to be lost; only secure the signora, and Allesandro Massaroni will soon accomplish the rest."

"What mean those words, Massaroni?" again demanded Melina; "do not keep me in doubt and suspense."

"Briefly, then, signora," answered the brigand, "we are pursued; I see a large body of troops approaching us; but, by the mass! they shall find us more than a match for them."

Melina turned deadly sick, but before she could make use of another observation, the vehicle was driven away with the speed of lightning, and was soon far away from Massaroni and the principal portion of the brigands.

The frequent flashes of lightning clearly revealed the approaching pursuers, who, it is needless to say, were the troops of the Prince Bianchi, who had arrived at the Villa Civetti so shortly after the abduction of our heroine.

"I do not know whether they have perceived us yet," said Massaroni; "but it is not at all unlikely that they have; however, we will give them a much warmer reception than they probably calculate upon. Our position is an excellent one, and if they are only hardy enough to venture to advance upon us, their destruction is inevitable."

"Ay, captain," returned Rubaldo; "I think there is not much reason to doubt upon whose side victory will be."

"Quick! quick! let us conceal ourselves, and wait in ambush for them," said our hero; "we have plenty of means at hand."

The brigands instantly obeyed the orders of their chief, and so adroitly was this performed, that with the quickness of thought they all disappeared as though they had sunk into the bowels of the earth.

The troops came on, and soon entered the place where their enemies were awaiting them.

"By the saints," said one of the officers in command, addressing himself to his companions, "I could have sworn that by the glare of the lightning I saw a large body of men on this very spot not many minutes ago; but there is not the least signs of a human being now, at any rate, and it is impossible, one would think, that they could vanish so suddenly."

"True, captain," said his friend; "but I also saw them, or else I will never trust my eyes again. It is most extraordinary."

"It is," coincided the captain; "and this is certainly not one of the most cheerful places in the world, especially on such a night as this. But come, let us push on, for something strikes me that we are on the right scent for the rascals, and I shall never rest satisfied until I have given Massaroni and his daring set of ruffians such a dressing as they have never experienced before. The Signora Melina must also be rescued from their power at all hazards; or his highness, the prince, will go mad to a certainty."

"Ay, in good truth will he," remarked the other officer; "but, confound it, this is not by any means an agreeable expedition."

"Well, we waste time," said the captain, "and every instant that we delay gives these brigands an additional opportunity to escape. Let us proceed."

"Yes," returned his companion, "and it is necessary that we should use caution, and keep a sharp look out; for I have had some dealings with these rascals before, and I know that they are in the habit of pouncing upon you and taking you by surprise when you least expect them."

The captain made no reply, and the soldiers moved farther on along the gloomy way, but were unable to make much progress in consequence of the darkness, and the ruggedness of the road. Suddenly they were startled by the shrill blast of a horn, and before they had time to recover themselves or to look around, a tremendous heavy fire was opened upon them from every side, and thirty of the soldiers, including the captain, were in an instant stretched lifeless upon the earth. This unexpected assault, as might be expected, threw them into the utmost state of confusion, and Massaroni, taking advantage of it, rushed out at the head of his band, from the different places where they been concealed, and made a desperate onslaught on the discomfited soldiers, dealing death and destruction around, and making the air resound again with their shouts of triumph. But notwithstanding the suddenness and fierceness of the attack, the troops quickly rallied, and went to the combat with much bravery and determination. While it lasted, it was most fierce and bloody, and the groans of the wounded, the wild shouts of the brigands, coupled with the voice of the tempest, rendered the scene one of the most frightful description that could well be imagined. But the brigands had every advantage, and at length the other officer being slain, the troops became disheartened; fell back, and ultimately fled in the utmost disorder, leaving Massaroni and his courageous band victors, with only three slain and two or three more wounded.

"Bravissimo! my brave comrades," said the brigand chief; "you have performed your work as you always do, most heroically. The survivors will have an agreeable tale to tell their princely master, and methinks this defeat will add much to his rage and disappointment, and prove to him how futile is the attempt to conquer Allesandro Masssaroni. Poor fellows! it is a pity that they should have been employed upon such a hopeless and desperate errand, and I deeply regret the loss of life that has taken place; but it was unavoidable. Our triumph is now complete. But come, we must not tarry here;—to horse, to horse,

and we shall probably overtake the vehicle containing the Signora Melina before they arrive at our secret haunt."

The brigands mounted their horses, and starting off at full speed, in a short time came in sight of the carriage, and rejoined their companions.

We need not attempt to describe the state of excitement and agitation that our heroine had been in while the terrific combat just described had been going on, and it was not without the greatest difficulty that Floretta could at all succeed in composing her feelings; her gentle nature shuddered with horror at the thought of the dreadful slaughter that was likely to take place; but her mind felt some degree of relief, when she again beheld Massaroni, for, independent of the interest she felt in his fate, she would have deeply regretted had he fallen a victim to his efforts to save and befriend her. Massaroni giving his horse in charge to one of his band, entered the vehicle and took a seat by her side, and endeavoured all he could to inspire her with confidence and hope.

"I have again triumphed, Signora Melina," he remarked; "the troops of the Prince Bianchi are defeated, and all danger is now at an end."

"Oh, signor," returned our heroine, again shuddering; "I would to Heaven that this fearful conflict could have been avoided; it shocks me much that any human life should be sacrificed in my defence."

"And believe me, signora,' observed the brigand, "that no one can feel more regret than myself when such desperate occasions arise; Massaroni delights not in the reckless shedding of human blood. But who is the real cause of all that has happened? The Prince Bianchi. But let me beg of you to dismiss all such painful thoughts as these from your breast, and to prepare yourself for the meeting which will shortly take place between you and Florio Clairville."

At the mention of that beloved name, the heart of Melina throbbed more violently than ever, and she could not return any answer.

"As I have before assured you, signora," said our hero, "you will find in my mountain home that everything has been prepared for your comfort and accommodation; no restraint will be put upon your actions, and who shall dare to insult one whom Massaroni has taken under his protection? Set, then, your mind at rest, and depend upon it that the time is not far distant when you will be able to look back upon the past without one pang of regret."

"Signor Massaroni," returned Melina, "I do place every confidence in you, for I can never believe that one who evinces so much innate nobleness of heart, could ever attempt to deceive a friendless and unprotected female.',

"Deceive you, signora?" replied the brigand; "I should despise myself if I could do so; I possess too much reverence for your sex, to harbour a single thought to their injury."

"Pardon me, Massaroni," ejaculated our heroine ; "but what a pity it is that a man possessing so many excellent qualities of head and heart, should be placed in the position of life that you are."

"Ah! lady !" said Massaroni, in melancholy accents ; "did you know the history of my wrongs, you would not condemn me ; it is no fault of mine that you see me as I am, an outcast and a robber; no, it is the work of villany of the blackest character. But enough of this ; why should I trouble you with the recapitulation of my misfortunes?—I cannot trust myself to dwell upon the subject."

Melina made no reply, and a silence of some minutes ensued.

"And have we much farther to travel before we reach the place of our destination?" she at last inquired. "The horrors of the night, and the dreariness of the scenery we are travelling among, strikes a chill to my heart, which I cannot conquer."

"It is indeed a fearful night ; but fear not signora, we shall soon be at our journey's end," replied Massaroni, "where you will find that all is prepared for your reception. Oh, you will see that the brigand's cavernous abode is not destitute of its comforts and even its luxuries; and that there is far more friendship and cordiality existing there than is to be found in the wide world, with all its allurements and temptations. You will also find there, as I have said before, companions of your own sex, companions in misfortune and unmerited persecutions."

"Yes," said our heroine, "the much wronged Signora Olympia and her offspring, I understand, are under your protection?"

"True," replied Massaroni; "and there is another who has suffered greater sorrows than herself, and who is far dearer to her than her very existence."

"Ah!" ejaculated Melina, with much curiosity ; "and who is that ?"

"Her mother," answered Massaroni.

"Her mother? Impossible! she never knew her parents ;—she was brought up by the benevolence of Count Alberti."

"True; but the Signora Olympia (as she has hitherto been called) knows her parents now ; and to the bosom of one, the only one whom she should regard, she is restored."

"Most extraordinary !" exclaimed Melina ; "how was this brought about? But her name?"

"The Signora Zitella!"

"Zitella!"

"Ay," replied the brigand chief; "one of the unfortunate, confiding beings who were basely and cruelly betrayed and deserted by the Prince Bianchi, your uncle, signora, in the days of his youth."

"Good God!" cried our agitated heroine, in accents of the most unbounded astonishment; "can this indeed be true? And the Signora Olympia?"

"Is proved beyond all doubt, not only by the revelation of her mother, but by the dying confession of a villain who was employed by your uncle in most of his nefarious transactions, to be no other than his own child !"

"Gracious Heaven !" ejaculated the horror-stricken Melina ; "how wonderful are Thy ways. Olympia, the hapless victim of the young Count Alberti, the daughter of the Prince Bianchi ?"

"Even so, signora," answered the brigand ; "and now with what other feelings than those of disgust and horror can you view that unnatural relative who would sacrifice you to the cowardly and heartless betrayer of his own child? Ought you not to rejoice that you have been enabled to frustrate his diabolical designs ?"

"Oh, I can scarcely believe the evidence of my senses," said Melina. "But is the Prince Bianchi aware of the fatal circumstances you have just stated to me?"

"Yes," replied Massaroni ; "I have made him acquainted with them."

"You, Massaroni ?"

"Yes, I poured the guilty tale into his ears at the hour of midnight in his own chamber, to which I obtained access by means that he could little imagine ; and he could not deny the truth of it."

"Alas, alas !" sighed our heroine ; "what a fearful disclosure is this ! Oh, my uncle, what hast thou not to answer for ?"

"Ay, signora," remarked Massaroni ; "you will pardon me, but the Prince Bianchi has proved himself to be a most consummate villain."

"But he will repent," she said ; "tell me, Massaroni, did he not appear to be stung with remorse when you repeated the guilty tale to him ?"

"No, signora, but with cowardly fear."

"Wretched uncle !" ejaculated our heroine, clasping her hands. "But the Count Alberti, tell me, is he yet restored to convalescence ?"

"Oh, no, signora," replied our hero, " or you may depend upon it the Prince Bianchi would have hastened your marriage with him ; in fact, I have been given to understand that he is still dangerously ill, his recovery being retarded by the irritability of his disposition, and his disappointment in being frustrated at the very time when he thought the moment of his complete triumph had arrived. But pardon me, signora ; I fear that I am intruding upon you, and I must see to the direction of my band."

Melina returned no answer, for her thoughts were too much occupied another way, and Massaroni again alighting from the vehicle, left Melina and her attendant to their own reflections.

"Oh, Floretta," said her mistress, when the brigand was gone; "what a fearful discovery is this. Can it, indeed, be true?"

"Ah, signora," replied Floretta, "after having read the melancholy narrative of the unfortunate Valentia, can you have any reason to doubt it?"

"Good God!" exclaimed our heroine; "from what a dreadful, what a revolting fate have I then escaped."

"Yes, signora," coincided Floretta; "and how grateful ought you to be to your preserver, Allesandro Massaroni."

"I am, indeed," said our heroine; "but surely my misguided uncle will repent. With all these proofs of his guilty transactions in existence, what can save him from confusion, infamy and disgrace? Is it not wonderful that the brigand chief should be made the instrument in the hands of Providence in bringing all these strange events and discoveries about?"

"It is, my dear lady," answered Floretta; "and should he prove to be the son of the much injured Signora Valentia——"

"Oh," remarked Melina, "I can scarcely dare trust myself with such an idea. And yet it is too probable, and I cannot, therefore, reject it. The more I gaze at Massaroni, the more his extraordinary likeness to the portrait of the Signora Valentia strikes me. Did you not particularly notice it, Floretta, when he was alluding to his own misfortunes just now?"

"I did, signora; the expression of the features is exactly the same; and had it not been for the difference of the sex, I could almost have imagined that the original of the portrait was before me."

"I cannot help thinking that some wonderful discovery is yet to be made," remarked our heroine; "and should the brigand chief really prove to be the son of the Prince Bianchi, the climax of his shame and misery will have arrived. Oh, what a scene am I about to experience at the retreat of Massaroni."

"Courage, signora, it will be one of joy: you will be restored to the arms of Signor Clairville, whose happiness will be all but complete when he once more beholds you, and knows that you are rescued from the terrible and revolting fate which was impending over your head."

"Ah!" sighed our heroine, "but with that happiness will be mingled the most melancholy feelings of despair, when he knows that there is but little hope that circumstances will ever permit us to be united."

"Say not so, my dear mistress," replied Floretta, "for surely after what has taken place, there is every prospect of your wishes being gratified. The Prince Bianchi, completely thwarted in his designs, will no longer attempt to offer any opposition; and after the cruel and unnatural manner in which he has abused the solemn and sacred trust reposed in him, you have no just right to submit to his authority."

"And yet, notwithstanding all the harsh and unjust treatment I have experienced from him, I would fain save him from disgrace," said Melina.

"He has the power in his own hands, my lady, if he will only act as justice dictates to him."

"Most freely could I forgive him all the injuries he has inflicted on me," observed our heroine; "but Zitella and her daughter——"

"Should he make atonement to them," returned Floretta, "it may not be too late to obtain their forgiveness also."

"But fear of the world's reproach will never permit him to acknowledge them in their real character."

"But even if he felt a repugnance in doing that, justice demands that he should make some ample provision for them, and to see to their future protection and comfort."

"True, but the Count Alberti?"

"The Prince Bianchi, as the father of Olympia, should demand that he makes her all the reparation in his power for the cruel injuries he has inflicted on her."

"And what reparation can he make her for the shame and misery he has brought upon her?" demanded Melina; "even if he should be willing to marry her, think you that Olympia would ever consent to become the wife of a man so unworthy of her, and whom she must now so thoroughly despise in her heart?"

"I know not, signora," answered Floretta, "no one ought to be better acquainted with the strength of woman's love than yourself; and should the Count Alberti be truly penitent, she might be induced to overlook the past, painful though it has been to her. Besides, Alberti would not dare to resist the demands of the Prince Bianchi for justice."

"Ah, Floretta," replied her mistress; "I know not that; is not my misguided uncle even more guilty than himself? Has he not more reason to fear exposure than the Count Alberti, who, knowing all the facts of his guilty history, has him completely at his mercy, and will laugh his threats to scorn? I know well the obstinate and hardened character of the count, and feel certain that nothing will subdue his haughty spirit, or bring him to a due sense of compunction. His disappointment in not being able to obtain my hand will only exasperate him the more, and goad him on to vengeance. Notwithstanding all that has taken place, I fear that there is much trouble yet to come, and I tremble at the anticipation of it."

"Indeed, signora," replied Floretta, " you must not give way to such sad and gloomy ideas as these, for I feel assured that they will turn out to be entirely groundless; let it suffice you that you are now rescued from all danger, and with such a powerful and sincere friend as Massaroni, you have everything to hope and nothing to fear. But wait patiently until you behold Signor Clairville again, and consult him on the important and delicate subject."

"Dear Florio," said our heroine, "how my heart palpitates with the mingled feelings of hope and fear when I think of you. Oh, what a meeting will be ours, after so long and painful a separation. And do you indeed still love me with the same ardent devotion that you ever professed to do?"

"Oh, signora," remarked her companion, "can you for a moment doubt the fidelity of Signor Clairville?—Depend upon it, the sentiments he has ever entertained towards you, must ever remain unaltered while life remains within his veins."

"Oh, yes, I do believe in the truth of what you say," ejaculated Melina; "it would be base ingratitude and injustice to harbour a thought to the contrary. Beloved Clairville, our's has been a severe trial, but let us hope that we shall be rewarded for all the troubles of the past in future happiness."

"And you will, my dear signora," said her faithful attendant; "Providence will surely reward you for the patience and resignation with which you have borne all the many bitter trials to which you have been subjected."

Melina returned no answer, and for a few minutes she relapsed into silence, reflecting seriously upon all that Massaroni had stated to her; and the longer she did so, the more her astonishment and anxiety increased. After she had read of the narrative of Valentia, and the proofs which the brigand chief had said he possessed of the truth of his assertions, she could no longer doubt him, and she felt greatly shocked at this additional proof of the guilt of her misguided uncle.

The storm which had been long subsiding, had now entirely ceased, and the first appearance of the sun in the eastern horizon gave token of a fine day. The aspect of the country they were travelling through was also changed, and though secluded and melancholy, presented many features for admiration. They had now pursued their journey for several hours, and our heroine imagined from what Massaroni had told her some time before that they could not be far from the place of their destination; and the nearer they approached towards it, the more her agitation increased,

and her bosom throbbed with the mingled feelings of hope and expectation. What would be the emotions of Clairville on beholding her? Although she was so anxious to again meet that man to whom her affections were so fervently devoted, she almost shrunk from the task, for she feared that she should not have the strength to support it, especially under such different circumstances to those which they had met before; but how great would be the joy and gratitude of Clairville at her escape from the disgusting fate with which her uncle had threatened her, and which for so long a period had seemed to be inevitable. She was still wrapped in these thoughts, when Massaroni again rode up to the carriage, and addressing himself to her, said—

"Fair signora, I trust that by this time your mind is more composed, seeing that the storm has ceased, and that we are no longer travelling amidst darkness and gloom; we have now almost arrived at the end of our journey, and I have sent a messenger forward to apprise Signor Clairville, and your other friends, of your approach, so that they will be prepared for your reception. You will find that Allesandro Massaroni will fulfil the promises he has made to you to the very letter."

"Indeed, signor," replied our heroine, "I do not doubt you, and again I return you my warmest thanks for the interest you seem to take in my fate; I trust that it will some time or other be in my power to repay you for the services you have rendered me, and the many risks you have run to rescue me from a fate which it is impossible that I can even reflect upon without feelings of the utmost terror and disgust."

"I pray you, signora," returned the brigand, "not to lavish upon me so many acknowledgments; I am amply rewarded in the satisfaction arising from the consciousness of having performed my duty towards an innocent and unprotected female; and if I should be made the humble instrument of bringing about your future happiness, I shall ever look back upon the circumstance as one of the most fortunate and gratifying epochs in my life."

"But Clairville," ejaculated Melina, "oh, what will be the ecstasy of his feelings when he hears of my deliverance from the revolting fate which was so long impending o'er my head, and that I am on my way to meet him?"

"True, signora," replied our hero; "his joy, no doubt, will be all that could be expected, and his presence will, I trust, give you every confidence in the security of your retreat. I feel confident that a few days only will elapse when a reconciliation will be effected with the Prince Bianchi, your uncle—

who must see the folly of longer obstinately persisting in his designs against you, knowing as he does, the power I hold over him, and the disgrace and infamy that would be brought upon his name, should all his vices be exposed to the world."

"The discovery you have made, signor, respecting the unfortunate Zitella, and more especially that Olympia is her daughter, is so extraordinary, that I can scarcely trust my senses to believe it."

"But, I repeat, signora," said the brigand

FRANSCISCO MALIETEVERA IN THE DEATH-CHAMBER OF HIS PARENTS.

"that it is no more extraordinary than true, as Zitella and daughter will confirm when you behold them. I have also the dying confession of Malvolio, the villain who was employed by the Prince Bianchi to execute his base designs, and to rid him of Zitella and her offspring. That confession was taken in the presence of a holy man, and, therefore, its authenticity is unquestionable. He acknowledged having left Olympia at the door of the palace of the late Count Alberti, and, therefore, her identity is proved beyond dispute."

No. 79.

"How miraculous are the ways of Providence!" observed our heroine; "and the deeply injured Olympia, too, to be the victim of the Count Alberti; the man to whom my uncle would so cruelly have sacrificed me! Oh, how horrible, disgusting, and torturing is that thought."

"Dismiss it from your mind, signora," said Massaroni, "and only anticipate the future happiness that is in store for you. But pardon me, I am intruding upon you: and will leave you to collect your thoughts and energies for the meeting which you are so shortly to experience."

Thus saying, the brigand chief, bowing with his accustomed gallantry, again quitted the vehicle, which proceeded on its way. The mind of Melina was too busily occupied to suffer her to enter into conversation; and the nearer they approached to the place of their destination, the more did her agitation increase. The change was so sudden and so remarkable, that she could scarcely persuade herself that she was not labouring under the delusion of a dream; but after the conduct he had evinced towards her, and the evident friendship he possessed for herself and Clairville, she could no longer doubt the truth of all that Massaroni had stated, and she looked forward with impatience for the issue of those various events.

The scenery through which they were journeying now assumed the most romantic and picturesque character, and the cheerful beams of the morning's sun added to the beauty and serenity of its aspect. They were now traversing an extensive valley, where several neat, but humble dwellings reared their heads, and the peasants were going to their daily labour, but seemed to take no notice of the brigands, for to them, as we have before frequently stated, Massaroni was a friend and benefactor, and they were all of them ready to lay down their lives for him.

At a short distance appeared that lofty chain of mountains, covered with verdure to the very summits, among which the retreat of the brigands was situated, and which our heroine knew, from the description which Massaroni had given of it, was the place of her destination. She strained her eyes to the utmost, almost expecting to see her lover eagerly approaching to meet her, and her heart throbbed so violently against her side that she could with difficulty support herself. Floretta, who had not offered to interrupt the train of her thoughts for some time by any observation of her own, entered fully into her feelings on that important occasion, and awaited with equal impatience their arrival at the cavernous abode of the brigand chief, and the interesting meeting that would be sure to take place between her mistress and Clairville.

There was something, too, of so romantic a nature in the adventure that well corresponded with the taste of Floretta, and she felt the deepest interest in all she at present saw, and all that she anticipated was in store for her.

At length the carriage reached the foot of one of the loftiest of the mountains, when it was suddenly stopped, and Massaroni once more appeared at the window.

"Fair lady," he observed, "at length we have arrived at our journey's end, but I must trouble you to alight, for it is impossible that the carriage can ascend the steep mountain's side."

Melina looked eagerly around her, and for a few moments her brain was so bewildered that she scarcely knew where she was, or understood what the brigand chief said to her. But, at length, without saying a word, and with considerable agitation, she suffered Massaroni to assist her from the carriage, and taking her arm, he supported her up the rugged mountain's side, followed by the brigands. This was a task of extreme labour to our heroine, who was unused to such travelling, and several times she was compelled to pause in order to rest herself, and to take breath; and at such times as these, the beautiful and extensive range of scenery that met her view from the elevated position could not fail to call forth her admiration and delight.

Again they proceeded, winding their way through the narrow mountain passes, and encountering fresh beauties at every turn; but at length Melina, raising her eyes, beheld a group of persons descending the mountain towards them, and one figure which was in advance of the others struck her in a moment, and she could not repress a faint scream of mingled astonishment and delight. He bounded with the speed of lightning towards her, and the next instant our heroine sank senseless in the arms of her beloved Florio Clairville!

With what indescribable emotions of transport and gratitude did he strain her to his bosom, and press warm kisses of the purest and most ardent affection upon her lips, while Massaroni and the others stood by, and, fully appreciating his feelings, did not offer to interrupt him.

"Melina! my own, my adored Melina!" he ejaculated, gazing fondly upon the beauteous and innocent countenance of her who was far more precious to him than his own existence; "and do I then, indeed, once more press thy beloved form to my bosom, and behold thee safe from the disgusting fate to which thy unnatural relative threatened to consign you? This is, indeed, a happiness which I never thought to experience. Oh, Massaroni, for this I owe you a debt of gratitude which I I shall never have it in my power to repay."

"Mention it not, Signor Clairville," replied the brigand. "I am perfectly satisfied to know that I have been successful in my designs, and that the Prince Bianchi and the Count Alberti are disappointed in the accomplishment of their hopes and wishes. But this is not the time or the place to talk further upon this subject. Bear the Signora Melina to the cave; the females will see to her recovery, and then she will require some short rest after the fatigue of the journey, before she will be in a fit state to hold any conversation with you."

Clairville made no reply, but supporting the form of his beloved Melina in his arms, and with feelings of rapture throbbing in his breast which he had not experienced for many a day, he conveyed her to the cavern, followed by Massaroni and the others. It was not without difficulty he, however, could be persuaded to resign her, even for a few minutes; and having left her in the care of Maria, Olympia, and Floretta, he retired with the brigand chief to another cavern, where he eagerly inquired all the particulars attending the rescue of Melina, and what had occurred on the journey from the Villa Civetti. Massaroni briefly informed him of all he wished to know, and Florio listened to him with the most eager curiosity and the deepest interest.

"Fortune has, indeed, been kind to us on this occasion," remarked Clairville; "but to your intrepidity, Massaroni, and the promptitude with which you acted, I owe everything. Melina is now safe under your protection, and may boldly set all her enemies at defiance."

"She may," answered the brigand; "and now that you have the beauteous and innocent Signora Melina near you, you ought to consider yourself one of the happiest and most fortunate of men in existence."

"And so I do," returned Clairville. "Oh, how anxious I am until I behold her again, and once more have the felicity of listening to the melodious tones of her voice. But how great will be the rage and disappointment of the prince and Alberti when they hear of the escape of Melina, and the subsequent defeat of the troops."

"True," coincided Massaroni, "it is a glorious revenge for the cruelty and injustice of their conduct; and, moreover, they know that it is useless their seeking to oppose me in this my mountain retreat; I should think they have had sufficient proof of that, and Bianchi will be glad enough to come to any terms, consequently, however repugnant they may be to his feelings."

"But think you the proud and haughty spirit of the Prince Bianchi will ever suffer him to submit?" said Clairville. "Do you believe that he will ever pardon his beauteous niece for having thus ventured to disobey his will, and set his authority at defiance?—or do you believe that he will so far forget his old prejudices as to give his consent to the union of myself and Melina?"

"And how can he help himself?" demanded the brigand; "have not yourself and your lover now everything in your power? and what occasion have you to heed his indignation and resentment?"

"Ah, no, Massaroni," said Florio, after a short pause, "I can never encourage such presumptuous ideas,—the disparity of our birth and station preclude the possibility of my ever becoming the husband of Melina."

"Pshaw, Clairville!" returned our hero, "I have no patience with such misgivings as those; and, besides, I cannot, for my own part, see the least cause for them."

"Melina would shrink from giving her consent, under such circumstances."

"Then she cannot love you."

"Not love me?"

"No, if she would suffer such scruples to have any influence on her mind. She will make any sacrifice for your sake; and what other course can she adopt, since to you alone she must look for that protection which she can no longer expect from the Prince Bianchi. Come, come, my young friend, you must learn to be less doubtful, and to look forward with the most sanguine hopes to the speedy consummation of your happiness, and rest assured you will not be disappointed. I have always predicted that I should have the pleasure and the honour of dancing at the wedding of yourself and the charming Signora Melina, and I feel confident that those predictions will be fulfilled."

"Thanks, Massaroni, for your good wishes," remarked Clairville; "though, I confess, that I cannot become so sanguine on that important subject as you have professed yourself to be. I am all impatience and anxiety till I behold Melina again, and we are enabled at once to communicate those thoughts to each other which glow within our breasts."

"That opportunity will, no doubt, be soon afforded you," replied Massaroni, "though, as I have said before, the signora will in the meantime require some rest after the fatigue of her long journey."

Clairville could not but acknowledge the reasonableness of this, and he, therefore, endeavoured to await patiently the result of his interview with Melina; though he had no doubt it would be of the most affectionate description, for he felt convinced that the sentiments which Melina had ever professed towards him had undergone no change, and, therefore, had he not every reason to encourage the hopes which the brigand chief had sought to inspire him with? He had; and as he came to this conclusion, he became more easy in his mind.

Old Montaldi and Zitella had been informed of the arrival of our heroine at the cavern, and they lost no time in hastening thither, so anxious were they to behold one in whose fate they felt so deep an interest, and who had experienced so many vicissitudes and acts of injustice from the persecutions of Bianchi. As might have been expected, from the nature of her unfortunate connexion with the prince, there was no one who felt a greater curiosity and anxiety to behold his fair niece, and to sympathies with her in the wrongs which had been inflicted on her, than Zitella; and when she thought of all the circumstances connected with her own and her daughter's history, the anguish that disturbed her mind may be far better imagined than described. But to return to our heroine: It was not many minutes ere she recovered from the fainting fit into which she had fallen from the power of her emotions on beholding Clairville, and found herself, as we have before intimated, attended upon by Maria Grazie, Floretta, and Mira. Her brain was bewildered and confused for the moment, and she scarcely knew where she was; and the novelty of her situation, as may be supposed, filled her bosom with no little astonishment. She looked around, in vain, for Florio Clairville, however, and then fixing her eyes upon the brigand's wife and Mira, whom she recognised in a moment, the whole truth flashed upon her recollection.

"Ah!" she ejaculated, "am I then, indeed, saved from shame and destruction? and am I near my beloved Clairville?"

"You are, signora," answered Maria; "you are now safe in the mountain abode of Allesandro Massaroni, the brigand chief, and surrounded by friends."

"Signora," said Mira, "do you not recollect me?"

"Yes, yes," replied our heroine, "it is Olympia."

"It is, indeed, her whom you have hitherto known as the unfortunate Olympia, but that is not my name; 'tis Mira."

"Ah!" exclaimed Melina, "I recollect now; Massaroni told me all—that you had discovered a mother living, and that that mother was the wretched victim of——"

"Your uncle, the Prince Bianchi," added Mira.

"And you are his daughter?"

"Oh, yes, signora," returned Mira; "I dare not doubt the truth of my mother's assertions. But, oh, signora, would but the Prince Bianchi repent of his evil ways, how freely could I forgive him for the past; and even my unfortunate mother entertains not the least vindictive feelings towards him. How sincerely do I congratulate you on your escape from the misery that was intended for you; may Heaven bring my guilty betrayer to a full sense of the enormity of his conduct, and forgive him for the past."

"My poor girl," said Melina, compassionately, "what a cruel destiny has yours been; but surely the Prince Bianchi and Count Alberti cannot much longer refuse to render you justice, and you will yet be restored to happiness."

"Alas! no, Signora Melina," sighed Mira, "pure happiness, I feel convinced, can never again be mine; for all the hopes which I had encouraged in my breast have long since been annihilated. But why should I trouble you with my sorrows and misfortunes, when you have so many of your own to contend with?"

"True, Mira," said the brigand's wife, "this is not the time to broach such dismal subjects as those. Signora Melina, you must need some refreshment after not partaking of any for so many hours; and then, if you would take my advice, you will endeavour to obtain an hour or two's repose; for after the fatigue you have undergone from the length of your journey, and the peculiar and exciting circumstances under which it was performed, you must greatly require it."

"I thank you, signora," replied our heroine, "but when shall I behold the Signor Clairville again?"

"Before many hours have elapsed," said Maria. "Signor Clairville is in the cavern, and is as anxious, no doubt, to behold you again as you can be to see him; but your mind is not yet sufficiently composed for the interview, and you had better follow the advice I have thought proper to offer you."

"I will do so, signora," said our heroine, "and I am grateful to you for the solicitude which you seem to feel in my welfare and happiness."

"Believe me, signora," returned Maria, "you will find no warmer or more zealous and sincere friends than Allesandro Massaroni and his wife, Maria Grazie. In this mountain retreat, though you will meet with none of those luxuries and superfluities which you have experienced at the Villa Rosa, and other mansions of the haughty prince, your uncle, you will find every comfort and enjoyment. Here the rules of order and decorum are enforced with a rigid hand, and, therefore, on that score, though surrounded by the daring band of the mountain chief, you may rest your mind contented; and feel yourself safe as if you were in your own palazzo, with nothing but the most well-tried friends around you."

"I do believe you, signora," said Melina, "and place the utmost confidence in you and your husband, to whom I am so largely indebted."

"Enough, signora," replied the brigand's wife, "then we understand each other; I will bring you some refreshments, in a few minutes, and then conduct you to the place which has been fitted up as a chamber for your accommodation."

Having thus spoken, Maria Grazie and Mira quitted the place, and left our heroine and Floretta to themselves.

"I am quite lost in wonder and admiration at all I have seen and heard since we came here, signora," remarked Floretta. "What a singular and romantic life is this to lead! I declare I am quite taken up with it—a brigand's cavern, or rather a succession of caverns, where there is every accommodation. I'm sure I don't wonder at their being so much attached to the life, wild though it is. Then what a handsome, graceful, and commanding-looking woman is the brigand's wife, and so generous, humane, and noble in the sentiments she expresses."

"True, Floretta," coincided her mistress; "but still, notwithstanding all these facts, I cannot yet feel myself entirely at ease in this place."

"Eh, my dear lady," said Floretta, "not when the Signor Clairville is so near to you? No danger can possibly befall you."

"Notwithstanding the severity and injustice with which the Prince Bianchi has treated me," observed Melina, "I cannot help feeling some regret at the chagrin and disappointment he will experience at my being rescued from his power, and that by one whom he has been accustomed to look upon (though with what reason I know not) as his most deadly foe."

"Indeed, signora," returned her attendant, "you will pardon me, but I cannot help thinking that that is a most preposterous and unreasonable idea. The Prince Bianchi has himself to blame for any disappointment he has experienced; and I cannot see that he who would not have hesitated to sacrifice you to a man whom you justly hate and dispise, the heartless betrayer of his own daughter, is worthy of any commiseration on your part."

"Alas!" sighed Melina, "he has indeed been most misguided."

"Misguided, my dear lady?" repeated her attendant; "you apply too mild a term to it by far; the Prince Bianchi has been most guilty, and it is only by a sincere repentance that he can hope to make atonement for the past, and to save himself from that disgrace and infamy which must otherwise inevitably overtake him."

"Would to Heaven that he would do so," replied Melina; "what an infinite source of gratification it would be to me. Oh, that I could have escaped the fate with which I was threatened by any other means than those I was compelled to adopt."

"Still, signora," remarked Floretta, "in spite of all you have said to the contrary, you seem to entertain some suspicion of the integrity of Massaroni's motives in risking so much to save you from the cruel persecution to which you were subjected."

"No, Floretta," answered her mistress, "you mistake me if you suppose that I doubt the honour of Massaroni for a moment. I should be most ungrateful and ungenerous were I to do so; but still the world is so censorious, and——"

"How often have we argued upon that subject, signora?" interrupted Floretta; "and I thought you had at last succeeded in banishing such erroneous ideas from your mind. The world surely must have blamed you more, had you tamely yielded to a fate so infamous and degrading. But time will, I trust, make you think differently; and now that you are restored to the arms of your lover, I have no doubt that he will be able to find arguments to persuade you to act as prudence and affection should dictate."

"What mean you, Floretta?" said our heroine, in a faltering voice, and blushing deeply.

"Pardon me, my dear lady," replied the faithful domestic; "but you and Signor Clairville love each other fervently, sincerely, do you not?"

Melina, by her looks, replied in the affirmative, and her bosom heaved with the intensity of her emotions.

"The only objection that the Prince Bianchi could ever offer to him," continued Floretta, "was that his birth was not so noble as your own. But Signor Florio possesses the true nobility of the soul; and what are rank and fortune when placed in contrast with superior virtues and endowments of the mind? I am certain, my dear mistress, that you would despise and loathe yourself could you suffer such false prejudices to enter your breast."

"Oh!" exclaimed Melina, energetically, "Heaven knows that I would."

"Why then, since your uncle has discarded you, and you possess sufficient of fortune's gifts in your own right, should you any longer hesitate to become the happy bride of the worthy man on whom your warmest affections are rivetted, and thus put a final end to the annoyances and persecutions with which you have hitherto been pursued?"

"Floretta!" said the still blushing damsel, "what a question is that which you have put to me! God knows that I love Florio for himself alone, and were he one of the wealthiest nobles in the universe, I could not love him with greater fervour; but I cannot make up my mind to——"

She was prevented from finishing the sentence, by the return of the brigand's wife and Mira with the refreshments, which they placed before Melina and her domestic, and requested them to partake of them freely. Melina again returned her acknowledgments to Maria, and then partook slightly of the repast, for she was in no disposition to eat, and Maria having remained silent during the meal, now arose, and addressing herself to our heroine, said :—

"And now, signora, allow me to show you to the chamber prepared for you, and to again advise you to seek a short interval of rest."

"Are your husband and Signor Clairville still in the cavern?" asked Melina.

"They are," answered the wife of Massaroni, "and when you have rested from the fatigue of your journey, they will both be most anxious to see you."

Melina made no reply, and having bade Mira good-bye for the present, she and Floretta followed Maria form the cavern. As they proceeded through the different cavernous apartments, the astonishment and admiration of Floretta and her mistress at all they saw increased, and they could not but marvel at the immense deal of labour, skill, money, and perseverance which had been bestowed upon every part of this secret and mountainous retreat. There seemed to be no end of the extent of the place; it was capable of giving shelter to some hundreds of individuals; and every cavern or room was furnished with something approaching even to taste.

Maria saw the amazement which was created in the breast of Melina by the contemplation of all these extraordinary particulars, and pausing, she remarked—

"Ay, signora, I marvel not at the surprise you evince at all you witness here. I told you the abode of the brigand chief was no trifling place, but one that can never be forgotten by those who have once seen it. Methinks it would take a large force and considerable trouble to make an attack upon us, with any chance of success. Thus you see that Allesandro Massaroni's power is even far greater than it does at first appear to be."

"True, signora," replied our heroine; "all that I gaze upon fills me with the most unbounded amazement. Who could imagine that such places at this exist in the bowels of the earth?"

"Or that there were secret passages leading from this place, which extend for miles?" said Maria.

"Is it possible?" demanded Melina.

"It is true," answered the brigand's wife, "and in a day or two, if you should feel so disposed, I will show you over them."

Melina expressed her curiosity to see them, and Maria then led the way through two or three more caverns, which were hung round with arms of every description, and had a good stock of amunition, and at last she stopped at a rude wooden door, and taking a key from her side, she applied it to the lock, and after some slight difficulty the door flew open, and dis-

covered a couple of caverns, which opened into each other, of pretty large dimensions, arched, and boarded. Melina and Floretta could not help being most forcibly struck by the extreme aspect of comfort which these singular places presented. They contained several useful articles of furniture, and each of them a bed and bedstead, which had a very clean and inviting appearance.

"These, signora," said Maria, "are the chambers fitted up for the accommodation of yourself and your attendant; and I hope you will be satisfied that we have made all the arrangements we could for your comfort. It is far removed from that part inhabited by the band; but whether it were or not, you would have nothing to fear from intrusion. I will wait upon you again in two or three hours to conduct you to the presence of Signor Clairville and my husband, whom, perhaps, by that time you may be anxious to see."

The Signora Melina again thanked her, and Maria then took her departure, and left Floretta and her mistress in such a state of astonishment for a few minutes, that they could not speak a word.

"What an extraordinary situation is this to be placed in!" at last said Melina; "it has so much the character of romance about it, that I am half inclined to doubt the evidence of my senses."

"For my own part," remarked Floretta, "I am quite delighted with it. Here will be something for us to talk about at some future period. Everything shows the respect and attention which Massaroni has paid to your comfort, signora, and should inspire you with still greater confidence."

"I entertain no doubt of him, believe me, Floretta," returned our heroine; "but, on the contrary, I am convinced that there is no risk he would hesitate to run to serve me and Florio; but still I cannot help entertaining some fears as to what may be the absolute result of all these events."

"Oh, doubt not but that they will terminate much more auspiciously than you seem at present to anticipate," said her domestic; "but the more I gaze upon the countenance of the brigand chief, the more forcibly am I struck with the strong resemblance which he bears to the representation of Signora Valentia."

"Yes," coincided our heroine; "and depend upon it there is something more to be revealed in respect to that than we at present know of."

"I am undoubtedly of opinion, signora," said Floretta, "that Massaroni will ultimately prove to be the son of Valentia Di Valori and the Prince Bianchi."

"Heaven forbid, for the sake of my unfortunate and guilty uncle!" ejaculated Melina;

"although it is too probable. Should Massaroni be goaded on by a spirit of revenge against the author of his mother's wrongs and sufferings, which it is not at all unlikely that he would, I shudder to think what the consequences might be."

"Nay, my lady, these fears are groundless," remarked Floretta; "it is not in Massaroni's nature to encourage such feelings of deadly and implacable revenge against any one, especially that man to whom he might discover to be the author of his being. But you will show Signor Clairville the manuscript of Valentia, which came into our possession in so singular a manner, and take his advice upon the subject?"

"Yes," answered Melina, "it is my intention, as I told you before, to do so; and I will be guided entirely by what he says."

"Very good, signora; but had you not better endeavour to obtain an hour or two's repose, for you must be fatigued? I do not feel inclined to sleep, so I will e'en sit here and watch by you, though I am satisfied that there is no danger to be apprehended."

"Well," remarked our heroine, "I do feel somewhat exhausted with the length of the journey and the anxiety of thought, so I will stretch my limbs upon the bed without undressing, and endeavour to tranquillise my mind to sleep."

With these words, Melina did as she said, and in a few minutes she had sunk off into a comfortable repose; Floretta watching by the side of her couch, and deeply immersed in the thoughts created by the extraordinary novelty of the situation in which she was placed.

Melina, however, slept little more than an hour, and awoke much refreshed, short even as the time had been, and did not feel inclined to sleep again. She was now most anxious for the time to arrive when she should again behold Clairville; though she knew not whether it would be prudent to encourage those hopes which, in all probability, he would entertain. And yet, she reflected, must she at once blight all the hopes and wishes he most likely had formed within his breast, now that her deliverance from the cruel persecution of her uncle had opened up fresh prospects? It would seem cruel and unjust to do so; and why, since the Prince Bianchi had forfeited all claim to her respect, had cast her from his bosom, and thrown her almost friendless and unprotected upon the world, should she hesitate to become the wife of the man of her heart, and who was every way so worthy of her?—Surely it was a false delicacy to hesitate; and yet she could not remove some feelings of doubt and alarm from her mind.

She was interrupted in the midst of her reflections by the return of Maria, who, having inquired how she felt, observed,—

"And, now, signora, I will, if you please, conduct you to the place where Florio Clairville waits most impatiently to see you; and I presume that you are equally anxious for an interview with him?"

"Oh, signora!" said our heroine, with much agitation, "what a moment of mingled sorrow and joy is this! Never did I expect that myself and Florio were destined to meet again in this world; and now that the moment has arrived, I almost shudder at the task, as though I were about to perform something wrong."

"Nay, signora," replied the brigand's wife, "there is no necessity for entertaining such thoughts and apprehensions as these; ought you not rather to encourage the most sanguine anticipations, sincere and faithful as you know Clairville to be, and ardent as is the love you feel towards him? Oh, Signora Melina, did you but know half the anguish of mind he has suffered since he has been here, and during your imprisonment by the Prince Bianchi, you could not for an instant doubt the strength of that passion, which your numerous personal charms and intrinsic virtues have created in his breast."

"Doubt my Florio's love!" ejaculated our heroine, fervently; "oh, that would, indeed, be impossible! Signora Maria, you misunderstand me; but at another time, I will explain myself more fully; prithee lead on to the place where Florio is waiting to see me."

Maria Grazie obeyed, and with a throbbing heart, and leaning on the arm of her faithful attendant for support, Melina followed her from the chamber by a different way to that which they had come, and which revealed fresh subjects for wonder and admiration at every turn. As our heroine proceeded, she acquired more confidence, and, presently, they stopped at the door of one of the cavernous apartments. Maria knocked at the door, which was speedily opened, and before Melina had time to recover herself, she was once more clasped to the throbbing heart of the delighted Florio. They both of them uttered a simultaneous cry of joy and affection, but were unable to utter a syllable, and, Massaroni having beckoned to his wife and Floretta, they abruptly retired from the place, and left the lovers to themselves.

For some moments they continued locked in each other's arms, and could only mingle their sighs together; but at length Florio partly disengaging himself from her embrace, and looking in her face with an expression of affection, nay, of adoration, which language must fail to describe in sufficiently glowing colours, he ejaculated—

"Oh, my beloved, suffering, much injured Melina! bright vision of my imagination, either sleeping or waking! and has, then, All-merciful Providence permitted us to meet again, and to breathe forth the sentiments of our hearts in each other's ears? This moment more than repays me for all the anguish and anxiety of mind I have so long endured. Speak to me, Melina, and tell me, do I still hold a place in your affections?"

"Florio," said the maiden, in a faint voice, and fixing upon him a look of gentle reproach, "why that question?"

"Because, Melina, it is one of life or death to me," replied Clairville.

"And can you doubt the fervour and sincerity of my love, Clairville? Indeed, indeed, you wrong me by encouraging for a moment thoughts such as these."

"Blest assurance, that has made me one of the happiest of human beings!" cried Clairville. "Melina loves me, and what else has Florio Clairville got to hope for in the world?"

"And yet, Florio," sighed our heroine in a hesitating and agitated voice.

"Yet what, my love?"

"Has not fate placed insurmountable obstacles in the way of our happiness?"

"Ah! I understand you now," said Florio, striking his forehead; "and I see the full extent of my misery and despair. The humble painter—the lowly born Florio Clairville, is no fitting match for the peerless Signora Melina, of the proud and noble house of Bianchi. No, no! presumptuous fool that I have been, how dared I thus aspire? I have flattered myself with false hopes, and have indulged in delusive visions. The Signora Melina despises the beggar Clairville, as her haughty uncle would term him, and she has only been sporting with his feelings!"

"Florio!" gasped forth Melina, in a still more agitated voice, and looking up in his face as if she would penetrate to his very soul, "are you mad? Or do you know what you say? Oh, how have I ever merited such cruel words as those you have just now made use of? Heaven knows that I love you with all that ardour and purity of spirit which can spring from the heart of woman; but my uncle——"

"Has he not proved himself unworthy of the name, Melina?" interrupted Florio, hastily; "has he not persecuted you with the heart of a fiend? And would he not, to gratify his own obstinate and unnatural wishes, have sacrificed you to one of the most abandoned miscreants in existence—nay, more, the betrayer of his own daughter—she whom you have hitherto known as the unfortunate Olympia? And is it for the authority of a man like this that you would entertain the least respect, and pay due deference to his will? By Heaven! the idea is monstrous!"

"Florio," said Melina, "your language is wild; I do not understand you. What would you have me do?"

"I would have you reflect calmly, Melina, on the painful circumstances connected with us, and decide accordingly," replied Clairville; "you owe the Prince Bianchi no allegiance; he has broken the solemn promise which he made to your mother on her death-bed, and treated you with unparalleled cruelty and injustice; and, therefore, should you hold his future authority at defiance. Will you be left alone in the world, without a lawful protector?"

"Ah!" ejaculated the blushing damsel, "I understand you now, Clairville; you would have me consent to a clandestine marriage!"

"And would there be anything criminal in that for two beings so fondly devoted as we are to one another?" eagerly interrogated Clairville. "Should we be to blame, situated as we are? But think not, my Melina, that I am prompted by sordid or mercenary motives; no—by all my hopes, if you can harbour such a thought to my prejudice, though it would probably cost me my life, I would immediately resign all pretensions to your hand, and fly your presence for ever. Say but the word, then, and we part for ever."

"Rash man!" cried Melina. "Oh, forbear!—How you torture me!—What would you have me do?"

"Promise me that in three months from the present time, if nothing particular occurs to prevent it, that you will become my wife," answered Florio; "and in the meantime I will watch your happiness with a jealous eye, and be to you all that the most affectionate brother can be towards an only and beloved sister."

"Florio," replied Melina, "I implore you, do not urge me upon a point over which it is impossible for me, at present, to make up my mind. My heart revolts from the idea of doing anything in secret, and what would the world think——"

"What would the world think?" repeated Clairville, impatiently; "who dare impugn your character or your motives? And as for the opinion of the world, bah!"

"And can this be Florio Clairville who gives utterance to such words as these?" said Melina. "I am surprised—I am shocked at you."

"Oh, pardon me, Melina, if in the agitation of my mind I have said anything that is painful to your feelings," he said; "but my brain is so distracted that, indeed, I scarcely knew what I gave utterance to! Will you grant me the promise I have requested of you?"

"Spare me, Clairville; indeed I cannot; my feelings revolt at the idea of making any such a vow."

"It is enough, then," ejaculated Florio,

striking his forehead with anguish. "I have cruelly deceived myself; you never loved me, Melina, and death alone can terminate my misery and despair."

"Hold! Florio, unless you would drive me to distraction," she exclaimed; "what can I say, how remove the terrible, the cruel doubts which you have suffered to take possession of your mind? How prove to you the strength and sincerity of the passion I have encouraged for you? And you now accuse me of the vilest hypocrisy, and infidelity! Alas!

THE APPARITION APPEARING TO THE PRINCE BIANCHI.

Clairville, how have I deserved this? Would to Heaven that we had never more met, since Florio Clairville, it now seems, takes delight to torture me!"

She covered her face with her hands as she thus spoke, and hysterical sobs choked her further utterance. Clairville approached her with much emotion and alarm, and placing his hand upon her arm, said—

"Wretch that I am! What have I said? What have I done? Oh, that I should cause one pang in the bosom of that fair and innocent being, for whose happiness I would gladly lay down my life! Melina, oh, look up, and forgive your headstrong and distracted Florio."

She raised her head and looked gently, though reproachfully at him through her tears, as she thus spoke—

"Oh, Florio, why accuse me as you have done of inconstancy and deception, when I always exerted myself to the utmost to satisfy you how different were the sentiments which held the most predominant sway in my breast? But you will not urge the request you have just now made? You must see the impolicy and the indelicacy of doing so in my present state of mind, and forbear."

Florio traversed the room for a few moments in a state of the greatest excitement, but at last turning to our heroine, he said:—

"Oh, Melina, dare I hope for forgiveness, for the wild and presumptuous language I have addressed to you? It was not dictated by vanity, or dishonour, but from the intensity of the love I bear you, and the anguish of despair, when I heard you express ideas that would annihilate all my hopes for ever. Could you but read my heart (as I had fondly flattered myself that you did,) you would know the sincerity with which I speak. But no more; my truant tongue has placed me, I am afraid, in a wrong position in your eyes, and I have nothing more to hope for now, than your pardon for my apparent boldness, and, since my presence has become painful and embarrassing to you, since——"

"Florio!" interrupted the agitated maiden, sinking on his bosom, and looking up in his face with such an expression beaming from her lovely and intelligent eyes, that spoke more, far more than any language could possibly have done the pure sentiments of her soul, and showed at once the intensity, the more than earthly love she bore towards him. "Oh, Florio, again I implore you to forbear giving utterance to observations that must eminate from the temporary distraction of your mind, and not from the more noble and generous dictates of your heart. Why seek to exact from me such a vow, convinced as you already are of my love?"

"Dearest Melina," replied her lover, pressing her fair hand (which she had presented to him) to his lips; "you do pardon me, then, for the hasty and imprudent words I uttered?"

"Pardon you, Florio?" said our heroine, and again she beamed upon him a look of the most unbounded affection. "Oh, most gladly!"

"And may I presume to put one question to you, Melina, on which all my hopes of future happiness depend?" asked Clairville, anxiously, and at the same time he looked in her face with that eager expression which showed plainly the thoughts that were passing in his mind.

"Name it, Florio," replied the damsel, in a faltering voice.

"Will you," said Florio, "promise me, that should at any time circumstances permit, you will consent to become mine, and mine only?"

"Oh, Clairville," answered the blushing Melina, "why put that question to me, which seems to imply a doubt of my candour and truth? I promise you, and with all sincerity I do so, that I will never, under any circumstances, become the wife of any other man but Florio Clairville."

"Enough, enough, beloved girl," ejaculated her lover, again pressing her with the fondest transport to his bosom. "I am satisfied, and you have now made me the happiest of human beings. Henceforth you shall never more hear me urge that which the impetuosity of my love just now urged me to do; but I will be your brother, friend, protector, until such time as it may please Providence to bring about the completion of my bliss; and sanguine hopes spring up in my breast, that that time is not far distant. Oh, Melina, what heavenly joys will then be ours, with what feelings of indifference shall we be able to look back upon the gloomy past as only some painful dream. Tell me, Melina, does not your heart throb, your hopes expand at the blissful anticipation?"

Melina could make no reply, but she hid her blushing face in his bosom, and her heart's palpitation showed plainly how fondly she participated in her lover's feelings. A silence of some minutes ensued, for they were both too much agitated to speak, but at length our heroine looked up, and in a timid and hesitating voice, she said—

"But, Florio, would it not have been much better and far more satisfactory had I been rescued from the fate with which my misguided uncle threatened me, by any other means than the interference of the brigand chief?"

"Nay, my dearest Melina," replied Clairville; "let not that idea disturb your mind; the Prince Bianchi has himself to blame for all that has happened, and who can censure you for adopting any means that presented themselves to you of escaping from such tyranny and persecution? Believe me, you will find that Allesandro Massaroni, although a brigand, is a man of the strictest honour, as I have experienced, and that he and his wife will treat you with the utmost respect and deference. The time that you may be compelled to remain here, will probably be brief; all may quickly be arranged to our satisfaction, and shall I not be near you? Oh, Melina, notwithstanding all the anxieties that at present press upon our mind, how happy may we not be in each other's society!"

"Your words reassure me, Florio," said our heroine, "and I will endeavour to wait with patience and fortitude the will of Providence."

"Well said, my beloved Melina," said Clairville, "and depend upon it you will have no cause to regret having formed that resolution. That All-merciful and Omnipotent power that has hitherto sustained you throughout so many trials, will not desert you on this occasion. Oh, my love, can you form any conjecture of the sufferings I have endured since our separation, and knowing the eminent danger by which you were on every side surrounded?"

"Yes, Florio," answered Melina; "it is impossible that any one could form a more just opinion of the anguish of mind to which you were subjected, than myself; and it was that conviction that rendered my own misery the more complete. But we are now restored to each other, and let us hope that the time is not far distant when all our troubles will be at an end."

"Oh, blessed words!" exclaimed her lover; "they impart fresh hope and confidence to me, and I feel as though I were another being, now that I am again gladdened by your sweet presence. Had you been consigned to the horrible and revolting fate with which you were threatened by your unnatural relative, life would have become insupportable to me, and madness and despair must have seized upon my brain. To Allesandro Massaroni I owe everything, and I hope that the time will yet arrive when we shall have it in our power to make him a due acknowledgment for the numerous and inestimable services he has from the most generous and disinterested motives rendered us."

"To that wish," observed our heroine, "you may believe me, Florio, I most heartily respond; and, moreover, nothing would afford me greater gratification than to see the brigand chief enabled to abandon his present course of life, and to enter into that position of society he is so eminently qualified to adorn."

"That wish, my beloved Melina," returned Clairville, "does honour to your heart. Massaroni is no insignificant or despicable individual, as I have had ample time and opportunities of discovering since I have been with him; he possesses a mind of the most noble quality, and might fairly put to the blush many who ostentatiously vaunt of their virtues, and who are considered by the ignorant and unthinking part of the community, as something superior to ordinary human beings."

"I agree with you in that opinion, Clairville," replied Melina: "I have much to communicate to you which will, I have no doubt, create your especial wonder; but not now; I do not feel myself disposed for the task."

It will be seen by this, that Melina alluded to the manuscript of Valentia, which she thought it would not be prudent to make Clairville acquainted with till they had both somewhat more recovered their composure. After a pause, however, she said—

"But there is one thing I wish to ask you, Florio."

"And what is that, my dear Melina?" interrogated Clairville, anxiously.

"Has it never struck you, that the brigand chief's features bear a most extraordinary resemblance to those of the portrait at the Villa Rosa?" said Melina.

"It has, indeed," replied her lover; "and I have frequently observed the same to Massaroni himself, but he has always seemed violently agitated, and anxious to avoid the subject. You also recollect the powerful emotion he evinced when he first accidently beheld the portrait?"

"True," said our heroine: "his history has been a strange, romantic, and unfortunate one, from all that I have heard of it."

"Yes," answered Clairville; "from all that I have been able to gather from him respecting it, his mother was betrayed, and afterwards abandoned, together with her offspring, by some wealthy nobleman; and after enduring some years of misery and remorse, she died of a broken heart."

"And refused to make her son acquainted with the name of her seducer?"

"She did; no doubt, fearing that he might be exasperated to revenge against his unnatural parent," answered Clairville.

"Did Massaroni ever mention the name of his mother to you?" asked Melina.

"He did not," returned Clairville. "But why are you so curious and so anxious upon this subject, Melina?"

"I have my reasons, Florio," she replied; "which at some other time I will explain. But do you believe in the identity of the Signora Zitella, and that Olympia is really her daughter?"

"I feel satisfied of the truth of it. I was present when the villain Malvolio made his dying confession, which fully corroborated all that Zitella stated, and proved that Olympia was the daughter who had been so inhumanly taken from her by the orders of the Prince Bianchi, beyond a doubt."

"Alas!" sighed our heroine, "how guilty has the prince been; would to Heaven that he could be awakened to a true feeling of compunction, and endeavour to make all the atonement in his power for the many errors he has committed against society."

"And I do not despair that he will be so," returned Clairville; "and in that belief I look forward to the most happy results. Oh, my Melina, when I reflect upon the dreadful sufferings, the anxiety of mind to which you have been subjected, and the disgusting fate from which you have escaped, my heart swells in gratitude to the Supreme for restoring you in safety to me. And to know that the sentiments with which you have honoured me, have undergone no change, is sufficient, indeed, to make me one of the happiest of human beings."

Melina, whose feelings entirely coincided with those of her lover, was about to return some answer, when she was prevented from doing so by the return of the brigand and his wife, who having once more congratulated them on their restoration to each other, invited them to accompany them to the cavern, where Montaldi, Zitella, and Mira, were waiting to receive them; and Clairville having taken the arm of our heroine, they obeyed.

The meeting that took place between the parties assembled, was of the most cordial description, and the Signora Zitella could not but the more admire the amiable qualities of the youthful and beauteous Melina, the longer she remained in her society. To our heroine also, as might have been expected, the unfortunate Zitella was an object of the deepest sympathy, and she could no longer entertain the smallest doubt of the truth of all she had stated while she bitterly condemned and deprecated the cruel and abandoned conduct of the Prince Bianchi, who had been the guilty cause of so much misery to his innocent and unsuspecting victims.

They continued in each other's company for the remainder of the day, and before they separated, they had become as much familiarized with each other as if they had been the members of one family, and had never been separated from each other.

When our heroine, with her faithful attendant, retired for the night, she felt more composed in her mind than she had been for some time past, and she began to look forward to the future with that degree of sanguine hope with which her friends had sought to inspire her.

"Something seems to whisper to me," she remarked, "that the clouds which have so long obscured the horizon of my destiny will shortly pass away, and that I shall at length be rewarded for the many troubles it has been my hard lot to endure, by experiencing complete happiness."

"Ah, my dear mistress," replied Floretta, "how it delights me to hear you talk thus! Persevere in encouraging such consolatory ideas, and depend upon it the time is not far distant when they will be realised. You see that Massaroni has kept his word, and that he has made the most judicious and ample arrangements for your accommodation and comfort."

"Oh, yes," coincided our heroine, "and I owe him an immense debt of gratitude for his disinterested kindness. Should my uncle relent, all may be amicably arranged, and then I shall have nothing to regret."

"True, signora; and after all, you see, it would have been madness for you to have rejected the aid of the brigand chief at the very moment when you were placed in such imminent peril. But have you mentioned anything to Signor Clairville respecting the manuscript of the Signora Valentia?"

"I have not," answered Melina, "for I considered that his mind was too much agitated with other subjects to enable him to listen with that calmness and attention which it requires. From what he has related to me, however, I feel more convinced than ever that Massaroni is the son of that unfortunate woman, and that, consequently, the Prince Bianchi is his father."

"May Heaven prompt him to look over the errors of his guilty father!" interrupted our heroine, "and may they be reconciled to each other!"

"To that wish I heartily respond, signora," remarked Floretta. "But surely Massaroni could never possess that unnatural, vindictive, and revengeful feeling as to be goaded to raise his hand against his own father?"

"Ah, Floretta," observed her mistress, "has he not ample cause to feel the most implacable hatred against the author of his mother's shame, misery, and untimely death, and he who has been the primary cause of plunging him into his present course of life? I tremble for the consequences, should that discovery which we anticipate ever take place."

"Dismiss such apprehensions from your mind, signora," said her attendant; "for, indeed, I trust that they will prove to be entirely groundless. Massaroni possesses too strong and generous a mind to commit himself in such a manner, and which must leave a stigma on his character, which nothing could ever eradicate."

Melina shook her head doubtingly, and after a pause, she observed—

"By this time, probably, the Prince Bianchi has been informed of the defeat of the troops sent in pursuit of us, and of the complete triumph of Massaroni; and how terrible will be his rage and disappointment! In spite of all I have so unjustly suffered from him, I cannot help pitying him."

"Ah, my lady," replied her domestic, "how little does he merit the kind and generous feelings you express towards him; have not all the sufferings of mind he may now be enduring been brought upon him entirely by his own vicious conduct?"

"True, Floretta," answered our heroine, "but still I bear no animosity towards him, nor do I wish to pursue him with a feeling of revenge and exultation. All that I want, and that I sincerely pray for, is that we may be brought in time to a due sense of the errors he has committed, and that he may again be restored to each other in a true spirit of harmony and friendship, forgetting the past, or, if we do indeed remember it, endeavouring by the future to make amends for its errors."

"Spoken like my own sweet mistress," remarked Floretta; "and may your hopes be realised, they deserve to be; and I have too good an opinion of the natural character of the Prince Bianchi, to belive that, when he has got rid of the fatal prejudices, and the unfornate infatuation which has so long beset it, he will any longer remain obstinate. He will be awakened to a sense of the great wrongs he has committed against yourself, signora, and others, and will only be too happy to effect a reconciliation, and to return once more to those paths of rectitude from which he has so long unfortunately deviated."

Melina could not deny the truth and force of the argument which her faithful domestic advanced, and after some further conversation, they retired to repose.

CHAPTER LII.

THE COUNT ALBERTI CONTINUES IN A STATE OF THE UTMOST DANGER.—THE PRINCE BIANCHI RECEIVES INTELLIGENCE OF THE DEFEAT OF THE TROOPS: HIS AGONY AND DESPAIR.—THE DESPERATE ATTEMPTED ACT OF SUICIDE PREVENTED.

WE left the Count Alberti and the Prince Bianchi at the time when the former had just, in the excitement of his feelings, ruptured the blood vessel, which placed his life in the most imminent danger, and increased the agony of Bianchi to an almost insupportable degree. That anguish of mind, as may be imagined, was not at all diminished by his second interview with Fransisco, and the state of doubt and uncertainty he was in respecting the result of the troops who had gone in pursuit of the brigands that had captured Melina; and all the remonstrances and advice of the doctor, Signor Giachomo, had but little effect in calming his feelings. It seemed to him as if some infernal spell had suddenly come upon him, and that whichever way he might attempt to counteract it, his destruction was inevitable.

After the lapse of some hours, Alberti revived to a state of consciousness, but was unable to speak, and Signor Giachomo still prohibited the visits of the Prince Bianchi to his chamber, for he thought that they might be fraught with the greatest danger to his patient; though he had the greatest difficulty in persuading the prince to follow his advice.

In his chamber, and when alone, the Prince Bianchi gave himself up to feelings of the most ungovernable rage and despair, and would suffer no one to approach him; indeed, the domestics were all afraid of him, and the Villa Rosa was in the utmost state of confusion.

"May the curses of hell light upon all those who have been the cause of bringing about this misery!" he said, in a hoarse voice, as he hastily paced his chamber, with his hands clasped to his temples; and the expression of his eyes and the distortion of his features fully evincing the tumultuous passions which at the time raged and struggled within his breast. "Ruin—destruction—disgrace, and infamy, stare me in the face, and I know not how to avoid them. Melina torn from my power—the Count Alberti in such a condition that precludes all chance of his recovery—Zitella and her daughter living, and that daughter proved to be, beyond all possibility of a doubt, Olympia the victim of that man whom I would have compelled my niece to become united to;—I shall go mad!—And then the sudden and unexpected appearance of the man whom I have so much cause to dread—Fransisco, the brother of the fair Florentia, whom, like my other victims, I so heartlessly betrayed and abandoned to the greatest misery. I am surrounded by enemies of the most fearful character, and yet I cannot help myself;—they held me at complete defiance, and mock and triumph in my anguish and despair! What is to be done?—How can I escape the ruin which stares me in the face?— I see too well that it is impossible for me to do so, and that my career is rapidly drawing to a close. But the brigand-chief is the principal cause of all this; that daring robber, who has ever been an insurmountable obstacle to the accomplishment of any designs I may have had in contemplation. In spite of all my efforts to the contrary, I shudder even at the mention of his name, and feel convinced that he is destined to be my ultimate destroyer. Would that I had the means of secretly destroying him; and is not that to be effected? Are the whole of his daring band invulnerable to the temptation of a rich bribe?—By all my hopes, I would not mind making the fortune of him who would do this service for me. Fool that I have been never to have thought of that before. But it is too late now; and even if it were not, such is the fidelity of the rascals to their chief—the terror in which he holds them, that I doubt much whether I could succeed in winning one of them to my purpose. And then, the extraordinary likeness which Massaroni bears to the portrait of the hapless and much wronged Valentia! By what cursed circumstance has that strange coincidence being brought about? The dream, too, which haunted my imagination the other night, and the phantom which I afterwards beheld!—My senses could not have deceived me! No, it was all as palpable as truth itself, and it is useless for me to endeavour to persuade myself to the contrary. What a remarkable and overwhelming accumulation of horrors is this, and there is no way for me to escape from them!"

He paused, for his emotion was so great that it choked his utterance, and the perspiration caused by the extraordinary excitement of his feelings, streamed copiously from every pore.

It was night, and the moon was shining brilliantly in the Heavens, surrounded by myriads of stars; but how little was the tranquil scene in accordance with the feelings of the wretched Prince Bianchi, and he almost in his heart cursed the serenity which reigned around, and which seemed to mock the bitter anguish of his thoughts. However, unable to remain any longer in the solitude of his own chamber, and with such torturing ideas crowding upon his brain, he walked forth into the open air, and wandered for some time among the beautiful and extensive grounds that surrounded the villa. Never before had he felt so lonely and wretched as he did on that occasion, and it was in vain that he endeavoured to find some degree of consolation. What was there indeed to console him or to lead him to hope?—It was a bitter mockery and delusion even to think of it. At length, tired with rambling about, he threw himself on one of the garden seats, which was placed beneath the umbrageous foliage of a noble tree, and gave himself up to the most gloomy and insupportable meditation.

"And this is the sure reward for a life of guilt," he muttered to himself; "retribution is sure sooner or later to overtake its votaries. And am I not justly punished?—Have I not been guilty of the most heartless villany towards those who confided in the honour and sincerity of my propositions, and whom it was my duty to cherish?—I have; and they now rise up in judgment against me. And would I not even now perpetuate my guilt, by the brutal sacrifice of Melina, if she were in my power?—I would! And can I wonder that the vengeance of Heaven should overtake me?—No; I merit all the misery that I meet with, and must still expect to encounter."

He was interrupted in the midst of this soliloquy by the sound of footsteps, and looking up, he beheld one of the domestics approaching him.

"Your pardon, excellenza," said the man, when he had got near him; "but I am glad that I have found you, though I have been searching for you everywhere."

"And what is your errand now you have found me?" demanded Bianchi, haughtily; "speak! quick! Do not keep me in suspense. Has any fresh trouble occurred to annoy me?"

"I know not, your highness," answered the servant; "but one of the soldiers who was despatched to the Villa Civetti——"

"Ah! what of him?" interrupted Bianchi, impatiently.

"He has just arrived at the villa, my lord," answered the man, "in great haste, and covered with dust; he appears to be in a state of great trepidation, and desires to see your highness immediately."

"By the infernal host!" cried the Prince Bianchi, starting to his feet, and his countenance exhibiting much excitement; "there is some more ill news for me; the fates have conspired against me, and seem resolved to drive me to madness!"

With these words, he darted precipitately from the spot, and in an instant gained the villa, and entered the room in which he had been given to understand the messenger was waiting to receive him. His clothes were disordered, as if he had been in some recent skirmish, and he appeared to be much fatigued with travelling.

"Now man, your business?" demanded Bianchi in peremptory tones. "What brings you here in such haste, and without your comrades?"

"Unfortunately, your highness, I am the bearer of bad news," replied the soldier.

"Ay, I foreboded as much," returned the prince, hastily; "let me know the worst at once. Where are your comrades?"

"Such as remain of them, your highness," replied the man, "are on their way hither, and will, doubtless, be here before long."

"Such as remain of them!" repeated Bianchi, and a frown overspread his features. "What mean you? Did they go in pursuit of the brigands?"

"They did, my lord," answered the man; "and overtook them in a lonely place some distance from the Villa Civetti."

"Ah! and what then?"

"Indeed I almost fear to tell you, excellenza."

"No trifling, rascal, but let me know the truth at once!" sternly and impatiently demanded Bianchi.

"The brigands were waiting in ambush for us, your highness, and took us by surprise, destroying a great number at the first fire. A determined combat then commenced, which lasted for some time, and our men fought with the greatest valour; but Massaroni had every advantage over us, and both our officers being unfortunately slain, our troops became disheartened, and unable to resist, were put to the rout, and Massaroni with his prize escaped."

"Hell and furies!" cried the distracted nobleman, "this is too much for human patience to endure! Massaroni escaped altogether, and with Melina in his power! All then is lost!

Nothing but shame, disappointment and contain surround me on every side! The cowards! had they done their duty, this could never have happened."

"Pardon me, your highness," said the soldier, "but our troops fought with the most indomitable courage, and——"

"Liar!" interrupted Bianchi, fiercely, "you have all conspired against me! Away with you, and think yourself lucky, if after a strict investigation of this dastardly affair, I do not punish yourself and your comrades severely! Begone, I say!"

The man needed no second order, but retired from the room, glad to escape from the fury of the excited nobleman, and for several minutes after he was gone, Bianchi paced the room to and fro in a state of the most indescribable agitation, and muttering dreadful curses to himself.

"The climax of my misery has arrived," he cried, "and madness and despair settle upon my brain!—My troops again defeated, and the brigand chief escaped, with Melina in his power! Oh! he is, indeed, triumphant, and she is lost to me for ever!—By this time she is probably restored to the arms of the presumptuous beggar, Clairville, and long before I can find any means to prevent it, she will have become his wife! His wife! Powers of darkness! are there no means to prevent that? Must all my authority be set at defiance, and the designs I have so long had in contemplation be thus frustrated, and that by a robber and a murderer, upon whose head a price is set?—I shall go distracted at the bare thought! And is my proud career to be thus brought to an ignominious termination? Oh, Melina, it is, indeed, your turn to exult now! Obstinate, disobedient girl, may every curse descend upon your head! And the Count Alberti, too, when he comes to hear of this, will it not, in his present dangerous condition, prove his death-blow?—The flames of perdition cannot be more torturing than are those thoughts to my mind!"

Again he threw himself upon a seat, and swaying his body to and fro with the agony of his feelings, smote his breast and forehead with his clinched fist, alternately. He was aroused from his gloomy and torturing meditations by the entrance of Signor Giachomo; and he started hastily to his feet, and gazed wildly at him.

"Pardon me, your highness, for this intrusion," said the doctor, "but I thought you would be anxious to know the state of the Count Alberti, and——"

"Ah!" hastily interrupted Bianchi, "what of him?—What of the Count Alberti? Have you some fresh intelligence with which to trouble me? Is he dead?"

"No, your highness," answered Giachomo;

"but I think he is rather worse than he was in the morning, and I would, therefore, have you be prepared for anything that may take place."

"Ay!" ejaculated Bianchi, with a bitter smile, "let it all come—let the fiends work their worst and fill the measure of my miseries to the brim. I am prepared for all, for I see that my career is fast drawing to a close. But I must see the count; I have much to say to him; and if there be any delay, it may be too late."

"Nay, your highness, if you would not endanger the life of the count," said Signor Giachomo, "let me beg of you not to persist in that determination; it can be productive of no possible good, and his lordship would not understand anything you might say to him, for he is totally unconscious of everything; besides, you seem to be in a great state of agitation, and——"

"Agitation!" repeated the prince, impatiently; "and would you not be in a state of agitation if you had that which I have to torture you?"

"Has, then, your highness received any fresh painful news?" asked Giachomo.

"Yes," answered Bianchi; "I have just heard that which is enough to rack my brain to madness. The troops who went in pursuit of the brigands have suffered a shameful defeat, and my niece is now securely in the power of the rascal, Massaroni."

"Indeed, my lord?" said the doctor; "that is a most unfortunate circumstance, and——"

"Unfortunate!" interrupted the prince, passionately; "it is madness! 'tis despair! And by my hopes, I will not rest until I have had revenge against all who have been the cause of it!—But leave me, signor; I must commune with my own thoughts, and desire that I may not again be interrupted."

Signor Giachomo returned no answer, for he saw plain enough that it would only tend to exasperate him, and bowing, he quitted the room.

"What is to be done?" said the Prince Bianchi, when he had quitted the room; "must I tamely submit to this without attempting to tear Melina from the brigand's power, and seeking a terrible revenge? No, by Heaven I will not! But, fool that I am to talk thus; what means have I at my command? Massaroni in his mountain retreat may set every enemy at defiance, and it would be certain destruction to approach him. I have already had sufficient proof of that, and it would be madness again to brave the danger. Melina is lost to me for ever, and I shall soon be denounced to the world as a villain of the blackest dye. And can I rebut the accusation? I cannot; the brigand chief possesses every proof to convict me. My soul shrinks appalled at the thought of the infamy and degradation that awaits me; and with the cowardice of guilt, I tremble to meet the charges that will be brought against me. And how can I avoid them? It is impossible, unless indeed, I coward-like take to flight, and abandon my present proud position. Psha! I will not, cannot entertain the thought for an instant; that would indeed render the triumph of my enemies complete."

Such were the torturing reflections that continued to distract the mind of the guilty Prince Bianchi; and it was not until a late hour that he made up his mind to seek his bed; and when he did so, he found it impossible to sleep, but lay tossing about till the morning, when he arose, and having sent a servant to inquire after the health of the Count Alberti, and ascertained that he was no worse, with a brain fevered by the intensity of thought, he quitted the house, and strolling from the city, he entered into the open country, and where from the earliness of the hour, and few individuals being yet about, he had not any cause to fear that he would be interrupted in his meditations. There was a wandering wildness and vacancy in the expression of his eye, which showed at once the disordered state of his mind; and his step was hesitating and trembling as though he faltered beneath some desperate purpose on which he had partly fixed his determination. Sometimes he stopped abruptly and looked behind him, as though he were fearful that some person was watching and following him, and then he would hurry on again, with renewed speed, and seemed to have succeeded in conquering his former hesitation. The conflicting thoughts, the tumult of passions that struggled in his breast, were of the most fearful description; and such a ghastly change had come over his countenance only within the last few hours, that no person could scarcely have believed that he was the same man.

The morning was dull and chilly, and the atmosphere was thick and hazy; but Bianchi took no notice of the weather, for his thoughts were too deeply engrossed by other subjects of far more importance to him, at any rate.

At length he reached a lonely part, and there he suddenly paused and once more looked around him, in order to ascertain whether he was observed by anybody.

"Why should I hesitate?" he at length said, after a pause; "has not Fortune turned her back upon me altogether? and can I dare to meet the world's scorn, disgrace, and opprobrium? No, by heaven I cannot! It is but the work of an instant; one bold step, and I shall at once put an end to this constant state of anguish, disappointment, and fear, and rid myself of a life which has now become a burthen and a misery to me. What have I to make me cling to existence? Within the last few days all the hopes that I had formed have been annihilated, and my guilt is threatened to be exposed to the world, by those who have the power to do so, and who, I am convinced, will not fail to keep their word. Should I not then be shorn of all my proud dignity and station in society, and looked upon as a thing of scorn? I cannot bear the thought; and my mind can no longer endure being kept in this constant state of excitement. There is no one near me; the hour befits the awful deed, and let me then at once put an end to all my earthly cares and anxieties. Heaven pardon me the desperate crime, and have mercy on my guilty soul! Valentia, Zitella, Florentia, and all my other unfortunate victims, your wrongs will now be avenged!"

As the wretched man gave utterance to these words, he took from his bosom a pistol, and was in the act of presenting it at his head, when his arm was suddenly arrested by some person from behind, the pistol was wrested from his grasp, and looking up, to the astonishment and consternation of the Prince Bianchi, he found himself in the hold of Fransisco.

"Rash fool! conscience-stricken wretch, what would you do?" exclaimed Fransisco, as he fixed upon the unhappy nobleman a stern look, "think you by an act of self-murder that you will make atonement for your other crimes?"

"Fransisco again here!" gasped forth Bianchi in a faint voice, and shrinking beneath his stern glance.

"Ay, Prince Bianchi," he answered, "it is indeed, your *friend*, Fransisco, who has done you far more service than you deserved, namely, saved your worthless life! Bah! get thee home, man, and advise your friends not to suffer you to go at large again, since these are your mad freaks."

"What devil's power guided your footsteps here at such a moment?" demanded the enraged prince, in a horse voice.

"Oh, that matters but little," replied Fransisco, carelessly; "I am here, you see, and it is a fortunate thing for you that I am, or you would now have been in another world, where, it strikes me, you are not quite prepared to make an appearance at present."

"By what right do you seek to control my conduct?" demanded Bianchi.

"Oh, your highness," returned Fransisco, with a sneer, "indeed, I cannot afford to lose you yet. You have much more to perform yet before you and I part company."

"Audacious scoundrel!" said the indignant and exasperated nobleman.

"Better language, my lord," said Fransisco; "methinks you forget who it is you are addressing."

"Leave me."

"Not so, your highness; at any rate, not till I have seen you safely enter your villa."

"You will not dare to follow me there?"

"Indeed, but I will."

"Confusion! This is not to be borne.'

"Nay, my lord, you may as well keep yourself cool, for I am not to be intimidated from the execution of anything upon which I have fixed my mind. So, your conscience at length reproaches you with the crimes you have committed? It is time that it did, and I trust

PRINCE BIANCHI SURPRISED AT BEHOLDING FRANSISCO MALIETEVERA.

that it will not allow you much rest or enjoyment in the midst of all your wealth."

"Fransisco," said the Prince Bianchi, in a tremulous voice, "I have acceded to all your demands; why, then, do you thus persist in seeking to torture me?"

"Oh, your highness," replied Fransisco, with a malignant grin; "indeed it affords me infinite delight and gratification to do so. Nor can you feel surprised to think it should do so, when you recall to mind all the many *favours* I have received from you."

"Provoking, taunting devil !" said Bianchi ; "I will no longer listen to you ; away, I say, and leave me to my own thoughts."

"Well," returned Fransisco, sarcastically, "I am sorry that I should be the means of interrupting the indulgence of them, since they must be so very agreeable. But I tell you again, that I shall not leave you until I see you safe at home ; so, if you wish to get rid of my company, the sooner you depart from this place the better. I do no expect that you will always be in the humour to commit suicide, and you will be much obliged to me when you are restored to your senses."

"Will nothing prevail upon you to retire from my presence ?" demanded Bianchi, "and to cease to persecute me in the manner you are now doing ?"

"I do not think it is very likely," answered Fransisco, with a disagreeable laugh. "But, come, come, my lord, we waste time. Will you allow me take your arm ?"

"This daring insolence is intolerable !" again ejaculated the prince ; "Fransisco, you may yet have bitter cause to repent this !"

"Indeed, your highness," he replied "these idle threats will have not the least effect on me ; there is no conduct that I may think proper to pursue towards you that I can have the least possible cause to repent. Come, come, we tarry."

The Prince Bianchi bit his lips with indignation, but finding that it was useless to remonstrate, or to offer any resistance to so determined a ruffian, and one, too, whom he had so much reason to dread, he walked away from the spot towards the villa, followed closely by Fransisco.

When they had arrived within sight of the house, Fransisco stopped, and addressing himself to Bianchi, said—

"There is now no occasion for me to accompany you further, my lord, so you may as well proceed at once to the villa, into which I can watch you. Once more, however, I advise you not to act the part of a madman a second time, by attempting to destroy yourself, until you are a little better prepared to give an account of your earthly actions. Adieu, Prince, Bianchi. I dare say before many days have elapsed, we shall have the pleasure of meeting each other again."

"Heaven forbid !" said Bianchi, vehemently. "Fransisco, beware of what you do, for, although you may think that I am in your power and at your mercy, you may find yourself mistaken."

"Pshaw, your highness," replied Fransisco, scornfully, "what a waste of breath is this ; have I not before told you that no idle threats will frighten me from anything that I may have in contemplation ? You will find that I am a man of my word, you may depend upon it."

The Prince Bianchi returned no answer, but fixing upon him a look of mingled hatred and fear, he slowly moved from the spot towards the villa, Fransisco watching him steadfastly till he entered the house, when, with a laugh of scorn and exultation, he also retired.

CHAPTER LIII.

THE BENIGHTED TRAVELLERS.—THE ATTACK BY THE BRIGANDS.—THE PRISONER.—A MOST REMARKABLE AND IMPORTANT DISCOVERY.—THE PROSPECTS OF FLORIO CLAIRVILLE BEGIN TO BRIGHTEN.

It now becomes necessary that we should, for a short time, deviate from the main thread of our narrative in order to introduce persons and incidents immediately connected with, and of the utmost importance to it.

It was a dark, wet, and miserable night, and although the season of the year had not far advanced, for the last few days the air had been particularly keen and piercing ; but on this particular night, the wind blew fiercely, and, added to the rapidly falling rain, rendered it remarkably unpleasant.

No night for travellers this, especially through a dismal and almost impenetrable wood bordering upon those stupendous mountains, among which the hero of our tale and his intrepid band had taken up their abode. It is to such a dreary scene as this we have briefly described, that we wish to direct the attention of the reader, and to the individuals who at that time, at an hour which was rapidly approaching midnight, were travelling through it.

These consisted of an elderly gentleman of noble person and general deportment, mounted on a fine and graceful horse, and a young man who rode by his side, and who probably might be his son, though there was not the least likeness existed between them. Two attendants followed behind, and the whole of the travellers were evidently drenched to the skin, and, as might have been expected, as most persons would be if placed in similar circumstances, they were in none of the best of humours.

"By the mass, Adolphus," observed the elder gentleman, addressing himself to his companion ; "this is a most unpleasant and vexatious situation to be placed in ; benighted in a gloomy, and apparently interminable forest, in the midst of such a storm as this, and without the least prospect of a human habitation where we might obtain a temporary shelter, and with no person to guide us on our way."

"You say truly, my lord," answered the young gentleman ; "it is not one of the most agreeable situations in the world to be placed in ;—and for my own part, I do not care how soon we are extricated from it; it is a pity that we did not remain at the town where we stopped for the night."

"Ay," remarked the other; "perhaps it would have been as well, as circumstances have turned out; but when we quitted there, there were no signs of an approaching storm, and I was anxious to push on my journey, with the hope that happily I may yet be able to discover some members of that unfortunate family which is connected with me by so many painful circumstances, still living."

The nobleman sighed, but he quickly recovered himself, and in gayer accents, said—

"Wheugh! what an abominable nuisance the rain is. I declare I am as wet as if I had been bathing in the ocean in my clothes for an hour. What is to be done? It is no use proceeding in this manner; this confounded forest appears to have no end, and the further we advance, the more we seem to become involved in its intricacies, and devious windings. Jaques, Henri, have you not the least knowledge of the way?"

"None whatever, my lord," answered Jaques.

"If I am not much mistaken," observed Henri, "we are in the Devil's Forest, as it is called, and which borders upon the mountains of the Abbruzzi."

"And a most remarkably consoling piece of information, too," said the young nobleman, with a laugh; "that is the neighbourhood, if I have heard aright, that is infested by the notorious brigand-chief, Allesandro Massaroni, and his desperate band, and if that should turn out to be the case, we may expect them to pay their respects to us every minute."

"The devil!" exclaimed his companion; "we want none of their company; though, by the by, if report speaks truly, this same brigand chief is one of the most polite and gentlemanly individuals in existence."

"That may be," returned Adolpus, "but for my part I do not see anything particularly polite or gentlemanly in picking a pocket or cutting a throat; at any rate, I have not the least wish to be experimentalized on in that way."

"Why no," said the other, "I must own myself that it would not be very agreeable; and as for one half of the romantic stories that I have heard respecting this said Massaroni, I do not believe them, and as you say, Adolphus, I have not the least wish to cultivate his acquaintance. I wish we were fairly out of this forest; for a better place for robbery and murder could not very well be imagined."

"I do not see much prospect of our getting out of it in a hurry," observed Adolphus, "for the more we proceed, the more do we seem to become involved and bewildered in its snares. What a delightful sight a human habitation would be just now, even if it were ever so humble."

"It would, indeed," answered his companion, "but it is not at all likely that we shall meet with one here; for a person must be mad who would ever choose to take up his residence in such a dismal place as this. However, it is no use complaining, for that won't bring us any relief, and as we are in a dilemma, all we can do is to put a good heart on the matter, and get out of it in the best way we can. We are wet through now, and it is, therefore, quite certain that we cannot be much worse, that is one consolation."

"And a fine consolation too," replied Adolphus, with a laugh. "But what is to be done now? It is no use proceeding in this state of doubt and uncertainty."

"What do you propose then?" demanded the nobleman; "that we should remain where we are, eh?"

"I confess that I am completely bewildered, and I know not what to propose."

"Why, we have no other alternative, but to proceed as fast as we can, and trust to Providence to release us from our difficulties. If it was not so confoundedly dark we might be able to form some idea whither we were going. If this be really the Devil's Forest, I must say that it does not belie its name; for a more frightful place I never had the misfortune to behold."

Adolphus returned no answer to this, and the travellers again pushed on their way as well as they could, though it was so dark that they were unable to distinguish objects the least distance before them. The storm rather increased in violence than abated, and the rain descended in such heavy and overwhelming torrents, that it was not without the greatest difficulty that the travellers could bear up against it at all.

In this manner, they proceeded for about another quarter of an hour, and still with no better prospect than ever of getting out of the forest, but on the contrary, their way seemed to be the more intricate and hopeless, and they at length again stopped, and considered what was best to be done.

"To me it seems most probable that we shall have to remain here till daylight," said the elder gentleman, "and then unless we should be fortunate enough to meet with some person who can direct us, we shall never find our way out of the forest. I wish I had bethought me to procure a guide from the town where we stopped."

"Yes, my lord," answered Adolphus, "it was a sad oversight on our part But, ah! did you not perceive that?"

"Perceive what?"

"I thought I distinguished a human form moving about yonder."

"It was only fancy, and your eyes must be remarkably good, if you can distinguish any thing in this darkness."

"Well, I could almost swear that I did," said Adolphus. "I have a strange presentiment that something is about to happen to us."

"Pshaw!" ejaculated his companion, with a laugh. "Why, Adolphus, I am surprised at you; you are quite qualmish."

"Well, this place is not at all calculated to impart the most lively sensations to a person's mind," returned Adolphus; "your lordship is well aware that I am not apt to give way to feelings of fear; but if this forest should be infested by Massaroni and his band, they may surround us sooner than we expect, and what chance should we then stand against them?"

"Not much, I dare say, though we are pretty well armed."

"If we attempted to resist such desperate men, depend upon it we should have to pay for our temerity with our lives," returned Adolphus.

"Well, well," remarked the other; "it is no use meeting troubles half way. Come, let us once more proceed."

They were about to do so, when suddenly a shrill whistle saluted their ears, and they paused in alarm, and looked anxiously around them, and endeavoured, but in vain, to penetrate the intense darkness.

"By the saints!" exclaimed his lordship, "I begin to think that your fears are not unlikely to be realised, Adolphus; I like not that signal at all, and we had better be prepared for the worst; for much may depend upon our firmness and presence of mind."

"They would avail us but little, my lord, against the numbers by whom we should probably be surrounded," said Adolphus.

A second whistle louder than the first, and nearer to them, now saluted their ears, and before they had time to recover themselves, they were surrounded by Rubaldo and about a dozen of the brigands, and instantly disarmed and dragged from their horses.

"Well, gentlemen," said his lordship, as coolly as he could; "you have made quick work of it, at any rate, though I must say that your conduct is anything but courteous and agreeable. May I ask what is your pleasure with us?"

"No doubt you can form a pretty shrewd guess, signor," replied Rubaldo; "it is bad travelling in such a storm as this; you doubtless want a shelter for the night, and, therefore, we will endeavour to accommodate you."

"You are very kind, signor," returned the nobleman, "but we would much rather decline your offer. I suppose it is money that you want, so you had better take it and then begone."

"Oh, no, signor," said Rubaldo, "we must not part on such terms as those. You are gentlemen of noble bearing, and our captain, Allesandro Massaroni, would like the honour of being introduced to you."

"Allesandro Massaroni, the brigand chief!" said his lordship; "I have heard of him frequently, but I must say, candidly, signor, that I have no desire to be introduced to him, at present, at any rate. Therefore, I must request you to allow us to proceed on our journey."

"I am sorry that I cannot comply with your wishes, signora," answered Rubaldo; "Massaroni would not lose the honour of your acquaintance upon any account. But your names?"

"What consequence can it be to you to know?"

"Oh, but indeed it is of every consequence, signor," returned Rubaldo; "so come, quick, for it is no use standing parleying here in the storm."

"Well, then, "answered the gentleman, "if you must know, I am the Count Eugene de Clairville, a nobleman of France; and this is Adolphus D'Aubigny, my friend."

"The Count de Clairville!" repeated the brigand, looking at him narrowly; "this is more surprising still."

"And why so?" demanded the count.

"That question Allesandro Massaroni will probably answer you, my lord," returned Rubaldo "But we tarry; come my lord, and you, signor, must allow me to escort you to our retreat among the mountains."

"Confusion!" exclaimed the count; "what would you with us?"

"Oh, you have nothing to fear, my lord," replied Rubaldo; "not the least harm will befall you, you may depend upon it; you will find that our captain is a perfect gentleman."

"I have no doubt of it," said the count; "but really I would much rather decline the pleasure of seeing him."

"Nonsense, my lord," said Rubaldo; "this is but a waste of time."

"Well," said the count, "I suppose it is no use to offer any resistance."

"I am sure your lordship's good sense will convince you it is not," answered the brigand.

"Lead the way then," remarked the count, himself and Adolphus mounting their horses, "and we will follow you, though I need not again tell you, I presume, it is against our inclination."

Rubaldo made no reply, and two of the brigands having laid hold of the horses' reins to prevent them from riding away, they led them in silence from the spot, the Count de Clairville and his companion entertaining the greatest doubts and apprehensions as to what would be the result of this adventure.

The storm now gradually subsided, and the darkness that had hitherto prevailed became less intense. The count and Adolphus conversed together in low tones, and mutually speculated on what would take place on their being introduced to the brigand chief, though they hoped from what Rubaldo had said, and the description they had heard of the character of Massaroni, that he would proceed to no further violence than that of plundering them of all the property they had about them, which being considerable, was no very pleasant reflection.

"It was an unfortunate job that we did not remain at the town where we had stopped for the night," observed the count; "but who could have suspected what was about to happen?"

"True," coincided Adolphus; "but your lordship laughed at my forebodings, and now you see they are verified to the very letter."

"Well, it cannot be helped," replied the Count de Clairville; "we must be firm, and, after all, it may not turn out so bad as we now anticipate. It is, however, very vexatious, this interruption and delay, so anxious as I am to arrive at the end of my journey, and to discover whether or not any of those whom I seek are still living. Should the brigand chief think proper to detain me—But no, he can have no reason to do that, and I will not, therefore, harass my mind upon the subject."

Adolphus D'Aubigny returned no answer to this, and they proceeded on their way through the forest, from which they shortly afterwards emerged, and entered upon an open tract of country, with the lofty mountains among which was the cavernous abode of the brigand chief in the distance.

"Have we much further to go?" asked the count, addressing himself to Rubaldo.

"No, my lord," answered the latter; "yonder mountains point to the place of our destination."

"It is a wild place," said the count.

"Ay, it is a fit retreat for Massaroni and his gallant band," returned Rubaldo; "you will find that his abode is no insignificant one, my lord, and it strikes me that you will have no cause to regret your visit."

"Indeed," said his lordship, in a doubtful tone; "but I rather suspect that I shall have to pay dearly for the gratification it may afford me."

"Perhaps not so dearly as you imagine, my lord," said Rubaldo; "but you will not long be kept in suspense."

He said no more, and in a few minutes afterwards they arrived at the foot of the mountain in which the retreat of our hero was situated. After ascending the mountain, which was a task of much difficulty to the unused feet of the travellers, they arrived at a broad ledge near the summit, and which commanded a most extensive view of the surrounding country; but they had not time to look around them, they were forced into what appeared to be the mouth of a cave, and then found themselves hurried along a narrow, winding, and descending passage, which was wrapped in the most impenetrable darkness. As they proceeded, their ears were frequently saluted by the shouts and loud bursts of merriment of men, no doubt the brigands, and they expected every moment to be in the presence of the brigand chief, and his daring band; and notwithstanding all that Rubaldo had said to them, they felt anything but easy and satisfied in their mind. However, at length they stopped at a low door, which Rubaldo opened with a key which he had brought with him, and they entered a cavernous apartment of moderate dimensions, from the roof of which a lamp was suspended, and which contained a few articles of furniture.

"I must leave you here for a few minutes, signors," said Rubaldo, "while I apprise our captain of your arrival, and he, no doubt, will shortly pay his respects to you."

"Well," replied the count, "I suppose it is no use complaining, as we have proceeded thus far: but I trust I shall not be detained here any longer than can be avoided, as I am travelling on business of the utmost and most urgent importance."

"I have no doubt that Massaroni will attend to your wishes, my lord," returned Rubaldo; "but he will have, I daresay, some important questions to put to you, which I trust you will not hesitate to answer with becoming candour."

"Questions to put to me?" repeated the count; "what can he have to inquire of me beyond the length of my purse?"

"Well, we shall see that, my lord," answered Rubaldo; "but I must again assure you that you will find Massaroni a perfect gentleman, and that you have nothing of a very serious nature to apprehend from him, however disparaging may be the circumstances under which you will have been introduced to him, and whatever may be the opinion you have formed of his character. But you will soon have an opportunity of judging for yourself. I must now leave you."

With these words Rubaldo and the other brigands returned, and left the count and his companion to their own reflections.

"Well," observed his lordship, looking around him, "a very agreeable situation we are placed in truly; if you are fond of the romantic, Adolphus, I should think that you would find quite enough in this adventure to gratify your taste."

"I would much sooner have been spared the gratification, my lord," replied Adolphus, "and I only hope this adventure may terminate no worse than the brigand has represented, though I have my doubts and misgivings on the subject. It is evident that robbery was not their only object, or they would have permitted us to proceed on our journey."

"And what other object can they have in view, any more than to gratify the curiosity of Massaroni?" demanded the count; "certainly not murder?"

"I know not," said Adolphus; "but should they have, we are entirely at their mercy, and cannot help ourselves."

"Oh, do not alarm yourself," said the count, "for I have a better opinion of the brigand chief than that. One thing, however, struck me most forcibly."

"And what was that, my lord?"

"Why, the astonishment which the man evinced when I mentioned my name."

"Yes," replied Adolphus, "I also noticed that, and am at a loss to understand it. Massaroni cannot know anything of you."

"Oh, no," said his lordship, "that is impossible, for I never saw him to my knowledge, and it is many years since I was anywhere in this part of the country before. But we shall soon know all about it, and we must, therefore, wait patiently the issue."

Thus saying, the count seated himself, and he and his companion awaited the appearance of the brigand chief with no little degree of anxiety.

"In the meantime, Rubaldo had sought the presence of Massaroni, and made him acquainted with what had taken place. He listened to him with the deepest interest and curiosity, but when Rubaldo made him acquainted with the name of the count, he started.

"The Count de Clairville?" he repeated; "are you certain that you were not mistaken, Rubaldo?"

"I am positive," answered the latter; "it is impossible that I could be so."

"And a French nobleman, you say?"

"Yes."

"It is most extraordinary," said our hero. "Should he prove to be in any way related to our young friend, Florio, it may turn out most fortunate. You did well to bring him hither, Rubaldo. I must see him immediately."

With these words, the brigand chief departed to the place where the count and his young friend were awaiting him. They arose on his entrance, and looked at the graceful, dignified, and handsome person of Massaroni with much curiosity.

"Your servant, signors," said our hero, bowing with his accustomed politeness. "I bid you a hearty welcome to my residence, and hope you have been put to no very serious inconvenience in being brought hither."

"Why, signor," replied the count, "to tell the truth, we are sadly annoyed by being obstructed in our journey, and trust we shall not be detained any longer than possible."

"Oh, certainly not, signor," returned Massaroni. "But you will pardon me if I take the liberty of putting a few questions to you; and, as I assure you that they are not dictated by any feeling of idle curiosity, I trust you will not hesitate to answer them with candour and sincerity."

"Proceed, signor," said the count; "what are the questions you wish to put to me?"

"You are the Count de Clairville, if I am informed rightly?"

"True."

"And a nobleman of France?"

"Yes, signor, though I have been away from it many years; it is there I am now travelling on business of importance, as I before informed you."

"You will pardon me, my lord," said our hero; "but should I be considered too impertinent and inquisitive were I to request to know the nature of that urgent business?"

"Indeed, signor," answered the count, "I must say that that sounds rather a bold question, coming from one who is an entire stranger to me."

"Well, well, it may appear to be so, but I have my reasons for it. Has your lordship any relations living in France?"

The count sighed, and an expression of the deepest melancholy passed over his features.

"I had relations living there," he replied, at last; "but I know not whether I have now; it is many years since I saw or heard from them, and it is with the hope of discovering some of them that I am now journeying to my native country."

"Were any of them poor?"

"Yes; I fear too poor."

"And yet you are wealthy?"

"True—true," replied the count, with much emotion and confusion; "but that is not to the purpose. I have answered all your questions, and it cannot concern you to know more."

"Perhaps," replied the brigand, "it may concern me more than you imagine, my lord."

"How?" interrogated the count, looking at him with increased astonishment.

"For some time past," continued our hero, "a young Frenchman, the victim of misfortune, has been under my protection; his name is Florio Clairville."

"Clairville!" repeated the count, starting, "and a native of France! I never knew one of that name who was not related to me. He is young and poor, you say? Has he any parents living?"

"He has not."

"He is living under your protection, you

say?" remarked the count; "am I to understand from that that he is one of your band?"

"No, my lord," answered Massaroni; "and I never wished or urged him to become so; he is good and honurable, and worthy of a much better fate than that which has hitherto befallen him."

"Can I see him?" asked his lordship, eagerly.

"Oh, yes, my lord," replied our hero, "I will conduct him to you immediately."

Thus saying, Massaroni retired, leaving the count and Adolphus in a state of the greatest amazement and anxiety. The count, in particular, paced backwards and forwards, muttering incoherent sentences to himself, and every muscle of his countenance evincing the extreme anguish of mind he was at the moment enduring.

"Most extraordinary!" he at length ejaculated, audibly, and addressing himself to Adolphus. "Should this young man prove to be connected with me, and not unworthy of my name, I shall, indeed, have no cause to regret the interruption I have experienced in my journey."

"True, my lord," said Adolphus; "but you have heard that this protogee of Massaroni calls himself Florio Clairville, not De Clairville."

"Ah, well can I understand that," replied the count, with another heavy sigh, and a still more melancholy expression of countenance; "I left them to —— But enough, at present; let me first question this young man, and from the facts I may elicit, the truth or erroneousness of my suppositions will appear. Oh, Antoine! Emile!—"

He took two or three more hasty strides across the cave, and then, once more throwing himself upon a seat, awaited the re-appearance of Massaroni and the young man he had mentioned to him, in a state of the greatest anxiety and suspense, and Adolphus D'Aubigny, who had long been anxious to obtain a full explanation of the circumstances that pressed so heavily upon the mind of his generous-hearted protector and friend, who had adopted him, and performed more, if possible, than the offices of a parent ever since he he had lost his own, did not attempt to interrupt him in his meditations.

Massaroni on quitting the presence of the count and his young friend, immediately made his way to the chamber of Florio, who, notwithstanding the earliness of the hour, (for the grey mists of morning had only just succeeded the sombre gloom of night upon the summits of the mountains) was already risen from his couch, and at his devotions. He started on beholding the brigand, and arising from his knees, grasped his hand, at the same time observing—

"Ah! my good friend, what means this early visit? Has anything particular happened?"

"Something, Florio," replied our hero, "that I imagine will prove to be of the utmost importance to yourself. You must with me immediately."

"Where? and upon what errand?"

"Oh, not from this cavern," replied the brigand, "and as for the errand, it is one which, it strikes me, will do you some service."

"You speak in problems, Massaroni," said Clairville; "it is impossible for me to understand you; pray explain yourself."

"I will do so," returned our hero, and he then briefly related what had happened; and Florio listened to him with the most breathless curiosity and astonishment.

"Good God!" he exclaimed, "can this be possible? Clairville! my name! and——"

"The Count de Clairville," interrupted Massaroni.

"Yes—yes; but still the coincidence is not the less remarkable; and strange ideas take possession of my mind when I reflect on it. But come, my good friend, Massaroni, conduct me to this gentleman immediately, and no doubt an explanation can be soon effected, and all anxiety removed."

"This way, then," returned Massaroni, "and all that I particularly hope is, that the wishes and ideas I have formed may be realised."

As he thus spoke, he took the arm of Florio, and led him away, and in a very few minutes afterwards they were in the presence of the count and Adolphus.

The former was wrapped in the same deep reverie as when we left him, and did not notice their entrance, but Adolphus D'Aubigny no sooner fixed his eyes upon Florio than he was struck with his noble and dignified figure, and the open manliness and candour of his countenance, and he saw at once that he was no common or insignificant individual, however humble his present circumstances might be.

"My lord Count de Clairville," said our hero, leading Florio forward, "allow me to introduce to you the youth of whom I spoke to you but a short time since—Monsieur Florio Clairville."

The count raised his head hastily, and fixed his eyes intently upon the person and countenance of the young painter, but no sooner did he behold his features, than he gave utterance to an exclamation of surprise, and the powerful emotion that struggled in his bosom was plainly visible in his whole demeanour.

"By Heaven!" he exclaimed, "can this be a dream? Or—oh, God! my brother, even such when about the same age didst thou appear. Tell me, young man, your name?"

"Florio Clairville, my lord," answered the young painter.

"And you were born?"

"But a short distance from the City of Paris.

"Your parents ?"

"Alas !" they are both dead; my father I never knew; I understand that he committed suicide when I was about a few months old."

"Gracious Heaven !" exclaimed the count, in a voice almost choked with the overpowering agony of his feelings; "and the names of those to whom you are indebted for your being?"

"Antoine and Emilie *de* Clairville," replied Florio.

"Merciful Providence! thy ways are wonderful!" cried the count Clairville, embracing him fondly in his arms. "Uunfortunate youth—offspring of those who were doomed to experience so much unmerited sorrow, it is your uncle, the Count Eugene de Clairville, who thus embraces you!"

"My uncle !" ejaculated the astonished and half-incredulous Florio; "have I indeed that happiness ?" As he spoke, he gently disengaged himself from the arms of the count, and knelt at his feet, and the latter raising his hands above his head, silently invoked a blessing upon him. Massaroni and Adolphus stood by, and gazed with feelings that may much better be imagined than described upon them.

CHAPTER LIV.

THE EXPLANATION.

It was several minutes ere the count and his newly discovered nephew could recover themselves sufficiently to speak, and Massaroni and Adolphus D'Aubigny did not offer to interrupt them. At length the Count de Clairville, raising Florio from his knees, and looking most earnestly in his face, said—

"Oh, youth—youth, the more I gaze upon your features the more poignant does become the anguish of my mind. Such as you now appear was that brother, whose melancholy fate I have so bitterly mourned, and which fate I was the primary cause of bringing about. Ay, you may well start, young man, and look upon me with feelings of suspicion, if not disgust and hatred ; if you are indeed the son of Antoine de Clairville, and my conscience tells me too forcibly that you are so, you should spurn me as one who has wrought your parents and yourself the greatest misery ; but, perhaps, there was some excuse to be offered for me, taking all the circumstances into consideration ; and God knows what agony of mind I have endured for months, for years past ; how anxious I have been to know whether fate had still left it in my power to make all the atonement I could for injuries done, and—oh, my brain !"

"My lord," said Florio, deeply commiserating the distress of the unfortunate nobleman, "far be it from me to add to the anguish of mind which you are evidently at the present moment enduring by reproaches which I know not I have any authority to make use of ; and if you should indeed prove to be my relation, it will be my pride to honour you as such, and to show that I am not unworthy of you."

"Spoken like my Antoine !" ejaculated the count. "Again I say that I could almost imagine he at this moment stood before me. But —your mother—I dare not trust myself to give utterance to her name—you say that she is no more !"

"Alas—alas !" sighed Florio, raising his hands, and tears, in spite of all his manly efforts to the contrary, starting to his eyes, "many years."

"And left you——"

"No other legacy but her beloved memory, and this faint resemblance of her heavenly self, which I treasure more than all that fortune could bestow upon me."

As the young man thus spoke, he drew from his bosom a miniature inclosed in a golden case, and which represented one of the most beautiful female countenances that imagination could conceive or the art of the most skilful limner pourtray. He bent one knee to the ground as he did so, and raising his eyes devoutly towards Heaven, pressed it fervently to his lips, then placed it in the hands of the Count. The moment that nobleman had fixed his eyes upon it, his whole frame became agitated in the most violent degree, and in a voice which told at once the powerful emotions that struggled in his breast, he exclaimed—

"Emilie ! beloved ! injured, persecuted Emilie, such didst thou once appear, ere sorrow had set its sad and unrelenting seal upon your heart. Oh, God ! and you are no more! It is forbidden me to seek your pardon on my knees ; to humble myself in the dust before you, to—to—my brain will go distracted !"

"My lord," interposed the deeply affected Florio ; "for Heaven's sake do not agitate yourself thus, you——"

"Oh, boy—boy, nephew, for such I am now convinced that you are, you little know half the injuries I have done you, or you would not thus talk to me. But there is one question I would ask you : Did your sainted mother ever mention to you the name of Eugene, Count de Clairville ?"

"I have heard her mention it in her prayers, my lord," answered Florio, "but never did I know from her lips that he was related to me, or hear her utter one word of reproach towards him."

"Immaculate being !" cried the count, "how worthy were you of a better fate.

Nor told she anything to you of your father's history?"

"No more than that which I have mentioned to you," answered Florio, "namely, that my unfortunate father, through some painful circumstances that pressed more heavily upon his mind than he could find fortitude sufficient to support, committed that rash and fatal act which consigned my mother to future misery, and, I have no doubt, hastened her passage to the grave. Oh, my lord, were I to describe to you the anguish of our final parting

MASSARONI SUPPORTING THE FAINTING MELINA.

on this earth, when she knew that I must be left alone, friendless, destitute in the world, it would——"

"Oh, hold—hold! in mercy!" groaned the Count de Clairville; "your words torture and wring my heart. It was to seek out her or any one that might be living of my unfortunate brother's relations, that I undertook my present journey, and there seems to be a Providence in it, in guiding me to the very place in which I was destined to encounter you. Allesandro Massaroni, I owe to you an eternal debt of gratitude."

"You owe me nothing, my lord," answered our hero, "and I am only too happy to think that I have indirectly been rendered the means of bringing yourself and your nephew together. I say your nephew, for, after what has taken place, I can scarcely believe him to be otherwise."

"Otherwise!" repeated the count; "oh, no, it would be mad infatuation to think so, after the corroborative proofs he has brought forward."

"Oh, am I then indeed so fortunate as to find, when I thought myself alone in the world, one so nearly allied to me?" ejaculated Florio, again sinking on his knees at the Count de Clairville's feet, and overpowered by the various emotions that crowded upon his brain. "Oh, my honoured uncle, let the humble individual before you, now for the first time in his life, pay that homage and reverence to you as the brother of the father he never knew, that is due to you; and think not that because I have discovered a relation in a nobleman that I thus kneel to you and ask your blesssng, but——"

"My blessing, youth!" interrupted the agitated nobleman; "alas! though given with sincerity, it would come with an ill grace from lips of mine. But spare me for a few hours; let me be alone, and endeavour to recover myself and to collect my thoughts after this extraordinary and unexpected occurrence; and then when my feelings become more calm, I will endeavour to enter into an ample explanation of all the remarkable and melancholy facts connected with my chequered history. Signor Massaroni, you spoke truly when you said that probably you had more to do with my name and title than I could imagine; will you allow me to be alone with my young friend here for a short time?"

"Certainly, my lord," replied our hero, "and most heartily do I hope that this unexpected event may be productive of the most beneficial and happy results to yourself and Signor Clairville. Your servant, signor; you will find every accommodation here, and in a few hours I will send a messenger here to know whether it may be your pleasure to see my young friend."

"My lord," said Florio, with the deepest emotion, for the longer he gazed upon the countenance of the count, the more his interest increased, "believe me I shall wait with the utmost anxiety the time when we shall meet again; and in the meantime, my best wishes be with you."

Thus saying, Massaroni and Florio quitted the place, and when they had regained the cavern which they had recently quitted, the latter threw himself on a seat, and for some moments gave himself up to the conflicting thoughts which rushed tumultuously upon his mind.

"What an extraordinary adventure is this, Massaroni," he said, at length; "at the very moment when I thought myself friendless and destitute in the world, to discover that I am so nearly related to one of noble birth, and who upon the simple facts I have already been able to adduce before him, has readily acknowledge me; by Heaven, it seems to by almost incredible."

"I firmly believe in its truth," said the brigand, "and I rejoice, Florio, in the favourable change which has so suddenly taken place in your fortune. But did you never hear your mother mention the name of this relation?"

"As I before stated," replied Florio, "when I have suddenly and unexpectedly obtruded upon her when she has been at her devotions, I have heard her breathe the name of Eugene de Clairville in her prayers; but whenever I have ventured to question her upon the subject, she has evaded it as much as possible, and appeared so violently agitated that I have regretted my forwardness in interrogating her."

"But you could gather from her that he was your relation?"

"Yes, that he was my uncle, and of noble origin."

"And yet you lived in poverty?"

"True."

"And you never could elicit from her why no intercourse existed between you?"

"Never."

"You never knew your father, you say?"

"I did not."

"He committed suicide?"

"Unfortunately he did."

"It must have been some great calamity that could have induced him to such a rash and desperate act," remarked the brigand chief.

"It must indeed," replied Florio, "but the dismal facts connected with it, I never heard from my mother's lips."

"From the observations which were made by the Count de Clairville at our recent interview," said Massaroni, "I should be inclined to infer that he had done him some injury, or at least, that he lays under the impression that he has done so."

"Heaven pardon him if he has," returned Florio, fervently and sincerely. "But we must not condemn him till we have heard the explanation he has promised to give us, and which I wait so anxiously to hear. But, Massaroni, should it indeed be proved beyond a doubt that I am the nephew of this nobleman, although I value not birth or fortune for their intrinsic worth, what a change will it be calculated to work in my pretensions to the hand of my beloved Melina. I may then indeed look forward with the fond and sanguine hope of surmounting the obstacles that have hitherto presented themselves to my union with her who is far more precious to me than my own existence, and even the proud and haughty Prince Bianchi may then raise no further objections to my alliance with his fair and peerless, and innocent niece."

"True, Florio," said the brigand; "and I sincerely congratulate you upon the prospects that open upon you,"

"Oh, what bliss is here even in the bare thought!" ejaculated Clairville, clasping his hands together, and his eyes beaming forth an expression, which shewed at once far more powerfully than any language could possibly express them, the feelings that were passing in his breast. "To be sure of such a consummation will more than reward me for any years of anxiety, doubt, and fear that I may have been destined to experience."

"Truly, so, my young friend," remarked our hero. "Oh, indeed, I am no prophet, if what I have always predicted since you and I have been acquainted be not verified, namely, that I shall have the pleasure and the honour of dancing at your wedding."

"But Melina," said Clairville; "what will be her feelings when she hears of the extraordinary circumstances that have taken place in the last few hours?"

"We can very well imagine them," said Massaroni; "to find that you are of noble origin will enable her to combat all the arguments and objections of the Prince Bianchi, and to overcome any scruples she may herself have entertained."

"The love of Melina is too pure and sincere to be biassed by the consideration of rank or wealth," observed Florio.

"I doubt it not, Signor Clairville," replied the brigand; "but still it is better, much better for you both should those obstacles be removed. I shall ever consider myself a fortunate man in having been made the means of assisting you in the gratification of your wishes, and in that will consist my greatest triumph over my haughty and implacable enemy, the Prince Bianchi."

"Massaroni," said Clairville, pressing his hand most cordially, "you have proved yourself my best and most disinterested earthly friend, and I am under obligations to you of such a weighty nature that I shall never be able to requite them. I trust that the time is not far distant when you will be restored to your proper position in society, and which you are so well calculated to adorn."

"For the matter of that, my young friend," returned the brigand chief, with a careless laugh, "I am happy and contented enough as I am, since it has been the will of fate to place me so. Allesandro Massaroni, thank the saints, can always rest his head upon his pillow with a far clearer conscience than those who boast of more superior virtues. One thing, I trust, Signor Clairville, as regards yourself."

"And what is that?" asked the latter eagerly.

"Why, that whatever may be the change in your circumstances, you will continue to remember me with feelings of friendship and to speak of the brigand chief as you have ever found him."

"And do you imagine that I can ever cease to do so, Massaroni?" asked Clairville. "I must be a most ungrateful scoundrel if I could. I will not only always remember you with the sincerest friendship, but should it ever lay in my power to release you from the dangers and difficulties by which you are at present surrounded, and the opprobrium which attaches itself to your name from those who know you not so well as I do, you shall find me most ready to do so."

"I am obliged to you, Signor Clairville, for your good wishes," said our hero, "and I believe you to be sincere; but I flatter myself that I shall yet obtain justice without the aid of any man, and if not, I am, as I said before, quite content to remain as I am. But I suppose you wish to be alone prior to your next interview with Count de Clairville, in order that you may prepare yourself for the extraordinary disclosure which I have no doubt he is about to make?"

"True, Massaroni," replied Clairville, "it is necessary that I should collect my thoughts, for the revelation I am about to hear is no doubt of the utmost importance, and probably upon it my future happiness depends. The melancholy fate of my unfortunate father has often been the subject of my thoughts, and most anxious have I been to be made acquainted with his history, and the particular circumstances that could have driven him to such a deplorable act; and the hints which the Count de Clairville has thrown out only serve to involve me still further in doubt and perplexity."

"Well," remarked Massaroni, "I will leave you for the present, hoping that all may terminate as our most anxious wishes can anticipate. In an hour or two, I will wait upon you again, and with your permission, will accompany you to the presence of his lordship."

"Be it so, Massaroni," said Florio. "I will await your coming. I should wish you to hear all that the Count de Clairville may have to reveal, that I may afterwards avail myself of your counsel and advice upon the subject, and I know that whatever of importance may transpire will be kept confided a profound secret to your own breast."

"Of that you may be certain," replied the brigand. "Massaroni is no tatler, especially upon the affairs which are of such importance to his friends."

"Enough," said Florio. "I know you will

believe me when I assure you that I am perfectly satisfied that I place the most implicit reliance on you."

Our hero pressed his hand cordially in silence, and then took his leave, and Clairville was left to the indulgence of his own thoughts, which, as the reader may imagine, were of the most varied and interesting description. But for some time his mind was so completely confused and bewildered by the extraordinary events that only the last few hours had given rise to, that he could not arrange them, and he paced his chamber in a state of the greatest excitement.

"And am I indeed of noble origin?" he said; "may I without any further appearance of undue presumption, aspire to the hand of the beauteous and innocent Melina, to whom my heart is devoted with the fondest adoration? What Heaven is there in that thought! But after what the Count de Clairville has already stated, can I any longer entertain a doubt upon the subject? Oh, no! Apart from his assertions, the voice of nature tells me I am related to him, and that this discovery will be the means of consummating my happiness."

Our hero was pleased to see him in this frame of mind, and after some more conversation upon the same subject, but not of sufficient importance to be recorded here, he left him for a short time, and on his return to the cavern which he had recently quitted, he found that Maria was there, and anxiously awaiting to see him, having heard from Rubaldo the particulars of the capture of the Count de Clairville, and the probability there was of his proving to be in some way connected with Florio.

"Well, Massaroni," she said, "what has taken place at the interview between you and your prisoner?"

"That which is most extraordinary and unexpected," replied her husband, "and which may turn out to be most fortunate indeed for our young friend, Florio."

"You have introduced the latter to the count, have you not?" asked Maria.

"I have," answered our hero, "and from what has already transpired, there seems to be but little doubt that Florio is the nephew of the Count de Clairville."

"Ah!" ejaculated the brigand's wife, "should that really prove to be the fact, and the Count de Clairville is ready to acknowledge him, the noble origin to Florio, may remove all the obstacles which have hitherto been placed in the way of his union with the Signora Melina, and dismiss from the mind of Bianchi all those scruples and prejudices he has hitherto entertained."

"Very true," coincided our hero; "and there can be but little or no doubt upon the subject, as regards the nature in which the count and Florio stand related to each other. The former, from what has already taken place, and the facts which our young friend has stated to him respecting his parents and the miniature likeness which he produced of his mother, has already acknowledged him for his nephew. The count accuses himself of having acted with injustice towards his brother and his wife, which accounts for their being allowed to live in poverty and obscurity, and urged the unfortunate father of Florio to commit suicide. He has long been absent from France, his native country, but being stung by remorse, he was on his way thither when captured by Rubaldo, with the hope of finding some of his relations living, so that he might make all the reparation in his power for the errors of the past."

"Most extraordinary," said Maria.

"Ay, you may well say so," returned Massaroni; "but an hour or two will explain everything, and until then it will be as well for us to suspend our judgment upon the matter."

"Fortune seems at last to smile upon the Signora Melina and her lover," remarked Maria, "and I feel sincerely gratified at it, for from all that I have seen of them, I consider that they are worthy of each other, and deserve to be rewarded for the many trials and difficulties they have had to encounter."

"Those sentiments do honour to your head as well as your heart, Maria," said her husband, "and proud and thankful indeed shall I feel to know myself to have been the instument in bringing about the consummation of the wishes and the happiness of such worthy beings as Florio Clairville and the Signora Melina."

"True," said Maria; "but what will be the feelings of Melina, when she is made acquainted with all these remarkable and unexpected circumstances?'

"It will be as well not to mention anything to her upon the subject, until we have heard everything upon the subject from the count, and it is proved beyond a doubt that the surmises at present entertained are correct," said our hero; "for it would be a pity to raise hopes in her breast, which after all might only be doomed to be disappointed."

To this Maria agreed, and after some further conversation they separated, Massaroni returning to Florio.

The Count de Clairville found it impossible to compose his feelings after what had already taken place at the interview between himself and Florio, and for some time after the brigand chief had left him he continued to traverse the cave in the most disordered and agitated manner, and regardless of the presence of his young friend, Adolphus D'Aubigny, to give free vent to the powerful emotions that crowded upon his mind. With the most eager eyes he continued to contemplate the miniature of Florio's mother, which he had left with him, and many were the sighs and melancholy exclamations he gave utterance to as he did so, and which Adolphus did not offer to interrupt.

"Oh, yes," he soliloquised, "there can no longer be any doubt upon my mind, after what this youth has stated, and while I contemplate this, the likeness of his mother. Dear, unfortunate, and much wronged Emilie, this is indeed a faint, but undeniable resemblance of thy beauteous features, such as they appeared in all the innocence of thy youth, and ere sorrow had set its gloomy stamp upon thy fair brow. By Heaven, I could almost imagine that the painting was animated with life, and that your eyes were beaming an expression of reproach upon me. My brother, too! Oh, what agony is there in the thoughts that crowd upon my brain, when your name arises to my memory, and I recall the dismal circumstances connected with thine untimely fate. Oh, Adolphus, I have been a villain of the blackest dye, and you should look with disgust and abhorrence upon me."

"My lord, my friend, my benefactor," said the young man, fervently, "you who have so generously, and so disinterestedly supplied to me the place of that beloved father whom I lost before I had arrived at those years of maturity that would have enabled me to protect myself, let me beg of you not to give way to those powerful feelings of anguish; indeed, you do, you must reproach yourself too severely; never, I am certain, could the Count de Clairville have been guilty of anything which he should be ashamed to acknowledge."

"Alas, Adolphus," replied the count, "you form by far too charitable an opinion of my character; but you will, I am certain, think far differently when you shall become acquainted with all the melancholy particulars of my history."

"Oh, no, my lord," returned his companion, "I can never look upon you with less feelings of reverence and gratitude than those I entertain towards you at present. I should, indeed, despise myself if I thought I could do so, for what am I not indebted to you?"

"Adolphus," said his lordship, pressing his hand warmly; "I well know and appreciate the feelings which you entertain towards me, and most happy am I to think I have been able to befriend you; but alas! it would be madness for me to attempt to conceal from myself the faults of which I have been guilty, and which have been productive of so much misery. But for me, my unfortunate brother and his wife might even now be living and surrounded by every earthly happiness; but I threw a blight upon all their prospects, and left them to poverty and sorrow."

"Calm your feelings, pray, my lord," said Adolphus; "surely the remorse you now express will more than amply atone for any error you may have committed in your youthful days, and with which you now so bitterly reproach yourself; and should this young man really prove to be your nephew, you will have the full opportunity afforded you of making to him that reparation which you seem to consider is due to him. But do you positively believe that he is so nearly allied to you?"

"Adolphus," replied the count, "after what Florio has stated regarding his parents, the place of his birth, and the fate which befel them, I cannot possibly any longer entertain a doubt. His extreme likeness to my unfortunate brother, Antoine, too, would be enough even in itself to satisfy me upon that point; besides this likeness, that of his mother,—oh, that impresses the truth more forcibly on my mind. Had you but known the heavenly countenance of the hapless Emilie, you could not have failed to recognise in it this miniature."

"And is it not wonderful, my lord," said Adolphus, "that Providence should have conducted your footsteps to the very place in which your relation was sheltered?"

"True," coincided Count Eugene; "but still, grateful as I am for the accident which has introduced me to him, I almost shudder at the idea of meeting him, knowing how richly I deserve his reproaches when he shall have been made acquainted with all the painful and guilty facts I have to reveal. He must look upon me with contempt, if not with absolute hatred."

"Impossible, my lord. I feel confident that you never can have been guilty of aught that should excite such sentiments in his breast. You take too warm a view of the subject, and torture yourself unnecessarily."

"My young friend," returned the count; "you are too ready to form excuses for me in your own generous mind, in consequence of the regard you bear me; but when you have heard the melancholy story I have to relate, I am much afraid that you will be induced to alter your opinion. But let me be firm, for justice demands that I should not shrink from the task that has devolved upon me. Would to Heaven that I had had the fortitude to perform it years since, Emilie might still have been living, and what a weight of care and self-reproach would it have been the means of removing from my conscience. Alas! alas! I have been much to blame, and bitterly do I now lament it. Those who should have been most dear to me have had to endure all the sufferings of poverty, whilst I have been basking in the sun of every earthly luxury, and of what use have my riches been to me?—I feel my own self-degradation and contemptible position as the thought arises to my mind."

Adolphus still endeavoured to argue him into composure, and at last he succeeded to a very considerable extent. Although the count had at different times harshly alluded to the misfortunes of his early life, and evidently suffered acutely from anxiety of mind, he had never related to him the particulars, although he had reason to believe that he had confided all the facts to his father, between whom and his lordship an almost brotherly friendship had existed for many years; and fearful of paining him, or seeming to be guided by imprudent and idle curiosity, he had never ventured to question him; but he now felt more anxious than ever to become acquainted with the secret which pressed so heavily upon the count's mind, and he therefore awaited impatiently for the time to arrive when he should think proper to make the disclosure.

Notwithstanding all that his lordship had said, he could not believe that he was so much to blame, as the manner in which he had upbraided himself would seem to imply; he thought that it was almost impossible that a man possessed of the many noble and amiable qualities of heart which the count might justly boast of, could ever have been guilty of any serious crime, and he was, therefore, the more eager to learn the secret, that he might contribute his humble share towards ameliorating his grief and anguish.

Adolphus D'Aubigny had been several years under the protection of the Count de Clairville, and he regarded him as much as if he had been his father. His own parent, through misfortune, at his death, had been enabled but to leave him very indifferently provided for, and his whose dependance was upon the excellent nobleman who had taken him under his protection; but let it not be supposed that Adolphus was guided by any mercenary motives; consequently, although, if Florio were fully proved to be the nephew of his benefactor, it must necessarily make a material alteration in his own pecuniary prospects, he was far from looking upon Clairville with feelings of jealousy, but on the contrary, was prepared to welcome him as a friend and companion, and to honour him as the relation of one from whom he had experienced so much disinterested kindness, and to whom he was so largely indebted.

The Count de Clairville read the thoughts that were passing in the mind of his young friend, but motives of delicacy prevented him from alluding to them at present, and he endeavoured to compose his feelings for the task which he had imposed upon himself, and succeeded much better than he had at first anticipated. In this manner two or three hours passed away, and at last a messenger arrived from Massaroni, as he had promised, in order that they might mutually enter into an explanation upon that subject which was of such importance and interest to them. His lordship expressed his readiness and anxiety for the interview, and the man who had brought the message having departed, in a few minutes afterwards Florio and the brigand chief entered.

The Count de Clairville advanced eagerly towards Florio, and pressing his hand vehemently in his, exhibited considerable emotion, and gazed earnestly in his features. Florio was no less affected and interested, and bending one knee to the ground, he pressed the hand of the nobleman respectfully to his lips. The count raised him, and for a few minutes he gazed at him earnestly in silence.

"Young man," he said at length, controlling his emotion as well as he was able; "the longer I look upon you, the more convinced do I become that I behold in you the son of those unfortunate beings who—but no, I cannot trust myself with the word;—your features bear so striking a resemblance to my late ill-fated brother, that I could almost imagine he stood before me, and I can no longer doubt that you are that nephew whom I never expected to behold, if, indeed, such an individual were in existence."

"Oh, my lord," said Florio; "and have I, indeed, the happiness and honour of being related to a nobleman like yourself? It seems scarcely possible; but should it prove to be so, most anxiously and constantly will I study to prove myself not unworthy of your acknowledgment."

"I do believe you, Florio," replied the count, "for truth and candour are in the expression of your countenance; but alas! I fear when you have heard all that I have to relate, you will be inclined to look upon me with very different sentiments to those which you now profess towards me."

"Indeed, my lord," returned Clairville, "I am certain that it will be impossible for me to ever view you with any other feelings than those of the utmost honour and regard."

"Am I intruding by remaining here during your conference?" asked our hero.

"By no means, Signor Massaroni," replied his lordship; "you have proved yourself to be the sincere friend of Florio, and, therefore, I should wish you to bear witness to all that may take place between us, and which may be of the utmost importance at some future period. Florio, you say that this miniature is the likeness of your mother, and from whom you received it?"

"'Tis true, my lord," answered Florio, a manly tear starting to his eye, as he thought of that revered and beloved woman to whom he owed his being; "may eternal blessings rest upon her memory."

The Count de Clairville was deeply affected; he pressed the miniature vehemently to his lips, and for a short time was unable to give utterance to a word. At length he said—

"And your father's name was—"

"The Chevalier Antoine de Clairville," replied Florio.

"Or rather," said the count, eagerly, "Antoine *de* Clairville! Oh, my ill-fated brother, how little did your numerous virtues merit so cruel a destiny as that which befel you! My nephew, for such indeed thou art, receive the blessing of your guilty but penitent relation.'

Florio again knelt, almost overpowered by his feelings, and the Count de Clairville, raising his hands towards Heaven, solemnly invoked a benediction upon his head. It was several minutes before either of them could sufficiently compose themselves to resume the conversation, but the Count de Clairville at last raised his nephew, and handing him to a seat by his side, said—

"Florio, this unexpected meeting has naturally taken me by surprise, and rendered me incapable of giving utterance to all that I wish. You have intimated to me that you have had many troubles to contend with, and I have no doubt but you have; but how is it that I behold you in your present situation, and why have you been compelled to seek the protection of Signor Massaroni?"

"Through no misconduct of my own, my lord, I assure you," returned Florio, "but entirely through misfortune and the injustice of others."

"I do believe you," remarked his lordship; "but I must confess that my curiosity is excited, and before I enter into any further explanation, I must request you to relate to me the particulars of your history."

"Willingly, my lord," said Florio, "for it is fit that you should know them; and if there should appear to you anything imprudent in my conduct, I trust that you will make every allowance for me, taking my youth into consideration."

"Certainly, Florio," answered his uncle. "Alas! I have been too much to blame myself not to make every charitable allowance for the errors of others."

Florio thanked him, and then as briefly as possible related all those particulars connected with himself, with which the reader has already been made acquainted. The Count de Clairville frequently interrupted him to give expression to his feelings, and when he had concluded, said—

"Florio, you have, indeed, had your share of the trials and misfortunes of this world. However, I see nothing in which your conduct merits reproach, and I feel delighted in finding myself related to one whose character is so unblemished and honourable."

"Oh, my lord, how highly honoured I must feel by the flattering opinion you are pleased to honour me with," observed Florio, "especially when I take into consideration the brief time that you have known me."

"Would to Heaven that I had known you before," returned the count: "it might have saved me many a sorrowful hour. But this Prince Bianchi—I have frequently heard of him before; and if report speaks truly of him, he is haughty, proud, and obdurate."

"Ay, my lord—you may well say that," remarked Massaroni. "The Prince Bianchi is all that report has spoken of him, and has ever proved himself to be one of my greatest enemies."

"And his niece, the Signora Melina," observed the count, "you say, is fair and amiable?"

"Oh, my lord," answered Florio, fervently, "Melina is all that can be lovely and amiable in woman, of which you will, I am certain, be satisfied, when you are introduced to her."

"And she returns the passion you feel for her?"

"With fervour, truth, and sincerity, my lord," replied the youth. "But the Prince Bianchi despises me, because of my humble circumstances, and the supposed meanness of my birth, and would fain sacrifice her to the Count Alberti, who is so unworthy of her—a libertine, a debauchee, and one whom Melina must ever look upon with abhorrence and disgust."

"But when he finds that your birth is noble," said the Count de Clairville, "will not the prince be likely to relent, and give his consent to that in which the happiness of his niece is so deeply involved?"

"Oh, yes, your lordship," said Florio; "and it is that thought which inspires me with hope. But pardon me, my lord, but will you not favour me with the narrative you promised, and in which I naturally feel so deep an interest and curiosity?"

"I must again claim your indulgence, Florio," answered the count, "for at present I do not feel myself sufficiently collected to accomplish the task; to-morrow, however, I will do so without fail, and in the meantime, you will see the fair Signora Melina, and making her acquainted with the extraordinary events that have taken place, prepare her for my introduction."

"I will, my lord," returned Florio; "and most delighted will my beloved Melina be, I know, at the unexpected intelligence I shall have to communicate to her."

They now continued to converse more freely for some time, and the admiration of the count was excited to a greater degree, the more the noble qualities of Florio's mind expanded themselves, whilst a reciprocity of sentiment in a short time established as firm and ardent a friendship between Florio and Adolphus D'Aubigny as if they had been acquainted for years. At length, however, they separated, and Florio, after exchanging a few observations with Massaroni, with a heart palpitating with hope and joy, made his way to Melina, in order that he might put her into possession of all the important particulars we have just recorded. Our heroine, however, was already aware of what had taken place, having been informed by Maria, and she was awaiting most anxiously and impatiently the appearance of her lover, in order that she might congratulate him, and to express her joy at the remarkable discovery he had made, and which was likely to effect such a material change in their prospects.

"But, dear Florio," she ejaculated, "Heaven knows that the circumstance of your being nobly born and connected can make not the least alteration in the sentiments I have ever entertained towards you; I should, indeed, be unworthy of you, did I suffer fortune, rank, or station to work any influence upon my mind; no, I love you for your virtues alone, and nothing can ever make you more valuable in my eyes. But still, this discovery is a source of the most infinite gratification to me, since it is calculated to remove at once those cruel prejudices, which the prince my uncle has so long encouraged, and will in all probability be the means of speedily effecting a reconciliation. Oh, what bliss is there in that thought! Heaven be praised for this happy change in our prospects, for now we may, indeed, with more confidence than ever, encourage hope."

She was interrupted by a knock at the door, and on opening it, Florio entered hastily, and threw himself in a transport of the most unbounded delight at her feet.

"Joy!—joy! my beloved Melina!" he exclaimed; "fortune does at last smile upon us; your Florio has made a discovery that will probably remove all the obstacles which have hitherto presented themselves to the completion of our happiness, and——"

"Maria has informed me of it, Florio," interrupted our heroine, "and most fervently do I hope that it may prove to be correct; not that any change of fortune can possibly render you more dear to my heart."

"Blissful assurance!" said Florio; "there spoke the true soul of my Melina. But all doubts upon the subject are removed; the recent explanation that has taken place between me and the Count de Clairville proves beyond all question that I am his nephew. He has acknowledged me as such, and has welcomed me with all the affection which should naturally inhabit his breast towards me. Now, Melina, can you any longer object to become my wife, and thus at once terminate the agony of fear and suspense which I have so long endured?"

"We must still be patient, Florio," replied the damsel, "rest satisfied with the solemn promise I have given you never to become the bride of any other man but yourself, and I feel assured that when the Prince Bianchi becomes acquainted with all the circumstances that have taken place, the past will be forgotten, and he will no longer withhold his consent to our union. But tell me, Florio, for you may be certain I am most anxious to know, what passed at the interview between yourself and the Count de Clairville?"

Florio informed her.

"This is indeed most extraordinary," she observed, "and what can have been the cause of the count's long separation from his family?"

"That he has promised to explain to-morrow, Melina," replied her lover; "he seems to accuse himself with having acted with cruelty and injustice towards my parents, but I can scarcely believe that one who appears to be possessed of principles the most noble and generous could ever have done so."

"And yet he is rich, and possesses a title, whilst your parents, you say, lived in a state of comparative poverty?"

"True," answered Florio.

"And your father committed suicide?"

"Alas! he did so."

"It must have been some dire calamity or insupportable wrong that could have driven him to such a desperate act," said our heroine.

"I scarcely know to what cause to attribute it," returned Florio, "though I have frequently reflected upon the subject."

"And did your mother never mention the name of your uncle to you?"

"No; she has told me that I had such a relation; but whenever I have questioned her upon the subject, she has evinced such emotion that I have always avoided it as much as possible. But the count will unravel the mystery to-morrow, and till then it is better that we should suspend our judgment. In the meantime, my dear Melina, I am requested by his lordship to prepare you for an introduction to him, which he hopes will take place in the course of to-day."

"I need not tell you, Florio," returned Melina, "that I shall be most happy to see his lordship, especially under all the circumstances. But is he aware of the nature of the sentiments that exist between us?"

"He is, Melina," answered her lover, "and therefore, on that account, is the more anxious to behold you. Well convinced I am that he cannot fail to be charmed with that fair and gentle being to whom my heart is devoted."

Melina blushed and hid her face in his bosom.

"Oh, my beloved Melina," added Florio, after a pause, "what scenes of future bliss now arise to my imagination! The gloomy past will be forgotten, and no troubles or anxieties will again oppress my mind. The Prince Bianchi will repent of his past conduct, and only be too happy to atone for it as far as lays in his power."

"Heaven grant that he may !" cried our heroine, fervently ; "Most happy should I be to forgive him all the misery and anguish he has caused me, and never reproach him by a single word."

"Spoken like my own sweet Melina," said Florio, ' and in that respect, most willingly

CLAIRVILLE AT THE FEET OF MELINA.

and zealously would I fellow her amiable example, and feel proud and happy to count him amongst the most ardent of my friends."

At this moment Floretta entered, with a message from Massaroni, requesting that Florio and Melina would join himself, his wife, and some of their other friends in the principal cavern ; and they immediately complied, and on entering it, found, in addition to the brigand and his wife, Montaldi, the Signora Zitella, and her daughter, awaiting them. They had been informed of all the remarkable circumstances that had transpired, and they congratulated Florio warmly on the change that had taken place in his fortune, and on the happy results of which it was likely to be productive. Florio thanked them, and after a few more remarks upon the same subject, the conversation became more general.

Melina felt somewhat disappointed that the Count de Clairville and his young friend, Adolphus D'Aubigny, of whom her lover had spoken in the highest terms, were not present; but Massaroni excused them by saying that they wished to be left to themselves for an hour or two, until they had recovered from the fatigue of the previous night, when they should feel most happy to have the honour of being introduced to those whom they had hitherto not seen.

The time passed quickly away in agreeable conversation, and towards the afternoon Massaroni quitted the company for a short time in order to ascertain whether or not the Count de Clairville and his friend were yet ready f.r the introduction. In a very few minutes he returned, accompanied by them, and the meeting which took place was of the most cordial and friendly description. The noble bearing, and benevolent countenance of the count greatly prepossessed him in the favour of our heroine, and he could not but feel the most unbounded admiration of her superlative charms, and her gentle, innocent, and unassuming manners. But there was one on whom they had a much more powerful and extraordinary effect, and that was Adolphus D'Aubigny. No sooner did he behold her than he felt his heart throb at double its wonted pace, and he was so confused that it was not without the greatest difficulty he could go through the ceremony without making his awkwardness and embarrassment plainly visible. He thought her the loveliest being he had ever beheld, and when he noticed the looks of affection which the maiden and Florio exchanged with each other, he could help encouraging a feeling of envy and jealousy towards the latter, which he was ashamed to acknowledge to himself, but which he was, at the same time, unable to conquer. He was so confused by the influence of these feelings, that he was unable to join in the conversation which followed, with the ease and vivacity he was accustomed to do, and although he felt the most unbounded delight in gazing at the personal charms of our heroine, and in listening to the elegance of her conversation, he, nevertheless, was anxious to retire from her presence, lest he should by any accident betray the thoughts which were passing in his mind.

The day passed away in the most agreeable manner, and they separated with regret at a late hour in the evening, the Count de Clairville promising the next day to reveal the secret which preyed upon his mind, though he requested that it should only be in the presence of Florio, Adolphus, and Massaroni.

On being conducted to the places which had been prepared for their repose, the Count de Clairville and Adolphus did not retire to rest immediately, and the latter, throwing himself upon a seat, gave himself up to the various and perplexing thoughts that crowded upon his mind. The beauteous form and innocent countenance of Melina, were still present to his imagination, and the more he reflected upon them, the greater became his uneasiness and anxiety. This did not escape the observation of the count, and he questioned him upon the subject.

"Why, how is this, Adolphus?" he said; "I never saw you look so dull and melancholy before, and certainly that ought not to be the case, after the delightful company we have just quitted."

"Excuse me, my lord," replied Adolphus, in a faltering voice, "but I feel rather indisposed; I suppose it is all owing to the unusual fatigue I experienced in the storm last night."

"Why, certainly," returned the count, "it was an exciting adventure altogether; but a night's rest will, doubtless, revive you. What think you of the Signora Melina?"

His lordship could not possibly have put a more perplexing or torturing question to his young friend, and Adolphus looked up vacantly in his face as he said,—

"The—the Signora Melina, my lord?"

"Yes, the Signora Melina," replied the count; "why, by the saints, man, your senses seem to wander. Do you not think she is a very paragon of beauty?"

"Alas!" sighed Adolphus, scarcely knowing what he said, "she is too beautiful."

"Too beautiful!" repeated the Count de Clairville, looking at him with an expression of astonishment; "that is a strange observation to make, Adolphus. Do you know what you are saying? Why, any one would imagine from the confusion and agitation of your manner that you were actually smitten with her yourself."

"I—I, my lord?" stammered Adolphus, more bewildered than ever; but quickly recovering himself, he added, with a faint smile, "upon my word, your lordship seems disposed to banter me."

"Well, do you not consider that the signora is very beautiful?" demanded the count; "for my own part I think she is one of the most lovely and fascinating maidens I ever beheld—with one exception," — and he sighed. "Florio has made an admirable choice, and they seem to love each other most fervently."

Adolphus could return no immediate answer, for every word that his lordship uttered went to his heart, and he sincerely wished that the conversation were at an end; but at length he said,—

"The Signora Melina, my lord, is, indeed, lovely, innocent, and accomplished, and happy will be the man who obtains her for a wife."

"That man will be no other than Florio de Clairville," said the count; "they love each other; he is proved to be her equal by birth, and would it not be the height of injustice and cruelty to attempt to separate them?"

"But the Prince Bianchi is obstinately opposed to their union," said Adolphus.

"True," replied his lordship, "but still I doubt not that he will be induced to yield now he finds that Melina is secure from his power, and when he discovers that Florio is not the insignificant being he thought he was. It shall be no fault of mine if the hopes and wishes of the lovers are not realised."

Adolphus again sighed; but struggling with the emotions that disturbed his breast, he endeavoured to change the conversation by observing,—

"To-morrow then, my lord, you think you will be prepared to relate the particulars of your past life?"

"Yes," answered the count, "the sooner I relieve my conscience of that weight the better."

"But are you still of opinion that this young man, Florio, is your nephew, my lord?" asked Adolphus.

"Oh, yes; after what I have heard, there can be no doubt of it," answered the count; "and most grateful am I to Providence for the accident which has led me to the discovery of him; it will enable me to do a tardy act of justice, and, perhaps, to pass the remainder of my days in peace; Florio appears good and honourable, and from what I have seen of him already, is every way calculated to do credit to my name. But oh, my unfortunate brother or Emilie, had either of you been living, I might then have made the atonement for the many injuries I had inflicted upon them complete."

"Surely, my lord," said Adolphus, "you must reproach yourself too severely."

"Alas! I do not, and so you will find when you hear the dismal narrative I have to relate," said the count. "But enough of this, at present; the time waxes late, and I need repose and meditation for the proper performance of my task to-morrow. Good-night, Adolphus."

The latter was glad enough to escape from any further conversation in the state his mind was in at that time, and responding to the wish of the count, they separated.

When Adolphus was alone, he gave himself up to the most racking thoughts, for, in spite of all his efforts to the contrary, he could not get rid of the powerful impression which the beauty of Melina had made upon his mind, and the more he thought of her, the greater became his agitation. He almost dreaded the time when he should again be in her presence, although he was still most anxious once more to behold her. Possessing the strictest honour and integrity of principle, he was ashamed of the thoughts which rushed irresistibly upon his brain; but still he was unable to conquer them, and that made him the still more restless and miserable.

Although so young, handsome, and accomplished, and with a heart susceptible to all the tenderest emotions, notwithstanding the society he had mingled in, Adolphus had never yet seen the damsel on whom he could fix his affections, and now the beauteous Melina came upon him like a spell, and, as it were, completely bewildered his senses; he could scarcely have believed there had been such a captivating being in existence; and still he could not help envying Florio the superlative happiness of possessing her love, and he had watched with feelings of the utmost emotion the looks of affection they had mutually exchanged with each other. He knew the injustice, the absolute sin of giving way to such ideas, and yet, he could not avoid them

"Alas, Melina!" he cried, "would that I had never beheld you, for I fear that it has destroyed my peace of mind for ever. It is impossible that I can banish your lovely image from my recollection, and yet am I fully sensible of the dishonour and madness of encouraging such thoughts. And were I to entertain such a presumptuous thought, could I ever expect to supplant Florio in her affections? Pshaw! the idea is preposterous as it is culpable! What would be the feelings of shame and contempt which my generous benefactor would entertain towards me, should he know the thoughts that are at present passing in my mind?—Would that we were away from this place, or that we had never entered it, for I feel that I am surrounded by danger, while I am anywhere near Melina. But I must, I will seek to conquer these feeling, or Heaven only knows what may be the consequences that may result from them."

Again he made a powerful effort to banish the dangerous and torturing impression, but with no better success than before; in fact, the more he tried, the greater had it seemed to gain upon him, and, his patience at last completely exhausted, he sought his pallet, with the hope of being enabled to drown his thoughts in sleep. It was some time, however, before he could sink off to repose, and when he did, still in his dreams the form of our heroine was presented to his imagination, and every observation she had made use of again saluted his eyes. When he finally awoke in the morning, he was as much fatigued in body and mind as before he had retired to bed, and he dreaded almost to see the count, lest he should observe it, and question him too narrowly upon the subject. However, at last he succeeded much better in conquering his emotion than might have been expected, and entered the chamber of his lordship, whom he found already risen, and at his morning devotions.

The count looked considerably more composed than he had been the night before, but he quickly noticed the pale looks and agitated demeanour of Adolphus, and said:—

"What is the meaning of this, Adolphus? You look more wan and haggard than you did last night even: something seems to prey upon your mind."

"Oh, my lord," replied Adolphus, affecting to smile, "what should prey upon my mind? Your lordship knows full well that I have nothing to trouble me."

"I don't know that you should have, my young friend; but if it is indeed so, I am entirely ignorant of it, and you should not hesitate to make a confidant of me."

"Indeed, my lord," replied Adolphus, scarcely able to conceal his confusion, and blushing at the thought of the subterfuge he was practising, "you must be aware that I have never had any secrets from you; surely there can be nothing I should wish to conceal from you."

"I trust not, Adolphus," returned the count, scrutinizing him narrowly; "but it surprises me that such a remarkable change should come over you, only since our interview with the Signora Melina yesterday."

"Your lordship cannot surely imagine that can be the cause of it?" said Adolphus, hesitating, for the count had touched the very chord which he so much dreaded; "the fact is that I do feel rather languid and ill, but perhaps that may be caused by the suddenness of this confined atmosphere. I hope your lordship does not intend to tarry here long?"

"Why," replied the count, "as circumstances have turned out, I am not quite certain about that. I have much to arrange, and it may take some time before I can accomplish what I want. This day I have a painful task to perform, but I have made up my mind to it, and I have no doubt that I shall be able to go through with it without much difficulty."

They now received a summons to attend the brigand-chief to breakfast, and Adolphus, on entering the cavern, felt his mind greatly relieved when he found that Melina was not there, (for he knew not how he should have met her without betraying his feelings); in fact, there was no one present with the exception of Massaroni and Florio; and having exchanged the usual compliments of the day, they seated themselves at the table, and the meal passed over in comparative silence.

"And now, my lord," said Massaroni, addressing the count, when the repast was done, 'are you prepared to fulfil the promise you made to us yesterday?"

"I am, signor," replied the count; "and I must claim the indulgence of yourself and Florio for any excitement which my feelings may undergo in the course of it. Alas! it is a sad narrative, and I am afraid that it will exhibit me in no very favourable light to you. Florio, from you I must particularly request patience and forbearance, as you are so deeply interested and connected with the facts I am about to disclose."

'Oh, my lord," answered Florio, "surely you can have no occasion to appeal to me?"

"But, indeed, I have too much reason to do so," said the count; "but for me you might have been spared the many years of vicissitude you have experienced;—but for me you would not have been looked upon with contempt by those whose equal you were by birth, and probably far their superior in natural worth and abilities; — but for me your parents — But enough of this; if I should attempt to enumerate all the reasons I have for seeking your indulgence, I should not only be laying a tax upon your patience, but likewise unfit myself for the task I am so anxious to accomplish. Let me then at once proceed."

CHAPTER LV.

THE COUNT DE CLAIRVILLE.—THE BROTHERS. THE COMPACT.

"The Chateau de Beauville," commenced the count, while his auditors listened to him with the most profound attention, "is situated in a beautiful and romantic spot near Abbeville. It is an extensive building of the most magnificent architecture, and has stood the brunt of the storm for many years, during the whole of which time it had been in the possession of my ancestors, who were the wealthiest and most powerful in the country.

"Lovely and picturesque is the scenery that surrounded this chateau, and it need scarcely be wondered that the neighbourhood is a source of the greatest attraction to all who travel that way.

"The interior of the building had undergone little or no change for centuries, and innumerable were its spacious apartments, extensive galleries, wide corridores, and winding, intricate, and subterraneous passages, with gloomy dungeons ranged on either side, in which, no doubt, in days of yore, many a deed of blood had been perpetrated. Often when a boy have I rambled with a kind of morbid feeling through these dismal places, and pictured to my vivid imagination the strange scenes that had been enacted in them; to my fancy, strange as it may appear, they presented an air of romance that was peculiarly attractive, and I have passed many solitary hours there when the members of my family knew not what had become of me. It is to this strange taste that I attribute that gloomy turn of mind which at times forms a part of my character, and probably has in a great measure tended to lead me into those errors which I now so deeply regret.

"There was one cell, however, among the rest which I had never at that time an opportunity of inspecting, for the door of it was always safely secured, barred and bolted. This dungeon I had a most burning curiosity to examine, for there were most curious tales connected with it, and I longed to penetrate the mystery which was concealed within it, notwithstanding it was probably of the most awful character. Alas! at a future time my curiosity was too fearfully gratified, for this dungeon you will find is most painfully connected with my history. But of this more anon.

"Not far from the chateau stood an ancient castle, which from time immemorial had been in the possession of the family of St. Almo, a proud and haughty race, who had great power in the country, and had always been looked upon with the deference of princes. This castle was situated in the midst of a deep impenetrable forest, and had a most solemn, impressive, and commanding appearance. You will pardon me for being thus particular, but you will find that the Castle of Almo and those who possessed it had a most important and fatal connection with my family, which led to many of the misfortunes I am about to recount.

"More than a century previous to the period at which my history commences, in consequence of some mysterious transactions that had taken place between them, the following curious compact was entered into by the Counts St. Almo and De Clairville, namely, that the second son of a De Clairville should always become the husband of the second daughter of a St. Almo, or in the event of his refusing, he should become disinherited and the whole of his property should go to the family of St. Almo."

"A most rash, unjust, and extraordinary compact," observed Florio.

"True," coincided the count; "but it was solemnly entered into by the two noblemen on their death-bed, (for they both died on the same day,) and a bitter curse was supposed to attend all those of their descendants who should dare to disobey it. Alas! I have too much reason to know that that idea was most fatally realised upon one occasion, at any rate. But to come to particulars.

"My parents (who had been united under the same circumstances as those which I have been describing, and had never entertained any sincere or fervent regard for each other) had three sons, of whom I am the eldest, Antoine (your father, Florio,) and Bertrand (who died in childhood) was the third.

"My mother was a most amiable woman, beloved and admired by all who had the pleasure of knowing her, but my father possessed many foibles, some of which I am compelled in truth to say, almost amounted to vices. He was proud, imperative, and vindictive, and woe to them who should attempt to oppose his will! My amiable mother could at times check the turbulent passions to which he was so often apt to give vent, but no argument, persuasion, or entreaty, however reasonable and just, could move him from any purpose upon which he had fixed his mind.

"The greatest pains was bestowed upon the education of myself and Antoine, though I was the favourite of the count, my father, from the fact, I suppose, that I assimilated to him in many respects, in point of disposition. At that time I possessed the same imperative and irritable temper, and being encouraged by him, and excused in all the errors I committed, it is no wonder that this evil disposition grew upon me, and was the cause of most of the faults with which I have now to reproach myself. I trust, however, that time and woful experience have wrought a moral change in my sentiments, and I am not without hope that I may yet, by my future conduct, make some atonement for the past.

"But how different was the disposition of Antoine to my own! Determined and energetic in what he considered to be right, he was still mild and submissive where he felt convinced it was his duty to be so. With the strongest passions were blended the most gentle nature, and he could forgive the deepest injury or insult, the moment the offender was brought to a sense of the wrong he had committed. In fact, in disposition he was the very counterpart of my mother. Towards me he bore the most brotherly affection, and it was only justice to myself to say, that in most points, I reciprocated his sentiments, though there were times when the worst parts of my character would gain the ascendancy, and cause me to exercise a species of tyranny over him which was unnatural, unjust, and uncalled for, but which was encouraged by my father, who had, in fact, ever made a marked distinction between us, treating me with every species of favouritism, and him at times with actual coldness and neglect.

"The first misfortune that befel us was the death of our beloved and excellent mother, which occurred suddenly and unexpectedly, through an accident she met with while out riding. It was some time ere my brother or myself could recover from the effects of this calamity, but it had but little effect upon my father, unless it was to make him more morose and overbearing than before. But it is now necessary that I should return to the castle of St. Almo.

The Count and Countess St. Almo were persons in the meridian of life, and possessed of all the pride of birth and station, although, at the same time, they were not without their good qualities. They were extremely benevolent, and by that means had gained the love and respect of their dependants, and all the poor for miles around their wide and valuable domains, and never was an appeal made to them in vain. My mother being the sister of the Count St. Almo, of course the utmost intimacy was kept up between the two families, which was strengthened by the fatal compact that bound them together.

"They had three daughters, all beautiful and amiable as nature could form them, but each of them varying materially in the character of their personal and intrusive charms. Marie, the eldest, was a beautiful brunette, tall, commanding, and dignified, possessing all the pride of her parents, but still affectionate, humane, and charitable. Lestelle, the second, was mild, and retiring, of studious habits, reserved in her manners, but possessed of every virtue that can adorn the breast of woman; but Emilie, the youngest, oh ! in what language shall I describe her ? Innocent and playful as a young fawn, and with a form and features which it would defy the skill of the most accomplished sculptor to do adequate justice to—But to you Florio, I need not attempt to describe your amiable mother !"

"Heaven rest her soul !" solemnly and fervently ejaculated Florio, at the same time raising his eyes and hands devoutly towards that fountain of grace and mercy to which he appealed. The Count de Clairville was deeply affected, and it was several moments ere he was enabled to proceed.

"When I reflect upon that lovely being," he said, at length, " and the misery I was afterwards the cause of inflicting upon her and an affectionate brother, how bitterly do I reproach myself, and my tongue almost hesitates to repeat the facts I am yet so anxious to reveal. From childhood I had felt for her the most ardent passion, but it was hopeless, for she loved me not, and if she had, I could never have made her mine, without bringing down upon my head the curse of my father, for I was destined to become the husband of her eldest sister, Marie, to whom I had been betrothed in childhood, and who loved me with a passion which I could not return, though I treated her with all the respect and admiration which was her due. Between Emilie and my brother, however, the most ardent and uncontrollable passion existed, which was the more unfortunate, as Antoine was bound by the fatal and cruel compact to become the husband of Lestelle, who from her heart entertained not the least regard for him, and looked forward with feelings of dread and anguish to the time when she would be compelled to become his wife.

"The love which I knew Emilie to bear towards my brother, now made me view him with feelings of jealousy, if not absolute hatred, and I avoided his society as much as I could, though, at the same time, I endeavoured to conceal from him as much as possible the fatal and dangerous sentiments that had taken possession of my breast. Emilie, however, perceived it, by the expression of my countenance whenever we met, and many a pang of regret no doubt it cost her ; she avoided my presence as much as she could, and that, if possible, added to the torture of my mind.

"Marie had no suspicion that my heart was another's, and every day her affection for me increased, and she looked forward to our nuptials with the most blissful anticipations. How bitterly did I reproach myself for thus deceiving her. But I dared not reveal the truth, or refuse her hand, for I well knew that the curse of my father and complete ruin would be sure to follow, and I had not the moral courage to meet such a fate.

"Thus two or three years rolled on without any important change taking place, but the more I beheld of Emilie my passion increased in strength, and it was not without the greatest difficulty that I could restrain my feelings sufficiently to prevent betraying myself, and not only that, but openly avowing to her the sentiments that glowed in my bosom towards her.

"At length the time arrived when it was decided that I should become the husband of Marie, and as it did so, despair settled upon my heart, and I know not how it was that I found myself enabled to bear myself with such common discretion as to drown the suspicions of those with whom I was connected, and who were constantly in my society, and watched narrowly my actions. Marie was full of hope and joyful anticipation, for, as I have before said, the love she entertained towards me was of the purest and most fervent character, and imagining that my sentiments were the same, she was indeed sincerely happy.

"There was one individual who, however, was far more wretched and melancholy than I could possibly be, and that was my brother, Antoine. He knew full well that, after the solemnization of my marriage, it would not be long before our father and the Count St. Almo would hasten his own with Lestelle, according to the compact ; and determined as he was to resist it, he well knew the sorrows that were in store for him and the beauteous being on whom he had fixed his affections. As for Emilie, she was as firm in resolution as her lover, for, in her opinion, death, even under the most torturing and lingering circumstances, would be far more preferable than a union with any other man but him on whom her whole soul's affection was rivetted. Shame mantles in my cheek while I acknowledge it, but at the time I could not help feeling a spirit of exultation and revenge at the suffering which I knew both my brother and Emilie were suffering, because there were no means of gratifying my own wishes; and it was this feeling that afterwards gained such a powerful ascendancy over me, and led me still deeper into the gulf of crime upon the verge of which I had so long been tottering. Alas! alas! when I recall all these deplorable facts to my mind, I feel ashamed and disgusted with myself, and wonder that a terrible retribution has not long ere now overtaken me.

"But poor Emilie, notwithstanding the determination she had formed, to die rather than become the wife of any other man but Antoine, as the time approached when the question of his marriage with her sister, Lestelle, should be urged by the parents of both, her spirits seemed to sink within her; and I frequently imagined (whether it was my own guilty conscience that prompted it or not, I will leave to others to decide) that she looked upon me with suspicion and dread, as if she could read my thoughts, and that rendered me the more wretched and fearful.

"Lestelle was completely passive; she knew no other earthly will than that of her parents, though she had taken no pains to conceal from them that she viewed my brother with the most stolid indifference, and, in fact, would rather have preferred leading a life of celibacy. But to be brief; the day arrived, and Marie St. Almo became my bride amid much pomp and festivity, which lasted for several days; and although I behaved towards my young bride with the greatest apparent affection, I felt truly wretched, and still envied my brother the affection of his beauteous and innocent Emilie. But yet I felt a sort of savage satisfaction at the idea that he must either abandon his hopes of Emilie and fortune, or become the husband of one whom he could never love, and who, for her part, viewed him with the same feelings of indifference. Now, Florio, do you not at once see what cause I have to claim your patience, forbearance, and indulgence, after the iniquity to which I have already pleaded guilty, and which is but a tithe of all the crimes I have been the author of? Do you not feel you ought to despise me, and look upon me with feelings of absolute abhorrence?"

"My dear lord," replied Florio, "my uncle, give not way to such thoughts, nor deem me so ungenerous or vindictive as to judge of you in the way you imagine. That fatal and monstrously extravagant compact has been the cause of all the evils that have occurred in our unfortunate family and that of the St. Almos, and——"

"Ah! no," interrupted the Count de Clairville, "indeed, you judge too charitably, although it is true that that detestable compact has been the primary cause of much that has arisen. But let me proceed.

"The honeymoon over, myself and my fair bride returned to the Castle of St. Almo, where it had been arranged that we should reside for the present, being so near the chateau, and which rendered a ready communication between the two families so easy. Here, of course, I had daily opportunities of beholding Emilie, and the unholy passion I entertained for her daily and hourly increased. Notwithstanding that I behaved to my Marie with the greatest attention and kindness, and she was all in her affections that man could desire, I could not help viewing her with feelings which almost amounted to disgust, and I took every opportunity of being alone, so that I might brood, without interruption, over my own thoughts.

"It was on one of those occasions, when I was seated in one of the most secluded parts of the forest, in the midst of which, as I have before said, the Castle of St. Almo was situated, that my brother suddenly startled me from my reverie by appearing before me, and I could not help feeling confused and abashed in his presence, knowing the injury and injustice I had done him by thought, if not by deed. He was pale and agitated, and the deepest melancholy was stamped upon his manly brow. My natural feelings overcame every other for the moment, and grasping his hand, I inquired anxiously what had happened to cause the emotion and excitement under which I saw he laboured.

"'Alas, Eugene!' he replied, in a melancholy voice, 'I am one of the most wretched of human beings.'

"'What do you mean, Antoine?' I interrogated, though at the same time I perfectly well guessed the feelings that were passing in his mind.

"'You know the cruel compact that exists in our family,' he replied, 'to the effect, that the second son of a de Clairville shall marry the second daughter of the Count St. Almo, or, in the event of his refusing, he shall become disinherited, and all his property shall go to the family of St. Almo?'

"'True,' I replied, 'such is the compact by which you are bound.'

"'And,' he rejoined, vehemently and determinedly, 'which I cannot, will not obey.'

"'Decide not rashly, Antoine,' I said, with apparent sympathy, though again, I must confess, a malicious feeling of exultation came over me at the agony he was enduring; 'you know the consequences.'

" 'I do,' he answered; 'our father has repeated them to-day, and has bidden me prepare to marry Lestelle St. Almo in a fortnight, or threatened that they shall descend upon my head.'

" 'And why should you object, my brother?' I demanded; 'is not Lestelle young, beautiful, and innocent?'

" 'Oh, yes,' he replied, 'but still I cannot love her; can never consent to make her my bride.'

" ''Tis strange,' I observed; 'you must have some other reason, Antoine, than that which you have assigned.'

" 'Yes,' he exclaimed, 'and that reason I will immediately explain to you, for I know full well that I can confide in you, and that you will prove my warmest and most sincere friend as far as your power extends.'

" How abashed I felt at these expressions, knowing the unnatural feelings I had so long entertained towards him, and I wonder that he did not perceive my emotions, though I endeavoured to conquer them as well as I was able, while I replied:

" 'Most happy, Antoine, shall I be to render you any service in my power to assist you from the dilemma in which you are placed; but you must be more explicit. Why do you object to become the husband of Lestelle?'

" 'Because I love another.'

" 'Ah!—beware!—beware!' I said.

" 'Nay, Eugene,' he returned, 'it is useless to expostulate with me thus; that love is implanted so deeply in my breast that nothing can eradicate it, and sooner than I can abandon my hopes I can perish! But why should I be forced into a compliance with this monstrous and ridiculous compact?—why should we be bound by anything which our ancestors in a fit of madness (for you can call it by no other name) may have performed? Besides, Lestelle loves me not; we have long since satisfied ourselves upon that point, and what, then, could a forced marriage so repugnant to both our feelings be productive of but the greatest misery?'

" 'And have you explained this to the Count St. Almo?' I asked.

" 'I have.'

" 'And what was his reply?'

" 'He insists upon the compact being fulfilled, or that I must take the consequences,' answered my brother.

" 'And who is the object of your affection?' I inquired, with apparent innocence, while at the same time I had the greatest difficulty to conceal the feelings which struggled in my breast.

" 'Oh, Eugene,' he replied, 'can you have been blind to the emotions that have so long throbbed within my bosom?—Surely you must have noticed the heavy grief and anxiety under which I have laboured?'

" 'I have noticed your depression of spirits,' I returned; 'but still I am at a loss to understand you; again I ask you who is the fair being whose superior charms to those of Lestelle St. Almo have so captivated you?'

" 'Her sister,' he replied; 'the beauteous, the all-innocent and accomplished Emilie!'

" 'Unfortunate passion!' I observed. 'And does she love you in return?'

" 'Oh, yes, and is willing to make any sacrifice for my sake. I can have no doubt of her sincerity or fidelity.'

" I bit my lips, and was obliged to avert my face to conceal the emotions which were passing in my mind.

" 'And how think you I can serve you, Antoine?' I inquired, 'under such peculiar circumstances?'

" 'By interceding with our father and the Count St. Almo.'

" 'The very idea is preposterous,' I replied; 'think you that they will either of them consent to cancel a compact which has existed for so many years, and to which they have themselves both subscribed?'

" 'Oh, Eugene,' he said, 'what law of heaven can sanction anything so revolting, so inhuman, and unnatural? But by the eternal judge I swear, that let whatever may be the consequences, I will not submit to it, and—'

" 'Nay,' I interrupted, 'say not anything rashly, but hear me patiently; I consent to do as you desire, though I much doubt whether or not I can meet with any success.'

" 'Oh, thanks! thanks! dear Eugene!" he said, grasping my hand vehemently; "this is indeed acting with the brotherly love you have ever evinced towards me, and heaven will most assuredly bless and reward you for it; and Emilie—'

" 'I have one request to make to you,' I interrupted.

" 'Name it,' he demanded, eagerly; 'there is no request that you can make which I can refuse compliance with.'

" 'It is this, then,' I answered, 'that you shall take no notice of any secret meetings that may take place between Emilie and myself, should you discover them, or inquire into the nature of them,'

" 'It is a most singular request, brother,' remarked Antoine, fixing upon me a look of astonishment; 'what can be the meaning of it?'

" 'No matter,' I returned, 'you have asked me to serve you, and I am anxious to do so, upon the only plan which I see most likely to succeed.'

" 'Explain yourself further.'

" 'Do you then doubt me?'

"'Oh, no.'

"'If you do, there's an end of the matter.'

"'But why so ambiguous?'

"'It is necessary to carry the point I have in view. Do you consent?'

"'I do,' he answered; 'for well do I know that my brother must always have my interest deeply at his heart.'

"What a villain must I have been to have been able to conceal the feelings that then held their empire in my breast," continued the count, "for at that very moment I was

THE BRIGANDS ON WATCH.

concocting and perfecting a plot which could scarcely have entered the mind of a fiend. I almost shudder to trace the full extent of my villany, and surely when you have heard all, you must shrink from me appalled."

"Oh, my lord," said Florio, "for Heaven's sake do not thus agitate and reproach yourself, for certainly you can never have been guilty of anything that should thus o'erburden your conscience."

"Florio," replied his lordship, "you judge me far too leniently; when you have heard all (if I have the courage to relate it to you) how different must be the opinion you will entertain of me, so deeply interested as you are in the circumstances, and so much injury as I have done all those with whom you are so immediately connected. But I must claim your indulgence for a few minutes, until I have recovered myself and collected my thoughts."

The Count de Clairville paused, and resting his head upon his hand, reflected deeply, while his bosom seemed to be agitated by the most violent emotions; but at length, having partaken of a glass of wine, he revived sufficiently to resume his narrative in the following words :

"'You do me no more than justice, Antoine,' I replied, after a brief pause, 'by entertaining that opinion; what else but the interest of my brother can I ever have at heart? But I have one more request to make of you.'

"'And what is that?' he demanded.

"'That you never divulge to any one, not even to Emilie, that which has taken place at this our meeting,' I replied.

"'Oh, that I most readily and easily can do,' he returned.

"'But that is not all.'

"'What, then?'

"'That you immediately absent yourself from the chateau,' I returned, 'and let no one, unless it is myself, know whither you are gone.'

"'That is a most singular request, Eugene,' he observed. 'I cannot understand it.'

"'It is necessary,' I said, 'in order to carry out my wishes; in the meantime I may succeed better than we both at present anticipate in the accomplishment of what we desire; at any rate, I can almost undertake to say that I will prevail upon the count, our father, to postpone the enforcement of the compact till a future period.'

"Enough, Eugene,' he said; 'I place every confidence in you, and will abide entirely by your counsel. But, by the love you bear me, make no delay, for my anxiety will be almost insupportable until I know the result of your generous intercession, for Emilie's happiness or misery depends upon it.'

"'I will not fail to attend to all your wishes, Antoine,' I replied, though the mention of the name of Emilie so excited me, that it nearly threw me off my guard.

"'But will not the count think my sudden disappearance from the chateau most extraordinary?' he asked.

'Leave everything to me,' I answered. 'I will form an excuse for you that will set all the suspicions of our father at rest.'

"'And Emilie, what can I say to her?'

"'You must endeavour to persuade her that some important business calls you from home for a few days, and during your absence, Emilie, fear not, will receive every consolation from myself and her sisters.'

"'I am satisfied,' said my brother, 'and hope again springs up in my bosom. Oh, Eugene, never before did I so duly appreciate your noble character as I do now; and should you succeed, I shall owe you a debt of gratitude, which no efforts on my part can ever repay.'

"'No thanks, my dear Antoine,' I replied, in accents of the greatest apparent sincerity; 'what I have undertaken to do, is no more than my duty and affection as a brother towards you should dictate; and should I indeed be enabled to accomplish my wishes, I shall be most sufficiently rewarded in witnessing the happiness of yourself and Emilie.'

"He fervently grasped my hand, and could not give utterance to the feelings which struggled in his breast, but his looks expressed far more than any language could possibly have done. I also pretended to be deeply affected, though in my heart I felt a deadly sensation of absolute hatred towards him, which I now shudder to think of, and blush to acknowledge. Oh, I must indeed have been a most consummate villain, thus to act the hypocrite towards one of the best of brothers, and who at the time had reason to believe me his dearest earthly friend.

"'Antoine,' I said, at length, 'compose yourself, and endeavour to await with fortitude the result, and should I fail——'

"'Should you fail!' he interrupted. 'Oh. what horror is there in that thought! I shudder to contemplate it! But let the worst come, so fervent and unconquerable is the love that myself and Emilie entertain for each other, that nothing shall prevent our coming together, even though the curses of our parents should descend upon our devoted heads, and we should be doomed to the direst poverty and suffering.'

"'Nay, Antoine,' I remarked, 'you must not give way to these sad and gloomy thoughts, for notwithstanding the apparently almost insurmountable difficulties that now present themselves to the gratification of your hopes and wishes, all may yet terminate much better than you now anticipate. But is Lestelle aware of the sentiments that you and her sister entertain for one another?'

"'Oh, yes,' he answered, 'and deeply does the generous girl sympathise with us, and most happy would she be could our parents be prevailed upon to cancel that cruel and monstrous compact, which is opposed to every law, human and divine, and give their consent to our union. She experiences no feeling of jealousy or wounded pride towards me in consequence of my rejection of her hand, but looks upon me with the fervent regard of a sister and a friend. That, then, is another argument in our favour, since the union of myself and Emilie could prove no outrage on her feelings.'

'Enough, Antoine,' I observed, 'thus far then we have arranged everything to our mutual satisfaction. To-morrow, then, you will take your departure from the chateau.'

"'To-morrow?'

"'Yes, the urgency of the circumstances will admit of no delay.'

"'I will do as you advise, Eugene,' he said; 'and will let you know as soon as possible where I am, so that we may constantly communicate with each other. May Heaven prosper you in your praiseworthy efforts, and reward you for the exemplary solicitude you feel in my fate. Oh, Emilie!—hope once more dawns upon me that we shall yet be able to surmount the obstacles that are at present placed in the way to the completion of our happiness, and if that hope is destined to be realised, all the bliss that can attend human beings will be ours.'

"I could scarcely refrain from giving candid expression to the feelings which his words excited in my breast; but I stifled them as much as possible, and after a few more words, we separated.

"I find myself almost incapable of describing the thoughts which crowded upon my brain when he was gone; in that brief interview, where I had pretended so much sympathy and interest in the fate of my unfortunate brother, I had made up my mind to his ruin, and the completion of the most diabolical designs against the lovely and innocent Emilie that ever entered the mind of man; and I was determined to pursue it, let the consequences be whatever they might. That plot I had so nicely contrived, that I thought it was utterly impossible it could fail to succeed, and I already looked forward to the time when Emilie should become my victim as almost certain.

"'She is mine!' I exclaimed, as I walked towards my home, 'she is mine, and nothing can save her. Why should I hesitate, or feel any repugnance to the accomplishment of my wishes?—Nature never designed me for her who is now my wife, whilst the beauteous Emilie is all that my fondest hopes could desire, and is formed to make me happy. She must, she shall be mine, even though I am afterwards stigmatised as a villain, and looked upon with disgust and hatred by the rest of my fellow-creatures.'"

Florio was shocked, and looked upon the count with astonishment, and almost incredulity. When he recalled to his memory the image of his beloved mother, and recollected all the sufferings she had endured—the constant agony of mind that wore her down, and the extraordinary emotion she had always

evinced, whenever he alluded to his relations, the most horrible ideas and suspicions rushed upon his imagination, and he looked at the Count de Clairville with an expression which seemed as though it would penetrate his very soul, as he exclaimed—

"Oh, my lord, even after what you have previously said, how little was I prepared for that which you have just now stated. But surely you must have exaggerated;—you could never have entertained such thoughts as those which——"

"Florio," interrupted the count, with much emotion, "I have spoken no more than the truth, and I am determined to do so, though you should curse and despise me afterwards. I told you that you had reason to hate me, for I have been the cause of all the misery that has attended yourself and your unfortunate parents, and no penitence of mine can ever make atonement for the wrongs I have done you. Oh, God! when I reflect upon the guilty past, it almost drives me mad! But I am determined to divulge everything, let the consequences to me be whatever they may. I can no longer exist with all this heavy and enormous weight of guilt upon my conscience. Thank God, however, that I have been enabled to discover the offspring of those whom I so deeply injured, for when I have rendered all that justice for the past which lies in my power, I can retire from that world which no longer possesses any charms for me, and in holy seclusion perhaps obtain that consolation which nothing else can bestow. The riches of the world I possess in abundance, but they cannot purchase me that peace of mind which I have lost through my own crimes; they are yours, my nephew, and may you, in a life of virtue and the strictest integrity, prosper with them; all that I ask of you in return is, that you will sometimes bestow a thought of mercy upon me, and offer up a prayer to heaven for my salvation."

Florio was deeply affected, and it was some moments before he could speak; but at length he said—

"Alas! my lord, how sincerely does it grieve me to see you suffer thus! Even after all that you have said, I cannot believe that you are so guilty as you have represented yourself to be, but that there are some extenuating circumstances for your past conduct. Heaven forbid that I should visit you with feelings of hatred or revenge, and I hope when all this is explained that you may live for many years to experience happiness and peace."

"Happiness and peace!" repeated the count. "Oh, no, they can never again be mine; it would be madness and presumption for one who has sinned as I have done to expect them."

"I trust, my dear uncle," said Florio, "that

nevertheless, you will experience them. But banish these gloomy thoughts from your mind, and proceed with your narrative, which I am so anxious to hear."

"Alas!" replied his lordship, "I fear I have imposed upon myself a task which I shall not be able to accomplish. At present, however, I feel myself entirely incapable of proceeding, and must request you to suspend the further gratification of your curiosity and anxiety for an hour or two, by which time I may probably be enabled to sufficiently collect my thoughts and compose my feelings to continue."

"Be it so, my lord," remarked Florio, "and, in the meantime, rest assured that all I have yet heard will not prejudice me against you."

"This is too kind, too generous, Florio," replied the Count de Clairville, grasping his hand; "there shone all the spirit of my ill-fated and deeply injured brother. But it is more than I deserve, and——"

"No more, my lord," interrupted Florio; "indeed I cannot listen to observations that cast such a bitter reproach upon yourself."

"Enough, then," said the count, struggling with his feelings as well as he could; "I will say no more. Excuse me, Florio, pardon me, Signor Massaroni, for thus taxing your patience, but I must be permitted to retire for a short time, and when I return I hope I shall be enabled to continue my sad and eventful history to the conclusion. Adolphus, you will be pleased to attend me, for I probably shall stand in need of your advice and consolation."

Adolphus made no reply, though the facts which his noble friend and benefactor had already disclosed had excited his deepest interest and curiosity, and for the time had diverted his thoughts from the torturing subject which had before engrossed them; and arising from his seat, he accompanied the Count de Clairville from the cavern.

CHAPTER LVI.

THE FURTHERANCE OF THE PLOT.—THE INEXORABLE PARENT.—THE DUNGEON.—THE LOVERS.—THE GUILTY CONFESSION.

For several minutes after the count and Adolphus D'Aubigny had retired, Florio, with folded arms, paced the cavern to and fro in a state of considerable agitation, and Massaroni did not offer to interrupt him in his reflections; but at length the former, turning to the brigand chief, said,—

"What think you of this strange confession of the Count de Clairville, Massaroni, so far as it has proceeded?"

"That it is most extraordinary," replied our hero, "to say the least of it."

"Surely the count can never have been so guilty as he has already represented," observed Florio.

"Judging from his present conduct," returned Massaroni, "it seems scarcely possible; and yet what reason have we to doubt him? It does not seem at all probable that he would falsely accuse himself of that which must bring shame and opprobrium upon his name, notwithstanding his present penitence."

"True," coincided Florio, "and when I remember the melancholy fate of my father, and the bitter anguish of mind that my poor mother constantly endured, have I not a right to imagine the worst? My God! should the count have succeeded in the accomplishment of his guilty designs and wishes, and my mother should have become the victim to—But no, it is impossible! I shudder with horror at the thought! Heaven would never permit so frightful and unnatural a sacrifice."

"I trust not," said our hero; "but you must endeavour to wait patiently and calmly the completion of the disclosure which the Count de Clairville has to make, and it may not turn out so bad as you now anticipate. Constant grief and meditation upon the past, and his singular and unexpected meeting with you, may have caused his lordship to exaggerate, and to accuse himself, in the disorder of his mind, of that of which he is not guilty, and you will, therefore, act wisely if you do not judge him too hastily, or till you have heard him to the conclusion of his narrative."

"Your observations are just and forcible, my friend," replied Florio, "and I will follow your advice. Fain would I acquit the count altogether in my own mind, for it is my wish to look up with reverence and esteem to one who is so nearly allied to me by blood."

"Those sentiments do honour to you, Signor Florio," remarked Massaroni; "and I hope that you may have every reason to give encouragement to your generous feelings. But the discovery of your noble origin must be hailed by you with the most infinite delight and gratification, for now you may without hesitation aspire to the hand of her you love, and even the haughty Prince Bianchi, it strikes me, will, when he becomes acquainted with the facts, no longer remain obstinate, but will yield that consent which he has so long unjustly withheld."

"Oh, what bliss is there in that thought, Massaroni," ejaculated Florio; "I can scarcely believe in the reality of what has happened, so great and extraordinary is the change that only in the course of a few short hours has come over my prospects; but to your friendship, and disinterested exertions in my welfare, I am indebted for everything, and never can I be sufficiently grateful to you."

"Do not mention it, my young friend," returned the brigand; "for you know I dislike thanks, and I am only too happy to think I have been the means of serving one who is so well deserving of it."

Florio pressed his hand cordially as he replied—

"I know your heart, Massaroni, and I will not, therefore, insult you by making any further use of what you might consider fulsome compliments. I hope, however, the time may come, and that it is not far distant, when I shall see you restored to your proper position in society, and——"

"Nay, Florio," interrupted our hero, "I do not wish it;—I am wedded to the wild life it has been my fate for so many years to lead, and I have not the least desire to leave it. By all my hopes, I would not abandon my bold and faithful comrades even though by so doing I could be promoted to the dignity of a prince. There were moments when I could have resumed my place in society, but they are passed now; I have around me all the enjoyment and freedom that man can wish for—I have wealth, I have power, I have the means of contributing to the necessities of the less fortunate, though, perhaps, more deserving portion of my fellow-creatures, and why should I sigh for change? But enough of this, Florio; it is necessary that you should sufficiently collect your feelings as to listen patiently to all that the Count de Clairville may have to disclose, so deeply and immediately as you are interested in it. I cannot help thinking that he has already reproached himself too severely, and that although he may have erred, and that greatly, it will be seen that there are, at any rate, some extenuating circumstances in his conduct."

"Heaven send that there may be," said Florio; "but when I take into consideration the untimely fate of my father, the continued anxiety and anguish of mind under which my beloved and affectionate mother laboured, and the observations which the Count de Clairville has already made, is it not natural that my apprehensions and suspicions should be aroused?"

"Very true," coincided our hero; "but I still trust that they will prove to be unfounded; at any rate, let the faults of his lordship be whatever they may, it is now evident that he sincerely repents of them, and is most anxious and willing to make all the atonement in his power. This extraordinary discovery, and at the time when you so much needed it, ought to inspire you with every hope, for, take my word for it, again I say that it will be the means of removing all those obstacles that have been hitherto placed in the way of the completion of your happiness."

"Yes," returned Clairville, "that thought does indeed reanimate my drooping spirits, and I will endeavour to encourage the idea you have suggested. The Prince Bianchi

surely will have no reason to object to my alliance with his fair and innocent niece, when he shall be satisfied that the blood which flows within my veins is as noble as his own? Unless, indeed, that the rage he may feel that his designs have been frustrated, should induce him to remain obstinate."

"And if he should," remarked Massaroni, "the conduct he has thought proper to pursue, has rendered it no longer imperative on the Signora Melina to acknowledge or submit to his authority. She loves you, there is every reason to believe, as fervently as you do her; and surely she can no longer possess any scruples in becoming your wife."

"I would fain hope not," replied Florio; "but still I would much rather that a reconciliation could be effected with the prince, for it would render everything much more satisfactory."

"If Bianchi acts wisely, he will not hesitate for a moment in what manner to act," remarked Massaroni, "but he will gladly come to an amicable arrangement, and endeavour to make all the reparation he can for the errors of which he has been guilty, and the misery he has caused. But, at any rate, let the result be whatever it may, you have ample occasion to congratulate yourself upon the favourable change that has so suddenly come over your prospects."

In this opinion, Florio Clairville could not but perfectly coincide, and he awaited with the greatest impatience and anxiety the return of the Count de Clairville, that he might hear what further he had to reveal; and he was not long kept in suspense, for his lordship made his re-appearance, accompanied by Adolphus, shortly afterwards, and it was evident that he had succeeded in greatly subduing the excitement under which he had recently laboured, and was prepared to continue his narrative to the conclusion.

"It is a painful task I have imposed upon myself, Florio," he observed, "but still it is indispensably necessary that the disclosure should be made, in justice to yourself and those who have suffered through my misconduct, and also to relieve my own conscience from a weight of anxiety and remorse that of late years has become almost insupportable to me. But again I say that I must appeal to your utmost patience and forbearance, to listen to that which I have unfortunately to reveal, and much I fear that when you have heard all the guilty particulars, you will not be able to view me with the clemency which you now do."

"Pardon me, my lord," returned Florio, "but you entertain a wrong opinion of me in that respect. Heaven forbid that I should view with such uncharitable feelings the failings of my fellow-creatures, when we are all so liable to error; but pray proceed, for, indeed, as you may imagine, I am all anxiety to become acquainted with all those particulars in which I am so deeply interested."

The count made no reply, but after a pause, he resumed his narrative in the following words—

" I am ashamed to acknowledge it, but it is nevertheless true, that after the guilty sentiments with which her sister had inspired me, I could not help viewing my young and amiable wife with something like repugnance, and I, therefore, shunned her company as much as I could ; but if she noticed the indifference with which I treated her, she never once alluded to it, or reproached me in the least degree. She was, of course, fully aware of the love which existed between Antoine and Emilie, and she deeply sympathised with them, the more so, as she felt convinced that there was no hope of their ever being united, unless they were so clandestinely, and then they would incur the certain and everlasting malediction of their parents.

" The next day Antoine departed from the chateau, and after a farewell interview with Emilie, during which he assured her that he would shortly return, and in the meantime that I had undertaken to espouse their cause, and to intercede with the Count de Clairville and the Count St. Almo, he quitted the immediate neighbourhood, making me acquainted whither he was gone, and begging of me, by the love I bore him, to lose no time in performing the generous offices I had undertaken, and to exert all the influence I possessed to forward his wishes and those of his beloved Emilie. I again promised him faithfully to do all that he requested, and he left me, elated with fresh feelings of hope and confidence. Oh, what a base hypocrite must I have been thus to deceive one of the best of brothers, and who, I knew, would have been willing to lay down his very life to serve me !

" As for Emilie, she was most unbounded in the expressions of her gratitude towards me, though she could scarcely dare to hope that my efforts would prove successful. It seemed but too improbable that our parents would cancel a compact that had existed for so many years, notwithstanding the cruelty, injustice, and extravagance of it.

" No one more deeply sympathised with the feelings of the lovers, than the gentle and amiable Lestelle; no sentiment of jealousy or mortified pride ever once entered her breast, but, on the contrary, she would willingly have done anything that laid in her power which might tend towards the gratification of their wishes. Her wish, as I have before stated, was to lead a life of celibacy, and, therefore, she could experience no disappointment at the rejection of her hand by Antoine.

" Before I commenced my plot, I sought a private interview with Emilie, which, of course, was granted without hesitation or suspicion, and I need not attempt to describe the feelings that predominated in my breast when I found myself alone with that lovely and innocent being. I prolonged the meeting as much as I could, and it required all my exertions and the deception I had at my command to enable me to restrain the guilty thoughts that held their sway in my bosom; but the beauteous Emilie penetrated them not, but, on the contrary, I firmly believe, on our separation, she had a more exalted opinion of the disinterestedness of my conduct than ever.

" This interview did but inflame my unholy and unnatural passions the more, and I was fully determined to carry my diabolical plot into execution, at all hazards. Ah, Florio ! I see well that the crimson blushes of shame and indignation mantle in your cheeks, and well they may ; but bear with me yet awhile, or I shall never be able to enter into that explanation which is of the greatest moment and importance to you, and which I am so anxious to give."

" Proceed, my lord," said Florio, " I will not attempt to interrupt you, and rest assured that I am ready to make every allowance for any errors which you may have been guilty of, but which I cannot believe to be of that heinous character you have represented them to be."

The count looked his thanks towards Florio, but returned no answer, and again continued—

" Emilie was anxious to know whither Antoine was gone, and the nature of his business; but I pleaded ignorance, and she did not urge her questions further. Several times I was on the point of throwing myself at her feet, and acknowledging the guilty sentiments that glowed in my breast towards her, but shame and fear restrained me, and I determined to await until some more favourable opportunity should present itself, though such an ascendancy had my unholy passions obtained over me, that I was fully resolved that they should be gratified at some future time at any cost.

" It was arranged between us that I should first seek an interview with my father, and endeavour to win him to my purpose, and then if I failed with him, to try my influence with the Count St. Almo ; and Emilie could not help entertaining a secret hope that when they found that the happiness of both their children was at stake, they would no longer remain inexorable, but in spite of the fatal compact, would at once yield their consent, and by so doing render the bliss of two beings who were so worthy of each other complete. But notwithstanding I did not seek to stifle these hopes in her breast, I felt convinced that they would not be realised, and I was fully determined that it should be no fault of mine if I did not succeed in the accomplishment of the diabolical wishes

I had formed. I had arranged all my infamous plans, which will be fully developed in the course of my narrative.

"The following day, according to my promise, I requested an interview with the count my father, which was granted, and I found him in his study, wrapped in deep meditation. He arose on my entrance, and advanced towards me.

" 'How, now, Eugene?' he demanded; 'what is it you seek in requesting this interview?'

" 'I would speak to you, my lord,' I replied, 'upon a subject of the greatest importance.'

" 'Indeed!' he said, 'and what may that be?'

" ''Tis one on which I must crave your lordship's indulgence,' I continued; 'the subject upon which I would speak is the fatal compact that exists in our family, and that of my father-in-law, the Count St. Almo.'

" 'And what of that?' he demanded, impatiently.

" 'My brother——'

" 'Ah! he has absented himself from the chateau,' said the count, 'and full well can I guess the cause; he has dared to object to the terms of the compact which has existed in our family for so many years, and to reject the hand of Lestelle St. Almo.'

" 'True, my father,' I said, in tones which might have led any one to suppose that I was sincere in advocating the cause of Antoine, 'it is true, my father,' I repeated, 'but Lestelle and my brother do not love each other, and surely you would not seek to sacrifice them, to consign them to misery, merely to fulfil the terms of a ridiculous and extravagant document, which ought never to have been in existence, or, at any rate, ought to have been abandoned years ago.'

" 'How!' said the count, frowning, 'and do you presume to question the justice and importance of that compact, Eugene?'

" 'My lord,' I replied, 'it is reason and justice that prompt me to do it.'

" 'Psha!' he exclaimed, 'reason and justice! I have no patience with you. You are here then, it seems, to advocate the cause of Antoine?'

" 'Even so, my lord,' I answered with the utmost respect in my tones and demeanour.

" 'Then, Eugene,' he returned, 'you may as well save yourself the trouble, for all the arguments you can possibly make use of, cannot have the least favourable effect on me. By the saints, man, think you I have become so weak and irresolute as to yield to the ridiculous caprices of a headstrong, giddy boy? What would the world say of me if I were now to cancel that compact which I was myself compelled to adhere to? Antoine knows the consequences of his refusal; and should he dare to deceive me, my curse——'

" 'Hold, my dear father,' I interrupted, with much apparent emotion; 'do not give utterance to anything rashly, and which you might afterwards have cause to regret. I repeat that Lestelle and my brother feel no more powerful sentiments towards each other than those of esteem and friendship.'

" 'Ridiculous, Eugene,' again said the count, in the same testy and impatient manner. 'Is not Lestelle young, innocent, and lovely?'

" 'She is, and possessed of every virtue,' I replied; 'but her sister, Emilie, and Antoine love each other to distraction, and they can never know what real happiness is, unless they are permitted to come together.'

" 'Confusion!' exclaimed the count, 'they must be absolutely mad to think of such a thing. It is impossible! They must banish all such ideas from their minds, or they know the consequences. Lestelle is the destined wife of your brother, and she must be so, or misery, poverty, and the curses of their parents will descend upon their heads and that of Emilie.'

" 'Oh, my father, say not so,' I observed, 'for such a decision would be the means of bringing about a scene of wretchedness which I shudder to contemplate.'

" 'It is the law laid down in the united families of de Clairville and St. Almo, and there is no departing from it. There is only one thing that I can yield to your supplications.'

" 'And what is that, my lord?' I asked.

" 'To extend the time when the marriage of Antoine and Lestelle shall take place to three months; and if at the end of that time they do not yield, be the consequences upon their own heads.'

" 'My lord,' I observed, 'it is not my duty to question or to interfere in your decision, but again I most humbly but earnestly implore you to reflect calmly upon the painful subject ere you come to any rash conclusion. I can have no other interest in this business than the love I bear my brother, and the—the esteem which I naturally feel for the transcendent virtues of the sister of my wife.'

" Who could have imagined for a moment," continued the Count de Clairville, " that I could be otherwise than sincere in that which I so plausibly argued? Who could suppose that I could be consummate villain and hypocrite sufficient to harbour one thought to the injury or prejudice of those whose cause I so eloquently advocated? But, alas! it was too truly so, and at the very moment when I was pretending to be their most ardent friend, I was maturing designs against their future happiness, which I now shudder to look back upon. Oh, I have indeed full cause to shrink abashed in the presence of the son of those whom I have so deeply injured. But let me endeavour to conquer my emotions, and to reveal the facts exactly as they occurred.

"'Eugene,' said the count, after a pause, during which interval he had paced the apartment backwards and forwards in a state of great agitation,; 'let me try to explain to you all the consequences that have attended those of our family who have been mad enough to disobey the compact. There have been those who have, by their own folly and obstinacy, been doomed to horrors so intense, that it is sufficient to make human nature recoil and shudder to reflect upon them. In their youth, taken from the busy and cheerful scenes of the world, they have been immured in a loathsome dungeon, into which the light of day never entered, and where hope and themselves have been fated to become henceforth strangers. There, imprisoned in a living tomb, they have had to endure such mental and bodily tortures, that made them pray for death, and from which they had not the smallest chance of extricating themselves.'

"'Oh, horrible!' I exclaimed with a shudder; 'and is it possible that such atrocities can ever have been perpetrated by any of the members of our family?'

"'It is true,' replied the count, 'and they were bound to do so by the oath they had taken.'

"'Fearful mockery of all that is just and sacred!' I observed; 'and that sincerely at the moment, 'what law, human or divine, could ever sanction an oath so monstrous?'

"'Woe be to those who should attempt to break it!' replied my father, in accents of solemnity, which showed to what an alarming and preposterous length he had permitted his superstitious ideas to carry him; 'an eternal curse would most assuredly follow them.'

"'Oh, my lord,' I remarked, 'you surely are too enlightened to believe in what you assert?'

"'Not only do I believe in it, Eugene,' he answered, seriously, 'but I shall be bound to put all I have stated into effect, if I were called upon by circumstances to do so. Do you doubt my word? If you do so, attend me, and I will soon convince you.'

"I returned no answer, for my most painful curiosity was excited to the greatest degree; and after a brief pause, he lighted a small table lamp, although it was broad day, and motioned me to follow him. I obeyed, and unlocking a small door in the room, concealed from observation by tapestry, and of the existence of which I was not aware before, he led the way, and I followed him with the most intense curiosity and anxiety. We entered upon a gloomy passage, at the end of which was a spiral flight of stairs, and which having descended, we found ourselves in a kind of court, upon either side of which were iron doors that seemed to open upon vaults or dungeons. At the termination of this, we turned abruptly round to the right, and then came upon another flight of stairs, or rather stone steps, which were narrow and winding, and which evidently communicated with some places on a level almost with the foundation of the building. We now arrived at a stone passage, low, narrow, and winding, and the vaults of which, as far as I could see from the light emitted by the lamp which my father carried, were dripping with unwholesome dew.

"I was astonished, for I had never formed the least idea of the existence of these places, and imagined that I had inspected all the subterranean horrors that were buried beneath the chateau.

"'Whither are you leading me, my lord?' I eagerly inquired, and entertaining a vague fear that he meant me some wrong.

"'You will see anon,' he answered.

"'What a fearful place is this,' I remarked 'Surely——'

"'You have nothing to dread, Eugene,' he interrupted; 'follow me, and the curiosity you no doubt feel, will soon be gratified.'

"I said no more, but followed in silence, and on gaining the end of this subterranean passage, which was terminated by an iron door, and descending a few broken steps beyond, we wound round a little to the left, and I then, to my astonishment, found myself in that dismal passage I had so often traversed, and which had the range of dungeons I have so often mentioned.

"My father paused for an instant, and looking narrowly in my countenance, he said,—

"'You have often visited this place, Eugene, and I have never offered to interrupt you, or to prohibit you from so doing, but there is one dungeon which you have never yet inspected, and which you have no doubt had some curiosity to examine. I am now about to show it you; it is that dungeon of horrors I have mentioned to you. This way.'

"I returned no answer, for my curiosity and anxiety were too much excited, and directly afterwards he stopped before the door of that cell to which I have alluded in the early part of my history, and whose hidden mysteries I had been so eager to penetrate. Having with difficulty removed the bolts, he took from his pocket a bunch of keys, one of which he applied to the lock, and after some resistance it yielded, and a cloud of dust met and almost suffocated us. This having dispersed, I found myself in a place the first aspect of which smote my mind with horror, and fully realised all that the count, my father, had described it to be. It was of very small dimensions, and its walls and low roof were blackened with age, and were covered with cobwebs and unwholesome dews. Upon the damp earth, the toad and adder sported in undisturbed security, and the whole place breathed a noisome vapour that was particularly oppressive, and, in fact, almost overpowering. My father held the lamp above his head to accelerate my view, and then I beheld that there were heavy chains and fetters upon the earth, secured to the walls by strong staples. There was nothing more to admit air, even such as could be procured in that frightful region, than a small chink in the wall, and it seemed utterly impossible for any one to exist even for

ANTOINE PERUSING THE LETTER FROM EMILIE.

the shortest space of time in such a horrible receptacle. I trembled as I gazed upon it, and a sickening sensation came over me.

"'Well, Eugene,' demanded my father, and he spoke in accents of triumph that excited my disgust; 'what think you of this place? Does it not fully realise the description I gave you of it? Is it not a fit place for thsoe who know not obedience?'

"'Good God!' I replied, 'is it possible that any unfortunate being could survive here for an hour? or that there could be found those inhuman enough to incarcerate any person in such a place of horror ?'

" 'It is even so, Eugene,' answered the count coolly, ' and such will be the doom of all those who should in future dare to resist the compact.'

" 'Oh, impossible !' I ejaculated, looking at him incredulously ; ' the bare idea is monstrous.'

" 'It may be so in your estimation, Eugene,' he returned, ' but it is nevertheless a fact. Here several of our ancestors have found a prison and a tomb. 'Twas here my own uncle perished.' "

" Most horrible !" exclaimed Florio, interrupting the Count de Clairville ; " is it possible that any one could ever have become so insensible to every feeling of humanity and justice, as to commit such barbarous acts ?"

" Alas !" replied his uncle ; " it is too true, as I have so much reason to know.'

" And such are the men who would call themselves noble," remarked our hero, " and who would be the first to designate Allesandro Massaroni monster, and to hunt him to the death ! Oh, what a cruel mockery it is to common sense, justice, and humanity !"

" True, Signor Massaroni," coincided the Count de Clairville ; " and I blush to think that any human being, boasting the name of man, should have been guilty of such atrocities. But to proceed.

" 'Your own uncle, my lord ?' I replied.

" 'Yes,' he answered, ' such was his fate, for refusing to comply with the demands of the compact, and such must inevitably be that of Antoine, should he be mad enough to remain obstinate.'

" 'What, my lord,' said I, again shuddering, and looking at him with mingled expressions of astonishment, incredulity, and horror, ' your own son ? You surely could never contemplate anything so hideously frightful and unnatural ?'

" 'I should have no other alternative,' he returned; ' but you have not yet seen all the horrors of this place, Eugene ; do you not observe something in yonder corner ?'

" I looked whither he pointed, and beheld an old cloak lying on the ground, and beneath a strong link of rusty iron chain that was fixed in the wall. The count advanced towards it, and raising it from the ground, what was my amazement and horror to behold that it had concealed the mouldering and blackened bones of a human skeleton.

' These are the ghastly remains of one of our ancestors, who perished here many years ago,' observed my father; 'here they have been left to moulder ever since, and to strie terror into the breasts of all those who were so frequently incarcerated here.'

" My heart sickened with disgust, and I turned away from the ghastly sight.

" 'No more of this, my lord,' I said, ' I can no longer bear to gaze upon such revolting horrors.'

" 'Be it so,' he replied ; ' but before you leave here, I must exact from you a promise.'

" 'And what is the nature of it ?' I asked.

" 'That you will never, while myself or the Count St. Almo are living, reveal to Antoine or any other person that which you have here seen, and what I have related to you.'

" I hesitated.

" 'Why do you not answer ?' he demanded impatiently.

" 'Why should you wish me to make such a promise ?'

" 'Because it is necessary, nay, indispensable,' he returned ; 'the secrets of this place must not become known to anyone. Do you comply with what I demand ?'

" 'I suppose it is useless to refuse,' I replied. ' I therefore promise to keep the horrible secrets of this place concealed within my own breast, until I am permitted to disclose them ; but I sincerely hope that they will in future be abolished.'

" 'You must swear this.'

" 'What necessity can there be for doing so ? Cannot you take my word ?'

" 'No, nothing less than your oath will satisfy me,' he answered.

" Finding that it was useless to deny him, I complied, and he having administered to me a solemn oath, we quitted the dungeon and returned to the room where we had held our previous conference, I filled with horror and astonishment at all I had seen and heard, entertaining very different feelings towards my father to those which I had experienced before, and for a time wavering in the guilty designs which I had formed against the peace and welfare of my unsuspecting brother, and the innocent Emilie. Would to God that I had adhered to the thoughts that at that time haunted my wavering mind, what a many years of bitter remorse would it have saved me. But, alas ! such was the powerful ascendancy which the charms of Emelie had obtained over my better principles, that I was unable to form the resolution.

" For some moments after our return to the room, I continued wrapped in deep meditation upon all the extraordinary and revolting things which I had seen, and my father did not offer to interrupt me, but at length he said—

" 'Eugene, you must now see the utter inutility of your brother opposing my will, and if you bear him that regard you profess to do, you will advise him accordingly.'

" 'Oh, my lord,' I replied, ' you must—you will think better of this.'

" 'I can never think differently or decide otherwise than I do now,' he returned.

"'Say not so, my dear father,' I observed, "you cannot be serious.'

"'Eugene, you ought to know me better. I am not much given to idle jesting, especially on such serious subjects as this. You will find that I shall keep my word.'

"'My lord, it is impossible that you can be guilty of anything so opposed to humanity and nature. Remember that Antoine is your own son, and that should you—

"'Enough upon that subject, Eugene,' he interrupted : 'it is useless to argue with me. It is enough that I give Antoine three months to make up his mind; and then, if he still remains obstinate, he must take the consequences. Even should he not place himself in my power, he will become disinherited, a beggar, a wandering outcast, and an alien to my blood.'

"'Surely this is most severe and unjust,' I remarked.

"'Such is the destiny that is unavoidably marked out for him,' returned the count. 'Had you not happened to be my eldest son, it would likewise have been your fate. But Antoine has acted prudently in leaving the neighbourhood ; for, probably, in absence from Emilie, he may be able to reflect calmly, and to banish her from his memory in any other character than that of a sister. I do not even ask you the place to which he has retired.'

"'But is the Count St. Almo acquainted with all those horrible facts you have informed me of, my lord?' I asked.

"'Most certainly he is,' returned the count; 'and he is bound in the same manner as I am to abide by them, however painful it may be to his feelings. You may appeal to him, if you think proper, on behalf of Antoine and Emilie ; but I promise you beforehand that it will be all to no purpose. Is Lestelle ready to yield to the wishes of her father, should your brother no longer object to become her husband ?'

"'I believe she is, my lord,' I replied, 'though, as I before informed you, I am convinced that she does not love him : in fact, her thoughts are fixed another way. The world possesses no charms for her ; and it is her anxious wish to be permitted to pass her life in holy seclusion.'

"'Strange taste,' remarked the count ; 'but one so young and beautiful must not be permitted to indulge in it. But this interview has lasted long enough, and I would now be alone. Bear in mind all that I have said, and rest assured that nothing whatever can alter me in my determination.'

"'I am heartily sorry to hear you say so, my lord,' I returned ; 'but I trust that you will think better of it, and allow me, at some future time, to repeat my appeal.'

"'You may do so if you think proper,' he said ; 'but I tell you again that it will be useless.'

"Here our interview ended, and I walked away from the chateau, buried in deep reflection upon all that had transpired. My feelings were of a mixed and conflicting nature, and sometimes I was half inclined to abandon my guilty designs, and sincerely to exert myself all I could to promote the happiness of Antoine and her to whom he was so devotedly attached ; but such was the powerful influence that the charms of Emilie had gained over me, that I found it quite impossible to relenquish my hopes. I had now every opportunity of seeing her daily alone, and I determined to avail myself of it to prosecute my designs to the utmost. The society of my unsuspecting wife had now become more tedious and painful to me, although she lavished upon me the greatest affection, and exerted herself to the utmost to make me happy. This was more embarrassing and annoying to me than all, and I often wondered that she did not observe there was something on my mind which I was anxious to conceal, and that she did not qunstion me upon the subject. However, in spite of all I could not help at times reproaching myself for the conduct I was pursuing, which was most unjust and despicable in the extreme. But to return to the part from which I have thus digressed. I continued for some time after I had quitted the chateau, rambling about, and giving myself up to the various thoughts which crowded upon my mind, and when at last I did return home, I retired to my own private apartment until I had sufficiently composed my feelings to meet my wife, who, knowing the business I had been upon to my father, would naturally question me as to the result. These questions when I did see her I evaded as much as possible, only informing her of such particulars as I could not very well avoid, and as soon as I could, I dropped the subject.

"At the first opportunity I sought an interview with Emilie alone, and she received me with much anxiety. The earnestness of her manner, and the language in which she spoke of my brother, greatly confused me, and at times I was at a loss how to answer her, and was afraid that she would discover from my looks and the hesitation of my manner the thoughts that were passing in my mind. When she heard of the result of my interview with my father, nothing could exceed the power of the emotions she exhibited, and she was unable to refrain from tears. This bewildered me more than all, and again the utmost feelings of jealousy and envy arose in my breast against my brother.

"'Alas !' she sighed, 'what a sad destiny is mine and Antoine's. Why should there be such cruel and insurmountable obstacles in the way of those who love each other so sincerely ? Oh, Antoine, if I am not permitted to become your wife, what is there left for me in this world but the most insupportable and torturing misery?'

"'Do not give way entirely to despair, Emilie,' I said, in tones as calm and collected as I could; 'do not forget, at least, that you have a sincere friend in me, who is anxious to do all he can to promote your happiness.'

"Oh, well do I know that, Eugene,' she answered, 'and most grateful do I feel towards you, you may rest assured; I must ever look upon you with the affection of a sister.'

"'With the affection of a sister, Emilie?' I repeated, for the moment forgetting myself, and a feeling coming over me at the same time, which I found it a most arduous task to subdue or conceal; but I quickly regained my self-possession, and in different accents added, 'With the affection of a sister, Emilie? Oh, how proud ought I to be of that distinction! And believe me that I do and ever must feel towards you all the warmest affection of a brother, and most happy shall I be if it should ever be in my power to serve one so lovely, so amiable, and so innocent.'

She blushed deeply, hid her face for a moment in evident confusion, and I began to fear that I had proceeded too far; however, she quickly recovered herself and observed,—

"'What a cruel and monstrous compact is that which consigns two beings to a mutual fate which may be so repugnant to their feelings.'

"'It is indeed, Emilie,' I coincided; 'and yet I see no means of avoiding it.'

"'Surely such a compact cannot be binding in the sight of Heaven?' she remarked.

"'Certainly not,' I answered; 'but still when you remember the fatal consequences that must attend an act of disobedience on your part, neither yourself nor Antoine dare to oppose the will of your parents.'

"'For my own part,' said Emilie, firmly, 'I am ready to suffer anything rather than yield to that which is so cruel, tyrannical, and unjust. Poverty and Antoine are far more preferable, than unbounded riches and a husband whom I cannot love.'

"I was obliged to turn away for a moment to conceal my emotion, and I bit my lips in the vexation of my soul. What would have been the horror and disgust of Emilie, could she have read the thoughts which at that moment were passing through my mind? However, I again recovered myself, and said—

"'I cannot but admire the rectitude and firmness of your feelings, Emilie; but still I am afraid it will all be of no avail.'

"'Oh, say not so, Eugene,' she returned, in a voice of increased agitation; 'for could I be confident of that, I should be sunk in the very abyss of despair. But our parents will never relent.'

"'Would to Heaven that they might,' I answered with apparent sincerity, 'but from what the count, my father, has said to me to-day, I am afraid it is almost hopeless.'

"'Alas! alas!' groaned Emilie, wringing her hands, 'then, indeed, will my misery be complete. Again, I say, that no other man but Antoine can ever possess my heart, and should we not be destined to come together, the sooner that Heaven takes me to itself the better.'

"I felt my confusion and my chagrin increase, and I almost wished myself away from her presence. It was wonderful how I could help betraying myself, and showing myself in my true character. How must Emilie have loathed and despised me, then! But the fatal and revolting discovery was not fated to be made at that time, and thus was I permitted every day and every hour to plunge myself still deeper into crime.

"At length, I again conquered my feelings sufficiently to reply—

"'Emilie,' I said, 'it pains me to hear you talk in that melancholy manner, for though I doubt not the anguish it would cause you were all your hopes of becoming the wife of Antoine to be annihilated, time and perseverance might teach you to remember him only as a friend, and you would meet with some one who would be equally worthy of your love.'

"'Oh, no, no!' she ejaculated, impatiently, 'that is impossible! It would be madness to encourage such a thought for a moment. Where could I ever meet with another man whom I could love with the same ardent affection as I do Antoine de Clairville? Eugene, did you thoroughly know my heart, it would be quite unnecessary for me to make such an assertion.'

"By Heaven! I thought to myself, it seemed as if she could really now penetrate what was passing in my mind, and was resolved to punish me for my presumption. However, I endeavoured to abate the warmth of the conversation, and said—

"'Well, Emilie, we must trust to time and the goodness of Providence, and in the meanwhile, again rest assured that I will do all in my power to serve you and to promote your wishes.'

"'Thanks, thanks, Eugene,' she replied, 'I place every confidence in you, for I know full well that you will ever act towards me with the zeal and affection of a brother.'

"'You do me no more than justice by such a supposition, Emilie,' I returned.

"'But will you not make another appeal to the Count de Clairville?' she asked.

"'I will do so in a day or two,' I replied, 'and when he has had sufficient time to weigh over in his own mind the arguments I made use of.'

"'And in the meantime I will throw myself

at the feet of my parents,' observed Emilie, 'and surely they will be unable to resist my earnest prayers and supplications?'

"'Most earnestly do I hope that they will not,' I returned, 'though I must acknowledge (for it would be cruel to attempt to deceive you) that I have the strongest doubts upon the subject, when I take all the painful and difficult circumstances of the case into consideration.'

"'I dare not think so,' said Emilie, 'for it would drive me to absolute madness and despair.'

"'Keep up your spirits, Emilie,' I said, 'and after all it may turn out better—far better than we now anticipate.'

"'What will be the anxiety of Antoine's mind till he knows the result of this interview?' she remarked.

"'I will immediately communicate to him the particulars,' I answered.

"'Ah, then!' she ejaculated, eagerly, 'you know where you brother at present is?'

"I replied in the affirmative, but at the same time added—

"'But it is necessary for the present I should conceal it from you; but you may rest assured, Emilie, that he is acting from perfectly prudential motives in absenting himself from the neighbourhood of the chateau, and in not revealing to you where he is at present staying. Let that satisfy you, and, at the same time, be certain that I have both your interests at heart in acting as I am now doing.'

"'I am satisfied, Eugene,' she answered; 'and may Heaven reward you for that which you have already done. But when shall I see Antoine again?'

"'Ere long, Emilie, depend upon it,', I returned; 'and, in the meantime, be contented to know that I shall be in constant communication with him, and also that I have persuaded my father to delay the marriage of your lover and Lestelle for three months; in the interim, something of importance that might turn the tide of fortune altogether, may occur; so, once more, I say, you must live in hopes.'

"'I will strive to do so,' said Emilie. 'But shall I not hear from him? Shall I not have the means of corresponding with him?'

"'Oh, yes,' I replied, and, at the same time a villanous idea flashed upon my mind, which I imagined was not only calculated to forward my nefarious designs, but likewise to gratify my curiosity; 'as I have before told you, I shall be in constant communication with him, and anything you may wish to write to him, I will safely deliver into his hands, and bring to you his answer. You will thus be in as ready an intercourse with him almost as if you were present to each other.'

"She grasped my hand fervently as I thus spoke, and pressed it to her lips (what an un-holy feeling of exultation thrilled through all my veins as she did so!) and in accents which spoke the sincerity of her heart, she ejaculated—

"'Kind, best of friends, as well as brothers, for this, in what language sufficiently powerful can I express my gratitude? But you will be rewarded for your generous and manly sympathy in——'

"'For the love of Heaven, Emilie, cease,' I interrupted, and I was stung with remorse and shame, though at the same time every word she uttered tended but to inflame the guilty passions she had excited in my breast; 'you overwhelm me by those flattering eulogies, which any service it is in my poor power to render you can but ill-deserve. But I must leave you, Emilie, for I have much to occupy my time and attention at the present moment, and to prolong this interview would only, perhaps, be embarrassing to us both. There is one thing, however, which I wish to request of you ere I depart.'

"'Name it, Eugene,' she said.

"I hesitated, for I almost feared to give utterance to my wishes, lest her suspicions should be aroused, and I should be foiled in the nefarious, the absolutely brutal designs which I had formed against the happiness of my brother and herself, while I was basely pretending to be their most sincere and devoted friend, and exposed to that shame, that infamy, and contempt which I so richly merited.

"'Nay, Eugene,' ejaculated Emilie, 'why should you hesitate? Surely there is no request that you can make, prompted as I know full well it must be by the purest motives, that I can refuse to you.'

"These observations confused me the more, and I almost regretted that I had proceeded so far, and would fain have equivocated, but her bright and penetrating eyes were fixed earnestly upon my countenance, and I saw that it would be useless. Little could the beauteous Emilie in the purity and innocence of her soul imagine at that moment the almost demoniacal thoughts which were passing in my mind, or one look, one word of hers only, must have sunk me into the earth. However, thus urged altogether, I had no means of evading an answer, and I therefore at last said—

'What I have to request of you is, Emilie, that, whatever conversation may occur between us, during the absence of my brother, you will never mention a word of it to him, but consider it as confidential and sacred between ourselves.'

'How, Eugene,' she remarked, fixing upon me a look of astonishment, 'this is surely a most singular requisition.'

'You may deem it so, at present, Emilie,' I replied, assuming as much coolness and plausibility as I could; 'but I am certain that you will ultimately be ready to admit that I have acted only as prudence dictates, and for the better furtherance of our wishes.'

'Why should we have any secrets from Antoine?' she demanded; 'I must confess that I am at a loss perfectly to understand you.'

'Did you know the sincerity with which I act in this important and difficult matter you would not hesitate for an instant to comply with the simple request I make of you,' I returned; 'a refusal might be the means of rendering all the plans I have formed in my own mind for the accomplishment of your wishes abortive, and I thought you said just now that you placed every confidence in me.'

"The subtlety of this query completely conquered her suspicions, and carried my point.

'Pardon me, Eugene,' she observed, 'if I have appeared for an instant to doubt you; you certainly can have nothing else but the welfare of your brother and myself at heart; I yield then to your request, without any further hesitation. Whatever conversation that may occur between us, I not only promise, but swear never to reveal to Antoine, *under any circumstances*, without your permission. I will rest everything in your hands and abide the consequences.'

"Wretch! monster, that I was," continued the Count de Clairville, with the greatest emotion. "I could scarcely conceal the exultation I felt at this triumph in my unholy designs. I considered it at that time as the grand stepping stone to the completion of my wishes, and was determined that nothing should prevent or intimidate me from my purpose, even though a curse should pursue me ever afterwards, and in spite of the misery which I knew it must produce. God of Heaven! why didst thou not strike me dead the moment I entertained such diabolical thoughts? It would have been no more than a just judgment upon me. Florio, do you not, can you possibly look upon me with any other feelings than those of disgust and hatred?"

"It is a sad, a melancholy disclosure, my lord," replied Florio; "but pray calm yourself; suffer me to hear you patiently to the end, and then I shall be enabled to form my own conclusions. At present I am inclined to view you with mercy and indulgence, making every allowance for the excitement under which you labour' from remorse, and which, probably, causes you to paint yourself in blacker colours than your errors deserve."

"Noble-hearted youth!" exclaimed the count, grasping his hand, "this is too generous, far too generous on your part; and in the observations you have just made use of, spoke all the spirit of your unfortunate and deeply-injured father. But still I have undertaken to give a just and unexaggerated revelation of the faults of my past life, and though it wring my brain to madness in doing so, I will not shrink from the performance of my promise, let the conse-

quences to myself be whatever they may. When you have heard me to the end, hate me, despise me, demand retribution, if you will; I place myself entirely in your hands, and to whatsoever descision you may arrive, I will submit without a murmur."

"Nay, my lord," replied Florio, "this is uncalled for; I feel satisfied, as I have before told you, that whatever faults you may have committed, they are not of that heinous nature which you represent them to be, and that there will be found to be extenuating circumstances in the facts you have to relate. But pray resume your narrative."

"Pardon me for this digression," said the count, "and I will do so."

He paused for a few minutes to refresh his memory, and then continued—

"'Enough, Emelie,' I said, 'this renewed confidence affords me every satisfaction, and you will have no cause to regret it. Tomorrow, then, we will meet again, and I will take charge of any letter your may think proper to write to my brother, and faithfully bring you back his answer.'

"What could appear more honest or disinterested? Was it not sufficient to quiet all suspicions on her part? Again she returned to me her thanks, and heaped her blessings upon my head, and every word to which she gave utterance, added to the unnatural sentiments with which she had inspired me. I imagined that she was now completely in my power, and I determined not to rest until I had achieved my nefarious object, let it cost what amount of misery it might; in fact, I was completely abandoned to every idea of virtuous principle, such was the fatal ascendancy that my evil passions had attained over me.

"'But, Emelie,' I said, after a brief pause, 'there are still one or two more requests that I have to make of you.'

"'And what are they, Eugene?' she asked.

"'First,' I answered, 'that you also keep it a secret from every one as well as Antoine whatever may transpire between us. Do you promise?'

"'I do, Eugene,' she returned; 'indeed, after what you have observed, I repeat that I place every reliance in you, and will leave everything to your judgment and discretion.'

"'Another thing I request is,' I said, 'that you do not make any appeal to your father at present, but leave that task to me. What I might say to him would probably have more effect upon him than anything you could advance.'

"'Be it as you advise, Eugene,' she replied; 'but surely when he knows the devoted affection that exists between myself and Antoine, and that my sister, Lestelle, is averse to a union between herself and your brother, he cannot be so cruel and unjust as to persist in the fulfilment of that monstrous compact, by which he must for ever sacrifice the happiness of two beings who ought to be dear to him.'

"'I would fain hope so, Emilie.' I returned with an air of sincerity which was well calculated to deceive; 'and it shall be no fault of mine if both he and my father do not yield to the force of argument and reason. We now then perfectly understand each other?'

"'We do.'

"'Till to-morrow, then, I must bid you adieu; I will call upon you previous to my communicating with Antoine, when I shall be ready to receive any letter you may feel inclined to write to him.'

"She once more warmly returned her acknowledgments, and we separated, I returning towards my home, exulting in the success of my plot so far as it had proceeded.

"I should have before informed you that on my marriage with Marie, I had taken up my residence at one of the estates of my father, which was situated between the chateau and the castle of St. Almo, and only a short distance from both. It may also be as well to mention that Antoine had retired to a secluded place, only about a couple of leagues from the neighbourhood, and where I could be in ready communication with him.

"As I slowly bent my way towards home, I reflected with feelings of satisfaction on all that had taken place at the interview between myself and Emilie, and prided myself upon the skill and adroitness with which I had commenced the operation of my designs.

"'My triumph is all but certain,' I ejaculated; 'she must, she shall be mine, in spite of all the obstacles which are at present placed in my way. She loves Antoine, but should she ever become his, it shall not be till after she has yielded to my wishes. They may preach of virtuous scruples, but I must be composed of adamant, if I could resist such superlative charms as those which Emilie possesses. Oh, what a contrast does she present to her to whom I am united! Why did fate ever link me to one who, however good and amiable, I cannot love?—But am I not acting the part of a villain in thus acting towards my innocent and faithful wife, who places every confidence in me, and who, I am convinced, loves me with the tenderest affection?—Am I not a heartless hypocrite and miscreant thus to deceive and endeavour to betray one of the best of brothers? Away with thought! The hope of possessing Emilie overcomes every other scruple, and let whatever may be the consequences, I will pursue my designs until they are accomplished.'

"I was aroused from these guilty reflections, by a scornful and unearthly laugh, and turning hastily round with astonishment and alarm, I beheld standing by my side a mysterious being known in the neighbourhood at that time by the name of Mad Jerome.

"He was, indeed, a strange and wild-looking man, and well calculated, from his singular habits and personal appearance, to inspire feelings of awe and dread in the breasts of all who encountered him. He was very aged, and his form was tall, lank, and bony, showing that he had in his more youthful days been possessed of much physical strength. His features were particularly ghastly and repulsive, and there was an expression in his small but brilliant eyes that caused a painful feeling to gaze upon. His hair, which was of iron-gray, hung wild and matted on his shoulders. His dress was of a most extraordinary description, dirty and ragged, and which added much to the general wildness of his appearance.

"This man was supposed by most persons to be mad, but the more vulgar and ignorant looked upon him with feelings of dread, supposing him to be possessed of supernatural powers; in fact, all the calamities that took place in the neighbourhood were supposed by those individuals to happen through him.

"Appearing to me at such a time, and imagining that he had overheard what I had said, you may naturally suppose that I was somewhat disconcerted and alarmed, and I looked at him in amazement for a few minutes, and was unable to speak, while he gazed at me with a mingled expression of scorn and triumph.

"'Well met, Eugene de Clairville,' he said at last, in harsh and disagreeable tones, 'though methinks thou art not well pleased to see me at a time like this, and when you were engaged in such agreeable reflections.'

"'Croaking old idiot!' I exclaimed passionately, 'are you not afraid to presume to address me thus?'

"'Afraid!' he repeated, with a scornful laugh; 'afraid of such a thing as thou art! Ha! ha! ha!—It is thou that ought to be afraid of me and all honest men, knowing the guilty thoughts that occupy thy mind.'

"'Begone, begone,' I tremulously replied, 'I would have no words with thee. If it be money that you seek, take it, and leave me.'

"'Money!' he returned, with another scornful look; 'it is dross! I need it not. But whether thou likest it or not, I must speak with thee.'

"'What wouldst thou?' I demanded.

"'I would warn thee to abandon thy guilty designs ere it be too late.' he answered.

"'Strange being,' I said, looking upon him with a feeling of astonishment and dread; 'what knowest thou of me?'

"'More—much more than it will please you to hear,' he replied; 'fools call me mad, but I am not so! Oh, no; it would gratify many if I were so: but I can penetrate the thoughts of those with whom I come in contact; wouldst try my skill, Eugene de Clairville?'

"You may well imagine the astonishment with which I gazed upon this extraordinary being as he gave utterance to these words; I still believed him to be a wretched maniac, but I thought it was best to humour him, in order that I might get rid of him the sooner, and I therefore said—

"'I do not doubt thy supernatural powers, good Jerome, but——'

"'*Good* Jerome!' he interrupted, and fixing upon me a look of anger; 'do not attempt to mock me, Eugene de Clairville, or, powerless though I may seem to be, it shall cost thee dear.'

"'Again I ask thee what thou wouldst with me?' I demanded, greatly alarmed at his words, although I attempted to conceal it; 'I never injured thee, why then should you possess any feeling of enmity towards me?'

"'You never injured me, it is true,' he replied, 'but you would injure others who should be dear to you, and therefore do I come to warn you.'

'How know you this?' I asked, in a tremulous voice; 'how can you know it?'

"'Ha! ha! ha!' he laughed, exultingly, 'that is the question. Have I not told thee that I can penetrate men's secret thoughts? and now will I give thee the proof. Dost thou not entertain guilty thoughts of the fair and innocent Emilie, and wouldst work her destruction, while at the same time thou pretendest to be her most sincere and ardent friend? Canst thou deny this?'

"I started and trembled, as you may well imagine, as he gave utterance to these words, and for a moment or two I found it impossible to make any reply, for I could scarcely believe the evidence of my senses."

"Most extraordinary and incredible," said Florio; "could you never ascertain who he really was, my lord, and how he had obtained his knowledge?"

"Never," answered the Count de Clairville, "and how he could have become acquainted with my secret designs I have ever been at a loss to conceive, for you may be very well assured that I had not made a confidant of any one."

"Well," observed Massaroni, "it certainly is most remarkable, and had it been stated by any other person but you lordship, I should almost have been inclined to doubt the truth of the statement."

"You may depend upon the accuracy of all I say," returned the count; "it could not benefit me to state a falsehood. That was the only meeting I had with Jerome, for immediately afterwards he disappeared from the neighbourhood, and no one knew whither he had gone, or what had become of him."

"More extraordinary still," said our hero, "But continue your narrative, my lord, for you may be sure that we are all most deeply interested."

"'Mysterious man!' I exclaimed," the count continued, "'how dare you accuse me thus?'

"'How dare I?' he replied; 'what is there that I dare not do?—But again I ask thee, canst thou deny that such are thy designs? Hast thou not even now just returned from an interview with Emilie, at which thou hast commenced the operation of thy plot? Art thou not basely, cruelly deceiving thy brother Antoine, at the very time when thou art pretending to espouse his cause?—Nay, 'tis useless for thee to deny that of which I accuse thee, for conscious guilt is stamped upon thy brow and thy quivering lip. Beware! for if thou dost persist in thy diabolical designs, the curse of offended Heaven will pursue thee, and years of bitter misery and remorse will be thy portion.'

"Alas! how fatally have his predictions been verified! Would to Heaven that I had taken his warning, I should not now be the wretched being that I appear before you; but alas! an infernal spell urged me on, and nothing could restrain me from the execution of my purpose. But I am digressing, and I am afraid that you will consider me tedious.

"'Strange man!' I ejaculated at length, 'you come to mock me and to torture me, but I will not be intimidated by you; what is your purpose?'

"'I have told it you, Eugene de Clairville,' he answered; 'and in spite of all you say, your looks betray the terror which I have struck into your guilty soul.'

"'Begone, begone,' I demanded, in an agitated and excited tone, 'I will listen to you no longer. Fool that I have been to suffer myself to be detained by you for an instant.'

"'You could not help yourself,' he returned, 'though, doubtless, that which I have told you has proved far from agreeable to you; for the present, however, I have done with you. Remember my words, and if you would save yourself and those connected with you from future misery, repent in time. Think of your innocent and affectionate wife, and shudder at the cruel injustice you are inflicting on her.—Again I say, beware, beware, for misery and destruction follow in the path you would pursue.'

"With these words, and before I could recover from the confusion and agitation into which this extraordinary adventure had thrown me, he hastened from the spot, and quickly disappeared from my sight.

"For some minutes after he was gone, I continued transfixed, as it were, to the spot on which I had been standing, and gazing towards the place whence he had disappeared, was completely overwhelmed with astonishment.

"'Is this a dream?' I said at last, 'or have my senses forsook me?—No, there was no mistaking the words of that mysterious man, and I am lost in amazement and alarm. What am I to imagine from them? How could he have penetrated the secret thoughts that were passing in my mind, when I have never revealed them to a human being? By

THE PRINCE BIANCHI AND COUNT ALBERTI IN CONSULTATION.

Heaven this is quite beyond by comprehension, and is almost enough to make me superstitious. But should he betray me, I should be exposed to shame and degradation. The thought is maddening; I must see this singular being again, and try to win him to my purpose.'

"You will thus perceive that, although I was alarmed and confounded by this extraordinary and almost incredible adventure, I was still determined to pursue my guilty designs; but for some time I was unable to leave the spot, fearing that if I returned home in my present state of mind, the agitation of my looks would be observed by my wife; and that she might put such questions to me as I should not know very well how to answer; and I gave myself up entirely to the most torturing and conflicting meditations.

"'But why should I suffer the words of this madman to torture me thus?' I at length ejaculated;—'it is impossible that he could have penetrated my thoughts, and he must have been listening to the observations I made use of, thinking that no one was near me.'"

"Ay, my, lord," remarked Florio, "that must have been it, for by no other means could he have arrived at his knowledge."

"I endeavoured to persuade myself that it was so," continued the count, "but that conclusion did not abate my alarm, for if it was so, had I not placed myself in his power? and he could at any time, if he felt so disposed, betray me, if I could not succeed in bribing him to silence.

"'But I will not be intimidated from my purpose,' I exclaimed aloud, thinking I was alone. 'Nothing whatever can conquer the powerful sentiments with which the lovely Emilie has inspired me, and I must and will gratify them, let whatever may be the consequences.'

"'Eugene,' said a well known and tremulous voice behind me. My God! how I started at the sound! And you may judge of my utter confusion and dismay when I beheld my wife, pale and trembling, standing by my side! I tried to speak, but I could not; and there I stood, staring vacantly upon her, with all the consciousness of guilt stamped upon my features. She had come out for a walk, and some cursed accident had guided her footsteps to the very spot on which I was standing; and it was plain, from the agitation of her manner, that she had overheard what I had said.

"'Marie,' I said at last, with as much composure as I could possibly assume, under the embarrassing circumstances, 'what brings you hither?'

"'Oh, Eugene,' she returned, with a sigh, and fixing upon me a look which was sufficient to penetrate to my very soul, and to sting me with remorse, 'what fearful and mysterious words were those I heard you utter just now?'

"'And have you had the meanness to listen to me?' I demanded, sternly.

"'It was accident that led me hither,' she replied. 'Would to Heaven that I had never heard what I just now did!'

"'What mean you, Marie?' I asked, hastily, but with a faltering voice, and trembling beneath the glances she fixed upon me.

"'You mentioned the name of Emilie,' she answered, 'and in such a manner that I shudder to think on. Oh, Eugene! in mercy remove,

if you can, the dark suspicions which those words have excited in my mind.'

"'Psha!' I exclaimed, impatiently, 'what outrageous fancies have you now suffered to enter your mind, Marie?'

"'Alas!' she sighed, 'I would fain persuade myself that my fears are erroneous, and it is, therefore, that I am so anxious to receive an explanation from you. Surely your wife has a right to demand it.'

"'What explanation have I to give,' I returned, 'not knowing that I have uttered anything that should alarm you? Of what do you suspect me?'

"'Surely, Eugene,' she replied, 'the manner in which you just now spoke of my sister was strange and unnatural. These were your words, and if you can explain them to my satisfaction, you will, indeed, remove a weight of dread and anxiety from my mind, and render me but too happy—'Nothing whatever can conquer the sentiments with which the lovely Emilie has inspired me, and I must and will gratify them, let whatever may be the consequences.' Such were your words, Eugene, and surely you cannot deny them?'

"'And in good truth, my jealous Marie,' I replied, with an affected laugh, 'I do not mean to attempt to do so, and do not believe that I should at all feel ashamed to acknowledge them.'

"'How, Eugene?' she ejaculated, with a faint voice, and gazing more earnestly upon me.

"'Pshaw!' I again exclaimed, having regained my self-possession; 'and pray what is there in the words you have quoted to excite your alarm and suspicions in so marvellous a manner? What other sentiments can you suppose that Emilie has excited in my breast but those of regard as a sister, and sympathy with the anxiety that at present presses upon her mind? Is it not my anxious wish to see her and my brother rendered happy?—and am I not also determined that it shall not be for the want of any exertion on my part, if these wishes are not gratified?'

"The countenance of Marie brightened as I gave utterance to those words, and throwing herself into my arms she ejaculated,

"'Pardon me, dear Eugene, if I have for a moment seemed to doubt your fidelity, and to put a wrong construction upon your words; I was wrong, very wrong; I ought to have known your honourable nature too well. But say that you will forgive me, and I shall again be happy.'

"These observations, and the sweet confidence she seemed to repose in me, ought to have aroused me to a sense of shame, but I was now becoming completely callous and indifferent; all the nobler feelings which had before characterised me were fast fading away beneath the influence of my evil passions, and it needed but little more to render me fully worthy of the character of a villain.

"With the most consummate hypocrisy I pressed my affectionate wife to my bosom, and while I imprinted a kiss upon her lips, I said—

"'Forgive you, my dearest Maria, for that which I know full well only emanated from the ardour and sincerity of the love you bear me?— oh, most willingly! I must, indeed, be an unworthy miscreant could I attempt to deceive one of the best of women and of wives.'

"'Blessed words!' she said, still entwining her fair arms around my neck, and looking through her tears with the most intense affection in my face. 'Eugene, I know, returns the love I feel for him with equal fervour, and I am happy. How grateful do I feel to you for the affectionate interest you take in the fate of my poor sister, and may Heaven prosper you in the praiseworthy efforts you are taking in her behalf. You have seen her to-day, have you not?'

"'I have,' I answered, 'and have managed to inspire her with hopes which, I trust, in spite of the obstacles which are at present placed in the way, will be realised; but there is one thing I must request of you, Marie.'

"'Oh, name it,' she returned; 'there is nothing I can refuse to my beloved Eugene.'

"'It is simply this, Marie,' I said, 'that you do not question me at present as to what may take place at the different private interviews it will be necessary for me to have with your sister; you may rest assured that I will act only as prudence and anxiety for her welfare shall dictate, and that when the fitting time shall come, you shall be made acquainted with everything.'

"'But why this secrecy, Eugene?' she asked, again looking half doubtfully in my face.

"'It is necessary,' I answered; 'and that I am certain you will be ready to admit when you shall know all.'

"'Well, Eugene,' she remarked, 'I will do all that you desire, for well convinced I am that you will do everything for the best.'

"'Enough, Marie,' I returned, 'this confidence and ready compliance with my wishes pleases me. But have you been to the castle to-day?'

"'I have,' she replied.

"'And has the count, my father, been there?'

"'He has, and for some time was closeted with the Count St. Alme.'

"'Ah!' I exclaimed; 'then doubtless he has made him acquainted with all that transpired at the interview which took place between myself and my father?'

"'It is more than probable that he has,' replied Marie; 'but my father said nothing to me, and I observed no difference in his behaviour.'

"'That augurs well,' I said; 'to-morrow, Marie, I shall be absent from home, and I shall not return till a late hour of the evening; you will visit your sister, and endeavour to keep up her spirits and to encourage her to hope?'

"'Oh, yes, most cheerfully will I do so,' she replied, 'and happy shall I be if I succeed. Poor Emilie, surely her numerous virtues entitle her to every reward, and why should all her young hopes and prospects be blighted, as they would be, should she not be permitted to become the wife of the only man to whom her fondest affections are devoted? Lestelle, too, she only regards Antoine as a brother, and, therefore, to compel her to become his wife, would be cruel in the extreme, and could only be productive of the greatest misery to them both.'

"'Very true, Marie,' I coincided; 'but come, it is useless for us to tarry here—let us return home.'

"She made no reply, and taking her arm, we departed from the place. But in spite of all my efforts, I could not help bitterly reproaching myself with the base and hypocritical part I was acting towards one of the most affectionate and faithful of wives, and who now seemed to place every confidence in me; and such being the nature of my thoughts, I felt embarrassed in her company, conversed but little with her as we proceeded, and was glad when we had arrived at home, where I made an excuse for retiring to my own apartment, so that I might, without interruption, indulge in the reflections that crowded upon my mind in such rapid succession.

"The extraordinary adventure, however, which I had had with old Jerome, was one of the uppermost subjects in my thoughts; and when I pondered again and again upon all he had said, it created the greatest uneasiness and apprehension in my mind.

"'He must have overheard what I said,' I ejaculated, 'and should he think proper to divulge it to my father or the Count St. Almo, all my plans will be rendered abortive, and I shall be plunged into the utmost disgrace. What would Marie then think of me? It would break her heart to discover the base deception and villany I have practised, and I should ever afterwards have to reproach myself with being her murderer. I must again see this singular being and endeavour to bribe him to silence. Fain would I conquer the guilty passions that have taken possession of my breast, and to abandon all thoughts of Emilie, but such is the powerful ascendancy they have gained over me, that I find it is impossible. But with what horror and disgust will that innocent damsel view me should I ever venture to disclose to her my unholy sentiments. Presumptuous fool and villain that I am, can I ever suppose that she will yield to my diabolical wishes? Would she not rather spurn and denounce me to the world as a miscreant of the blackest dye? She would, and the vengeance of Heaven must, most assuredly, pursue me for it. Would to God that I had never seen her, or that she had been formed less beautiful, or could I have inspired her with love towards me instead of my brother, I might have continued honourable, and have been one of the happiest of human beings!—How can I meet the unsuspecting Antoine, with these thoughts upon my mind? Will not my looks betray me?—But away with these ideas! it is necessary that I should become firm, or I shall bring ruin and disgrace upon myself without having done anything to achieve the objects I have in view. Emilie has gained such a hold upon me that life would become valueless to me unless I could possess her. She shall be mine, in spite of all that may result from it.'

"Such were the thoughts that continued to haunt and torture my mind, and kept me waking nearly the whole of the night; but in the morning I exerted myself to the utmost to compose my feelings, and I succeeded so well as to appear before my wife in more apparent cheerful spirits than I had been for some time, and that was sufficient to quiet any suspicions that might still be lurking in her mind.

"The morning repast being over, I was about to prepare myself for my departure to Antoine, when the Count St. Almo was announced. I felt confused and uneasy, for I had no doubt what the purport of his visit was, and shortly afterwards he entered the room, and was received by myself, and his daughter with our usual cordiality. There was nothing in his manner to excite any apprehension in my breast, and he conversed for some time on indifferent subjects in his usual affable and agreeable manner; but at length turning to me, he said—

"'Eugene, I would speak with you awhile in private.'

"I guessed what he meant, but having by this time prepared myself for it, I assented to his wishes, and desiring him to attend me to my study, we quitted the room.

"When we had entered the study, he took a seat, and remained for a few minutes silent, and apparently endeavouring to collect his thoughts; but at length he said—

"'I presume, Eugene, that you can guess why it is that I seek the present interview?'

"'Indeed, my lord,' I replied, hesitatingly, 'I must request you to be more explicit, for I must confess that I do not exactly understand you.'

"'When I inform you that I saw your father yesterday,' said the count, 'and that he explained to me all that had taken place between himself and you the day before, I should imagine that you must perfectly understand me.'

"'Oh, yes, my lord,' I replied, 'perfectly; but I trust that you will not deem me too bold and officious in interesting myself for those for whom I naturally possess so much esteem.'

"'Eugene,' he returned, 'I am disposed to treat this important business calmly and dispassionately. It pains me, however, exceedingly to hear that Emilie and your brother have contracted a fatal passion for each other, the more so, because it is impossible that it can ever be gratified; and should my daughter obstinately persist in encouraging it, she will bring down upon her head my severest wrath and indignation.'

"'Oh, my lord,' I said, with apparent sincerity, 'surely you will think better of this?'

"'It is impossible,' answered the count; 'Lestelle is the destined bride of Antoine, and nothing whatever but death can set aside their union.'

"'But, my lord, consider, they do not love each other, and should you and my father force them to become united, you will doom them to certain misery, which you may afterwards have bitter cause to repent when it is too late.'

"'Remember the compact, Eugene,' he said, 'that must be obeyed; there is no alternative.'

"'But surely your lordship cannot persist in enforcing the fulfilment of that monstrous and unnatural document?' I remonstrated.

"'There is no avoiding it,' he answered, 'if even I were so inclined; it must be obeyed to the very letter, let the consequences be whatever they may. The mutual interests of our families demand it. But I am willing to agree to the arrangements of the count, your father, namely, to defer the union of Lestelle and your brother for three months, in the hope that in the meantime he and Emilie will be able to bring their reasoning faculties to bear upon, and to conquer their hopeless and unfortunate passion. In the meantime, to show the goodness of my feelings towards Emilie, I will place no restraint upon her, but she shall receive the same kind and affectionate indulgence that she has ever experienced. I think Antoine has acted wisely in absenting himself from home, for whilst away he will have an opportunity to reflect calmly, and to be enabled to forget Emilie in any other character than that of the sister of his betrothed wife.'

"'Indeed, my lord,' I returned, 'I am certain that is impossible; too well I know the strength of the passion which my brother entertains for Emilie, to believe that anything will ever induce him to consent to become the husband of Lestelle, much as he may esteem her for her numerous virtues.'

" ' Then,' said the Count St. Almo, ' he knows the consequences that will follow. Emilie, too, if she does not consent to abandon all thoughts of Antoine, I will immure her for the rest of her days within the walls of a convent.'

" ' Nay, my lord,' I remarked, ' surely that would be most cruel and unjust.'

" ' You may deem it so, Eugene,' he answered, ' but such nevertheless is my firm determination, and nothing whatever can move me from it. And hark ye, Eugene if you would not incur the utmost displeasure of the Count de Clairville and myself, you will refrain from exciting hopes in the breasts of Emilie and your brother, which it is impossible can ever be realised.'

" ' My lord,' I ejaculated, ' again I must beg of you not to decide harshly, but to reflect calmly and seriously before you proceed to extremities.'

" ' There is no occasion for me to reflect, Eugene, upon that to which I have already made up my mind. But you have heard my determination, and will, therefore, act accordingly. You can, if you please, communicate the same to Emilie and Antoine ; I am not disposed to talk to them upon the subject at present.'

" ' One word more, my lord,' I said.

" ' No more,' he replied ; ' you have heard what I have had to say, and if we were to argue for a month, it could not alter my deter mination.'

" With these words, the Count St. Almo arose from his seat and stalked from the room, and I followed him. I must confess that, notwitstanding I affected to the contrary, I felt the utmost satisfaction at the determination he had evinced, for I considered that it would all tend towards the furtherance of my designs, which I determined to put into execution with as little delay as possible.

" The count only had some trifling conversation with myself and wife, and he then took his departure.

" ' Eugene,' said Marie, when he was gone, ' I can form a pretty shrewd guess as to the nature of the interview which has just taken place between yourself and my brother. It was, if I imagine rightly, on the subject of the unfortunate loves of Emilie and Antoine.'

" ' True, Marie,' I replied.

" ' And what is his determination ?' she inquired.

" ' The same as that of my father,' I answered.

" ' Ah !' ejaculated Marie, ' it is no more

than I anticipated. Poor Emilie! I see too plainly that your sorrows have only just began. But will you communicate these painful facts to her, Eugene ?'

" ' Undoubtedly I shall, Marie,' I returned. ' It would be cruel and unjust of me to keep her in ignorance of them; and your father says that he is not disposed to speak to her upon the subject at present.'

" ' That is strange,' observed my wife ; ' but still it is better that he does not do so, for the present excited state of her feelings might not suffer her to reply to him with that calmness and propriety that she ought to do.'

" ' True, Marie,' I coincided ; ' but you will see your sister to-day, and you will then endeavour to impart to her all the consolation and advice that you can.'

" ' You may be sure that I will do so, Eugene. But will you not see her yourself to-day ?'

" ' Yes,' I replied ; ' in about an hour we are to meet by appointment. But I must be gone, for I have much business of the greatest importance to transact to-day, and it will not admit of any delay.'

" Thus saying, I departed from the house, heartily glad to escape from the presence of my wife, who, in spite of what she had said, I could not help imagining still entertained some suspicions of the sincerity of my conduct, though she hesitated to give expression to her feelings. I should before have mentioned that the place in which myself and Emilie had appointed to hold our secret meetings was in a small cottage situated but a short distance from the Castle of St. Almo, and which I had hired for the purpose; and on my arrival there I found her most anxiously awaiting to receive me, and the expression of her countenance plainly shewed the agony of mind she had been enduring since we had last met. She advanced eagerly to meet me, and ejaculated—

" ' You are punctual, Eugene ; but you look excited. Has anything particular happened since we met yesterday ?'

" ' I have this morning seen the Count St. Almo, your father, Emilie,' I replied.

" She turned pale as I stated this, and trembled violently.

" ' Ah !' she ejaculated, ' then the Count de Clairville, who was with him yesterday, has doubtless told him all ?'

" ' He has,' I returned.

" ' And is there no hope for me from him ?'

" ' For the present, I fear there is not,' I replied ; ' he has expressed his determination to adhere to the compact to the very letter.'

" ' Then I am lost,' sighed Emilie, and clasping her hands together in the most agitated manner.

" ' Nay, say not so, Emilie,' I remarked ; ' your father has agreed as well as my parent to postpone the union of Antoine and Lestelle for three months, and in that interim there is no knowing what may take place to forward the wishes of yourself and my brother.'

"'Ah! no!' she answered; 'alas! I have too much reason to fear that they will both remain inexorable, and that there is nothing but the greatest misery inevitably before us. I tremble at the idea of meeting my father, for will he not heap upon me his bitterest wrath and reproaches, and——'

"'No, Emilie,' I interrupted, 'do not thus unnecessarily alarm yourself, for your father has promised me that during the three months he will place no restraint upon you, and indeed he has expressed a wish not to speak to you at all upon the subject.'

"'Oh, that is indeed some relief to me,' she eagerly ejaculated; 'but at the expiration of that brief time of grace, what may I not expect?'

"I did not answer.

"'Ah!' she said, 'you are silent! I see by your looks that you anticipate the worst, although you would fain inspire me with hopes to the contrary.'

"'Emilie,' I returned, fixing upon her a look which I could not repress, 'shall I reveal to you my real sentiment upon the subject?'

"'Oh, yes!' she answered. 'I would indeed have you confide to me your real thoughts, for I look upon you as my best friend and without your advice I know not how to act.'

"I could not but feel confused and abashed by the innocent and unsuspecting confidence she reposed in me while I harboured such guilty thoughts against her. At length I replied—

"'If, then, I must candidly speak my mind, I do regret the love that you and Antoine entertain for each other; I consider that it would have been far better had you never met, or that you could now forget one another, and seek to place your affections upon some other objects.'

"'Love any other man than Antoine de Clairville!' ejaculated Emilie, vehemently. 'Oh, that is impossible! He is, by his numerous virtues, so entwined around my heart, that that nothing whatever can remove him, and death would be far more preferable to me than to be compelled to become the bride of any other man. Eugene, you cannot possibly duly appreciate my feelings, or you would not talk to me thus.'

"I could not, without the greatest difficulty, conceal the rage with which these observations inspired me, and for a moment or two I was almost resolved boldly to acknowledge the guilty sentiments she had excited in my breast, and thus at once unmasking myself; but, by a powerful effort, I restrained myself

though I was at the same time fully determined to leave no means or stratagem untried to obtain the accomplishment of my diabolical wishes.

"'Pardon me, Emilie,' I at length said, 'if I appear too bold and unreasonable in what I have observed; but it is the interest I feel in your fate, and the esteem I bear you which prompt what I say. Surely, there are other men in the world who are equally as deserving of the affections of Emilie as Antoine.'

"'How, Eugene?' she ejaculated, with a look of surprise; 'this from you?'

"'Nay, Emilie,' I returned, hastily, for I began to fear that I had probably proceeded too far; 'do not misunderstand me; I am sure you will acquit me of having a wish to say anything to the prejudice of my brother, but still when I reflect upon all the obstacles that are thrown in your way, and the consequent misery that is likely to accrue to you both, I must repeat that I regret you are not able to conquer this unfortunate passion in your breasts. However, think not that I begin to hesitate to perform my promise, but on the contrary I will do all that lies in my power to promote your wishes. There is one question, notwithstanding, that I wish to put to you.'

"'And what is that, Eugene?' she inquired.

"'Should my brother at the expiration, of the three months, still remain determined to brave all the consequences of his refusing to become the husband of your sister Lestelle, and in spite of the wrath of both your parents should propose a clandestine union, would you yield compliance with his wishes?'

"'It is a delicate question to put to me, Eugene,' she replied with a blush; 'but still I cannot say what the ardour of my passion might tempt me to do; Heaven forbid that I should incur the wrath of my parents; but surely it would be enough to drive me to madness and despair to see Antoine compelled to become the husband of another woman. Providence would pardon us for that into which we should have been precipitated by circumstances over which we had no control. Could you blame us, Eugene?'

"This was a question which it greatly perplexed me to answer, but I conquered my feelings as well as I could, and at last replied in the negative.

"'But still, Emilie,' I remarked, 'I must advise you not to do anything precipitately, and without well considering the circumstances that would follow. Should my father and the Count St. Almo persist in adhering to the principles of that harsh and extravagant compact, Antoine would be disinherited—you would both be discarded, and consigned to misery and the most abject poverty.'

"'Oh,' returned Emilie, 'they could surely never act in so cruel and unnatural a manner; and if they did, even poverty would not possess half so many terrors for me as the disappointment of my hopes. But you are now going to visit Antoine, are you not?'

"'I am,' I returned, 'and will consult with him on what is best to be done. Have you any communication that you wish me to convey to him?'

"'Oh, yes,' she replied, placing a letter in my hand; 'this epistle will make him entirely acquainted with all my thoughts and wishes; if you, Eugene, will deliver it safely into his hands, and bring back to me any answer he may think proper to write, you will confer on me a favour which I can never sufficiently repay.'

"'You may depend on me, Emilie,' I said.

"'I am convinced I can,' she returned. 'Oh, how anxious I am to hear from Antoine, though I can well imagine, by my own, what his feelings are at the present moment. When shall I see you again, Eugene?'

"'To-morrow morning I will again meet you here; and, in the meantime, you will receive every advice and consolation from your sister Marie, though I must caution you not to make her acquainted with anything which has and may still take place between us.'

"'Why this precaution, Eugene?' she demanded with a look of surprise.

"'It is necessary,' I replied, 'in order to forward me in my designs; do you promise to comply with my request?'

"'I do,' she returned, 'for I am satisfied that you only act from the best of motives.'

"'You do me justice by that supposition, Emilie,' I observed, 'and will have no cause to regret the confidence you repose in me.'

"Base hypocrite that I was, and at the very moment I was plotting her destruction, and inwardly exulting in the anticipation of the gratification of my wishes, I wonder that, led on by my guilty passions, I did not betray myself; but innocent as Emilie was, how could she for a moment suspect me of such base perfidy? But I am becoming tedious, and I fear that I have already intruded upon your time and patience too far."

"Oh, no, my lord," answered Florio, who, as may be imagined, was deeply interested in that which so immediately concerned him, and who was anxious to hear what the result of this extraordinary and complicated narrative would be; "indeed you are not; there is not a word you have uttered but is of the deepest importance; but let me request you not to agitate your feelings too violently, but to proceed as calmly as you can."

"I thank you, Florio, for your forbearance and consideration," said the Count de Clairville,

"and Heaven knows that I shall much require them; but to resume:—

"After some further conversation, which is of too little importance to relate here, I quitted Emilie, and made my way towards the place of Antoine's concealment, brooding on the road upon my guilty and unnatural designs, and more determined than ever to accomplish them at all hazards, and at any cost of misery to my unsuspecting victims.

"'Why should I suffer any feelings of compunction to unnerve me?' I soliloquised; 'the ardent love which Emilie professes for Antoine, ought to strengthen my determination. Curses light upon him! A deadly feeling of hatred and jealousy now rises in my breast against him which I cannot control. Had he never existed, I might have won her affections, instead of being united to one whom I cannot help viewing with feelings almost amounting to repugnance.'

"Oh, Marie, most amiable of human beings and faithful of wives, how deeply did I wrong you! Surely no punishment that I can receive can be ever too severe for the systematic and cold-hearted villany with which I acted towards you.

"I had determined to peruse the contents of the letter which the unsuspecting Emilie had entrusted to me to deliver to my brother, and, therefore, having arrived at an inn which was on my road, I entered, and having requested to be shown into a private room, I eagerly broke the seal, and unfolding the letter, impatiently scanned every line. It was couched in the most affectionate language that could well be imagined; vowed eternal constancy, and solemnly promised to encounter anything, even the most torturing death, rather than she would ever consent to become the wife of any other man than Antoine. You may well conceive the feelings of hatred and envy that every word of this affectionate letter excited in my breast. I was almost inclined to destroy it, but then the the recollection that that would at once expose the villany of my thoughts, and be the certain means of frustrating my nefarious designs, and of holding me up to shame and degradation, restrained me, and after having again and again perused the contents, until every word was vividly stamped upon my memory, I folded and resealed it carefully, so that it was impossible to detect that it had been opened. I returned it to my pocket, and emerging from the inn, resumed my journey.

"Many were the curses that I invoked upon the head of my unoffending brother, and I vowed that I would disappoint him in the gratification of his hopes, even at the hazard of my life. It was not without the most powerful efforts on my part that I could conquer my feelings sufficiently before my arrival at the retreat of my brother to prevent betraying myself, but at length I was enabled to assume a greater degree of composure than might have been expected, and in a few minutes afterwards I was in the presence of Antoine.

"He advanced eagerly to meet me, and his looks sufficiently testified the nature of the feelings which predominated in his breast.

"'Oh, welcome, Eugene,' he ejaculated; 'how anxious have I been to see you. My beloved Emilie—tell me how is she? Our father, too, and the Count St. Almo—what of them?'

"'Patience, Antoine,' I returned, 'and I will answer all your questions. I have seen the Count St. Almo, as well as our father, and they are both determined that the terms of the compact shall be fulfilled to the very letter; three months is all they will allow you to consider, and then, if you still refuse to become the husband of Lestelle, they say that you must prepare yourself to take the consequences. You will be disinherited, and Emilie will be immured within the walls of a convent for the rest of her days.'

"'Oh, this is surely most monstrous!' he said; 'but no matter—I will be firm; let whatever may be the consequences, I will never submit to so unjust and unnatural a demand.'

"'Nay, Antoine,' I remarked, 'do not form any hasty resolutions which you may afterwards see the prudence and necessity of abandoning.'

"'And think you I can ever abandon my hopes of Emilie?' he demanded, impatiently; 'do you imagine for an instant that I can ever cease to love that amiable and gentle being, or consent to become the husband of one whom I can never regard with any other feelings but these of friendship and esteem? It is impossible! The very idea is madness, and I am determined to resist the tyrannical and cruel demands of our father and the Count St. Almo at all risks. Eugene, you entertain a wrong opinion of my sentiments if you think that I can ever act differently to what I say. But tell me, what took place at your interview with our father and the Count St. Almo?'

"I related to him such particulars as I thought proper, and he listened to me with the deepest interest and anxiety.

"'How cruel, inexorable, and unreasonable is this,' he said, when I had concluded; 'am I not justified in resisting it to the utmost of my power? But you say that neither of them attach any particular blame to me for absconding from the chateau, or have expressed any wish to know whither I have retired?'

"'They do not,' I answered, 'but, on the contrary, they commend you for so doing, thinking that it will enable you to banish Emilie from your thoughts, and to abandon your wishes.'

"'Never!' he exclaimed, vehemently; 'absence does but render her the more dear to me, and but strengthens me in my determination to possess her at all risks.'

"'But,' I remarked, 'should Emilie herself be enabled to conquer the unfortunate passion you have excited in her breast, and to behold some other man to whom she could transfer her affections, and who would not be objected to by——'

"'My fond, my gentle Emilie forget me—cease to love me!' he hastily interrupted; 'oh, what a cruel slander is it upon her truth and constancy to imagine such a thing. Oh, too well I know the anguish she must now be enduring at our separation. But you have seen her, you say, Eugene? Tell me, how is she? What did she say to you? Did she not send any message by you? Do not keep me in suspense.'

"I hesitated for a minute, for I well knew the effect which the letter would have upon him, and I was fearful that my manners would reveal the thoughts which were passing in my mind; but at length I placed it in his hand, and he pressed it eagerly to his lips, and feasted his eyes upon the well-known delicate characters of the superscription. At last he broke the seal, and eagerly perused the contents, while I retired to another part of the room, and watched his powerful emotions with feelings of rage and jealousy, such as I need not attempt to describe.

"'Beloved, adored Emilie,' he at last ejaculated, 'in this fond epistle you do, indeed, speak the sentiments of your soul, and this inspires me with fresh confidence and determination. Heaven evidently created us for each other, and why should man seek to separate us? Dearest, most faithful of girls, with what feelings of transport do I ponder over every word, and almost imagine that you are now present, and speaking to me! You have inspired me with fresh hope; and while I possess the secret assurance of your constancy, I am fully prepared to encounter all the dangers and obstacles that may threaten me.'

"'Be not too sanguine in your hopes, Antoine,' I remarked, 'lest you should be doomed to be disappointed. Faithfully, even, as Emilie may love you, there is no chance of her becoming your wife, unless you make her so clandestinely, and thus bring upon yourself inevitable misery.'

"'Oh,' he replied, impatiently, "I am ready to brave all that may befal me, rather than abandon the bright and heavenly hopes I have formed. What misery can I ever experience, if possessed of the beauteous Emilie? But, deprived of her, life would become an insupportable burthen to me, and the sooner I am rid of it the better.'

"'Indeed, Antoine,' I returned, scarcely able to conceal the feelings that were passing in my mind, 'it is little short of madness to talk thus. Would you consign Emilie, as well as yourself to all the horrors of poverty as well as the malediction of her parent?'

"'Oh, Providence would surely not suffer us to experience so cruel and unmerited a fate as that you have depictured,' he replied.

'But, Eugene, you do not speak so encouragingly as you formerly did; why is this?'

"'It is not because I have the welfare of yourself and Emilie less at heart, Antoine,' I answered, in accents of well-feigned sincerity;

EMILIES REPUGNANCE AT THE ADDRESSES OF EUGENE.

'but at the same time I would not flatter you with hopes that are too likely only to end in disappointment. The Count St. Almo and our father I have too much reason to believe will not be moved to alter their determination, and when you reflect upon all the conse-quences that would be certain to ensue should you act in disobedience to their will, it is necessary you should not act too precipitately, or plunge yourself and the innocent damsel to whom you are attached into that from which you may not be able to extricate yourselves.'

No. 87.

" ' Do you, then, decline to aid us further ?' he demanded.

" ' Oh, no !' I answered; 'you misunderstand me. All that I can possibly do to aid you and further your wishes I will most readily ; and I sincerely hope that I may succeed ; but I must request that you will not do anything rashly, or without consulting me.'

" ' That I most faithfully promise you, Eugene,' he replied, grasping my hand ; ' and you have my heartiest feelings of gratitude for the brotherly interest you express in my happiness and welfare. But I mus. see Emilie, and in her own ears pour forth my thoughts and wishes. Absence from her presence is most insupportably torturing to me.'

" ' No, Antoine,' I returned, ' that must not be.'

" ' And why not ?' he demanded, impatiently.

" ' Because it may be fraught with more danger than you can now anticipate,' I repeated ; 'and would probably tend to render all my anxious efforts abortive, should it be discovered by our father or the Count St. Almo. Besides, whatever communications you may have to make, you may safely entrust to me, and surely you can place every confidence in me ?'

" ' Oh, yes,' he said, ' and pardon me if I have for a moment appeared to doubt you ;—I will yield to your advice, and leave everything to you. I will return an answer to the affectionate letter of Emilie, which, I trust, you will faithfully deliver to her, as soon as you behold her again.'

" ' You may depend upon me, Antoine,' I said ; ' and can I be only instrumental in the promotion of your wishes, I shall be amply rewarded for any trouble which it may cost me.'

" He again grasped my hand and looked his thanks, and he then retired to an ante-room for a few minutes, for the purpose of writing the answer to the letter of Emilie. While he was gone I gave myself up to all the various and guilty thoughts which crowded upon my mind, and every moment the determination to work his ruin and to accomplish my nefarious designs gained fresh strength in my mind.

" ' The fool !' I thought to myself, 'he little imagines the bitter enemy he has in his own brother, or the nefarious designs he has formed against his peace. Emilie become his ! Pshaw ! the thought is preposterous ! If he does, indeed, ever possess her, it shall not be until after I have obtained the gratification of my wishes, and already the impression is strong upon my mind that I shall succeed in accomplishing them. Situated as they both are, I have them completely in my power ; and although I may afterwards be denounced as an unnatural villain, I will brave the worst, and it shall not make me falter in the execution of my purpose.'

" I was interrupted in the midst of this soliloquy by the return of Eugene to the apartment, and I received him with the same air of sincerity and cordiality which I had before assumed.

" ' Here is the letter, Eugene,' he observed, placing it in my hand, ' and may it serve to inspire my beloved Emilie with hope and confidence. Oh, my brother, I leave everything to you ; on your affection I depend, for well I know that you would not attempt to deceive me.'

" ' Deceive you, Antoine !' I repeated, in accents of hypocrisy that only the most consummate villany could assume ; " no, Heaven is my witness that I would not do so, but that my whole study shall be to promote the happiness of yourself and Emilie, and if I can only succeed, my gratification will be complete.'

" ' Thanks, Eugene,' he returned. ' Oh, how grateful am I to think that I at least possess one so faithful and enthusiastic a friend in you. But you will see me often, and let me know all that takes place ?'

" ' I will see you daily,' I replied, ' if nothing occurs to prevent it.'

" ' To your protection, Eugene,' he continued, ' I commit my Emilie, during my absence from her presence, and I know you will be as anxious and watchful of her safety and welfare as if she were under my own immediate care.'

" I know not how I must have looked as my unfortunate brother gave utterance to these words, but a feeling of reproach shot across my mind, and I could not help acknowledging to myself the miscreant I was. However, I soon conquered the emotion, and we then conversed more freely upon our future plans until it getting towards evening, I took my departure, and proceeded on my way home, exulting in the success which had attended my diabolical plot thus far.

" ' Everything goes on as well as I could wish it,' I muttered to myself ; ' Antoine so far from entertaining any suspicion of my sincerity, believes me to be his most ardent friend, and that I am ready to make any sacrifice for his sake and that of Emilie. That delusion is all that I could have wished, and renders my ultimate triumph all but certain. But am I not a heartless scoundrel to entertain such monstrous designs as these against those who are so closely united to me by blood ? But away with remorse ! I cannot resign my hopes of Emilie, and I have advanced too far to recede. Marie, with what feelings of disgust and horror must you view me did you but know what is at present passing in my mind.'

" I paused, for a strange foreboding of something that was about to happen, and for which

I was at a loss to account, at that moment crossed my mind, and I slowly pursued my way for some distance further in silence. At length I arrived at the same inn at which I had stopped in the morning, and being determined to peruse the contents of Antoine's letter, I entered it, and was ushered into the same private room. Here I broke the seal of the letter which had been entrusted to my care by my brother, and perused the contents with a greedy eye. There was very little in it, however, to gratify my curiosity. It was written in the same affectionate terms as that of Emilie's, and it passed some high eulogiums on my disinterested friendship, and the zeal with which I had espoused their cause, requesting her to place every confidence in me, and to be guided by me entirely in anything which I might advise. I could scarcely repress a laugh as I perused these lines, for it showed to me the success with which I had hitherto conducted my nefarious designs, and the manner in which it would be advisable for me in future to proceed for the final completion of my wishes.

" 'How he is deceived,' I said, 'how easily does he fall into the snare I have laid for him and the beauteous Emilie, and from which it is almost impossible that they can escape. Eugene de Clairville, thou hast already proved thyself to be an accomplished villain, and it will be strange indeed if thou dost not succeed to the full extent of thy wishes.'

"Again I paused, for once more a strange foreboding, coupled with a feeling of self-reproach and shame for the infamous thoughts I entertained, darted across my mind, and resealing the letter in the same careful manner as I had done that of Emilie's, I left the house.

"It would have been a just judgment and punishment upon me, had I at that moment have been struck a corpse, ere I could have had the opportunity of further attempting to put my wicked plans into execution. What a multiplicity of crimes it would have prevented me from rushing into, and what infinite misery would have been spared to others who so ill-merited the sufferings to which they were afterwards subjected. As I now recal to my memory the guilty past, my heart is stung with the most bitter and painful remorse, and I feel myself a degraded wretch, only worthy of the world's scorn and reprobation. Oh, Florio, what a pitiable example do I present to the rest of mankind, of the awful results that ensue from suffering your evil passions to obtain the ascendancy over you. Had it not been for that, I might now have looked with confidence for the respect of all my fellow-creatures; but as it is, I feel myself a wretch unworthy of anything else but hatred, and my own conscience is a perpetual hell to me. Of what use

has been my wealth to me ? Could it purchase for me ease and contentment of the mind ? Oh, no, it could not; and the only consolation I now feel is in having been fortunate enough to meet with the offspring of those whom I have so deeply injured, that I may, by placing him in that rank and station which he should always have enjoyed, make at least some atonement for the errors (or rather crimes, for the former is by far too mild a term to apply to them) of my past life. This disclosure made, and the resignation of my property made to one whom I have no doubt will know how to make a better use of it than I have done, there will be nothing left for me to do than to retire from the world, and in holy seclusion, seek by penitence and prayer to fit myself for appearing in the presence of that Almighty Judge whose laws I have so greatly violated."

"Oh, my noble relative," remarked Florio, deeply affected by the seriousness of the Count de Clairville's manner, "again I beseech you not to talk thus, or to reproach yourself so severely. I trust that when all is explained, there will be found to be many extenuating circumstances for the errors of your youth, and that you may live for many years to come in the society of your friends and relations, adding to their enjoyment and your own, by proving to them how worthy you are of their veneration."

"No, Florio," returned the count, "though I would fain have your prayers, I have no wish to remain in the world, for I feel that seclusion is the fitting place for me, and while I remained in the world, it would only, perhaps, divert my thoughts from that which is right and necessary for me for my soul's welfare hereafter. You are now Florio, but too ready to treat me with leniency, and to believe that I exaggerate my faults; but I imagine that when you have heard me to the conclusion of my guilty narrative, you will be disposed to look upon me in a far different light, and to view me with contempt and abhorrence."

"That is impossible," replied Florio. "Notwithstanding all that you have said, my lord, I feel convinced that you must ever possess my esteem and sympathy."

"Noble youth," ejaculated the count, again deeply affected, "this is too kind, too generous, and is a more painful, a more bitter reproach to me than anything you could possibly have uttered. But allow me to pause for a short time, in order that I may collect my thoughts, and compose my feelings sufficiently to continue my narrative to the conclusion."

Florio and the others nodded assent, and the Count de Clairville having partaken of a glass of wine, remained wrapt in meditation for a short time, when he resumed his silgular and eventful story in the following words :—

" I walked slowly on towards home, still buried in profound meditation, and alternately wavering between the feelings of remorse and exultation; but all of a sudden I was aroused by hearing the hurried tramp of horse's hoofs approaching me, and looking up, I beheld by the light of the moon (for it had now arisen) a man riding breathlessly towards me, in whom I recognised as he approached me nearer, one of my own domestics. He distinguished me almost at the same time as I did him, and riding close up to me, he hastily dismounted from his horse, and stood before me, apparently in a state of great agitation.

"'How now, Francois?' I demanded, 'where are you riding to?—and what brings you here in such a hurry?'

"'Oh, my lord,' he answered, 'I am so glad to think I have met you; I have been sent to search for you, and have been everywhere that I could think of in quest of you. Your presence is required at home immediately; so, mount my horse, an it please you, and make all haste thither. I can follow on foot at my leisure.'

"'What means all this, Francois?' I again demanded; 'has anything particular happened?'

"'Madame de Clairville, your lordship's lady,' he replied.

"'Ah!' I ejaculated, eagerly. 'What of her? Speak!'"

"'She was seized with a fit of apoplexy about two hours ago,' he replied, 'and it is feared that she is dying.'

" I waited to hear no more, but leaping upon the horse's back, galloped away as fast as I could, and in a state of agitation you may readily imagine. Here was the strange foreboding that had crossed my mind fully accounted for; but as I proceeded on my way, how shall I do justice to the mingled emotions that crowded on my brain? Pity for the amiable being whom I had by thought so deeply wronged, and bitter self-reproach, superseded every other in my breast, and yet I could not, at the same time, help experiencing a kind of inward and unnatural gratification at the thought of being probably soon released from one whom I could not love, and who only presented an insurmountable obstacle to the accomplishment of my designs against the innocent Emilie. Still, in spite of all this, I must have been a heartless monster, indeed, had I not felt a sensation of sorrow and regret at the melancholy situation of that devoted and unsuspecting wife, who, notwithstanding the coldness with which I had ever treated her, had always bestowed upon me the most unbounded affection. All the numerous virtues she possessed rushed vividly upon my recollection, as if to reproach me for my guilty conduct, and I could not but feel uneasy and sad. But how could I appear in the presence of my dying wife, knowing the base hypocrisy and villany with which I had acted towards her, and the diabolical thoughts which I at the present moment harboured in my breast? How could I listen to her last words, probably invoking a farewell blessing upon my head, without a feeling of shame, remorse, and self-upbraiding? Could I gaze upon her fading looks of affection without a shudder?

" Such were the thoughts that tortured and distracted my brain, as I rode towards the castle of St. Almo (for it was there that my poor wife was lying, having been seized with her last fatal illness while on her usual early visit there); and when I had arrived within a short distance of it, I was compelled to pause in order to endeavour to compose myself. At that time the most distracting and conflicting thoughts crowded upon my mind, and I could not help experiencing a feeling of compunction. At one moment I was half resolved to acknowledge my guilt, and to sue for forgiveness; but why should I torture the last moments of my unfortunate wife by such a revolting disclosure? And should I not be looked upon with horror and disgust by all with whom I was connected? That idea changed at once my mind, and let the consequences be whatever they might, I resolved to brave them out. However, it was with a sad and trembling heart that I entered the castle, and the silence that reigned within it added to the melancholy impression upon my mind. I inquired of a servant for my father or the Count St. Almo, and was informed that they were both in the chamber of my wife, whose death seemed rapidly approaching, and who had several times inquired and wondered that I was not by her bed-side in such an awful moment. This was another painful shock to my feelings, and my conscience reproached me bitterly. I still hesitated, and dreaded to encounter this last awful trial; but at length by a powerful effort I conquered my emotions and felt composed at least, as much so as I could be expected to be on such a melancholy occasion. and I then made my way to the chamber in which poor Marie was lying, and with a trembling and faltering step I entered it. I found the whole of the members of my family (of course with the exception of Antoine) assembled there, and they greeted me in melancholy silence. I approached the bed, and gazed upon the features of my wife, who at that time was lying in a state of unconsciousness, and terrible was the pang that shot through my heart as I did so. What a fearful change had only a few short hours wrought! It seemed scarcely possible that it was the same being whom I had left in all the bloom and freshness of health in the morning. The features were ghastly and shrivelled, the cheeks sunken, the eyes hollow, and everything, in fact, bore the appearance of suffering old age, rather than that of one so youthful, and who but a few hours previously had presented all the appearance of vigorous health. The sight was too much for me; a deathly sickness came upon my heart, and I covered my face with my hands. Those around naturally attributed my emotion to the feelings which the fatal situation of a faithful and affectionate wife had excited in my breast and they did not offer to interrupt me. Had they known the real thoughts which were passing in my mind, with what feelings of horror and disgust must they have viewed me! Emilie, too, was there, my innocent intended victim, helping to perform the last sad duties to my dying wife. I dared not look at her, for that must have excited me to such a degree that I should, in all probability, have betrayed the truth, and what a scene of anguish would then have ensued. Never can I forget the horrors of that moment, and yet in spite of this terrible warning to me, I could afterwards be the villain to persist in my diabolical designs, and to be the cause of the greatest misery to those whose happiness should have been as dear and as precious to me as my own life. I must again pause, for the recollection of these events overpowers me."

The Count de Clairville once more became silent, and covering his face with his hands, sunk into melancholy and profound meditation, from which no one attempted to arouse him, knowing that the free indulgence of his own thoughts would go farther to tranquillise his feelings than any advice or consolation which they could offer.

They felt deeply interested in all that he had hitherto related, and while they could not but regret the errors of which he had been guilty, it was impossible that they could help deeply sympathising with him, seeing the remorse which he now experienced. Florio felt the deepest sorrow at the sufferings of his unfortunate parents, and he was naturally most anxious to hear the conclusion of the count's narrative, though no feeling of revenge was excited in his breast towards him, for he could not bring his mind to believe that he was altogether so guilty as he had represented himself to be.

At length the Count de Clairville sufficiently subdued his feelings as to be able to proceed.

" Let me hasten over this dismal part of my story as quickly as possible, for the remembrance of it now harrows up my feelings, and quite unmans me.

" My wife had been in a state of stupor for some time, and from which it was at first thought she would never again arouse; in fact, frequently was it so difficult to discover the pulsation of her heart, or to trace her breathing, that it was imagined the vital spark had fled. However, only a short time after my arrival she partly revived, and opening her eyes, every moment becoming more dim and glassy, she called upon my name. This was a moment of fearful trial to me, and I have often wondered since how I could find fortitude sufficient to support it. But the sound of her voice aroused me from my lethargy, and I turned my looks towards her. On recognising me, a faint and melancholy smile of satisfaction overspread her pale features, and she extended her hand towards me, which I tremblingly raised to my lips.

" ' This is a terrible affliction for you, my dear Eugene,' she said, ' for you are about to lose a faithful wife, whose whole study has been to make you happy, and to prove herself worthy of your exalted virtues. I am dying, Eugene; God ordains that we should thus early be separated on earth, but I trust that we may meet again in Heaven, where sorrow never enters. Bless you, my lord, my husband, for all the love and attention you have ever bestowed on me, and may you enjoy many years of happiness after I am taken from you.'

" Good Heaven! what words were those to address to a wretch like me, who had never felt for her that affection which her devoted attachment and immaculate soul had merited, but, on the contrary, had for weeks past been plotting the destruction of her own sister. I must have been a hardened miscreant, or they would have sunk me into the earth. As it was, I scarcely knew what answer to make, and guilty conscience made me tremble in every limb.

" ' Oh, my Marie, my unfortunate and too affectionate and confiding wife,' I said at length, ' what a bitter moment of trial is this! And can you indeed invoke a blessing upon the head of one who has ever been so unworthy of your love? You should rather curse me, Marie, for——'

" Curse you, Eugene,' she interrupted. ' Oh, Heaven forbid! What terrible words are these to which you have just now given utterance? But grief has disordered your brain, and you know not what you say. My poor Eugene, I fear it will be some time ere you will recover from this shock, and I myself could have wished to live for your sake; but we must not murmur at the decrees of the Almighty, who orders everything for the best. I go to a happier and a better world, for my conscience cannot accuse me of ever having committed any wilful sin. Eugene, should you ever become the husband of another, may she be worthy of you, and love you as fondly and as faithfully as your Marie has done!'

"I covered my face with my hands, and sobbed aloud in the anguish and remorse of my feelings, and the grief of every one present may be much better imagined than I can possibly describe it.

"'Do not weep for me, Eugene,' said my poor dying wife, 'for that is sinful. You will find some one else when I am no more to render you as happy, perhaps happier, than I have done; it is my fervent wish, my dying prayer that you may do so, and my spirit shall hover around you and bless your union. Ah! it is approaching! I feel that my time is getting short—my eyes grow dim.—Husband, parents, come nearer. Let me embrace you. Bless you—bless you all!—Ah, now I am happy and prepared to die.'

"'Oh, my wife, my affectionate wife!' I ejaculated, unable to control my feelings, 'and must I, indeed, lose you thus? Oh! if it would please Heaven yet to spare you, it should, indeed, be my future study to endeavour to render myself worthy of you, and to make atonement for the past.'

"'Atonement for the past!' she repeated with difficulty, in a faint voice, and fixing her dying eyes with an indescribable expression full upon me, and which it will be impossible for me ever to forget; 'oh, my Eugene, what have you to atone for?—You have been everything to me, and I know you could never harbour a thought but for my happiness.'

"My very soul shrunk appalled at her words, and at that moment I felt myself to be one of the most heartless monsters that had ever disgraced society. I took her thin hand; I looked piteously in her pale face, but my tongue clove to the roof of my mouth, and I could not utter a syllable.

"I feel it would be a totally fruitless task for me to attempt adequately to pourtray the varied feelings which in that solemn moment crowded upon my mind, and distracted and bewildered my brain. I must rather leave it to your imaginations, and dwell no longer than possible upon the painful subject. When I now, after the lapse of so many years, recal the circumstances to my memory, I shudder appalled and wonder that I have so long been able to retain my senses. Shame, remorse, and the bitter reproaches of my guilty conscience weighed me down, and again I was about to confess all, and to sue for mercy and forgiveness. I must, indeed, have been a monster, could I have witnessed unmoved the Christian patience and resignation with which that most excellent of women supported herself in her dying moments; my heart must have been made of adamant could I have listened to her last words, the innocent confidence she reposed in me, and the boundless love she evinced towards me, with indifference. But still I dared not to acknowledge the truth, and that

in the presence of those who were so immediately interested in it, and who must look upon me with feelings of the utmost horror and detestation.

"Fearful was the silence which now reigned within that chamber of death, and which was only interrupted by the sobs of agony from those who were gathered round the bed of the unfortunate sufferer. I threw myself once more frantically on my knees, and looked mournfully and distractedly in the pale face and fast glazing eyes of poor Marie, but speech was still denied me. She extended her hands towards me and smiled benignly upon me, but although she made several efforts to speak, she could not. I saw plain enough that the last fatal hour was fast approaching, and what I felt at that moment I dare not, cannot venture to say. For a few minutes her eyes were intently fixed upon all around, and her lips moved as if she were engaged in earnest prayer; probably invoking the blessings of that Omnipotent Power in whose dread presence she was so shortly to appear upon my head, and those of all her relatives. Oh, God! what a bitter pang did that thought convey to my mind! Suddenly her features and her frame became convulsed, and she made an effort to raise herself in bed. It was the last death struggle. One more earnest look she fixed upon me, which I can never forget, then her eyes closed for ever; one faint sigh escaped her bosom, and her gentle and spotless spirit hastened to join its native Heaven! My feelings could endure no more; and I sank insensible on the couch by the side of my wife."

Here the feelings of the Count de Clairville again overpowered him, and for a short time he was unable to proceed, while Florio and the others, who were deeply impressed by the melancholy and important facts he had related, did not attempt to interrupt him in his reflections, by making use of a single remark.

CHAPTER LVII.

THE COUNT DE CLAIRVILLE CONCLUDES HIS NARRATIVE.

AFTER awhile, the Count de Clairville, having sufficiently recovered himself, continued his confession in the following words:—

"When I was restored to consciousness, I found myself in my own chamber, reclining upon my couch, with my father and the medical attendant watching anxiously by my couch. In a moment my fears suggested to me that I might probably in the wanderings of insensibility have divulged the guilty truth, and for a minute or two shame and terror overwhelmed me, and I shrunk abashed and conscience-stricken from my father's gaze ; but he quickly undeceived and re-assured me, and taking my hand, he kindly inquired of me how I felt.

"'Oh, my lord,' I said, ' tell me, is it true that my pror Marie is no more ? or have I only experienced some frightful vision ?'

"'Alas, Eugene !' he answered, in melancholy accents; 'it is too true; your wife has been summoned to eternity, and her guileless soul is an inmate of Heaven. This is a terrible calamity for you, coming so sudden and so unexpected; but I trust that you will find fortitude to support it with calmness and resignation, and——'

"'Calmness! resignation!' I interrupted; 'oh, that is impossible ; father, I feel that I am a wretch, and that I was totally unworthy of the devoted and immaculate being who is taken from me.'

"'How, Eugene !' said the count, with a look of surprise ; 'these are surely strange and unaccountable words. But you know not what you say; grief has distracted you brain. Be calm——be calm, and console yourself with the thought that your poor Marie is happy.'

"I made a powerful effort, and recovered myself sufficiently not to betray the fatal truth, but the mingled feeling of shame, horror, and remorse, that agitated my bosom, were almost too much to bear. After some further conversation, I requested that my father would leave me to the indulgence of my own thoughts for a short time, and after he had again exerted himself to impart consolation to me, he complied, and I was left alone.

"What the nature of my feelings were, it is needless for me to attempt to describe, for I am certain that you will be able to form a ready conception of them. I arose from my couch, and with my hands clasped to my burning temples, I paced to and fro across the apartment in a state of mind bordering upon absolute distraction. The dying words of my wife still seemed to ring in my ears, and I feared to look around me, lest I should encounter her ghastly and reproachful spirit.

"'Wretch !——monster ! that I am,' I ejaculated, in hoarse accents ; ' can I ever again be happy, knowing how brutally I have deceived one of the best of women ? Surely a curse will pursue me, and there is no atonement I can make for the guilty thoughts which I have harboured in my breast. Emilia, too, and my brother Antoine, how can I ever again meet them, knowing how deeply I have wronged them, in thought, if not by deed ? But I will abandon my wicked and diabolical designs, and by penitence seek to obtain forgiveness for the past.'

"Could it be believed, after these promises, I could ever again encourage the base thoughts and wishes that had hitherto inhabited my bosom ? Could it be supposed that I could so soon banish from my memory the dying words of my sainted wife ? But I did so, and surely a terrible retribution must sooner or later overtake me for my villany.

"In the course of an hour or so my father returned to me, and with much difficulty persuaded me to repair with him to the apartment of the Count St. Almo, who, as might naturally be expected, I found overwhelmed with grief; but it was some relief to me to find that neither Emilie nor her sister were present, for I must have shrunk abashed before them, especially the former. The nature of the conversation that passed between us it is unnecessary for me to describe; but I could not on any account be persuaded for the present to visit the chamber in which the corpse of my much wronged wife was lying, for how could I have dared to contemplate her livid features ? I should have expected that she would have risen up in death to curse me !"

"But your brother, my lord ?" inquired Florio, eagerly; "surely you could not help informing him of the melancholy event which had so suddenly and so unexpectedly taken place ?"

"Oh, no," replied the Count de Clairville, "though I almost trembled to meet him again under the circumstances. My father and the Count St. Almo were the first to propose that he should be made acquainted with the circumstances, at the same time requesting him to return home without delay, and promising that all relating to himself and Emilie should be waived for the present, and that he should be received with every mark of affection. I accordingly despatched a messenger to the place of his retreat immediately, and in an hour or two he arrived at the castle. His astonishment and grief at the painful event which had taken place so suddenly, may be anticipated, and the words of sympathy and condolence which he offered to me went to my conscience more than all. What took place at the meeting between him and Emilie, I am unable to describe.

"It was not till the second day after the death of Marie that I could be persuaded to enter the chamber in which her sad remains were lying, and I went alone. Oh, God ! what were the mingled feelings of dread, sorrow, and remorse which struggled in my breast on that awful occasion ! I have often wondered since that I could find courage for the dreadful task. When I arrived at the door of the chamber of death, an overpowering sensation came over me, and I was compelled to hesitate, and several times I was half induced to return ; but at last I mustered all my resolution, and opening the door, entered the room. The mournful trappings with which the apartment was hung were sufficient to inspire awe in any breast; what then must have been my emotions, guilty wretch as I was? With trembling steps, and a palpitating heart, I slowly approached the coffin, and throwing myself on my knees, I clasped my hands together, and continued for some time in silent prayer—yes, I dared venture to pray, guilty wretch though I knew myself to be.

"It was some time ere I could find courage to remove the lid of the coffin, and then I almost expected the phantom of my wife to rise up before me, and to heap curses upon my head. With what emotions of dread did I gaze upon the pale features, so lovely, so calm, and so placid even in death;—a sweet angelic smile seemed to play upon them, and to bespeak the pure and spotless spirit in heavenly rest; and yet while I continued to gaze they seemed to change, and an expression of reproach to encircle her bloodless lips. The profound silence of all around added to the solemnity of the scene, and my emotion increased every moment. A shuddering sensation came over me; hastily I replaced the lid of the coffin, and covering my face with my hands, with a groan of agony I rushed from the room. That was the last time that I ventured to gaze upon the cold remains of my wife; though her image was never absent from my sight for some time afterwards, either sleeping or waking.

"At length the funeral obsequies were performed, and I returned to my chateau, and for some days kept myself almost entirely secluded to my own chamber, buried in deep and solemn meditation. Antoine was treated with the utmost attention by my father and the Count St. Almo, and no allusion was ever made to his marriage, though they took good care that himself and Emilie should meet as seldom as possible, and then it was always in their presence; so that they had no opportunity of communicating their thoughts to each other.

"For some weeks my grief at the death of my wife was sincere, but at last it abated, and to my shame and disgrace, I must acknowledge that the guilty thoughts I had before entertained once more entered my mind. Whenever I beheld her, Emilie appeared more lovely and irresistible to me; and now that I was at liberty, what should prevent me from persisting in the prosecution of my designs?—I found that it was impossible for me to resign my hopes of her; all those feelings of remorse and compunction which I had lately experienced, gradually became stifled within my breast, and, wretch that I was, the memory of my unfortunate wife almost faded from my recollection, Do you not now perceive, Florio, what a villain I must be at heart, and how little deserving I am of your mercy and forbearance? I should tremble in your presence, for I have injured you and your unfortunate parents past atonement."

"Still, my lord," returned Clairville, "though much as you may have erred, I am inclined to treat you with every indulgence; for I am not able to believe that you can have been so guilty as you represent yourself."

"Ah, Florio," said the count, "how can you consider me anything else than as a wretch worthy of the severest reprobation for even for a moment entertaining the unholy and unnatural thoughts which I have stated? But they daily and hourly gained strength upon me, and the more I beheld Emilie, the more did my heart become insensible to every feeling of virtue and integrity, and it was with difficulty that I could conceal from your father the diabolical thoughts that were passing in my mind whenever he consulted me as his best friend on the passion that existed between himself and Emilie.

"'It is no use attempting to stifle the sentiments that have so long predominated in my breast,' I would soliloquise to myself, when I was alone. 'Emilie must and shall be mine, though perdition be my lot. The love she bears Antoine does but goad me on to desperation, and triumphs over every other feeling within my breast. Shall I see her become his, until at any rate she has yielded to my desires? By all my hopes, never! Let me stifle all foolish and delicate scruples, and my triumph is secure. I am at liberty now; I have no one to watch over or to question my conduct, and why should I then longer hesitate?—Courage, courage, Eugene, and all your wishes shall be accomplished.'"

Florio was much shocked when the Count de Clairville came to this passage, and yielding to the natural doubts and fears that beset his mind, he said—

"Oh, my lord, surely you exaggerate. Can it be possible that you ever entertained such wicked thoughts as those, and against your own brother, and one who should have been almost equally dear to you?"

"I did, I did," replied his lordship, in a voice of the deepest emotion, "and that too so soon after the death of one of the best and most faithful of wives, and at the very time when they imagined that they could repose every confidence in me. Ah! Florio, I am prepared for your scorn and indignation, for I know how richly I merit them. When I reflect upon the guilty past, I hate, loathe, and despise myself; but let whatever may be the consequences I am determined to unburthen all without the least reserve."

"Oh, my lord and benefactor," remarked Adolphus de Aubigny, and at the same time he reproached himself for the sentiments he had so suddenly allowed to take possession of his breast towards our beauteous heroine, and which, if not conquered in time, might be productive of such serious consequences; "what a painful disclosure, indeed, is this you are now making; but—"

"Patience, good Signoras Adolphus and Florio," interrupted Massaroni, "and hear the Count de Clairville to the conclusion of his eventful narrative, when I trust that you will find that you have no reason to judge so harshly of him as you do at present."

"I thank you, Signor Massaroni, for that suggestion," remarked the count; "but alas! I fear that I shall be found to be unworthy of any such indulgence."

EUGENE AND ANTOINE GALLOPING AT FULL-SPEED TO THE FIRE.

"Answer me, Count de Clairville," said Florio, breathlessly, and his cheeks glowing with the power of his emotions—"answer me, I beseech you, and banish at once the doubts and suspense which at the present moment torture my mind—if such were really the designs you entertained against the honour and happiness of my lamented mother, did you succeed?"

"Heaven be praised, I did not!" answered his lordship, energetically.

"Ah!" exclaimed Florio; "that is enough.

That assurance has removed a weight of anxiety from my mind, and I can hear you with patience to the termination of your narrative."

"But," returned the count, "am I scarcely the less culpable because I did not triumph in my nefarious designs? Was I not the means of inflicting the greatest misery upon two most deserving individuals, and of bringing my unfortunate brother to an untimely end? When I reflect upon that, I can look upon myself in scarcely any better light than that of an assassin, and I feel that I am deserving of the greatest punishment that can overtake me."

"You are stung with remorse, my lord, for the errors of which you unfortunately acknowledge yourself to have been guilty," replied Florio, "and are willing to make all the atonement in your power for the past."

"Heaven knows that I am, and at any cost of humiliation to myself."

"Enough, my lord," remarked Florio. "Such sincere and earnest repentance will most certainly be accepted by the Eternal Judge of all; and it is not, therefore, for weak and erring mortals to presume to visit you with their vengeance."

"Noble—generous youth!" ejaculated the Count de Clairville, firmly grasping his hand, "how grateful should I be to you for this clemency, although it conveys a more bitter reproach to me for the wrongs I have committed. But to proceed.

"The three months' grace which my father and the Count St. Almo had originally granted to Antoine and Emilie had now expired; but still they did not urge the union of the former and Lestelle, and they began to hope that they had relented, and would ultimately yield to their wishes, though they prohibited their meeting as much as possible, and during that period I had frequent opportunities of seeing Emilie; and while I pretended to be endeavouring to promote the happiness of herself and my brother as much as possible, I was secretly cherishing my nefarious hopes, and endeavouring to devise some means for the final accomplishment of my wishes. In this I was further encouraged by some hints which my father had two or three times thrown out, and from which I was led to infer that he would be very well satisfied if I could supplant Antoine in the affections of Emilie.

"Another month wore away, when one morning, while my brother and myself were engaged in serious conversation together, our father abruptly entered the room, and it was evident, from the expression of his features, that he had come upon some important errand, the nature of which we could both readily guess.

"'Well met, Antoine and Eugene,' he said. 'I have long wished to converse with you upon a subject which concerns us all so materially, but which I have delayed doing till now in consequence of the heavy calamity which has recently taken place. I must desire you to listen to me calmly and patiently, Antoine,' he added, observing the emotion which my brother evinced; 'this not the moment for trifling. You have already received sufficient indulgence from me; Lestelle St. Almo is your destined wife. She is young and beautiful; besides, the compact that exists between the two houses of de Clairville and St. Almo leaves you no alternative, whatever objections you may entertain, or whatever rash and imprudent sentiments you may have suffered to take possession of your mind. I, therefore, command you to prepare for your union on this day fortnight, for on no consideration whatever can it longer be delayed.'

"'Oh, my lord,' replied Antoine, in a voice of extreme agitation, 'you surely and the Count St. Almo cannot be so cruel and unjust as to force myself and Lestelle into an union which is so repugnant to both our feelings, and which could only be productive of the greatest misery. No one is more ready than myself to acknowledge the numerous and exalted virtues of Lestelle, but we cannot feel for each other any stronger sentiments than those of esteem, and——'

"'No more,' interrupted the count, sternly, 'I have no patience with such egregious folly as this, and if I had, I have no power to yield to your wishes. You, perhaps, will need not to be told the consequences of disobedience.'

"'Eugene, my brother,' said Antoine, turning to me with supplicating looks; 'plead for me; you know my feelings upon this delicate subject, and I am certain that the affection you bear me will prompt you still, as you have ever hitherto done, to espouse and advocate my cause.'

"I felt the embarrassment of my situation to the full extent, but I conquered my real feelings as well as I could, and with the most consummate hypocrisy, I said——

"'My dear father, suffer me to intercede with you for my brother, Antoine, and to——'

"'Hold, Eugene!' he interrupted, impatiently and determinedly; 'hold, as you value my favour. There is no argument that can be made use of that can have the smallest weight with me.'

"'My lord,' replied Antoine, with a determined air, 'let whatever may be the consequences, I can never—I will never consent to become the husband of a woman whom I do not love, and who possesses no affection for me.'

"'Rash boy!' said the count, passionately, 'beware! Remember the inevitable fate that must attend you should you remain obstinate. You will be cast forth a beggar upon the world, discarded for ever from my bosom, and with my heaviest maledictions upon your head.'

" 'Oh, this is most unjust and cruel, my lord,' replied Antoine, 'and such as no law, human or divine, can sanction. You will think better of this, and not condemn your own son, who never yet wilfully offended you, to a fate so terrible and revolting.'

" 'Again I tell you that I have no alternative,' said my father. 'But I see plainly how it is—you still dare to encourage your fatal passion for Emilie.'

" ' 'Tis true, my lord,' answered Antoine, 'and the lovely and innocent Emilie entertains the same ardent sentiments for me—our vows are registered in Heaven, and it would be madness to suppose that we can ever fail to fulfil them.'

" 'Fool!' exclaimed my father, passionately, 'would you bring destruction upon the head of Emilie as well as yourself? The Count St. Almo has spoken to her upon the subject this morning, and told her what will be the consequences should she not banish you from her thoughts—seclusion in a convent of the severest order for the rest of her days, and the curses of all with whom she is connected will descend upon her head.'

" 'Oh, monstrous!' ejaculated the agitated Antoine; 'it is impossible that Heaven will ever permit so inhuman an outrage. Oh, my father, reflect what it is yourself and the Count St. Almo would do, and relent in time.'

" 'We have both reflected long enough, and you now know our determination. But I waste words with you, and all your supplications and arguments can have no more effect on me than the idle wind. In a fortnight from the present you must prepare yourself to become the husband of Lestelle, or nothing can save you from the fate which I have pointed out to you.'

" 'Never!' cried Antoine, firmly; 'there is no fate that I will shrink from encountering sooner than I will resign my hopes of Emilie.'

" 'Obdurate boy!' exclaimed my father, 'then you rush madly on your own destruction. But I will leave you to your own reflections, and I trust that reason and duty will induce you to alter your mind. In the meantime, I charge you not to seek the presence of Emilie, but to seek to banish her from your thoughts in any other character than that of the sister of your intended bride. Disobey those injunctions, and the consequences will be equally fatal to Emilie as yourself.'

" With these words, he quitted the room in the same abrupt brutal manner as he had entered it, and left Antoine in the greatest possible state of excitement. He clasped his forehead with his hands, and for some minutes he continued to traverse the apartment, mutter-

ing incoherent expressions to himself. Heartless and unnatural wretch as I was, I must confess that the agony of mind he was at that time enduring afforded me gratification, for the love which Emilie so ardently and devotedly felt for him had inspired me with a feeling almost amounting to hatred towards him, and the stern determination of the count, my father, had strengthened the guilty hopes I entertained. However, I saw that there was no time to be lost, and I resolved to hazard everything without the least possible delay, though in what manner exactly to set about my diabolical task I had not exactly made up my mind. At length Antoine turned towards me, and with a look, in which all the violence of his grief was depicted, he said—

" 'Oh, Eugene, is not this a melancholy situation to be placed in? Do you not pity me?'

" 'Indeed, I do, Antoine,' I replied, with a look and in a tone of voice which only a most consummate hypocrite could possibly have assumed.

" 'But how would you advise me to act?' he eagerly demanded.

" 'Alas!' I answered, 'for the present I scarcely know how.'

" 'Do you think that our father and the Count St. Almo will remain inexorable?' he said.

" 'It does not appear very probable to me, taking all the circumstances into consideration, that they will be induced to relent,' I returned. 'But have you weighed all the consequences of disobedience maturely in your mind?'

" 'Oh, yes; and nothing can make me yield to a demand so cruel and unjust.'

" 'You cannot then conquer your love for Emilie?' I said.

" 'Conquer my love for Emilie, Eugene!' he returned, fixing upon me a look of astonishment. 'Oh, what a question is that to put to me! Sooner, much sooner could I resign my life, than relinquish my hopes of her to whom my whole soul is devoted. Eugene, my mind is made up; no power on earth shall ever compel me to become the husband of Lestelle.'

" 'Do not determine hastily, Antoine,' I remarked, 'for your refusal to comply with this demand, which I am ready to admit is harsh and unreasonable, would bring incalculable misery upon yourself and Emilie, from which I fear no one, however so disposed, could extricate you.'

" 'I will place myself in the hands of Providence,' he replied, 'and I cannot believe that it will ever desert us in a moment of such unmerited trial. What madness is this compact! And is there any law, human or divine, that can render it binding? But my poor Emilie, what anguish must she now be enduring after this interview with her father, and hearing from his lips his stern and unnatural decree. And I am not permitted to see her, that I might endeavour to console her and inspire her with hope.'

" 'And what could you say to encourage her to hope?' I demanded.

" 'Alas! I know not,' he answered; 'but you will still be our friend, Eugene, will you not?'

" 'Most certainly I will,' I replied; 'surely you can have no reason to doubt the sincerity of my friendship?'

" 'Oh, no, indeed, I do not,' he returned; 'but my brain is bewildered and distracted; and the time allowed is so short, that I know not what course to adopt for the best.'

" 'You would not clandestinely unite yourself to Emilie, even were she to consent to it?' I interrogated.

" 'I know not scarcely what in my despair I might be tempted to do,' he said. 'Again I swear that I can never resign my hopes of Emilie; and to possess her, I would be willing to encounter any fate.'

" 'But you forget, Antoine,' I remarked, 'that whatever misery you might bring upon yourself, Emilie would in that case be compelled to be a partaker of it.'

" 'Too well do I know the fervour and sincerity of my Emilie's love, not to be convinced that she could endure no greater misery than to see me become the husband of another. No, Eugene, our vows are solemnly plighted to each other, and let whatever may be the result, they can never be broken. It were madness to suppose so.'

" 'But think you not, Antoine, when Emilie should discover that fate was against you, she would endeavour to banish your image from her bosom, and to place her affections on another?'

" 'It is impossible, Eugene,' he replied, vehemently; 'it would be a monstrous scandal on the truth and fidelity of that innocent damsel to imagine so. Oh, my brother, you are but little acquainted with the heart of Emilie if you can believe that she could ever love any man but myself.'

" I bit my lips with inward rage as he gave utterance to these words, and turned away for a moment or two in order that I might conceal the expression of my features from his observation; at the same time I resolved more firmly than ever that if I could not win the love of Emilie, which I had very little hope of doing, I would leave no means untried to obtain the accomplishment of my licentious wishes, even though I should afterwards be denounced to the world as a villain. Little could the too confiding Antoine imagine the dark thoughts which at that moment were passing in my mind, or with what feelings of indignation and detestation must he have viewed me.

" 'I had hoped, after this long delay,' he said, 'and the silence which they maintained upon the subject, that my father and the Count St. Almo would have seen the severity and injustice of their conduct, cancelled the fatal and preposterous compact, and no longer have opposed the wishes of myself and my beloved Emilie.'

" 'You must have been very sanguine to have done so, Antoine,' I answered; 'especially after what I told you had transpired between the count, our father, and myself, at the first interview we held together upon the subject. I am satisfied that no arguments or entreaties will ever induce them to change their mind; and although I do not wish to throw a damp upon your spirits, I would advise you not to encourage hopes which may never by any possibility be realised.'

" 'Alas!' returned my brother, 'and must I then give myself up entirely to despair? But, no—in spite of everything, I repeat, that no earthly power shall ever compel me to unite my fate with one on whom I cannot bestow my heart; and I place that confidence in you, Eugene, to believe that although our father should discard me, and consign me to poverty and misery, you, at least, would never desert me in my hour of need.'

" 'You do me no more than justice, Antoine,' I returned, 'by that supposition; all that I could possibly do to serve you and the fair Emilie, you may be sure I would most willingly, though I am fearful that my means would be but limited on such an occasion. But come to—try to compose yourself, and to await the result of this painful and difficult business with patience and fortitude.'

" 'I will, indeed, try to do so,' he remarked, 'but I am prohibited from meeting Emilie, and that of itself is sufficient to cause me the greatest anguish.'

" 'Let not that trouble you so seriously,' I replied, with a look of candour and sincerity that was sufficient to deceive any one; 'I will see her as often as possible, and communicate all your thoughts and wishes to her, at the same time I will try to impart to her all the consolation that is in my power.'

" 'Oh, thanks—thanks, Eugene,' he ejaculated, warmly grasping my hand, 'you are the kindest and best of brothers, and may the curse of Heaven overtake me whenever I act with ingratitude towards you.'

" 'Enough—enough of this, Antoine,' I said, for his words confused and abashed me, knowing how basely I was deceiving him, and imposing upon his generous and unsuspecting nature; 'I am doing no more than my duty, and that everything may turn out as I would have it, is my most sincere and fervent wish. But we must now separate, for the count, our father's, suspicions might be excited, should we prolong our interview, and he might adopt steps that would be calculated in all probability to mar our designs.'

"'True,' coincided Antoine, and after a few more words of no importance, we separated. When out of his presence, I could not help laughing exultingly at the manner in which I had deceived him, and the confidence he placed in me; and I was more determined than ever to proceed in my designs to their accomplishment, and of which I entertained the most sanguine anticipations. It would seem as if I had banished from my breast every feeling of humanity and nature; and even now when I reflect upon the degraded state to which I had sunk, I cannot help feeling a shuddering sensation of horror. The memory of my late unfortunate and amiable wife now never once haunted my imagination, and my whole thoughts were fixed upon the obtaining of one object, and that was the destruction of the innocent Emilie. But pardon me, Florio—let me not disgust your ears with language such as this, connected as it is with your unfortunate mother.

" I made my way, on leaving Antoine, towards the Castle of St. Almo, and as I did so, I pondered deeply upon all that had taken place between myself and him. The stern determination of my father pleased me well, for I considered that it would hasten my designs, and it gratified me, as I said before, by the torture which it inflicted upon my brother. I had often thought of the frightful dungeon beneath the chateau which my father had exhibited to me, and I own that it would have given me pleasure had Antoine been secretly incarcerated therein, for it would have given me, as I imagined, more power over Emilie.

"'The vain fool!' I soliloquised, as I proceeded on my way, 'how he prides himself upon the influence he possesses over the affections of Emilie, and imagines that no one can supplant him; but if I cannot win her love, I will at least triumph over her innocence, let it cost me whatever it may. My plans are laid so ingeniously that no one can possibly suspect them, and let me but once succeed, I will brave all that may afterwards take place. Oh, Emilie, thou hast made that powerful impression upon my ravished senses that I would risk any danger to possess thee, and nothing whatever can daunt me in my purpose.'

" Thus giving myself up to such guilty and disgusting thoughts as these, I arrived at the Castle of St. Almo, where I hoped by some means or other to obtain a private interview with Emilie, and entering the spacious gardens by which it was surrounded, I walked rapidly on. I had reached a small alcove about the centre, when my footsteps were suddenly arrested by hearing some one talking in a low tone of voice, and listening attentively, I was gratified to find that it was Emilie. Her voice was frequently half stifled by sobs of anguish, but at length I distinguished the following words:—

"'Alas! alas! what a melancholy fate is mine, when I am thus forbidden to think upon the only man who ever did or can possess my affections. But in vain the stern decrees of a too inexorable parent, dear Antoine, thou must ever be uppermost in my fondest thoughts while the purple current of life continues to circulate through my veins; and if I cannot possess thee, I will never, never become the wife of any other man. They may inflict what tortures upon me they please, but nothing, no nothing can ever eradicate the passion thou hast inspired in my breast; and if I am not fated to become thine, life will become a burthen to me which I should be but too happy to get rid of.'

" She ceased, and stepping forward, she beheld me, and blushed deeply. Her eyes were humid with tears, and her whole frame was violently agitated, yet I could not help thinking that she had never looked more beautiful than she did at that moment, and I felt a sensation in my breast which I knew not scarcely how to control.

" She partly arose from her seat on recognising me, and I thought she seemed somewhat embarrassed; however, she extended her hand to me with her usual affability and innocent confidence, and I respectfully raised it to my lips.

"'In tears, fair Emilie?' I said; 'indeed it grieves me to see you thus. It is a pity that sorrow should ever wring so gentle a bosom.'

"'Ah! Eugene,' she replied, with a sigh; 'Heaven knows that I have cares enough upon my mind to cause me to weep. But you are the ardent, confidential, and sincere friend of myself and your brother Antoine, and it affords me some consolation to see you, that I may make you acquainted with the thuoghts that at present torture my mind, and seek your advice.'

"'And that you shall most willingly have, Emilie,' I answered. 'But I know what you would say; you have this morning had an interview with your father, and it is the result of that which has agitated you thus.'

"'Ah!' she ejaculated, 'how know you that, Eugene?'

"'From the Count de Clairville, my father,' I returned, 'who has also seen me and Antoine this morning, and has commanded the latter to prepare himself for his union with your sister, Lestelle, this day fortnight.'

" ' Cruel decree !' she sighed. ' But Antoine can never, will never obey it.'

" 'But unfortunately, Emilie, should he not do so,' I remarked, ' nothing awaits for himself and you but the most abject misery. The Count St. Almo and my parent are both inexorable, and nothing, I am confident, will move them from their purpose. Your father threatens you, I understand, that unless you banish my brother from your affections altogether, he will immure you within the dreary walls of a convent.'

" ' Cruel and unnatural threat !' said Emilie, 'it is too true; but let them beware, lest they urge us to do that which they might afterwards have cause to regret.'

" ' What mean you, Emilie ?'

" ' No matter; time and circumstances will explain all,' she replied. ' But anything is preferable to the inhuman fate to which they would consign myself and your brother; and as to cease to love each other, that is impossible, whilst opposition to our wishes, which are sanctioned by virtue and justice, will only tend to fan the flame.'

" These observations, spoken with such candour, fervour, and sincerity, went to my heart, and it was not without the greatest difficulty that I could conceal my chagrin from her observation.

" ' I guess to what you, allude, Emilie,' I said at length ; ' but beware, and do not act with impetuosity. Do you not know that a clandestine marriage would be certain to entail the greatest poverty on you both ?'

" ' Yes,' answered Emilie, ' and I should be prepared to encounter it without a murmur if shared with the man to whom my heart is devoted. What enjoyment can the most boundless wealth produce if unaccompanied by pure and genuine affection ?'

" ' But, Emilie,' I remarked, 'how little is your gentle nature fitted to encounter the vicissitudes of life and the frowns of fortune.'

" ' The love of the man of my heart would give me strength and fortitude to support anything,' she returned ; ' Providence, too, would surely not desert me altogether. But what would you have me do, Eugene ? Resign my hopes of Antoine, and tamely submit to the harsh will of my father ?'

" ' I would have you avoid those dangers, Emilie,' I answered, ' of which you can form so faint a conception.'

" ' And how can that be done, if the Count de Clairville and my father remain inexorable ?' demanded Emilie; ' my sister, Lestelle, and Antoine cannot love each other, or Heaven knows, though a ever so great a sacrifice, I would present no obstacle, and think you that your brother will ever consent to be forced into a marriage which is so repugnant to his feelings, unless he know that he could be

happy ? Oh, no, Eugene, full well I know that that is impossible, and, therefore, do I put my trust in Heaven to assist us. But Antoine is prohibited from meeting me, is he not ?'

" ' He is,' I replied, ' and it might be fraught with the most imminent danger should either of you attempt to break those injunctions,'

" ' True,' coincided Emelie, ' and I will not attempt to do so, thought it will be a great trial to my patience. But you will be suffered to see me as usual, will you not ?'

" ' Oh, yes,' I answered, eagerly.

" ' That, indeed, is some consolation to me,' she observed. I felt a sensation of delight thrill through my veins at these innocent observations, and I said—

" " And do my visits afford any pleasure and gratification to the fair and gentle Emilie ?'

" ' Oh, yes !' she returned, ' as the brother of my Antoine, and one who takes so deep and friendly an interest in us both.'

" I felt somewhat vexed and disappointed at this reply, and did not make any immediate observation.

" ' You will communicate all the thoughts and wishes of Antoine to me, will you not ?' she continued ; ' and act with the same degree of friendship you have hitherto evinced towards us ?'

" ' You may depend upon me, Emilie,' I replied, ' there can be nothing that can afford me such infinite gratification as to be able to save, or in any way contribute to the happiness of one whom I so much esteem.'

" She looked her thanks, and I felt my admiration of her transcendent charms every moment increase. She now questioned me more minutely as to what had taken place between Antoine and my father, and I satisfied her as far as I thought prudent. She listened to me with much attention ; but the particulars I related, I saw, caused her the greatest emotion, and when I had concluded, she said—

" ' Alas ! what strange infatuation, or rather obstinate bigotry, is it that drives our parents in this important business, and induces them rather to consult their own prejudices in favour of a monstrous deed, worthy of the darkest days of barbarism, than the happiness of their children ? Surely a compact entered into in a moment of madness by their ancestors, ought not to be binding upon us now.'

" ' It should not, I am ready to admit, Emilie,' I replied, ' but unless there was any chance of doing away with those prejudices from the minds of those who hold authority over you, it is almost hopeless to resist, when the consequences that must follow are taken into consideration.'

" ' It may appear so, but tell me,' she

added, eagerly, ' is Antoine still prepared to resist them?—Does he waver or hesitate?'

"'I should imagine not, from what he said,' I returned, in a half hesitating half doubtful tone: 'but——'

"'But,' interrupted Emilie, fixing upon me a penetrating glance, ' surely; Eugene, you cannot doubt the sincerity of my Antoine?'

"'No, Emilie,' I answered, 'I do not doubt the sincerity of my brother; I believe he loves you, perhaps as fervently as you do him, but you have accepted me as the adviser between you both, and as such, I must in all candour speak my mind.'

"'What, then, would you advise, Eugene?'

"'That you make an heroic sacrifice of your feelings, and yield to the painful necessity that occurs,' returned I. 'Time will enable you to forget Antoine in any other character but that of a dear friend, and Antoine and Lestelle—'

'Hold, Eugene!' she interrupted, hastily rising from her seat, and flashes of indignation darting from her beautiful and expressive eyes; 'I will hear no more;—and is this the advice that you, whom I thought my best friend, give to *me*? Can you think so meanly of me and your brother, as to suppose that our love is of that evanescent description, that it can pass away like the fleeting hour?—Think you that your brother regards me so lightly that he will consent to resign me at the bidding and the threats of tyrannical authority, and passively submit, like a child, to that which is repugnant to his feelings and those of my sister? Enough—enough, Eugene; I find, to my deep regret, that I can no longer confide in you; henceforth myself and Antoine must depend upon our own fidelity and fortitude on each other for the accomplishment of our wishes. You have deceived me.'

"As she thus spoke she fixed upon me a look of the keenest reproach, and made a movement to depart abruptly from the spot; but I detained her. I saw that the impetuosity of my passions had led me to go much further than I had intended to do at that time; but, nevertheless, since it was so, I determined no longer to conceal the real sentiments I entertained towards her, let the result be whatever it might, and to this bold and presumptuous step I was further urged by the jealous feelings she excited in my breast by speaking i such terms of ardent affection of my brother. The time and the spot were suited to my guilty purpose; there was no one near, or likely to interrupt us; a demoniac feeling, (for I can term it nothing else) urged me on—I knew that both she and Antoine were in my power, and, therefore, taking her hand, which she endeavoured to withdraw from me, I said—

"'Stay, Emilie; you judge me too hastily. Deceived you? Oh, I must be a villain, indeed, could I even for a moment contemplate doing

so. But for your own sake, I would urge you to endeavour to resign you hopes of Antoine; remember, that unless you do, your father has threatened to immure you for the rest of your days within the gloomy walls of a convent.'

"'And even that would be far preferable than to relinquish the love of Antoine,' she returned.

"'And yet,' I remarked, and at the same time fixing upon her a look she could scarcely fail to understand, ' it were indeed a pity that one so young, so lovely, and so fascinating as Emilie St. Almo, should be banished from the world, when there are those who can love her as fondly as Antoine de Clairville, and on whom——'

"'Forbear, Eugene!' she interrupted, crimson blushes mantling in her cheeks, while mingled expressions of astonishment and resentment flashed from her eyes; 'is this the language that the husband of my late lamented sister—the brother of Antoine, should address to me? Fearful misgivings flash upon my mind; and yet my soul would fain reject the thought. Unhand me, and let me away to the solitude of my own apartment, where I will endeavour to conquer the torturing suspicions you have excited in my breast.'

"'Nay, Emilie,' I said, still detaining her, 'you must not—shall not leave me thus; since it has proceeded thus far, I will disclose everything.—Forbear!—do not venture to raise any alarm, for that would only recoil upon yourself and Antoine. Listen to me patiently, for I can no longer conceal the feelings that are excited in my breast towards you.'

"'Good God!' she exclaimed, with a look of astonishment and alarm, blushing more deeply than before, and her fair bosom heaving with emotion, ' what fearful meaning do your words convey? Why do you look upon me so strangely?'

"As she uttered these words, I bent one knee to the earth, still retaining the hold of her hand, which she in vain sought to extricate; and looking in her face with all the eloquence of expression I could command, I said—

"'Beauteous Emilie, if man is to be blamed for worshipping all that is transcendently lovely, then, indeed, am I most criminal, for I have ever adored you above all earthly beings, though never till this moment have I ventured to reveal to you the secrets of my heart. Nay, frown not, nor shrink from me as though I were something repulsive and hideous to look upon; fate ordained that you should not reciprocate my sentiments, and Heaven knows the many hours of agony that it has cost me; but now I am unshackled, free, and as you are convinced that you can never become the wife of the man whom you have honoured with your affections without entailing the greatest misery on yourselves, may I hope that——'

"'Hold!' she interrupted, in a voice almost

stifled by the power of her emotions, her astonishment, and disgust; 'I will listen to no more. Oh, Eugene, cruel, heartless, designing man, how monstrously have you deceived me and your brother, who placed such implicit confidence in you, believing you to be our best friend. How basely do you scandalize the memory of my poor sister! I can scarcely believe it possible that it is Eugene de Clairville, whom I imagined to be all that is good and honourable, who has thus addressed me. What has there ever been in my conduct towards you, to give encouragement to this boldness of speech?'

"'You may call it boldness, if you will, beauteous Emilie,' I replied, 'but I speak the sincere sentiments of my heart. From the earliest days of childhood you have been the object of my affections, although I never till now dared to give utterance to my thoughts, for I saw with anguish the most poignant that Antoine held that place in your heart which I so much coveted. Your sister I esteemed, but nothing more, and ever treated her with the greatest respect; why, then, should you reproach me as you have done? Oh, Emilie, the love I bear you is of that intense description that nothing can conquer it; every time that I behold your superlative charms it increases in strength, and by all my hopes I swear, that I will never rest till I have obtained the gratification of my wishes, let the consequences to myself be what they may.'

"'Villain!' she exclaimed, in tones which I had never before heard her assume, and her bosom swelling with indignation and offended modesty, 'you have unmasked yourself, and now stand confessed before me in your true character. I have hitherto viewed you with sisterly regard, but what can you now expect must be my feelings towards you? Begone, begone, and if you have one feeling of shame left within your breast, abandon your guilty and unholy thoughts, and blush to look on me again.'

"As she thus spoke, she again tried to disengage herself, and to retreat from the spot. But I still forcibly detained her, and overpowered by the terror and disgust of her feelings, she could offer but little resistance.

"'Emilie,' I replied, 'the scorn with which you treat me does but add to the strength of the passion with which you have inspired me; by heaven, you look more beautiful than ever in your indignation, and I could worship you as something superhuman. Nay, you may frown, but nothing whatever will induce me to abandon my hopes of you, fair object of my every thought and wish, I——'

"'Good God!' she again interrupted, 'and am I to be compelled to listen to language such as this? Unhand me, Eugene, or dread the vengeance of offended heaven. Your looks shock and alarm me. Oh, Antoine, where art thou that thou dost not fly to my rescue from such a brutal insult as this?'

"'And think you, Emilie,' I returned, 'that Antoine could restrain me in the expression of my sentiments? Need I remind you that he is entirely powerless, and that were I so disposed I could plunge him into such an abyss of misery from which he could not extricate himself? But what is he so superior to myself that he should monopolise the whole of your affections? He can never love you with half that strength and fervour that I do, and by this kiss I swear—"

"'Villain! hypocrite! audacious libertine!' cried Emilie, as I entwined my arms around her slender waist, and endeavoured to pollute her lips with my unholy kisses. 'My cries shall bring some persons to my aid, and expose you to shame and indignation. Oh, help! help!'

"But in spite of her cries, and violent efforts to extricate herself, I continued to clasp her in my arms, and again and again I pressed warm kisses of unholy passion upon her lips. Wretch that I was, my brain seemed to be on fire, and I felt at that moment as if I could have proceeded to any desperate length; but Providence watched over the safety of Emilie and frustrated me in my diabolical designs. Still she continued to rend the air with her cries for aid, and I became alarmed lest they should reach the ears of the inmates of the castle, and I should thus be exposed in my true character, that of a consummate villain.

"'Hold, Emilie,' I said at length, 'the very safety of yourself and Antoine depend upon your silence. Should your cries reach the ears of any of the inmates of the castle, though it might be the means of bringing upon me temporary disgrace, it would be the signal for the destruction of Antoine. You have called me villain, hypocrite, libertine; those are harsh terms, but at present I can bear them all, coming from the lips of the lovely Emilie. I was prepared for your reproaches, but notwithstanding the disadvantage under which I at present labour, I do not despair of yet being enabled to conquer your prejudices, and to convince you of the fallacy of entertaining any hopes of Antoine. However, be that as it may, I can never cease to love you with the same ardour that I do now, and I feel satisfied that I have at last confessed to you the real sentiments that predominate in my breast towards you.'

"'Unhand me, ruffian,' she exclaimed, her cheeks glowing with the indignation of her feelings; 'alas! did I ever expect to be thus insulted, and that by the brother of Antoine the pretended friend and advocate of our cause, Have you no regard for sex and the painful!

situation in which I am placed, but you must seize such a moment as this to outrage my feelings? Release me from your hold, and—oh!'

"Her strength would not permit her to say more, and she fainted in my arms. I now began to fear that I had proceeded too far, and regretted that I had been so precipitate; but still as she lay insensible in my arms, I could not help gloating, with feelings which I now am ashamed to acknowledge, over her various beauties, and again I polluted her lips with

EUGENE SEEKS OLD GERVOISE FOR NEWS OF THE ABSENT LOVERS.

my kisses, and remained firm to my guilty determination to obtain, at all hazards, the accomplishment of my wishes, though I saw that it would be necessary for me to endeavour for the present to tranquillise her fears, and to exact a promise from her to keep what had taken place a secret; for if she did not do so, all my plans would be certain to be frustrated, and my hopes annihilated.

"My situation was now most embarrassing, for should any one be led to the spot while Emilie remained in a state of insensibility, the whole truth would be discovered, and I should be exposed to that disgrace and execration which I so richly merited. I tried every means that I could think of to recall her to animation, but for some time without the least success, and again I bitterly reproached myself for the brutal extravagance of my conduct, and would have given anything could I have recalled it; not that I felt the least remorse, nor had the sinful sentiments I entertained towards her undergone the slightest change.

"It was some time ere I could relinquish her delicate and beauteous form, but at length I gently placed her on the seat, and then looked cautiously forth from the alcove, to see whether any person was approaching, but the place was quite clear, and my apprehensions in a great measure abated.

"I returned to Emilie, and again endeavoured to recall her to sensibility, and at last I succeeded, for she opened her eyes, and gazed vacantly around her, for the moment unconscious of where she was, or what had happened; but at length beholding me, she started hastily to her feet with a look of terror and disgust, and exclaimed—

"'Ah! am I then still in the presence of he who has dared to shock the feelings and insult the ears of her whom he had promised, and whom he was bound to protect? Gracious Heaven! what have I done, that I should thus be subjected to such degradation?'

"She covered her face with her hands as she spoke, and sobbed bitterly. I must confess that I was somewhat moved by the agitation she displayed, and approaching nearer to her, I said—

"'Emilie, will you grant me but a few words in explanation?'

"She again started at the sound of my voice, and looking up with an expression of the keenest reproach, she hastily ejaculated—

"'Approach me not, for the sight of you now inspires me with dread, and can excite nothing but feelings of disgust and shame in my bosom. Alas! alas! little did I ever expect to have experienced such cruel, such unmanly, such dishonourable treatment from the husband of my deceased sister, and that too at a time when both myself and Antoine so much needed and depended on his consolation and advice. But let me begone; I feel myself contaminated and degraded by your presence; I leave you to the bitter reproaches of your own conscience, if you have not become entirely callous to every sense of proper feeling.'

"'Emilie,' I said, in a subdued and supplicating tone, and assuming all the remorse I possibly could; 'I again beseech you to listen to me but for a moment, and not to condemn me too hastily.'

"'Condemn you too hastily,' she replied,

'after the manner in which you have proceeded? What can you possibly say in extenuation of your conduct?'

"'I acknowledge,' I returned, 'that the impetuosity of my feelings have led me too far, and caused me to conduct myself in a manner which I now sincerely regret. But do not altogether condemn me because the superiority of your charms have made an impression upon my heart which I have found it impossible to resist. You have called me villain and deceiver, and I own you have been justified by the circumstances in doing so; but can you forgive me for this my first offence against the delicacy of your feelings?'

"'Forgive you. Eugene?' she ejaculated; 'oh, surely it is no easy task to forgive such an unmerited insult as I have this day received from you. It is painful to have that implicit confidence which I reposed in you destroyed.'

"'Say not so, Emilie, I implore you,' I said, 'it is my first offence against the modesty of your nature, and bitterly—most bitterly, do I repent it. You will not repeat what has so unfortunately happened to any one? Promise me that you will not.'

"'Should I not appear criminal were I to do so?' she demanded.

"'No,' I replied, 'you would only be exhibiting the generous forbearance of your nature, and such mercy on your part would be the fittest reproof you could give me for the error I have committed.'

"She hesitated, and then fixing upon me a keen and penetrating look, she said—

"Are you sincere, Eugene?"

"'By my soul's hopes, I am, Emilie,' I returned with the most unblushing appearance of truth and candour.

"'You will stifle the unholy and fatal passions you have unfortunately encouraged towards me in your breast,' she added, 'and never again give utterance to a word that can call a blush upon my cheek?'

"'Most solemnly I promise you that I never will,' I answered.

"'On those conditions, then, Eugene,' she said, 'I do forgive you what has happened, and will endeavour to banish it from my recollection altogether.'

"With the most generous and unexampled confidence, she extended her hand to me as she thus spoke, which, bending one knee to the earth, I raised respectfully to my lips, at the same time that I ejaculated—

"'Most amiable of women, how can I ever sufficiently testify to you my gratitude for this condescension? You promise me, then, that you will never mention a word of what has this day so unfortunately happened between us to my brother or any other individual?'

"'If you adhere to your promise I will to mine,' she answered.

"'And you will still repose the same confidence in me as if I had never revealed the unfortunate sentiments which I had suffered to take possession of my mind?'

"'I will endeavour to do so,' she said, 'and I hope that I may have no cause to repent my having done so.'

"'Enough, Emilie,' I cried, 'I am satisfied, and again do I return to you my most fervent thanks for the noble and generous forbearance with which you have acted towards me.'

"'No more, Eugene,' she remarked, 'let us endeavour to banish the painful circumstance from our memory.'

"'But you will not avoid me?' I interrogated. 'You will allow me to see you as usual at every opportunity?'

"'Have I not assured you that I will place the same reliance on your honour and friendship as I did before?' she returned. 'And you, in return, Eugene, will do all you can do to promote the wishes of myself and your brother?'

"'Most earnestly I will, Emilie,' I replied, 'and by that endeavour to prove my sincere remorse for the anguish I have caused you.'

"'I am satisfied,' she observed; 'but suffer me now to depart, for should we be observed here by any of the inmates of the castle, it might excite the worst suspicions.'

"'Be it as you wish, Emilie,' I returned. 'I have now no will but yours, and henceforth I trust that you will at least allow me to use the respectful familiarity of a brother.'

"'Yes—yes,' she said, hastily, and evidently much embarrassed; 'on the terms that I have proposed, and which you have promised to accede to. But this interview has already been protracted long enough, and the count, my father, will begin to feel surprised at the length of my absence. Farewell, and may nothing again occur to interrupt that friendship and harmony which ought to exist between us.'

"I reciprocated her wishes with much apparent sincerity, though at the same time the worst feelings were rankling at my heart, and as I thought it would not be prudent to appear before the Count St. Alme in my present state of mind, I suffered Emilie to leave me. I watched her fair and graceful form with a palpitating heart, as she made her way to the castle, and when it was hidden from my sight. I returned to the alcove, and throwing myself upon the seat, I abandoned myself to the thoughts to which the circumstance had naturally given rise within my breast. My mind felt somewhat relieved by the daring disclosure of my sentiments, and the result was no more than I had anticipated; but still, notwithstanding the solemn promises I had made to Emilie, I was determined not to abandon my nefarious designs, and I flattered myself, in spite of the many obstacles that were at present thrown in my way, I should yet succeed.

"'Yes, scornful beauty,' I muttered to myself, as I quitted the garden, and retraced my steps towards my own dwelling, 'in spite of all your opposition, and the solemn promises I have made, I will never resign my hopes of you, even at the risk of being denounced to the world as a villain. What can ever subdue the violence of the passions your superlative charms have engendered in my breast? Nothing but the gratification of them, and that object once achieved, I shall be satisfied, and Antoine may then possess you as soon as he likes.'

"But still, although this was my wicked design, I knew that it would be necessary for me to act with the utmost precaution and hypocrisy in order to obtain the achievement of my object, and to drown the suspicions of those whom I was plotting against, and I therefore endeavoured to calm my real feelings as much as possible. I knew that I should have a difficult task to perform in doing that, but I set myself boldly and determinedly about it, and was resolved not to stop at anything which was calculated to lead to my success.

"That night I had but little rest in thinking of the events of the day and in arranging my plans for the future, and in the morning I repaired to the chateau, in order that I might ascertain whether or not my father was in the same state of mind, though I felt fully convinced that nothing whatever would alter him. My father, however, was from home, and I had, therefore, every opportunity of conversing freely with my brother; and so well did I succeed in concealing my real thoughts from his observation, that he believed that I sympathised more deeply than ever with himself and Emilie, and was unbounded in the feelings of gratitude he expressed towards me. What would have been his feelings of horror and indignation, had he known what had taken place between myself and Emilie on the day before? Most anxious were the inquiries he made respecting her, and I answered him with apparent truth and candour, but, of course, only just as suited my own purpose. He informed me that he had had another interview with our father that morning, and that he still turned a deaf ear to his arguments and expostulations, and had commanded him peremptorily to prepare for his union with Lestelle at the time he had appointed, or to take the consequences.

"'But, terrible though I know them to be,' he added, 'I will brave them all rather than consent to that which my heart abhors.'

"'I can duly appreciate and sympathise with your feelings, Antoine,' I observed, 'but at the same time you must bear in mind the misery into which Emilie will be plunged by your refusal.'

"'Oh, no,' he returned, 'I know the heart of my beloved Emilie too well to believe that she could experience any greater misery than in seeing me become the husband of another.'

"'She will be incarcerated within the gloomy walls of a convent,' I observed; 'such is the stern determination of the Count St. Almo, her father.'

"'Oh, never!' he exclaimed, resolutely. 'I would sooner encounter death than suffer her to be consigned to such a fate.'

"'But how are you to prevent it?' I demanded.

"'I will do so, at all hazards,' he replied. 'Eugene, I may depend upon you? Whatever may take place, you, at any rate, will not desert me, but will extend a brother's hand to aid me in any difficulties in which I may become involved?'

"'I will do so to the best of my power, Antoine,' I replied; 'though I fear that my means would be limited; and should I excite the wrath of the count, our father, I need not remind you that I should be placed in a similar position to yourself. But do not resolve on anything hastily, and probably something may yet be done to avert the evils you apprehend.'

"'But the time allowed us for consideration is so limited,' he remarked; 'but a fortnight. Some prompt and decisive step must be taken ere that time expires, should our father and the Count St. Almo remain inexorable, of which there appears to be every probability. Plainly speaking, Eugene, Emilie must and shall become my wife, let the consequences be whatever they may, so long as she is willing to encounter them.'

"'Well, Antoine,' I replied, 'since such is your determination, and I speak it with every feeling of sincerity and truth, it is no use arguing the point with you any further, at present; but of this I once more assure you, namely, that I have the interest of yourself and Emilie deeply at heart.'

"'I am convinced that you have, my dear brother,' he returned, 'and need I likewise assure you how grateful I am for your generous sympathy?'

"'I am aware of it, Antoine,' I answered; 'but I must leave you now, and will repair to the castle with the hope of seeing Emilie.'

"'Thanks, Eugene,' he observed. 'Oh! you are indeed my best friend, and without you I should sink into a state of absolute despair!'

"I know not how I looked as he gave utterance to these words, but I could not help feeling a pang of shame and remorse steal upon my heart, and I hurried away as quickly as I could, fearful that I might betray myself.

In the interview that I had with the Count St. Almo, he never once broached the subject of Emilie and my brother, and I had no opportunity of seeing her till the evening, when I was about to take my departure, when I met her in the same place I had done the day before, and she was again immersed in tears. I could not help feeling somewhat confused and abashed when I encountered her glance, but I quickly recovered myself, and inquired, with much apparent solicitude and anxiety, if anything else particular had occurred to excite her grief.

"'Alas! Eugene,' she replied, 'how can I be otherwise than truly wretched when I reflect upon the untowardness of my fate? My father has again seen me this morning, and not only does he remain invulnerable to all my appeals, but he has threatened me that if I do not at once abandon all thoughts of Antoine he will use such coercive measures as he considers will compel me to yield. But banish Antoine from my mind! Oh, that is impossible! Every day, every hour, does but render him more dear to me; and sooner than I can resign my hopes of him, I can encounter the greatest tortures that it is possible can be inflicted upon me.'

"I need not attempt to describe the sensations which her words imparted to me, but I maintained my self-possession with remarkable skill, and in accents that were sufficient to deceive even the most penetrating observer, I replied:—'Do not abandon yourself entirely to despair, Emilie, for sad and gloomy as your prospects now appear to be, the result of all these trials may be far less painful than you now anticipate.'

"'And do you sincerely wish that what you have just now expressed may be realised, Eugene?' she eagerly demanded.

"'You surely cannot doubt me, Emilie,' I returned, 'after the explanation that has taken place between us?'

"She blushed deeply as I made use of these observations, and in a faltering voice replied:

"'Believe me, Eugene, I meant not to make any allusion to that painful subject, which I wish to be banished from our memory altogether. I place every reliance upon the solemn promise you have made me.'

"'Generous confidence!' I returned, and at the same time I could scarcely conceal the exultation I felt at the manner in which I had been enabled to quiet the apprehensions which my conduct of the previous day had naturally excited in her breast; 'you shall find that I will not abuse it—that I will not deceive you, but that all I can do to promote the happiness of yourself and my brother, I will.'

"'Enough, Eugene,' she ejaculated, 'I am satisfied, and your words inspire me with hope. But, Antoine, oh, tell me what is the state of his mind at the present moment?'

"'All that you can imagine,' I answered; 'he has again made an earnest appeal to my father, but with no better prospect of success than before.'

"'Alas! I feared as much,' she remarked; 'but does Antoine still remain determined to resist the unnatural union into which our parents would compel him and Lestelle?'

"'He does.' 'But your sister, Lestelle?'

"'Oh, you know well the sentiments she entertains, and how deeply she sympthises with me and Antoine. She has also most strongly protested against the union, and remonstrated with my father, but all to no purpose. It would seem as if the Count de Clairville and my parent were labouring under some singular and fearful infatuation, and were determined to create misery to both our families.'

"'Obstinate, headstrong, and disobedient girl!' at that moment exclaimed a stern and well-known voice, and looking up, what was our astonishment, alarm, and confusion, on beholding the Count St. Almo standing near us, his countenance flushed with anger, and his whole demeanour evincing the excitement of his feelings. Emilie uttered a faint exclamation of terror, and sinking back on her seat, almost became insensible, whilst I was so embarrassed that I could not give utterance to a syllable.

"'Obstinate, headstrong, and disobedient girl!' the count repeated; 'and is it thus that you dare to break through my injunctions, and to brave my wrath? And you, Eugene, it well becomes you and the duty you owe to your father, to thus become the counsellor and the abettor of my daughter in her opposition to my will. From this moment I prohibit your visits to the castle till after the union of your brother with my daughter, Lestelle.'

"'Pardon me, my lord,' I answered, proudly, 'but you judge me too harshly, and misconstrue my objects. This meeting with Emilie has taken place by accident, and not from any preconcerted plan; and I would merely interpose to save both your daughter and Antoine from misery.'

"'And who gave you authority to presume so much?' he demanded, haughtily; 'but I have no wish to bandy words with you: you have heard my determination, and I must insist that you comply with it. That which the Count de Clairville and myself have decreed is irrevocable, and all the arguments, persuasions, and supplications in the world, cannot have the least effect. Emilie, return to the castle, and prepare yourself to explain to me, if you can, and make atonement for this act of disobedience.'

"'Oh, my father!' ejaculated Emilie, sinking on her knees at his feet, and bursting into tears, 'do not, I implore you, pursue me with a cruelty and severity which is beyond my strength to bear, but——'

"'No more, girl,' he interrupted, sternly, 'but do as I command, lest you would encounter my utmost indignation.'

"'My lord,' I interposed, 'I wish not to appear impertinent, or to question your authority for a moment; but I would implore you to act with mercy and forbearance towards your unfortunate daughter on this occasion, when indeed she is not to blame.'

"'I need not your advice, young man,' he replied, in the same haughty tones; 'I am, I presume, the master of my own actions, and if I needed counsel, methinks I should be disposed to apply for it to sager heads than your own. Good day, sir; I have nothing more to say to you.'

"With these words he took the arm of the trembling Emilie, and led her abruptly from the spot; whilst I remained for a few minutes completely bewildered, and rivetted to the earth; but at length, muttering a curse to myself, I walked slowly from the place.

"This event caused me the greatest uneasiness and vexation, for I feared that it might be productive of the worst consequences, and be the means of retarding, if not ultimately frustrating my designs, and again and again I regretted that it had taken place. I well knew the stern and determined character of the Count St. Almo, and I had not the least doubt but that he would now keep the unfortunate Emilie strictly confined to the castle until after the marriage of Antoine and Lestelle had taken place, and although that gratified me in one respect, as it would completely annihilate the hopes of the lovers, and thus afford me a better opportunity of accomplishing my designs on some future occasion, it would deprive me of the chance of seeing Emilie in the meantime, and feeding my evil passions in the contemplation of her charms, and in listening to the fascinating allurements of her conversation.

"'What cursed accident led him to the spot?' I soliloquised, as I proceeded on my way home; 'or, rather, why did I not suggest to Emilie the propriety of proceeding to some place away from the castle where we might have conversed without the fear of interruption? This accident may be the cause of incalculable mischief, and it is calculated to bring down upon my head the utmost indignation of my father when he comes to hear of it, which he will be sure to do. But, nevertheless, I will brave everything, and will not rest until the deep-laid schemes which I have formed in my own mind are accomplished. The beauteous Emilie shall not escape me, in spite of all the apparently insurmountable obstacles that are thrown in my way.'

"Thus meditating, I had nearly arrived at my chateau, when looking up, I beheld my brother advancing towards me. This annoyed me, for I was in no state of mind to see him at present, and I hesitated whether or not I should inform him what had taken place; but before I had time to form any positive determination, he had come up to me, and eagerly saluted me.

"'What brings you here, Antoine?' I inquired.

"'My anxiety to learn whether you have seen Emilie,' he replied, 'and to hear what may have taken place at the interview. I have been waiting some time for you at the chateau, until my patience was exhausted, and I thought that I would walk forth, with the hope of meeting you.'

"'Has the count, our father, returned home yet?' I asked.

"'He has not,' answered Antoine.

"'That is well,' I remarked; 'for I have no wish to see him at present; though I have no doubt that it will not be long before he will demand an interview with me.'

"'What mean you, Eugene?' he demanded; 'you look excited. Has anything particular taken place?'

"'Yes,' I returned, 'something that has annoyed me greatly.'

"'You alarm me,' he remarked; 'tell me what it is. What of Emilie?'

"I briefly informed him.

"'Alas! alas!' he ejaculated, with much emotion, 'how unfortunate is this. Poor Emilie, are your misfortunes never to be at an end? She will now be visited with the utmost severity by her father; and as your visits to the castle are prohibited, I shall have no means of communicating with her. But, by heavens I will be firm in my determination, and though destruction should be my inevitable fate, I will never be forced into a union that is so repugnant to my feelings.'

"'Be calm, Antoine,' I said, 'and all may yet terminate according to your wishes.'

"'Ah, Eugene,' replied my brother, 'I have too much reason to fear that that is hopeless; our father and the Count St. Almo will never consent to the union of myself and Emilie, and if that is at all accomplished, it will be by clandestine means.'

"'And can you contemplate such a step?' I demanded.

"'What other alternative is there left to me and the innocent damsel to whom my very soul is devoted?' he interrogated.

"'Know you that by adopting such a course you would plunge yourselves into the most abject poverty and misery?'

"'I can brave anything, encounter any hardship, rather than resign my hopes of Emilie,' he replied. 'Oh, Eugene, did you really know the full intensity of my love, you would not marvel at my determination, when my wishes are so strongly opposed by the obstinacy and injustice of our father and the Count St. Almo. But what is now to be done? I know not. Emilie will doubtless be confined a close prisoner in the castle, and all correspondence between us entirely prevented.'

"'It would be a folly to attempt to flatter you with a hope to the contrary,' I returned. 'But wait patiently, and I will consider what is best to be done.'

"'Oh, how futile it is to talk to me of patience under such circumstances,' he observed; 'but I must see the Count St. Almo, and that without delay.'

"'Nay, Antoine,' I said, 'it would be folly for you to attempt to do so, and might be attended by the most dangerous consequences after the stern and peremptory injunctions you have received from our father. Besides, I am satisfied that the mind of the Count St. Almo is inaccessible to any persuasions or arguments that you could make use of.'

"'Can he be so cruel and unnatural as to seek to consign his beauteous and affectionate child to misery?' said Antoine.

"'His conduct proves that he will not hesitate or feel the least repugnance upon that point,' I replied.

"'Then she is fully justified in resisting to the utmost of her power anything so opposed to reason and humanity,' he observed; 'he has forgotten his duty as a parent, and has retrograded into the tyrant, and the consequences, whatever they may be, will assuredly rest upon his own head. Oh, my Emilie, that I could behold you, that I might be enabled to impart to you that consolation of which you stand so much in need under the painful trials to which you are now so cruelly and unjustly subjected.'

"'It is useless thus to give way to lamentations, Antoine,' I remarked, at the same time I could not help secretly exulting at the anguish of mind he was enduring, notwithstanding that I appeared so deeply and sincerely to sympathise with him, that it was impossible for him to suspect the real thoughts that were passing in my mind; 'all that can be done is to consider maturely what course it will be most prudent and practical to adopt; and I need not, I believe, assure you, that in anything which may seem calculated to obtain the consummation of your wishes, you shall have my most zealous and hearty co-operation.'

"'I believe you, my dear brother,' he said, vehemently grasping my hand; 'you have ever proved yourself to be my best earthly friend, and but for you I must long since have resigned myself to the blackest despair. Heaven will reward you as you deserve, for much I fear it will never be in my power to do so.'

"What an unnatural miscreant I must have been, to listen to these observations unmoved! But they made not the least impression on me; on the contrary, I secretly chuckled to myself at the easy manner in which he was deceived, and the implicit confidence he placed in me, which was so well calculated to advance the nefarious plans I had so long had in contemplation.

"After some further conversation, having by this time reached my chateau, we parted, I promising to see him on the following day, when I would endeavour to advise with him what was best to be done.

"The circumstance I have just related, caused me much reflection, and it was impossible that I could divest my mind entirely of the doubts and apprehensions it excited, as all future communication between myself and Emilie would now be entirely prevented; but there was one circumstance, at the same time, connected with it, which afforded me infinite satisfaction, and that was that Antoine and Emilie would have no power of eloping, and thus setting the power of their parents at defiance; and I was resolved that I would take advantage of that circumstance, and leave no means untried to triumph over the stubborn virtue of the poor and innocent girl who had excited such guilty and ungovernable passions within my breast.

"Such were the thoughts that occupied my breast during the night, and my determination to achieve my base object increased with the obstacles that presented themselves in my way. I had scarcely finished my morning meal, and was about to prepare myself to leave the chateau, when the Count de Clairville was announced, and soon afterwards entered the room. I guessed very well what the purport of his visit was, and as soon as I beheld the expression of his features my suspicions were confirmed. However, I was prepared for everything, and met his stern glance with the utmost composure.

"'Eugene,' he said, at length, 'I always, till now, imagined that in you I had at least one son who was anxious to act in accordance with my will, and to do nothing which might be calculated to obstruct or annoy me.'

"'True, my lord,' I replied composedly, 'and you calculated rightly; may I be permitted to inquire what cause you have to alter that opinion?'

"'Your question, I should conceive, is answered, when I inform you that I have seen the Count St. Almo since your meeting with him yesterday,' he returned; 'what reply have you to make to that?'

"'Simply this, my lord,' I said, in the same firm tone, 'that I have done nothing which I conceive to be inconsistent with my duty to you as a son, or that I should raise the ire of the Count St. Almo.'

"'What,' observed my father hastily, 'not after my strictest injunctions to the contrary, not only encouraging Antoine and Emilie in their headstrong and hopeless passion, but likewise abetting them in their designs to evade our authority? Beware, Eugene, for you are taking a course, which, if you do not speedily abandon, may involve you in ruin.'

"'My lord,' I answered, losing none of my firmness or self-possession, 'I am ready to admit that I have from my heart espoused the cause of my brother and the fair Emilie, because I consider that the enforcement of a compact so ridiculous and monstrous in its nature is not only unjust but tyrannical.'

"'How!' he exclaimed, passionately, 'dare you thus speak to me? And think you, by opposition so foolish as this, to divert myself and the Count St. Almo from our purpose? I have strictly commanded you not to encourage Antoine or Emilie to indulge in hopes which can never be realised. Answer me, sir: are you prepared to obey those injunctions or not?'

"I felt gratified at the stern determination with which he pursued his designs against the happiness of my brother and Emilie; nevertheless, to give a better colouring to my own plans, I continued to act the hypocrite with the most consummate skill, and I therefore replied:—

"'My dear father, I presume that I need not remind you that I have ever been obedient to your will, and that I would most willingly yield to your injunctions, were it not that sympathy for my brother and the gentle Emilie prevented me. They love each other, while, on the other hand, no such sentiment as that exists between Lestelle St. Almo and Antoine; what I would then request is, and pardon me if I appear too bold or presumptuous in so doing, that you should yet take some further time for consideration, ere you demand the fulfilment of the compact, and——'

"'Hold, Eugene,' he interrupted, impatiently, 'hold, I command you, as you value my favour; these fruitless solicitations and objections to my will do but serve to excite my wrath. It has been madness and obduracy on the part of Antoine and Emilie to encourage hopes which they well knew could never be realised; and if they are doomed to misery and disappointment, they have only their own headstrong folly to blame. As for Lestelle, she is patient and submissive; she can esteem Antoine, and do her duty towards him as a wife, if she cannot love him, and time will, no doubt, strengthen their sentiments towards each other. Is she not in every way more than worthy of him? Young, amiable, accomplished, and virtuous? Fair, too, as her sister Emilie? Bah! I have no patience with the ridiculous objections of your brother, and I am determined that they shall have no effect upon me. Moreover I once more warn you, Eugene, that you will only involve yourself in trouble by presuming to advise me to that with which it is impossible for me to comply. Your boldness in holding secret meetings with Emilie, and encouraging her in opposing the will of her father, also excites my indignation, and any repetition of such conduct may place you in a more critical position than you can at present form any conception of. Remember well what I have said, and do not again attempt to disobey my injunctions. I also command you for the present to refrain from visiting the castle of St. Almo, and on no account to seek to hold any communication with Emilie, though you will have no opportunity of doing so, as the count has now commanded her to keep herself closely confined to her own apartments, and to dare not to leave the castle without his express permission.'

" ' My lord,' I said, ' I believe I need not assure you that I have ever looked upon the Count St. Almo with feelings of the utmost respect and friendship ; but I cannot help considering that his present conduct towards his beauteous and innocent daughter, Emilie, is most harsh, if no to say tyrannical.'

" ' How,' he exclaimed, angrily, ' dare you arraign the conduct of my noble friend ? By what right do you question his authority over his own daughter ? This presumption on your part is intolerable, and if persisted in, can only involve you in trouble, without assisting those whose cause you seem so warmly to advocate. But I will not waste time in bandying words with you ; you know my will, and if you are wise you will not provoke my wrath by seeking to oppose it. You cannot have forgotten the dungeon beneath the old chateau ?'

" ' And why remind me of that fearful place ?' I demanded, eagerly.

" ' No matter,' he returned, ' I merely wished to throw out the hint to you, and I trust that you will have the good sense and prudence to profit by it."

" With these words, and without waiting for me to return a reply, he abruptly quitted the house and left me to my own reflections. Notwithstanding that I felt satisfied at his stern determination to oppose the unfortunate passion of my brother and Emilie, my pride was mortified by the haughty and authoritative tone which he had addressed to me, and I was resolved, in spite of the manner in which I might appear to submit to his will, to oppose him by every means in my power, and to leave no plan untried in order to obtain the gratification of my own sinful and secret wishes. In the course of the day I had an opportunity of seeing Antoine alone, and the agitation and excitement of his feelings on being informed of what had taken place between myself and our father may be readily imagined, although he was fully prepared for it, the count having seen

him previous to his visiting me, and reading him a severe lecture.

" ' Eugene,' he remarked, ' the manner in which myself and Emilie are persecuted by our parents, I think that every reasonable person must be ready to admit, is most cruel and unjust, and notwithstanding all the threats that have been held out to us, I am determined to resist it by every means in my power, while I am satisfied of the unabated fidelity of that dear girl to whom my heart is devoted. No power on earth shall compel me to enter into a marriage which is so repugnant to my feelings ; and convinced as I am that I could not render that justice to the amiable Lestelle which her numerous and unquestionable merits entitle her to.'

" ' I cannot but admire your firmness, Antoine,' I said, with much apparent sincerity, ' though it is impossible for me to close my eyes to the utter inutility of opposing the stern decree of our father and the Count St. Almo, which can only bring down upon yourself and Emilie the utmost wrath and vengeance of them both. It is needless for me to repeat to you the consequences that will follow your disobedience, for they have already been sufficiently explained to you, and all that has been threatened I have no doubt will be put into execution.'

" ' By Heaven that shall never be,' he returned, vehemenly, ' though I lose my life in attempting to prevent it. Of course, should my father think proper to carry his unnatural feelings so far as to discard me from his bosom, and to send me forth upon the world an outcast and a beggar, I have no power to prevent him ; but Emilie shall never be consigned to the fate with which her father has threatened her, but she shall become my wife, in spite of all the many and apparently insurmountable obstacles that are at present thrown in my way.'

" ' Calm yourself, Antoine,' I returned, ' and reflect upon the utter impracticability of accomplishing that which you threaten. Should you contemplate a clandestine marriage, which I imagine is that at which you have just now hinted, you may depend upon it that the Count St. Almo will take every precaution to prevent it. There is no doubt that he will keep Emilie closely confined till after the day appointed for your union with Lestelle, and should you then remain obstinate, the fate that awaits her is certain ; she will be forced into a convent, buried from the world for the rest of her days, and——'

" ' Oh, dreadful thought !' he interrupted, with increased emotion ; ' Providence will surely never permit so monstrous a sacrifice. But even should it do so, it will be far preferable to my breaking the solemn vows I have so often plighted to her, and becoming the husband of another. But tell me, my dear brother, have you no advice to offer me in this terrible dilemma?'

"'The only advice that I can at present offer you, Antoine,' I answered, 'is what I know you will reject. I would have you struggle with your feelings, and yield to stern necessity, leaving the future to chance.'

"'What,' ejaculated Antoine, impatiently, 'would you then persuade me to become the

THE BRIGAND AND FLORIO DE CLAIRVILLE.

husband of Lestelle, and thus at once to annihilate the hopes of my beloved Emilie?'

"'Yes,' I replied, 'it is the only way by which you can save yourself and her from the most incalculable misery.'

"'Never! by all my hopes!' he cried; 'sooner could I perish by the most lingering and torturing of deaths, than I could yield to such monstrous and unnatural demands. Emilie, I am convinced, will remain as firm as myself, and be prepared to encounter all the consequences that may follow resistance to the tyrannical will of our parents, and I will leave the rest to the will of the Almighty, who will not, I trust, desert us in the hour of need. Remember, Eugene, that Lestelle is as much opposed to this union as myself, and, therefore, what else could be expected to result from it, than the most inconceivable misery? No, reason, honour, and justice are opposed to it, and I will never, never be forced into a compliance with that which would be productive of so many evils. Alas! my faithful, devoted Emilie, what must be the anguish you are now enduring!'

"'True,' I coincided, 'and it is that which induces me to advise you to endeavour to conquer your unfortunate passions, and thus to rescue her and yourself from the fate which otherwise inevitably awaits you.'

"'You surprise me, Eugene,' he said, 'in urging me to that from which every feeling of my nature recoils with a sentiment almost approaching to horror and disgust.'

"'The regard with which I hold both you and Emilie, prompts me to do so,' I replied, in the same hypocritical accents. 'But I will leave you to reflect calmly and maturely upon this painful subject, and I trust that you will see the absolute necessity of abandoning the hopes you have so long encouraged, since fate is evidently against you.'

"'But may I not still depend upon your friendship and sympathy?' he eagerly demanded.

"'You may, indeed, Antoine,' I answered, 'and that with confidence. What reason have you to doubt me?'

"'And you will still aid me in the accomplishment of my wishes?'

"'As far as my limited means will permit me.'

"'Thanks—thanks,' he ejaculated. 'With such assurances as these, I will not give way entirely to despair. Emilie, notwithstanding the dark clouds which at present obscure the horizon of our happiness, they will yet pass away, and the hopes which we have from earliest childhood indulged in, and which virtue and every sacred feeling sanction, will be realised.'

"'Fool!' I thought to myself, 'how bitterly are you doomed to be disappointed. Little do you imagine the dark plot that I have laid to defeat you in your hopes, and the determination I have formed to triumph over the innocence of that fair being, to obtain possession of whom you are ready to sacrifice your life.'

"Such were the guilty thoughts that occupied my mind, while I still remained in the presence of my unsuspecting brother; but at length we separated, and after I had passed a short time in reflection, I wandered towards the castle, notwithstanding the stern prohibition of the Count St. Almo, with the hope of being enabled to learn the real situation of Emilie. Again and again I regretted what had taken place the day before, which had, at least, deprived me of the pleasure of the society of her who held so powerful an influence over my passions, and might be the means of retarding the accomplishment of the diabolical and nefarious designs I had in contemplation; but still I resolved not to relax in my efforts, and I flattered myself with the thought that in the end I should be triumphant.

"I could not make up my mind to seek an interview with the Count St. Almo, and endeavour to remonstrate with him, after the peremptory commands I had received from him; but at length I beheld a female domestic, whom I knew to be in the confidence of Emilie, emerge from the castle, and I instantly advanced towards her, and placing a purse of money in her hand, I requested her to make me acquainted with all the particulars she knew of her mistress. She readily complied, and informed me that after the return of the Count St. Almo and his daughter to the castle on the day before, they had been closeted together for some time, until Emilie was removed in a state of great agitation and excitement to her own chamber, in which she was now held a close prisoner, and was only permitted to hold intercourse with her (her domestic). This was no more, of course, than I had expected after what the Count St. Almo and my father had stated to me; but still it caused me the greatest vexation and uneasiness, and I could not help secretly cursing the austerity with which she was treated, and feeling a most anxious wish to release her from their power. That, however, I knew could only be a work of time, and that it would likewise be indispensably necessary for me to act with caution, or I might otherwise not only betray myself, but be foiled in my designs. One thing, however, afforded me much gratification, and that was the opportunity I at least had of communicating with her through the means of Jeanette, who readily undertook to deliver any messages I might have for her, and to convey her reply; and on this understanding we parted, I requesting that Jeanette would assure her mistress of the continued sympathy I felt in her fate, and the firm determination I had to serve her all that was in my power.

"Thus day after day passed away, and I had frequent interviews with Jeanette, and kept up a secret correspondence with her mistress, who sent repeated letters to Antoine, couched in the most affectionate language, assuring him of the unabated strength of the sentiments she entertained towards him, and endeavouring to inspire him with hope. But it was in vain he sought to encourage it, as the time rapidly approached at which his union with Lestelle was fixed to take place, and the Count St.

Almo and our father still remained inexorable. Lestelle, too, was in scarcely a less agitated state of mind than himself, and had made several most earnest appeals to her father, but in vain; and it seemed as if nothing whatever could avert the fate of herself and Antoine, the preparations for the marriage going on with all possible expedition.

"It is needless for me to say that I viewed the probability of the speedy consummation of that important event with the most infinite satisfaction, for then the hopes of Emilie and my brother would be crushed for ever, and I flattered myself that my triumph would be all but certain. But let me not dwell any longer than is necessary upon all the guilty facts connected with my history, for I begin to fear that I have already tired your patience too far.

"My father kept a strict watch over the actions of Antoine as the time approached nearer, for his suspicions were excited that he might, in order to avoid the union that was so obnoxious to his feelings, be induced to depart from the chateau, and the consequence was that he was never permitted to absent himself even for the shortest period without being under the strict surveillance of some of the most trustworthy of the domestics; and I was not even allowed to see him only in the presence of our father. This restraint upon his actions was, as you may imagine, a source of great annoyance to him, but still he remained firm in his determination, and not all the threats, the persuasions, or the remonstrances of the Count de Clairville could move him. But an event was now about to occur as awful as it was unexpected, and which was not only the means of preventing the marriage from taking place, but was also productive of the most important results.

"I believe I have before given you to understand that my mother was the sister of the Count St. Almo, and between her and his wife the most intimate friendship had always existed, for no two individuals could be more assimilated in manners and disposition. It wanted but three days to the time fixed for the union of Antoine and Lestelle to take place, when the Countess St. Almo was taken seriously ill, and the physicians shortly afterwards pronounced her to be in a state of great danger, and, in fact, that unless a speedy and remarkable change took place, they saw no chance of her recovery. This circumstance, of course, caused a postponement of the marriage to an indefinite period, and the hopes of Antoine were again revived. Emilie was also released from confinement, to attend upon the sick couch of her mother, and the lovers had an opportunity of meeting each other again, though they were never permitted to be alone.

"My mother was in constant attendance upon the Countess St. Almo, and for the present took up her residence at the castle. It was at this time that Emilie and her sister, Lestelle, took the opportunity to plead their cause with their mother, with the hope that she would be induced to interpose in their behalf with the Count St. Almo in that solemn moment, and they could not believe it possible that he could remain insensible to her supplications when they were probably so soon to be separated by death; but, alas! in that they were doomed to be disappointed; such was the powerful and extraordinary influence which that monstrous compact had obtained over her reason, that she not only refused to interpose in any way, but also strictly enjoined Emilie and her sister, as they feared her dying curse, to submit without a murmur to that which fate had rendered inevitable."

"Strange infatuation," remarked Florio; "it seems scarcely possible that any person in their rational moments, and with their reasoning faculties about them, could yield to it."

"True," coincided the count, "but believe me, I am not exaggerating in any of the statements I have made to you. You may well imagine the agony of your mother and her sister, Florio, at this result, for they now saw plainly that all hope was at an end, and that all they had to depend upon was the merciful interposition of Providence. As for Antoine, he could scarcely be kept within the bounds of reason, and bitterly did he lament the cruel and unmerciful fate which had attended him and her he so fondly loved. He feared, however, to communicate his thoughts except to me, for he well knew that they could now expect no forbearance from either our father or the Count St. Almo.

"The condition of the Countess St. Almo every day became more alarming, and it was quite evident that her illness must before long terminate fatally. My mother, as I have before stated, never quitted her for a moment from the time when she was first attacked, and had taken up her residence for the present altogether at the castle; but little did we any of us anticipate the extent of the calamity that was about to befall us.

"The Countess St. Almo had now been confined to her bed for more than a week, and every day was looked forward to as her last, for her physician had given up all hopes of her recovery. It was on the night of the day to which I am now about to refer, that myself and Antoine were seated in the parlour of the old chateau, where we had been conversing during the whole of the afternoon, the Count de Clairville being at the castle. My brother was more than usually low-spirited, and he gave himself up entirely to the melancholy fears and forebodings that beset his mind, and of which, I must confess, I greatly partook, though I affected to smile at them, and endeavoured to inspire Antoine with hopes which I felt satisfied, and was far from wishing should be realised. The night was black as pitch, the atmosphere was dense and oppressive, and everything seemed to betoken that something fearful was about to happen.

"Myself and Antoine had been wrapt in silence for a short time, which neither of us seemed disposed to break, and that silence added to the general solemnity which reigned around ; but suddenly a lurid glare shot across the sky, and startled us from the reverie into which we had fallen. At first we imagined it to be lightning, but we were soon convinced, from the broad reflection which quickly spread itself across the heavens in a certain direction, that we were mistaken ; and immense clouds of sparks, and volumes of flames, now proved beyond a doubt that a terrific fire was raging at no great distance. We watched its progress more narrowly, and our apprehensions increased.

"'By Heaven !' exclaimed Antoine, at length, 'it is in the direction of the Castle of St. Almo! Should anything have happened there, and the count, our father, not returned ! My Emilie, my mother!—Good God! these apprehensions, I——'

"'Nay, Antoine,' I remarked, 'do not give way to fears that afterwards may turn out to be entirely groundless.'

"'Groundless, Eugene!' he repeated ; 'oh, no, there is too much reason to believe that my worst surmises are correct. There is no other building for some distance, you are aware, in the direction of the castle, and the devouring element marks out the scene of destruction too vividly to be easily mistaken !'

"Higher and higher the flames shot into the sky, dispersing the darkness which had previously reigned, and rendering every object for some distance around the chateau as clear and distinct as in the broad light of day. In spite of all I affected to the contrary, a deadly sickness came over me, and I was perfectly of the same opinion as Antoine, namely, that the fire was raging at the Castle of St. Almo; but still I was so awe-struck, and so taken by surprise, that I had not the power to move or to give utterance to a word.

"'Why do we remain here thus inactive?' at length said Antoine, 'when our services may be so much needed? Oh, my beloved Emilie!—my unfortunate mother!—my heart misgives me! Come, come, Eugene, it is criminal—it is cruel—it is unnatural for us to remain here longer. Let us alarm the domestics in the chateau, and hasten to the castle ; Heaven only knows how much their service may be required, and it may not yet be too late to rescue from a frightful death those who should be so precious to us.'

"As he thus spoke, he was about to pull the parlour bell violently, when looking across the lawn, we beheld, by the reflection of the conflagration, a man mounted on horseback galloping at a most furious speed towards the chateau. He soon arrived at the door, and dismounting, he was immediately admitted, and ushered into our presence.

"'Now, Andre,' said my brother breathlessly, 'what brings you in such haste ? Tell us the worst at once, and do not keep me in suspense.'

"'Alas, monsieur,' replied Andre, 'I grieve to be the messenger of such melancholy intelligence to you, but a terrific fire is at present raging at the Castle of St. Almo, which threatens its entire destruction.'

"'Good God !' exclaimed Antoine, in a voice of agony it would be impossible to describe, 'my worst fears are realised. But the inmates—Mademoiselle Emilie—my mother—tell me, as you value your life, and would save me from distraction, are they all safe ?'

"'The Count de Clairville, the Count St. Almo, and his daughters were all safe when I left the burning pile,' answered the man; 'but the fire had evidently broken out in the chamber of the dying countess, the Countess de Clairville, your honoured mother, being the only individual in attendance upon her at the time, and the flames had so rapidly gained an ascendancy, that I fear all communication with them was cut off, though the utmost exertions were being used to rescue them.'

"'Gracious Heaven !' cried Antoine, his feelings wound up to the utmost pitch of horror, 'what a frightful calamity is this ! But why do we waste time in talking here, when our services are so much required at the dreadful scene of devastation? Come, Eugene, let us immediately away !'

"I own that I was so completely horror-struck by this fearful and unexpected event, that I scarcely knew what I was about, but the next minute I found myself on horseback by the side of Antoine, and galloping at full speed towards the terrific scene of destruction. The horrors increased the nearer we approached, and numerous individuals were rushing about in a state of the utmost confusion and dismay.

"In a very short time we arrived at the spot, and the scene that presented itself was such as can never be erased from my memory. The fine old castle was enveloped in flames, from the top to the bottom, and so intense was the heat that it was impossible to approach within some distance of it. The roaring of the fire, the hissing of the clouds of sparks as they rushed into the heavens, the noise of the falling ruins, and the shouts of the multitude that had gathered together, rendered the scene doubly awful, and caused the senses to reel for a moment or two in confusion.

"A small group of persons at a short distance attracted our attention, and hastening towards it, we beheld the Count St. Almo and our father supporting the inanimate forms of Emilie and Lestelle in their arms, while they seemed to be in scarcely better condition themselves. Antoine and I myself rushed forward and threw ourselves at their feet, but we were too much agitated to speak, while they gazed upon us with looks of vacant horror. It needed no words to tell their dreadful tale; our unfortunate mother and the Countess St. Almo had both perished in the flames, it being impossible to reach them or to render the least assistance, the chamber in which they were being situated in one of the upper stories of the castle, and where it was supposed the fearful calamity had by some means originated.

"All attempts to stop the progress of the devouring element, it was evident, would be vain; the work of destruction was rapidly proceeding, and in a very short time it was clear that there would be nothing left of that once noble pile of buildings but a heap of smoking ruins.

"By this time a vehicle was procured, but it was with great difficulty, after we had placed the insensible forms of Emilie and Lestelle in it, that we could persuade our father and the Count St. Almo to follow. In the most frantic and piteous manner they called upon the names of their unfortunate and ill-fated wives, and bitterly reproached those around for not rescuing them, though it was too painfully evident that any such attempt would be madness and perfectly hopeless. However, we at length persuaded them to enter the carriage, and then following ourselves, with feelings of the utmost agony, and the most inexpressible horror, we were driven in the direction of the chateau.

"I should fail were I to attempt to give anything like an adequate description of the scene which followed this frightful calamity; our senses were all completely bound up in horror, and we were totally incapable of imparting the least consolation to each other under so awful a visitation. Emilie and her sister were conveyed to a chamber, and every means immediately adopted towards their recovery; but we almost feared what effect the terrific shock might have upon their feelings when they should be restored to their senses.

"It was some time ere we could any of us sufficiently compose ourselves to speak; but at last Antoine observed—

"'Oh, God! what a terrible visitation of Thy wrath is this! My poor mother—the unfortunate Countess St. Almo, to meet with such a terrible fate as this!'

"'It surely cannot be!' exclaimed the Count St. Almo, suddenly starting from his lethargy, and staring vacantly around him; 'it can only be some hideous dream. Oh! my beloved wife, my poor sister, Henriette! and have you, indeed, perished thus?—Could no friendly hand be stretched forth to save you?—Ah! no; I remember, now, it was impossible; the flames were raging with terrific fury up every passage and staircase which led to the chamber of death. But my children, where are they?'

"'Emilie and Lestelle are safe, my lord,' answered Antoine.

"'Thank Heaven for that!' ejaculated the count, clasping his hands together. He then relapsed into silence, and seemed to be completely overwhelmed by the intensity of his agony. As for our father, he appeared to be quite stupified with the horror of the event, and could only give utterance at intervals to broken and incoherent sentences.

"It would be impossible to describe the agony of mind we all endured on that awful night; never can it be eradicated from my memory; and frequently has it haunted me in my visions since. We could none of think of retiring to rest, but continued together, vainly endeavouring to impart consolation to each other.

"How the fire occurred we had never any means of ascertaining, though it was evident that it took place in the sick chamber, the first alarm being given by the domestics who resided in that wing of the castle; but so rapid was the progress of the flames that all communication with that apartment, as I have before stated, was immediately cut off.

"Emilie and her sister were restored to sensibility; but, as may be imagined, so great was the shock which their feelings had sustained that they were unable to leave their chamber for a day or two afterwards, and, in fact, the fearful event cast a gloom of despondency over every one.

"As the morning approached, the fire was subdued, but not until a great portion of the castle was laid in ruins, destroying valuable property to an immense amount, and thus compelling the Count St. Almo and his daughter, for the present, to take up their residence at the chateau.

"When the ruins were sufficiently cooled, a search was made for the bodies of the unfortunate ladies, and their blackened remains were found, so frightfully burned and disfigured that it was impossible to recognise them. Let me pass over this frightful part of my narrative as quickly as possible. The Countess St. Almo and our mother were both interred in one tomb with due solemnity, and a monument was erected to their memory recording the particulars of their dreadful and untimely fate.

"It was some time ere we could any of us recover the least tranquillity after this awful shock, and the Count St. Almo, in particular, was inconsolable for his loss, he being devotedly attached to his wife. Our father, in fact, was the first to gain his composure; for, as I have before intimated, no great amount of affection had ever existed between him and my unfortunate mother; their union having been one of compulsion and not of love.

"Of course this event caused the marriage of my brother and Lestelle to be postponed for an indefinite period; it seemed, indeed, as if Heaven were opposed to it, and allusion was never so much as made to it. Emilie, Antoine, and myself were allowed full intercourse with each other, and the hopes of the lovers revived. I watched them narrowly, and with jealous eyes, and I never allowed them to be alone any more than I could possibly help. All my guilty resolutions were revived in full strength, and every look, every word of affection they interchanged with each other was poison to my soul. I saw now the necessity more than ever of proceeding with the utmost caution in my designs, but I was fully determined not to be foiled, even at all hazards.

"Any one would have imagined that the frightful circumstance I have just related would entirely have changed the determination of the Count St. Almo and our father, and that they would no longer have urged a marriage that could not be productive of anything but the greatest misery to those concerned; but it did not do so; in a few months the Castle of St. Almo was restored, and the count and his daughters removed to it. The same restrictions as before were put upon myself and Antoine; it was seldom that we were permitted to see Emilie, and never alone, and once more the day was fixed for the marriage of my brother and Lestelle to take place, and preparations were made for it accordingly; therefore, as you may suppose, the anguish of Antoine and Emilie was renewed with tenfold force. In vain they remonstrated and supplicated their parents; they could make not the least impression in their favour upon them, and, in fact, only met with reproaches and threats in return. I was the only adviser and confident of my brother, and with the most consummate skill and deliberate villany did I play the hypocrite towards him, for he believed me all that was good, and generous, and honourable, while at the same time I was plotting the misery and destruction of himself and her on whom his affections were so firmly, so unmovably fixed. Notwithstanding the apparent resolution and the resistance of Antoine, I imagined that he would, when the moment of trial arrived, never be able to meet the consequences that would follow his disobedience, but would be compelled to yield and once united to Lestelle, all his hopes of Emilie would be at an end, and then there would be every opportunity for me to carrry my villanous schemes into effect. I exulted at this thought, and looked forward to the future with the brightest prospects of success. Heartless miscreant that I was, nothing could move me from my infamous purpose; no sense of shame or compunction could enter my guilty soul.

"Time wore rapidly away, and it now wanted only a month to the day on which the marriage was appointed to be solemnised. There were vast preparations making at the chateau and the Castle of St. Almo, and Antoine and Emilie watched them with sad and revolting hearts; but I little imagined the even more serious thoughts that were passing in their minds. They had ceased to expostulate with, or to appeal to their parents, for they saw that it was entirely useless, and Lestelle now ceased to murmur at the harsh decree which was so repugnant to her feelings, though despair and misery were settled upon her heart. This made the Count St. Almo and my father imagine that they had triumphed over their scruples, and they looked forward to the union with the most sanguine expectations. They relaxed considerably in the restriction they had placed upon the lovers, and thus they had frequent opportunities of communicating their thoughts to each other; but I watched them with the same jealous and suspicious eye that I had done before, and would not suffer them to enjoy each other's society alone any more than I could help, or without appearing impertinent and intrusive. But, in spite of all my artifices, they managed to deceive me, as you will find presently.

"I had been staying for a few days at the chateau, and one morning my father and myself were seated at an early hour in the library, conversing. My brother had not yet made his appearance, nor had I seen him since an early hour the previous evening, when I noticed nothing whatever unusual in his manners. There was nothing, however, remarkable in this, for he was in the habit of taking early walks before breakfast, and that hour had not yet arrived.

"We were suddenly, however, interrupted by the entrance of a servant, who informed us that the Count St. Almo was waiting in the parlour, and wished to see us immediately on business of the utmost importance. My fears and suspicions were aroused, but I did not mention them to my father, but accompanied him to the parlour, where we found the Count St. Almo hurriedly pacing the room in a state of the greatest excitement.

"'My lord,' said my father, 'to what are we indebted for the honour of this early visit?

You look agitated; I hope nothing serious has happened?'

"'Where is Antoine?' demanded the count, hastily.

"'He has not yet made his appearance,' returned the Count de Clairville; 'but why do you put that question so eagerly?'

"'We are duped, we are deceived, betrayed!' exclaimed the Count St. Almo, passionately. 'Emilie—'

"Ah! what of her?' inquired myself and my father in a breath, and the whole truth in a moment flashed upon my mind.

"'The disobedient, obstinate, headstrong girl!' exclaimed the count, 'she is gone, fled, left the castle!'

"'Left the castle?' said my father, starting.

"'Yes,' replied the count, 'and my bitterest curses go with her, for she is no longer child of mine!'

"'Calm your feelings, my dear friend,' said my father, 'and explain; for your communication has so taken me by surprise, that I can scarcely believe the evidence of my ears.'

"'The whole disgusting affair is soon explained,' answered the Count St. Almo; 'Emilie not making her appearance at her usual hour this morning, a servant was sent to her chamber, when she found the room door standing wide open, Emilie not there, and the appearance of the bed showed that she had not slept in it on the previous night. The disappearance of her jewels, and the principal portion of her wardrobe, prove beyond a doubt that she has eloped.'

"'Is it possible?' ejaculated my father, while I could with difficulty conceal the rage and disappointment under which I laboured.

"'It is no less possible than it is true,' replied the Count St. Almo; 'but to be thus duped, and my authority set at defiance by an obstinate girl! Oh, I will not rest until I have had the most ample vengeance. But where is Antoine?'

"'I am not certain whether he has left his chamber yet,' answered my father; 'though it is his usual custom to take a walk before breakfast; but as you seem anxious, and suspect that something of a serious nature has indeed happened, I will despatch a domestic to him immediately. Should your lordship's apprehensions prove to be correct, may the heaviest malediction that can descend upon their heads, pursue the fugitives to destruction.'

"My father now summoned a domestic into his presence and ordered him to desire his son to come to him without delay. During the brief period that he was absent, the excitement and agitation of the Count St. Almo increased, whilst I awaited the result of this event with the greatest impatience; though I could not but apprehend the worst.

"We were not long kept in suspense, for the domestic returned and informed us that Antoine was not in his chamber, and, moreover, it was quite clear that the bed had not been slept in at all on the previous night.

"'Confusion!' cried my father in furious accents, 'it is, then, too evident that they have thus foiled us in our designs. And have they then thus presumed to set our authority at defiance? Rash and headstrong as they are, they will have bitter cause to repent this. But be the consequences upon their own heads. From this moment I discard Antoine from my breast; and though he may be exposed to the greatest poverty and misery, I swear by all my hopes that he shall neither meet with assistance nor sympathy from me. Rash idiot! what does he expect will become of him, friendless as he now is? And into what bitter misery has he plunged her whom he professes to love!'

"'To be thus deceived and defied,' remarked the Count St. Almo, passionately; 'by Heaven! it is almost too much for human patience to endure. Eugene,' he added, looking at me with an expression of suspicion; 'were you not aware of their guilty designs, since in you I know, they placed the most implicit confidence?'

"'My lord,' I answered, and with the utmost sincerity, too, 'if you have suffered such surmises to enter your breast, you do me wrong. I knew nothing of their intentions, though I was fully aware that they were resolved to oppose your will to the utmost of their power. But we waste that time which should be employed in pursuit. If we act promptly it may not yet be too late to prevent that marriage from taking place which they too probably have in contemplation.'

"'Alas!' returned the Count St. Almo, 'where can we pursue them? How form the least idea as to whither they have shaped their course?—May eternal curses pursue them, I say again, and every misery overtake them for this daring act of disobedience!'

"Thus the Count St. Almo and my father continued in the same state of agitation and excitement for some time, while the rage and disappointment which filled my breast you may readily picture to your imagination. But at length we all repaired to the chamber of Antoine, and examined it minutely, with the hope of being able to discover some clue to the place whither he had gone, but without the least success, though we saw sufficient in the room to convince us, if we could possibly have entertained any further doubt upon the subject, that Antoine and Emilie had indeed eloped together, and that as their plans had in all probability been preconcerted for some time, no doubt that ere this they were indissolubly united, and, therefore, all the wishes of their parents were completely frustrated The servants were all closely interrogated upon the subject, but they could give no information whatever, as they had seen nothing of my brother after he had retired to his chamber the previous night. The servants at the castle were in the same state of ignorance as regarded Emilie, and Lestelle appeared to be as much astonished as any one, but tried to abate the wrath of her father, and to move him to pity and forbearance towards her sister. Her remonstrances, however, had no other effect upon him than to increase his indignation, and again and again he invoked curses upon the head of the unfortunate girl who had dared to act in opposition to his will, and vowed if ever the opportunity should present itself, to pursue her with his utmost vengeance.

"The excitement which this event created amongst the domestics at the castle and the chateau, was, as might have been expected, of the most intense description; but it was evident to be seen that every one deeply sympathised with the fugitives, and strongly deprecated the tyrannical and unreasonable conduct of my father and the Count St. Almo, and were gratified to think that they were defeated in their designs.

"'And thus,' remarked my father, and the expression of his features showed at once the rage and disappointment which predominated in his breast, 'the compact which has for so many years existed in our families has been set at defiance by those who had a right to yield implicit obedience to our will. But they shall have to pay dearly for their daring, and will have bitter cause to repent it when it is too late. Henceforth they will become wretched outcasts and beggars in the world. You, my lord, I presume, can never forgive your daughter, for the conduct she has thus thought proper to pursue?'

"'Forgive her!' replied the count, and his countenance became more flushed than ever with anger; 'by all my hopes never. From this moment she is an alien from my breast, and it will be well for her if she does not again venture to cross my path. My lord, we have acted with too much forbearance in this matter altogether; had we not yielded to persuasion and delayed the union of Antoine and Lestelle, this could never have happened.'

"'Well,' returned my father, 'we have, I fear, acted imprudently, but it is too late to regret it now. When I reflect upon the manner in which we have been duped and defeated, my patience is quite exhausted, and were Antoine again to cross my path I should forget that my blood flows within his veins, and wreak upon his head the full measure of my most terrible vengeance.'

"These observations afforded me the ut- most satisfaction, though I thought it would be the more prudent for me to continue to act the hypocrite in order that I might drown their suspicions, and the better to forward my own guilty designs, and I therefore said—

"'Of course, my lord, I am not going to attempt to defend the conduct of my brother in this unfortunate affair; but still I trust that you will not come to any hasty determination, but that a reconciliation may be effected between——'

"'A reconciliation!' he interrupted, impatiently; 'know you what you say, Eugene? And think you that a reconciliation can ever be effected between me and that headstrong, obstinate boy, who has dared to set all my authority at defiance? Bah! the thought is preposterous. I tell you again, that henceforth he is a stranger to me. He well knew what the consequences of his disobedience would be, and it is now useless for him to murmur at them. And mark my words, Eugene: should you ever discover the place of his concealment, I charge you, as you fear my utmost wrath, not to sympathise with him, or to render him the least assistance. Do you mark me?'

"'My lord,' I answered, 'it is my duty to obey you, and you will, I trust, have no cause to complain of me. But at the same time, I would again implore of you not to do anything hastily, and which you might afterwards have cause to regret.'

"'Eugene,' he replied, haughtily and impatiently, 'I need not your advice upon a subject on which I can much better use my own judgment and discretion. Retire! The Count St. Almo and myself would be alone!'

"I bowed and quitted the room, for I was glad to be left to the undisturbed indulgence of my own reflections, and hastening to my own apartment, I gave myself up entirely to the various and conflicting thoughts which crowded upon my brain.

"'I am defeated,' I muttered to myself, as I paced the room to and fro in a state of the greatest agitation; 'by this time the beauteous Emilie has doubtless become the wife of Antoine, and he has thus obtained a triumph over me which I was little prepared for. But I will have revenge; yes, and that much sooner than he could well anticipate, for he believes me to be his most zealous friend, and could never for a moment suspect the base and unnatural designs I have all along had against the happiness of himself and Emilie. But to think that he should possess that fair being whose transcendent charms have so inflamed my passions! The thought is madness! But no matter: in spite of all that has taken place, I will not rest until I have at least made her yield to my wishes. They will not be able to withstand the horrors of poverty and misery, and I will make her compliance with my desires the price of my assistance, notwithstanding the stern injunctions of my father. Oh, Emilie, thou art too beauteous a prize for me to abandon all thoughts of you. But whither have they gone? Shall I ever be able to discover them? Yes, doubtless Antoine will take the earliest opportunity of making me acquainted with the place where they are concealed, for he will much need my counsel and advice, in which he

EUGENE, DISGUISED, GAZING THROUGH THE COTTAGE WINDOW ON EMILIE.

places so much confidence, and then I will lose no time in putting my well-laid schemes into effect.'

"Thus I continued to reflect for some time longer, but notwithstanding all my efforts to the contrary, I could not help feeling fearful and uneasy at the elopement of my brother and Emilie, and regretted that I had deferred the execution of my nefarious plot so long, let the consequences have been whatever they might.

"The Count St. Almo and my father remained in deep consultation together for several hours, and when the former took his departure from the chateau, I could see that his excitement had increased, and that he had made up his mind to some desperate and determined course.

"The strictest inquiries had been made during the day for several miles around the neighbourhood, but not the least clue could be obtained as to the route which the lovers had pursued, and everything remained wrapt in the same state of mystery. It was quite evident that all hopes of preventing the secret marriage of Antoine and Emilie was at end, and the rage and disappointment of my father became almost insupportable. To such a state of excitement did he suffer his feelings to carry him, that the servants feared to come near him, and I felt not the least inclination to be in his presence, for I was fearful that I might inadvertently betray myself, and that would be attended with the most disagreeable consequences.

"That night and the following day passed away without our being able to obtain the least intelligence of Antoine and Emilie, and we began to think that they had made up their minds to abandon us altogether, and to leave their future fate in the hands of Providence; but still I was resolved to leave no means untried to discover them, and I flattered myself that by perseverance I should not fail to succeed, though I felt surprised that Antoine should not have made a confidant of me; and sometimes I was inclined to think he either had begun to doubt my sincerity, or else that Emilie had made him acquainted with what had taken place between us on a former occasion. Notwithstanding the solemn promise I had exacted from her, I could not believe that she could ever forget the boldness of my advances, or could continue to view me with the same confidence and friendship that she had done before, and that idea filled me with numerous doubts and apprehensions.

"'But should she even have forfeited her word and revealed everything,' I muttered to myself, 'it shall not save her from my power; the disgust and vengeance of my brother I have no cause to fear, for he is powerless to harm me; and should he attempt to do so, it can only recoil upon himself. They are both discarded by their parents, and, therefore, it is not likely that any conduct I may think proper to pursue towards them would meet with the censure of my father and the Count St. Almo. No, I have nothing to fear in that respect, and, therefore, I will proceed boldly and determinedly, and I have no doubt but that in the end I shall be successful.'

"These diabolical feelings hourly grew upon me, and nothing could awaken me to a sense of shame or remorse; every natural feeling was stifled in my breast; the elopement of my brother and Emilie only served to inflame my evil passions, and I was anxious not only to gratify my desires, but likewise the deadly feeling of revenge that was now kindled within my bosom. Do you not blush, my friends, to hear me make this guilty acknowledgment? But I have undertaken to give a full disclosure of my errors, and whatever may be the feelings of hatred, contempt, and disgust you may entertain towards me, I am determined not to shrink from the task.

"On the third day after the disappearance of the lovers, while the Count de Clairville, the Count St. Almo, and myself, were seated in the library of the chateau, conversing on all the stirring events that had so recently taken place, one of the male domestics suddenly entered the room with a couple of letters in his hand, one of which was for my father, and the other for the Count St. Almo, and it needed but a glance at the characters of the superscription of each to tell who they were from. We all immediately started to our feet, and my father hastily demanded—

"'Who brought these letters?—and why did you not usher him immediately into our presence?'

"'My lord,' replied the domestic, 'they were brought here by a person on horseback, whom I do not remember to have ever seen before; he delivered them into my hands without uttering a word, and before I had time to interrogate him, he rode off with all expedition, and was speedily out of sight.'

"'Confusion!' exclaimed the Count St. Almo, 'this is unfortunate. Had the fellow been detained we might probably have elicited from him the place where the fugitives are concealed. But what can they have to say to us? What excuse can they make for their daring and disobedient conduct?'

"They now opened the letters, and I waited most anxiously to know the contents. When they had hastily perused them, they both gave utterance to a bitter and simultaneous oath, and throwing them towards me, they retired to the farther end of the room, where they entered into earnest conversation together, and I could see by there gestures that they were in a state of much excitement.

"I cast my eyes hastily over the contents of the two epistles, and read them with feelings of no small agitation and rage. They were both brief, and contained no address, or the least clue to the place to where they had retired. That from my brother merely contained the following words, evidently written with a trembling hand—

"'My lord, my father,—For such I must still call you, though you may have discarded me from your breast, and look upon me with hatred—I have been compelled to yield that to unconquerable love which I could not do to duty, (as you thought proper to interpret the word). Emilie is now my wife, and although the course we have been compelled to adopt may be productive of much misery and anguish to us both, I will still place my trust in Providence to ultimately remove us from the difficulties by which we are at present surrounded. May I fervently hope that time will move the heart of yourself and the Count St. Almo towards us in mercy, and that we may yet receive your forgiveness? In the meantime, believe me to be your affectionate but unfortunate son,   'ANTOINE.'

" The following were the contents of Emilie's epistle :—

" ' My honoured father,—Surely you cannot view with an unnatural feeling of revenge that poor child who has ever been to you all that love and reverence could command. You knew well the sentiments of my heart; I never for an instant attempted to disguise them from you; the object which had inspired those sentiments was worthy of me, and why, then, did you oppose that mutual love which heaven seemed to sanction, and thus compel me to that step I would fain have avoided? But the deed is done, past recall; Antoine is my husband, and while I am convinced of the sincerity of his love, I cannot regret it. For the love of Heaven, my lord, let reason and humanity guide you in your decision, and extend your pardon to your affectionate daughter,

" ' EMILIE DE CLAIRVILLE.'

" It is, I presume, perfectly needless for me to attempt to describe our feelings on the perusal of these letters. For my own part, my rage was most unbounded. I felt my pride mortified; I considered myself insulted and treated with contempt, inasmuch as neither my brother nor Emilie had made the slightest allusion to my name, and I could not help muttering a bitter curse between my teeth, while at the same time I secretly vowed to have a terrible revenge at the first opportunity that presented itself.

" ' Forgive them! presumptuous wretches!' cried the Count St. Almo, passionately; ' by all my hopes, never! Let them endure the greatest misery, it will be but a fitting punishment for the act of disobedience of which they have been guilty. May they experience all the horrors of the most abject poverty and privation, they shall have no sympathy from me. Even though I saw them perishing of hunger, it should not excite one feeling of pity in my breast. Again I say, may my bitterest curses light upon their heads! As for Emilie, should she ever again dare to cross my path, I will have a terrible revenge.'

" ' Ay,' remarked my father, in the same unnatural tones of indignation; ' and by every power I swear that should I ever be able to discover the place where he is concealed, I will wreak upon him the full weigh of my wrath. Fit inmate is he for the dungeon of the chateau, and should I once be enabled to place him there, he shall never more behold the light of day.'

" These observations opened a new idea to my mind, and it was not without the greatest difficulty I could conceal the deadly feelings of hatred and revenge it engendered. Could Antoine be trepanned, waylaid, and incarcerated in that frightful place, Emilie would have no opportunity of discovering him, and she would then be entirely at my mercy, and nothing whatever could prevent the accomplishment of my wishes. I resolved to leave no means untried to discover the place of his present retreat, and that once effected, he might easily be led into the snare I had laid for him. Another thing, I no longer saw any necessity for concealing my real sentiments from the Count St. Almo and my father, and so far from their disapproving of them, I felt convinced they would do all to aid me in my nefarious and unnatural designs, as it would at once gratify their own feelings of revenge.

" ' And what, candidly, think you of this unfortunate business, Eugene?' inquired my father, after a pause; ' surely you cannot now pretend to defend the conduct of Antoine?'

" ' No, my lord,' I answered, ' it is impossible that I can approve of this act of disobedience on the part of my brother, although I have endeavoured to prevail upon you to treat him with all possible indulgence. I had indeed hoped that Emilie, too, could have subdued her passion for Antoine, for no one could possibly feel more regret that they should ever entertain such sentiments towards each other than myself.'

" ' What mean you, Eugene?' demanded my father, with a look of surprise; ' your words seem to imply something which I do not exactly understand.'

" ' I almost hesitate to explain to you my meaning, my father, and you, Count St. Almo,' I replied, ' lest you should deem me bold and presumptuous for encouraging the thoughts I have, and may heap upon me your reproaches.'

" ' Be more explicit, Eugene,' said the Count St. Almo; ' I do not believe that you can have entertained any ideas that should deserve our reprobation."

" ' Thus encouraged, my lord,' I remarked, ' it emboldens me to speak, and I will now reveal a secret which probably I have too long kept confined to my own breast. What will you think of me or say to me when I inform you that the beauteous Emilie has made an impression upon my heart, that, notwithstanding her clandestine marriage with Antoine, nothing whatever can eradicate?'

" ' How! is it possible, Eugene?' said the

two noblemen in a breath, and looking at me with increased amazement.

"'I speak the truth, my lords,' I returned, 'whether it must meet with your displeasure or not. I repeat, that I have long loved—nay, worshipped the charming Emilie, and those sentiments, I am convinced, must ever remain unchanged, although she is now the wife of another.'

"'And yet you have always appeared to espouse their cause,' remarked my father.

"''Tis true,' I answered; 'and there I must plead guilty to having acted the part of the hypocrite; for I feared that I might offend yourself and his lordship, here, had I acknowledged the truth.'

"'Mistaken idea,' said the Count St. Almo; 'had the count, your father, and myself, have been acquainted with the secret of your heart, after the death of your wife, my poor Marie, I am certain that we should not only have approved of and given you every encouragement to your passion, but have forced Emilie to yield, for that would have prevented all the mischief that has now taken place.'

"'Most undoubtedly it would have done so,' coincided my father, 'and Antoine, seeing then that all his hopes of Emilie were annihilated, would have yielded to our wishes, and thus every obstacle would have been readily surmounted. Oh, why did you keep yourself so reserved, Eugene?'

"'I have stated my reasons to you, my lord, for doing so,' I replied; 'but I now sincerly regret it.'

"'But have you ever confessed to Emilie the sentiments you entertain towards her?' asked the Count St. Almo.

"'I have, my lord,' I returned.

"'And she rejected your vows?'

"'She did.'

"'And was Antoine ever aware that you loved her?' interrogated my father.

"'Not that I am aware of,' I answered; 'affecting to regret that I had made the acknowledgment to her, I exacted a solemn promise from her that she would never reveal the circumstance to my brother; but the silence they have maintained in these letters respecting me, leads me to suspect that she has broken that promise, now that she has become his wife.'

"'What is to be done?' said St. Almo, after another pause; 'oh, most happy should I have been could a union have been effected between you and Emilie, after the death of Marie. But could we succeed in discovering them, a separation must by some means be brought about; for I am determined that they shall never continue to live together. Emily is not yet of age, and, therefore, the union in illegal.''

"Monstrous!" observed Massaroni; "I never heard of such unnatural conduct in a parent before."

"True, signor," observed the Count de Clairville; "but what must I have been that I could exult at the thought of the approbation which the Count St. Almo and my father bestowed upon my unholy passion? Their observations had inspired me with fresh courage and resolution, and I made up my mind to lose no time in endeavouring to trace them to the place of their concealment. I could not help thinking that Antoine would yet make me acquainted, in confidence, where they were, for they would much need my counsel and advice; and then they would be completely in my power, and my ultimate triumph, both as regarded the gratification of my revenge and my diabolical wishes, would be certain.

"But in that idea I was mistaken; day after day, and week after week vanished, and still we heard nothing more from, nor could we gain the least information of, my brother and Emilie, and we began to despair that we ever should.

"Three months had now elapsed, and nothing occurred to solve the mystery; Lestelle had been permitted to follow the bent of her inclination and to retire into a convent, and the Count St. Almo and my father gave free indulgence to the sullen mood that had come over them, being almost constantly together, and seldom mingling in society. They scarcely ever mentioned the names of Antoine and Emilie, and it would almost seem as if they had banished them from their memory altogether: But not so had I. I daily became more impatient, and had my agents employed in all parts of the country to endeavour to track their footsteps, but without success. I began to think that something serious had happened to them, for I was well convinced that what little property they had had in their possession when they absconded must by this time be nearly, if not altogether exhausted, and how were they then to live, friendless as they were, and unfitted as they were to follow any employment, if even they could obtain it?

"Several more months passed away, and still no light was thrown on the matter; but an accident now occurred which was calculated to divert our thoughts for awhile from the subject. The Count St. Almo was thrown from his horse in riding from the chateau to his castle, and so seriously injured that he only survived a few hours. This circumstance was likely to work a considerable change in our affairs, though I considered that it would be to my advantage, for the count might have been some impediment in the way of the gratification of my designs against Emilie, notwithstanding the sentiments he had expressed upon the subject, and the Count de Clairville, I was well convinced, would have no such delicate scruples upon the subject.

"The title of the Count St. Almo had now become extinct, but I found to my surprise that he had made a will in which he had bequeathed to me the whole of his large property, whilst to the unfortunate Emilie and my brother he had not left a single fraction, nor even so much as mentioned their names. Thus did he carry his revenge and animosity to the grave, and rendered my guilty power over my intended victims tenfold

"'I now determined to leave home for awhile, and to travel to different parts of the country with the hope that accident would at last guide me to the place of Antoine and Emilie's concealment, and in which case I resolved that the wishes I had so long in contemplation should be accomplished at all hazards, and without delay.

"I visited all the most secluded spots where I thought they were most likely to go, and made the strictest inquiries on the road, but without being able to ascertain anything that was at all calculated to gratify my hopes, and I was about to give up the attempt in despair, when an accident occurred which discovered to me all that I wished when least expected.

"I was accompanied in my travels by only two faithful attendants, and one night we were overtaken by a violent storm in the midst of a deep and gloomy forest. We urged on our way with all the speed we could, in the hope of meeting with some shelter, but there did not appear to be much chance of that, and we suddenly paused and consulted what was best to be done.

"It was too far to return to the town we had recently quitted, and now looking around us, it became quite evident that we had wandered from the right track in the darkness of the night, and the confusion that the storm had naturally created, and had lost our way. This discovery was most vexatious, and we knew not what do, and we could not see any signs of a human being who might direct us right. There seemed to be no other prospect for us than to ramble about the forest till daylight, and, consequently, our situation, as you may very well imagine, was of the most unpleasant description. However, knowing that it was of no use for us to remain where we were, we walked on, several times shouting aloud, in the hope that our voices might reach the ears of some individual who might be travelling near the same dismal spot.

"Breaking through a deep cluster of trees, we came upon a more open space, and looking eagerly around us, one of my attendants suddenly exclaimed—

"'Ah, my lord—look! Do you not observe that light glimmering in the distance?'

"I did look anxiously in the direction whither he pointed, and then beheld a faint light glimmering, as he said; but it was at a great distance, and while I was still engaged in watching it, it disappeared, and all was again involved in complete darkness.

"'That light proceeded from a human habitation, my lord,' said my domestic; 'let us make haste towards it as quick as we can, and no doubt we shall be enabled to obtain the temporary shelter we seek.'

"'It is a strange, wild place for anyone to choose for a dwelling,' I observed; 'but come, let us, at any rate, hasten towards the place from whence it seemed to proceed.'

"We increased our speed accordingly, and we had not proceeded far when we again beheld the light, and perceived that we were approaching it nearer, and we had now but little or no doubt that it did proceed from a human dwelling. In about ten minutes we came up to it, and found it to be a commodious-looking cottage, and that it presented a more comfortable looking aspect than might have been expected in such a place.

The light we had seen proceeded from the window of a room up-stairs; and opening a small gate, we knocked loudly at the door. In a short time the casement was gently raised, and a man protruding his head, inquired who was there. The voice sounded familiar to my ears, but without any hesitation, I replied—

"'We are travellers, my good friend, who are benighted in this forest, and seek a temporary shelter from the storm. We will reward you well for your kindness and hospitality.'

"The casement was closed again in an instant, the man not returning any answer, and I began to fear that he had declined to admit us; but I was not long kept in suspense, for in a few minutes we heard some one descending the stairs, the door was opened, and an old man appered; but no sooner did he behold me, than he uttered a mingled exclamation of astonishment and alarm, and darted back into the parlour of the cottage. I quickly followed him, raised the lamp he had carried, and looked narrowly in his features, but my astonishment you may imagine was as great as his own, when I recognised in him old Gervoise, who had been for many years in the service of my father, and who had only quitted it a short time before the elopement of my brother and Emilie.

"'Oh, Monsieur Eugene,' said the old man, when he had partially recovered himself from his amazement and trepidation, 'who, in the name of all the saints, would have thought of seeing you?—And yet, I don't know, but it may be fortunate that your footsteps have been guided hither, for——'

"'What do you mean, Gervoise?' I demanded; 'why do you evince so much agitation on beholding me?'

"'Pardon me, Monsieur Eugene,' he faltered out; 'but, but——'

" 'Does this cottage belong to you?' I asked.

" 'No—no—yes, that is to say——' he again stammered hesitatingly.

" 'Know you aught of my brother and—and his wife?'

" 'Alas! alas!' he replied.

" 'Has anything serious happened to them?' I eagerly demanded; 'do not keep me in suspense. Do you know where they have so long concealed themselves?'

" 'Yes, yes, monsieur,' he returned; 'but you will pardon them, will you not, and me, for having befriended them? You will not betray them to the vengeance of the Count de Clairville?'

" 'No, no,' I answered, 'you ought to know me better than that. But where have they secreted themselves? Answer me that question, for my patience is nearly exhausted.'

" 'In this cottage, monsieur,' replied Gervoise.

" 'Ah!' I exclaimed; 'then Fortune has at last guided my footsteps to them. But tell me, are they here at present?'

" 'No, monsieur,' he returned; 'they went to the town in the afternoon, and I suppose that they have been detained by the storm. When that has subsided they will return, and, oh, how astonished they will be to see you.'

" You may imagine my feelings of exultation at this sudden and unexpected discovery, and for some minutes I continued wrapt in deep thought.

" 'But what is the reason that my brother never communicated to me where he was?' I demanded at length.

" 'Why, monsieur,' answered Gervoise, ' perhaps he was wrong in not doing so; but he was fearful that your father might discover it, and he therefore thought it was better to leave your meeting to chance.'

" 'And how have they existed all this time?' I demanded.

" 'Why, monsieur,' answered the old man, 'you know that they had some little property when they absconded, and I had saved a considerable sum during the many years I was in the service of your father, so I would not allow them to touch that.'

" And are they aware of the death of the Count St. Almo?'

" 'Oh, yes, they heard of that fatal calamity soon after it happened,' replied Gervoise, 'and grieved enough poor lady Emilie was about it. The count, I am afraid, never forgave his unfortunate daughter and her husband in his last moments?'

" 'He did not,' I returned, 'and the whole of his property he bequeathed to me.'

" 'Thank God!' ejaculated Gervoise; 'then they will not, at any rate, be left entirely destitute.'

" I returned no answer to this, and the old man busied himself in placing a repast before me; but my mind was too busily occupied with the thoughts that crowded upon it to suffer me to eat; and I awaited with the utmost impatience the return of my brother and Emilie. What would be their surprise on beholding me! I could never be sufficiently grateful for the accident which had guided my footsteps hither, and at the very time when I had nearly given up all hope of ever being able to discover them again. But how could I meet with Emilie, now that I knew her to be the wife of Antoine? Would not my looks betray the feelings of jealousy and disappointment that were passing in my mind? Oh, no! I was determined to exert myself, and to act the hypocrite with all my skill, for on the prudence and artifice of my conduct on this important occasion depended, in a great measure, the success of my plans; and I was fully determined that now I had once more discovered the object of my base and unnatural passions, and my father would be favourable to my plans, even though they might involve her destruction, she should not again escape me.

" I put several more questions to old Gervoise, and he answered me without any further hesitation. From him I gathered many important particulars that I was anxious to know, and which I might not so easily be able to elicit from Antoine; and I treasured them in my memory, resolved to make every use of them in the accomplishment of my purpose.

" I had been at the cottage above an hour, and I began to grow impatient. I had despatched my attendants to another apartment at the back of the cottage, as, of course, I did not wish them to be witnesses of what took place at the meeting between myself and my brother and his wife.

" At length the storm subsided, and shortly afterwards there was a knock at the door, which announced the return of those whom I had so anxiously expected. My heart palpitated with impatience, but Gervoise would have persuaded me to retire to another room, until he had announced to them my unexpected arrival, and prepared them for the meeting, but I could not think of such a thing, and he, therefore, hastened to the door. I heard him mention my name, which was followed by a faint exclamation of astonishment and emotion from Emilie, and the next instant they were in my presence.

" I should fail were I to seek to pourtray in the colours it deserves the scene which followed. Emilie could not speak, and for a few minutes Antoine could only press my hand in silence.

" Emilie was more pale than she formerly was, and her form was somewhat attenuated, while there was a melancholy languor in the expression of her eyes that showed she had lately suffered much from anxiety of mind; but still she was very lovely, and as I gazed upon her, I felt all my guilty passions revive with tenfold force, while envy, hatred, and a spirit of revenge occupied my mind towards my brother.

" 'Oh, Eugene,' at length he ejaculated, 'and do we then again meet? It will be a most invaluable blessing to myself and my dear Emilie to have the benefit of your advice.'

" These observations satisfied me, for they proved to me that my suspicions were unfounded as regarded Emilie having revealed to him what had taken place between myself and her in the garden of the castle, and I was, therefore, inspired with renewed confidence.

" 'Accident has brought me to the place of your retreat, Antoine,' I at last replied; 'but surely you have not treated me well in acting with so much secrecy towards me. What have I done to forfeit your confidence?'

" 'Pardon me, Eugene,' he answered, 'but I meant not to offend you, neither did I entertain a thought or wish to the prejudice of the sincerity of your friendship. At some future period I intended to have made you acquainted with the place of our concealment, and all that has happened to us since we last met; but I wished to wait awhile in hopes that our father would relent; and I thought that in the meantime, if you were to know where to find me, it might lead to some discovery that probably would involve you in trouble. But my father—oh, tell me, Eugene, have not the sentiments he formerly entertained towards me and my Emilie undergone no change?'

" 'They have not, Antoine,' I answered, and I was pleased to see the anguish it caused him; 'and it would be wrong to flatter you with the hope that they ever will. He has discarded you from his breast altogether, and it would be madness to attempt to persuade him to alter his determination.'

" 'Alas!' sighed Antoine, 'I have never deserved this unnatural severity at his hands. It is not for myself that I so much care, but for the sake of that fair and innocent being who has linked her fate with mine, and will thus be compelled to become a partaker of my sorrows.'

" 'Nay, my Antoine,' said his wife, fixing upon him a look of the most unbounded affection,' do not suffer any thought of me to torture your mind. Providence, I feel assured, will yet watch over us, and shield us from any of the dangers and the sorrows that now seem to threaten us. But my poor, misguided father to meet with such a fate, and to breathe his last without pronouncing his forgiveness on my head! That thought tortures me even more than all.'

" 'It was, indeed, a sad thing, Emilie,' I remarked; 'and Heaven knows how ardently and sincerly I pleaded your cause with him, but without the least effect, so strongly had your conduct prejudiced him against yourself and my brother.'

" 'But surely, Eugene,' said the latter, ' you do not condemn the step that I and Emilie have taken?'

" This was a question that greatly perplexed me; but could I have ventured to speak the real sentiments of my mind, I should have found no difficulty in answering it. However, at length I said—

" ' Why, the fact is, Antoine, that I must say I think you acted too precipitately, and that I fairly expected, after the confidence you had professed to repose in me, that you would at least have consulted me previous to your adopting a course which was fraught with so much danger, and which required such due consideration.'

" 'Believe me, Eugene,' he replied, 'it was from no want of confidence in your sincerity, your friendship, and affection as a brother, that I did not do so; but I feared from what you had previously remarked to me, that you would have opposed my designs, and I wished not to enter into any controversy with you upon the subject. The determination of myself and Emilie was fixed; we could not live without each other; there was no time for delay; in a few days our parents had resolved that my marriage with Lestelle should take place, and, consequently, we finally made up our minds to elope without delay, though it was my intention to have informed you of the place of our retreat, as soon as the excitement consequent upon our clandestine marriage should in some degree have abated. This, Eugene, is the only explanation I have to give you, and I trust when you take into consideration all the peculiar circumstances in which we were placed, the many dangers by which we were surrounded, and the irresistible power of the sentiments that existed between us, you will accept it.'

" 'Oh, yes,' remarked Emilie, fixing upon me a look of supplication and confidence which added to the embarrassment and secret chagrin I experienced; 'Eugene, I am certain, is too generous, and sympathises to deeply in our fate, to withdraw his friendship from us on any such grounds, especially when our only reliance for the future is upon him. Say, Eugene, am I mistaken in the opinion I have formed?'

" 'You are not, Emilie,' replied I, with as much appearance of candour and sincerity as I could assume; 'though I cannot attempt to disguise from you the perilous circumstances in which you have placed youreslves, by thus opposing the will of my father and the late Count St. Almo. The latter carried his wrath to his death-bed, and I know too much of the character of the count, my father, to imagine that he will relent. All argument and expostulation, I am afraid, will be lost upon him, though for your sake and that of my brother, I will continue to exert myself to the utmost to effect that desirable object.'

"'Oh, thanks, thanks!' ejaculated Antoine and Emilie, in a breath, and the former then added:—'but you will not desert us, let whatever may be the result of your efforts?'

"'I will not, Antoine,' I returned, 'though the count, our father, has threatened me with his eternal wrath should he find that I am rendering you any assistance.'

"'This is indeed most kind,' said my brother, again clasping my hand, and pressing it to his heart; 'how shall we ever be able to repay the manifold obligations we are under to you? But do you think it advisable to make our father acquainted with your having accidentally discovered the place of our concealment?'

"'Certainly not,' I answered; 'that would, in all probability, be the means of rendering all the designs I have in contemplation for your welfare abortive.'

"'What, then, do you for the present advise?' he asked.

"'That you remain where you are,' I returned, 'and leave the rest to me. I will visit or communicate with you as frequently as possible, and in the meantime, all the pecuniary assistance you may require from me shall be at your command.'

"Again Antoine and Emilie returned their acknowledgments to me, and I received them with an air that might very well have deceived the most penetrating of individuals; though I need not tell you that my heart was burning with jealousy, and was I more determined than ever, since I had discovered them, to carry out my infamous projects to the fullest extent.

"'Alas!' sighed Emilie, after a pause; 'how does it torture and afflict my mind to think that my father should have retained the same implacable feeling of animosity towards myself and Antoine upon his deathbed. Surely his reasoning faculties must have forsaken him, or he would never have remained so obstinate. Why should he oppose that love which had its origin in the greatest purity of sentiment, and which heaven itself seemed to sanction?'

"'It was unfortunate that he did so, Emilie,' I replied; 'but no doubt he was guided in what he considered to be right according to the compact which binds our families together.'

"'Ah! that fatal, that monstrous compact!' remarked Antoine; 'it is that extravagant and unnatural document which has ever been the curse of all the families of De Clairville and St. Almo. Those who entered into it at the time, must have had some private and sinister motives to serve by so doing, or have otherwise been in a state of insanity; and why should we, their descendants, pay the least respect to it, to the sacrifice of our own happiness, and, I must say, our mutual interests? The bare idea is preposterous, and is opposed to every sentiment of justice and reason. But the Count de Clairville, our father, will surely think better of this painful and important business, and notwithstanding all that has taken place, I do not despair of yet being enabled to obtain his forgiveness.'

"'My brother,' I said, 'anxious as you know I am that your wishes should be gratified, I, at the same time, must advise you not to encourage any such hopes, which I have too much reason to believe will be only doomed to be disappointed.'

"'But,' said Antoine, 'when he knows that the deed is done past recall, surely he will not adhere to the terrible and unnatural threats he has held out, should we throw ourselves at his feet and implore his mercy?'

"'Do not contemplate such a thing,' I replied hastily, 'for you can form no conception of the danger of so doing; nor of the awful consequences that might ensue to yourselves.'

"'What mean you?' he demanded, with a look of astonishment.

"'I cannot at present explain myself,' I answered; 'but you will take my advice, will you not, and leave everything to me?'

'I will,' returned Antoine, 'for I know, Eugene, that all you advise, and will ever advise, is for the best, and most gratified am I that Providence has guided your footsteps to the place of my concealment before I made it known to you, since it has happened at the time when I most need your counsel and assistance. Oh, Eugene, did you but know the real intensity of the sentiments I and my beloved Emilie entertain for one another, you would not wonder at the course we have adopted, and which has brought down upon our devoted heads the vengeance of those whom we have always revered, and whose authority we have ever obeyed, when reason, justice, and duty commanded it. You will not desert us, Eugene, let the consequences be whatever they may?'

"'I tell you again, Antoine,' I answered, and at the same time with the greatest difficulty concealing the real feelings that predominated in my guilty breast, 'that I will not; but it is necessary that the greatest precaution should be used, and that you should be guided entirely by me in everything which I may propose, however strange it may appear at the moment.'

'We will,' he observed; 'for very well convinced am I that you would not propose anything which honour and affection did not dictate.'

"'You judge me rightly,' I remarked, in the same hypocritical tone, and inwardly chuckling at the success of my nefarious designs, and the manner in which I had deceived him.

"'Enough,' said Antoine; 'but you will remain here for a few days, until we have further consulted upon and arranged this important matter, will you not?'

"Nothing could be more in unison with my feelings and designs, since I should be near Emilie, and I, therefore, replied in the affirma-

THE SPIRIT OF MARIE APPEARING TO EUGENE.

tive. We then slightly partook of the refreshment that was before us, and after some further conversation, which was not of sufficient importance for me to particularize, Antoine conducted me to my chamber, where we separated for the night.

"When I was left alone, I gave myself up to those feelings of exultation which my unexpected discovery of the retreat of Antoine and his lovely wife naturally excited in my breast, and it was long ere I thought of retiring to my couch. I threw myself on a seat, and for some time pondered upon the course it would be most prudent for me to pursue, now that so glorious an opportunity for the gratification of my diabolical wishes was afforded me, and I was fully resolved that no consideration of the consequences that would be likely to ensue should restrain me; no feelings of compunction should be permitted to obtain a place in my breast. To behold Emilie the wife of my brother, and to perceive that their union had served to increase the love she had before entertained towards him, was poison to my very soul, and goaded me on in the accomplishment of my nefarious designs for the purpose of revenge; and I could not help applauding my own sagacity for the manner in which I had succeeded in deceiving them, and apparently quieting all suspicions that might, from previous circumstances, naturally have been engendered in Emilie's breast. I saw plainly that it would be bad policy on my part to make my father acquainted with the discovery I had made, as he might wish to adopt a course that would interfere with the objects I had in view, if it did not entirely frustrate them, while, at the same time, by maintaining such a secrecy I should be enabled to blind and deceive my brother and his wife as to the real feelings of my father, the more readily prejudice him against them, and thus advance my views. They would, indeed, fall into the snare I had laid for them without the least suspicion, and when they discovered it, it would be too late for them to extricate themselves. Whichever way I directed my attention, the prospect of my success seemed all but certain, my triumph complete; and again I exulted in the deep-laid schemes I had so long formed for the destruction of the happiness of my unsuspecting victims. It is a dark and hideous epoch in my life to look back upon, and I shudder with shame and remorse when I recall it to my memory.

"'Beauteous, but scornful Emilie,' I muttered to myself, as I arose from my seat, and traversed the narrow precincts of my chamber with hasty strides; 'thou art the bride of the man on whom you have bestowed your most ardent affections, but, nevertheless, that shall not prevent me from accomplishing the designs I have formed against you. No, by all my hopes I swear that, let the consequences be whatever they may to myself, thou shall not escape me. The preference thou hast shown to my brother does but goad me on, and I will not rest until my triumph is complete. Situated as you are, I hold you both in my power, and I will not fail to take advantage of the opportunity which is thus affording me of gratifying the designs I have so long encouraged. You may denounce me as an hypocrite, a villain, if you will, but nothing whatever shall stay me in the resolution I have formed;

nothing whatever shall deter me from the completion of that which has so long held a paramount place in my mind. It is for weak fools to tremble and relent: I am not the man."

"Such were the guilty thoughts in which I continued to indulge for some time before I thought of retiring to bed, and when I did, and sleep took possession of my faculties, my dreams were of Emilie. But my narrative has extended to a greater length than I at first anticipated it would, and as the hour is now getting late, and I feel myself rather fatigued, I must claim your patience and indulgence for the conclusion of it till to-morrow."

To this request neither Florio nor the others could, of course, raise any reasonable objection, though they were most anxious to hear the whole of the painful particulars; and after a few observations of no importance, the Count de Clairville and Adolphus D'Aubigny retired, and left Florio and the brigand chief to themselves.

"Well, Massaroni," said Florio, after they had sat together for some time in silence, "what think you of the particulars which the Count de Clairville has related, so far as he has proceeded?"

"He certainly has been most guilty," replied our hero, "but the remorse he now expresses is evidently sincere, and, therefore, I should think you would be inclined to forgive him, notwithstanding the many sufferings to which he subjected your unfortunate parents, and the dark designs he contemplated against them."

"Oh, yes," returned Florio; "Heaven forbid that I should bear any revengeful feelings towards one who is so nearly related to me, especially when he evinces such sincere contrition for the errors of his past life. But when I reflect upon all the troubles it was the hard lot of my ill-fated parents to have to encounter, it is only natural that I should feel the deepest regret, and that I should likewise wish that they had lived to receive that atonement which their misguided relative is now so willing to make. But may Heaven rest their souls; I trust they are better off."

"True, Florio," said Massaroni; "but did not your mother ever hint to you any of the particulars which the Count de Clairville has related?"

"She did not," answered Clairville. "I was very young when she died, and shame would, doubtless, restrain her tongue, though, as my uncle has asserted, she was as innocent as purity itself."

"But she intimated that you had a noble relative whom she believed to be still in existence?"

"She did, though she never mentioned his title."

"And did it never occur to you that you

were connected with the noble house of De Clairville?" asked the brigand chief.

"No," answered Florio, "for the place where I was born, and where I passed my youthful days, was in a remote part of the country, and I had never so much as heard of the family."

"It is strange," observed Massaroni; "but still it was a most fortunate as well as singular accident which brought the Count de Clairville hither, and led to the discovery of your being so nearly related to him; for it has wrought a wonderful change in your prospects, and you may now safely aspire to the hand of the fair Signora Melina, without running the risk of being considered presumptuous, as you are equal by rank; and if your uncle keeps his word, which I do not think he is likely to forfeit, you will also be her equal by fortune."

"But such is the prejudice which the Prince Bianchi entertains towards me," returned Florio, "that I do not believe he will ever give his consent to my becoming the husband of his beauteous niece."

"And if he should refuse," said our hero, "it matters not, as the signora is now removed from his power, and if she loves you as sincerely as I believe she does, after the tyranny and persecution she has experienced from him, she will no longer hesitate."

"Alas! I know not," remarked Florio; "sincere as I know the affection which Melina entertains for me to be, she entertains the most delicate scruples, and would hesitate to act in opposition to her uncle's will, notwithstanding the severity and injustice with which he has behaved towards her."

"Pardon me, Florio," replied the brigand chief, "but I cannot help thinking that this is a false delicacy. However, I feel satisfied that Bianchi will yield that to necessity which he might not be disposed to do from choice, when he finds that your connection with the Count de Clairville is firmly and satisfactorily established."

"You are sanguine, Massaroni."

"And taking all the circumstances into consideration, have I not a right to be so?"

"To your generous and disinterested exertions in my behalf, and those who are so dear to me, I am indebted for everything," observed Florio; "I am afraid that I shall never be able to return the obligation as I ought."

"A truce with compliments, my worthy young friend," returned Massaroni; "for you know full well that they are not to my taste. I am only too happy to think that it has been my good fortune to serve you and others in the manner I have done; and I do not despair of seeing the whole of my wishes accomplished. With all the evidence there is against him of the crimes he has committed in former days,

the Prince Bianchi must succumb, and he will only be too glad to do so, to avoid the exposure that must otherwise take place."

"And his vengeance; can you avoid it, Massaroni?"

"And think you, Clairville," answered the brigand, "that Allesandro Massaroni fears the vengeance of such a man as the Prince Bianchi? Have I not proved often enough that he is powerless to harm me? But it is only a waste of time to talk further upon this subject at present. As the time is getting late, we had better separate for the night."

Florio said no more, and shaking hands with the brigand chief, he took his departure to the cavernous apartment in which he slept.

In the morning Florio took the opportunity of seeing Melina before he again met the Count de Clairville, and he found her most anxious to see him, though he refrained from relating to her any particulars until he had heard the whole of his uncle's narrative; but he told her sufficient to convince her that there could now be no doubt that he was the nephew of that nobleman, and exulted in the thought that as he was now proved to be her equal by birth, it must do away with the principal objections of the Prince Bianchi to their union.

"Oh, Melina," he observed, "never did I feel the value of rank and fortune so much as I do at present, since it may be the means of removing those obstacles to our union that were before placed in our way, though I know full well that it can make no difference in those sentiments you have ever professed towards me."

"Ah, no," replied the gentle Melina, "rank and influence can have no effect upon my heart, Florio; I can never love you less than I do at present, and I am convinced that my Clairville will never be less worthy of it; and even if it be the will of Fate that we shall not be united, no other man can ever supplant you in those pure affections which your merits have inspired in my breast."

"Blessed words!" exclaimed Florio, rapturously embracing the blushing and innocent maiden; "they fall like heavenly music on my senses. May a terrible curse descend upon my head if ever I abuse the sweet confidence you repose in me. But should your uncle remain obstinate, and refuse his consent to our union?"

"He will yield, Florio," answered our heroine; "I feel satisfied that he will be awakened to a full sense of the injustice with which he has treated me, and only be too happy in making all the atonement in his power, by complying with my wishes."

"And should he not do so, dear Melina," said Florio, anxiously, "will you any longer hesitate to become mine?"

"Do not urge that question at present,

Florio," answered Melina; "but wait with patience until we see what decision my uncle will come to. I need not assure you how anxious I am to effect a reconciliation with him; and if I can succeed in doing that, I shall indeed be one of the happiest of human beings."

"Enough, my beloved Melina," exclaimed Florio, "I am satisfied, and for the present will urge you no further. Your observations have inspired me with fresh hopes, and I will look forward to the future with the most sanguine anticipations."

With these words he once more embraced her, and they then separated, and Florio made his way to the cavern in which our hero was seated, and they were shortly afterwards joined by the Count de Clairville and his young friend.

The count appeared much refreshed after his night's rest, and in much better spirits than he had been the day before ; and after they had partaken of the morning meal, he resumed, and concluded his narrative in the following words :

"I should become tedious were I to par-ticularise all that took place during the few days that I remained at the residence of my brother and his wife; let it suffice, that, by the most insidious means, I availed myself of the opportunity to mature my evil designs, without in the least exciting their suspicions of my honesty and sincerity; and on my departure, in order to impress them still more strongly in my favour, I presented Antoine with a considerable sum of money, sufficient to supply their wants for some time, and promised to see them again in a week or two, and in the meantime to correspond with them, and to communicate to them all that took place between me and my father, and to exert myself to the utmost in their behalf, even at the risk of incurring his displeasure, a promise which I need not say it was never my intention to fulfil. Having accomplished more than I had anticipated, I returned home, much sooner than my father had expected, and he eagerly inquired whether I had been able to obtain any information which would be likely to lead to 'a discovery of the place where Antoine and his wife had concealed themselves. To this, of course, I replied in the negative, and he seemed for the moment vexed and disappointed.

"'But why should I trouble myself any more about them?' he said, at length; 'have they not, by their rash, presumptuous, and disobedient conduct, rendered themselves un-worthy of a thought?—But they will be severely punished for it, and will learn to repent it when it is too late.'

"'True, my lord,' I coincided, 'for their limited means will soon be exhausted, and how are they to exist afterwards?'

"'Let them perish!" he replied, with a savage and unnatural look ; 'it is a fit reward for the conduct of which they have been guilty. When poverty in all its terrible forms comes upon them, which assuredly it must, it will bring them to their senses, and they will be glad to come to me and sue for money and relief.'

"'And will you not grant it them, my lord?' I inquired.

"'Eugene,' he replied passionately, 'are you mad to ask me such a question?—By all my hopes, I would not relieve or commiserate them if even I saw them perishing of hunger at my feet. Let them not again cross my path. or I may be tempted to do that which I might afterwards repent. Again I say, may my ever-lasting curses pursue them.'

"His cruel observations afforded me the utmost gratification, though, of course, the better to carry out my plans, I pretended to the contrary, and even ventured to intercede for them ; but finding that it was likely to bring down his indignation upon my head, I thought it was most prudent to desist, and soon afterwards quitted his presence, in order that I might give free indulgence to my guilty thoughts alone.

"In this manner several days elapsed, and my father seldom or never mentioned the name of Antoine or his wife, and it appeared to me as if he wished to banish them from his memory altogether, and I plainly perceived that so far as my nefarious projects went, I had it my own way altogether, and I was determined to take advantage of it. I forwarded several letters to my brother, in which I represented myself as using all my powers of persuasion with my father in his favour, and even gave him some reason to hope that in time I should succeed; for I knew that by holding out such expecta-tions to him, it would more readily induce him to place confidence in me, and would thus give me an agreeable opportunity of prosecuting my designs.

"The count, my father, was seldom at home, and thus I had every opportunity of indulging in my own cogitations, and secretly maturing my plans ; but I could not long rest in this way : I was anxious to perform a more active part ; I felt restless and doubtful while I was absent from Emilie, and I, therefore, resolved to visit them again, and, if possible, to put my designs into execution. I resolved not to give them any notice of my intentions, so that I might take them by surprise, and hoping that in all probability I might catch Emilie alone, and I resolved at all hazards to make known to her my diabolical wishes, imagining that fear of the consequences that might attend her husband would induce her to yield; if not, I was determined that force should make her. Base wretch that I was to form so disgusting, so revolting, so degrading an opinion of Emilie! Vain idiot that I must be to imagine that all the arts I could practice could ever induce that amiable woman to forget her love and duty to her husband, to stifle every feeling of virtue in her breast, and wantonly yield to my unholy desires! But mad infatuation, jealousy and revenge, goaded me on, and I determined to stick at nothing which would be likely to forward my wishes. Oh, when I think of all the revolting thoughts that filled my bosom at that time, and urged me on to the destruction of one of the most innocent and lovely of nature's fair creations, my guilty soul shrinks with horror and shame, and I wonder how my lips dare to give utterance to the monstrous truth, and that to the son of those whom I have so deeply injured. Florio, notwithstanding all that you have said to me, and the patience and forbearance with which you have listened to me, I cannot but blush and tremble in your presence. You should curse and abhor me, Florio; and rather than show any mercy and indulgence to me, you should wreak your vengeance on my head. Would to Heaven that I had died years ago, for I feel myself unfit to live; a disgrace, a pollution to human society, and that I must cast a blight upon all whom I approach or contaminate by my presence."

Here the Count de Clairville again became so violently agitated that he was again compelled to pause.

"I beseech you, my lord," said Florio, "not to agitate yourself so violently. Heaven forbid that I should entertain one feeling o revenge against you after the penitence for your past errors which you so fervently express, and the atonement you are so willing to make."

"Ah, Florio," replied his uncle, "the words you have expressed do but add to the agony and self-reproach of my mind, for they remind me so much of the character of my amiable, but deeply-injured brother. Just like you, noble, generous, confiding, and honourable, was he when he was about your age; and as I gaze upon you, I could almost imagine that he again stood before me; and the remembrance of his melancholy and untimely fate, and my own villany which brought him to it, rushes with tenfold force upon my brain, and almost overwhelms me."

"Alas!" sighed Florio, "it was indeed a sad fate, and many a pang has the dismal recollection of it caused me, though he died before I knew him. My poor mother never, I am convinced, could banish him from her thoughts; and had it not been for my sake, so intense was her grief, so great her hatred of life, that she would long before she was summoned into the presence of her Maker have rid herself of it."

"Oh, God!" groaned the count, beating his breast with the most indescribable agony of feelings, "and this was all the work of my accursed hands. Surely, for crimes such as mine have been, there can be no forgiveness."

"Nay, my lord," remarked Florio, "do not give way to those feelings of despair. There is mercy even for the greatest sinner who sincerely repents, and you ought to feel grateful to Providence for permitting you to live to make all the reparation you can for your past transgressions, by a future life of integrity and virtue."

"True, Florio," replied the count, "and Heaven knows that the remorse I now feel, and which I have for so many years experienced, is sincere. But you have not yet heard the most guilty and painful part of my narrative, and I tremble to relate it."

"Muster courage, my dear uncle," said Florio; "and after you have disburthened your conscience of all the weight of cares that have so long oppressed it, I trust that you may find tranquillity and consolation."

"Alas! I fear they will never be mine," said the count; "I have sinned too much ever to know again that peace of mind which, had I pursued a virtuous and honourable course, would have been the just reward of my declining years. Oh, may giddy, thoughtless youth take warning by my fate, and stifle those evil passions in their breast which inevitably lead to shame and misery, and bring so many curses upon their unoffending fellow creatures. But to resume, and hasten to a conclusion of that guilty narrative, the recital of which causes me such uncontrollable anguish.

"Having stated to my father that I felt my health declining, and thought a change of scene and climate necessary to its restoration, I took my departure from the chateau, accompanied by one confidential attendant, who was in all my secrets, and expressing my intention to travel into Italy, and stating that I might probably be absent for a few months. This, I knew would give me every opportunity of prosecuting my designs unmolested, or without the least suspicion on the part of my father; and I started on my journey, fully confident of success. It was not my intention, however, to go direct to the residence of my brother, but to put up at some hotel a short distance from it, where I could the better watch an opportunity of stealing upon Emilie during the absence of her husband, and while remaining there incog, mature my plans, Antoine and Emilie still believing me to be at the chateau.

"On arriving at the town on the borders of the forest in which the cottage of Gervoise was situated, I found an hotel of that retired description which just suited my purpose, and from there I despatched a letter by my faithful domestic to my brother, as though it had come from the chateau, and in which I assured him and his wife that their welfare and future happiness was the constant subject of my thoughts; that I left no opportunity escape me of interceding with the Count de Clairville in their behalf, and that though for the present he remained stern and inflexible, I had the strongest hopes that in time I should be able to make some impression on him, and to move him to relent, but that in the meanwhile they might depend upon my unabated friendship and affection. How I smiled to myself with fiendish exultation as I penned those lines, and knew the effect they would have upon my brother and Emilie, and how well they were calculated to promote my own infamous wishes, and to work their ruin at the very time when they imagined that everything was being done to release them from the difficulties by which they were then surrounded.

"The answer that I received to this epistle from my brother was couched in the most affectionate language, and himself and Emilie were unbounded in their gratitude, and invoked every blessing upon my head; expressing a wish at the same time that they should shortly have the happiness of seeing me again. Certainly I must have been the most consummate hypocrite that ever imposed upon the credulity of the unsuspecting, or I could never have acted the base part I was doing.

"'Weak, fool!' I ejaculated, when I had perused the contents of the unfortunate Antoine's letter; 'how easily do you fall into the snare that is laid for your destruction. Little do you think that you are nurturing a serpent in your breast who will sting you in the most tender and vital part; but you will soon be awakened from your dream of unconsciousness to the false and stern reality, and when it will be too late to help yourself. I have you completely in my power, and even now I could place you in a position from which you could never escape, and forcibly make your beloved Emilie, that fair but scornful beauty who has ravished my senses, mine. But no, I will rather adopt the course upon which I have fixed my mind, fully confident as I am that my success is certain.'

"Although I thought it would not be prudent for me to visit my brother and his wife for the present, I was most anxious to do so, and Emilie was never for a moment absent from my thoughts, the unholy passion I had dared to encourage for her every hour gaining fresh strength within my breast. Every evening, so disguised that it was impossible for any one to recognise me, I wandered round the cottage of Gervoise, and when by accident I caught a glance of her through the parlour casement, seated in affectionate converse with her husband, or beheld her standing at the cottage door, having placed myself in such a position that I was completely concealed from observa-

tion, my feelings became so strong that I could scarcely contain them.

"At length, however, my patience was exhausted, and I determined again to visit my brother and his sister, so that I might at least have the opportunity of listening to the conversation of Emilie, and thus giving some indulgence to the guilty passions I had suffered to take possession of my guilty breast. I, therefore, forwarded a note to Antoine, informing him of that intention, and at the same time intimating that in all probability I should remain in the neighbourhood for some weeks, or until such time as I could see some means of adjusting the difficulties with which they were surrounded.

"Two days after I had forwarded this letter, I repaired to the cottage of Gervoise, as if I had just arrived off a long journey, and was received by Antoine and Emilie with the utmost cordiality and affection. The hopes that the several flattering letters I had written to them had inspired her with, had revived her spirits; her eyes sparkled with all their wonted animation, and the roses had once more replaced the lilies in her cheeks. To my imagination she had never appeared half so lovely as she did at that moment.

"They eagerly inquired concerning all the particulars that had taken place between myself and my father since I had been away, and, of course, I replied in such a way as was calculated to answer my own purpose and to forward my views. I made it appear that I had been unremitting in my exertions to move the count to relent, and to raise them once more to his bosom, and I made them to believe that I did not altogether despair of being enabled in time to succeed. They were, as you may imagine, unbounded in their gratitude, and placed more confidence in me than ever.

"'Oh, Eugene,' said my brother, grasping my hand, 'how shall I find words to express the feelings with which your noble conduct has inspired me? Without you, what would have become of me and my beloved Emilie, whose happiness is far more precious to me than my own existence? But Heaven will reward you for it, though we cannot, only with our warmest feelings of gratitude.'

"'Antoine,' I answered, in accents of the greatest apparent truth and sincerity, 'you should know me, and that whatever I do is only by the promptings and the dictates of my heart; I have done no more than a brother's duty, and require not your thanks.'

"'Noble-minded man,' ejaculated Emilie, tears of gratitude starting to her eyes, and extending her fair hand to me, which I eagerly but respectfully raised to my lips; 'the sentiments you have just expressed do honour to your head and heart. Could I find language sufficiently powerful or eloquent to express my feelings, how gladly would I do so; but as it is, rest assured, that while I live the brother of my husband must always hold the warmest place in my regard, and I shall never cease to offer up my prayers to Heaven for his welfare!'

"'You overwhelm and embarrass me, Emilie, by those affectionate acknowledgments,' I replied, still retaining my hold of her hand, and looking in her beauteous face with an expression which I could not control, and which, under ordinary circumstances, was sufficient to have excited suspicion; 'to deserve the esteem of so amiable and gentle a being as my brother's wife, is the height of my ambition, and I trust that she will never see cause to regret the generous confidence she has reposed in me, or the flattering opinion she has condescended to form of me.'

"'It is impossible that she can do so, Eugene,' remarked my brother; 'and need I assure you that in all that she has said, I most fully and fervently coincide? But the count, our father, does not entertain any suspicion of the place where we are at present concealed, does he?'

"'He does not,' I answered, 'and for the present I thought it would be more prudent not to discover it to him.'

"'You acted wisely, Eugene,' he said, 'and I leave everything to your discretion, knowing full well that you will do everything for the best.'

"'You may depend upon me, Antoine,' I returned; 'it shall be no fault of mine if I do not move the inflexible spirit of the count; and in the meantime, all that you may require for your pecuniary necessities and comfort, are at your command.'

"Again he pressed my hand to his heart, and gave utterance to his feelings of gratitude in the most fervent language. In this manner the day passed away, and so deeply interested were we with each other's society, that we did not separate till a late hour of the night.

"When I found myself again alone in my chamber, I gave free indulgence to the feelings of exultation which occupied my bosom, and I could not help laughing in very triumph at the manner in which I had deceived them, and the prospect there was of my speedily being enabled to accomplish all that I desired. But I must quickly come to the darkest and most painful part of my history, and when you have heard it, Florio, I cannot but believe that your utmost disgust and indignation will be excited against me.

"As there was not sufficient room at the cottage of old Gervoise for the accommodation of myself and my domestic, I proposed that, during the time I remained in the neighbourhood, I should put up at the hotel in the adjacent town (the very one where I had been secretly staying already), so that being near them, I might visit them daily, and consult with them what was best to be done. To this, of course, they could raise no objection, and, accordingly, I once more took up my residence at that establishment, passing every day in their society, and feasting my guilty passion in contemplating the charms and in listening to the conversation of the innocent Emilie, professing towards her the utmost esteem and friendship, while at the same time I was plotting her destruction, and only awaited impatiently the time when I could put it into effect.

"In this manner more than a week passed away, and I daily grew in the favour and confidence of Emilie, and anxiously longed for the chance to be with her alone; and the opportunity I thirsted for was, unfortunately, too soon afforded me.

"Antoine informed me on one of the occasions of my visit, that he had promised old Gervoise (who was very feeble) to accompany him the following day on some business he had to transact in a town about a league from the cottage, and which he expected would engage them for some hours; he, therefore, requested that I would come as early as possible to the cottage, in order to dissipate the loneliness of Emilie during his absence by my society.

"You may imagine the secret satisfaction with which I heard this; it was with the greatest difficulty only that I could conceal the real feelings which predominated in my breast; but having promised to comply with my brother's request, after some further conversation, I took my departure, and returned towards the hotel.

"As I proceeded on my way, I gave free vent to the feelings of ecstasy that filled my breast, and I looked forward to the arrival of the following day, which I was resolved should decide the fate of Emilie, at all hazards, with the greatest anxiety and impatience.

"'By all my hopes!' I ejaculated, 'Fortune smiles upon me, and the opportunity I have so long panted for has now arrived. The beauteous Emilie shall now be mine; no prayers, no tears, no reproaches shall induce me to abandon my designs. Alone, unprotected, and with no one nigh who might fly to her aid, all attempts at resistance on her part will be vain. She cannot escape me; and that conviction fills my soul with such feelings of transport that I never experienced before. Oh, I have played the game most adroitly! how cleverly have I deceived them, and now I am about to reap the rich reward. Emilie, most beautiful of women, to possess thee I would forfeit my soul's welfare, and brave any danger that might beset me,'

" But let me not dwell on the revolting thoughts which crowded upon and inflamed my guilty mind ; they were such only as a villain of the blackest dye could indulge in, and I wonder only that the vengeance of outraged Heaven did not strike me dead in the midst of them ; though a terrible, it would have been but a just punishment for my enormous guilt, and oftentimes since, in the moments of my bitterest remorse, when the recollection of the fearful past has become almost insupportable, I have regretted that that retribution did not overtake me. But the Almighty extended more mercy to me than I deserved, by not depriving me of life in the midst of my sins, but in giving me time to repent, and in discovering to me the son of those unfortunate beings whom I so monstrously and recklessly injured, and affording me the opportunity of humbling myself before him and making him all the atonement in my power. Florio, do you not blush for me ?"

" My lord,' said Clairville, " why do you continue to agitate yourself thus, after the assurances I have given you ?"

" Because I feel myself unworthy of anything but your hatred and contempt," answered the count. Oh, Florio, to one who has been as guilty as I have been, how terrible it is to look back upon the past ; and yet my mind feels some relief by the disclosures I am making, and which for years have pressed with an overwhelming weight upon my conscience."

" Think no more of it, my lord," said Florio, " but proceed with your narrative."

After a pause of a few minutes, to regain his composure, the Count de Clairville resumed—

" The whole of that night sleep never once closed my eyelids, so intently were my thoughts fixed upon the events that were likely to take place on the following day, and so impatient was I to put my villanous designs into execution ; and as soon as the first streak of day appeared in the eastern horizon, I arose from my couch, and summoning my attendant, I dressed with more than usual care, and then quitted the hotel, telling him to follow me in the course of an hour or two, and to wait near the cottage of Gervoise, within call, in case I should require his assistance.

" It was yet much too early for me to make my appearance at the cottage, for I expected that Antoine and Gervoise had not yet taken their departure, and, I therefore, rambled slowly on through the forest, buried in deep reflection, and maturing my wicked designs against the innocent Emilie. My resolution was unshaken, and I only awaited impatiently for the time when I should put it into execution.

" ' And what will be the reception I am likely to meet with ?' I ruminated ; ' will she not be overwhelmed with horror and disgust ? Can I expect anything else but her bitterest reproaches, when I unmask myself as the hardened and consummate villain that I am ? I cannot. I am prepared for all ; the passion which her superlative charms has engendered in my breast has gained such ascendancy over me, that I might as well attempt to stay the waters of the mighty ocean as to resist its power. Even though the bitterest curses should pursue me ever afterwards, I must proceed to the completion of my wishes. Emilie, couldst thou have loved me as thou dost my brother, and smiled upon my suit, this shame and misery might now have been spared thee ; as it is, I have no alternative but to persist in the designs I have formed against thee, let the consequences be what they may.'

" But in spite of these reflections, a sudden feeling of compunction came over me, and I paused, and deliberated for a few minutes within myself. In that brief interval all the terrible consequences of my diabolical crime were presented vividly to my imagination, and I could not help shuddering, and for a moment feeling abashed and horror-struck at myself. Suddenly the predictions of that mysterious man, old Jerome, flashed upon my recollection, and I hastily looked around me, almost expecting to behold him standing before me. But this feeling of hesitation and remorse quickly passed away, and my guilty determination became as firm as ever.

" ' Why should I suffer these qualms of conscience to overcome me ?' I soliloquised ; ' or the wild predictions of a wandering maniac to have any effect on me ? The game is now secure in my hands, and I must be weak, indeed, if after all the trouble I have taken, and the many anxious thoughts it has cost me, I do not persist in playing it out. Yes, I will be firm and resolute, and obtain the fair prize I have so long coveted, let the consequences be whatever they may.'

" Having come to this determination, I moved from the spot, and slowly made my way in the direction of the cottage, though it was still too early for me to make my appearance there. I arrived at it, and looked up at the different casements, but the blinds were all down, and I felt satisfied that they had not left their chambers. I took my station in a secluded spot opposite the cottage, and throwing myself upon the grass, being concealed from observation, I gave myself up to the various and conflicting thoughts that crowded upon my mind.

" ' This is the eventful day which decides all,' I muttered to myself ; ' and on my own determination depends my triumph or defeat. Whichever it proves to be, my disgrace is certain ; I am sure to be denounced to the world as a villain, and, therefore, as it is so, why should I longer hesitate what course to pursue ? I will be firm. The desperate nature of the circumstances will admit of no faltering or delay, for such another opportunity might never again be afforded me. In this lonely and unfrequented spot, I need not apprehend any interruption; Emilie will be completely in my power and at my mercy, and any resistance she may offer will be useless! By all my hopes, I will achieve my object at all hazards. Emilie, this day shall see thee mine! Oh, what would be the feelings of Antoine did he but know the dark designs which that brother whom he

THE DEATH-BED OF THE COUNT DE CLAIRVILLE.

looks upon as his only friend contemplates against him! But it is the completion of my triumph that I have deceived him in the manner I have, or he would have taken ready and certain means to frustrate my nefarious designs, and hold me up to the scorn and infamy of the world. Bah! what care I for the opinion of the world? And is he not completely powerless to do me harm? Let not such thoughts annoy me, or restrain the ardour of my determination; it is enough for me to know that he possesses the loch of Emilie to make me hate him, and to entertain towards him a feeling of deadly jealousy and revenge. I will persevere, and this day shall accomplish all the wishes I have so long indulged in, or witness my ruin altogether.'

"I arose from my recumbent posture, and once more walked round the cottage, and even ventured to open the little gate and approach the door, to ascertain for a certainty whether any of the inmates were yet stirring; but all was profoundly still, and I once more returned to the spot I had just quitted, and awaited most patiently to see my brother and old Gervoise depart, for I was most anxious at once to put my diabolical designs into execution.

"In this manner more than another hour passed away, and I continued to watch the cottage from the place of my concealment with the greatest anxiety. But I was not much longer kept in suspense; presently I saw the blinds of the various casements withdrawn, and that convinced me that they had left their chmabers, and that the departure of my brother and old Gervoise would take place immediately after they had partaken of their morning meal.

"In that conjecture I was right, for in less than half an hour afterwards I saw the cottage door opened, and Antoine and his aged companion issue from it, Emilie following them to the door. My brother and she embraced affectionately, and that was wormwood to my heart; but at the same time I exulted within myself, knowing how soon I should have her in my power, and that there would then be no one nigh to prevent the completion of the diabolical plot I had so long contemplated against her. Again they embraced and exchanged some words together, and then they departed. Emilie watched her husband with anxious and affectionate eyes until he was hidden from her sight, and she then returned into the cottage, and closed the door.

"I now endeavoured to regain my composure ere I ventured to appear before her; and thinking it most prudent not to do so too soon after the departure of Antoine, I restrained my impatience as well as I could, and arising to my feet, I took another ramble in the forest, weighing in my mind maturely the course I should adopt in my approaching important interview with my intended victim, the sight of whom that morning, and the fond endearments she bestowed upon her husband, had inflamed my unholy passions more than ever.

"'Beauteous woman,' I soliloquised, 'little do you suspect the fate that awaits you—the demon who is lurking near to destroy your peace, and to bring infamy, sorrow, and shame, upon him who is rivetted in your heart's fondest affections.'

"As these thoughts flashed across my brain,

I once more felt a sensation of remorse, and hesitated.

"'What a wretch I must be,' I exclaimed, 'to contemplate such a hellish deed as this. Shall I persist in the destruction of one of the most lovely, amiable, and innocent of her sex, and she, too, the wife of my own brother? Oh, the thought is worthy only of the mind of a fiend, and the vengeance of offended Heaven must pursue me ever afterwards.'

"I walked for some distance from the spot, and deeply did I weigh these arguments in my mind; would to Heaven that they had had the effect that they should have had, I should never have been the guilty and unfortunate wretch that I am at present. I should then have seen at once the utter hideousness of the crime I was in the act of committing, I should have felt horrified and disgusted at my own depravity, and abandoned my wicked and unnatural designs. But some strange, some unaccountable fatality seemed to lead me on, and it appeared as if I were to be immolated on the very shrine which I had formed for the destruction of others.

"'Away with these weak and idle thoughts,' I said; 'there is no reason in them. Shall I allow them to bear any influence upon the designs that have so long occupied my mind and which I have sacrificed so much to accomplish? No, by all my hopes I will not; Eugene de Clairville will ever be the same determined character he has professed to be, let the consequences to himself be whatever they may. Emilie, thou hast scorned me, and given thine hand to my brother; and now, since I have no other means of gratifying the passion with which thy superlative charms have inspired me, I will resort to that violence which, under different circumstances, I might have avoided, and which, indeed, my heart would have revolted from.'

"Thus, hypocrite as I was, I sought to reason with myself, and to find an excuse for my own iniquity, instead of receiving that true conviction, which a rational and well formed mind would have been anxious to arrive at. Oh, Florio, I must repeat, often as I have done so throughout this painful and guilty disclosure, that I feel disgusted with myself; that I am sensible I am a wretch whom every person should despise and reprobate, and that, therefore, you, who are so immediately interested in the facts I am relating, should not only despise and hate me, but that you should also wreak your vengeance upon my head for the wrongs inflicted upon your unfortunate parents by the guilty individual now before you."

"My lord," replied Florio, solemnly, "vengeance is for God, who is the master of all our actions, and not for us, his humble erring creatures. That Almighty Power you have by your actions, according to you own acknowledgment, offended; and it is for you to sue to Him for mercy, and not to me."

"Noble-hearted youth!" said the count, much affected, and grasping his head in the most vehement manner; "every word you give utterance to is a severe, but wholesome monitor to me. Thus would my poor brother have spoken, I am convinced, had he been now living and could have seen me, even after all the manifold and terrible wrongs that I did him. I have detained you long in this tedious chronicle of my guilt, but I could not help the indulgence, the free indulgence, of the real feelings which, after the lapse of so many years, predominate in my breast, and to endeavour to convince you of the sincerity of the remorse which I feel at the enormities of my past life, and how anxious I am to make atonement for them, though, alas! I fear that it will never be in my power to do so."

"My dear uncle," returned Florio, "you much mistake my character if you imagine that I can possibley feel any gratification in seeing you humble yourself in the manner you are doing now. Great as your errors have been, which I must in truth and candour admit they have been, the penitence you now evince ought to be to me ample atonement for the wrongs you inflicted upon my parents, and I am certain, if their spirits can now witness what is taking place between us, they will approve of the sentiments to which I now give utterance."

"Well spoken, Florio," remarked the brigand chief; "such sentiments do honour to your head and heart, and I respect you more than ever I did for them. Where is there the man who is immaculate—who has never erred? And we must be wretches indeed, unworthy to live, if we judge each other by the strict code of our moral laws. It may appear strange, and as yourself and your noble uncle would probably say, rather *outre*, to hear a brigand, a robber, a cutthroat,—*par excellence!* ha! ha!—discuss upon subjects of morality, but such happens to be my humour now, and you must take my opinions only at their fair valuation. I have had to encounter the misfortunes and vicissitudes of life in their severest characters; but for the guilt of him who was the author of my being, I should not have been where you see me now; nor could the world have had the opportunity of casting one stigma on my character. But those who know me well will not even now attempt to say that Allesandro Massaroni is anything less than a man; that he has not a bumping heart, ay, a bumping heart, brimful of love and good wishes towards his fellow creatures; and that if there be any rancour in his constitution, that rancour is poured upon the tyrants and oppressers of his fellow men."

"Massaroni," said the Count de Clairville, taking the hand of our hero, and cordially pressing it within his own, "I do, I must admire your sentiments. I believe you to be a man, and am convinced that it must have been some cruel system of oppression, of villany, and tyranny, that has placed a man of your superior abilities and endowments of mind in your present position."

"You judge me rightly, my lord," replied the brigand; "but for one whose name I knew not, but whom nature would compel me to call father, I might have lived in this bright world of ours, honoured and respected as much as any of its denizens, and not have been driven to commit those outrages upon society which my heart revolts at. But he has been my curse, my bane, and do not all the errors I have committed rest upon his head? By the saints! there is not a human being whom I would in cold blood injure but him who is the author of my existence, and all my misfortunes."

"Massaroni," said the Count de Clairville, solemnly, "and would you, if you were to discover your parent, so far forget the feelings of nature as to raise your hand against him?"

"Raise my hand against him!" repeated the brigand chief determinedly, and his fine eyes flashing fire. "I would strike him dead!" and, as the brigand uttered these words, he *looked* his determination.

"Oh, horrible!" ejaculated the Count de Clairville and Florio, in a breath.

"Horrible!" returned Massaroni, "what, to inflict a just retribution upon the head of my poor mother's betrayer and murderer, and the cause of all my own misfortunes and degradation! By all my hopes, there is no man who is more opposed to the shedding of human blood than Allesandro Massaroni, but in that case he could forget that it was his father who was before him, and would wreak his most terrible vengeance upon his head. Heaven guard him from my knowledge, if he be still living, that is all I can say."

"And if those are your sentiments towards your own parent," observed the count, "what ought to be those that yourself and Florio should entertain respecting me?"

"My lord," replied our hero, "you have never erred as he whom I blush to call by the name of father has done."

"But my thoughts were equally criminal," said the count.

"That may be," remarked Massaroni; "but were they productive of the same evil consequences?"

"Alas! alas!" replied his lordship, "have I not already shown to you in what I have related that they were? Did not my guilty transactions cause my brother to hurry himself, unsummoned, into the presence of his Maker, and send his broken-hearted wife, with her tender offspring, on the world to starve ? Oh, I feel too keenly that no villany can possibly exceed that of which I have been guilty, and that nothing I can possibly endure can be an adequate punishment for it. You, Florio, should hate and despise me, as I have frequently before said ; and the patience and forbearance you have shown to me throughout my narrative is even a more bitter reproach to me than all the words of invective you could possibly have given utterance to ; for it recalls so vividly to my mind's eye, and my own self-reproving conscience, the hapless and unsuspecting victims of my atrocious guilt, that, by that High Heaven whose holy laws I have so grossly violated, I could almost imagine they stood before me in your person, to reproach and curse me for my past iniquities. Oh, what a terrible monitor is a guilty conscience !"

" My lord," said Florio, " how it pains me to hear you give utterance to words such as these, while they at the same time convince me of the sincerity of your penitence, and are a sufficient atonement for that with which you so bitterly reproach yourself. God forbid that I should pursue you with any vindictive feelings ; but compose yourself, and hasten as quickly as possible towards the completion of your painful task ; such digressions as those only serve to aggravate your agony of mind."

" True, Florio," replied the Count de Clairville ; " but pardon me for a few minutes, although I have already intruded upon your time and patience too long. My thoughts wander, and I scarcely remember the point of my guilty and painful narrative at which I had arrived. I must request a short time for reflection, and to tranquillise my feelings."

Florio returned no answer to this, but nodded assent, and he and our hero retired for a few minutes to another part of the cavern, and discoursed together, leaving the count to his own meditations. It required, however, but a short time for the latter to recover himself, and he then resumed his long and painful history in the following words :—

"'In the state of mind which I have described, I continued for some time, and still hesitated to enter the cottage ; but at length I was aroused from my lethargy by some one repeating my name, and looking up I beheld that it was my faithful and confidential servant, Victor, who, it appeared, by what he afterwards stated, had been watching me for several minutes, and had overheard my observations. When I term him my faithful and confidential servant, I presume I need not inform you that he was as great a villain as myself ? He was, indeed, a complete adept in all those arts which so well suited my infamous purposes, and was capable of committing almost any crimes, however atrocious, so long as he met with an adequate reward, and in that particular he had nothing to complain of in me.

" ' Ah, Victor, my trusty friend,' I observed when I beheld him, ' I am glad' you have arrived, for I much needed your counsel and advice. They have just left the cottage.'

" ' I know they have, Monsieur,' he answered. ' for I watched them, though I took especial good care that they should not observe me ; pardon me, too, if I acknowledge that I have also listened to your soliloquies, and am surprised that you should now hesitate at the very moment when the opportunity is afforded you in gratifying those wishes you have so long entertained.'

" ' But, Victor,' I returned, ' must I not be a consummate villain to entertain such atrocious thoughts against the wife of my own brother, and one so pure and innocent, and who places such implicit confidence in my friendship, my honour, and integrity ?'

" ' The more fortunate for you that she does so,' replied the scoundrel, ' for it has given you an opportunity you might not otherwise have obtained of accomplishing your designs.'

" ' And shall I betray that confidence ?' I demanded.

" ' Has she not inflamed your passions?' replied Victor ; ' and after all the trouble you have been at, the many hours of anxiety you have experienced, are you now to suffer any false scruples of conscience to induce you to abandon your designs ? Pshaw, my lord, I repeat, that I am surprised at you. Arouse yourself ; be firm, and the hour of triumph which you have so long panted for has arrived.'

" ' But the future consequences, Victor,' I suggested.

" ' Heed them not,' he answered ; ' what have you to fear ? You have wealth ; you have power ; they are beggars, dependant on you for their very means of existence, and though they may murmur, they cannot do you any injury. Come, come, bethink yourself and be firm.'

" The words of this villain had that due effect upon me they were intended to have ; I walked with him for a few minutes in the forest, and ultimately all my worst passions and determinations gained their former ascendancy in my breast.

" ' I will no longer hesitate,' I said ; ' thus far I have hazarded everything for that gratification of my wishes, and shall I pause now that the opportunity is afforded me of doing so ? No, by all my hopes I will not ; no consideration whatever shall restrain me. Emilie shall be mine, even though my own destruction were to follow.'

" ' Well said, Monsieur,' remarked Victor, ' that is spoken like yourself, and far more becomes you than those feelings of remorse which you previously expressed. This is a glorious day of triumph for you, and you have good reason to praise yourself for the ability with which you have conducted your plot.'

" 'Ay, Victor,' I answered, 'I do ; but you will be within call in case I should require your assistance, or to give me notice should any one approach to interrupt me?'

" 'You may depend upon me, Monsieur,' he returned, ' though I am satisfied you have nothing to apprehend ; this is a lonely and unfrequented spot, and as for your brother and the old man, I suppose you are certain that they will not return for some time ?'

" 'Oh, yes,' I replied.

" 'Then the game is your own,' he remarked ; 'away with you to the accomplishment of your ardent desires, and may success attend you.'

" I pressed the hand of the villain as he thus spoke, and having regained all my self-possession and confidence, I left him, and advanced with a bold step towards the cottage ; but when I arrived at the door I again paused, and then ventured to peep in at the parlour window.

' Emilie was seated there in a melancholy attitude, with her elbow resting upon the table, and her head reclining upon her hand, evidently wrapped in deep thought. The sight of her aroused all my energies, and inflamed the revolting passions I had so long harboured in my breast.

" Unconscious beauty,' I muttered to myself, ' thou art there, and completely at my mercy. Little do you suspect the wretch who is now awaiting to accomplish your destruction ; little can you conceive the fate that is in store for you. Antoine, you will return to—But let me not think,' I added, after a pause ; ' this is not the time to waste in idle speculations, but to act.'

" As I gave utterance to these words, I knocked at the door, and immediately heard the light footsteps of Emilie approaching it.

" Who is there ?' she inquired, in a gentle voice.

" 'It is I, Eugene, sweet Emilie,' I replied.

" She opened the door immediately, and my intended victim stood before me, looking, if possible, more lovely than ever.

" 'Oh, Eugene,' she said, smiling through the tears that had before dimmed her eyes. ' I am so glad you are come—so punctual too ; for I need not tell you that I felt very sad and lonely in the absence of my dear Antoine, and in reflecting upon the troubles and difficulties by which we are surrounded.'

" 'Be mine the task, then,' I said, ' to endeavour to alleviate your anguish, and inspire you with hope ; come, Emilie, we must have no sadness to-day.'

" 'Oh, Eugene,' she replied, fixing upon me a look which spoke the sincerity of her soul,

and was a bitter reproach upon the treacherou and villanous part I was acting ; ' how much are both myself and Antoine indebted to you for your disinterested friendship. How can we ever repay it as we ought to do ?"

" 'Name it not, Emilie,' I answered ; " I must be insensible to every feeling of nature and humanity, did I not feel an interest in all that concerns your welfare. There is nothing that is within my humble power that I would not do, no sacrifice that I would not willingly make, to serve Emilie and—*my brother.*'

" 'I believe you, Eugene,' she said ; 'I place every confidence in you, and it is that which makes me feel still more the weight of obligation I am under to you.'

" 'Where favour, esteem, and friendship are deserved, there is no obligation, Emilie,' I returned ; ' it becomes a duty, and I should despise myself were I to shrink from the performance of it. But Antoine, will he be absent long ?'

£." 'I do not expect that he will return till the evening,' she replied ; 'but there was something in his manner on leaving me, which I cannot comprehend, and which has caused me many painful reflections since.'

" 'Indeed,' I said, anxiously ; ' what mean you ?'

" 'He appeared more than usually sad,' she answered ; ' seemed loth to leave me, and stated that he had some melancholy forebodings on his mind that something of a serious nature was about to happen to us.'

" I started, and could not conceal the emotions which those observations created in my breast ; but I quickly recovered myself, and said :

" ' Nay, Emilie, that was a weakness on his part, natural enough at the thought of being separated from you even for the shortest period. What harm can befal you whilst I am present ?'

" ' Oh, no, Eugene,' she returned, with the sweetest confidence, ' I place every reliance on you.'

" ' You do me no more than justice by so doing, Emilie,' I answered, with the most unblushing effrontery ; ' but Antoine is but a young husband yet, and the time will come, I dare say, when a temporary separation from you will not cause him so much care and anxiety.'

" ' Eugene,' she returned hastily, ' you surprise me ; but such observations cannot have escaped you with a serious thought. Can you believe that Antoine will ever cease to love me less than he does at present ?'

" This question was sufficient to confuse me ; but I quickly recovered myself, and replied :

" ' No, no, Emilie, indeed you misunderstand me. I do not doubt the fervour and sincerity of my brother's love towards you, or th…

will ever prove inconstant to you. Pardon me for giving utterance to words that were meant only in a joke. But Antoine's sadness, as I said before, is easily to be accounted for, and you ought not to suffer it to disturb your mind for a moment.'

" ' Well, Eugene,' she observed, " I will endeavour to think as you do, though I must confess that I could not help the words and demeanour of Antoine making an impression upon me, and but for your opportune arrival, I should have been sad indeed. Surely we have already suffered enough, and Providence in its infinite mercy will not afflict us more. We have never given cause for the enmity of any one, and they must be base, indeed, who would seek to injure us.'

" I know not how I looked as she said this, but I felt a pang of shame and remorse shoot through my heart, and I was so confused that for a few minutes I knew not what to reply; at length I said:

" Oh, no, Emilie, it is impossible that any tindividual can entertain a feeling of animosity owards you or my brother, unless, indeed, unrtunately, it be my father.'

" Alas! alas! how sad is that thought,' ejaculated Emilie; 'but may we not hope that time will change his sentiments towards us, and that he will receive us again to his bosom?'

" ' I sincerely trust that he will,' I replied, 'though at present I see little or no room to hope.'

" ' Oh, Eugene,' Emilie observed, ' say not so, for that, indeed, will plunge me into the lowest depths of misery and despair. But the Count de Clairville can never be so cruel as to close his heart against us altogether.'

" ' If persuasion, argument, and supplication on my part can prevent it, he will not, Emilie,' I returned; 'but you know my father's disposition as well as I do; he is stern and inflexible, and when he has once made up his mind to anything, it is difficult to move him from it.'

" ' But you will be unremitting in your exertions in our behalf, will you not, Eugene?' she asked, eagerly.

" ' And why should Emilie put such a question to me,' I answered, ' after the confidence she has expressed in me?'

" ' Forgive me, Eugene,' she returned, ' if from anything that I have said I have seemed to doubt you. Heaven knows how sincerely I depend upon and value your friendship.'

" ' And when I abuse it,' I returned, with an air of truth and candour which it would seem almost impossible for even the most consummate hypocrite to assume, ' denounce me as a villain of the blackest dye.'

" ' Oh, no,' she ejaculated, ' Eugene de Clairville can never be worthy of so opprobrious

an epithet; he is the soul of honour and integrity, and would blush to be guilty of a single act which would disgrace his unsullied name.'

" I was compelled to avert my face in order to conceal the real feelings which these observations from the innocent and confiding Emilie excited in my guilty bosom. Monster that I was, and yet I could still contemplate the ruin of her, for whom I professed so much esteem and sympathy; and I only awaited a fitting opportunity to put my villanous designs into execution. Some demon seemed to urge me on, and every proper feeling was stifled in my breast. But afraid to trust myself any longer for the present, and thinking it not prudent to be too hasty in my advances, I changed the topic of conversation, and thus for several hours we continued to discourse upon various subjects, which I should become tedious were I to particularise. However, the moment for my infamous attempt had arrived; Emilie having accidentally made some allusion to the scene which had formerly taken place between herself and me in the gardens of the Castle of St. Almo, afforded me the opportunity I had long been so anxiously waiting for, and aroused all my guilty energies into action.

" ' And can Emilie reproach me for having acknowledged the sentiments with which her superior charms and mental quailities had inspired me?' I said.

" ' Eugene,' she replied, blushing, and turning upon me a look of gentle reproach, ' did you not solemnly promise me never to repeat that painful subject upon which you so well know my sentiments? Surely you do not forget that I am the wife of your brother, Antonie?'

" ' No, Emilie,' I answered, ' alas! I do not; and it is that thought which drives me to madness and despair.'

" She started from her seat, and fixed upon me a look of mingled astonishment and indignation, as she replied—

" ' Good God! can I believe my ears? Is this the same Eugene de Clairville, who, but a few minutes since, was expressing to me such sentiments of sympathy, respect, and friendship? It is impossible!'

" ' It is true, Emilie,' I returned, attempting to take her hand. ' I am the same Eugene de Clairville that I have ever been to you!'

" ' Your looks and words alarm me,' she said, in a faint voice, and retreating towards the door which led into an adjoining room, but against which I placed my back; ' you have cruelly, basely deceived me, and I must not, will not listen to you any longer; I feel that I am not safe in your presence; leave me, and let me endeavour to forget that this ever took place.'

" ' Leave you Emilie?' I returned; ' by

Heaven, never! until you and I have come to a proper understanding. I own my fault, namely, that I have deceived you, and endeavoured to conceal the real feelings that I always have, and ever must, entertain towards you; but I now throw away the mask, and again confess to you the ardent, the unconquerable sentiments of love, nay, adoration, that I entertain towards you. The flames you have kindled in my breast nothing can ever extinguish, and——'

"'Villain!' she interrupted, and her eyes flashing with disgust and indignation; 'I do indeed know you now, and loathe and despise you as you merit. Oh, God! and am I to be thus brutally insulted by the brother of my unsuspecting husband? Begone, 'nor dare again contaminate me by the presence of one so utterly devoid of every feeling of virtue, shame, and honour! Begone, I repeat, or dread the vengeance of my injured husband.'

"'The vengeance of your husband, Emilie?' I replied, with a scornful laugh; 'and think you that I fear one so utterly powerless and abject as he is? But this is no time to trifle in idle words. I courted your love when I could do so with honour, but you rejected me, and became the wife of my brother. That has only tended to strengthen the passion your charms had engendered in my breast, and that passion I have determined shall be gratified, let the consequences be whatever they may. Fortune now smiles upon me, and at length the opportunity is afforded me, which I have so long panted for. We are alone—there is no one near to interrupt us, and all resistance on your part will be fruitless; so thus, most lovely of women, idol of my very soul, I seal my happiness!'

"As I thus spoke, I rushed towards her, and enfolded her in my arms, she struggling violently, but in vain, to release herself.

"'Monster!' she shrieked, 'unhand me, cowardly ruffian! Oh, God! help! help!'

"'Your cries are fruitless,' I exclaimed; 'there is no one here to assist you, and by all my hopes I swear that I will not be foiled; Emilie, beauteous, but scornful Emilie, thou art mine! Thou art mine!'

"'Merciful God assist me!' she cried, still struggling to release herself, whilst I polluted her fair cheeks with my odious and unholy kisses, and endeavoured to force her into the adjoining room; 'help! help! mercy! mercy! as you dread the terrible vengeance of Heaven, spare me, Eugene!'

"But I remained deaf to her supplications, and forced her into the room; her strength was almost exhausted, and there seemed to be every probability of the accomplishment of my diabolical designs; but just at the critcial moment, when the ruin of Emilie appeared certain, the outer door of the cottage was burst hastily open, and Antoine rushed into the room, and tearing his wife from my arms, he exclaimed in a furious voice—

"'Villain! black-hearted scoundrel! and is this the friendship and esteem you professed towards me, and which I had a right to expect from a brother?—Oh, shameless hypocrite! begone from my sight, lest I forget that the same blood flows within our veins, and wreak my vengeance on your head!'

"'Villain in your teeth, weak, drivelling idiot!' I cried fiercely, and drawing my sword, I was rushing upon him, when Emilie interposed between us, and in a voice of the greatest agony she exclaimed :

"'Forbear! forbear! guilty, misguided man would you add murder to your other crimes?'

"'For your sake, fair, but scornful Emilie, I spare him now!' I answered; 'but mark my words, you will both have bitter cause to repent this! Antoine, we shall meet again.'

"Without waiting to receive any reply from my brother, bursting with rage and disappointment, I rushed from the cottage, and giving utterance to the most fearful curses, I hurried towards the hotel, followed by my attendant, who had not noticed the return of Antoine and Gervoise. Thus Florie, I have at last disclosed the most guilty part of my history, and I am prepared to meet your utmost indignation."

"No, my lord," replied Florie, "I have already expressed my sentiments upon that painful subject, and believe, me, they remain unchanged. My poor parents! But thank Heaven that my mother was saved from the awful and revolting fate that was intended her."

"Oh, what a relief is it to my guilty conscience to think she was," said the count; "but it would have been a just retribution on my guilty head, had I been struck dead in making the diabolical attempt."

"It was the mercy of Providence that spared you, my lord," replied Florio; "but was it not most extraordinary that my poor father should return just at the critical moment when his interposition was so much required?"

"It was," coincided the Count de 'Clairville, and I have often thought that, although he concealed it, your father must have had some suspicion of my integrity and sincerity and his journey with old Gervoise was only a preconcerted plan to discover me."

"It is not at all improbable, my lord," said his nephew. "But you have not yet concluded your narrative."

"I have not," answered the count; "but I will do so as quickly as I can, for it has already extended to greater length than I expected it would, and I am afraid you will think me tedious.

"On reaching the hotel, and retiring to my

own apartments, you may readily conceive the state of mind under which I laboured. I gave vent to my rage and disappointment by the most fearful oaths, and would suffer no one to come near me. By turns I invoked the most bitter curses on the head of my deeply injured brother, and then I vowed to have a terrible revenge at the finest opportunity, at the same time that I was still determined that Emile should not escape me. In the same state of agitation I continued throughout the night, and sleep never for a moment descended upon my eyelids. I was not at a loss what course to pursue, but I know full well that it would not be prudent for me to remain any longer in the neighbourhood, though I was, notwithstanding what had taken place, fully determined not to abandon my designs, and was also resolved never to rest until I had gratified my revenge. I was half disposed to brave everything, and at once make my re-appearance at the cottage of Gervoise; but when I more calmly reflected upon the consequences that were likely to ensue, I dismissed the thought from my mind. Previous, however, to my departure from the neighbourhood, which I determined should take place on the following day, I despatched my attendant to reconnoitre near the place of my brother and his wife's retreat, in order that he might endeavour to ascertain whether or not anything particular had happened since my guilty interview with Emilie, and you may judge of my astonishment and rage, when, on his return, he informed me that the cottage was closely shut up, and that it was evident they had abruptly quitted the place, and had thus, for the present, at any rate, foiled me in any designs which I might contemplate against them.

"I will not attempt to describe the power of my feelings on receiving this information. I raved like a madman, and vented the most terrible curses upon the heads of those whom I had so cruelly wronged; vowing that I would leave no means untried still to discover them, and to accomplish my diabolical wishes, and to gratify my revenge, even though in seeking to do so I should involve myself in the greatest dangers.

"'They shall not escape me," I muttered to myself determinedly, 'though for the present fortune frowns upon me. Had I adopted a different course to that which I have done, my triumph would have been certain; why did I not adopt some means to secure the person of Antoine, which I might easily have done, and then Emilie would have been completely in my power and at my mercy, and must have yielded to my wishes, though by doing so it might have broken her heart? But what is to become of them, destitute as they are of all means of support? They cannot long remain concealed, and in spite of all that has taken place, they will be compelled to succumb and to sue to me for relief, and then will that moment of revenge I have so anxiously sought for, that hour of triumph which I have so eagerly panted for, have arrived.'

"Presumptuous, guilty fool that I was, to suffer such thoughts as these to enter my mind; but such was the power, the fatal ascendancy which my nefarious passions had obtained over me, that I found it impossible to resist them, and I was hurried on, as it were, headlong to my own destruction as well as the happiness of those who ought to have been so dear to me, and whom I had already so irreparably injured."

"I now resolved to postpone my departure from the hotel for a day or two, in order that I might endeavour to recover my composure, previous to my return home and meeting again the count, my father; and I trusted that, in the meantime, I might be able to obtain some intelligence of the fugitives, whose abrupt flight had caused me so much surprise and disappointment. I left the hotel, however, for awhile, and walked forth into the forest, rambling towards the cottage, and which I found to be, as my domestic had represented it, completely deserted; and looking through the parlour casement, I saw that every article of furniture had been removed, which surprised me the more, as it convinced me that their departure must have occupied some time, and that it could not have been accomplished very easily without assistance. 'And shall I be defeated,' I said, as I threw myself upon the grass, 'and that at the very time when I thought my success was certain? By all my hopes, that thought is more than I can find patience to endure. But it shall not be; I am determined it shall not: I will arouse myself into action, and set all my ingenuity to work to accomplish my wishes, let the consequences to myself be whatever they may.'

"In this state of mind I continued throughout the day, and did not offer to move from the spot. The gloom and silence that reigned around were in perfect unison with my feelings, and night unconsciously advanced before I was aware altogether where I was. But I now felt a sensation of dread gradually steal over me which I found it impossible to resist, and though I was anxious to retire from the place, I could not; my limbs seemed to fail me; my brain turned giddy, strange phantoms rose before my perturbed imagination, and I almost feared to look around me. I do not remember ever to have experienced such an extraordinary sensation before, and yet it was in vain that I tried to conquer it.

"'But what weakness and folly is this,' I said at length; 'what have I to fear? There is no one here who would seek to harm me, and, therefore, why should I entertain such childish apprehensions? The gloom of this place has taken an effect upon my spirits; let me retire from it, and no doubt I shall soon be able to regain my usual state of mind.   Bah! I have no patience with myself!'

"Thus saying, I walked slowly away from the spot, but notwithstanding all my efforts, I could not banish the remarkable and unaccountable impression from my mind. It seemed as if something of a painful and fearful nature was about to happen to me.

FLORIO DE CLAIRVILLE AND ADOLPHE D'AUBIGNY.

"The night was particularly dark; there was not a star to be seen, and it was not without the greatest difficulty I could trace my way amidst the profound gloom which reigned around.   Florio, I am now about to relate a circumstance of such a mysterious and awful nature, that I have never been able to reflect upon it since without a sensation of horror. You may probably doubt the accuracy of my statement, and that I was either labouring under the influence of some frightful dream, or that I had suffered the horrors of my imagination to deceive me; but I solemnly assure you that what I am about to relate to you actually occurred to me, and that I was as completely awake and sensible to all that was passing around me, as I am at this present moment. I had now just entered upon a long avenue of the most lofty trees, and which I knew was the nearest way out of the forest, when I was suddenly startled by beholding a sickly light glimmering in the distance, and which seemed to be gradually advancing towards me. I at first imagined it to proceed from a lantern, carried by some traveller, and I, therefore, took but little notice of it.'

"And a very natural conclusion, too," remarked Florio.

"Hear me out," said the Count de Clairville; "and I rather imagine that you will then be disposed to change that opinion. As I proceeded on my way, the light seemed also to move towards me, and gradually it expanded until it filled the whole width of the pathway, became suddenly stationary, and had a most singular and indescribable appearance altogether. I felt a kind of tremor come over me, and hesitated for a minute or two ere I could proceed, for again the impression was strong upon my mind that some danger threatened me. The effect of this strange light, as I have said before, was most remarkable; but suddenly I perceived it change; it appeared to divide itself, and from the centre a shadowy form emerged, which glided noiselessly and solemnly towards me. The feelings of astonishment and alarm I had before experienced, now gained strength in my breast, and I was completely rivetted to the spot, and awaited the result of this most extraordinary adventure in a state of great suspense and anxiety. I had not to await long, and oh, God! never shall I be able to efface from my memory the horror of that moment. Nearer and nearer the object of my amazement and alarm approached, and as it did so, I perceived it was that of a female, clad in long flowing garments of white, and the features completely hidden from the view beneath a veil, which descended to the waist. There was something so unearthly about the appearance of this form altogether, that I could not contemplate it, as it advanced towards me, without the deepest awe; and when at length it stood before me—so still, so solemn, and so statue-like, while, to my imagination, a supernatural light seemed to play around it, all my faculties appeared to forsake me, and I would have given anything had I been released from its presence. But still it moved not, and at length making a desperate effort to conquer my emotions, I said :—

"'Stranger, who art thou that appearest thus so mysteriously and so suddenly before me? and what is the purport of thy visit to me at this hour and in such a place?'

"Not a word was spoken in answer to this, but slowly raising her veil, powers of mercy! judge of the feelings of horror which froze the very blood in my veins, when I beheld the pale, ghastly, and reproachful features of my late wife !"

"Oh, impossible! my lord," remarked Florio; "you can never be so superstitious as to believe in such supernatural visitations. You must have suffered your imagination to deceive you, or to have been labouring under the influence of some fearful dream.''

"Oh no!" answered his lordship; "it is impossible that I could do so, situated as I was when the awful adventure occurred to me. Do I not tell you that I was on my way through the forest when the phantom appeared before me? Could I then be labouring under the influence of sleep? The very idea is preposterous. But could I contemplate the pale shade of that amiable wife whom I had so deeply wronged, without the greatest of terror and remorse? It was impossible that I could do so. I tried to speak, but my tongue clave to the roof of my mouth; faculty seemed for the moment suspended; the perspiration stood in large drops upon my quivering temples; and with a groan of agony, I sank upon the earth in a state of temporary unconsciousness.

"How long I remained in that condition I know not; but when I recovered, I found myself supported by my faithful attendant, who, feeling surprised and alarmed at my protracted absence, had came in search of me. He eagerly inquired of me what had happened; but I stared vacantly at him for a moment or two, and was incapable of returning any answer. Then I looked wildly and fearfully around me, expecting again to behold the phantom of my wife, and I continued to tremble convulsively in every limb. Finding that it was useless for him to seek to obtain from me any explanation as to the cause of my serious alarm, he persuaded me to allow him to conduct me to my hotel, and I yielded without saying a word, though in a state of mind which you may readily imagine. On reaching the hotel where I was staying, I immediately retired to my chamber, when I threw myself upon the bed and for some time I gave myself up entirely to the racking thoughts that crowded upon my distracted brain. My guilty conscience was aroused to madness; I reproached myself for a villain of the blackest dye, and almost feared to be alone, lest I should again behold the ghastly phantom of my late wife, and have to listen to her solemn curses ringing in my ears

"'And are the dead permitted to revisit this earth,' I ejaculated, in a hoarse and hollow voice, 'and to blast me with their presence? But is it not a punishment that my numerous and heinous crimes have merited? Shall such a wretch as I am ever expect to escape with impunity? Oh, my poor, confiding, cruelly injured wife, my gentle, amiable Marie, what a miscreant I must be to deceive thee in the manner in which I did. No wonder that thy sainted spirit should now look down from its heavenly abode and curse me.'

"I remained in this state of mind during the night, but by the morning I had become more tranquil, and I blush to own that the same unnatural and guilty feelings I had so long harboured in my breast against my brother and Emilie resumed their influence in my breast, and rage and disappointment at their abrupt flight, and the consequent present frustration of my nefarious designs, were the principal passions that predominated in my mind.

"'Away with these cowardly feelings of remorse,' I exclaimed; 'I have proceeded too far to repent now; and I am determined to discover them and obtain the gratification of my desires, even though my own destruction should ultimately follow. I am no weak boy to be easily daunted from the execution of any purpose upon which I have fixed my mind; and these frequent disappointments do but add fresh energy to my desires. Let the world look upon me as a villain, I scorn its opinion, and mock at its reproaches. I possess the power to carry out my prospects to any extent, and I will not fail to take advantage of it, and something seems to assure me that, notwithstanding the Fates at present seem to have conspired against me, I shall yet accomplish all my desires. At any rate, I will boldly proceed, and leave the result to chance.'

"By arguments such as these, I endeavoured to fortify and encourage my nefarious hopes, and to stifle the voice of conscience, and I succeeded far better than might have been expected; I tried hard to persuade myself that I must have been labouring under some fearful delusion when I imagined I had seen the spectre of my late wife, on the previous night in the forest, but so palpable did everything appear to me to be, that I found it was impossible for me to do so; and in spite of all my efforts to the contrary, my mind alternated between doubt and fear, and bitter self-reproach.

"The day after the extraordinary and fearful adventure I have just related, I was seated in my own private room at the hotel, buried in deep thought, when I was suddenly aroused from my lethargy by the entrance of my servant, who placed a letter in my hand, which he said had just been brought to the hotel by a strange man, habited as a peasant, and who had taken his departure again immediately, without waiting for an answer, and before any question could be put to him. I hastily glanced at the letter, and instantly saw that it was in the handwriting of Antoine.

"'Ah!' I exclaimed, 'why was not this man detained? He might have been induced by threats, or the promise of a reward, to have revealed the place to which they had fled.'

"'He had no sooner placed the letter in the hand of one of the servants of the hotel, monsieur,' answered my domestic, 'than he departed, and, of course, the person to whom he had delivered it saw no necessity for his putting any question to him, or to detain him.'

"I could not help muttering a curse at this disappointment, and then hastily opening the letter, I read the following words:—

"'This is probably the last communication he whom I blush to call a brother will ever receive from that man whom he has so cruelly deceived and bitterly injured. Your villany has destroyed the happiness and ruined the prospects of those who loved and honoured you as their best friend, and who would willingly have laid down their lives to serve you. If you have not become callous to every sense of shame and humanity, the remembrance of the crimes you have committed against those who reposed every confidence in you, must be a terrible reproach to your conscience for the rest of your days. That we may never meet again, and that you may be brought to a full sense of the enormity of your conduct, and repent ere it is too late, is the sincere wish of—

"'ANTOINE AND EMILIE.'

"No sooner had I perused the contents, than I crumpled the letter up passionately in my hand, and paced the room for several moments in the most excited manner.

"'And does he then think that his reproaches or threats can have any other effect upon me than excite my utmost scorn?' I cried. 'Fool! he imagines that I will now dismiss all further thoughts against the happiness of himself and Emilie from my mind, and that I shall find it impossible to discover them; but if fortune does not frown upon me altogether, he will find himself most wofully deceived. There are no means that I will leave untried to bring about the completion of my wishes: there is no danger that shall intimidate me, or move me from my purpose; and I do not despair of seeing him compelled to humble himself before me; for want and misery, no doubt, will crush his scornful spirit.'

"However," continued the count, "I will not detain you, or shock your ears by detailing all the abominable thoughts in which I indulged, and the many vows of vengeance which I uttered to myself against my unfortunate brother, if the opportunity should ever be afforded me. The day after the receipt of this epistle, having sufficiently recovered myself, I took my departure from the hotel, being determined to return to the chateau, for I had strong suspicions that Antoine had likewise made the count acquainted with what had taken place, and that he would require some explanation from me for having deceived him, and the conduct I had thought proper to pursue. It was not long before I arrived there, and I found that my surmises were correct, and that he had received a letter from Antoine, informing him of all the disgusting particulars, and appealing to his sense of honour, nature, and humanity, to visit the dastardly outrage I had committed with the indignation it deserved, and to relent in the harsh conduct he had pursued towards himself and the innocent being who was now his wife, and whose only fault had been, if such it were, in loving him too well.

" 'And is all that is stated in that letter correct, Eugene?' demanded my father, after he had placed it in my hands, and suffered me to peruse it.

"It is, my lord," I answered, with perfect firmness; "accident discovered to me the place where Antoine and Emilie were concealed, and I have to crave your forgiveness for not having made you acquainted with it; but I was fearful that you would not approve of the designs which I had formed, and which the passion inspired in my breast by the charms of Emilie induced me to contemplate. But if you consider that I have acted with too much impetuosity and——"

" 'Eugene,' interrupted my father, 'I have before told you that I approve of the sentiments you entertain for Emilie, and only regret that you did not acknowledge them to myself and the late Count St. Almo years ago; all the misery that has since taken place might probably then have been prevented; Emilie should have been compelled to become your wife instead of her sister Marie, and no doubt, by perseverance, you would have been enabled to have won a return of her affections. But we will talk further upon this subject on a future occasion. The place to which Antoine and Emilie have fled must be discovered, if possible; and when that is accomplished, we will arrange the course it will be best to adopt for the future.' "

"And is it possible," said Florio, "that any man could so far forget the feelings of nature and humanity, as to pursue his own son with such implacable hatred and revenge, and even to give his sanction to a crime so revolting and atrocious?"

"He did," answered the Count de Clairville, "and I cannot but shudder when I reflect upon it. May God in His infinite mercy forgive him, for, indeed, his crime was great; but the judgment of Heaven was about to overtake him much sooner than could have been expected; that same night I had only just retired to my bed, when I received a hasty summons to attend the chamber of my father, as he was taken suddenly and alarmingly ill,

and on entering the room I was completely shocked to behold the awful change which only a brief hour or two had effected in his appearance; he was then in robust health, and looked like a man who would in all probability live to a great age; but now he was pale, and haggard, and ghastly to look upon, and was writhing in the intense agony of his sufferings. He seemed perfectly conscious, and recognised me with a look which I can never forgot, but all power of utterance was denied him, and it was too evident that the hand of death had struck him; indeed, the significant looks of the physician sufficiently confirmed those suspicions.

"During the whole of that night his sufferings were most excruciating, and his groans were quite painful to hear; and it was also quite evident that he had something on his mind which he wished to divulge, but still he was deprived of the power of speech, and his mind was too bewildered and distracted, and his hand too nervous to render him capable of making use of writing materials in order to communicate that which he wished. I never left his bedside for a moment, and I must confess that the suddenness of this visitation, and the contemplation of his sufferings, which were evidently greatly aggravated by the keen reproaches of his own conscience, awakened me to some sense of remorse. From the very first moment that he was seized with this fatal illness to the time of his dissolution, the power of speech was taken from him; and it was truly painful to witness the powerful, but fruitless efforts he made to give utterance to his feelings.

"In less than four and twenty hours after his attack, my unfortunate, but guilty and misguided father breathed his last, in the greatest bodily and mental agony; and unable any longer to control the indescribable and conflicting feelings that agitated my breast, I retired to my own apartment, where I gave free indulgence to them.

" I was now the Count de Clairville; the whole of the immense property was mine, as well as the proud estates of St. Almo, whilst my poor brother was a beggar, and exposed to all the miseries and sufferings consequent upon poverty. But could I hope to be happy with all my riches? Could I expect to have one moment's peace with such an overwhelming weight of guilt upon my conscience? I could not. The last moments of my father had made an indelible impression upon me; I must, indeed, have been callous to every sense of feeling had they failed to do so; the whole of the enormities of which I had been guilty were presented to my mind's eye in the most vivid colours, and I shrank appalled at myself, while pity and anxiety for the fate of my injured brother and his innocent wife took possession of the former disgusting feelings that had predominated in my breast, and made me feel doubly wretched and hopeless.

"'Good God!' I exclaimed, striking my forehead in the anguish of my feelings, what a miscreant have I been to have acted the part that I have done towards those whom I ought to have valued and cherished with the same affection as I did my own existence. The curses of outraged Heaven must ever pursue me for it, and bring upon me shame, misery, and destruction. Of what value is all my wealth to me? Can it purchase me peace of mind, and restore me to that state of honour and happiness I might have enjoyed had I not suffered my evil, my diabolical passions to prevail? It cannot; and better, therefore, would it be for me—But,' I added, suddenly recollecting myself, and shuddering with a sensation of horror, 'what was I about to say? Is such a guilty wretch as I am fit to die? Oh, no! How can I meet the presence of that Almighty and awful Judge, whose holy laws I have so greatly violated? Let me not die with all this weight of sin upon my wretched soul, but rather live for repentance. But I will find out the much-wronged Antoine and Emilie, and make them all the atonement in my power, even though I search for them in the remotest corner of the globe. I will throw myself at their feet; I will humble myself in the dust before them, and supplicate their forgiveness. Their forgiveness? Dare I hope to obtain that, after the manifold injuries I have inflicted on them? Dare I again venture into their presence? Must not the sight of me be odious to them? And what could I expect but that they would heap their bitterest maledictions upon my head? Oh, I am, indeed, a miserable and hopeless being!'

"Such were the conflicting thoughts that continued to harass my mind; but I had no right to murmur, for it was no more than a just punishment to me, for the crimes of which I had been guilty.

"The whole of the day on which the count, my father, breathed his last, I secluded myself in my chamber, and would not suffer any one to approach me; and it was in vain that I endeavoured to obtain the least degree of peace or consolation. The last sufferings of the count were sufficient to prove to me how keenly his conscience upbraided him for the cruelty and injustice of his conduct towards those who ought to have been the objects of his greatest care and solicitude; and how anxious he was to behold them that he might implore their forgiveness, ere his soul was summoned into the presence of the Supreme. That wish was not granted him, and it was an awful warning to me to repent in time. The awful appearance of the shade of my wife, now made a more powerful impression upon my mind than

before, and urged me still further on towards endeavouring to discover the victims of my guilt, and to make all the reparation in my power, while, at the same time, I was afraid that the opportunity would never be afforded me; and, alas! too fatally were my fears doomed to be realised.

"All the guilty passions that had before held their sole influence in my breast were now entirely banished, and were replaced by feelings of the deepest and most sincere remorse. I awakened from an hideous dream, and beheld the infamy of my guilt in all its deformity. I shuddered, and shrunk from myself with feelings of shame, regret, and disgust. What would I not have given could I but have recalled the past!

"'Alas! Antoine, but is it possible that you can ever more look upon me with any other feelings than those of shame and abhorrence? or, that I can dare to enter your presence, or that of your innocent and amiable wife, or to encounter your bitter, but justifiable reproaches? I tremble at the thought, and am ashamed of myself. But surely when you hear of the death of our parent, you will endeavour to stifle the feelings of indignation and animosity, which have naturally been engendered in your breast against me, by my villanous conduct towards you, and will seek me out, and then I will quickly convince you of the sincerity of my repentance, by restoring you to those rights of which you have been so cruelly deprived, and doing all that is in my power to contribute to your happiness. It was, I am certain, the wish of my misguided father to have done so in his last moments, had speech not been denied him, and I should now loathe and despise myself were I not to follow what his wishes dictated.'

"Having come to this resolution, I felt somewhat more easy in my mind, and after some short time longer passed in serious reflection, I slowly made my way to the chamber in which the corpse of my father was lying. I felt a sensation of mingled awe, regret, and fear, on entering the room of death, which I cannot adequately describe, and for some moments I paused, and drew in my breath without venturing to raise my eyes towards the place where the coffin was standing. At length fresh courage nerved me, and approaching the bier upon which the coffin rested, and raising the lid, I fixed my gaze, with the most intense earnestness, upon the ghastly features of the corpse of that man to whom I owed my being, and who but a few short hours previous was in full vigour of life and health. I then knelt down by the side of the coffin, and clasping my hands together, in fervent and solemn tones I supplicated the forgiveness of the Supreme for the heinous offences of which I had been guilty, and besought him to strengthen the resolution I had formed, and enable me to accomplish all that which in my penitence I was so anxious to do.

"Having thus given utterance to the sentiments that now occupied my breast, I felt much more happy in my mind than I had done for some time; and when I again gazed upon the pale countenance of my father, I could almost imagine that a smile of approbation overspread his fixed and ghastly features. Slowly I quitted the chamber of death, and once more returned to my own apartment.

"During the time that the corpse of my father remained in the chateau, I looked forward with the greatest anxiety, expecting every moment that Antoine would return, in order that he might pay due respect to the remains of the count, and at the same time with the hope of bringing me to a due sense of the errors of my past life, and effecting a reconciliation. But I was doomed to be most woully disappointed, and at length the day appointed for the funeral to take place arrived, and I still heard nothing of my brother and his wife. That mournful ceremony over, I again shut myself up in the chateau, and for a few days I would not see any one, but abandoned myself entirely to my own distracting feelings. But at length I aroused myself into action, and was determined to lose no time in endeavouring to discover the place where the unfortunate Antoine and his wife were at present concealed, and to bring about that reconciliation and restitution of his rights which I was now so anxious to effect. With that view I dispatched persons in different directions all over the country, and I promised a large reward to any one who might be able to furnish me with such information as was calculated to lead to their discovery. I, however, for the present resolved not to leave the chateau myself, but to await and see what results these inquiries would have, entertaining strong hopes as I did that they would be attended with success. But when several weeks elapsed and I was not enabled to obtain the least intelligence, my impatience and anxiety became almost insupportable, and I again began to give myself up to despair.

"But, at length, I received a communication from one of the men whom I had sent in search of the unfortunate fugitives, informing me that he had received the fatal intelligence, from a source on which he could place the utmost reliance, that Antoine (who, with his wife, had been residing in a state of great poverty in the same neighbourhood as the informant) had, in the utter despair of his feelings, committed a desperate act of suicide, and that his wife had immediately afterwards absconded from the neighbourhood, and no one could tell or form the slightest conjecture what had become of her.

"You may imagine the utter horror and anguish of my feelings on receiving this information; I clasped my forehead in agony, and throwing myself on a seat, madness almost seized upon my brain. In this state of mind I insisted upon being left to myself, and the excitement of my feeling every moment obtained additional strength. I raved, I swore, and cursed my very existence, accused myself of being his murderer, and called down the vengeance of heaven upon my head.

"'Monster that I am!' I cried; 'surely now the measure of my crimes is at last full! Oh, Antoine! unfortunate, cruelly-used brother, what a dreadful fate has been thine, and what have I not to answer for for the wrongs, the infamous and revolting wrongs which I have inflicted on you? Alas! what must have been the horrors and tortures that you suffered, that you should have been driven to commit so rash and dreadful an act!—And what has become of her whose happiness I have for ever destroyed?—Whither can she have gone, penniless, friendless, and broken-hearted as she must now be?—And I, heartless miscreant that I am, have been the cause of all this!—I shall go mad!'

"I beat my breast and groaned aloud, and it was in vain that I sought to regain the least composure. For several days after the receipt of this fatal and awful intelligence I was unable to leave my chamber, and it was found necessary for a couple of servants to remain in charge of me, for it was feared, from the alarming state of excitement I was in, that if I were to be left alone, I also might lay violent hands upon myself. But, at length, I sufficiently recovered myself to prosecute my search after Emilie. I had placards posted all over the country, offering an immense reward for any intelligence I might receive which would be likely to give a clue to the place of her concealment; I likewise dispatched agents to all quarters, and set forth myself in the search, though it was with a heavy and hopeless heart that I did so.

"I visited the neighbourhood where my brother and his wife had resided after their flight from the forest, and made the most minute inquiries I could. The particulars I there ascertained wrung my heart with grief and despair; Antoine and Emilie had been reduced to the most abject state of want and destitution, almost entirely subsisting upon such scanty relief as the charity of their kind neighbours, who were almost as poor as themselves, could afford them, and——"

"But my lord," interrupted Florio, "what became of old Gervoise?"

"I was informed that the poor old man was taken seriously and suddenly ill, immediately after their arrival in the neighbourhood, and that he died in a few days," answered the Count de Clairville; "no doubt the little money he had accumulated was exhausted, and he had nothing to leave them, so that the state of utter wretchedness to which they must have been reduced, may be easily conceived. Would to heaven that they could have conquered the natural feelings of disgust and indignation they entertained towards me, and had sought me out; all the horrors that followed might have been spared them, and probably, when time should have banished the remembrance of the past from our minds, we might all have lived to have experienced the most uninterrupted happiness.'

"Alas! my unfortunate parents," said Florio, "what a melancholy fate was thine! How terrible must have been your sufferings."

"Yes," returned the count, "and what punishment is there that can be sufficiently severe for that man who was the cause of them all? You, Florio, must look upon me, in spite of all you have said, with feelings amounting to disgust and detestation. But let me hasten to the conclusion of my narrative, for I have but little more to add.

"Before I quitted the neighbourhood, I left sufficient instructions for the erection of a monument over the grave of my ill-fated brother, and I then journeyed on in my fruitless search, though I scarcely knew in what direction to bend my course; and terrible, indeed, were the sufferings I endured, most painful and insupportable the upbraidings of my own conscience. Sometimes I was driven to such a state of madness and despair, that, had it not been for the attendance of my servants, I am certain I should have terminated that existence which had now not only become hateful, but a burthen to me. But all my efforts to discover the retreat of Emilie were ineffectual, and I could not help at times thinking that she also had committed some act of suicide, for how was she to exist, left destitute as she was, and without a friend or protector?

"I passed away some months in the prosecution of this melancholy and hopeless task, during which time I travelled all over France, Switzerland, and Italy, but not the least clue could I obtain which was likely to lead to any discovery, and, at length, I gave it up in despair, and with a sorrowful heart I returned to the chateau, the very sight of which, however, had now become hateful to me; as it reminded me so strongly of all the painful events that had taken place, and of which I had been one of the principal and guilty causes. I determined to quit that part of the country altogether, and to endeavour by travelling to ameliorate the poignant anguish of my mind. The Castle of St. Almo I had already let; and placing the chateau in the charge of a faithful old servant and his wife, I then commenced my melancholy perambulations, in which I was accompanied

only by two confidential and trustworthy servants, and partly resolved never more to return to my native home. I cannot enumerate all the different places I travelled to, nor the adventures I encountered, as I have already detained you too long, and I am inclined to believe that you would not be much interested by the recital. For several years, I never remained long in any place, and I lost no opportunity of making all the inquiries that were likely to assist me in my wishes, but without the least success, and I at length gave it up in despair, and endeavoured to reconcile my mind to my fate; but that was a difficult task to accomplish, and I succeeded but indifferently. In vain I rushed into society, and tried to drown the anguish of my mind in the wine-cup; nothing whatever could banish the remembrance of the past from my mind, and I every day, if possible, became more and more miserable.

"At length, tired of travelling, I took up my residence in Switzerland, near Lausanne, and so pleased was I with the beauty and retirement of the place, which was so much in unison with my feelings, that I resolved no more to leave it, and I accordingly wrote to the old people whom I had left in charge of the chateau, that, as it was quite uncertain when I should return to France, they might let it on any terms they chose, only letting me know from time to time all those particulars it was necessary for me to be made acquainted with.

"It was here that I became acquainted with the father of my young friend, D'Aubigny, and a more excellent man never existed. In tastes and dispositions we very much assimilated, and we, therefore, soon became as ardent friends as if we had known each other, and been on the most intimate terms from childhood. I took up my residence in the same mansion with the Chevalier D'Aubigny and his lady (a most amiable woman); and as they seldom or never received any company, my time was wholly occupied in their society. This served to divert my thoughts in a great measure from the dismal and painful subjects that had before engrossed them, and I became comparatively resigned and tranquil. The first interruption that took place to our happiness was the death of Madame D'Aubigny, (which took place rather suddenly and unexpectedly), and it was a severe blow to her husband, for she was, as I have said before, a most amiable woman, and they loved each other most affectionately. It was some time ere my friend could recover from this severe loss; but my friendly efforts at length served to restore him to some degree of composure, and this affliction, if possible, cemented our friendship more firmly than ever together. In order to seek to banish the melancholy thoughts that, notwithstanding all our endeavours to the contrary, would at times steal over us, we entered somewhat more freely into society than we had previously done, and extended our pursuits. We frequently took long rambles in the most romantic part, of the country, and in that we found more real enjoyment than anything else. The wild scenery of Switzerland well accorded with our tastes and feelings, and saved in no small measure to ameliorate the sorrows that laboured in our breasts. Had the chevalier and I been brothers, we could not have been more firmly attached to each other than we were; our thoughts, our wishes were mutual; we never dissented from each other in opinion; nor did we ever exchange a word together which could have been misconstrued into one of anger, or anything approaching to ill-feeling. Oh, D'Aubigny, my excellent, my amiable, my devoted friend, when can I ever cease to cherish and revere thy memory? Never while the purple current of life shall continue to circulate throughout my veins."

Young D'Aubigny here raised his hands and eyes solemnly towards Heaven, and mentally invoked a blessing to the memory of his father; and the Count de Clairville again paused for a moment or two, in order that he might indulge in the feelings which this sad reminiscence created in his breast.

"Let me hasten to the conclusion of my long and dismal story," he at last resumed. "But notwithstanding this change in the course of my life, and the pleasures I enjoyed from the society and friendship of D'Aubigny, it was impossible I could entirely forget the past. At times the recollection of the heinous offences of which I had been guilty, would rush upon my memory with such overwhelming force, that I wonder my reason did not sink beneath its influence, and at such times even the society of D'Aubigny was irksome to me, and I would rush into the seclusion of my own chamber, where I would lock myself for hours together, and would not permit myself to be intruded upon. These were indeed moments of the severest, the most inexpressible agony to me, and I cannot even now look back upon them without feelings of horror. When I thought of the melancholy and untimely fate of my deeply injured brother, and the dreadful uncertainty of that of Emilie, all brought about by my deep designing villany, I could not help shrinking appalled at the enormities I had committed, and cursing and hating myself. What would I not have given could I but have recalled the past, and have been as free from guilt as I once was!—Oh, that I could have again beheld Emilie, that I might have humbled myself in the dust before her, and have sued for her forgiveness for the manifold wrongs I had inflicted on her head! —Her forgiveness! could I ever dare hope for

that?—Could I expect to blot out from her memory those guilty transactions which had deprivd her of a fond and affectionate husband, to whom she was sincerely, fervently devoted? Could I think that even I could erase from her memory the monstrous designs I had had upon her honour? The thought was presumptuous; it was such a one as could only emanate from the conscience-stricken brain of a madman!

"One of the greatest relaxations of mind from gloomy thought that myself and the Chevalier D'Aubigny found, was in attending to the education and cultivation of his son, and to that task we both applied ourselves with equal energy and assiduity. My young friend can testify to the care and attention we bestowed upon him, and the mutual delight we felt at the readiness with which he received our instructions, and the early promises he gave of that future excellence which has since characterised him, and has rendered him as dear to me as if he were my own son."

"Oh, my kind friend, my benefactor," exclaimed young D'Aubigny, fervently; "how can I find words sufficiently powerful to express the gratitude I feel for all the manifold favours I have received from you?—the heavy debt of obligation which I owe to you?—I can alone endeavour by my actions to prove the sincerity of my words."

"My dear boy," replied the count, "well am I convinced of the truth and fervour of all you speak, and I am satisfied that I have been enabled to keep the solemn promise I made to one of the best of friends. I now come to another most melancholy part of my story, and one which I cannot look back upon without feelings of the most peignant anguish and regret; but I will dwell upon it as briefly as possible.

"In the manner that I have described, several years passed away, and I heard nothing whatever of the fate which had befallen Emilie, though I belived she was no more; that she had either perished of want or of a broken heart.

"Myself and my friend continued to live in the same harmony together, and we hoped whenever it should please Heaven to end our mortal career it might be on the same day, and that the same tomb might hold our remains; but such was not destined to be the case, and the time was now fast approaching when we were to be separated from each other, and I was again to be left, as it were, almost alone in the world.

"On leaving my chamber one morning at my usual hour, I was somewhat surprised to find that my venerable friend was not in the room where we always met at breakfast; I say, I was surprised, for he was always punctual almost to the moment: but thinking that he had probably overslept himself, I went to his chamber, and was still more astonished to find that he was not there, nor had any of the domestics seen him that morning. This made me rather uneasy, for he was not accustomed to walk forth from the house till I accompanied him, and a dismal foreboding of something about to happen crossed my mind. Myself and my young friend here, however, resolved to go in search of him, and with that view we first

D'AUBIGNY UNVEILS HIS PASSION FOR MELINA TO THE COUNT DE CLA... ...LLE.

examined the gardens attached to the house, and it was not long ere we discovered him, but in such a state as filled us both with the most indescribable anguish and alarm. He was lying on his back in a state of complete insensibility, and at first we thought he was dead; but we soon discovered that he was in a fit, and the ghastly paleness of his countenance, and the distortion of his features, convinced us that he was in a state of the greatest danger, and that there was not an instant to be lost. With all possible care and expedition we raised him in our arms and conveyed him into the house, where medical assistance was quickly in attendance; but it was some time ere he showed the least signs of returning animation, and you may imagine the deep and overpowering agony with which myself and Adolphe hung over him during that time. I anticipated the worst, and could not but think that my revered friend was struck with death, and, in fact, the physician gave me no hopes to the contrary. At length D'Aubigny was restored to some degree of consciousness, and perceiving me and his son by his bed-side, he extended his hands towards us, which we pressed fervently to our lips, and inquired eagerly how he was. He shook his head in a melancholy manner, and then in a faint voice replied:

"'It is useless to deceive you or to flatter you with delusive hopes, my dear friend and beloved son; I feel that the hand of death is upon me—that my mortal career is fast drawing to a close. For your sakes, I wish that my life might have been prolonged, for I know well how severely you will feel my loss; but it is the will of Heaven, and it is not for me, poor erring mortal, to dare to murmur at its wise decrees. I go to join my sainted wife!'

"'Oh, my best, my only friend,' I ejaculated with the deepest emotion, 'and must I indeed be deprived thus suddenly and unexpectedly of your society and sympathy? This is indeed the severest blow that I have experienced for many, many years. But it will not be; the Almighty will surely, in mercy to me and your son, spare you to us yet a few years longer, and——'

"'De Clairville,' he interrupted, in a solemn voice, 'compose yourself, and learn to submit with fortitude to the will of the Most High; it is sudden, but, notwithstanding, I feel myself fully prepared for the awful change I am so soon about to undergo. I have never wilfully done any person an injury, and I trust that God will pardon me for those errors I have in my lifetime committed.'

"'He will, my poor friend,' I returned, and I found it impossible to restrain the tears of anguish that gushed to my eyes; 'oh, would to Heaven that I had nothing more to answer for than you have! How shall I, with all the weight of guilt I have upon my conscience, be able to meet the terrible hour of death?'

"'Tremble not, my dear friend,' replied D'Aubigny; 'but continue firm in your penitence, and so shall your last moments be those of peace and resignation. We all have sinned, but God is merciful, and will not abandon those of this creatures who feel sincere compunction for the errors they have committed. But there is one request I have to make, and it is one which I know you will not fail to comply with.'

"Oh, name it, my friend!' I exclaimed, vehe-

mently, 'and by all my hopes I solemnly swear to obey it to the very letter.'

"'My son, my poor Adolphe,' he replied; 'when I am no more, he will have no other friend in the world but you; will you, then, promise me that, while he continues to deserve it, you will never desert him; but that you will endeavour to be to him the father he will have lost?'

"'I swear it, most solemnly I swear it,' I answered, 'and as I keep my oath, may God prosper me!'

"'Enough! enough! De Clairville,' he said, 'and may Heaven's blessings light upon you for this assurance. And you, my beloved Adolphe, let me solemnly enjoin you, as you hope to prosper in the world and for future happiness, never to act in disobedience to the will or wishes of the Count de Clairville, but to look upon him with the reverence and affection of a son, and to endeavour by your conduct to make up in some measure for the loss he will experience in me.'

"'My beloved father,' exclaimed Adolphe, sinking on his knees by the side of the bed, and raising his hands and eyes solemnly and devoutly towards Heaven; 'I swear to obey your injunctions, and if I break my oath, may every curse pursue me!'"

"And have I not kept the solemn promise I then made, my lord?" asked young D'Aubigny.

"You have, my dear young friend, most sacredly," answered the Count de Clairville, "and have proved to me a solace in the midst of the heavy sorrows with which my mind is afflicted. But let me proceed.

"After some few more words, my friend D'Aubigny became exhausted, and sunk into a state of apathy, during which time myself and Adolphe watched by him in a state of the most unspeakable anguish and anxiety. We consulted with the medical gentlemen who were in attendance, and the observations they made in reply to the interrogatories we put to them fully confirmed our worst fears; they considered, according to the present symptoms he evinced, that it was impossible for him to survive many hours, and certainty that all chance of recovery was at an end, it being a severe attack of appoplexy, which his advanced years rendered it most unlikely he would be able to contend against for any lengthened period.

"Need I tell you what intense grief this dismal intelligence was productive of to both myself and Adolphe? I am satisfied that I have no occasion to attempt to do so, for I could find no language at all adequate to the task; I will, therefore, leave it to your own imaginations, and hasten to the close of the melancholy scene, which neither time nor circumstance can ever efface from my memory, as quickly as I possibly can.

"For several hours, poor D'Aubigny remained in the same deplorable state; he was at times evidently conscious of what was passing around him, recognised myself and his son, and smiled faintly upon us as if in recognition of the attention we paid him, and the deep grief in which we were immersed at his hopeless condition; but he was unable in these moments to give utterance to that which he wished to express, and it was but too clear that death would soon claim his victim. The medicine gentlemen advised us to leave the chamber for awhile, but it was not likely that we could be persuaded to do so even for a moment, and the looks of the poor suffering patient, in those intervals when reason and susceptibility held their sway, showed plainly enough that he approved of our determination, and duly appreciated the motives that prompted it, and seeing that, they no longer urged their advice. During this painful interval, I recalled to my memory, in the most vivid colours, all the many acts of kindness and sympathy I had experienced from him; and the loss, the irreparable loss I was about to sustain, swelled into such magnitude, that my heart was fit to break, and I was frequently compelled to retire to a remote part of the chamber in order that I might conceal from observation the powerful and overwhelming emotions that swelled my breast. Towards the evening, however, the acuteness of his pain seemed to be greatly abated, and my hopes for a short time once more revived, especially when he recovered the use of speech.

"He motioned me to his bedside (from which, as I have said before, I had for a short time retired, in order to conceal the violence of my anguish), and I immediately obeyed the summons, and took hold of his thin, damp hand, which he had extended towards me, and pressed it fervently to my heart.

"'You are weeping, De Clairville,' he ejaculated; 'it is in vain that you seek to hide from my observation, though my eyes are now growing dim, the deep, the uncontrollable anguish that corrodes your heart. Arouse yourself, my dear friend; be collected and firm; it is sinful to take on thus; we do but part for a season, and we shall meet again, I trust, in that world where sorrow is unknown. I am happy, and shrink not from the approach of death, whose hand is now upon me. But a short time, and all will be over; you will remember my injunctions, I know, and adhere to the solemn promises you have made, and in that assurance I shall die content. Let my son emulate the conduct of his parents, and he will be happy; my spirit and that of his mother shall hover and watch over him and you, and, heaven permitting, shield you from every danger that might threaten you. God bless

you, my son: God bless you, my dear friend, and may that happiness in future be your lot in the world, which hitherto it has not been your fate to experience.

"He could say no more for a moment or two, for his strength was again exhausted, and clasping his hands together piously across his breast, and raising his eyes meekly towards heaven, he was evidently engaged in silent, but earnest prayer.

"Can I ever forget the impression which the last words of that excellent man made upon my mind? It would be impossible for me to do so; but my heart was full to bursting, and, again for a few moments I was compelled to avert my face, so that I might conceal the intense agony of mind I was undergoing.

"''Oh, D'Aubigny,' I said, at length, turning towards him; 'and must I so soon and so suddenly be deprived of you, at the very time when I feel your inestimable value the most? Cruel decree of fate! But it will not be; Heaven, in its infinite mercy, will still preserve you to your son and me.

"''De Clairville,' he said, after a brief pause, and in the same solemn accents in which he had before spoken; 'arraign not the justice of heaven, but rather learn to yield with humble resignation and fortitude. Death is a debt we must all some time pay, and it is our duty to prepare ourselves for the awful change that we must one day undergo. Again, I say, I feel happy; and now that my soul is firm in confidence and reliance upon the mercy of the Almighty Judge, I would not wish to live. But a short time since, I beheld the sainted spirit of my wife, surrounded by the bright halo of heavenly glory, and she smiled benignantly upon me, and welcomed me to join her in the realms of eternal bliss; and shall I any longer cling to this world, and all the cares, the anxieties, and the temptations that exist in it? No, no: Almighty God, it is thy will that I should quit it, and I cheerfully submit, and eagerly court the moment of my emancipation. Oh, I am indeed so very, very happy.'

"A sweet and unearthly smile spread itself over his countenance as he gave utterance to these words, and again he sunk into a state of unconsciousness.

"We anxiously questioned the medical gentlemen in attendance, as to whether or not there was any hope in his recovery, for we could not make up our minds to the certainty of the dreadful event, and they candidly assured us that there was not, and desired us to be prepared for the worst, though it was not at all improbable, they thought, from the symptoms he then evinced, that he might continue to linger several days longer; but they would have persuaded us to retire from the chamber for a short time, in order that we might collect ourselves, and be enabled to be in a condition to meet the final moment with becoming fortitude. To this we, however, could no listen with any degree of patience, and we continued in the chamber of the dying gentleman, and watched every change in his pale countenance that came over it, and indicated the rapid approach of death, with such feelings as only those can duly appreciate who have been placed in similar awful and impressive circumstances. But I fear that I am harrowing up the feelings of my young friend, by dwelling thus long upon the melancholy subject, though I found it was utte impossible for me to refrain from giving ssion to the feelings which the remembra of it naturally gave rise to in my breast; but I will hasten to the conclusion.

"M. D'Aubigny remained much in the same condition till about ten o'clock at night, and did not appear to be suffering much, if any pain; he did not, however, speak, and we feared that we should never hear his voice again. But suddenly he started from his lethargy, and raising himself up in the bed, with more strength than we could have thought it possible for him to do, in the exhausted state in which he was, he gazed vacantly around him for a moment or two, with the dew of death standing upon his brow. Myself and Adolphe each seized his hands, and again he smiled faintly upon us, and made an effort to speak, but for an instant the words were stifled in his throat, and it was then evident that the fatal moment was at hand.

"'It has come,' he gasped forth, at length. 'Heaven opens upon my vision. Bless you, my son! bless you. De Clairville. Let my ashes repose in the same tomb as that which incloses those of my Clarisse, and——'

"He could say no more, a gentle sigh escaped his bosom, he fixed one impressive glance upon myself and Adolphe, which it is impossible that we can either of us forget to the latest moment of our existence, and then the eyes of one of the best of men, and warmest hearted of friends, closed in death for ever!"

Here the Count de Clairville was once more compelled to pause to give vent to the powerful emotions that agitated his bosom, and young D'Aubigny especially, and all those who were present, were deeply affected, and made no effort to conceal the feelings that sprang from so pure and manly a source. In a few minutes, however, the Count de Clairville was sufficiently recovered to proceed as follows—

"The sufferings of myself and Adolphe that night may easily be conceived; it was some time ere we could be prevailed upon to quit the chamber of death, but continued to hang over the corpse in a state bordering upon frenzy, scarcely being able to persuade ourselves of the truth of the fatal calamity which

had so suddenly and unprepared for come upon us; and when we did retire to another apartment, it was only to give vent to the most melancholy lamentations, at the sad and irreparable bereavement we had sustained.

"What occurred for two or three days after the death of the lamented D'Aubigny I know not, for I was in a state of unconsciousness; and when I recovered my senses, I could scarcely believe in the truth of that which had taken place. But too soon the whole fatal facts rushed upon my recollection with the most painful and overwhelming force, and I became perfectly inconsolable; I found that I had lost one of the most faithful, fervent, and devoted of friends, and what could ever replace him? Nothing! it was sheer madness to think of such a thing, and the more I sought to do so, the more powerful and insupportable became my emotions. But at length I summoned religion to my aid, and by its genial influence became more calm and resigned, remembering the words of my deceased friend, and resolving to adhere to his last injunctions even to the very letter.

"In due time the remains of the lamented D'Aubigny were consigned, with all proper solemnity and respect, according to his request, to the same tomb which contained those of his wife; and by my instructions a monument was erected to their joint memory. For several weeks afterwards, myself and Adolphe D'Aubigny kept ourselves entirely secluded to the house, with the exception of twice every day, morning and night, paying our visits to the tomb of D'Aubigny and his amiable lady, and in offering up our prayers to Heaven for the repose of their souls; but at length our physicians gave it as their opinion that it was absolutely necessary, in order to the restoration of our health, that we should travel for awhile, so that by change of scene and society we might probably be able to recover somewhat from the severe shock our feelings had sustained in the recent and deplorable loss we had experienced, and at last we yielded to their advice, though it was with very little hope of receiving the relief which was expected. We travelled to Italy and various other parts of the Continent, and were absent for several months, but without its having any material effect upon our spirits; it was impossible that we could forget the bitter sorrows that were preying upon our hearts; and, if possible, the more we sought to do so, the more poignant and insupportable they became. What added to my anguish was the fact that my mind was never free from the remembrance of those errors of which I had formerly been guilty, and though Heaven knows how truly penitent I was, I could not hope for forgiveness, or look forward to the future with any other feelings than those of the utmost horror and dread. During the time that we had been travelling, I again made all the inquiries I could which might possibly lead to the discovery of Emilie, if she were still living, but without the least success ; and I now concluded, beyond all doubt, that she was no more, and that thus I was deprived of every means I was so anxious for, namely, to make her all the atonement that was in my power for the many and terrible injuries I had inflicted on her.

"More than two years passed away, and myself and Adolphe continued to reside at the house where his parents had expired ; but though we persevered to the best of our ability, nothing could assuage the grief we experienced at the heavy and irremediable loss we had sustained, and at length we resolved again to travel with the same hope that had induced us to do so before. I will not tire your patience by particularizing all that occurred to us in the course of our peregrinations ; we seldom remained long in one place, and in order to try what effect that would have, we mingled in society as much as possible, and I must say that we derived considerable benefit by so doing ; our sorrows were ameliorated, though nothing whatever could entirely eradicate them from our mind. But by accident I now obtained such important information as entirely altered the plans I had so long adopted, and inspired me with hopes which, I thank Heaven, have been partly realised. Never resting in my inquiries after the unfortunate Emilie, notwithstanding the lapse of so many years, I at length succeeded in meeting with a person who said he had known her when she resided with her child near Paris, but that was several years previously, and as he had been away from there some time, he knew not whether she was still in existence or had removed.

"From the description which this man gave of her, I had no reason for an instant to doubt the accuracy of his statement, and you, Florio, may, therefore, judge the state of my feelings when I received the important particulars from his lips. When he recounted such of the sufferings and privations she had endured as had come to his knowledge, with what bitter feelings of remorse and self-reproach did I listen to him ; and mentally I cursed myself, and considered that I was worthy of any punishment that might overtake me ; but at the same time my mind was made up ; I was determined to visit France without delay, with the hope of either finding Emilie or her offspring, and Hope whispered to me that I should not be entirely unsuccessful. With as little delay as possible, myself and Adolphe took our departure from the place where we were staying, and Heaven be praised, my errand has not been altogether a failure, for Providence has guided my footsteps to you, my nephew, and although

your unfortunate mother was not permitted to live to witness my repentance for my past crimes, and to receive from my hands all the reparation I could make for the dreadful wrongs I inflicted upon her and my poor brother, I have at last been able to relieve my conscience from the heavy burthen which before pressed upon it, and made me one of the most wretched of human beings."

CHAPTER LVIII.

YOUNG D'AUBIGNY AND MELINA.—THE FATAL PASSION.—AN UNEXPECTED SCENE, AND THE CONSEQUENCES.

IN these words the Count de Clairville finished his very lengthy, but deeply interesting and important recital, and the whole of the persons present remained silent for a few minutes, for the effect it had had upon them, especially on Florio, may easily be imagined. The count having concluded, sighed deeply, and then folding his arms across his chest, he walked to a remote part of the cavern, where he sank into a state of abstraction, in which he was permitted to indulge for some time without interruption.

There were many passages in the narrative which could not but fill the mind of Florio with shame and disgust ; and when he reflected upon the cruel sufferings to which his unfortunate parents had been so unjustly subjected, his heart was stung with pity and anguish ; still, he could not witness the sincere penitence and remorse of his misguided uncle without pity ; and the feelings he would otherwise naturally have experienced towards him subsided into those of regret and commiseration.

Massaroni remained silent, but the sentiments he entertained upon the subject were similar to those of Florio, and he also felt gratified to think that so strange and fortunate an accident had guided the Count de Clairville to his mountainous retreat, otherwise his young friend, Florio, might for ever have remained in ignorance of the true nobility of his birth, and thus one great obstacle to his union with the beauteous Signora Melina would have continued unremoved.

The thoughts of young D'Aubigny were of the most varied and conflicting description. The narrative of his benefactor, the Count de Clairville, had not only surprised but deeply interested him ; but still, in spite of all his efforts to the contrary, he could not banish the fair image of Melina from his mind ; and when he reflected upon the position in which she and the nephew of that nobleman to whom he owed such an immense debt of gratitude, stood together, he could not help entertaining feelings of regret and remorse. He trembled for himself, and heartily did he wish that he had never beheld her, for that circumstance might be productive of the most serious and dangerous consequences; and those feelings were strengthened when he recalled to his mind the principal incidents in the narrative of the Count de Clairville, and he recollected that most of the errors he had so unfortunately committed had been caused by his entertaining similar sentiments which he, D'Aubigny, had suffered to take possession of his mind on beholding Melina. He, however, stifled his real feelings as well as he was able, lest they should meet the observation of those present, and excite their surprise and curiosity, and awaited with eager impatience for the time to arrive when he should be permitted to retire to the privacy of his own chamber, that he might there indulge his thoughts alone.

At length the Count de Clairville, having apparently succeeded in somewhat conquering the emotions which the recital of his eventful story had naturally excited in his breast, turned to Florio and the others, and said—

"Thus, you see, Florio and my friends, that I have made a candid confession of the many and heinous errors of which I have been guilty; and although the confession has greatly relieved my mind, I almost blush to appear before you; for what else, when you take all the circumstances of my conduct into consideration, can you think me than a most consummate villain? Are you not prepared to curse me, Florio, as the destroyer—the fell destroyer of your parents, and to visit me with your most implacable vengeance?"

"Oh, my lord," answered Florio, "how ungenerous is the opinion you seem to have formed of my character; and why will you still persist in distracting yourself with thoughts such as those you have just now expressed? Have I not frequently in the course of your narrative assured you of my forgiveness, and why should you doubt my sincerity? It is impossible that I can do otherwise than regret the misfortunes of my parents, and that they should in any way have been caused by one so nearly related to me; but I believe you to be truly penitent, and I should hate and despise myself if I could now entertain the slightest feeling of animosity towards you."

"Generous, noble hearted young man," exclaimed the Count de Clairville; "this unmerited kindness overwhelms me; how shall I ever be able sufficiently to evince my gratitude for your forbearance? Never did I feel my own guilt and degradation so keenly as I do at present."

"Compose your feelings, my dear uncle," returned Florio, "and in time, I trust, that you will be able to bury the painful past in oblivion."

"Florio says right, my lord," observed Massaroni, "and I hope you will follow his advice; time will enable you to think of the past only as some painful dream."

"No, no," replied the count, impatiently, "that is impossible; the terrible facts are stamped in characters too powerful upon my conscience ever to be effaced. But my mind is made up; I will but wait to see my nephew placed in that position in society to which his birth entitles him, and to endeavour to bring about his union with the fair Signora Melina, to whom it seems his heart is so fondly devoted, and then I will retire into holy seclusion, and try to find that consolation and tranquillity in religion which I cannot hope to meet with in the world."

"Oh, no, my lord," remarked Florio, "you will think beter of thus; there are, indeed, believe me, many days of happiness in store for you yet, and why should you, who are so well calculated to adorn society, seek to immure yourself in the gloomy walls of a monastery?"

"The world has long possessed no charms for me, Florio," returned his uncle.

"But now that you have discovered your nephew, my lord," observed the brigand chief, "and everything is explained, surely you may be able to reconcile your mind, and to look forward to the future with hope?"

"Shall I not be pointed at as a villain?" demanded the count.

"No," answered Florio; "all that is past is known only to ourselves, my lord, and who dare cast an aspersion on your name? But come, my dear uncle, you are at present in no frame of mind to discuss this painful subject; you require rest and calm reflection after the task you have had to undergo, and to-morrow you may be better prepared to enter calmly and dispassionately into this question."

"Exactly so," coincided Massaroni, "and my word for it, that his lordship will then see the prudence and necessity of abandoning the hasty resolutions which he had formed."

"Well," replied the Count de Clairville, "I do feel my mind fatigued and harassed by the conflicting thoughts that crowd upon it, and will, therefore, avail myself of your kind suggestion, and retire. To-morrow we will meet again, when we will further discuss this subject, which is of so much importance to us."

The Count de Clariville now bade his nephew and our hero farewell, and he then retired from the cavern, accompanied by D'Aubigny, who, however, was in no state of mind to enter into conversation with him, for his thoughts were too much occupied with the image of the beauteous Signora Melina.

"And what think you of this narrative, Massaroni?" asked Florio, when they were gone.

"Why, it is certainly a most extraordinary one," answered the brigand; "but you may consider yourself most fortunate, Signor Florio, in having made the discovery you have, for it not only raises you to wealth and station, but almost secures your union with the fair object of your affection."

"Upon that important point, Massaroni," replied Clairville, "I must confess I am not so sanguine in my expectations as you seem to be. I have experienced enough of the obduracy and vindictiveness of the Prince Bianchi's disposition to make me doubtful. He will never break the promise he has made to the Count Alberti, and he will be further goaded on in his determination by a feeling of revenge."

"Nay, my young friend," remarked Massaroni, "it is sheer nonsense to talk thus, when we have everything in our power, and Bianchi cannot help himself. Besides, will he not fear the exposure it is in our power to make, by producing the victims of his guilt, and that man to whom he would sacrifice his beauteous and innocent niece? Believe me, Clairville, as I have often said before, and I repeat it now, that your union with the Signora Melina is as certain as if it had already taken place, unless you are both resolved to relinquish the consummation of your hopes from any false scruples of delicacy."

"For my own part," returned Clairville, "I am ready to brave anything rather than resign that beloved being on whom all my fondest hopes are fixed; but Melina's sense of honour and delicacy, and the reverence she still entertains for her uncle, notwithstanding the cruelty and oppression with which he has acted towards her, are too keen and powerful, I am afraid, to permit her to consent to become my wife without his consent."

"If she really loves you with the sincerity and ardour which I believe she does, she will not hesitate," replied the brigand. "Pardon me, Signor Clairville, but still I must again say that it is ridiculous to talk thus. You love each other; the principal objection which the Prince Bianchi had against you is now removed, by this fortunate and extraordinary discovery you have made; you are proved to be of noble birth, and, believe me, that Bianchi, when he is satisfied upon that point, which he will soon be, will no longer remain obstinate, in spite of the power and influence which the Count Alberti holds over him, but will be only too happy to come to an amicable arrangement, and to render some atonement for the many wrongs he has committed by consenting to the union of yourself and his fair niece. But if he should remain obstinate, he will have no one but himself to blame for the consequences that may take place."

"Very true, Massaroni," agreed Florio "but you, my friend, to whom I am so greatly indebted for the manifold services you have rendered me—will he not ever pursue you with the same implacable spirit of hatred and revenge he has ever evinced towards you?"

"If he be wise he will not," answered our hero; "methinks he should already have had sufficient proofs of my power, and how fruitless it is for him to seek to triumph over me; it has already cost him dear in his attempts to do so; and by the saints I swear, that should he persist in trying to hunt me down like some beast of prey, not all the power he possesses shall shield him from my vengeance."

"Hold, Massaroni," said Clairville, "you forget that, should myself and my Melina then be united, any feuds that might arise between the prince and you, whom we have so much reason to respect, must prove a source of the greatest misery and regret to us."

"Well—well," observed the brigand chief, "we will talk further upon that subject on a future occasion; time and circumstances may effect all that we can wish, and to that we will leave it; but whatever may happen, Florio Clairville, and all those immediately connected with him, shall always possess the warmest friendship and esteem of Allesandro Massaroni."

"I know that full well, my generous and disinterested friend," replied Florio, cordially pressing his hand, "and believe me that nothing would grieve me more than that any misfortune should happen to you."

"Oh," returned our hero, "I fear not that. In all the many difficulties which it has been my lot to experience, kind fortune has never forsaken me yet, and I feel confident that she will not do so now."

"I trust not," said Florio, "and I sincerely hope that the time is not far distant when you will be restored to that position in society you are formed to adorn."

"No, my young friend," answered Massaroni, "I do not expect that, nor, in truth, do I much wish it; I have been so long connected with my present adventurous life, that I have become attached to it, and have not the least desire to leave it, or the bold associates who have devoted themselves so zealously to my cause. What value does the world and all the vanities, frivolities, and vices it contains possess in my eyes? None! Here, in my mountain home, I am free, and unshackled as the air I breathe; I have a world of my own, and those who move in the proudest circles of life, as it is called, are often compelled to pay tribute to me, and to acknowledge my power, while, at the same time, they affect to despise the brigand chief. Oh, it is a glorious life to lead! and I would not exchange it for the noblest station that could be offered to me."

"But could you discover the author of your being, and he should be willing to acknowledge you, and to make you all the atonement in his

power for the injuries he has done you?"
suggested Florio.

"What!" replied Massaroni, and his fine
eyes flashed with fearful determination as he
spoke, "the base seducer and destroyer of my
excellent and ill-fated mother——he who was
the base cause of driving me from society, and
exposing me to all the many troubles and vicissitudes I have since had to encounter! By all
my hopes, it will be well for him if he never is
revealed to me, for better then would it have
been for him had he never been born."

"Massaroni," said Clairville, "surely you
could not raise your hand in vengeance against
your own father?"

"My own father?" repeated the brigand
chief; "has he not rendered himself totally
unworthy of the name? What mercy should
I show towards the murderer of my mother?
All the cruel wrongs I have received at his
hands would arise to my memory on beholding
him, and fierce hatred and revenge would
supersede every other feeling in my breast. It
is the hope of discovering him, and hurling
upon his head the just, though terrible revenge
for the injuries inflicted upon the innocent and
confiding being whom he so remorselessly
betrayed and abandoned, that has principally
sustained me through the many dangers and
difficulties I have experienced; and should we
meet, by Heaven no thought of nature shall
restrain my hand from the perpetration of that
which justice and outraged innocence so loudly
calls for.'

"I would fain hope that you will yet think
better of this, Massaroni," said Florio. "Vengeance is for Heaven, not for man; and should
he of whom you speak prove to be penitent,
and ready to make atonement——"

"Atonement!" hastily interrupted our
hero; "what atonement, think you, could he
make for the base, the monstrous wrongs of
which he has been guilty? Could he recall to
life and happiness the innocent being whom he
destroyed?—could he repay me for all the
miseries I have suffered?—could he remove
from me the stigma of a dishonourable birth?
Oh, Clairville, had you experienced that which
it has been my lot to endure, methinks you
would not talk thus; you would feel as I do,
that is, if your mind had not become insensible
to every manly passion."

"Pardon me, Massaroni," observed Florio,
"if I appear too bold in thus obtruding upon
your private sorrows, but it is only the sincere
friendship and sympathy I feel for you that
induces me to do so."

"I know it, Clairville," replied the brigand
chief, again pressing his hand; "and, believe
me, I sincerely thank you for the kind solicitude you so warmly express; but it is impossible that I can ever forget the cruel injuries
that have been inflicted on myself and that

beloved being whose cold remains have long
since mouldered to dust in a premature grave,
that grave prepared for her by the heartless
villain who betrayed her. Her spirit has long
called for retribution on the head of her murderer; and, by all my future hopes, should it be
my fate to discover him, if he be living, I will
not fail to execute that which I consider to be
a sacred duty."

"Reflect calmly on this, Massaroni," said
Florio, "and I feel certain that you will think
better of it."

"Reflect calmly!" repeated the brigand,
impatiently; "oh! how easy it is for one who
has never experienced what I have to advise
thus. Have I not reflected till madness has
nearly seized upon my brain? But no more
of this, at present; the subject only tortures
me, and we had, therefore, better waive it. I
must leave you now, Clairville, and, no doubt,
you are anxious to see the Signora Melina, who
will be impatient to hear something more of
what has transpired between ourselves and
your uncle, the Count de Clairville."

"And do you think it would be prudent to
make her acquainted with all the particulars of
the count's melancholy and eventful history?"
asked Clairville.

"Yes," answered Massaroni. "I do not see
the least necessity for concealing them from
her. Situated as you are, there should be no
secrets between you."

"Very true," coincided Florio; "and the
facts will satisfy her that the Count de Clairville and myself are really as nearly related as
we were at first led to suppose."

"Certainly," returned the brigand, "and
she will then at once perceive that one of the
principal obstacles to your union is removed,
and will no longer entertain any objection to
its taking place, should the Prince Bianchi
obstinately persist in refusing to give his
consent."

"I would indeed fain hope so," said Florio,
"but I have my doubts upon the subject."

"Nonsense, signor," replied our hero;
"she cannot possibly advance any reasonable
objection. Besides, the Count de Clairville
will, no doubt, take the earliest opportunity
of communicating with the Prince Bianchi, and
of advocating your cause, which, I imagine, can
now be accomplished with all due effect, and
that a perfect reconciliation may be brought
about."

"God grant that your surmises may prove
to be correct, Massaroni," said Clairville,
fervently, "but, indeed, I have still my doubts
upon the subject."

"They will shortly be removed, take my
word for it," said Massaroni, "and you will
be one of the happiest of men—at least, you
should be so in possessing so fair a being as
the Signora Melina. But we have talked

sufficient just now upon that point; trust to Providence, my young friend, put a bold heart upon the matter, live in hopes, and, depend upon it, you will not be doomed to be disappointed. Farewell for the present; by-and-by we shall see each other again, and then we will consult with the count, your uncle, as to the course it will be most prudent to adopt in order to bring about a speedy and satisfactory termination to this important business."

Clairville again thanked him for his good

THE MYSTERIOUS APPEARANCE OF THE TWO MASKED FIGURES.

wishes, and the interest he took in his welfare, and Massaroni having quitted him, he made his way to the cavern in which he knew he should find Melina.

Melina had been for some time enjoying the society of the Signora Zitella and her daughter, who expressed the warmest and most sincere interest in her welfare, and she had been most anxiously waiting to see her lover, with the hope that he would impart to her all the particulars of the history of the Count de Clairville, which, she had no doubt, would disclose some important facts. On the entrance of Clairville, Zitella and Mira, after exchanging a few complimentary words with him, retired, and left them to themselves, well knowing that their presence might be embarrassing to them.

The meeting of the lovers was of the most affectionate description, and it was several minutes ere they could sufficiently regain their composure to talk freely; but at length Clairville said—

"Dearest Melina, how it glads me to be once more in your sweet society, and to listen to the music of your voice. No doubt you have been most anxious to see me, and to know the result of the interview between me and the Count de Clairville, for on that, probably, depended our future happiness. But everything has been proved to my satisfaction, my love; there can now no longer be any doubt that I am the nephew of that nobleman whom Providence has guided hither in so extraordinary and unexpected a manner, and, therefore, one of the principal obstacles to the consummation of our happiness is removed; and by equality of rank I may not be considered presumptuous in aspiring to your hand, though too well do I know my own unworthiness in other respects."

"Florio," said the maiden looking into his face with an expression of the most innocent affection, while, at the same time, it was not unmingled with one of gentle reproach, "you wrong me much if you imagine that any change in your fortunes (though for your sake it affords me the most inexpressible satisfaction), can at all strengthen the sentiments which I have ever entertained towards you, for your intrinsic merits alone. Florio Clairville would always have been the same in my estimation, though he had never been proved to be allied to nobility. Honour and virtue are the true spirits of nobility; and it is to these in the humble and friendless painter, Florio Clairville, that I have ever yielded my warmest admiration and love."

"Sweetest and purest of human beings," ejaculated her lover, fervently, and clasping her with the most inexpressible fondness to his bosom; "what transport do those blessed words impart to my senses. How, oh! how shall I ever be able to prove my worthiness of the flattering admiration you are pleased to bestow upon me? In what words can I ever express to you my gratitude? And may I, indeed, hope to call so inestimable a treasure mine own?—May I, after all the cares and anxieties it has been my lot to contend with, look forward to the time when we shall be united in those bonds that nothing but death can sever?"

Melina hid her blushing face on his shoulder, but could return no answer.

"Enough, my sweet Melina," said Florio, "those looks, that gentle sigh assure me, and I am happy."

"Florio," said our heroine, in a faint voice, and after a brief pause, "I need not again repeat the sincerity of the sentiments I entertain towards you, and how anxious I am that the hopes we have mutually encouraged should not be disappointed; but——"

"But!" interrupted her lover, with a melancholy expression of countenance; "ah! I know too well what you would say, and it is that which diminishes my happiness, and throws a blight upon those fond hopes I should otherwise entertain. Should your uncle still refuse to sanction our union, you cannot, will not consent to become my bride?—Say, is it not so?"

"Florio," replied the maiden, "you put a painful and delicate question to me, but I will endeavour to answer it with all the candour and sincerity that becomes me. I, therefore, confess then, that I am most anxious to effect a reconciliation with my uncle, and that, should he remain inflexible, though great as would be the disappointment to my hopes, and painful though the sacrifice would be that I should have to make to my feelings, I should still hesitate to consent to a clandestine union."

"Alas! alas!" sighed Clairville, "that assurance is the annihilation of all the bright hopes I had so fondly, but so rashly indulged in. Ah! Melina, I fear, if that is your determination, knowing the unnatural, but powerful prejudice which the prince your uncle entertains towards me, that all chance of our happiness ever being completed is at an end. But, surely, reason will prompt you to think better of this. My uncle will, no doubt, plead our cause with the Prince Bianchi; he can raise no real objection to my character, and should he still determine to oppose our wishes, merely from obstinacy's sake, and wish to sacrifice you to such a man as the Count Alberti, it will show that he cannot entertain a proper regard for you, and you certainly would not then, I should imagine, any longer acknowledge his authority, nor refuse to place yourself under the lawful protection of one who loves you to adoration, and whom you have been pleased to admit holds a similar place in your affections?"

"No, Florio," replied Melina; "of this rest assured, that should my uncle, after due and reasonable argument and persuasion, still remain inflexible, I shall consider myself at liberty to act as my inclinations lead me, and in that manner which I am persuaded will contribute to my happiness."

"Blessed words!" cried Clairville, pressing her still more closely to his bosom, "they have again made me one of the happiest of human beings. I am satisfied, my Melina, and will not again urge the question, but trust to that kind Providence which ever watches over those who are so fondly devoted by virtuous love to one another as you and I are, and still will I encourage the sweet hope, that all the sanguine wishes we now, and have ever entertained towards each other, will be gratified, unpromising though our prospects may at present seem to be."

Melina returned no answer, but her looks sufficiently testified that she ardently responded to the wish which her lover had just now uttered, and a pause of several minutes ensued, during which they were both evidently giving free indulgence to the various thoughts that crowded upon their minds, and which neither of them seemed disposed to interrupt.

"But," said Melina, at last, "has the Count de Clairville yet finished his narrative?"

"He has," answered Clairville, "and an eventful, though melancholy one it is. I will, if you please, my love, relate to you the particulars, for it may, perhaps, be necessary for you to know them; but I must claim your kind and generous indulgence for the errors which the count, my uncle, has committed, and which he now so truly repents."

"Oh, yes, Florio," returned our heroine, "you may be sure that I shall view them with a lenient eye; Heaven forbid that I should judge too severely of any of my fellow-creatures."

"Spoken like my own sweet Melina," observed her lover, "and I am satisfied that you will find, when you are better acquainted with my uncle, that he is every way worthy of your indulgence and regard."

"Oh, indeed I do not doubt it," said the beauteous and innocent damsel; "he is the uncle of my Florio, and as such I am confident that he must be ever worthy of my esteem and reverence."

Clairville once more embraced her fondly, and then seating himself by her side, he proceeded to relate all those important, but painful particulars, with which the reader has already been made acquainted, in as few words as possible. Melina listened to him with the most profound attention and deepest interest, but was frequently compelled to interrupt him in order to give vent to her feelings, being frequently affected to tears, when she heard of the many sufferings it was the cruel destiny of the parents of her lover to experience; and when he had come to the conclusion, she was for some minutes absorbed in thought, and which he did not seek to interrupt.

"Dear Melina," he observed at last, "such is the dismal history of the Count de Clairville, and those beloved beings to whom I am indebted for my existence; and though I know your virtuous and innocent heart must condemn the conduct of my noble relative, still I trust, when you take into consideration all the singular and unexampled circumstances by which that conduct was brought about, and the years of bitter remorse which the count has since endured, you will be inclined to pardon him and to pity him for a weakness which he could not control."

"Oh, yes," replied our heroine; "but still how fearful were the results which that misconduct was productive of. What an untimely fate was that which befel your unfortunate father, and how terrible must have been the sufferings which your mother had to endure."

"Alas! they were," returned Clairville, "and had you but seen the christian patience and resignation with which she bore them, it could not have failed to have excited the warmest feelings of sympathy and admiration in your gentle bosom."

"But surely the parents of the Count de Clairville and Antoine, and those of your mother and her sisters were principally to blame for all that took place," said Melina; "such a monstrous compact as that which you have mentioned I never before heard of, and could only have originated in a species of monomania or brutal tyranny."

"Very true, my dear Melina," coincided her lover; "and it was calculated to be productive of the greatest misery to those who were unfortunately bound by it."

"Yes," said Melina, "had it not been for that, probably none of the misfortunes that afterwards attended your parents would have happened to them. But what does the Count de Clairville now propose to do?"

"He has stated that he is tired of the world," answered Clairville, "that he wishes to end his days in holy seclusion; and that after he has settled his affairs, and resigned his title and estates to me, it is his determination to enter the walls of a monastery."

"And a pious resolve, too," remarked Melina; "showing the deep and earnest contrition of his soul; but still it is a pity that one who seems now to be so eminently favoured to ornament society should thus seclude himself from it, especially when he has the means of doing so much good in the world; and I trust that, on mature consideration, he will be induced to change his mind."

"I hope so, too, Melina," said Florio, "for I calculate, if he should remain amongst us, upon much enjoyment from his society. But now, my love, since my claim to noble origin is fairly established, do you not think that it may work some influence in my favour in the mind of the Prince Bianchi?"

"I would fain think so, Florio," replied our heroine; "but while the Count Albert, still exists, I am afraid it will not. Besides, my uncle will be more prejudiced against you in consequence of my rescue from his power by the brigand chief, and knowing that you and I are now together. It would, perhaps, have been more prudent to have suffered me to remain his prisoner at the Villa Civetti."

"What," returned Clairville, "to endure all the acts of oppression and coercion to which you were subjected? No, that would have been monstrous, and I cannot think of it with any degree of patience."

"Had I been suffered to remain there," observed Melina, "now that you have made this discovery as regards yourself, the prince might have been induced to listen to the arguments and persuasions of the Count de Clairville with a more favourable ear, and not have been exasperated, as he now doubtless is, to a feeling of revenge."

"Indeed, Melina," said her lover, "I entertain no such thoughts; but, on the contrary, I firmly believe that, notwithstanding the illness of the Count Alberti, he would have forced you to become his wife ere this, and thus all our hopes would have been annihilated."

"He surely would never have gone to such cruel extremities," said Melina.

"Experience, my beloved Melina," replied Clairville, "ought to convince you that he would not have hesitated to have done so. Thank Heaven that you are not now in his power, for I cannot but flatter myself that he will yet see the justice and the necessity of coming to terms."

"God grant that he may," ejaculated the damsel, "for it would remove a heavy weight of care and anxiety from my mind. But the Count de Clairville, I presume, will now not much longer remain here, and Massaroni can have no motive or inclination to detain him?"

"Certainly not," answered Clairville.

"And when he departs from this mountain retreat," added Melina, looking anxiously in his face, "I presume, Florio, that you will accompany him?"

"What, without you, Melina?" returned Florio. "Oh, never! that is impossible! How could you ever entertain such a thought? But myself, the Count de Clairville, and Massaroni, must hold a consultation upon that subject, ere we can decide what course it will be best to pursue."

Melina acquiesced in this opinion; and after some time passed in further conversation, they separated, and Melina was left to the indulgence of her own thoughts, which were of the most complicated and conflicting description, and tortured her to come to any satisfactory conclusion.

"Dear Florio," she ejaculated, "what a strange and chequered fate is ours, and how uncertain is it in what manner it will yet terminate! This discovery of your noble birth, and all the other circumstances that are attached to it, is a most extraordinary and important one, and may be productive of the most favourable results—and, therefore, is it that I hail it with feelings of satisfaction, and not from any idea of the manner in which it will aggrandise Florio, for he must ever be as precious to my heart for his intrinsic virtues, as he is now, were he even steeped in the lowest depths of poverty. It is not riches that can purchase happiness and content, and Florio possesses noble qualities that are beyond all price. The Count de Clairville will, no doubt, lose no time in pleading our cause with the Prince Bianchi, my uncle; and should he be able to move him to relent, and to seek to make all the atonement in his power for the many acts of injustice he has inflicted on me, and the cruel sufferings he has subjected me to, and give his consent to the union of myself and Florio, my happiness would indeed be complete, and freely could I forgive and forget the past. Oh, blissful thought! should it be realised; but, alas! I fear that my uncle will remain inflexible. And should he do so, shall I refuse to grant my hand to the only being who possesses my heart, out of any false notions of prudence?—shall I thus sacrifice my hopes, and consign Florio to misery and despair? Reason and justice revolt at the idea. Let me be firm and resolute, and wait with patience the result, and should the Prince Bianchi still persist in refusing to give his sanction to our vows, may Heaven teach me in what way to act for the best. Florio, I cannot resign you, so worthy as you have ever proved yourself to be of my love by your exalted virtues, let the consequences be whatever they may."

Having come to this resolution, she felt her mind more at ease, and sat herself down to reflect upon all the remarkable circumstances of the Count de Clairville's narrative. The more she pondered over them, the more astonished she became and the deeper she sympathised with the misfortunes that had attended the parents of her lover. She could not but deprecate the errors of the Count de Clairville, which had been productive of so many fatal consequences; yet she was moved to pity him from the contrition he evinced, and which she had every reason to believe was sincere; and she could never enough admire the wisdom of Providence which had directed his footsteps in such a miraculous manner to the very place in which one of those beings whom he was so anxious to discover was residing. She was interrupted in the midst of her cogitations, however, by the entrance of Floretta, and to her she confided all those extraordinary particulars with which her lover had made her acquainted.

The astonishment of the faithful Floretta as she listened to them, may easily be conjectured;

and when her mistress had concluded, she said—

" Well, my dear signora, I declare that this is, without exception, one of the most remarkable narratives I ever listened to. Poor Signor de Clairville and his wife, Emilie! what terible misfort unes did untoward fate subject them to, and so unmerited likewise."

"True, Floretta," remarked Melina, " they were, indeed, the victims of adverse fate."

" Ah, signora," said her attendant, " they were, indeed. much to be pitied; and who would have thought such an amiable looking gentleman as the Count de Clairville is, could ever have been so guilty?"

" No, Floretta," said our heroine; " but he is now truly penitent, and no doubt has suffered many years of bitter remorse."

"Yes, my dear mistress," observed the loquacious Floretta; " a guilty conscience is a terrible monitor, I should think. But what a fortunate thing it is that Signor Clairville is discovered to be of noble birth, for that removes the only barrier to your union; and when the Prince Bianchi comes to hear of it, I should think he would no longer withhold his consent, especially when he knows that your future happiness depends on it."

" I hesitate to entertain such a hope," said Melina, " so prejudiced is my uncle against Florio, and after the opposition that has been offered to his stern decree."

" Then pardon me, signora," returned Floretta; " if he does refuse his consent, he must be even more cruel than I take him to be."

"He has pledged his word to the Count Alberti, and he is too scrupulous to break it," answered her mistress.

" What, signora! sacrifice you to the heartless betrayer of his own daughter? The thought is monstrous in the extreme."

" I am afraid that no feelings of compunction would move him to change his mind."

" But should the Count Alberti die?"

" I am afraid that circumstance would make very little difference in regard to his inflexibility," replied our heroine. " His mind is too much exasperated at my escape from his power; and he will never forgive the opposition he has experienced to his authority."

" Well, then, signora. I suppose you have decided how you shall act?" remarked Floretta.

" What mean you?" demanded her mistress.

" Why," returned her attendant, " if the Prince Bianchi will not relent, and come to a reconciliation, I presume, since you are no longer responsible to his authority, and he will prove himself so unworthy of your regard, you will at once avail yourself of the protection of the Signor de Clairville by becoming his wife?"

" I dislike the idea of doing anything in a clandestine manner," answered Melina, " and should hesitate to do so."

" And who could blame you for so doing, my dear signora?" interrogated Floretta. " Is not your lover good and honourable? and is he not also now proved to be your equal in birth and station?"

" True; but still, the world is too ready to censure."

" You may set it at defiance, signora," said Floretta; "and I'm sure, when you come to reflect more seriously upon the subject, you will never be able to make up your mind to abandon your lover to misery and despair, merely because of the cruel prejudices and stern opposition of your uncle."

"Do not question me any more upon the subject, Floretta," said our heroine, " for it racks and perplexes my mind almost beyond endurance. I scarcely know how to act. I would fain conciliate the favour of my misguided uncle; and I could, if he would yield, freely and gladly pardon him all the sufferings he has so undeservedly inflicted on me; but to abandon my hopes of becoming the wife of Florio—oh! that I feel to be utterly impossible."

" Well said, signora," remarked her attendant. " There you spoke like yourself, and I sincerely trust that you will continue in the same mind. The opposition of the Prince Bianchi is unnatural and unjust, and Heaven will sanction you in the determination you have come to. But mark my words, your uncle will yet be aroused to his senses, more particularly when he hears of the circumstances connected with Signor de Clairville, and will only be too happy to yield that consent to the gratification of your wishes which he has too long withheld."

" You are most sanguine in your expectations, Floretta," said her mistress, with a faint smile.

" No less so, signora, than the circumstances warrant," she answered; " and if you could only persevere in encouraging the same ideas, you would not experience half the anxiety of mind you now do."

" Well, my good girl," said our heroine, " I will endeavour to do so, and Heaven send that the hopes you have expressed may be fulfilled."

" I have no doubt but that they will. But I have been thinking, signora, that perhaps the Count de Clairville will propose taking you under his protection until matters are settled with the Prince Bianchi, and for you and Signor Florio to remove with him to his chateau, in France."

" Ah!" ejaculated Melina, " that idea never occurred to me, and it is not at all improbable."

" And would you consent to leave the protection of Massaroni?" asked Floretta;

"especially after he has been so kind to you?"

"Why," replied our heroine, "I should not like to do so; but still I should not be so likely to meet with censure under his protection as in the brigand's cavernous abode.''

"You would be more safe here, signora," said her attendant; "besides, Massaroni would be offended, I should imagine, were you to adopt such a course, which would appear to be treating him with ingratitude."

"Well, probably he might," returned Melina; "however, we must consult with each other upon the subject, and we shall probably then be able to come to a decision that will be satisfactory to all parties."

After some further conversation of no importance, Floretta, having some business to attend to, took her departure, and Melina was left once more to the undisturbed indulgence of her meditations, which were of the most busy and perplexing nature.

We must now return, however, to Adolphus D'Aubigny, who, on being left alone after the Count de Clairville had left him, gave himself up to a variety of thoughts of the most painful description, and in vain endeavoured to tranquillise his feelings and to banish the beauteous and dangerous image of Melina from his mind; but that he found to be a task that he was wholly inadequate to accomplish. The longer he thought of her, the more powerful and alarming became the impression which her numerous and transcendent charms had made upon his feelings, and he found that it was utterly impossible for him to divert his thoughts from the delicate subject which so completely engrossed them. And yet how bitterly did he reproach himself for encouraging ideas that were fraught with so much danger, and especially after the terrible example which had been presented to him in the narrative of his benefactor, the Count de Clairville; and already he accused himself of acting a base and treacherous part towards Florio, which, if he did not quickly abandon, must end in destruction. He paced his apartment backwards and forwards in the most disordered manner, and still the form of Melina haunted his imagination, and he recalled to his memory every word she had uttered when they had been together in each other's company; and every word that he remembered added its influence to the feelings that agitated his bosom. He longed to behold her again, and yet he feared to enter into her society, lest he should by a single look or expression betray himself. Then feelings of a far different nature came over him to those that we have described, and which he in vain tried to conquer; they were those of jealousy and almost hatred towards the man with whom he had so recently become acquainted, and who had never offended him, but, on the contrary,

had evinced the same friendship towards him as if they had been acquainted for years. Need we say that this was Florio Clairville? He could not but envy him his good fortune in possessing the love of so beauteous a being as Melina; and when he rememberd the looks of ardent affection she had bestowed upon him, the fond expressions that had passed between them, it was like wormwood to his soul. He felt surprised and shocked at himself for the sinful thoughts that had crowded upon his brain; but still, the more he sought to conquer them the stronger they became, until his brain was completely distracted, and he scarcely knew what he was about. And what would be the disgust and indignation of the Count de Clairville, did he but know the feelings in which he was indulging, after the warning he had received from him? He could not help shuddering as this reflection crossed his mind, and again he traversed the place in which he was in a more agitated state, if possible, than before.

"What cursed and dangerous infatuation is this that has taken possession of my senses?" he said; "am I going mad, that I should thus let this weakness overcome every feeling of honour and virtue? Let me banish the demon from my breast, ere it involves me in the meshes of destruction. But no, it is impossible! That angelic form, so far surpassing everything that I have before seen, can never be banished from my imagination. It haunts me like a vision, and tortures my senses to distraction. Oh, she is most lovely, and methinks that I could kneel down and worship her as some deity. But, fool that I am, why do I give way to such thoughts as these? I must never dare venture to breathe in her ear the sentiments with which she has inspired me, for is not her love bestowed upon another, and one more worthy of her than I can ever hope to be? Oh, Florio de Clairville—Florio de Clairville, how do I envy thee the bliss that is in store for thee!"

He paused, and beat his breast in the agony and despair of his feelings. But it was to no purpose that he endeavoured to banish the maddening thoughts from his mind; and the more he tried to do so, the more powerful and torturing became their influence over him.

"What will become of me," he said, "if I continue to encourage the feelings that I have suffered to take possession of my breast, and that in so sudden a manner? It will end in my ruin, and probably destroy the happiness of those who never offended me. Oh, my respected, but unfortunate benefactor, how do I tremble when I reflect upon your fatal passion for the innocent and confiding Emilie, and find myself just on the brink of a similar precipice! Beauteous Melina, thou wert surely formed to captivate all who encounter thee; but would to Heaven that I had never beheld thee, then should I have been spared the anguish of mind I am now enduring. Where will this end? I tremble to think. But, weak fool that I am, I must not give way to this infatuation; I must struggle with my feelings, and endeavour to banish the image of this fair enchantress from my breast, or the consequences will be to me of the most fatal and disgraceful nature."

He paused, and for a short time was wrapped in deep meditation; but all his efforts to conquer the feelings that had so unfortunately taken possession of his mind were in vain, and, in fact, the longer he reflected upon the numerous captivating personal graces, and the transcendent qualities of mind possessed by our heroine, the greater became his agitation, and the more powerful the influence she obtained over him. It was in vain that all the evils that must naturally follow such a hopeless passion, and the injustice he was doing to the noble-minded nephew of his friend and benefactor, by encouraging it, were presented in the most vivid and glowing colours to his imagination; he could not succeed in subduing those feelings which he knew too well were fraught with so much danger, and which, in all probability, must end in his own disgrace and ultimate ruin, whilst they also at the same time would so greatly disturb the pleace of those who were so eminently entitled to his respect and regard. Short as had been his acquaintance with the beauteous Signora Melina, so powerful was the impression that she had made upon him, that he felt confident, notwithstanding all the virtuous and honourable exertions he might make, even though he should tear himself away from her presence, and by mingling in other scenes, and seeking the society of other maidens who might possibly possess attractions equal to hers, if not surpassing her own, nothing could have the power to eradicate. But the bare idea of being separated from her distracted his mind, and he was so bewildered and tortured by the variety of conflicting thoughts that crowded with overwhelming force upon his brain, that he knew not how to act, or what decision to come to. He thought it not at all unlikely, now that the Count de Clairville had made the extraordinary discovery he had, he would wish to take Melina and Florio under his protection until such time as a reconciliation might be effected with the Prince Bianchi; and he could not but look forward with a feeling of dread to the consequences which might follow his being thus constantly in her presence. He placed not the least confidence in his own strength of mind; and he thus saw that there were no other means of preventing that from taking place, the bare idea of which his better feelings revolted from, than by withdrawing himself from her presence altogether; but that was a task which he knew not how to accomplish.

"Alas!" he again soliloquised, "what a miserable wretch have a few brief hours made me, when I was before so happy and contented. Beauteous Melina, I fear that it was a fatal moment for us both which first introduced us to each other. Would to heaven that we had never met, or that Florio de Clairville had never existed, or at least became acquainted with you, and made such a powerful impression upon your heart, then might I have dared to entertain some hope of obtaining your affections, and aspiring to your hand; but now, even to encourage the thought is guilty and presumptuous, and while I am compelled to acknowledge the power which you have obtained over me, I cannot but shudder and feel ashamed of myself when I reflect upon the misery which my hopeless and unlicensed passion may be productive of. What can I do? How shall I act? Oh, my excellent friend, thou who hast ever been to me more than a father, what would be thy feelings of regret and indignation, did you but know the thoughts which at the present moment occupy my mind? With what base ingratitude must you consider that I have treated you. And shall I not receive any warning from the fatal and painful example you have shown me of encouraging a hopeless and unlawful passion, in your own melancholy history? Shall I rush madly into that vortex of shame and misery which must surely be my fate if I do not conquer the dangerous feelings and wishes which at present hold their dominion in my breast? Alas! however anxious I am to do so, something seems to whisper to me that it will be impossible for me to accomplish the task. Florio de Clairville, most honourable of men, did you but know the base and presumptuous passions that have gained such a powerful and unconquerable ascendancy over me, how wouldst thou despise me; what a villain must thou consider me; and how justly would thy utmost indignation be excited against me. And how must I quail beneath thy reproaches; what could I say in extenuation of my conduct? Nothing; nor could I dare to offer any resistance to thy vengeance. I feel that I have debased myself, and by such conduct as that I am now pursuing, degraded my father's memory. Had he been living, how bitter, yet how merited, would have been the reproaches he would have heaped upon my guilty head. I feel ashamed of myself, and yet, weak wretch that I am, I cannot stifle the feelings that have usurped my breast, and which must end in my own ruin."

He beat his breast in the agony of his feelings, and continued to pace the cavern which formed his chamber with the most disordered steps. In vain he tried to rush away from thoughts so painful, or, at least, divert them into another channel, but the more he sought to do so, the greater became the influence they obtained over him, until he was worked up to a pitch that actually bordered upon madness. He trembled even to remain where he was, though there was no one to observe his agitation, or to listen to the thoughts to which he was giving utterance. He would have left the cavern, and, wandering amidst the solitude of the night, have tried to gain some respite to his cares and anxieties, but he knew it would be impossible for him to do so without being seen by some of the brigands who were on guard, and who would be sure to obstruct him, and to prevent his egress, and he had, therefore, no alternative but to remain where he was, and to give himself up to all that torturing anguish which at the present occupied his mind. How he wished for morning, and yet he, at the same time, dreaded its arrival, for he should then probably behold the fair and innocent Melina again, and he could not but tremble with feelings of shame in her presence and that of her lover, and probably betray the guilty feelings which her charms had engendered in his breast.

"Oh, Florio," he ejaculated, "how do I envy you your happiness in the possession of the love of one so lovely, so innocent, and so fascinating, as Melina! Proud, indeed, ought you to be of the conquest thou hast made, and how amply ought it to repay you for all the troubles thou hast endured. As for me, now that I have beheld her, all my prospects of future happiness are destroyed, and I feel hateful to myself. But where is all that firmness and rectitude of mind upon which I once so greatly prided myself? Can I not form the virtuous resolution to crush this hopeless and guilty passion in its infancy? Arouse yourself, D'Aubigny, and let your better feelings once more predominate ere it be too late. But, alas! no—I feel it is impossible; the fatal spell has obtained too powerful an ascendancy over me for me to destroy it, and the more I seek to do so, the deeper do I become involved in the miseries by which I am now on every side surrounded. Oh, God! why, oh! why didst Thou ever permit so fair and irresistible a being to cross my path!"

Thus for some time longer did he continue to meditate, and his mind could not gain the least relief from the cares and anxieties that corroded it. At length, completely worn out with thinking, he threw himself, undressed, upon his couch, but it was long ere sleep descended upon his eyelids, and when it did, it afforded him little or no relief. Dreams of the most conflicting and torturing description haunted his perturbed imagination, and he frequently started from it, and staring wildly and alarmed around the place, he gave utterance to the most strange and incoherent exclamations, scarcely knowing where he was. The image of Melina was presented to his disordered fancy in a

variety of shapes. Sometimes he imagined that she smiled affectionately and approvingly upon him, and that she uttered words of the fondest love in his ears. But quickly her countenance changed its expression, dark frowns overspread her beauteous features, and words of the keenest reproach escaped her lips. Then he imagined himself in deadly combat with Florio de Clairville, and just as his weapon was about to penetrated the body of his innocent and much-injured rival, the lovely Melina rushed in between them, received the fatal wound, and sunk bleeding and dying to the earth. He beheld the ghastly expression of her features, now distorted with agony; he saw the awful looks of reproach which she fixed upon him; he heard her painful groans, and witnessed the dreadful anguish and despair with which her lover stooped over her, and endeavoured in vain to stay the departure of that life which was so precious to him; and in the horror of the feelings which this frightful vison naturally engendered in his breast, he awoke, and started from the bed, gazing distractedly around him, and for a few moments being scarcely able to persuade himself that it was not reality. The lamp still burnt dimly, and the faint and sickly light which it shed around the cavern rendered everything upon which his eyes rested more dismal and indistinct, and added to the impression which his dream had created in his mind. It was several minutes ere he could at all recover himself, and then the perspiration stood in large drops upon his temples, and his limbs trembled with convulsive emotion.

"Oh, God!" he gasped forth at length, "should this fearful vision be realised, into what misery and crime shall I be plunged! And if I do not make a bold and manly effort to conquer the fatal sentiments that I have suffered to take possession of my senses, what is more likely to occur? Should Florio de Clairville discover that I have presumed to raise my thoughts towards that lovely and innocent being to whom his whole soul is devoted, what can I expect, but that he will seek to inflict his vengeance upon my head? But should it be so, I beseech thee, Heaven, to let me be the victim, for it would be no more than I should deserve; but Melina to perish, and by such awful means, oh, the thought is madness, and as I think of it, my brain becomes distracted, and I feel appalled at myself."

He struck his forehead as he thus spoke, and then once more he paced the cave backwards and forwards in a state of mind which it is unnecessary for us to attempt to describe. To attempt to sleep again he knew would be fruitless, and he feared that even if he could do so so, the same kind of frightful visions would disturb and torture his imagination. The gloom and silence that reigned around added to the terror and agitation of his feelings; and so strongly were they wrought upon by his own thoughts, and the dreams that had occurred to him, that he almost feared to look around him, lest he should behold some terrific object.

"Alas!" he again soliloquised, "what a fearful change has come over me only within the last few days. I can scarcely persuade myself that I am the same individual. How happy and contented was my mind, how free from any thought which I should be ashamed

SIGNOR MONTALDI CONDOLING D'AUBIGNY.

to acknowledge, before I beheld Melina; her boundless charms and numerous virtues seem to have worked a complete revolution in my nature, and I hate and despise myself when I reflect upon the guilty passions I have suffered to gain such powerful ascendancy in my breast.

But could I injure that lovely and immaculate being? No, Heaven forbid; I must, indeed, be a monster of the blackest dye could I contemplate such a deed; and yet, if I do not learn to triumph o'er the dangerous sentiments that now hold their dominion in my breast, to what

No. 97.

fatal consequences may they not give rise? I shudder at the thought; but still I cannot but anticipate that the worst will occur, unless I persevere, and struggle with my feelings. Oh, D'Aubigny, little did I expect that you could so far forget yourself, and those inestimable and virtuous principles instilled into your mind by the best of parents, and the most valuable of friends and benefactors, who has ever behaved towards you with the same affection as if you had been his own son, as thus to commit yourself. But how shall I avoid the temptation that is thus thrown in my way, and which I have not the strength of mind to resist? It will be impossible for me to do so while Melina remains near me' and now that the Count de Clairville has made the remarkable discovery he has, it is impossible that I can avoid her presence, unless I abandon this part of the country, and my benefactor altogether. And what would be his opinion should I do so without assigning any cause? And whither can I go, totally friendless as I am, and almost a stranger to society from the all but secluded life I have led? I am lost and bewildered, and know not in what manner to act for the best. I dread to meet the Count de Clairville and his nephew again, for surely my guilty, self-upbraiding conscience must betray the thoughts that are passing in my mind. I feel wretched and miserable, and when I weigh all the circumstances in my mind, I am driven to the lowest depths of misery and despair. But have I become a child, that I thus suffer my worst and most dangerous passions to triumph? I feel the burning blushes of shame mantling in my cheeks when I reflect upon it. Again, I say, let me arouse myself and endeavour to devise some means of extricating myself from the imminent dangers and difficulties in which I have involved myself."

Once more he paused, and sought to collect his thoughts sufficiently to reason himself into some prudent and judicious mode of action; but it was all to no purpose—the more he tried to do so, the stronger became the influence of his unfortunate passion upon his senses. In this way two or three hours of the greatest anxiety and perplexity of mind passed away, and he judged from the time which had elapsed, and the bustle that prevailed among the brigands in the other parts of the cavernous retreat, that it was daylight, and he tried to compose himself as much as possible prior to his beholding any one who might notice the agitation of his demeanour, and put such questions to him upon the subject as he might find it difficult and embarrassing to answer. This he, however, succeeded but indifferently in accomplishing, and he would have given anything could he but have issued from the cavern without being observed, and tried to have drowned his thoughts, by wandering amongst the solitudes by which the mountain home of the brigand chief and his daring associates was surrounded but that he knew was impossible, and he had no alternative but to await the issue with all the confidence and fortitude he could muster.

He again recalled all the circumstances of the Count de Clairville's melancholy recital to his memory in the most powerful and vivid colours; and as he did so, and compared the principal incidents with his own case, his uneasiness increased, and most keenly did he upbraid himself for having suffered himself to become involved in the same dilemma which had been the sole cause of all the errors and misfortunes that his benefactor had experienced, and productive of so much misery to others.

"What a painful example is here before me," he said; "and yet it is no warning to me. It would seem as if some fatal spell were upon me, and that it would impel and urge me on to my own destruction and that of others. No, I have hitherto revolted at the bare idea of a dishonourable act, and now I find myself as weak and irresolute as an infant. Again, I say, let me arouse myself; I will be firm, and by perseverance I may learn to triumph over those unholy thoughts, which, if encouraged much longer, cannot fail to lead to the most awful results. Melina can never be mine; she can never entertain no other feeling towards me but one of friendship and respect; it would be madness to think so, and the height of presumption and vanity to entertain such an idea; and, therefore, let me at once battle with my guilty feelings, and I may yet hope to conquer, and to retain the same character for honour and virtue which I now possess."

Thus did the young man waver between virtue and crime; but his passions, which were powerful, had never before been properly tested, and it need not be wondered, therefore, that he should find the task he wished to impose upon himself, one of the most trying and difficult he had ever before encountered. He was interrupted in the midst of his meditations by the sudden and abrupt entrance of the Count de Clairville, and he started on beholding him, and although he tried hard to do so, he found it impossible to conceal the agitation and confusion under which he laboured, and which he found did not escape the keen and penetrating observation of his benefactor.

The count looked much better than he had done the day before, and seemed to have entirely recovered from the agitation and excitement into which his recital had naturally thrown him, and advancing towards his young friend, he took him by the hand, and greeted him warmly, which D'Aubigny in vain tried to return with the same freedom and cordiality.

"Come, Adolphus," he remarked, "it is later than our usual time of rising, and I have been long expecting you in my chamber. I am anxious to see my nephew, Massaroni, and the fair and gentle Signora Melina; in whom I cannot help feeling the deepest interest, not only from her own intrinsic merits, and the sufferings she has so undeservedly experienced, but also in consequence of the virtuous and ardent attachment which exists between her and Florio."

Adolphus turned pale and trembled on the mention of our heroine's name, and he found it impossible to conceal the emotion it caused him from the observation of the count, who looked at him with no small degree of surprise, as he said—

"Why, how is this, Adolphus?—Why are you so agitated and confused? I confess that you look as if some great trouble weighed upon your mind, and—"

"Pardon me, my lord," interrupted D'Aubigny, with as much composure as he could; "but—but I do not feel myself exactly well this morning; I have had a bad night's rest, though from what cause it originated, I have no means of ascertaining."

"Indeed," said the count; "I am sorry to hear that; but probably the society of our friends may serve to revive you, so, if you please, we will join them directly, for I have much to consult them about, and I may most likely need your advice on the occasion."

"I must request, my lord," replied Adolphus, "that you will excuse me to-day; I am sadly out of spirits as well as being indisposed, and I am afraid that you would find me but a sorry companion."

The Count de Clairville looked at him narrowly for a moment or two, and then with a smile observed—

"Well, I must acknowledge, my young friend, that you astonish me, by conduct which is so unusual with you; any one would be inclined to think from your present appearance, and the melancholy tenor of your observations, that you were in love."

We need not state that the embarrassment of Adolphus D'Aubigny was very much increased by these remarks, and he turned away his head, and for some seconds was at a loss what answer to return.

"Your lordship has a mind to be jocose with me," he said at last, with a faint smile; "but indeed you have judged wrong if you have suffered yourself to entertain any such suspicion."

"Well," returned the count, laughingly, "probably I have; but we will say no more upon the subject at present. Will you not accompany me to our friends? Their cheerful conversation, especially that of the amiable Signora Melina, may serve to revive your spirits."

"Indeed, your lordship," answered D'Aubigny, again exhibiting the most violent emotion at the mention of the name of that fair being who was the subject of his thoughts, "I must again beg to be excused; in fact, I should feel obliged to Massaroni if he would permit me to walk a short distance from the cavern, for probably the air, and the change of scene, will do more than anything else to refresh me, and restore me to my wonted spirits, and I would thank you to make the request of him."

"Very well, my young friend," said the Count De Clairville, after a moment's hesitation, "be it so; since you are so anxious, I will comply with your request; though I would much rather that you were present at our conference, for I have some proposals to make as regards my nephew and the Signora Melina."

"Your lordship approves of the sentiments that exist between Florio and the signora?" interrogated D'Aubigny, in a tremulous voice, and scarcely daring to look at the count, lest he should read what was passing in his mind.

"Most undoubtedly," replied his lordship, "for I am fully convinced that they are both equally worthy of each other. Melina, from all that I have seen of her, is most amiable and virtuous; and as for her personal attractions, I think you must admit, my young friend, that you have never yet seen them surpassed. But bless me, Adolphus, how extremely agitated you do seem again; what can be the cause of this?"

"Nothing, my lord," returned his companion, in a confused and faltering voice, "it was but a slight spasm that at the moment affected me; I am better now. The Signora Melina is all and much more than you have described her, and is deserving of the happiest fate that can fall to the lot of a human being."

"Very true," coincided the count, "and it shall be no fault of mine if she does not experience it. She and Florio, I am satisfied, love each other with a sentiment as pure as it is fervent, and they must be united together."

"You, then, intend to plead their cause with the Prince Biancha, my lord?" said Adolphus, in a hesitating tone, and at the same time feeling the greatest and almost insupportable anguish of mind.

"Undoubtedly I do," replied the count.

"But the prince is strongly opposed to their union, and greatly prejudiced against Florio?" remarked D'Aubigny.

"I know it," returned his lordship, "but, nevertheless, I do not despair; when he finds that Florio's birth is equal to that of his fair niece, and that he is related to me, I have no doubt that he will yield, and only be too happy to effect a reconciliation, and to obtain the restoration of Melina."

"And in the meantime, what is it you propose to do, my lord, as regards the signora?" asked Adolphus.

"Take her under my protection, and remove her to the chateau, for the present," answered the count; "this mountain retreat is no fitting place for a maiden like her."

"True, my lord," coincided Adolphus; "but think you that Massaroni will resign her, after all the trouble he has been at? And will it not appear like ingratitude for his generous and disinterested conduct?"

"Argument will, I trust, convince him to the contrary," returned the Count de Clairville; "however, that will soon be decided, and whichever way it may be, I am determined not to relax in my efforts until the happiness of my nephew and the beauteous maiden to whom he is so devotedly attached is accomplished. Should the Prince Bianchi remain obstinate, then must their union take place under my sanction, and without his consent."

Adolphus D'Aubigny again felt a severe pang at his heart as the Count de Clairville gave utterance to these words, and it was not without the most painful effort on his part that he could avoid revealing to him his real feelings; but after some further remarks of no importance, his lordship quitted him, and he was left again to the indulgence of his gloomy and torturing meditations. Every word that the count had spoken to him had gone like a dagger to his heart, and now that he reflected on them, he reproached himself more bitterly than before, and his agitation increased every moment.

"Should Massaroni consent to the proposition of his lordship," he ejaculated, "and suffer Melina to accompany him, I shall be exposed to that danger and temptation which I shudder to think upon; and yet I cannot think upon a separation from that lovely being who has inspired me with such unconquerable and unfortunate sentiments with any degree of composure. Would to Heaven that fate had never have introduced me to her, I might then have avoided that misery and shame which my heart now forebodes is in store for me. But what a terrible and fatal weakness is this, and how shall I longer be able to conceal it from the count? What will be his thoughts should he indeed ever become acquainted with it? How painful, but how merited will be the reproaches that I must expect he will bestow upon me! It makes me wretched, and fills my mind with despair to reflect upon it. And in what way can I avoid the danger which I apprehend? In no other way but by flight. Yes, should I retire to some part of the country where I have no possibility of encountering Melina, I might in time learn to drive her image from my mind; to think of her only as a friend, or to forget her altogether. Forget her? Ah, no! that I feel to be utterly impossible. Who that has once beheld the beauteous and innocent Signora Melina can ever banish her again from their memory? And should I adopt the course that has suggested itself to me, must I not reveal everything to my benefactor? And how will he then hate and despise me? The thought tortures me, and my brain every moment becomes more distracted. I know not what to do for the best. Can I ever again grasp the hand of Florio in friendship, knowing the thoughts that I have dared to encourage against his peace of mind? Must I not expect that he can read my baseness in my eyes, and in the expression of my countenance? And he, too, is the nephew of him from whom I have ever experienced the affection and attention of a father. Oh, I feel myself one of the most degraded and ungrateful of human beings, and I despise myself as one unworthy of the respect of my fellow-creatures. Adolphus D'Aubigny, who would have thought that you could ever sink so low?"

At that moment there was a knock at the door which opened into the cavern, and one of the brigand's entered, with a message from Massaroni that he was to conduct him from the cavern, according to his request, but at the same time enjoining him not to ramble to any great distance for fear of danger, and desiring that he would not prolong his walk to any unreasonable time. These injunctions D'Aubigny of course promised to obey, and then immediately followed his conductor, who led him from the cavern, and having seen him to the secret entrance, left him to pursue his ramble alone.

On finding himself in the open air, Adolphus paused for a minute, and folding his arms across his chest, he gazed around him, and the beautiful, romantic, and picturesque scenery which met his view on every side for a brief period diverted his thoughts from the melancholy subjects that had hither engrossed them. The morning was particularly fine, and the golden sun was shining in full splendour in a cloudless sky, while the air was light, pure, and refreshing, as it came breathing over the lofty summits of the vast range of mountains. The extensive panoramic view that was commanded from the spot on which Adolphus stood, was beautiful and striking in the extreme, and the painter's pencil, however skilful he might have been, must have failed to do adequate justice to it. A range of the most lovely and fertile country, extending many miles, the eye might rest upon at a single glance, and all the principal beauties of fair Italy seemed to be concentrated in that one view. D'Aubigny, who was an ardent admirer of the wonders of Nature, could not fail to gaze upon such a scene with the most enthusiastic feelings ; but it was not long that he could do so ; the same painful thoughts that had before occupied his mind returned, and, with a sigh, he averted his looks, and with a slow step descended the mountain's side.

He made his way towards the forest, the gloom of which being best in accordance with his thoughts; and when he had reached a most secluded point he paused, and gave himself up entirely to his gloomy meditations.

"My doom, I fear, is sealed," he said ; "a fatal spell seems to rest upon me, and I see no means of extricating myself from the danger which threatens me from the ungovernable strength of my own passions. Oh, Melina, why did nature form thee so lovely and irresistible ? What man could ever behold thee without loving thee ? He must, indeed, possess a heart insensible to every tender feeling if he could. Florio de Clairville, what a fortunate and happy man thou should'st consider thyself to know that you alone possess her most pure and ardent affections. Can I help envying you your lot ? It is impossible ! Let the consequences be to me whatever they may, Melina must ever hold a predominant sway over my heart."

"D'Aubigny," said a solemn voice at that moment by his side. He started, and looking up, his confusion and alarm may be readily imagined when he beheld old Montaldi standing by his side, and gazing at him with a mingled expression of surprise, regret, and reproach. He was completely paralysed, for he was satisfied that Montaldi had overheard the words he had uttered, and if so, his painful and guilty secret was out.

"Signor Montaldi," he at length gasped forth, in a faltering voice, "what brings you here ?"

"Accident, young man," answered the old man, in the same serious and impressive accents ; "but I am glad that it has done so, for I may be enabled by my advice to snatch you from a precipice, upon the brink of which I perceive, to my astonishment, you are now tottering."

"Ah !" said Adolphus, in a faint voice, "then you have heard the observations to which I just now gave utterance ?"

"I have," replied Montaldi, "and I know not which I feel the most, surprise or regret."

"But you will not betray me ?" ejaculated D'Aubigny, eagerly.

"No," returned Montaldi ; "on one condition your secret shall never pass my lips."

"Name it," said Adolphus, in a voice of the greatest agitation.

"That you stifle the fatal and unholy passion you have suffered to take possession of your breast," answered Montaldi, "and that you banish the image of Signora Melina from your mind, in every other character but that of a friend."

"Alas !" ejaculated D'Aubigny, with a deep sigh, "what a painful situation is mine. I own my weakness, Signor Montaldi, for it would be useless to deny it to you who have overheard the secret from my unguarded lips ; but, alas ! what man could behold so angelic a being as the Signora Melina without loving, without adoring her ? Would that we had never met, then should I have been spared the bitter anguish I am now enduring."

"Beware, young man," said Montaldi, solemnly ; "divest your mind of such thoughts, for by encouraging them you will place yourself in a position which it is terrible even to reflect upon."

"Alas ! alas !" groaned Adolphus, "it is too true."

"Know you not," continued Montaldi, "that Melina loves another ? and that he is the nephew of your benefactor, the Count De Clairville ? Know you not that they are betrothed to each other in the sight of Heaven, and, therefore, to indulge such thoughts as those you have permitted to take possession of your mind is criminal in the extreme, and can only end in shame and misery ?"

"Oh, yes, signor," replied D'Aubigny, "too well do I know all that you have said, and severely do I feel the fatal truth ; but such is the impression that the incomparable charms and virtues of Signora Melina have made upon me, that I fear it will be impossible for me to eradicate it or subdue it."

"Hold, Signor D'Aubigny," said Montaldi, "I must not listen to language such as this. Do you not see the fearful danger in which you are involving yourself ?—What would be the anguish of the Count De Clairville did he know the feelings that at present occupy your breast ?"

"Oh," answered Adolphus, with increasing emotion, "I dare not think of it ; he must despise and loathe me."

"Then why not form a virtuous resolution, and learn to conquer your hopeless passion ere it is too late, and before it has plunged you into that gulph of infamy and misery from which you will find it impossible to extricate yourself ?" demanded Montaldi.

"Would to God that I could," answered his companion. "Would that I could cease to remember there was such a being as Melina in existence. How grateful to Heaven should I be !"

"You have but to exert yourself earnestly, and with sincerity," remarked Montaldi, "and the task may be easily accomplished."

"Alas ! I fear not," returned D'Aubigny. "Melina has taken too firm a hold of my heart, even in the short time that I have become acquainted with her, for me to dare hope ever to love her less than I do at present."

"What madness is this!" said Montaldi. "Could you be base enough, if even there were a chance of your succeeding, to seek to supplant the nephew of that nobleman to whom you are so much indebted, and upon whom his every hope is fixed?"

"I know not how to answer. My brain is bewildered with anxious and conflicting thoughts."

"Reason and honour should at once dictate to you what to do," remarked Signor Montaldi. "There requires not a moment's hesitation upon the painful subject. Signora Melina and Florio de Clairville have loved each other with a pure affection from childhood; and it would not only be criminal but presumptuous in you to aspire to her affections. But this is ridiculous, and, but for the danger by which it is surrounded, is unworthy of a serious thought. Again I warn you to stifle your guilty passion in the bud, or depend upon it the consequences that will ensue to you will be of a far more terrible nature than you can possibly now form any conception of."

"I see plain enough the danger by which I am surrounded," said D'Aubigny; "but yet I have not the power to assist my feelings."

"What a strange and unaccountable infatuation is this!" returned the old man. "There are no feelings, however powerful, when honour does not sanction them, that virtuous resolutions cannot overcome. But attend me to my cottage, signor, where we will talk further upon this disagreeable subject, and where we may confer without the danger of being overheard."

D'Aubigny returned no answer, and Signor Montaldi led the way in silence to his cottage, which was no great distance from the spot where they were standing. When they had arrived there, the old man made use of all the most powerful friendly arguments and persuasions that were at his command, and he did succeed in making a strong impression on D'Aubigny's mind. He found it impossible to deny the truth or force of all to which Montaldi gave utterance, had he been ever so disposed; but still he was unable at present to stifle entirely the feelings that had obtained such a powerful hold of him; and when he arose to depart, after the kind and sensible advice which Montaldi had given him, it was with a heavy and foreboding heart that he did so.

"I will, my kind friend," he said, "struggle to the utmost to conquer the unhappy passion which the irresistible charms of the Signora Melina have inspired me with, and I trust that Providence will give me strength sufficient to do so."

"Call reason, honour, and virtue to your aid," replied Signor Montaldi, "and you cannot fail to triumph; but lose sight of them, and your ruin and disgrace are inevitable. Let not a look or a word betray you to Melina or her lover, or be sure that the consequences will be terrible."

"Oh, yes," answered Adolphus, "I will be most careful, though the task is one which I fear I shall find most difficult to accomplish. I will avoid their presence as much as possible."

"That is a wise determination," observed Montaldi; "and if you only adhere to it, I have not much doubt that you will soon be able to conquer the painful and unlawful sentiments which, with all the impetuosity and thoughtlessness of youth you have suffered to triumph over your better feelings."

"But I may depend upon your secrecy, Signor Montaldi?" again asked D'Aubigny, eagerly.

"Why should you doubt me, after what has taken place between us?" returned Montaldi. "Act as I have advised, and you will ever find in me a sincere friend; but if you pursue a contrary course of conduct, you will find no greater opponent than in Signor Montaldi."

"Your assurances satisfy me, my good friend, and I will endeavour to follow your injunctions strictly,' said D'Aubigny, "although, alas! I fear that the beauteous Melina has made too powerful, too lasting, and too favourable an impression on my heart for me to be able to succeed entirely as reason and justice should dictate, and as you advise."

"Again, young man," said his companion, at the same time he fixed upon him a mingled look of regret and gentle remonstrance, "I caution you to beware of the fatal consequences which will be almost sure to ensue should you not persist in conquering the hopeless and unlawful sentiments which you have unfortunately permitted to obtain such powerful ascendancy in your breast. Remember the fatal example you have before you, in your noble benefactor and friend, and pause ere it be too late, and you may be guilty of that which can scarcely fail to plunge you into the most unspeakable shame and misery, while at the same time it may be the cause of so greatly interrupting, if not of entirely destroying, the happiness of those who ought to be most dear to you. Florio De Clairville is the chosen of the amiable and virtuous Signora Melina's heart; no one can ever hope to supercede him in her affections, and, therefore, what madness and folly it would be for you to encourage any such thoughts. Come—come, Signor D'Aubigny, arouse yourself, reflect seriously, and my word for it, you will yet be able to conquer the unfortunate passion which has taken possession of your senses."

"Would to Heaven that I could," said

Adolphe, fervently; "but, alas! I fear that the charms, and numerous intrinsic perfections of the too fancinating Signora Melina have taken so firm a hold of my senses, that all the efforts I may make to destroy their influence will be in vain. Nay, Signor Montaldi, I know full well what you would say, and I am fain to acknowledge the justice of all which you advance; no one honours the feelings of my venerable and excellent friend and benefactor, the Count de Clairville, more than I do; no one can feel greater respect for him whom he has so recently discovered to be his nephew; but I am satisfied that my having beheld the beauteous Melina will prove the destruction of all my future hopes of happiness, that time can but serve to strengthen those sentiments, and——"

"Hold, Signor Adolphe!" interrupted Montaldi; "I cannot hear you thus express yourself without remonstrating with you, and again impressing on your mind the fatal consequences that must inevitably ensue should you not stifle all such thoughts within your breast, and that, too, immediately."

"Alas—alas!" said the young man, and his countenance assumed even a more powerful and melancholy expression of despair than it had yet done before. "I admit the truth, Signor Montaldi, of all that you have said, but I feel as weak and as powerless as an infant to act as you advise me."

"Did you not but a few minutes since solemnly promise me that you would obey my injunctions to the very letter?" said Montaldi; "and yet you now declare that to do so would be impossible. How am I to reconcile such inconsistences as these?"

"Oh, I know not," replied D'Aubigny; "their inconsistency—their imprudence—nay, their culpability, I am ready to admit; but, at the same time, I see no means of avoiding that danger with which this fatal passion threatens me, and all those with whom I have unfortunately become connected, than by flight. Absence will prevent any evil consequences from ensuing to those who are connected with me, though it can never change the feelings that at present inhabit my breast towards that fair being whom it is most unfortunate that I ever beheld."

"What extravagant nonsense is this, Signor D'Aubigny," remarked old Montaldi, with an expression of impatience. "You much unman yourself, I must say, by giving way to any such thoughts. What! can you for a moment think of abandoning that venerable nobleman to whom you admit you are so largely indebted, and who evidently still is, and ever has been, so warmly attached to you, and would do anything to serve you? For shame, signor; I could not have believed you capable of such thoughts."

"Indeed," returned Adolphe, "I do not shrink from your reproaches, for I know that I deserve them; but what other way than that which I have hinted at have I of avoiding the mischief and trouble that must otherwise ensue? How can I meet the Count de Clairville, his nephew, and Melina, daily, and stifle the unfortunate passion which has taken possession of my breast, and seems, as it were, to have become a portion of my very nature? I acknowledge my error—my weakness—my culpability; but how can I act for the best?"

"As you have promised me," replied Signor Montaldi, "and, although everything at present appears to you to be so gloomy and so cheerless, depend upon it all will yet be well, and you will learn to look back upon the past without a pang. But should you abandon your noble friend, he must become acquainted with all, and you will probably be the means of embittering his future days, when they might otherwise be rendered serene and happy."

"Heaven forbid that I should!" cried Adolphe, emphatically; "I should, indeed, then most thoroughly despise myself. Would to God that I and the Signora Melina had never met, then would all this danger and anguish and anxiety of mind have been avoided, but now—"

"And what is to prevent you from yet being happy and contented?" demanded Montaldi, "if you do not foolishly reject the means that are offered to you? Come—come, compose yourself; put a bold resolution upon the matter, and, my word for it, you will be enabled to succeed much better than you now anticipate."

"You are most sanguine in your expectations, Signor Montaldi," observed D'Aubigny.

"Because," answered the old man, "reason tells me beyond a doubt that they will be realised; that is, if you act according to my wishes and the advice which I have, in the most friendly spirit, given to you. But should you not, then the consequences be upon your own head, and you will pardon me, signor, if I give it as my opinion that you will fully deserve all that may befall you."

"But you will say nothing to the Count de Clairville or to any one else as to what has come to your knowledge?" said D'Aubigny.

"Have I not repeatedly assured you that I will not?" answered Montaldi; "and can you not take my word? I am a man of peace, and Heaven forbid that I should ever seek to wound where I may have the power to heal, and I think that the party is deserving of my sympathy. This is a feeling which I trust you will soon be able to conquer, Signor Adolphe, and you will be able to view the Signora Melina with no other sentiments but those of friendship, esteem, and admiration, which every one must experience who has once beheld her."

D'Aubigny shook his head, as he replied,—

"I would fain do as you advise, Signor Montaldi; but I almost fear that I should be unable to accomplish the task, while I remain in the presence of that too lovely being. And should the Count de Clairville succeed in persuading her and the Signor Florio to accompany him to the chateau (which, after the extraordinary and unexpected discovery he has made, in all probability he will), will not the angelic form of Melina be ever present to my eyes? Shall I have any opportunity of escaping from her presence? And think you that I can continue to notice the transcendent accomplishments of her mind, as well as the glowing charms of her person, and yet turn with a stoical feeling of indifference away from her, and cease to remember her with the same ardent sentiments that——"

"Forbear, Signor D'Aubigny," interrupted his aged companion. "I must not listen to language such as this; it is criminal in you to encourage such thoughts, and if you do not banish them from your mind, the consequences that may most likely follow will be of the most serious nature."

"Signor Montaldi," returned Adolphe, "you will pardon me, but were you ever in love?"

"Ay, signor," answered Montaldi, evincing considerable emotion, "and with one of the most gentle and amiable of human beings; but mine was a virtuous and honourable love, signor and—But no more of this; I have already said sufficient, I should think, to convince you not only of the folly, but likewise the danger and the sin of encouraging such thoughts as those to which I have heard you give utterance; and if you act with prudence and propriety, you will at once exert all your energies to banish them from your mind. But has the Count de Clairville expressed any determination to endeavour to persuade the Signora Melina to accompany him to France?"

"He has," answered D'Aubigny, "and I should think there is nothing remarkable in that, since the Signor de Clairville, will of course, attend him, and it is not likely that they will agree to a separation; neither would it seem very prudent for the signora to remain in this lawless retreat of the brigands, when she could have the protection of such a nobleman as the Count de Clairville."

"Very true," coincided Montaldi; "but still I much doubt whether they will not have great difficulty in persuading Massaroni to relinquish his charge. He is most deeply interested in her fate; he is the very soul of honour, and would scorn to betray those to whom he has once proffered the hand of friendship. But this is not the time or the place to talk upon a subject of so much importance. No doubt that everything will be arranged for the best; and of one thing I am certain, namely, that there is no sacrifice which Massaroni would hesitate to make in order to serve those to whom he has promised his friendship. But we wander from the subject of our meeting. I ask you again, Signor D'Aubigny, if you are prepared to act according to the advice which I have tendered to you?"

"I repeat, Signor Montaldi," replied the young man, though the melancholy of his features plainly showed the emotions that agitated his breast, "that I will endeavour to the best of my abilities to do so, though, at the same time, I am thoroughly convinced I shall have a severe struggle with my feelings to enable me to accomplish the task."

"Take courage, my young friend," remarked Montaldi, "bring reason and the force of your own sound judgment to bear upon the point, and fear not but you will succeed much better than you can now anticipate. I must admit the superior accomplishments and personal attractions of the Signora Melina, and marvel not that she should create such feelings as those you have expressed in any youthful and sensible breast; but it is indispensibly necessary that we should learn to control our passions, especially when we know that the object who has engaged our attention is not only the affianced bride of another, but that her heart is also sincerely devoted to him, and that even if honour and virtue did not forbid it, it would be utterly impossible for us to supplant him in her affections. Indeed, young man, you may believe me when I declare that I cannot contemplate the misery of which the encouragement of your hopeless passion must be productive to those whose happiness it is your bounden duty to study without shuddering. I am an old man, who has experienced much of the world, and had to encounter all the numerous vicissitudes, temptations, and trials with which it is pregnant, and, therefore, I entertain too high an opinion of your good sense not to suppose that you will take my remonstrances and advice in good part."

"I do indeed, Signor Montaldi," replied D'Aubigny, grasping his hand; "and most fervently do I thank you for the interest you seem to take in me, and the good feelings you have expressed towards me, and which it shall be my study to show my sense of. I am fully aware of the danger of encouraging a passion which reason tells me can never be gratified; and it is on that account that, for a time, at any rate, I should leave my benefactor, and, by change of scene and mingling in other society, endeavour, if I cannot forget that such a being as the beauteous Signora Melina ever existed (for that I feel convinced is utterly impossible), at least so far to conquer my unfortunate passion as to be enabled to meet her without a blush, without a fear for myself."

"Abandon the Count de Clairville," said Montaldi, "and in your present state of mind? Oh, no, that must not be; it must appear to be the height of ingratitude on your part; and when you take into consideration the anguish and anxiety of mind it must cause him. I feel confident that you will persevere and banish all such thoughts from your breast. Had you not better reveal to him the whole truth, and receive his advice upon the painful subject?"

"Oh, no, no," answered Adolphe, impa-

FLORIO REMONSTRATES AGAINST THE COUNT'S RETIREMENT FROM THE WORLD.

tiently; "I dare not do so; I dread to meet his stern but just reproaches. What would be the bitter and poignant regret and anguish of his feelings, did he but know the real nature of my thoughts at the present moment? It is that which makes me fear to meet him, Melina, or Florio, lest in their presence I should, by the agitation of my manner, betray myself. With what feelings of disgust and contempt must they then view me; and how keen would be the reproaches, nay, the curses that they would lavish upon my devoted head. My brain is bewildered—I know not how to act. You are an old man, Signor Montaldi, you profess to sympathise with me in my peculiar situation, and I have every reason to place the utmost reliance upon the truth and sincerity of your assertions; I look upon you as a friend, and in you, then, will I place every confidence, and once more I say that I will throw myself upon your generosity, and, in spite of any personal sacrifice it may cost me, I will be guided alone by what you shall advise and propose."

"Well said, my young friend," replied Montaldi, "and, depend upon it, you will have no cause to repent of your confidence. I duly appreciate your feelings, and am ready and willing to make every allowance for the impetuosity of youth; but at the same time, I must enjoin you to be firm, for on that depends in a great measure the honour and happiness of yourself, and of those who ought now to be dear to you. Fear not but that in time you will meet with some other maiden whom you may love equally as well as the fair and gentle Signora Melina, and who will be as worthy of you."

"Oh, no," returned D'Aubigny, hastily, and striking his forehead; "that I feel to be utterly impossible! Where is there another damsel whom I can ever love with half the ardour that I do Melina, even from the short time that we have been acquainted? And—"

"Forbear, signor!" interrupted his aged companion; "such language as this must not escape your lips; to encourage such thoughts is sinful in the extreme."

"I know it! I know it! but, alas! I cannot help it, such is the fatal influence that Melina has obtained over my senses."

"You must struggle with your feelings, signor, or all my counsel and friendly efforts will be of no avail. Compose yourself, and let us repair to the cavern, for doubtless Massaroni and your other friends will begin to feel surprised and somewhat alarmed at your protracted absence, and it will be necessary that you should meet them with an unruffled demeanour, or they will probably put such questions to you as it may be embarrassing and difficult for you to answer, and thus you will betray that which you are so anxious, and it is absolutely imperative on you to conceal."

"Alas!" said D'Aubigny, "I know not how I shall accomplish that. I dread to meet them again."

"Nay," said Montaldi, "you must, indeed, conquer this worse than weakness, or I know not what can be done to extricate you from the difficulty in which you have involved yourself."

"You will accompany me, thither, will you not?" asked Adolphe.

"I will," answered Montaldi, "and they will not feel surprised or inquisitive when they hear that you have visited me at my cottage. Come—come, be firm, my young friend, and all will yet terminate much better than you can now anticipate."

"I must endeavour to excuse myself from their presence, and probably, when left to the undisturbed indulgence of my own thoughts, I may in some measure be able to tranquillise my feelings."

"Be it so," observed Montaldi; "but you will bear in mind what I have said to you, and endeavour to profit by the friendly advice I have offered to you?"

"I will do so, my kind friend," replied D'Aubigny, "and Heaven grant that it may have the desired effect."

"I have no doubt that it will, and be productive of the most desirable results, if you do but persevere," returned Montaldi. "In me you may depend; and if I can only be the means of serving you in the way that I wish, I shall be most happy."

D'Aubigny pressed the old man's hands fervently in his, as he replied—

"Your kindness to me, Signor Montaldi, to one who is almost an entire stranger to you, nearly overpowers me. But you do not think any the worse of me for that which you now know?"

"I do not," said Montaldi, in reply. "I am not one of those austere and inconsiderate beings, who can make no allowances for the impetuous passions of youth; but still it is necessary that they should be controlled and restrained, or fearful are the consequences of which they are too frequently productive. Florio de Clairville is good and amiable, and every way worthy of her to whom his whole soul is devoted, and it would indeed be a calamity, should any ill-feeling arise between you and the nephew of your noble friend and benefactor."

"Oh, Heaven forbid that there should," ejaculated Adolphe, emphatically; "if I thought that there could, I would at once fly from the spot, and thus prevent the evil consequences that might otherwise take place. Florio de Clairville I respect as ardently and as sincerely as if we had been acquainted from our earliest days of childhood; and it is that which makes me regret still more the feelings with which the Signor Melina has inspired me, as I feel that I am doing him an almost irreparable injury, by encouraging such unholy thoughts. With what contempt and detestation must he look upon me were he but aware of them."

"But," returned Signor Montaldi, "if you act with proper prudence and precaution, and adhere to the advice I have already and will still give you, you will have no occasion to entertain any fear upon that subject. Florio will have no suspicion of you, and all will end much better, I trust, than you now seem to anticipate."

"God grant that it may!" said Adolphe, in tones that fully showed the sincerity with which he spoke, and how anxious he was to avoid the evils which his encouraging a hopeless passion for our heroine were calculated to engender. "Could I but learn to view the Signora Melina with no other sentiments but those of friendship and admiration, I should indeed be happy; but, at any rate, let the consequences be whatever they may, however great the sacrifice that I may have to make, I will never disgrace myself by any act that might cause any of my friends a single pang." "Nobly spoken, signor," returned Montaldi. "Keep in the same state of mind, and you will have nothing to fear. You will find that I, at any rate, will not betray your secret."

D'Aubigny again thanked him, and they then slowly bent their way towards the retreat of the brigands, at which they soon arrived, and Adolphe, pressing the hand of Montaldi in silence, he having previously requested him to excuse him to Massaroni and the others, made his way to his own apartment (if so it might be called), flung himself upon a seat, and gave himself up to the various torturing reflections that crowded upon his brain in such rapid succession, that they completely bewildered him. He did not regret his meeting with Montaldi, for he felt satisfied that he could place every confidence in him, and that he would not betray him; but still he could not so easily conquer the sentiments which the beauteous Melina had inspired in his breast, and when he thought of the criminality of his doing so, he reproached himself most bitterly for so doing, and his agitation, if possible, increased every moment. He arose from his seat, and traversed the place in the most disordered state of mind it was possible to conceive, and striking his aching forehead with his clenched fists, he gave vent to his feelings in the most wild and incoherent words.

"It is impossible to stifle the passion with which the transcendent beauties of that amiable being has inspired me," he soliloquised; "and the more I think of her, the stronger and more uncontrollable become the sentiments which glow in my breast towards her. Oh! what a contemptible villain do I feel myself to be to encourage such thoughts as these! And yet I cannot banish them from my mind. I feel as if some spell were upon me, and that I could not extricate myself from its power, although destruction stares me in the face. Oh, Melina, why did nature ever form you half so lovely, or why—oh! why did we ever meet? And she loves another, and that other the nephew of my benefactor and best earthly friend. And she will become his bride! What madness is there in that thought! Methinks I could content myself, even though I knew that I

could never hope to obtain her love, could I be assured that no other man could ever possess that hand which I so much envy. But that will not be, and I must be mad to think of such a thing. Montaldi advises me to patience and resignation; to abandon the thoughts which have taken possession of my mind, and to look upon Melina in no other character but that of a friend. A friend! Oh, how cold and unreasoning is that name to one who loves with the fervour that I do! It is a task which I feel it utterly impossible for me to accomplish. How easy it is to advise; he could never have experienced the feelings that burn and consume me, or he could not have talked in the manner he has done to me. But am I not ungrateful and uncharitable? He has only acted from the purest motives of friendship towards me, and I must be a villain if I abuse his kindness. My benefactor, should you ever become acquainted with the thoughts that at present occupy and torture my mind, what bitter anguish will it cost you—how must you reproach me—and with what contempt must you view that man to whom you have ever been even more than a father, and who has so cruelly repaid your generosity and kindness, and abused those virtuous and noble precepts you have taken such pains to instil into my breast. How shall I venture to behold you again? And how shall I dare again venture into the presence of Melina and Florio Clairville? Shall I not be sure to betray myself? Will they not be certain to read my guilt in my looks? I tremble at the thought, and feel that I am on the verge of a precipice from which I cannot extricate myself. There is nothing left for me but flight, notwithstanding all the arguments which old Montaldi has made use of, and the advice which he has offered. Flight! Whither can I go? Where hide myself, or banish from my breast the thoughts that have taken possession of it? Will not the form of that immaculate being who has so enslaved my heart, and who holds such an unconquerable influence over my feelings, ever be present to my imagination? Nothing whatever can banish it from my memory, and absence would but tend to strengthen the sentiments with which she has inspired me. And she would then probably be the bride of Florio, and all my hopes, if I dare be so presumptuous as to entertain any, would be for ever annihilated. I know not what to do—how to act! I am indeed now one of the most wretched beings in existence, and could almost wish myself dead, rather than have to live to endure this insupportable weight of misery and racking thought."

Again he threw himself on the seat, and became completely absorbed in the agony of his thoughts. Here we will leave him for awhile, and return to the cavern in which the

Count de Clairville, his nephew, and Massaroni were seated in consultation.

CHAPTER LIX.

THE CONSULTATION.—THE PROPOSAL.—THE DECISION.—THE PROJECTED DEPARTURE TO THE OLD CHATEAU.

THE Count de Clairville met the brigand chief and his nephew, according to appointment, in much better spirits than he had been in since his recital of his long and interesting narrative, and they entered freely into a discussion upon the course it would now be most prudent for them to adopt.

" The friendship and kindness I have experienced, Massaroni," said the count, " since I have been an inmate of your cavernous retreat, I can never forget, and I hope that it may yet be in my power to make you some adequate return for it."

"Do not mention that, my lord," replied the brigand; " all you have received from me, you may depend upon it, you are heartily welcome to ; your acknowledgment of your satisfaction at the treatment you have received at my hands is a sufficient reward for me, and I am only too happy to think that fortune directed your footsteps hither, or you might never have made the extraordinary discovery that you have now done, and my young friend here might still have remained in ignorance of the nobility of his birth, and the removal, consequently, of one of the principal obstacles to his union with the fair Signora Melina."

" Very true," coincided the Count de Clairville, " and I might still have been fated to support the heavy weight which pressed upon my mind, and rendered me miserable. Had I found that all my unfortunate relations whom I had so cruelly injured were dead, and that I had no means left of making any atonement for my past errors, what an unhappy wretch should I have been ! But now, however, we will not talk further upon that subject, since we have other important matters to discuss, and it might unsettle my mind to do so."

" Very true, my dear uncle," said Florio, "and let me endeavour to persuade you to banish the painful recollections of the past from your mind, since you have already suffered sufficient for those youthful indiscretions of which you were guilty."

" Youthful indiscretions, Florio ?" said the count, with a sigh ; " alas! you apply so far too mild a term to them, when the manifold and terrible evils of which they were productive are taken into consideration. But enough of this at present. I hope that my future conduct will show how willing and anxious I am

to make all the atonement in my power. But, Massaroni, I am most anxious to make you some acknowledgment for the services you have rendered myself and those who are connected with me. What return can I make you ?"

" I seek no other return, my lord, but your friendship and good wishes," replied the brigand chief. " I trust that when you have departed from hence, you will condescend sometimes to bestow a friendly thought upon Allesandro Massaroni."

" A friendly thought !" returned the count. " Oh, yes, you may depend upon me doing that. But that is not enough ; I would make you some more tangible and permanent acknowledgment than that. Would you not like to abandon your present wild and perilous course of life ?"

" No, my lord," answered Massaroni ; "years have so inured me to it, that I have not the slightest wish to leave it, and the world beyond it has but few charms for me."

" It is a pity that a man possessing your accomplishments and natural nobility of spirit, should be lost entirely to that society you are so well calculated to adorn," returned the count.

" I am a proscribed man," said the brigand chief, " a price is set upon my head, and, therefore, I do not think it would be exactly wisdom on my part to place myself in the hands of those who are thirsting for my blood."

" But if you were to accompany me," remarked the Count de Clairville, " away from this country, you would be safe, and probably my influence might obtain a pardon for you."

" No," said the brigand chief, proudly, " Allesandro Massaroni never yet condescended to crouch to and beg of any man, and I do not think it very likely that he is going to do so now. My lord, I thank you for your kind offers, which I know are made in the pure spirit of friendship, but I cannot accept of them. I am content to remain here in my mountain home, and among my brave companions, who have always continued so faithful to me, and would shed the last drop of their blood in my service. The life I lead is one of freedom, and by the saints I would not exchange situations with the wealthiest and proudest nobleman in the land. They call me brigand, robber ! Well, be it so ; I do not disown it ; but it is upon the rich and the oppressive that I alone prey ; the poor and helpless always command my aid and protection, and my conscience is more free from crime than those who pride themselves so much upon their virtues and other noble qualities."

" I believe you, Massaroni," said his lordship ; " but yet would I persuade you to yield to my wishes, and to quit your present life, which I fear will some day end in your destruction. I would regard you as my friend and equal, and I have no doubt that, by exertion, all the past might be forgotten and forgiven, and that——"

"No, my lord," interrupted our hero, "you will pardon me, but my mind is made up, and nothing whatever can change it. I could never hope for forgiveness from my implacable enemies, if even I sought it, especially while the Prince Bianchi exists, and, therefore, why should I humble myself to sue for a favour which I do not want? There is but one thing more I seek, and then I shall be content."

"And what is that, Massaroni?"

"Revenge!"

"Revenge?"

"Ay," replied the brigand, and his fine black eyes sparkled with more than usual animation. "Revenge, and that I will yet have, if there is a possibility of my obtaining it."

"Against whom?" eagerly inquired the Count de Clairville.

"The base destroyer of my unfortunate mother," replied Massaroni. "I have been seeking it for many a year, and I do not yet despair of ultimately obtaining it."

"But you know not his name?"

"True; my poor mother would not reveal it to me; but something strikes me that I shall yet discover it, and that he is still in existence, and then let him tremble, for here I swear, as I have often done before, that, whatever his rank may be, he shall not escape me."

"But could you lay violent hands on your own father, Massaroni?" demanded the count.

"My father!" repeated our hero. "No, I would not acknowledge him by such a title; I should recognise him only as the murderer of my mother, and the destroyer of my prospects, and deal with him accordingly. Oh, that I had him now before me; how speedily would I gratify the wishes I have so long indulged in!"

"Dreadful!" said the count, with a shudder.

"It may seem so, in your lordship's opinion," returned the brigand, "but retributive justice would demand the deed, and I should be worse than coward, and unworthy of the name I bear, if I hesitated to perform it."

"It is a pity, Massaroni," observed the count, "that with all your other noble qualities you do not endeavour to banish such fearful thoughts from your mind."

"Banish them from my mind!" repeated our hero; "oh, no, I should hate myself if I could: they are my principal food, and I should never rest until the deed is performed. B [illegible] pardon me in [illegible] if you [illegible] change the subject, which I know must be any thing but agreeable to you. What were you about to say?"

"Why," answered his lordship, "that having rested myself for a day or two, it is my intention to depart for France, so that I might finally arrange my affairs. My plans are already settled. I will but wait to bestow my title and estates upon my nephew, making a suitable provision for my young friend, Adolphe D'Aubigny, and to adopt some means to bring about the union of Florio and the fair Signora Melina, and then it is my intention to abandon the world altogether, and to retire within the walls of a monastery."

"Oh, my lord," said Florio, "I pray you to abandon such a gloomy and unnecessary design as that. Surely the world has not become so hateful to you that you should thus seclude yourself from it, and deprive society of the pleasure it must ever derive from your virtues and manifold accomplishments."

"Nay, Florio," returned his uncle, "my mind is made up, and nothing whatever can move me from my resolution. I have experienced enough of the world to render me disgusted with it, and it is only within the walls of the sanctuary that I can hope to find that tranquillity and repose of which I so much stand in need."

"It would not become me, my lord, to question or to murmur at your will," said Florio; "but still I trust that you will think better of this, and that it may be many years ere we may be deprived of the pleasure of your society, and your experienced advice."

"We will talk further on that subject anon," remarked his lordship; "but you will be prepared to accompany me and D'Aubigny to the chateau of your ancestors, in which so many strange and painful scenes have been enacted, and which it is so many years since I have seen. Signor Massaroni will, I know, excuse me depriving him of your society under the circumstances."

"But Melina?" said Florio, with an anxious look."

"Oh, I propose that she should also accompany us," answered the count. "She will be safe under my protection, and scandal will not be so ready to point its envious finger at her at the chateau as it it might be here. When we have arrived safe, and our other arrangements are made, I will take the earliest opportunity of communicating with the Prince Bianchi, and I have very little doubt with a favourable result."

Massaroni looked displeased, and for a moment or two he remained silent; but at length he said—

"Pardon me, my lord, but I had hoped that Signora Melina would have been permitted to [illegible] under my protection, until the union of her and your nephew should have been brought about, by fair and amicable means, if possible. She cannot be more secure than she is here, and I think I need not assure you that she will receive; as she has hitherto done, every kindness and attention, and be treated with the utmost respect."

"I am fully aware of that, Massaroni," answered the count, " and how much we are all indebted to you for the many services you have rendered her; but it is not likely that my nephew could endure a separation from her, and it is indispensably necessary that he should accompany me; besides, you must admit that the chateau will be a far more fitting residence for her than this place; although I am satisfied that she would be safe from every insult while under your protection."

"She has ever been so, my lord," said our hero; "for Massaroni would scorn and hate himself could he ever be guilty himself, or suffer others to be guilty of an insult towards a young and innocent female. However, if it be your lordship's desire, I do not know that I have any right to complain or object; though I hope that should you require my assistance, you will not think Allesandro Massaroni altogether unworthy of being employed."

"You judge me very uncharitably, Massaroni," answered the count, " if you think that I could be guilty of such ingratitude or incivility. In all things we will consult you; and should we require your assistance, we will not fail to avail ourselves of it."

"That is enough, my lord," said the brigand chief, " and even after Signora Melina and your nephew have quitted my cavern, you shall find that I am not idle in endeavouring to promote that in which we all feel so deep an interest. But have you arranged any plan with regard to the Prince Bianchi?"

"I have not at present," replied the count; "but I will lose no time in doing so, after I have become settled a few days at the chateau, and of which I will give you early notice."

"I am satisfied, my lord," said our hero. " But the journey is a long one, and there is no knowing what accident might occur to you on the road; you will probably, therefore, allow myself and a trusty portion of my band to accompany you it least a part of the way?"

"To that," answered the count, " I cannot have the least objection. But it may, perhaps, be as well to hear what the Signora Melina has to say upon the subject."

"True," coincided Massaroni, " Signor Florio will probably go and escort her hither?"

This Florio, as course, readily assented to do, and left the place for that purpose, just as old Montaldi entered the cavern, and in a few words informed them that Adolphe D'Aubigny had visited him at his cottage, and had returned with him to the cavern, but felt so indisposed that he begged to be excused from visiting them for the present.

"I cannot think what can be the matter with my young friend," said the Count de Clairville; " I never saw him so dull and disordered in his manner as he was this morning, and any one to see him would take him to be in love."

"Well, probably he may be so, my lord," returned Montaldi, with a smile. "Do you know of any young maiden to whom he was attached, and from whom he is now separated?"

"Oh, no," answered the count, " he never made me acquainted with any; but that is not suprising, for lovers are very tenacious of revealing the secrets of their hearts to we old folks. However, perhaps there is nothing of the kind, after all."

Signora Melina now entered the cavern, accompanied by Florio, and that put an end to the conversation upon the subject. The count advanced towards her with a kind and encouraging look, and taking her hand, he said—

"Dear Signora Melina, I feel delighted to see you looking so well; we sent for you to consult you upon a business of some importance which concerns you; but I presume my nephew has told you all about it?"

"He has, my lord," answered Melina, in a timid voice, and still blushing deeply, " and I await your pleasure.'

"Before I proceed any further, fair Signora Melina," said the Count de Clairville, " I must take the present opportunity of talking to you upon a subject which is still more closely connected with your heart. Nay, blush not, my sweet girl, for modesty should never scruple for a moment to acknowledge a virtuous and sincere passion, especially when it is excited for a worthy object. You love my nephew, and he, I am convinced, entertains sentiments equally sincere and ardent. You are worthy of each other. Providence has discovered that Florio's birth is equal to your own; Heaven seems to approve of your passion, though the foolish obstinacy of the Prince Bianchi, your uncle, renders him averse to it; that obduracy on his part, I trust, may be conquered; what, then, should prevent the consummation of your happiness? Say, signora, have you any objection to offer?"

"Oh, my good lord," replied our heroine, in a faltering voice, " how can I return an adequate answer to you on so delicate a subject? You must well know the nature of the sentiments that exist between myself and Florio towards each other, and, therefore, I am satisfied that you will spare me the embarrassment of repeating them. No other man but Florio de Clairville can ever possess the heart of Melina."

The eyes of Florio sparkled with delight, and fervently he pressed the fair hand to his lips, but was unable to articulate a syllable.

"Nobly spoken, sweet Melina," said the

count; "those few words express a volume, and Florio ought to consider himself one of the happiest men in existence. Need I say, how warmly I approve of your attachment, and that it will be my future study to promote your union, and to endeavour to win the consent of the Prince Bianchi? Florio,—Melina," he added, taking their hands, and speaking in a voice of considerable emotion; "you have loved each other for many years; neither time nor trouble have wrought any change in your sentiments, which proves at once that you are worthy of each other, and that nature ordained you to come together. Let the decree of Prudence be fulfilled, and may the choicest blessings of heaven descend upon your heads, my children."

Melina and Florio were much affected by the energy of the count's manner, and kneeling down, they received his solemn benediction. They then arose, and seating themselves by his side, a silence of some minutes' duration ensued, which no one during that period seemed inclined to break.

"Signora Melina," at length remarked his lordship, "you say that you have heard from my nephew the particulars of the business upon which I wished to see you; you will, therefore, be aware that in a day or two it will be necessary for me to depart from hence to my own paternal estate in France, which I have not seen for so many years, and where——"

He paused, and a painful expression of emotion passed over his features; but he soon recovered himself, and, after a brief interval, went on to say—

"As it is my determination to arrange my affairs with as little delay as possible, and to reinstate Florio in those possessions which he should long since have enjoyed, of course he must accompany me, and I know full well that neither he nor yourself can bear the idea of a separation from each other, even for a short time. Besides, under my protection, you would be more secure from the slander of the world than you can possibly be, situated as you at present are, and, therefore, I have been proposing to our generous and disinterested friend here, Massaroni, that he should resign his trust to me, and that you should accompany me and Florio to my chateau, where you can remain until I have probably succeeded in bringing the Prince Bianchi to some amicable arrangements, which I do not despair of doing."

Melina hesitated, and fixed a look of anxious inquiry and reluctance upon the brigand chief, which showed plainly the thoughts that were passing in her mind.

"Signora Melina," observed our hero, "I know well what you would say, and duly appreciate the feelings which naturally hold possession of your breast. 'Tis true that a brigand's cavernous abode may not seem to be the most proper dwelling place for a young and innocent maiden, though here you are as secure from insult, nay, even more so than you might probably be in the palace of the prince, your uncle, and I feel confident that you will be ready to admit that since you have been under my protection, you have been treated with the utmost respect and attention, and—"

"Oh, yes, Signor Massaroni," interrupted Melina, fervently, "yourself and all those who are connected with you have ever been most kind and considerate towards me, and I owe you a debt of gratitude for the inestimable services you have, from the most disinterested motives, rendered me, which I much fear it will never be in my power to repay. But I must at the same time acknowledge the force and reasonableness of that which the Count de Clairville has proposed, and of my anxiety to agree to it; but still I trust that by so doing, you may not imagine me unmindful of the favours I have received from you, that it may not lower me in your good opinion, but that you will still consider me entitled to your esteem and friendship."

"Enough, fair and gentle signora," replied the brigand chief; "I am satisfied, and will no longer offer any objection, though I must confess that I had flattered myself with the hope that I should have been the sole cause of promoting and establishing your happiness, and that you would have remained under my protection until I could have effected an amicable adjustment of your peculiar affairs."

"And you will still be the sole cause of bringing about the happiness of my nephew and the Signora Melina, Massaroni," remarked the Count de Clairville; "for had it not been for your noble and generous interposition in their behalf, would not their misery have even now been consummated? and nothing whatever could have saved Melina from being sacrificed to the Count Alberti."

"Oh, most true," said our heroine; "and when I reflect upon that fact, and picture to myself all the horror that would have accrued to me from an union with that man, can I ever sufficiently estimate that which I owe to Signor Massaroni? But for him I should have been one of the most miserable and hopeless beings in existence, while now, with the blessing of Heaven, all the bright hopes I have ever so fondly cherished seem fated to be realised, and the sorrows of the past bid fair to be forgotten in the happiness that is in store for me. Tell me, Massaroni, are you satisfied?"

"How can I be otherwise, signora?" replied our hero; "how is it possible for me to be otherwise, after what you have said? Need I say, how highly flattered I feel by the gentle expressions of commendation you have been pleased to bestow upon me, and of my anxiety, to prove to you in future how well I deserve them? Go, then, signora; accompany the Count de Clairville and your lover, and may every blessing attend you; and rest assured, that though far away from you, the watchful eye of Allesandro Massaroni will ever be upon your safety, and that, should occasion require his arm will be the first that will be raised in your defence."

With a sweet smile of gratitude and friendship, our heroine extended her fair hand towards him, which he raised respectfully to his lips, and again a silence of a few minutes ensued, in which each person present gave indulgence to the varied thoughts that crowded upon their mind.

"Signor Massaroni," at length said Florio, "it might seem ungrateful in me were I not also to give expression to the feelings of esteem and obligation which I owe towards you, for the manifold kindness and services which I myself, and she who is far more precious to me than my own existence, have ever experienced from you. You have acted from the purest and most disinterested motives, and, therefore, does it make the obligation more weighty. Believe me, that, wherever I may be, and under whatever circumstances, I shall never forget that to Allesandro Massaroni I am indebted for the principal-portion of the blessings it may be my lot to enjoy."

"Enough, signor," returned the brigand, cordially grasping his hand; "I am overwhelmed with these flattering encomiums, and scarcely know what answer to make; I have done no more than my duty, and am only too happy to think that the opportunity has been afforded me, since it has enabled me to render such important services to others, and to frustrate the designs of those who would have trampled on their happiness."

"Well said, Massaroni," observed the count; "and so there is an end of the matter, since we are all agreed. In three days from the present, then, I propose that we should take our departure from hence, and the Signora Melina will, therefore, hold herself in readiness for the journey."

"I will do so, my lord," answered our heroine.

"It will be a painful trial to me," continued his lordship, with a sigh, "to revisit those scenes from which I have been so many years separated, and with which are associated some of the most melancholy circumstances of my life. But it will not be for long that I shall mingle amongst them. I have but to arrange my affairs, see the happiness of yourself, Melina, and my nephew complete, and then I will bid adieu to the world and all its foibles for ever, and in holy seclusion endeavour to prepare

myself for that dread Eternity into which I must ere long be summoned."

"Oh, my good lord," ejaculated Melina, and looking earnestly into his face as she spoke, "I prithee talk not thus. Why should you, who are well calculated to adorn society, and to impart happiness to all who may have the honour and advantage of your friendship, think of retiring from the world? There are, I trust, many years of rational enjoyment left for you yet, and why, then, should you reject the blessings that are offered by an all-bounteous Providence to you?"

"Ah! no, signora," returned his lordship, "I fear that there is no more enjoyment for me in the busy scenes of the world, and, therefore, am I anxious to seek that sacred asylum, where, in the calm reflections that religion never fails to inspire, I may hope to become, at least, contented, if I cannot be happy."

"I trust, my lord," said Florio, "that you will think better of this, for I cannot contemplate the idea of your being separated from us, so soon after I have discovered that I was so fortunate as to have one so dearly and nearly related to me living, with any degree of patience."

"Yes," observed Massaroni, "his lordship will change his mind, and learn to view the world with a less jaundiced eye. I admit that he has experienced enough of its vicissitudes; but still there are others in the world who have suffered much more—I, myself, for instance, Driven from society—made an outcast—hunted like some wild beast of the forest—a price set upon my head, and all through the villany of that unknown man, whom I blush to call by the name of father; and yet it has not thrown such a cloud upon my feelings, as to disgust me with the world altogether, and to tempt me to bury the rest of my days in gloomy seclusion. No, I live, buoyed up with the hope that I shall yet experience better things. But I confess that I shall feel for a time somewhat sad and cheerless when I am deprived of the society of the Signora Melina and Signor Florio."

"I regret, Massaroni," replied the Count De Clairville, "that I should be the means of depriving you of any such pleasure; but you know the motives that prompt me to do so, and that it is unavoidable?"

"Certainly I do, my lord," said our hero, "and it is impossible but that I must approve of them. I should have been better satisfied had the distance which will separate us not been so great; but I trust that you will contrive some means of speedily communicating with me, should anything occur which may seem to require my interference and assistance."

"You may depend upon my doing so," answered his lordship; "although I trust that everything will be settled in an amicable and satisfactory manner."

"And should the Prince Bianchi still remain obdurate," said the brigand, "shall the union of the Signora Melina and your lordship's nephew then longer be delayed?"

"You will pardon me, Massaroni," replied the count; "but that question is somewhat premature; however, I trust that there will be no necessity to go to extremities. The Prince Bianchi, I cannot persuade myself, can be so blind to reason and justice as to remain obstinate when all his objections to the marriage of his fair niece to my nephew are removed."

MASSARONI SWEARS TO AVENGE THE WRONGS OF HIS MOTHER.

"I know not," returned our hero; "but you must bear in mind that the Count Alberti possesses the greatest influence over him, and his prejudice against Signor Florio, especially since Melina has been taken from his power, and his authority set at defiance, is so strong, that I fear it will be a difficult matter to overcome it. However, time will prove everything, and I think that I need not assure you I sincerely wish it may terminate as well as you seem to anticipate. One promise, however, that I have frequently made to Florio, if I live, I am determined to keep, and that is, that I will dance at their wedding."

Melina blushed, but could not help smiling at the well-intended jocose manner of the brigand.

"You, Massaroni!" said the count; "unfortunately proscribed as you are? It is impossible! Do you not consider the consequences?"

"I do," answered Massaroni; "and let them be whatever they may, I will not fail to keep my word—that is, if you have no objection. So, my lord, that business is settled. There is a long account of justice, however, for the Prince Bianchi to perform; Signora Zitella and her daughter's wrongs must not go unredressed."

"My poor unfortunate and misguided uncle!" ejaculated Melina; "but I trust that he will be awakened to a due sense of remorse, and endeavour to make all the atonement in his power for the injuries he has inflicted. Signora Zitella and her daughter will still remain under your protection, Massaroni?"

"Yes, signora," replied our hero; "and in whom can they better confide? They will, however, I fear, be sadly grieved to think they are so soon to be deprived of the pleasure of your society."

"I trust," said Melina, "that it will not be long ere we shall meet again, and under far different and happier circumstances."

"The journey you are about to take is a long one," remarked Massaroni; "and as there is no knowing what dangers might beset you on the road, I have proposed to the Count de Clairville to accompany you, with a few of the most trusty of my band, part of the way."

"But might there not be danger in so doing?" suggested Florio.

"No," answered the brigand, "none whatever. I propose that the journey should be commenced at night, to prevent any curiosity being excited. Once beyond these mountains, you will be in safety, and fearing my passport, none of my band who may happen to meet you will dare to interrupt or molest you."

The Count de Clairville thanked him for his kindness and consideration, and they then conversed more freely upon their future plans and prospects.

"The chateau, for anything that I know to the contrary, may be inhabited," observed the count; "but I intend to despatch a messenger forward there immediately to inform them of my intended return, so that there will be no confusion on our arrival. I have no doubt that the place is greatly altered since I saw it last, which is many years ago, and that I shall meet with no one that can recognise me. I hope that it may be so; for, alas! when I recall to my mind the guilty events of the past, and reflect upon the villanous part which I——"

"Forbear, my lord, I beseech you," interrupted Florio, "do not suffer such torturing thoughts to enter your mind; why do you continue thus bitterly to reproach yourself? For every error you may in your youth have committed, you are now anxious to make all the reparation that you possibly can, and you should, therefore, seek to bury the gloomy past in oblivion."

"I do seek to do so, Florio," returned the count, "but—alas! with all my efforts, I find it to be impossible. It is that which strengthens me in my determination to fly from society, and in the walls of the cloister to seek that relief and consolation of mind, which I cannot hope to meet with in the world."

"Would to heaven, my dear uncle," said Florio, "that I could wean you from this gloomy mode of thinking, and lead you to look forward to the future with brighter and more sanguine anticipations."

"Time and circumstances will, doubtless, work an alteration in his lordship's mind," said Massaroni, "and he will learn to look back upon the past with indifference."

"With indifference, Massaroni!" repeated his lordship, and the expression of his features clearly showed the violence of the emotions that agitated his bosom. "Oh, no, that is impossible; I must indeed have become callous to all sense of feeling if I could. Forget the untimely fate of that brother, who was urged into the commission of the rash and desperate act by the wrongs I had heaped upon him? Banish from my memory the sufferings of Emilie? Oh, no, no, no! that can never be; and, therefore, happiness and myself must ever henceforward be strangers."

He covered his face with his hands as he gave utterance to these melancholy words, and walked to the other side of the cave, in a state of the greatest excitement. Florio and Massaroni had touched upon a tender chord, at the same time that they had only been anxious to impart consolation, and they deeply regretted it; but they thought that it would be most prudent to remain silent, and to allow the unfortunate nobleman to indulge freely in his own meditations, and after the lapse of a few minutes he turned towards them with a much more composed aspect of countenance, and said—

"Pardon me, my dear friends, for giving way to this emotion, which may look like weakness; but it is over now, and we will drop the subject. We will leave the lovers to themselves, for probably they may have something more to talk about than it may be agreeable to them for us to hear."

Melina and her lover smiled, and the Count de Clairville, Massaroni, and old Montaldi left the place. The latter immediately made his way to the cavern in which D'Aubigny was anxious to converse with him further upon the subject which had engaged their attention in the morning. He found him seated moodily in one corner of the place, and apparently absorbed in the most gloomy meditations; but he arose from his seat on the entrance of Montaldi, and advanced towards him.

"I am sorry still to see you in this depressed state of mind, my young friend," remarked Montaldi; "and had hoped that calm reflection would have convinced you of the folly and danger of your conduct. Come—come, arouse yourself, and exert all your energies to banish from your bosom that fatal passion, which reason must assure you can never be gratified."

"Alas!" replied Adolphe, "I would fain do as you exhort me to do, for I know that it is dictated by prudence and anxiety for my welfare. But it is a task from which I shrink with a cowardice that I never remember to have experienced before, and I fear that even were I to exert myself ever so, I should never be able to accomplish it."

"What madness is this?" said Montaldi; "for I cannot call it by any milder term; would you plunge yourself into ruin and disgrace, and inflict misery and shame upon the head of your benefactor?"

"Oh, not for the world!—sooner would I perish!"

"Then," returned Montaldi, "the only way you have of avoiding it, is by stifling those dangerous feelings which you have permitted to take possession of your mind, and endeavour to look upon the Signora Melina with no other feelings than those of respect and friendship."

"Would to Heaven I could do so," cried D'Aubigny.

"Pshaw!" replied his aged companion, impatiently; "you can do so, if you will but persevere. Think what would be the horror and disgust of the Count de Clairville, and your other friends, should they become acquainted with the thoughts that at present occupy your mind."

"Oh, not for the world would I that it should come to their knowledge!" said D'Aubigny, energetically.

"But if you do not conquer the dangerous feelings to which you at present give way," observed Montaldi, "you will betray yourself. Already your strange behaviour and extraordinary emotions, I iamgine, have attracted the attention and excited the curiosity of the count; and I know not what may be the consequences if you persist in the same line of conduct."

"Well—well, I will try," said Adolphe; "though I much fear that I shall succeed but indifferently. But have you been present at the interview?"

"I have," answered Montaldi; "the Signora Melina and Florio were also there."

"Melina?"

"Yes," returned the old man; "and it is finally settled, that, in three days from the present, the Count de Clairville will depart from hence to his own estate in France, accompanied by yourself, Florio, and Melina."

"Melina!" again gasped forth Adolphe, with emotion.

"Yes," said Montaldi; "the count thinks, and I agree with him, too, that it will be much more prudent for her, and better calculated to quiet the voice of calumny, for her to be placed under his protection than that of Massaroni; besides, Florio will accompany him, and it is not at all likely that the lovers could ever have made up their minds to a separation."

"It is no more than I anticipated," ejaculated D'Aubigny, "and that at once convinces me that I must act with decision."

"What mean you?"

"It is impossible that, under such circumstances, I can accompany his lordship to France!" answered Adolphe; "I see no other alternative but to fly to some distant part of the country, where I may brood over my sorrows alone, and be out of the reach of temptation and danger."

"Are you mad?" demanded Montaldi; "by so doing, you would at once betray the secret of your heart, and———"

"And," hastily rejoined D'Aubigny, "should I not at least evince by so doing an honourable and virtuous resolution?"

"Nay, Adolphe," said the old man, "this course, which is a desperate one, must be avoided, if possible, for it is fraught with numerous dangers. You surely, upon calm reflection, may succeed in at least so far subduing your unfortunate and hopeless passion, as not to betray yourself."

"And think you," returned Adolphe, "that it is possible I can ever conquer the sentiments which now consume me, while I am constantly in the presence of the lovely being who has inspired them? It would be the height of madness to entertain such a thought for a moment. No, Signor Montaldi, you may think me rash and obstinate, but I see no other way of avoiding those consequences which I shudder to think upon, than by the course that I have suggested. The more frequently I behold her—the oftener I listen to the heavenly music of her voice, is it not only reasonable to suppose that my passion will become more inflamed; and I might be precipitated into the perpetration of some rash act, which I should afterwards have bitter reason to repent. There is nothing left for me but flight!"

"Headstrong young man," demanded Montaldi, "whither would you go?"

"Alas!" said D'Aubigny, "I know not; and it matters not; all places are now alike to me; but near where the beauteous Signora Melina is, it is impossible for me to remain."

"Signor D'Aubigny," observed Montaldi, "I cannot but confess that I feel the deepest interest in your fate, and there is scarcely anything that I would not do to serve you; but I cannot advise you to do that which will be sure to cause so much misery to the Count de Clairville, whom you acknowledge has ever treated you with the attention and affection of a father."

"Oh, yes," replied Adolphe, "he has indeed most truly done so, and never can I feel sufficiently grateful to him for it."

"Will you promise me one thing, D'Aubigny?"

"Name it."

"It is this," answered Montaldi. "The time fixed for the departure of the Count de Clairville is three days from the present; that interval will afford sufficient time for calm reflection; will you promise me that you will do nothing rashly without again consulting me?"

D'Aubigny hesitated for a moment or two, and seemed to reflect seriously within himself.

"Why should you pause, D'Aubigny?" said the old man; "surely there is nothing unreasonable in the request; and I thought that you reposed some confidence in me."

"Ah, yes, Signor Montaldi," answered Adolphe, "indeed I do. I believe you to be my friend."

"You do me no more than justice by such an opinion," said Montaldi, "and it is the anxiety I feel to serve you that induces me to make the request I have done. You, at any rate, cannot meet with any harm by consulting an old man like me, and receiving my advice. Will you promise me?"

"I do," returned D'Aubigny.

"Enough," said his companion, "I am satisfied, and do not fear but that I shall yet be able to extricate you from the difficulties by which you are at present surrounded, and to restore your mind to its wanted tranquillity."

Adolphe shook his head.

"Would to God that you could," he said; "but I feel confident that is a task which will baffle all your skill and powers of eloquence. The impression which the lovely and amiable Signora Melina has made upon my heart, I feel too plainly can never be eradicated."

"Hold, young man!" said Montaldi, solemnly. "I must not hear you give utterance to such language as that. It is sinful even to harbour such thoughts for an instant."

"I know it, Montaldi," replied Adolphe, "and, therefore, do I hate and despise myself, knowing the cruel injustice with which I am acting towards Melina and Florio de Clairville. But so powerful is the spell that is upon me,

that I cannot break it; and the more I endeavour to do so, the stronger my unfortunate and guilty passion seems to become."

"Still bear in mind the melancholy circumstances of the Count de Clairville's history," observed Montaldi; "and be warned in time."

"Oh, yes," replied Adolphe; "and it is the remembrance of them that makes me tremble, and anxious to fly from the temptation, lest I should fall into the same fatal errors."

"If you follow my advice, you will be rescued from any such a fate," said Montaldi. "But you must not give way to a weakness which is highly reprehensible. Again I say, persevere, and you will yet be able to triumph, and to laugh to scorn the present infatuation which holds possession of your senses, and seems to drive every other feeling before it."

"I know the excellence of your advice, Montaldi," said D'Aubigny, "and the motives of friendship towards me that dictate it. But anxious as I am to follow it, I know not how to do so. It would indeed have been a most fortunate thing for me, had I never have beheld the beauteous Melina, who has so completely ravished my senses; and it is quite useless to deny it."

"Well, perhaps it would be," remarked Montaldi; "but still, fate has ordained it otherwise; and as her heart is irrevocably another's, and there is not the least possibility of her ever becoming yours, there is nothing left for you to do but to make an heroic effort to conquer your passion; and to forget that there was ever such a being as Melina in existence."

"What!" exclaimed D'Aubigny, passionately; and, should I accompany them to the chateau, I shall be daily in her presence? Such an idea is preposterous. Besides, even were it not so, her image is so firmly ingrafted in my heart that I feel confident nothing can ever banish it from my memory. I know not what to do; I am truly miserable."

"Again I warn you to arouse yourself," said Montaldi, "and at least seek to put on some semblance of composure, lest you should excite the suspicions of the Count de Clairville, and he may put such questions to you as you may find it difficult to answer."

"I trust sincerely that I shall not see his lordship, for the present," returned Adolphe; "for, in my present excited state of mind, the questions he would probably put to me would indeed be most embarrassing."

"Certainly," coincided the old man; "and it is therefore that I would have you be the better prepared to meet him, for he will be sure to visit you before long, as he imagines that you are ill. I would not that he should become acquainted with the fatal secret which disturbs your mind, for the world; for how terrible would be the shock to him, recalling as it would be sure to do all the melancholy circumstances of his own history to his memory in the most vivid colours. For his sake, then, exert yourself, and stifle those dangerous passions ere it be too late."

"Believe me, my excellent friend," returned Adolphe, warmly grasping his hand, "that not one word you utter is lost upon me, and that I am only too anxious to be able to follow your advice. Yet, when you take all the peculiar circumstances into consideration, I think you must be ready to admit that I have enough to bewilder and distract me, and that the task is a most arduous one to accomplish. However, I will exert myself to the utmost to do so; and, with the aid of Providence, I trust that I shall yet be able to succeed."

"Well said, Signor D'Aubigny," remarked Montaldi; "persevere and keep in the same state of mind that you are now, and there is no doubt that, difficult even as it may at present seem to be, you will succeed. But I must leave you, for I have some business to transact with Massaroni. To-morrow morning you will, perhaps walk again to my cottage, where we can consult together, without any danger of being overheard or interrupted."

"I will do so, signor," answered D'Aubigny, "and I cannot but express my thanks to you for the interest you seem to take in my fate."

"I am, indeed, most anxious to serve you, D'Aubigny," said Montaldi, "and I think I cannot better do so than by rendering you my advice and assistance, in your present painful and embarrassing situation. Farewell, signor, and I beseech you to bear seriously in your mind all that I have said to you."

"I will not fail to do so," answered Adolphe; "and most heartily do I wish that I may be able to profit by the advice you have given. Adieu till we meet again to-morrow."

Montaldi now quitted the cavern, and left D'Aubigny to his own meditations. He threw himself on a seat, and for some time his mind was in that state of excitement, that he scarcely knew how to contain himself. At length he started to his feet, and folding his arms across his chest, he paced the place backwards and forwards in the most disordered manner.

"Forget Melina!" he ejaculated at length; "ah! old man, you could never have known what it was to love as I do now, or you could not thus coolly advise. Forget her! by Heaven! her image is so closely entwined round my heart, even from the short time that I have known her, that I feel it is utterly impossible for me to do so. And yet what a consummate villain I must be to encourage such thoughts; and what would be the anguish of my aged and excellent friend and benefactor should he by any chance become acquainted with them?

Oh, I shudder to think of it! How would he loathe and despise me, too! But it is not likely that I can long keep concealed from him that which is passing in my mind, if I remain with him, and I dare not meet the bitter and well-merited reproaches he will not then fail to heap upon my head! Oh, Montaldi, it is that thought which half tempts me to reject your advice, and to fly ere it be too late. But then, what will be the opinion of, the Count de Clairville, from whom I have experienced the most unexampled kindness, and who has ever placed the most unlimited confidence in my honour and integrity? Will he not consider that I have acted with the basest ingratitude towards him, and denounce me to the world accordingly? Again, can I hope to be able to banish my unhappy passion from my breast, and to forget Melina by my absence? No, that would be impossible, and it is madness for me to think about it. I am completely lost and bewildered, and know not how to act. Alas! Melina, too beauteous maiden, had I never beheld you, these painful and conflicting passions would never have distracted my bosom. How do I envy Florio de Clairville his happiness! To possess the love of one so young, so fair, and gentle as the Signora Melina, is indeed a blessing that may be designated inestimable; and no one can for a moment doubt the ardour of the sentiments she entertains towards him. And she will become his bride; nothing now can possibly prevent the consummation of all their fondest wishes, and he will revel in every earthly felicity, while I—Oh, there is madness in the very thought, and I know not how I can find patience or fortitude to endure it! But he is noble, honourable, and generous, and every way worthy of her; he is the nephew of him who has proved himself to be my best earthly friend, and should I not prove myself a villain of the blackest dye, if I were to contemplate any design against his happiness? I should, indeed!—Away with such thoughts from my mind! I despise myself for ever for a moment entertaining them. Florio de Clairville has long been the chosen of her who has made such an indelible and fatal impression upon my heart, and why should I attempt, why should I have the unparalleled presumption to attempt to supplant him in her affections? Fool! could I, almost a stranger to her, and with none of his pretensions and claims upon her affection, hope to succeed, if even I dared to make the attempt? No—no, the very idea is preposterous; and yet I feel at present that it is in vain for me to attempt to banish it from my mind! And being constantly in her society, as I must be if I accompany them to the chateau, it will but serve to add to the fire which at present rages within my breast, and drives me almost to distraction. My conduct, I am convinced, must betray me, and how can I dare venture to enter into any explanation, which I know must bring down their disgust, their indignation, and their keenest reproaches upon my head, and make me shrink appalled within myself? There are no other means of avoiding this except by flight. And whither can I go? Where can I fly where I can hope to find an oblivion to my anguish? Heaven send me how to act in this painful dilemma, for I know not."

Thus did the unfortunate young man continue to soliloquise, and the longer he reflected even more agitated did his mind become, and more disordered his brain. He saw all the evil consequences that must arise from his encouraging his fatal passion—he could not help seeing them even on a moment's reflection, and yet he had no means of avoiding them. It seemed to him as if he were marked out by fate to be the victim of some cruel destiny, and to be the means of not only bringing misery upon himself, but upon all those who were unfortunately in any way connected with him; and for a short time he was wrought up to such a pitch of frenzy, that he was almost urged to lay violent hands on himself. He continued to pace the room in the most disordered manner; and any one to have noticed the wild delirious expression of his eyes at that moment, and the distortion of his features, would naturally have imagined that madness had seized upon his brain.

"This is insupportable," he said at length; "and surely it would be better to hazard any fate rather than to endure this. What have I to tempt me to life, now that I find that happiness without the possession of that fair being whom I know it is impossible for me ever to obtain, can never be mine? Let me, then, by one bold effort, at once end this misery, and prevent myself from committing that which must ever stamp my name with infamy. Thus then," he added, as he drew a poniard from his bosom, "let me——"

He was interrupted in that moment of desperation, by hearing some one at the door of the cavern which formed his apartment, and hastily concealing the weapon, he endeavoured, to regain his composure in some measure, but before he could do so, the door was thrown open, and, to his confusion, the Count de Clairville stood before him, and fixed upon him a keen and penetrating glance, which only seemed to confuse him the more.

"Adolphe!" at length said the count.

"My lord," replied D'Aubigny in a faltering voice, and not looking towards him.

"What strange words were those that saluted my ears as I reached this door?"

"Words, my lord?" stammered out Adolphe, still more confounded, and perfectly at a loss what answer to make; "I do not understand you."

"Nay, D'Aubigny," returned his lordship, with a look of reproach, "this is equivocating. The words I heard, but could not understand distinctly, were uttered by you."

"Oh, my lord," replied Adolphe, affecting to smile, "they were probably merely the expression of some foolish thoughts that at the moment came over me, but which I do not now recollect."

"You look confused and agitated, Adolphe, and I have noticed the same for this last day or two; what is the meaning of this?"

"I have felt indisposed, my lord," replied D'Aubigny; "as you are aware. But—but I trust I shall soon be better."

"Come, Adolphe," said his lordship, seriously; "this will not do; you must not endeavour to evade my questions thus; there was a time when I believe you had no secrets from me, and why should you now?"

"Secrets, my lord? Oh, indeed you wrong me by such a supposition. What secrets can I possibly have that I should wish to conceal from you?"

"Nay, but I am confident from your manner and the expression of your countenance," said the Count de Clairville, "that you have something on your mind that you wish to conceal from me. Impart it, then, to me, and if my advice and consolation can be of any service to you, you know that you can freely have them."

D'Aubigny hesitated; the count had addressed him so pointedly and at a moment when it was so totaly unexpected, that he knew not what answer to make.

"Indeed, my lord," he said at last, "you are entirely labouring under a mistake. I have no secrets to impart to you, or you know full well that you are the only person to whom I would first apply for consolation and advice. But I feel ill, dull, low spirited, and unfit for society, though perhaps a few days may restore me to my wonted spirits."

"And is that really the cause of the agitation of demeanour, and perturbation of mind that you evince?" demanded his lordship, again fixing upon him a penetrating glance.

"It is, my lord," answered Adolphe, somewhat recovering himself, for he saw that unless he persevered he should betray himself, and thus be exposed at once to the count's reproaches. "But probably change of scene may serve to revive me."

"Well, well," returned the count, "probably it may be so; though I seldom knew a young man to take these fits of melancholy unless he was in love, or something else of an equally serious and tormenting nature affected him."

"In love, my lord!" repeated Adolphe in a faint voice, and averting his looks, for his lordship, as may be supposed, had touched upon one of the tenderest chords that he possibly could, and he felt more extremely agitated than he had done before.

"In love? Yes," replied the count with a smile, "is there anything surprising in a young man like you falling a prey to the tender passion? And should it be bestowed upon a worthy object, by the mass, man, why should you be ashamed to acknowledge it? Come, come, D'Aubigny, out with this tender secret, and make me acquainted at once with the fair and gentle being who has taken your heart captive."

"Indeed, my lord," faltered Adolphe, in the same hesitating tone, "this raillery is uncalled for, and unmerited by me; there is no—no one who has yet made any impression of the warm description to which you allude, upon my heart."

"What!" cried his lordship, "not among all the fair and accomplished damsels whom we have encountered in the course of our travels? Well, I must say, Adolphe that, if you speak the truth, your heart must be made of far more adamantine materials than mine was at your age. However, I do not exactly believe you, nevertheless. But come, you must arouse yourself from this dismal mood, for I declare it is quite painful to behold you. Why, you look as melancholy as if you had just met with some dreadful calamity, which had sunk you to the very lowest depths of despair. However, as you say, change of scene may serve to revive you, and you will soon have that, for three days from the present we depart from this place to the mansion of our ancestors, which I have not seen for so many years, though the old chateau must be strangely altered if it is now at all calculated to disperse the horrors when they have once taken possession of a person's mind."

"In three days from the present, my lord?" said D'Aubigny, affecting some surprise.

"Yes," replied the Count de Clairville, "it is all settled, and Florio and the Signora Melina will accompany us."

At the mention of Melina's name, D'Aubigny turned pale, and, notwithstanding all his efforts to conceal it, fearful of betraying himself, trembled violently. The count looked at him with some degree of surprise.

"Why, how now, Adolphe," he said, "what is the meaning of this emotion?"

"Noth—nothing, my lord," stammered D'Aubigny, as may be imagined, scarcely knowing what to say; "it was only the pleasure I felt at hearing that the signora was to be our companion, and—"

"Ay, Adolphe," interrupted his lordship, "the Signora Melina will, indeed, be an invaluable acquisition to our society, for never did I behold one more good, more fair, and amiable. She and my newly discovered nephew love each other ardently and sincerely, and as they are both so worthy of each other, it shall be no fault of mine if they are not shortly united."

The feelings of Adolphe as the Count de Clairville gave utterance to these words may easily be conceived; they went like daggers to his heart, and for a few moments he was so confused that he knew not how to reply; but at length he struggled with his emotions, and said—

"The Signora Melina is, indeed, most good and amiable, and must render any man supremely happy who has the honour to possess her for his bride. But think you, my lord, that you will be able to overcome the scruples of the Prince Bianchi, her uncle?"

"Oh, no doubt of it," answered his lordship; "pride has alone hitherto prevented him from sanctioning their union; but when he finds that Florio's birth is equal to that of his niece, he will not, I think, raise any further objection."

"I know not that, my lord," said D'Aubigny; "if all be true that we have heard, the prince is very obstinate, and is greatly prejudiced in favour of the Count Alberti, and against Florio."

"It shall be my task to remove that prejudice," observed the count; "and should I fail, why then I do not see why the happiness of the lovers should be longer delayed, or that their union should not at once take place."

"But is Massaroni willing that the signora should quit his protection?" asked Adolphe.

"Why, of course he objected to it at first," answered his lordship, "for he takes the deepest and most honourable interest in her fate; but he is not blind to reason, and, consequently, he quickly saw the propriety of her being removed from this place, and entrusted to my future protection. When we are finally settled at the chateau, I will lose no time in communicating with the Prince Bianchi, and I have not the least doubt but that we shall be able to bring this important and delicate business to a favourable issue. But come, Adolphe, I must again enjoin you to arouse yourself from this state of melancholy, for although you deny it, I feel convinced that it arises from nothing else but something you have that weighs heavily upon your mind."

"How can I convince your lordship to the contrary?" said Adolphe, who avoided the keen glance of the Count de Clairville as much as he could, and felt extremely hurt that he was thus compelled to play the hypocrite.

"By at once reasuming your usual spirits, and mingling freely in society as formerly," answered his lordship. "By the saints, I never saw any one who more resembled a poor lovesick swain than you do at present."

"Your lordship is, indeed, disposed to banter me," said Adolphe, though he could with difficulty help betraying the confusion he felt as he spoke.

"No," returned the count; "I speak seriously, and give that as my candid opinion, and I will acknowledge myself no prophet, if my words do not ultimately prove to be true. But will you not join us this evening in the large cavern, where Massaroni, his wife, Montaldi, the Signora Zitella and her daughter, my nephew and the Signora Melina, will be present? and we shall, therefore, have a most delightful party; and that, I should think, would tend more than anything else to restore you to spirits."

"No, my lord," answered Adolphe, "I must beg of you to excuse me, for, indeed, I feel so severely indisposed, that I should prove but a sorry addition to your company."

"Well," returned the Count de Clairville, "I suppose that I must yield to your request; but remember that I shall expect you to exert yourself, and to get rid of this ennui, for it is nothing else, or I shall feel it my duty to lecture you severely on the subject."

Adolphe bowed, but made no reply, and his lordship then retired, much to his relief, and left him to his own secret and painful meditations. He remained silent for some minutes after he was gone, and, with his arms folded across his chest, he sat buried in gloomy thought, whilst a variety of the most painful emotions agitated his breast; but at length he started up and paced the room in a most agitated manner, and exclaimed—

"What torture has this interview with the Count de Clairville cost me, and what a consummate hypocrite I must be, thus to conceal my real feelings, and to return the answers I did to the questions he put to me. By Heaven! by what he said, I could almost swear that he read my very thoughts. But no, it is impossible that he could form the slightest conjecture of them; he could never for a moment believe me so base as to have formed an unhappy passion for the beauteous Melina, or would not his utmost indignation have been aroused, and he would have loaded me with his reproaches? It is my own guilty conscience that awakens the suspicion in my mind, and thus tortures me. Alas! I am truly miserable! But had he distinguished the words to which I gave utterance, when he had arrived at the door, he would have discovered all. What a desperate and guilty act was my rash hand about to commit; and yet would it not have been better that I had done so, and thus have rid myself of a life that has now become insupportable to me? It is impossible for me to remain much longer in his society without betraying myself, and then what can I expect but to be looked upon as a villain, and to be overwhelmed with the scorn and reproaches of all who know me? And Melina is to be the

companion of our journey, too; I might have expected as much. How can I ever again enter her presence, with those thoughts passing in my mind? How can I ever more meet Florio without blushing and betraying myself? I am completely lost and bewildered, and am now completely reckless as to what may become of me. And what if I were to acknowledge the truth to the Count de Clairville, and throw myself upon his mercy and forbearance? Would he not pity and forgive me, and advise me how to act? Ah! no! I can never acquire sufficient firmness to do so, and surely he would spurn me from his feet, and look upon me with loathing. And yet am I not surely worthy of some little pity and sympathy? Is it at all surprising that charms and accomplishments so transcendent as those which Melina possesses should make such a powerful impression upon my heart, notwithstanding I knew that she was the betrothed of another, and could never by any possibility be mine? Ah, no! that knowledge ought to have restrained my passions, especially when I had the terrible example of my benefactor before me. I have been, I am much to blame. Would that I were dead; for only within the space of a few short days I have become hateful to myself. After all, I see no other means of escaping the evil I dread than by flight. And yet I cannot form the resolution to do so."

He continued to pace the cavern backwards and forwards in the same disordered manner, and without being able to bring his mind to any satisfactory conclusion, or to obtain that least degree of composure. And in this manner the time passed away until night approached, and not receiving any further interruption, he retired to bed at an early hour, but his mind was too much disturbed to suffer him to sleep, and he lay tossing about on his couch in a state of excitement which we need not attempt to describe. When, at length, sleep descended upon his eyelids, his brain was disturbed by the most frightful and painful visions, and he frequently started from it in a state of the greatest alarm. But at length he became more composed, and slept soundly and undisturbed till the morning.

* * * * *

Floretta and her mistress, after the interview between her and the Count de Clairville, sat for some time in that part of the cavern which was appropriated to their accommodation, conversing on the prospects that were now before them.

"I declare, signora," said the loquacious but faithful domestic, "that I am all anxiety for the journey, and to see what sort of a place this old chateau is. I dare say it is a large, gothic, gloomy old edifice, full of secret passages and haunted chambers, which will be very romantic, you know, and there is nothing in the world that I like so well as——"

"For goodness sake cease, you silly girl," interrupted Melina, "your tongue far outstrips your wits. There may be something very romantic, according to your fancy, in haunted chambers and secret passages; but I must confess that such places are not at all suited to my taste. However, I am anxious for us to go to this old chateau, for I shall feel myself much more comfortable under the protection of the Count de Clairville than that of Massaroni,

INTERVIEW IN THE GARDEN BETWEEN MELINA AND THE COUNT.

although it would be both unjust and ungrateful of me to deny that the latter has ever behaved to me with the utmost respect and attention."

"True, signora," coincided Floretta; "and I'm sure that I shall ever esteem the brigand chief for it, let the world say whatever it may of him. No doubt he feels very great regret at parting with you."

"Yes," replied our heroine, "that, of course,

was to be expected; but he sees the prudence and the necessity of the step, and, therefore, offers no opposition."

"Exactly so, my lady," remarked her attendant; ".I declare I am quite taken up with the Count de Clairville, he is such a very amiable nobleman, and has met with so many misfortunes, though, for the matter of that, they were o' his own seeking. However, that's of no consequence. He will be as a father to you, signora, no doubt; and only to think that he should prove to be the uncle of Signor Clairville! Ah! he will quickly communicate with the Prince Bianchi; and when he becomes acquainted with the fact that your lover is of such noble origin, he will no longer remain obstinate, but will at once give his consent to your union with Signor Florio."

"Nay, Floretta," said her mistress, "I do not entertain any such sanguine expectations; the prince, my uncle, has already given me sufficient proofs of his obduracy, if I could ever indeed have doubted it, to make me fear that he will not yield: besides, his prejudice is so strong against Florio, that I fairly believe nothing will ever be able to conquer it, and all the influence of the count will not, I think, have any effect upon him."

"And suppose it should not, signora, how do you then intend to act?"

"I know not; I am yet undecided."

"Dear me, signora, I am surprised at that. Of course, you will then no longer hesitate to become the wife of Signor Clairville, since you will do so under the sanction of his noble uncle?'

"I really cannot say," answered Melina, "it is a delicate point to decide."

"Why, so it is, signora," coincided Floretta; "but if the Prince Bianchi will not yield, why should you resign your happiness for that? You and Signor Clairville love one another sincerely; you are worthy of each other, and what is there, then, to prevent your union?"

"True," said our heroine; "but I would that it could be solemnized under different circumstances. I should feel most happy could we come to some amicable arrangement with the Prince Bianchi."

"Why, that would be better, to be sure," said Floretta; "but still, if that cannot be effected, I suppose you will not refuse to become the bride of Florio?"

"You put questions to me, Floretta, that I know not how to answer."

"Pardon me, signora, but I do not consider that there can be any difficulty in answering that question. You are your own mistress; the prince, your uncle, has abused his authority, and I do not see that you have any business to study him. As for refusing to become the wife of Signor Clairville, because he will not give his consent, that would be preposterous.

But, however, all these obstacles will be removed by the intervention of the count, and before many weeks have elapsed, take my word for it, all your wishes will be gratified."

"I hope to Heaven that they may," said our heroine, fervently, "for, indeed, I have had my share of trials, and I have endeavoured to bear them patiently."

"You have, indeed, my dear lady," replied Floretta, "and you deserve to be rewarded for it. But the journey we are about to take is a long one, and there is no knowing what might happen on the road, if we have not some protection."

"Massaroni and a few of the most trusty of his band will accompany us part of the way," said her mistress; "and when we have got beyond these mountain fortresses, I believe that we shall have nothing to fear."

"Oh, that is all right," remarked Floretta; "oh, how anxious I am for the journey, not but that I have enjoyed myself very well since we have been here, but I expect that we shall meet with some fresh adventures, and if there is anything in the world that I am fond of it is romantic adventures, that is, if there is no danger attached to them. How astonished the Prince Bianchi will be when he comes to hear of all these wonderful events. And Florio is to be the Count de Clairville too, is he not?"

"Yes," answered Melina, "at least, if the count does not change his present resolution, but which I sincerely hope he will."

"And what is that, my dear signora?" interrogated her attendant.

"Why," replied our heroine, "he has stated it as his determination to resign his title and estates to Florio, and retire into a monastery for the rest of his days."

"Oh, signora," said Floretta, "it would indeed be a great pity for him to do that, so well calculated as he is to adorn society. What if he was a little imprudent in his youthful days, he has endeavoured to make all the atonement in his power since, and there is no one who will reproach him for it."

"True, Floretta; but, as I said before, I hope he will change his mind, for it would grieve both Florio and myself and all who know him to be deprived of his society."

"Well," remarked Floretta, "seclusion may be all very well for those who like it, but for myself I must confess that I have no fancy that way. I don't see the wisdom of burying yourself within the gloomy walls of a cloister, while there is such a beautiful world for our enjoyment."

"Very true," said Melina; "but still, I would willingly have entered the walls of a convent rather than become the wife of the odious Count Alberti."

"Well, I do not wonder at that, for, of two

evils, a convent would certainly have been the last. However, thank the saints, you have not been compelled to take any such a step, and it is not likely that you will be now. The Count Alberti is a very bad man; his conduct to the poor Signora Olympia, or rather Mira, as she is now discovered to be, proves that. Is it not wonderful the way events have been brought about, signora? To think that she whom we have so long known as Olympia should prove to be the daughter of your uncle! I wonder what his feelings will be when he comes to know the secret, and that the unfortunate Zitella is still living?"

"Heaven only knows," answered our heroine; "but I should think that he would be stung with remose, and would endeavour to render them all the justice in his power."

"Yes, signora, that is the least he can do. But there is another question I have to ask you."

"And what is that, Floretta?"

"The manuscript we found in the Villa Civetti; do you intend to show it to Signor Florio?"

"Not at present," replied Melina; "I have changed my mind, and think it is better not to do so until after my own affairs are a little more settled."

"Well," observed Floretta, "perhaps that will be the most prudent plan. But does it not appear, from all the circumstances connected with Massaroni, that the unfortunate and deeply injured writer of that manuscript was his mother? And if so, there can scarcely be any doubt that the brigand chief is also the son of the Prince Bianchi."

"It does, indeed," said our heroine; "and it is that belief that renders me fearful of the secret being discovered at present; Massaroni has sworn, you know, to reak his vengeance upon the head of his misguided father, should he ever be revealed to him; and should he have sufficient proof that the prince is his parent, in his present state of mind, and so inveterate as he otherwise is against him, nothing whatever, depend upon it, could prevent him from keeping his word."

"Very true, signora," said Floretta, "and that would, indeed, be a terrible thing. But I trust that no such calamity will take place, but that, on the contrary, all the important matters that have so long troubled you, and kept your mind in a continual state of anxiety, fear, and suspense, will terminate happily, and that we shall many a time in future be able to converse upon what has past only as some wonderful romance. Dear me! I cannnot for the life of me help imagining the time when you, my dear signora, will be the Countess de Clairville; happy as the days are long in the love of your husband, and surrounded by a family of lovely little ——"

"Hush! my silly girl!" interrupted her mistress, blushing, though she could not help smiling at her faithful attendant's loquacity. "I cannot allow you to give your tongue such free licence on so delicate and important a subject. To what extreme lengths do you suffer your garrulity to lead you!"

"Well, I beg your pardon, signora," returned Floretta, "if I should seem too bold, but my spirits are so exceedingly elevated to-day, that I cannot help giving expression to my feelings. But surely there can be no particular horror in anticipating what is sure to take place? Come, come, signora, you must be cheerful, for your prospects brighten, and I firmly believe that you will never more have to encounter those severe storms and misfortunes you have hitherto been so unfortunate as to experience."

"Well, Floretta," said our heroine, "I know the sincerity of your heart, and I thank you most heartily for your good wishes. Should all the hopes you have expressed in such sanguine terms be realised, I shall, indeed, be one of the happiest of human beings."

"And they will be, my dear mistress, depend upon it," said Floretta; "I flatter myself that I am not often out in my conjectures, and if what I predict on this occasion does not come true, I will acknowledge myself at once to be no prophetess. As for the Prince Bianchi, your uncle, he must be composed of something more than human materials, if he continues to remain obdurate, that's all I have to say about it. He will be friends with you again—he will be brought to a full sense of the injustice he has done you, and I feel convinced that it will be his future study to render you all the atonement in his power. Oh, yes, I see it all, signora, as if it had but just taken place; you will be as happy as the days are long; and I shall be happy, and we shall all be happy, and——"

"But the Count Alberti?" interrupted Melina.

"Oh, it matters little what becomes of him," answered Floretta; "his power and influence over his Excellenza, the Prince Bianchi, will soon be at an end, and you will have nothing more to fear from him. The best thing he can do, I should think, after the manner in which he has disgraced himself, and the crimes he has committed, will be to hide himself in obscurity, and try to repent of his sins. But let us think no more about him, my lady; all that we can say of him is, that he is a very bad man, and that he deserves to suffer, and that severely, for the injuries he has done to others."

"And what a strange and unfortunate infatuation must my uncle have laboured under to be so prejudiced in his favour," remarked Melina.

"Yes," coincided Floretta, "and in one sense he is to be pitied for it. But I have no doubt he will be brought to a full sense of the olly and injustice of which he has been guilty, and that the principal study of his future days will be to show the sincerity of his repentance."

"But when he is convinced that the Signora Zitella is still living," said our heroine, "and that that unfortunate and deeply-injured being, the victim of that man to whom he would have sacrificed my happiness, whom he has hitherto known as Olympia, is his own daughter, what must be his feelings? I cannot but pity him for the anguish he will feel."

"Very true, signora," returned her companion; "but the past cannot be recalled, and the only reparation he can make is by his future conduct towards those unfortunate beings."

"It is, Floretta," agreed her mistress; "but I fear the discovery will overwhelm him, and that his reason will never be able to sustain the sudden shock. Besides, the disgrace it will heap upon him when his crimes become known."

"But there will be no necessity for that, signora," suggested Floretta; "neither the Signora Zitella nor her daughter, you know, entertain any vindictive feelings towards him, and their connexion with him is not obliged to be publicly known, if he amply provides for them, which it is his duty to do. But come, my dear lady, let us talk no more upon this disagreeable subject; I am all upon the *qui vive* for the commencement of our journey, and anticipate a host of adventures of the most happy and romantic description. This old chateau of which we have heard so much, and with which there are so many remarkable and important events connected, haunts my imagination like a vision, and I am all anxiety to behold it. My word for it, when all other important matters are settled, we will soon change the gloomy character of the place. But I must lose no time in making all the necessary arrangements for the journey."

"For goodness sake, Floretta," again interposed our heroine, "do not suffer your tongue to run so glibly, for, indeed, I have too many other and more serious thoughts upon my mind to suffer me to listen to such nonsense."

"Nonsense!" repeated her attendant; "indeed, I do not think it such nonsense as you seem to consider it. But, however, signora, if it be disagreeable to you I will e'en say no more about it; though I cannot help thinking that you will be much happier under the protection of the Count de Clairville than you could possibly be under that of the brigand chief, although he has behaved with such extraordinary attention and respect towards you."

"True," replied Melina, "Massaroni has acted a most generous, disinterested, and honourable part towards me, and I feel that I owe him a debt of gratitude for the same, which it shall be my constant study to endea-

vour to repay. It is that feeling which ma[..] me the more anxious to see Massaroni plac[..] in a different situation to what he is at prese[..] —to have the wrongs he has received redresse[..] —to be forgiven for the lawless life he has fo[..] so many years led, and to be restored to tha[..] position in society which his mental qualifica-tions so well fit him to adorn."

"Truly spoken, my lady," said her maid; "and in those feelings, I think I need not assure you that I most heartily concur. There is every excuse to be offered for Allesandro Massaroni, for had it not been for the cruelty and neglect of those whose duty it was to provide for him and to protect him, he would never have been driven to adopt the dangerous and guilty course he is at present pursuing. But I am afraid that he has offended the laws of his country too greatly ever to hope for forgiveness, and, besides, he is so warmly attached to his present wild and romantic life, and his old and faithful associates, ever to quit it, if even he had the opportunity."

"Alas!" said Melina, "I fear so too; after the services which the brigand chief has rendered me, it cannot but be supposed that I feel no inconsiderable interest in his fate; and should he indeed prove to be the unfortunate son of the Prince Bianchi, my uncle, which, after what we have read, and taking the strange coincidences of his history into consideration, it is not at all unreasonable to suppose he is, that interest must, of course, be naturally increased. And yet, after the feelings of revenge he has expressed against the author of his being, should he ever discover him, almost tempts me to hope that he may not prove to be so, for the consequences that would then be likely to follow would be of the most lamentable description."

"Nay, signora," remarked Floretta, "your apprehensions upon that painful and delicate subject, I am inclined to think, are far too powerful and groundless. Should Massaroni discover that the Prince Bianchi is his father, he would, I am convinced, prompted by nature, forget the revengeful feelings that at present inhabit his breast, especially if he found that his highness was fully and sincerely penitent, and was ready and willing to acknowledge him as his son."

"I know not," remarked our heroine; "the wrongs that a beloved mother has received are hard to forget. Massaroni naturally feels warmly upon the melancholy subject, and I tremble to think what he might in the excitement of the moment be tempted to do. God grant that my fears may be wrong, and that that which I now anticipate may not be realised."

"It will not, signora," said Floretta, "you may depend upon it. Should that important and extraordinary discovery be made, after the first burst of passion is over, all will terminate amicably; a reconciliation will be effected, and the past will be buried in oblivion."

"Oh, no," returned Melina, " that I feel to be impossible; the past may be forgiven, but where the offences have been of so serious a nature they can never be forgiven."

"Well, signora," answered her companion, " it is useless to dwell any longer upon so disagreeable a subject, since we can come to no other conclusion. Entertain no vague fears, but trust in the wisdom and goodness of Providence for the happy issue of events."

Our heroine was about to return some reply, when she was prevented from doing so by a gentle tap at the door, and having opened it, Florio entered.

Floretta curtseyed to him and her mistress, and immediately retired from the place.

"My dearest Melina," said her lover, gently and fondly encircling her slender waist with one arm, and drawing her towards him, " I hope you will not consider me intrusive, but I could no longer deprive myself of your society for a short time, that I might breathe in your ear the feelings that at present occupy my mind; feelings of happiness and joyful anticipation. The observations you made use of in the presence of my uncle can never be effaced from my memory, and have convinced me, if, indeed, I required any further proof, of the ardour and sincerity of the sentiments you entertain towards me. Oh! what a happy, what a doubly fortunate man I ought to consider myself to be, to possess the love of such a being as Melina."

"Florio," replied the blushing maiden, " why this extraordinary display of feeling on the present occasion, because I have merely acknowledged to your noble relative the true feelings of my heart? Could you for one moment doubt the sincerity of those vows which I have so often repeated to you?"

"Oh, no, no!" returned Florio, emphatically, " Heaven forbid that I should, for then how truly unworthy should I prove myself to be of that sweet confidence you have reposed in me —of the unswerving constancy you have ever evinced towards me, in spite of the numerous trials and difficulties by which you have been surrounded; difficulties that were more than sufficient to crush the strongest spirit. Pardon me, I beseech you, if my words have seemed to imply any doubt; but, alas! I fear that I shall never be able to prove myself worthy of the preference you have shown me, even when you supposed me to be humble, friendless, poor, and obscure."

"Oh, Florio!" said the maiden, with a look of gentle reproach, " and think you that wealth or station could have had any influence over my affections, or that I could have felt any warmer sentiments towards you had I known you to have been rich and noble? No, you wrong me

by supposing that I could ever have suffered such a sordid passion to enter my breast. I loved you for your intrinsic merits alone, and the Count de Clairville can never be more dear to me than the humble and friendless Florio, the painter."

"Oh, blesssed assurance!" ejaculated her lover, embracing her rapturously; " what truth, what innocence and sincerity are expressed in those words! Pardon me, Melina, if I have seemed not duly to appreciate your feelings; but, indeed, I meant not to convey any such idea. I know the noble, the generous, and virtuous mind of my beloved Melina too well to entertain such an opinion. Notwithstanding all the difficulties it has been our lot to encounter, and the numerous and apparently insurmountable obstacles that have been thrown in our way, fortune seems to smile upon our loves, and to point to us with certainty the consumption of our happiness. In a few days we shall be removed from this cavernous retreat, and placed in far more favourable circumstances than we have hitherto been; the Count de Clairville will take the earliest opportunity to plead our cause with your uncle; he will use all the arguments that truth and reason can suggest to induce him to yield to our wishes; but should the Prince Bianchi still remain obstinate, and refuse to relent, say, Melina, will you any longer refuse to consent to our union taking place, and——"

"Florio," interrupted the blushing Melina, at the same time the expression of her beautiful eyes spoke far more than any language, however eloquent, could possibly convey, " you already know my sentiments upon that subject, and, therefore, I beg of you not to question me further. I trust that there will be no necessity to put my resolution to the test; but I firmly hope, and feel confident, that should such an occasion arrive, I shall be found adequate to the task, and enabled to act as reason, honour, and virtue shall dictate."

"Enough, my sweet Melina," said Florio, again clasping her fervently to his heart, and imprinting a kiss upon her fair cheek, " that assurance is everything to me, and I have nothing more to hope for. Oh, how supremely happy have you made me! The change in our situation, I feel confident, will be productive of great good, though, at the same time, I cannot but deeply regret the necessity which compels us to quit the protection of Massaroni, to whom we are so much indebted."

"True, Florio," said our heroine, " we owe the brigand chief much for the almost inestimable services he has rendered us, and which, I hope, we may yet have it in our power to repay. Would that he could be prevailed upon to quit his present course of life; he probably might obtain a pardon for the offences he has committed; and I confess that I feel the deepest interest in his fate."

"And in that feeling, Melina," said her lover, "I most warmly participate. Massaroni possesses mental qualities that would render him an ornament to society, instead of being, as he is looked upon now, its scourge. There is something in his personal appearance, and his general demeanour, too, which convinces me that he is of no mean origin."

"Such, Florio," replied our heroine, "is the opinion I have formed. Have you ever noticed the extraordinary resemblance he bears to the mysterious portrait in the Villa Rosa?"

"Oh, frequently," answered Florio, "and I have often marvelled at it; had it been the representation of his own mother, it could not have been expected to be more like him."

"His own mother!" replied Melina, in a faint and agitated voice.

"Yes, Melina," returned her lover; "but why should that observation cause you so much emotion?"

"Florio," replied our heroine, "it is quite evident that the original of that portrait was connected with the Prince Bianchi in a most delicate and particular manner; and it is not impossible that the father of her child, if indeed, she had one, was my uncle."

"And should it be so?"

"And that child should prove to be no other than Massaroni?"

"Oh, no, that is impossible," said Florio.

"And why so?" demanded Melina.

"Well, I know not; but even should the brigand chief prove to be the son of the Prince Bianchi, would it not be the means of rescuing him from his present perilous situation, and of restoring him to that society from which he has been so long excluded?"

"Ah, no!" returned Melina. "I tremble for the consequences that would be most likely to ensue, should Massaroni discover that the prince is his father; for do you remember that he has sworn to have a deadly revenge upon him for the injuries he inflicted upon his mother?"

"True," answered Florio; "but I trust that he would be able to conquer those vindictive and unnatural feelings, especially if his father were ready to acknowledge him as his son, and to make him all the atonement that he could for the wrongs he had suffered from him."

"But think you that the Prince Bianchi would ever acknowledge the brigand chief, and one who has ever been so strongly opposed to, and frustrated his designs, for a son?" demanded our heroine.

"My dear Melina," remarked Florio, "how singular are the observations you make upon this subject, and how powerful is the interest you seem to take in it."

"Believe me, Florio," returned the maiden, "it is no common interest that I feel. You have heard the name of the original of that portrait, I presume?"

"Yes," said Florio. "I did hear it accidentally, though I believe I never told it to you before. It was Zerlina."

"Ah!" ejaculated our heroine; "the very same; and I am now all but convinced of the truth of my surmises."

"What mean you, my dear Melina?" interrogated Florio, with a look of surprise.

"When I was confined in the Villa Civetti," answered Melina, "I accidentally discovered a manuscript, which purports to be the history of an unfortunate being named Zerlina. She loved the prince my uncle, and he professed to return her passion with equal fervour and sincerity. Under the pretext of marriage, he triumphed over her innocence, and afterwards confined her in the Villa Civetti. A son was the offspring of this unfortunate connexion, and the similarity that exists between the history of this unfortunate individual and that of Massaroni, and then the strong resemblance that he bears to the portrait—Oh, how it grieves me to have to mention the crimes of one so nearly allied to me by blood; but—"

"This is most extraordinary, dear Melina," said her lover. "But why did you not mention this circumstance to me before?"

"I frequently thought of doing so," replied our heroine, "and to ask your advice upon the subject; but still something made me hesitate to do so. I was fearful lest Massaroni should become acquainted with it, and that should Zerlina prove to be his mother, in his present state of mind he might be led to wreak his vengeance on the head of the Prince Bianchi, and thus be the cause of that which I shudder to think upon."

"Oh, no," observed Florio, "nature and reason would surely conquer those revengeful feelings. But have you the manuscript by you, Melina?"

"I have," she answered, going to a small cabinet and producing it; "it is here."

Florio eagerly took it from her hand, and hastily glanced over its contents, and as he did so, the emotion he felt was clearly visible on his countenance.

"How extraordinary is this," he said, after he had hurriedly perused some of the main incidents recorded in the manuscript;—"there can be no doubt of the truth of your surmises, Melina."

"Ah!" cried our heroine, "do you then believe that Allesandro Massaroni is the son of the Prince Bianchi, and the ill-fated writer of that melancholy history?"

"I do," answered Florio, "and the more I reflect upon such particulars of his history as I have been able to elicit from the brigand chief, the stronger becomes my conviction that it is so."

"But do you think it would be safe or prudent to make Massaroni acquainted with the facts?" interrogated Melina.

"Not at present, at any rate," replied Florio; "it will be advisable to wait to see whether time will effect any change in his feelings. He might, in the state of mind he is in now, be urged to some act of violence and desperation, which he would afterwards repent."

"Very true," coincided our eroine; "that is exactly my opinion; but, oh, what will be the feelings of remorse and anguish that my uncle must experience when he becomes acquainted with these facts. Wretched, misguided man! how manifold are his offences; how much has he got to answer for. All the crimes that Massaroni may have been guilty of will assuredly rest upon his head, for had he not so cruely deserted his mother and himself, he would never, in all probability, have been placed in the situation he now is."

"May Heaven bring Bianchi to repentance," observed Florio, "for indeed he stands in much need of it."

"And is it not horrible to think that my uncle has ever viewed Massaroni with the most deadly feelings of hatred and revenge?" said Melina; "and I verily believe that he now thirsts for his blood!"

"True," said her lover, "it is a fearful thought; but you must endeavour to banish it from your mind, and to live in hopes that everything will yet terminate happily."

"God grant that it may," fervently returned Melina; "but when I weigh all the peculiar circumstances in my mind, I can scarcely help resigning myself to despair."

"Indeed, my sweet Melina," Florio replied, "you must not talk thus, for that will only serve to distress and harass your mind more than it is at present. Until some future occasion, I think it will be prudent to keep this secret to ourselves, and we shall then probably see how it will be best to act."

"Oh, yes," coincided our heroine; "that is exactly my opinion; and when we are away from Massaroni we shall not be so likely to betray it."

"Exactly so," said her lover. "But enough upon that subject just now, for I see that it distresses your mind. I confess that I am now most eager for our departure from this place, for I am naturally anxious to behold that spot which is connected with me by so many melancholy recollections and associations. My unfortunate parents! little, I dare say, did you imagine that your son would ever tread the halls of his ancestors, or reign the lord of his paternal estates! Would to Heaven that you had lived to have seen that day, then

might my misguided uncle have obtained your forgiveness, and a heavy weight of care and bitter self-reproach would have been removed from his conscience."

"But the Count de Clairville surely will not adhere to the resolution he has expressed," said Melina, "namely, to retire from the world, and to bury his future days within the gloomy walls of a monastery?"

"I trust not," answered Florio, "though his mind at present appears to be firmly made up. But I hope that we shall be able to dissuade him from that determination, and that we may experience many happy years of his society."

"In that wish I most heartily coincide," said our heroine; "and I trust that we shall be able to divert his thoughts from the dismal retrospect of the past."

"No doubt the efforts of my sweet Melina will be attended with the desired effect," observed her lover. "Oh, my beloved girl, what days of bliss do I anticipate are in store for us; what an ample reward will they be for all the troubles it has been our fate to undergo. To know that I possess my Melina's love, will be enough for me; and what care, what anxiety, what trouble can then beset my mind? The proudest monarch that reigns upon his throne might envy me my happy lot, for Melina is a treasure that kingdoms could not purchase."

The blushing maiden hid her face on his shoulder, and her emotions prevented her from returning any answer, though the throbbing of her heart told how fervently she responded to the feelings Florio had expressed. They remained for some time longer wrapped in the most blissful conversation; but at length they separated, and Melina a short time afterwards retired to rest, her mind feeling more calm and happy than it had been some time before.

* * * *

The time that intervened prior to the departure from the cavernous retreat of Massaroni, was occupied in making preparations for the journey, which were at length completed, and our heroine and her lover looked forward to the hour when they were to commence their journey with considerable anxiety, for they could not help looking upon it as one of the most important events of their lives

Melina felt the deepest regret at being compelled to part from the Signora Zitella and her daughter, for they had ever evinced towards her the greatest esteem and friendship, and she had always derived much consolation from their society, and the sympathy they had expressed for her fate; but she consoled herself with the idea that it would not be long ere they would meet again, and that it would be under far different and happier circumstances.

The brigand also felt that he should be lost when Florio and Melina had taken their departure from his retreat; but, of course, knowing that it was done for the best, he could raise no further objection, and was resolved that he would still leave no means untried to serve them and to forward their wishes; and he was satisfied that they fully appreciated the feelings he entertained towards them, and respected him for that which he had already been able to accomplish to promote their happiness, and to frustrate the designs of their enemies.

As for Adolphe D'Aubigny, he continued in much the same unhappy state of mind as we have previously described him to be, and it was in vain that he endeavoured to arouse himself from it. He excused himself from all society as much as possible, and had never once seen the beauteous object of his thoughts. He dreaded the journey, and the arrival at the chateau, when he must so frequently be in her presence; and as these thoughts crowded upon his mind, he became still more agitated and irresolute. Old Montaldi saw him frequently, and endeavoured all that he could to combat his feelings, but his efforts met with very little, if any success; D'Aubigny could not yet divert his mind of the impression that the only way he could avoid the evils he apprehended was by flight; thinking that when he was far away, if he could not entirely forget her, he might, at least, so far conquer his unfortunate and hopelesss passion as to venture again to return, without being guilty of any act of impropriety; and that the Count de Clairville, and Melina and her lover would then, when they were convinced of his sincerity, so far from reproaching him, commend him for the virtuous and honourable resolution he had formed.

"After all that you have said to the contrary, Signor Montaldi," he observed, at one of their interviews, "and the arguments you have advanced, I am convinced that that is the only course that I should adopt, and which reason and honour seem to sanction. While I am near the too lovely Melina, it will be impossible to conquer my feelings, and I know not to what lengths my fatal passion may not in a moment of frenzy and despair urge me to go. Should I tear myself away, and thus avoid the danger to which I am now exposed, they must commend me; and let whatever may be the circumstances that may happen to me, I can at least console myself with the reflection that I did my best to save myself from being precipitated into that fatal abyss, upon the brink of which I found myself standing."

"I admire your motives, Signor Adolphe," said Montaldi; "but still it is my firm belief that such a step would not be productive of any good. I fear the idea of your being left to your own solitary thoughts and actions in the present state of your mind, and without a friend nigh you to control you with his arguments and advice. Besides, the grief that it would cost your aged and noble benefactor, who, I am convinced, regards you with the same affection as if you were his own son?"

"Ah!" ejaculated D'Aubigny, "it is that which tortures me more than all. The shame, the grief that the knowledge of my fatal passion must cost that venerable nobleman to whom I am so greatly indebted, after all the years of anxiety and attention he has bestowed upon me since the death of my late lamented father, more especially when it will revive in his memory all the circumstances of his own melancholy history."

"Then," said Montaldi, "since you know the agony which your abrupt departure will cost the Count de Clairville, had you not better remain and combat everything? Would it not better become you to remain, and exercise a proper and manly fortitude to conquer the fatal and hopeless passion which has unfortunately taken possession of your breast, and by never betraying the painful feelings of your heart, save your benefactor those pangs which you now apprehend? Come, D'Aubigny, do not give way to a weakness which cannot but be productive of the most lamentable consequences; but arouse yourself from this state of despair and irresolution, and my word for it, you will succeed, and all will again be well."

"Your advice is good, my kind friend," answered Adolphe, "and I know that it is tendered to me in the best spirit; but, alas! I feel most painfully the great difficulty of following it. Heaven knows how keenly I feel the danger and delicacy of my situation, and how plainly I see the fatal consequences that are attendant on it; but still I feel incompetent to the task you would impose upon me, and seem to be hurried irresistibly on to destruction. My brain becomes the more bewildered the longer I reflect upon it, and I know not how to act. Would that I had never beheld the too-captivating Signora Melina, then might I still have remained as happy and contented as I was before; but now, with all these thoughts upon my mind, life has become a burthen to me."

"How it grieves me, Signor D'Aubigny," said his aged companion, "to see one so young, and with such happy prospects before him, thus yield himself up entirely to despair, when, by the proper exercise of his energies, he might triumph over everything, and without for a moment ever giving cause to those who must be dear to him to suspect the thoughts that are at present torturing his mind. Come, come, I say again, it needs but resolution, and the painful task I would impose upon you will be accomplished."

"Alas!" sighed D'Aubigny, " and that resolution, unfortunately, I feel it impossible to call to my aid. I dread the idea of again beholding Melina; for can I possibly gaze upon her superlative charms—can I listen to the glowing eloquence of her tongue—without feeling that the unfortunate passion she has inspired me with must increase in strength instead of abating, and that there is nothing left for me but the greatest misery and anguish?

MELINA PLEADS THE CAUSE OF HER UNCLE TOMASSARONI.

Think you, Montaldi, that I can behold the smiles of affection she bestows upon the too fortunate Florio de Clairville unmoved? Or that I can help feeling all the corroding pangs of envy and jealousy? No, by Heaven, I must be less than man, and insensible to all that is lovely in womankind, if I could. My very looks must at once betray the feelings that are struggling in my breast, and I should stand confessed as a despicable scoundrel, and receive the scorn and reproaches of all those who are connected with me. It is that I so much dread—it is this that I wish to avoid; and I see no other means of doing so than by at once flying from the scene of danger, and indulging in my agonising thoughts alone."

"You have given me your word that you would abandon such an idea, D'Aubigny," remarked Montaldi.

"'Tis true, I have," he answered, pressing his hand upon his forehead; "but my mind was so distracted that I knew not what I said. Oh, Montaldi, do not judge me harshly, or condemn me altogether; Heaven knows how anxious I am to avoid the dangers that beset me, and that I would not wrong the gentle and beauteous Melina by a word or deed; but still, I am the victim of a passion which I fear it will never be in my power to conquer, and while L remain near her, I tremble for the consequences that may ensue. When we reach the chateau, it will be impossible for me to avoid the presence of Melina; and that I have too much reason to fear will bring about the crisis of my fate."

"Unfortunate young man," said Montaldi, "I know not what to say to you, since all the arguments I can make use of seem to have no effect on you. But again I caution you to beware, ere you take any rash step which you may afterwards have bitter cause to repent, and when it will be too late for you to recal the past."

D'Aubigny returned no answer, but paced the cavern with disordered steps.

"Will you give me your word, Signor D'Aubigny," continued the old man, "that you will do nothing rashly, or adopt any course without previously consulting me?"

Adolphe hesitated, and seemed for a moment at a loss what answer to return.

"You hesitate," said Montaldi, "and that excites my doubts and suspicions."

"Oh, Signor Montaldi," replied Adolphe, in a voice of emotion, "do you not pity me?"

"I do; but I am anxious to arouse you from this state of misery and anguish."

"Would to God that I could!"

"It requires but determination, and the task is accomplished. But will you grant me the request I have made?"

"I—I will," answered D'Aubigny, after a pause, "for I am convinced that you are sincerely my friend."

"Enough," said Montaldi. "I will take your word, and do not yet despair of seeing you restored to your former state of mind."

"Alas! I fear that can never be."

"Nonsense! say not so; there is no knowing what fortune has in store for you. But will you promise me also, that when you have quitted this place you will communicate with me, and let me know all that takes place?"

"I will," answered Adolphe, taking his hand, and speaking earnestly, "for who is there in whom I can so strictly confide?"

"And that confidence," returned Montaldi, "depend upon it, you shall find that I will never abuse. Bear well in mind all that I have said, and the advice I have given you, and you will profit by it. I trust that, whenever we shall meet again, which I sincerely hope we shall, that it will be under far different and much happier circumstances than the present, and that your mind will be restored to its wonted state of peace and tranquillity."

"I can but again thank you for your good wishes," observed D'Aubigny; "and believe me, my venerable and excellent friend, that I shall never cease to remember you with feelings of the utmost gratitude."

"I know it, signor," replied Montaldi, cordially returning the pressure of his hand, "and I am satisfied. I must now leave you, but again request a private interview with you previous to your departure from the cavern."

"I shall be prepared to meet you whenever you please," replied D'Aubigny, and Signor Montaldi then quitted his presence.

D'Aubigny stood for a moment or two after he was gone, and reflected deeply. There was so much force and truth in all that Montaldi had said, that he found it impossible to combat it by any reasonable argument of his own, and he, therefore, notwithstanding all his deliberations, still remained in the same unsettled and undecided state of mind, and was tortured and distracted by the various and conflicting thoughts that crowded upon his brain.

"Signor Montaldi spoke the truth, and I cannot but acknowledge it," he observed, "when he said that my flying from the temptation which is presented to my imagination would display a weakness on my part, and that I ought to remain, and, by exerting all my manly fortitude, to conquer the unfortunate and fatal passion which has taken possession of my breast. But, alas! how difficult is the task to accomplish; and although I may try every means which reason can suggest, I feel too thoroughly convinced that I should never be able to succeed. Most easy is it to advise. And Melina is a maiden, whom once to behold it is impossible ever to forget. In spite of all my efforts, and the evil consequences which I know are almost certain to ensue, I feel that every moment her image obtains still greater influence over me, and, therefore, that if I remain near her, and constantly in the way of beholding her, that it must end in my shame, if not in my entire destruction. What, then, can I do? How avoid the evils that I apprehend? Should I fly, will it not, to the Count de Clairville, appear like the basest ingratitude? And even should I be able to conquer my unhappy passion, should I be able to effect a reconciliation with him again? No, he would then loathe and despise me, and consider me no longer worthy of his friendship and esteem. It is a critical position in which I stand. I am involved in a dilemma from which I do not know how to extricate myself; and the longer I attempt to devise some means of doing so, the more bewildered I become. Heaven only knows how this will end, for I do not. It seems as though some cursed spell were upon me, and that I must become the victim, in spite of all that I can do to the contrary. Oh, Melina, why did nature ever form you so lovely?—or why was I fated to behold you? Hitherto my character has remained unblemished; but should I not be able to form an honourable resolution, into what shame and misery may I not be plunged!— The very thought unmans me, and I know not how to act."

He threw himself into a chair, and placing his elbow on the table, and reclining his chin disconsolately upon his hand, he abandoned himself to all the overwhelming melancholy of his oppressive thoughts. Every moment that he reflected, he become more wretched and miserable ; whichever way he directed his thoughts, the more dark and painful became the prospect that was presented to his distem-dered imagination, until he was at last worked up to such a pitch of excitement, that he scarcely knew in what way to contain himself.

How long he had remained in this state of melancholy he knew not, but he was suddenly aroused by hearing a knock at the door or cavern in which he was, and starting hastily to his feet, his confusion and agitation may be imagined, when the door opened, and the Count de Floriville entered. He, however, made a strong effort to recover himself, and partially succeeded, but not sufficiently to prevent the count from observing his emotion.

"Well, Adolphe," he said, "how are you now ?—But I need not put the question, for I perceive that you are still pale and agitated. Come, man, explain yourself to me, at least. for I think that I have a right to demand it, Connected as we are together, you should have no secrets from me."

"Secrets, my lord !" replied Adolphe, in a hesitating voice, and still more confused and agitated than before.

"Yes," returned the count, " I am certain that you must have some other cause for this depression and excitement than that which you have stated to me."

"Indeed, my lord," said D'Aubigny, in a faltering voice, " I have explained everything to you. I have been very ill for the last four days, and it is, therefore no wonder, I presume, that my spirits should be depressed."

"Now, then, would I wager one-half my fortune that you are in love," said the count. with a smile. " I am no novice in these

matters, Adolphe, and am not easily to be deceived. Why should you hesitate to acknowledge the truth to me, and to furnish me with the name of your fair inamorato ? I warrant me, that the damsel who has conquered your heart is a very paragon of beauty and accomplishments, and I should not only like to behold her, but to have the pleasure of being introduced into her society."

"Your lordship is still disposed to banter me," said D'Aubigny, assuming as much composure as he possibly could, but doing so with a very bad grace. "Indeed, you mistake my feelings altogether. and—"

"Adolphe," interrupted the count, seriously, and fixing his eyes keenly upon him, "I trust that you will not attempt to deceive me, for that would be unworthy of you, and I am not deserving of it."

The agony of Adolphe on hearing these pointed observations put to him may well be imagined, and he knew not what answer to make. To act the part of the hypocrite was most abhorrent to his feelings ; but how could he help doing so unless he revealed the truth? and that he could not find the courage to do. He had never felt himself placed in a more awkward position, and how to extricate himself from it, he knew not.

"You are silent, Adolphe," at last said his lordship ; " you look still more confused and agitated ; what am I to conclude from that ? Ah! I see plain enough that I am right in my surmises—that the little blind god has at last made a captive of your heart, and that love is the cause of all the emotion you evince. Come, come, confess it, Adolphe, at once, and by divulging the whole matter to me, ease your mind of the weight which seems at present to oppress it, and thus bring the business at once to a happy conclusion."

"Indeed, my lord," replied Adolphe, in as firm a voice as he could, " you are mistaken in the idea you have formed. Had such, indeed, been the case, you may depend upon it that I should not have kept it concealed from you ; but——"

"But," interrupted the count, " in spite of all your assertions to the contrary, I must adhere to my original opinion. I never knew what the tender passion was, Adolphe, if you are not in love now ; and you must have some particular reason, which I cannot fathom, for wishing to keep it concealed from me. However, I have no doubt that you will yet see the necessity of making a confidant of me, and, therefore, I will give you a few days more grace. The day after to-morrow, you know, we depart on our journey to France, and I trust that I shall find you in better spirits than you are at present, or you will form but a sorry companion ; though I should think if anything could serve to reanimate you, it would be the presence of the beauteous Signora Melina, whose charming conversation and sweet urbanity of manners are quite sufficient of themselves to make the most powerful impression upon even the most insensible heart."

Had the Count de Clairville at that moment have thrust a dagger in the heart of Adolphe D'Aubigny, he could scarcely have felt a greater pang than he did at the mention of that name. It was with difficulty that he could suppress a sigh, and he was compelled to avert his face in order to conceal his emotion ; but, notwithstanding, the count, whose eyes were keenly fixed upon him, and watching his every action, noticed it, and he said, in a half jocose, half serious manner—

"Why, hey-day, Adolphe, I declare you seem to get worse instead of improving upon it. Your heart seems to be so entirely gone, that even the bare mention of a female's name agitates you. You could not be more confused if even the fair Melina were the object of your affections, which is not at all likely, although it is impossible that she can do otherwise than possess your most unbounded esteem and admiration."

"Oh, my lord," said the abashed Adolphe, in a tremulous voice, "did you but really know how ill I am, how thoroughly indisposed I am for mirth or raillery, you would pity me, and forbear to tantalize me thus."

"Well," remarked his lordship, "this is a mystery which I am perfectly at a loss to comprehend. There is more in it, I am convinced, than you think proper at present to make me acquainted with, and I feel surprised that you should hesitate for a moment to make me your confidant."

"My lord," answered D'Aubigny, "you judge me too hastily and harshly. Have you ever yet had reason to suspect that I had any secrets from you, or that I would do anything that I should be ashamed to acknowledge to you ?"

"True," returned the count ; "hitherto I have not, and I trust that I never shall. But when I see the singular alteration in your behaviour within the last few days, has it not a right to make me doubtful and suspicious ?"

"Suspicious, my lord, of what ?"

"That you have something on your mind which you have not imparted to me. However, as I do not wish to appear to be too pressing, I will say no more upon the subject just now, with the hope that in a few days, at any rate, I shall see you restored to your accustomed spirits."

"Bear with me, my lord, for a short time," said D'Aubigny, "and I trust that my conduct will prove satisfactory to you, and do away with the impression which seems at present to have taken possession of your mind."

"Well, be it as you say," replied the Count de Clairville, "but I must request you to prepare yourself for our journey, and probably the change of scene may have a favourable effect upon your spirits."

"I sincerely hope that it may, my lord," returned Adolphe ; "at any rate, I will exert myself to the utmost to meet your lordship's wishes."

"Well said, Adolphe," observed his lordship ; "I do not yet despair of you ; and if it is indeed love which has had such an effect upon you, I hope, if the object is worthy of you, that you may meet with no obstacle to the consummation of your happiness."

Adolphe attempted to thank him, but his feelings were too powerfully agitated to suffer him to speak, and the Count de Clairville, having cordially shaken hands with him, took his leave, much to his relief.

For a few minutes after he was gone, D'Aubigny paced the apartment backwards and forwards in a state of the greatest agitation, and was unable to collect his thoughts or to compose his feelings in the slightest degree.

"How torturing it is," he said at length, "to be thus compelled to act with such duplicity, and that towards one who has ever been my best friend, and acted towards me with the most unexampled kindness. And what will be his feelings of astonishment, regret, and disgust, should he ever discover the manner in which I have deceived him ; and that I feel convinced he must ultimately do. I shudder even to think of it. But can he have any suspicion of the unfortunate passion which I entertain for Melina ? His observations, so pointed, would almost induce me to think that he did ; and yet if it were so, would he not at once challenge me with it, instead of taunting me in the idle and frivolous manner he has done ?—He would ; and, therefore, I must banish all such ideas from my mind. But how it tortures me to think that I must thus continue to act the hypocrite, if I would save myself from his reproaches. More than all do I dread this journey, for how can I possibly comport myself in the presence of Melina ? The glance of her eye, the sound of her voice, will overwhelm me, and at once, I fear, reveal the sentiments which now hold their empire in my breast. And then, how can I witness unmoved the fond endearments she will be sure to bestow upon Flerio ? What bitter anguish, nay, feelings of jealousy, will it impart to my soul ! And mingled with that feeling must be one of regret and self-reproach, for having dared to encourage a passion for one who has so long been affianced to him, and who loves him with all the sincerity and ardour that woman's heart can ever experience.—Oh, whichever way I turn my eyes, I see no means of escaping from the fatal dilemma in which I am placed. But have I become a child again," he continued, after a minute or two's reflection, " that I should thus abandon myself to despair?—Let me take the advice of my kind friend, Signor Montaldi ; exert all my natural energies, and arouse myself from this state of apathy and weakness. I will not give way to the torturing feelings that have so long oppressed me, and borne down my spirit. I will be firm, and I may yet be able to triumph over everything, and the Count de Clairville may never be put to the anguish of knowing the thoughts that have so long occupied my breast."

As these ideas arose to his imagination, he did become somewhat more composed, and in that state he continued for some time ; but at length his former painful feelings resumed their sway in his breast, and he became, if possible, more wretched and miserable than he had been before.

" It is to no purpose," he said ; " all my exertions are useless ; nothing whatever can banish the image of the beauteous Melina from my mind, or stifle this fatal, this guilty and hopeless passion in my breast. The more I endeavour to do so, the more powerful becomes the impression which she has made upon me ; and should I remain near her, Heaven only knows into what guilt and danger the impetuosity of my passion may lead me. I am, indeed, a wretched and unfortunate being, and it seems to me as if my doom were sealed, and that nothing whatever can rescue me from it. Had I never encountered the Signora Melina I might now have been as happy as I formerly was, and have held up my head without a blush ; but now I feel as if I had already committed some heinous crime, and am ashamed and afraid almost to meet the gaze of my fellow-men. What a life of misery, and constant fear, and suspense is this to lead, and I know not which way to alter it—how to escape from it. Would to Heaven that I could banish these racking thoughts from my mind, then I might be as happy and contented as I formerly was."

He clasped his forehead as he thus spoke, and throwing himself in a chair, became completely lost in the bitter and overwhelming anguish of his own feelings.

CHAPTER LX.

THE DEPARTURE FROM THE RETREAT OF MASSARONI.—THE JOURNEY.—THE ARRIVAL AT THE OLD CHATEAU, AND WHAT OCCURRED THERE.

AT length the day arrived for the departure from the cavernous retreat of the brigand chief ; and the whole of the persons so deeply connected with this history, and who had at present sought refuge there, had assembled in the principal cavern, having resolved to pass a pleasant day together previous to the parting in the evening, as had been agreed upon. All the preparations had been completed, and Massaroni had secured horses and a couple of vehicles, which were to be in waiting near the cavern as soon as darkness had descended upon the earth.

Adolphe D'Aubigny had been compelled to join the party, and the reader may very well imagine the state of his mind on doing so, and it cost him the greater pain as he was compelled to exert all his energies to stifle his emotions, and to conceal his real thoughts from the observation of the persons present. It was the first time that he had been in the company of Melina for several days, and the agitation he experienced on that occasion was of an almost insupportable character. He scarcely dared to raise his eyes towards her, lest her glance should meet his, and she should be able to penetrate the fatal secret of his heart, and thus betray him ; but when he did so, he could not help thinking that she looked, if possible, far more lovely than ever, and he could not help feeling his admiration for her every moment increase. When she spoke, the music of her voice thrilled to his very soul, and every observation that fell from her lips, charmed and captivated, while at the same time it bewildered his senses. But when he noticed the fond looks which she bestowed upon De Clairville, and listened to the words of affection that she ever and anon addressed to him, they went like so many daggers to his heart, and he could scarcely help betraying the powerful excitement under which he was labouring, and heartily wished that he might be allowed to retire from their presence, and indulge, in secret and unseen, in the anguish of his own thoughts. He entered as little as he could into the conversation that passed, and when he did, his observations were as brief as possible, and it was with considerable embarrassment, for he well knew that the Count de Clairville's eyes were fixed upon him, and that he was narrowly watching his conduct on that occasion, in order that he might be able to penetrate the secrets of his thoughts, and probably to ascertain the cause of the melancholy under which he had been labouring for so many days.

Our heroine was in excellent spirits, as was also her lover, and they entered freely into the conversation that prevailed, and expressed the most sanguine hopes and anticipations as to the future, in which the Count de Clairville took good care to encourage them, and pointed out to them in the most glowing colours that his imagination could depicture the prospects that were before them.

"Once settled at the chateau," he said, "I will lose no time in communicating with the Prince Bianchi and in pleading the cause of the Signora Melina and my nephew; and something seems to assure me that my success will be equal to my wishes, or else his highness must be one of the most obstinate and unreasonable of men in existence ; that's all I have to say."

"Well, my lord," returned Massaroni, "I suppose I need not assure you that I heartily hope you may not be disappointed ; though I confess that I have many doubts upon the subject. We have all of us experienced enough of the prince's character to know the strength of his obduracy ; and the manner in which all his plans have been hitherto defeated will but add to his feelings of indignation and revenge."

"Alas!" sighed Melina, "what Massaroni has just now stated is too true, as I have too painfully experienced. I am fearful that no arguments that it is possible for any person to make use of, can ever persuade him to give his consent to the marriage of myself and Florio."

"But you love each other, do you not?" demanded the count, impatiently. Our heroine blushed and hung down her head, and Florio could not help smiling at the honest abruptness of his uncle's manner.

"Silence gives consent," said his lordship, "so I may conclude that you are both now agreed upon that point, if even I had entertained any doubts before, which I certainly did not. You are worthy of each other ; that is also pretty well known to every one ; so the whole of it is, if the Prince Bianchi remains obstinate, and refuses to make two worthy beings happy when it is in his power, I don't see why I should follow his example. So the whole of it is, if he will not grant his sanction, as I said before, seeing that we have the whole of the power in our own hands, we must marry you without it, and then, perhaps, we may win his approbation afterwards. By the saints! there are more ways than one of overcoming a difficulty."

"Wisely spoken, my lord," remarked the brigand chief, "and I perfectly agree with everything you have said."

"And what says the fair Signora Melina?" interrogated the count.

"Why, my lord," answered our heroine "it would be a much greater satisfaction to my mind, if a reconciliation could be effected with my uncle, and his consent could be obtained ; but——"

"But," added his lordship, with a smile, "if it cannot, you are willing to agree to that which I propose, are you not?"

Melina returned no answer, and again hid her face, which was crimsoned with blushes

"Ah !" said the count, "I see how it is, your thoughts are in perfect unison with what I propose, and a very wise decision too. Florio, you are a happy and a fortunate fellow, and so there ends that important business."

While this brief but interesting conversation was passing, the feelings of Adolphe D'Aubigny may easily be conceived. How he envied Florio the happiness that was in store for him, and what a painful contrast did it present to his own fate! And then when he noticed the soft smiles of ardent affection that were exchanged between the lovers, his anguish of mind increased, and he would have given the world had he been permitted to retire. Signor Montaldi had taken good care to seat himself next to him, and he took the opportunity when the attention of the company was diverted from them, to whisper a few words of consolation and advice in his ear, which, however, passed unheeded by D'Aubigny, so deeply were his thoughts occupied another way.

"I sincerely regret the departure of the Signora Melina from this place," observed Zitella, "for in her society have I felt more gratification and happiness than I have before experienced for many years. But I trust that it will not be long ere we shall meet again, and that under more favourable circumstances than we have hitherto seen each other."

"Oh, there is no doubt you will, signora," answered the Count de Clairville ; "and I trust, too, that the time is not far distant when you will be completely restored to that happiness which you so well deserve to experience, and that the misguided Prince Bianchi will be ready to make you all the atonement in his power for the injuries he has done you."

"God grant that he may," ejaculated our heroine, "and that your daughter may also be recognised by him, and no more be subjected to those heavy trials which it has been her hard lot to experience."

"Many thanks, signora, for your kind wishes," said Mira, "for I know full well that they spring from your heart. Could the Count Alberti be brought to a sense of repentance. I could most freely forgive him for all the wrongs that I have suffered from him."

"And Heaven knows how gladly could I pardon the Prince Bianchi," remarked Zitella ; "notwithstanding the severe cruelties he has inflicted upon me. But then, I would willingly bury the past in oblivion, and never once reproach him for his conduct towards me."

"Nobly and generously spoken, Signora Zitella!" said the count; "and I have no doubt that all your wishes will in time be gratified; and when all the differences that at present exist are removed, justice will be rendered to every one, and that you will be restored to tranquillity and your proper position in society, if not to happiness."

"Real happiness I can never more hope to enjoy," said Zitella; "but still, if all is ultimately arranged in the manner which we anticipate, I shall be content. Oh, what will be the feelings of the Prince Bianchi when we meet again?"

"And when he discovers that her whom he has hitherto known as the foundling Olympia, and the victim of the villain, Count Alberti, is his own daughter," suggested Massaroni. "Surely that ought to bring him to shame and remorse, if anything can; and he must then be thankful that he was saved the crime of sacrificing his fair and innocent niece to the base betrayer of his daughter. It shall be my task to bring about that consummation, if it be possible."

"Well said, Massaroni," remarked the Count de Clairville; "the determination that you have just expressed does credit to your head and heart, and I do not wonder at the interest you take in the fate of the Signora Zitella and her daughter, similar as their history is to that of your unfortunate mother. I also hope that you may discover your parent, and that you may be restored to that position in society, which you are so well calculated to adorn."

"No," answered the brigand; "I again assure you that I have not the least wish to quit the course of life I am at present leading, if even I had the opportunity of so doing; but I do sincerely hope that I may discover the base and guilty destroyer of my mother, if he be still living, that I may wreak my vengeance on his head."

Melina shuddered as Massaroni gave utterance to these words, and exchanged a significant glance with Florio, who well understood her meaning.

"But, Massaroni," said Florio "surely if you were to discover the author of your being, and he was sincerely penitent, you would forgive him? You could never commit any act of violence upon your own father?"

"My father!" repeated our hero; "I tell you again that I could never recognise him in that character; my poor mother's wrongs would be uppermost in my thoughts, and nothing whatever could unnerve my hand for vengeance on the head of him who was her destroyer. It will be well for him if fate never suffers me

to encounter him, for that moment would be his last."

"Oh fatal resolve," said Melina, shuddering; "Massaroni, you will think better of this; you can never, I am certain, so fearfully commit yourself."

"Had you experienced what I have, signora," returned Massaroni, "you would not marvel at my feelings."

"But," observed Florio, "suppose that your father should prove, as you believe him to have been, rich and noble, that he was truly penitent, and was willing to snatch you from your present perilous situation, would you not——"

"No," hastily interrupted the brigand, "I would scorn his wealth; I should hate and despise myself could I accept of any favours from him. Vengeance, deep and deadly vengeance, would occupy my thoughts, and every other feeling would fade before the power of its influence."

"Hold, Massaroni!" interrupted the Count de Clairville; "it shocks my ears to hear you thus express yourself. Vengeance is for Heaven, not for man. But you will think better of this, should it be the will of Providence that you should ever discover your misguided parent."

"No, my lord," answered Massaroni, "you deceive yourself if you entertain any such ideas; my mind is fixed. But let us drop this subject, which only serves to excite my feelings, and cannot be of any interest to those who are present, who have other business of more importance to them to think of. I hope you are satisfied with the arrangements I have made for your journey?"

"Perfectly so," replied his lordship, "and I feel obliged to you for the trouble you have taken."

"Oh, as for the trouble," said our hero, "it is not worth mentioning. As soon as it is dark we can take our departure from hence in safety, and without any fear of exciting any curiosity or suspicion."

"Very true," said the count; "but I have not much fear of receiving any violence on the road."

"I do not know that," said Massaroni; "however, you will have nothing to fear, as myself and some of the most trusty of my band will accompany you to some distance from this place, and until you have got beyond the most dangerous part of the country."

"Enough," said his lordship; "then all so far is arranged, and we have nothing now to think of but the future. You may depend upon my keeping my word with you, Massaroni, and communicating with you at the earliest opportunity, to make you acquainted with all that may happen."

"I thank you, my lord," said the brigand

chief, "and you will always find me most ready and willing to serve you."

"I do not doubt it," answered his lordship, "and I hope the time is not far distant when the whole of our wishes will be gratified, and the anticipations which we now entertain will be realised."

"I need not tell you, I suppose, my lord," said our hero, "that in the whole of those wishes I most heartily concur; and I do not entertain any apprehensions that they will be disappointed. No time must be lost in communicating with the Prince Bianchi; and, perhaps, when you have considered the best way of doing that, you will let me know, and receive my advice upon the subject?"

"I will do so, Massaroni," replied the count; "for I place the greatest confidence in your advice upon this important subject. And now, my fair Melina, do you feel yourself fully prepared for the journey?"

"Oh, yes, my lord," answered our heroine; "I am fully prepared for everything, and anticipate the most favourable results."

"I am afraid you will find the old chateau but a gloomy place," said the count, "but I dare say your lover and my young friend D'Aubigny here, will be able by their society to render it agreeable to you. What say you, Adolphe? I should think the society of so amiable and agreeable a young lady as the Signora Melina will have the effect of dissipating some of that ennui which has so long troubled you."

The count could not possibly have put a more embarrassing question to Adolphe, who scarcely knew how to reply without betraying his real feelings. At length he conquered his emotion as well as he could, and in a faltering voice, and without daring to raise his eyes to our heroine, he said—

"I trust that I shall be fortunate enough, my lord, to be able to make my society as agreeable to the fair signora Melina, as I am sure hers will be to me."

"Well said," remarked his lordship; 'oh, I have hope of you yet, Adolphe, in spite of all the horrors in which you have lately indulged."

D'Aubigny turned away his head to hide his confusion, and he was glad when the subject of the conversation was changed, though he felt not a little surprised that he had been enabled to conduct himself with so much composure.

"I deeply regret," remarked Massaroni, after a pause, "that I am so soon to be deprived of the pleasure of Signora Melina's company; but I trust that she will, at least, sometimes condescend to think of me with respect when absent."

"Oh, yes, Signor Massaroni," replied our heroine, fervently; "I must, indeed, be most ungrateful could I ever forget one from whom I have ever experienced so much kindness,

and to whom I am under such a weight of obligation. Should it ever be in my power, you may depend upon my anxiety to return it."

"I require no return but your esteem, fair signora, and to know that I possess that is enough," said the brigand. "May all your wishes be speedily gratified, and may you be placed in that position of happiness and prosperity which you so well deserve to enjoy! That is the sincere hope of Allesandro Massaroni, and I have not the least doubt but that it will be realised."

Melina again returned her thanks; and after some further conversation, as the evening was advancing, and the hour of departure approached, it was agreed that they should separate for a short time, in order that the travellers might make their final preparations for the journey. This was a great relief to D'Aubigny, who wanted a short time to be alone, in order that he might collect himself; and hastening to his own apartment, he threw himself in a chair, and gave himself up to the most busy reflections. He pondered over every word that our heroine had uttered, and recalled to his memory every expression of her eyes; and as he did so, so far from his emotion abating, it increased. He thought that he had never seen her look half so beautiful and so fascinating as she did on that occasion; and he dreaded the time to arrive when he should be in her company again, lest he should commit himself, and the real state of his feeling should be revealed to the Count de Clairville and his nephew.

"What a torturing situation is this to be placed in," he ejaculated; "and how difficult, nay, impossible a task do I find it to conquer the emotions which fill my bosom and distract my brain. Oh, Florio, fortunate man! how much are you to be envied, possessed as you are of the love of one of the fairest and most innocent of human beings. And yet, is he not worthy of her? Has he not proved the sincerity of his attachment, his fond devotion to her, amidst all the severe trials to which he has been subjected? He has; and it is only a fitting reward for his fidelity that he should possess her hand. Even if her hand was not engaged, what pretensions have I to her love? None! Is it not the greatest presumption in me to entertain such a thought? It is, and I deserve to be punished in the way that I am for giving way to a passion which is not only hopeless, but guilty to encourage. The longer I reflect upon my weakness, the greater does my culpability appear to be, and the more does my shame increase. But away with these sinful thoughts, which tempt me on to destruction. Let me be firm, and I may yet triumph over my unfortunate passion, and again be able to show my face without a blush. Am I not a man?—and shall I not boldly, resolutely exert the energies which nature has given me, rather than thus give way to feelings which can never be gratified, and can only bring me to inevitable destruction? I will persevere, and, I trust, with the aid of Providence that I shall yet be able to succeed, and that I may still be enabled to look back upon the past with composure."

As these reflections arose to his mind, young D'Aubigny became much more firm and tranquil than he had been for some time before, and he set about preparing himself for the journey he was so shortly to commence in the com

THE JOURNEY FROM THE RETREAT OF THE BRIGAND CHIEF.

pany of the fair being who had excited such unfortunate feelings in his breast.

By the time the hour had arrived for them o depart from the cavernous retreat of the rigand chief, he had so far succeeded in his fforts to regain tranquillity and resolution, that he evinced not the least symptoms of excitement; and he was preparing to rejoin his friends, when Signor Montaldi entered the apartment, and advancing towards him, and gazing eagerly in his countenance, was agreeably surprised at the favourable change which so short a time had wrought in its expression and his general appearance.

"Well, my young friend," he said, "how do you feel now? You conducted yourself much better in the presence of Melina than I had expected; and I am highly gratified to perceive from your appearance that your feelings are far less excited than they so lately were."

"True, Montaldi," replied Adolphe, "I do, indeed, feel more firm and tranquil than I lately did, and for which favourable change I am bound to acknowledge myself indebted to you for the excellent advice you have given me, and the sympathy and interest you have expressed in my fate. I trust that I shall be able to keep in the same state of mind, and finally to conquer the fatal and hopeless passion which I had suffered to gain possession of my breast."

"How gratifying it is to my feelings, Signor D'Aubigny, to hear you say so," remarked the old man. "I sincerely hope that your praise worthy efforts will be crowned with success, and that you may be restored to the same state of happiness and content which you formerly enjoyed."

"I most cordially thank you, my venerable and excellent friend, for your kind wishes," said Adolphe; "and, though we are now about to separate, I hope the time will not be long distant when we shall meet again, and under far more propitious circumstances than we do at present. I consider myself greatly indebted to you for the trouble you have taken with me; and believe me, wherever I am, or whatever the length of time that may elapse, I must ever entertain a lively and grateful sense of the many obligations I am under to you."

"I know it, signor," said Montaldi, warmly pressing his hand, "and I require no further acknowledgments for the little service it has been in my power to render you. I am only too happy to think that my efforts have been so far crowned with success. When you are away from here, may I hope that you will communicate with me as often as circumstances will permit? for I need not, I think, assure you how anxious I shall be to hear how you are getting on."

"I will not neglect to do so, you may believe me," answered D'Aubigny, "and I hope the intelligence I may have to communicate to you may be all that you could wish."

"I trust that it may," returned Montaldi, "and that you may continue in the same state of mind that you are at present. It requires but a firm resolution, and all is accomplished."

"And that resolution I hope that Providence will enable me to acquire," said Adolphe "Heaven knows how anxious I am to be able to view the beauteous Signora Melina only

with that respect, esteem, and admiration which are due to her great merits."

"Well spoken, D'Aubigny," remarked Signor Montaldi; "and I am satisfied that you will not fail. You must now, I think, perceive the folly, the rashness, and even ingratitude with which you would have acted had you deserted your excellent friend and benefactor, the Count de Clairville, and left him in a state of painful suspense and doubt as to what had become of you."

"I do indeed," answered D'Aubigny; "but I scarcely knew what I said in the agony of my despair. But, at least, I trust that I may confide in you, Signor Montaldi, and that, let whatever may transpire, you will never reveal what has passed between us?"

"Indeed, my young friend," replied his aged companion, "you may depend upon me; why should you entertain a doubt, after all the pains I have taken to compose your feelings, and to conquer the unhappy passion which you had suffered to gain such powerful ascendancy over you? Montaldi is no hypocrite, and he never yet professed anything which he was not fully prepared to perform."

"Pardon me, signor," said Adolphe, "if my observations should have sounded harsh and ungenerous. I will, I do place every confidence in you; and it shall be my future study to endeavour to prove to you that I am not altogether unworthy of the deep interest you have taken in my welfare."

"Enough," observed the old man; "I am satisfied; and should you be able to regain your wonted peace and serenity of mind, I shall be fully repaid for any trouble I may have been put to in this delicate and important business. But all is now ready for your departure, and your friends await you in the principal cavern. Here, then, while we are alone, we will take our leave of each other; and it is my fervent hope that before many weeks have elapsed all these important affairs which have so long agitated us will be brought to a favourable crisis, and that we may meet again."

"God grant that your wishes may be gratified, Signor Montaldi," said D'Aubigny, fervently; "for the happiness of the amiable Signora Melina is as dear to me as my own existence. Farewell, my kind and venerable friend; and rest assured that, wherever I may be, I shall never cease to remember you with those feelings of gratitude and respect which the many obligations I am under to you entitle you to."

"Adieu, signor," responded Montaldi, "and believe me that no one will ever continue to hold a warmer place in my esteem than yourself. God keep you in the same state of mind that you are at present, is what I fervently wish, and then I do not fear but that all will be well."

D'Aubigny pressed his hand with the most sincere respect to his lips, and then kneeling down, the old man invoked a blessing upon his head. He then arose, and taking his arm, they hastened towards the principal cavern, where they found Melina, her lover, the Count de Clairville, and the brigand chief, all ready equipped for the journey, and only awaiting his arrival to take their departure. Melina was engaged with Florio in deep conversation in another part of the cavern, so that D'Aubigny did not behold her face, and he scarcely ventured to direct his eyes towards her; and the Count de Clairville perceiving him enter, advanced towards him, and, taking his hand, said,—

"Now, Adolphe, the moment for the commencement of our journey has arrived, and it gratifies me much to see you looking so much better and in more cheerful spirits than you were a short time since. Oh, depend upon it, my young friend, that change of scene, and the society of your friends, will speedily banish this ennui from your mind, and that you will become yourself again."

"I trust, my lord," replied Adolphe, "that I shall not disappoint your expectations, and that in future you will have no cause to complain of me."

"Ah," remarked his lordship, with a good-humoured smile, "this love is a most terrible thing, as I know from experience. But, mark me, Adolphe, it is not my intention to let you off so easily as you seem to imagine; and when we are settled, I shall really insist upon your unfolding to me the whole of the secrets of your breast, and your revealing to me the name of the tender inamorato who seems to have made so powerful an impression upon your heart."

"Your lordship will, indeed, be disappointed, if you think to elicit any such secret from me," replied D'Aubigny, himself endeavouring to smile, though he felt much confused by the observations of the count; "you are decidedly wrong in your surmises if you attribute the cause of the melancholy depression of spirits under which I have lately laboured, to love. To that passion I am yet a stranger."

"Ay," said his lordship, "it is the natural modesty of youth which always prompts them to make those denials. However, there will be a more fitting opportunity for us to discuss that subject. Signor Massaroni, is all in readiness for our departure?"

"Yes, my lord," answered the brigand, "all is ready; the vehicles are waiting at the foot of the mountain, and myself and that portion of my band which I have selected for the duty are ready to attend you."

"Enough, then," said his lordship; "as the evening is advancing, it will be better for us not to delay our departure any longer."

We will pass over the scene which took place at the parting between Melina and the Signora Zitella, her daughter, the brigand's wife, and Signor Montaldi. It is enough to say, that it was one of the most affectionate, friendly, and cordial description; and that over, Massaroni led the way to the secret entrance of the cavern, and our heroine, supported by her lover and the Count de Clairville, following, and Floretta and D'Aubigny taking up the rear. They soon emerged from the cavern, and descending the mountain, found the two carriages which Massaroni had mentioned, waiting at the foot, into one of which Melina, Florio, and the faithful Floretta got; and the Count de Clairville, Adolphe D'Aubigny, and our hero, entered the other; and the brigands (who were all disguised) having mounted their horses, at a signal from the chief, the whole cortege rapidly departed, and had soon got some distance from the spot.

Melina and her lover conversed but little during the early part of the journey, though their minds, as may be expected, were busily occupied by the various thoughts that crowded upon them. The night was particularly fine, the moon shone serenely in an almost cloudless sky; and having emerged from the wilder part of the country, the scenery among which they found themselves travelling was of the most picturesque and romantic description; and the blinds of the carriage being up, Melina and her lover found sufficient to amuse and divert their thoughts in the lovely prospect which on every side met their eyes.

"How calm and beautiful is everything around," said Melina, at length; "who can gaze on such a scene as this without feelings of awe and admiration?"

"True, my dearest Melina," replied Florio; "and God grant that, after all the storms which it has been our lot to encounter, we may experience such a calm as this. Our troubles, I trust, are now at an end, and that ere long all our fondest hopes will be realised, and that our happiness will be complete."

"I need not tell you," returned our heroine, "how heartily and sincerely I respond to that wish; but still I cannot help entertaining some apprehensions that our happiness will not so soon be completed as we now anticipate."

"Oh banish such gloomy thoughts from your mind, my love," said Florio; "for what occasion is there for your fears? Our prospects have assumed the brightest aspect, and everything promises a happy future. The Count de Clairville will lose no time in communicating with the Prince Bianchi, and I entertain the most sanguine hopes that he will have little or no difficulty in bringing about a reconciliation with him."

"Alas!" observed our heroine, "when I take into consideration all the obstinate and vindictive traits in my uncle's character, I fear not."

"Nonsense, Melina," returned her lover; "the prince must be little better than a madman any longer to hold out when he finds that all his plans are defeated, and that there is not the least chance of his ever again getting you in his power. He will only be too happy to discover you, and to find that you are willing to bestow upon him the same affection that you have hitherto done, and to bury the past in oblivion."

"Pardon me," remarked Floretta; "but I cannot help saying that that is decidedly my opinion. And I'm sure he ought to consider himself a most fortunate man to find that he can effect a reconciliation so easily."

"Oh, how gladly, how willingly I can forgive him all that has taken place," ejaculated Melina; "and never would I upon any occasion remind him of the past. But still I fear that his pride will not suffer him to yield, and that he will never give his consent to our union."

"And what could his obstinacy avail him?" demanded Florio; "he no longer possesses any authority over you, you are out of his jurisdiction, and how could he prevent our marriage from taking place, if even he were to refuse his consent?"

"True," replied our heroine; "but still it would be more consonant with my feelings, if his sanction could be obtained, and then, at any rate, I should have nothing to reproach myself with afterwards."

"And what would you have to reproach yourself with, Melina," demanded her lover, "if even you should be compelled to act without his permission? Have we not proved by time, and the bitter experience of so many trials, that we are worthy of each other, and that Heaven, at least, sanctions our union? What, then, have we to fear? Come, come, my dear girl, banish such gloomy thoughts from your mind, and look forward with hope for the best. My word for it, that the result of the mission which the count, my uncle, will undertake, will be all that our fondest wishes could anticipate."

"God grant that it may," ejaculated Melina, earnestly. "But the Count Alberti?"

"Oh, we have nothing to fear from him," answered Florio. "He is completely powerless, and he may think himself fortunate if he be not brought to a severe account for the crimes he has committed."

"No," said Melina, "I would not visit even him with a feeling of revenge. All that I wish is, that he may be brought to a full sense of compunction for the numerous offences of which he has been guilty, and that the will

at last be anxious to render to the unfortunate Mira and her hapless child that justice and atonement which is so undeniably their due."

"And that he will be compelled to do," returned Florio, "or he will be held up to the world in his true character—that of a villain of the blackest dye."

"I am afraid," remarked Melina, "that he has become so inured to crime, that he is perfectly indifferent as to what the world thinks of him. But what must be the feelings of my uncle when he discovers that Mira is his own daughter, and that he would have sacrificed me to her destroyer?"

"Ay, Melina," answered her lover, "it is that circumstance which, I am convinced, will bring the Prince Bianchi more to remorse than anything else, and that he will demand of the Count Alberti that he shall render justice to his innocent and unfortunate victim."

"Alas!" sighed Melina, "so many discoveries of so astounding a description will completely overwhelm my unfortunate but misguided uncle, and I fear that his reason can never withstand the shock. And then, if the brigand chief, Massaroni, should also prove to be his son—"

"And of that, my dear Melina," returned her lover, "after what I have read, and bearing in mind the circumstances of Massaroni's history, as gathered from his own lips, I cannot entertain the least doubt."

"But should Massaroni become acquainted with the extraordinary and important fact, has he not sworn to have a terrible revenge? And with such power as he possess, what can prevent him from carrying his fearful threats into execution? My God! should my uncle, indeed, perish by his hands!"

"Nay, Melina, again I tell you that you must not give way to such terrible apprehensions," said Florio; "should the brigand chief make the discovery, and the Prince Bianchi prove to be truly penitent, Massaroni will abandon his fearful and unnatural designs, and all may terminate as happily as we could wish it."

"Heaven send that it may," said our heroine. "But is it your intention to communicate the contents of the manuscript to Massaroni?"

"At present it would be imprudent to do so," answered Florio; "it will be better to wait till our own important business is settled, and to watch the opportunity when Massaroni shall be in a perfectly calm state of mind, and more prepared to receive the remarkable disclosure with composure."

"Unfortunate, much injured man," ejaculated Melina; "how greatly is he to be pitied."

"He is, indeed," coincided Florio, "and I sincerely hope that the time may come when he will be placed in for different circumstances to what he is at present; for it is a pity that a man so highly gifted by nature, so accomplished, and possessed of so many excellent and noble qualities, should be lost to society."

"It is, indeed," said our heroine; "to him we are all much indebted, and I sincerely hope that before long, full and ample justice will be rendered him."

"True," coincided Melina; "and yet when I come to weigh all the circumstances in my mind as connected with the brigand chief and the Prince Bianchi, I cannot still help entertaining some misgivings of a fatal result should they happen to discover that they are, indeed, so closely related as we believe them to be. After the horrible threats that Massaroni has so frequently uttered against his misguided father, should fate ever reveal the fact to him, and so implacable as that feeling of revenge appears to be within him, I am compelled, notwithstanding all my efforts to the contrary, to apprehend the worst."

"Nay, my dear Melina," replied Florio, "it is useless for you to disturb your mind with these painful thoughts. I trust that Massaroni will think better of this, and that should circumstances happen to turn out as we anticipate they will, all may terminate as happily as we could wish them to do. But enough on that subject; we have now much that is bright and cheerful to look forward to. Ere long I have no doubt that all the troubles, the cares, and anxieties, the severe trials and disappointments it has been our lot to experience, will be at an end, and that all the hopes we have so fondly encouraged will be realised."

"Heaven grant that they may," ejaculated our heroine, fervently and her eyes beaming with the most ardent and undisguised affection upon her lover. He pressed her fair hand vehemently to his lips, his looks sufficiently expressing the feelings which throbbed at his heart, and they then relapsed into silence for some time, and their minds were sufficiently occupied and amused by the varied and romantic scenery amongst which they were travelling.

In the meantime the travellers in the other vehicle had been deeply engaged in conversation of the most interesting description, which served to while away the tediousness of the journey, and D'Aubigny joined in it with much more freedom and cheerfulness than might have been anticipated, though his mind, at the same time, was ill at rest, and he looked forward to the future with fear and anxiety.

Suddenly, after they had been journeying for about a couple of hours, they entered a much more gloomy part of the country, and Rubaldo having rode up to the window of the carriage in which the brigand and his companions were seated, said—

"Some danger threatens us, Massaroni; I perceive a considerable number of men advancing this way, and it is my opinion they contemplate no good."

"Well," replied Massaroni, coolly; "we are fully prepared to meet them; no doubt they are some of the band of Gaspard Guiacolo, who infest this part of the country; but if they venture to make an attack on us, we will give them such a reception as they little anticipate. Be not alarmed, my lord, for there is not the least doubt that we shall soon be enabled to put the fellows to the rout."

"Oh," replied the count, "you may believe me that I entertain no fear; but the Signora Melina,' she will be much terrified, it is only reasonable to suppose. What course do you propose to adopt?"

"Why, to meet them boldly, man to man," answered our hero; "and there is not much reason to fear on whose side the triumph will be. Let two or three of our men guard the carriage in which the Signora Melina is, and the rest conceal themselves in the best manner they can, until these fellows arrive upon the spot, then suddenly rushing out, taking them by surprise and attacking them with courage and determination, they will soon be glad enough to take to flight, I'll warrant. Do you hear me, Rubaldo?"

"Ay, captain," answered the latter; and he immediately quitted the carriage to put the orders he had received into execution, and Massaroni, the Count, and D'Aubigny put themselves in readiness for any desperate emergency that might arise.

Alarmed by the brigand riding up to the carriage, Melina started from her seat, and hastily inquired what was the matter; and on being informed, the terror of her and Floretta may easily be conceived; but Florio exerted himself to compose them, reminding them that they were under the protection of Massaroni, and also that he, himself, was fully prepared to defend them to the last, and he succeeded much better than, under all the circumstances, could have been expected. He put his head from out the carriage window, and then perceived a number of men only a short distance off, who had evidently observed the vehicles and were making towards them; and he had scarcely had time to make this observation, when the vehicle in which himself and Melina were seated was summoned, and one of the ruffians riding up to the window thrust in his head, and in a coarse and determined voice demanded their money or their lives; the next instant he was stretched bleeding on the earth by a well directed shot from the pistol of Florio, and the brigands immediately rushing from their place of concealment, headed by Massaroni, Rubaldo, the Count de Clairville, and Adolphe D'Aubigny, the combat commenced with great fury, both parties fighting with desperate determination, while the scene that prevailed was of that fearful description, and the shouts of the combatants were so appaling that Melina fainted, overcome by her terrors, and was supported in the arms of her lover.

The combat, however, was not of long duration, for although the assailants greatly outnumbered Massaroni and his companions, the latter fought with such determined bravery that there was no resisting them, and at length, several of the ruffians having fallen, the rest took to flight in all directions, and in the greatest confusion, and left them completely masters of the field. Florio, the Count and Massasoni now congratulated themselves on the termination of this adventure, and returning to their vehicle, they resumed their journey. By the exertions of Florio and Floretta our heroine was soon restored to consciousness, and on being informed of what had taken place, she speedily regained her composure, although she had suffered considerably from fright. They proceeded on their way for about another hour, when they came in sight of an inn at a short distance off.

"It is now too late, I should imagine," said Massaroni, "for you to think of proceeding any farther on your journey to night, and I would therefore, advise you to put up at this inn, where you may receive every accommodation, I know. In the morning I would have you resume your journey at an early hour, before there are many persons about, whose curiosity might be excited."

"And you, and your companions?" asked his lordship.

"Why," replied the brigand, "it would not, of course, be prudent for us to accompany you to the inn, and as I have seen you safe through the most dangerous part of the country, it is my intention to separate from you here, with the hope that we snall shortly meet again, and under far more favourable circumstances than we have known each other at present."

The count returned his thanks for the many marks of friendship he had received from Massaroni, and the latter having alighted from the carriage, took a respectful leave of them all, and immediately took his departure, followed by his band, and the travellers proceeded towards the inn, at which they shortly afterwards arrived, and found, as the brigand chief had informed them, everything for their accommodation.

Having partaken of some refreshment, and after a short time passed in conversation, they separated for the night, and retired to their chambers with a determination to resume their journey as soon as it was daylight in the morning.

We should become tedious were we to enter into a minute detail of their journey; it may be sufficient to state that nothing particular occurred to them, and at the end of the fifth day from the time they had left the retreat of Massaroni they found themselves not far from the place of their destination; and the anxiety, impatience, and curiosity of Melina and her lover every moment increased.

As the Count de Clairville drew near to that place from which he had been absent for so many years, and with which were associated so many painful events of his life, the melancholy feelings which beset his mind may readily be imagined, and he relapsed into silence, indulging in his own thoughts, which no one offered to interrupt, well imagining as they did, the nature of his meditations. All the fearful events which he detailed in his dismal, but interesting narrative, recurred to his memory in the most vivid colours, and it seemes to his disturbed imagination as if they had occurred but yesterday. But under what different circumstances was he now returning to his maternal dwelling to those under which he had left it! He could scarcely believe in the reality of all that had taken place, and, in fact, it appeared more like a dream than anything else. How deeply he lamented the fate which had befallen his unfortunate brother, and the beauteous Emilia, and at the same time how bitterly did he reproach himself with being the cause of it. But, still, he was most grateful to the Supreme for having enabled him to discover their son, and thus giving him the opportunity he had so long prayed for, namely, that of making all the atonement in his power for his past errors.

In a very short time the travellers arrived in sight of the old chateau, and a gloomy, ancient-looking building it was, as the count had described it to be, and one that was not at all calculated to inspire any pleasurable feelings in the breasts of those who beheld it. No sooner did his lordship gaze once more upon its ivy-covered walls than the deep emotion he experienced was perfectly visible in his countenance, and the most painful sighs escaped his bosom.

Every preparation had been made for their arrival, the Count de Clairville, as we have before stated, having despatched a messenger to the chateau for that purpose; and as the vehicles drove into the court-yard of the building, there were several domestics waiting to receive them; but the Count de Clairville could only find composure enough to make a slight acknowledgment of their presence, and having seen his companions to the principal dining-room, where the cloth was already laid for the repast, he retired to another apartment, where he could indulge his feelings without interruption, giving free vent to the various and agonising thoughts that crowded upon his brain. He was not absent long, and when he rejoined his young friends they were pleased to observe that, from the expression of his countenance, he had completely regained his composure. He entered freely into the conversation that ensued, and the meal being over, he undertook to conduct them over the different apartments of the building, which was of considerable extent, and had evidently existed for many ages. It was a trying scene to the count, and as they entered the different rooms in which the most important and melancholy events connected with his history had taken place, he was unable to control the expression of the deep emotion that laboured at his breast, and in which feelings every one so sincerely sympathised with him, and none more so than the gentle and amiable Signora Melina. There was much in the old chateau, however, to gratify their curiosity, and even the wild and cheerless scenery by which it was surrounded, was not without its interest to them.

The day passed quickly away, and as they were rather fatigued with their journey, they retired early to rest, their minds agitated by a varity of feelings.

Several days passed away, and nothing more particular than that we have already recorded took place. The Count de Clairville had become perfectly composed and tranquil, and our heroine felt herself far more composed, and even cheerful, than she had done for some time before, and was seldom absent from the society of Florio, with whom she rambled over the different apartments of the chateau, and the grounds attached to it, conversing on their future prospects, and picturing to themselves the happiness, which, after the many trials they had had to encounter, were yet in store for them.

But what was the state of D'Aubigny's feelings? In spite of all the praiseworthy efforts he had made to the contrary, and the manner in which he seemed likely to succeed, the fatal passion he had suffered to take possession of his breast for the beauteous Melina still held the most predominant sway over his feelings, and it seemed, in fact, now to be aroused with more irresistible strength in his bosom, and he felt convinced that nothing less than its gratification would satisfy him. And yet how he shuddered and blushed for himself, as these guilty thoughts arose to his imagination, and he saw no means of conquering them or of avoiding the danger be apprehended, except it was by flight. The more he beheld of our heroine, the more powerful and insupportable did his passion become, and he now regretted that he had not, instead of following the advice of old Montaldi, at once have adhered to the resolution he had once formed to abscond from the Count de Clairville, for the present, at any rate, and by absence seek to forget her and to fix his mind upon some other being.

Such were the thoughts that harassed and distressed D'Aubigny for several days after their arrival at the chateau, and he could find but very little consolation or relief. It was impossible for him to find any plausible excuse to escape from the presence and society of Melina, without exciting some feeling of suspicion in the breasts of his friends; and every hour passed in that manner did but serve to increase his anguish and likewise to add to the fatal passion which had so unfortunately been engendered in his bosom. He did, however, avoid her presence, and that of Florio, and the Count de Clairville, as much as possible, and would take the most solitary walks in the extensive gardens belonging to the chateau, where he could indulge his gloomy thoughts alone, and without any fear of being interrupted

It was evening, and Adolphe D'Aubigny was seated in a retired part of the garden indulging in the thoughts we have described, and in vain endeavouring to hit upon some scheme to avoid the danger which he apprehended.

"Alas!" he murmured in his rumination, after a pause; "what will become of me, if I do not succeed in conquering the unfortunate and guilty passion which at present inhabits my breast? Oh, Melina! that nature should have formed you so lovely, so enchanting! Would to Heaven that I could form the resolution to forget you, and to stifle the sentiments with which you have inspired me; but now, I feel convinced that, whatever the consequences may be, the beauteous Melina must ever hold the same place in my heart that she does at present, and——"

He was interrupted by hearing a faint scream, and turning hastily round, what was his surprise and confusion on beholding our heroine standing pale, trembling, and awestruck before him. It was evident to him, though she could not speak a word, that she had heard all he had said; the fearful secret that had so long tortured his mind was divulged, and, filled with shame, remorse, and despair, he covered his face, and with a groan of anguish he rushed wildly from the spot, before Melina could attempt to detain him, if she had even been ever so inclined. She stood, in fact, completely paralysed to the spot, and was so completely astonished and terrified by all that she had seen and overheard, that she could not, without the greatest difficulty, trust the evidence of her senses; and before she had in the slightest degree recovered from her emotion, Florio, who had been surprised at the length of her absence from the chateau, and had started forth in search of her, arrived at the spot. His amazement and alarm at the paleness of her countenance, and her fixed attitude, may be readily imagined, and impatiently he hastened towards her, and enfolding her in his arms, begged her to inform him, without a moment's delay, what had happened to cause her such violent agitation. It was several minutes before the poor girl could find sufficient strength to speak, or to make any reply; but at length, hiding her blushing face on her lover's bosom, and bursting into tears, she sobbed—

"Oh, Florio, why do you ask the torturing question? What answer can I make to your natural interrogatories? Oh, I have heard that which has astonished me, and filled my mind, at the same time, with grief and shame."

"For Heaven's sake what mean you?" said her lover, fixing upon her a look of the most impatient curiosity and credulity.

"D'Aubigny!" gasped forth our heroine.

"Ah! what of him?" interrogated Florio, with increased impatience. "Speak! tell me! for my mind is on the rack."

"Oh, I tremble, I blush to do so," she once more faltered out.

"Nay," he returned, "this does but serve to excite my worst apprehensions. What of D'Aubigny?"

It was not until after Melina had had a most violent struggle with her feelings, that she was enabled to make her lover acquainted with all the painful circumstances, and when she did so, the emotion of Florio may be much better imagined than we could describe it. Adolphe D'Aubigny entertain a guilty passion for his beloved Melina? He could scarcely believe the evidence of his senses, and for a few moments his feelings of surprise, emotion, and indignation were so great, that he could not give utterance to his emotions.

"Good God!" he exclaimed at last, "can this be possible?—D'Aubigny, the young friend of the count, my uncle, who has ever believed him to be the very soul of probity and honour, in love with my Melina? And dare he encourage such guilty hopes, knowing the sentiments that exist between us? But you must have been deceived, my Melina; he could never have——"

"Ah, no!" interrupted our heroine; "it is, alas! too true; it is impossible that I could have been deceived!—Just in the language which I have stated to you did I overhear him express himself; and, probably overwhelmed with shame and confusion when he found that he had betrayed himself, he rushed precipitately from the spot."

"I can still scarcely believe the evidence of my senses," said Florio; "and no wonder at the extreme agitation you evince. But I must see him immediately, and insist upon his giving me an explanation of this most extraordinary and unpardonable conduct."

"Oh, no," said Melina; "had you not better see his lordship upon the subject, and making him acquainted with all the circumstances, seek his advice upon the subject?"

"I will do as you say, my beloved Melina," answered her lover; "and what will be the astonishment and disgust of his lordship when he hears it! Alas! I almost dread to communicate it to him, for will it not revive the most harrowing recollections in his breast, and cause him the most unbounded misery when he recalls to his memory the melancholy circumstances of his own fate, so analogous to it?"

"It is a matter of the deepest regret to me that this has happened," returned Melina; "but still it is absolutely necessary that he should be made acquainted with it, without a moment's delay."

"I will do as you advise, dear Melina," said her lover; "and I only hope that D'Aubigny will be able to explain himself, and to offer some reasonable excuse for his conduct, though I do not see how he is to do so. Compose yourself, my love, for surely this is enough to shock and agitate your feelings."

Melina returned no answer, though the agitation of her feelings may be readily conceived, and suffering her lover to take her arm, they hastened into the chateau. They found the count seated alone, and apparently buried in deep meditation, on entering the apartment where he was; but he quickly arose on their entrance, and greeted them with his usual kindness and affection, but beholding the agitation of their manner, he eagerly inquired what was the matter. It was several minutes before Florio could find strength or confidence to inform him, and the blushing Melina was so much confused, and so violently agitated, that she was compelled to avert her looks from those of his lordship, and to retire to another part of the room in order to conceal her feelings. But when the count did hear the fatal truth, his astonishment and the excitment he evinced may be easily conceived; and striking is forehead, he paced the room for a moment or two in the most disordered manner, and totally unable to give vent to his feelings in words.

"Good God!" he exclaimed at last; "and has it indeed came to this? Adolphe D'Aubigny, he to whom I have behaved with the same kindness and attention as if he had been my own son, thus to disgrace himself, and to bring shame and misery on me? Oh, Melina! what must be the anguish of your soul on discovering this! How great must be your indignation at the presumption of one whom I never could have supposed would have suffered such guilty feelings to have entered his breast! But I must see this rash, this headstrong and presumptuous boy; and——"

"Let me beg of you," interrupted our heroine, "not to be too harsh with him, but to advise with him mildly. He will surely see at once the folly and imprudence of his conduct, and no longer give way to a passion which can only be productive of the worst consequences."

"Signora Melina," returned his lordship, "I fear you are too charitable. Ought not the melancholy example he has had in my sad history have been sufficient to warn him? His strange behaviour of late is now indeed most easily accounted for; but little did I imagine that he would ever suffer such guilty thoughts to enter his mind. But I must see him. Remain here until my return, and I still hope that everything may yet be satisfactorily explained, and that D'Aubigny may be brought to a

THE FLIGHT OF D'AUBIGNY AND HIS VALET FROM THE CHATEAU.

full sense of the imprudence and folly of his conduct."

Neither Florio nor Melina returned any reply, and the Count de Clairville quitted the room, and with an impatient step he hastened to the apartment in which he ex-pected to find D'Aubigny. In a few minutes he returned, much disordered in his manner, and holding a note in his hand.

"What is the matter, my lord?" hastily inquired Florio; "what is it that agitates you so violently? Have you seen Adolphe?"

"Seen him!" repeated the count; "no, he has gone! Deserted me, his benefactor! He has acknowledged all; but his note will explain everything. I saw it lying upon the table in his room. Read—read!"

Florio and Melina did so eagerly. The note was composed of a few brief words, and it will be unnecessary to explain them more fully to the reader than to state, that the unfortunate Adolphe confessed all in the most impressive language; expressed his determination too leave the neighbourhood until such time as he might be able to conquer his unfortunate passion; at the same time he most earnestly and eloquently implored the forgiveness of his lordship, Melina, and Florio, for the error into which he had unhappily fallen; at the same time expressing a hope that he might by absence still be able to conquer his fatal passion, and that at some future period he might again be restored to their friendship, esteem, and confidence.

"Unfortunate D'Aubigny," said Florio, when he had perused aloud this epistle; "I do indeed pity him, for I am convinced, short even as our acquaintance has been, that he is possessed of natural honour, goodness, and integrity of heart. But my dear Melina?"

"Oh, Florio," replied our blushing heroine, "you know full well what the nature of my feelings must be on this painful occasion. But from the bottom of my soul I forgive Signor D'Aubigny, and sincerely hope that in time he may be able to conquer this hopeless passion, and be able to return with confidence to those friends who are all so anxious for his welfare."

"Dear Melina," observed the Count de Clairville, "that sentiment does honour to your head and heart, and must, if possible, entitle you still more to the love and admiration of myself and Florio. Wretched Adolphe! what cruel fate can have created this unfortunate and hopeless passion in your breast? But whither can he have gone? What course does he intend to adopt? May he not, in the frenzy of his despair, be hurried into the perpetration of some fatal act, and thus——"

"Oh, no, my dear lord," interrupted Florio, "I trust that he will be enabled to muster sufficient fortitude and manly determination to resist any such fatal temptation, and that in a few weeks he will return, having succeeded in triumphing over those feelings which he has unhappily suffered to enter his breast. Compose yourself, my dear uncle, and all will yet end well."

"May your anticipations be realised," returned his uncle, "for that is, believe me, my most sincere wish, though this event has rekindled, for the time being, all those melancholy feelings and recollections in my breast

which it has been my most anxious wish to bury in oblivion."

"Banish those dismal thoughts from your mind, my lord, I beg," said Florio, "and let the past be forgotten."

The count sighed deeply, but returned no other answer, and it was some time ere they could recover their composure. They then made a more strict inquiry into the abrupt flight of D'Aubigny, but none of the domestics had seen him leave the chateau, though he was accompanied by his faithful valet; and, therefore, they were at a perfect loss to imagine what direction he had taken, or where to go in search of him.

CHAPTER LXI.

THE PRINCE BIANCHI AND COUNT ALBERTI AGAIN.—THE REMORSE AND DESPAIR OF THE FORMER.—THE DEATH OF FRANSISCO.—THE LETTER OF THE COUNT DE CLAIRVILLE.—THE RESOLUTION OF BIANCHI, AND THE CONSEQUENT RUPTURE BETWEEN HIM AND ALBERTI.

IT is now due time that we should return to the Prince Bianchi and the Count Alberti, who, during the period that the events were taking place recorded in the preceding chapters, were subjected to all the torturing feelings of doubt, suspense, hope, and disappointment. Bianchi was at times the victim of rage, remorse, and bitter self-reproach; he was fully awakened to a sense of the cruelty and injustice with which he had acted towards his fair and innocent niece, yet the manner in which all his plans had been foiled, and his authority set at defiance, mortified his pride, and at times rendered him almost incapable of controlling his guilty passions within the bounds of reason. But both himself and Alberti were driven to despair when they saw the hopelessness of getting Melina in their power, and reflected upon the probability that she had already become the wife of Florio, through the aid and machinations of Allesandro Massaroni, and that thus all their hopes would be annihilated, and their designs rendered abortive.

The Count Alberti, after the rupture of the blood-vessel, remained for several weeks in an almost hopeless condition, when a favourable change took place, and his restoration to almost complete convalescence was most extraordinary and sudden; and he then consulted with the Prince Bianchi upon the best means it would be advisable for them to adopt with the hope of being able to discover the present place of our heroine's retreat, and to get her once more in their power. But, as we have said before, the mind of Bianchi frequently wavered upon that point, and he could not but accuse himself of the greatest injustice towards his niece, who had ever behaved to him with the most exemplary duty and affection. He would have given anything could she but be restored to him, and a reconciliation brought about, though his pride and ambition would never suffer him to give his consent to her union with one whom he imagined to be so humble and ignobly born as Florio Clairville. Conscience, that fearful monitor, frequently upbraided him for the cruelty and injustice he had practised towards the unfortunate Zerlina, Zitella, and the sister of Fransisco, and he was inconstant fear, should it indeed be true that Zitella was living, and under the protection of the brigand chief, she would one day come forward to confront him, and to denounce him to the world in his true colours. In order that he might give uninterrupted indulgence to these thoughts, he frequently absented himself from the society of the Count Alberti; secluded himself in his own chamber, or took long and solitary walks in the neighbourhood of the villa, buried in the most gloomy meditation, and most intense and torturing was the anguish of mind which he endured on those occasions, while, at the same time, he was unable to come to any satisfactory conclusion as to the course it would be better for him to adopt.

The frequent appearance of Fransisco, and the threats he had held out to him, held him in a constant state of alarm and doubt, but at the same time he was fearful of attempting to adopt any proceedings against him, as he knew not to what his secret power extended, and what might be the consequences of his setting him at defiance. He had, however, seen nothing of him for more than a week, and he began to hope that something had either happened to remove him, or that he had abandoned his designs, though there did not seem to be much probability of the latter, when he took into consideration the advantage he had over him, and the means which it afforded him of extorting money from him.

It was in one of those gloomy rambles, a short distance from the villa, that the Prince Bianchi, feeling somewhat fatigued, threw himself on the grass in a retired spot, and gave himself up entirely to those melancholy and painful reflections that almost constantly haunted his mind, and rendered him so truly miserable.

"How can I act?" he said; "how extricate myself from the difficulties and fears by which I am on every side surrounded, and which threaten at last to overwhelm me? Melina torn from me, probably now the wife of the plebeian Clairville—all my proud and ambitious hopes annihilated—what is there left for me but misery, vexation, and disappointment? Zitella living, too, and her child; at least, so I am told, and I have too much reason to fear it is the truth; should they make their appearance and denounce me, I should be exposed to the world as a villain, and not even my position in society would be able to save me from the shame and degradation that would be sure to follow. I know not what course to adopt; how to release my-from the dilemma in which I have placed myself. Oh, I have been most guilty; my conscience tells me that I have been so, and I am only justly punished for the crimes I have committed."

"True," exclaimed a coarse and well-known voice close to his ear; "but your punishment is not yet half complete, unless you agree to the terms which I have now to propose to you."

Bianchi looked hastily up, and the reader may easily imagine his agitation and alarm, when he beheld the villain Fransisco standing before him, and gazing upon him with a mingled expression of triumph and revenge.

"Francisco!" he said, in a tremulous voice, and starting to his feet.

"Ay," replied the ruffian, with an exulting and sardonic grin; "you see I have called once more to pay my respects to you;—no doubt you have been most uneasy at the length of my absence, and was afraid that something had happened to me."

"What want you now?" impatiently demanded Bianchi.

"Oh, something more than I have hitherto had of you," replied Fransisco; "and you must yield to my demands, too, or you can form but little idea of the consequences."

"What mean you, villain?" said the prince, in stern and haughty tones.

"Nay, your highness," returned Franissco, "I would advise you to make use of different and better language when you are addressing yourself to me, for you aught, by this time, to know that I am a man who will not tamely brook an insult, even though it be offered by the proud and mighty Prince Bianchi. Do you forget what I have so frequently told you? Can you deny that I have you completely in my power, and that one word from me would consign you to shame, and misery, and degradation?"

"This insolence is insupportable," ejaculated Bianchi; "Fransisco, I repeat, what is it you now demand, and why do you thus again appear before me?"

"Oh," answered the ruffian, "that question may be answered in a very few words; briefly, then, I am tired of receiving these drivelling sums of money that I have hitherto had from you, and which are so inadequate to my wants.

My ambition soars to something higher, and it must be gratified, too, at all hazards."

"Hold !" cried Bianchi, passionately ; " I will not be intimidated by you ; I have already too tamely submitted to your base and extravagant extortions, but I will do so no longer."

" You had better reflect calmly ere you decide," said Fransisco, coolly ; " you know the power which I possess over you, and that I am not the sort of man to be tampered or trifled with. Yield to the demands that I am about to make, and you may rid yourself of me altogether, and so prevent that mischief which it is otherwise in my power to work you."

"Fransisco, you are a dangerous man," said the prince.

"True," coincided the former, with a malicious grin, " and those act the wisest who do not attempt to offend me. But are you prepared to do as I require of you ?"

"Explain yourself," returned Bianchi, in a faltering voice, and looking timidly and apprehensively at his determined and repulsive companion.

" Well, then," answered Fransisco ; " it is simply this ; I have been too long buffeting with the world, and despised by my fellow creatures, though my birth is scarcely less noble than that of the Prince Bianchi ! I wish to regain my position in society and to be courted and honoured by those who have hitherto scorned and avoided me. You have the means of gratifying my ambition, and if you study your own welfare you will not for a moment hesitate to do so. What I demand, then, from you is, that you give me a sufficient sum of money to keep me in affluence for the rest of my days, and that should I in future appear before you, you recognise me in my assumed character of the Count Fransisco D'Gasparino !"

"Outrageous insolence !" cried Bianchi indignantly ; " and think you that I will ever be intimidated into a compliance with any such bold and extravagant demands ?"

" If you are not absolutely mad you will," answered Fransisco, in the same cool and determined accents. " Come, you highness, call a little reason to your aid, and you will then see the policy of not remaining obstinate, when by so doing you will plunge yourself into inevitable destruction. What can be the pecuniary object of such an arrangement to you ? Are you not the richest nobleman in all Italy, and, therefore, cannot miss the sacrifice that I require ? The whole of it is, as I told you before, that I must have it, and, consequently, resistance on your part is useless. Yield readily to my demands, and you will make me your sworn slave for ever, and the secrets which are in my possession, and which it would ruin you should they become known to the world, shall for ever remain unrevealed."

"By Heaven, never !" exclaimed Bianchi, mustering up all the resolution and determination he could, although he could not help inwardly trembling at the threats that the villain Fransisco held out, and which he so well knew he had both the power and the will to execute. "I will risk anything rather than thus be forced into a compliance with that which is so repulsive to my feelings."

" Fool !" cried the fellow, fiercely ; " are you determined to brave my vengeance which, of you reject my propositions, in spite of the power which you possess, you know will be certain to overtake you ? Do not exasperate me, for I am in no humour to be trifled with or delayed in the accomplishment of my desires. Once more I ask you, will you agree to that which I demand ?"

" Fransisco, hear me," said Bianchi, with the most undisguised alarm ; " do not act unreasonable, but be satisfied with that which I have already done for you, and what I am still willing to do ; but——"

"Bah !" interrupted Fransisco, impatiently. " I am not to be put off on any such terms—of that you may rest assured. What is the paltry assistance I have received from you ? What atonement have you made me for the wrongs you have done me, and your innocent victim, my unfortunate sister ? Beware—beware ! for if you offend me, you will arouse a sleeping lion, who will never be satisfied until he has inflicted the most terrible vengeance on your head !"

" Miscreant !" exclaimed the prince, unable any longer to control the rage and indignation of his feelings, and at the same time rushing upon Fransisco, and grasping him by the collar. " I will no longer brook this daring insolence, but——"

" Ah !" interrupted Fransisco, his eyes at the same time flashing with the violent rage and excitement of his feelings, " dare you thus assault me, and brave my vengeance ? Idiot ! take, then, the consequences !"

As he spoke these words, he released himself from the weak hold of the Prince Bianchi, and dashed him fiercely to the earth ; and he was about to follow up the same by a blow, when the loud report of a pistol was suddenly heard, and Fransisco, with a terrible oath, sank bleeding to the earth ; and the next instant, the Count Alberti, who had left the villa in search of the Prince Bianchi, and was accidentally led to the spot, stood before them. It was from his hand that Fransisco had received the fatal wound.

"Villain !" he exclaimed, as he fixed his stern gaze upon the distorted features of the ruffian ; " thus have you received the just reward of your daring. My lord," he added, turning to Bianchi, who was completely astounded and bewildered at the suddenness of the event, "I am happy to think that Providence guided my footsteps hither at so critical a moment. This wretch is punished as he deserved; and I trust that you have now nothing more to apprehend from him."

Fransisco was bleeding profusely, and his features were frightfully distorted with the agony he was enduring. It was evident that he had received a mortal wound, and that he could not survive many minutes. By a powerful effort, he raised himself slightly from the ground on his elbow; and fixing a ghastly look upon the Count Alberti, in a hoarse and hollow voice he, with the utmost difficulty, exclaimed--

"Ah, I am slain! But to perish thus, when I had so much to do to complete my vengeance! May the curses of hell light upon thee, Count Alberti, and—oh!—I—I—"

The finish of the sentence was stifled in his throat; a livid and ghastly hue overspread his features; his eyes closed, and he sank back upon the earth a corpse, just as several domestics, who had been alarmed by the report of the pistol, arrived at the spot, and, by the commands of the Count Alberti, they conveyed the corpse away, while he, taking the arm of the Prince Bianchi, who was completely confounded by all that had taken place, led him to the villa.

*   *   *   *

This remarkable event caused no little sensation and conversation among the domestics at the villa, and the persons in the neighbourhood, and various were the speculations that were formed upon the subject, though the particulars were, of course, not permitted to transpire, and it was generally supposed that the man who was slain was some desperate robber who had met with his just reward in attempting to plunder the Prince Bianchi.

As for the latter nobleman, it was several days before he could recover from the excitement into which the circumstance had naturally thrown him; but when he did so, he could not but congratulate himself that he had at least got rid of one so desperate and dangerous an enemy. But his mind continued in a state of the greatest uneasiness, as he could gain no information whatever as to what had become of Melina; his conscience bitterly reproached him for the manner in which he had treated her, and there were times when he was fully determined, if he could discover her, that he would solicit her forgiveness, abandon the designs he had hitherto entertained against her, and when he thought that he could even so far conquer his prejudices as to yield to her wishes, in spite of the promises he had given to the Count Alberti. The latter could not but perceive the wavering thoughts that were passing in his mind, and it caused him much anxiety and apprehension. He endeavoured all that he could to argue him out of it, but

his efforts met with but little, if any success, and his agitation and apprehension in consequence increased.

In this manner several days passed away, without any change taking place in the manners of the Prince Bianchi, nor could the least intelligence be obtained, which might lead them to conjecture the place where our heroine was concealed, though they entertained but little doubt that she was under the protection of Massaroni, and they were perfectly at a loss what course to adopt.

They had been one afternoon seated in the parlour discussing this important subject, when a servant suddenly entered the room, and informed his master that a courier had at that moment arrived at the villa, apparently from a long journey, who stated that he had a letter which he would not deliver into the hands of any other person than the Prince Bianchi.

"Ah!" exclaimed the latter, rising from his seat in considerable anxiety; "what can this mean? Can it be a communication from Melina? Conduct the courier instantly to my presence."

The servant left the room, and in a few minutes returned, conducting in the courier, who having respectfully bowed to Bianchi and the Count Alberti, placed a sealed packet in the hands of the former.

"Let this stranger retire to another room," said the Prince Bianchi, "and I desire that he will not leave the villa till he knows my further pleasure."

The man bowed and obeyed, and then Bianchi, glancing at the superscription on the letter, started and evinced the greatest astonishment.

"Why, how is this?" he exclaimed; "this handwriting is unknown to me! From whom can it come?"

He hastily broke the seal, and unfolding the packet, he proceeded to peruse the contents, but he had scarcely glanced over half a dozen lines, when he uttered a mingled exclamation of astonishment, and sinking back in his chair, covered his face with his hands.

"What is the meaning of this agitation, my lord?" eagerly interrogated Alberti.

"Read—read!" replied Bianchi; "read aloud, for I cannot. Melina is safe, under the protection of a stranger, the Count de Clairville, who acknowledges himself to be the uncle of Florio. Zitella living, and her daughter too, and—oh, God!—that daughter—my daughter, your unfortunate victim, Count Alberti, she whom we have hitherto known as the poor girl Olympia! Oh! I am indeed most justly punished."

With a trembling hand the bewildered and conscience-stricken Alberti picked up the packet which the Prince Bianchi had cast on the floor, and proceeded, as well as he could, to read the contents, though he was frequently compelled to pause in order to give vent to his feelings. It is needless to particularise them here, as they were merely a recapitulation of the extraordinary events with which the reader has been already made acquainted; but, in addition, they contained an earnest appeal to the Prince Bianchi, in behalf of his niece and Florio, and stating that upon his solemn promise to receive them amicably, he would loose no time in introducing them to the prince. There was also a most affectionate letter from Melina to her uncle, to prove the truth of the statements of the Count de Clairville, and in which she most solemnly promised to bury the past in oblivion if he would only agree to the propositions there set forth.

To attempt to describe the various feeling that distracted the brain of Bianchi, as he listened to these remarkable and important facts, would be a fruitless task, while the agitation, rage, and disappointment of the Count Alberti exceeded all bounds.

"It is all false!" he exclaimed; "it is nothing more than a base attempt to impose on your credulity, and to thwart us in our designs. Surely, your highness, you are not going to suffer yourself to be thus deceived?"

"Deceived!" replied Bianchi. "Oh, no; my conscience tells me it is too true. I have too long given way to my evil passions, and trampled on honour and justice, but now that an opportunity is afforded me of repentance and atonement, I must not—will not neglect to avail myself of it. Oh, Melina! how deeply have I injured you! But let me not neglect a moment writing her to and the Count de Clairville, to assure them of——"

"What would you do?" hastily demanded Alberti.

"That which justice demands," replied the prince, "and which I have too long neglected to perform. But let me not delay a moment."

"And do you forget the solemn compact entered into between yourself and me?" asked Alberti, in a hoarse voice, and half choked with rage.

"No!" answered Bianchi; "and most bitterly does my conscience now upbraid me for it. Remember, my lord, that you have atonement to make as well as myself, and do not neglect doing so, lest the vengeance of Heaven should descend upon your head. Think you that I could ever be so base and unnatural, as to bestow the hand of my niece upon the seducer of my own child?"

The eyes of the Count Alberti flashed with rage, and it was not without the greatest difficulty that he exclaimed—

"'Tis well, Prince Bianchi; you have deceived me, and trifled with my feelings, and this moment I owe you nothing, but the most deadly and implacable revenge. I leave the villa this very hour; but, beware! for when next we meet, my hour of retribution will have arrived!"

With these words, shaking his fist in a threatening manner at the Prince Bianchi, and his whole frame convulsed with the powerful excitement of his feelings, the Count Alberti started from the room, and hastily summoning his attendants, at once quitted the villa.

For a short time after his departure, the Prince Bianchi remained in the most indescribable state of agitation, and his brain was so distracted, that he scarcely knew what he was about; but at length he hastily summoned the attendance of his domestic, and commanded him to re-conduct the carrier to his presence, which he having obeyed, he put such questions as were necessary to him, and which being promptly and explicitly answered, he once more dismissed him, and then with much more composure than could have been expected, he proceeded to write letters to the Count de Clairville and Melina, in which he earnestly and sincerely expressed his sorrow for the past; his willingness to agree to their wishes, and, entreating them to use no more delay than possible in hastening to the villa, but at the same time requested that the time of his interview with the unfortunate Signora Zitella and her daughter should be deferred until he had somewhat recovered from the painful excitement into which these extraordinary events had naturally thrown him. This task accomplished, he felt more easy and satisfied in his own mind than he had been for many a long day; and having sealed all the letters, and delivered them into the hands of the carrier, he dismissed him from the villa on his important mission, and locking himself up in his own apartment, would not suffer himself to be intruded upon by any one.

CHAPTER LXII

THE RAGE OF ALBERTI.—HIS DESIGNS.—THE RESTORATION OF MELINA TO THE VILLA ROSA.—THE MEETING.—THE PENITENCE OF THE PRINCE BIANCHI.—THE SUDDEN APPEARANCE OF THE BRIGAND CHIEF.—THE CATASTROPHE.—THE DISCOVERY,

THE state of mind under which the Prince Bianchi now laboured, may be more readily imagined than described. The events of the last few hours were of that extraordinary description that he could scarcely persuade himself that he was not labouring under the influence of a dream, but when he was convinced of their reality, his feelings of anxiety, and dread to behold his beauteous and much wronged niece again, were almost too powerful for his senses to withstand. And then what must be the emotion of his feelings, when he once more beheld Zitella and her daughter? shame and remorse, he felt convinced, must overwhelm him. But still he was encouraged by the assurance which the Count de Clairville had given him in his letter, and he was fully determined to exert himself to the utmost to make all the atonement in his power for the past; and that resolution inspired him with more confidence than he could have otherwise have experienced. He was somewhat disturbed at the threats to which the Count Alberti had given utterance, and at the abrupt manner in which he had quitted the villa; but still he consoled himself with the reflection that he was now only acting as justice dictated, and trusted that Providence would protect him from any danger that might threaten him.

The news of what had taken place quickly spread, and caused no inconsiderable sensation among the domestics of the Prince Bianchi, and in the neighbourhood of the villa, and the return of the Signora Melina and her lover was looked forward to with much impatience and joyful anticipation, for it is almost needless to say that their numerous virtues, and the condescending urbanity of their manners, had endeared them to all who knew them, and who sincerely commiserated with them in the numerous troubles to which they had been subjected.

The Count Alberti, on leaving the villa, retired to an inn for the present, a short distance off, where he resolved to remain secluded, until the result of this disappointment of his hopes should be seen. To say that he was bursting with rage at the sudden and unexpected change that had taken place in his affairs, would only be to give an appropriate term to the character of the feelings that raged within his breast. The weakness of the prince, as he designated his penitence and remorse, filled him with disgust and indignation, and he determined, at all hazards, to have a terrible revenge. But to find that Florio, after all, was of noble origin, and that one of the principal objections of Bianchi was consequently removed, and that he would probably at length give his consent to the union of him and Melina, tortured and exasperated him more than all, and for some time his rage was so great that he could not keep it within the bounds of reason. But there was another circumstance that astonished and agitated him almost as much as those we have mentioned, and that was the discovery that Olympia was the daughter of the Prince Bianchi. Yet with that there was coupled a feeling of revenge and satisfaction, since the disgrace and misery

he had brought upon her must be a source of the greatest anguish and regret to Bianchi, and which he thought it was impossible that anything could remove. He had his spies about to give him every information of all that took place at the villa; he had also the means of entering it unknown to any one, and he determined to be present at the meeting which was about to take place, and to arrange his plans of revenge accordingly.

More than a week elapsed after the circumstances had taken place which we have recorded in the previous chapter, when Alberti was informed that a messenger had arrived at the villa Rosa, to apprise the Prince Bianchi that the Count de Clairville and his companions were on their way thither, and that if nothing important happened to prevent them, they might be expected to arrive there the following day. This fixed the determination of Alberti, and having the means of gaining admittance to the villa, unknown to any one, as we have said before, he resolved to conceal himself there that night, and to await the issue of all that might take place. He armed himself for the occasion, and desired his servants to be in attendance in the vicinity of the villa on the following day, in case their assistance should be required, and when night had approached, he set forward on his expedition, where we will leave him for the present, and return to the Prince Bianchi.

That nobleman passed a sleepless night, the one which intervened between the day on which he expected that the interesting and important meeting would take place, and the hours never appeared half so long and tedious to him, although at the same time he could not help entertaining some misgivings as to what would be the result of it. But could he doubt the sincerity of Melina's assertions, and her eagerness and anxiety to assure him of her forgiveness when she was convinced of his penitence? Oh, no, he knew her gentle and generous nature too well to entertain any such doubts, and what, therefore, had he to fear? Oh, he reflected, that he had come to this resolution before what a world of anxiety and anguish would it have saved him! At length, the morning dawned, and at an early hour the prince quitted his couch, and descending into his private room, awaited with the utmost impatience and anxiety of mind the important arrival.

About the middle of the day a messenger rode at full speed up to the villa, and informed Bianchi that the travellers were within a short distance of the villa, and that they might be expected to arrive there in a few minutes. The agitation of the prince may now be easily conjectured; his heart beat quick, and throwing himself on his knees, he fervently supplicated the support of Omnipotence throughout the trying scene. In a few minutes afterwards, he heard the rolling of carriage-wheels driving up to the door of the villa, and a servant immediately afterwards entered the room, and announced that the Count Eugene de Clairville awaited the honour of seeing his highness. With agitated steps, and palpitating heart, Bianchi made his way to the apartment in which his lordship was, and which he understood was the one which contained the portrait, behind the curtain, of which so much has been said in the course of this narrative. The count met him with the utmost respect and politeness; the Prince Bianchi, who was much prepossessed in his favour, could not help gazing upon him with some feelings of shame and confusion; but he soon recovered himself, and said—

"My lord, I cannot help expressing to you my heartfelt gratitude for the great interest and trouble you have taken in this painful and important business; but, pardon my anxiety, my much injured niece, and your nephew—say, are they not with you?"

"They are, your highness," replied the Count de Clairville; "and anxious to crave your blessing."

Immediately he advanced towards the folding doors, which he threw open, and Melina and her lover rushing forward, threw themselves at the prince's feet. With a burst of emotion such as no language can describe, he raised them, and pressing the beauteous form of our heroine to his heart, tears of mingled delight and remorse gushed from his eyes, and he was unable for some minutes to give utterance to a syllable.

It would be a useless task for us to attempt to describe the scene which followed, and the Count de Clairville stood by and watched it with the deepest interest and satisfaction. But what was the rage of the Count Alberti? He could not without the greatest difficulty help betraying himself, and several times he grasped his pistol, and pointed it towards Florio, half resolved to sacrifice the life of his hated rival on the spot; but some instinctive power, over which he had no control, withheld his hand, and saved him from the perpetration of his deadly purpose.

"Oh, Melina!" at length ejaculated the Prince Bianchi, in a tone of voice which sufficiently told the extreme agony of his feelings; "how dare I meet your reproachful gaze after the unexampled cruelty and injustice with which I have behaved towards you? Can you, oh, can you forgive me, when I assure you that I am stung with remorse for what I have done?"

"Can I forgive you, my beloved uncle?" replied Melina, and her eyes spoke the sincerity of her feelings; "with what delight and gratitude to Heaven can I do so, and how cheerfully shall be my task to bury the painful past

in oblivion! Oh, my lord, you have made me but too happy."

"Generous, noble-minded girl!" cried the prince, again straining her to his bosom, "how little deserving were you of the injuries I inflicted on you. May Heaven heap its choicest blessings upon your head and pardon me."

"And may I venture to approach your highness," said Florio, in the most respectful accents, "and to solicit your forgiveness for any boldness or presumption of which I may seem to have been guilty, and for any trouble, disappointment, and anxiety I may have caused you?"

"Florio de Clairville," replied the prince, "it is I who should solicit to you for pardon, for I have treated you with the greatest harshness and injustice. But it is now my determination to make you all the atonement in my power, and I thank Heaven that I have the means of doing so, so readily at my hands. You and Melina, I know, have long sincerely loved one another, and your unabated constancy throughout so many trials proves how worthy you are of each other. Take her—take her, and may you both be happy."

As he thus spoke, he placed the fair hand of the blushing Melina in that of her enraptured lover, and both kneeling at his feet, he invoked the blessing of Heaven upon their heads; and they were all of them too much overpowered by their feelings for a few moments to be able to speak a word. As for the Count Alberti, he was ready to burst with rage and jealousy, and muttered the most terrible curses to himself on beholding a scene which he had never expected to witness.

"Thank Heaven!" at length ejaculated the Count de Clairville, "that all has ended even much happier than my most sanguine anticipations led me to expect, and I cannot but express my thanks to your highness for that which you have done, and which has rendered happy and contented the hearts of those who are so dear to each other. But I have to crave your highness's indulgence for a moment, while I beg of you a favour."

"A favour, my lord?" said the Prince Bianchi; "name it, for there is no favour which it is possible I can refuse to grant to a nobleman to whom I am so largely indebted."

"Thanks, excellenza," returned the count; "the favour I have, then, to ask of you is, that you will allow me to introduce to you one to whom we are all under a weight of obligation; and that you will be pleased to banish from your mind any prejudices that you may have entertained towards him."

The Prince Bianchi looked surprised, but after a pause, he said—

"Well, my lord, e'en be it as you wish; let me have the honour of being introduced to this friend of yours; and I trust that I may have no cause to refuse to comply with your wishes to the full extent."

The Count de Clairville bowed; and then again advancing to the folding doors, he threw them open, and there entered the room the tall and commanding figure of a man who was en-veloped in a large cloak, and whose hat was so slouched down over his brow as to conceal his features from immediate observation. He advanced towards the spot where the Prince Bianchi and his fair niece were standing, and was in the act of bowing to them, when the report

MARIA MOURNING THE DEATH OF THE BRIGAND CHIEF.

of a pistol was heard, and with a groan he sank bleeding on the floor.

In an instant the room was filled with men, some the brigands, and the others the soldiers and attendants of the Prince Bianchi. The perpetrator of the foul deed was seen, for it was the Count Alberti, who emerged from the place of his concealment, and received the contents of a pistol in his breast, discharged by Maria Grazia.

Nothing could possibly exceed the astonishment and consternation that prevailed amongst all the guests assembled, and they immediately flocked around the wounded man.

"Rash, headstrong man!" exclaimed the Prince Bianchi, addressing himself to the Count Alberti, who was writhing with agony, and had evidently received a mortal wound; "what cursed fate brought you here, and what have you done?"

"Slain one who has foiled me in all my designs," replied Alberti, with a ghastly smile of exultation, "and whom you have in vain tried to capture—Allesandro Massaroni, the Brigand Chief!"

"Massaroni!" cried the Prince Bianchi. "Wretched man, have you then at last met with the fate that your crimes have so long invoked?"

"Hold! hold! my lord!" exclaimed Florio, starting suddenly forward; "exult not over that which you should so deeply and so bitterly deplore. What, I solemnly ask you, was the name of the original of that portrait?"

"Why do you put that question, your highness?" replied Bianchi, in a faint and faltering voice, while Massaroni, gently raised in the arms of his wife, fixed upon him a dying look of the most intense and earnest expression.

"Answer the question, your highness," replied Florio, "for there is not a moment to be lost. The name of the original of that portrait is ——"

"Zerlina!" gasped forth Bianchi, covering his face with his hands, and groaning convulsively.

"And in Allesandro Massaroni," interrupted Florio, producing the manuscript—"read! read!—you behold Zerlina's son!"

"My son! my son!" groaned the wretched and unfortunate Prince Bianchi, and he sunk into the arms of his attendants. But to attempt to describe the effect it had upon the dying brigand chief would be a fruitless task. He seemed to muster more than human strength upon the occasion, and breaking from the hold of his wife, he staggered up towards the Prince Bianchi, and unsheathing his poniard, he exclaimed—

"Ah! the cursed betrayer and destroyer of my mother—have I, then, discovered you at last? This to your heart, and so be the cruel wrongs of Zerlina and her son avenged!"

His arm was raised, and in another moment his dagger would have penetrated the breast of the unfortunate and unconscious nobleman, had not Melina started between them, and averted the blow.

"Hold! Massaroni!" she exclaimed; "vengeance is for God, and not for man! You have performed your duty to the memory of your mother, and that Almighty Power in whose presence you must shortly appear, will judge you accordingly."

Massaroni fixed upon her a look of admiration and respect, and sunk back in the arms of his wife. The brigands were about to rush upon the Prince Bianchi, but he commanded them back with a wave of his hand.

"Forbear!" he said; "you have ever obeyed my orders in life, and will do so now in death: The curse of Massaroni rest upon the head of he that attempts to injure that old man. He has sinned, he is penitent—he is sufficiently punished, and I sincerely forgive him, and may Heaven do so likewise. Sainted spirit of my mother, I hasten to join you! Maria, my wife, Melina, Florio, comrades, all farewell; Allesandro Massaroni, the brigand chief, and the son of his excellenza, the Prince Bianchi, has ended his career; respect his memory, and let his bones moulder in the earth of his mountain home! I—I——"

He could not finish the sentence, his eyes closed, and, sinking back in the arms of his wife, with a gentle sigh, the soul of Allesandro Massaroni, the Mountain Chief, departed to the realms of Eternity!

To describe the scene which followed would indeed be a difficult task. The Prince Bianchi, overpowered by the violent emotion of his feelings, had become insensible to all that was passing around him; our heroine and her lover stood and gazed at the corpse of that brave and unfortunate man, to whom they were so much indebted, with feelings of the most profound sorrow, awe, and regret; Maria still supported the lifeless body of her husband in her arms, and was as fixed and inanimate as a statue; while the brigands gathered around, and by the mournful expression of their countenances, said much more than it would have been at all possible for any language to convey. But suddenly they were all aroused by a deep groan of the most intense agony, proceeding from the Count Alberti, to whom, in the excitement of the moment, consequent upon the extraordinary catastrophe that had occurred, and the discovery which had been made, no attention had been paid; and it was then evident to all that he was in the last agonies of death. But who commiserated that guilty young nobleman? No one. In fact, the brigands were so exasperated with him, that, had it not been for the dying injunctions of their lamented chief, they would have rushed upon him like so many bloodhounds, and have hastened his death. He, with a last convulsive struggle, raised himself on his elbow, and looking wildly around him, he ejaculated in tones that were sufficient to thrill the souls of all who heard them with horror:

"Death! death! and must I perish thus? Am I thus at last to be triumphed over? Melina become the wife of him whom I so thoroughly detest and despise! Oh, torture most unutterable! Massaroni, the brigand chief, is proved to be the son of the haughty Prince Bianchi; I, too, am the seducer of his own daughter; I have caused a wreck around me, and leave behind me that which will cause him future agony and grief. I am revenged! Ha! ha! ha! But eternity! I am entering upon it! No—no, I must not die! I dare not meet that fearful judge, whose laws I have so grossly violated! Hold me up! stop the blood that is flowing round my heart! Let not my breath escape me! Wretches! do you not witness my agony, and yet you stand tamely and unpitying by? Ah! that pang! I —I, save me! Oh!"

And with one frightful groan, the wretched and guilty man sank back in the arms of the attendants who had gathered round him, a corpse.

——

CONCLUSION.

IT was several weeks ere the Prince Bianchi, and the other persons interested, could at all recover from the shock which the appalling events we have just recorded had occasioned, and then a deep feeling of regret pervaded the breasts of them all for the fate of the noble-hearted and unfortunate Massaroni. He was buried according to his wish, with due solemnly and respect, in the immediate vicinity of his mountain retreat, and a marble monument was erected by the Prince Bianchi over the spot, to his memory. His wife would have been handsomely provided for by the father of her ill-fated partner; but her happiness was gone, and for the rest of her days she secluded herself in that retreat where she had passed so many years of her life, and unceasing were the tears which the devoted woman shed to the memory of her husband.

The meeting of Zitella and her daughter with the Prince Bianchi, we are certain that we need not attempt to describe. Bianchi made Zitella all the compensation for the injuries he had inflicted upon her which it was in his power to do; he fixed upon her and her daughter a handsome fortune, and in a few months afterwards the former and Mentaldi were united, and thus the old man was sufficiently rewarded for the many acts of kindness he had performed for one who but for him would probably have perished.

When the excitement of the events we have detailed had somewhat abated, Florie led his beloved and beauteous Melina to the altar, the Prince Bianchi presenting him her hand, and that was a day of universal happiness and enjoyment throughout Rome. Years of the most uninterrupted bliss crowned their union; and if they ever thought of the past, it was almost without one pang of regret. A numerous and lovely family added to the felicity of their union; and it may be sufficient to say, that, as they increased in years, they endeavoured to emulate the transcendent virtues of their parents, and were beloved by all who knew them.

The Count de Clairville abandoned his former intention of secluding himself in a monastery; took up his residence with his nephew and his wife; was the constant companion of the Prince Bianchi, and lived for many years, honoured and respected, and died regretted by a wide circle of friends and acquaintances.

Adolphe D'Aubigny, having succeeded in conquering his hopeless passion, returned to his venerable benefactor, by whom and all the others he was received with the utmost kindness and welcome. In a few months a mutual passion arose between him and Mira, and they were united in the presence of all to whom they were so dear, and who were so anxious for their happiness.

PUBLISHED BY E. LLOYD, SALISBURY SQUARE, LONDON.

www.ingramcontent.com/pod-product-compliance
Lightning Source LLC
Chambersburg PA
CBHW081136020726
47504CB00009B/1889